Hal Lambell
Christmas 1997
With Love from
Your Daughter,
Julie

More Praise for John leCarré

"I don't think anyone is likely to write
a better suspense novel."
—*The New York Times*

"LeCarré is the premier spy novelist of his time.
Perhaps of all time."
—*Time*

"LeCarré is writing at the top of his form."
—*The Los Angeles Times*

"Extraordinary."—*USA Today*

JOHN LE CARRÉ

A NEW COLLECTION OF THREE COMPLETE NOVELS

JOHN LE CARRÉ

A NEW COLLECTION OF THREE COMPLETE NOVELS

A PERFECT SPY

THE RUSSIA HOUSE

THE SECRET PILGRIM

WINGS BOOKS

New York · Avenel, New Jersey

This 1996 edition is published by Wings Books,
a division of Random House Value Publishing, Inc., 40 Engelhard Avenue, Avenel, New Jersey 07001, by arrangement with Alfred A. Knopf, Inc.

Random House
New York • Toronto • London • Sydney • Auckland

Printed and bound in the United States of America

Library of Congress Cataloging-in-Publication Data

LeCarré, John, 1931–
   [Selections. 1995]
   John leCarré: three complete novels.
     p.   cm.
   Contents: A perfect spy—The Russia House—The secret pilgrim.
   ISBN 0-517-15019-0
   1. Spy stories, English. I. Title.
PR6062.E33A6   1996
823'.914—dc20   96-10282
                                       CIP

8 7 6 5 4 3 2 1

CONTENTS

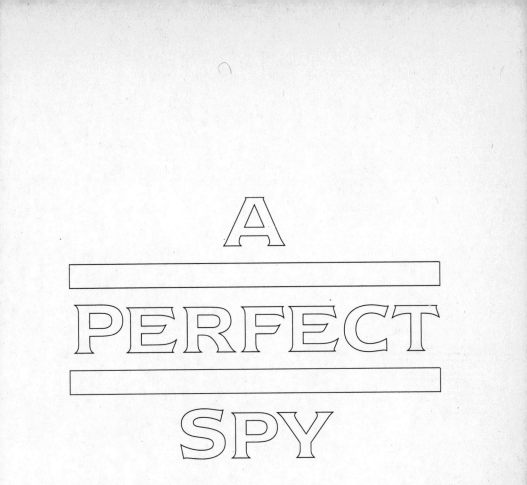

A PERFECT SPY

*For R, who shared the journey, lent me his dog,
and tossed me a few pieces of his life*

A man who has two women loses his soul.
But a man who has two houses loses his head.

PROVERB

1

In the small hours of a blustery October morning in a south Devon coastal town that seemed to have been deserted by its inhabitants, Magnus Pym got out of his elderly country taxi-cab and, having paid the driver and waited till he had left, struck out across the church square. His destination was a terrace of ill-lit Victorian boarding-houses with names like Bel-a-Vista, The Commodore and Eureka. In build he was powerful but stately, a representative of something. His stride was agile, his body forward-sloping in the best tradition of the Anglo-Saxon administrative class. In the same attitude, whether static or in motion, Englishmen have hoisted flags over distant colonies, discovered the sources of great rivers, stood on the decks of sinking ships. He had been travelling in one way or another for sixteen hours but he wore no overcoat or hat. He carried a fat black briefcase of the official kind and in the other hand a green Harrods bag. A strong sea wind lashed at his city suit, salt rain stung his eyes, balls of spume skimmed across his path. Pym ignored them. Reaching the porch of a house marked "No Vacancies" he pressed the bell and waited, first for the outside light to go on, then for the chains to be unfastened from inside. While he waited a church clock began striking five. As if in answer to its summons Pym turned on his heel and stared back at the square. At the graceless tower of the Baptist church posturing against the racing clouds. At the writhing monkey-puzzle trees, pride of the ornamental gardens. At the empty bandstand. At the bus shelter. At the dark patches of the side streets. At the doorways one by one.

"Why Mr. Canterbury, it's you," an old lady's voice objected sharply as the door opened behind him. "You bad man. You caught the night sleeper again, I can tell. Why ever didn't you telephone?"

"Hullo, Miss Dubber," said Pym. "How are you?"

"Never mind how I am, Mr. Canterbury. Come in at once. You'll catch your death."

But the ugly windswept square seemed to have locked Pym in its spell. "I thought Sea View was up for sale, Miss D," he remarked as she tried to pluck him into the house. "You told me Mr. Cook moved out when his wife died. Wouldn't set foot in the place, you said."

"Of course he wouldn't. He was allergic. Come in this instant, Mr. Canterbury, and wipe your feet before I make your tea."

"So what's a light doing in his upstairs bedroom window?" Pym asked as he allowed her to tug him up the steps.

Like many tyrants Miss Dubber was small. She was also old and powdery and lopsided, with a crooked back that rumpled her dressing-gown and made everything round her seem lopsided too.

"Mr. Cook has rented out the upper flat, Celia Venn has taken it to paint in. That's you all over." She slid a bolt. "Disappear for three months, come back in the middle of the night and worry about a light in someone's window." She slid another. "You'll never change, Mr. Canterbury. I don't know why I bother."

"Who on earth is Celia Venn?"

"Dr. Venn's daughter, silly. She wants to see the sea and paint it." Her voice changed abruptly. "Why Mr. Canterbury, how dare you? Take that off this instant."

With the last bolt in place Miss Dubber had straightened up as best she could and was preparing herself for a reluctant hug. But instead of her customary scowl, which nobody believed in for a moment, her poky little face had twisted in fright.

"Your horrid black tie, Mr. Canterbury. I won't have death in the house, I won't have you bring it. Who is it for?"

Pym was a handsome man, boyish but distinguished. In his early fifties he was in his prime, full of zeal and urgency in a place that knew none. But the best thing about him in Miss Dubber's view was his lovely smile that gave out so much warmth and truth and made her feel right.

"Just an old Whitehall colleague, Miss D. No one to flap about. No one close."

"Everyone's close at my age, Mr. Canterbury. What was his name?"

"I hardly knew the fellow," said Pym emphatically, untying his tie and slipping it into his pocket. "And I'm certainly not going to tell you his name and have you hunting the obituaries, so there." His eye as he said this fell on the visitors' book, which lay open on the hall table beneath the orange nightlight that he had fitted to her ceiling on his last visit. "Any casuals at all, Miss D?" he asked as he scanned the list. "Runaway couples, mystery princesses? What happened to those two lover-boys who came at Easter?"

"They were not lover-boys," Miss Dubber corrected him severely as she hobbled towards the kitchen. "They took single rooms and in the evenings they watched football on the television. What was that you said, Mr. Canterbury?"

But Pym had not spoken. Sometimes his gushes of communication were like phone calls cut off by some inner censorship before they could be completed. He turned back a page and then another.

"I don't think I'll do casuals any more," Miss Dubber said through the open kitchen doorway as she lit the gas. "Sometimes when the doorbell goes I sit here with Toby and I say: 'You answer it, Toby.' He doesn't of course. A tortoiseshell cat can't answer a door. So we go on sitting here. We sit and we wait and we hear the footsteps go away again." She cast a sly glance at him. "You don't think our Mr. Canterbury is smitten, do you, Toby?" she enquired archly of her cat. "We're very *bright* this morning. Very *shiny*. Ten years younger, by the look of our coat, Mr. Canterbury is." Receiving no helpful response from the cat, she addressed herself to the canary. "Not that he'd ever tell us, would he, Dickie? We'd be the last to know. Tzuktzuk? Tzuktzuk?"

"John and Sylvia Illegible of Wimbledon," said Pym, still at the visitors' book.

"John makes computers, Sylvia programs them, and they're leaving tomorrow," she told him sulkily. For Miss Dubber hated to admit there was anyone in her world but beloved Mr. Canterbury. "Now what have you done to me this time?" she exclaimed angrily. "I won't have it. Take it back."

But Miss Dubber was not angry; she would have it, and Pym would not take it back: a thickly knitted cashmere shawl of white and gold, still in its Harrods box and swathed in its original Harrods tissue paper which she seemed to treasure almost above their contents. For having taken out the shawl she first smoothed the paper and folded it along its creases before replacing it in the box, then put the box on the cupboard shelf where she kept her greatest treasures. Only then did she let him wrap the shawl round her shoulders and hug her in it, while she scolded him for his extravagance.

Pym drank tea with Miss Dubber, Pym appeased her, Pym ate a piece of her shortbread and praised it to the skies although she told him it was burned. Pym promised to mend the sink plug for her and unblock the waste-pipe and take a look at the cistern on the first floor while he was about it. Pym was swift and over-attentive and the brightness she had shrewdly remarked on did not leave him. He lifted Toby on to his lap and stroked him, a thing he had never done before, and which gave Toby no discernible pleasure. He received the latest news of Miss Dubber's ancient Aunt Al, when normally the mention of Aunt Al was enough to hurry him off to bed. He questioned her, as he always did, about the local goings-on since his last visit, and listened approvingly to the catalogue of Miss Dubber's complaints. And quite often, as he nodded her through her answers, he either smiled to himself for no clear reason or became drowsy and yawned behind his hand. Till suddenly he put down his teacup and stood up as if he had another train to catch.

"I'll be staying a decent length of time if it's all right with you, Miss D. I've a bit of heavy writing to do."

"That's what you always say. You were going to live here for ever last time. Then it's up first thing and back to Whitehall without your egg."

"Maybe as much as two weeks. I've taken some leave of absence so that I can work in peace."

Miss Dubber pretended to be appalled. "But whatever will happen to the country? How shall Toby and I stay safe, with no Mr. Canterbury at the helm to steer us?"

"So what are Miss D's plans?" he asked winningly, reaching for his briefcase, which by the effort he needed to lift it looked as heavy as a chunk of lead.

"Plans?" Miss Dubber echoed, smiling rather beautifully in her mystification. "I don't make plans at my age, Mr. Canterbury. I let God make them. He's better at them than I am, isn't he, Toby? More reliable."

"What about that cruise you're always talking about? It's time you gave yourself a treat, Miss D."

"Don't be daft. That was years ago. I've lost the urge."

"I'll still pay."

"I know you will, bless you."

"I'll do the phoning if you want. We'll go to the travel agent together. I looked one out for you as a matter of fact. There's the *Orient Explorer* leaves Southampton just a week away. They've got a cancellation. I asked."

"Are you trying to get rid of me, Mr. Canterbury?"

Pym took a moment to laugh. "God and me together couldn't dislodge you, Miss D," he said.

From the hall Miss Dubber watched him up the narrow stairs, admiring the youthful springiness of his tread despite the heavy briefcase. He's going to a high-level conference. A weighty one too. She listened to him step lightly along the corridor to room 8 overlooking the square, which was her longest let ever, in her whole long life. His loss has not affected him, she decided in relief as she heard him unlock the door and close it softly behind him. Just some old colleague from the Ministry, no one close. She wanted nothing to disturb him. He was to remain the same perfect gentleman who had appeared on her doorstep years ago, looking for what he had called a sanctuary without a telephone even though she had a perfectly good one in the kitchen. And had paid her in advance six-monthly, ever since, cash-cash, no receipts. And had built the little stone wall beside the garden path for her, all in an afternoon to surprise her on her birthday, bullied the mason and the bricklayer. And had put the slates back on the roof with his own hands after the storm in March. And had sent her flowers and fruit and chocolates and souvenirs from amazing foreign places without properly explaining what he did there. And had helped her with the breakfasts when she had too many casuals, and listened to her about her nephew who had all the schemes for making money that never came to anything: the latest was starting up a bingo hall in Exeter but first he needed the capital for his overdraft. And received no mail or visitors and played no instrument except the wireless in foreign, and never used the telephone except for local tradesmen. And never told her anything about himself except that he lived in London and worked in Whitehall but travelled a lot, and that his name was Canterbury like the city. Children, wives, parents, sweethearts—not a soul on earth had he ever called his own, except his one Miss D.

"He could have a knighthood by now for all we know," she told Toby aloud as she held the shawl to her nose and inhaled its woolly smell. "He could be Prime Minister and we'd only ever hear it from the television."

Very faintly Miss Dubber heard above the rattle of the wind the sound of singing. A man's voice, tuneless but agreeable. First she thought it was "Greensleeves" from the garden, then she thought it was "Jerusalem" from the square, and she was halfway to the window to yell out. Only then did she realise it was Mr. Canterbury from upstairs, and this amazed her so much that when she opened her door to rebuke him, she paused instead to listen. The singing stopped of its own accord. Miss Dubber smiled. Now *he's* listening to *me,* she thought. That's my Mr. Canterbury all over.

In Vienna three hours earlier, Mary Pym, wife of Magnus, stood at her bedroom window and stared out upon a world which, in contrast to the one elected by her husband, was a marvel of serenity. She had neither closed the curtains nor switched on the light. She was dressed to receive, as her mother would have said, and she had been standing at the window in her blue twin-set for an hour, waiting for the car, waiting for the doorbell, waiting for the soft turn of her husband's key in the latch. And now in her mind it was an unfair race between Magnus and Jack Brotherhood which of them she would receive first. An early autumn snow still covered the hilltop, a full moon rode above it, filling the room with black and white bars. In elegant villas up and down the avenue, the last camp fires of diplomatic entertainment were going out one by one. Frau Minister Meierhof had been having a Force Reduction Talks dance with a four-piece band. Mary should have been there. The van Leymans had had a buffet dinner for old Prague hands, both sexes welcome and no *placement.* She should have gone, they both should, and swept up the stragglers for a scotch-and-soda afterwards, vodka for Magnus. And put on the gramophone, and danced till now or later—the swinging diplomatic Pyms, so popular—just the way they had entertained so famously in Washington when Magnus was Deputy Head of Station and everything was absolutely fine. And Mary would have made bacon and eggs while Magnus joked and picked people's brains and acquired new friends, which he was so tirelessly good at. For this was Vienna's high season, when people who have clammed up all year talked excitedly of Christmas and the Opera, and tossed out indiscretions like old clothes.

But all that was a thousand years ago. All that was until last Wednesday. The only thing that mattered now was that Magnus should drive up the avenue in the Metro he had left at the airport and beat Jack Brotherhood to the front door.

The telephone was ringing. By the bed. His side. Don't run, you idiot, you'll fall. Not too slowly or he'll ring off. Magnus, darling, oh dear God, let it be you, you've had an aberration and you're better, I'll never even ask what happened, I'll never doubt you again. She lifted the receiver and for some reason she couldn't work out sat in a heap on the duvet, plonk, grabbing the pad and pencil with her spare hand in case of phone numbers to take down, addresses, times, instructions. She didn't blurt "Magnus?" because that would show she was worried about him. She didn't say "Hullo" because she couldn't trust her voice not to sound excited. She said their whole number in German so that Magnus would know it was she, hear that she was normal and all right and not angry with him, and that everything was just fine to come back to. No fuss, no problems, I'm here and waiting for you like always.

"It's me," said a man's voice.

But it wasn't me. It was Jack Brotherhood.

"No word of that parcel, I suppose?" Brotherhood asked in the rich, confident English of the military classes.

"No word from anyone. Where are you?"

"Be there in about half an hour, less if I can. Wait for me, will you."

The fire, she thought suddenly. My God, the fire. She hastened downstairs, no longer capable of distinguishing between small and large disasters. She had sent the maid out for the night and forgotten to bank up the drawing-room fire. It was out for sure. But it was not. It was burning merrily, and all that was needed was another log to make the early morning hour less funereal. She put it on, then floated round the room prinking things—the flowers, the ashtrays, Jack's whisky tray—making everything outside herself perfect because nothing inside herself was perfect in the least. She lit a cigarette and puffed out the uninhaled smoke in angry kisses. Then she poured herself a very large whisky, which was what she had come down for in the first place. After all, if we were still dancing I'd be having several.

Mary's Englishness, like Pym's, was unmistakable. She was blonde and strong-jawed and forthright. Her one mannerism, inherited from her mother, was the slightly comic stoop from which she addressed the world, and foreigners in particu-lar. Mary's life was a record of fine deaths. Her grandfather had died at Passchenda-ele, her one brother, Sam, more recently in Belfast, and for a month or more it had seemed to Mary that the bomb that had blown Sam's jeep to pieces had killed her soul too, but it was her father, not Mary, who had died of a broken heart. All of her men had been soldiers. Between them they had left her with a decent inheri-tance, a fiercely patriotic soul and a small manor house in Dorset. Mary was ambitious as well as intelligent, she could dream and lust and covet. But the rules of her life had been laid down for her before she entered it and had been entrenched with every death since: in Mary's family the men campaigned while the women lent succour, mourned and carried on. Her worship, her dinner parties, her life with Pym had all been conducted on this same sturdy principle.

Until last July. Until our holiday in Lesbos. Magnus, come home. I'm sorry I raised a stink at the airport when you didn't show up. I'm sorry I bellowed at the British Airways clerk in what you call my six-acre voice and I'm sorry I waved my diplomatic pass around. And I'm sorry—I'm terribly sorry—I phoned Jack to say where the hell's my husband? So please—just come home and tell me what to do. Nothing matters. Just be here. Now.

Finding herself standing before the double doors to the dining room, she pushed them open, switched on the chandeliers, and, whisky in hand, surveyed the long empty table glistening like a lake. Mahogany. Eighteenth-century repro. Counsel-lor's grade, nobody's taste. Seats fourteen with comfort, sixteen if you double up on the curved ends. That bloody burn mark, I've tried everything. Remember, she told herself. Force your mind back. Get the whole story straight in your stupid little head before Jack Brotherhood rings that doorbell. Step outside yourself and look in. *Now.* It is a night like this one was, crisp and exciting. It is Wednesday and our night for entertaining. And the moon is like the moon tonight except for a bite out of one side. In the bedroom, that fool Mary Pym who notched up one A-level and never went to university stands with her feet too wide apart putting on her family pearls while brilliant Magnus her husband, a First at Oxford and already in his dinner-jacket, kisses the nape of her neck and does his Balkan gigolo number to try to get her in the party mood. Magnus of course is in whatever mood he needs to be in.

"For God's sake," Mary snaps more roughly than she intends. "Stop fooling and fix this bloody clasp for me."

Sometimes my military family gets the better of my language.

And Magnus obliges. Magnus always obliges. Magnus mends and fixes and carries better than a butler.

And when he has obliged he puts his hands over my breasts and breathes hotly on my bare neck: "Please, my dullink, have we not time for most divine perfect moment? No? Yes?"

But Mary is, as usual, too nervous even to smile and orders him downstairs to make sure Herr Wenzel the hired manservant has fetched the ice from Weber's fish-shop. And Magnus goes. Magnus always goes. Even when a sharp smack across Mary's chops would be the wiser course, Magnus goes.

Pausing, Mary lifted her head and listened. A car engine. In this snow they come up on you like bad memories. But, unlike a bad memory, this one passed.

It is dinner; it is the diplomatic happy hour, it is as good as Georgetown in the days when Magnus was still an upwardly mobile Deputy Head of Station with the post of Chief of Service squarely in his sights and everything is mended between Magnus and Mary except for a black cloud that night and day hangs over Mary's heart, even when she is not thinking of it, and that cloud is called Lesbos, a Greek island in the Aegean wholly surrounded by monstrous memories. Mary Pym, wife to Magnus, Counsellor for Certain Unmentionable Matters at the British Embassy in Vienna and actually the Head of Station here as everyone unmentionable knows, proudly faces her husband across Mary's silver candelabra while the servants hand round Mary's venison, jugged according to her mother's recipe, to twelve unmentionably distinguished members of the local intelligence community.

"Now you also have a daughter," Mary firmly reminds an Oberregierungsrat Dinkel from the Austrian Ministry of Defence in her well-learned German. "Name Ursula—right? She was studying piano at the Conservatorium when last heard of. Tell me about her." And to the servant, quietly as she passes: "Frau Wenzel. Mr. Lederer two down has no red sauce. Fix."

It was a pretty night, Mary had decided as she listened to a recitation of the Oberregierungsrat's family woes. It was the sort of night she worked for, had worked for all her married life, in Prague and Washington while they were rising and now here where they were marking time. She was happy, she was flying the flag, the black cloud of Lesbos was as good as blown away. Tom was doing well at boarding-school and would soon be home for the Christmas holidays, Magnus had rented a chalet in Lech for skiing, the Lederers had said they would join them. Magnus was so resourceful these days, so attentive to her despite his father's illness. And before Lech he would take her to Salzburg for *Parsifal* and, if she pressed him, to the Opera ball because, as they liked to say in Mary's family, a gal loves a hop. And with luck the Lederers could join them for that too—the children could spend the night together and share a baby-sitter—and somehow with Magnus these days extra people were a comfort. Glimpsing Pym down the candlelight she darted a smile at him just as he slipped away to engage a deaf mute on his left. Sorry about being touchy earlier, she was saying. All forgotten, he was telling her. And when they've gone we'll make love, she was saying, we'll stay sober and make love and everything will be fine.

Which was when she heard the phone ring. Exactly then. As she was transmitting those loving thoughts to Magnus and having a desperately happy time with them. She heard it ring twice, three times, she started to get cross, then to her relief she heard Herr Wenzel answer it. Herr Pym will return your call later unless it's urgent, she rehearsed in her mind. Herr Pym should not be disturbed unless it is essential. Herr Pym is far too busy telling a funny story in that perfect German of his which so annoys the Embassy and surprises the Austrians. Herr Pym can also do you an Austrian accent on demand, or funnier still a Swiss one, from his days at school there. Herr Pym can put you a row of bottles in a line, and by pinging them with a table-knife, make them chime like the bells of the old Swiss railway, while he chants the stations between Interlaken and the Jungfraujoch in the tones of a local stationmaster and his audience collapses in tears of nostalgic mirth.

Mary lifted her gaze to the far end of the empty table. And Magnus—how was he doing at that moment, apart from flirting with Mary?

Going great guns was the answer. On his right sat the dread Frau Oberregierungsrat Dinkel, a woman so plain and rude, even by the standards of official wives, that some of the toughest troopers in the Embassy had been reduced to stunned silence by her. Yet Magnus had drawn her to him like a flower to the sun and she could not get enough of him. Sometimes, watching him perform like this, Mary was moved to involuntary pity by the absoluteness of his dedication. She wished him more ease, if only for a moment. She wanted him to know that he had earned his peace whenever he chose to take it, instead of giving, giving all the time. If he were a real diplomat, he'd be an Ambassador easily, she thought. In Washington, Grant Lederer had privately assured her, Magnus had exerted more influence than either his Station Chief or the perfectly awful Ambassador. Vienna—though of course he was enormously respected here and enormously influential too—was an anticlimax, obviously. Well it was meant to be, but when the dust settled, Magnus would be back on course, and the thing here was to be patient. Mary wished she was not so young for him. Sometimes he tries to live down to me, she thought. On Magnus's left, similarly mesmerised, sat Frau Oberst Mohr, whose German husband was attached to the Signals Bureau at Wiener Neustadt. But Magnus's real conquest, as ever, was Grant Lederer III, "he of the little black beard and little black eyes and little black thoughts," as Magnus called him, who six months ago had taken over the American Embassy's Legal Department, which meant of course the reverse, for Grant was the Agency's new man, though he was an old friend from Washington.

"Grant's a piss artist," Magnus would complain of him, as he complained of all his friends. "He has us all round a big table once a week inventing words for things we've been doing perfectly well for twenty years without them."

"But he is fun, darling," Mary would remind him. "And Bee's *terribly* dishy."

"Grant's an alpinist," Magnus said another time. "He's stacking us all in a neat line so he can climb over our backs. You just wait and see."

"But at least he's bright, darling. At least he can keep up with you, can't he?"

For the truth was, of course, that given the limitations of any diplomatic friendship, the Pyms and the Lederers were one of the great quartets, and it was just

Magnus's perverse way of liking people to kick at them and pick holes in them and swear he would never talk to them again. The Lederers' daughter Becky was the same age as Tom and they were practically lovers already; Bee and Mary got on like a house on fire. As to Bee and Magnus—well frankly Mary did wonder sometimes whether they weren't the tiniest bit *too* friendly. But, on the other hand, she had noticed that with quartets there was always one strong diagonal relationship even if it never came to anything. And if it ever *did* come to something between them —well, to be absolutely *totally* frank, Mary would be quite willing to take her revenge with Grant, whose lurking intensity she found increasingly to be rather a turn-on.

"Mary, cheers, okay? A great party. We're loving it."

It was Bee, for ever toasting everyone. She was wearing diamond earrings and a décolleté which Mary had been eying all evening. Three children and breasts like that: it was bloody unfair. Mary lifted her glass in return. Bee has typist's fingers, she noticed, crooked at the tips.

"Now Grant, old boy, come on now," Magnus was saying, in his half-serious banter. "Give us a break, be fair. If everything your gallant President tells us about the Communist countries is true, how the devil can we do a deal with any of them?"

Out of the corner of her eye Mary saw Grant's droll smile stretch until it looked like snapping in itchy admiration of Pym's wit.

"Magnus, if I had my way, we'd set you up on a big Embassy carpet with a shaker full of dry Martinis and an American passport and magic you right back to Washington and have you pick up the Democratic ticket. I never heard a seditious case put so well."

"Draft Magnus for President?" Bee purred, sitting up straight and pressing out her breasts as if somebody had offered her a chocolate. "Oh goody."

At which point the ostentatiously menial Herr Wenzel appeared and, bowing elaborately over Magnus, murmured in his left ear that he was required urgently —forgive, Excellency—on the telephone from London—Herr Counsellor, excuse.

Magnus excused. Magnus excuses everybody. Magnus picked his way delicately between imaginary obstacles to the door, smiling and empathising and excusing, while Mary chatted all the more brightly to provide him with covering fire. But as the door closed behind him something unforeseen occurred. Grant Lederer glanced at Bee, and Bee Lederer glanced at Grant. And Mary caught them at it and her blood ran cold.

Why? What had passed between them in that one unguarded look? Was Magnus really sleeping with Bee—and had Bee *told* Grant? Were they momentarily joined, the two of them, in perplexed admiration of their departed host? In all the turmoil since, Mary's answer to those questions had not budged an inch. It wasn't sex, it wasn't love, it wasn't envy and it wasn't friendship. It was conspiracy. Mary was not fanciful. But Mary had seen and she knew. They were a pair of murderers telling each other "soon" and the soon was about Magnus. Soon we shall have him. Soon his hubris will be purged and our honour restored. I saw them hate him, thought Mary. She had thought it then, she thought it now.

"Grant is a Cassius looking for a Caesar," Magnus had said. "If he doesn't find a back to stab soon, the Agency will give his dagger to someone else."

Yet in diplomacy nothing lasts, nothing is absolute, a conspiracy to murder is no grounds for endangering the flow of conversation. Chatting busily, talking children and shopping—hunting frantically for an explanation for the Lederers' bad look—waiting, above all, for Magnus to return to the party and re-enchant his end of the table in two languages at once—Mary still found time to wonder whether this urgent telephone call from London might be the one her husband had been waiting for all these weeks. She had known for some while that he had something big going on, and she was praying it was the promised reinstatement.

And it was at this moment, as Mary remembered it while she was still chatting and still praying for her husband's luck to change, that she felt his fingertips skip knowingly over her naked shoulders as he returned to his place at the head of the table. She hadn't even heard the door, though she'd been listening for it.

"Everything all right, darling?" she called to him over the candelabra, playing it openly because the Pyms were so frightfully happily married.

"Her Maj in good shape, Magnus?" she heard Grant enquire in his insinuating drawl. "No rickets? Croup?"

Pym's smile was radiant and relaxed but that didn't always mean too much, as Mary knew. "Just one of Whitehall's little rumbles, Grant," he replied with magnificent casualness. "I think they must have a spy here who tells them when I'm giving a dinner party. Darling, are we out of claret? Jolly mingy rations, I must say."

Oh, Magnus, she had thought excitedly: you chancer.

It was time to get the women upstairs for a pee before coffee. The Frau Oberregierungsrat, who held herself to be modern, was inclined to resist. A scowl from her husband dislodged her. But Bee Lederer, who by this time in the evening was disposed to become the great American feminist—Bee left like a lamb, peremptorily handed out by her sexy little husband.

"Now comes the punch," says Jack Brotherhood contentedly, in Mary's imagination.

"There is no punch."

"Then why are we shaking, dear?" says Brotherhood.

"I'm not shaking. I'm just pouring myself a small drink waiting for you to arrive. You know I always shake."

"I'll have mine straight, please, same as you. Just give it me the way it happened. No ice, no fizz, no bullshit."

Very well then, damn you, have it.

The night is ending as perfectly as it began. In the hall Mary and Magnus help the guests to their coats and Mary cannot help noticing how Magnus, whose life is service, stiffens his arms and curls his fingers with each successfully negotiated sleeve. Magnus has invited the Lederers to linger but Mary has covertly countermanded this by telling Bee, with a giggle, that Magnus needs an early night. The hall empties. The diplomatic Pyms, ignoring the cold—they are English after all—stand valiantly on their doorstep and wave farewell. Mary has an arm around Pym's waist and she is secretly poking her thumb inside the waistband of his trousers at the back and down the partition of his buttocks. Magnus does not resist her. Magnus does not resist. Her head rests affectionately on his shoulder as she whispers sweet nothings into the same ear Herr Wenzel employed to summon him to the telephone and she hopes that Bee will notice their lovey-doveyness. Under the porch light—Mary luminously youthful in her long blue dress, Magnus so distinguished in his dinner-jacket—we must have looked the picture of harmonious married life. The Lederers leave last and are the most effusive. "Dammit, Magnus, I don't remember when I had such a good time," says Grant, with his quaint, rather faggy indignation. They are followed by their bodyguard in a second car. Side by side the very English Pyms enjoy a moment of shared disdain for the American way.

"Bee and Grant are terrific fun, really," says Mary. "But would *you* have a bodyguard if Jack offered you one?" There is more to her question than mere curiosity. She has been wondering recently about the odd people who seem to loiter outside the house with nothing to do.

"Not bloody likely," Pym retorts with a shudder. "Not unless he'll promise to protect me from Grant."

Mary extracts her thumb, they turn and arm in arm go indoors. "Is everything all right?" she asks, thinking of the phone call. Everything is absolutely fine, he replies. "I want you," Mary whispers boldly and lets her hand brush across his thighs. Smiling, Pym nods and pulls at his tie, loosening it apparently in preparation. In the kitchen the Wenzels are waiting to leave. Mary can smell cigarette smoke but decides to ignore it because they have worked so hard. On her deathbed she will remember that she took the conscious decision to ignore their cigarette smoke: that her life at that moment was so relaxed, Lesbos so far away, her sense of service so complete, that she was able to consider matters of such massive triviality. Pym has the Wenzels' money ready for them in an envelope plus a handsome tip. Magnus will tip with his last fiver, thinks Mary indulgently. His generosity is something she has learned to love even when her more frugal upper-class approach tells her he overdoes it: Magnus is so seldom vulgar. Even when at times she wonders whether he is overspending and she should offer him some from her private income. The Wenzels leave. Tomorrow night they will do another party at another house. The Pyms in close harmony move to the drawing-room, hands linking and breaking and ranging freely for the ritual foreplay of a nightcap and a gossipy post-mortem. Pym pours a scotch for Mary and a vodka for himself but unusually does not remove his jacket. Mary is fondling him explicitly. Sometimes in these cases they don't manage to get up the stairs.

"Super venison, Mabs," says Pym. Which was what he always does first: congratulate her. Magnus congratulates everyone all the time.

"They all thought Frau Wenzel cooked it," says Mary, feeling for the top of his zip.

"Then sod them," says Pym gallantly, rejecting the whole fatuous diplomatic world for her with a sweep of his forearm. For a moment Mary fears that Magnus has had one too many. She hopes not for she is not pretending: after the worries and fatuities of the evening she wants him very much. Handing Mary her glass, Magnus raises his own and drinks to her silently: well done, old girl. He is smiling straight down at her, his knees are almost touching hers and steady. Affected by the tension in him Mary wants him urgently here and now and gives him further clear evidence of this with her hands.

"If Grant Lederer is the *third,*" she asks, thinking again for a moment of that murderous look, "what on earth were the first two like?"

"I'm free," says Pym.

Mary fails to understand. She thinks he is capping her joke in some way.

"I don't get it," she says a little shamefacedly. I'm so slow for him, poor love. A sudden awful thought. "You don't mean they've sacked you?" she says.

Magnus shakes his head. "Rick's dead," he explains.

"Who?" Which Rick does he mean? Rick from Berlin? Rick from Langley? Which Rick is dead who can be setting Magnus free and, who knows, making space for his promotion?

Magnus begins again. Perfectly reasonably. Clearly the poor girl has not understood. She is tired from her long evening. She's had a couple too many. "Rick, my father, is dead. He died of a heart attack at six this evening while we were changing. They thought he was okay after the last one but it turns out he wasn't. Jack Brotherhood phoned from London. Why the hell Personnel gave it to Jack to break to me rather than break it to me themselves is a secret not ours to share, presumably. But they did."

And Mary even then doesn't get it right.

"What do you mean—free?" she shouts wildly as all constraint leaves her. "Free of what?" Then very sensibly she bursts out weeping. Loud enough for both of them. Loud enough to drown her own dreadful questions from Lesbos all the way here.

And she has half a mind to weep again now, for Jack Brotherhood, as the front doorbell sounds through the house like a bugle call, three short peals as ever.

Pym briskly drew the curtains and switched on the light. He had stopped singing. He felt nimble. Setting down his briefcase with a little grunt, he peered gratefully around him, letting everything greet him in its own good time. The brass bedstead. Good morning. The embroidery picture above it exhorting him to love Jesus: I tried, but Rick always got in the way. The roll-top desk. The bakelite wireless that had listened to dear old Winston Churchill. Pym had imposed nothing of himself on this room. He was its guest, not its coloniser. What had drawn him here, back in those dark ages, all those lives ago? Even now, with so much else clear to him, a sleepiness came over him when he tried to make himself remember. So many lonely journeys and aimless walks in foreign cities led me here, so much fallow, solitary time. He had been catching trains, looking for somewhere, escaping from somewhere else. Mary was in Berlin—no, she was in Prague—they had been transferred a couple of months earlier, and it was being made clear to him even then that if he kept his nose clean in Prague, the Washington appointment would be next on the list. Tom was—good God, Tom was scarcely out of nappies. And Pym was in London for a conference—no, he wasn't, he was attending a three-day course on the latest methods of clandestine communication in a beastly little training house off Smith Square. The course over, he had taken a cab to Paddington. Mindlessly, the instinct guiding him. His head still crammed with useless knowledge about anodes and squash transmissions. He jumped on a train that was about to pull out and at Exeter crossed the platform and took another. What greater freedom than not knowing where you are going or why? Finding himself in the middle of nowhere, he spotted a bus bearing a vaguely familiar destination and boarded it.

This was granny-land. This was Sunday, when aunts rode to church with collection coins inside their gloves. From his spaceship on the upper deck, Pym gazed down fondly on chimney-pots, churches, dunes and slate roofs that looked as though they were waiting to be lifted up to Heaven by their topknots. The bus stopped, the conductor said "Far as we go, sir," and Pym alighted with a most curious sense of accomplishment. I'm there, he thought. I've found it at last, and I wasn't even looking for it. The very town, the very beach, exactly as I left them all those years ago. The day was sunny and the world empty. Probably it was lunch-time. He had lost count. What was certain was that Miss Dubber's steps were scrubbed so white it was a shame to tread on them, and a hymn tune issued from the house, together with a smell of roast chicken, blue bag, carbolic soap and godliness.

"Go away!" a thin voice shouted. "I'm on the top step and I can't reach the fuse and if I stretch any more I'll pop."

Five minutes later this room was his. His sanctuary. His safe house away from all the other safe houses. "Canterbury. The name is Canterbury," he heard himself say as, the fuse safely mended, he pressed a deposit on her. A city had found a home.

Stepping to the desk, Pym now slid back the top and began turning the contents of his pockets on to the leatherette surface. As a stocktaking preparatory to a shift in personality and premises. As a retrospective examination of today's events till now. One passport in the style of Mr. Magnus Richard Pym, colour of eyes green, hair light brown, member of Her Majesty's Foreign Service, born far too long ago. There was always something rather shocking after a lifetime of symbols and code-names, about seeing his own name, naked and undisguised, splurged over a travel document. One calfskin wallet, a Christmas present from Mary. In the left side credit cards, in the right two thousand Austrian schillings and three hundred English pounds in various and elderly notes, his escape money cautiously assem-bled, more available in the desk. The Metro car keys. She's got the other set. Photo of family on Lesbos, everybody absolutely fine. Scribbled address of girl he had met somewhere and forgotten. He put the wallet aside and, continuing with his inven-tory, drew from the same pocket one green airport boarding-card still valid for last night's British Airways flight to Vienna. The sight and touch of it intrigued him. This was when Pym voted with his feet, he thought. In all his life till now, perhaps the first completely selfish gesture he had made, with the noble exception of the room where he now sat. The first time he had said "I want" rather than "I ought."

At the cremation in a silent suburb he had had a suspicion that the tiny number of mourners was unnaturally inflated by somebody's watchers. There was nothing he could prove. He could hardly as chief mourner stand at the door of the chapel challenging each of his nine guests to state his business. And it was true that Rick's erratic path through life had attracted a host of people Pym had never set eyes on and never wished to. All the same the suspicion remained with him and grew as he drove to London Airport, and became a near certainty when he returned his car to the hire company, where two grey men were taking much too long to fill in their contract forms. Undeterred, he checked his suitcase to Vienna and, with this very boarding-card in his hand, passed through immigration and sat himself in the insanitary lounge behind his *Times*. When his flight was delayed, he almost con-cealed his irritation, but still contrived to let it show. When it was called, he hurried obediently forward to join the straggling crowd on its walk to the departure gate, the very picture of a dutiful conformer. As he did so he could almost feel, if he could not see, the two men peel away for tea and ping-pong back at base: let the Vienna bastards have him and good riddance, they were saying to each other. He turned a corner and advanced towards a moving walkway but did not board it. Instead he ambled, peering behind him as if in search of a delayed companion, then imperceptibly allowing himself to be borne backward by the opposing flow of passengers. Moments later he was showing his passport at the arrivals desk and receiving the quiet "Welcome home, sir" that is reserved for those with certain serial numbers. As a last and spontaneous precaution he had taken himself to the domestic airlines counter and enquired in a loose and general way that was calculated to annoy the busier clerk about flights to Scotland. Not Glasgow, thank you, just Edinburgh. Well hang on, you'd better give me Glasgow as well. Ah, a printed timetable, fantastic. Look, thank you *very* much. And you can issue me with a ticket if I buy one? Oh I see. Over there. Great.

Pym tore the boarding-card into small pieces and put them in the ashtray. How much did I plan, how much was spontaneous? It scarcely mattered. I am here to act, not brood. One coach ticket, Heathrow-Reading. It had rained on the journey. One single rail ticket, Reading-London, unused, bought to deceive. One night-sleeper ticket, Reading-Exeter, issued on board the train. He had worn a beret and kept his face in shadow while buying it from the drunk attendant. Tearing these also into small pieces, Pym added them to the pile in the ashtray and, whether out of habit or for some more aggressive reason, set a match to them and gazed into the flames with an unblinking fixity. He'd half a mind to burn his passport, too, but a residual squeamishness restrained him, which he found quaint about himself and rather endearing. I planned it to the last detail—I who have never taken a conscious decision in my life. I planned it on the day I joined the Firm in a part of my head I never knew about until Rick died. I planned everything except Miss Dubber's cruise.

The flames dwindled, he broke up the ash, took off his coat and hung it over the back of the chair. From a chest of drawers he hauled an old cardigan, hand-knitted by Miss Dubber, and put it on.

I'll talk to her about it again, he thought. I'll think of something she'd like more. I'll pick my moment better. The important thing for her is to have a change of scene, he thought. Somewhere she doesn't have to worry.

Suddenly needing an activity, he switched out the lights, slipped quickly to the window, opened the curtains and set to work checking out the little square, life by life and window by window as the morning woke it, while he searched for tell-tale signs of watchers. In her kitchen, the wife of the Baptist minister, wearing her lovat dressing-gown, is unpegging her son's football gear from the washing line in preparation for today's match. Pym draws back swiftly. He has caught a glint of steel in the manse gateway, but it is only the minister's bicycle still chained to the trunk of a monkey-puzzle tree as a precaution against unchristian covetousness. In the frosted bathroom window of Sea View a woman in a grey slip is stooped over a handbasin soaping her hair. Celia Venn, the doctor's daughter who wants to paint the sea, is evidently expecting company today. Next door to her at number 8 Mr. Barlow the builder and his wife are watching breakfast television. Pym's eye passes methodically on, until a parked van holds his attention. The passenger door opens, a girlish figure flits stealthily through the central gardens and vanishes into number 28. Ella, the daughter of the undertaker, is discovering life.

Pym closed the curtains and put the lights back on. I will make my own daytime and my own night. The briefcase stood where he had left it, strangely rigid from its steel lining. Everybody carried cases, he remembered, as he stared at it. Rick's was pigskin, Lippsie's was cardboard, Poppy's was a scruffy grey thing with marks printed on it to look like hide. And Jack—dear Jack—you have your marvellous old attaché case, faithful as the dog you had to shoot.

Some people, you see, Tom, they leave their bodies to a teaching hospital. The hands go to this class, the heart to that one, the eyes to another, everyone gets something, everyone is grateful. Your father, however, has only his secrets. They're his provenance and his curse.

With a bump, he sat down at the desk.

To tell it straight, he rehearsed. Word for word the truth. No evasions, no fictions, no devices. Just my overpromised self set free.

To tell it to no one in particular, and to everyone. To tell it to all of you who own me, to whom I have given myself with such unthinking liberality. To my handlers and paymasters. To Mary and all the other Marys. To anyone who had a piece of me, was promised more and duly disappointed. And to whatever of myself remained after the great Pym share-out.

To all my creditors and co-owners incorporated, here once and for all the settlement of arrears that Rick so often dreamed of and that shall now be achieved in his only acknowledged son. Whoever Pym was to you, whoever you are or were, here is the last of many versions of the Pym you thought you knew.

Pym took a deep breath and puffed it out again.

You do it once. Once in your life and that's it. No rewrites, no polishing, no evasions. No would-it-be-better-this-ways. You're the male bee. You do it once, and die.

He took up a pen, then a single sheet of paper. He scribbled some lines, whatever came into his head. All work and no play makes Jack a dull spy. Poppy, Poppy, on the wall. Miss Dubber must a-cruising go. Eat good bread, poor Rickie's dead. Rickie-Tickie father. His hand ran smoothly, not a crossing-out. Sometimes, Tom, we have to do a thing in order to find out the reason for it. Sometimes our actions are questions, not answers.

2

A black and gusty day then, Tom, as sabbaths in these parts mostly are, I saw a crop of them as a child and I don't remember a sunny one. I hardly remember outdoors at all except when I was hurried through it like a child criminal on my way to church. But I am running ahead already, for Pym on this particular day was not yet born. The time is all your father's life ago plus half-a-dozen months, the place a seaboard town not too far from this one, with more of a slope to it and a thicker tower—but this one will do quite as well. A swirling, sopping doom-laden mid-morning, take my word for it, and myself, as I say, an unborn ghost, not ordered, not delivered and certainly not paid for: myself a deaf microphone, planted but inactive in any but the biological meaning. Old leaves, old pine needles and old confetti stick to the wet church steps as the humble flow of worshippers files in for its weekly dose of perdition or salvation, though I never saw that much to choose between the two of them. And myself a mute and foetal spy, unconsciously fulfilling his first mission in a place normally devoid of targets.

Except that today something is up. There's a buzz around, and its name is Rick. There's a spark of mischief to their piety today they can't keep dim and it comes from inside themselves, from the smouldering centre of their dark little sphere, and Rick is its owner and its origin and its instigator. You can read it everywhere: in the portentous, rolling tread of the brown-suited deacon, in the fluttering and exhaling of the hatted women who arrive in a rush imagining they are late, then sit blushing through their white face-powder because they are early. Everyone agog, everyone on tiptoe and a first-class turn-out, as Rick would have remarked proudly, and probably he did, for he loved a full house whatever happened, never mind it was his own hanging. A few of them have come by car—such wonders of the day as Lanchesters and Singers—others by trolley-bus, and some have walked; and God's sea rain has given them beards of cold inside their cheap fox stoles, and God's sea wind is cutting through the threadbare serge of their Sunday best. Yet there is not one of them, however he has come, who does not brave the weather a second longer to pause and goggle at the noticeboard and confirm with his own eyes what the bush telegraph has been telling him these several days. Two posters are fixed to it, both smeared by rain, both to the passer-by as dreary as cups of cold tea. Yet to those who know the code they transmit an electrifying signal. The first in orange proclaims the five-thousand-pound appeal, mounted by the Baptist Women's League, to provide a reading-room—though all of them know that no book will ever be read in it, that it will be a place to set out homemade cakes and photographs of leprous children in the Congo. A plywood thermometer, designed by Rick's best craftsmen, is fastened to the railings revealing that the first thousand has already been achieved. The second notice, green, declares that today's address will be given by the minister, all welcome. But this information has been corrected. A rigid bulletin has been pinned over it, typed in full like a legal warning, with the comically misplaced capital letters that in these parts signal omens.

Due to unforeseen Circumstances, Sir Makepeace Watermaster, Justice of the Peace and Liberal Member of Parliament for this Constituency, will provide today's Message. Appeal Committee please to Remain behind Afterwards for an Extraordinary meeting.

Makepeace Watermaster himself! And they know why!

Elsewhere in the world, Hitler is winding himself up to set fire to the universe, in America and Europe the miseries of the Depression are spreading like an incurable plague, and Jack Brotherhood's forebears are abetting them or not according to whatever spurious doctrine of the day prevails in the deniable corridors of Whitehall. But the congregation doesn't presume to hold opinions on these impenetrable aspects of God's purpose. Theirs is the dissenting church and their temporal overlord is Sir Makepeace Watermaster, the greatest preacher and Liberal ever born, and one of the Highest in the Land, who gave them this very building out of his own purse. He didn't, of course. His father Goodman gave it to them, but Makepeace, having succeeded to the fiefdom, has a way of forgetting that his father existed. Old Goodman was a Welshman, a preaching, singing, widowed, miserable potteryman with two children twenty-five years apart of whom Makepeace is the elder. Goodman came here, sampled the clay, sniffed the sea air and built a pottery. A couple of years later he built two more and imported cheap migrant labour to man them, first Low Welsh like himself and afterwards and cheaper still and lower, the persecuted Irish. Goodman lured them with his tied cottages, starved them with his rotten wages, and beat the fear of Hell into them from his pulpit before himself being taken off to Paradise, witness the unassuming monument to him six thousand feet high that stood in the pottery forecourt until a few years ago when the whole lot was ripped down to make way for a bungalow estate and good riddance.

And today *due to unforeseen Circumstances* that same Makepeace, Goodman's only son, is coming down from his mountain-top—though the circumstances have been foreseen by everyone except himself, the circumstances are as palpable as the pews we wait in, as immovable as the Watermaster tiles the pews are bolted to, as fateful as the rasping clock that wheezes and whistles between every chime like a dying sow fighting off the awful end. Picture the gloom of it—how it stultified its young and dragged them down, its prohibition of everything exciting that they cared about: from Sunday newspapers to Popery, from psychology to art, from flimsy underwear to high spirits to low spirits, from love to laughter and back again, I don't think there was a corner of the human state where their disapproval did not fall. Because if you don't understand the gloom of it, you'll not understand the world that Rick was running away from or the world he was running towards, or the twisting relish that buzzes and tickles like a flea in every humble breast this dark sabbath as the last chimes merge with the drumming of the rain and the first great trial of young Rick's life begins. "Rick Pym's for the high jump at last," says the word. And what more awesome executioner than Makepeace himself, Highest in the Land, Justice of the Peace and Liberal Member of Parliament, to adjust the noose around his neck?

With the last chime of all, the strains of the voluntary die also. The congregation holds its breath and starts counting to a hundred while it seeks out its favourite actors. The two Watermaster women have arrived early. They sit shoulder to shoulder in the pew for notables directly beneath the pulpit. On almost any other Sunday, Makepeace would have been roosting there between them, all six foot six of him, his long head cocked to one side while he listened to the voluntary with his moist little rosebud ears. But not today because today is extra, today Makepeace is in the wings conferring with our Minister and certain worried trusties from the Appeal Committee.

Makepeace's wife, known as Lady Nell, is not yet fifty but already she is hunched and shrivelled like a witch, with a habit of flicking her greying head without warning as if she were shaking off flies. And next to her—a tiny, earnest statue beside Nell's pecking and stupidity—perches Dorothy, rightly called Dot, an immaculate speck of a lady, young enough to be Nell's daughter instead of Makepeace's sister—and she is praying, praying to her Maker, she is pushing her tiny scrumpled fists into her eyes while she pledges her life and death to Him if only He will hear her and make it right. Baptists do not kneel before God, Tom. They squat. But my Dorothy would have stretched herself flat on the Watermaster tiles and kissed the Pope's big toe that day if God would have let her off the hook.

I have one photograph of her and there have been times—though no longer, I swear it, she is dead for me—when I would have given my soul for just one more. I found it in an old scuffed Bible when I was Tom's age, in a suburban mansion we were hastily vacating. "To Dorothy with all my special love, Makepeace," runs the inscription on the inside page. One in all the world. One spotted sepia-brown photograph is all, taken like a pause in flight as she steps down from the taxi, licence number not in frame, clutching a homemade posy of small flowers that could be wild, and her big eyes have too much behind them for our comfort. Is she on her way to a wedding? To her own? Is she calling on a sick relative—on Nell? Where is she? Where is she escaping to this time? She has the flowers to her chin and her elbows pressed together. Her forearms form a vertical line from waist to neck. Long sleeves nipped at the wrist. Muslin gloves, therefore no rings visible, though I have a suspicion of a bulge in the third joint of the third finger of the left hand. A cloche bonnet covers her hair and throws a shadow like a mask across the scaring eyes. Shoulders on a slant, as if she is on the point of losing her balance, and one tiny foot tipped sideways to prevent her. Her pale stockings have the zigzag sheen of silk; her shoes are of patent leather, pointed, buttoned. And somehow I know they pinch her, that they were bought against the clock like the rest of her outfit, in a shop where she is not known and does not wish to be. Her lower face pale as a plant grown in the dark—think of The Glades, the house she was brought up in! An only child, as I was, you can see it at a glance—never mind she has a brother twenty-five years ahead of her.

Shall I tell you what I found once, in the summerhouse in the Watermasters' great dark orchard, where I myself, a child like her, was wandering? The colouring book she had won at Bible class, *The Life of Our Saviour in Pictures*. And do you know what my darling Dot had done with it? Scored out every saintly face with savage crayoning. I was shocked at first, until I understood. Those faces were the dreaded ones from the real world she had no part of. They enjoyed all the companionship and kindly smiles she never had. So she coloured them out. Not in rage. Not in hate. Not even in envy. But because their ease of living was beyond her grasp. Look again at the photograph. The jaw. The stern unsmiling jaw locking out expression. The little mouth clamped shut and downward to keep its secrets safe. That face cannot discard a single bad memory or experience, because it has nobody to share them with. It is condemned to store every one of them away until the day when it will break from overloading.

Enough. I'm running out ahead. Dot, a.k.a. Dorothy, family name Watermaster. No connection with any other firm. An abstraction. Mine. An unreal, empty woman permanently in flight. If she had had her back to me and not her face, I could not have known her less or loved her more.

And behind the Watermaster women, far behind, by chance as far as the great long aisle allows, at the very back of the church, in their chosen pew directly beside the closed doors, sits the flower of our young men, their neckties pulled up and outward from their stiff collars, their slicked hair parted in a razor slash. These are the Night School Boys, as they are affectionately known, our Tabernacle's apostles of tomorrow, our white hopes, our future ministers of religion, our doctors, missionaries, and philanthropists, our future Highest in the Land, who will one day go out into the world and Save it as it has never been Saved before. It is they who by their zeal have acquired the duties customarily entrusted to older men: the distributing of hymn books and special notices, the taking of collection money and the hanging up of overcoats. It is they who once a week, by bicycle, motorcycle and kindly parents' motorcars, distribute our church magazine to every god-fearing front door, including that of Sir Makepeace Watermaster himself, whose cook has standing orders that a piece of cake and a glass of lemon barley be always waiting for the bringer; they who collect the few shillings of rent from the church's poor cottages, who pilot the pleasure boats on Brinkley Mere at children's outings, host the Band of Hope's Christmas bunfights and put fire into Christian Endeavour action week. And it is they who have taken upon themselves as a direct commission from Jesus the burden of the Women's League Appeal, target five thousand pounds, at a time when two hundred would maintain a family for a year. Not a doorbell they have not pressed along their pilgrimage. Not a window they have not offered to clean, flower-bed to weed and dig for Jesus. Day after day the young troops have marched out, to return, reeking of peppermint, long after their parents are asleep. Sir Makepeace has sung their praises, so has our minister. No sabbath is complete without a reminder to Our Father regarding their devotion. And bravely the red line on the plywood thermometer at the church gates has climbed through the fifties, the hundreds to the first thousand, where for a while now, for all their efforts, it has seemed to stick. Not that they have lost momentum, far from it. Failure is not in their thoughts. No need for Makepeace Watermaster to remind them of Bruce's spider, though he often does. The Night School Boys are "crackerjack," as our saying goes. The Night School Boys are Christ's own vanguard and they will be the Highest in the Land.

There are five of them and at their centre sits Rick, their founder, manager, guiding spirit and treasurer, still dreaming of his first Bentley. Rick, full names Richard Thomas after his dear old father, the beloved TP, who fought in the Great War trenches before he became our mayor, and passed away these seven years ago, though it seems like only yesterday, and what a preacher *he* was before his Maker took him back! Rick, your grandfather without portfolio, Tom, because I would never let you meet him.

I have two versions of Makepeace's Message, both incomplete, both shorn of time or place or origin: yellowed press-cuttings, hacked apparently with nail-scissors from the ecclesiastical pages of the local press, which in those days reported our preachers' doings as loyally as if they were our footballers. I found them in Dorothy's same Bible with her photograph. Makepeace accused nobody outright, Makepeace framed no charge. This is the land of innuendo; straight speaking is for sinners. "M.P. sounds Stern Warning against Youthful Covetousness, Greed," sings the first. "Perils of young Ambition splendidly Highlighted." In Makepeace's imposing person, the anonymous writer declares, "are met the poet's Celtic grace, the Statesman's eloquence, the lawgiver's Iron sense of Justice." The congregation was "spellbound unto the Meekest of its Members," and none more so than Rick himself, who sits in an enraptured trance, nodding his broad head to the cadences of Makepeace's rhetoric, even though every Welsh note of it—to the excited ears and eyes of those around him—is hurled at Rick personally down the length of the aisle, and rammed home with a botched stab of the lugubrious Watermaster forefinger.

The second version takes a less apocalyptic tone. The Highest in the Land was not ranting against youth's sinfulness, far from it. He was offering succour to the youthful falterer. He was extolling youth's ideals, likening them to stars. To believe this second version, you would suppose Makepeace had gone star crazy. He couldn't get away from the things, nor could the writer. Stars as our destiny. Stars that guide Wise Men across deserts to the very Cradle of Truth. Stars to lighten the darkness of our despair, yea even in the pit of sin. Stars of every shape, for every occasion. Shining above us like God's very light. The writer must have been Makepeace Watermaster's property, body and soul, if it wasn't Makepeace himself. Nobody else could have sweetened that awesome, forbidding apparition in the pulpit.

Though my eyes were not yet open on this day, I see him as clearly as I saw him later in the flesh, and shall see him always: tall as one of his own factory chimneys, and as tapered. Rubbery, with weak pinched shoulders and a wide bendy waist. One jointless arm tipped out at us like a railway signal, one baggy hand flapping on the end of it. And the wet, elastic little mouth that should have been a woman's, too small even to feed him by, stretching and contracting as it labours to deliver the indignant vowels. And when at long, long last, enough awesome warnings have been uttered, and the penalties of sin outlined in sufficient detail, I see him brace himself and lean back and moisten his lips for the kiss-off, which we children have been begging for these forty minutes while we crossed our legs and died for a pee however often we had peed before we left home. One cutting gives this final preposterous passage in full, and I will give it again now—their text, not mine—though no Watermaster sermon I ever heard later was complete without it, though the words became part of Rick's very nature, and remained with him all his life and consequently mine, and I would be amazed if they did not ring in his ears as he died, and accompany him as he strode towards his Maker, two pals reunited at last:

"Ideals, my young brethren . . ." I see Makepeace pause here, shoot another glare at Rick and start again: "Ideals, my beloved brethren all, are to be likened unto those splendid stars above us"—I see him lift his sad, starless eyes to the pine roof—"we cannot reach them. Millions of miles separate us from them." I see him hold out his drooping arms as if to catch a falling sinner. "But oh my brethren, how greatly do we profit from their presence!"

Remember them, Tom. Jack, you'll think I'm mad, but those stars, however fatuous, are a crucial piece of operational intelligence, for they lend a first image to Rick's unquenchable conviction of his destiny, and it didn't stop with Rick either; how could it, for what is a prophet's son but himself a prophecy, even if nobody on God's earth ever discovers what either one of them is prophesying? Makepeace, like all great preachers, must do without a final curtain or applause. Nevertheless, quite audibly in the silence—I have witnesses who swear to it—Rick is heard to whisper "beautiful" twice over. Makepeace Watermaster hears it too—slurs his big feet and pauses on the pulpit steps, blinking round him as if somebody has called him a rude name. Makepeace sits down, the organ strikes up "what purpose burns within our hearts?" Makepeace stands again, unsure where to put his ridiculously tiny backside. The hymn is sung to its dreary end. Night School Boys, with Rick star-struck at their centre, process down the aisle and in a practised drill movement fan out to their appointed posts. Rick, smart as paint today and every Sunday, proffers the collecting plate to the Watermaster ladies, his blue eyes glistening with divine intelligence. How much will they give? How quickly? The silence lends tension to these massive questions. First comes Lady Nell, who keeps him waiting while she pecks in her handbag and curses, but Rick is all forbearance, all love, all stars today, and each lady regardless of age or beauty receives the benefit of his thrilled and saintly smile. But where daft Nell simpers at him and tries to muss his slicked hair and pull it forward over his broad, Christian brow, my little Dot is looking nowhere but at the ground, still praying, praying even while she stands, and Rick has actually to touch her forearm with his finger in order to alert her to his Godlike nearness. I can feel his touch now upon my own arm, and it sends a healer's charge through me of weak-kneed loathing and devotion. The boys line up before the Lord's table, the minister accepts the offerings, says a perfunctory blessing, then orders everyone but the Appeal Committee to leave at once and quietly. The unforeseen Circumstances are about to begin, and with them the first great trial of Richard T. Pym—the first of many, it is true, but this is the one that really whetted his appetite for Judgment.

I have seen him a hundred times as he stood that morning. Rick alone, brooding at the doorway of a crowded room. Rick his father's son, the glory of a great heritage creasing on his brow. Rick waiting, like Napoleon before the battle, for Destiny to sound the trumpets for his assault. He never made a lazy entrance in his life, he never fluffed his timing or his impact. Whatever you had in mind till then, you could forget it: the topic of the day had just walked in. So it is in the Tabernacle on this rainy sabbath, while God's wind booms in the pine rafters high above and the disconsolate huddle of humanity in the front pews waits awkwardly for Rick. But stars, we know, are like ideals and elusive. Heads begin to crane, chairs creak. Still no Rick. The Night School Boys, already in the dock, moisten their lips, tip nervously at their ties. Rickie's done a bunk. Rickie can't face the music. The deacon in his brown suit hobbles with an artisan's mysterious discomfort towards the vestry where Rick may have hidden. Then a thump. Round whips every head to the sound, till they stare straight back down the aisle at the great west door, which has been opened from outside by a mysterious hand. Silhouetted against the grey sea clouds of adversity, Rick T. Pym, until now David Livingstone's natural heir if ever we knew one, gravely bows to his judges and his Maker, closes the great door behind him, and all but vanishes once more against its blackness.

"Message from old Mrs. Harmann for you, Mr. Philpott." Philpott being the name of the minister. The voice being Rick's and everyone as usual remarking its beauty, rallying to it, loving it, scared and drawn by its unflinching self-assurance.

"Oh yes then?" says Philpott, very alarmed to be addressed so calmly from so far away. Philpott is a Welshman too.

"She'd be glad of a lift to Exeter General to see her husband before his operation tomorrow, Mr. Philpott," says Rick with just the tiniest note of a reproach. "She doesn't seem to think he'll pull through. If it's any bother to you I'm sure one of us can take care of her, can't we, Syd?"

Syd Lemon is a cockney whose father not long ago came south for his arthritis and in Syd's view will shortly die of boredom instead. Syd is Rick's best-loved lieutenant, a small, punchy fighter with the townie's nimbleness and twinkle, and Syd is Syd for ever to me, even now, and the nearest I ever came to a confessor, excluding Poppy.

"Sit with her all night if we have to," Syd affirms with strenuous rectitude. "All next day too, won't we, Rickie?"

"Be quiet," Makepeace Watermaster growls. But not to Rick, who is bolting the church doors from the inside. We can just make him out among the lights and darks of the porch. Clang goes the first bolt, high up, he has to reach for it. *Clang* the second, low down as he stoops to it. Finally, to the visible relief of the susceptible, he consents to embark on his forward journey to the scaffold. For by now the weaker of us are dependent on him. By now in our hearts we are begging a smile from him, the son of old TP, sending him messages assuring him that there is nothing personal, enquiring of him after the dear lady his poor mother—for the dear lady, as everybody knows, does not feel sufficiently herself today and nobody can budge her. She sits with a widow's majesty at home in Airdale Road behind drawn curtains under the tinted giant photograph of TP in his mayoral regalia, weeping and praying one minute to have her late husband given back to her, the next to have him stay put exactly where he is and be spared the disgrace, and the next rooting for Rick like the old punter she secretly is—"Hand it to them, son. Fight them down before they do the same to you, same as your dad did and better." By now the less worldly officers of our improvised tribunal have been converted if not actually corrupted to Rick's side. And as if to undermine their authority still further, Welsh Philpott in his innocence has made the error of placing Rick beside the pulpit in the very spot from which in the past he has read us the day's lesson with such brio and persuasion. Worse still, Welsh Philpott ushers Rick to this position and twitches the chair for Rick to sit on. But Rick is not so biddable. He remains standing, one hand rested comfortably on the chair's back as if he has decided to adopt it. Meanwhile he engages Mr. Philpott in a few more easy words of talk.

"I see Arsenal came a cropper Saturday, then," says Rick. Arsenal, in better times, being Mr. Philpott's second greatest love, as it was TP's.

"Never mind that now, Rick," says Mr. Philpott, all of a flurry. "We've business to discuss, as well you know."

Looking poorly the minister takes his place beside Makepeace Watermaster. But Rick's purpose is achieved. He has made a bond where Philpott wanted none; he has presented us with a feeling man instead of a villain. In recognition of his achievement Rick smiles. On all of us at once: grand of you to be among us here today. His smile sweeps over us; it is not impertinent, it is impressive in its compassion for the forces of human fallibility that have brought us to this unhappy pass. Only Sir Makepeace himself and Perce Loft the great solicitor from Dawlish, known as Perce the Writ, who sits beside him with the papers, preserve their granite disapproval. But Rick is not awed by them. Not by Makepeace and certainly not by Perce, with whom Rick has formed a fine relationship in recent months, based it is said on mutual respect and understanding. Perce wants Rick to read for the bar.

Rick is bent upon it but meanwhile wants Pierce to advise him on certain business transactions he is contemplating. Perce, ever an altruist, is supplying his services free.

"That was a wonderful sermon you gave us, Sir Makepeace," says Rick. "I never heard better. Those words of yours will ring inside my head like the bells of Heaven for as long as I'm spared, sir. Hullo, Mr. Loft."

Perce Loft is too official to reply. Sir Makepeace has had flattery before, and receives it as no more than his due.

"Sit down," says our Liberal Member of Parliament for this Constituency and Justice of the Peace.

Rick obeys at once. Rick is no enemy of authority. To the contrary he is a man of authority himself, as we waverers already know, a power and a justice in one.

"Where's the Appeal money gone?" Makepeace Watermaster demands without delay. "There was close on four hundred pound donated last month alone. Three hundred the month before, three hundred in August. Your accounts for the same period show one hundred and twelve pound received. Nothing put by and no cash in hand. What have you done with it, boy?"

"Bought a motor coach," says Rick, and Syd—to use his own words—seated in the dock with all the rest of them, has a hard time not corpsing.

Rick spoke for twelve minutes by Syd's dad's watch and when he'd done only Makepeace Watermaster stood between him and victory, Syd is sure of it: "The minister, he was won over before your dad ever opened his mouth, Titch. Well he had to be, he gave TP his first pulpit. Old Perce Loft—well, Perce had fish to fry by then, didn't he? Rick had stitched him up. The rest of them, they was going up and down like a tart's knickers from waiting to see which way The Lord High Makewater's going to jump."

First of all, Rick magnanimously claims full responsibility for everything. Blame, says Rick, if blame there be, should be laid squarely at his own door. Stars and ideals are nothing to the metaphors he flings at us: "If a finger is to be pointed, point it here." A stab at his own breast. "If a price is to be paid, here's the address. Here I am. Send me the bill. And leave them to learn by his mistakes who got them into this, if such there have been," he challenges them, beating the English language into submission with the blade of his plump hand by way of an example. Women admired those hands till the end of Rick's days. They drew conclusions from the girth of his fingers, which never parted when he made a gesture.

"Where did he get his rhetoric form?" I once asked Syd reverently, enjoying what he and Meg called "a small wet" at their fireside in Surbiton. "Who were his models, apart from Makepeace?"

"Lloyd George, Hartley Shawcross, Avory, Marshall Hall, Norman Birkett and other great advocates of his day," replied Syd promptly, as if they were the runners and starters for the two-thirty at Newmarket. "Your dad had more respect for the law than any man I ever knew, Titch. Studied their speeches, followed their form better than what he did the geegees. He'd have been a top judge if TP had given him the opportunities, wouldn't he, Meg?"

"He'd have been Prime Minister," Meg affirms devoutly. "Who else was there but him and Winston?"

Rick next passes to his Theory of Property which I have since heard him expound many times in many different ways but I believe this was its unveiling. The burden is that any money passing through Rick's hands is subject to a redefinition of the laws of property, since whatever he does with it will improve mankind, whose principal representative he is. Rick, in a word, is not a taker but a giver and those who call him otherwise lack faith. The final challenge comes in a mounting bombardment of passionate, grammatically unnerving pseudo-Biblical phrases. "And if any one of you here present today—can find evidence of a single advantage—one single benefit—be it in the past, be it stored away for the future—directly or indirectly from this enterprise—which I have derived—ambitious though it may have been, make no two ways about it—let him come forward now, with a clear heart—and point the finger where it belongs."

From there it is but a step to that sublime vision of the Pym & Salvation Coach Company Ltd., which will bring profit to piety and worshippers to our beloved Tabernacle.

The magic box is unlocked. Flinging back the lid Rick displays a dazzling confusion of promises and statistics. The present bus fare from Farleigh Abbott to our Tabernacle is twopence. The trolley-bus from Tambercombe costs threepence, four-up in a cab from either spot costs sixpence, a Granville Hastings motor coach costs nine hundred and eight pounds discounted for cash, and seats thirty-two fully loaded, eight standing. On the sabbath alone—my assistants here have made a most thorough survey, gentlemen—more than six hundred people travel an aggregate of over four thousand miles to worship at this fine Tabernacle. Because they love the place. As Rick does. As we all do, every man and woman here present—let's make no bones about it. Because they want to feel *drawn from the circumference to the centre,* in the spirit of their faith. (This last is one of Makepeace Watermaster's own expressions and Syd says it was a bit cheeky of Rick to throw it back in his face.) On three other days in the week, gentlemen—Band of Hope, Christian Endeavour and Women's League Bible Group—another seven hundred miles are travelled leaving three days clear for normal commercial operation, and if you don't believe me watch my forearm as it beats the doubters from my path in a series of convulsive elbow blows, the cupped fingers never parting. From such figures it is suddenly clear there can be only one conclusion.

"Gentlemen, if we charge *half* the standard fare *and* give a free ticket to every disabled and elderly person, to every child under the age of eight—with full insurance—observing all the fine regulations which rightly apply to the operation of commercial transport carriages in this increasingly hectic age of ours—with fully professional drivers with every awareness of their responsibilities, god-fearing men recruited from our own number—allowing for depreciation, garaging, maintenance, fuel, ticketing and sundries, and assuming a fifty-percent capacity on the three days of commercial operation—there's a forty-percent clear profit for the Appeal and room left over to see everybody right."

Makepeace Watermaster is asking questions. The others are either too full or too empty to speak at all.

"And you've bought it?" says Makepeace.

"Yes, sir."

"You're not of age, half of you."

"We used an intermediary, sir. A fine lawyer of this district who in his modesty wishes to remain anonymous."

Rick's reply draws a rare smile from the improbably tiny lips of Sir Makepeace Watermaster. "I never knew a lawyer who wished to remain anonymous," he says.

Perce Loft frowns distractedly at the wall.

"So where is it now?" Sir Makepeace continues.

"What, sir?"

"The coach, boy."

"They're painting it," says Rick. "Green with gold lettering."

"With whose permission, at any stage, have you embarked on this project?" asks Watermaster.

"We're asking Miss Dorothy to cut the tape, Sir Makepeace. We've drafted the invite already."

"Who gave you permission? Did Mr. Philpott here? Did the deacons? Did the committee? Did I? To spend nine hundred and eight pounds of Appeal funds, widows' mites, on a motor coach?"

"We wanted the element of surprise, Sir Makepeace. We wanted to sweep the board with them. Once you spread the word beforehand, talk it round town, you take the air out of it. P.S.C. is going to be sprung upon an unsuspecting world."

Makepeace now enters what Syd calls the dicey part.

"Where are the books?"

"Books, sir? There's only one Book I know of—"

"Your files, boy. Your figures. You alone kept the accounts, we heard."

"Give me a week, Sir Makepeace. I'll account for every penny."

"That's not keeping accounts. That's fudging them. Did you learn nothing at all from your father, boy?"

"Rectitude, sir. Humbleness before Jesus."

"How much have you spent?"

"Not spent, sir. Invested."

"How much?"

"Fifteen hundred. Rounded up."

"Where's the coach at present?"

"I said, sir. Being painted."

"Where?"

"Balham's of Brinkley. Coach-builders. Some of the finest Liberals in the county. Christians to a man."

"I know Balham's. TP sold timber to Balham's for ten years."

"They're charging cost."

"You propose to ply for trade in public, you say?"

"Three days a week, sir."

"Using the public coach stages?"

"Certainly."

"Are you familiar with the likely attitude to be taken by the Dawlish & Tambercombe Transport Corporation of Devon to this venture?"

"A popular demand like this—those boys can't block it, Sir Makepeace. We've got God driving for us. Once they see the ground-swell, feel the pulse, they'll back away and give us our heads all the way to the top. They can't stop progress, Sir Makepeace, and they can't stop the march of Christian people."

"Can't they," says Sir Makepeace, and scribbles figures on a piece of paper in front of him. "There's eight hundred and fifty pound in rent money missing as well," he remarks as he writes.

"We invested the rent money too, sir."

"That's more than the fifteen hundred then."

"Call it two thousand. Rounded up. I thought you only meant the Appeal money."

"What about the collection money?"

"Some of it."

"Counting all monies from any source, what's the total capital? Rounded up."

"Including private investors, Sir Makepeace—"

Watermaster sat up straight: "So we've private investors too, have we? My gracious, boy, you've been going it a bit. Who are they?"

"Private clients."

"Of whom?"

Perce Loft looks as though he is about to fall asleep out of sheer boredom. His eyelids are two inches long, his goatish head has slipped forward on his neck.

"Sir Makepeace, I am not at liberty to reveal this. When P.S.C. promises confidentiality, that's what she delivers. Our watchword is integrity."

"Has the company been incorporated?"

"No, sir."

"Why not?"

"Security, sir. Keep it under wraps. Like I said."

Makepeace begins jotting again. Everybody waits for more questions. None come. An uncomfortable air of completeness settles over Makepeace, and Rick senses it faster than anybody. "It was like being up the old doctor's, Titch," Syd told me, "when he's made up his mind what you're dying of, only he's got to write out this prescription before he gives you the good news."

Rick speaks again. Unprompted. It was the voice he used when he was cornered. Syd heard it then, I heard it later only twice. It was not a pretty tone at all.

"I could bring those accounts up to you this evening, as a matter of fact, Sir Makepeace. They're in safekeeping, you see. I'll have to get them out."

"Give them to the police," says Makepeace, still writing. "We're not detectives here, we're churchmen."

"Miss Dorothy might think a bit different, though, mightn't she, Sir Makepeace?"

"Miss Dorothy has nothing to do with this."

"Ask her."

Then Makepeace stops writing and his head comes up a bit sharpish, says Syd, and they look at each other, Makepeace with his little baby eyes uncertain. And Rickie, suddenly his gaze has the glint of a flick-knife in the dark. Syd does not go as far as I shall in describing that stare because Syd won't touch the black side of his lifelong hero. But I will. It looks out of him like a child through the eyeholes of a mask. It denies everything it stood for not a half-second earlier. It is pagan. It is amoral. It regrets your decision and your mortality. But it has no choice because you cannot go back.

"Are you telling me Miss Dorothy is an investor in this project?" says Makepeace.

"You can invest more than money, Sir Makepeace," says Rick, from far away but close.

Now the point is, says Syd rather hastily here, Makepeace should never have driven Rick to use that argument. Makepeace was a weak man acting hard and they're the worst, says Syd. If Makepeace had been reasonable, if he'd been a believer like the rest and thought a little better of poor TP's boy instead of lacking faith and undermining everybody else's into the bargain, things could have been settled in a friendly, positive way and everyone could have gone home happy, believing in Rick and his coach the way he needed them to. As it was, Makepeace was the last barrier and he left Rickie no alternative but to knock him down. So Rickie did, didn't he? Well he had to, Titch.

I strain and stretch, Tom, I shove with every muscle of my imagination as deep as I dare into the heavy shadows of my own pre-history. I put down my pen and stare at the hideous church tower across the square, and I can hear as plain as Miss Dubber's television downstairs the ill-contrasted voices of Rick and Sir Makepeace Watermaster matched against each other. I see the dark drawing-room of The Glades where I was so seldom admitted and I picture the two men closeted together there that evening alone, and my poor Dorothy trembling in our murky upper room reading the same hand-stitched homilies that now adorn Miss Dubber's landings as she tries to suck comfort from God's flowers, God's love, God's will. And I could tell you, I think near enough to a sentence or two, what passed between them by way of continuing their unfinished chat of that morning.

Rick's spirits are back, because the flick-knife never shows for long and because he has already achieved the object that is more important to him than any other in his human dealings, even if he himself does not yet know it. He has inspired Makepeace to hold two totally divergent opinions of him and perhaps more. He has shown him the official and unofficial versions of his identity. He has taught him to respect Rick in his complexity and to reckon as much with Rick's secret world as with his overt one. It is as if in the privacy of that room each player revealed the many cards, fake or real is of no account, that comprised his hand: and Makepeace was left without a chip in front of him. But the fact is, both men are dead, both took their secret to the grave, Sir Makepeace going ahead by thirty years. And the one person who may still know it cannot speak, because if she exists at all any more, then it is only as a ghost, haunting her own life and mine, killed long ago by the very consequences of the two men's fateful dialogue that evening.

History records two meetings between Rick and my Dorothy before that sabbath. The first when she made a royal visit to the Young Liberals Club, of which Rick was at that time an elected officer—I believe, God help them, treasurer. The second when Rick was captain of the Tabernacle's football team and one Morrie Washington, a Night School Boy and another of Rick's lieutenants, was goalie. Dorothy, as sister of the Sitting Member, was invited to present the cup. Morrie remembers the line-up ceremony, with Dorothy walking along the troops and pinning a medal to each victorious breast, starting with Rick himself as captain. It seems she fumbled the clasp, or that Rick pretended she did. Either way, he let out a playful cry of pain and went down on one knee, clutching his bosom and insisting she had pierced him to the heart. It was a bold and rather naughty number and I am surprised he took it so far. Even in burlesque, Rick was normally very protective of his dignity, and at fancy-dress balls, which were the rage until the war came, he preferred to go as Lloyd George rather than risk ridicule. But down he went, Morrie remembered it like yesterday, and Dorothy laughed, a thing nobody had ever seen her do: laugh. What assignations followed we can never know, except that, according to Morrie, Rick did once boast that there was more than cake and lemon barley waiting for him up at The Glades when he delivered the church magazine.

Syd, I think, knows more than Morrie. Syd saw a lot. And people tell him things because he keeps his counsel. Syd, I believe, knows most of the secrets that lurked in the wooded house that Makepeace Watermaster called his home, even if in old age he has done his best to bury them six foot under. He knows why Lady Nell drank and why Makepeace was so ill-at-ease with himself, and why his damp little eyes were so tormented, and his mouth unequal to his appetites, and why he was able to castigate sin with such passionate familiarity. And why he wrote of a special love when he put his wretched name in my Dorothy's Bible. And why it was that Dorothy had taken herself to the furthest corner of the house to sleep, far from Lady Nell's rooms and further still from Makepeace's. And why Dorothy was so accessible to the smart-tongued upstart from the football team who spoke as if he could build her a road to anywhere, and drive her there in his coach. But Syd is a good man and a Mason. He loved Rick and gave the best years of his life, now to roistering with him, now to hanging on to his coat-tails. Syd would have a laugh, he would tell a story, provided it hurt nobody too much. But Syd won't touch the black side.

History records also that Rick took no account books to that meeting, though Mr. Muspole the great accountant, another Night School Boy, offered to help him write some and probably did. Muspole could invent accounts the way others can write postcards on holiday or rattle off anecdotes into a microphone. And that in order to prepare himself, Rick took a stroll over Brinkley Cliffs, alone, which I believe is the first known walk of this kind, though Rick, like myself after him, was always a one for striding out in search of a decision or a voice. And that he returned from The Glades wearing an air of high office not unlike Makepeace Watermaster's, except that it had more of the natural radiance in it that comes, we are told, of inner cleanliness. The matter of the Appeal had been attended to, he informed his courtiers. The problem of liquidity had been solved, he said. Everybody was going to be seen right. How? they begged him; how, Rickie? But Rick preferred to remain their magician and allowed nobody to look up his sleeve. Because I am blessed. Because I steer events. Because I am destined to become one of the Highest in the Land.

His other good news was not vouchsafed to them. This was a cheque drawn on Watermaster's personal account in the sum of five hundred pounds to set himself up in life—presumably, said Syd, in outer Australia. Rick endorsed it, Syd cashed it, since Rick's own bank account, as so often in later years, was temporarily indisposed. A few days afterwards, on the strength of this subsidy, Rick presided over a lavish if sombre banquet at the Brinkley Towers Hotel, attended by the entire court as then composed and several local Lovelies who were always an off-screen feature. Syd recalls a mood of historic change pervading the occasion though no one knew precisely what was over or what was about to begin. Speeches were made, mostly on the theme of old pals sticking together and keeping a straight bat through life, but when Rick's health was drunk he responded with uncharacteristic brevity, and it was whispered that he was in the grip of an emotion, for he was seen to weep, which he did often, even in those days; he could weep buckets, on the drop of a handkerchief. Perce Loft, the great lawyer, attended the gathering to the surprise of some, and to their greater surprise brought with him a beautiful, if incongruous, young music student named Lippschitz, first name Annie, who put the other Lovelies in the shade even though she'd hardly a coat to cover her back. They dubbed her "Lippsie." She was a refugee from Germany who had come to Perce in some immigration matter, and Perce in his goodness had decided to extend a helping hand to her, much as he had extended one to Rick. To close proceedings Morrie Washington the court jester sang a song, and Lippsie joined the other women in the chorus, though she sang too well and didn't fully appreciate the dirty bits, being foreign. It was by then dawn. A sleek taxi took Rick away, and he was not seen in those parts for many years.

History records further that one Richard Thomas Pym, bachelor, and Dorothy Godchild Watermaster, spinster, both very temporarily of this parish, were the next day solemnly and discreetly married in the presence of two co-opted witnesses in a newly opened registry office off the Western by-pass, just where you turned left for Northolt Aerodrome. And that a little boy christened Magnus Richard and weighing in at very few pounds at all was born to them not six months later, whom the Lord protect. The Companies Registry, which I have consulted, also records the event, though in different terms. Within forty-eight hours of the birth, Rick had unveiled the Magnus Star Equitable Insurance Company Ltd., with a share capital of two thousand pounds. Its stated purpose was the Provision of life insurance to the Needy, Disabled, and Elderly. Its accountant was Mr. Muspole, its legal adviser Perce Loft. Morrie Washington was company secretary, and the late Alderman Thomas Pym, affectionately known as TP, its patron saint.

"So was there really a coach then or was it all flannel?" I ask Syd.

Syd is always cautious in how he replies. "Now there *could* have been a coach, Titch. I'm not saying there wasn't, I'd be a liar if I did. I'm just saying I never heard about a coach till your dad happened to mention it in church that morning. Put it that way."

"So what had he done with the money—if there was no coach?"

Syd really doesn't know. So many thousands of pounds have floated under the bridge since then. So many great visions come and gone. Maybe Rick gave it away, Syd says awkwardly. Your dad couldn't say no to anyone, specially the Lovelies. Never right with himself unless he was giving. Maybe a con came and took it off him, your dad always loved a con. Then to my amazement Syd blushes. And I hear faintly but clearly from the side of his mouth the ratta-tat-tat he used to make for me when I was a child and wanted him to do the clip of horses' hoofs.

"You mean he used the Appeal money to lay bets?" I ask.

"Titch, I'm only saying that that coach of his could have been horse-drawn. That's all I'm saying, isn't it, Meg?"

Oh but there was a coach all right! And it was not horse-drawn at all. That coach was the most splendid, powerful ever made. The golden lettering of the Pym & Salvation Coach Company shone from its lustrous sides like the illuminated chapter headings of all the Bibles of Rick's youth. Its green was the racing green of England. Sir Malcolm Campbell himself was going to drive it. The Highest in the Land would ride in it. When the people of our town saw that coach they were going to go down on their knees and put their hands together and thank God and Rick in equal portion for it. The grateful crowds would gather outside Rick's house and call him out on to his balcony till late into the night. I have seen him practising his wave in expectation of them. With both hands as if rocking me above his head, while he beams and weeps into the middle distance: "I owe it all to old TP." And if, as doubtless happened, it turned out that Balham's of Brinkley, some of the finest Liberals in the county, had never strictly speaking heard of Rick's coach, let alone painted it for cost out of the goodness of their hearts, then they were in the same state of provisional reality as the coach was. They were waiting for Rick's wand to beckon them into being. It was only when meddlesome unbelievers such as Makepeace Watermaster had difficulty accepting this state of affairs that Rick found himself with a religious war on his hands, and like others before him was compelled to defend his faith by unpleasant means. All he demanded was the totality of your love. The least you could do in return was give it to him blindly. And wait for him, as God's Banker, to double it over six months.

M ary had prepared herself for everything except for this. Except for the pace and urgency of the intrusion and the number of the intruders. Except for the sheer scale and complexity of Jack Brotherhood's anger, and for his bewilderment, which seemed greater than her own. And for the awful comfort of his being there.

Admitted to the hall he had barely looked at her. "Did you have any inkling of this?"

"If I had I'd have told you," she said, which was a quarrel before they had even begun.

"Has he phoned?"

"No."

"Has anybody else?"

"No."

"No word from *anyone*? No change?"

"No."

"Brought you a brace of house guests." He jabbed a thumb at two shadows behind him. "Relatives from London, come to console you for the duration. More to follow." Then he swept through her like a great ragged hawk on its journey to another prey, leaving her one frozen impression of his lined and punctured face and shaggy white forelock as he stormed towards the drawing-room.

"I'm Georgia from Head Office," said the girl on the doorstep. "This is Fergus. We're so sorry, Mary."

They had luggage and she showed them to the foot of the stairs. They seemed to know the way. Georgie was tall and sharp-edged, with straight, sensible hair.

Fergus was not quite Georgie's class, which was the way the Office worked these days.

"Sorry about this, Mary," Fergus echoed as he followed Georgie up the stairs. "Don't mind if we take a look round, do you?"

In the drawing-room Brotherhood had switched out the lights and wrenched open the curtains to the French windows. "I need the key for this thing. The Chubb. The whatever they have here."

Mary hastened to the mantelpiece and groped for the silver rose bowl where she kept the security key. "Where is he?"

"He's anywhere in the world or out of it. He's using tradecraft. Ours. Who does he know in Edinburgh?"

"No one." The rose bowl was full of pot-pourri she had made with Tom. But no key.

"They think they've traced him there," said Brotherhood. "They think he took the five-o'clock shuttle from Heathrow. Tall man with a heavy briefcase. On the other hand, knowing our Magnus as we do, he might just be in Timbuctoo."

Looking for the key was like looking for Magnus. She didn't know where to begin. She seized the tea-caddy and shook it. She was getting sick with panic. She grabbed the silver Achievement Cup that Tom had won at school and heard something metal skid inside it. Taking the key to him, she barked her shin so hard her eyes blurred. That bloody piano stool.

"The Lederers ring?"

"No. I told you. No one did. I didn't get back from the airport till eleven."

"Where's the holes?"

She located the top keyhole for him and guided his hand to it. I should have done it myself then I wouldn't had to touch him. She knelt and began fumbling for the lower one. I'm practically kissing his feet.

"Has he ever vanished before and you not told me?" Brotherhood demanded while she continued to grope.

"No."

"I want it level, Mary. I've got the whole of London at my throat. Bo's having the vapours and Nigel's cloistered with the Ambassador now. The RAF doesn't fly us out in the middle of the night for nothing."

Nigel is Bo Brammel's hangman, Magnus had said. Bo says three-bags-full to everyone and Nigel pads behind him chopping off their heads.

"Never. No. I swear," she said.

"Did he have a favourite place anywhere? Some hideaway he talked of going to?"

"He said once Ireland. He'd buy a croft overlooking the sea and write."

"North or south?"

"I don't know. South, I suppose. As long as it was sea. Then suddenly the Bahamas. That was more recent."

"Who does he have there?"

"Nobody. Not as far as I know."

"Did he ever talk of going over to the other side? Little dacha on the Black Sea?"

"Don't be a fool."

"So Ireland, then the Bahamas. When did he say the Bahamas?"

"He didn't. He just marked the property advertisements in *The Times* and left them for me to see."

"As a sign?"

"As a reproach, as a come-on, as a signal that he wanted to be somewhere else. Magnus has a lot of ways of talking."

"Has he ever talked about doing away with himself? They'll ask you, Mary. I might as well do it first."

"No. No, he hasn't."

"You don't sound sure."

"I'm not. I'll have to think."

"Has he ever been physically frightened for himself?"

"I can't answer it all at once, Jack! He's a complicated man—I've got to think!" She steadied herself. "In principle, no. No to all of it. It's all a total shock."

"But you still rang very fast from the airport. As soon as he wasn't on that plane, you were on the phone: 'Jack, Jack, where's Magnus?' You were right, he'd vanished."

"I saw his suitcase going round the bloody apron, didn't I? He'd checked himself in! Why wasn't he on the plane?"

"How about his drinking?"

"Less than before."

"Less than Lesbos?"

"Miles less."

"What about his headaches?"

"Gone."

"Other women?"

"I don't know. I wouldn't know. How could I? If he says he's out for the night, he's out for the night. It could be a woman, it could be a Joe. It could be Bee Lederer. She's always after him. Ask her."

"I thought wives could always tell the difference," said Brotherhood.

Not with Magnus they can't, she thought, beginning to settle to his pace.

"Does he still bring papers back at night to work on?" Brotherhood asked, peering into the snow-clad garden.

"Now and then."

"Any here now?"

"Not that I know of."

"American papers? Liaison stuff?"

"I don't read them, Jack, do I? So I don't know."

"Where does he keep them?"

"He brings them at night, takes them back in the morning. Just like everyone else."

"And keeps them where, Mary?"

"By the bed. In the desk. Wherever he's been working on them."

"And Lederer hasn't rung?"

"I told you. No."

Brotherhood stood back. Two men, muffled against the night, tumbled into the room. She recognised Lumsden, the Ambassador's private secretary. She had recently had a row with his wife, Caroline, about starting a bottle-bank in the

Embassy forecourt as an example to the Viennese. Mary thought it essential. Caroline Lumsden thought it irrelevant and explained why in an angry outburst to an inner caucus of the Diplomatic Wives Association: Mary was not a real Wife, said Caroline. She was an Unmentionable, and the only reason she was accepted as a Wife *at all* was to protect her husband's half-baked cover.

They must have soldiered up the bridlepath from the school, she thought. Waded through half a metre of snow in order to be discreet about Magnus.

"Hail, Mary," Lumsden said brightly in his best scoutmaster's voice. He was a Catholic but that was how he always greeted her, so he did it tonight. To be normal.

"Did he bring any papers back on the night of the party?" Brotherhood asked, closing the curtains once more.

"No." She put on the light.

"Know what's in this black briefcase of his that he's carrying?"

"He didn't take it from here so he must have collected it at the Embassy. All he took from here was the suitcase that's at Schwechat."

"Was," said Brotherhood.

The second man was tall and sickly-looking. He carried a bulging bag in each gloved hand. Enter the abortionist. It was practically a full plane, she thought stupidly; Head Office must have a permanent defection team on twenty-four-hour standby.

"Meet Harry," Brotherhood said. "He's going to put some clever boxes on your telephones. Use them normally. Don't think of us. Any objection?"

"How can I?"

"You can't, you're right. I'm being polite, so why don't you do the same? You've got two cars. Where are they?"

"The Rover's outside, the Metro's in the airport carpark waiting for him to pick it up."

"Why did you go to the airport if he had a car there?"

"I just thought he might like me to be there so I took a taxi and went."

"Why not take the Rover?"

"I wanted to ride back with him, not drive in convoy."

"Where's the Metro key?"

"In his pocket presumably."

"Got a spare?"

She searched her handbag till she found it. He dropped it in his pocket.

"I'll get it lost," he said. "If anybody asks, it's gone for repair. I don't want it kicking round the airport."

She heard a heavy thud from upstairs.

She watched Harry pull off his gumboots and place them neatly on the mat beside the French windows.

"His father died Wednesday. What's he been up to in London apart from burying him?" Brotherhood continued.

"I assumed he'd be dropping in at Head Office."

"He never did. He didn't ring, he didn't visit."

"Then probably he was busy."

"Did he have any plans for London—anything he told you of?"

"He said he'd go and see Tom at school."

"Well, he did that. He went. Anything else? Friends—dates—women?"

She was suddenly very tired of him. "He was burying his father and tidying up, Jack. The whole visit was one long date. If you'd had a father and he died, you'd know how it was."

"Did he phone you from London?"

"No."

"Steady, Mary. Think now. That's five days already."

"No. He didn't. Of course he didn't."

"Would he usually?"

"If he can use the Office phone, yes."

"And if he can't?"

She thought for him. She really tried. She had been thinking for so long. "Yes," she conceded. "He'd phone. He likes to know we're all right, all the time. He's a worrier. I suppose that's why I went off with such a bang when he didn't show up. I think I was worried already."

Lumsden was stalking round the room in his stockinged feet, pretending to admire Mary's water-colours of Greece.

"You're so, so talented," he marvelled, his face pressed against a view of Plomari. "Did you go to art school or simply do it?"

She ignored him. So did Brotherhood. It was a tacit bond between them. The only decent diplomat is a deaf Trappist, Jack liked to say. Mary was beginning to agree.

"Where's the servant?" said Brotherhood.

"You told me to get rid of her. On the phone. When I rang."

"She smell a rat?"

"I don't think so."

"It mustn't get out, Mary. We've got to sit on it as long as we possibly can. You know that, don't you?"

"I guessed."

"There's his Joes to think of, there's everything to think of. Far more than you can know. London's stiff with theories and begging for time. You quite sure Lederer hasn't phoned?"

"Jesus," she said.

His eye fell on Harry, who was unpacking his clever boxes. They were grey-green and possessed no apparent controls. "You can tell the servant they're transformers," he said.

"*Umformer*," Lumsden piped helpfully from the wings. "Transformer is *Umformer*. '*Die kleinen Büchsen sind Umformer.*' "

Once again they ignored him. Jack's German was almost as good as Magnus's, and about three hundred times better than Lumsden's.

"When's she due back?" Brotherhood asked.

"Who?"

"Your servant, for God's sake."

"Tomorrow lunchtime."

"Be a good girl and see if you can get her to stay away a couple more days."

She went to the kitchen and phoned Frau Bauer's mother in Salzburg. Sorry about the outrageous hour but with a death that's how it goes, she said. Herr Pym is remaining in London for a few days, she said. Why don't you take advantage of Herr Pym's absence and have a nice rest? she said. When she came back it was Lumsden's turn to say his piece. She got his drift immediately and after that she deliberately stopped hearing him. "Just to fill in any awkward blanks, Mary . . . So that we're all speaking the same language, Mary . . . While Nigel is still closeted with Ambass . . . In case, which God forbid, the odious press gets on to it before it's all cleared up, Mary . . ." Lumsden had a cliché for every occasion and a reputation for being nimble-minded. "Anyway, that's the route Ambass would like us all to go," he ended, using the very latest in daring jargon. "Not unless we're asked, naturally. But if we are. And Mary he sends terrific love. He's with you all the way. And with Magnus too naturally. Terrific condolences, all that."

"Just nothing to Lederer's crowd," said Brotherhood. "Nothing to anyone but for God's sake nothing to Lederer. There's no disappearance, nothing abnormal. He's gone back to London to bury his father, he's staying on for talks at Head Office. End of message."

"It's the same route I've been going already," Mary said, appealing to Brotherhood as if Lumsden didn't exist. "It's just that Magnus didn't apply for compassionate leave before taking it."

"Yes, well now I think that's the part Ambass wants us *not* to say, if you don't mind," said Lumsden, showing the steel. "So I think we won't, please."

Brotherhood squared to him. Mary was family. Nobody messed her around in front of Brotherhood, least of all some overeducated flunkey from the Foreign Office.

"You've done your job," said Brotherhood. "Fade away, will you? Now."

Lumsden left the way he had come, but faster.

Brotherhood turned back to Mary. They were alone. He was as broad as an old blockhouse and, when he wanted to be, as rough. His white forelock had fallen across his brow. He put his hands on her hips the way he used to, and drew her into him. "God damn it, Mary," he said as he held her. "Magnus is my best boy. What the devil have you done with him?"

From upstairs she heard the squeak of castors and another loud thud. It's the bow-fronted chest of drawers. No, it's our bed. Georgie and Fergus are taking a look round.

The desk was in the old servants' room next to the kitchen, a sprawling, spidery half-cellar to which no servant had been consigned for forty years. Near the window among Mary's plant pots stood her easel and water-colours. Against the wall, the old black-and-white television and the agonising sofa for watching it. "There's nothing like a little discomfort," Magnus liked to say primly, "for deciding whether a programme is worth its salt." In an alcove under lanes of piping stood the ping-pong table where Mary did her bookbinding and on it lay her hides and buckram and glues and clamps and threads and marbled end-papers and powering knives, and the bricks in Magnus's old socks that she used instead of lead weights, and the wrecked volumes she had bought for a few schillings at the flea market. Beside it, next to the defunct boiler, stood the desk, the great, crazy Hapsburg desk bought for a song at a sale in Graz, sawn up to get it through the door and glued together again all by clever Magnus. Brotherhood pulled at the drawers.

"Key?"

"Magnus must have taken it."

Brotherhood lifted his head. "Harry!"

Harry kept his lock picks on a chain the way other men keep keys, and held his breath to help him listen while he probed.

"Does he do all his homework here or is there somewhere else?"

"Daddy left him his old campaign table. Sometimes he uses that."

"Where is it?"

"Upstairs."

"Where upstairs?"

"Tom's room."

"Keep his documents there too, does he? . . . Firm's papers?"

"I don't think so. I don't know where."

Harry walked out smiling with his head down. Brotherhood pulled open a drawer.

"That's for the book he was writing," she said as he extracted a meagre file. Magnus keeps everything inside something. Everything must wear a disguise in order to be real.

"Is it though?" He was pulling on his glasses, one red ear at a time. He knows about the novel too, she thought, watching him. He's not even pretending to be surprised.

"Yes." And you can put his bloody papers back where you got them from, she thought. She did not like how cold he had become, how hard.

"Gave up his sketching, did he? I thought you two were in that together."

"It didn't satisfy him. He decided he preferred the written word."

"Doesn't seem to have written much here. When did he switch?"

"On Lesbos. On holiday. He's not writing it yet. He's preparing."

"Oh." He began another page.

"He calls it a matrix."

"Does he though?"—still reading—"I must show some of this to Bo. He's a literary man."

"And when we retire—when he does—if he takes early retirement, he'll write, I'll paint and bookbind. That's the plan."

Brotherhood turned a page. "In Dorset?"

"At Plush. Yes."

"Well, he's taken early retirement all right," he remarked not very nicely as he resumed his reading. "Wasn't there sculpture, too, at some point?"

"It wasn't practical."

"I shouldn't think it was."

"You encourage those things, Jack. The Firm does. You're always saying we should have hobbies and recreations."

"What's the book about, then? Anything special?"

"He's still finding the line. He likes to keep it to himself."

"Listen to this: 'When the most horrible gloom was over the household; when Edward himself was in agony and behaving as prettily as he knew how.' Not even a main verb, far as I can make out."

"He didn't write that."

"It's in his handwriting, Mary."

"It's from something he read. When he reads a book he underlines things in pencil. Then when he's finished it he writes out his favourite bits."

From upstairs she heard a sharp snap like the cracking of timber or the firing of a pistol back in the days when she had been taught.

"That's Tom's room," she said. "They don't need to go in there."

"Get me a bag, dear," Brotherhood said. "A bin bag will do. Will you find me one?"

She went to the kitchen. Why do I let him do this to me? Why do I let him march into my house, my marriage and my mind and help himself to everything he doesn't like? Mary was not usually compliant. Tradesmen did not rob her twice. In the English school, the English church, in the Diplomatic Wives Association, she was regarded as quite the little shrew. Yet one hard stare of Jack Brotherhood's pale eyes, one growl of his rich, careless voice, was enough to send her running to him.

It's because he's so like Daddy, she decided. He loves our kind of England and the rest can go hang.

It's because I worked for Jack in Berlin when I was an empty-headed schoolgirl with one small talent. Jack was my older lover at a time when I thought I needed one.

It's because he steered Magnus through his divorce for me when he was dithering and gave him to me "for afters" as he called it.

It's because he loves Magnus too.

Brotherhood was flipping the pages of her desk diary.

"Who's P?" he demanded, tapping a page. " 'Twenty-fifth September, six-thirty P.M. P.' There's a P on the sixteenth too, Mary. That's not 'P' for Pym, is it, or am I being stupid again? Who's this P he's meeting?"

She began to hear the scream inside herself and had no whisky left to quell it. Of all the entries, the dozens and dozens, and he has to pick that one. "I don't know. A Joe. I don't know."

"You wrote it, didn't you?"

"Magnus asked me to. 'Put down I'm meeting P.' He didn't keep a diary of his own. He said it was insecure."

"And he made you write the entries for him."

"He said if anybody looked, they wouldn't know which were his dates and which were mine. It was part of sharing." She felt Brotherhood's stare. He's making me speak, she thought. He wants to hear the quaver in my voice.

"Sharing what?"

"His work."

"Explain."

"He couldn't tell me what he was doing, but he could show me that he was doing it and when."

"Did he say that?"

"I could feel it."

"What could you feel?"

"That he was proud! He wanted me to know!"

"Know what?"

Brotherhood could drive her mad even when she knew he meant to. "Know that he had another life! An important one. That he was being used."

"By us?"

"By you, Jack. By the Firm! Who do you think—the Americans?"

"Why do you say that—the Americans? Did he have a thing about them?"

"Why should he? He served in Washington."

"Needn't stop him. Might even encourage him. Did you know the Lederers in Washington?"

"Of course we did."

"But better here, eh? I hear she's quite an armful."

He was turning forward to the days yet to be endured. Tomorrow and the day after. To the weekend, which was already gaping at her like a hole in her shattered universe.

"Mind if I keep this?" he asked.

Mary damn well did mind. She possessed no spare diary and no spare life either. She snatched it back and let him wait while she copied out her future on a sheet of paper: Drinks Lederer . . . dinner Dinkels . . . Tom's school term ends. . . . She came to "meet P" and left it out.

"Why's this drawer empty?" he asked.

"I didn't know it was."

"So what was it full of?"

"Old photographs. Mementoes. Nothing."

"How long's it been empty?"

"I don't know, Jack. I don't know! Get off my back, will you?"

"Did he put papers in his suitcase?"

"I didn't watch him pack."

"Did you hear him down here while he was packing?"

"Yes."

The telephone rang. Mary's hand shot out to take it, but Brotherhood was already grasping her wrist. Still holding her, he leaned towards the door and yelled for Harry while the phone went on ringing. It was rising four A.M. already. Who the hell calls at four in the morning except Magnus? Inside herself Mary was praying so loud she hardly heard Brotherhood's shout. The phone kept calling her, and she knew now that nothing mattered except Magnus and her family.

"It might be Tom!" she shouted while she struggled. "Let go, damn you!"

"It might be Lederer, too."

Harry must have flown downstairs. She counted two more rings before he was standing in the doorway.

"Trig this call," Brotherhood ordered, loud and slow. Harry vanished. Brotherhood released Mary's hand. "Make it very, very long, Mary. Spread it right out. You know how to play those games. Do it."

She lifted the phone and said, "Pym residence."

Nobody answered. Brotherhood was conducting her with his powerful hands, willing her, pressing her to talk. She heard a metallic ping and crammed her hand over the mouthpiece. "It could be a call code," she breathed. She held up one finger for one ping. Then a second. Then a third. It was a call code. They had used them in Berlin: two for this, three for that. Private and prearranged between the Joe and base. She opened her eyes to Brotherhood to say what shall I do? He shook his head to say I don't know either.

Speak, he mouthed.

Mary drew a deep breath. "Hullo? Speak up, please." She took refuge in German. "This is the residence of Counsellor Magnus Pym of the British Embassy. Who is that? Will you speak, please? Mr. Pym is not here at the moment. If you wish to leave a message, you may do so. Otherwise, please call later. Hullo?"

More, Brotherhood was urging. Give me more. She recited her telephone number in German and again in English. The line was open and she could hear a noise like traffic and a noise like scratchy music played at half speed, but no more pings. She repeated the number in English. "Speak up, please. The line is dreadful. Hullo. Can you hear me? Who's that calling, please? Do—please—speak—up." Then she couldn't help herself. Her eyes closed and she screamed, "Magnus, for God's sake say where you are!" But Brotherhood was miles ahead of her. With a lover's knowledge he had felt her outburst coming and clapped his hand over the cradle.

"Too short, sir," Harry lamented from the doorway. "I'd need another minute at the least."

"Was it foreign?" Brotherhood said.

"Could be foreign, could be next door, sir."

"That was naughty, Mary. Don't do those things again. We're on the same side in this and I'm boss."

"Someone's kidnapped him," she said. "I know they have."

Everything froze: herself, his pale eyes, even Harry in the doorway. "Well, well," said Brotherhood at last. "That would make you feel better, would it? A kidnapping? Now why do you say that, dear? What's worse than kidnapping, I wonder?"

Trying to meet his gaze Mary experienced a violent time warp. I don't know anything. I want Plush. Give me back the land that Sam and Daddy died for. She saw herself as a school-leaver seated in front of the careers mistress in the middle of her last term. A second woman is with her, London and tough. "This lady is a recruiting officer for the Foreign Service, dear," says the careers mistress. "A special bit of it," says the tough woman. "She's terribly impressed by the way you *draw,* dear," says the careers mistress. "She so admires your draughtsmanship, as we all do. She wonders whether you'd be interested in taking your folder to London for a day or two, so that some other people can look at it." "It's for your country, dear," the tough woman says with meaning, to the child of English patriots.

She remembered the training house in East Anglia, girls like herself, our class. She remembered the jolly lessons in copying and engraving and colouring, in papers and cardboards and linens and threads, how to make watermarks and how to alter them, how to cut rubber stamps, how to make paper look older and how to make it look younger, and she tried to remember just when it was exactly that they had realised they were being taught to forge documents for British spies. And she saw herself standing before Jack Brotherhood in his rickety upstairs office in Berlin, not a stone's throw from the Wall, Jack the Stripper, Jack the Stoat, Jack the Black and all the other Jacks he was known as. Jack who had charge of Berlin Station and liked to meet all newcomers personally, particularly if they were pretty girls of twenty. She remembered his bleached gaze running slowly over her body while he guessed her shape and sexual weight and she remembered again hating him on sight, as she was trying to hate him now as she watched him flip through a folder of family correspondence he had pulled from the desk.

"You realise half of those are Tom's letters from boarding-school, I suppose," she said.

"Why doesn't he write to both of you?"

"He does write to both of us, Jack. Tom and I have one correspondence. Magnus and Tom have a separate correspondence."

"No interconsciousness," said Brotherhood, using a bit of trade talk he had taught her in Berlin. He lit one of his fat yellow cigarettes and watched her theatrically through the flame. There's a poseur in all of them, she thought. Magnus and Grant included.

"You're absurd," she said in nervous anger.

"It's an absurd situation and Nigel will be here any minute to make it more absurd still. What caused it?" He opened another drawer.

"His father. If it's a situation at all."

"Whose camera's this?"

"Tom's. But we all use it."

"Any other cameras around?"

"No. If Magnus needs one for his work he brings it from the Embassy."

"Any here from the Embassy now?"

"No."

"Maybe his father caused it or maybe a lot of things did. Maybe a marital tiff I don't know about caused it."

He was examining the camera's settings, turning it over in his big hands as if he were thinking of buying it.

"We don't have them," she said.

His knowing eyes lifted to her. "How do you manage that?"

"He doesn't offer a fight, that's why."

"You do though. You're a right little demon when you get going, Mary."

"Not any more," she said, mistrusting his charm.

"You never met his dad, did you?" said Brotherhood as he wound the film through the camera. "There was something about him, I seem to remember."

"They were estranged."

"Ah."

"Nothing dramatic. They'd drifted apart. They're that sort of family."

"What sort, dear?"

"Scattered. Business people. He'd said he'd let them in on his first marriage and once was enough. We hardly talked about it."

"Tom go along with that?"

"Tom's a child."

"Tom was the last person Magnus saw before he vanished, Mary. Apart from the porter at his club."

"So arrest him," Mary suggested rudely.

Dropping the film into the bin bag Brotherhood picked up Magnus's little transistor radio.

"This the new one they do with all the shortwave on it?"

"I believe so."

"Take it with him on holiday, did he?"

"Yes, he did."

"Listen to it regularly?"

"Since, as you once told me, he runs Czechoslovakia single-handed out here, it would be fairly startling if he didn't."

He switched it on. A male voice was reading the news in Czech. Brotherhood stared blankly at the wall while he let it continue for what seemed like hours. He switched off the radio and put it in the bag. His gaze lifted to the uncurtained window, but it was still a long while before he spoke. "Not displaying too many lights for the time of morning, are we, Mary?" he asked distractedly. "Don't want to set neighbours chattering, do we?"

"They know Rick's dead. They know it's not a normal time."

"You can say that again."

I hate him. I always did. Even when I fell for him—when he was taking me up and down the scale and I was weeping and thanking him—I still hated him. Tell me about the night in question, he was saying. He meant the night they heard of Rick's death. She told it to him exactly as she had rehearsed it.

He had found the cloakroom and was standing before the worn dufflecoat that hung between Tom's loden and Mary's sheepskin. He was feeling in the pockets. The din from upstairs was monotonous. He extracted a grimy handkerchief and a half-consumed roll of Polo mints.

"You're teasing me," he said.

"All right, I'm teasing you."

"Two hours in the freezing snow in his dancing pumps, Mary? In the middle of the night? Brother Nigel will think I'm making it up. What did he do in them?"

"Walked."

"Where to, dear?"

"He didn't tell me."

"Ask him?"

"No, I didn't."

"Then how do you know he didn't take a cab?"

"He'd no money. His wallet and change were upstairs in the dressing-room with his keys." Brotherhood replaced the handkerchief and mints in the duffle.

"And none in here?"

"No."

"How d'you know?"

"He's methodical in those things."

"Maybe he paid the other end."

"No."

"Maybe someone picked him up."

"No."

"Why not?"

"He's a walker and he was in shock. That's why. His father was dead, even if he didn't particularly like him. It builds up in him. The tension or whatever it is. So he walks." And I hugged him when he came back, she thought. I felt the cold on his cheek and the trembling of his chest and the hot sweat clean through his coat from his hours of walking. And I'll hug him again, as soon as he comes through that door. "I said to him: 'Don't go. Not tonight. Get drunk. We'll get drunk together.' But he went. He had his look." She wished she hadn't said that, but for a moment she was as cross with Magnus as she was with Brotherhood.

"What look is that, Mary? 'Had his look.' I don't think I follow you."

"Empty. Like an actor without a part."

"A *part*? His father takes up and *dies* and Magnus doesn't have a *part* any more? What the hell does that mean?"

He's closing in on me, she thought, resolutely not answering. In a minute I'm going to feel his sure hands on me, and I'm going to lie back and let it happen because I can't think of any more excuses.

"Ask Grant," she said, trying to hurt him. "He's our tame psychologist. He'll know."

They had moved to the drawing-room. He was waiting for something. So was she. For Nigel, for Pym, for the telephone. For Georgie and Fergus upstairs.

"You're not doing too much of this, are you?" Brotherhood asked, pouring her another whisky.

"Of course not. When I'm alone, almost never."

"Well, don't. It's too damn easy. And when Brother Nigel's here, nothing. Keep it under wraps completely. Yes, Jack?"

"Yes, Jack." You're a lecherous priest scavenging the last of God's grace, she told him, watching his slow purposeful movements as he filled his own glass. First the wine, now the water. Now lower your eyelids and lift the chalice for a sanctimonious word with Him who sent you.

"And he's free," he remarked. " 'I'm free.' Rick's dead, so Magnus is free. He's one of your Freudian types who can't say 'Father.' "

"It's perfectly normal at his age. To call a father by his Christian name. More normal still, if you haven't seen each other for fifteen years."

"I do like you to defend him," Brotherhood said. "I admire your loyalty. So will they. And you never let me down. I know you didn't."

Loyalty, she thought. Keeping my silly mouth shut round the Station in case your wife finds out.

"And you wept. Quite the old weeper, you are, Mary, I didn't know. Mary weeps, Magnus consoles her. Odd, that, to the casual observer, seeing as how Rick was *his* daddy, not yours. A rôle reversal with a vengeance, that is: you doing his mourning for him. Who were the tears for exactly? Any idea?"

"His father had died, Jack. I didn't sit down and say 'I'll cry for Rick, I'll cry for Magnus.' I just cried."

"I thought it might be for yourself."

"What's that supposed to mean?"

"You're the one person you didn't mention. That's all. Defensive: that's how you sound."

"I am not being defensive!"

She was too loud. She knew it and once more so did Brotherhood and he was interested.

"And when Magnus is done with consoling Mary," he continued, picking a book from the table and flipping through it, "he slips on his duffle and he goes for a walk in his dancing pumps. You try to restrain him—you beg him, which is hard for me to visualise, but I'll try—but no, he will go. Any phone calls before he leaves?"

"No."

"No incoming, no outgoing?"

"I said no!"

"Direct dial, after all, you'd think a bereaved man would want to share the bad news with other members of his family."

"They're not that kind of family. I told you."

"There's Tom for a start. What about him?"

"It was much too late to ring Tom and anyway Magnus thought it better to tell him himself."

He was looking at the book. "Another gem he's underlined. 'If I am not for myself who is for me; and being for my own self what am I? If not now when?' Well, well. I'm enlightened. Are you?"

"No."

"Nor am I. He's free." He closed the book and put it back on the table. "He didn't take anything with him on his walk, did he? Like a briefcase?"

"A newspaper."

You're going deaf. Admit it. You're worried that a hearing-aid will spoil your self-image. Speak, damn you!

She *had* said it. She knew she had. She had been waiting all evening to say it, prepared it from every possible angle, practised it, rehearsed it, denied it, forgotten it, revived it. And now it was echoing in her head like an explosion while she took a frightfully careless pull at her whisky. Yet his eyes, straight at her, were still waiting.

"A newspaper," she repeated. "Just a newspaper. What of it?"

"Which newspaper?"

"The *Presse*."

"That's a daily."

"Correct. *Die Presse* is a daily."

"A local daily newspaper. And Magnus took it with him. To read in the dark. Dressed in his dancing pumps. Tell me about it."

"I just did, Jack."

"No, you didn't. And you're going to have to, Mary, because when we get the heavy guns here you're going to need all the help you can get."

She had perfect recall. Magnus was standing by the door, a step from where Brotherhood stood now. He was pale and untouchable, the dufflecoat flung crookedly over his shoulders while he glared round in stiff phases: fireplace, wife, clock, books. She heard herself telling him the things she had already recounted to Brotherhood, but more of them. For God's sake, Magnus, stay. Don't get the blacks, stay. Don't sink into one of your moods. Stay. Make love. Get drunk. If you want company, I'll get Grant and Bee back, or we'll go there. She saw him smile his rigid, bright-lit smile. She heard him put on his awfully easy voice. His Lesbos voice. And she heard herself repeat his words exactly, to Brotherhood, now.

"He said, 'Mabs, where's the bloody paper, darling?' I thought he meant *The*

Times for looking at the Scottish property market, so I said, 'Wherever you put it when you brought it back from the Embassy.'"

"But he didn't mean *The Times*," said Brotherhood.

"He went over to the rack—there—" She looked at it but didn't point, because she was terrified of giving too much importance to the gesture. "And helped himself. To *Die Presse*. From the rack, where the *Presse* is kept. Till the end of each week. He likes me to keep the back numbers. Then he walked out," she ended, making it all sound perfectly normal, which of course it was.

"Did he look at it at all when he took it out?"

"Just the date. To check."

"What did you suppose he wanted it for?"

"Maybe there was a late-night film." Magnus had never gone to a late-night film in his life. "Maybe he wanted something to read in the café." With no money on him, she thought, as she filled the void of Brotherhood's silence. "Maybe he was looking for distraction. As we all might be. Have been. Anyone might when they're bereaved."

"Or free," Brotherhood suggested. But he did not otherwise help her.

"Anyway, he was so upset he took the wrong day's," she said brightly, clinching the matter.

"You looked, did you, dear?"

"Only when I was throwing away."

"When were you doing that?"

"Yesterday."

"Which one did he take?"

"Monday's. It was all of three days old. So I mean obviously he was in considerable shock."

"Obviously."

"All right, his father wasn't the great love of his life. But he was still dead. Nobody's rational when a thing like that happens. Not even Magnus."

"So what did he do next? After he'd looked at the date and taken the wrong day's?"

"He went out. As I told you. For a walk. You don't listen. You never did."

"Did he fold it?"

"Really, Jack! What does it matter how somebody carries a newspaper?"

"Just tuck in your ego a minute and answer. What did he do with it?"

"Rolled it."

"And then?"

"Nothing. He carried it. In his hand."

"Did he carry it back again?"

"Here to the house? No."

"How do you know he didn't?"

"I was waiting for him in the hall."

"And you noticed: no newspaper. No rolled newspaper, you said to yourself."

"Purely incidentally, yes."

"Incidentally nothing, Mary. You had it in your mind to look. You knew he'd gone out with it and you spotted at once he'd come back without it. That's not incidental. That's spying on him."

"Please yourself."

He was angry. "It's you who's going to have to do the pleasing, Mary," he said, loud and slow. "You're going to have to please Brother Nigel in about five minutes from now. They're in spasm, Mary. They can see the ground opening up at their feet again and they do not know what to do. They literally do not know what to do." His anger passed. Jack could do that. "And later—as soon as you had a chance—you incidentally searched his pockets. And it wasn't there."

"I didn't *look* for it, I simply noticed it was missing. And yes, it wasn't there."

"Does he often go out with old newspapers?"

"When he needs to keep abreast—for his work—he's a conscientious officer— he takes a newspaper with him."

"Rolled up?"

"Sometimes."

"Bring them back ever?"

"Not that I remember."

"Ever remark on it to him?"

"No."

"He to you?"

"Jack. It's a habit he has. Look, I'm not going to have a marital row with you!"

"We're not married."

"He rolls up a newspaper and walks with it. The way a child carries a stick or something. As a comforter or something. Like his Polos. There. He had Polos in his pocket. It's the same thing."

"Always the wrong date?"

"Not always—don't make so much of everything!"

"And always loses it?"

"Jack, stop. Just stop. Okay?"

"Does he do it on any special occasion? Full moon? Last Wednesday of the month? Or only when his father dies? Have you noticed a pattern to it? Go on, Mary, you have!"

Beat me, she thought. Grab me. Anything is better than that ice-cold stare.

"It's sometimes when he meets P," she said, trying to sound as if she were pacifying a spoilt child. "Jack, for God's sake, he runs Joes, he lives that life, you trained him! I don't ask him what his tricks are, what he's doing with who. I'm trained too!"

"And when he came back—how was he?"

"He was absolutely fine. Calm, completely calm. He'd walked it out of himself, I could feel. He was absolutely fine in every way."

"No phone calls while he was out?"

"No."

"None after?"

"One. Very late. But we didn't answer it."

It was not often she had seen Jack surprised. Now he almost was. "You didn't answer it?"

"Why should we?"

"Why shouldn't you? It's his job, as you said. His father had just died. Why shouldn't you answer the phone?"

"Magnus said don't."

"*Why* did he say don't?"

"We were making love!" she said, and felt like the worst whore ever.

Harry was looming in the doorway again. He was wearing blue overalls and had a red face from his exertions. He was holding a long screwdriver in his hand and he looked shamefully joyful.

"Care to pop upstairs a jiffy, Mr. Brotherhood?" he said.

It's like our bedroom before the Diplomatic Wives' jumble sale, with our cast-off clothes all over the bed, she thought. "Magnus, darling, do you really need three worn-out cardigans?" Clothes over the chairs. Over the dressing-table and the towel-horse. My summer blazer that I haven't worn since Berlin. Magnus's dinner-jacket hung from the cheval mirror like a drying hide. There was nothing on the floor because there was no floor. Fergus and Georgie had removed the carpet and most of the floorboards underneath it, and stacked them like sandwiches beneath the window, leaving the joists and the odd plank for a walkway. They had taken the bedside lamps to pieces and the bedside furniture and the telephone and the wake-up wireless. In the bathroom, it was the floor again, and the panel to the bath, and the medicine chest, and the sloped attic door that led to the sloped attic where Tom had hidden for a whole half hour last Christmas playing Murder, and nearly died of fright from being so brave. At the basin, Georgie was working her way through Mary's things. Her face-cream. Her diaphragm.

"What's yours is his, for them, dear, and vice versa," said Brotherhood as they paused to stare in from the doorless doorway. "There's no his and hers, not for them—there can't be."

"Not for you either," she said.

Tom's bedroom was across the corridor from theirs. His luminous Superman lay sprawled over the bed, together with his thirty-one Smurfs and three Tiggers. Her father's campaign table was folded against the wall. The toy chest had been pulled to the centre of the floor, revealing the marble fireplace behind. It was a fine fireplace. Works Department had wanted to board it over to reduce draughts but Magnus hadn't let them. Instead he had bought this old chest to put across the opening, leaving the mantel visible over it, so that Tom could have a bit of old Vienna all his own. Now the fireplace stood free and the girl Georgie knelt respectfully before it in her fifty-guinea freedom fighter's tunic. And before Georgie lay a white shoe box with its lid off, and inside the shoe box was a rag bundle, then several smaller bundles around it.

"We found it on the ledge up above the grate, sir," said Fergus. "Where it joins the main flue."

"Not a speck of dust on it," said Georgie.

"Reach up and it's there," said Fergus. "Dead handy."

"You don't even have to shove the chest out really, once you get the knack," said Georgie.

"Seen it before?" Brotherhood asked.

"It's obviously something of Tom's," said Mary. "Children will hide anything."

"Seen it before?" Brotherhood repeated.

"No."

"Know what's in it?"

"How could I if I haven't seen it?"

"Easily."

Brotherhood did not stoop but held his arms out. Georgie passed the box up to him and Brotherhood took it to the table where Tom did his Spirograph and his Lego and his endless drawings of German aeroplanes being shot down against a Plush sunset, with family in the background, everybody waving, everybody absolutely fine. Brotherhood picked out the biggest bundle first and they looked on while he started to unwrap it and changed his mind.

"Here," he said, handing it to Georgie. "Woman's fingers."

She's one of his mistresses, Mary suddenly realised. She wondered why on earth it hadn't dawned on her before.

Georgie rose elegantly to her full height, one leg, other leg, and having fixed her straight hair behind her ears, applied her woman's fingers to unwinding the strips of bedsheet that Magnus had said he wanted for the car, revealing at last a small, clever-looking camera with a clever steel harness round it. And after the camera a thing like a telescope with a bracket on it which, when you pulled it to its full length, made a stand that you could screw the camera to, face downwards and at a fixed distance, for photographing documents on your father-in-law's campaign table. After the telescope came a succession of films and lenses and filters and rings and other bits of equipment she could not identify offhand. And underneath these a pad of flimsy cloth-paper with columns of numbers on the top sheet and thickly rubberised edges so that you could only see the top page. Mary knew the type of paper. She had worked on it in Berlin. It shrivelled into fern the moment you put a match near it. The pad was half used. Underneath the pad again, an aged cardboard-backed military jotting pad marked "W.D. Property," standing for War Department and consisting of unwritten-on lined paper of blotchy wartime quality. And inside it, when Brotherhood continued searching, two pressed red flowers of great age, poppies, but just possibly roses, she was not entirely certain, and anyway by then she was shouting.

"It's for the Firm! It's for his work for you!"

"Of course it is. I'll tell Nigel. No problem."

"Just because he didn't tell me about it, it doesn't mean it's wrong! It's for in case he gets landed with documents in the house! At weekends!" And then, realising what she had said: "It's for his Joes—if they bring him documents, you fool! If Grant does, and he's got to turn them round at short notice! What's so fucking sinister about that?"

Fergus was fingering the half-used pad, turning it over and over, tilting it in the beam of Tom's Anglepoise lamp.

"Looks more like your Czech, sir, frankly," said Fergus, tilting the pad to the light. "It could be Russian but I think Czech's more likely, frankly. Yes," he said pleasantly as his eye caught some unexplained feature of the rubber edge. "That's it. Czech. Mind you, that's only where they're made. Who's dishing them out is another matter. Specially these days."

Brotherhood was more interested in the pressed flowers. He had laid them on his palm and was staring at them as if they told his future.

"I think you're a bad girl, Mary," he said deliberately. "I think you know a lot more than you told me. I don't think he's in Ireland or the bloody Bahamas. I think that was a lot of smoke. I think he's a bad man and I'm wondering whether you're bad together."

All constraint left her. She screamed "You shit!" and hit at him with her open hand but he blocked her. He put an arm round her and swung her off the ground as if she had no legs left. He carted her across the corridor to Frau Bauer's bedroom which was the only room that hadn't so far been ripped apart. He dumped her on the bed and whisked her shoes off exactly as he used to in the squalid safe flat where he did his screwing. He rolled her into the eiderdown, making a straitjacket of it. Then he lay on her, grappling her into submission while Georgie and Fergus looked on. But somehow, amazingly, throughout all these antics and dramatics, Jack Brotherhood had still contrived to keep hold of the two pressed poppies in his left fist, and kept hold of them even when the doorbell went again, one long peal for authority.

To be above the fray," Pym wrote to himself on a separate sheet of paper. "A writer is King. He should look down with love upon his subject, even when the subject is himself."

Life began with Lippsie, Tom, and Lippsie happened long before you came along or anyone else did, and long before Pym was what the Firm calls of marriageable age. Before Lippsie all Pym remembered was an aimless trek through different-coloured houses and a lot of shouting. After her everything seemed to flow in the one unstoppable direction and all he had to do was sit in his boat and let the current carry him. From Lippsie to Poppy, from Rick to Jack, it was all one jolly stream, however much it wriggled and divided itself along the way. And not only life but death began with her as well, for it was actually Lippsie's dead body that got Pym going, though he never saw it. Others saw it, and Pym could have made the journey because it was in the bell yard and no one covered it for ages. But the little fellow was going through a squeamish and self-centered period at the time and had a notion that if he didn't see it she might not be dead after all, but pretending. Or that her death was a judgment upon himself for taking part in the recent killing of a squirrel in the empty swimming-pool. The hunt had been led by a wall-eyed maths master called Corbo the Crow. When the squirrel was safely trapped, Corbo sent three boys down the pool ladder with hockey sticks, and Pym was one. "On you go, Pymmie. Give it to him!" Corbo urged. Pym had watched the crippled creature limp towards him. Scared by its pain he had caught it a great swipe, harder than he meant. He had seen it catapult to the next player and lie still. "Good man, Pymmie! Good shot."

His other thought was that the Sefton Boyd gang had made the whole thing up to tease him, always possible. So as a stopgap Pym gave himself the desk job of gathering descriptions and forming, in that first rush before the school went silent, a mind's picture of her that was probably as clear as anybody's. She lay in a running position, sideways on the flagstones, her forward hand punched towards the finishing line and her rear foot pointing the wrong way. Sefton Boyd, who made the original sighting and alerted the Headmaster during school breakfast, actually thought she *was* running, he said, until he saw the wonky foot. He thought she was doing a special exercise on her side, a sort of kicking, bicycling exercise. And he thought the blood round her was a cape or a towel that she was lying on until he noticed how the old chestnut leaves stuck to it and wouldn't blow away. He didn't go close because bell yard was out of bounds, even to sixth-formers, on account of the dangerous roof above it. And he didn't throw up, he boasted, because us Sefton Boyds own simply masses of land and I've done a lot of shooting with my father and I'm accustomed to seeing blood and innards all the time. But he did run up sixth-form staircase to the tower window, which the police said later was where she had fallen from; she must have been leaning out to do something. And it must have been something urgent and important she was leaning out for because she had been wearing her nightdress, having bicycled up the mile-long drive from the Overflow House in the middle of the night. Her bicycle with its tartan cover on the saddle was still leaning against the dustbin shed behind the kitchens.

Sefton Boyd's theory, excitedly culled from his father's life-style, was that she was drunk. Except that he didn't call her "she" but "Shitlips," which was his gang's witty play on Lippschitz. But then again, as he had been suggesting for some time, Shitlips may have been a German spy who had slipped up the tower to send messages after blackout, sir. Because from tower window you can see right the way across the valley to the Brace of Partridges, so it would be a wizard place for signalling to German bombers, sir. The trouble was she had no light with her except her bike lamp, which was still securely on the handlebars. So perhaps she had hidden it in her vagina, which Sefton Boyd claimed to have seen clearly because the fall had ripped her nightdress off.

Thus the stories went round that morning while Pym stood on the fine wood seat of the staff lavatory which he had made his safe house after the first furore, and held his breath and blushed and turned white in front of the mirror in a series of puzzled efforts to make his face appropriate to his grief. Using the Swiss Army penknife from his pocket, he had sawn off a bit of his forelock as a sort of useless tribute, then loitered, fiddling with the taps and hoping someone was looking for him. Where's Pym? Pym's run away! Pym's dead, too! But Pym hadn't run away, nor was he dead, and in the chaos of having Lippsie's body lying in bell yard and ambulance and police arriving, nobody was looking for anybody, least of all in the staff lavatory which was the most out-of-bounds place in the school, so forbidden that Sefton Boyd himself was in awe of it. Classes were cancelled and what you were supposed to do after all the shouting and the clamour was go quietly to your form room and revise—unless, like Pym, you were in the second form which overlooked bell yard, in which case you were to go to the arts hall. This was the converted Nissen hut built by Canadian soldiers where Lippsie taught music and painting and drama and held remedial exercises for boys with flat feet. It was also where she did her typing and paperwork in her capacity as school dogsbody: collecting school fees, paying school bills for the Bursar, ordering taxis for boys in confirmation class and, as such people do, just about running the place single-handed and unthanked. But Pym wouldn't go to the arts hall either, though he had a half-finished balsa model of a Dornier to work on with his penknife, as well as a half-made plan to copy out some obscure poems from an old book there and claim they were his own. What he had to do, when he found his courage and the moment, was get back to the Overflow House where he had lived till now with Lippsie and the eleven other Overflow Boys. Until he had done that and done something about the letters, he daren't go anywhere because Rick would go back to prison.

How he had got himself into this pass, how he had acquired the training that was to stand him in such fine stead in this, his first clandestine operation, was pretty much the story of his life this far, which was ten years and three terms of boarding-school old.

Even today, trying to trace Lippsie through Pym's life is like pursuing an errant light through an impenetrable thicket. For Perce Loft, now dead himself, she was simply deniable—"Titch's figment" he called her, meaning my invention, my fabrication, my nothing. But Perce the great lawyer could have made a figment out of the Eiffel Tower after he had banged his nose on it, if he needed to. That was his job. And this despite the testimony of Syd and others that it was Perce himself who first had the use of her, Perce who had introduced her to the court back in the dark ages before Pym's birth. Mr. Muspole, that marvel with the books—also now passed on —understandably backed Perce up. He would. He was up to his neck in the business himself. Even Syd, the one surviving source, is not much more helpful. She was a German Four-by-Two, he said, using the affectionate cockney rhyming slang for Jew. He thought she came from Munich, could have been Vienna. She was lonely, Titch. Adored the kids. Adored you. He didn't say she adored Rick but in the court that was taken for granted. She was a Lovely and in court ethic that was what Lovelies were there for: to be seen right by Rick and to bathe in his glory. And Rick in his goodness had her learn secretarial and qualify, says Syd. And your Dorothy, she thought the world of Lippsie and taught her English, which was meant, says Syd—after which he clams up, remarking only that it was a shame and we should all learn from it, and maybe your dad worked her a bit too hard because she never had your advantages. Yes, he admits, she was a looker. And she had a drop of class to her which some of the others, let's face it, didn't always have, Titch. And she loved a joke till she started to think of her poor family and what had been done to them by those Jerries.

My furtive record checks have not been more enlightening. Finding myself with the run of Registry during a stint as night duty officer not too many years back, I chased Lippschitz, first name Annie, right through the general index but drew a blank on all spellings. Old Dinkel in Vienna, who heads up the personnel side of the Austrian service, recently ran a similar search for me when I spun him a story; so, on another occasion, did his German counterpart in Cologne. Both reported no trace.

In my memory, however, she is anything but no trace. She is a tall, soft-haired, vital girl with large scared eyes and an air of flounce about her stride, nothing happening slowly. And I remember—it must have been a summer holiday in some house where we were temporarily sheltering—I remember how Pym longed more than anything to see her naked, and devoted his waking hours to contriving it. Which Lippsie must have guessed somehow for one afternoon she suggested he share her bath with her to save hot water. She even measured the water with her hand: patriots were allowed five inches and Lippsie was never less than a patriot. She stooped, naked, and let me watch her while she put her hand's span in the tub, I'm sure she did, and brought it out again: "See, Magnus!"—showing me the wet spread hand—"how we may be sure we do not help the Germans."

Or so I fervently believe, though try as I may I cannot to this day remember what she looked like. And I know that in the same house or one like it her room was opposite to Pym's own across a corridor, and that it contained her cardboard suitcase and photographs of her bearded brother and solemn sisters in black hats and silver frames which stood like tiny polished gravestones on her dressing-table. And there was the room where she screamed at Rick and warned him she would rather die than be a thief, and where Rick laughed his brown rich laugh, the one that went on longer than it needed and made everything all right again until next time. And though I do not remember a single lesson, she must have taught Pym German because years later when he came to learn the language formally he discovered that he possessed a repository of information about her—*Aaron war mein Bruder. Mein Vater war Architekt*—all in the same past tense to which she herself by then belonged. He also realised still later in life that when she had called him her *Mönchlein* she had meant her "little monk" and was referring to the hard path of Martin Luther—"little monk, go your own way"—whereas at the time he had thought she had cast him as the organ-grinder's tethered monkey and Rick as his organgrinder. The discovery raised his self-respect no end, until he realised she had been telling him that he must get along without her.

And I know she was in Paradise with us because without Lippsie there was no Paradise. Paradise was a golden land between Gerrard's Cross and the sea, where Dorothy wore an angora pullover for her ironing and a blue ulster for her shopping. Paradise was where Rick and Dorothy fled after their runaway marriage, a Metroland of new beginnings and exciting futures, but I don't remember a day of it without Lippsie flouncing somewhere at the edge, or telling me what was right and wrong in a voice I didn't mind. One hour eastward by Bentley motorcar lay Town and in Town lay the West End and that was where Rick had his office; the office had a big tinted photograph of Granddad TP wearing his mayor's necklace, and the office was what kept Rick late at night, which was the infant Pym's best thing because he was allowed to climb into Dorothy's bed and keep her warm, she was so small and shivery even to a child. Sometimes Lippsie stayed behind with us, sometimes she went to London with Rick because she had to qualify and, as I now understand, justify her own survival when so many of her kind were dead.

Paradise was a string of shiny racehorses that Syd called "neverwozzers" and a succession of even shinier Bentleys which, like the houses, wore out as fast as the credit they were bought on and had to be changed with thrilling rapidity for yet newer and more expensive models. Sometimes the Bentleys were so precious they had actually to be driven round the side of the house and hidden in the back garden for fear they might become tarnished by the gaze of the Unfaithful. At other times Pym drove them at a thousand miles an hour sitting on Rick's lap, down sandy unmade roads lined with cement mixers, hammering the big deep horn at the builders while Rick shouted "How are you, boys?" and invited them all back to the house for a glass of bubbly. And Lippsie was there beside us in the passenger seat, straight as a coachman and as distant, until Rick chose to speak to her or make a joke. Then her smile was like holiday sunshine and she loved us both.

Paradise was also St. Moritz where Swiss Army penknives come from, though somehow the Bentleys and those two pre-war winters in Switzerland become fused in my memory as one place. Even today I have only to sniff the leather interior of a grand car and I am wafted willingly away to the great hotel drawing-rooms of St. Moritz in the wake of Rick's riotous love of festival. The Kulm, the Suvretta House, the Grand—Pym knew them as a single gigantic palace with different sets of servants but always the same court: Rick's private household of jesters, tumblers, counsellors, and jockeys; he barely went anywhere without them. In the daytime, Italian doormen with long brooms flipped the snow off your boots every time you went through the swing doors. In the evenings, while Rick and the court banqueted with local Lovelies and Dorothy was too tired, Pym would venture on Lippsie's hand through snowy alleys clutching his penknife in his pocket while he pretended to himself he was some kind of Russian prince protecting her from everyone who laughed at her for being serious. And in the morning after an early levee, he would tiptoe unescorted to the landing and gaze down through the banisters on his army of serfs toiling in the great hall below him, while he sniffed the stale cigar smoke and women's perfume and the wax polish that glistened like dew on the parquet as they buffed it with long sweeps of their mops. And that was how Rick's Bentleys smelt ever after: of the Lovelies, of beeswax, of the smoke of his millionaire's cigars. And very faintly, from sledge rides through the freezing forest at Lippsie's side, of the cold and the horse dung, while she chatted away in German to the coachman.

Back home again, and Paradise was pyramids of polished tangerines in silver paper, and pink chandeliers in the dining-room and roaring visits to distant race-tracks to flash our Owners' badges and watch the neverwozzers lose, and a tiny black-and-white television set in a huge mahogany case that showed the boat race behind a sky of white spots, and when we watched the Grand National the horses were so far off that Pym wondered how they ever found their way home, but I'm afraid now that Rick's very often didn't which was why Syd called them neverwozzers. And cricket in the garden with Syd, sixpence if he didn't get Titch out in six balls. And boxing in the drawing-room with Morrie Washington, the court expert on the Fight Game, for Morrie was our Minister for the Arts: he had spoken to Bud Flanagan and shaken hands with Joe Louis, he had played conjuror's stooge for the Man with X-Ray Eyes. And having half-crowns pulled out of your ears by Mr. Muspole the great accountant, though Mr. Muspole was never my favourite; there was too much of making me do arithmetic in my head. And watching sugar-knobs vanish from under Perce Loft's legal Homburg: they were being turned to figments before my very eyes. And piggybacks round the garden on the waistcoated shoulders of the jockeys, who had names like Billie and Jimmy and Gordon and Charlie and were the best magic-makers in the world, the best elves, and read all my comics and left me theirs when they'd finished them.

But always somewhere in this pageant I can still find Lippsie, now mother, now typist, musician, cricketer and always Pym's own private moral tutor, flouncing through the outfield in pursuit of a high catch while everyone yelled *"Achtung!"* at her, and "Whoopsie, mind the flower-beds!" It was in Paradise too that Rick kicked a brand-new full-size football slap into Pym's young face, which was like being hit by the inside of all the Bentleys at once, the same leather travelling at the same breakneck speed. When he came round, Dorothy was bending over him with a handkerchief crammed between her teeth, whimpering "Oh, don't, please, dear God, don't," because the blood was everywhere. The football had only cut his forehead but Dorothy insisted it had shoved the whole eyeball deep into his head never to be got out again. The poor heart, she was too scared to dab away the blood so Lippsie had to do it for her, because Lippsie could touch me as she touched wounded animals and birds. I never met a woman since with so much touching in her hands. And I believe now that was what I meant to her: a thing to touch and cherish and protect, after everything else had been removed from her. I was her bit of hope and love in the gilded prison where Rick kept her.

In Paradise when Rick was in residence there was no night and nobody went to bed but Dorothy, the court's self-appointed Sleeping Beauty. Pym could join the festival any time he chose and there they all were, Rick and Syd and Morrie Washington and Perce Loft and Mr. Muspole and Lippsie and the jockeys, lying on the floor amid piles of money, watching the roulette ball hopping over the tin walls while TP in his regalia looked down on them, so there must have been a picture of him in the houses too. And I see us all dancing to the gramophone and telling stories about a chimpanzee called Little Audrey who laughed and laughed at jokes that were beyond Pym's intellectual reach. But he laughed louder than anyone because he was learning to be a pleaser, with funny voices, acts and anecdotes to make himself attractive. In Paradise everybody loved everybody because once Pym found Lippsie sitting on Rick's lap and another time he was dancing cheek to cheek with her, a cigar between his teeth, while he sang "Underneath the Arches" with his eyes shut. And it seemed a pity that Dorothy was once again too tired to put on the frilly dressing-gown Rick had bought her—pink for Dorothy, white for Lippsie—and come on down and have some fun. But the louder Rick yelled to her up the stairs the deeper Dorothy slept, as Pym discovered for himself when he was dispatched on Rick's instruction to talk her round. He knocked and had no answer. He tiptoed to the enormous bed and brushed what looked at first like cobwebs from her cheek. He whispered to her, then he tried shouting at her, but with no useful result. Dorothy was crying in her sleep, he reported when he returned downstairs. But next morning everything was all right again because there they were the three of them in bed together with Rick in the middle, and Pym was allowed to wriggle in beside Lippsie while Dorothy went down and made the toast and Lippsie held him gravely to her, and gave him her troubled, moral frown, which I suppose now was her way of telling me she was ashamed of her weakness and infatuation, and wished to cleanse it with her concern for me.

In Paradise, it was true, Rick roared but never at Pym. He never once raised his voice at me; his will was strong enough without it and his love was stronger still. He roared at Dorothy, he cajoled and warned her about things Pym could not understand. More than once he carted her bodily to the telephone and made her talk to people—to Uncle Makepeace, to shops, and to others who were threatening us somehow, and only Dorothy could appease them, because Lippsie refused to do that, and anyway her accent wasn't right. I believe now that this was the first time Pym heard the name Wentworth, for I remember Dorothy holding my hand for courage while she told Mrs. Wentworth it would be all right about the money if only everyone would stop pressing. So the name Wentworth was ugly to Pym from early. It became synonymous with fear and an end to things.

"Who's Wentworth?" Pym asked Lippsie, and it was the only time she told him to be quiet.

And I remember how Dorothy knew all the operators' names at the exchange, and what their husbands and fiancés did, and where their children were at school, because when she was alone with Pym and shaky in her angora pullover, she'd pick up the white phone and have a good chat with them, she seemed to find comfort in a world of disembodied voices. Rick roared at Lippsie too when she stood up to him, and I think now that she stood up to him more as I grew up. And sometimes he roared at Dorothy and Lippsie together, making them both weep at the same time until they all patched it up in the great bed where he had his toast for breakfast and dripped the butter on the pink sheets. But no one hurt Pym or made him cry. I think, even in those days, Pym understood that Rick measured his relationships with women against his relationship with Pym, and found them wanting by comparison. Sometimes Rick took Dorothy and Lippsie skating. Rick wore a black tail suit and a white tie, but Dorothy and Lippsie dressed like pantomime boys, each holding an arm of him, and avoiding one another's eye.

The Fall occurred in darkness. We had been moving house a great deal recently, in what must have been a giddy ascent through the local real-estate market, and our palace of the day was a mansion on a hill and the day was a black winter afternoon near Christmas. Pym had been making paper decorations with Lippsie, and I have a notion that if I could ever find the place, if it is not a council estate or a bypass by now, they would still be hanging there exactly as we left them, stars of David and stars of Bethlehem—she taught me the difference precisely—twinkling in enormous empty rooms. First the lights went out in Pym's vast nursery, then the electric fire faded, then his brand-new ten-track Hornby O electric train set wouldn't work, then Lippsie gave a kind of shriek and vanished. Pym went downstairs and pulled open the walnut lid of Rick's brand-new de-luxe cocktail cabinet. The mirrored interior refused to light up and it wouldn't play "Someone's in the Kitchen with Dinah."

Suddenly, in the whole house, the brass balls of the barometric perpetual clock were the only thing that had retained their energy. Pym ran to the kitchen. No Cookie and no Mr. Roley the gardener, whose children stole his toys but couldn't be blamed because they hadn't his advantages. He ran upstairs again and feeling very cold made an urgent reconnaissance of the long corridors, calling "Lippsie, Lippsie," but no one answered. From the arched landing window of stained glass, he glared into the garden and made out black cars in the drive. Not Bentleys but two police Wolseleys. And police drivers with peaked caps sitting at the wheel. And men in brown mackintoshes standing round them talking to Mr. Roley while Cookie twisted her handkerchief and wrung her hands like the dame in the Crazy Gang pantomime that Rick had taken the court to see only a week before. People under siege go upwards, I now know, which may explain why Pym's reaction was to race up the narrow staircase to the attic. There he found Rick in a great flurry, with files and papers on the floor all round him, and he was loading them by the armful into an old chipped green filing cabinet that Pym in all his explorations had never seen before.

"The electricity's broken and Lippsie's scared and the police have come and they're in the garden arresting Mr. Roley," Pym told Rick in one breath.

He said this several times, louder each time, because of the great moment of his message. But Rick wouldn't hear him. He was rushing between the papers and the cabinet, loading up the drawers. So Pym went to him and punched him hard on the upper arm, as hard as he could on the soft bit just above the steel spring he wore to keep his silk shirt sleeve straight, and Rick flung round on him and his hand went back to strike him, and his face looked like Mr. Roley's when he was about to make a huge last heave at a log to split it: red and strained and damp. Then he dropped into a crouch and seized Pym by each shoulder with his thick cupped hands. And his face worried Pym much more than the axe-heave, because his eyes were scared and crying without the rest of his face knowing it and his voice was smooth and holy.

"Don't ever hit me again, son. When I'm judged, as judged we shall all be, God will judge me on how I treated you, make no bones about it."

"Why are the police here?" said Pym.

"Your old man's got a temporary problem of liquidity. Now clear a way to that cupboard and open the door for us like a good chap. Quick."

The cupboard was in a corner behind a pile of old clothes and attic junk. Somehow Pym fought his way to the door and hauled it open. With a series of crashes Rick was slamming shut the drawers of the filing cabinet. He turned the lock, grabbed Pym by the arm and poked the key deep into his trouser pocket, which was small and woolly and only big enough for a key and a small bag of sweets.

"You give that to Mr. Muspole, do you hear, son? Nobody but Muspole. Then you show him where this cabinet is. You bring him here and you show him. No one else. Do you love your old man?"

"Yes."

"Well then."

Proud as a sentry, Pym held back the door while Rick swivelled and rolled the cabinet past him on its castors into the cupboard, then into the dark wainscotting beyond. Then he threw in a lot of junk after it, which hid it completely.

"See where it went, son?"

"Yes."

"Close the door."

Pym did so, then stomped downstairs with his chest out because he wanted to take another look at the police cars. Dorothy was in the kitchen dressed in her new fur coat and her new fluffy bedroom slippers, stirring a tin of tomato soup. She had one of those bubbles over her mouth that people get when they are too choked to speak. Pym loathed tomato soup, so did Rick.

"Rick's mending the water-pipes," he announced grandly, in order to keep his secret intact. This was the only meaning he could place on Rick's reference to liquidity. Yelling even louder for Lippsie he charged into the corridor, straight into the path of two policemen labouring under the weight of a great desk that was Rick's office when he was at home.

"That's my dad's," he said aggressively, putting a hand over the pocket where he had the key.

The first policeman is the only one I remember. He was kindly and had a white moustache like TP's, and he was taller than God.

"Yes, well, I'm afraid it's ours now, lad. Hold open that door for us, will you, and mind your toes."

Pym the official door-holder obliged.

"Your dad got any more desks, has he?" the tall policeman asked.

"No."

"Cupboards? Anywhere he keeps his papers?"

"They're all in there," said Pym, pointing firmly at the desk while he kept his other hand over the pocket.

"Do you want a wee then?"

"No."

"Where's some rope?"

"I don't know."

"Yes you do."

"It's in the stable. On a big saddle hook next to the new mower. It's a halter."

"What's your name?"

"Magnus. Where's Lippsie?"

"Who's Lippsie?"

"She's a lady."

"She work for your dad?"

"No."

"Slip and fetch the rope for us, will you, Magnus, there's a lad. Me and my friends here we're going to take your dad on a working holiday for a bit and we need his papers or nobody can work."

Pym raced off to the shed which was across the other side of the grounds between the pony paddock and Mr. Roley's cottage. On the shelf stood a green tea-tin where Mr. Roley kept his nails. Pym put the key into it, thinking: green tin, green filing cabinet. By the time he returned with the halter Rick was standing between two men in brown raincoats. And I picture it still exactly: Rick so pale that not all the holidays in the world would see him right, commanding loyalty of me with his eyes. And the tall policeman letting Pym try his flat cap on and push the button that made the silver bell ring under the hood of the black Wolseley. And Dorothy looking as though she needed a holiday even more than Rick did, not choking any more, but standing still as an effigy with her white hands folded across her fur coat.

Memory is a great temptress, Tom. Paint the tragic tableau. The little group, the winter's day, Christmas in the air. The convoy of Wolseleys bumping away down the lane that Pym has spent so long patrolling with his new Harrods six-shooter. Rick's desk lashed to the last car with the aid of the halter from the stable. Motionless they stare after the cortège as it vanishes into the tunnel of the trees, taking our one Provider to Lord knows where. Mrs. Roley weeping. Cookie howling in Irish. Pym's little head pressed against his mother's bosom. A thousand violins playing "Will Ye No Come Back Again?"—there is no limit to the pathos I could squeeze out of that lemon if I worked on it. Yet the truth, when I make the effort to recall it, is different. With the departure of Rick a great calm descended over Pym. He felt refreshed and freed of an intolerable burden. He watched the cars leave, Rick's desk last. And he continued to stare anxiously after them, but only for fear that Rick would talk them into turning back. As he watched, Lippsie stepped out of the woods wearing her headscarf and struggled towards him weighed down by the cardboard suitcase that contained her life's possessions. The sight of her made Pym even more furious than he'd been when he'd found Dorothy making soup. You hid, he accused her in the secret dialogue he constantly conducted with her. You were so scared you hid in the woods and missed the fun. I realise now, of course, but could not at the time, that Lippsie had seen people taken away before: her brother Aaron and the architect her father, to mention only two. But Pym in common with the rest of the world cared little about pogroms in those days and all he could feel was a deep resentment that his life's love had failed to rise to a historic moment.

Muspole came that evening. He arrived at the side door with a cooked chicken for us and a rhubarb pie and thick custard and a thermos of hot tea, and he said he was making arrangements for us and everything would be fine tomorrow. To get him on his own, Pym said "Come and see my Hornby" and at once Dorothy cried because by then there was no Hornby: the distraining bailiffs had fought a pitched battle with the repossessing shopkeepers and the Hornby had been one of the first things to go. But Mr. Muspole went with Pym anyway and Pym took him to the shed and gave him the key, then led him to the attic and showed him the secret. And everybody watched again while Mr. Roley and Mr. Muspole heaved and puffed and loaded the cabinet on to Mr. Muspole's car. And waved again when Mr. Muspole drove into the twilight in his hat.

After the Fall came, very properly, Purgatory, and Purgatory possessed no Lippsies —I guess she was trying to make one of her breaks from me, using Rick's absence to cut herself off. Purgatory was where Dorothy and I served out our sentence, Tom, and Purgatory is just over the hill from here, a few of Rick's fare-stages along the coast, though the new time-share apartments have removed much of its sting. Purgatory was the same wooded hollow of clefts and chines and dripping laurels where Pym had been conceived, with red windswept beaches always out of season, and creaking swings and sodden sandpits that were closed to enjoyment on the sabbath and for Pym on any other day as well. Purgatory was Makepeace Water-master's great sad house, The Glades, where Pym was forbidden to leave the walled orchard if it was dry or enter the main rooms if it was raining. Purgatory was the Tabernacle with the Night School Boys written clean out of the history books; and Makepeace Watermaster's frightful sermons; and Mr. Philpott's sermons; and ser-mons from every aunt, cousin and neighbourhood philosopher who felt moved to words by Rick's misfortune and saw the young criminal as the proper person to address.

Purgatory possessed no cocktail cabinets, television sets, jockeys, Bentleys or neverwozzers, and served bread and margarine instead of buttered toast. When we sang, we droned, "There Is a Green Hill Far Away," and never "Underneath the Arches" or one of Lippsie's *Lieder*. Contemporary photographs show a grinning toothy child, well grown and well looking enough, but stooped as if from living under low ceilings. All are out of focus; all have a furtive, stolen look about them, and I try to love them only because I believe Dorothy must have taken them, though it was Lippsie whom Pym was missing. In a couple the child is tugging at the arm of whatever mother happens to attend him, probably trying to persuade her to come away with him. In one he is wearing sloppy white gloves like puppets' hands, so I suppose he suffered from some skin disease, unless Makepeace was worried about fingerprints. Or perhaps he was intending to become a waiter.

The mothers, all large, all dressed in the same strict uniform, have such an air of the wardress about them that I seriously wonder whether Makepeace obtained them from an agency specialising in the care of delinquents. One wears a medal like an Iron Cross. I do not mean they are without kindness. Their smiles are alight with pious optimism. But there is something in their glance that assures me they are alert at all times to the latent criminality of their charge. Lippsie is not featured, and my poor Dorothy, Pym's one cellmate in the dark rear wing to which the two of them were confined, was even more useless than before. If Pym was thrashed, Dorothy would dress his wounds but never question the need for them. If he was put into shameful nappies as a punishment for wetting his bed, Dorothy would urge him not to drink in the second part of the day. And if he was denied tea altogether, Dorothy would save him her biscuits and pass them to him in the privacy of their upper room, poking them one by one between the invisible bars. In Paradise on good days Pym and Dorothy had managed to share the occasional joke together. Now the guilty silence of her house reclaimed her. Each day drove her further into herself and though he told her his best jokes and did his best acts for her, and painted the best pictures for her that he knew, nothing he could do was able to wake her smile for long. At night she moaned and ground her teeth and when she switched the light on, Pym lay awake beside her, thinking of Lippsie and watching Dorothy's unblinking eyes staring up at the parchment star of Bethlehem that was their lampshade.

If Dorothy had been dying Pym could have gone on nursing her for ever, no question. But she wasn't so he resented her instead. In fact soon he began to weary of her altogether and wonder whether the wrong parent had gone on holiday, and whether Lippsie was his real mother and he had made an awful mistake, the one that accounted for everything. When war broke out Dorothy was incapable of rejoicing at the marvellous news. Makepeace turned on the wireless and Pym heard a solemn man saying he had done everything he could to prevent it. Makepeace turned off the wireless and Mr. Philpott, who had come for tea, asked mournfully where, oh where, would the battlefield be? Makepeace, never at a loss, replied that God would decide. But Pym, spilling over with excitement, for once presumed to question him.

"But Uncle Makepeace! If God can decide where the battlefield is, why doesn't He stop the battle altogether? He doesn't want to. He could if He wanted to, easy. He doesn't!" Even to this day, I do not know which was the greater sin: to question Makepeace or to question God. In either case the remedy was the same: put him on bread and water like his father.

But the worst monster in The Glades was not rubbery Uncle Makepeace with his little rose ears, but mad Aunt Nell in her liver-coloured spectacles, who chased after Pym with no reason, waving her stick at him and calling him "my little canary" because of the yellow pullover Dorothy had managed to knit him while she wept. Aunt Nell had a white stick for seeing with and a brown stick for walking with. She could see perfectly well, except when she carried her white stick.

"Aunt Nell gets her wobblies out of a bottle," Pym told Dorothy one day, thinking it might make her smile. "I've seen. She's got a bottle hidden in the greenhouse."

Dorothy did not smile but became very frightened, and made him swear never to say such a thing again. Aunt Nell was ill, she said. Her illness was a secret and she took secret medicine for it, and nobody must ever know or Aunt Nell would die and God would be very angry. For weeks afterwards Pym carried this wonderful knowledge round with him much as, briefly, he had carried Rick's, but this was better and more disgraceful. It was like the first money he had ever owned, his first piece of power. Who to spend it on? he wondered. Who to share it with? Shall I let Aunt Nell live or shall I kill her for calling me her little canary? He decided on Mrs. Bannister, the cook. "Aunt Nell gets her wobblies out of a bottle," he told Mrs. Bannister, careful to use exactly the form of words that had so appalled Dorothy. But Aunt Nell did not die, and Mrs. Bannister knew about the bottle already and cuffed him for his forwardness. Worse still, she must have taken his story to Uncle Makepeace who that night made a rare visit to the prison wing, swaying and roaring and sweating and pointing at Pym while he talked about the Devil who was Rick. When he had gone Pym made his bed across the door in case Makepeace decided to come back and do some more roaring, but he never did. Nevertheless the burgeoning spy had acquired an early lesson in the dangerous business of intelligence: everybody talks.

His next lesson was no less instructive and concerned the perils of communication in occupied territory. By now Pym was writing to Lippsie daily and posting his letters in a box that stood at the rear gate of the house. They contained to his later shame priceless information, almost none of it in code. How to break into The Glades at night. His hours of exercise. Maps. The character of his persecutors. The money he had saved. The precise location of the German guards. The route to be followed through the back garden and where the kitchen key was kept. "I have been kidnapped to a dangerous house, please get me quick," he wrote, and enclosed a drawing of Aunt Nell with canaries coming out of her mouth as a further warning of the hazards that surrounded him. But there was a snag. Having no address for Lippsie, Pym could only hope that somebody at the post office would know where she was to be found. His confidence was misplaced. One day the postman delivered the whole top-secret bundle to Makepeace personally, who summoned the prevailing mother, who summoned Pym, and led him like the convict he was to Makepeace for chastisement, though he simpered and begged and blandished him for all he was worth, for Pym somewhat unsportingly hated the lash and was seldom gallant about receiving it. After that he contented himself with looking for Lippsie on buses and, where he could do so deniably, asking people who happened to be passing the rear gate whether they had seen her. Particularly he asked policemen, whom he now smiled at richly wherever he found them.

"My father's got an old green box with secrets in," he told a constable one day, strolling in the memorial gardens with a mother.

"Has he then, son? Well, thanks for telling us," said the constable and pretended to write in his notebook.

Meanwhile word of Rick, though not of Lippsie, reached Pym like the unfinished whispers of a distant radio transmitter. Your father is well. His holiday is doing him good. He has lost weight, lots of good food, we're not to worry, he's getting exercise, reading his law books, he's gone back to school. The source of these priceless snippets was the Other House, which lay in a poorer part of Purgatory down by the coking station and must never be mentioned in front of Uncle Makepeace, since it was the house that had spawned Rick and brought disgrace on the great family of Watermaster, not to mention the memory of TP. Hand in hand, Dorothy and Pym rode there in fireside darkness, sticky mesh against bomb blast on the windows of the trolley-bus, and the lights inside burning blue to baffle German pilots. At the Other House, a steadfast little Irish lady with a rock jaw gave Pym half-a-crown out of a ginger jar and squeezed his arm muscles approvingly and called him "son" like Rick, and on the wall hung a copy of the same tinted photograph of TP, framed not in gold but in coffin wood. Jolly-faced aunts made sweets for Pym out of their sugar ration, and hugged and wept and treated Dorothy like the royalty she once had been, and hooted when Pym did his funny voices and clapped when he sang "Underneath the Arches." "Go on, Magnus, give us Sir Makepeace then!" But Pym dared not for fear of God's anger, which he knew from the Aunt Nell affair to be swift and awful.

The aunt he loved most was Bess. "Tell us, Magnus," whispered Aunt Bess to him, alone in the scullery, drawing his head close to her own. "Is it true your dad ever owned a racehorse called Prince Magnus, after you?"

"It's not true," said Pym without a second's thought, remembering the excitement as he sat beside Lippsie on her bed, listening to the commentary of Prince Magnus coming nowhere. "It is a lie made up by Uncle Makepeace to hurt my father."

Aunt Bess kissed him and laughed and wept in relief, and held him even tighter. "Never say I asked you. Promise."

"I promise," said Pym. "God's honour."

The same Aunt Bess, one glorious night, smuggled Pym out of The Glades and into the Theatre Pier, where they saw Max Miller and a row of girls with long bare legs like Lippsie's. On the trolley-bus back, brimming over with gratitude, Pym told her everything he knew in the world, and made up whatever he didn't. He said he had written a book by Shakespeare and it was in a green box in a secret house. One day he would find and print it and make a lot of money. He said he would be a policeman and an actor and a jockey, and drive a Bentley like Rick, and marry Lippsie and have six children all called TP like his granddad. This pleased Bess enormously, except for the bit about the jockey, and sent her home saying Magnus was a card, which was what he wanted most. His gratification was short-lived. This time Pym had made God very angry indeed, and as usual He was not slow to do something about it. On the very next day before breakfast the police came and took away his Dorothy for ever, though the reigning mother said they were only ambulance.

And once again—though Pym dutifully wept for Dorothy—and refused food for her, and flailed with his fists at the long-suffering mothers—he could not but see their rightness in removing her. They were taking her to a place where she would be happy, the mothers said. Pym envied her luck. Not to the same place as Rick, no, but somewhere nicer and quieter, with kind people to look after her. Pym planned to join her. Escape, till now a fantasy, became his serious aim. A celebrated epileptic at Sunday school acquainted him with his symptoms. Pym waited a day, ran into the kitchen with his eyes rolling, and collapsed dramatically before Mrs. Bannister, shoving his hands into his mouth and writhing for good measure. The doctor, who must have been a rare imbecile, prescribed a laxative. Next day in a further attempt to draw attention to himself, Pym hacked off his forelock with paper scissors. No one noticed. Improvising now, he released Mrs. Bannister's cockatoo from its cage, sprinkled soap flakes into the Aga cooker and blocked the lavatory with a feather boa belonging to Aunt Nell.

Nothing happened. He was beating the air. What he needed was a great dramatic crime. All night he waited, then early in the morning when his courage was highest, Pym walked the length of the house to Makepeace Watermaster's study in his dressing-gown and slippers and relieved himself prolifically over the centre of the white carpet. Terrified, he threw himself on to the patch he had created, hoping to dry it out with the heat of his body. A maid entered and screamed. A mother was summoned and from his anguished position on the carpet Pym was treated to a formative example of how history rewrites itself in a crisis. The mother touched his shoulder. He groaned. She asked him where it hurt. He indicated his groin, the literal cause of his distress. Makepeace Watermaster was fetched. What were you doing in my study in the first place? The pain, sir, the pain, I wanted to tell you about the pain. With a screech of tyres the doctor returned and now everything was remembered while he bent over Pym and probed his stomach with his stupid fingertips. The collapse before Mrs. Bannister. The nightly moans, the daily pallor. Dorothy's madness, discussed in hushed terms. Even Pym's bed-wetting was taken down and used in evidence on his behalf.

"Poor boy, it's got him here as well," said the mother as the patient was lifted cautiously to the sofa and the maid was hurried off to fetch Jeyes disinfectant and a floor-cloth. Pym's temperature was read and grimly observed to be normal. "Doesn't mean a thing," said the doctor, now battling to make good his earlier negligence, and ordered the mother to pack the poor boy's things. She did so and in the course of it must inevitably have discovered a number of small objects that Pym had taken from other people's lives in order to improve his own: Nell's jet earrings, Cook's letters from her son in Canada and Makepeace Watermaster's *Travels with a Donkey* which Pym had selected for its title, the only part he had read. In the crisis even this black evidence of his criminality was ignored.

The outcome was more effective than Pym could have hoped. Not a week later, in a hospital newly fitted to receive victims of the approaching blitz, Magnus Pym, aged eight and a half years, yielded up his appendix in the interests of operational cover. When he came round, the first thing he saw was a blue and black koala bear larger than himself seated on the end of his bed. The second was a basket of fruit bigger than the bear, which looked like a piece of St. Moritz that had landed by mistake in wartime England. The third was Rick, slim and smart as a sailor, standing to attention with his right hand lifted in salute. Beside Rick again, like a scared ghost dragged unwillingly from the shades of Pym's chloroformed realm, came Lippsie, hunched at the shoulders by a new fur cape, and supported by Syd Lemon looking like his own younger brother.

Lippsie knelt to me. The two men looked on while we embraced.

"That's the way then," Rick kept saying approvingly. "Give him a good old English hug. That's the way."

Softly, like a bitch recovering her pup, Lippsie picked me over, lifting the remains of my forelock and staring gravely into my eyes as if fearing that bad things had got into them.

How they celebrated their release! Shorn of all possessions except the clothes they stood up in and the credit they could muster as they went along, Rick's reconstituted court took to the open road and became crusaders through wartime Britain. Petrol was rationed, Bentleys had vanished for the duration, all over the country posters asked "Is Your Journey Really Necessary?" and every time they passed one they slowed down to yell back, "Yes, it is!" in chorus through the open windows of their cab. Drivers either became accomplices or left in a hurry. A Mr. Humphries threw them all into the street in Aberdeen after a week, calling them crooks, and drove away without his money, never to be seen again. But a Mr. Cudlove whom Rick had met on holiday—and who got the court a week's tick at the Imperial at Torquay on the strength of an aunt who worked in the accounts department—he stayed for ever, sharing their food and fortunes and teaching Pym tricks with string. Sometimes they had one taxi, sometimes Mr. Cudlove's special friend Ollie brought his Humber and they had day-long races for Pym's sole benefit, with Syd leaning out of the back window giving the car the whip. Of mothers they had a dazzling and varying supply and often acquired them at such short notice they had to cram them into the back two deep, with Pym squeezed into an exciting, unfamiliar lap. There was a lady called Topsie who smelt of roses and made Pym dance with his head against her breast; there was Millie who let him sleep with her in her siren-suit because he was frightened of the black cupboard in his hotel bedroom, and who bestowed frank caresses on him while she bathed him. And Eileens and Mabels and Joans, and a Violet who got carsick on cider, some into her gas-mask case and the rest over Pym. And when they were all got out of the way, Lippsie materialised, standing motionless in the steam of a railway station, her cardboard suitcase hanging from her slim hand. Pym loved her more than ever, but her deepening melancholy was too much for him and in the whirl of the great crusade he resented being the object of it.

"Old Lippsie's got a touch of the what's-its," Syd would say kindly, noting Pym's disappointment, and they'd heave a bit of a sigh of relief together when she left.

"Old Lippsie's on about her Jews again," said Syd sadly another time. "They keep telling her another lot's been done."

And once: "Old Lippsie's got the guilts she isn't dead like them."

Pym's intermittent enquiries after Dorothy led him nowhere. Your mum's poorly, Syd would say; she'll be back soon, and the best thing our Magnus here can do for her meantime is not fret over her, because it will only get to her and make her worse.

Rick took a wounded line. "You'll just have to put up with your old man for a while. I thought we were having fun then. Aren't we having fun?"

"All the fun in the world," said Pym.

On the subject of his recent absence Rick was as sparing as the rest of the court, so that soon Pym began to wonder whether they had ever been on holiday at all. Only the occasional hint convinced him that they had shared a cementing experience. Winchester had been worse than Reading because of those bloody gypsies off of Salisbury Plain, Pym once overheard Morrie Washington tell Perce Loft. Syd backed him up. "Those Winchester gyppos was rough you wouldn't believe," said Syd with feeling. "The screws was no better, either." And Pym noticed that their holiday had made hearty eaters of them. "Eat your peas now, Magnus," Syd urged him amid much laughter. "There's worse hotels than this one, *we* can tell you."

It wasn't till a year or more later, when Pym's vocabulary had grown equal to his intelligence gathering, that he realised they had been talking about prison.

But their leader did not share these jokes and they ceased abruptly, for Rick's *gravitas* was something no man tampered with lightly, least of all those appointed to uphold it. Rick's superiority was manifest in everything he did. In the way he dressed even when we were very broke, his clean laundry and clean shoes. In the food he required and the style to eat it in. The rooms he had in the hotel. In the way he needed brandy for his snooker, and scared everyone into silence with his brooding. In his preoccupation with good works, which involved visiting hospitals where people had taken bad knocks and seeing the old people right while their children were away at the war.

"Will you see Lippsie right too, when the war's over?" Pym asked one day.

"Old Lippsie's crackerjack," said Rick.

Meanwhile we traded. What in, Pym never rightly knew and nor do I now. Sometimes in rare commodities, such as hams and whisky, sometimes in promises, which the court called Faith. Other times in nothing more solid than the sunny horizons that sparkled ahead of us down the empty wartime roads. When Christmas approached somebody produced sheets of coloured crêpe paper, thousands of them. For days and nights on end, augmented by extra mothers recruited for this vital war-work, Pym and the court crouched in an empty railway carriage at Didcot, twisting the paper into crackers that contained no toys and would not crack, while they told each other wild stories and cooked toast by laying it on top of the paraffin stove. Some of the crackers, it was true, had little wooden soldiers inside them, but these were called "samples" and kept separate. The rest, Syd explained, was for decoration, Titch, like flowers when there isn't any. Pym believed it all. He was the most willing child labourer in the world, so long as there was approval waiting for him round the corner.

Another time they towed a trailer filled with crates of oranges which Pym refused to eat because he overheard Syd saying they were hot. They sold them to a pub on the road to Birmingham. Once they had a load of dead chickens that Syd said they could only move at night when it was cold enough, so perhaps that was what had gone wrong with the oranges. And there is a clip of film running forever in my memory. It shows a scraggy moonlit hilltop on the moors, and our two cabs with their lights out winding nervously to the crest. And the dark figures standing waiting for us on the back of their lorry. And the masked lamp that counted out the money for Mr. Muspole the great accountant while Syd unloaded the trailer. And though Pym watched from a distance because he hated feathers, no night frontier crossing later in his life was ever more exciting.

"Can we send the money to Lippsie now?" Pym asked. "She hasn't got any left."

"Now how do you know a thing like that, old son?"

From her letters to you, Pym thought. You left one in your pocket and I read it. But Rick's eyes had their flick-knife glint so he said "I made it up," and smiled.

Rick did not come on our adventures. He was saving himself. What for was a question nobody asked within Pym's hearing and certainly he never asked it for himself. Rick was devoting himself to his good works, his old people and his hospital visiting. "Is that suit of yours pressed, son?" Rick would say when as a special privilege father and son embarked together on one of these high errands. "God in heaven, Muspole, look at the boy's suit, it's a damned shame! Look at his hair!" Hastily a mother would be ordered to press the suit, another to polish his shoes and get his fingernails proper, a third to comb his hair till it was orderly and sensitive. With flimsy patience Mr. Cudlove tapped his keys on the car roof while Pym was given a final check-over for signs of unintentional irreverence. Then away at last they sped to the house or bedside of some elderly and worthy person, and Pym sat fascinated to see how swiftly Rick trimmed his manner to suit theirs, how naturally he slipped into the cadences and vernacular that put them most at ease, and how the love of God came into his good face when he talked about Liberalism and Masonry and his dear dead father, God rest him, and a first-class rate of return, ten percent guaranteed plus profits for as long as you're spared. Sometimes he brought a ham with him as a gift and was an angel in a hamless world. Sometimes a pair of silk stockings or a box of nectarines, for Rick was always the giver even when he was taking. When he was able Pym threw his own charm into the scales by reciting a prayer he had composed, or singing "Underneath the Arches," or telling a witty story with a range of regional accents that he had picked up in the course of the crusade. "The Germans are killing all the Jews," he said once, to great effect. "I've got a friend called Lippsie and all her other friends are dead." If his performance was wanting, Rick let him know this without brutality. "When somebody like Mrs. Ardmore asks you whether you remember her, son, don't scratch your old head and pull a face. Look her in the eye and smile and say, 'Yes.' That's the way to treat old people, *and* to be a credit to your father. Do you love your old man?"

"Of course I do."

"Well then. How was your steak last night?"

"It was super."

"There's not twenty boys in England ate steak last night, do you know that?"

"I know."

"Give us a kiss then."

Syd was less reverent. "If you're going to learn to shave people, Magnus," he said over a lot of winks, "you've got to learn how to rub the soap in first!"

Somewhere near Aberdeen, without warning, the court became interested only in chemists' shops. We were a limited company by then, which to Pym was as good as being a policeman. Rick had found a new banker with Faith, Mr. Cudlove's live-in friend Ollie signed the cheques. And our product was a concoction of dried fruit that we pulped with a handpress in the kitchens of a great country house belonging to a dashing new mother called Cherry. It was a large house with white pillars at the front door and white statues all like Lippsie in the garden. Even in Paradise the court had never stayed anywhere so grand. First we stewed the fruit and pulped it in the press, which was the best bit; then we added gelatine to make lozenges out of it, which Pym rolled round and round in Company sugar with his bare palm, licking it clean between batches. Cherry had evacuees and horses, and gave parties for American soldiers who presented her with cans of petrol in the tithe barn. She owned farms and a great park with deer, and an absent husband in the Navy whom Syd referred to as "the Admiral." In the evenings before dinner, a pack of King Charles spaniels was whipped by an old gamekeeper. They swarmed over the sofas yapping till they were whipped out again. At Cherry's, for the first time since St. Moritz, Pym saw silver candles on the dinner table lighting bare shoulders.

"There's a lady called Lippsie who's in love with my father and they're going to marry and have babies," Pym told Cherry helpfully one evening as they walked together down the ride; and was greatly impressed by how seriously Cherry took this news, and how intently she questioned Pym concerning Lippsie's accomplishments. "I've seen her in the bath and she's beautiful," said Pym.

And when they left a few days later, Rick took something of the dignity of the place with him, and something of its proprietor also, for I remember him striding down the great stone steps with a white hide suitcase in each hand—Rick always loved a fine suitcase—and sporting a smart country outfit of the sort no admiral would wear to sea. Syd and Mr. Muspole followed after him like circus midgets, clutching the chipped green filing cabinet between them and shouting, "Your end, Deirdre!" and "Gently down the stairs, Sybil!"

"Don't you ever talk to Cherry about Lippsie again, son," Rick warned him, in his heaviest moralistic tone. "It's high time you learned it's not polite to mention one woman to another. Because if you don't learn that, you'll waste your advantages and that's a fact."

It was through Cherry also, I suspect, that Rick formed the determination to turn Pym into a gentleman. Until now it has been assumed that Pym was already of the aristocracy. But Cherry, a forceful and superior woman, taught Rick that true English privilege was obtained by hardship, and that the best hardship was to be found at English boarding-schools. She also had a nephew at Mr. Grimble's academy by the name of Sefton Boyd, but better known to her as my darling Kenny. A second and less tender influence was the army. First Muspole became its casualty, then Morrie Washington, then Syd. Each with a rueful smile of failure packed his little suitcase and disappeared, returning only seldom and with very short hair. Then one day to his hurt surprise Rick himself was summoned to the flag. In later life he took a more tolerant view of the pettiness of the society entrusted to his care, but the sight of his call-up papers on the breakfast table provoked an outburst of righteous anger.

"God damn it, Loft, I thought we'd taken care of all that," he raged at Perce, who was exempt from everything.

"We did take care of it," said Perce, jabbing a thumb in my direction. "Delicate kid, mother in the nut-house, it's watertight compassion."

"Well where the devil's their compassion now then?" Rick demanded, shoving the buff document under Perce's nose. "It's a damn shame, Loft. That's what it is. Get after it."

"You never ought to have told old Cherry about Lippsie," Perce Loft fumed at Pym later. "She went and peached on your dad out of spite."

But the army declined to surrender, and the depleted court, consisting of Perce Loft, a clutch of mothers, Ollie and Mr. Cudlove, duly uprooted itself to a drab hotel in Bradford, where Rick was obliged to reconcile the ignominy of the parade ground with the burdens of financial generalship. Using the hotel's coin box and the hotel's credit, typing and filing in the hotel's bedrooms, storing their mysterious wares in the hotel's garage, the court fought a gallant rearguard action against dissolution, but in vain. It was Sunday evening in the hotel. Rick in his private's uniform, freshly pressed, was preparing to return to barracks. A new dartsboard was wedged under his arm, which he planned to present to the sergeants' mess, for Rick had his heart set on the post of catering clerk, which would enable him to see us right in the shortages.

"Son. It's time for you to set those fine feet of yours on the hard road of becoming Lord Chief Justice and a credit to your old man. There's been too much lazy fare about and you're part of it. Cudlove, look at his shirt. No man ever did business in a dirty shirt. Look at his hair. He'll be an airy-fairy before you can say Jack Robinson. It's boarding-school for you, son, and God bless you and God bless me too."

One more bear-hug, a final staunching of the tears, one noble handshake for the absent cameras as, dartsboard at the ready, the great man rode away to war. Pym watched him out of sight, then stealthily climbed the stairs to the provisional State Apartments. The door was unlocked. He smelt woman and talc. The double bed was in disarray. He pulled the pigskin briefcase from beneath it, tipped out the contents and, as he had often done before, puzzled over unintelligible files and correspondence. The Admiral's country suit, donned for a few hours and still warm, was hanging in the wardrobe. He poked in the pockets. The green filing cabinet, more chipped than ever, lurked in its habitual darkness. Why does he always keep it in cupboards? Pym tugged vainly at the locked drawers. Why does it travel separately from everything as if it had a disease?

"Looking for money, are we, Titch?" a woman's voice asked him, from the bathroom doorway. It was Doris, typist elect and good scout. "Spare yourself the trouble, I would. It's all tick with your dad. I've looked."

"He told me he'd left me a bar of chocolate in his room," Pym replied resolutely, and continued delving while she watched.

"There's three gross of army milk-and-nut sitting in the garage. Help yourself," Doris advised. "Petrol coupons too, if you're thirsty."

"It was a special kind of bar," said Pym.

I have never fathomed the machinations that sent Pym and Lippsie to the same school. Were they infiltrated singly or as a package, the one to be taught, the other to supply her labour in payment? I suspect as a package but have no proof beyond a general knowledge of Rick's methods. All his life, Rick maintained a work-force of devoted women whom he regularly discarded and revived. When they were not required in the court they were put out to work for him in the great world, easing his crusade with remittances they could ill afford, selling their jewellery for him, cashing their savings and lending their names to bank accounts from which Rick's name was banned. But Lippsie had no jewellery and no credit with the banks. She had only her lovely body and her music and her brooding guilt, and a little English schoolboy who held her to the world. I suspect now that Rick had already read the warning signs collecting in her, and decided to give her to me to look after. Nevertheless there was profit to our partnership and Rick was nothing if not an opportunist.

If Pym possessed any learning by the time he presented himself to Mr. Grimble's country academy for the sons of gentlemen, then he owed it to Lippsie and not to any of the dozen or so infant schools, Bible schools and kindergartens scattered along the hectic road of Rick's progress. Lippsie taught him writing, and to this day I write a German "t" and put a stroke through my small "z"s. She taught him spelling, and it was always a great joke between them that they could not remember how many "d"s there were in the English version of "address," and to this day I can't be sure of the answer until I have written out the German first. Whatever else Pym knew, apart from meaningless passages of the Scriptures, was contained in her cardboard suitcase, for she never came to see him anywhere without whisking him to her room and foisting some piece of geography or history on him, or making him play scales on her flute.

"See, Magnus, without informations we are nothing. But with informations we can go anywhere in the world, we are like turtles, our houses always on our backs. You learn to paint, you can paint anywhere. A sculptor, a musician, a painter, they need no permits. Only their heads. Our world must be inside our heads. That is the only safe way. Now you play Lippsie a nice tune."

The arrangement at Mr. Grimble's was the perfect flowering of this relationship. Their world was inside their heads, but it was also contained in a brick-and-flint gardener's cottage at the end of Mr. Grimble's long drive, designated the Overflow House and occupied by the Overflow Boys of whom Pym was the newest recruit. And Lippsie, his lovely lifelong Lippsie, their best and most attentive mother. They knew at once they were outcasts. If they didn't, the eighty boys up the drive made it plain to them. They had a pallid grocer's son without an "h" to his name, and tradesmen were ridiculous. They had three Jews whose speech was spattered with Polish, and a hopeless stammerer called M-M-Marlin, and an Indian with knock-knees whose father was killed when the Japanese took Singapore. They had Pym with his spots and wet beds. Yet under Lippsie they contrived to glory in all these disadvantages. If the boys up the drive were the crack regiment, the Overflow Boys were the irregulars who fought all the harder for their medals. For staff, Mr. Grimble took what he could get, and what he could get was whatever the country didn't need. A Mr. O'Mally punched a boy so hard across the ear he knocked him out cold, a Mr. Farbourne beat heads together and fractured someone's skull. A science master thought the marauding village boys were Bolsheviks and fired his shotgun into their retreating rumps. At Grimble's, boys were flogged for tardiness and flogged for untidiness, flogged for apathy and flogged for cheek, and flogged for not improving from the flogging. The fever of war encouraged brutality, the guilt of our non-combatant staff intensified it, the intricacies of the British hierarchical system provided a natural order for the exercise of sadism. Their God was the protector of English country gentlemen and their justice was the punishment of the ill-born and disadvantaged, and it was meted out with the collaboration of the strong, of whom Sefton Boyd was the strongest and most handsome. It is the saddest of all the ironies of Lippsie's death, as I see it now, that she died in the service of a Fascist state.

Each leave-out day, on Rick's standing orders, Pym presented himself at the entrance to the school drive in readiness for Mr. Cudlove's arrival. When nobody appeared, he hurried gratefully to the woods in search of privacy and wild strawberries. Come evening he returned to the school boasting of the great day he had had.

Just occasionally the worst happened and a carload would appear—Rick, Mr. Cudlove, Syd in private's uniform, and a couple of jockeys crammed in anyhow— all well refreshed after a pause at the Brace of Partridges. If a school match was in progress they would roar support for the home side and hand round unheard-of oranges from a crate in the boot of the car. If none, then Syd and Morrie Washington would press-gang any boy who happened to be passing on his bicycle, and mount a handicap race round the playing fields while Syd belted out the commentary through his cupped hands. And Rick personally, dressed in the Admiral's suit, would start them off with a mayoral wave of his handkerchief, and Rick personally would present an unimaginable box of chocolates to the winner, while the pound notes changed hands around the court. And when evening came Rick never failed to install himself at the Overflow House, bringing a bottle of bubbly along to cheer old Lippsie up because she seemed so glum—"What's got into her, son?" And Rick cheered her up all right; Pym heard it going on, thump, creak and scream, while he crouched outside her door in his dressing-gown wondering whether they were fighting or pretending. Back in bed, he would hear Rick tiptoeing down the stairs, though Rick could tread as lightly as a cat.

Till a morning came when Rick did not leave quietly at all. Not for Pym, not for the rest of the Overflow Boys, who were greatly excited to be woken by the clamour. Lippsie was bawling and Rick was trying to quell her, but the nicer he was to her the more unreasonable she became. "You made me to be a *teef!*" she was yelling between great big whoops while she took another gulp of air. "You made me *teef* to punish me. You were bad priest, Rickie Pym. You made me to steal. I was honest woman. I was refugee but I was honest woman." Why did she speak as if it was all last year? "My father was honest man. My broder also was honest man. They was good men, not bad like me. You made me to steal until I was criminal like you. Maybe God punish you one day, Rickie Pym. Maybe He make you to weep, too. I hope He will. I hope, I hope!"

"Old Lippsie's having a touch of her wobblies, son," Rick explained to Pym, finding him on the stairs as he made to leave. "Slip in there and see if you can make her laugh with one of your stories. Is old Grimble feeding you up there?"

"It's super," said Pym.

"Your old man is seeing them right, know that? The healthiest school in Britain, this is. Ask them at the Ministry. Want a half-crown? Well then."

To reach Lippsie's bicycle Pym used a walk he had acquired from Sefton Boyd. You kept your hands lightly linked behind your back, shoved your head forward and fixed your eyes upon some vaguely pleasing object on the horizon. You stalked wide and high, smiling slightly, as if listening to other voices, which is how the flower of us wear authority. He was too small to sit on the tartan saddle but a lady's bicycle has a hole and not a bar, as Sefton Boyd was always happy to point out, and Pym swayed through the hole pumping his legs from side to side as he swung the handlebars between the rainfilled craters in the tarmac. I am the official bicycle collector. To his right was the kitchen garden where he and Lippsie had Dug for Victory, to his left the coppice where the German bomb had fallen, hurling bits of blackened twig against the window of the bedroom he shared with the Indian and the grocer's boy. But behind him in his terrified imagination was Sefton Boyd with his lictors in full cry, mimicking Lippsie at him because they knew he loved her: "Vere are you goink, mein little black market? Vot are you doink mit your sweetheart, mein little black market, now she be dead?" Ahead of him was the gate where he had waited for Mr. Cudlove, and to the left of the gate was the Overflow House with its iron railings ripped away for the war effort, and a policeman standing in the gap.

"I've been sent to collect my nature-study book," said Pym to the policeman, looking him straight in the eye as he leaned Lippsie's bicycle against a brick post. Pym had lied to policemen before and knew you must look honest.

"Your nature book, have you?" said the policeman. "What's your name, then?"

"Pym, sir. I live here."

"Pym who?"

"Magnus."

"Hop along then, Pym Magnus," said the policeman but Pym still walked slowly, refusing to show any sign of eagerness. Lippsie's silver-framed family was queued up on the bedside table, but Rick's heavy head dominated the lot of them, sensitive and political in its pigskin frame, and Rick's sage eyes followed him wherever he went. He opened Lippsie's wardrobe and breathed the smell of her, he shoved aside her frilly white dressing-gown, her fur cape and the camel-hair overcoat with the pixie's hood that Rick had bought her in St. Moritz. From the back of her wardrobe he pulled out her cardboard suitcase. He set it on the floor and opened it with the key she kept hidden in the Toby jug on the tiled mantelpiece next to the soft toy chimp who was Little Audrey who laughed and laughed and laughed. He took out the book like a Bible that was written in little black sword blades, and the music books and reading books he didn't understand and the passport with her picture in it when she was young, and the wads of letters in German from her sister Rachel, pronounced "Ra-ha-el," who no longer wrote to her, and from the very bottom of the case Rick's letters, tied into bundles with bits of harvest twine. Some he knew almost by heart, though he had difficulty unravelling the portent seething beneath their verbiage:

"It is a matter of weeks no days my darling before the present besetting clouds will be dispersed away as a permanency. Loft will have obtained my Discharge and you and I can enjoy our well-deserved Reward. . . . Look after that boy of mine who regards you as a Mother and make sure he doesn't turn out airy-fairy. . . .

"Your doubts regarding Trust completely misplaced . . . you should not trouble your Head as it is a further worry to me here waiting for the Bugle's summons Perhaps never to Return . . . what is involved here will bring untold benefits to Many such as Wentworth . . . don't go on at me about W or his wife, that woman is a professional troublemaker of the worst kind out. . . .

"My regards to Ted Grimble whom I consider a great Educationist and Headmaster. Tell him a further Hundred-weight of prunes on its way . . . he should prepare kitchen for Two gross best fresh oranges also. Loft has got me Out on three weeks compassionate which means I Recommence my basic from scratch if I am recalled. Regarding Another Matter, Muspole says to continue sending items as before. Please oblige quickly owing purely Temporary problem of liquidity this end which is preventing decent people like Wentworth being seen right. . . .

"If you don't send more fee cheques immediately, you may as well send me back to Prison and all the Boys excepting Perce as usual and that's a Fact. . . . Talk about killing yourself is Foolishness with so many Killing each other round the World in this Senseless and Tragic war. . . . Muspole says if you send poste restaurant express Tomorrow he will be at P.O. when they open Saturday and send on to Wentworth immediately. . . ."

Lippsie's letter, which he had left till last, was by contrast a marvel of conciseness:

"My dear darling Magnus,
"You must be good boy always, darling, play your music and be strong like a man to your father, I love you.

Lippsie"

Pym made a bundle of them, Lippsie's included, stuffed them inside his nature book and the nature book inside his belt. He rode past the policeman slowly, feeling cats' claws on his back. The school boiler was a brick furnace built into the basement, fed by a chute in the kitchen yard. To approach the chute was a beatable offence, to burn paper was a Quisling act and sailors would drown for it. A fierce rain was blowing from the Downs, the chalk hills were olive against the storm-clouds. Standing before the open chute, shoulders high against his neck, Pym shoved the letters into it and watched them disappear. A dozen people must have seen him, staff and inmates, and some for sure were allies of Sefton Boyd. But the openness with which he had proceeded convinced them he was acting on authority. Certainly it convinced Pym. He shoved in the last letter, which was the one that told him to be strong, and walked away without once turning to see if he was being noticed.

He needed the staff lavatory again. He needed his secret St. Moritz with its panelled seclusion, he needed the secret majesty of its brass taps and mahogany-framed mirror, for Pym loved luxury as only those can who have had love taken from them. He gained the forbidden staircase to the staffroom; he reached the half-landing. The lavatory door was ajar. He pushed it, slipped inside, locked it behind him. He was alone. He stared at his face, making it harder, then softer, then harder. He ran the taps and washed his cheeks till they shone. His sudden isolation, added to the grandeur of his achievement, made him unique in his own eyes. His mind whirled with the vertigo of greatness. He was God. He was Hitler. He was Wentworth. He was the king of the green filing cabinet, TP's noble descendant. Henceforth, nothing on earth need happen without his intervention. He took out his penknife, opened it and held its big blade uppermost before his face in the mirror, taking an Arthurian vow. By Excalibur I swear. The lunch bell rang but there was no roll-call for lunch and he was not hungry; he would never be hungry again, he was an immortal knight. He thought of cutting his throat but his mission was too important. He thought of names. Who has the best family in the school? I have. The Pyms are crackerjack and Prince Magnus is the fastest horse in the world. He pressed his cheek against the wood panelling, smelling cricket bats and

Swiss forests. The knife was still in his hand. His eyes went hot and blurred, his ears sang. The divine voice inside him told him to look, and he saw the initials "KS-B" carved very deeply into the best panel. Stooping, he gathered the splinters at his feet and put them into the lavatory where they floated. He pulled the plug but they still floated. He left them there, went to the arts hut and completed his Dornier bomber.

All afternoon he waited, confident nothing had happened. I didn't do it. If I went back it wouldn't be there. It was Maggs in third form. It was Jameson who owns a kukri. I saw him go in. An oik from the village did it, I saw him sneaking round the grounds with a dagger in his belt, his name is Wentworth. At evensong he prayed that a German bomb would destroy staff lavatory. None did. Next day, he presented Sefton Boyd with his greatest treasure, the koala bear Lippsie had given him after his appendix operation. In break he buried his penknife in the loose earth behind the cricket pavilion. Or as I would say today, cached it. It was not until evening line-up that the full name of the Honourable Kenneth Sefton Boyd was called out in a voice of doom by the duty master, the sadist O'Mally. Mystified, the young nobleman was led to Mr. Grimble's study. Mystified himself, Pym watched him go. Whatever can they want him for—my friend, my best friend, the owner of my koala bear? The mahogany door closed, eighty pairs of eyes fixed upon its fine workmanship, Pym's also. Pym heard Mr. Grimble's voice, then Sefton Boyd's raised in protest. Then a great silence while God's justice was administered, blow by blow. Counting, Pym felt cleansed and vindicated. So it wasn't Maggs, it wasn't Jameson and it wasn't me. Sefton Boyd did it himself, otherwise he would not have been beaten. Justice, he was beginning to learn, is only as good as her servants.

"It had a hyphen," Sefton Boyd told him next day. "Whoever did it gave us a hyphen when we haven't got one. If I ever find the sod I'll kill him."

"So will I," Pym promised loyally and meant every word. Like Rick he was learning to live on several planes at once. The art of it was to forget everything except the ground you stood on and the face you spoke from at that moment.

The effects of Lippsie's death upon the young Pym were many and not by any means all negative. Her demise entrenched him as a self-reliant person, confirming him in his knowledge that women were fickle and liable to sudden disappearances. He learned the great lesson of Rick's example, namely the importance of a respectable appearance. He learned that the only safety was in seeming legitimacy. He developed his determination to be a secret mover of life's events. It was Pym, for instance, who let down Mr. Grimble's tyres and poured three six-pound bags of cooking salt into the swimming-pool. But it was Pym who led the hunt for the culprit too, throwing up many tantalising clues and casting doubt on many solid reputations. With Lippsie gone, his love for Rick became once more unobstructed and, better, he could love him from a distance, for Rick had once more disappeared.

Had he gone back to prison, as he had promised Lippsie that he would? Had the police found the green filing cabinet? Pym did not know then and Syd, I suspect by choice, does not know now. Army records grant Rick an abrupt discharge six months before the period in question, referring the reader to the Criminal Records Office for an explanation. None is available, perhaps because that Perce had a friend who worked there, a lady who thought the world of him. Whatever the reason Pym floated out alone once more, and had a fair amount of fun. For weekend leave Ollie and Mr. Cudlove received him at their basement flat in Fulham and pampered him in every imaginable way. Mr. Cudlove, fit as ever from his exercises, taught him how to wrestle, and when they all went out for a toot on the river together, Ollie wore ladies' clothes and did a squeaky voice so well that only Pym and Mr. Cudlove in all the world ever knew there was a man inside them. For his longer holidays, Pym was obliged to trek over Cherry's vast estates with Sefton Boyd, listening to ever more awful stories about the great public school of which he would soon become a member: how new boys were tied into laundry baskets and flung down flights of stone stairs, how they were harnessed to pony traps with fish-hooks through their ears and made to haul the prefect round school yard.

"My father's gone to prison and escaped," Pym told him in return. "He's got a pet jackdaw that looks after him." He imagined Rick in a cave on Dartmoor, with Syd and Meg taking him pies wrapped in a handkerchief while the hounds sniffed his trail.

"My father's in the Secret Service," Pym told him another time. "He's been tortured to death by the Gestapo but I'm not allowed to say. His real name is Wentworth."

Having surprised himself by this pronouncement Pym worked on it. A different name and a gallant death suited Rick excellently. They gave him the class Pym was beginning to suspect he lacked and made things right with Lippsie. So when Rick came bouncing back one day, not tortured or altered in any way, but accompanied by two jockeys, a box of nectarines and a brand-new mother with a feather in her hat, Pym thought seriously of working for the Gestapo and wondered how you joined. And would have done so, too, for sure, had not the peace ungraciously robbed him of the chance.

A last word is also needed here about Pym's politics during this instructive period. Churchill sulked and was too popular. De Gaulle, with his tilted pineapple head, was too much like Uncle Makepeace, while Roosevelt, with his stick and spectacles and wheelchair, was clearly Aunt Nell in disguise. Hitler was so wretchedly unloved that Pym had more than a fair regard for him, but it was Joseph Stalin whom he appointed to be his proxy father. Stalin neither sulked nor preached. He spent his time chuckling, and playing with dogs, and picking roses in news cinemas while his loyal troops won the war for him in the snows of St. Moritz.

Putting down his pen, Pym stared at what he had written, first in fear, then gradually in relief. Finally he laughed.

"I didn't break," he whispered. "I stayed above the fray."

And poured himself a Poppy-sized vodka for old times' sake.

5

Frau Bauer's bed was as narrow and lumpy as a servant's bed in a fairy-tale and Mary lay in it exactly as Brotherhood had dumped her there, roly-polyed in the eiderdown, knees drawn up in self-protection, clutching her shoulders with her hands. He had slid off her, she could no longer smell his sweat and breath. But she could feel his bulk at the foot of the bed and sometimes she had a hard time remembering that they had not made love a few moments earlier, for his habit in those days had been to leave her dozing while he sat as he was sitting now, making his phone calls, checking his expenses or doing whatever else served to restore the order of his all-male life. He had found a tape-recorder somewhere and Georgie had a second in case his didn't work.

For a hangman Nigel was small but extremely dapper. He wore a waisted pinstripe suit and a silk handkerchief in his sleeve.

"Ask Mary to make a voluntary statement, will you, Jack?" Nigel said, as if he did this every week. "Voluntary but formal is the tone. Could be used, I'm afraid. The decision is not Bo's alone."

"Who the hell says voluntary?" said Brotherhood. "She signed the Official Secrets Act when she joined, she signed it again when she left. She signed it again when she married Pym. Everything you know is ours, Mary. Whether you heard it on top of a bus or saw the smoking gun in his hand."

"And your nice Georgie can witness it," said Nigel.

Mary heard herself talking but didn't understand a lot of what she said because she had one ear in the pillow and the other was listening to the morning sounds of Lesbos through the open window of their little brown terrace house halfway up the hill that Plomari was built on, to the clatter of mopeds and boats and bouzouki music and lorries revving in the alleys. To the scream of sheep having their throats cut at the butcher's and the slither of donkey hoofs on cobble and the yells of the vendors in the harbour market. If she squeezed her eyes tight enough, she could look over the orange rooftops across the street, past the chimneys and the clotheslines and the roof gardens full of geraniums, down to the waterfront and out to the long jetty with its red light winking on the point and its evil ginger cats soaking themselves in the sunshine while they watched the tramper putter out of the mist.

And that was how Mary saw her story henceforth as she told it to Jack Brotherhood: as a nightmarish film she dared look at only piecemeal, with herself as the meanest villain ever. The tramper draws alongside, the cats stretch, the gangway is lowered, the English family Pym—Magnus, Mary and son Thomas— file ashore in search of yet another perfect place away from it all. Because nowhere is far enough any more, nowhere is remote enough. The Pyms have become the Flying Dutchmen of the Aegean, scarcely landing before they pack again, changing boats and islands like driven souls, though only Magnus knows the curse, only Magnus knows who is pursuing them and why, and Magnus has locked that secret behind his smile with all his others. She sees him striding gaily ahead of her, clutching his straw hat against the breeze and his briefcase dangling from his other hand. She sees Tom stalking after him in the long grey flannels and school blazer with his Cub colours on the pocket, which he insists on wearing even when the temperature is in the eighties. And she sees herself still doped with last night's drink and oil fumes, already planning to betray them both. And following them in their bare feet she sees the native bearers with the Pyms' too-much-luggage, the towels and bed linen and Tom's Weetabix and all the other junk she packed in Vienna for their great sabbatical, as Magnus calls this once-in-a-lifetime family holiday they have all apparently been dreaming of, though Mary cannot remember it being mentioned until a few days before they left, and to be honest she would rather have gone back to England, collected the dogs from the gardener and the long-haired Siamese from Aunt Tab, and spent the time in Plush.

The bearers set down their burdens. Magnus, generous as ever, tips each of them from Mary's handbag while she holds it open for him. Stooped gawkily over the reception committee of Lesbos cats, Tom declares they have ears like celery. A whistle sounds, the bearers hop up the gangway, the tramper is returned to the mist. Magnus, Tom and Mary the traitor stare after it like every sad story of the sea, their life's luggage dumped around them and the red beacon dripping slow fire on their heads.

"Can we go back to Vienna after this?" asks Tom. "I'd like to see Becky Lederer."

Magnus does not answer him. Magnus is too busy being enthusiastic. He will be enthusiastic for his own funeral and Mary loves him for this as she loves him for too much else, does still. Sometimes his sheer goodness accuses me.

"This is it, Mabs!" he cries, waving an arm grandly at the treeless conical hill of brown houses that is their newest home. "We've found it. Plush-sur-mer." And he turns to her with the smile she has not seen until this very holiday—so gallant, so tired-bright in its despair. "We're safe here, Mabs. We're okay."

He throws an arm around her, she lets him. He draws her to him, they hug. Tom squeezes between, an arm round each of them. "Hey, let me have some of that," he says. Locked together like the closest allies in the world, the three move off down the jetty, leaving their luggage till they have found a place to put it. Which they achieve within the hour, for clever Magnus knows just the right taverna to go to first time, whom to charm and whom to recruit in the surprisingly passable Greek identity he has somehow cobbled together for himself on their journeying. But there is the evening yet to come and the evenings are getting worse and worse, they hang over her from when she wakes, she can feel them creeping up on her all through her day. To celebrate their new home Magnus has brought a bottle of scotch though they have agreed several times in the last few days to lay off the hard stuff and stick to local wine. The bottle is nearly empty and Tom, thank God, is finally asleep in his new bedroom. Or so Mary prays, for Tom has recently become a fag-ender, as her father would have said, hanging around them for whatever he can pick up.

"Hey, come on, Mabs, that's a bit of a bad face, isn't it?" says Magnus, jollying her up. "Don't you like our new Schloss?"

"You were being funny and I smiled."

"Didn't look like a smile," says Magnus, smiling himself to show her how. "More like a bit of a grimace from where I sits, m'dear."

But Mary's blood is rising and as usual she cannot stop herself. The prospect of her uncommitted crime is already laying its guilt on her.

"That's what you're writing about, is it?" she snaps. "How you waste your wit on the wrong woman?"

Appalled by her own unpleasantness Mary bursts out weeping and drives her fists on to the arms of the rush chair. But Magnus is not appalled at all. Magnus puts down his glass and comes to her, he taps her gently on the arm with his fingertips, waiting to be let in. He puts her glass delicately out of reach. Moments later the springs of their new bed are pinging and whining like a brass band tuning up, for a desperate erotic fervour has latterly come to Magnus's aid. He makes love to her as if he will never see her again. He buries himself in her as if she is his only refuge and Mary goes with him blindly. She climbs, he draws her after him, she is shouting at him—"Please, oh Christ!" He hits the mark for her, and for a blessed moment Mary can kiss the whole bloody world goodbye.

"We're using Pembroke, by the way," Magnus says later but not quite late enough. "I'm sure it's unnecessary but I want to be on the safe side in case."

Pembroke is one of Magnus's worknames. He keeps the Pembroke passport in his briefcase, she has already located it. It has an artfully muddy photograph that might be Magnus or might not. In the forgery workshop in Berlin they used to call photographs like that floaters.

"What do I tell Tom?" she asks.

"Why tell him anything?"

"Our son's name is Pym. He might take a little oddly to being told he's Pembroke."

She waits, hating herself for her intractability. It is not often that Magnus has to hunt for an answer even when it concerns guidance on how to deceive their child. But he hunts now, she can feel him do it as he lies wakefully beside her in the dark.

"Yes, well tell him the Pembrokes own the house we're in, I should. We're using their name to order things from the shop. Only if asked, naturally."

"Naturally."

"Those two men are still there," says Tom from the door, who turns out to have been part of their conversation all this while.

"What men?" says Mary.

But her skin is pricking on her nape, her body is clammy with panic. How much has Tom heard? Seen?

"The ones who are mending their motorbike by the river. They've got special army sleeping-bags and a torch and a special tent."

"There are campers all over the island," says Mary. "Go back to bed."

"They were on our ship too," says Tom. "Behind the lifeboat, playing cards. Watching us. Speaking German."

"Lots of people were on the ship," says Mary. Why don't you say something, you bastard? she screams at Magnus in her head. Why do you lie dead instead of helping me when I'm still wet from you?

With Tom on one side of her, Magnus on the other, Mary listens to the bells of Plomari tolling out the hours. Four more days, she tells herself. On Sunday, Tom flies back to London for the new school term. And on Monday I'll do it and be damned.

Brotherhood was shaking her. Nigel had said something to him: ask her about the beginning—pin her down.

"We want you to come back a stage, Mary. Can you do that? You're running ahead of yourself."

She heard murmuring, then the sound of Georgie changing a reel on her tape-recorder. The murmuring was her own.

"Tell us how you came to be taking the holiday in the first place, will you, dear? Who proposed it? . . . Oh Magnus, did he? I see. And was that here in this house?

. . . It was. . . . Now what time of day would that have been? Sit up, will you?"

So Mary sat up and began again where Jack had told her: on a sweet, early summer evening in Vienna when everything was still absolutely fine and neither Lesbos nor all the islands that came before it were a glint in clever Magnus's eye. Mary was in the basement in her overalls, binding a first edition of *Die letzten Tage der Menschheit,* by Karl Kraus which Magnus had found in Leoben while meeting a Joe there and Mary—

"That a regular one—Leoben?"

"Yes, Jack, Leoben was regular."

"How often did he go there?"

"Twice a month. Three times. It was an old Hungarian he had, no one special."

"He told you that, did he? I thought he kept his Joes to himself."

"An old Hungarian wine dealer from way back, with offices in Leoben and Budapest. Mostly Magnus kept his secrets to himself. Sometimes he told me. Now can I go on?"

Tom was at school, Frau Bauer was out praying, said Mary. It was some kind of Catholic bean feast, Assumption, Ascension, Prayer and Repentance, Mary had lost count. Magnus was supposed to be at the American Embassy. The new committee had just started meeting and she wasn't expecting him back till late. She was bang in the middle of glueing when suddenly, without hearing a sound, she saw him standing in the doorway—God knows how long he'd been there—looking very pleased with himself and watching her the way he liked to.

"How was that, dear? Watched you how?" Brotherhood cut in.

Mary had surprised herself. She faltered. "Superior, somehow. Pained superiority. Jack, don't make me hate him, please."

"All right, he's watching you," said Brotherhood.

He is watching her and when she catches sight of him he bursts out laughing and shuts her mouth with passionate kisses doing his Fred Astaire number, then it's upstairs for a full and frank exchange of views, as he calls it. They make love, he hauls her to the bath, washes her, hauls her out and dries her, and twenty minutes later Mary and Magnus are bounding across the little park on the top of Döbling like the happy couple they nearly are, past the sandpits and the climbing-frame that Tom is too big for, past the elephant cage where Tom kicks his football, down the hill towards the Restaurant Teheran which is their improbable pub because Magnus so adores the black-and-white videos of Arab romances they play for you with the sound down while you eat your couscous and drink your Kalterer. At the table he holds her arm fiercely and she can feel his excitement racing through her like a charge, as if having her has made him want her more.

"Let's get away, Mabs. Let's really get away. Let's live life for a change instead of acting it. Let's take Tom and all our mid-tour leave and bugger off for the whole of the summer. You paint, I'll write my book, and we'll make love until we fall apart."

Mary says where to, Magnus says who cares, I'll go to the travel agent on the Ring tomorrow. Mary says what about the new committee. He is holding her hand inside his own, touching it with his fingertips into little peaks, and she is going mad for him again, which is what he likes.

"The new committee, Mary," Magnus pronounces, "is the most stupid bloody charade I've been mixed up in, and believe me, I've seen a few. All it is, it's a talking-shop to goose up the Firm's ego and allow them to tell whoever will listen to them that we're hugger-mugger in bed with the Americans. Lederer can't possibly imagine we're going to unveil our networks to him, and as for Lederer, he wouldn't tell me the name of his tailor, let alone his agents—assuming he's got either, which I doubt."

Brotherhood again: "Did he tell you *why* Lederer mightn't be inclined to talk to him?"

"No," said Mary.

Nigel for a change: "And no other reasons offered as to why or how the committee might be a charade?"

"It was a charade, it was a sham, it was makework. That's all he said. I asked about his Joes, he said the Joes could look after themselves and if Jack was bothered about them he could send a locum. I asked what Jack would think—"

"And what *would* Jack think?" said Nigel, all open curiosity.

"He said Jack's a sham too: 'I'm not married to Jack, I'm married to you. The Firm should have retired him ten years ago. Sod Jack.' Sorry. That's what he said."

Hands shoved in his pockets, Brotherhood took a stroll round the little room, poking at Frau Bauer's photographs of her illegitimate daughter, poring over her shelf of paperback romances.

"Anything else about me?" he asked.

"Jack's had too many miles in the saddle. The Boy Scout era's over. It's a new scene and he's not up to it."

"Any more?" said Brotherhood.

Nigel had lowered his chin into his hand and was studying one small but perfectly formed shoe.

"No," said Mary.

"Did he go for a walk that night? Meet P?"

"He'd been the night before."

"I said that night. Answer the bloody question!"

"And I said the night before!"

"With a newspaper. The whole bit?"

"Yes."

His hands still in his pockets, his head high against his shoulders, Brotherhood turned stiffly to Nigel. "I'm going to tell her," he said. "You want to throw a fit?"

"Are you asking me formally?" Nigel asked.

"Not particularly."

"If you are, I'll have to pass it to Bo," said Nigel and looked respectfully at his gold watch as if he took orders from it.

"Lederer knows and we know. If Pym knows too, who's left?" Brotherhood insisted.

Nigel thought about this. "Up to you. Your man, your decision, your tail-end. Frankly."

Brotherhood leaned over Mary and put his head close to her ear. She remembered his smell: tweedy and paternal. "Listening?"

She shook her head. I'm not, I never will be, I wish I never had.

"The new committee that your Magnus derided was shaping up to be a very high-powered outfit. Maybe the best potential working relationship at field level that we've had with the Americans for years. The name of the game was mutual trust. Not as easy to establish these days as it used to be, but we managed it. Are you going to sleep?"

She nodded.

"Your Magnus was not only aware of this, he was one of the prime movers in getting the committee off the ground. If not *the* prime mover. He even went so far as to complain to me, when we were negotiating the deal, that London was being small-minded in its interpretation of the barter terms. He thought we should give the Americans more. In exchange for more. That's number one."

I have absolutely nothing else to say. You can have my home address, my next of kin and that's your lot. You taught me that yourself, Jack, in case they ever grabbed me.

"Number two is that for reasons which I regarded at the time as specious and insulting, the Americans objected to your husband's presence on that committee not three weeks after it met, and asked me to replace him with somebody more to their liking. Since Magnus was kingpin of the Czecho operation and of several other little shows in Eastern Europe besides, this was a totally unrealistic demand. They'd raised the same objections about him in Washington the year before and Bo had bowed to them, in my view mistakenly. I wasn't about to let them do it again. I happen not to care for American gentlemen or anybody else telling me how to run my shop. I said no and ordered Magnus to take himself off on mid-tour leave and stay clear of Vienna till I told him to come back. That's the truth, and I think it's time you heard some."

"It's also very secret," said Nigel.

She waited in vain to be amazed. No surge of protest, no flash of the celebrated family temper. Brotherhood had taken himself to the window and was staring out. Morning had come early because of the snow. He looked old and beaten. His white hair was fluffed against the light and she could see the pink skin of his scalp.

"You defended him," she said. "You were loyal."

"Seems as if I was a bloody fool as well."

The house had turned itself upside down. The thump of shifting furniture came from below them in the drawing-room. The safest place to be was here. Upstairs with Jack.

"Oh don't be so hard on yourself, Jack," Nigel said.

Brotherhood had sat Mary in the chair and handed her a whisky. You get one only, he had said; make it last. Nigel had taken over the bed and was lounging on it with one suited little leg stuck out in front of him as if he'd sprained it trying to get up the steps of his club. Brotherhood had turned his back on both of them. He preferred the view from the window.

"So first you go to Corfu. Your auntie has a house there. You borrowed it from her. Tell that bit. Carefully."

"Aunt Tab," said Mary.

"In full, I think," said Nigel.

"Lady Tabitha Grey. Daddy's sister."

"Sometime member of the Firm," Brotherhood murmured to Nigel. "There's hardly a member of her family hasn't been on our books at one time or another, come to think of it."

She had telephoned Aunt Tab as soon as they got back from their drink that evening, and by a miracle there'd been a cancellation and her house was free. They took it, phoned Tom's school and arranged for him to fly there direct when term ended. As soon as the Lederers heard, they wanted to come too of course. Grant said he would drop everything but Magnus wouldn't hear of it. The Lederers are exactly the kind of social prop I need to kick away, he had said. Why the hell should I take my work with me on holiday? Five days later they were settled into Tab's house and everything was absolutely fine. Tom took tennis lessons at the hotel up the road, swam, fed the landlady's goats and pottered around the boat with Costas who looked after it and watered the garden. But his best thing was the crazy cricket matches on the edge of town that Magnus took him to in the evenings. Magnus said the Brits had brought the game to the island when they were defending it against Napoleon. Magnus knew those things. Or pretended to.

At the cricket in Corfu Magnus was closer to Tom than he had ever been. They lay on the grass, munched ice creams, rooted for their favourite players and had those mannish chats that were so crucial to Tom's happiness: for Tom loved Magnus to distraction; he was a man's boy, always had been. As to Mary, she had taken up pastels because Corfu in summer was really too hot for her style of water-colours, the paint just dried on the page before she could get near it. But she was drawing well, getting nice likenesses and shapes, and playing hostess to half the dogs on the island because the Greeks don't feed them or look after them or *anything*. So everyone was happy, everyone absolutely fine and Magnus had a cool conservatory to write in, and inland walks for his restlessness, which came to him first thing in the morning and again in late evening after he had held it off all day. They lunched late, usually in a taverna—and often rather a liquid affair, to be honest, but why not, they were on holiday. Then long sexy siestas while Mary and Magnus made love on the balcony and Tom lay on the beach studying the nudies across the bay with Magnus's binoculars, so as Magnus put it everybody was getting his pound of flesh. Until one day the clock stopped dead and Magnus came back from a late walk and confessed he had hit a bit of a block with his writing. He just strode in, poured himself a stiff ouzo, flung himself into a chair and said it straight out:

"Sorry, Mabs. Sorry, Tom, old chap. But this place is too damned idyllic. I need roughing up a bit. I need *people,* for Christ's sake. Smoke and dirt and a bit of suffering around us. It's like being on the moon here, Mabs. Worse than Vienna. Truly."

He was sweet about it but he was adamant. He'd been drinking, obviously, but that was because he was upset. "I'm going bonkers, Mabs. It's really getting to me. I told Tom. Didn't I, Tom? I said I really can't take much more of this and I feel a shit because you two are having such a good time."

"Yes, he did," said Tom.

"Several times. And today it's just hit me, Mabs. You've got to help me out. Both of you."

So of course they both said they would. Mary rang Tab at once, so that she could put the house back on the market, they all had a bear-hug and went to bed feeling resolved, and next day Mary packed while Magnus went off to town to do tickets and fix the next stage of their odyssey. But Tom, over washing-up which was always a talkative time for him, had a different version of why they were leaving Corfu. Daddy had met this mystery man at cricket. It was a really super match, Mum, the best two teams on the island, a real vendetta. We were watching it like mad and suddenly there was this wise, stringy man with a sad moustache like a conjuror's and a limp, and Dad got all uptight. He came up to Dad smiling, they talked a bit, they walked round and round the ground together with the thin man going slowly like an invalid, but he was terribly kind to Dad although Dad got so emanated.

"Animated," Mary corrected him automatically. "Don't talk too loud, Tom. I think Daddy's working somewhere."

And there was this really incredible batsman, said Tom. Called Phillippi. Just the absolute best batsman Tom had seen *ever*. "He scored eighteen in one over and the crowd went absolutely ape, but Dad didn't notice, he was so busy listening to the kind man."

"How do you know he was so kind?" said Mary with a strange irritation. "Keep your voice down." There was no light in the conservatory, but sometimes Magnus sat there in the dark.

"He was like a father with him, Mum. He's senior to him but sort of calm. He kept offering Dad a ride in his car. Dad kept saying no. But he didn't get angry or anything, he was too wise. He gentled him and smiled."

"What car? It's just a great big romance, Tom. You know it is."

"The Volvo. Mr. Kaloumenos's Volvo. One man was driving and another man in the back. They kept up with them on the other side of the fence when they went round and round talking. Honestly, Mum. The thin man never lost his temper or anything, and he really likes Dad, you can tell. It's not just holding arms. They're friends to each other. Much more than Uncle Grant. More like Uncle Jack."

Mary asked Magnus that night. They'd packed, she was excited to be moving, and really looking forward to the Athens museums.

"Tom says you were harassed by some tiresome man at the cricket match," said Mary while they enjoyed a rather stiff nightcap after their heavy day.

"Was I?"

"Some little man who chased you round and round the ground. Sounded like an angry husband to me. He had a moustache, unless Tom imagined it."

Then vaguely Magnus did remember. "Oh that's right. He was some boring ancient Brit who kept pressing me to go and see his villa. Wanted to flog it. Bloody little pest actually."

"He spoke German," said Tom, next day at breakfast while Magnus was out walking.

"Who did?"

"Dad's thin friend. The man who picked Dad up at the cricket. And Dad spoke German back to him too. Why did Dad say he was an ancient Brit?"

Mary flew at him. She hadn't been so angry with him for years. "If you want to listen to our conversations, you bloody well come in and listen to them and don't skulk outside the door like a spy."

Then she was ashamed of herself and played tennis with him till the boat left.

On the boat Tom was sick as a dog and by the time they reached Piraeus he had a temperature of a hundred and three so her guilt was unconfined. At the Athens hospital a Greek doctor diagnosed shrimp rash which was absurd because Tom loathed shrimps and hadn't touched a single one; by now his face was swollen like a hamster's, so they took expensive rooms and put him to bed with an icepack and Mary read fantasy to him while Magnus listened or sat in Tom's room to write. But mainly he liked to listen because the best thing in his life, he always said, was watching her comfort their child. She believed him.

"Didn't he go out at all?" Brotherhood asked.

"Not to begin with. He didn't want to."

"Make any phone calls?" said Nigel.

"The Embassy. To check in. So that you'd know where he was."

"He tell you that?" said Brotherhood.

"Yes."

"You weren't there when he made them?" Nigel said.

"No."

"Hear him through the wall?" Nigel again.

"No."

"Know who he spoke to?" Still Nigel.

"No."

From his place on the bed Nigel lifted his eyes to Brotherhood. "But he phoned *you*, Jack," he said encouragingly. "Little chats from out-of-the-way places with his old boss now and then? That's practically mandatory, isn't it? Check on the Joes —'How's our old buddy from you-know-where?' "

Nigel is one of the new non-professionals, Mary remembered Magnus telling her. He's one of the idiots who are supposed to be introducing a breath of Whitehall realism. If ever I heard a contradiction in terms, that's it, said Magnus.

"Not a peep," Brotherhood was replying. "All he did was send me a string of stupid postcards saying 'Thank God you're not here' and giving me his latest address."

"When did he start going out?" said Nigel.

"When Tom's temperature went down," Mary replied.

"A week?" said Nigel invitingly. "Two?"

"Less," said Mary.

"Describe," said Brotherhood.

It was evening, probably their fourth day. Tom's face was normal again so Magnus suggested Mary go shopping while he baby-sat Tom to give her a break. But Mary wasn't keen on braving the Athens streets alone so Magnus went instead; Mary would do a museum in the morning. He came back around midnight very pleased with himself saying he'd found this marvellous old Greek travel agent in a basement opposite the Hilton, a tremendously cultured fellow, and how they had drunk ouzo together and solved the problems of the universe. The old man ran a villa-renting service for the islands and hoped to turn up a cancellation in a week or so when they'd all had enough of Athens.

"I thought islands were out," Mary said.

For a moment it seemed that Magnus had forgotten the reason they had left Corfu. He smiled lamely and said something about not every island being the same.

After that, she seemed to lose count of the days. They moved to a smaller hotel; Magnus wrote and wrote, went out in the evenings and when Tom was well enough took him swimming. Mary sketched the Acropolis and took Tom to a couple of museums but he preferred swimming. Meanwhile they waited for the old Greek to come up with something.

Brotherhood was once more interrupting. "This writing of his. How much did he talk about it exactly?"

"He wanted to preserve his secrecy. Scraps. That was all he gave me."

"Like his Joes. The same," Brotherhood suggested.

"He wanted to keep me fresh for when he'd really got something to show me. He didn't want to talk it out of himself."

It was a quiet and, as Mary now remembered it, strangely furtive time until one night Magnus vanished. He went out after dinner saying he was going to give the old boy a prod. Next morning he hadn't come back and by lunchtime Mary was scared. She knew she should phone the Embassy. On the other hand she didn't want to start a scare unnecessarily or do anything that might get Magnus into trouble.

Yet again Brotherhood cut in. "What sort of trouble?"

"If he'd gone on a bender or something. It wouldn't exactly have looked well on his file. Just when he was hoping for promotion."

"Had he gone on benders before?"

"Absolutely not. He and Grant got drunk together occasionally but that was as far as it went."

Nigel sharply lifted his head. "But why should he be expecting promotion? Who said anything about promotion to him?"

"I did," said Brotherhood without a whiff of repentance. "I reckoned after all the messing him around he was about owed it with his reinstatement."

Nigel made a neat little note in his book and smiled mirthlessly as he wrote. Mary went on.

Anyway, she waited till evening then took Tom up to the Hilton and together they explored all the houses opposite until they found the cultured old Greek in his basement, exactly as Magnus had described him. But the Greek hadn't seen Magnus for a week and Mary wouldn't stay for coffee. When they got back to the taverna they found Magnus with two days' beard, dressed in the clothes he had disappeared in, sitting in the courtyard and eating bacon and eggs, drunk. Not silly drunk, he couldn't do that. Not angry drunk, or maudlin, or aggressive, and least of all indiscreet, because drink only ever fortified his defences. Courteous drunk, therefore, and amiable to a fault as ever, and his cover story perfectly intact except for one rare mistake.

"Sorry, gang. Got a bit pissed with Dimitri. Swine drank me clean under the table. Hullo, Tom."

"Hullo," said Tom.

"Who's Dimitri?" Mary asked.

"You know who Dimitri is. Old Greek travel agent who does his beads across the road from the Hilton."

"The cultured one."

"That's him."

"Last night?"

"Far as I can remember, old girl, last night as ever was."

"Dimitri hasn't seen you since last Monday. He told us himself an hour ago."

Magnus considered this. Tom had found a copy of the *Athens News* and was standing at the next table intently studying the film page.

"You checked on me, Mabs. You shouldn't have done that."

"I wasn't checking on you, I was looking for you!"

"Don't make a scene now, girl. Please. Other people eating here, you see."

"I'm not making a scene. You are. It's not me who disappears for two days and comes back with a lie. Tom, go to your room, darling. I'll be up in a minute."

Tom left, smiling brightly to show he hadn't heard anything. Magnus took a long drink of coffee. Then he grasped Mary's hand and kissed it and gently pulled her down on to the chair beside him.

"Which would you rather I told you, Mabs? I was carousing with a whore or I've got problems with a Joe?"

"Why don't you just tell me the truth?"

The suggestion amused him. Not cruelly or cynically. Merely, he received it with the rueful indulgence that he would show towards Tom when he came through with one of his solutions for ending world poverty or the arms race.

"Know something?" He kissed her hand again and held it against his cheek. "Nothing goes away in life." To her surprise she felt moisture in his stubble and realised he was weeping. "I'm in Constitution Square, right? Coming out of the Grande Bretagne bar. Minding my own business. What happens? I walk straight into the arms of a Czech Joe I used to run. Real tough egg, fabricator, caused us a lot of problems. Holds my arm like this. 'Colonel Manchester! Colonel Manchester!' Threatens to call the police, expose me as a British spy if I don't give him money. Says I'm the only friend he's got left in the world. 'Come and drink with me, Colonel Manchester. Like we used to.' So I did. Drank him right under the table. Then gave him the slip. I'm afraid I got a bit pissed myself. Line of duty. Let's go to bed."

And they do. And make love. The desperate screwing of strangers while Tom reads fantasy next door. And two days later they leave for Hydra, but Hydra is too cramped, too ominous, there is suddenly nowhere to go but Spetsai: at this time of year we'll have no problem. Tom asks if Becky can join them, Magnus says no she absolutely can't because they'll all want to come and he's not going to have a pride of Lederers sitting on his head while he's trying to write. Otherwise, apart from his drinking, Magnus has never been more caring and polite than now.

She had stopped. Like standing back from a painting halfway. Studying the story so far. She drank some whisky, lit a cigarette.

"Christ," said Brotherhood softly. Then nothing.

Nigel had found a bit of dead skin on the back of one undersized finger and was picking it off meticulously.

It is Lesbos again, it is another dawn but the same Greek bed and Plomari is once more waking up though Mary is praying it will go back to sleep again, that the sounds will fade and the sun flop behind the rooftops where it came from, because it is Monday and yesterday Tom went back to school. Mary has the evidence under her pillow where she promised to put the rabbitskin he gave her to keep her safe

—and as if she needed it to strengthen her resolve—the terrible memory of his last words to her before he left. Mary and Magnus have driven him to the airport, weighed him in for yet another departure. Tom and Mary are standing about unable to touch each other while they wait for the flight to be called, Magnus is at the bar buying Tom a bag of pistachios for the journey and an ouzo for himself while he's about it. Mary has six times confirmed that Tom has his passport and his money and his letter to Matron about his shrimp rash, and his letter to Granny to be handed to her the *moment* you meet her at London Airport, darling, so that you don't forget. But Tom is even more than usually distracted; he is looking back to the main entrance, watching the people going through the swing doors, and there is something desperate in his face, so desperate that Mary really wonders whether he is thinking of making a dash for it.

"Mums?" Sometimes, when he is distracted, he still calls her that.

"Yes, darling."

"They're here, Mums."

"Who are?"

"Those two campers from Plomari. They're sitting in the airport carpark on their motorbike, watching Dad."

"Now darling just *stop,*" Mary retorts firmly, determined to drive away these shadows, one and all. "Just completely stop, okay?"

"Only I've recognised them, you see. I worked it out this morning. I remembered. They're the men who drove the car round the outside of the cricket ground at Corfu while Dad's friend tried to make him come for a drive."

For a moment, though Mary has been through this agonising procedure a dozen times before, she wants to scream out: "Stay—don't go—I don't care a damn about your bloody education—stay with me!" But instead the fool waves him through the barrier and saves her tears for the journey back while Magnus is absolutely sweet to her as ever. And now it is next morning, Tom is just about arriving at his school, and Mary is staring at the prison bars of Kyria Katina's rotting shutters while the sky remorselessly whitens through the cracks and she is trying not to hear the clanking of the water-pipes beneath her and the rush of water free-falling onto the flagstones as Magnus celebrates his morning shower.

"Wowee! Christ! You awake, girl? It's brass monkeys down here, believe me!"

Believe you, she repeats to herself and draws deeper into the bedclothes. In fifteen years he never called me girl till here. Now suddenly she is girl all day as if he has woken to her gender. A single width of floorboard separates her from him and if she dares look over the bedside she will glimpse his stranger's naked body through the gaps between the planks. Receiving no reply from her, Pym starts singing his one piece of Gilbert and Sullivan while he sloshes water.

" 'Rising early in the morning. We proceed to light the fire . . .' How'm I doing?" he calls when he has sung all he knows.

Mary in another life has a small reputation for her music. In Plush she led a passable group in madrigals. When she was doing her stint at Head Office she sang solo in the Firm choir. It's just that nobody's ever played records for you, she used to tell him in a veiled criticism of his first wife, Belinda. One day your singing voice will be as good as your spoken one, darling.

She summons her breath. "Better than Caruso!" she shouts.

The exchange is accomplished, Magnus can resume his showering.

"It went well, Mabs. Really well. Seven pages of deathless prose. Undercoat but good."

"Great."

He has started shaving. She can hear him empty the kettle into the plastic washing-up bowl. Contour blades, she thinks: Oh God, I forgot to buy him his bloody Contour blades. All the way to the airport and back she had known there was something she had forgotten, for little things are as dreadful to her as big things these days. Now I will buy cheese for lunch. Now I will buy bread to go with the cheese. She closes her eyes and takes another enormous breath.

"Did you sleep?" she asks.

"Like the dead. Didn't you notice?"

Yes, I noticed. I noticed how you slipped out of bed at two in the morning and crept downstairs to your workroom. How you paced and stopped pacing. I heard the creak of your chair and the whisper of your felt-tipped pen as you began to write. Who to? In what voice? Which one?

A boom of music drowns the sound of his shaving. He has switched on his clever radio for the BBC *World News.* Magnus knows the time to the minute, all through the day and night. If he looks at his watch it is only to confirm the schedules in his brain. She listens numbly to a recitation of events no one is able to control. A bomb has gone off in Beirut. A town has been wiped out in El Salvador. The pound has fallen. Or risen. The Russians are out of the next Olympics—or into them after all. Magnus follows politics like a gambler who is too wise to bet. The noise grows steadily louder as Magnus carries the radio upstairs, slop, slop, naked except for his sandals. He bends over her and she smells his shaving soap and the flat Greek cigarettes he has taken to smoking while he writes.

"Still sleepy?"

"A bit."

"How's Rat?"

Mary has been tending a half-eviscerated rat she found in the garden. It is lying in a straw box in Tom's room.

"I haven't looked," she says.

He kisses her close to the ear, an explosion, and starts to fondle her breast as a sign to her to take him, but she grunts an awkward "Later" and rolls over. She hears him slop to the wardrobe, she hears the old door resist and jolt open. If he chooses shorts he's going for a walk. If he chooses jeans he's going into town to drink with the deadbeats. Colonel call-me-Parkie Parker, with my Greek fancy-boy and my Sealyham dog that I hold on the lead like a teapot. Elsie and Ethel, retired dyke schoolteachers from Liverpool. Jock somebody, I've a wee business in Dundee. Magnus pulls out a shirt and slips it on. She hears him fastening his shorts.

"Where are you going?" she says.

"For a walk."

"Wait for me. I'll come with you. You can tell me about it."

Who was this speaking out of her suddenly—this mature straight-to-the-point woman?

Magnus is as surprised as she is: "About what, for heaven's sake?"

"Whatever it is that's worrying you, darling. I don't mind. Just tell me, whatever it is, so that I don't have to . . ."

"Don't have to what?"

"Bottle it up. Look away."

"Nonsense. Everything's fine. We're just both a bit blue without Tom." He comes to her and lays her back on the pillow as if she were an invalid. "You sleep it off, I'll walk it off. See you at the taverna round three."

Only Magnus can make Kyria Katina's front door close so softly.

Suddenly Mary is strong. His departure has released her. Breathe. She goes to the north window, everything planned. She has done these things before and remembers now that she is good at them, often steadier than the men. In Berlin when Jack needed a spare girl Mary had kept watch, gulled room keys out of concierges, replaced stolen documents in dangerous desks, driven scared Joes to safe flats. I knew the game better than I realised, she thought. Jack used to praise my coolness and my sharp eye. From the window she sees the new tarmac road winding into the hills. Sometimes he goes that way, but not today. Opening the window, she leans out as if savouring the place and morning. That witch Katina has milked her goats early; that means she's gone to market. Only one fleeting glance does Mary allow herself towards the dried-up river bed where, in the shadow of the stone footbridge, the same two boys are tinkering with their German-registered motorbike. If they had appeared outside the house in Vienna like this, Mary would have been on to Magnus in an instant—phoned him if need be at the Embassy. "Looks like the angels are flying rather low today," she'd have said. And Magnus would have done whatever he did—alerted the diplomatic patrol, sent his people down to check them out. But now in their separated lives it is as if they have agreed between them that angels, even suspected ones, are not to be remarked upon.

His workroom is on the ground floor. He does not lock the door on her but there is an ethic between them that she does not enter except at his specific beckoning. She turns the handle and steps inside. The shutters are closed but they do not cover the upper window panes and there is light for her to see by. Tread heavily, she tells herself, remembering her training. If you have to make a noise, make a bold one. The room is sparse, which is what Magnus likes. A desk, a chair, a single bed to crash on between bursts of creative matrix-writing. She pulls back the chair and sends a bottle of vodka skidding. The desk is covered with books and papers but she touches nothing. His old buckram-bound copy of *Simplicissimus* occupies pride of place as usual. His mascot. His something. It is a source of permanent offence to Mary that he will never let her bind it. Because I like it the way it is, he says stubbornly. That's how it was given to me. By some woman no doubt. "For Sir Magnus who will never be my enemy" reads the inscription in German. Screw her. And screw fancy nicknames.

Brotherhood had again interrupted.

"Where's it now, this book?"

With difficulty and a slight resentment Mary returned to time present.

But Brotherhood insisted: "It's not in his desk downstairs. I didn't see it lying about in the drawing-room either. It's not in the bedroom or in Tom's room. Where is it?"

"I told you," she said. "He takes it everywhere."

"You didn't, but thank you," Brotherhood retorted.

She is wearing a pair of cotton gloves against sweat and grime marks. He'll use a trick. He does those things instinctively. His old briefcase lies on the floor, wide open, but she doesn't touch that either. Other books are strewn like paperweights to hold down the manuscript and seemingly at random. She reads a title. It is in German: *Freedom and Conscience* by someone she has never heard of. Beside it, a copy of Madox Ford's *Good Soldier,* which Magnus reads incessantly these days; it has become his Bible. Beside this again, an old photograph album. Gently she lifts the unfamiliar cover and without moving it turns a few pages. Magnus aged eight in football gear, a team group. Magnus aged five in alpine setting holding a toboggan. Magnus at Tom's age already with his overwilling smile, inviting you in but not expecting to be invited. Magnus on honeymoon with Belinda, neither of them looking more than about twelve years old. She has not seen these photographs before. Letting the cover fall, Mary steps back and again surveys the arrangement on the desk. As she does so his bit of tradecraft becomes apparent to her. Each of the three books, lying seemingly haphazardly across the papers, is aligned to the point of the paper scissors at their centre. Going to the kitchen Mary grabs the tablecloth, comes back and lays it on the floor beside the desk, then measures the distances between each object on the desk with her gloved hand. As gently as if she is lifting bandages from a wound she lays them in the same pattern on the table-cloth. The papers on the desk now lie free for her inspection. She has not reckoned with so much dust. Just by crossing the floor she has set up clouds of it. I'm a tomb robber, she thinks, as the dust burns her throat. She is gazing at a wad of handwritten manuscript. The top page is dark with crossings-out. She picks up the wad, leaving everything else lying. She takes it to the little bed, sits down. At Plush when she was a girl they had called it "Kim's Game" and played it every New Year's Eve along with acting games and Murder and reels. At the training house, when she was supposed to be adult, they called it Observation and played it round the sleepy villages of Dedham, Manningtree and Bergholt: who's had their door painted this week, pruned their roses, bought a new car; how many bottles of milk did No. 18 have on its doorstep? But wherever they play it Mary always comes top by miles; she is cursed with a snapshot memory from which very little ever goes away.

Bits of novel, she told Brotherhood, all beginnings.

A dozen Chapter Ones, some typed and some in longhand, all stiff with crossings-out. Mostly they told about the orphan childhood of a boy called Ben.

Doodles. Drawings of an arm stretched out to steal. A woman's crotch.

Notes to himself, all abusive: "sentimental crap" . . . "rewrite or destroy" . . . "You've missed the curse we pass from man to child" . . . "One day a Wentworth will get us all."

A pink folder marked "Random Passages." Ben gives himself up to the authorities. Ben discovers there is another, real Secret Service, and joins it in the nick of time. A blue folder marked "Final Scenes," several of them addressed to "Poppy, dear bloody Poppy." A sheet of cartridge paper stolen from her sketch block on which Magnus has drawn a pattern of linked think-bubbles to form a flow chart of his ideas, exactly as Tom is taught to prepare his essays at school. Bubble: "If all Nature abhors a vacuum, how does a vacuum feel about all Nature?" Bubble: "Duplicity is when you please one person at the expense of another." Bubble: "We are patriots because we are afraid to be cosmopolitan, cosmopolitan because we are afraid to be patriots."

There was a tapping at the door but Brotherhood shook his head at Georgie, telling her to ignore it.

"It wasn't his true writing," Mary said. "It was all spiky. It ran for a while then seized up. It seemed to hurt him to go on."

Brotherhood didn't give a damn whom it hurt.

"More," he said. "More. Hurry."

"It's me, sir," Fergus called through the door. "Urgent message, sir. Very."

"I said wait," Brotherhood ordered.

" 'The systems of Ben's life are all collapsing,' " Mary continued. " 'All his life he's been inventing versions of himself that are untrue. Now the truth is coming to get him and he is on the run. His Wentworth is standing at the door.' "

"More," said Brotherhood, towering over her.

" 'Rick invented me, Rick is dying. What will happen when Rick drops his end of the string?' "

"Keep going."

"A quotation from Saint Luke. I never saw him open a Bible in his life. 'He who is faithful in a very little is faithful also in much.' "

"And?"

" 'He who is dishonest in a very little is dishonest also in much.' He'd illuminated the edges of the page for hours on end. Different inks."

"And?"

" 'Wentworth was Rick's Nemesis. Poppy was mine. We each spent our lives trying to put right what we'd done to them.' "

"And again!"

" 'Now everyone's after me. The Firm's after me, the Americans are after me, you're after me. Even poor Mary is after me, and she doesn't know you exist.' "

"*You* being who? Who's *you* in this poem?"

" 'Poppy. My destiny. Dearest Poppy, best of best friends, get your bloody dogs off my doorstep.' "

"Poppy like the flowers," Brotherhood suggested, shoving away Georgie's microphone as he knelt beside her. "Like the flowers in the chimney. But singular. One Poppy."

"Yes."

"And Wentworth like the place. Sunny Wentworth, in tasteful Surrey?"

"Yes."

"Know him—her—anyone of that name?"

"No."

"Or Poppy?"

"No."

"On."

"There was a Chapter Eight," she said. "Out of the blue. No Two to Seven, but this Chapter Eight, all in his own handwriting and without a crossing-out. Titled 'Overdue Bills,' whereas the Chapter Ones were untitled. Describing a day when Ben revolts against all his promises. Slipping from third to first person and staying there, whereas the Chapter Ones were 'he' and 'Ben.' 'The creditors are beating at the door, Wentworth to the fore, but Ben doesn't give a damn. I lower my head and lift my shoulders, I wade at them, I punch and flail and butt them while they smash my face in. But even with no face left I am doing what I should have done thirty-five years ago, to Jack and Rick and all the mothers and fathers, for stealing my life off my plate while I watched you do it. Poppy, Jack, the rest of you, driving me into a lifetime's—a lifetime's—a lifetime's—' "

She had stopped. Iron clamps had squeezed the breath out of her. The door opened and Fergus gatecrashed, a flouting of discipline for which he would surely be punished. Nigel was staring at him expressionlessly. Georgie was rolling her eyes at him, pointing at the door and mouthing Get out, get out, but Fergus stood his ground.

"A lifetime's what, for God's sake?" Brotherhood was shouting in her ear.

She was whispering. She was screaming. She was fighting the word inside her mouth, heaving and pressing at it but nothing came out. Brotherhood shook her, at first gently, then much harder, then very hard indeed.

"Betrayal," she said. " 'We betray to be loyal. Betrayal is like imagining when the reality isn't good enough.' He wrote that. Betrayal as hope and compensation. As the making of a better land. Betrayal as love. As a tribute to our unlived lives. On and on, these ponderous aphorisms about betrayal. Betrayal as escape. As a constructive act. As a statement of ideals. Worship. As an adventure of the soul. Betrayal as travel: how can we discover new places if we never leave home? 'You were my Promised Land, Poppy. You gave my lies a reason.' "

And that was the very phrase she had got to in her reading, she explained—the one about Poppy and the Promised Land—when she turned round and saw Magnus in his shorts standing in the open doorway to his workroom, holding a big blue envelope in one hand and the telegram in the other, smiling like the head boy of one of his schools.

"There was someone else inside him," Mary said, shocking herself. "It wasn't him."

"What the hell does that mean? You just said it was Magnus, standing in the doorway. What are you getting at?"

She didn't know either. "It was something that had happened to him when he was young. Someone standing in doorways watching him. He was doing it back somehow. I could see the recognition in his face."

"What did he say?" Nigel suggested helpfully.

She had a voice for Magnus, or perhaps it was just a facial expression. Empty yet impenetrable. Tirelessly polite: "Hullo, old love. Catching up with the great novel, are we? Not exactly Jane Austen, I'm afraid, but some of it may be usable when I get a proper run at it."

The tablecloth was spread on the floor, his books and half his papers on it. But his smile flashed victory and relief as he held the telegram towards her. She took it from his hand and walked with it to the window in order to read it. Or to distract his attention from the desk.

"It was from you, Jack," she said, "using your cover name of Victor. Addressed to Pym care of Pembroke. Return at once, you said. All is forgiven. Committee reassembles Vienna Monday 10 A.M. Victor."

Taking his time, Brotherhood had turned to Fergus at last.

"What the hell do you want?" he said.

Fergus spoke the way Tom did when he had been holding back too long, waiting for the grown-ups to let him in.

"Crash message from the Station clerk at the Embassy, sir," he blurted. "He phoned it through in word code. I've just unbuttoned it. The Station burnbox is missing from the strongroom."

Nigel had a funny little gesture designed to ease a charged atmosphere. He raised his beloved hands and, with the fingertips pointing loosely toward Heaven, flapped them as if he were drying his nails. But Brotherhood, still kneeling at Mary's side, seemed suddenly to have been seized by lethargy. He rose slowly, then slowly passed his hand across his mouth as if he had a bad taste on the tip of his tongue.

"Since when?"

"Not known, sir. Not signed out. They've been searching for it for this last hour. They can't find it. That's all they know. There's a diplomatic courier card that goes with it. The card's disappeared too."

Mary had not yet grasped the mood. The synchronisation has gone wrong, she thought. Who is in the doorway, Fergus or Magnus? Jack's gone deaf. Jack who questions in salvoes has run out of ammunition.

"Chancery guard says Mr. Pym called at the Embassy first thing Thursday morning on his way to the airport, sir. The guard hadn't thought to mention it because he hadn't put him into his log. It was upstairs, down again and sorry about your father, sir. But when he came down the stairs he was carrying this heavy black pouch."

"And the guard didn't think to question him at all?"

"Well he wouldn't sir, would he? Not with his father dead and him being in a hurry."

"Anything else missing?"

"No, sir, just the burnbox, sir, so far as he's got. And the card like I said."

"Where are you going?" said Mary.

Nigel was on his feet, tugging at the points of his waistcoat, while Brotherhood was loading things into his jacket pocket for a long journey on his own. His yellow cigarettes. His pen and notebook. His old German lighter.

"What's a burnbox?" Mary said, close on panic. "Where are you going? I'm talking! Sit down!"

Finally Brotherhood remembered her, and stared down at her where she sat.

"You wouldn't know, would you," he said. "Of course you wouldn't. You were grade nine. You never got high enough to find out." Explaining was a chore but he managed it for old times' sake. "A burnbox is what it says. Little metal box. In this instance it's a diplomatic pouch, steel-lined. Burns whatever is inside it as soon as you tell it to. It's where a Station Chief keeps his crown jewels."

"So what's in it?"

Nigel and Brotherhood exchanged glances. Fergus still had his eyes wide open.

"What's in it?" she repeated as a different and more elusive fear began to grip her.

"Oh. Not much," said Brotherhood. "Agents in place. All our Czechs. A few Poles. Hungarian or two. Just about everything we have that's run from Vienna. Or used to be. Who's Wentworth?"

"You asked. I don't know. A place. What else is in the burnbox?"

"So it is. A place."

She had lost him. Jack. Gone. Lost him as a lover, as a friend, as an authority. His face was her father's face when she took him the news of Sam's death. The love had gone out of him and the last of his faith with it.

"You knew," he said casually. He was halfway to the door, not even looking at her. "You bloody knew, for years and years."

We all did, she thought. But she hadn't the heart to say it to him or, for that matter, the interest.

As if the bell had rung for the end of visiting time, Nigel also prepared to make his exit. "Now, Mary, I'm leaving you Georgie and Fergus for company. They'll agree their cover with you and tell you how to play everything. They'll report to me all the time. From now on, so will you. Only to me. Do you understand? If you need to leave a message or anything like that, I'm Nigel, I'm Head of Secretariat, my P.A. is called Marcia. Don't talk to anybody else in the Firm at all. I'm afraid that's an order. Even Jack," he added, meaning Jack particularly.

"What else is in the burnbox?" she repeated.

"Nothing. Nothing at all. Routine stores. Don't you worry yourself." He came to her and, emboldened by Brotherhood's intimacy with her, placed a hand awkwardly on her shoulder. "Listen. This needn't all be as bad as it sounds. We have to take precautions, naturally. We have to assume the worst and cover ourselves. But Jack does have a rather Gothic way of looking at things sometimes. The less dramatic explanations are often a lot closer to home. Jack's not the only one with experience."

6

A dark sea rain had enveloped Pym's England and he strode in it warily. It was early evening and he had been writing for longer than he had written in his whole life and now he was empty and accessible and afraid. A foghorn sounded—one short, two long—a lighthouse or a ship. Pausing under a lamp he again studied his watch. A hundred and ten minutes to go, fifty-three years gone. Bandstand empty, bowling green awash. Shop-windows still wearing their fly-blown yellow cellophane against the summer's sun.

He was heading out of town. He had bought a plastic cape from Blandy the haberdasher. "*Good* evening, Mr. Canterbury, sir, what can we be doing *you* for?" In the rain its hood pattered round him like a tin roof. Inside its skirts he carried his shopping for Miss Dubber: the bacon from Mr. Aitken, only mind and tell him he's to cut it on number five, give him half a chance he'll make it thicker. And tell that Mr. Crosse three of his tomatoes were rotten last week, not just bad, *rotten*. If I don't have replacements I'll never go to him again. Pym had followed her instructions to the letter, though not with the ferocity she would have wished, for both Crosse and Aitken were recipients of his secret subventions, and for years had been sending Miss Dubber bills for only half what she had spent. From Farways the travel agent he had also obtained details of a senior citizens' tour of Italy departing Gatwick in six days. I'll phone her cousin Melanie in Bognor, he thought. If I offer to pay for Melanie as well, Miss Dubber won't be able to refuse.

A hundred and six minutes. Only four gone. From countless pressing memories in his head clamouring to be acknowledged, Pym selected instead Washington and the balloon. Of all the crazy ways we ever had of talking, really that balloon took the biscuit. You wanted a chat, I wouldn't meet you. I was running scared and had appointed you my unperson. But you wouldn't be put down, you never would. To humour me, you launched a miniature silver-coated gas balloon over the rooftops of Washington, D.C. Half a metre diameter; sometimes Tom gets them free at the supermarkets. As we drove our separate cars on either side of town, you told me in German what a fool I was to do a Garbo on you. Over matched handsets that hopped like bedbugs between the frequencies and must have sent the listeners just as frantic.

He was climbing the cliff path, past lighted bungalows cut from the gardens of a great house. I'll phone that doctor of hers and get him to persuade her that a break is what she needs. Or the vicar, she'd listen to him. Below him the fairy lights of the Amusement Palace glowed like fat berries in the mist. Alongside them he could make out the blue-white neons of the Softa Ice Parlour. Penny, he thought. You'll never see me again unless it's my face in the newspaper. Penny belonged to his secret army of lovers, so secret she didn't know she was a member. Five years ago she was selling fish and chips from a Portacabin on the promenade and was in love with a leather-boy called Bill who beat her up, until Pym ran the licence number of Bill's motorbike across the Firm computer and established he was married and had kids in Taunton. In a disguised hand he sent the details to the local vicar and a year later Penny was married to a jolly Italian ice-cream seller called Eugenio. But not tonight she wasn't. Tonight, as Pym had approached her café for his regular two scoops of Cornish, she was head to head with a burly man in a trilby whom Pym hadn't liked the look of one bit. It was just an ordinary traveller, he told himself as a gust of wind filled his cape. A food salesman, a taxman. Who hunts alone these days apart from Jack? And Jack it isn't, not by thirty years. It was the car, he thought. Those clean wings, the smart aerial. The pitch of his head as he listened.

"Any callers, Miss D?" said Pym, setting out his packages on the sideboard.

Miss Dubber was sitting in the kitchen watching American soap-opera and having her one of the day. Toby sat in her lap.

"They're so wicked, Mr. Canterbury," she said. "There's not one among them we'd have here even for a night, would we, Toby? What's that tea you bought? I said Assam, you silly man, take it back."

"It is Assam," Pym said gently, stooping to show her. "They've put it in a new packing and given you three pence off. Any callers while I was out?"

"Only the gasman for the meter."

"That usual? Or someone new?"

"New, dear. They're all new these days." Lightly kissing her cheek he straightened her new shawl over her shoulders. "Give yourself a nice stiff vodka, darling," she said.

But Pym declined, saying he must work.

Regaining his room he checked the papers on his desk. Stapler to handle of teacup. Book matches to pencil. Burnbox aligned to desk leg, ignore. Miss Dubber is no Mary. Shaving, he caught himself thinking of Rick. I saw your ghost, he thought. Not here but in Vienna. Just as I used to see you in the flesh in Denver, Seattle, San Francisco, Washington. I saw your ghost in every shop-window and autumn doorway while I tried to clear my itchy back. You were wearing your camel-hair coat and smoking the cigar you never drew on without frowning.

Following me, you were, and your blue eyes shadowed like a drowned man's, the pupils stuck against the upper lids to scare me. "Where are you off to, old son, where are those fine legs of yours taking you so late at night? Got a nice lady, have you? Someone who thinks the world of you? Come on, old son. You can tell your old man. Give us a hug." In London you were lying on your deathbed but I wouldn't go to you, I wouldn't know about you or talk about you, it was my way of mourning you. "No, I will not. No, I will not," I used to say each time my heel hit the cobble. So you came to me instead. To Vienna and did a Wentworth on me. Every corner I turned you were there. Until I felt your loving stare like a heat on the back I could never clear. Get off me, damn you, I whispered. What death was I wishing you? All of them by turns. Die, I told you. Do it on the pavement where everyone can see. Stop adoring me. Stop believing in me. Did you want money? Not any more. You had waived your claim to it in favour of the greatest claim of all. You wanted Magnus. You wanted my living spirit to enter your dying body and give you back the life I owed you. "Having a bit of fun, are we, son? Old Poppy's crackerjack, I can see that for openers. What are you two hatching up together there? Come on, you can tell your old pal! Got some piece of business, have you? Putting a few bob in your pockets, are you, the way your old man taught you?"

Three minutes. I always like to cut it fine. Pym wiped his face clean and from an inside pocket drew his faithful copy of Grimmelshausen's *Simplicissimus,* bound in worn brown buckram and much travelled. He laid it ready on the desk beside a pad of paper and a pencil, crossed the room and knelt down in front of dear old Winston's wireless, spinning the bakelite tuning dial until he had the wavelength.

Volume down. Switch on. Wait. A man and a woman discussing in Czech the economics of a fruit cooperative. Discussion fades in midsentence. Time signal announces evening news. Stand by. Pym is calm. Operational calm.

But he is also a little bit transported. There is a serenity here that is not quite of this world, a hint of mystical affinity in his youthful loving smile that says "Hullo there" to someone not quite of this earth. Of all those who have known him, other than this extraterrestrial stranger, perhaps only Miss Dubber has seen the same expression.

Item one, harangue against American imperialists following breakdown of latest round of arms talks. Sound of page turning, signal for get ready. Noted. You are going to talk to me. I am thankful. I appreciate this gesture. Item two coming up. Presenter introduces college professor from Brno. Good evening, Professor, and how is the Czech Secret Service this evening? The professor speaks, a passage for translation. All nerves extended, the all of me at full stretch. First sentence: THE TALKS HAVE ENDED IN DEADLOCK. Ignore. IN ANOTHER BID. Write it down. Slowly. Don't rush. Patience again while we wait for the first numeral. Here it is. A FIFTY-FIVE-YEAR-OLD WELDER FROM PLZEŇ. He switched off the wireless and, pad in hand, returned to his desk, eyes straight ahead of him. Opening his Grimmelshausen at page 55, he found five lines down without even counting and on a fresh sheet of paper wrote out the first ten letters of that line, then converted them to numerals according to their position in the alphabet. Subtract without carrying. Don't reason, do it. He was adding again, still not carrying. He was converting numbers into letters. Don't reason. NEV . . . VER . . . RMI . . . IND . . . DEW . . . There's nothing here. It's gobbledegook. Tune in again at ten and take a fresh reading. He was smiling. He was smiling like a saint when the agony is over. The tears were starting to his eyes. Let them. He was standing, holding the page in both hands above his head. He was weeping. He was laughing. He could scarcely read what he had written. NEVER MIND, E. WEBER LOVE YOU ALWAYS. POPPY.

"You cheeky sod," he whispered aloud, punching away more tears. "Oh Poppy. Oh my."

"Is anything wrong, Mr. Canterbury?" Miss Dubber demanded sternly.

"I came to take that vodka off you, Miss D. Vodka," he explained. "Vodka and something."

He was already mixing it.

"You've only been upstairs an hour, Mr. Canterbury. We don't call that working, do we, Toby? No wonder the country's in a fuss."

Pym's smile widened. "What fuss is that?"

"The football crowds. Setting such a bad example to the foreigners. *You'd* never have let that happen, would you, Mr. Canterbury?"

"Of course I wouldn't."

Warm orange juice from the bottle, oh glory! Chalky water from the tap, where else would you find it? He sat with her for an hour, bubbling on about the charms of Naples, before he returned to his task of saving the country.

How Rick won the peace I'll never rightly know, Tom, but win it he did, overnight as usual, and none of us will ever have to worry again, son, there's plenty for everyone and your old man's made it. In the zeal of the new prosperity father and son took up the profession of country gentleman. With victory in Europe still wet on the hoardings the newly adolescent Pym bought himself a charcoal Harrods suit with its coveted long trousers, a black tie and a stiff white collar, all on the account, and steeled himself to have Sefton Boyd's promised fish-hooks poked through his earlobes. Rick meanwhile in his immense maturity acquired a twenty-acre mansion in Ascot with white fencing down the drive, and a row of tweed suits louder than the Admiral's, and a pair of mad red setters, and a pair of two-toned country shoes for walking them, and a pair of Purdey shotguns for his portrait with them, and a mile-long bar to while away his rustic evenings over bubbly and roulette, and a bronze bust of TP's head on a plinth in the hall beside a larger one of his own. A platoon of displaced Poles was hauled in to staff the place, a new mother wore high heels on the lawn, bawled at the servants and gave Pym tips on the hygiene and diction of the upper classes. A Bentley appeared and was not changed or hidden for several weeks though a Pole with a grudge contrived to fill it with water from a hose-pipe through a crack in the window and drench Rick's dignity when he opened the door next morning. Mr. Cudlove got a mulberry uniform and a cottage in the grounds where Ollie grew geraniums, sang *The Mikado,* and painted the kitchen for his nerves. Livestock and a surly cowman supplied the character of a farm, for Rick had become a taxpayer which I know now marked the summit of his heroic struggle for liquidity: "It's a damn shame, Maxie," he declared proudly to a Major Maxwell-Cavendish who had been brought in to advise on matters of the Turf. "Lord in Heaven if a man can't enjoy the fruits of his labours these days what the devil did we fight the war for?" The Major, who wore a tinted monocle, said "What indeed?" and pursed his lips into a holly leaf. And Pym, agreeing wholeheartedly, topped up the major's glass. Still waiting to be sent to school, he was going through a faceless period and would have topped up anything.

Up in London the court commandeered a pillared Reichskanzlei in Chester Street staffed by a troupe of Lovelies who were changed as often as they wore out. A stuffed jockey in the Pym sporting colours waving his little whip at them, photographs of Rick's neverwozzers, and a Tablet of Honour commemorating the unfallen companies of the latest Rick T. Pym & Son empire completed the Wall of Fame. Their names live in me for ever more, apparently, for it took me years of sworn statements to disown them and I have most of them by heart to this day. The best celebrate the victory at arms that Rick by now was convinced he had obtained for us single-handed: the Alamein Sickness & Health Company, the Military & Permanent Pensions Fund, the Dunkirk Mutual & General, the T.P. Veteran Alliance Company—all seemingly unlimited, yet all satellites of the great Rick T. Pym & Son holding company, whose legal limitations as a receptacle of widows' mites were only gradually revealed. I have enquired, Tom. I have asked lawyers who know things. A hundred pounds of capital was enough to cover the lot. And we had books, fancy! Winfield on Tort, MacGillivray on Insurance, Snell on Equity, somebody else on Rome, hoary old lawyers that they were, they were always the first to disappear in adversity and the first to come back smiling when the struggle was won. And beyond Chester Street lay the clubs, tucked like safe houses around the quieter corners of Mayfair. The Albany, the Burlington, the Regency, the Royalty —their titles were nothing to the glories that awaited us inside. Do such places exist today? Not on the Firm's expenses, Jack, that's for sure. And if so, then in a world already dedicated to pleasure, not austerity. They don't sell you illegal petrol coupons at the bar, illegal steaks in the grill-room or take illegal bets in the illegal sporting room. They don't have illegal mothers in low gowns who swear you'll break a lot of hearts one day. Or real live members of our beloved Crazy Gang leaning gloomily at the bar, an hour before reducing us to tears of laughter in the stalls. Or jockeys scurrying round the snooker table that was too high for them, a hundred quid a corner and Magnus why aren't you at school yet and where's that bloody jigger? Or Mr. Cudlove standing outside in his mulberry, reading *Das Kapital* against the Bentley steering wheel while he waited to whisk us to our next important conference with some luckless gentleman or lady requiring the divine touch.

Beyond the clubs again lay the pubs: Beadles at Maidenhead, the Sugar Island at Bray, the Clock here, the Goat there, the Bell at somewhere else, all with their silver grills and silver pianists and silver ladies at the bar. At one of them Mr. Muspole was called a bloody profiteer by a small waiter he was insulting and Pym contrived to leap in with a funny word in time to stop the fight. What the word was I don't remember, but Mr. Muspole had once shown me a brass knuckleduster he liked to take to the races and I know he had it with him that night. And I know the waiter's name was Billy Craft and that he took me home to meet his underfed wife and children in their Bob Cratchit flat on the edge of Slough, and that Pym spent a jolly night with them and slept on a bony sofa under everybody's woollies. Because fifteen years later at a resources conference at Head Office who should loom out of the crowd but this same Billy Craft, supremo of domestic surveillance section. "I thought I'd rather follow them than feed them, sir," he said with a shy laugh as he shook my hand about fifty times. "No disrespect to your father, mind. He was a great man, naturally." Pym, it turned out, had not been the only one to redress Mr. Muspole's ill-behaviour. Rick had sent him a case of bubbly and a dozen pairs of nylons for Mrs. Craft.

After the pubs, if we were lucky, came a dawn raid on Covent Garden for a nice touch of bacon and eggs to perk us up before the hundred-mile-an-hour dash to the stables where the jockeys put on brown caps and jodhpurs and became the Knights Templar Pym had always known they were, galloping the neverwozzers down frosty runways marked by pine sprigs, till in his loyal imagination they rode off into the sky to win the Battle of Britain for us all over again.

Sleep? I remember it just the once. We were driving to Torquay for a nice weekend's rest at the Imperial, where Rick had set up an illegal game of chemin de fer in a suite overlooking the sea, and it must have been one of those times when Mr. Cudlove had resigned, for suddenly we found ourselves in the middle of a moonlit cornfield that Rick, smelling strongly of the cares of office, had mistaken for the open road. Stretched side by side on the Bentley roof, father and son let the hot moon scorch their faces.

"Are you all right?" Pym asked, meaning, are you liquid, are we on our way to prison?

Rick gave Pym's hand a fierce squeeze. "Son. With you beside me, and God sitting up there with His stars, and the Bentley underneath us, I'm the most all-right fellow in the world." And he meant it, every word as ever, and his proudest day was going to be when Pym was at the Old Bailey on the right side of the rails wearing the full regalia of the Lord Chief Justice, handing down the sentences that had once been handed down to Rick in the days we never owned to.

"Father," said Pym. And stopped.

"What is it, son? You can tell your old man."

"It's just that—well, if you can't pay the first term's boarding fees in advance, it's all right. I mean I'll go to day school. I just think I ought to go somewhere."

"Is that all you've got to say to me?"

"It doesn't matter. Really."

"You've been reading my correspondence, haven't you?"

"No, of course not."

"Have you ever wanted for anything? In your whole life?"

"Never."

"Well then," said Rick and nearly broke Pym's neck with an armlock embrace.

"So where did the money come from, Syd?" I insist again and again. "Why did it ever end?" Even today in my incurable earnestness I long to find a serious centre to the mayhem of these years, even if it is only the one great crime that lies, according to Balzac, behind every fortune. But Syd was never an objective chronicler. His bright eye mists over, a far smile lights his birdy little face as he takes a sip of his wet. Deep down he still sees Rick as a great wandering river which each of us can only ever know the stretch that Fate assigns to us. "Our big one was Dobbsie," he recalls. "I'm not saying there wasn't others, Titch, there was. There was fine projects, many very visionary, very fantastic. But old Dobbsie was our big one."

With Syd there must always be the big one. Like gamblers and actors he lived for it all his life, does still. But the Dobbsie story as he told it to me that night over God knows how many wets can serve as well as any, even if it left the darkest reaches unexplored.

For some time, Titch—says Syd while Meg gives us a drop more pie and turns the log fire up—as the ebb and flow of war, Titch, with God's help, naturally, increasingly favours the Allies, your dad has been very concerned to find a new opening to suit those fantastic talents of his that we are all fully aware of and rightly. By 1945 the shortages cannot be counted on to last for ever. Shortages have become, let's face it, Titch, a risk business. With the hazards of peace upon us, your chocolate, nylons, dried fruit and petrol could flood the market in a day. The coming thing, Titch, says Syd—out of whom Rick's cadences ring like tunes I cannot shake off—is your Reconstruction. And your dad, with that brain of his he's got, is as keen as any other fine patriot to get his piece of it, which is only right. The snag, as ever, is to find the toehold, for not even Rick can corner the British property market without a penny piece of capital. And quite by accident, says Syd, this toehold is provided through the unlikely agency of Mr. Muspole's sister Flora— well *you* remember Flora! Of course I do. Flora is a good scout, a favourite with the jockeys on account of her stately breasts and the generous use she puts them to. But her true allegiance, Syd reminds me, is pledged to a gentleman named Dobbs, who works for Government. And one evening in Ascot over a glass—your dad being away at a conference at the time, Titch—Flora casually lets slip that her Dobbsie is by vocation a city architect and that he has landed this important job. What job is that, dear? the court enquires politely. Flora falters. Long words are not her suit. "Assessing the compensation," she replies, quoting something she has not fully understood. Compensation for what, dear? the court asks, pricking up its ears, for compensation never hurt anyone yet. "Bomb-damage compensation," says Flora and glowers round her with growing uncertainty.

"It was a natural, Titch," says Syd. "Dobbsie hops on his bicycle, slips round to a bombed house, picks up the blower to Whitehall. 'Dobbs here,' he says. 'I'll have twenty thousand quids' worth by Thursday and no backchat.' And Government pays up like a lady. Why?" Syd jabs my upper knee with his forefinger— Rick's gesture to the life. "Because Dobbsie is impartial, Titch, and never you forget it."

Dimly I remember Dobbsie too, a whipped, untruthful little man plastered on two glasses of bubbly. I remember being ordered to be nice to him—and when was Pym ever not? "Son, if Mr. Dobbs here asks you for something—if he wants that fine picture off the wall there—you give it to him. Understand?"

Pym eyed the picture of ships on a red sea in a different light from that day on but Dobbsie never asked for it.

With Flora's amazing secret on the table, Syd continues, the wheels of commerce are flung into top gear. Rick is recalled from his conference, a meeting with Dobbsie is arranged, a mutuality established. Both men are Liberals or Masons or the Sons of Great Men, both follow Arsenal, admire Joe Louis, think Noël Coward is a sissy or share the same vision of men and women of all races marching arm in arm towards the one great Heaven which, let's face it, is big enough for all of us, whatever our colour or creed may be—this being one of Rick's set speeches, guaranteed to make him weep. Dobbs becomes an honorary member of the court and within days introduces a loved colleague named Fox, who also likes to do good for mankind, and whose job is selecting building land for the post-war Utopia. Thus the ripples of conspiracy multiply, find each other and spread.

The next to be blessed is Perce Loft. While pursuing a line of business in the Midlands Perce has heard voices about a moribund Friendly Society that is sitting on a fortune, and makes enquiries. The Chairman of the Society, name of Higgs—Destiny has decreed that all conspirators bear monosyllables—turns out to be a lifelong Baptist. So is Rick; he could never have got where he is today without it. The fortune derives from a family trust watched over by a country solicitor named Crabbe, who went off to the war the moment it became available, leaving the trust to watch over itself as it thought best. As a Baptist, Higgs can fiddle no funds without Crabbe to cover him. Rick secures Crabbe's release from his regiment, whisks him by Bentley to Chester Street where he can inspect the Wall of Fame, the law books and the Lovelies, and thence to the dear old Albany where he can have a nice talk and relax.

Crabbe turns out to be a cantankerous, idiotic little man who sticks out his elbow to take his drink, sir, wiggles his moustache to demonstrate his military shrewdness and after a few glasses demands to know what you stripe-arsed civilians were doing while I was taking part in a certain contest, sir, risking one's neck amid shot and shell? At the Goat some drinks later, however, he declares Rick to be the kind of chap he'd have liked to have as commandant and if need be die for, which one damn nearly did a few times but mum's the word. He even calls Rick "Colonel," thus triggering a bizarre interlude in the great man's rise, for Rick is so taken with the rank that he decides to award it to himself in earnest, much as in later life he convinces himself he has been knighted secretly by the Duke of Edinburgh and keeps a set of calling-cards for those admitted to this confidence.

Yet none of these added responsibilities holds up Rick's breathless waltz for one minute. All night long, all weekend, the house in Ascot receives a pageant of the great, the beautiful and the gullible, for Rick has become a collector of celebrities as well as fools and horses. Test cricketers, jockeys, footballers, fashionable Counsel, corrupt parliamentarians, glistening Under Secretaries from helpful Whitehall Ministries, Greek shipowners, cockney hairdressers, unlisted maharajahs, drunk magistrates, venal mayors, ruling princes of countries that have ceased to exist, prelates in suède boots and pectoral crosses, radio comedians, lady singers, aristocratic layabouts, war millionaires and film stars—all pass across our stage as the bemused beneficiaries of Rick's great vision. Lubricious bank managers and building-society chairmen who have never danced before throw off their jackets, confess to barren lives and worship Rick the giver of their sun and rain. Their wives receive unobtainable nylons, perfumes, petrol coupons, discreet abortions, fur coats and if they are among the lucky ones, Rick himself—for everyone must have something, everyone must be taken care of, everyone must think the world of him. If they have savings, Rick will double them. If they like a flutter, Rick will get them better odds than the bookies—slip me the cash, I'll see you right. Their children are passed to Pym for entertainment, exempted from National Service by the intervention of dear old somebody, given gold watches, tickets to the Cup Final, red setter puppies and, if they are ailing, the finest doctors to attend them. There was a time when such liberality dismayed the growing Pym and made him envious. Not today. Today I would call it no more than normal agent welfare.

And among them, casual as cats, stalk the quiet men of the enlarged court, the men from Mr. Muspole's side, in broad-shouldered suits and brown pork-pie hats, calling themselves consultants and holding the telephone receiver to their ear but not speaking into the mouthpiece. Who they were, how they came there, where they went—to this day only the Devil and Rick's ghost know, and Syd refuses point-blank to speak of them, though with time I think I have put together a fair idea of what they did. They are the axemen of Rick's tragicomedy, now yielding at the knees and covered in false smiles, now posted like Shakespearean sentries round his stage, white-eyed in the gloom as they wait to disembowel him.

And tiptoeing between this entire menagerie—as if between their legs, although he was already as tall as half of them—I glimpse Pym again, willing potboy, blank page, Lord Chief Justice designate, clipping their cigars and topping them all up. Pym the credit to his old man, the diplomat in embryo, scurrying to every summons: "Here, Magnus—what have they done to you at that new school of yours, poured fertiliser over you?" "Here, Magnus, who cut your hair then?" "Here, Magnus, tell us the one about the cabbie who puts his wife in the family way!" And Pym—the most compelling raconteur for his age and weight in all of Greater Ascot—obliges, smiles and sidesteps between their anomalous, colliding masses, and for relaxation attends late-night classes in radical politics with Ollie and Mr. Cudlove in their cottage, at which it is heartily agreed over stolen canapés and cocoa that all men are brothers but nothing against your dad. And though political doctrines are at root as meaningless to me today as they were to Pym then, I remember the simple humanity of our discussions as we promised to mend the world's ills, and the truthful goodheartedness with which, as we went off to bed, we wished each other peace in the spirit of Joe Stalin who, let's face it, Titch, and nothing against your dad *ever,* won the war for all these capitalist bastards.

Court holidays are restored to the curriculum, for no man can give of his best without relaxation. St. Moritz is off the map following Rick's unsuccessful bid to buy the resort as a substitute for paying his bills there, but as compensation, now a favourite word, Rick and his advisers have espoused the South of France, sweeping down on Monte in the Train Bleu, banqueting the journey away in a brass-and-velvet dining-car, only pausing to tip the Froggie engine driver, who's a first-rate Liberal, before dashing off to the Casino, illicit currency at the ready. There, standing at Rick's shoulder in the *grande salle,* Pym can watch a year's school fees vanish in seconds and nobody has learned a thing. If he prefers the bar he can exchange views with a Major de Wildman of Lord knew whose army, who calls himself King Farouk's equerry and claims to have a private telephone link to Cairo so that he can report the winning numbers and take royal orders inspired by soothsayers on how to dissipate the wealth of Egypt. For our Mediterranean dawns we have the sombre march to the all-night pawnbroker on the waterfront, where Rick's gold watch, gold cigarette case, gold swizzle-stick and gold cufflinks with the Pym sporting colours are sacrificed to the elusive god liquidity. For our reflective afternoons, we have the *tir aux pigeons* at which the court, well lunched, lies face down in the butts and pots away at luckless doves as they emerge from their tunnels and start out into the blue sky before crashing into the sea in a crumpled swirl. Then home again to London with the bills all taken care of, which meant signed, and the concierges and headwaiters seen right, which meant tipped lavishly with the last of our cash, to resume the ever-mounting cares of the Pym & Son empire.

For nothing may stand still, too much is not enough, as Syd himself admits. No income is so sacrosanct that expenditure cannot exceed it; no expenditure is so great that more loans cannot be raised to hold the dam from breaking altogether. If the building boom is put temporarily out of service by the passing of an unfriendly Building Act, then Major Maxwell-Cavendish has a plan that speaks deeply to Rick's sporting soul: it is to buy up everyone who has drawn a horse in the Irish Sweep and so win first, second and third prizes automatically. Mr. Muspole knows a derelict newspaper proprietor who has got in with a bad crowd and needs to sell out fast; Rick has ever seen himself as a shaper of the human mind. Perce Loft the great lawyer wants to buy a thousand houses in Fulham; Rick knows a building society whose chairman has Faith. Mr. Cudlove and Ollie are on intimate terms with a young dress designer who has acquired the donkey-ride concession for the projected Festival of Britain; Rick likes nothing better than to give our English kids a break, and my God, son, if anybody has earned it they have. An amphibious motorcar has been designed by Morrie Washington's nephew, a National Cricket Pool is envisaged to complement the winter Football Pools, Perce has yet another scheme for contracting an Irish village to grow human hair for the wig market which is expanding fast thanks to the munificence of the newly formed National Health Service. Automatic orange-peelers, pens that can write under water, the spent shell cases of temporarily discontinued wars: each project engages the great thinker's interest, attracts its experts and its alchemists, adds another line to the Pym & Son Tablet of Honour at the house in Chester Street.

So what went wrong? I ask Syd again, glancing ahead to the inevitable end. What quirk of fate, this time round, Syd, checked the great man's stride? My question sparks unusual anger. Syd sets down his glass.

"Dobbsie went wrong, that's what. Flora wasn't enough for him any more. He had to have the lot. Dobbsie went woozy in the head from all his women, didn't he, Meg?"

"Dobbsie done his little self too well," says Meg, ever a stern student of human frailty.

Poor Dobbs, it transpires, became so lulled that he awarded a hundred thousand pounds of compensation to a housing estate that had not been built till a year after the bombing ended.

"Dobbsie spoilt it for everyone," says Syd, bristling with moral indignation. "Dobbsie was selfish, Titch. That's what Dobbsie was. Selfish."

One later footnote belongs to this brief but glorious high point of Rick's affluence. It is recorded that in October 1947 he sold his head. I chanced upon this information as I was standing on the steps of the crematorium covertly trying to puzzle out some of the less familiar members of the funeral. A breathless youth claiming to represent a teaching hospital waved a piece of paper at me and demanded I stop the ceremony. "In Consideration of the sum of fifty pounds cash I, Richard T. Pym of Chester Street W., consent that on my death my head may be used for the purposes of furthering medical science." It was raining slightly. Under cover of the porch I scribbled the boy a cheque for a hundred pounds and told him to buy one somewhere else. If the fellow was a confidence trickster, I reasoned, Rick would have been the first to admire his enterprise.

And always somewhere in this clamour the name of Wentworth ringing softly in Pym's secret ear like an operational codename known only to the initiated: Wentworth. And Pym—the outsider, not on the list—struggling to join, to know. Like a buzzword passed between older hands in the senior officers' bar at Head Office and Pym the new boy, hearing from the edge, not knowing whether to pretend knowledge or deafness: "We picked it up on Wentworth." "Top Secret and Wentworth—have you been Wentworth-cleared?" Till the very name became to Pym a teasing symbol of wisdom denied, a challenge to his own desirability. "The bugger's doing a Wentworth on us," he hears Perce Loft grumble under his breath one evening. "That Wentworth woman's a tiger," says Syd another time. "Worse than her stupid husband ever was." Each mention spurred Pym to renew his searches. Yet neither Rick's pockets nor his desk drawers, not his bedside table or his pigskin address book or pop-up plastic telephone book, not even his briefcase, which Pym reconnoitred weekly with the key from Rick's Asprey key chain, yielded a single clue. Nor did the impenetrable green filing cabinet which like a travelling icon had come to mark the centre of Rick's migrant faith. No known key fitted it, no fiddling or prising made it yield.

And finally there was school. The cheque was sent, the cheque was cleared.
    The train lurched. In the window Mr. Cudlove and other people's mothers dipped their faces into handkerchiefs and vanished. In his compartment, children larger than himself whimpered and chewed the cuffs of their new grey jackets. But Pym with one turn of his head glanced backward on his life thus far, and forward to the iron path of duty curling into the autumn mist, and he thought: here I come, your best recruit ever. I'm the one you need so take me. The train arrived, school was a mediaeval dungeon of unending twilight, but Saint Pym of the Renunciation was on hand immediately to help his comrades hump their trunks and tuck-boxes up the winding stone staircases, wrestle with unfamiliar collar-studs, find their beds, lockers and clothes-pegs and award himself the worst. And when his turn came to be summoned before his housemaster for an introductory chat Pym made no secret of his pleasure. Mr. Willow was a big homely man in tweeds and a cricket tie, and the Christian plainness of his room after Ascot filled Pym at once with an assurance of integrity.
    "Well, well, what's in here then?" Mr. Willow asked genially as he lifted the parcel to his great ear and shook it.
    "It's scent, sir."
    Mr. Willow misunderstood his meaning. "Sent? I thought you brought it with you," he said, still smiling.
    "It's for Mrs. Willow, sir. From Monte. They tell me it's about the best those Frenchies make," he added, quoting Major Maxwell-Cavendish, a gentleman.
    Mr. Willow had a very broad back and suddenly that was all Pym saw. He stooped, there was a sound of opening and closing, the parcel vanished into his enormous desk. If he'd had a nine-foot grappling iron he couldn't have treated Pym's gift with greater loathing.

"You want to watch out for Tit Willow," Sefton Boyd warned. "He beats on Fridays so that you have the weekend to recover."

But still Pym strove, bled, volunteered for everything and obeyed every bell that summoned him. Terms of it. Lives of it. Ran before breakfast, prayed before running, showered before praying, defecated before showering. Flung himself through the Flanders mud of the rugger field, scrambled over sweating flagstones in search of what passed for learning, drilled so hard to be a good soldier that he cracked his collarbone on the bolt of his vast Lee-Enfield rifle, and had himself punched to kingdom come in the boxing ring. And still he pulled a grin and raised his paw for the loser's biscuit as he tottered to the dressing-room and you would have loved him, Jack; you would have said that children and horses needed to be broken, public school was the making of me.

I don't think it was at all. I think it damn near killed me. But not Pym—Pym thought it all perfectly wonderful and shoved out his plate for more. And when it was required of him by the rigid laws of a haphazard justice, which in retrospect seems like every night of the week, he pressed his limp forelock into a filthy washbasin, clutched a tap in each throbbing hand, and expiated a string of crimes he didn't know he had committed until they were thoughtfully explained to him between each stroke by Mr. Willow or his representatives. Yet when he lay at last in the trembling dark of his dormitory, listening to the creaks and kennel coughs of adolescent longing, he still contrived to persuade himself that he was a prince in the making and, like Jesus, taking the rap for his father's divinity. And his sincerity, his empathy for his fellow man flourished unabated.

In a single afternoon, he could sit down with Noakes the groundsman, eat cake and biscuits in his cottage beside the cider factory and bring tears to the old athlete's eyes with his fabricated tales of the antics of the great sportsmen who had let their hair down at the Ascot feasts. All nonsense, yet all perfectly true to him as he spun his magic. "Not the Don?" Noakes would cry incredulously. "The great Don Bradman himself, dancing on the kitchen table? In your house, Pymmie? Go on!" "And singing 'When I Was a Child of Five' while he was about it," said Pym. Then while Noakes was still glowing from these insights, straight up the hill went Pym to faded Mr. Glover, the assistant drawing master, who wore sandals, to help him wash palettes and remove the day's daubs of powder paint from the genitals of the marble cherub in the main hall. Yet Mr. Glover was the absolute opposite of Noakes. Without Pym the two men were irreconcilable. Mr. Glover thought school sports a tyranny worse than Hitler's and I wish they'd throw their bloody football boots into the river, I do, and plough up their games fields and get on with some Art and Beauty for a change. And Pym wished they would as well and swore his father was going to send a donation to rebuild the arts school to twice its size—probably millions, but keep it secret.

"I'd shut up about your father if I were you," said Sefton Boyd. "They don't like spivs here."

"They don't like divorced mothers either," said Pym, biting back for once. But mainly his strategy was to pacify and reconcile, and keep all the threads in his own hands.

Another conquest was Bellog the German master who seemed physically crumpled by the sins of his adopted country. Pym beleaguered him with extra work, bought him an expensive German beer mug on Rick's account at Thomas Goode's, walked his dog and invited him to Monte all expenses paid, which by a mercy he declined. Today I would blush for such an unsophisticated pass and agonise about whether Bellog had gone sour and been turned. Not Pym. Pym loved Bellog as he loved them all. And he needed that German soul, he had been hard on its path since Lippsie's day. He needed to give himself away to it, right into Mr. Bellog's startled hands, though Germany meant nothing whatever to him, except escape to an unpopular preserve where his talents would be appreciated. He needed the embrace of it, the mystery, the privacy of another side of life. He needed to be able to close the door on his Englishness, love it as he might, and carve a new name somewhere fresh. He even went so far on occasion as to affect a light German accent which drove Sefton Boyd to paroxysms of fury.

And women? Jack, no one was more alive than Pym to the potential virtues of a female agent well handled, but in that school they were the devil to come by and handling anybody, including yourself, was a beatable offence. Mrs. Willow, though he was prepared to love her any time, appeared to be permanently pregnant. Pym's languishing glances were wasted on her. The house matron was personable enough but when he called on her late at night with a fictitious headache in the vague hope of proposing marriage to her, she ordered him sharply back to bed. Only little Miss Hodges who taught the violin showed a shortlived promise: Pym presented her with a pigskin music case from Harrods and said he wished to turn professional, but she wept and advised him to take up a different instrument.

"My sister wants to do it with you," said Sefton Boyd one night as they lay in Pym's bed embracing without enthusiasm. "She read your poem in the school rag. She thinks you're Keats."

Pym was not altogether surprised. His poem was certainly a masterpiece, and Jemima Sefton Boyd had several times scowled at him through the windscreen of the family Land Rover when it came to collect her brother for weekends.

"She's panting for it," Sefton Boyd explained. "She does it with everybody. She's a nympho."

Pym wrote to her at once, a poet's letter.

"A tale must linger in your soft hair. Do you ever have the feeling beauty is a kind of sin? Two swans have settled on the Abbey moat. I watch them often, dreaming of your hair. I love you."

She replied by return, but not before Pym had suffered agonies of remorse at his recklessness.

"Thank you for your letter. I get a long exeat from school starting twenty-fifth which is one of your exeat weekends also. How fateful that they coincide. Mama will invite you for Sunday night and obtain Mr. Willow's permission for you to sleep with us. Are you considering elopement?"

A second letter was more precise:

"The servants' staircase is quite safe. I will kindle a light and have wine waiting in case you get thirsty. Bring any work you have in progress and please caress me first. On my door you will find the red rosette I won last holidays for jumping Smokey."

Pym was scared stiff. How could he acquit himself with a woman of such experience? Breasts he knew about and loved. But Jemima appeared to have none. The rest of her was an unintelligible thicket of dangers and disease, and his memories of Lippsie in the bath became hazier by the minute.

A card came:

> "We would all be so pleased if you would visit us at Hadwell for the weekend of the twenty-fifth. I am writing separately to Mr. Willow. Don't worry about clothes as we do not dress in the evenings during summer.
> Elizabeth Sefton Boyd"

On the hill above Mr. Willow's house stood a girls' school peopled by brown vestals. Boys who penetrated its grounds were flogged and expelled. But Elphick in Nelson House maintained that if you stood beneath the footbridge when the girls were crossing on their way to hockey much could be learned. Alas, all Pym saw when he followed this advice was a few cold knees that looked much like his own. Worse, he had to suffer the coarse humour of a games mistress who leaned over the bridge and invited him to come and play. Disgusted, Pym stalked back to his German poets.

The town library was run by an elderly Fabian, a Pym agent. Pym skipped lunch and hunted his way unchecked through the section marked "Adults Only." *Guidance on Marriage* appeared to be a handbook on mortgages. *The Art of the Chinese Pillow Book* started well but descended into a description of games of darts and leaping white tigers. *Amor and Rococo Woman,* on the other hand, richly illustrated, was a different matter, and Pym arrived at Hadwell expecting naked Graces frolicking with their gallants in the park. At dinner, which to his relief was taken dressed, Jemima cut Pym dead, hiding her face in her hair and reading Jane Austen. A plain girl called Belinda, billed as Jemima's dearest friend, declined speech in sympathy.

"That's how Jem gets when she's horny," Sefton Boyd explained within Belinda's hearing, at which Belinda tried to punch him, then stormed off in a rage.

Dispatched to bed Pym wound his way up the great staircase while a dozen clocks tolled his death knell. How often had Rick not warned him against women who wanted nothing but his money? How dearly he longed for the safety of his bed at school. Crossing the landing he saw a rosette glinting like blood in the low light. He climbed another flight and saw Belinda's head scowling at him round her door. "You can come in here if you like," she said rudely.

"It's all right, thanks," said Pym. He entered his room.

On his pillow lay his eight love letters and four poems to Jemima, bound with ribbon and smelling of saddle soap.

> "Please take back your letters which I find oppressive since I regret we are no longer compatible. I do not know what possessed you to slick down your forelock like an errand boy but henceforth we meet as strangers."

Dashed down by humiliation and despair Pym hastened back to school and the same night wrote to every mother, active or retired, whose name and address he could put his hands on.

"Dearest Topsie, Cherry, darling Mrs. Ogilvie, Mabel, darling Violet, I am being beaten mercilessly for writing poetry and I am very unhappy. Please take me away from this awful place." But when they answered his appeal, the readiness of their love revolted him and he threw away their letters scarcely read. And when one of them, the best, dropped everything and travelled a hundred expensive miles to buy him a mixed grill at the Feathers, Pym met her enquiries with a remote politeness. "Yes, thank you, school is super, everything is absolutely fine. How are *you?*" Then led her an hour early to the railway station so that he could be a good chap at kickabout.

"Dear Belinda"—he wrote in his poet's cursive hand—"Thanks very much for your letter explaining that Jem is unstable. I know girls are terrifically sensitive at this age and going through all sorts of changes so it's really all right. Our house side won Juniors which is a bit of a sensation here. I often think of your beautiful eyes. Magnus."

"Dear Father"—he wrote in a gruff Edwardian manner copied from Sefton Boyd—"I am doing lots of essential entertaining here which is very much the thing and gets me on. Everyone is very grateful for what I do, but prices at the tuckshop have risen and I wondered whether you could send me another five pounds to see me right."

To his surprise, Rick sent him nothing, but came down from the mountain in person, bringing not money but love, which was what Pym had written to him for in the first place.

It was Rick's first visit. Until now Pym had forbidden him the place, explaining that distinguished parents were considered bad form. And Rick with unwonted diffidence had accepted his exclusion. Now with the same diffidence he came, looking trim and loving and mysteriously humble. He didn't venture into the school but sent a letter in his own hand proposing a rendezvous on the road to Farleigh Abbott, which was on the sea. When Pym arrived by bicycle as instructed, expecting the Bentley and half the court, round the corner instead rode Rick alone, also on a bicycle, with a lovely smile that Pym could see from miles off and humming "Underneath the Arches" out of tune. In the bicycle basket he had brought a picnic of their favourite things, a bottle of ginger pop for Pym, bubbly for himself and a football left over from Paradise. They rode their bicycles on the sand and skimmed pebbles on the waves. They lay in the dunes munching foie gras and Ryvita. They wandered through the little town and wondered whether Rick should buy it. They stared at the church and promised never to forget their prayers. They made a goal out of a broken gateway and kicked the football at each other all the way across the world. They kissed and wept and bear-hugged and swore to be pals all their lives and go bicycling every Sunday even when Pym was Lord Chief Justice and married with grandchildren.

"Has Mr. Cudlove resigned?" Pym asked.

Rick just managed to hear, though his face had already acquired the dreamy expression that overcame it at the approach of a direct question.

"Well, son," he conceded, "old Cuddie's been having his ups and downs over the years and he's decided it's time to give himself a bit of a rest."

"How's the swimming-pool coming along?"

"Nearly done. Nearly done. We must be patient."

"Super."

"Tell me, son," said Rick, now at his most venerable. "Have you got a pal or two who might like to do you the favour of supplying you with a bed and some accommodation during the school holidays that are already looming on the horizon?"

"Oh, masses," said Pym, striving to sound careless.

"Well I think you would be well advised to accept their invitations, because with all that rebuilding going on at Ascot, I don't think you're going to enjoy the rest and privacy that fine mind of yours is entitled to."

Pym at once said he would, and made an even greater fuss of Rick in order to persuade him that he did not suspect anything was amiss.

"I'm in love with a rather super girl too," said Pym when it was nearly time to part, in a further effort to persuade Rick of his happiness. "It's quite amusing. We write to each other every day."

"Son, there's no finer thing in this life than the love of a good woman and if anybody's earned it, you have."

"Tell me, boy," said Willow one evening, during an intimate confirmation class. "What does your father do, exactly?"

To which Pym with a natural instinct for the way to Willow's heart replied that he appears to be some kind of, well, free-wheeling businessman, sir, I don't know. Willow changed the subject but at their next session obliged Pym to give an account of his mother. His first instinct was to say she had died of syphilis, an ailment that featured large in Mr. Willow's lectures on Sowing the Seed of Life. But he restrained himself.

"She just sort of vanished when I was young, sir," he confessed with more truth than he intended.

"Who with?" said Mr. Willow. So Pym, for no particular reason he could afterwards think of, said, "With an army sergeant, sir, he was already married so he took her off to Africa to elope."

"Does she write to you, boy?"

"No, sir."

"Why not?"

"I suppose she's too ashamed, sir."

"Does she send you money?"

"No, sir. She hasn't any. He swindled her out of everything she had."

"We are speaking of the sergeant still, I take it?"

"Yes, sir."

Mr. Willow pondered. "Are you familiar with the activities of a company known as The Muspole Friendly and Academic Limited?"

"No, sir."

"You appear to be a director of this company."

"I didn't know, sir."

"Then you also have no knowledge, presumably, as to why this company should be paying your school fees? Or not paying them, perhaps?"

"No, sir."

Mr. Willow pushed up his jaw and narrowed his eyes, indicating a sharpening of his interrogation technique. "And does your father live in some luxury, would you say, by comparison with the kind of standards that apply to other parents here?"

"I suppose he does, sir."

"Suppose?"

"He does, sir."

"Do you disapprove of his life-style?"

"I do a bit, I suppose."

"Does it occur to you that you may one day be obliged to choose between God and Mammon?"

"Yes, sir."

"Have you discussed this with Father Murgo?"

"No, sir."

"Do so."

"Yes, sir."

"Have you ever thought of entering the Church?"

"Often, sir," said Pym, putting on his soulful face.

"We have a fund here, Pym, for impecunious boys wishing to enter the Church. It occurs to the Bursar that you might be eligible to benefit from this fund."

"Yes, sir."

Father Murgo was a toothy, driven little soul whose unlikely task, considering his proletarian origins, was to act as God's itinerant talent-spotter to the public schools. Where Willow was thunderous and craggy, a sort of Makepeace Watermaster without a secret, Murgo writhed inside his habit like a ferret roped into a bag. Where Willow's fearless gaze was unruffled by knowledge, Murgo's signalled the lonely anguish of the cell.

"He's nuts," Sefton Boyd declared. "Look at the scabs on his ankles. The swine picks them while he's praying."

"He's mortifying himself," said Pym.

"Magnus?" Murgo echoed in his sharp northern twang. "Whoever called you that? God's Magnus. You're Parvus." His quick red smile glinted like a stripe that would not heal. "Come this evening," he urged. "Allenby staircase. Staff guestroom. Knock."

"You mad bugger, he'll touch you up!" Sefton Boyd shouted, beside himself with jealousy. But Murgo never touched anyone as Pym had guessed. His lonely hands remained lashed inside his sleeves by invisible thongs, emerging only to eat or pray. For the rest of that summer term Pym floated on clouds of undreamed freedom. Not a week earlier Willow had sworn to flog a boy who had dared to describe cricket as a recreation. Now Pym had only to mention that he proposed to take a stroll with Murgo to be excused what games he wished. Neglected essays were mysteriously waived, beatings vaguely due to him deferred. On breathless walks, on bicycle rides, in little teahouses in the country, or at night crammed into a corner of Murgo's miserable bedroom, Pym eagerly offered versions of himself that alternately shocked and thrilled them both. The shiftless materialism of his home life. His quest for faith and love. His fight against the demons of self-abuse and such tempters as Kenneth Sefton Boyd. His brother-and-sister relationship with the girl Belinda.

"And the holidays?" Murgo proposed one evening as they loped down a bridlepath past lovers fondling in the grass. "Fun, are they? High living?"

"The holidays are a desert," said Pym loyally. "So are Belinda's. Her father's a stockbroker."

The description acted on Murgo like a goad.

"Oh, a desert, are they? A wilderness? All right. I'll go along with that. Christ was in the wilderness too, Parvus. For a bloody long time. So was Saint Anthony. Twenty years he served, in a filthy little fort on the Nile. Perhaps you've forgotten."

"No I hadn't at all."

"Well he did. And it didn't stop him talking to God or God talking to him. Anthony didn't have privilege. He didn't have money or property or fine cars or stockbrokers' daughters. He prayed."

"I know," said Pym.

"Come to Lyme. Answer the call. Be like Anthony."

"What the fuck have you done to the front of your hair?" Sefton Boyd screamed at him the same evening.

"I've cut it off."

Sefton Boyd stopped laughing. "You're going to be a monkey Murgo," he said softly. "You've fallen for him, you mad tart."

Sefton Boyd's days were numbered. Acting on information received—even now I blush to contemplate the source of it—Mr. Willow had decided that young Kenneth was getting a little too old for the school.

So there's yet another Pym for you, Jack, and you had better add him to my file even if he is neither admirable nor, I suspect, comprehensible to you, though Poppy knew him inside out from the first day. He's the Pym who can't rest till he's touched the love in people, then can't rest till he's hacked his way out of it, the more drastically the better. The Pym who does nothing cynically, nothing without conviction. Who sets events in motion in order to become their victim, which he calls decision, and ties himself into pointless relationships, which he calls loyalty. Then waits for the next event to get him out of the last one, which he calls destiny. It's the Pym who passes up a two-week invitation to stay with the Sefton Boyds in Scotland, all found including Jemima, because he is pledged to hurl himself over the Dorset hills in the wake of a tortured Mancunian zealot, preparing for a life he has not the smallest intention of leading, among people who chill him to the root. It's the Pym who writes daily to Belinda because Jemima has cast doubts on his divinity. It's Pym the Saturday night juggler bounding round the table and spinning one stupid plate after another because he can't bear to let anyone down for one second and so lose their esteem. So off he goes and half chokes himself on incense and sleeps in a cell that stinks like a wet dog and nearly dies of nettle stew in order to become pious and pay his school fees and be adored by Murgo. Meanwhile he heaps fresh promises on old and convinces himself that he is on the path to Heaven while he digs himself deeper into his own mess. By the end of a week he is promised to a boys' camp in Hereford, a pan-denominational retreat in Shropshire, a Trade Unionists' pilgrimage in Wakefield and a Celebration of Witness in Derby. By the end of two weeks there isn't a county in England where he hasn't pledged his holiness six different ways—which is not to deny that intermittently he has visions of himself as a haggard apostle of the life renounced, converting beautiful women and millionaires to Christian poverty.

It was a full month before God provided the escape that Pym was waiting for.

YOUR IMMEDIATE PRESENCE CHESTER STREET ESSENTIAL IN MATTER OF VITAL NATIONAL AND INTERNATIONAL IMPORTANCE RICHARD T. PYM MANAGING DIREC-TOR PYMCORP.

"You must go," said Murgo with tears of misery rolling down his hollowed cheeks as he handed him the fatal telegram after Terce.

"I don't think I can face it," said Pym, no less affected. "It's just money, money all the time."

They walked past the print shop and the basket shop, through the kitchen gardens to the little wicker gate that kept Rick's world at bay.

"You didn't send it to yourself, did you, Parvus?" Murgo asked.

Pym swore he had not, which was the truth.

"You don't understand what a force you are," Murgo said. "I don't think I'll be the same again."

It had never occurred to Pym until now that Murgo was capable of change.

"Well," said Murgo with a last sad writhe.

"Goodbye," said Pym. "And thanks."

But there is cheer in sight for both of them. Pym has promised to be back for Christmas, when the tramps come.

Mad swings, Tom. Mad leaps and loves, madder round the corner. I wrote to Dorothy too somewhere in that time. Care of Sir Makepeace Watermaster at the House of Commons, though I knew he was dead. I waited a week then forgot until one day out of the blue my ploy was rewarded with a tatty little letter, blotchy with tears or drink, on ruled paper torn from a notepad, no address but postmark East London, a country I had never visited. It is before me now.

> "Yours was a voice down many Coridors of Years, my dear, I put it in the kitchen cuboard with my Tableware to view at leasure. I will be at Euston Station the up platform 3 P.M. Thursday without my Herbie and I will be carrying a posy of lavender which you always loved."

Already greatly regretting his decision, Pym arrived at the station late and placed himself in the gunman's corner beneath an iron arch close to some mail bags. Quite a bevy of mothers was milling about, some eligible, some less so, but there was none he wanted and several who were drunk. And one of them seemed to be clutching a posy of flowers wrapped in newspaper but by then he had decided he had the wrong platform. It was his darling Dorothy that Pym had wanted, not some lolloping old biddy in a pantomime hat.

A weekday evening, Tom. The traffic in Chester Street burps and crackles in the rain, but inside the Reichskanzlei it is a Green Hill Sunday. Still pious from his monastery Pym presses the bell but hears no answering chime. He drives the great brass door knocker against its stud. A lace curtain parts and closes. The door opens, but not far.

"Cunningham's the name, squire," says a heavy man in a thick expatriate cockney, as he shuts the door fast after him as if scared of letting in germs. "Half cunning, half ham. You'll be the son and heir. Greetings, squire, Salaams."

"How do you do," says Pym.

"I'm optimistic, squire, thank you," Mr. Cunningham replies with a Middle-European literalness. "I think we're on a road to understanding. Some resistance at first is to be expected. But I believe I see a light begin to shine."

It is more than Pym does for the passage down which Mr. Cunningham leads him with such assurance is pitch black and the only light comes from the pale patches on the wall left by the departed law books.

"You're a German scholar, I understand, squire," says Mr. Cunningham more thickly, as if the exertion has affected his adenoids. "A fine language. The people, I'm not sure. But a lovely tongue in the right hands, you can quote me."

"Why are we going upstairs?" says Pym, who has by now recognised several familiar omens of impending pogrom.

"Trouble with the lift, squire," Mr. Cunningham replies. "I understand an engineer has been sent for and is at this moment hastening on his way."

"But Rick's office is on the ground floor."

"But upstairs has the privacy, squire," Mr. Cunningham explains, pushing open a double door. They enter a gutted State Apartment lit by the glow of street lamps. "Your son, sir, fresh from his worship," Mr. Cunningham announces, and bows Pym ahead of him.

At first Pym sees only Rick's brow glinting in the candlelight. Then the great head forms round it, followed by the broad bulk of the body as it advances swiftly to envelop him in a damp and fervent bearhug.

"How are you, old son?" he asks urgently. "How was the train?"

"Fine," says Pym who has hitchhiked owing to a temporary problem of liquidity.

"Did they give you a bit to eat then? What did they give you?"

"Just a sandwich and a glass of beer," says Pym who has had to make do on a piece of rocklike bread from Murgo's refectory.

"My own boy, as you see me!" Mr. Cunningham exclaims with zest. "Never satisfied unless he's eating."

"Son, you want to watch that drinking of yours," says Rick in an almost unconscious reflex, as he clutches Pym under the armpit and marches him over bare floorboards towards an imperial-sized bed. "There's five thousand pounds for you in cash if you don't smoke or take liquor until you're twenty-one. All right, my dear, what do you think of this boy of mine?"

A darkly dressed figure has risen like a shade from the bed.

It's Dorothy, thinks Pym. It's Lippsie. It's Jemima's mother lodging a complaint. But as the darkness lifts, the aspiring monk observes that the figure before him is wearing neither Lippsie's headscarf nor Dorothy's cloche hat, nor has she the daunting authority of Lady Sefton Boyd. Like Lippsie she sports the antiquarian uniform of pre-war Europe but there the comparison ends. Her flared skirt has a nipped waist. She wears a blouse with a lace ruff and a feathery bit of hat that makes the whole outfit jaunty. Her breasts are in the best tradition of *Amor and Rococo Woman,* and the dim light flatters their roundness.

"Son, I want you to meet a noble and heroic lady who has known great advantages and misfortunes and fought great battles and suffered cruelly at the hands of fate. And who has paid me the greatest compliment a woman can pay a man by coming to see me in her hour of need."

"Rot-schilt, darling," the lady says softly, lifting her limp hand to a level where Pym may kiss or shake it.

"Heard that name anywhere, have you, son, with your fine education? *Baron* Rothschild? *Lord* Rothschild? *Count* Rothschild? Rothschild's *Bank?* Or are you going to tell me you're not conversant with the name of a certain great Jewish family with all the wealth of Solomon at its fingertips?"

"Well yes, of course I've heard of it."

"Well then. Just you sit yourself here and listen to what she has to say because this is the baroness. Sit down, my dear. Come here between us. What do you think of him, Elena?"

"Beautiful, darling," says the baroness.

He's selling me to her, thinks Pym, not at all unwilling. I'm his last desperate deal.

So there we all are, Tom. Everyone on the go and madness here to stay. Your father and grandfather seated buttock to buttock with a Jewish baroness in the half-furnished director's knocking-shop of a West End palace without electricity, and Mr. Cunningham, as I gradually realise, keeping guard at the door. An air of daft conspiracy comparable only with later daft conspiracies mounted by the Firm, as her soft voice embarks on one of those patient refugee monologues that your Uncle Jack and I have listened to more times than either of us can remember, except that tonight Pym is a virgin in these matters, and the baroness's thigh is pressed cosily against that of the aspiring monk.

"I am a humble widow of simple but pious family, married happily but oh so briefly to the late Baron Luigi Svoboda-Rothschild, the last of the great Czech line. I was seventeen, he twenty-one, imagine our pleasure. My greatest regret is I bore him no child. Our country seat was the Palais of Nymphs at Brno, which first the Germans then the Russians rape worse than a woman literally. My Cousin Anna she marry to the head man from De Beers diamonds Cape Town, got houses like you not imagine, too much luxury I don't approve." Pym does not approve either, as he tries to tell her with a monkish smirk of sympathy. "With my Uncle Wolfram I never speak and thanks God I say. He collaborate with the Nazis. The Jews hang him upside down." Pym sets his jaw in grim approval. "My Granduncle David give all his tapestries to the Prado. Now he is poor like a kulak, why don't the museum give him something so he can eat?" Pym rolls his head in despair at the baseness of the Spanish soul. "My Auntie Waldorf—" She breaks down beautifully while Pym wonders whether the agitation of his body is visible to her in the darkness.

"It's a damn shame!" cries Rick, while the baroness composes herself. "My God, son, those Bolsheviks could swoop down on Ascot tomorrow without a by-your-leave and help themselves to a fortune. Go on, my dear. Son, tell her to go on. Call her Elena, she likes it. She's not a snob. She's one of us."

"*Weiter, bitte,*" says Pym.

"*Weiter,*" the baroness echoes approvingly and pats her eyes with Rick's handkerchief. "*Jawohl,* darling. *Sehr gut!*"

"Oh but you should hear his accent," Mr. Cunningham calls from the door.

"Not a wrinkle, you can quote me, same as my own boy."

"What does she say, son?"

"She can manage," says Pym. "She can handle it."

"She's a damned gem. I'm going to see her right, you mark my words."

So is Pym. He is going to marry her at least. But meanwhile, to his irritation, he must hear more praise for my dear late husband the baron. My Luigi was not only the proprietor of a great palace, he was a financial genius and until the outbreak of war the Chairman of the House of Rothschild in Prague.

"They were the richest of the lot," says Rick. "Weren't they, son? You've read your history. What's your verdict?"

"They couldn't even count it," Mr. Cunningham confirms from the door with the pride of an impresario. "Could they, Elena? Ask her. Don't be shy."

"We give such concerts, darling," the baroness confides to Pym. "Princes from all countries. We got house from marble. We got mirrors, culture. Like here," she adds graciously, indicating a priceless oil painting of Prince Magnus in his paddock, done from a photograph. "We lose everything."

"Not quite everything," says Rick under his breath.

"When the Germans come, my Luigi he refuse to flee. He face the Nazi pigs from the balcony, got a pistol in his hand, don't never been heard of since."

Another necessary break follows in which the baroness allows herself a delicate sip of brandy from a row of crystal decanters on the floor, and Rick to Pym's fury takes over the story, partly because Rick is already tired of listening, but more particularly because a secret is approaching, and secrets in court etiquette are Rick's alone to divulge.

"That baron was a fine man and a fine husband, son, and he did what any fine husband would do, and believe me, if your mother was in a position to appreciate it, I'd do the same for her tomorrow—"

"I know you would," says Pym hastily.

"That baron got some of the best treasures out of that palace, he put them in a box and he gave that box to certain very good friends of his and friends of this fine lady here, and he gave orders that when the British won the war this same box should be handed over to his lovely young wife, with everything it contained, however much it may have risen in value in the meantime."

The baroness knows the menu from memory and again selects Pym as her audience, for which purpose it is necessary for her to arrest his attention with a delicate hand placed on his wrist.

"One Gutenberg Bible, nice condition, darling, one Renoir early, two Leonardo medical. One first edition Goya caprices, artist annotation, three hundred best gold American dollar, Rubens a couple cartoons."

"Cunningham says it's worth a bomb," says Rick when she seems to have finished.

"It's Hiroshima," says Mr. Cunningham from the door.

Pym contrives an ethereal smile intended to indicate that great art knows no price. The baroness intercepts it and understands.

It is an hour later. The baroness and her protector have departed, leaving father and son alone in the great unlighted room. The traffic below the window has subsided. Shoulder to shoulder on the bed they are eating fish and chips which Pym has been dispatched to buy with precious pound notes from Rick's back pocket. They wash it down with a bottle of Château d'Yquem from a Harrods crate.

"Are they still there, son?" says Rick. "Did they see you? Those men in the Riley. Heavy built."

"I'm afraid they are," says Pym.

"You believe in her, don't you, son? Don't spare my feelings. Do you believe in that fine woman or do you think she's a black-hearted liar and adventuress to boot?"

"She's fantastic," says Pym.

"You don't sound convinced. Spit it out, son. She's our last chance, I'll tell you that for nothing."

"It's just I wasn't quite sure why she hadn't gone to her own people."

"You don't know those Jews the way I do. They're some of the finest people in the world. There's others, they'd have the coat off her back as soon as look at her. I asked her the same question. I didn't pull my punches either."

"Who's Cunningham?" says Pym, barely able to conceal his distaste.

"Old Cunnie's first class. I'm bringing him into the business when this is over. Exports and Foreign. He'll be a tearaway. His sense of humour alone is worth five thousand a year to us. He wasn't on form tonight. He was tense."

"What's the deal?" says Pym.

"Faith in your old man, that's the deal. 'Rickie,' she says to me—that's what she calls me, she doesn't pull her punches either—'Rickie, I want you get that box for me, sell the contents and invest the money in one of your fine enterprises, and I want you to take the cares off my shoulders and give me ten percent a year for life for as long as I'm spared, with all the necessary provisions of insurance and endowment if you go before me. I want that money to be yours to see the world right in whatever way you deem in your wisdom.' That's a big responsibility, son. If I had a passport I'd go myself. I'd send Syd if he was available. Syd would go. Cattle and pigs. That's what I'm going to do after this. Just a few acres and some livestock. I'm retiring."

"What's happened to your passport?" said Pym.

"Son, I'm going to level with you, which I always do. That airy-fairy school of yours are hard bargainers. They want cash and they want it on the due day and that's it. You speak her language, that's the point. She likes you. She trusts you. You're my son. I could send Muspole but I'd never be sure he'd come back. Perce Loft's too legal. He'd scare her. Now slip to the window and see if that Riley's gone. Don't get the light on your face. They can't come in. They haven't got a warrant. I'm an honest citizen."

Half hidden behind the chipped green filing cabinet, Pym squints steeply downward into the street in covert counter-surveillance. The Riley is still there.

There are no blankets for the bed so they make do with curtains and dust-sheets. Pym sleeps fitfully and freezes, dreaming of the baroness. Once Rick's arm falls violently across him, once he is roused by Rick's strangled voice calling out invective against a bitch called Peggy. And some time in the early hours he feels the soft female weight of Rick's nether body in silk shirt and underpants backing inexorably against him, which persuades him it is more restful on the floor. In the morning Rick still will not leave the house, so Pym walks alone to Victoria Station carrying his few possessions in a splendid white box-calf suitcase with Rick's initials in brass underneath the handle. He wears one of Rick's camel-hair coats though it is too large for him. The baroness, looking more delectable than ever, is waiting on the platform. Mr. Cunningham is there to wave them off. In the train lavatory, Pym opens the envelope Rick gave him and extracts a wad of white ten-pound notes and his first-ever instructions for a clandestine encounter.

> "You are to proceed to Bern and take Rooms at the Grand Palace Hotel. Mr. Bertl the under-manager is first Rate, the Bill is taken care of. Signor Lapadi will Contact the Baroness and guide you to the Austrian border. When Lapadi has given you the Box and you have Confirmed in our Language that it's all there, see him right with the Enclosed and not until. This is going to be the Saving of us, son. That Money you are Carrying took a lot of earning, but when this is over none of us will ever have to Worry again."

I shall be brisk with the operational details of the Rothschild assignment, Jack— the days of hope, the days of doubt, the sudden leaps from one to the other. And I truly forget which street corners or codewords preceded the slow descent into inconclusion that has been my memory of so many operations since—just as I forget, if I ever knew, in what quantities of skepticism and blind faith Pym pursued his mission to its inevitable end. Certainly I have known operations since that have been mounted on quite as little likelihood of success, and have cost a great deal more than money. Signor Lapadi spoke only to the baroness, who relayed his information with disdain.

"Lapadi he talk mit his *Vertrauensmann,* darling." She smiles indulgently when Pym asks what a *Vertrauensmann* is. "The *Vertrauensmann* is man we are trusting. Not yesterday, maybe not tomorrow. But today we are trusting him for ever."

"Lapadi he need one hundred pound, darling"—a day or two later—"the *Vertrauensmann* know a man whose sister know the head from customs. Better he pay him now for friendship."

Remembering Rick's instructions Pym offers token resistance but the baroness already has her hand out and is rubbing her finger and thumb together with delightful insinuation. "You want to paint the house, darling, first you got to buy the brush," she explains and to Pym's amazement lifts her skirts to the waist and pops the banknotes into the top of her stocking. "Tomorrow we buy you nice suit."

"Gave her the money, son?" Rick roars that night across the Channel. "God in Heaven, what do you think we are? Fetch me Elena."

"Don't shout me, darling," the baroness says calmly into the telephone. "You got lovely boy here, Rickie. He very strict with me. I think one day he be great actor."

"The baroness says you're first rate, son. Are you talking our language with her out there?"

"All the time," says Pym.

"Have you had an honest-to-God English mixed grill yet?"

"No, we're sort of saving it."

"Well have one on me. Tonight."

"We will, Father. Thanks."

"God bless you, son."

"And you too, Father," says Pym politely and, butler-like, keeps his knees and feet together while he puts the phone down.

More important to me by far are my memories of Pym's first platonic honeymoon with a wise lady. With Elena beside him, Pym wandered Bern's old city, drank the light small wines of the Valais, watched *thés dansants* in the great hotels and consigned his past to history. In scented, frilly boutiques that she seemed to find by instinct, they exchanged her battered wardrobe for fur capes and Anna Karenina riding boots that slithered on the frosty cobble, and Pym's dismal school habit for a leather jacket and trousers without buttons for his braces. Even in her disarray, the baroness would insist on Pym's judgment, beckoning him into the little mirrored box to help her choose, and permitting him, as if unknowingly, delicious glimpses of her Rococo charms: now a nipple, now the cup of a buttock carelessly uncurtained, now an amazing shadow at the centre of her rounded thighs as she whisked from one skirt to another. She is Lippsie, he thought excitedly; she is how Lippsie would have been if she hadn't thought so much of death.

"*Gefall' ich dir,* darling?"

"*Du gefällst mir sehr.*"

"One day you have pretty girl, you talk to her just like this, she go crazy. You don't think too tarty?"

"I think perfect."

"Okay, we buy two. One for my sister Zsa-Zsa, she my size."

A tilt of the white shoulders, a careless pull at a straying hem of lingerie, the bill was brought, Pym signed it and addressed it to the provident Herr Bertl, turning his back on her and crouching forward in order to conceal the evidence of his perturbation. From a jeweller in the Herrengasse they bought a pearl necklace for another sister in Budapest and as an afterthought a topaz ring for her mother in Paris which the baroness would take to her on her way home. And I see that ring now, winking on her freshly manicured finger as she traces a trout back and forth across the fish tank in the grill-room of our grand hotel while the headwaiter stands above her with his net poised to strike.

"*Nein, nein,* darling, *nicht* this one, *that* one! *Ja, ja, prima.*"

It was at one such dinner, in the event their last, that Pym was so moved by love and confusion that he felt obliged to confide to the baroness his intention of leading a monastic life. She put down her knife and fork with a clatter.

"Don't tell me no more from monks!" she commanded him angrily. "I see too many of monks. I see monks of Croatia, monks of Serbia, Russia. God He ruin the damn world with monks."

"Well, it's not completely certain," said Pym.

It took a lot of funny voices from him, and a lot of intimate fabrications, before the light came cautiously back to her brown eyes.

"And her name was Lippsie?"

"Well that's what we called her. I mustn't tell you her real name."

"And she slept with such a young boy like you? You made love with her so young? She was a whore, I think."

"Probably just lonely," said Pym wisely.

But her thoughtfulness remained and when Pym as usual saw her to her bedroom door she studied him closely before taking his head between her hands and kissing him on the mouth. Suddenly her mouth opened, Pym's also. The kiss became intense, he felt an unfamiliar mound plying irresistibly against his thigh. He felt its warmth, he felt soft hair slipping against silk as she pressed more rhythmically. She whispered *"Schatz,"* he heard a squeak and wondered whether he had hurt her somehow. Her head twisted, her neck pressed against his lips. With confiding fingers she handed him the key to her bedroom door and looked away while he opened it. He found the keyhole, turned the key and held the door for her. He put the key into her palm and saw the light in her eyes fade.

"So, my dear," she said. She kissed him, one cheek other cheek, she stared at him as if searching for something she had lost. It was not till next morning that he discovered she had been kissing him goodbye.

> "Darling"—she wrote—"You are good man, got body from Michelangelo but your Papi got bad problems. Better you stay in Bern. Never mind. E. Weber love you always."

In the envelope were the gold cufflinks we had bought for her cousin in Oxford, and two hundred of the five hundred pounds that Pym had given her for the invisible Mr. Lapadi. I wear the cufflinks as I write. Gold with tiny diamonds in a crown. The baroness always loved a touch of royalty.

It was morning at Miss Dubber's also. Through the closed curtains, Pym heard the milk van clinking on its rounds. Pen in hand he drew a pink file towards him marked simply "R.T.P.," licked his forefinger and thumb and began methodically turning through the entries until he had extracted some half dozen.

Copy letter Richard T. Pym to Father Guardian, Lyme Regis, dated 1 October 1948, threatening legal proceedings for the abduction of his son Magnus. (Ex R.T.P.'s files.)

Memorandum of 15 September 1948, Fraud Squad to Passport Control Department, recommending impounding of R.T.P.'s passport pending criminal investigations in the matter of one J. R. Wentworth. (Obtained informally through Head Office police liaison section.)

Letter from school bursar to R.T.P. declining to accept either dried fruit, tinned peaches or any other commodity in part or full payment of fees and regretting that the governing board cannot see its way to educating Pym for nothing. "I note also with regret that you refuse to describe yourself as an impecunious parent whose son is destined for the clergy." (Ex R.T.P.'s files.)

Furious letter from lawyers representing Herr Eberhardt Bertl, sometime under-manager of the Grand Palace Hotel in Bern, addressed to Colonel Sir Richard T. Pym, D.S.O., one of a succession, demanding payment in the order of eleven thousand and eighteen Swiss francs forty centimes, plus interest at four percent per month. (Ex R.T.P.'s files.)

Extract from London *Chronicle* dated November 8, 1949, declaring personal bankruptcy R.T.P., and compulsory liquidation of the eighty-three companies of the Pym empire including, no doubt, The Muspole Friendly & Academic Ltd.

Extract from *Daily Telegraph* dated October 9, 1948, recording the death in Truro Hospital, Cornwall, of one John Reginald Wentworth, after a long illness resulting from his injuries, beloved husband to Peggy.

And a quaint little cutting, culled from God knows where, recording the arrest at sea, on the cruise ship S.S. *Grande Bretagne,* of the notorious confidence tricksters Weber and Woolfe alias Cunningham, masquerading as the Duke and Duchess of Seville.

One by one, with a red pen, Pym numbered each document in the top right corner, then entered the same numbers at the appropriate points in his text by way of reference. With a bureaucrat's neat manners he stapled the exhibits together and inserted them in a file marked "Annexe." Closing the file he stood up, gave an unrestrained sigh and thrust down his arms behind him like a man slipping off a harness. The ghostly formlessness of adolescence was over. Manhood and maturity beckoned, even if he never made the distance. He was in his beloved Switzerland at last, the spiritual home of natural spies. Crossing to the window he made a last inspection of the square, the tired lights of England fading as he watched. Gravely he undressed, drank a last vodka, gravely took a look at himself in the mirror and prepared to put himself to bed. But lightly, very lightly. Almost on tiptoe. Almost as if he were afraid to wake himself up. On his way he paused at the desk and read again the decoded message that for once he had not bothered to destroy.

Poppy, he thought, stay exactly where you are.

7

Five years ago Jack Brotherhood had shot his Labrador bitch. She was in her basket, rheumatic and shaking; he'd given her the pills but she'd sicked them up, then shamed herself by messing the carpet. And when he threw on his windcheater and took his 12-bore from behind the door, willing her, she looked at him like a criminal because she knew she was finally too sick to find for him. He ordered her to get up but she couldn't. When he yelled "Seek!" she rolled herself on to her forepaws and lay down again with her head stuck stupidly over the basket. So he put down the gun and got a shovel from the shed and dug her a hole in the field behind the cottage, a bit up the slope with a decent view across the estuary. Then he wrapped her in his favourite tweed jacket and carried her up there and shot her in the back of the head, smashing the spinal cord at the nape, and buried her. After that he sat beside her with a half-bottle of scotch while the Suffolk dew settled itself over him and he decided she had probably had the best death anyone was likely to have in a world not distinguished by good deaths. He didn't leave a headstone or a coy wood cross for her but he had taken bearings on the spot, using the church tower, the dead willow tree and the windmill, and whenever he passed it by he'd send her a gruff mental greeting, which was as near as he had ever come to pondering on the afterlife, until this empty Sunday morning as he drove through deserted Berkshire lanes and watched the sun lifting on the Downs. "Jack's had too many miles in the saddle," Pym had said. "The Firm should have retired him ten years ago."

And how long ago should we have retired you, my boy? he wondered. Twenty years? Thirty? How many miles have you had in the saddle? How many miles of exposed film have you rolled into how many newspapers? How many miles of newspaper have you dropped into dead letter boxes and tossed over cemetery walls? How many hours have you listened to Prague radio, seated over your code pads?

He lowered his window. The racing air smelt of silage and wood smoke and it thrilled him. Brotherhood was country stock. His forebears were gypsies and clergymen, gamekeepers and poachers and pirates. With the morning wind pouring into his face, he became a raggedy-arsed boy again, galloping Miss Sumner's hunter bareback across her park and getting the hiding of his life for it. He was freezing to death in the flat mud of the Suffolk fens, too proud to go home without a catch. He was making his first drop from a barrage balloon at Abingdon Aerodrome and discovering how the wind kept his mouth open after he yelled. I'll leave when they throw me out. I'll leave when you and I have had our word, my boy.

He had slept six hours in forty-eight, most of them on a lumpy camp bed in a room set aside for typists with the vapours, but he was not tired. "Can we have you for a minute, Jack?" said Kate, the Fifth Floor vestal, with a look that stayed on him a beat too long. "Bo and Nigel would like another small word." And when he wasn't sleeping or answering the telephone or thinking his usual puzzled thoughts about Kate, he had watched his life go by in a kind of bewildered free fall into enemy territory: so this is what it's like, this is badland and these are my feet spinning towards it like a sycamore twig. He had contemplated Pym in all the stages he had grown up with him, drunk with him and worked with him, including a night in Berlin he had totally forgotten until now when they had ended up screwing a couple of army nurses in adjoining rooms. He had remembered contemplating his own mangled arm on the winter's day in 1943 when it had hung beside him embellished with three German machine-gun bullets, and he had experienced the same feeling of incredulous detachment.

"If you could only have let us know a little earlier, Jack. If only you could have seen it coming."

Yes, I'm sorry, Bo. Careless of me.

"But Jack, he was practically your own son, we used to say."

Yes, we did, didn't we, Bo. Silly really, I agree.

And Kate's reproving eyes, as ever, saying, Jack, Jack, where are you?

There had been other cases in his lifetime, naturally. Ever since the war had ended, Brotherhood's professional life had been regularly turned upside down by the Firm's latest terminal scandal. While he was Head of Station in Berlin, it had happened to him not twice but three times: night telegrams, flash, for Brotherhood's eyes only. Phone call—where is he? Jack, get off your elbows and get in here *now*. Race through wet streets, dead sober. Telegram one, the subject of my immediately following telegram is a member of this service and has now been revealed as a Soviet Intelligence agent. You will inform your official contacts of this in confidence before they read it in the morning papers. Followed by the long wait beside the codebooks while you think: is it him, is it her, is it me? Telegram two, spell a name of six letters, who the hell do I know who's got six letters? First group M—Christ, it's Miller! Second group A—oh my God, it's Mackay! Until up comes a name you never heard of, from a section you didn't know existed, and when the expurgated case history finally arrives on your desk all you have is a vision of an under-welfared little nancy-boy in the cypher room in Warsaw who thought he was playing the world's game when what he really wanted was to shaft his employers.

But these distant scandals had been till now the gunfire of a war he was certain would never come his way. He had regarded them not as warnings but as confirmation of everything he disliked about the way the Firm was going: its retreat into bureaucracy and semi-diplomacy, its pandering to American methods and example.

By comparison his own hand-picked staff had only looked better to him, and when the witch-hunters had gathered at his door, led by Grant Lederer and his nasty little Mormon bag-carriers, baying for Pym's blood and brandishing fanciful suspicions based on nothing more than a few computerised coincidences, it was Jack Brotherhood who had banged his open hand upon the conference table and made the water-glasses hop: "Stop this *now*. There's not a man or woman in this room who won't look a traitor once you start to pull our life stories inside out. A man can't remember where he was on the night of the tenth? Then he's lying. He *can* remember? Then he's too damn flip with his alibi. You go one more yard with this and everyone who tells the truth will become a barefaced liar, everyone who does a decent job will be working for the other side. You carry on like this and you'll sink our service better than the Russians ever could. Or is that what you want?"

And God help him, with his reputation and his anger and his connections and with his section's record, in the modern jargon that he loathed, of low cost and high productivity, he had carried the day, never thinking for a moment that another day might come where he wished he hadn't.

Closing his window Brotherhood stopped the car in a village where no one knew him. He was too early. He had needed to get out of London, out of touch, away from Kate's brown stare. Give him one more hopeless damage-limitation conference, one more session on how to keep it from the Americans, one more glance of pity or reproach from Kate, or of plain hatred from Bo's grey army of suburban mandarins, and possibly, just possibly, Jack Brotherhood might have said things that everyone, but most of all himself, would afterwards have regretted. So he had volunteered for this errand instead, and Bo with rare promptness had said what a good idea, who better? And he knew as soon as he cleared Bo's doorway that they were as glad to see him go as he was to leave. Except for Kate.

"Just do keep phoning in if you don't mind," Bo called after him. "Three-hourly at most. Kate will know the score. Won't you, Kate?"

Nigel followed him down the corridor. "When you phone in, I want you coming through Secretariat. You're not to use his direct line and I shall need to speak to you first."

"And that's an order," Brotherhood suggested.

"It's a temporary licence and it can be withdrawn at any time."

The church had a wooden porch, a footpath led beside a playing field. He passed a farmyard with brick barns and smelt warm milk on the autumn air.

"We evacuate them in echelons, Jack," Frankel is saying in his hand-pressed Euro-English. "That's if we evacuate them at all."

"And on my say-so," Nigel adds from the wings.

The room is low and windowless and overlit. A uniformed guard mans the peephole. Spaced along the wall sit Frankel's greying female assistants at their trestle desks. They have brought thermos flasks and share each other's cigarettes. They have done it all before, like a day at the races. Frankel is fat and ugly, a Latvian headwaiter. Brotherhood recruited him, Brotherhood promoted him. Now he was taking over Brotherhood's mess. So it goes. It is three in the morning. It is today, six hours ago.

"Day one, Jack, we move only head agents," says Frankel with a doctor's false assurance. "Conger and Watchman in Prague, Voltaire in Budapest, Merryman in Gdansk."

"When do we begin?" says Brotherhood.

"When Bo waves the flag, and not before," says Nigel. "We're still evaluating and we still regard Pym's loyalties as *quite possibly impeccable,*" says Nigel, like somebody mastering a tongue-twister.

"We move them very quietly, Jack," says Frankel. "No goodbyes, no flowers for the neighbours, no finding somewhere for the cat. Day two radio operators, day three the cut-outs, subagents. Day four whoever's left."

"How do we reach them?" Brotherhood asks.

"You don't, we do," says Nigel. "If and when the Fifth Floor says it's necessary, which at the moment, I repeat, is pure hypothesis."

Kate has followed them in. Kate is our widowed English spinster, pale and sculptural and beautiful, who at forty mourns the loves she never had. And Kate is still Kate, he can see it as clear as ever in her eyes.

"Maybe we pick them off the street when they go to work," Frankel continues. "Maybe we bang on the door, tell a friend, leave a note somewhere. Just anything we think of, so long as it wasn't done before."

"That's where you'll be able to help if we get that far," Nigel explains. "Telling us what's been done before."

Frankel has paused before a map of Eastern Europe. Brotherhood waits a step behind him. Head agents red, subagents blue. So much easier to kill a pushpin than a man. Still gazing at the map Brotherhood remembers an evening in Vienna. Pym is playing host, Brotherhood is Colonel Peter bringing London's thanks for ten years' service. He remembers Pym's gracious speech in Czech, the champagne and medals, the handshakes, the assurances, the quiet waltzes to the gramophone. And this dumpy couple in brown, he a physicist, she a senior lady in the Czech Ministry of the Interior, lovers in betrayal, their faces glistening with excitement as they whirl round the drawing-room to the strains of Johann Strauss.

"So when do you start?" Brotherhood asks again.

"Jack, that is Bo's judgment," Nigel insists, dangerously patient.

"Jack, the Fifth Floor has ruled that the most important thing is to look busy, act natural, keep everything normal," says Frankel, picking a sheaf of telegrams from his desk. "They use letter boxes? So clear the letter boxes like normal. They got radio? So send radio like normal, stick to all the normal schedules, hope the opposition are listening."

"That's the most important thing at the moment," Nigel says, as if anything Frankel says is invalid until he says it too. "Total normality in all areas. One premature step would be fatal."

"So would a late one," Brotherhood says as his blue eyes start to catch fire.

"They're waiting for you, Jack," Kate says, meaning, come away, there's nothing you can do.

Brotherhood does not move. "Do it now," he tells Frankel. "Take them into the embassies. Broadcast a warning. Abort."

Nigel doesn't say a word. Frankel looks to him for help but Nigel has folded his arms and is looking over the shoulder of one of Frankel's women while she types a signal.

"Jack, no way do we take those Joes into embassies or consulates," Frankel says, making faces in Nigel's direction. *"Verboten.* The most we can do when we get the order from the Fifth Floor is fresh escape papers, is money, transport, a couple of prayers. That right, Nigel?"

"If you get the order," Nigel corrects him.

"Conger will head east," Brotherhood says. "His daughter's at university in Bucharest. He'll go to her."

"Okay, so where does he go from Bucharest?" says Frankel.

Brotherhood is nearly shouting. There is nothing Kate can do to stop him. "South into bloody Bulgaria, what do you think! If we give him a date and place, we can put a plane in, hedgehop him into Yugoslavia!"

Now Frankel also lifts his voice. "Jack. Hear me, okay? Nigel, confirm this for me so I don't sound too negative all the time. No little planes, no embassies, no frontier crashes of any kind. This is not the sixties any more. Not the fifties, not the forties. We don't drop planes and pilots around Eastern Europe like birdseed. We are not enthusiastic about reception committees for ourselves or our Joes that are laid on by the opposition."

"He's got it straight," Nigel confirms with just enough surprise.

"I got to tell you this, Jack. Your networks are so contaminated at this moment that the Foreign Office wouldn't even drop them in the trash can, would they, Nigel? You are isolated, Jack. Whitehall's got to cover itself in polythene before it shakes your hand. Is this correct, Nigel?" Frankel hears himself and stops. He looks to Nigel yet again but receives no comforting word. He catches Brotherhood's eye and stares at him with a long and unexpected fearfulness, the way we look at monuments and find ourselves contemplating our own mortality. "I take orders, Jack. Don't look at me that way. Cheers."

Brotherhood slowly climbs the stairs. Climbing them ahead of him, Kate slows down and trails a couple of fingers for him to take hold of. He pretends he hasn't seen.

"When will I see you?" she says.

Brotherhood has gone deaf as well.

The responsibilities that rested on the shoulders of Tom Pym that morning were as heavy as any he had been obliged to face during his first month as a school prefect and captain of Pandas. Today was the first of Pandas' duty week. Today, and for the six awesome days to follow, Tom must ring the morning bell, assist Matron to supervise showers and call the roll before breakfast. Today being Sunday he must keep charge of letter-writing in the day room, read the Lesson in chapel and inspect the changing rooms for untidiness and impropriety. When evening came at last he must preside over the boys' committee that receives suggestions about the management of school life and, after editing, submit them to the agonised consideration of Mr. Caird the Headmaster, for Mr. Caird could do nothing lightly and saw all sides of every argument. And when he had somehow got through all this and rung the bell for lights out, there was Monday to wake up to. Last week it had been Lions' turn for duty and Lions had done well. Lions, Mr. Caird had pronounced in a rare show of conviction, had displayed a democratic approach to power, holding votes and forming committees on every contentious issue. In chapel, waiting for the last lines of the hymn to die, Tom prayed earnestly for his dead grandfather's soul, for Mr. Caird and for victory in Wednesday's squash match against St. Saviour's, Newbury, away, though he feared it would be another humiliating defeat, for Mr. Caird was divided on the merits of athletic competition. But most fervently he prayed that come next Saturday—if Saturday ever did come—Pandas too would earn Mr. Caird's favour, because Mr. Caird's disappointment was actually more than Tom could bear.

Tom was a very tall boy and affected already the British administrator's bobbing walk that characterised his father. His receding hairline gave him an air of maturity that may have accounted for his advancement to high position in the school. To watch him, hands linked behind his back, detach himself from the prefect's pew, step into the aisle, duck his head at the altar and mount the two steps to the lectern, you could have been forgiven for wondering whether this was a pupil at all and not a member of Mr. Caird's impressively youthful staff. Only his froggy voice as he barked the day's text betrayed the changeling inside the senatorial exterior. Tom heard little of what he was reading. The Lesson was the first he had read and he had practised it till he knew it by heart. Yet now that he came to perform it, the red and black print before him had neither sound nor meaning. Only the sight of his chewed thumbs stuck either side of him on the lectern, and the white head floating above them in the back row of the congregation, held him to the world at all. Without them, he decided, he could have taken off, smack through the chapel ceiling and into the sky, and thereafter levitated, like his gas balloon on Commemoration Day, which flew all the way to Maidenhead and landed with his name on it in an old lady's back garden, earning him five pounds in book tokens and a letter from her saying she too had a son called Tom, who worked at Lloyd's.

"I have trodden the winepress alone," he bellowed to his surprise. "And of the people there was none with me: for I will tread them in mine anger and trample them in my fury." The threat alarmed him and he wondered why he had uttered it and to whom. "And their blood shall be sprinkled upon my garments, and I will stain all my raiment."

Still reading, feeling the backs of his knees batting against his trousers, Tom considered a number of other matters that turned out to be weighing on his mind, some of which were new to him until this moment. He had no expectation any more that his mind would be ruled by what was going on around it, even in work. In Friday's gym class he had found himself thinking out a problem of Latin grammar. In yesterday's Latin he had worried about his mother's drinking. And in the middle of French construe he had discovered that he was no longer in love with Becky Lederer, despite their ardent correspondence, but preferred instead one of the Bursar's daughters. Under the pressures of high office his mind had become a slice of undersea cable like the one in the science lab. First there was this bunch of wires, all carrying their proper messages and doing their appointed jobs; and then, swimming around them like a shoal of invisible fish, ran a whole lot more messages which for some reason did not need wires at all. And that was how his mind felt now, while he honked out the sacred words in his deepest possible voice only to hear them tinkling like cracked bells in a distant room.

"For the day of vengeance is in mine heart, and the year of my redeemed is come," he said.

He thought of gas balloons and of the Tom who worked in Lloyd's, and of the forthcoming apocalypse when he failed his common entrance examination, and of the Bursar's daughter when she rode her bicycle with her blouse flattened against her chest by the wind. And he fretted about whether Carter Major, who was Pandas' vice-captain, had the qualities of democratic leadership to handle afternoon kickabout. But there was one thought he refused to have at all because really all these other thoughts were surrogates for it. There was one thought he could not put in words or even pictures, because it was so bad that even thinking it could turn it into truth.

"How's your beef, son?" Jack Brotherhood asked, what seemed about twenty seconds later, over lunch in the Digby Hotel where they always went.

"Super, Uncle Jack, thank you," said Tom.

Otherwise they ate in the silence that they mostly observed till lunch was past. Brotherhood had his *Sunday Telegraph,* Tom a fantasy novel he was reading over and over again, because it was a book in which everything came right and other books could be dangerous. Nobody understands better than Uncle Jack how you take people out from school, Tom decided, while he read and ate and thought of his mother. Not even his father had such a clear idea of how everything should be the same each time yet exquisitely different in tiny ways. How you had to be completely calm and unfussed yet draw out the day by doing masses of different things until the last moment. How school was a place that for most of the day must not exist, so that there was never any question of going back there. Only during the last countdown must it be sufficiently reconstructed to make return a possibility.

"Want a second?"

"No, thank you."

"More Yorkshire?"

"Yes, please. A bit."

Brotherhood lifted his eyebrows to the waiter and the waiter came at once, which was what waiters did for Uncle Jack.

"Heard from your father?"

Tom did not answer at once because his eyes suddenly hurt and he couldn't breathe.

"Here, now," said Brotherhood softly, putting down his newspaper. "What's this, then?"

"It's just the Lesson," said Tom, fighting away his tears. "It's all right now."

"You made a damn good job of reading that Lesson. Anyone tells you different, knock him down."

"It was the wrong day's," Tom explained, still fighting to get back above water. "I should have turned to the next bookmark and I forgot."

"Bugger the wrong day's," Brotherhood growled, so emphatically that the old couple at the next table swung their heads round at him. "If yesterday's Lesson was any good, it won't do anyone an ounce of harm to hear it twice. Have another ginger beer."

Tom nodded and Brotherhood ordered it before once more taking up his *Sunday Telegraph.* "Probably didn't even understand it the first time anyway," he said with contempt.

But the real trouble was Tom had not read the wrong Lesson; he had read the right one. He knew very well he had, and he had a suspicion Uncle Jack knew it too. He just needed something easier to cry about than the fish that were swimming round the cable in his head and the thought he refused to have.

They agreed to do without pudding so as not to waste the fine weather.

Sugarloaf Hill was a chalky hump in the Berkshire Downs with Ministry of Defence barbed wire round it and a warning to the public to keep out, and probably in all Tom's life there was nowhere better in the world to be, except at home in Plush at lambing time. Not Lech and skiing with his father, not Vienna and riding with his mother: nowhere he had ever been or dreamed of was as private, as amazingly privileged, as this secret hilltop compound with barbed wire to keep out enemies, where Jack Brotherhood and Tom Pym, godfather and godson and the best friends ever, could take turns to loose off clay pigeons from the launcher, and shoot them down or miss them with Tom's 20-bore. The first time they had come here, Tom hadn't believed it. "It's all locked, Uncle Jack," he had objected as Uncle Jack stopped the car. It had been a good day till then. Now suddenly it had gone all wrong. They had driven ten miles by the map and to his chagrin ended at a pair of high white gates that were locked and forbidden by order. The day was over. He had wished he could be back at school again, doing his voluntary-punishment prep.

"Then go over and yell 'Open sesame!' at it," Uncle Jack had advised, handing Tom a key from his pocket. And the next thing was, the white gates of authority had closed again behind them and they were special people with a special pass to be up here on the hilltop with the boot open, pulling out the rusted launcher that Uncle Jack had kept secret all through lunch. And the next thing after *that* was that Tom scored nine clays out of twenty, and Uncle Jack nineteen, because Uncle Jack was the best shot ever, the best at everything, although he was so old, and he wouldn't give away a match to please anybody, not even Tom. If Tom ever beat Uncle Jack, he would beat him fair, which was what they both wanted without needing to say it. And it was what Tom wanted more than anything today: a normal exchange, a normal competition, with normal conversation, the kind that Uncle Jack was brilliant at. He wanted to hide his worst thoughts in a deep hole and not have to show them to anybody ever until he died for England.

It was the outdoors that set Tom free. Uncle Jack had nothing to do with it. He didn't like too much talk and certainly not about things that were private. It was the sense of daytime that was like a resurrection. It was the din of gunfire, the clatter of the October wind that buffeted his cheeks and slid inside his school pullover. Suddenly these things got him talking like a man instead of whimpering under the bedclothes with the stuffed animals which progressive Mr. Caird encouraged. Down in the river valley there had been no wind at all, just a tired autumn sun and brown leaves along the towpath. But up here on the bare chalk hilltop the wind was going like a train through a tunnel, taking Tom with it. It was clanking and laughing in the new Ministry of Defence pylon that had gone up since they had last come here.

"If we shoot the pylon down we'll let the bloody Russians in!" Uncle Jack yelled at him through cupped hands. "Don't want to do that, do we?"

"No!"

"All right, then. What do we do?"

"Pitch the launcher right next to the pylon and shoot away from it!" Tom had shouted back joyfully, and as he shouted he felt the last bits of worry go out of his chest, and his shoulders settle on his back, and he knew that with a wind like this whipping over the hilltop he could tell anything he wanted to anybody. Uncle Jack launched ten clays for him and he brought down eight with eleven cartridges, which was his absolute best yet considering the wind. And when it was Tom's turn to launch, Uncle Jack had a fight on his hands just to match him. But match him he did and Tom loved him for it. He didn't want to beat Uncle Jack. His father maybe, but not Uncle Jack; there would be nothing left. In his second ten Tom did less well but he didn't mind because his arms were aching, which wasn't his fault. But Uncle Jack stayed steady as a castle. Even when he was reloading, the white head stayed forward to meet the rising butt.

"Fourteen eighteen to you," Tom shouted as he galloped about collecting empty cartridges. "Well shot!" And then, just as loud and cheerful: "And Dad's all right, is he?"

"Why wouldn't he be?" Brotherhood shouted back.

"He seemed a bit down when he came to see me after Granddad's funeral, that's all."

"I should think he bloody well *was* down. How would you feel if you had just buried *your* old man?"

Still shouting in the wind, both of them. Small talk while they loaded the 20-bore and cranked back the launcher for another go.

"He talked about freedom all the time!" Tom yelled. "He said nobody could ever give it to us, we've got to grab it for ourselves. I got rather bored with it, actually."

Uncle Jack was so busy reloading that Tom even wondered whether he had heard. Or if he had, whether he was interested.

"He's dead right," said Brotherhood snapping the gun shut. "Patriotism's a dirty word these days."

Tom released the clay and watched it curl and burst to powder under Uncle Jack's perfect aim.

"He wasn't talking about patriotism exactly," Tom explained, delving for another couple of cartridges.

"Oh?"

"I think he was telling me that if I was unhappy I should run away. He said it in his letter too. It's sort—"

"Well?"

"It's as if he wanted me to do something he hadn't done himself when *he* was at the school. It's a bit weird actually."

"I shouldn't think it's weird at all. He's testing you, that's all. Saying the door's open if you want to bolt. More like a gesture of trust by the sound of it. No boy had a better father, Tom."

Tom fired and missed.

"What do you mean letter, anyway?" said Brotherhood. "I thought he came and saw you."

"He did. But he wrote to me as well. A great long letter. I just thought it was weird," he said again, unable to get away from a favourite new adjective.

"All right, he was cut up. What's wrong with that? His old man dies, he sits down and writes to his son. You should feel honoured—good shot, boy. Good shot."

"Thanks," said Tom and looked on proudly while Uncle Jack marked a hit on his scorecard. Uncle Jack always kept the score.

"That's not what he said, though," Tom added awkwardly. "He wasn't cut up. He was pleased."

"He wrote that, did he?"

"He said Granddad had gobbled up the natural humanity in him and he didn't want to gobble it up in me."

"That's just another way of being cut up," said Brotherhood, unbothered. "Your dad ever talk about a secret place, by the by? Somewhere he could find his well-earned peace and quiet, ever?"

"Not really."

"He had one though, didn't he."

"Not really."

"Where is it?"

"He said I was never to tell anyone."

"Then don't," said Uncle Jack firmly.

Suddenly, after that, talking about one's father became the necessary function of a democratic prefect. Mr. Caird had said it was the duty of people of privilege to sacrifice what they held most dear in life, and Tom loved his father beyond bearing. He felt Brotherhood's gaze on him and was pleased to have aroused his interest even though it did not seem to be particularly approving.

"You've known him a very long time, haven't you, Uncle Jack?" said Tom, getting into the car.

"If thirty-five years is a long time."

"It is," said Tom, for whom a week was still an age. Inside the car there was suddenly no wind at all. "So if Dad's all right," he said with false boldness as he buckled on his seat belt, "why are the police looking for him? That's what *I* want to know."

"Going to tell our fortunes today, Mary Lou?" Uncle Jack asked.

"Not today, darling, I'm not in the mood."

"You're always in the mood," said Uncle Jack, and the two of them had a huge laugh while Tom blushed.

Mary Lou was a gypsy, Uncle Jack said, though Tom thought her more like a pirate. She was fat-bottomed and black-haired and had false lips drawn over her mouth like Frau Bauer in Vienna. She cooked cakes and served cream teas in a wooden café at the edge of the Common. Tom asked for poached eggs on toast and the eggs were creamy and fresh like the eggs at Plush. Uncle Jack had a pot of tea and a piece of her best fruitcake. He seemed to have forgotten everything Tom had been talking about, which Tom was grateful for, because he was feeling headachey from the fresh air and embarrassed by his own thoughts. It was two hours and eight minutes till he had to ring the bell for evensong. He was thinking he might take his father's advice and run away.

"So what was all this about the police again?" said Brotherhood a little vaguely, long after Tom had decided he had forgotten or not heard.

"They came and saw Caird. Then Caird sent for me."

"*Mr.* Caird, son," Brotherhood corrected him perfectly kindly and took a grateful pull of tea. "When?"

"On Friday. After house rugger. Mr. Caird sent for me and there was this man in a raincoat sitting in Mr. Caird's armchair, and he said he was from Scotland Yard about Dad, and did I by any chance have his leave address because in his absent-mindedness after Granddad's funeral Dad had taken leave and not told anyone where he was."

"Bollocks," Brotherhood said after a long time.

"It's true, sir. It really is."

"You said they."

"I meant he."

"Height?"

"Five foot ten."

"Age?"

"Forty."

"Colour of hair?"

"Like mine."

"Clean-shaven?"

"Yes."

"Eyes?"

"Brown."

It was a game they had played often in the past.

"Car?"

"He took a taxi from the station."

"How do you know?"

"Mr. Mellor brought him. He takes me to cello and works from the station cab-rank."

"Be accurate, boy. He came in Mr. Mellor's car. Did he tell you he'd come by train?"

"No."

"Did Mellor?"

"No."

"So who says he was a policeman?"

"Mr. Caird, sir. When he introduced me."

"What was he wearing?"

"A suit, sir. Grey."

"Did he give his rank?"

"Inspector."

Brotherhood smiled. A wonderful, comforting affectionate smile. "You silly chump, he was a *Foreign Office* inspector. That's just a flunkey from your dad's shop. That's not a *policeman,* son; that's a half-arsed clerk from Personnel Department with too little to do. Caird got it wrong as usual."

Tom could have kissed him. He nearly did. He straightened up and felt about nine feet taller, and he wanted to bury his face in the thick tweed of Uncle Jack's sports coat. Of course he wasn't a policeman! He didn't talk like a policeman, he didn't feel like a policeman, he didn't have big feet or short hair like a policeman, or a policeman's way of being separate from you even when he was being nice. It's all right, Tom told himself in glory. Uncle Jack's made it right, the way he always can.

Brotherhood was holding out his handkerchief and Tom scrubbed his eyes with it.

"So what did you tell him anyway?" Brotherhood said. And Tom explained that he didn't know where his father was either, he'd talked about losing himself in Scotland for a few days before returning to Vienna. Which had made Dad somehow seem at fault, a sort of criminal or worse. And when Tom had told his Uncle Jack everything else he remembered about the interview, the questions, and the telephone number in case Dad surfaced—Tom didn't have it, but Mr. Caird did—Uncle Jack went to the phone in Mary Lou's parlour and rang Mr. Caird, and got an extension for Tom till nine o'clock, on the grounds that there were family matters that needed talking about.

"But what about my bells?" said Tom in alarm.

"Carter Major's doing them," said Uncle Jack, who understood absolutely everything.

He must have rung London too, because he took a long time and gave Mary Lou an extra five pounds to fill what he called her Christmas stocking, which had them both in fits again, and this time Tom joined in.

How they came to be talking about Corfu, Tom was afterwards never sure and perhaps there was no real path to their conversation any more; it was just chat about what they had both been up to since they had last met, which after all was before the summer holidays so there was masses to talk about if you were in a talking mood. And Tom was; he hadn't talked like this for ages, maybe ever, but Uncle Jack had the ease, he had that mixture of tolerance and discipline that for Tom was the perfect blend, for he loved to feel the strength of Uncle Jack's frontiers as well as the safe ground inside.

"How's your confirmation going?" Brotherhood had asked.

"All right, thanks."

"You're of an age now, Tom. Got to face it. In some countries you'd be in uniform already."

"I know."

"Work still a problem?"

"A bit, sir."

"Still got your eye on Sandhurst?"

"Yes, sir. And my uncle's regiment says they'd take me if I do all right."

"Well you'll have to swot, won't you?"

"I'm really trying actually."

Then Uncle Jack drew nearer and his voice dropped. "I'm not sure I should tell you this, son. But I'm going to anyway because I think you're ready to keep a secret. Can you do that?"

"I've got lots of secrets I've never told to anyone, sir."

"Your father is rather a secret man himself actually. I expect you knew that, didn't you?"

"You are too, aren't you."

"Quite a great man as well, he is. But he's got to keep it quiet. For his country."

"And for you," said Tom.

"A lot of his life is blocked off completely. You could almost say from human gaze."

"Does Mummy know?"

"In principle, yes, she does. In detail, next to nothing. That's the way we work. And if your father has ever given the impression of lying, or being evasive, less than truthful sometimes, you can bet your boots it was his work and his loyalty that were the reason. It's a strain for him. It is for all of us. Secrets are a strain."

"Is it dangerous?" Tom asked.

"Can be. That's why we give him bodyguards. Like boys on motorbikes who follow him round Greece and hang about outside his house."

"I saw them!" Tom declared excitedly.

"Like tall thin men with moustaches who come up to him at cricket matches—"

"He did, he did! He had a straw hat!"

"And sometimes what your dad does is so secret he has to disappear completely. And not even the bodyguards can have his address. *I* know. But the rest of the world doesn't and it mustn't. And if that inspector comes to you again, or to Mr. Caird, or if anybody else does, you must tell them whatever you know and report to me immediately afterwards. I'm going to give you a special phone number and have a special word with Mr. Caird too. He deserves a lot of help, your father does. And gets it."

"I'm really glad," said Tom.

"Now then. That letter of his he wrote to you. The long one that came after he'd gone. Did it talk about things like that?"

"I don't know. I haven't read it all. There was a whole lot of stuff about Sefton Boyd's penknife and some writing in the staff loo."

"Who's Sefton Boyd?"

"He's a boy in the school. He's my friend."

"Is he your dad's friend too?"

"No, but his father was. His father was in the school too."

"Now what have you done with this letter?"

Punished himself with it. Squidged it up till it was tight and prickly and kept it in his trousers pocket where it jabbed his thigh. But Tom didn't say that. He just handed the remnants gratefully to Uncle Jack, who promised to take proper care of them and talk everything over with him next time—if there was anything that needed talking over, which Uncle Jack very much doubted that there would be.

"Got the envelope, have you?"

Tom hadn't.

"Where did he post it from then? There's a clue there, I expect, if we look for it."

"The postmark was Reading," said Tom.

"What day?"

"The Tuesday," said Tom unhappily, "but it could have been after post on Monday. I thought he was going back to Vienna on Monday afternoon. If he didn't go to Scotland, that is."

But Uncle Jack didn't seem to hear because he was talking about Greece again, playing what the two of them called report writing about this weedy fellow with a moustache who had shown up at the cricket ground in Corfu.

"I expect you were worried about him, weren't you, son? You thought he was up to no good with your dad, I expect, although he was so friendly. I mean, if they knew each other *that* well, why didn't your dad ask him home to meet your mum? I can see that would have bothered you on reflection. You didn't think it very nice your dad should have a secret life on Mum's doorstep."

"I suppose I didn't," Tom admitted, marvelling as ever at Uncle Jack's omniscience. "He held Dad's arm."

They had returned to the Digby. In the great joy of his release from worry, Tom had rediscovered his appetite and was having a steak and chips to fill the gap. Brotherhood had ordered himself a whisky.

"Height?" said Brotherhood, back at their special game.

"Six foot."

"All right, well done. Six foot exactly is correct. Colour of hair?"

Tom hesitated. "Sort of mousy fawny with stripes," he said.

"What the hell's that supposed to mean?"

"He wore a straw hat. It was hard to see."

"I know he wore a straw hat. That's why I'm asking you. Colour of hair?"

"Brown," said Tom finally. "Brown with the sun on it. And a big forehead like a genius."

"Now how the hell does the sun get under the brim of a hat?"

"Grey brown," said Tom.

"Then say so. Two points only. Hatband?"

"Red."

"Oh dear."

"It was red."

"Keep trying."

"It was red, red, red!"

"Three points. Colour of beard?"

"He hasn't got a beard. He's got a shaggy moustache and thick eyebrows like yours but not so bushy, and crinkly eyes."

"Three points. Build?"

"Stoopy and hobbly."

"What the hell's hobbly?"

"Like chumpy. Chumpy's when the sea is choppy and bumpy. Hobbly is when he walks fast and hobbles."

"You mean limps."

"Yes."

"Say so. Which leg?"

"Left."

"One more try?"

"Left."

"Certain?"

"Left!"

"Three points. Age?"

"Seventy."

"Don't be damn stupid."

"He's old!"

"He's not seventy. I'm not seventy. I'm not sixty. Well only just. Is he older than me?"

"The same."

"Carry anything?"

"A briefcase. A grey thing like elephant skin. And he was stringy like Mr. Toombs."

"Who's Toombs?"

"Our gym master. He teaches aikido and geography. He's killed people with his feet, though he's not supposed to."

"All right, stringy like Mr. Toombs, carried an elephant skin briefcase. Two points. Another time, omit the subjective reference."

"What's that?"

"Mr. Toombs. You know him, I don't. Don't compare one person I don't know with another I don't know."

"You said you knew him," said Tom, very excited to catch Uncle Jack out.

"I do. I'm fooling. Did he have a car, your man?"

"Volvo. Hired from Mr. Kaloumenos."

"How do you know that?"

"He hires it to everyone. He goes down to the harbour and hangs about and if anyone wants to hire a car Mr. Kaloumenos gives them his Volvo."

"Colour?"

"Green. And it's got a bashed wing and a Corfu registration and a fox's tail from the aerial and a—"

"It's red."

"It's green!"

"No points," said Brotherhood firmly, to Tom's outrage.

"Why not?"

Brotherhood pulled a wolfish smile. "It wasn't his car, was it? How do you know it was the bloke with the moustache who hired it when two other blokes were riding in it? You lost your objectivity, son."

"He was in charge!"

"You don't *know* that. You're guessing it. You could start a war, making up things like that. Ever met an Auntie Poppy at all, son?"

"No, sir."

"Uncle?"

Tom giggled. "No, sir."

"A Mr. Wentworth a name to you?"

"No, sir."

"No bells at all?"

"No, sir. I thought it was a place in Surrey."

"Well done, son. Never make it up if you think you don't know and ought to. That's the rule."

"You were teasing again, weren't you?"

"Maybe I was at that. When did your dad say he'd see you again?"

"He didn't."

"Does he ever?"

"Not really."

"Then there's no fuss, is there?"

"It's just the letter."

"What about the letter?"

"It's as if he's dead."

"Bollocks. You're imagining. Want me to tell you something else you know? That secret hideaway of your dad's that he's gone to. It's all right. We know about it. Did he give you the address?"

"No."

"Name of the nearest Scottish town?"

"No. He just said Scotland. On the sea in Scotland. A place to write where he's safe from everyone.

"He's told you all he can, Tom. He's not allowed to tell you any more. How many rooms has he got?"

"He didn't say."

"Who does his shopping then?"

"He didn't say. He's got a super landlady. She's old."

"He's a good man. And a wise man. And she's a good woman. One of us. Now don't you worry any more." Uncle Jack glanced sideways at his watch. "Here. Finish that up and order yourself a ginger beer. I need to see a man about a dog." Still smiling, he strode to the door marked toilets and telephone. Tom was nothing if not an observer. Points of happy colour on Uncle Jack's cheeks. A sense of merriness like his own and everybody absolutely fine.

Brotherhood had a wife and a house in Lambeth, and in theory he could have gone to them. He had another wife in his cottage in Suffolk, divorced it was true but given notice willing to oblige. He had a daughter married to a solicitor in Pinner and he wished them both to the devil and it was mutual. Nevertheless they would have had him as a duty. And there was a useless son who scratched a living on the stage and if Brotherhood was feeling charitable towards him, which oddly enough these days he sometimes was, and if he could stomach the squalor and the smell of pot, which he sometimes could, he would have been welcome enough to the heap of greasy coverlets that Adrian called his spare bed. But tonight and for every other night until he had had his word with Pym he wanted none of them. He preferred the exile of his stinking little safe flat in Shepherd Market with sooty pigeons humping each other on the parapet and the tarts doing sentry go along the pavement below him, the way they used to in the war. Periodically the Firm tried to take the place away from him or deduct the rent from his salary at source. The desk jockeys hated him for it and said it was his fuck-hutch, which occasionally it was. They resented his claims for hospitality booze and cleaners he didn't have. But Brotherhood was hardier than all of them and more or less they knew it.

"Research have turned up more stuff about the use of newspapers by Czech Intelligence," Kate said into the pillow. "But none of it's conclusive."

Brotherhood took a long pull of his vodka. It was two in the morning. They had been here an hour. "Don't tell me. The great spy pricks the letters of his message with a pin and posts the newspaper to his spymaster. Said spymaster holds the newspaper to the light, and reads the plans for Armageddon. They'll be using semaphore next."

She lay white and luminous beside him on the little bed, a forty-year-old Cambridge débutante who had lost her way. The grey-pink glow through the grimy curtains cut her into classic fragments. Here a thigh, here a calf, here the cone of a breast or the knifeline of a flank. She had turned her back to him, one leg slightly bent. God damn it, what does she want of me, this sad, beautiful bridge-player of the Fifth Floor, with her air of lost love and her prim carnality? After seven years of her, Brotherhood still had no idea. He'd be out touring the stations, he'd be in Bonga-bonga land. He'd not speak or write to her for months. Yet he'd hardly unpacked his toothbrush before she was in his arms, demanding him with her sad and hungry eyes. Does she have a hundred of us—are we her fighter pilots, claiming her favours each time we limp home from another mission? Or am I the only one who storms the statue?

"And Bo's called in some top shrink to join the feast," she said, in her impeccable vowels. "Somebody who specialises in harmless nervous breakdowns. They've thrown Pym's dossier at him and told him to assemble the profile of a loyal Englishman under severe stress who is arousing anxiety in other people, particularly Americans."

"He'll be calling in a medium next," said Brotherhood.

"They've checked flights to the Bahamas, Scotland and Ireland. That's as well as everywhere else. They've checked ships, car-hire firms and goodness knows what. They've got warrants running on every telephone he ever used and a blanket warrant for the rest. They've cancelled leave and weekends for all transcribers and put the surveillance teams on twenty-four-hour alert, and they still haven't told anybody what it's about. The canteen's a funeral parlour, nobody talking to anybody. They're questioning anyone who shared an office with him or bought a secondhand car from him, they've turned the tenants out of the Pym's house in Dulwich and stripped the place from top to bottom pretending to be woodworm experts. Now Nigel's talking of moving the whole search team to a safe house in Norfolk Street, it's getting so big. Including the help, that's about a hundred and fifty staff. What's in the burnbox?"

"Why?"

"There's a shadow over it. Not in front of the children. Bo and Nigel clam up as soon as anybody mentions it."

"Press?" said Brotherhood, as if he had answered her question instead of deflecting it.

"Sewn up as usual. From *TitBits* downwards. Bo had lunch with the editors yesterday. He's already written their leaders for them in case anything gets out. How rumours weaken our security. Uninformed speculation as the true Enemy Within. Nigel's been leaning his full weight on the radio and television people."

"All two stone of it. What about the phoney copper?"

"Whoever called on Tom's Headmaster wasn't family. He wasn't from the Firm and he wasn't police."

"Maybe he was from the competition. They don't have to ask us first, do they?"

"Bo's terror is that the Americans are launching their own manhunt."

"If he'd been American there'd have been three of him. He was a cheeky Czech.

That's the way they work. Same as they used to fly in the war."

"The Headmaster describes him as up-market English, not a whiff of foreign. He didn't come or leave by train. He gave his name as Inspector Baring of Special Branch. There isn't one. The taxi bill return between the station and the school was twelve pounds and he didn't ask the driver for a receipt. Imagine a policeman not wanting a receipt for twelve pounds. He left a fake visiting card. They're looking for the printer, the paper-maker and for all I know the ink manufacturers, but they won't bring in police, the competition or liaison. They'll make any enquiry they can think of as long as it doesn't frighten the horses."

"And the London phone number he gave?"

"Bogus."

"I could nearly laugh about that if humour was my mood. What does Bo think about the moustachioed gentleman with a handbag who holds Pym's arm at cricket matches?"

"He refuses to take a view. He says if we all had our friends checked at cricket matches, we'd have no friends and no cricket. He's drafted extra girls to comb the Czech personalities index and he's signalled Athens Station to send someone to Corfu to talk to the car-hire man. It's delay and pray, and Magnus please come home."

"Where do I stand? In the corner?"

"They're terrified you'll pull down the Temple."

"I thought Pym had done that already."

"Then perhaps it's guilty contact," Kate said in her crisp Queen Bee voice.

Brotherhood took another long swallow of vodka. "If they'd get the bloody networks out. If they'd do the obvious thing, just for once."

"They won't do anything that might alert the Americans. They'd rather lie all the way to the grave. 'We've had three major traitors in three minor years. One more and we might as well admit the party's over.' That's Bo speaking."

"So the Joes will die for the Special Relationship. I like that. So will the Joes. They'll understand."

"Will they find him?"

"Maybe."

"Maybe's not enough. I'm asking you, Jack. Will they find him? Will you?"

She sounded suddenly imperious and urgent. She took the glass from his hand and drank the rest of his vodka while he watched her. She leaned over the side of the bed and fished a cigarette from her handbag. She handed him the matches and he lit it for her.

"Bo's put a lot of monkeys in front of a lot of typewriters," Brotherhood said, still watching her intently. "Maybe one of them will come up with the goods. I didn't know you smoked, Kate."

"I don't."

"You're drinking well too, I'm pleased to see. I don't remember you hitting the vodka as hard as this, I'm sure I don't. Who taught you to drink vodka that way?"

"Why shouldn't I?"

"More to the point is why should you? You're trying to tell me something, aren't you? Something I don't think I like at all. I thought you were spying for Bo for a minute there. I thought you were doing a bit of a Jezebel on me. Then I thought, no, she's trying to tell me something. She's attempting a small and intimate confession."

"He's a blasphemer."

"Who is, dear?"

"Magnus."

"Oh he is, is he? Magnus a blasphemer. Now why is that?"

"Hold me, Jack."

"Like hell I will." He pulled away from her and saw that what he had mistaken for arrogance was a stoical acceptance of despair. Her sad eyes stared straight at him, and her face was set in resignation.

" 'I love you, Kate,' " she said. " 'Get me clear of this and I'll marry you and we'll live happily ever after.' "

Brotherhood took her cigarette and drew on it.

" 'I'll dump Mary. We'll go and live abroad. France. Morocco. Who cares?' Phone calls from the other end of the earth. 'I rang to say I love you.' Flowers, saying 'I love you.' Cards. Little notes folded into things, shoved under the door, personal for my eyes only in top-secret envelopes. 'I've lived too long with the what-ifs. I want action, Kate. You're my escape-line. Help me. I love you. M.' "

Once again, Brotherhood waited.

" 'I love you,' " she repeated. "He kept saying it. Like a ritual he was trying to believe in. 'I love you.' I suppose he thought if he said it to enough people enough times, one day it might be true. It wasn't. He never loved a woman in his life. We were enemy, all of us. Touch me, Jack!"

To his surprise he felt a wave of kinship overcome him. He drew her to him and held her tightly to his chest.

"Is Bo wise to any of this?" he said.

He could feel the sweat collecting on his back. He could smell Pym's nearness in the crevices of her body. She rolled her head against him but he gently shook her, making her say it aloud: Bo knows nothing. No, Jack. Bo's got no idea.

"Magnus wasn't interested till he was calling the whole game," she said. "He could have had me any time. That wasn't enough for him. 'Wait for me, Kate. I'm going to cut the cable and be free. Kate, it's me, where are you?' I'm here, you idiot, or I wouldn't be answering the phone, would I? . . . He doesn't have affairs. He has lives. We're on separate planets for him. Places he can call while he floats through space. You know his favourite photograph of me?"

"I don't think I do, Kate," Brotherhood said.

"I'm naked on a beach in Normandy. We'd stolen the weekend. I've got my back to him, I'm walking into the sea. I didn't even know he had a camera."

"You're a beautiful girl, Kate. I could get quite hot about a picture like that myself," said Brotherhood, pulling back her hair so that he could see her face.

"He loved it better than he loved me. With my back to him I was anyone—his girl on the beach—his dream. I left his fantasies intact. You've got to get me out of it, Jack."

"How deep in are you?"

"Deep enough."

"Write him any letters yourself?"

She shook her head.

"Do him any little favours? Bend the rules for him? You better tell me, Kate." He waited, feeling the increasing pressure of her head against him. "Can you hear me?" She nodded. "I'm dead, Kate. But you've got a while to go. If it ever comes out that you and Pym so much as had a strawberry milkshake together at McDonald's while you were waiting for your bus home, they will shave your head and post you to Economic Development before you can say Jack anybody. You know that, don't you?"

Another nod.

"What did you do for him? Steal a few secrets, did you? Something juicy out of Bo's own plate?" She shook her head. "Come on, Kate. He fooled me too. I'm not going to throw you to the wolves. What did you do for him?"

"There was an entry in his P.F.," she said.

"So?"

"He wanted it taken out. It was from long ago. An army report from his National Service time in Austria."

"When did you do this?"

"Early. We'd been going for about a year. He was back from Prague."

"And you did it for him. You raided his file?"

"It was trivial, he said. He was very young at the time. A boy still. He'd been running some low-grade Joe into Czechoslovakia. A frontier crosser, I think. Really small stuff. But there was this girl called Sabina who'd got in on the act and wanted to marry him and defected. I didn't listen to it very clearly. He said if anybody picked through his file and came on the episode he'd never make it to the Fifth Floor."

"Well that's not the end of the world now, is it?"

She shook her head.

"Joe have a name, did he?" Brotherhood asked.

"A codename. Greensleeves."

"That's fanciful. I like that. Greensleeves. An all-English Joe. You fished the paper from the file and what did you do with it? Just tell it to me, Kate. It's out now. Let's go."

"I stole it."

"All right. What did you do with it?"

"That's what he asked me."

"When?"

"He rang me."

"When?"

"Last Monday evening. After he was supposed to have left for Vienna."

"What time? Come on, Kate, this is good. What time did he ring you?"

"Ten. Later. Ten-thirty. Earlier. I was watching *News at Ten*."

"What bit?"

"Lebanon. The shelling. Tripoli or somewhere. I turned the sound down as soon as I heard him and the shelling went on and on like a silent movie. 'I needed to hear your voice, Kate. I'm sorry for everything. I rang to say I'm sorry. I wasn't a bad man, Kate. It wasn't all pretend.'"

"Wasn't?"

"Yes. Wasn't. He was conducting a retrospective. Wasn't. I said it's just your father's death, you'll be all right, don't cry. Don't talk as if you're dead yourself. Come round. Where are you? I'll come to you. He said he couldn't. Not any more. Then about his file. I should feel free to tell everyone what I'd done, not try to shield him any more. But to give him a week. 'One week, Kate. It's not a lot after all those years.' Then, had I still got the paper I took out for him? Had I destroyed it, kept a copy?"

"What did you say?"

She went to the bathroom and returned with the embroidered spongebag she kept her kit in. She drew a folded square of brown paper from it and handed it to him.

"Did you give him a copy?"

"No."

"Did he ask for one?"

"No. I wouldn't have done that. I expect he knew. I took it and I said I'd taken it and he should believe me. I thought I'd put it back one day. It was a link."

"Where was he when he rang you on Monday?"

"A phone box."

"Reverse charges?"

"Middle distance. I reckoned four fifty-pence pieces. Mind you, that could still be London, knowing him. We were on for about twenty minutes but a lot of the time he couldn't speak."

"Describe. Come on, old love. You'll only have to do it once, I promise you, so you might as well do it thoroughly."

"I said, 'Why aren't you in Vienna?' "

"What did he say to that?"

"He said he'd run out of small change. That was the last thing he said to me. 'I've run out of small change.' "

"Did he have a place he ever took you? A hideaway?"

"We used my flat or went to hotels."

"Which ones?"

"The Grosvenor at Victoria was one. The Great Eastern at Liverpool Street. He has favourite rooms that overlook the railway lines."

"Give me the numbers."

Holding her against him, he walked her to the desk and scribbled down the two numbers to her dictation, then pulled on his old dressing-gown and knotted it round his waist and smiled at her. "I loved him too, Kate. I'm a bigger fool than you are." But he won no smile in return. "Did he ever talk about a place away from it all? Some dream he had?" He poured her some more vodka and she took it.

"Norway," she said. "He wanted to see the migration of the reindeer. He was going to take me one day."

"Where else?"

"Spain. The north. He said he'd buy a villa for us."

"Did he talk about his writing?"

"Not much."

"Did he say where he'd like to write his great book?"

"In Canada. We'd hibernate in some snowy place and live out of tins."

"The sea—nothing by the sea?"

"No."

"Did he ever mention Poppy to you? Someone called Poppy, like in his book?"

"He never mentioned any of his women. I told you. We were separate planets."

"How about someone called Wentworth?"

She shook her head.

" 'Wentworth was Rick's Nemesis,' " Brotherhood recited. " 'Poppy was mine. We each spent our lives trying to put right the wrong we'd done to them.' You heard the tapes. You've seen the transcripts. Wentworth."

"He's mad," she said.

"Stay here," he said. "Stay as long as you like."

Returning to the desk, he wiped the books and papers off it with a single sweep of his arm, switched on the reading lamp, sat down and laid the sheet of brown paper beside Pym's crumpled letter to Tom, postmark Reading. The London telephone directories were on the floor at his side. He chose the Grosvenor Hotel, Victoria, first and asked the night porter to put him through to the room number Kate had given him. A drowsy man answered.

"House detective here," Brotherhood said. "We've reason to believe you've got a lady in your room."

"Of course I've got a fucking lady in my room. This is a double room I'm paying for, and she's my wife."

It wasn't any of Pym's voices.

He laughed for her, rang the Great Eastern Hotel, and got a similar result. He rang Independent Television News and asked for the night editor. He said he was Inspector Markley of Scotland Yard with an urgent enquiry: He wanted the time of transmission of the item on the Lebanese bombing story on Monday night *News at Ten*. He held on for as long as it took, while he continued to leaf through the pages of Pym's letter. Postmark Reading. Posted Monday night or Tuesday morning.

"Ten-seventeen and ten seconds. That's when he rang you," he said, and glanced round to make sure she was all right. She was sitting up against the pillow, head back like a boxer between rounds.

He rang the post office investigation unit and got the night officer. He gave her the Firm's codeword and she responded with a doom-laden "I hear you," as if the third world war was about to happen.

"I'm asking the impossible and I want it by yesterday," he said.

"We'll try our best," she said.

"I want a backtrack on any cash call to London made from a Reading area telephone box between ten-eighteen and ten-twenty-one on Monday night. Duration around twenty minutes."

"Can't be done," she said promptly.

"I love her," he told Kate over his shoulder. She had rolled over and was lying on her stomach with her face buried in her arm.

He rang off and addressed himself in earnest to Kate's purloined pages from Pym's personal file. Three of them, extracted from the army record of First Lieutenant Magnus Pym, number supplied, of the Intelligence Corps, attached No. 6 Field Interrogation Unit, Graz, described in a footnote as an offensive military intelligence-gathering unit with limited permission to run local informants. Dated 18 July

1951, writer unknown, relevant passage sidelined by Registry. Date of entry to Pym's P.F., 12 May 1952. Reason for entry, Pym's formal candidature for admission to this service. The extract was from his commanding officer's conduct report at the close of Pym's tour of duty in Graz, Austria: ". . . exceptional young officer . . . popular and courteous in the mess . . . earned a high reputation for his skilful running of source GREENSLEEVES who over the last eleven months has supplied this unit with secret and top-secret intelligence on the Soviet Order of Battle in Czechoslovakia."

"You all right there?" he called to Kate. "Listen. You did nothing wrong. Nobody even missed this stuff. Nobody would have been the wiser for it. Nobody ever tried to follow it up."

He turned a page: ". . . close personal relationship established between source and case officer . . . Pym's calm authority during crisis . . . source's insistence on operating through Pym only . . ." He read fast to the end then began again at the beginning more slowly.

"His C.O. was in love with him too," he called to Kate. " '. . . his excellent memory for detail,' " he read, " '. . . lucid report writing, often done in the early hours of the morning after a long debriefing . . . high entertainment value . . .'

"Doesn't even mention Sabina," he complained to Kate. "Can't see what the devil he was so worried about. Why risk his hotline to you to suppress a bit of paper from the Dark Ages that did him nothing but credit? Must be something in his own nasty little mind, not ours at all. That doesn't surprise me either."

The phone was ringing. He glanced round. The bed was empty, the bathroom door closed. Scared, he sprang up and pulled it quickly open. She was standing safely at the basin, chucking water in her face. He closed the door again and hastened back to the telephone. It was a mossy green scrambler with chrome buttons. He picked up the receiver and growled "Yes?"

"Jack? Let's go over. Ready? Now."

Brotherhood pressed a button and heard the same tenor voice trilling in the electronic storm.

"You'll enjoy this, Jack—Jack, can you hear me? Hullo?"

"I can hear you, Bo."

"I've just had Carver on the line." Carver was the American Head of Station in London. "He insists his people have come up with fresh leads concerning our mutual friend. They want to reopen the story on him immediately. Harry Wexler's flying over from Washington to see fair play."

"That all?"

"Isn't it enough?"

"Where do they think he is?" said Brotherhood.

"That's exactly the point. They didn't ask, they weren't worried. They assume he's still coping with his father's affairs," said Brammel, very pleased. "They actually made the point that this would be an excellent time to meet. While our friend is occupied with his personal affairs. Everything is still in its place as far as they're concerned. Except for the new leads of course. Whatever they are."

"Except for the networks," Brotherhood said.

"I'll want you with me at the meeting, Jack. I want you in there punching for me, just like your usual self. Will you do that?"

"If it's an order, I'll do anything."

Bo sounded like someone organising a jolly party: "I'm having everyone we'd normally have. Nobody's to be left out or added. I want nothing to stick out, not a ripple while we go on looking for him. This whole thing could still be a storm in a teacup. Whitehall is convinced of it. They argue that we're dealing with follow-on from the last thing, not a new situation at all. They've got some awfully clever people these days. Some of them aren't even civil servants. Are you sleeping?"

"Not a lot."

"None of us is. We must stick together. Nigel's over at the Foreign Office at this moment."

"Is he though?" said Brotherhood aloud as he rang off. "Kate?"

"What is it?"

"Just keep your fingers away from my razor blades, hear me? We're too old for dramatic gestures, both of us."

He waited a second, dialled Head Office and asked for the night duty officer.

"You got a rider there?"

"Yes."

"Brotherhood. There's a War Office file I want. British Army of Occupation in Austria, old field case. Operation Greensleeves, believe it or not. Where will it be?"

"Ministry of Defence, I suppose, seeing that the War Office was disbanded about two hundred years ago."

"Who are you?"

"Nicholson."

"Well, don't bloody suppose. Find out where it is, fetch it and phone me when it's on your desk. Got a pencil, have you?"

"I don't think I have actually. Nigel has left instructions that any request from you has to be processed by Secretariat first. Sorry, Jack."

"Nigel's at the Foreign Office. Check with Bo. While you're about it, ask Defence to give you the name of the Commandant of Number Six Interrogation, Graz, Austria, on July 18, 1951. I'm in a hurry. Greensleeves, have you got it? Maybe you're not musical."

He rang off and pulled Pym's battered letter to Tom savagely towards him.

"He's a shell," Kate said. "All you have to do is find the hermit crab that climbed into him. Don't look for the truth about him. The truth is what we gave him of ourselves."

"Sure," said Brotherhood. He set a sheet of paper ready to jot on while he silently read: *"If I don't write to you for a while, remember I'm thinking of you all the time."* Maudlin slush. *"If you need help and don't want to turn to Uncle Jack, this is what you do."* He continued reading, writing out Pym's instructions to his son, one by one. *"Don't worry your head so much about religious things, just try to trust in God's goodness."* "Damn the man!" he expostulated aloud for Kate's sake and, slamming down his pencil, pressed both fists against his temple as the phone rang again. He let it ring a moment, recovered and picked it up, glancing at his watch, which was his habit always.

"Anyway the file you want went missing *years* ago," said Nicholson with pleasure.

"Who to?"

"Us. They say it's marked out to us and we never returned it."

"Who of *us* in particular?"

"Czech section. It was requisitioned by one of our own London desk officers in 1953."

"Which one?"

"M.R.P. That would be Pym. Do you want me to ring Vienna and ask him what he did with it?"

"I'll ask him myself in the morning," he said. "What about the C.O.?"

"A Major Harrison Membury of the Education Corps."

"The *what?*"

"He was on secondment to Army Intelligence for the period 1950 to '54."

"Christ Almighty. Any address?"

He wrote it down, remembering a quip of Pym's, paraphrased from Clemenceau: "Military intelligence has about as much to do with intelligence as military music has to do with music."

He rang off.

"They haven't even indoctrinated the poor bloody duty officer!" Brotherhood expostulated, again for Kate.

He went back to his homework better pleased. Somewhere beyond Green Park a London clock was striking three.

"I'm going," Kate said. She was standing at the door, dressed.

Brotherhood was on his feet in a moment.

"Oh no you're not. You're staying here until I hear you laugh."

He went to her and undressed her again. He put her back to bed.

"Why do you think I'm going to kill myself?" she said. "Has somebody done that to you once?"

"Let's just say once would be too often," he replied.

"What's in the burnbox?" she asked, for the second time that night. But for the second time, too, Brotherhood appeared too busy to reply.

$$8$$

M y memory gets selective here, Jack. More than usual. He's in my sights as I expect he begins to be in yours. But you are in them too. Whatever doesn't point to you both slips by me like landscape through a railway window. I could paint for you Pym's distressing conversations with the luckless Herr Bertl in which, on Rick's instruction, he assured him repeatedly it was in the post, it was taken care of, everybody would be seen right, and his father was on the point of making an offer for the hotel. Or we could have some fun with Pym, languishing for days and nights in his hotel bedroom as a hostage to the mountain of unpaid bills downstairs, dreaming of Elena Weber's milky body reflected in its many delightful poses in the mirrored changing rooms of Bern, kicking himself for his timidity, living off hoarded continental breakfasts, running up more bills and waiting for the telephone. Or the moment when Rick went off the air. He did not ring and when Pym tried his number the only response was a howl, like the cry of a wolf stuck on one note.

When he tried Syd he got Meg, and Meg's advice was strikingly similar to E. Weber's. "You're better off where you are, dear," she said in the pointed voice of someone who is telling you she is overheard. "There's a heat wave here and a lot of people are getting burned." "Where's Syd?" "Cooling himself, darling." Or the Sunday afternoon when everything in the hotel fell mercifully silent and Pym, having packed together his few possessions, stole heart in mouth down the staff staircase and out through a side door into what was suddenly a hostile foreign city —his first clandestine exit, and his easiest.

I could offer you Pym the infant refugee, though I never starved, had a valid British passport and in retrospect seldom wanted for a kindly word. But he did dip tallows for a religious candlemaker, sweep the aisle of the Minster, roll beer barrels for a brewer and unstitch sacks of carpets for an old Armenian who kept urging him to marry his daughter, and come to think of it he might have done worse; she was a beautiful girl and kept sighing and draping herself over the sofa but Pym was too polite to approach her. All those things he did and more. All of them at night, a night animal on the run through that lovely candlelit city with its clocks and wells and cobble and arcades. He swept snow, carted cheeses, led a blind dray-horse and taught English to aspiring travel agents. All under cover while he waited for Herr Bertl's hounds to sniff him out and bring him to justice, though I know now the poor man bore me no grudge whatever, and even at the height of his rage avoided mentioning Pym's part in the affair.

"Dear Father,
"I am really happy out here and you must not worry about me at all as the Swiss are kindly and hospitable and have all sorts of remarkable bursaries for young foreigners keen on reading law."

I could sing of another great hotel, not a stone's throw from the first, where Pym went to earth as a night waiter and became a schoolboy again, sleeping under avenues of lagged piping in a basement dormitory as big as a factory where the lights never went out; how he took gratefully once more to his little iron bed and how he jollied his fellow waiters as he had jollied his fellow new boys, for they turned out to be peasants from Ticino who wanted only to go home. How he rose willingly with every bell and donned a white dicky that, though thick with last night's grease, was not half as constricting as Mr. Willow's collars. And how he took trays of bubbly and foie gras to ambiguous couples who sometimes wanted him to stay, Amor and Rococo beckoning from their glances. But once again he was too polite and too unknowing to oblige. His manners in those days were a barbed-wire cage. He only lusted when he was alone. Yet even as I allow my memory to brush past these tantalising episodes, my heart is hurtling ahead to the night I met the saintly Herr Ollinger in the third-class buffet of Bern railway station and, through his charity, stumbled into the encounter that altered all my life till here— and I fear your life as well, Jack, though you have yet to learn by how much.

Of the university, how Pym enrolled there and why, my recollections are equally impatient. It was for cover. All for cover as usual, leave it there. He had been working in a circus at its winter home, which was a patch of land just beneath the same railway station where his footsteps so often finished after his all-day walks. Somehow the elephants had drawn him. Any fool can wash an elephant, but he was surprised to learn how hard it was to dip the head of a twenty-foot brush into a bucket when the only light comes in shafts from the spotlights in the apex of the marquee. Each dawn when his work was done he made his way home to the Salvation Army hostel that was his temporary Ascot. Each dawn he saw the green dome of the university rising above him through the autumn mist like an ugly little Rome challenging him to convert. And somehow he had to get inside the place, for he had a second terror, greater than Herr Bertl's hounds: namely that Rick despite his problems of liquidity would appear in a cloud of Bentley and whisk him home.

He had fabricated for Rick handsomely and imaginatively. *I have won that foreigners' scholarship I was talking about. I am reading Swiss law and German law and Roman law and all the other laws there are. I am attending night school on the side to keep myself out of mischief.* He had praised the erudition of his non-existent tutors and the piety of the university chaplains. But Rick's systems of intelligence, though erratic, were impressive. Pym knew he was not safe until he had given substance to his fictions. One morning therefore he found the courage and marched up there. He lied first about his qualifications and then about his age, for the one could not have been earned without an adjustment to the other. He paid out the last of E. Weber's white banknotes to a crew-cut cashier, and in return received a grey cloth-card with his photograph on it, describing him as legitimate. *I have never in my life been so gratified by the sight of a false document.* Pym would have given his whole fortune for it, which was a further seventy-one francs. *Philosophie Zwei* was Pym's faculty and I still have only the sketchiest notion of what it comprised, for Pym had asked for law but somehow been rerouted. He learned more from translating the students' bulletins on the notice-board, which invited him to a string of unlikely forums and gave him his first rumblings of political gunfire since Ollie and Mr. Cudlove had vented their anger against the rich and Lippsie had warned him of the hollowness of possessions. You remember those forums too, Jack, though from a different aspect, and for reasons we shall come to soon enough.

It was from the university notice-board also that Pym discovered the existence of an English church in Elfenau, the diplomatic fairyland. Along he went—he could hardly wait—often two or three Sundays running. He prayed, he hovered outside the doors afterwards, shaking hands with anything that moved, though little did. He gazed soulfully at elderly mothers, fell in love with several, consumed cake and lifeless tea in their thickly curtained houses and charmed them with extravagant accounts of his parentless upbringing. Soon the expatriate in him couldn't get along without its weekly shot of the English banality. The English church with its iron-back diplomatic families, ancient Britons and dubious Anglophiles became his school chapel and all the other chapels he had defected from.

Its counterpart was the third-class railway buffet where, if he wasn't working, he could sit all night smoking himself sick on Disque Bleus over a single beer and fancying himself the most stateless, world-weary globe-trotter he had ever met. Today the station is an indoor metropolis of smart boutiques and plastic-coated restaurants, but in the immediate post-war years it was still an ill-lit Edwardian staging post, with stuffed stages in the concourse and murals of freed peasants waving flags, and a scent of Bockwurst and fried onion that never went away. The first-class buffet was full of gentlemen in black suits with napkins round their necks, but the third class was shadowed and beery, with a whiff of Balkan lawlessness and drunks who sang out of tune. Pym's favourite table was in a panelled corner near the coats where a sacred waitress called Elisabeth gave him extra soup. It must have been Herr Ollinger's favourite also for he homed on it as soon as he entered and having bowed lovingly at Elisabeth, who wore a low-cut *Tracht* with perforated smocking, bowed at Pym too, and fidgeted with his poor briefcase, and hauled at his disobedient hair, and asked, "Do we disturb you?" in a tone of breathless anxiety while he stroked an old yellow chow dog that hung grumbling on its lead. Thus as I now know does our Maker disguise His best agents.

Herr Ollinger was ageless but I guess now fifty. His complexion was doughy, his smile regretful, his cheeks were dimpled and pendulous like an old man's bottom. Even when he did finally allow that his chair was not taken by superior beings, he lowered his round body so gingerly into it that you would think he expected to be shooed away any minute by someone more deserving. With the assurance of an habitué Pym took the brown raincoat from his unresisting arm and threaded a hanger into it. He had decided he needed Herr Ollinger and his yellow chow dog urgently. His life was going through a fallow period at the time and he had not exchanged more than a few words with anyone for a week. His gesture threw Herr Ollinger into a vortex of hopeless gratitude. Herr Ollinger beamed and declared Pym most friendly. He grabbed a copy of *Der Bund* from the rack and buried his face in it. He whispered to the dog to behave itself and tapped it ineffectually on the snout, though it was behaving with exemplary tolerance. But he had spoken, which gave Pym reason to explain, in a set sentence, that unfortunately I am foreign, sir, and not yet equal to your local dialect. So please be kind enough to speak High German and excuse me. After this, as he had learned to, he added his surname, "Pym," at which Herr Ollinger confessed that he was Ollinger, as if the name implied some frightful slur, and afterwards presented the chow as Herr Bastl, which for a moment rang uncomfortably of the luckless Bertl.

"But you speak excellent German!" Herr Ollinger protested. "I would immediately have thought you are from Germany! You are not? Then where do you come from, if I may be so impertinent?"

And this was kind of Herr Ollinger for nobody in his right mind, in those days, could have confused Pym's German with the real thing. So Pym told Herr Ollinger the story of his life, which was what he had intended from the first, and dazzled him with tender questions about himself, and in every way he knew laid upon Herr Ollinger the full burden of his sensitive charm—which as it later turned out was a totally needless exertion on Pym's part since Herr Ollinger was unselective in his acquaintance. He admired everybody, pitied everybody from below—not least for their dreadful misfortune in having to share the world with him. Herr Ollinger said he was married to an angel, and possessed three angel daughters who were musical prodigies. Herr Ollinger said he had inherited his father's factory in Ostermundigen, which was a great worry to him. And so indeed it should have been, for in retrospect it is clear that the poor man rose diligently every morning in order to run it further into the earth. Herr Ollinger said Herr Bastl had been with him three years but only temporarily, because he was still trying to find the dog's owner.

Reciprocating with equal generosity, Pym described his experiences in the blitz, and the night he had been visiting his aunt in Coventry when they hit the cathedral; how she lived but a hundred yards from the main doors and her house by a miracle was unscathed. When he had destroyed Coventry, he described himself in an imaginative tour de force as an admiral's son standing at his dormitory window in his dressing-gown, calmly watching the waves of German bombers flying over his school and wondering whether this time they were going to drop the parachutists dressed as nuns.

"But did you have no shelters?" Herr Ollinger cried. "That's a disgrace! You were a child, my God! My wife would be completely furious. She is from Wilderswil," he explained, while Herr Bastl ate a pretzel and farted.

Thus Pym skipped on, piling one fiction on another, appealing to Herr Ollinger's Swiss love of disaster, enthralling the neutral in him with the dire realities of war.

"But you were so young," Herr Ollinger protested again when Pym related the rigours of his early military training at the Signals Depot in Bradford. "You had no nest warmth. You were a child!"

"Well, thank God they never had to use us," said Pym in a throwaway voice as he called for his bill. "My grandfather died in the first one, my father was given up for dead in the second, so I can't help feeling it's time our family had a break." Herr Ollinger would not hear of Pym paying. Herr Ollinger might be breathing the free air of Switzerland, he said, but he had three generations of English to thank for the privilege. Pym's sausage and beer were a mere step in the mercurial progress of Herr Ollinger's generosity. It was followed by the offer of a room, for as long as Pym wished to do him the honour, in the narrow little house in the Länggasse that Herr Ollinger had inherited from his mother.

It was not a big room. It was actually a very small room indeed. An attic, one of three, and Pym's was in the middle, and only the middle of it was big enough for him to stand in, and even then he was more comfortable with his head poked through the skylight. In summer the daylight lasted all night, in winter the snow blacked out the world. For heating he had a great black radiator cut into the party-wall, which he heated from a wood stove in the corridor. He had to choose between freezing and boiling, depending on his mood. Yet, Tom, I have not been so content anywhere until I found Miss Dubber. Once in our lives, it is given us to know a truly happy family. Frau Ollinger was tall and luminous and frugal. On a routine patrol of the house Pym once watched her through a crack in a doorway while she slept, and she was smiling. I am sure she was smiling when she died. Her husband fussed round her like a fat tug, upsetting the economy, dumping every waif and sponger on her that he came upon, adoring her. The daughters were each plainer than the next, played musical instruments atrociously, to the fury of the neighbours, and one by one they married even plainer men and worse musicians whom the Ollingers thought brilliant and delightful—and by thinking made them so. From morning till night a trail of migrants, misfits and undiscovered geniuses drifted through their kitchen, cooking themselves omelettes and treading out their cigarettes on the linoleum. And woe if you left your bedroom unlocked, for Herr Ollinger was quite capable of forgetting you were there—or, if need be, of persuading himself you would be out tonight, or that you wouldn't mind a stranger just until he's got somewhere. What we paid I don't remember. What we could afford was next to nothing and certainly not enough to subsidise the factory in Ostermundigen, for the last I heard of Herr Ollinger he was working happily as a clerk in Bern's main post office, enchanted by the erudite company. The only possession I associate with him apart from Herr Bastl is a collection of erotica with which he consoled himself in his shyness. Like everything else about him it was there to be shared, and it was a great deal more revealing than *Amor and Rococo Woman*.

Such then was the household on which Pym's crow's-nest was built. For once his life was as good as complete. He had a bed, he had a family. He was in love with Elisabeth in the third-class buffet and contemplating marriage and early fatherhood. He was locked in a tantalising correspondence with Belinda, who felt it her duty to inform him of Jemima's love affairs, "which I'm sure she only has because you are so far away." If Rick was not extinct he was at least quiescent, for the only sign of him was a flow of homilies on Being Ever True to your Advantages, and avoiding the Foreign Temptations and the Snares of Synicism, which either he or his secretary could not spell. These letters had the distinct air of being typed on the run, and never came from the same place twice: "Write care Topsie Eaton at the Firs, East Grinstead, no need to put my name on envelope." "Write to Colonel Mellow post restaurant the main G.P.O. Hull who obliges by collecting my mail." On one occasion a handwritten love letter varied the diet, beginning: "Annie, my sweet Pet, your body means more to me than Riches of the earth." Rick must have put it into the wrong envelope.

The only thing Pym missed therefore was a friend. He met him in Herr Ollinger's basement on a Saturday at midday, when he took down his laundry for his weekly wash. Upstairs in the street the first snowfall was driving out the autumn. Pym had an armful of damp clothes in front of his face and was concerned about the stone steps. The basement light was operated by a time switch; any second he could be plunged into darkness and trip over Herr Bastl, who owned the boiler. But the light stayed on and as he brushed past the switch he noticed that somebody had ingeniously jammed a matchstick into it, a very sleek matchstick trimmed with a knife. He smelt cigar smoke but Bern was not Ascot—anyone who had a few pence could smoke a cigar. When he saw the armchair he mentally assigned it to the junk Herr Ollinger set aside as a gift to Herr Rubi the rag-and-bone man who came on Saturdays on his horse-drawn float.

"Don't you know it is forbidden for foreigners to hang their clothes in Swiss basements?" said a male voice, not in dialect but in a crisp High German.

"I'm afraid I didn't," said Pym. He peered round for someone to apologise to and saw instead the unclear form of a slender man curled on the armchair, clutching a patchwork blanket to his neck with one long white hand and a book with the other. He wore a black beret and had a drooping moustache. No feet showed, but his body had the look of something spiky and wrongly folded, like a tripod that had stuck halfway. Herr Ollinger's walking-stick was propped against the chair. A small cigar smouldered between the fingers that clutched the blanket.

"In Switzerland it is forbidden to be poor, it is forbidden to be foreign, it is *completely* forbidden to hang clothes. You are an inmate of this establishment?"

"I am a friend of Herr Ollinger's."

"An English friend?"

"My name is Pym."

Discovering the moustache, the fingers of one white hand began stroking it reflectively downward.

"Lord Pym?"

"Just Magnus."

"But you are of aristocratic stock."

"Well, nothing very special."

"And you are the war hero," the stranger said, and made a sucking noise that in English would have sounded skeptical.

Pym did not like the description at all. The account of himself that he had given to Herr Ollinger was obsolete. He was dismayed to hear it revived.

"So who are you, if I may ask?" said Pym.

The stranger's fingers rose to claw at some irritation in his cheek while he appeared to consider a range of alternatives. "My name is Axel and since one week I am your neighbour, so I am obliged to listen to you grinding your teeth at night," he said, drawing on his cigar.

"*Herr* Axel?" said Pym.

"Herr Axel Axel. My parents forgot to give me a second name." He put down the book and held out a slim hand in greeting. "For God's sake," he exclaimed with a wince as Pym grasped it. "Go easy, will you? The war's over."

Too challenged for his comfort Pym left his washing for another day and took himself upstairs.

"What is Axel's other name?" he asked Herr Ollinger next day.

"Maybe he hasn't one," Herr Ollinger replied mischievously. "Maybe that's why he has no papers."

"Is he a student?"

"He is a poet," said Herr Ollinger proudly but the house was stiff with poets.

"They must be very long poems. He types all night," said Pym.

"Indeed he does. And on my typewriter," said Herr Ollinger, his pride complete.

My husband found him in the factory, Frau Ollinger said while Pym helped her prepare vegetables for the evening meal. That is to say, Herr Harprecht the night-watchman found him. Axel was sleeping on sacks in the warehouse and Herr Harprecht wanted to hand him over to the police because he had no papers and was foreign and smelly, but thank goodness my husband stopped Herr Harprecht in time and gave Axel breakfast and took him to a doctor for his sweating.

"Where does he come from?" Pym asked.

Frau Ollinger became uncharacteristically guarded. Axel comes from *drüben*, she said—*drüben* being across the border, *drüben* being those irrational tracts of Europe that were not Switzerland, where people rode in tanks instead of trolley-buses, and the starving had the ill manners to pick their food from rubble instead of buying it from shops.

"How did he get here?" Pym asked.

"We think he walked," Frau Ollinger said.

"But he's an invalid. He's all crippled and thin."

"We think he had a strong will and a great necessity."

"Is he German?"

"There are many sorts of German, Magnus."

"Which sort is Axel?"

"We don't ask. Maybe you should not ask either."

"Can you guess from his voice?"

"We don't guess either. With Axel it is better we are completely without curiosity."

"What's he ill of?"

"Maybe he suffered in the war, as you did," Frau Ollinger suggested with a smile of rather too much understanding. "Don't you like Axel? Is he disturbing you up there?"

How can he disturb me when he doesn't speak to me? thought Pym. When all I hear of him is the clicking of Herr Ollinger's typewriter, the cries of ecstasy from his lady callers in the afternoons and the shuffle of his feet as he hauls himself to the lavatory on Herr Ollinger's walking-stick? When all I see of him is his empty vodka bottles and the blue cloud of his cigar smoke in the corridor and his pale empty body disappearing down the stairs?

"Axel's super," he said.

Pym had already appointed Christmas to be the jolliest of his life and so it was —despite a letter of appalling misery from Rick describing the privations of "a small Private hotel in the wilds of Scotland where the meagrest of life's Necessities are a Godsend." He meant, I discovered later, Gleneagles. Christmas Eve came. Pym as youngest lit the candles and helped Frau Ollinger lay the presents round the tree. It had been wonderfully dark all day and in the afternoon thick snowflakes began swirling in the streetlights and clogging the tramlines. The Ollinger daughters arrived with their escorts, followed by a shy married couple from Basel over whom some shadow hung, I forget what. Next a French genius called Jean-Pierre who painted fish in profile, always on a sepia background. And after him an apologetic Japanese gentleman called Mr. San—enigmatically so since, as I now know, San is itself a term of Japanese address. Mr. San was working at Herr Ollinger's factory as some sort of industrial spy, which in retrospect strikes me as very funny indeed, because if the Japanese ever tried copying Herr Ollinger's methods, they must have set back their industrial output by a decade.

Finally Axel himself came slowly down the wood stairs and made his entry. For the first time Pym could regard him at his leisure. Though desperately thin, his face was by nature rounded. His brow was tall but the hank of brown hair that grew sideways over it gave it a curved and saddening air. It was as if his Maker had put His thumb and forefinger to either temple and yanked the whole face downward as a warning to his frivolity: first the hooped eyebrows, then the eyes, then the moustache which was a shaggy horseshoe. And somehow inside all this was Axel himself, his eyes twinkling out of their own shadows, the grateful survivor of something Pym was not allowed to share. One of the daughters had knitted him a sloppy cardigan which he wore like a cape over his wasted shoulders.

"*Schön guten Abend*, Sir Magnus," he said. He was carrying a straw bonnet upside down. Pym saw parcels in it, beautifully wrapped. "Why do we never speak to each other up there? We could be kilometres apart instead of twenty centimetres. Are you still fighting the Germans? We are allies, you and I. Soon we shall be fighting the Russians."

"I suppose we shall," said Pym feebly.

"Why don't you bang on my door once when you are lonely? We can have a cigar together, save the world a little. You like to talk nonsense?"

"Very much."

"Okay. We talk nonsense." But on the point of shuffling away to greet Mr. San, Axel stopped and turned. And over his caped shoulder he vouchsafed Pym a quizzical, almost challenging glare, as if asking himself whether he had invested his trust too easily.

"Aber dann können wir doch Freunde sein, Sir Magnus?"—then we may be friends after all?

"Ich würde mich freuen!" Pym replied heartily, meeting his gaze without fear —I would be happy!

They shook hands again, but this time lightly. At the same moment Axel's features broke into such a smile of sparkling good fun that Pym's heart filled for him in response, and he promised himself that he would follow Axel anywhere for all the Christmases that he was spared. The party began. The girls played carols and Pym sang with the best, using English words where he lacked the German. There were speeches and after them a toast to absent friends and relations, at which Axel's long eyelids almost hid his eyes and he fell quiet. But then, as if shaking off bad memories, he stood up abruptly and began unpacking the bonnet he had brought while Pym hovered at hand to help him, knowing that this was what Axel had always done at Christmas, wherever Christmas was. For the daughters he had made musical pipes, each with her name carved along the underneath. How had he carved with such wispy white hands? So exquisitely, without Pym hearing him through the partition? Where had he found his wood, his paint and brushes? For the Ollingers he produced what I later realised was another emblem of prison life, a matchstick model. This one was an ark with painted figures of our extended family waving from the portholes. For Mr. San and Jean-Pierre he had squares of cloth of a sort that Pym had once made for Dorothy on a homemade handloom between nails. For the Basel couple a patterned woollen eye to ward off whatever was afflicting them. And for Pym—I still take it as a compliment that he left me until last—for Sir Magnus he had a much used copy of Grimmelshausen's *Simplicissimus,* bound in old brown buckram, which Pym had not heard of but could not wait to read since it would give him an excuse to bang on Axel's door. He opened it and read the inscription. "For Sir Magnus, who will never be my enemy." And in the top left corner, in an older ink but in a younger version of the same hand: "A.H. Carlsbad August 1939."

"Where is Carlsbad?" Pym asked before he had allowed himself a second's thought, and noticed at once an awkwardness round him as if everybody had heard the bad news except for himself who was deemed not old enough to receive it.

"Carlsbad no longer exists, Sir Magnus," Axel replied politely. "When you have read *Simplicissimus* you will understand why."

"Where was it?"

"It was my home town."

"Then you have given me a treasure from your own past."

"Would you prefer me to give you something I did not value?"

And Pym—what had he brought? God help him, the Chairman and Managing Director's son was not used to ceremonies with meaning, and had thought of nothing better than a box of cigars to see dear old Axel right.

* * *

"Why does Carlsbad no longer exist?" Pym asked Herr Ollinger as soon as he could get him alone. Herr Ollinger knew everything except how to run a factory. Carlsbad was in the Sudetenland, he explained. It was a beautiful spa city and everybody used to go there: Brahms and Beethoven, Goethe and Schiller. First it was Austria, then it became Germany. Now it was Czechoslovakia and had a new name and the Germans had all been chucked out.

"So who does Axel belong to?" Pym asked.

"Only to us, I think," said Herr Ollinger gravely. "And we must be careful of him or they will take him away from us, you may be sure."

"He has women in his room," said Pym.

Herr Ollinger's face turned pink with impish pleasure. "I think he has all the women of Bern," he agreed.

A couple of days passed. On the third Pym banged on Axel's door and found him standing smoking at the open window with several heavy-looking books before him on the sill. He must have been freezing but he seemed to need the open air to read by.

"Come for a stroll," said Pym boldly.

"At my speed?"

"Well we can't go at mine, can we?"

"My constitution dislikes crowded places, Sir Magnus. If we are to walk, better we stay out of town."

They borrowed Bastl and wandered with him along the empty towpath beside the racing Aare while Herr Bastl peed and refused to follow and Pym did his best to keep an eye open for anyone who looked like a policeman. In the sunless river valley the frost drifted about in evil clouds and the cold was merciless. Axel seemed not to notice. He puffed at his cigar while he tossed out questions in his soft, amused voice. If this is how he walked from Austria, thought Pym, shivering in his wake, he must have taken years.

"How did you reach Bern, Sir Magnus? Were you advancing or retreating?" Axel asked.

Never able to resist an opportunity to portray himself on a fresh page, Pym went to work. And though, as was his wont, he took care to improve upon the reality, rearranging the facts to fit his prevailing image of himself, an instinctive caution nevertheless counselled him restraint. True, he endowed himself with a noble and eccentric mother, and true, when he came to describe Rick he awarded him many of the qualities Rick unsuccessfully aspired to, such as wealth, military distinction and daily access to the Highest in the Land. But in other respects he was frugal and self-mocking and when he came to the story of E. Weber, which he had not told anyone till now, Axel laughed so much he had to sit on a bench and light another cigar to get his wind back, while Pym laughed with him, delighted by his success. And when he showed him her very letter saying, "Never mind. E. Weber love you always," he shouted, "*Nochmal!* Tell it again, Sir Magnus! I order you! And make sure it is completely different this time. Did you sleep with her?"

"Of course."

"How many times?"

"Four or five."

"All in one night? You are a tiger! Was she grateful?"

"She was very, very experienced."

"More than your Jemima?"

"Well, jolly nearly."

"More than your wicked Lippsie who seduced you when you were still a little boy?"

"Well, Lippsie was in a class of her own."

Axel slapped him gaily on the back. "Sir Magnus, you are a prince, no question. You are a dark horse, you know that? Such a good little boy, yet you sleep with dangerous adventuresses and young English aristocrats. I love you, hear me? I love all English aristocrats, but you best."

Walking again, Axel had to shove his arm through Pym's to support himself, and from then on used him unashamedly as his walking-stick. For the rest of our lives we have seldom walked in any other way.

Somewhere that evening under a bridge, Pym and Axel found an empty café and Axel insisted on paying for two vodkas from the black purse he kept on a leather thong round his neck. Somewhere on the freezing journey home they agreed that Axel and Pym must begin the education they had never had, and that they would appoint tomorrow the first day of the world, and that Grimmelshausen would be their first subject because he taught that the world was a mad place and getting madder by the moment, with everything that appeared right almost certainly wrong. They agreed that Axel would take charge of Pym's spoken German and not rest till he spoke it to perfection. Thus, in a day and an evening, Pym became Axel's legs and Axel's intellectual companion and, though it was not initially meant that way, Axel's pupil, for over the next few months he unveiled for Pym the German muse. If Axel's knowledge was greater than Pym's, his curiosity was not less, his energy equally relentless. Perhaps by resuscitating his country's culture for an innocent, he was reconciling himself to its recent past.

As to Pym, he was gazing at last on the glories of the kingdom he had dreamed of for so long. The German muse had no particular draw for him, then or later, for all his loud enthusiasm. If she had been Chinese or Polish or Indian, it would have made no earthly odds. The point was, she supplied Pym with the means, for the first time, to regard himself intellectually as a gentleman. And for that Pym was eternally grateful to her. By willing Pym night and day to accompany Axel on his explorations, she gave him the world inside his head that Lippsie had said he would be able to take with him anywhere. And Lippsie was right, because when he went down to the warehouse in Ostring where Herr Ollinger had obtained illegal nightwork for him at the hands of a fellow philanthropist, he neither walked nor took the tram but rode with Mozart in his coach to Prague. When he washed his elephants at night he endured the humiliations of Lenz's *Soldaten*. When he sat in the third-class buffet bestowing soulful looks on Elisabeth, he imagined himself as the young Werther, planning his wardrobe before committing suicide. And when he considered all his failures and hopes together, he was able to compare his *Werdegang* with Wilhelm Meister's years of apprenticeship, and planned even then a great autobiographical novel that would show the world what a noble sensitive fellow he was compared with Rick.

And yes, Jack, the other seeds were there, of course they were: a crash diet of

Hegel, as much as they both could swallow at a time, a burst of Marx and Engels and the bad bears of Communism—for after all, said Axel, this was the first day of the world. "If we are to judge Christianity by the misery it has caused mankind, who would ever be a Christian? We accept no prejudices, Sir Magnus. We believe everything as we read it and only afterwards reject it. If Hitler hated these fellows so much, they can't be all bad, I say." Out came Rousseau and the revolutionaries, and *Das Kapital,* and *Anti-Dühring,* and in went the sun for several weeks, though I swear we came to no conclusions that I remember, except that we were glad when it was over. And I honestly doubt now whether the substance of Axel's teaching was of importance beside Pym's joy that he was teaching him at all. What counted was that Pym was happy from the moment he got up until the early hours of the following morning; and that when they finally went to bed on either side of their black radiator, sleeping, to use Axel's phrase, like God in France, Pym's mind went on exploring in his sleep.

"Axel's got the Order of the Frozen Meat," Pym told Frau Ollinger proudly one day, carving bread for family fondue.

Frau Ollinger gave an exclamation of disgust. "Magnus, what nonsense are you talking now?"

"It's true! It's German soldiers' slang for a Russian campaign medal. He volunteered from his *Gymnasium.* His father could have got him a safe post in France or Belgium. A *Druckposten,* somewhere he could keep his head down. Axel wouldn't let him. He wanted to be a hero like his classmates."

Frau Ollinger was not pleased. "Then better you keep quiet about where he fought," she said sternly. "Axel is here to study, not to boast."

"He has women up there," said Pym. "They creep up the stairs in the afternoons and scream when he makes love to them."

"If they give him happiness and help him to study they are welcome. Do you wish to invite your passionate Jemima?"

Furious, Pym stalked to his room and penned a long letter to Rick about the unfairness of the average Swiss in daily matters. "Sometimes I think the law here does duty for common kindness," he wrote stuffily. "Particularly where women are concerned."

Rick wrote back by return, urging chastity: "Better you remain Clean until you have made the choice that is Meant for you."

"Dear Belinda,

"Things are a bit sticky here at the moment. Some of the foreign students in the house are taking things a bit far with their womenfolk and I have had to step in or I'll never get my work done. Perhaps if you adopted the same firm line with Jem, you might in the long run be doing her a favour."

A day came when Axel fell ill. Pym hurried back from the zoo full of funny stories about his adventures to find him in bed, where he hated most to be. His tiny room was heavy with cigar smoke, his pale head darkened with stubble and shadows. A girl was hanging about but Axel ordered her out when Pym arrived.

"What's wrong with him?" Pym asked Herr Ollinger's doctor, peering over his shoulder, trying to decipher the prescription.

"What is wrong with him, Sir Magnus, is that he was bombed by the heroic

British," said Axel savagely from the bed, in a barbed unfamiliar voice. "What is wrong with him is that he got half a British shell up his arse and is having trouble shitting it out."

The doctor was sworn not just to secrecy but to silence and with a friendly pat for Pym departed.

"Maybe it was you who fired it at me, Sir Magnus. Did you land in Normandy, by any chance? Perhaps you led the invasion?"

"I didn't do anything like that at all," said Pym.

So Pym became Axel's legs again, fetching his medicines and cigars and cooking for him and ransacking the university libraries for ever more books which he could read aloud to him.

"No more Nietzsche, thank you, Sir Magnus. I think we know enough about the cleansing effect of violence. Kleist is not as bad but you don't read him properly. You must bark Kleist. He was a Prussian officer, not an English hero. Get the painters."

"Which ones?"

"Abstractionists. Decadents. Jews. Anyone who was *entartet* or forbidden. Give me a holiday from these mad writers."

Pym consulted Frau Ollinger. "Then you must ask the librarian for whomever the Nazis did not like, Magnus," she explained in her governess voice.

The librarian was an émigré who knew Axel's needs by heart. Pym brought Klee and Nolde, Kokoschka and Klimt, Kandinsky and Picasso. He stood their picture books and catalogues open on the mantelshelf where Axel could see them without moving his head. He turned the pages and read the captions out loud. When women came, Axel again sent them away. "I am being attended to. Wait till I am well." Pym brought Max Beckmann. He brought Steinlen, then Schiele and more Schiele. Next day the writers were reinstated. Pym fetched Brecht and Zuckmayer, Tucholsky and Remarque. He read them aloud, hours of them. "Music," Axel commanded. Pym borrowed Herr Ollinger's wind-up gramophone and played him Mendelssohn and Tchaikovsky until Axel fell asleep. He woke delirious, the sweat falling off him like raindrops while he described a retreat through snow with the blind hanging on to the lame and the blood freezing in the wounds. He talked of a hospital, two to a bed and the dead lying on the floor. He asked for water. Pym fetched it and Axel took the glass in both hands, shaking wildly. He lifted the glass till his hands froze, then he lowered his head in jerks until his lips reached the brim. Then he sucked the water like an animal, spilling it while his fevered eyes kept guard. He drew up his legs and wetted himself and sat shaking and grumpy in an armchair while Pym changed his sheets.

"Who are you afraid of?" Pym asked again. "There's no one here. It's just us."

"Then I must be afraid of you. What's that poodle in the corner?"

"It's Herr Bastl and he's a chow chow, not a poodle."

"I thought it was the Devil."

Till a day when Pym woke to find Axel standing fully dressed at his bedside. "It is Goethe's birthday and it's four in the afternoon," he announced in his military voice. "We must go into town and listen to the idiot Thomas Mann."

"But you're ill."

"Nobody who stands up is ill. Nobody marches who is ill. Dress."

"Was Mann on the forbidden list too?" Pym asked as he pulled on his clothes.

"He never made it."

"Why's he an idiot?"

Herr Ollinger supplied a raincoat that could have gone twice round Axel's body, Mr. San provided a broad black hat. Herr Ollinger drove them to the door in his broken car two hours early and they took their places at the back before the great hall filled. When the lecture was over, Axel marched Pym backstage and hammered on the dressing-room door. Pym had not cared for Thomas Mann till now. He found his prose perfumed and unwieldy, though he had tried his best for Axel's sake. But now, there stood God Himself, tall and angular like Uncle Makepeace. "This young English nobleman wishes to shake your hand, sir," Axel advised him with authority from underneath Mr. San's broad hat. Thomas Mann peered at Pym, then at Axel so pale and ethereal from his fever. Thomas Mann frowned at the palm of his own right hand as if asking himself whether it could take the strain of an aristocratic embrace. He held out his hand and Pym shook it, waiting to feel Mann's genius flow into him like one of those electric shocks you used to be able to buy at railway stations—hold this knob and let my energy revive you. Nothing happened, but Axel's enthusiasm was enough for both of them:

"You touched him, Sir Magnus! You are blessed! You are immortal!"

Within a week, they had saved enough cash to take themselves to Davos to visit the shrine of Mann's diseased souls. They travelled in the lavatory, Pym standing and Axel, in his beret, sitting patiently on the seat. The conductor knocked on the door and yelled, *"Alle Billette, bitte"*; Axel gave a girlish whimper of discomfort and pushed their one ticket under the door. Pym waited, his eyes fixed on the shadows of the conductor's feet. He felt the conductor stoop, he heard him grunt as he straightened up. He heard a snap that felt like his own nerve breaking as the ticket reappeared under the door with a hole punched in it. The shadows moved on. This is how you walked here, thought Pym with admiration, as they silently shook hands. These are the tricks that got you to Switzerland. In Davos that evening Axel told Pym all about his nightmare journey from Carlsbad to Bern. Pym felt so proud and rich he decided that Thomas Mann was the best writer in the world.

"Dear Father"—he wrote jubilantly as soon as he was back in the attic—"I am having a really wizard time here now and getting some first-rate instruction. I cannot tell you how much I miss your worldly counsel and how grateful I am for your wisdom in sending me to Switzerland for my studies. Today I met lawyers who really seem to know life in all its aspects, and I am sure they will be a help in furthering my career."

"Dear Belinda,

"Now that I have put my foot down, things are much better."

Meanwhile there was good old you, wasn't there, Jack? Jack the other war hero, Jack the other side of my head. I will describe to you who you were because I don't expect we know the same person any more. I will describe what you were to me and what I did for you and as best I can why, because there again I doubt whether we share the same interpretation of events and personalities. I doubt it very much. To Jack, Pym was just another baby Joe, one more addition to his private army in the making, not broken and certainly not trained, but with the halter already slipped nicely round his neck and willing to run a long way for his lump of sugar. You probably don't remember—why should you?—how you picked him up or made your overtures to him. All you knew was he was the type the Firm liked, and so did you, and so did part of me. Short back and sides, speaks the King's English, decent linguist, good country public school. A games player, understands discipline. Not an arty chap, certainly not one of your overintellectual types. Level-headed, one of us. Comfortably off but not too grand, father some sort of minor tycoon—how typical that you never bothered to check Rick out. And where else should you meet this paragon of tomorrow's men but at the English church, where the flag of Saint George fluttered victorious in the neutral Swiss breeze?

How long you had been tracking Pym I don't know. I'll bet you don't either. You liked the way he read the Lesson, you said, so you must have had your eye on him from at least before Christmas because it was an early Advent text. You seemed surprised when he told you he was studying at the university, so I guess your first enquiries were made before he enrolled there and you hadn't topped them up. It was on Christmas Day after matins that Pym shook your hand for the first time. The church porch was like a crowded lift with everyone rattling umbrellas and making rah-rah English noises, and the diplomatic kids pelting each other with snowballs in the street. Pym was wearing his E. Weber jacket, and you, Jack, you were a tweedy, unscalable English mountain of twenty-four. In terms of war and peace the seven years between us were a generation, more like two. Much as they were with Axel, as a matter of fact; you both had those crucial years on me, still do.

Do you know what else you wore apart from your good brown suit? Your Airborne tie. Prancing silver-winged horses and crowned Britannias on a maroon field, congratulations. You never told me where you had been for it, but the reality as I now know it is no less impressive than my imaginings: with the Partisans in Yugoslavia and the Resistance in Czechoslovakia, behind the lines with the Long Range Desert Group in Africa and even, if I remember right, in Crete. You are an inch taller than I, but I remember as if it were yesterday how, as Pym grasped your great dry hand, that Airborne tie looked him in the eye. He lifted his head, he saw your rock jaw and your blue eyes—the ferocious bushy eyebrows even then—and he knew he was standing face to face with the character he was supposed to have become at all his schools, and sometimes in his fancy had: a straight-backed English brave of the officer class, the one who keeps his head when all about him are losing theirs. You wished him Happy Christmas and when you spoke your name he thought you were making a sort of Everyman's joke to do with Christmas Day—you are Good Fellowship and I will be Brotherhood.

"No, no, old boy, it's real," you insisted with a laugh. "Why should a nice chap like me use a false name?"

Why indeed, when you had diplomatic cover? You invited him for a glass of sherry before lunch tomorrow, Boxing Day, and you said you would have sent him an invitation if you'd known his address, which was clever of you, because of course you knew it perfectly well: address, date of birth, education and all the other nonsense we imagine gives us ascendancy over those we seek to obtain. Then you did an amusing thing. You took an invitation card from your pocket and in the crammed porch while everyone went on woof-woofing you spun Pym round and, using his back to press on, wrote his name along the middle line and handed it to him: "Captain and Mrs. Jack Brotherhood request the pleasure." You scratched out the "RSVP" to emphasise that the deal was done, and you scratched out the "Captain" to show what pals we were. "If you want to stay on afterwards you can help us eat up the cold turkey. Rough clothes," you added. Pym watched you stride off through the rain exactly as he knew you had carried yourself through the gunfire of all the battlefields where you had triumphed single-handed over Jerry, while Pym was doing nothing braver than carve Sefton Boyd's initials on the wall of the staff lavatory.

Next day he presented himself punctually at your little diplomatic house, and as he pressed the bell he read your visiting card framed in the panel above it. "Captain J. Brotherhood, Assistant Passport Officer, British Embassy, Bern." You were married to Felicity in those days, you may remember. Adrian was six months old. Pym played with him for hours in order to impress you, a habit that soon became a feature of his dealings with the younger members of your trade. You questioned him in a perfectly agreeable way and, where you left off, Felicity as the good Secret Service squaw took over, God forgive her: "But what *friends* have you got, Magnus, you must be so *lonely* here?" she cried. "What do you do for *fun*, Magnus?" And was there much in the way of an extracurricular life at the university, for instance—she asked—political groups and so forth? Or was it all a bit flat and dreary like the rest of Bern? Pym didn't find Bern flat or dreary at all, but for Felicity he pretended he did. In the chronology, Pym's friendship with Axel was by now twelve hours old, but he didn't give him a thought—why should he when he was so taken up with impressing you both with himself?

I remember asking what crowd you fought with, sir, expecting you to say "Fifth Airborne," or "Artists' Rifles" so that I could look suitably awed. Instead you went a bit gruff and said, "General List." I know now that you were exercising the double standard of diplomatic cover: you wanted it to cover you, but you also wanted Pym to see through it. You wanted him to know you were an irregular, and not one of those intellectual little ponces from the Foreign Office, as you call them. You asked him whether he got around the country and suggested that, on occasions when you were making an official car journey somewhere, he might like to come aboard and amuse himself the other end. The two of us put on boots and went for what you called a bash: meaning a forced march through the Elfenau woods. In the course of it you told Pym he needn't call you "sir," and when we came back, Felicity had fed Adrian, and there was an older, smirking man sitting talking to her. You introduced him as Sandy from the Embassy and Pym sensed you were colleagues and vaguely that Sandy was your boss. I know now that he was your Station Head and you were his number two, and that he was performing his standard task of looking over the property before allowing you to buy your way any further in. But at the time Pym just thought of Sandy as headmaster and you as housemaster, a construction you would not have disapproved of.

"How good's your German, by the by?" Sandy asked Pym through his smirk while the three of us munched Felicity's mince pies. "Bit hard to learn here, isn't it, with all this Swissie dialect about?"

"Magnus knows rather a lot of university émigrés," you explained for me, underlining a selling point. Sandy let out a silly laugh and slapped his knee.

"Does he, does he though? I'll bet there's some rum characters among *that* crowd!"

"He could probably tell us a good deal about them too, couldn't you, Magnus?" you said.

"You wouldn't mind?" said Sandy quizzically, still smirking.

"Why should I?" said Pym.

Sandy forced the card cleverly. He sensed that Pym liked taking rash decisions in front of people, and he used this knowledge to press a commitment out of him before he knew what he was committing to.

"No high-minded scruples about the sanctity of academic study or anything like that?" Sandy insisted.

"None at all," said Pym boldly. "Not if it's for my country," and was rewarded by Felicity's smile.

What version of himself Pym supplied that day, and had to live with for the coming months, I do not remember, which means it must have been a fairly restrained one, short on those awkward story-points that too often had to be paid for later. As best he could, he gave you what he thought you were looking for. He was prudent enough not to admit he was earning money, which went down well with you, for you knew already he was working "black," as the Germans call it— meaning illegally, and at night. Shrewd chap, you thought; resourceful; not above a bit of larceny. He played down family life with the Ollingers since proxy parents undermined his self-image as a mature exile. When you asked him whether he knew any girls—the shadow of homosexuality, is he one of those?—Pym got the message at once, and wove a harmless fantasy around an Italian beauty called Maria whom he had met at the Cosmo Club and was keen on, but only as a stopgap for his regular girlfriend Jemima, back in England.

"Jemima who?" you asked, and Pym said Sefton Boyd, which produced an audible sigh of social satisfaction. A real Maria did indeed exist and was indeed beautiful but Pym's adoration of her was private to himself, for he had never spoken to her.

"Cosmo?" said you. "Don't think I've heard of that one. Have you, Sandy?"

"Can't say I have, old boy. Sounds fishy to me."

Pym explained that the Cosmo was a sort of foreigners' political forum, and Maria was some sort of officer of it, like treasurer.

"Any particular complexion?" Sandy asked.

"Well she's dark," said Pym ingenuously and you and Felicity and Sandy laughed and laughed, like Little Audrey, and Felicity remarked that it was *quite* clear what Magnus's politics were. After that no meeting was complete without somebody asking after Maria's complexion, and everyone cracking up over such a marvelously healthy misunderstanding. It was evening by the time Pym left your house and you had given him a present of a duty-free bottle of scotch to keep out the cold. Cost to the Firm in those days: I guess around five shillings. You offered to run him home but he said he loved to walk, thus earning further Brownie points. And walk he did, on air. He skipped and laughed and hugged his bottle and himself; he hadn't felt so blessed in all his seventeen years. In a single Christmas, God had dished him up two saints. The one was on the run and couldn't walk, the other was a handsome English warlord who served sherry on Boxing Day and had never had a doubt in his life. Both admired him, both loved his jokes and his voices, both were clamouring to occupy the empty spaces of his heart. In return he was giving to each man the character he seemed to be in search of. His decision to keep them secret from each other was never taken. Let each be the mistress that keeps the other home intact, Pym thought. If he thought at all.

"From whom did you steal it, Sir Magnus?" Axel asked in his formal English, looking curiously at the label.

"The chaplain," said Pym without a second's hesitation. "He's a terrific bloke. Ex-army. I didn't steal it. He gave it me, actually. A free bottle for regular attenders. They get it at diplomatic rates, of course. They don't have to pay like in the shops."

"He didn't offer you cigarettes as well, did he?" said Axel.

"Why should he?"

"A bar of chocolate for a night with your sister?"

"I haven't got a sister."

"Good. Then let's drink it."

Do you remember our car journeys, Jack? I begin to think you do. Have you ever wondered how our forebears managed to run their agents in the days before the motorcar? Our first trip could not have come more handy. You had a date in Lausanne. You would need three hours. You gave no reason why you needed three hours in Lausanne, though you could have given me any cover story under the sun. Once again with the advantage of hindsight I know that you were deliberately admitting me to the secrecy of your work without letting on what the work was. You asked nothing of Pym on that occasion. You were building intimacy. The most you did was give him a rendezvous and a fallback and see whether he managed them. "Look here, it's just possible I'll have to make another call. If I'm not outside the Hotel Dora at three, be at the west side of the main post office at three-twenty." Pym wasn't good at east and west but he asked about six people till one of them got it right for him, and he made the fallback at three-twenty exactly, even if he was panting his heart out. You circled the square and the second time round you kept the car rolling and pushed open the door, and Pym hopped in like an airborne soldier to show you how able he was.

"I've been talking to Sandy," you said as we drove to Geneva a week later. "He wants you to do a job for him. Mind?"

"Of course not."

"You any good at translation?"

"What sort?"

"Can you keep your mouth shut?"

"I think so."

You gave him his first Target for Tonight: "We get technical stuff in from time to time. Mainly about funny little Swissie firms that are manufacturing things we don't much like. Nasty things that blow up," you added with a smile. "It's not exactly secret, but we hire a lot of local labour in the Embassy so we'd rather have it done by someone outside. Preferably a Brit. Someone we trust. You game?"

"Of course."

"We pay. Not much, but it'll buy you a dinner with Maria now and then. Heard from Jemima recently?"

"Jem's fine, thanks."

Pym had never been so scared in his life. You handed him the envelope, he put it in his pocket, you gave him your Master of Intrigue look and said "Good luck, old chap"—Yes, Jack, you did! We talked to each other like that—and Pym walked home changing that damned envelope from one pocket to another so many times he must have looked like a bookie on the run. And what was in it? Don't tell me, I'll tell you: junk. Photocopied junk from out-of-date armaments catalogues. It was Pym's soul you were after, not the piffling translation. He lost the envelope about six times in his attic too. Under the bed, under the mattress, behind the mirror, up the chimney. He translated its contents in hours even Axel didn't know he had. You paid Pym twenty francs. The technical dictionary had cost twenty-five but he knew that gentlemen didn't mention things like that, even if Rick's cheques, if they came at all, tended to meet with failure.

"Been to the Cosmo Club recently?" you enquired lightly as we headed towards Zurich, where you said you had a man to see about a dog. Pym confessed he had not. With Axel and Jack Brotherhood as his cosmos, who needed another?

"I'm told some of the people who go along there are a bit outspoken. Nothing against Maria, mind. Those outfits always have a broad spectrum. Part of democracy. Might be a good idea all the same if you took a closer look," you said. "Don't stick out. If they expect you to be a Leftie, let them think you are one. If they're looking for a Right-of-centre Brit, give 'em one. If necessary give 'em both. But don't go overboard. We don't want you getting into trouble with the Swissies. Any other Brits there, apart from you?"

"There are a couple of Scottish medical students but they told me they come for the girls."

"A few names would help," you said.

With that one conversation, looking back, Pym was Pym no longer. He was our man in the Cosmo, don't use the telephones for anything delicate. He was a symbolised agent, graded semi-conscious, which is our sweet way of saying he sort of half knows what he is sort of doing and sort of why. He was seventeen years old, and if he needed you urgently he was to ring Felicity and say his uncle was in town. If you needed him you'd phone the Ollingers from a callbox and say you were Mac from Birmingham passing through. Otherwise it was meeting-to-meeting, which means we always fix the next one at this one. Float, Magnus, you said. Get in there and be your own charming self, Magnus. Keep your ears and eyes open, see what sticks, but for God's sake don't get us into trouble with the Swissies. And here's your next month's alimony, Magnus. And Sandy sends his love. I tell you, Jack: we reap as we sow, even if the harvest is thirty-five summers in the growing.

The secretary of the Cosmo was a vapid Rumanian royalist called Anka who wept unaccountably in lectures. She was gangly and wild and walked with her wrists turned inside out, and when Pym stopped her in the corridor she scowled at him with red eyes and told him to go away because she had a headache. But Pym was on spy's business and brooked no rejection.

"I'm thinking of starting a Cosmo newsletter," he announced. "I thought we might include a contribution from each group."

"The Cosmo don't got no groups. The Cosmo don't want no newsletter. You are stupid. Go away."

Pym pursued Anka to the tiny office that was her lair.

"All I need is a list of members," he said. "If I have a list of members I can send out a circular and find out who is interested."

"Why don't you come to next meeting and ask them?" Anka said, sitting down and putting her head in her hands as if she were about to be sick.

"Not everyone comes to meetings. I want to test all shades. It's more democratic."

"Nothing is democratic," said Anka. "Is all illusion."

"He is an English," she explained to herself aloud as she hauled open a drawer and began to pick through its chaotic contents. "What does an English know about illusion?" she demanded of some private confessor. "He is mad." She handed him a grimy sheet of names and addresses. Most of them, it turned out later, were misspelt.

"Dearest Father" wrote Pym excitedly—"I am having one or two amazing successes here despite my youth, and I gather the Swissies are considering offering me some kind of academic honour."

"I love you"—he wrote to Belinda—"I've never written that to anyone before."

It is night. It is Bern's darkest winter. The city will never see day again. A smothering brown fog rolls down the wet cobble of the Herrengasse and the good Swiss hurry dutifully through it like reservists headed for the front. But Pym and Jack Brotherhood sit snugly in a corner of their little restaurant and Sandy has sent his extra-special love, together with his absolutely warmest congratulations. It is the first time agent and controller have eaten together in public in their target city. An ingenious cover story has been agreed in the event of a chance encounter. Jack has appointed himself secretary of the Embassy's Anglo-Swiss Christian Society and wishes to attract elements of the university. What more natural than he should turn to Magnus whom he knows from the English church? For deeper cover still he has brought the lovely Wendy who works in Chancery and is honey-haired and well-born, and has a slight but prominent protrusion of the upper lip as if she is permanently blowing out a candle just below her chin. Wendy loves both men equally; she is a natural and spontaneous toucher, with shallow, unfrightening breasts. When Pym has finished describing how he landed his great coup, Wendy cannot resist laying a hand along his cheek and saying, "God, Magnus, that was so brave. I mean marvellous. Wouldn't Jemima be proud if she was allowed to know. Don't you think so, Jack?" But all very quietly, in the soft-fall voice that even the horsiest must learn before they are let out of the paddock. And going very near to Jack with her hair to speak to him.

"You did a damn good job," says Brotherhood with his military smile. "Church should be proud of you," he adds, straight at his agent. They drink to Pym's good job for the church.

It is coffee time and Brotherhood has taken an envelope from one jacket pocket and from the other a pair of steel-framed half-moon spectacles which give a mysteriously finite authority to his British-brave face. Not alimony this time, for alimony comes in a white unwatermarked envelope, not a mousy-brown one like this. He does not hand it to Pym but opens it himself in full view of everyone who cares to watch, and asks Wendy for a pencil, dear, your flashy gold one, don't tell me how you earned *that*. And Wendy says, "For you, darling, anything," and drops it into his cupped hands, which close on hers. Jack spreads the paper out before him.

"Just want to check on a few of these addresses," he says. "Don't want to start sending out literature till we're sure. Okay?"

"Okay" meaning: Have you decoded this brilliant *double entendre?*

Pym says absolutely fine and Wendy trails a loving fingernail down the list, stopping at one or two lucky names that are marked with ticks and crosses.

"Only it seems that one or two members of our choir have been quite unduly modest about their personal particulars. Almost as if they wanted to hide their lights under a bushel," says Brotherhood.

"I didn't really look," says Pym.

Brotherhood's voice drops. "Nor should you. That's our job."

"We couldn't find your lovely Maria *anywhere*," says Wendy, frightfully disappointed. "What have you done with her?"

"I'm afraid she has gone back to Italy," says Pym.

"Not looking for a replacement, Magnus, are you, darling?" says Wendy, and all laugh uproariously, Pym loudest, though he would have given the rest of his life just for the sight of one of her breasts.

Brotherhood mentions names that have no addresses. Pym can help with none of them, cannot put faces to them, cannot supply character descriptions. In other circumstances, he would gladly have made some up but Brotherhood has an uncomfortable way of knowing answers before he asks questions and Pym is getting wise to this. Wendy refills the men's glasses and keeps the dregs for herself. Brotherhood passes to addresses that have no names.

"A.H.," he says carelessly. "Ring a bell? A.—H.?"

Pym confesses it does not. "I really haven't been to enough meetings yet," he says apologetically. "I've been having rather a hard slog at my work before exams."

Brotherhood is still smiling, still perfectly relaxed. Does he know that Pym is sitting no exams? Pym notices that Wendy's pencil has nearly vanished inside his closed fist. Its sharp end peaks out of it like a tiny gun barrel.

"Think a bit," Brotherhood suggests. And says it again, mouthing it slowly like a password: "A.—H."

"Perhaps it's A.H. somebody else," says Pym. "A. H. Smith. Schmidt. I could find a way of asking if you like. It's all quite open really."

Wendy has frozen in the way you freeze in party games when the music stops. Her smile has frozen with her. Wendy has the private secretary's art of suspending her personality until it is required and something has told her it is not required at present. The waiter is clearing plates. Brotherhood's fist is covering the paper so that quite by accident no names are visible to the passer-by.

"Would it help if I told you that A.H., whoever he is—or she is—shares a certain address in the Länggasse. Or says he does. Care of Ollinger. That's your place too, isn't it?"

"Oh you mean Axel," says Pym.

Somewhere a cock was crowing but Pym didn't hear it. His ears were full of a kind of waterfall, his heart was bursting with a sense of righteous duty. He was in Rick's dressing-room, looking for a way of stealing back the love he had given to a wrong cause. He was in the staff lavatory, doing a knife job on the classiest boy in the school. There were the stories Axel had told him when he was delirious and spilling his drinking water with both hands. There were the stories he had told him in Davos when they went to visit Thomas Mann's sanatorium. There were the crumbs he had gleaned for himself on his occasional precautionary inspections of Axel's room. And there was Brotherhood's clever prompting that dragged things out of him he hadn't realised he knew. Axel's father had fought with the Thälmann brigade in Spain, he said. He was an old-style Social Democrat, so he was lucky to die before the Nazis could arrest him.

"So he's a Leftie?"

"He's dead."

"I meant the son."

"Well not really, not that he's said. He's just catching up on his education. He's uncommitted."

Brotherhood pressed his eyebrows together and pencilled "Thälmann" on his choir list. Axel's mother was Catholic but his father had been a member of the anti-Catholic *Los von Rom* movement, which was Lutheran, Pym said. His mother lost her right to confession because she had married a Protestant.

"And a Socialist," Brotherhood reminded Pym, under his breath, as he wrote.

At the *Gymnasium* Axel's friends all wanted to fly planes against England but Axel was persuaded by the visiting recruiting teams to volunteer for the army. He was posted to Russia, taken prisoner and escaped, but when the Allies invaded France he was pulled out to fight in Normandy where he was wounded in the spine and hip.

"Did he tell you *how* he escaped from the Russians?" Brotherhood cut in.

"He said he walked."

"Like he walked to Switzerland," said Brotherhood with a hard smile and Pym began to see a pattern that he had not thought of until Brotherhood suggested it.

"How long was he there?"

"I don't know. But long enough to learn Russian anyway. He's got books in Cyrillic in his room."

Back in Germany he went ill from his wounds but as soon as he was well enough to walk he was sent to fight the Americans. He was wounded again and sent back to Carlsbad where his mother was laid up with jaundice, so he put her on a cart with her possessions and pushed her to Dresden, a beautiful city that the Allies had recently bombed flat. He took his mother to the district where the Silesian refugees had gathered but she died soon after he got her there, so he was alone. By now Pym's head was swimming. The colours on the wall behind Brotherhood's head were merging and sliding. It's not me. It's me. I'm doing my duty for my country. Axel, help me.

"Right-ho, now it's peacetime. 'Forty-five. What does he do?"

"Gets out of the Soviet Zone."

"Why?"

"He was scared the Russians would find him and put him back in prison. He didn't like them and he didn't like prison and he didn't like the way the Communists were taking over Eastern Germany."

"Good story so far. What does he do about it?"

"He burns his paybook and buys another one."

"Where from?"

"A soldier he met in Carlsbad. Somebody who came from Munich who looked fairly like him. He said that in 1945 nobody in Germany looked like their photograph anyway."

"Why didn't this accommodating soldier want his papers?"

"He wanted to stay in the East."

"Why?"

"Axel didn't know."

"Bit thin, isn't it?"

"I suppose it is."

"On we go."

"He boarded the repatriation train to Munich and everything worked fine till he got to the other end, when the Americans pulled him straight off the train and put him into prison and beat him up."

"Why'd they do a thing like that?"

"It was because of his papers. He'd bought the papers of a wanted man. He'd just walked completely into a trap."

"Unless of course they were his own papers in the first place and he never bought them from anybody," Brotherhood suggested, writing again. "Sorry, old boy. Didn't mean to shatter your illusions. Way of the world, I'm afraid. How long did he do?"

"I don't know. He got ill again and they put him into hospital and he escaped from hospital."

"Pretty good at escaping, I must say. You say he walked here?"

"Well, walked and bummed rides on trains. They had to shorten one of his legs. The Germans did. After he came back from Russia. That's why he limps. I should have said that earlier. So I mean even with trains it was quite a walk. Munich to Austria, then Austria over the border at night to Switzerland. Then to Ostermundigen."

"To where?"

"That's where Herr Ollinger has his factory." Pym heard himself trying to make excuses. "He hasn't any papers at all, you see. He destroyed his own in Carlsbad. The Americans kept the ones he bought and he can't find anyone to give him a new set. Meanwhile he's still on the Allied wanted list. He says he'd have confessed everything the Americans asked if only he'd known what he was supposed to have done wrong. But he didn't, so they went on beating him."

"Heard that one before too," said Brotherhood under his breath, once more writing. "How does he spend his days here, Magnus? Who are his buddies?"

Far, far too late, voices were whispering Pym caution.

"He's afraid to go out in case the *Fremdenpolizei* arrest him. If he goes into town he borrows a big hat. It isn't only the *Fremdenpolizei*. If the ordinary Swissies knew about him they'd inform against him too. He says they do that. It's a national sport. He says they do it out of envy and call it civic-mindedness. It's just household gossip I'm telling you."

"Pity you didn't tell it to us earlier."

"It didn't mean anything. It wasn't anything you were interested in. Herr Ollinger told me most of it. He gossips all the time."

Brotherhood had his car outside. Man and boy were sitting in it but Brotherhood didn't drive anywhere. Wendy had gone home. Brotherhood asked about Axel's politics. Pym said Axel despised established attitudes. Brotherhood said, "Describe." He wasn't writing any more and his head was very still in the window frame. Pym said Axel had once remarked that pain was democratic.

"Reading habits?" said Brotherhood.

"Well, everything really. Everything he's missed from the war. He types a lot. Mostly at night."

"What does he type?"

"He says it's a book."

"What does he read?"

"Well, everything. Sometimes when he's ill I get books out of the library for him."

"In your own name?"

"Yes."

"That's a bit rash. What do you get?"

"The whole spectrum."

"Describe."

Pym described and came inevitably to Marx and Engels and the bad bears, and Brotherhood wrote all of them down, asking him who Duhring was when he was at home.

Brotherhood asked about Axel's habits. Pym said he liked cigars and vodka and sometimes kirsch. He didn't mention whisky.

Brotherhood asked about Axel's sex-life. Sweeping aside his own limitations in this respect, Pym declared it mixed.

"Describe," said Brotherhood again.

Pym did his best, though he knew even less about Axel's sexuality than his own, except that whatever form it took, unlike Pym he was on terms with it.

"He does sometimes have women," said Pym deprecatingly, as if that were something all of us did. "Usually she's some token beauty from the Cosmo, cooking for him or polishing his room. He calls them his Marthas. I thought at first he meant martyr."

"Dearest Father"—Pym wrote that night, alone and miserable in his attic—"I am absolutely fine and my head is buzzing from all the seminars and lectures, though I miss you terribly as ever. One bad thing however is that I had a pal who recently let me down."

How Pym loved Axel in the weeks that followed! For a day or so, it was true, he would not go near him, he resented him so much. He resented everything about him, every move on the other side of the radiator. He patronises me. He sneers at my ignorance without respecting my strengths. He is an arrogant German of the worst sort and Jack is right to keep his eye on him. Pym resented the mail he received, Herr Axel care of Ollinger. He resented more than ever the Marthas tiptoeing like shy disciples up the stairs to the great thinker's sanctum, and down again two hours later. He is dissolute. He is unnatural. He is turning their heads for them, exactly as he tried to turn mine. Diligently he kept a log of these developments to give to Brotherhood at their next meeting. He also spent a lot of time in the third-class buffet wearing his clouded look for the benefit of Elisabeth. But these exercises in separation did not endure and the line to Axel grew tighter with every day. He discovered he could gauge his friend's mood from the tempo of his typing: whether he was excited or angry or tired. He is reporting on us, he told himself without conviction. He is selling out the foreign students to his German paymaster. He is a Nazi war criminal turned Communist spy in the image of his Leftie father.

"When do we ever get to read it?" Pym had asked him once shyly in the days when they were close.

"If I ever finish it, and the publisher ever publishes it."

"Why can't I read it now?"

"Because you will take the cream off it for me, and leave me with the curds."

"What's it about?"

"Mysteries, Sir Magnus, and if they are spoken aloud they will never be written down."

He's writing his Wilhelm Meister autobiography, thought Pym indignantly. That was my idea, not his.

He could tell when Axel could not sleep by the striking of his matches as he lit his cigars. He could tell when his body was driving him mad. He told it by the altered rhythm of his movements and the determined gaiety of his singing as he clomped the wooden corridor to crouch for hours in their shared lavatory with its porcelain footprints. After several nights had passed that way Pym was able to loathe Axel for his incontinence. Why doesn't he go back to hospital? "He sings German marching songs," he wrote to Brotherhood in his notebook. "Tonight he sang the whole Horst Wessel Lied in the lavatory." On the third night, long after Pym had gone to bed, his door suddenly flew open and there stood Axel wrapped in Herr Ollinger's dressing-gown.

"Well? Have you forgiven me yet?"

"What have I got to forgive you for?" Pym replied, discreetly pushing his secret logbook under the bedclothes.

Axel stayed in the doorway. The dressing-gown was ridiculously large for him. Sweat had made black fangs of his moustache. "Give me some of your priest's whisky," he said.

After that Pym couldn't let Axel go until he had wiped the shadows of suspicion from his face. The weeks passed and spring began and Pym knew that nothing was happening, and that he had never betrayed Axel in the first place, because if he had they would have done something long ago. Occasionally Brotherhood asked a couple of follow-up questions but they had the ring of routine. Once he asked, "Can you tell me an evening when you know for certain he will be out?" But Pym was able to answer that there were no certainties in Axel's life. "Well look here. Why don't you take him out to a slap-up dinner at our expense?" said Brotherhood. One night Pym tried. He told Axel he had had a windfall from his father and wouldn't it be fun to put on disguise again like the time they called on Thomas Mann? Axel shook his head with a wisdom Pym dared not explore. After that Pym studied and strove for Axel in every way he knew, now denying to himself that Brotherhood existed anywhere but in his mind, now congratulating himself on Axel's continued survival, which was owed entirely to Pym's nimble manipulation of irresistible forces.

* * *

They came in the small hours of a spring morning, just when we fear them most: when we want to live the longest and are most afraid of dying. Soon, unless I make their journey unnecessary, they will come for me in the same way. If so, I trust I shall see the justice of it and relish the circularity of life. They had acquired a key to the front door and some method of detaching Herr Ollinger's chains which were not unlike Miss Dubber's. They knew the house inside out because they had been watching it for months, photographing our visitors, sending in their bogus meter men and window cleaners, delaying the mail while they read it and no doubt listening to Herr Ollinger's forlorn telephone conversations with his creditors and lame ducks. Pym knew there were three of them because he could count their stealthy Father Christmas footsteps on the squeaky top stair. They looked in the lavatory before they placed themselves outside Axel's door. Pym knew this because he heard the lavatory door squeak and stay open. He also heard a rattle as they removed the lavatory-door key in case their desperate criminal should attempt to lock himself inside. But Pym could do nothing personally because at the time he lay deeply dreaming in all the scared beds of his childhood. He dreamt about Lippsie and her brother Aaron and how he and Aaron together had pushed her off the rooftop at Mr. Grimble's school. He dreamt that an ambulance was waiting outside the house like the one that called at The Glades for Dorothy, and that Herr Ollinger was trying to stop the men coming up the stairs but was being ordered back to his quarters in a fury of Swiss dialect. He dreamt that he heard a shout of "Pym, you bastard, where are you?" from the direction of Axel's room and directly afterwards the awful brief thundering noise of a man with uneven legs struggling against three healthy intruders and the furious opposition of Bastl whom Axel had once accused of being his Faustian Devil. But when he lifted his head from the pillow and listened to the real world, there was silence and everything was absolutely fine.

I held it against you, Jack, I confess. I argued with you in my head for years, uphill, downhill, and long after I had joined the Firm. Why had you done it to him? He wasn't English, he wasn't a Communist, he wasn't the war criminal the Americans claimed he was. He was nothing to do with you. His only crimes were his poverty, his illegal presence and his lameness—plus a certain freedom in his way of thinking, which in the eyes of some is what we are there to protect. But I did nurse a grudge and I'm sorry. Because now of course I know you hardly gave it a thought. Axel was another bit of barter material. You wrote him up; he came back into your in-tray looking formidable and sinister in Wendy's flawless type. You lit your pipe and admired your handiwork, and you thought: Hullo, I'll bet the old Swissies will like a smell of this one; I'll pop it down to them and earn myself a Brownie point. You made a phone call or two and invited some contact in the Swiss Security Service to join you for an extended luncheon at your favourite restaurant. Over the coffee and the schnapps you slipped him an anonymous brown envelope. As an afterthought you slipped a copy to your American colleague too, because if you're going to earn one favour, why not earn a second while you're about it? After all, it was the Yanks who put him in the cooler, even if they got his record wrong.

You were junior then, too, weren't you? You had your way to make. As we all have. Maturer now, both of us. Sorry to be so lengthy in the remembering, but the episode took me rather a long time to forget. I've got it straight now. Served me right for having a friend outside the service.

"Mr. Canterbury! Mr. Canterbury! You've got a man!"

Pym had put down his pen. He had not looked towards the door. Almost before he was aware of it, he had leapt to his slippered feet and was flying across the room to where the metal-lined black briefcase, still locked, stood against the wall. Dropping to a crouch beside it, he inserted the complicated key in the first lock and sprung it. Then the second: anti-clockwise or it fires.

"What man's that, Miss D?" he said in his softest and most reassuring tone, one hand already in the case.

"With a *cabinet,* Mr. Canterbury," Miss Dubber replied with disapproval through the keyhole. "You've never had a cabinet before. You've never had anything. You've never locked your door either. What's wrong?"

Pym laughed. "Nothing's wrong. It's just a cabinet. I ordered it. How many of them are there?"

Taking the briefcase with him, he tiptoed to the window and squared his back against the wall while he squinted cautiously through the gap in the curtain.

"Just one—isn't that enough? A great green ugly one made of iron. If you'd wanted a cabinet why didn't you tell me? You could have had Mrs. Tutton's cupboard from room two."

"I meant how many men?"

It was daylight. A yellow taxi-truck was parked outside the house, the driver at the wheel. He glanced round the rest of the square. Fast. Checking everything. Then slowly. Checking everything again.

"What does it matter how many men, Mr. Canterbury? Why do we have to count the men when it's a cabinet?"

Relaxing, Pym replaced the briefcase in its corner and relocked it. Clockwise or it fires. He returned the keys to his pocket. He opened the door.

"Sorry, Miss D. I think I must have been dozing."

She watched him down the stairs, then went after him and watched again as he looked first at the two men, then shyly at the green cabinet, lightly touching its chipped paintwork, up and down, tugging at each drawer in turn.

"It's a bloody weight, governor, I'll tell you," said the first.

"Who's it got in it then?" said the second.

She watched him lead the men up to his room, the cabinet between them, and lead them down again. She watched him pay their bill in cash from his back pocket, and give them an extra five pounds for themselves.

"Sorry about that, Miss D," he said as they drove off. "Some old Ministry archives I'm working on. Here. This is for you." He handed her a travel brochure he had brought down with him from his room. There was a whiff of Rick about the capitals. "Discover Tunisia in the Luxury of our air-conditioned Coach. Seniors a Speciality. Shades of the East in the Mediterranean. Enough to make your mouth Water."

But Miss Dubber would not accept the brochure. "Toby and I aren't going anywhere any more, Mr. Canterbury," she said. "Whatever's troubling you won't go away with us. That's for sure."

9

B rotherhood had bathed and shaved and cut himself and put on a suit. He had listened to the news on the BBC and afterwards tuned to the Deutsche Welle because sometimes the foreign press got hold of stories while Fleet Street was still obediently suppressing them. But he had heard no lighthearted mention of a senior officer of the British Secret Service going walkabout or turning up in Moscow. He had eaten a piece of toast and marmalade, he had made a few phone calls but six till eight of an English morning were the dead hours when nobody except himself was about. On a normal day he would have walked across the park to Head Office and given himself a couple of hours at his desk reading the night's crop of Station reports and preparing himself for the ten-o'clock prayer session in Bo's sanctum. "So how's our Eastern Front this rainy morning, Jack?" Bo would say in a tone of jokey veneration, when Brotherhood's turn came round. And a respectful quiet would follow while the great Jack Brotherhood gave his chief the score. "Some quite nice stuff from Conger on the Comecon trading figures for last year, Bo. We've sent it up to Treasury by special bag. Otherwise it's the silly season. Joes are on holiday, so's the opposition."

But this was not a normal day and Brotherhood was no longer the grand old man of covert operations that Bo cracked him up to be when he introduced him to visiting firemen from Western liaison services. He was the latest unperson in the latest looming scandal and, as he stepped into the street below his flat, his quick gaze was more than usually vigilant. It was eight-thirty. First he headed south across Green Park, walking as fast as ever and perhaps a little faster, so that Nigel's watchers, if they were on him, would either have to gallop or radio for somebody to get ahead of him. The night's rain had stopped. Warm, unhealthy mist hung over the ponds and willows. Reaching the Mall he hailed a cab and told the driver Tottenham Court Road. He walked again and took a second cab to Kentish Town. His destination was a grey hillside of Victorian villas. The lower reaches were still run down, their windows plugged with corrugated iron against squatters. But higher up Volvo estate cars and teak-framed dormer windows testified to the safe arrival of the middle classes, and the long gardens boasted coloured climbing frames and half-made dinghies. Here Brotherhood was no longer in a hurry. He trudged up the hill slowly, noting everything at his leisure: this is the pace I have earned in life, this is the smile. A pretty girl passed him on her way to work and he greeted her indulgently. She winked pertly back at him, proving for all time that she was not a watcher. At number 18 he paused and in the manner of a prospective purchaser stood back and surveyed the house. Bach and a smell of breakfast issued from the ground-floor kitchen. A wooden arrow marked "18A" pointed down the basement steps. A man's bicycle was chained against the railings, a poster for the Social Democratic Party hung in the bay window. He pressed the bell. A girl in a blazer opened the door to him. At thirteen she already wore an air of superiority.

"I'll get Mummy," she said before he could speak, and turned sharply so that he could watch her skirt swing. "Mummy. It's a man. For you," she said and, sweeping past him down the steps, set off for her decent school.

"Hullo, Belinda," Brotherhood said. "It's me."

Coming out of the kitchen, Belinda paused at the foot of the stairs, drew a breath and yelled up them at a closed door. "Paul! Come down at once, please. Jack Brotherhood is here. I assume he wants something."

Which more or less was what he knew she'd shout—though not quite so loud —because Belinda had always reacted badly first and put it right rather sweetly later.

They sat in a pine drawing-room on low basketwork chairs that creaked like swings when you moved. A gigantic lampshade of white paper rocked crookedly above them. Belinda had made coffee in hand-thrown mugs and sweetened it with natural sugar. Her Bach still played defiantly in the kitchen. She was dark-eyed and angry about something in her childhood—at fifty her face was still set ready for another quarrel with her mother. She had greying hair bound in a sensible bun and wore a necklace of what looked like nutmeg. When she walked, she waded through her kaftan as if she hated it. When she sat, she spread her knees and scraped at the knuckles of one hand. Yet her beauty clung to her like an identity she was trying to deny and her plainness kept slipping like a bad disguise.

"They've already been here in case you don't know, Jack," she said. "At ten at night as a matter of fact. They were waiting for us on the doorstep when we got back from the cottage."

"Who's they?"

"Nigel. Lorimer. Two more I didn't know. All men, of course."

"What did they say they were here for?" Brotherhood asked, but Paul stopped him.

You could never be angry with Paul. He smiled so wisely through his pipe smoke even when he was being rude. "What is this actually, Jack?" he said, taking his pipe from his mouth and lowering it until it became a hand microphone. "Interrogations about interrogations? You people have no constitutional position, you know, Jack. You're only a chartered body even under this government, I'm afraid."

"You probably don't know it, but Paul has written extensively on the rise and rise of the para-military services under the Tories," Belinda said in a voice that struggled to be harsh. "You'd know if you'd bother to read The Guardian, but you don't. They gave him a whole page for the last one."

"So screw you actually, Jack," said Paul just as pleasantly.

Brotherhood smiled. Paul smiled. An old English sheepdog wandered in and settled at Brotherhood's feet.

"Do you want to smoke, by the way?" said Paul, ever sensitive to people's needs. "I'm afraid Belinda draws the line at fags but I can offer you a nifty little brown one if you're pushed."

Brotherhood pulled out a packet of his foul cigarettes and lit one. "Screw you too, Paul," he said equably.

Paul had peaked early in life. Twenty years ago he had written promising plays for fringe theatres. He wrote them still. He was tall but reassuringly unathletic. Twice, to Brotherhood's knowledge, he had applied to join the Firm. Each time he had been turned down flat, even without Brotherhood's intervention.

"They came here because they were vetting Magnus for a top appointment, if you want to know," Belinda said all in one breath. "They were in a hurry because they wanted to promote him immediately so that he could get on with the job."

"Nigel?" Brotherhood echoed with an incredulous laugh. "Nigel and Lorimer plus two other men? Doing their own vetting at ten o'clock at night? You've got half the brass of secret Whitehall on your doorstep there, Bel. Not a vetting team of old crocks on half pay."

"It's a senior appointment so he has to be vetted by senior people," Belinda retorted, blushing scarlet.

"Did Nigel tell you that?"

"Yes, he did!" said Belinda.

"Did you believe it?"

But Paul had decided it was time to show his mettle. "Actually, fuck off will you, Jack?" he said. "Get out of the house. Now. Darling, don't answer him. It's all too theatrical and stupid for words. Come on, Jack. Out. You're welcome for a drink any time, as long as you phone first. But not for this nonsense. Sorry. Out."

He had opened the door and was flapping his big soft hand as if scooping water but neither Brotherhood nor the sheepdog stirred.

"Magnus has jumped ship," Brotherhood explained to Belinda, while Paul put on his I-can-be-violent glower. "Nigel and Lorimer sold you a load of cock. Magnus has bolted and gone into hiding while they cook up a case against him as the big traitor of the Western world. I'm his boss so I'm not quite as enthusiastic as they are. I think he's strayed but not lost and I'd like to get to him first and talk to him." Addressing Paul, he didn't even bother to turn his head. He just lifted it far enough to make the difference. "They've put a muzzle on your editor for the time being, same as everybody else, Paul. But if Nigel has his way, in a few days' time your colleagues will be plastering Belinda's previous marriage all over their nasty little columns and taking your picture every time you go to the launderette. So you'd better start thinking about how to get your act together. In the meantime, fetch us some more coffee and leave us in peace for an hour."

Alone, Belinda was much stronger than when protected by her mate. Her face, though dazed, had relaxed. Her gaze had fixed itself steadfastly on a spot a few feet from her eyes, as if to suggest that although she might not see as far as others, her faith in what she saw burned twice as bright. They sat at a round table in the window bay and the Venetian blind sliced the Social Democratic Party into strips.

"His father's dead," Brotherhood said.

"I know. I read. Nigel told me. He asked me how it might have affected Magnus. I suppose that was a trick."

Brotherhood took a moment to answer this. "Not entirely," he said. "No. Not a complete trick, Belinda. I think they're reasoning that it could have turned his head a little."

"Magnus always wanted me to save him from Rick. I did my best. I tried to explain that to Nigel."

"How save him, Belinda?"

"Hide him. Answer the phone for him. Say he was abroad when he wasn't. I sometimes think that's why Magnus joined the Firm. As a hiding place. Just as he married me because he was scared to risk it with Jemima."

"Who's Jemima?" said Brotherhood, playing ignorant.

"She was a close friend of mine at school." She scowled. "Too close." The scowl softened and became melancholy. "Poor Rick. I only ever saw him once. That was at our wedding. He turned up uninvited in the middle of the reception. I never saw Magnus look happier. Otherwise he was just a voice on the telephone. He had a nice voice."

"Magnus have any other hiding places in those days?"

"You mean women, don't you? You can say it if you want. I don't mind any more."

"Just somewhere he might have hidden. That's all. Little cottage somewhere. An old buddy. Where would he go, Belinda? Who'd have him?"

Her hands, now that she had unlocked them, were elegant and expressive. "He'd have gone anywhere. He was a new man every day. He'd come home one person, I'd try to match him. In the morning he'd be someone else. Do you think he did it, Jack?"

"Do you?"

"You always answer one question with another. I'd forgotten. Magnus had the same trick." He waited. "You could try Sef," she said. "Sef was always loyal."

"Sef?"

"Kenneth Sefton Boyd. Jemima's brother. 'Sef's too rich for my blood,' Magnus used to say. That meant they were equals."

"Could Magnus have gone to him?"

"If it was bad enough."

"Could he have gone to Jemima?"

She shook her head.

"Why not?"

"I understand she's gone off men these days," she said and blushed again. "She's not predictable. She never was."

"Ever heard of anyone called Wentworth?"

She shook her head, still thinking of something different. "Since my time," she said.

"Poppy?"

"My time ended with Mary. If there's a Poppy, that's Mary's bad luck."

"When did you last hear from him, Belinda?"

"That's what Nigel asked me."

"What did you say to Nigel?"

"I said there was no reason to hear from him after we divorced. We'd been married six years. There were no children. It was a mistake. Why relive it?"

"Was that the truth?"

"No. I lied."

"What were you concealing?"

"He rang. Magnus did."

"When?"

"Monday night. Paul was out, thank God." She paused, listening for the sound of Paul's typewriter, which was tapping reassuringly from upstairs. "He sounded strange. I thought he was drunk. It was late."

"What time?"

"It must have been around eleven. Lucy was still doing her homework. I won't let her work after eleven as a rule but she was doing a French mock O-level. He was in a phone box."

"Cash?"

"Yes."

"Where?"

"He didn't say. He just said, 'Rick's dead. I wish we'd had a child.' "

"That all?"

"He said he'd always hated himself for marrying me. Now he was reconciled. He understood himself. And he loved me for trying so hard. Thanks."

"That all?"

" 'Thanks. Thanks for everything. And please forgive the bad parts.' Then he rang off."

"Did you tell Nigel this?"

"Why do you keep asking me that? I didn't think it was Nigel's business. I didn't want to say he was being drunk and sentimental on the phone late at night just at the time when they were considering him for promotion. Serves him right for deceiving me."

"What else did Nigel ask you?"

"Just character stuff. Had I ever had any reason to suppose Magnus might have had Communist sympathies. I said Oxford. Nigel said they knew about that. I said I didn't think university politics meant much anyway. Nigel agreed. Had he ever been erratic in any way? Unstable—alcoholic—depressive? I said no again. I didn't reckon one drunken phone call constituted drunkenness, but if it did I wasn't going to tell four of Magnus's colleagues about it. I felt protective of him."

"They ought to have known you better, Belinda," said Brotherhood. "Would you have given him the job yourself, by the way?"

"What job? You said there wasn't one." She was being sharp with him, belatedly suspecting him too of duplicity.

"I meant suppose there had been a job. A high-level, responsible job. Would you give it to him?"

She smiled. Very prettily. "I did, didn't I? I married him."

"You're wiser now. Would you give it to him today?"

She was biting her forefinger, frowning angrily. She could change moods in moments. Brotherhood waited but nothing came so he asked her another question: "Did they ask you about his time in Graz, by any chance?"

"Graz? You mean his army time? Good heavens, they didn't go back *that* far."

Brotherhood shook his head as if to say he would never be equal to the wicked ways of the world. "Graz is where they're trying to say it all started, Bel," he said. "They've got some grand theory he fell among thieves while he was doing his National Service there. What do you make of that?"

"They're absurd," she said.

"Why are you so sure?"

"He was happy there. When he came back to England he was a new man. 'I'm complete,' he kept saying. 'I've done it, Bel. I've got my other half together.' He was proud he'd done such good work."

"Did he describe the work?"

"He couldn't. It was too secret and too dangerous. He just said I would be proud of him if I knew."

"Did he tell you the name of any of the operations he was mixed up in?"

"No."

"Did he tell you the names of any of his Joes?"

"Don't be absurd. He wouldn't do that."

"Did he mention his C.O.?"

"He said he was brilliant. Everyone was brilliant for Magnus when they were new."

"If I said 'Greensleeves' to you in a loud voice, would that ring any bells?"

"It would mean English traditional music."

"Ever hear of a girl called Sabina?"

She shook her head. "He told me I was his first," she said.

"Did you believe him?"

"It's hard to tell when it's the first for you too."

With Belinda, he remembered, the quiet was always good. If her charges into the lists had something comic about them, there was always dignity to the calm between.

"So Nigel and his friends went away happy," he suggested. "Did you?"

Her face against the window was in silhouette. He waited for it to lift or turn to him, but it didn't.

"Where would you look for him?" he said. "If you were me?"

Still she did not move or speak.

"Some place by the sea somewhere? He had these fantasies, you know. He chopped them up and gave a bit to each person. Did he ever give a version to you? Scotland? Canada? The migration of the reindeer? Some kind lady who'd take him in? I need to know, Belinda. I really do."

"I won't talk to you any more, Jack. Paul's right. I don't have to."

"Not whatever he's done? Not to save him perhaps?"

"I don't trust you. Specially when you're being nice. You invented him, Jack. He'd have done whatever you told him. Who to be. Who to marry. Who to divorce. If he's done wrong it's as much your fault as his. It was easy to get rid of me—he just gave me the latch key and went to a lawyer. How was he supposed to get rid of you?"

Brotherhood moved towards the door.

"If you find him, tell him not to ring again. And Jack?" Brotherhood paused. Her face was soft again, and hopeful. "Did he write that book he was always on about?"

"Which book was that?"

"The great autobiographical novel that was going to change the world."

"Should he have done?"

" 'One day I'm going to lock myself away and tell the truth.' 'Why do you have to lock yourself away? Tell it now,' I said. He didn't seem to think he could. I'm not going to let Lucy marry early. Nor's Paul. We're going to put her on the pill and let her have affairs."

"Lock himself away *where*, Belinda?"

The light once more faded from her face. "You brought it on yourselves, Jack. All of you. He'd have been all right if he'd never met people like you."

Wait, Grant Lederer told himself. They all hate you. You hate most of them. Be a clever boy and wait your turn. Ten men sat in a room inside a room. In the false walls, false windows looked onto plastic flowers. From places like this, thought Lederer, America lost her wars against the little brown men in black pyjamas. From places like this, he thought—from smoked-glass rooms, cut off from humankind —America will lose all her wars except the last. A few yards beyond the walls lay the placid diplomatic backwaters of St. John's Wood. But here inside they could have been in Langley or Saigon.

"Harry, with the greatest *possible* respect," Mountjoy of the Cabinet Office piped with very little respect at all. "These early indicators of yours could perfectly easily have been dumped on us by an unscrupulous opposition, as some of us have been saying all along. Is it really fair to trot them out yet again? I thought we put all this stuff to bed back in August."

Wexler stared at the spectacles he was holding in both hands. They are too heavy for him, thought Lederer. He sees too clearly through them. Wexler lowered them to the table and scratched his veteran's crew cut with his stubby fingertips. What's holding you up? Lederer demanded of him silently. Are you translating English into English? Are you paralysed by jet-lag after flying Concorde all the way from Washington? Or are you in awe of these English gentlemen who never tire of telling us how they set up our service in the first place and generously invited us to sup at their high table? You're a top man of the best intelligence agency in the world, for Christ's sake. You're my boss. Why don't you stand up and be counted? As if in response to Lederer's silent pleading, Wexler's voice started functioning again with all the animation of a machine that speaks your weight.

"Gentlemen," Wexler resumed—except that he said "junnlemen." Reload, aim again, take your time, thought Lederer. "Our position, Sir Eric," Wexler resumed, with something unpleasantly close to a bow in the direction of Mountjoy's knight-hood, "that is—the ah Agency position overall on this thing—at this important meeting, and at this moment in time—is that we have here an accumulation of indicators from a wide range of sources on the one hand, and new data on the other which we consider pretty much conclusive in respect of our unease." He moistened his lips. So would I, thought Lederer. If I'd spoken that mouthful, I'd spit at least. "It looks to us therefore that the ah logistics here require us to go back over the ah course a little distance and—when we've done that—to ah slot the new stuff in where we can all take a good look at it in light of what has—ah latterly gone before." He turned to Brammel and his lined but innocent face broke into an apologetic smile. "You want to do it different in any way, Bo, why don't you just say so and see if we can accommodate you?"

"My dear chap, you must do exactly whatever makes you feel most comfort-able," said Brammel hospitably, which was what he had been saying to everybody all his life. So Wexler went back to his brief, first centering the folder before him on the table then tilting it cautiously to the right, as if landing it on one wingtip. And Grant Lederer III, who has the impression that the inside surfaces of his skin have been afflicted by an itchy rash, tries to lower his pulse rate and his blood heat and believe in the high level of this conference. Somewhere, he argues to himself, there is worth and secrecy and an all-knowing intelligence service. The only trouble is, it's in Heaven.

The British had fielded their usual intractable, over-fluent team. Hobsbawn, seconded from the Security Service, Mountjoy from the Cabinet Office and Dorney from the Foreign Office all lolled in varying positions of disbelief or outright contempt. Only the placement had changed, Lederer noticed: whereas Jack Brotherhood had hitherto been placed symbolically at Brammel's side, today that position had gone to Brammel's bagman, Nigel, and Brotherhood had been promoted to head of the table, where he presided like an old grey bird glowering down on his prey. On the American side of the table they were a mere four. How typical that in our Special Relationship the Brits should outnumber the Americans, thought Lederer. In the field the Agency outguns these bastards by about ninety to one. In here we're a persecuted minority. To Lederer's right, Harry Wexler, having cleared his throat not before time, had at last begun wrestling with the intricacies of what he insisted on calling the ongoing ah situation. To Lederer's left lounged Mick Carver, Head of the London Station, a spoilt Bostonian millionaire considered brilliant on no evidence Lederer was aware of. Below him the egregious Artelli, a distraught mathematician from Signals Intelligence, looked as though he had been hauled from Langley by his hair. And, between them, here sit I, Grant Lederer III, unlovable even to myself, the pushy law boy from South Bend, Indiana, whose tireless efforts in the interest of his own promotion have dragged everyone together this one more time to prove what could have been proved six months ago: namely, that computers do not fabricate intelligence, do not sidle over to the opposition in return for favours, do not voluntarily compose slanders against men in high standing in the British service. They tell the disgraceful truth without regard to charm, race or tradition and they tell it to Grant Lederer III, who is busy making himself as unpopular as possible.

As Lederer listened impotently to Wexler's floundering, he decided that it was himself not Wexler who was the alien. Here is the great Harry E. Wexler, he reasoned, who in Langley sits at the right hand of God. Who has been featured in *Time* as America's Legendary Adventurer. Who played a star part in the Bay of Pigs and fathered some of the finest intelligence fuck-ups of the Vietnam War. Who has destabilised more bankrupt economies in Central America than are dreamed of, and conspired with the greatest in the land from the heads of the Mafia downwards. And here is me, an ambitious jerk. And what am I thinking? I am thinking that a man who cannot speak clearly cannot think clearly. I am thinking that self-expression is the companion to logic and that Harry E. Wexler is by this criterion circumcised from the neck up, even if he does hold my precious future in his hands.

To Lederer's relief, Wexler's voice suddenly acquired new confidence. This was because he was reading directly from Lederer's brief. *"In March '81 a reliably assessed defector reported that . . ."* Cover name Dumbo, Lederer remembered automatically, himself becoming the computer: resettled Paris with a hooker supplied by Resources Section. A year later, it was the hooker who defected. *"In May '81 Signals Intelligence reported that . . ."* Lederer glanced at Artelli, hoping to catch his eye, but Artelli was hearing signals of his own. *"In March again of '82 a source*

inside Polish Intelligence while on a liaison visit to Moscow was advised that . . ."
Cover name Mustapha, Lederer recalled with a fastidious shiver: died of overen-
thusiasm while assisting Polish security in its enquiries. With a fumble and a near
fall the great Wexler delivered his first punchline of the morning and managed not
to fluff it. "And the burden of these indicators, junnlemen, is in every case the
same," he announced, "namely *that the entire Balkan effort of an unnamed Western
intelligence service is being orchestrated by Czech Intelligence in Prague, and that
the leak is occurring under the noses of the Anglo-American intelligence fraternity
in Washington."* Nobody leaps in the air however. Colonel Carruthers does not
remove his monocle to exclaim "By God, the fiendish cunning!" The sensational
force of Wexler's revelation is six months old. The sedge is withered from the case
and no spooks sing.

Lederer decided to listen instead to what Wexler does not say. Nothing about
my interrupted tennis training, for example. Nothing about my imperilled marriage,
my truncated sex-life, my total noncontribution as a father, starting the morning
they hauled me off all other duties and assigned me to the great Wexler as his
superslave for twenty-five hours a day. "You have a lawyer's training, you have
Czech language and Czech expertise," Personnel had told him in as many words.
"More appropriately you have a thoroughly sleazy mind. Apply it, Lederer. We
expect terrible things of you." Nothing about the night hours in front of my
computer while I typed my damned fingers off, feeding in acres of disconnected
data. Why did I do it? What got into me? Mom, I just felt my talent striding out
inside of me, so I got on its back and rode away to my destiny. Names and records
of all Western intelligence officers past or present in Washington with access to the
Czech target, whether central or peripheral consumers: Lederer cans the whole
ridiculous assembly in four days cold. Names of all their contacts, details of their
travel movements, behavior patterns, sexual and recreational appetites: Lederer
nets them all in a manic Friday-to-Monday while Bee does the praying for both of
us. Names of all Czech couriers, officials, legal and illegal travellers passing in and
out of the United States, plus separately entered personal descriptions to counteract
false passports. Dates and ostensible purpose of such journeys, frequency and
duration of stay. Lederer delivers them bound and gagged in three short days and
nights while Bee convinces herself he is making it with Maisie Morse from Colla-
tion, who has pot smoke coming out of her ears.

Still disdaining these and the many other noble sacrifices of his subordinate,
Wexler has embarked on a disastrous paragraph about "incorporating our general
awareness of the Czechoslovak methodology in regard to the servicing *of* and the
ah communication *with* their agents in the field." An impressed silence follows
while the meeting mentally paraphrases.

"Ah, you mean *tradecraft,* Harry," says Bo Brammel, who never could resist a
quip if he thought it would adorn his reputation, and little Nigel next to him
restrains his laughter by patting down his hair.

"Well, yes, sir, I guess that is what I do mean," Wexler confesses, and Lederer
to his surprise feels a yawn of nervous excitement pass over him as the tousled
Artelli takes the stage.

* * *

Artelli uses no notes and has a mathematician's frugality with words. Despite his name, he speaks with a slight French accent that he disguises beneath a Bronx drawl. "As the indicators continued to multiply," he says, "my section was ordered to make a reappraisal of clandestine radio transmissions beamed from the roof of the Czech Embassy in Washington as well as from certain other identified Czech facilities in the United States, throughout the years '81 and '82, notably their consulate in San Francisco. Our people reconsidered skip distances, frequency variations and probably reception zones. They backtracked over all intercepts of that period though we had not been able to break them at the time of their original transmission. They prepared a schedule of such transmissions so that they could be matched against the movements of eligible suspects."

"Hold on a minute, will you?"

Little Nigel's head snaps round like a weathervane in a gale. Even Brammel shows distinct signs of human interest. From his exile at the end of the table, Jack Brotherhood is pointing a .45-calibre forefinger straight at Artelli's navel. And it is symptomatic of the many paradoxes of Lederer's life that of all the people in the room, Brotherhood is the one whom he would most wish to serve, if ever he had the opportunity, even though—or perhaps because—his occasional efforts to ingratiate himself with his adopted hero have met with iron rebuff.

"Look here, Artelli," Brotherhood says. "You people have made rather a lot out of the point that every time Pym left the precincts of Washington, whether on leave or in order to visit another town, a particular series of coded transmissions from the Czech Embassy was discontinued. I suspect you are going to make that point again now."

"With embellishments, yes, I am," says Artelli pleasantly enough.

Brotherhood's forefinger remains trained on its mark. Artelli keeps his hands on the table. "The assumption being that if Pym was out of range of their Washington transmitter, the Czechs wouldn't bother to talk to him?" Brotherhood suggests.

"This is correct."

"Then every time he came back to the capital they'd pop up again. " 'Hullo it's you and welcome home.' Correct?"

"Yes, sir."

"Well turn it round for a moment, will you? If you were framing a man, isn't that precisely what you would do too?"

"Not today," he says equably. "And not in 1981 or '82. Ten years ago, maybe. Not in the eighties."

"Why not?"

"I wouldn't be that dumb. We all know it's standard intelligence practice to continue transmitting whether or not the party is listening the other end. It's my hunch they—" He stops. "Maybe I should leave this one to Mr. Lederer," he says.

"No you don't—you tell it to them yourself," Wexler orders without looking up.

Wexler's terseness is not unexpected. It is a feature of these meetings, known to everybody present, that a curse, if not an outright embargo, hangs over the use of Lederer's name. Lederer is their Cassandra. Nobody ever asked Cassandra to preside over a meeting on damage limitation.

Artelli is a chess-player and takes his time. "The communication techniques we were required to observe here were out of fashion even at the time of their use. You get a feel. A smell. A smell of age. A sense of long habituation, one human being to another. Years of it maybe."

"Well now that's *very* special pleading," Nigel exclaims, quite angry, and continues to sit bolt upright before kneeling towards his master, who appears to be trying to shake his head and nod at the same time. Mountjoy says "Hear, hear." A couple of Brammel's supporters' club are making similar farmyard noises. There is hostility in the air, and it is forming on national lines. Brotherhood says nothing but has coloured. Whether anyone apart from himself has noticed this, Lederer does not know. He has coloured, he has lowered his fist, and for a second he appears to have dropped his guard entirely. Lederer hears him growl, "Fanciful twaddle," but misses the rest because Artelli has decided to continue.

"Our more important discovery relates however to the types of code in these transmissions. As soon as we had the notion of an older type of system, we subjected the transmissions to different analytical methods. Like you don't immediately look for a steam engine inside the hood of a Cadillac. We decided to read the messages on the assumption they were being received by a man or woman in the field who is of a certain generation of training, and who cannot or dare not store modern coding materials. We looked for more elementary keys. We looked in particular for evidence of non-random texts that would serve as base keys for transposition."

If anybody here understands what he's saying, they are not showing it, thinks Lederer.

"When we did this, we at once began to detect a progression in the structure. Right now it's still algebra. But it's there. It's a logical linguistic progression. Maybe it's a piece of Shakespeare. Maybe it's a Hottentot nursery rhyme. But there is a pattern emerging that is based upon the continuous text of some such analogue. And that analogue is in effect the codebook for those transmissions. And we feel —maybe it's a little mystical—that the analogue is—well, like a bond between the field and base. We see it as having almost a human identity. All we need is one word. Preferably but not necessarily the first. After that it's only a question of time before we identify the rest of the text. Then we'll break those messages wide open."

"So when will that be?" says Mountjoy. "About 1990, I suppose."

"Could be. Could be tonight."

Suddenly it becomes apparent that Artelli means more than he is saying. The hypothetical has become the specific. Brotherhood is the first to take him up on his innuendo.

"So why tonight?" he says. "Why not 1990?"

"There's something very peculiar going on with the Czech transmissions overall," Artelli confesses with a smile. "They're throwing stuff out at random everywhere. Last night Prague Radio put out a world-wide spook call using some phoney professor who doesn't exist. Like a cry for help to somebody who's only in a position to receive spoken word. Then all around the clock we get Mayday calls— for example a high-speed transmission from your Czech Embassy here in London. For four days now, they've been bumping high-speed signals into your mainline BBC transmissions. It's as if the Czechs had lost a kid in the forest and were shouting out any messages that might conceivably get through to him."

Even before Artelli's echoless voice has died, Brotherhood is speaking. "Of *course* there's a London transmission," he declares vehemently, laying his fist on the table like a challenge. "Of course the Czechs are stirring it. My goodness, how many times do we have to put this to you? For two damned years, there have been Czech transmissions in any part of the globe where Pym sets foot and they do, naturally, coincide with his movements. It's a radio game. That's how you play the radio game when you're framing a man. You persist and you repeat and you wait till the other fellow's nerve cracks. The Czechs are not fools. Sometimes I think we are."

Unbothered, Artelli turns his twisted smile to Lederer as if to say, "See if *you* can impress them." At which Grant Lederer allows himself an irrelevant memory of his wife Bee splayed above him in her naked glory, making love to him like all the angels in Heaven.

"Sir Michael, I have to start the other end," Lederer says brightly in a prepared opening, straight at Brammel. "I have to pick up in Vienna just ten days ago, if you don't mind, sir, and track back from there to Washington."

Nobody is looking at him. Start wherever you must, they were saying, and get it over with.

A different Lederer has broken loose inside him and he greets this version of himself with pleasure. I am the bounty hunter, shuttling between London, Washington and Vienna with Pym perpetually in my sights. I am the Lederer who, as Bee vociferously complained when we were safe from microphones, took Pym into bed with us every night, woke sweating with self-doubt in the fitful hours, woke again in the morning with Pym once more firmly between us: "I'll get you, boy. I'll nail you." The Lederer who for the last twelve months—ever since Pym's name began to wink at me from the computer screen—has tracked him first as an abstraction, then as a fellow screwball. Has posed with him on spurious committees as his earnest and admiring colleague. Shared jolly drunken picnics with family Pym in the Vienna woods, then rushed back to my desk and set to work with fresh vigour to rip apart what I have just enjoyed. I am the Lederer who too easily attaches himself, then punishes whatever holds him tight; the Lederer who is grateful for every wiry smile and casual pat of encouragement from the great Wexler, my master, only to round on him minutes later, lampooning him, degrading him in my overheated mind, punishing him for being yet another disappointment to me.

Never mind that I am twenty years Pym's junior. What I recognise in Pym is what I recognise in myself: a spirit so wayward that, even while I am playing a game of Scrabble with my kids it can swing between the options of suicide, rape and assassination. "He's one of *us,* for Christ's sake!" Lederer wants to scream at the sleeping potentates around him. "Not one of you. One of *me.* We're howling psychopaths, the both of us." But of course Lederer doesn't scream that or anything else. He talks sanely and wisely about his computer. And about a man named Petz, also known as Hampel and Zaworski, who travels almost as much as Lederer and exactly as much as Pym, but takes more trouble than either of us to conceal his tracks.

But first, in the same perfectly balanced and dispassionate voice, Lederer describes the situation as it had stood in August, when it was agreed on both sides —Lederer casts a respectful glance towards his hero Brotherhood—that the Pym case should be abandoned and the committee of investigation dissolved.

"But it wasn't abandoned, was it?" Brotherhood says, not bothering this time to give warning of his interruption. "You kept a watch going on his house and I don't mind betting you left a few other meters ticking too."

Lederer glances at Wexler. Wexler scowls into his hands to say keep me ah out of this. But Lederer has no intention of fielding that ball, and waits boorishly for Wexler to do it for him.

"The determination on our side, Jack, was that we should capitalise the ah existing appropriation of resources," Wexler says reluctantly. "We opted here for a gradual reduction of a—ah phased and undramatic running down."

In the silence Brammel gives a sporting smile. "So you mean you did keep the surveillance going? Is that what you're saying?"

"On a limited basis only, very low key, very minimal at all levels, Bo."

"I rather thought we said we'd all call off our dogs at once, Harry. We certainly kept *our* half of the bargain, I know."

"The ah Agency decided here to honour that agreement in spirit, Bo, but also in light of what was deemed operationally expedient having regard to ah all the known facts and indicators."

"Thanks," says Mountjoy and tosses down his pencil like a man refusing food.

But this time Wexler bites back and Wexler can do that: "I think you may find your gratitude is well placed, sir," he snaps, and pushes his knuckles combatively across the tip of his nose.

The case of Hans Albrecht Petz, Lederer continues, surfaced six months ago in a context that at first sight had nothing whatever to do with the case against Pym. Petz was simply another Czech journalist who had appeared at an East-West conference in Salzburg and been talent-spotted as a new face. An older man, withdrawn but intelligent, passport details supplied. Lederer put his name on watch and signalled Langley for a routine background check. Langley signalled "nothing recorded against" but warned that it was irregular that a man of Petz's age and profession should not have come to notice. A month later Petz surfaced again in Linz, purportedly to cover an agricultural fair. He didn't hobnob with other journalists, didn't try to ingratiate himself, was seen seldom at the tents and contributed nothing. When Lederer had his press readers comb the Czech press for contributions by Petz, the most they came up with was two paragraphs in the *Socialist Farmer,* signed "H.A.P.," on the limitations of Western heavy tractors. Then, just when Lederer was disposed to forget about him Langley came back with a positive identification. Hans Albrecht Petz was identical with one Alexander Hampel, a Czech intelligence officer, who had recently attended a conference of non-aligned journalists in Athens. Do not approach Petz-Hampel without an authorisation. Stand by for more information.

Hearing himself say "Athens," Lederer has a feeling that the air pressure has dropped inside the safe room.

"Athens *when?*" Brotherhood growls irritably. "How can we follow this stuff without dates?"

Nigel's hair has become a sudden and intense worry to him. He is shaping the greying horns above one ear again and again with his immaculate fingertips while he frowns in pain.

Wexler once more cuts in, and to Lederer's pleasure he is beginning to shed his shyness and respect. "Athens conference was July 15 to 18, Jack. Hampel was sighted on the first day only. He kept his hotel room the three nights but didn't sleep in it once. Paid cash. According to Greek records he arrived Athens on July 14 and never left the country. Most likely he went out on a different passport. Looks like he flew to Corfu. Greek flight lists are the usual pig's breakfast, but looks like he flew to Corfu," he repeats. "By this time we're getting very interested in this man."

"Aren't we running ahead?" says Brammel, whose sense of the proprieties is never sharper than in moments of crisis. "I mean damn it, Harry, it's the same old game. It's guilt by coincidence. It's no different to the radio stuff. If *we* were looking to frame a man, we'd play the same game on them. We'd get some old member of the Firm, a bit tarnished but nothing discreditable, and we'd run him parallel to some poor chap's movements and wait for the opposition to say "Whoo-hoo, our man's a spy." Get them to shoot themselves in the foot. Dead easy. All right. Hampel is trailing Pym around. But what's to show that Pym's an active partner?"

"At that point in time nothing, sir," Lederer confesses with false humility, stepping in on Wexler's behalf. "However we had by then established a retrospective link between Pym and Hans Albrecht Petz. At the time of the Salzburg conference, Pym and his wife were attending a music festival there. Petz was staying about two hundred yards from the Pyms' hotel."

"Same story over again," says Brammel doggedly. "It's a set-up. Sticks out a mile. Right, Nigel?"

"It's awfully tenuous actually," Nigel says.

The air pressure again. Maybe the machines kill the oxygen as well as the sound, thinks Lederer. "Do you mind telling us the date when that Athens trace came through?" asks Brotherhood, still on the matter of the timing.

"Ten days ago, sir," says Lederer.

"Bloody slow about advising us, weren't you?"

In anger Wexler finds his words faster: "Well now, Jack, we were pretty damn reluctant to present you people prematurely with yet another series of computerised coincidences." And to Lederer, his whipping boy: "What the hell are you waiting for?"

It is ten days ago. Lederer is crouched in the communications room in the Station in Vienna. It is night and he has bowed out of two cocktail invitations and one dinner by pretending a light flu. He has phoned Bee and let her hear the excitement in his voice and he has half a mind to rush back and tell her then and there, because he has always told her everything anyway—and sometimes when trade was poor a little more than everything in order to keep the image going. But he holds on to himself. And though his fingers are frozen in the joints from the sheer tension of it, he keeps on typing. First he calls up the most recent schedules of Pym's known movements in and out of Vienna and establishes, almost as a matter of course, that he visited both Salzburg and Linz on precisely the same dates as Petz alias Hampel.

"Linz too?" Brotherhood interrupts sharply.

"Yes, sir!"

"You followed him there, I suppose—contrary to our agreement?"

"No, sir, we did not follow Magnus to Linz. I had my wife Bee call Mary Pym.

Bee elicited the information in the course of an innocent conversation, woman to woman, on another matter, Mr. Brotherhood."

"He might still not have gone to Linz. Could have told his wife a cover story."

Lederer is at pains to concede that this is possible but gently suggests that it hardly matters, sir, in view of Langley's signal of that same night, which signal he now reads aloud to his assembled Anglo-American lords of intelligence. "It arrived on my desk five minutes after we had the Linz connection, sir. I quote: 'Petz-Hampel also identical with Jerry Zaworski, born Carlsbad 1925, West German journalist of Czech origin who made nine legal journeys to United States in 1981, '82.' "

"Perfect," says Brammel under his breath.

"Birthdates are of course approximations in these cases," Lederer continues undaunted. "It is our experience that alias passports have the tendency to give the bearer a year or two."

The signal is hardly on Lederer's desk, he says, before he is typing in the dates and destinations of Herr Zaworski's visits to America. And then it was—says Lederer, though not in as many words—that with one touch of the button everything came together, continents merged, three journalists in their late fifties became a single Czech spy of uncertain age, and Grant Lederer III, thanks to the flawless insulation of the signals room, was able to scream "Hallelujah!" and "Bee, I love you!" to the padded walls.

"Every American city visited by Petz-Hampel-Zaworski in 1981 and 1982 was visited by Pym on the same dates," Lederer intones. "During those dates the relevant clandestine transmissions from the Czech Embassy roof were discontinued, the reason in our estimation being that a personal encounter was occurring between the agent in the field and his visiting controller. Radio transmissions were accordingly superfluous."

"It's beautiful," says Brammel. "I'd like to find the Czech intelligence officer who thought this one up and give him my private Oscar immediately."

With a pained discretion Mick Carver lifts a briefcase gently to the table and extracts a bunch of folders.

"This is Langley's profile as of now on Petz-Hampel-Zaworski, Pym's presumed controller," he explains in the patient manner of a salesman bent on showing off a new technology, despite the obstruction of the older element. "We expect a couple more updates in the next immediate while, maybe even tonight. Bo, when does Magnus return to Vienna, do you mind telling us, please?"

Brammel like all the rest of them is peering into his folder, so it is natural he should not reply at once. "When we tell him to, I suppose," he says carelessly, turning a page. "Not before, that's for certain. As you say, his father's death was rather providential. Old man left quite a mess, I gather. Magnus has a lot to sort out."

"Where is he now?" says Wexler.

Brammel looks at his watch. "Having dinner, I should imagine. Nearly time, isn't it?"

"Where's he staying?" Wexler insists.

Brammel smiles. "Now Harry, I don't think I'm going to tell you that. We do have some rights in our own country, you know, and your chaps have been a bit overeager on the surveillance stakes."

Wexler is nothing if not stubborn. "Last we heard of him, he was at London Airport checking in to his flight to Vienna. Our information is he'd wrapped up his affairs over here and was heading back to his post. What the hell happened?"

Nigel has clasped his hands together. He sets them, still clasped, on the table to indicate that, small or not, he is speaking. "You haven't been following him over here too, have you? That really would be going it."

Wexler rubs his chin. His expression is rueful but undefeated. He turns again to Brammel. "Bo, we need a piece of this. If this is a Czech deception operation it's the damnedest, most ingenious case I ever heard of."

"Pym is a most ingenious officer," Brammel countered. "He's been a thorn in the Czechs' side for thirty years. He's worth a lot of trouble on their part."

"Bo, you've got to pull Pym in and you've got to interrogate the living shit out of him. If you don't, we're going to go around and around this thing till we've all got grey hairs and some of us are in our graves. Those are our secrets he's been fooling with as well as yours. We have some very heavy questions to put to him and some fine people trained to put them."

"Harry, you have my word that when the moment is ripe, you and your people shall have as much of him as you want."

"Maybe the moment's right now," Wexler says, sticking out his jaw. "Maybe we should be there from when he starts to sing. Hit him while he's soft."

"And maybe you should trust sufficiently in our judgment to bide your time," Nigel purrs sleekly in reply, and casts Wexler a very reassuring glance over the top of his reading spectacles.

A most strange impulse, meanwhile, is taking hold of Lederer. He feels it rising in him and can no more check himself than if it were an urge to vomit. In this self-renewing cycle of compromise and double-think he needs to externalise the secret affinity between himself and Magnus. To assert his monopoly of understanding of the man and underline the personal nature of his triumph. To be at the centre still, and not shoved out to the bleachers where he came from.

"Sir, you mentioned Pym's father," he bursts out, talking straight at Brammel. "Sir, I know about that father. I have a father who is not in certain ways dissimilar, only in degree. Mine's a small-time iffy lawyer and honesty is not his strong suit. No, sir. But that father of Pym's was a total crook. A con artist. Our psychiatrists have assembled a really disturbing profile of that man. Do you know that when Richard T. Pym was in New York he faked a whole *empire* of bogus companies? Borrowed money from the most unlikely people, really some important people? I mean listed. There's a serious strain of controlled instability here. We have a paper on this." He was overrunning himself but couldn't stop. "I mean Jesus, do you know Magnus made the most wild pass at my own wife? I don't grudge him that. She's an attractive woman. What I mean is the guy's everywhere. He's all over the place. That English cool of his is just veneer."

Not for the first time Lederer has just committed suicide. Nobody hears him, nobody shouts "Wow, you don't say!" And when Brammel speaks, his voice is as cold as charity and as late in arriving.

"Yes, well, I always assume that businessmen are crooks, don't you, Harry? I'm sure we all do." He glances round the table at everyone but Lederer and comes back to Wexler. "Harry, why don't you and I get our heads together for an hour, shall we? If there's to be a hostile interrogation at some stage, I'm sure we should agree on some guidelines in advance, Nigel, why don't you come along to see fair play? The rest of us—" His gaze falls on Brotherhood and he awards him a particularly confiding smile. "Well, we'll simply say see you all later. You will leave in pairs, won't you, when you've done your reading? Not all at once, it scares the local peasants. Thank you."

Brammel leaves, Wexler waddles boldly after him, a man who has made his point and doesn't care who knows it. Nigel waits till they have all left, then like a busy undertaker hastens round the table and takes Brotherhood's arm in a fraternal gesture.

"Jack," he whispers. "Well put, well played. We absolutely stymied them. A word in your ear away from the microphones, yes?"

It was early afternoon. The safe house where they had met was a pseudo-Regency villa with jewelers' screens across the windows. A warm fog hung over the gravel drive and Lederer loitered in it like a murderer waiting for Brotherhood's hulk to fill the lighted porch. Mountjoy and Dorney passed by him without a word. Carver, accompanied by Artelli and his briefcase, was more explicit. "I have to live here, Lederer. I just hope that this time either you make it stick or they post the hell out of you."

Bastard, thought Lederer.

At last Jack Brotherhood emerged, speaking cryptically to Nigel. Lederer watched them jealously. Nigel turned and went back inside. Brotherhood walked forward.

"Mr. Brotherhood, sir? Jack? It's me. Lederer."

Brotherhood came slowly to a halt. He was wearing his usual grimy raincoat and a muffler, and he had lit one of his yellow cigarettes.

"What do you want?"

"Jack. I want to tell you that whatever happens, and whatever he's done or not done, I'm sorry it's him and I'm sorry it's you."

"Probably hasn't done anything at all. Probably recruited one of the other side and hasn't told us, knowing him. My guess is you've got the story inside out."

"Would he do that, Magnus? Play a lone hand with the enemy and not tell anybody? Jesus, that's dynamite! If I ever tried that, Langley would skin me."

Unbidden, he fell in beside Brotherhood. A policeman stood at the gate. They passed the Royal Horse Artillery Barracks. The sound of hoofs clattered at them from the parade ground but the horses were hidden in the fog. Brotherhood was striding fast. Lederer had difficulty keeping up.

"I feel really bad, Jack," Lederer confessed. "Nobody seems to understand what it's been like for me to have to do this to a friend. It's not just Magnus. It's Bee and Mary and the kids and everybody. Becky and Tom are real sweethearts. It kind of made all of us consider ourselves in many ways. There's a pub right here. Can I buy you a drink?"

"Got to see a man about a dog, I'm afraid."

"Can I drop you somewhere? I have a car and driver right here around the corner."

"Prefer to walk if you don't mind."

"Magnus told me a lot about you, Jack. I guess he broke some of the rules but that's how we were. We really shared. It was a great liaison. That's the crazy thing. We really *were* the Special Relationship. And I believe in that. I believe in the Anglo-Saxon alliance, the Atlantic Pact, the whole bit. You remember that burglary you and Magnus did together in Warsaw?"

"Don't think I do, I'm afraid."

"Oh come on, Jack. How you lowered him through a skylight? Like in the Bible? And you had these fake Polish cops downstairs on the doorstep in case the quarry came home unexpectedly? He said you were like a father to him. You know how he referred to you once? 'Grant,' he said to me. 'Jack is the true champion of the great game.' You know what I feel? I think if Magnus's writing had ever worked for him, he'd have been okay. There's just too much inside him. He has to put it somewhere." He was breathing a little hastily between his words, but he insisted on keeping up; he had to get it right with Brotherhood. "You see, sir, I've read a great deal recently about the creativity of the criminal mind."

"Oh he's a criminal now, is he?"

"Please. Let me quote you something I read." They had reached a crossing and were waiting for the lights. " 'What is the difference, in morality, between the totally anarchic criminality of the artist, which is endemic in all fine creative minds, and the artistry of the criminal?' "

"Can't do it, I'm afraid. Too many long words. Sorry about that."

"Hell, Jack, we're licensed crooks, that's all I'm saying. What's our racket? Know what our racket is? It is to place our larcenous natures at the service of the state. So I mean why should I feel different about Magnus just because maybe he got the mix a little wrong? I can't. Magnus is still exactly the same man I spent these great times with! And I'm still the same man who had these times with Magnus. Nothing's changed except we've landed on different sides of the net. You know we talked about defection once? Where we would go if we ever cut and run? Left our wives and kids and work, and just stepped into the blue? We were that close, Jack. We literally thought the unthinkable. We really did. We were amazing."

They had entered St. John's Wood High Street, and were heading towards Regent's Park. Brotherhood's pace had increased.

"Where did he say he'd go, then?" Brotherhood snapped. "Back to Washington? Moscow?"

"Home. He said there was only ever one place. Home. I mean this shows you. The man loves his country, Mr. Brotherhood. Magnus is no renegade."

"Didn't know he had a home," said Brotherhood. "Vagrant childhood, he always told me."

"Home is a little seaside town in Wales. It has a very ugly Victorian church. It has a very strict landlady who shuts him in at 10 P.M. And one of these days Magnus is going to lock himself in that upstairs room and write his ass off till he comes out with all twelve volumes of Pym's answer to Proust."

Brotherhood might not have heard. He strode faster.

"Home is childhood re-created, Mr. Brotherhood. If defection is a self-renewal, it requires also a rebirth."

"That his stupid phrase or yours?"

"Mine and his equally. We discussed all this and we discussed much, much more. Know why so many defectors redefect? We had that one straight too. It's in and out of the womb all the time. Have you ever noticed that about defectors—the one common factor in all that crazy band? They're immature. Forgive me, they are *literally* motherfuckers."

"Have a name, this place?"

"Pardon?"

"This Welsh paradise of his. What's it called?"

"He never said a name. All he said was it was near the castle where he grew up with his mother, in an area with great houses, where he and his mother used to go to the hunts, dance at the Christmas balls and mix quite democratically with the servants."

"Have you ever come across Czechs using back numbers of newspapers?" Brotherhood asked.

Momentarily thrown by the change of tack, Lederer was obliged to pause and consider.

"It's a case a colleague of mine is running," Brotherhood said. "He asked me. Czech agent always grubbing around for last week's newspapers before he takes a walk up the road. Why would he do that?"

"I'll tell you why. It's a standard thing," said Lederer, recovering. "Old hat, but standard. We had a Joe like that, a double. The Czechs trained him for days, just in how to roll exposed film into newspaper. Took him out into the streets at night, made him find a dark area. Poor bastard nearly froze his fingers off. It was twenty below."

"I said back numbers," Brotherhood said.

"Sure. There's two ways. One way they use the day of the month, the other way they use the day of the week. Day of the month is a nightmare: thirty-one standard messages to be learned by heart. It's the eighteenth of the month so it's 'Meet me behind the gentleman's convenience in Brno at nine-thirty and don't be late.' It's the sixth so 'Where the hell's my monthly pay cheque?' " He giggled breathlessly but Brotherhood did not reciprocate. "The days of the week, that's a shortened version of the same thing."

"Thanks, I'll pass it on," said Brotherhood, drawing to a halt at last.

"Sir, I can imagine no greater honour than taking you out to dinner tonight," Lederer said, now quite desperate for Brotherhood's absolution. "I cast aspersions on one of your men, that's duty. But if I were ever able to separate the personal and the official sides, I'd be a happy man, sir. Jack?"

The taxi was already drawing up.

"What is it?"

"Do you think you could give Magnus a message for me—a friendly one?"

"What is it?"

"Tell him any time—when it's over—any place. I'll be there as his friend."

With a nod Brotherhood climbed into the taxi and rode away before Lederer could hear his destination.

What Lederer did next should go into history, if not into the larger history of the Pym affair then at least into his own exasperating personal chronicle of seeing everything with perfect vision and being repeatedly dismissed as an unwelcome prophet. Lederer struggled into a phone box intending to call Carver, only to discover he had no English coins. He dived into the Mulberry Arms, fought his way to the bar and bought a beer he did not want in order to have change. He returned to the phone box to find it didn't work, so he pelted back down the road in search of his driver, who, having watched Lederer march by with Brotherhood, had assumed he was no longer required and had driven home to Battersea where he had a friend. At nine o'clock, Lederer burst in upon Carver at the U.S. Embassy, where Carver was drafting a signal on the day's events.

"They're lying!" Lederer shouted.

"Who are?"

"The fucking Brits! Pym's flown the coop. They don't know where he is from the man in the fucking moon. I asked Brotherhood to pass him this totally subversive message and he sweet-mouthed me to keep me off the track. Pym jumped ship at London Airport and they're looking for him the same way we are. Those Czech radio transmissions are kosher. The Brits are looking for him, we're looking for him. And the fucking Czechs are looking for him all over. Listen to me!"

Carver had listened. Carver continued to listen. He took Lederer through his conversation with Brotherhood and concluded it should not have taken place and that Lederer had exceeded his competence. He did not say this to Lederer but he made a note of it, and later that night in a separate telegram to the Agency's personnel people he took care that this note was added to Lederer's file. At the same time he accepted that Lederer might well have stumbled upon the truth, even if by the wrong route, and said this also. Thus Carver covered his back all ways, while at the same time knifing an unpleasing interloper. Never bad.

"The British are not playing this straight," he confided to people he knew at the top. "I am going to have to watch this very carefully."

The Headmaster's study smelt of killing bottles. Mr. Caird, though he hated violence, was a passionate lepidopterist. A grim portrait of our founder G. F. Grimble glowered down on cracked leather chairs. In one of them sat Tom. Brotherhood sat opposite him. Tom was looking at the photograph from the Langley folder on Petz-Hampel-Zaworski. Brotherhood was looking at Tom. Mr. Caird had shaken Brotherhood's hand and left them to it.

"That the one who walked your dad round the cricket ground in Corfu?" said Brotherhood, watching Tom.

"Yes, sir."

"You weren't far wrong with your description then, were you?"

"No, sir."

"I thought you'd be amused."

"I am."

"He doesn't limp in the photograph, so he doesn't look so hobbly. Had any more letters from your dad? Phone calls?"

"No, sir."

"Written to him?"

"Don't know where to send it, sir."

"Why don't you give it to me?"

Tom delved inside his grey pullover and unearthed a sealed envelope with no name or address on it. Brotherhood took it from him, and took back the photograph too.

"That inspector fellow hasn't been back to trouble you, has he?"

"No, sir."

"Anyone else been?"

"Not really, sir."

"What does that mean?"

"It's just so odd you coming tonight."

"Why?"

"It's maths prep," said Tom. "It's my worst thing."

"I expect you'd like to get back to it then." He took Pym's crushed letter from his pocket and handed it across the gap. "Thought you might like this back, too. It's a fine letter. You should be proud."

"Thank you, sir."

"Your dad talks there about an Uncle Syd. Who's that? 'If you're ever down on your luck,' he says, 'or if you need a warm meal and a laugh or a bed for the night, don't forget your Uncle Syd.' Who's Uncle Syd, when he's at home?"

"Syd Lemon, sir."

"Where does he live?"

"Surbiton, sir. By a railway."

"Old man, is he? Youngish?"

"He looked after Dad when he was small. He was a friend of Granddad's. He's got a wife called Meg but she's dead."

They both stood up.

"Dad's still all right, isn't he, sir?" said Tom.

Brotherhood's shoulders stiffened. "You're to go to your mother, d'you hear? Your mother or me. No one else. That's if things get tough." He pulled an old leatherbound box from his jacket pocket. "This is for you."

Tom opened it. A medal lay inside with a piece of ribbon attached to it—crimson with narrow dark blue stripes on either side.

"What did you get it for?" said Tom.

"Sticking out dark nights alone." A bell was ringing. "Now run along and do your job," said Brotherhood.

The night was foul. Gusts of rain tore across the windscreen as Brotherhood negotiated the narrow lane. The car was a souped-up Ford from the Firm's pool and he had only to stroke the accelerator for it to lunge towards the hedge. Magnus Pym, he thought: traitor and Czech spy. If I know, why don't they? How many times, in how many ways, do they need the proof before they act on it? A pup loomed suddenly out of the rain. He pulled into the forecourt and drank a scotch before going to the phone. Call me on my private line, old boy, Nigel had said expansively.

"The man in the picture is our friend from Corfu. No question about it," Brotherhood reported.

"You're sure?"

"I'm sure. The boy's sure. I'm sure he's sure. When are you going to give the order to evacuate?"

A muffled crackle while Nigel put his fist over the mouthpiece the other end. But not, presumably, the earpiece.

"I want those Joes out, Nigel. Get them out. Tell Bo to get his head out of the sand and give the order."

Long silence.

"We're tuning in at 0500 tomorrow," said Nigel. "Come back to London and get some sleep." He rang off.

London was east. Brotherhood headed south, following the signs to Reading. In every operation there is an above the line and a below the line. Above the line is what you do by the book. Below the line is how you do the job.

The letter to Tom was postmarked Reading, he rehearsed. Posted Monday night or first thing Tuesday morning.

He rang me on Monday evening, Kate had said.

He rang me on Monday evening, Belinda had said.

Reading station resembled a low redbrick stable set at one end of a tawdry square. A poster in the concourse gave the times of coaches to and from Heathrow. That's what you did, he thought. That's what I'd do. At Heathrow you put up your smokescreen about planes to Scotland, then you hopped a coach to Reading to keep things nice and private. He considered the coach stop, then cast a long slow look around the square until his eye fell at last on the ticket kiosk. He wandered over to it. The clerk wore a small metal wheel in the buttonhole of his jacket. Brotherhood put five pounds in the tray.

"I'd like some change, please, to telephone."

"Sorry, mate. Can't do," the clerk said, and went on with his newspaper.

"You could do it last Monday night though, couldn't you?" The clerk's head came up fast.

Brotherhood's office pass was green with a red diagonal line drawn in transparent ink across his photograph. A notice on the back said that if found it should be returned to the Ministry of Defence. The clerk looked at both sides of it and gave it back.

"I haven't seen one like that before," he said.

"Tall fellow," Brotherhood said. "Carried a black briefcase. Probably wore a black tie as well. Well spoken, nice manner. Had a lot of calls to make. Remember?"

The clerk vanished, to be replaced a minute later by a tubby Indian with exhausted, visionary eyes.

"Were you on duty here Monday evening?" Brotherhood said.

"Sir, I was the man who was on duty on Monday evening," he replied warily, as if he might not be that man any more.

"A pleasant gentleman in a black tie."

"I know, I know. My colleague has acquainted me with all the details."

"How much change did you give him?"

"Good heavens above, what does that matter? If I elect to give a man change, that is my personal preference, a matter for my pocket and my conscience that has nothing to do with anybody."

"How much change did you give him?"

"Five pounds exactly. Five he wanted, five he got."

"What in?"

"Fifty p's exclusively. He wished to make no local calls at all. I questioned him about this and he was entirely consistent in his answers. I mean where is the hardship in this? Where is the sinister element?"

"What did he pay you with?"

"To my recollection, he gave me a ten-pound note. I cannot be completely certain but that is my imperfect recollection: that he gave me a ten-pound note from his wallet, accompanied by the words 'Here you are.' "

"Did the ten pounds cover his rail ticket too?"

"This was totally unproblematical. The price of a second-class single fare to London is four pounds and thirty pence exactly. I gave him ten fifties and the balance in small change. Now have you further questions? I seriously hope not. Police, police, you know. If it's one enquiry a day, it's half a dozen."

"Is this the man?" said Brotherhood. He was holding a photograph showing Pym and Mary at their wedding.

"But that is you, sir. In the background. I think you are giving the bride away. Are you sure you are engaged in an official enquiry? This is a most irregular photograph."

"Is this the man?"

"Well I'm not saying it is not, put it that way."

Pym would take him off perfectly, thought Brotherhood. Pym would catch that accent to a tee. He stood at the barrier studying the timetable of trains leaving Reading station after eleven o'clock on a weekday night. You went anywhere except to London because London is where you bought your ticket to. You had time. Time to make your maudlin telephone calls. Time to write your maudlin letter to Tom. Your plane left Heathrow at eight-forty without you. By eight o'clock latest you had done your turnaround. By eight-fifteen, according to the testimony of the airport travel clerk, you had put up your little smokescreen about planes to Scotland. After that you hightailed it to the Reading-bound coach, pulled down the brim of your hat and said goodbye to the airport as quickly and quietly as you knew how.

Brotherhood walked back to the coach timetable. Time to kill, he repeated to himself. Say you caught the eight-thirty from Heathrow. Between nine- and ten-thirty there were half a dozen trains in both directions out of Reading but you caught none of them. You wrote to Tom instead. Where from? He went back to the square. In the neon-lit pub there. In the fish-and-chip shop. In the all-night café where the tarts sit. Somewhere in this dowdy square you sat down and told Tom what to do when the world ended.

The telephone box stood at the station entrance, under a bright light that was supposed to deter vandals. Smashed glass and paper cups cluttered the floor. Graffiti and promises of love defaced the awful grey paint. But it was a good telephone, for all that. You could watch the whole square from it while you said your goodbyes. A mail box was let into the wall close by. And that's where you posted it, saying whatever happens, remember that I love you. After which you went to Wales. Or to Scotland. Or you popped over to Norway to watch the migration of the reindeer. Or you hightailed it to Canada and prepared to eat out of tins. Or you did something that was all these things and none of them, in an upstairs room with a view of the church and the sea.

Reaching his flat in Shepherd Market, Brotherhood was still not quite done. The Firm's official police contact was a Detective Superintendent Bellows at Scotland Yard. Brotherhood rang his home number.

"What have you got for me on that ennobled gentleman I mentioned to you this morning?" he asked, and to his relief detected no note of reservation in Bellow's voice as he read him out the details. Brotherhood wrote them down.

"Can you do me another one for tomorrow?"

"It'll be a pleasure."

"Lemon, believe it or not. First name Syd or Sydney. Old chap, widowed, lives in Surbiton, close to a railway."

Reluctantly Brotherhood phoned Head Office and asked for Nigel of Secretariat. Belatedly, and in the teeth of more larcenous instincts, he knew he must conform. Just as he had conformed this afternoon when he poured scorn on the Americans. Just as in the end he had always conformed, not out of slavishness but because he believed in the fight and, despite everything, the team. A lot of atmospherics followed while Nigel was located. They went over to scramble.

"What's the matter?" said Nigel rudely.

"The book Artelli was talking about. The analogue, he called it."

"I thought he was perfectly ridiculous. Bo is going to take it to the *highest* level."

"Tell them to try Grimmelshausen's *Simplicissimus*. On a hunch. Tell them to be sure to use an early text."

A long silence. More atmospherics. He's in the bath, thought Brotherhood. He's in bed with a woman, or whatever he likes.

"Now how are you spelling that?" said Nigel warily.

10

Once again a willed brightness was overtaking Pym as he listened to the many voices in his mind. To be king, he repeated to himself. To look with favour on this child that was myself. To love his defects and his strivings, and pity his simplicity.

If there was such a thing as a perfect time in Pym's life, a time when all the versions of himself were appreciated and playing nicely and he would never want for anything again, then surely it was his first few terms at Oxford University whither Rick had dispatched him as a necessary interlude to having him appointed Lord Chief Justice and thus securing him a place among the Highest in the Land. The relationship between the two pals had never been better. Following Axel's departure, Pym's final lonely months in Bern had seen a dramatic flowering of their correspondence. With Frau Ollinger barely speaking to him and Herr Ollinger increasingly absorbed in the problems of Ostermundigen, Pym walked the city streets alone, much as he had done at the beginning. But at night, with the wall beside him silent, he penned long and intimate letters of affection to Belinda and his one true anchor, Rick. Stimulated by his attentions, Rick's letters in reply took on a sudden stylishness and prosperity. The anguished missives from outer England ceased. The stationery thickened, stabilised and acquired illustrious headings. First the Richard T. Pym Endeavour Company wrote to him from Cardiff, advising him that the Clouds of Misfortune which had appeared to Gather had been swept Away one and All by a Providence I can only regard as crackerjack. A month later, the Pym & Partners Property and Finance Enterprise of Cheltenham was advising him

that certain Steps were now in Hand for Pym's future with a view to Insuring that
he would never want for Anything again. Most recently a printed card of regal
elegance was pleased to announce that following a Merger Agreeable to all Parties,
matters relating to the above Companies should henceforth be referred to the Pym
& Permanent Mutual Property Trust (Nassau), of Park Lane W.

Jack Brotherhood and Wendy treated him to a farewell fondue on the Firm;
Sandy came and Jack gave him two bottles of whisky and hoped their paths would
cross. Herr Ollinger accompanied him to the railway station and they drank a last
coffee. Frau Ollinger stayed home. Elisabeth served them but she was distracted. She
had put on bulk around the tummy, though she wore no ring. As the train pulled
out of the station, Pym took a look downward at the circus and its elephant house,
then a look upward at the university and its green dome and by the time he reached
Basel he knew that Bern had sunk with all hands. Axel was illegal. The Swiss
informed against him. I was lucky to get out myself. Standing in the corridor
somewhere south of Paris he observed tears on his cheeks and vowed not to be a
spy again. At Victoria Mr. Cudlove was waiting for him with a new Bentley.

"What do we call you now, sir? Doctor or Professor?"

"Just Magnus will do fine," said Pym handsomely as they pumped hands.
"How's Ollie?"

The new Reichskanzlei in Park Lane was a monument to prosperous stability.
The bust of TP was back in place. Law books, glass doors and a new jockey with
the Pym colours winked assurance at him while he waited on leather cushions for
a Lovely to admit him to the State Apartments.

"Our Chairman will see you now, Mr. Magnus."

They bear-hugged, both for a moment too proud to speak. Rick palmed Pym's
back, moulded his cheeks and wiped away his tears. Mr. Muspole, Perce and Syd
were summoned by separate buzzers to pay homage to the returning hero. Mr.
Muspole produced a sheaf of documents and Rick read the best bits of them aloud.
Pym was appointed International Legal Adviser for life and awarded five hundred
pounds a year to be reconsidered as appropriate on the strict understanding he
worked for no other firm. His law studies at Oxford were thus taken care of; he
need never want for anything again. A second Lovely brought bubbly. She seemed
to have nothing else to do. Everybody drank the health of the company's newest
employee. "Come on, Titch, let's have it in the parley-voo!" cried Syd excitedly, and
Pym obliged by saying something fatuous in German. Father and son hugged again,
Rick wept again and said if only he had had the advantages. The same evening, at
a mansion in Amersham called The Furlong, his homecoming was again celebrated
by an intimate party of two hundred old friends, few of whom Pym had seen before,
including the heads of several world-famous corporations, leading stars of stage and
screen and several Great Barristers who one by one took him aside and claimed the
credit for obtaining a place for him at Oxford. The party over, Pym lay wakefully
in his fourposter listening to the expensive slamming of car doors.

"You did a fine job out there in Switzerland, son," said Rick from the dark
where he had been standing for some while. "You fought a good fight. It's been
noticed. Enjoy your dinner?"

"It was really good."

"A lot of people said to me, 'Rickie,' they said, 'you've got to get that boy back.

Those foreigners will make a whore of him.' You know what I said to them?"

"What did you say to them?"

"I said I had faith in you. Have you got faith in me, son?"

"Masses."

"What do you think of the house?"

"It's wonderful," said Pym.

"It's yours. It's in your name. I bought it from the Duke of Devonshire."

"Thank you very much, anyway."

"Nobody can ever take it away from you, son. You can be twenty. You can be fifty. Where your old man is, that's home. Did you talk to Maxie Moore at all?"

"I don't think I did."

"The fellow who scored the winning goal for Arsenal against Spurs? Go on. Of course you did. What do you think of Blottsie?"

"Which one was he?"

"G. W. Blott? One of the most famous names in the retail grocery world you'll ever meet. That marvellous dignity. He'll be a lord one day. So will you. What do you think of Sylvia?"

Pym recalled a bulky, middle-aged woman in blue with an aristocratic smile that could have been the bubbly.

"She's nice," he said cautiously.

Rick seized on the word as if he had been hunting for it half his life: "Nice. That's what she is. She's a damned nice woman with two first-class husbands to her credit."

"She's really attractive, even for my age."

"Did you get yourself involved out there? There's nothing can't be put right in this world by good pals."

"Just the odd affair. Nothing serious."

"No woman's ever going to come between us, son. Once those Oxford girls know who your old man is, they'll be after you like a pack of wolves. Promise you'll keep yourself clean."

"I promise."

"And learn your law as if your life depended on it? You're being paid, remember."

"I promise."

"Well, then."

The stealthy weight of Rick's body landed like a sixteen-stone cat at Pym's side. He pulled Pym's head towards his own until their two cheeks were pressed stubble to stubble. His fingers found the fatty parts of Pym's chest under his pyjama top and kneaded them. He wept. Pym wept too, thinking again of Axel.

The next day Pym moved hastily into his college, claiming a variety of urgent reasons for going up two weeks early. Declining the services of Mr. Cudlove, he travelled by bus and gazed in mounting wonder on flowing hills and mown corn-fields glowing in the autumn sunlight. The bus passed through country towns and villages, down lanes of russet beech trees and dancing hedgerows, till slowly the golden stone of Oxford replaced the Buckinghamshire brick, the hills flattened and the city's spires lifted into the thickening rays of afternoon. He dismounted, thanked the driver, and drifted through the enchanted streets, asking his way at every corner, forgetting, asking again, not caring. Girls in bell skirts skimmed past him on their bicycles. Dons in billowing gowns clutched their mortarboards against the wind; bookshops beckoned to him like houses of delight. He was lugging a suitcase but it weighed no more than a hat. The college porter said staircase five, across the Chapel Quad. He climbed the winding wooden stairs until he saw his name written on an old oak door: M. R. Pym. He pushed the door and saw darkness and another door beyond. He pushed the second door and closed the first. He found the switch and closed the second door on his whole life till now. I am safe inside the city walls. Nobody will find me, nobody will recruit me. He tripped over a case of legal tomes. A vaseful of orchids wished him "Godspeed, son, from your best pal." A Harrods invoice debited them to the newest Pym consortium.

University was a conventional sort of place in those days, Tom. You would have a good laugh at the way we dressed and talked and the things we put up with, though we were the blessed of the earth. They shut us in at night and let us out in the morning. They gave us girls for tea but not for dinner and God knows not for breakfast. The college scouts doubled as the Dean's Joes and ratted on us if we broke the rules. Our parents had won the war—or most people's had—and since we couldn't beat them our best revenge was to imitate them. Some of us had done national service. The rest of us dressed like officers anyway, hoping no one would notice the difference. With his first cheque, Pym bought a dark blue blazer with brass buttons. With his second, a pair of cavalry twill trousers and a blue tie with crowns that radiated patriotism. After that there was a moratorium because the third cheque took a month to clear. Pym polished his brown shoes, sported a handkerchief in his sleeve, and groomed his hair like a gentleman's. And when Sefton Boyd, who was a year ahead of him, feasted him in the exalted Gridiron Club, Pym made such strides with the language that in no time he was talking it like a native, referring to his inferiors as Charlies, and to our own lot as the Chaps, and pronouncing bad things Harry Awful, and vulgar things Poggy, and good things Fairly Decent.

"Where did you pick up that Vincent's tie, by the by?" Sefton Boyd asked him kindly enough as they sauntered down the Broad for a game of shove-ha'penny with some Charlies at the Trinity pub. "Didn't know you were a boxing blue in your spare time."

Pym said he had admired it in the window of a shop called Hall Brothers in the High Street.

"Well, put it on ice for a bit, I should. You can always get it out again when they elect you." Carelessly he put a hand on Pym's shoulder. "And while you're about it, get your scout to sew some ordinary buttons on that jacket. Don't want people thinking you're the Pretender to the Hungarian throne, do we?"

Once more Pym embraced everything, loved everything, stretched every sinew to excel. He joined the societies, paid more subscriptions than there were clubs, became college secretary of everything from the Philatelists to the Euthanasians. He wrote sensitive articles for university journals, lobbied distinguished speakers, met them at the railway station, dined them at the society's expense and brought them safely to empty lecture halls. He played college rugger, college cricket, rowed in his college eight, got drunk in college bar and was by turn rootlessly cynical towards society and stalwartly British and protective of it, depending on whom he happened to be with. He threw himself afresh upon the German muse and scarcely faltered when he discovered that at Oxford she was about five hundred years older than she had been in Bern, and that anything written within living memory was unsound. But he quickly overcame his disappointment. This is quality, he reasoned. This is academia. In no time he was immersing himself in the garbled texts of mediaeval minstrels with the same energy that, in an earlier life, he had bestowed on Thomas Mann. By the end of his first term he was an enthusiastic student of Middle and Old High German. By the end of his second he could recite the *Hildebrandslied* and intone Bishop Ulfila's Gothic translation of the Bible in his college bar to the delight of his modest court. By the middle of his third he was romping in the Parnassian fields of comparative and putative philology, where youthful creativity has ever had its fling. And when he found himself briefly transported into the perilous modernisms of the seventeenth century, he was pleased to be able to report, in a twenty-page assault on the upstart Grimmelshausen, that the poet had marred his work with popular moralising and undermined his validity by fighting on both sides in the Thirty Years' War. As a final swipe he suggested that Grimmelshausen's obsession with false names cast doubt upon his authorship.

I shall stay here for ever, he decided. I shall become a don and be hero to my pupils. To entrench this ambition he worked up a selective stammer and a self-denying smile, and at night sat long hours at his desk keeping himself awake on Nescafé. When daylight came he ventured downstairs unshaven so that all might see the lines of study etched upon his eager face. It was on one such morning that he was surprised to find a case of vintage port waiting for him, accompanied by a note from the Regius Professor of Law:

"Dear Mr. Pym,

"Yesterday, Messrs. Harrods delivered the enclosed to me, together with a charming letter from your father which appears to commend you to me as my pupil. While it is not my habit to turn away such generosity, I fear that the gesture is better directed to my colleague in the Modern Languages school, since I understand from your Senior Tutor that you are reading German."

For half the day, Pym did not know where to put himself. He turned up his collar, wandered miserably in Christ Church Meadows, cut his tutorial for fear of being arrested and wrote letters to Belinda who was working as an unpaid secretary to a London charity. In the afternoon he sat in a dark cinema. In the evening, still in despair, he carted his guilty parcel to Balliol, determined to tell Sefton Boyd the whole story. But by the time he got there he had thought of a better version.

"Some rich shit in Merton is trying to get me to go to bed with him," he protested, in the tone of healthy exasperation he had been practising all the way to the gates. "He sent me a Harry great case of port to buy me over."

If Sefton Boyd doubted him he did not let it show. Between them they carried their booty to the Gridiron Club where six of them drank it at a sitting, fitfully toasting Pym's virginity till morning. A few days later Pym was elected a member. When the vacation came he took a job selling carpets at a shop in Watford. A lawyers' vacation course, he told Rick. Similar to the holiday seminars he had attended in Switzerland. In reply Rick sent him a five-page homily, warning him against airy-fairy intellectuals, and a cheque for fifty pounds that bounced.

* * *

A summer term was devoted entirely to women. Pym had never been so in love. He swore his love to every girl he met, he was so anxious to overcome what he assumed would be their poor opinion of him. In intimate cafés, on park benches or strolling beside the Isis on glorious afternoons, Pym held their hands and stared into their puzzled eyes and told them everything he had ever dreamed of hearing. If he felt awkward today with the one, he swore he would feel better tomorrow with the next, for women of his own age and intelligence were a novelty to him and he became disconcerted when they did not assume a subordinate position. If he felt awkward with all of them he wrote to Belinda, who never failed to reply. His love-talk was never duplicated; he was not a cynic. To one he spoke of his ambitions to return to the Swiss stage, where he had been such a runaway success. She should learn German and come with him, he said; they would act together. To another he painted himself as a poet of the futile and described his persecution at the hands of the murderous Swiss police.

"But I thought they were so terrifically neutral and humane!" she cried, appalled by his descriptions of the beatings he had received before being marched over the border into Austria.

"Not if you're different," Pym said grimly. "Not if you refuse to conform with the bourgeois norm. Those Swissies have two laws that really matter out there. Thou shalt not be poor and thou shalt not be foreign. I was both."

"You've really been through it," she said. "It's fantastic. I haven't done anything at all."

And to a third he portrayed himself as a novelist of the tortured life, with work that he had yet to show his publishers, all stashed away in an old filing cabinet at home.

One day Jemima came. Her mother had sent her to an Oxford secretarial college to learn typing and go to dances. She was long-legged and distraught like someone always late. She was more beautiful than ever.

"I love you," Pym told her, handing her bits of fruitcake in his room. "Wherever I was, whatever I was having to endure, I loved you all the time."

"But what were you having to endure?" Jemima asked.

For Jemima an extra kind of specialness was needed. Pym's reply took him by surprise. Afterwards, he decided that it had been lying in wait inside him and leapt out before he could prevent it. "It was for England," he said. "I'm lucky to be alive. If I tell anyone about it they'll kill me."

"Why ever will they do that?"

"It's secret. I swore never to tell."

"Then why are you telling me?"

"I love you. I had to do awful things to people. You can't imagine what it's like, carrying secrets like that alone."

As Pym heard himself saying this he remembered something that Axel had told him shortly before the end: There is no such thing as a life that does not return.

The next time he met Jemima, he described a brave girl he had worked with when he was doing his terribly secret work. He had in mind one of those muddy war photographs of beautiful women who win George Medals for being parachuted weekly into France.

"Her name was Wendy. We did secret missions into Russia together. We became partners."

"Did you do it with her?"

"It wasn't that kind of relationship. It was professional."

Jemima was fascinated. "You mean she was a tart?"

"Of course she wasn't. She was a secret agent like me."

"Have you ever done it with a tart?"

"No."

"Kenneth has. He's done it with two. One each end."

Each end of what? thought Pym, in rampant indignation. Me a secret hero, and she talks to me about sex! In his despair he wrote Belinda a twelve-pager about his platonic love for her, but by the time her reply came he had forgotten the context of his feelings. Sometimes Jemima came uninvited, wearing no make-up and her hair shoved behind her ears. She lay on the bed and read Jane Austen on her tummy, while she kicked a bare leg in the air or yawned.

"You can put your hand up my skirt if you like," she said.

"I'm fine, thanks," said Pym.

Too polite to disturb her further he sat in the chair and read *A Handbook of Old High German Literature* till she made a grimace and left. For a while after that, she didn't visit him. He kept glimpsing her in cinemas of which there were seven so he got round them nicely in a week. Always she was with another man and once, like her brother, she had two. Once during this same period Belinda came to stay with her, but told Pym she should keep away from him because it wasn't fair on Jem. Pym's need to impress Jemima now took on wild dimensions. He ate his meals alone and looked haunted, but she still didn't come to him. One evening, passing a brick wall, he deliberately dashed his knuckles against it until they bled, then hurried to her expensive lodgings in Merton Street, where he found her drying her long hair before the electric fire.

"Who've you been fighting?" she asked as she dabbed on iodine.

"I can't talk about it. Some things never go away."

Laying the fire on its back she cooked him toast while she went on brushing her hair and watching him through the strands.

"If *I* were a man," she said, "I wouldn't waste my energy hitting anybody. I wouldn't play rugger, I wouldn't box, I wouldn't spy for people. I wouldn't even ride. I'd save everything I had for fucking, again and again and again."

Pym departed, once more smouldering at the frivolity of those who failed to perceive his higher calling.

"Dearest Bel,

"Is there nothing you can do for Jemima? I simply cannot bear to see her go to the devil like this."

Did Pym know that he had tempted God? Certainly I know it now, this blowy night beside the sea as I try to write it so many years later. Whom else but his Maker was he provoking as he spun his stupid stories? Pym was calling down his fate on himself as surely as if he had begged for it by name in his prayers, and God dealt him the favour as God often did. Pym's fantasy version of himself waited out there like a decoy that no celestial eye could overlook, and the divine response was lying in his cubbyhole in the porter's lodge not twenty-four hours later when he came down to see who loved him this Saturday morning before breakfast. Ah! A letter! Blue in colour! Can it be perhaps from Jemima? Or is it from the virtuous Belinda, Jemima's friend? Is it from Lalage, perhaps—or Polly, or Prudence, or Anne? The answer, Jack, was none of them. It came, like so many bad things, from you. You were writing to Pym from Oman, care of the Trucial-Oman Scouts, though the stamp was true-blue British and the postmark Whitehall, because it had come to England by bag.

"My dear Magnus,

"As you will see from the letter heading, I have abandoned the fleshpots of Bern for harsher fare and am presently attached to the Military Mission here, where life is certainly a little more exciting! I still do the odd spot of church work, and I must say some of these Arabs sing pretty nicely. The purpose of my letter is twofold.

"1. To wish you all the best with your studies and to repeat my interest in your progress.

"2. To tell you that I have passed your name to our sister church back in the old country, since I gather they are a bit short of tenors in your region. So if you should chance to hear from a chap called Rob Gaunt, who tells you he is a friend of mine, I trust you will allow him to buy you a meal on my behalf, and make sure he does you proud! Incidentally, he is a Lieutenant Colonel, nominally a Gunner."

Pym had not long to wait, though every minute seemed a year. On the following Tuesday, returning from a testing tutorial on the theory of Ablaut, he found a second envelope waiting for him. This one was brown and of exceptional thickness, of a type I never saw in later years. Faint lines ran across it, giving it the appearance of corrugated cardboard though the texture was oily and smooth. There was no crest on the back, no address of sender. Even the manufacturer was secret. Yet Pym's name and address were immaculately typed, the stamp perfectly centered, and when he probed at the flap in the safety of his room, he discovered that it was stuck down with a rubberised bonding, which smelt of acid drops and parted in sticky threads like chewing gum. Inside lay a single sheet of thick white paper that was not so much folded as ironed. Prising it open the great spy observed at once the absence of a watermark. The type was large, as if for the partially sighted, the alignment faultless:

Box 777
The War Office
Whitehall S.W. 1

My dear Pym,

Our mutual friend Jack tells me excellent things about you and I would greatly like the opportunity to get to know you, as there are important matters of mutual interest that you might help us out with. Unfortunately I have a full programme at the moment, and shall be abroad by the time you receive this letter. I wonder therefore whether as an interim measure you would care to have a conversation with a colleague of mine who will be down your way on Monday of next week. If you are willing, why not take the bus to Burford and be in the saloon bar of the Monmouth Arms a little before midday? For ease of recognition he will be carrying a copy of Rider Haggard's *Allan Quatermain,* and I suggest you provide yourself with a *Financial Times,* which has a distinctive pink. His name is Michael and, like Jack, he had a valuable war. I have no doubt the two of you will hit it off famously.

With all good wishes,

Yours sincerely,

R. Gaunt

(Lt. Col., R.A., ret.)

For the next five days Pym abandoned work. He paced the back streets of the city, turning in his tracks to see who was following him. He bought a sheath knife and practised throwing it at trees until the blade broke. He wrote a Will and sent it to Belinda. When he entered his rooms he did so with circumspection, never descending or climbing his staircase without first listening for unfamiliar sounds. Where should he hide the secret letters? They were far too precious to throw away. Remembering something he had read, he gouged out the centre of his brand-new copy of Kluge's *Etymological Dictionary* to make a nest for them. From then on, his eviscerated Kluge became the first thing his eye fell upon when he returned from his sorties. To buy his copy of the *Financial Times* without attracting notice, he walked all the way to Littlemore but the village post office had never heard of it. By the time he returned to Oxford everything was shut. After a sleepless night he made a dawn raid on the Junior Common Room before anyone was up, and stole a back number from the racks.

Two buses went to Burford on weekday mornings but the second left him only twenty minutes to find the Monmouth Arms, so he took the first and got there at nine-forty, only to discover that the bus dropped him at the door. In his overalert condition the inn sign with its bold lettering struck him as a breach of national security and he strode past it with averted eyes. The rest of the morning crawled by on feet of lead. By eleven o'clock his notebook was already crammed with the number of every parked car in Burford, as well as copious notes on suspicious passers-by. By two minutes to twelve, duly seated in the saloon bar of the Monmouth Arms, he was seized by panic. Was he in the Monmouth Arms or the Golden Pheasant? Had Colonel Gaunt said the Horn of Plenty? In the furnace of Pym's mind these possibilities fused themselves into a brilliant and appalling alloy. He stepped into the forecourt and covertly reread the inn sign before hastening to the outdoor gentlemen's to throw cold water in his face. Standing at a stall he heard the sound of wind breaking and divined a bulky figure in a navy-blue mackintosh standing at his side. The body was tilted backwards and sideways, the eyes were cast upward in agony. For a frightful moment Pym feared the man was shot, until he realised that these contortions were caused by the difficulties of retaining a thick volume wedged under his armpit. Unable to perform, Pym buttoned himself, hurried back to the saloon and, laying *Financial Times* on the bar, ordered himself a bitter.

"Make that two, will you, sport?" a breezy voice told the barman. "Uncle's in the chair today. How are you? What about over there in the corner? Don't forget your paper."

I won't give you much of our courtship, Jack. When two people have decided to go to bed with each other, what passes between them before the event is a matter of form rather than of content. Nor do I remember very clearly what justifications we cooked up, for Michael was a shy man who had spent most of his life at sea, and his rare snatches of philosophy came out of him like escaping steam signals while he pummelled his mouth with a check handkerchief. "Somebody's got to dredge the drains, o'boy—fire with fire, only way. Unless we want the buggers to steal the ship from under us, which I *don't,* thank you." This last being a tensely underplayed statement of personal faith, which he at once smothered with a swig of beer. Michael was the first of your surrogates, Jack, so let him do duty for the rest. After Michael, if I remember, came David, and after David an Alan, and after Alan I forget. Pym would see no flaw in any of them. Or if he did, he translated it at once into a fiendishly clever piece of deception. Today of course I know the poor souls for what they were: members of that large, lost family of the British unprofessional classes that seems to wander by right between the secret services, the automobile clubs and the richer private charities. Not bad men by any means. Not dishonest men. Not stupid. But men who see the threat to their class as synonymous with the threat to England and never wandered far enough to know the difference. Modest men, practical, filling in their expense accounts and collecting their salaries, and impressing their Joes with their quiet expertise beneath the banter. Yet still, in their secret hearts, nourishing themselves on the same illusions that in those days nourished Pym. And needing their Joes to help them do it. Worried men, touched with an odour of pub meals and club squash, and a habit of looking round them while they paid, as if wondering whether there was a better way to live. And Pym, as he was passed from hand to hand, did his best to honour and obey each one of them. He believed in them; he cheered them with witty stories from his ever-increasing store. He strained to give them treats and make their day exciting. And when it was time for them to go he was always careful to have saved for them some last nugget of information to take home to their parents, even if he sometimes had to make it up.

"How's the colonel?" Pym ventured one day, belatedly recalling that Michael was still officially the stand-in for a Colonel Gaunt.

"Not a question I ever ask, personally, old boy," said Michael and to Pym's surprise began snapping his fingers as if he were summoning a dog.

Did Rob Gaunt exist? Pym never met him and later, when he was in a better position to ask, he could find nobody who would admit to having heard of him.

Now the brown envelopes flow in thick and fast, often two or three a week. The college porter grows so used to them he chucks them into Pym's pigeonhole without reading the address and Pym has to gouge out the centre of another dictionary to accommodate them. Always they contain instructions, and sometimes they contain small sums of cash, which the Michaels call his hard-lying money. Better still is Pym's float for operational expenses, which is kept at a fabulous twenty pounds: to entertaining secretary O. U. Hegelian Society, seven and ninepence . . . contribution to Peace in Korea campaign, five shillings . . . bottle of sherry for Society of Cultural Relations with the USSR get-together, fourteen shillings . . . coach trip to Cambridge for good-will visit to C.U. Branch members, plus entertainment, one pound fifteen shillings and ninepence. At first Pym is timid of these claims, fearing that by making them he is straining his masters' indulgence. The colonel will find someone cheaper, someone richer, someone who knows that gentlemen do not count the cost. But slowly he comes to realise that, far from displeasing his masters, his expenditures are taken as evidence of his industry.

"Dear Old Friend," wrote Michael—observing his own dictum that names must be avoided lest the enemy intercept our correspondence—

"Eleven. Thanks for your Eight safely to hand, a pearl as usual. I took the liberty of passing your rendering of the clans' latest choral to our lord and master upstairs and I haven't seen the old boy laugh so much since his aunt caught her left doo-dah in the you've-got-it. Brilliant and informative, dear sir, and be advised that the great man himself remarked upon your perseverance. Now to the usual shopping list.

"1. Are you certain that our distinguished clan treasurer spells his name with a Z and not an S? The Doomsday Book contains an Abraham S, mathematician, late of Manchester Grammar School who fits the bill, but definitely no Z. (Though it's always possible of course that a gentleman of his tartan spells it both ways anyway . . .) Don't force it, as the Bishop said, but if Lady Luck pushes the answer your way, let us know. . . .

"2. Please keep your Eversharp ear open for talk about our gallant Scottish brethren getting up a delegation to attend the Sarajevo Youth Festival in July. The powers that be are getting unaccountably miffed about gents who accept large government grants only to oil off abroad and spit on said government's shadow.

"3. Regarding the distinguished visiting vocalist from Leeds University who is slated to address the clan on March 1st, do please keep an eye and an ear open for his faithful spouse, Magdalene (God bless us!), who by repute is quite as musical as her old man, but prefers to keep her head down owing to her delicate scientific interests. All comments gleefully received . . ."

Why did Pym do it, Tom? In the beginning was the deed. Not the motive, least of all the word. It was his own choice. It was his own life. No one forced him. Anywhere along the line, or right at the start of it, he could have yelled no and surprised himself. He never did. It took another ten university generations before he threw in the sponge, and by then the lines were drawn for good, all the lines. Why chuck away his freedom and good luck, you will ask, his good looks and good humour and good heart, just when they were coming into their own at last? Why befriend a bunch of grimy and unhappy people of alien background and mentality, press himself upon them, all smiling and obliging—because, believe me, there was no glamour to the university Left by then; Berlin and Korea had put paid to that for good—merely in order to be able to betray them? Why sit whole nights away in back rooms among sullen girls from the provinces who scowled and ate nut cutlets and took Firsts in Economics, in order to profess a view of the world that he had to learn as he went along, twisting his mind inside out, killing himself on cheap cigarettes while passionately agreeing that everything that was fun in life was a damn shame? Why do a Father Murgo on them, offering his bourgeois origins for their condemnation, abasing himself, revelling in their disapproval, yet gaining no absolution from it—only to rush off and bang the scales down the other way in a gush of embellished reports of the night's proceedings? I should know. I have done it and I have made others do it, and I was never less than cogent in my persuasion. For England. So that the free world can sleep safely in its bed at night while the secret watchers guard her in their rugged care. For love. To be a good chap, a good soldier.

Abie Ziegler's name, whether with a Z or an S, was written, you may be sure, in capitals on every left wing poster in every college lodge of the university. Abie was a publicity-crazed pipe-smoking sex maniac about four feet high. His one ambition in life was to be noticed and he saw the depleted Left as a fast lane to this end. There were a dozen painless ways in which Michael and his people could have found out whatever they wanted about Abie, but Pym had to be their man. The great spy would have walked all the way to Manchester just to look up Siegler or Ziegler in the phone book, such was the drive with which he had flung himself into his secret mission. This is not betrayal, he told himself when he was being the Michaels' man; this is the real thing. These strident men and women with their college scarves and funny accents who refer to me as our bourgeois friend are my own countrymen planning to upset our social order.

For his country, or whatever he called it, Pym addressed envelopes and memorised the addresses, played steward at public meetings, marched in dispirited processions, and afterwards wrote down whoever came. For his country he took any menial job going if it earned him favour. For his country or for love or for the Michaels, he stood at street corners late at night, offering unreadable Marxist pamphlets to passersby who told him he ought to be in bed. Then dumped the surplus copies in a ditch and put his own money into the Party kitty because he was too proud to reclaim it from the Michaels. And if occasionally, as he sat up still later writing his meticulous reports on tomorrow's revolutionists, the ghost of Axel materialised before him and Axel's cry of "Pym you bastard where are you" whispered in his ear, Pym had only to wave him away with a combination of the Michaels' logic and his own: "You were my country's enemy even if you were my friend. You were unsound. You had no papers. Sorry."

"Hell are you running with all those Reds for?" Sefton Boyd asked drowsily one day, face downward in the grass. They had driven out to Godstow in his sports car for lunch, and were lying in a meadow above the weir. "Somebody told me they'd seen you at the Cole Group. You made a piss-awful speech about the madness of war. Hell's the Cole Group when it's at home?"

"It's a discussion group run by G.D.H. Cole. It explores avenues of Socialism."

"Are they queer?"

"Not that I know of."

"Well, explore somebody else's avenue. I also saw your nasty name on a poster. College secretary of the Socialist Club. I mean, Christ, you're supposed to be in the Grid."

"I like to see all sides," said Pym.

"They're not all sides. We are. They're one side. They've pinched half Europe and they're a band of absolute shits. Take my words for it."

"I'm doing it for my country," Pym said. "It's secret."

"Bollocks," said Sefton Boyd.

"It's true. I get instructions from London every week. I'm in the Secret Service."

"Like you were in the German Army at Grimble's," Sefton Boyd suggested. "Like you were Himmler's aunt at Willow's. Like you fucked Willow's wife and your father carried messages for Winston Churchill."

A day came, long spoken of and frequently postponed, when Michael took Pym home to meet his family. "Double First material," Michael warned him in an advance write-up of his spouse. "Mind like a dart. No mercy." Mrs. Michael turned out to be a ravenous, fast-fading woman in a slashed skirt and a low blouse over an unappetising chest. While her husband did things in his shed, where he appeared to live, Pym inexpertly mixed the Yorkshire pudding and fought off her embraces until he was obliged to take refuge with the children on the lawn. When it rained he marched them to the drawing-room and posted them round him in self-defence while he pushed their Dinky toys.

"Magnus, what are your father's initials?" Mrs. Michael said bossily from the doorway. I remember her voice, querulous and interrogative, as if I had just eaten her last chocolate instead of refusing to pop upstairs with her to bed.

"R.T.," said Pym.

She was trailing a copy of a Sunday newspaper in her hand and must have been reading it in the kitchen.

"Well, it says here that there's an R. T. Pym standing as Liberal Candidate for Gulworth North. He's described as a philanthropist and property broker. There can't be two, can there?"

Pym took the paper from her. "No," he agreed, staring at Rick's Portrait of Self with Red Setter. "There can't."

"Only you could have told us. I mean you're terribly rich and superior, I know, but a thing like that is jolly exciting if you're people like us."

Sick with apprehension Pym returned to Oxford and forced himself to read, if only glancingly, the last four letters from Rick that he had tossed unopened in his desk drawer, next to Axel's copy of Grimmelshausen and other unpaid bills.

Inside his camel-hair dressing-gown Pym at fifty-three was shivering. It had come over him suddenly, as it sometimes did, a fever without a temperature. He had been writing for as long as he had been awake, which to judge by his beard was a long time. The shiver turned to a shake, which was how it went. It twisted his neck muscles and gnawed at the backs of his thighs. He started to sneeze. The first sneeze was long and speculative. The second followed it like an answering shot. They're fighting over me, he thought: the good guys and the bad guys are shooting it out inside me. Whoops: O God receive my soul. Whoops: O Lord forgive him, for he knew not what he did. Rising, he held one hand over his mouth and with the other turned up the gas fire. Clutching himself, he began a prisoner's tour of the room's perimeter, dipping into his knees with each stride. From a corner of Miss Dubber's carpet he paced ten feet, made a right angle and paced eight more. He stopped and surveyed the rectangle he had measured. How did Rick endure it? he asked himself. How did Axel? He raised his arms, comparing the cell's breadth with his own wingspan. "Christ," he whispered aloud. "I'll hardly fit."

Picking up the reinforced briefcase which he had still not opened, he carried it to the fire and sat there, brows drawn, eyes glowering at the flames while the shaking grew more violent. Rick should have died when I killed him. Pym whispered the words out loud, daring himself to hear it. "You should have died when I killed you." He returned to his desk and took up his pen. Every line written is a line behind me. You do it once, then die. He wrote fast. And as he wrote, he began to smile again. Love is whatever you can still betray, he thought. Betrayal can only happen if you love.

Mary too was praying. She was kneeling on her school hassock with her eyes plunged into the night-time of her palms and she was praying that she was not at school any more but at their little Saxon church in Plush that went with the estate, with her father and brother kneeling protectively to either side of her and their Colonel the Reverend High Anglican vicar barking out his fire orders and rattling the incense like a mess-gong. Or that she was kneeling at her own bedside in her own room in her nightdress with her hair brushed and her bottom pushed out, praying that nobody would make her go to boarding-school again. Yet however much Mary prayed and begged, she knew that she wasn't going anywhere but where she was: in the English church in Vienna where I come every Wednesday for early service, in common with the usual band of upwardly mobile Christians led by the British Ambassadress and the American Minister's wife and supported by Caroline Lumsden, Bee Lederer and a heavy contingent of Dutch, Norwegians and also-rans from the German Embassy next door. Fergus and Georgie are roosting in the pew behind me without a pious thought between them, it's Tom not me who is at boarding-school and it is Magnus not God who is all-pervasive, all-knowing yet invisible and who holds the keys to all our destinies. So Magnus you bastard, if there is any truth left in you at all, do me a favour will you and lean out of your firmament and advise me, of your infinite goodness and wisdom—just for once with no lies, evasion or decoration—what the hell I am supposed to do about your dear old friend from Corfu cricket ground who is sitting not praying in the same pew as myself just across the aisle on the bride's side—is slender and drooping with a pepper-and-salt moustache and bottleneck shoulders, exactly as Tom described him right down to the cobwebby lines of laughter round his eyes and the grey raincoat wrapped around his shoulders like a cape. For this is neither the first appearance of your grey angel nor the second. It is the third and the most imaginative in two days, and each time that I do nothing about it I feel him draw a step nearer to me, and if you don't come back soon and tell me what to do, you may very well find us in bed together, because after all, as you used to assure me in Berlin, you can't beat a little sex for breaking the tension and removing social barriers.

Giles Marriott the English chaplain was inviting all those of a pure heart and humble mind to draw near with faith. Mary stood up, straightened her skirt and stepped into the aisle. Caroline Lumsden and her husband were ahead of her but the ethics of piety required that they greet one another after and not before the Sacrament. Georgie and Fergus stayed firmly in their pew, too high-minded to sacrifice their agnosticism for cover. More likely they just don't know what to do, thought Mary. Clasping her hands to her chin, she quickly ducked her head again in prayer. Oh God, oh Magnus, oh Jack, tell me what to do now! He is standing a foot behind me, I can smell his stale cigar smoke. Tom had mentioned that too. At the airport, as an afterthought: "He smoked little cigars, Mum, like Dad used to when he was giving up cigarettes!" And he has *limped* along his pew. He has *limped* into the aisle. A dozen people or more had fallen in behind Mary, including the Ambassadress, her spotty daughter and a flock of Americans. Yet a limp is a limp and good Christians stop for it and smile and let it go ahead, and there he was behind her, the privileged recipient of everybody's charity. And still each time the queue takes a pace nearer to the altar he *limps* as intimately as if he were patting me on the bum. Mary had never known such an insinuating, impudent, flagrant limp in all her life. His merry eyes were burning her back, she could feel them. She could feel her neck burning and her face heating as the moment of divine consummation approached. At the altar rail Jenny Forbes, the Administration Officer's wife, was genuflecting before retiring to her seat. As well she might, the way she's carrying on with the new young Chancery guard. Mary stepped forward gratefully and kneeled in her place. Get off my back you creep, stay your own side. The creep did, but by then his softly murmured words were bellowing inside her head like a bullhorn. "I can help you find him. I will send a message to the house."

In choral unison the questions were shrieking inside Mary's head. Send how? A message saying what? To instruct her in the causes of her disloyalty? To explain to her why, as she was leaving yesterday's International Ladies' bunfight, she had not flung out an accusing arm at him as he smiled at her from across the street? Why she had not screamed "Arrest that man!" to Georgie and Fergus who were parked not forty feet from the doorway he emerged from—jauntily, no hood was ever like that? Or again when he appeared not six yards from her at Swab's supermarket?

Giles Marriott was gazing down at her in puzzlement, offering her for the second time the body of Christ which was given for her. Hastily Mary placed her hands as she had been taught since childhood—right over left and make a cross with them. He laid the wafer on her palm. She raised it to her lips and felt it stick, then lie like a log on her dry tongue. No, I am not worthy, she thought wretchedly as she waited for the chalice. It's true. I am not worthy to come to this Thy table or anybody else's table either. Every moment I fail to denounce him is another moment of disloyalty. He is tempting me and I am hearing him for all I am worth. He is drawing me to him and I am saying yes please. I am saying, "I will come to you for the sake of Magnus and my child." I am saying, "I will come to you if you are clarity, even if you are evil. Because I am searching for a light, any light at all, and going half off my head in the darkness. I will come to you because you are the other half of Magnus, and therefore the other half of me."

As she walked back to her seat she caught Bee Lederer's eye. They exchanged pious smiles.

11

There was never a by-election like it, Tom, there was never an election like it. We are born, we get married, we divorce, we die. But somewhere along the way, if we get the chance, we should also stand as Liberal Candidate for the ancient fishing and weaving constituency of Gulworth North situated in the remoter fens of East

Anglia in the unlit post-war years before television replaced the Temperance Hall, and communications were such that a man's character could be born again by removing it a hundred and fifty miles north-east of London. If we do not have the luck to stand ourselves, then the least we can do is drop everything from crypto-Communism to unconsummated sexual exploration and, forgetting the later *Minnesänger,* hasten to our father's side in the Hour of his Greatest Test to shiver on icy doorsteps for him, and charm votes out of old ladies in the manner in which he has instructed us, and see them right if it kills us, and tell the world by loudspeaker what a crackerjack fellow he is, and that they will never want for anything again, and promise ourselves, and mean it, that as soon as polling day is over we will forsake all other lives and take our place among the working classes where our hearts and origins have always been, as witness our clandestine espousal of the workers' cause during the formative years of our studentship.

It was deep winter when Pym arrived and it is winter still, for I have never been back, I never dared. The same snow lies over the fens and marshes and freezes Quixote's windmills to a standstill against the cindery Flemish sky. The same steepled towns dangle from the sea's horizon, the Brueghel faces of our electorate are as pink with zeal as they were those three decades ago. Our Candidate's convoy, led by the lifelong Liberal Mr. Cudlove and his precious cargo, still bears the message from chalky schoolroom to paraffin-heated hall, skidding and cursing over country lanes while Our Candidate broods and downs another wet, and Sylvia and Major Maxwell-Cavendish fight in undertones over the Ordnance Survey map. In my memory our campaign is a drama tour of the theatre of the politically absurd as we advance across snow and marshland upon Gulworth's majestic Town Hall itself—hired against all advice from those who said we'd never fill it, but we did —for Our Candidate's Positively Last Appearance. There suddenly the comedy stops dead. The masks and fools' bells come clattering to the stage as God in one simple question presents us with His bill for all our fun till here.

Evidence, Tom. Facts.

Here is Rick's rosette of yellow silk that he wore for his great night. It was run up for him by the same luckless tailor who made his racing colours. Here is the centre-page spread from the *Gulworth Mercury* next day. Read all about it for yourself. CANDIDATE DEFENDS HIS HONOUR. SAYS LET GULWORTH NORTH BE THE JUDGE. See the picture of the podium with its illuminated organ pipes and curving staircase? All we need is Makepeace Watermaster. See your grandfather, Tom, centre stage, hacking at the speckled beams of the spotlights, and your father peeking coyly from behind him, forelock at the slope? Hear the thunder of the great saint's piety rising into the wagon roof, do you? Pym knows every word of Rick's speech by heart, every hammy gesture and inflection. Rick is describing himself as an honest trader who will devote "my life for as long as I am spared, and as long as you deem in your wisdom that you require me," to the service of the constituency, and he's about five seconds from making a swipe with his left forearm to cut off the heads of the Unbelievers. Fingers closed and slightly curled as ever. He is telling us that he's a humble Christian and a father and a straight dealer, and he's going to rid Gulworth North of the twin heresies of High Toryism and Low Socialism, though sometimes in his teetotal fervour he gets them the wrong way round. He also hates excess. It really churns him up. Now comes the good news. You can hear it from the faith in his voice. With Rick as its Member of Parliament, Gulworth North will undergo a Renaissance beyond its dreams. Its moribund herring trade shall rise from its bed and walk. Its decaying textile industry shall bring forth milk and honey. Its farms shall be freed of Socialist bureaucracy and become the envy of the world. Its crumbling railways and canals shall be miraculously cut loose from the toils of the Industrial Revolution. Its streets shall run with liquidity. Its aged shall have their savings protected against Confiscation by the State, its menfolk shall be spared the ignominies of conscription. Pay-As-You-Earn taxation shall go and so shall all the other iniquities that are featured in the Liberal Manifesto which Rick has partly read but believes in totally.

So far so good, but tonight is our final curtain and Rick has worked up something special. Daringly he turns his back to the punters and addresses his faithful supporters ranged behind him on the dais. He is about to thank us. Watch. "First my darling Sylvia, without whom nothing could have been accomplished— thank you, Sylvia, thank you! Let's have a big hand for Sylvia my Queen!" The punters oblige with enthusiasm. Sylvia pulls the gracious smile for which she is retained. Pym is expecting to be called next but he is not. Rick's blue gaze has steel in it tonight, the glow is on him. More voice and less breath to his bombast. Shorter sentences but the champ throws them harder. He thanks the Chairman of the Gulworth Liberal Party and *his* very lovely lady wife—Marjory, my dear, don't be shy, where are you?—He thanks our miserable Liberal agent, an unbeliever called Donald Somebody, see the caption, who since the court's arrival on his territory has retired into a fuming sulk from which he has only tonight emerged. He thanks our transport lady whom Mr. Muspole claims to have favoured in the snooker room, and a Miss Somebody Else who made sure Your Candidate was never once late for a meeting—laughter—though Morrie Washington swears she isn't safe to be sat with in the back. He passes "to these other gallant and faithful helpers of mine." Morrie and Syd leer like a pair of reprieved murderers from the back row, Mr. Muspole and Major Maxwell-Cavendish prefer to scowl. It is there in the photograph, Tom, look for yourself. Next to Morrie roosts an inebriated radio comedian whose failing reputation Rick has contrived to harness to our campaign, just as in the last weeks he has wheeled in witless cricketers and titled owners of hotel chains and other so-called Liberal personalities, marching them through town like prisoners and tossing them back to London when they have served their brief span of usefulness.

Now take another look at Magnus seated on the right hand of his maker. Rick arrives at him last and every word he shouts at him is replete with secret knowledge and reproach. "He won't tell you himself so I will. He's too modest. This boy of mine here is one of the finest students of law this country has yet seen and not only this country either. He could hold this speech in five different languages and do it better than I can in any one of them." Laughter. Cries of "Shame!" and "No, no." "But that never stopped him from working his feet off for his old man throughout this campaign. Magnus, you've been crackerjack, old son, and your old man's best pal. Here's to you!"

But the dinning ovation does nothing to alleviate Pym's anguish. In the lonely reality of being Pym and listening to Rick resume his speech, his heart is beating in terror while he counts off the clichés and waits for the explosion that will destroy the candidate and his bold tissue of deceptions forevermore. It will blow the wagon roof and its gilded bearings into the night sky. It will smash the very stars that provide the grand finale of Rick's speech.

"People will say to you," cries Rick, on a note of ever-mounting humility, "and they've said it to me—they've stopped me in the street—touched my arm—'Rick,' they say, 'what is Liberalism except a package of ideals? We can't *eat* ideals, Rick,' they say. 'Ideals don't buy us a cup of tea or a nice touch of English lamb chop, Rick, old boy. We can't put our ideals in the collection box. We can't pay for our son's education with ideals. We can't send him out into the world to take his place in the highest law courts of the land with nothing but a few ideals in his pocket. So what's the point, Rick?' they say to me, 'in this modern world of ours, of a party of ideals?' " The voice drops. The hand, till now so agitated, reaches out palm downward to cup the head of an invisible child. "And I say to them, good people of Gulworth, and I say to you too!" The same hand flies upward and points to Heaven as Pym in his sickly apprehension sees the ghost of Makepeace Watermaster leap from its pulpit and fill the Town Hall with a dismal glow. "I say this. Ideals are like the stars. We cannot reach them, but we profit by their presence!"

Rick has never been better, more passionate, more sincere. The applause rises like an angry sea, the faithful rise with it. Pym rises with the faithful, pummelling his hands together loudest of us all. Rick weeps. Pym is on the brink. The good people have their Messiah, the Liberals of Gulworth North have too long been a flock without a shepherd; no Liberal candidate has stood here since the war. At Rick's side our local Liberal Party Chairman is smacking his yeoman's paws together and rhubarbing ecstatically into Rick's ear. At Rick's back, the whole court is following Pym's example, standing, clapping, rah-rahing "Rick for Gulworth!" Thus reminded, Rick turns to them yet again and, taking his cue from any number of the variety shows he loves, indicates the court to the people, saying: "You owe it to them, not to me." But once more his blue eyes are on Pym, saying, "Judas, patricide, murderer of your best pal."

Or so it seems to Pym.

For this is exactly the moment, this is exactly where everyone is standing and beaming and clapping, when the bomb that Pym has planted goes off: Rick with his back to the enemy, his face upon Pym and his beloved helpers, half ready, I think, to break into a rousing song. Not "Underneath the Arches," it is too secular, but "Onward, Christian Soldiers" will be first rate. When suddenly the din takes sick and dies on its feet in front of us, and a freezing silence slips in after it as if somebody has flung open the great doors of the Town Hall and let in the vengeful angels of the past.

Someone unreliable has spoken from under the minstrel gallery where the press sits. At first the acoustics are so lousy they do not allow us more than a few querulous notes, but already the notes are subversive. The speaker tries again but louder. She is not a person yet, merely a damned woman, with the kind of piping, strident Irish voice that menfolk instinctively detest, wheedling you with its impotence in the same breath as its cause. A man shouts "Silence, woman," then "Be quiet," and then "Shut up, you bitch!" Pym recognises the port-fed voice of Major Blenkinsop. The major is a Free-Trader and a rural Fascist from the embarrassing

Right of our great movement. But the scratchy Irish voice prevails like a door squeak that will not go away, and no amount of slamming or oiling seems able to silence it. Some tiresome Home-Ruler probably. Ah good, somebody has got hold of her. It is the major again—see his bald head and yellow rosette of office. He is calling her "My good *madame*," of all things, and manhandling her towards the door. But the freedom of the press prevents him. The hacks are leaning over the balcony shouting "What's your name, miss?" and even "Yell it at him again!" Major Blenkinsop is suddenly neither a gentleman nor an officer but an upper-class lout with a screaming Irishwoman on his hands. Other women are yelling "Leave her be!" and "Get your hands off her, you dirty swine." Somebody shouts "Black and Tan bastard!"

Then we hear her, then we see her, both clearly. She is small and furious in black, a widowed shrew. She wears a pill-box hat. A bit of black veil hangs from it by a corner, ripped aside by herself or someone else. With the perversity of a crowd, everybody wants to hear her. She begins her question for perhaps the third time. Her brogue comes from the front of the mouth and appears to be spoken through a smile, but Pym knows it is no smile but the grimace of a hatred too powerful to be kept inside her. She speaks each word as she has learned it, in the order she has arranged them. The formulation is offensive in its clarity.

"I wish to know please—whether it is true—if you would be so kind, sir—that the Liberal Parliamentary Candidate for the Constituency of Gulworth North—has served a prison sentence for swindle and embezzlement. Thank you very much for your consideration."

And Rick's face on Pym while her arrow shoots him in the back. Rick's blue eyes opening wide on impact, but still steady on Pym—exactly as they were five days ago, when he lay in his ice-bath with his feet crossed and his eyes open, saying, "Killing me is not enough, old son."

Come back ten days with me, Tom. The excited Pym has arrived from Oxford light of heart, determined as a protector of the nation to throw his changeful weight behind the democratic process and have some fun in the snow. The campaign is in full cry but the trains to Gulworth have a way of petering out at Norwich. It is weekend and God has ruled that English by-elections be held on Thursdays, even if He has long forgotten why. It is evening: the Candidate and his cohorts are on the stomp. But as Pym alights bag in hand at Norwich's imposing railway station, there stands faithful Syd Lemon at the barrier with a campaign car plastered with the Pym regalia waiting to whisk him to the main meeting of the evening, scheduled for nine o'clock in the village of Little Chedworth-on-the-Water, where according to Syd the last missionary was eaten for tea. The car's windows are darkened with posters saying "PYM THE PEOPLE'S MAN." Rick's great head—the one, as I now know, that he had quite likely sold—is pasted to the boot. A loudspeaker bigger than a ship's cannon is wired to the roof. A full moon is up. Snow covers the fields and Paradise is all around.

"Let's drive to St. Moritz," Pym says as Syd hands him one of Meg's meat pies, and Syd laughs and musses Pym's hair. Syd is not an attentive driver but the lanes are empty and the snow is kind. He has brought a ginger ale bottle filled with whisky. As they meander between the laden hedges they swallow big mouthfuls.

Thus fortified, Syd briefs Pym on the state of the battle.

"We favour free worship, Titch, and we're mustard for Home Ownership for All with Less Red Tape."

"We always were," says Pym, and Syd gives him the hairy eyeball in case he's being cheeky.

"We take a poor view of ubiquitous High Toryism in all its forms—"

"Iniquitous," Pym corrects him, sipping again from the ginger ale bottle.

"Our Candidate is proud of his record as an English Patriot and Churchman. He's a Merchantman of England who has fought for his country, Liberalism being the only right road for Britain. He's been educated in the University of the World, he's never touched a drop of the hard stuff in his life, nor have you, and don't forget it." He grabbed back the ginger ale bottle and took a long, teetotal draught.

"But will he win?" said Pym.

"Listen. If you'd have come in here with ready money on the day your dad announced his intention, you could have had fifty to one. By the time me and Lord Muspole showed up he was down to twenty-fives and we took a ton each. Next morning after he done his adoption you couldn't get tens. He's nine to two now and shrinking and I'll have a small wager with you that come polling day he's evens. Now ask me whether he'll win."

"What's the competition?"

"There isn't any. The Labour boy's a Scottish schoolmaster from Glasgow. Got a red beard. Small bloke. Looks like a mouse peering out of a red bear's backside. Old Muspole sent a couple of the lads round the other night to cheer up one of his meetings. Put them in kilts and gave them football rattles and had them roaring round the streets till morning. Gulworth doesn't hold with rowdiness, Titch. They take a very poor view of the Labour Candidate's drunken friends singing 'Little Nellie of the Glen' at three in the morning on the church steps."

The car slides gracefully towards a windmill. Syd rights it and they proceed.

"And the Tory?"

"The Tory is everything a Tory candidate should be with knobs on. He's a landed pukka sahib who toils one day a week in the City, rides to hounds, gives beads to the natives and wants to bring back the thumbscrew for first offenders. His wife opens garden fêtes with her teeth."

"But who's our traditional mainstay?" asks Pym, remembering his social history.

"The God-thumpers are solid for him, so's the Masons, so's the Old Nellies. The teetotallers are a cakewalk, so's the anti-betting league so long as they don't read the form books and I'll thank you not to mention the neverwozzers, Titch, they've been put out to grass for the duration. The rest are a pig in a poke. The sitting member was a Red but he's dead. The last election gave him five thousand majority on a straight race with the Tory, but look at the Tory. The total poll was thirty-five thousand but since then another five thousand juvenile delinquents have been enfranchised and two thousand geriatrics have passed on to a better life. The farmers are nasty, the fishermen are broke and the hoi polloi don't know their willies from their elbows."

Switching on the interior light Syd allows the car to steer itself while he reaches into the back and fishes out an imposing red-and-black pamphlet with a photograph of Rick on the front cover. Flanked by somebody's adoring spaniels, he is reading a book before an unfamiliar fireside, a thing he has never done in his life. "A Letter to the Electorate of Gulworth North," runs the caption. The paper, in defiance of the prevailing austerity, is high gloss.

"We are also supported by the ghost of Sir Codpiece Makewater, V.C.," Syd adds with particular relish. "Peruse our rear page."

Pym did so and discovered a ruled box resembling a Swiss obituary notice:

A FINAL NOTE

Your Candidate derives his proudest political inspiration from his childhood Mentor and Friend, Sir Makepeace Watermaster, M.P., the World Famous Liberal and Christian Employer whose stern but Fair hand following his Father's untimely Death guided him past Youth's many Pitfalls to his present Highly consolidated position which brings him into daily Contact with the Highest in the Land.

Sir Makepeace was a man of God-fearing Family, an Abstainer, an orator who knew no Equal without whose Shining inspiration it is safe to say Your Candidate might never have presumed to put myself forward for the Historic Judgment of the people of Gulworth North which has already become a Home from home for me, and if elected I shall obtain a Major property here at the earliest convenience.

Your Candidate proposes to Dedicate himself to your interests with the same Humility as was ever displayed by Sir Makepeace, who went to his grave preaching Man's moral right to Property, free Trading and a fair Crack of the Whip for Women.

Your future Humble Servant,

Richard T. Pym

"You've got the learning, Titch. What do you think of it?" asks Syd, with vulnerable earnestness.

"It's beautiful," says Pym.

"Of course it is," says Syd.

A village, then a church spire glide towards them. As they enter the main street a yellow banner proclaims that Our Liberal Candidate will be speaking here tonight. A few old Land Rovers and Austin Sevens, already snowbound, stand dejectedly in the carpark. Taking a last pull from the ginger ale bottle, Syd carefully parts his hair before the mirror. Pym notices that he is dressed with unaccustomed sobriety. The frosted air smells of cow dung and the sea. Before them rises the archaic Temperance Hall of Little Chedworth-on-the-Water. Syd slips him a peppermint and in they go.

The ward chairman has been speaking for some time but only to the front row, and those of us at the back hear nothing. The rest of the congregation either stares into the rafters or at the display cards of the Common Man's Candidate: Rick at

Napoleon's desk with his law books ranged behind him. Rick on the factory floor for the first and only time in his life, sharing a cup of tea with the Salt of the Earth. Rick as Sir Francis Drake gazing towards the misted armada of Gulworth's dying herring fleet. Rick the pipe-sucking agriculturalist intelligently appraising a cow. To one side of the ward chairman, under a festoon of yellow bunting, sits a lady officer of the ward committee. To the other runs a row of empty chairs waiting for the Candidate and his party. Periodically, while the chairman labours on, Pym catches a stray phrase like the Evils of Conscription or the Curse of Big Monopolies—or worse still an apologetic interjection such as "as I was saying to you only a moment ago." And twice, as nine o'clock becomes nine-thirty, then ten past ten, an elderly Shakespearean messenger hobbles painfully from a vestry, clutching his earlobe to tell us in a quavering voice that the Candidate is on his way, he has a busy schedule of meetings tonight, the snow is holding him up. Till just when we have given up hope, Mr. Muspole strides in accompanied by Major Maxwell-Cavendish, both prim as beadles in their greys. Together the two men march up the aisle and mount the dais, and while Muspole shakes hands with the chairman and his lady, the major draws a sheaf of notes from a briefcase and lays them on the table. And though Pym by the end of the campaign had heard Rick speak on no less than twenty-one occasions between that night and his Eve of Poll address in the Town Hall, he never once saw him refer to the major's notes or so much as recognise their presence. So that gradually he concluded they were not notes at all, but a piece of stage business to prepare us for the Coming.

"What's Maxie done with his moustache?" Pym whispers excitedly to Syd, who has sat up with a jolt after a bit of a nap. "Mortgaged it?" If Pym expects a witticism in return, he is disappointed.

"It's not deemed appropriate—that's what he's done with it," says Syd shortly. In the same moment Pym sees the light of pure love suffuse Syd's face as Rick sweeps in.

The order of appearance never changed, neither did the allocation of duties. After Muspole and the major come Perce Loft and poor Morrie Washington who is already getting bother with his liver. Perce holds open the door. Morrie steps through and sometimes, as tonight, gets a bit of a clap because the uninitiated mistake him for Rick, which is not surprising since Morrie, though a third Rick's size, spends most of his life and all his money in an effort to achieve Total Assumption with his idol. If Rick buys a new camel-hair coat, Morrie rushes off and buys two like it. If Rick is in two-tone shoes, so is Morrie, and white socks as well. But tonight Morrie has dressed like the rest of the court in churchy grey. For love of Rick he has even managed to get some of the booze out of his complexion. He steps in, he takes up his place across the door from Perce and fiddles with his rosette to make sure it is working properly. Then Morrie and Perce together crane their heads back in the direction they have come from, straining, as the audience is, to catch a first sight of their champion. And look!—they are clapping! And look, so are we! —as enter Rick, at a spanking pace, for we statesmen have no time to lose, and even as he comes striding up the aisle he is earnestly conferring with the Highest in the Land. Is that Sir Laurence Olivier with him?—looks more like Bud Flanagan to me. It is neither, as we shall quickly learn. It is none other than the great Bertie Tregenza, the Radio Bird Man, a lifelong Liberal. On the dais Muspole and the major present the other notables to the chairman and guide them to their seats. At last the moment we have come for is upon us when the only man left standing is the man in the photographs around him. Syd leans forward, listening with his eyes. Our Candidate begins speaking. A deliberate, unimpressive opening. Good evening and thank you for coming here in such numbers on this cold winter's night. I am sorry to have had to keep you waiting. A joke for the Nellies: they tell me I kept my mother waiting a whole week. Laughter from the Nellies as the joke is turned to account. But I'll promise you this, people of Gulworth North: nobody here is going to be kept waiting by your next Member of Parliament! More laughter and some applause from the faithful as the Candidate's tone stiffens.

"Ladies and Gentlemen, you have ventured out on this inhospitable night for one reason only. Because you care about your country. Well that makes two of us, because I care about it too. I care about the way it's run and the way it's not run. I care because Politics are People. People with hearts to tell them what they want, for themselves and for one another. People with minds to tell them how to achieve it. People with the Faith and Guts to send Adolf Hitler back to where he came from. People like ourselves. Gathered here tonight. The Salt of the Earth and make no bones about it. English people, root and bough, worried about their country, and looking for the man to see them right."

Pym peers round the little hall. Not a face but is turned flowerlike towards Rick's light. Save one, a little woman in a veiled pill-box hat, sitting like her own shadow, all apart and the black veil hiding her face. She is in mourning, Pym decides, moved at once to sympathy. She has come here for a spot of company, poor soul. On the dais Rick is explaining the meaning of Liberalism for the benefit of those unfamiliar with the differences between the three great parties. Liberalism is not a dogma but a way of life, he says. It is faith in the essential goodness of man regardless of colour, race or creed in a spirit of all pulling together to one end. The fine points of policy thus dispatched, he can proceed to the solid centre of his speech, which is himself. He describes his humble origins and his mother's tears when she heard him vow to follow in the footsteps of the great Sir Makepeace. If only my father could be here tonight, seated among you good people. An arm lifts and points to the rafters, as if picking out an aeroplane, but it is God whom Rick is indicating.

"And let me say this to the voters of Little Chedworth tonight. Without a certain person up there acting night and day for me as my senior partner—laugh if you will, because I would rather be the object of your mockery than fall prey to the cynicism and Godlessness that is sweeping through our country—without a certain person's helping hand and you all know who I mean, oh yes you do!—I wouldn't be where I am today, offering myself—be it never so humbly—to the people of Gulworth North." He speaks of his understanding of the export market and his pride at selling British products to those foreigners who will never know how much they owe us. His arm strikes out at us again and he issues a challenge. He is British to the core and he doesn't care who knows it. He can bring British common sense to every problem you throw at him. "Bar none," says Syd approvingly under his breath. But if we know a better man for the job than Rickie Pym, we had better speak up now. If we prefer the airy-fairy class prejudices of the High Tories who think they own the people's birthright, whereas in reality they are sucking the people's blood, then we should stand up here and now and say so without fear or favour and let's have it out once and for all. Nobody volunteers. On the other hand, if we would rather hand over the country to the Marxists and Communists and the bully-boy trade unions who are bent on dragging this country to its knees—and let's face it, that's what the Labour vote is all about—then better to come out with it in the full glare of the public gaze of the voters of Little Chedworth and not skulk in the dark like miserable conspirators.

Once again, nobody volunteers, though Rick and everyone on the dais glowers around the room in search of a miscreant hand or guilty face.

"Now press button B for Beautiful," Syd whispers dreamily and closes his eyes for extra pleasure as Rick starts the long climb towards the stars, which like Liberal ideals we cannot reach but can only profit from their presence.

Again Pym looks round. Not a face but is wrapt in love for Rick, save the one bereaved woman in her veil. This is what I came for, Pym tells himself excitedly. Democracy is when you share your father with the world. The applause fades but Pym goes on clapping until he realises he is the only one. He seems to hear his name being called, and observes to his surprise that he is standing. Faces turn to him, too many. Some are smiling. He makes to sit but Syd shakes him back to his feet with a hand under his armpit. The ward chairman is speaking and this time he is recklessly audible.

"I understand our candidate's celebrated young son Maggus is among us here tonight, having interrupted his legal studies at Oggsford in order to assist his father in his great gampaign," he says. "I'm sure we'd all appreciate a word from you, Maggus, if you'll favour us. Maggus? Where is he?"

"Over 'ere, governor!" Syd yells. "Not me. Him."

If Pym is resisting, he is not aware of it. I have fainted. I am an accident. Syd's ginger ale has knocked me out. The crowd separates, strong hands bear him towards the dais, floating voters gaze down on him. Pym ascends, Rick seizes him in a bear-hug; a yellow rosette is nailed to Pym's collarbone by the ward chairman. Pym is speaking, and a cast of thousands is staring up at him—well, sixty, at least —smiling at his first brave words.

"I expect you are all asking yourselves," Pym begins long before anything has occurred to him. "I expect that many of you here tonight, even after that fine speech, are asking yourselves, what manner of man my father is."

They are. He can see it in their faces. They want the confirmation of their faith, and Maggus the Oggsford lawyer supplies it without a blush. For Rick, for England, and for fun. As he speaks he believes as usual every word he says. He paints Rick as Rick has painted himself, but with the authority of a loving son and legal brain who picks his words but never splits them. He refers to Rick as the plain man's honest friend—"and I should know, he's been the best friend I've had these twenty years or more." He depicts him as the reachable star in his childlike firmament, shining before him as an example of chivalrous humility. The image of the singer Wolfram von Eschenbach wanders through his mind and he considers offering them Rick as Little Chedworth's soldier-poet, wooing and jousting his way to victory. Caution prevails. He describes the influence of our patron saint TP, "marching on long after the old soldier has fought his last fight." How whenever we had to move house—a nervous moment—TP's portrait was the first thing to be hung up. He speaks of a father blessed with a fair man's sense of justice. With Rick as my father, he asks, how could I have contemplated any other calling than the law? He turns to Sylvia, who roosts at Rick's side in her rabbitskin collar and stay-press smile. With a choke he thanks her for taking up the burdens of motherhood where my own poor mother was obliged to lay them down. Then, as quickly as it all began, it is over, and Pym is hastening after Rick down the aisle towards the door, brushing away his tears and clasping hands in Rick's wake. He reaches the door and takes a misty look back. He sees again the woman in the veiled pill-box hat, seated by herself. He catches the glint of her eye inside the mask and it seems to him baleful and disapproving just when everyone else is being so admiring. A guilty fret replaces his elation. She is not a widow, she is the risen Lippsie. She is E. Weber. She is Dorothy, and I have wronged them all. She is an emissary of the Oggsford Communist Party here to observe my treacherous gonversion. The Michaels sent her.

"How was I, son?"

"Fantastic!"

"So were you, son. By God, if I'm spared to be a hundred, I'll never be a prouder man. Who cut your hair?"

Nobody has cut it for a long time, but Pym lets this go. They are crossing the carpark with difficulty for Rick is holding Pym's arm in an ambulant bear-hug and they are advancing at an angle like a pair of crookedly hung overcoats. Mr. Cudlove has the Bentley door open and is weeping a teacher's tears of pride.

"Beautiful, Mr. Magnus," he says. "It was Karl Marx come alive, sir. We shall never forget it."

Pym thanks him distractedly. As so often when on the crest of a phoney triumph, he is gripped by an unfocussed sense of God's approaching retribution. What have I done wrong to her? he keeps asking himself. I'm young and fluent and Rick's son. I'm wearing my new unpaid-for suit from Hall Brothers, the tailor. Why won't she love me like the rest of them? He is thinking, like every artist before or since him, of the only member of the audience who did not applaud.

It is the following Saturday, it is approaching midnight. Campaign fever is mounting fast. In a few minutes, it will be Eve of Poll Day minus three. A new poster saying "He Needs YOU on Thursday" is stuck to Pym's window, yellow bunting with the same message is strung from the sash, across the street to the pawnbroker's opposite. Yet Pym is lying fully dressed and smiling on his bed, and not a thought of the campaign is going through his mind. He is in Paradise with a girl called Judy, the daughter of a Liberal farmer who has lent her to us to drive Old Nellies to the booths, and Paradise is the front of her parked van on the way to Little Kimble. The taste of Judy's skin is on his lips, the smell of her hair is in his nostrils. And when he cups his hands over his eyes they are the same hands that for the first time in human history enclosed a young girl's breasts. The bedroom is on the first floor of a run-down corner house called Mrs. Searle's Temperance Rest, though rest and temperance are the last things it sells. The pubs have closed, the shouts and sighs have taken themselves to another part of town. A woman's voice shrieks from the alley, "Got a bed for us, Mattie? It's Jessie. Come on, you old bugger, we're freezing." An upper window bangs open and the blurred voice of Mr. Searle advises Jessie to take her client behind the bus shelter. "What do you think we are, Jess?" he complains. "A bloody doss house?" Of course we aren't. We are the Liberal

Candidate's campaign headquarters and dear old Mattie Searle our landlord, though he didn't know it till a month ago, has been a Liberal all his life.

Careful not to wake himself from his erotic reverie, Pym tiptoes to the window and squints steeply downward into the hotel courtyard. To one side the kitchen. To the other the residents' dining room, now the campaign's committee rooms. In its lighted window Pym makes out the bowed grey heads of Mrs. Alcock and Mrs. Catermole, our tireless helpers, as they determinedly seal the last envelopes of the day.

He returns to his bed. Wait, he thinks. They can't stay up all night. They never do. His conquest in one field is inspiring him to conquest in another. Tomorrow being the sabbath, Our Candidate rests his troops and contents himself with pious appearances at the best-attended Baptist churches where he is disposed to preach on simplicity and service. Tomorrow at eight o'clock Pym will stand at the bus stop for Nether Wheatley and Judy will meet him there in her father's van and in the boot she will have the toboggan the gamekeeper made for her when she was ten. She knows the hill, she knows the barn beside it, and it is agreed between them without fallbacks that somewhere around ten-thirty, depending on how much tobogganing they do, Judy Barker will take Magnus Pym to the barn and anoint him her full and consummated lover.

But in the meantime Pym has a different slope to scale or descend. Beyond the committee rooms lies a staircase to the cellar, and in the cellar—Pym has seen it —stands the chipped green filing cabinet that he has aspired to for three-quarters of his life and too often tried in vain to penetrate. In Pym's wallet beneath his pillow nestles the pair of blue steel dividers with which the Michaels have taught him to spring cheap locks. In Pym's mind, heated by voluptuous ambitions, is the calm conviction that a man who can gain access to Judy's breasts can burst open the fortress of Rick's secrets.

His hands over his face once more, he relives each delicious moment of the day. He was bounced from sleep as usual by Syd and Mr. Muspole, who have taken to shouting Crazy Gang obscenities through his bedroom door.

"Come on, Magnus, give it a rest. You'll go blind, you know."

"It'll drop off, Magnus, dear, if you don't let it grow. Doctor will have to strap it up with a matchstick. What will Judy say then?"

Over early breakfast, Major Maxwell-Cavendish bawls out Saturday's orders to the court. Pamphlets are obsolete, he announces. The only thing we can hit them with now is loudspeakers and more loudspeakers, backed by frontal attacks on their own doorsteps. "They know we're here. They know we mean business. They know we've got the best candidate and the best policy for Gulworth. What we're after now is every single, individual vote. We're going to pick them off one by one and drag them to the polls by sheer force of will. Thank you."

Now the detail. Syd will take number one loudspeaker and two ladies—laughter—down to that bit of scrubland beside the race course where the gyppos hang out—gyppos have votes same as everyone else. Shouts of "Put a fiver on Prince Magnus for us while you're about it!" Mr. Muspole and another lady will take loudspeaker number two and pick up Major Blenkinsop and our miserable agent from the Town Hall at nine. Magnus will take Judy Barker again and cover Little Kimble and the five outlying villages.

"You can cover Judy too while you're about it," says Morrie Washington. The joke, though brilliant, receives only token laughter. The court is uneasy about Judy. It distrusts her composure and resents her claim on their mascot. Barker looks down her nose at you, they complain behind her back. Barker's not the good scout we thought she was. But Pym these days cares less than he used to about the court's opinion. He shrugs off their gibes and, while the committee rooms are unguarded, slips down the steps to the cellar where he inserts the Michaels' dividers in the lock of the chipped green filing cabinet. One prong to hold back the spring, one to turn the chamber. The lock pops open. I am in the presence of a miracle and the miracle is me. I will return. Quickly relocking the cabinet he hastens back upstairs and not one minute after establishing his ascendancy over life's secrets he is standing innocently on the hotel doorstep in time for Judy's van to pull up beside him, the loudspeaker fixed to its roof with harvest twine. She smiles but does not speak. This is their third morning together but on the first they were accompanied by another lady helper. Nevertheless Pym contrived several times to brush his hand against Judy's as she changed gear or passed him the microphone, and when they parted at lunchtime and he made to kiss her cheek, she boldly redirected him to her lips by placing a long hand on the back of his neck. She is a tall, sunny girl with fair skin and an agricultural voice. She has a long mouth and playful eyes inside her serious spectacles.

"Vote for Pym, the People's Man," Pym booms into the loudspeaker as they head through Gulworth's suburbs towards open country. He is holding Judy's hand quite openly, first on her lap and now, at Judy's instigation, on his own. "Save Gulworth from the scourge of party politics." Then he recites a limerick about Mr. Lakin the Conservative Candidate, composed by Morrie Washington the great poet, which the major vows is winning votes everywhere.

> *"There's a bossy old buffer called Lakin,*
> *Whose manners are frightfully takin'.*
> *But if he thinks Rickie Pym*
> *Can be beaten by him,*
> *It's a deuce of a bloomer he's makin'."*

Reaching across him, Judy switches off the instrument. "I think your dad's got a cheek," she says cheerfully when the city is safely behind them. "Who does he think we are? Bloody idiots?"

Steering the car into an empty side lane, Judy turns off the engine, unbuttons her jacket and then her blouse. And where Pym had been expecting more impediments he discovers only her small and perfect breasts with nipples rigid from the cold. She watches him proudly as he puts his hands over them.

For the rest of the day, Pym walked on clouds of light. Judy had to return to the farm to help her father with the milking, so she dropped him at an inn on the road to Norwich, where he had agreed to meet up with Syd and Morrie and Mr. Muspole for a discreet wet on neutral territory clear of the constituency. With polling day so near, an end-of-term hilarity has infected the gathering and, having remained upright until closing time, the four of them piled into Syd's car and sang "Underneath the Arches" over the loudspeaker all the way to the border, where they once more put on their jackets and their pious faces. In the early evening Pym attended Rick's final Saturday pep talk to his helpers. Henry V on the eve of Agincourt could have done no better. They should not flinch from the final push. Remember Hitler. They should carry a straight bat to victory, they should keep the left elbow up through life, praise God and give her the whip in the final straight. Their ears ringing with these exhortations, the team scrambled for the cars. By now Pym's speech is a fully incorporated feature of the programme. The punters love him and inside the court he has the status of a star. In the Bentley, the two champions can squeeze each other's hands and exchange notes over a glass of warm bubbly to keep them going between triumphs.

"That gloomy woman was there again," said Pym. "I think she's following us round."

"What woman's that, son?" said Rick.

"I don't know. She wears a veil."

And somewhere, amid these pressures and activities, Pym contrived to under-take the most perilous foray of his sexual career till now. Having located an all-night chemist in Ribsdale on the other side of town, he took a tram there and made a series of passes to check his back before marching boldly to the counter and purchasing a packet of three contraceptive sheaths from an old reprobate who neither arrested him nor asked whether he was married. And there is his prize now, winking at him in its mauve-and-white wrapping from its hiding place at the centre of a stack of "Vote Pym" circulars as he tiptoes once more to his bedroom window and looks down.

The committee rooms are in darkness. Go.

The way is clear but Pym is too old a hand to make straight for his target. Time spent on reconnaissance is never time wasted, Jack Brotherhood used to say. I will fight my way to the heart of the enemy and earn her. He begins in the hall, affecting to read the day's notices. The ground floor is by now deserted. Mattie's filthy office is empty, the front door chained. He begins his slow ascent. Two doors past his own on the next floor lies the residential lounge. Pym opens the door and smiles in. Syd Lemon and Morrie Washington are playing a four of snooker against a couple of dear old friends of Mattie Searle who look like horse thieves but they could be sheep rustlers. Syd wears his hat. Two locally obtained Lovelies are chalking cues and dispensing comfort. The mood is fraught.

"What are you playing?" says Pym as if hoping for a game.

"Polo," says Syd. "Piss off, Titch, and don't be funny."

"I meant how many frames."

"Best of nine," says Morrie Washington.

Syd misses his shot and swears. Pym closes the door. They are settled. No danger there for at least an hour. He continues his patrol. Another flight upwards the atmosphere tightens, as it will in any secret building. Here is the quiet room where invited guests may kick off their shoes and take part in a relaxing hand of poker with Our Candidate and his circle. Pym enters without knocking. At a table strewn with cash and brandy glasses, Rick and Perce Loft are locked in a sharp piece of betting with Mattie Searle. The pot is a stack of petrol coupons, which in the court are preferred as hard currency. Mattie raises Rick and Rick sees him. Rick looks on with forbearance while Mattie scoops the pool.

"They tell me you and Colonel Barker had a crack at Little Kimble this morning, old son."

I forget exactly why Rick called Judy Colonel. I have an idea it was a reference to a celebrated lesbian who had been involved in a court case. Whatever the reason, Pym did not care for it.

"The boy had them kissing the ground, Rickie," Perce Loft confirms.

"Not the only thing he's been kissing, if you ask me," says Rick and everybody laughs because it is Rick's joke.

Pym leans in for the good-night bear-hug and hears Rick sniff his cheek, which has Judy's smell on it.

"Just you keep that old mind of yours on the election, son," he says, patting the same cheek in warning.

Down the corridor lies Morrie Washington's publicity department which doubles as disinformation section. Cases of whisky and nylons are stacked against the wall waiting to pave the way to the last electoral favours. It was from Morrie's desk that the baseless rumours went out regarding the Tory Candidate's support of Sir Oswald Mosley, and the Labour Candidate's overaddiction to his pupils. Springing the locks with his dividers, Pym flicks quickly through the drawers. One bank statement, one set of indecent playing cards. The statement is in the name of Mr. Morris Wurzheimer and is overdrawn by a hundred and twenty pounds. The playing cards would be impressive if Judy's reality did not eclipse them. Relocking everything neatly after him Pym climbs halfway up the last flight, then hovers listening to Mr. Muspole murmuring on the telephone. The top floor is the sanctum. It is safe room, cypher room and operations centre combined. At the end of the corridor lie Our Candidate's State Apartments which not even Pym has penetrated so far, for Sylvia now spends erratic hours in bed having headaches or trying to grill herself brown with a mysterious hand lamp she has bought from Mr. Muspole. He can therefore never be sure of a safe run. Next door resides the so-called Action Committee, where big money and support are mustered and promises traded. What promises is still half a mystery to me, though Syd once spoke of a plan to fill the ancient harbour with cement and make a carpark of it, to the pleasure of many influential contractors.

Abruptly Mr. Muspole rings off. Without a sound, Pym swivels on his heel and prepares to beat an orderly retreat down the stairs. He is saved by the whirr of Mr. Muspole dialling again. He is talking to a lady, asking tender questions and purring at the answers. Muspole can carry on like this for hours. It is his little pleasure.

Having waited till his voice has settled to a reassuring flow Pym returns to the ground floor. The darkness of the committee rooms smells of tea and deodorant. The door to the courtyard is locked from the inside. Pym softly turns the key and pockets it. The cellar staircase stinks of cat. Boxes are stored on the steps. Groping his way down, unwilling to put on the light lest it be visible from the courtyard, Pym has an unmistakable mental reprise of a day in Bern when he carried his damp washing down the stone steps to another cellar and was scared of tripping over Herr Bastl. And as he reaches the bottom step he does indeed miss his footing. Lurching forward he falls heavily on to the cellar door and pushes it open with both hands as he tries to steady himself. The door screeches in the grime. The impetus of his body is enough to carry him into the cellar which to his surprise is lit by a pale light.

By its glow Pym makes out the green filing cabinet and standing before it a woman holding what appears to be a chisel, examining its locks by the ailing beam of a bicycle lamp. Her eyes, which are turned to him, are dark and pugnacious. There is not a flicker of guilt about her. And it is a thing I wonder at still that it never seriously occurred to him to doubt that she was the same woman, with the same gaze, and the same intense and disapproving quietness, whose veiled face had fixed on him after his triumph on the hustings of Little Chedworth, and stalked him through a dozen meetings since. Even asking her name Pym realises that he knows it already though he is blessed with no faculty of premonition. She wears a long skirt that could have been her mother's. She has a hard, pebble face and young hair turned to grey. Her eyes are disconcertingly straight and bright, even in the gloom.

"My name is Peggy Wentworth," she replies defiantly in a tough Irish brogue. "Shall I spell it for you, Magnus? Peggy short for Margaret, have you heard that? Your father, Mr. Richard Thomas Pym, killed my husband John, and as good as killed me too. And if it takes me the rest of my living death till they put me in the grave beside him, I'll find the proof of it, and bring the brute to justice."

Seeing a flicker of moving light Pym glances sharply behind him. Mattie Searle is standing in the doorway with a blanket over his shoulders. His head is hung sideways to favour his good ear while he squints first at Pym then at Peggy over the top of his spectacles. How much has he heard? Pym has no idea. But his mind is made fertile by alarm.

"This is Emma from Oxford, Mattie," he says boldly. "Emma, this is Mr. Searle who owns the hotel."

"Pleased to meet you," says Peggy calmly.

"Emma and I are in a college play next month, Mattie. She came up to Gulworth so that we could rehearse together. We thought we'd be out of your way down here."

"Oh yes," says Mattie. His eyes slip from Peggy to Pym and back again, with a knowledge that makes nonsense of Pym's lies. They hear his lazy shuffle going up the stairs.

I can't tell you very accurately any more, Tom, which bits she told Pym where. His first thought on escaping the hotel was to keep going, so they hopped a bus and went as far as it took them, which turned out to be the oldest, most broken-down bit of waste dockland you could imagine: gutted warehouses with windows you could see the moon through, idle cranes that rose like gallows straight out of the sea. A bunch of roving knife-bladers had pitched camp there, they must have worked at night and slept by day, because I remember their Romany faces rocking over their wheels as they trod their treadles, and the sparks gushing over the watching children. I remember girls with men's muscles flinging fish baskets while they yelled ribaldries at each other, and fishermen strutting among them in their oilskins, too grand to be bothered with anyone but themselves. I remember with a leap of gratitude every flash of face or voice outside the windows of the prison she had locked me in with her relentless monologue.

At a tea-stall on the waterfront while they stood shivering with a crowd of down-and-outs, Peggy told Pym the story of how Rick had stolen her farm. She had begun it the moment they got on the bus, for the benefit of anyone who'd care to hear it, and had continued it without a comma or a full stop since, and Pym knew that it was all true, all terrible, even if quite often the sheer venom in her drove him secretly to Rick's protection. They walked to get warm but she didn't stop talking for one second. When he bought her beans and egg at a Seamen's Mission hut called the Rover, still she went on talking as she spread her elbows and sawed the toast and used her teaspoon to get up the sauce. It was at the Rover that she told Pym about Rick's great trust fund that took possession of the nine thousand pounds of insurance money paid to her husband John after he fell into the thresher and lost both legs below the knee and all the fingers of one hand. As she told this part she drew the lines of amputation on her own scant limbs without looking at them, and Pym sensed her obsession again and was scared of it. The one voice I never did for you, Tom, is Peggy's Irish brogue dropping into Rick's chapel cadences as she repeated his silver-tongued promises: twelve and a half percent plus profits, my dear, year in and year out, enough to see dear old John right for as long as he's spared, and enough for yourself when he's gone, and enough left over after that, my dear, to put some by for that first-rate boy of yours for when he goes to college and reads his law just the way my own son will—they're birds of a feather. It was a Thomas Hardy story that she told, full of casual disasters that seemed to have been timed by an angry God to obtain the maximum of misfortune. And she was Hardy's woman to go with it: lured forward by her obsession, and only her own destiny left to deal with.

John Wentworth, as well as being a victim, was an ass, she explained, and was ready to be swayed by the first charmer who walked into the room. He went to his grave convinced that Rick was a saviour and a pal. His farm was a Cornish manor called Tamar Rose where every grain of wheat had to be wrestled from the sea wind. He had inherited it from a wiser father, and Alastair their son was his only heir. When John died there was not a penny for anybody. Everything signed away, every bloody thing mortgaged to the neck, Magnus—on which word Peggy passed her bean-stained knife across her throat. She told about Rick visiting John in hospital soon after his accident and the flowers and the chocolates and the bubbly —and Pym in his mind's eye saw the basket of black-market fruit beside his own hospital bed when he woke up after his operation. He remembered Rick's noble caring for the aged and decrepit that he had helped him with during the war years of the great crusade. He remembered Lippsie's sobbing voice calling Rick a *teef*, and Rick's letters to her promising to see her right.

"And a free train ticket for myself," Peggy is saying, "to come up to Truro Hospital to visit him. And your father driving me home after, Magnus, nothing too much trouble for him until he has our man's money." The documents he made John sign, Magnus, always witnessed by the prettiest nurses. How your father always had the patience for John, always explaining to him whatever he couldn't understand, over and again if necessary, but John won't listen, the deluded man is too trusting and lazy in his mind.

A fit of fury seizes her: "Me up at four in the morning for the milking and falling asleep over my accounts at midnight!" she shouts as sleepy heads turn to her from other tables. "And that stupid husband of mine lying warm in his bed in Truro signing it all away behind my back while your father sits by his bedside playing the saint to him, Magnus. And my Alastair needing a pair of shoes to walk to school in, while you're living on the hog there with your fine schools and your fine clothes, Magnus, God save you!" For it turns out, of course, on John's death, that for reasons outside everyone's control the great trust fund has suffered a purely temporary problem of liquidity and can't pay the twelve and a half percent plus profits after all. It can't refund the capital either. And that to tide everyone over this sticky patch, John Wentworth took the wise precaution, just before his death, of mortgaging the farm and land and livestock, and bloody nearly his wife and child as well, so that nobody will ever want for anything again. And had given the proceeds to his dear old pal Rick. And that Rick has brought down a distinguished lawyer, name of Loft, all the way from London with him, just to explain the implications of this smart move to John on his deathbed. And John, to please everyone as usual, has written out a special long letter all in his own hand, assuring whom it may concern that his decision has been taken while he was of sound mind and in full possession of his mental faculties and was not in any manner subjected to undue influence by a saint and his lawyer while he was lying gasping out his last. All this in case Peggy, or for that matter Alastair, should later have the bad manners to dispute the document in court or try to get John's nine thousand pounds back, or should otherwise show a lack of faith in Rick's selfless stewardship of John's ruin.

"When did all this happen?" says Pym.

She tells him the dates, she tells him the day of the week and the hour of the day. She pulls a wad of letters from her handbag signed by Perce and regretting that "our Chairman, Mr. R. T. Pym, is unavailable, being absent indefinitely on a mission of national necessity," and assuring her that "the documents relating to the Freehold of Tamar Rose are at present being processed with a view to acquiring a large Figure in your interest." And she watches him with her mad cold eyes as he reads them by the light of a street lamp while they sit huddled on a broken bench. She takes back the letters and returns them to their envelopes lovingly, careful of the edges and the folds. As she continues talking, Pym wants to close his ears or slap a hand over her mouth. He wants to get up and run to the sea-wall and throw himself over. He wants to scream "Shut up!" But all he does is ask her, please, I beg you, if you would be so kind, don't continue with your story.

"Why not, pray?"

"I don't want to hear it. It's not my business, this part. He robbed you. The rest doesn't make any difference," says Pym.

Peggy doesn't agree. She is flailing her Irish back with her Irish guilt and using Pym's presence as the excuse to do it. She is talking in a gush. It is what she has been waiting to tell him best.

"And why not—seeing as the bloody man possesses you anyway? If he's already got his filthy arms around you sure as if he had you in his fancy bed with the frills and the fancy mirrors"—it is Rick's bedroom in Chester Street she is describing—"seeing as he's already got the power of life and death over you and you're a foolish lonely woman in the world with a sickly boy to care for and a bankrupt farm to mind, and not a soul but the stupid bailiff to say nice day to for a week at a time?"

"It's enough to know he's done you wrong," Pym insists. "Please, Peggy. The rest is private."

"Seeing as he can beckon you up to London first-class, send the tickets, just with a flick of his fingers the moment he gets back from his national necessity, because he thinks you're going to put the lawyers on him? Well you go, don't you? If you haven't had a man for two years and more and only your own body to look at withering in the mirror every day, you go!"

"I'm sure you do. I'm sure there was every reason," Pym says. "Please don't tell me any more."

She is doing Rick's voice again: " 'Let's sort this matter out once and for all, Peggy my dear. I'm not having a sour bit of business come between us when all I ever wanted was to see you right.' Well, you go, don't you?" Her voice is echoing in the empty square and out over the water. "My God, you go. You pack your bag, you take your boy and lock the door because you're off to get your money and some justice. You scurry up there bursting to have the fight of your life just the moment you set eyes on him. You leave the washing and the dishes and the milking and the penny-pinching life he's put you to. And you tell the stupid bailiff to mind the shop for you, me and Alastair we're going up to London. And when you arrive, instead of a business conference with Mr. Percy Loft and Mr. Bloody Muspole and the gang of them, the man buys you fine clothes in Bond Street and treats you like a princess, with the limousines and the restaurants and the fancy petticoats and silks—well you can always have your row with him later, can't you?"

"No," says Pym. "You can't. You've got to have it then or never."

"If he's trodden you into the mud these years the least you can do is get a bit back from him, in exchange for all the misery, take him for every penny he's robbed you of." Yet again she does Rick's voice: " 'I always fancied you, Peggy, you know that. You're a good scout, the best. Always had my eye on that pretty Irish smile of yours and not only the smile either.' So all right, he's got a treat prepared for the boy as well. Takes him to the Arsenal and we sit up there like gods in the special box with the lords and grandees, and dinner at Quaglino's after, him the People's Man, with a two-foot cake with the boy's name written on it, you should see Alastair's face. And next day a Harley Street specialist laid on to listen to his cough and a gold watch for the boy after, for being the brave one, with his initials on it, 'From RTP to a fine young man.' Come to think of it, it's not at all unlike the one you're wearing now—is that a gold one too? So when a man's done all that for you and been a bastard—well you have to admit to yourself after a couple of days of it, there's many worse bastards than him in the world. Most of them wouldn't split their bloody Bath bun with you, let alone a two-foot cake at Quaglino's and somebody to take the boy home to bed after, so that the grown-ups can go to a nightclub and have a bit of fun—why not if he always fancied me? There's not many women wouldn't put off a fight for a day or two for some of that, I suppose —so why not?"

She is speaking as if Pym is no longer there and she is right. She has deafened him but he can still hear her. As I hear her still, an endless, needling babble of destruction. She is speaking to the derelict cattle market with its broken pens and stopped clock, but Pym is numb and dead and anywhere but here. He is in the Overflow House at his prep school and Rick's raised voice and Lippsie's weeping keep waking him in his sleep. He is on Dorothy's bed at The Glades and bored to bloody death, with his head against her shoulder staring at the white sky through the window all day long. He is in an attic somewhere in Switzerland, wondering to God why he has killed his friend to please an enemy.

She is describing Rick's madness with her own. Her voice is a nagging querulous torrent and he hates it to distraction. The way the man boasted. He'd not a foot on the earth when he started with his lying. How he had been Lady Mountbatten's lover and she'd assured him he was better than Noël Coward. How they'd wanted him for Ambassador in Paris but he'd turned it down; he'd no patience with the airy-fairies. And about the stupid green filing cabinet with his rotten secrets in it, imagine the madness of a fellow who spends his hours weaving the rope they ought to hang him with! How he'd led her bare-foot to it in her nightdress, look at this my child. The record, he called it. All the rights and the wrongs he'd done. All the evidence of his innocence—his bloody righteousness. How, when he was judged, as judged he would surely be, everything in this stupid cabinet would be put into the balance, rights and wrongs together, and we would see him for what he was, up alongside of the angels while us poor sinners down here bleed and starve for the glory of him. It's what he's put together to con the Almighty with and that's the short of it—imagine the impertinence, and him a bloody Baptist too!

Pym asks her how she has known where to find it. I saw the stupid thing being delivered, she says. I was keeping a watch on Searle's hotel the first day of the campaign. The pansy Cudlove drove it up specially in his limousine, the cost alone. The bastard Loft helped him carry it to the cellar, first time he's got his hands dirty. Rick didn't dare leave it in London while they were all up here. "I have to put the proof on him, Magnus," she keeps repeating as he leads her through the dawn to her miserable lodging-house, her voice whining and insisting in his ear like a machine that nobody can stop. "If he's got the proof there like he says, I'll have it off of him and turn it back on him, I swear I will. All right, I've taken a drop of money off him, it's true. But what's the money when he's cheated me in love? What's the money when he can walk down the street a grandee and there's my John rotting in his grave? And the people in the street all clapping for him, for Rickie boy? And con his way to Heaven into the bargain? What's the use of a poor deluded victim like me who let him have his will with her and will burn in Hell for it, if she won't do her duty by the world and point him up for the devil that he is? Where's the proof? I'm asking."

"Please stop," said Pym. "I know what you want."

"Where's the justice? If he's got it there I'll have it from him, thank you. I've no letters above a couple of procrastinators from Perce Loft, and what do they say? It's like trying to nail a raindrop to the wall, I tell you."

"Try to be calm now," Pym said. "Please."

"I took myself to that stupid Lakin, the Tory. Half a day it took of waiting but I got to him. 'Rick Pym's a shark,' I tell him. What's the good of telling that to a Tory when they're all sharks anyway? I told the Labour but they kept saying 'What's he done?' They said they'll enquire and thank you, but what will they find, the poor innocents?"

Mattie Searle is sweeping the courtyard. Pym is indifferent to his scrutiny. Pym carries himself with authority, using the same walk that got him to Lippsie's bicycle and past the policeman to the Overflow House. I am authority. I am British. Will you kindly get out of my way.

"I left something in the cellar," he says carelessly.

"Oh yes," says Mattie.

Peggy Wentworth's bandsaw voice is cutting into his soul. What dreadful echoes has it woken in him? In what empty house of his childhood is it nagging and whining at him? Why is he so abject before its dredging insistence? She is the risen Lippsie, speaking out from the grave at last. She is the world inside my head made strident. She is the sin I can never expiate. Put your head in the basin, Pym. Hold these taps and listen to me while I explain why no punishment will ever be enough for you. Put him on bread and water, his father's child. Why do you wet your bed, old son? Don't you know there's a thousand quid in cash waiting for you at the end of your first dry year? He switches on the committee-room lights, throws open the door to the cellar steps and stomps heavily down them. Cardboard boxes. Commodities. A glut to fill the shortages. The Michael's dividers to the fore again, better than a Swiss penknife. He trips the lock of the green cabinet and pulls out the first drawer as the glow begins to spread over him.

Lippschitz first name Anna, two volumes only. Why Lippsie, it's you at last, he thinks calmly. Well it was a short life, wasn't it? No time now, but rest where you are and I'll come back and claim you later. Watermaster Dorothy, Marital, one volume only. Well it was a short marriage too, but wait for me, Dot, for I've other ghosts I must attend to first. He closes the first drawer and pulls open the second. Rick, you bastard, where are you? Bankruptcy, the whole drawer full of it. He opens the third. The imminence of his discovery is setting his body on fire: the eyelids, the surfaces of his back and waist. But his fingers are light and quick and agile. This is what I was born for, if I was born at all. I am God's detective, seeing everybody right. Wentworth, a dozen of them, tagged in Rick's handwriting. Foremost in his mind Pym has the dates of Muspole's letter regretting Rick's absence for his national necessity. He remembers the Fall and Rick's long healthy holiday while he and Dorothy were sweating out their imprisonment in The Glades. Rick you bastard where were you? "Come on, old son, we're pals, aren't we?" In a minute I shall hear Herr Bastl barking.

He opens the last drawer and sees Rex versus Pym 1938, three fat files, and beside it Rex versus Pym 1944, one only. He pulls out the first of the 1938 batch, replaces it and selects the last instead. He turns to the final page first and reads the judge's summing-up, verdict, sentence, the immediate disposal of the prisoner. In calm ecstasy he turns back to the beginning and starts again. No camera in those days. No copier, no tape-recorders. Only what you can see and hear and memorise and steal. He reads for an hour. A clock strikes eight but it means nothing to him. I am following my vocation. Divine service is in progress. You women want nothing but to drag us down.

Mattie is still sweeping the courtyard but his outlines are blurred.

"Find it then?" says Mattie.

"Eventually, thanks, yes."

"That's the way then," says Mattie.

He gains his bedroom, turns the key in the lock, pulls a chair to the washstand, starts writing at once, from the memory straight on to the paper, not a thought for style. A clock strikes again and once he hears a knock, first timid then louder. Then a soft and pessimistic "Magnus?" before the feet slowly descend the stairs. But Pym is at the heart of things, women are temporarily abhorrent to him, even Judy is irrelevant to his destiny. He hears her feet clip across the forecourt and the sound of her van driving away, slow at first, then suddenly much faster. Good riddance.

"Dear Peggy"—he is writing—"I hope that the enclosed will be of use to you."

"Dear Belinda"—he is writing—"I really must own to being fascinated by this glimpse of the democratic process at work. What seems at first to be such a rough instrument turns out to be equipped with all sorts of refined checks and balances. Do let's meet as soon as I return to London."

"Dearest Father"—he is writing—"Today is Sunday and in four days we shall know our fate and yours. But I do want you to know how much I have learned to admire the courage and conviction with which you have fought your arduous campaign."

On the dais, Rick had not moved. His flick-knife stare was still fixed on Pym. Yet he appeared quite calm. Nothing had happened behind him in the hall that could not be dealt with, apparently. His preoccupation was with his son, whom he was regarding with dangerous intensity. He was wearing his statesman's silver tie that night and a handmade shirt of cream silk with double cuffs and the great big RTP links from Asprey's. He had had his hair cut earlier in the day, and Pym could smell the barber's lotion as father and son continued to face each other. Once, Rick's gaze switched to Muspole and it was Pym's later impression Muspole nodded to him in some signal. The silence in the hall was absolute. No coughs or creaks that Pym could hear, not even from the Old Nellies whom Rick, as always, had appointed to the front row where they could remind him of his dear mother and his beloved father who had died so many heroes' deaths.

At last Rick turned, and advanced towards the audience with the dutiful Goodman Pym walk that so often preceded an act of particular hypocrisy. He reached the table but did not stop. He reached the microphone and switched it off: let no machine come between us at this moment. He went on walking till he had reached the edge of the dais, at the point where it meets the fine curving staircase. He set his jaw, he looked out over the faces, he allowed his features to betray a moment's soul-searching before he set himself to speak. Somewhere on his way between Pym and the audience he had unbuttoned his jacket. Strike me here, he was saying. Here is my heart. At last, he spoke. His voice higher than usual. Hear the emotion clenching it.

"Would you mind repeating that question, please, Peggy? Very loudly, my dear, so that everyone can hear?"

Peggy Wentworth did as she was bidden. But as Rick's guest now as well as his accuser.

"Thank you, Peggy." Then he asked for a chair for her so that she could sit down like everybody else. It was brought by Major Blenkinsop himself. Peggy sat on it in the aisle, obediently, a child in disgrace, waiting to hear some home truths. So it seemed to Pym, and still does, for I have long believed that everything Rick did this night was prepared in advance. If they had popped a dunce's cap on her head Pym would not have been surprised. I believe they had seen Peggy haunting them and Rick had laid out his mental defences in advance of her, as he had often done before. Muspole's people could have snatched her for the evening. Major

Blenkinsop could have been advised she was not welcome inside the hall. There were a dozen ways in the court's book to keep a crazed and penniless little black-mailer like Peggy at bay for a crucial night. Rick used none of them. He wanted the trial, as ever. He wanted to be judged and found spotless.

"Ladies and gentlemen. This lady's name is Mrs. Peggy Wentworth. She is a widow whom I have known and tried to help for many years, who has been desperately wronged in life, and who blames me for her misfortune. I hope that after this meeting you will all hear whatever Peggy has to tell you, give her every indulgence at your command, show her every patience. And in your wisdom judge for yourselves where the truth may lie. I hope you will show charity to Peggy, and to me, and remember how hard it is for all of us to accept misfortune without pointing the finger of blame."

He placed his hands behind his back. His feet were close together.

"Ladies and gentlemen, my old friend Peggy Wentworth is quite right." Not even Pym, who thought he knew all the instruments in Rick's orchestra, had heard him so straight and simple in his delivery, so bereft of rhetoric. "Many years ago, ladies and gentlemen, when I was a very young man, striving to get on in life—as we all were once, overeager, ready to cut a few corners—I found myself in the position of the office boy who had borrowed a few stamps from the till and been caught before he had a chance to put them back. I was a first offender, it is true. My mother, like Peggy Wentworth here, was a widow. I had a great father to live up to and only sisters in the family. The responsibilities that weighed upon me, I will admit, blew me across the borders of what Justice, in her blind wisdom, deemed right. Justice exacted her penalty. I paid it in full measure. As I shall pay for it all my life."

Then the jaw went up and the thick hands untied themselves, and one arm struck out towards the Old Nellies in the front while his eyes and voice reached into the darkness at the back.

"My friends—Peggy, my dear, I still count you as one too—my loyal friends of Gulworth North, I see among you here tonight men and women still young enough to be impulsive. I see others with the experience of life upon them, whose children and grandchildren have gone out into the world to follow their impulses, to strive and make mistakes and overcome them. I want to ask you older people this. If one of these young people—children, grandchildren, or if this son of mine who sits behind me here, poised to collect some of the highest prizes the law of this country can offer—if one of them should ever make a mistake, and pay the price that society exacts, and come home and say, 'Mum, it's me. Dad, it's me'—which one of you sitting here among us tonight is going to slam the door in his face?"

They were standing. They were calling his name. "Rickie—good old Rickie— you get our vote, Rickie boy." On the dais behind him were standing too, and Pym saw through his own tears that Syd and Morrie were embracing each other. For once Rick did not acknowledge the applause. He was casting round theatrically for Pym and calling "Magnus, where are you, son?" though he knew perfectly well where he was. Affecting to find him he seized his arm, raised it and drew him forward, almost lifting him off the ground even as he offered him as champion to the jubilant crowd, shouting "Here's one, here's one!" I suppose he meant a penitent who has paid the price and come home, though I'll never be certain because of the roar, and perhaps he said, "Here's my son." As to Pym, he could no longer contain himself. He had never adored Rick more. He was choking and clapping, he was shaking Rick's hand for them with both of his, bear-hugging him and patting his great shoulder for them and telling him he was crackerjack. As he did so, he thought he saw Judy's pale face and big pale eyes behind their serious spectacles, watching him from the centre of the crowd. My father needed me, he wanted to explain to her. I forgot where the bus stop was. I lost your phone number. I did it for my country. The Bentley was waiting at the front steps. Cudlove at the door. Riding away at Rick's side, Pym imagined he heard Judy calling out his name: "Pym. You bastard. Where are you?"

It was dawn. Unshaven, Pym sat at his desk, not wanting the daylight. Chin in hand he stared at the last page he had written. Change nothing. Don't look back, don't look forward. You do it once, then die. A miserable vision assailed him of the women in his life vainly waiting at every bus stop along his chaotic path. Rising quickly he mixed himself a Nescafé and drank it while it was still too hot for him. Then took up his stapler and marker pen and set himself busily to work —I am a clerk, that is all I am—stapling his cuttings and cross-indexing the helpful references.

Extracts from *Gulworth Mercury* and *Evening Star* reporting Liberal Candidate's fighting stand on Eve of Poll night in the Town Hall. For libel reasons writers omit direct reference to Peggy Wentworth's accusations, referring only to Candidate's spirited self-defence against personal attack. Enter at 21a. Bloody stapler doesn't work. This sea air rusts everything.

Cutting from London *Times* giving results of Gulworth North by-election:

McKechnie (Labour) 17,970
Lakin (Cons.) 15,711
Pym (Lib.) 6,404.
Semi-literate leader ascribes victory to "Miscalculated intervention" of Liberals. Enter at 22a.

Extract from Oxford University *Gazette* notifying waiting world that Magnus Richard Pym has been awarded a B.A. Hons. degree in Modern Languages, Class I. No reference to night hours spent studying previous examination papers, or informal exploration of tutor's desk drawers with the aid of the Michael's ever-handy steel dividers. Entered at 23a.

But actually not entered at all, for in the act of marking this cutting, Pym set it down before him and stared at it, head in hands, with an expression of revulsion.

Rick knew. The bastard knew. His head still between his hands, Pym returns himself to Gulworth later the same night. Father and son are riding in the Bentley, their favourite place. The Town Hall lies behind them, Mrs. Searle's Temperance Rest is approaching. The tumult of the crowd still rings in their ears. It will be another twenty-four hours before the world will learn the name of the winning candidate, but Rick knows it already. He has been judged and applauded for all his life till now.

"Let me tell you something, old son," he says in his mellowest and kindest voice. The passing streetlights are switching his wise features on and off, making his triumph appear intermittent. "Never lie, son. I told them the truth. God heard me. He always does."

"It was fantastic," says Pym. "Could you possibly let go of my arm, please?"

"No Pym was ever a liar, son."

"I know," says Pym, taking back his arm anyway.

"Why couldn't you have come to me, son? 'Father,' you could have said— 'Rickie' if you like; you're old enough—'I'm not reading law any more. I'm building up my languages because I want the gift of tongues. I want to go out into the world like my best pal, and be heard wherever men gather regardless of colour, race or creed.' Because do you know what I'd have answered if you'd come to me and said that to your old man?"

Pym is too mad, too dead to care.

"You'd have been super," he says.

"I'd have said: 'Son, you're grown up now. You take your own decisions. All your old man can do is play wicket-keeper while Magnus here bats and God does the bowling.'" He grasps Pym's hand, nearly breaking the fingers. "Don't shrink away from me like that, old son. I'm not angry with you. We're pals, remember? We don't have to tiptoe round each other looking in one another's pockets, poking in drawers, talking to misguided women in hotel cellars. We come out with it straight. On the table. Now dry those old peepers of yours and give your old pal a hug."

With his monographed silk handkerchief the great statesman magnanimously wipes away the tears of Pym's rage and impotence.

"Want a good English steak tonight, son?"

"Not much."

"Old Mattie's cooking us one with onions. You can invite Judy if you like. We'll all have a game of chemmy afterwards. She'd like that."

Raising his head, Pym recovered his marker pen and went back to work.

Extract of Branch minutes of Oxford University Communist Party regretting departure of Comrade M. Pym, tireless worker on behalf of cause. Fraternal thanks for his tremendous efforts. Entered at 24a.

Pained letter from Bursar of Pym's college enclosing his cheque for his last term's battles, marked "Refer to Drawer." Similar letters and cheques from Messrs. Blackwell, Parker (Booksellers), and Hall Brothers (Tailors), entered at 24c.

Pained letter from Pym's bank manager regretting that following return of cheque drawn in Pym's favour by the Magnus Dynamic & Astral Company (Bahamas) Ltd., in the sum of two hundred and fifty pounds, he has had no alternative but to refer to drawer the cheques as at 24c.

Extract from London *Gazette* dated March 29, 1951, appointing official receiver in yet another petition for bankruptcy of R.T.P. and eighty-three associated companies.

Letter from Director of Public Prosecutions inviting Pym to present himself for interview on named date in order to explain his relationship with above companies. Entered at 36a.

Military call-up papers offering Pym sanctuary. Grabbed with both hands.

* * *

"If I could just sit with you for a bit, Miss D," said Pym, softly pushing open her kitchen door.

But her chair was empty and the fire out. It was not evening as he had thought, but dawn.

12

It was the same dawn. It was time minus ten minutes. It was the moment Brotherhood had lain wakeful and alone for in his rotten flat that was becoming a solitary cell for him, staring at the images of his past in the restless London sky. It was an outdoor game being played by indoor people who didn't know they were awake. How many times had he sat like this, in rubber boats, on arctic hillsides, pressing the headphones into his ears with kapok mittens to catch the whisper that meant life was not extinct? Here in the communications room on the top floor of the Head Office there were no headphones, no subzero winds to rip through sodden clothing and freeze the operator's fingers off, no bicycle generator that some poor bastard had to pump at till his legs failed. No aerial that collapsed on you when you most needed it. No two-ton suitcase to be cached in iron-hard soil while the Huns were breathing down your neck. Up here we have dimpled grey-green boxes freshly dusted, with pretty pin-lights and shiny switches. And tuners and amplifiers. And dials to cut out atmospherics. And comfortable chairs for the barons here assembled to rest their candy arses on. And a mysterious compression of the air that clenches your scalp while you watch the green numerals sliding through their prison window as quickly as the later years of life: now I am forty, now I am forty-five, now I am seventy, now I am ten minutes to being dead.

On the raised platform two boys in headphones were patrolling the dials. They'll never know what it was like, thought Brotherhood. They'll go to their graves thinking life came out of a packet. Bo Brammel and Nigel sat below them like producers at a preview. Behind them a dozen shadows that Brotherhood had barely bothered with. He noticed Lorimer, Head of Operations. He saw Kate and thought thank heaven she's alive. At the edge of the stage, Frankel was lugubriously reporting a string of failures. His mid-European accent has thickened.

"Nine-twenty yesterday morning local time, Prague Station has its chief cut-out dial the Watchman household from a callbox, Bo," he said. "Number engaged. He makes five calls in two hours from round town. Still engaged. He tried Conger. Number out of order. Everybody vanished, everybody out of touch. Midday the Station sends a little girl they own to the canteen where Conger's daughter goes for lunch. Conger's daughter is conscious so maybe she knows where her father is. Our little girl is a sixteen-year-old kid, very small, very hardy. She hangs around two hours, checks both sittings, checks the queue. No daughter. She checks the attendance sheets at the factory gate, tells the guards she is the daughter's room-mate. She's so innocent they let her. Conger's daughter is not reported present, is not reported sicklisted. Vanished."

In the tension nobody spoke to anybody. Everyone spoke to himself. The room was still filling up. How many people does it take to give a network a decent burial? thought Brotherhood. Eight minutes to go.

Frankel continued his dirge. "Seven o'clock yesterday morning local time, Gdansk Station puts two of their local boys to mend a telegraph pole at the end of the street where Merryman lives. His house is in a cul-de-sac. He's got no other way out. Every day normally he goes to work by car, leaves his house seven-twenty. But yesterday his car is not outside his house. Every other day it is parked outside his house. Not yesterday. From where the boys work they can see his front door. The front door stays closed. No Merryman, nobody at all leaves or enters that house by that door. Downstairs is curtained, no lights, no fresh tracks in the drive. Merryman's good friend is an architect. Merryman likes to take a coffee with him sometimes on his way to work. This architect is not a Joe, he is not whitelisted."

"Wenzel," said Brotherhood.

"Wenzel is the architect's name, Jack. One of the boys calls up Mr. Wenzel and tells him Merryman's mother is ill. 'Where can I get hold of him to give him this bad news?' he says. Mr. Wenzel says try the laboratory, how ill? The boy says she's maybe dying, Merryman ought to get to her fast. 'Give him this message,' the boy says. 'Tell him please that Maximilian says he better get to his mother's bedside fast.' Maximilian, that's the codeword for it's all over. Maximilian means abort, means run, means get the hell out by any known means, don't bother with customary procedures, run. The boy is resourceful. When he has ceased to speak to Mr. Wenzel, he calls the laboratory where Merryman works. 'This is Mr. Maximilian. Where's Merryman? It's urgent. Tell him Maximilian got to speak to him about his mother.' Merryman don't come in today, they tell him. Merryman got a conference in Warsaw."

Brotherhood was already objecting. "They wouldn't say that," he growled. "The labs don't give out details of staff movements. They're a top-secret installation, for Christ's sake. Somebody's playing games with us."

"Sure, Jack. My own reaction entirely. You want I go on?"

A couple of heads turned to locate Brotherhood at the back of the room.

"When the line to Merryman went dead we instructed Warsaw to try to reach Voltaire direct," Frankel continued. He paused. "Voltaire is sick."

Brotherhood let out an angry laugh. "Voltaire? He hasn't had a day's sickness in his life."

"His Ministry says he's sick, Jack, his wife says he's sick, his mistress says he's sick. He ate some bad mushrooms, gone to hospital. He's sick. Official. They all say the same."

"I'll say it's official."

"What do you want me to do, Jack? Tell me something I should do that you would do yourself and I have not done. Okay? It's a blackout, Jack. Like a silence everywhere. Like a bomb fell."

"You said you'd keep filling the letter boxes," Brotherhood said.

"We filled for Merryman yesterday. Money and instructions. We filled."

"So what happened?"

"Still there. Money and instructions so much he want. Fresh papers, maps, you name it. For Conger we put up two visuals, one for call us, one for evacuate. One curtain on a first floor, one light in a basement window. Is that correct, Jack? Does that accord with the agreed procedures?"

"It accords."

"Okay. So he doesn't answer. He doesn't call, he doesn't write, he doesn't run."

For five minutes there was no sound but the sounds of waiting: the sighing of soft chairs, the striking of lights and matches and the squeaky-soled footsteps of the boys. Kate glanced at Brotherhood and he smiled confidence back. Bo said, "We're thinking of you, Jack," but Brotherhood did not reply and he was certainly not thinking of Bo. A bell rang. From the platform a boy said, "Conger, sir, on schedule," and trimmed some dials. A white pin-light winked above his head. The second boy dropped a switch. Nobody clapped, nobody got to his feet or cried, "they're alive!"

"Conger operator's come in and say he's ready to send, Bo," Frankel said gratuitously. Behind him, the boys were moving automatically, deaf to everything outside their headphones. "Now we make our first transmission. We use all tape, no handwriting. Conger does the same. Accelerated Morse, we unroll it both ends. Transmission takes maybe one and a half minutes, two. Unroll and decode takes maybe five. . . . See that? . . . 'We are ready to receive you. Talk.'—this is what we say to him. Now Conger is talking again. Watch the red light left, please. It burns, he's talking—he's finished."

"Wasn't very long, was it?" Lorimer drawled, not to anyone in particular. Lorimer had buried agents before.

"Now we wait for the decode," Frankel told his audience a little too brightly. "Three minutes, maybe five. Time to smoke a cigarette, okay? Everybody relax. Conger's alive and well."

The boys were transferring spools, resetting instruments.

"Let's just be grateful he's alive," said Kate, and several heads turned sharply, remarking this unaccustomed display of feeling from a Fifth Floor lady.

The grey spools were rolling, one on to the other. For a moment they heard the unrhythmic piping of Morse code. It stopped.

"Hey," said Lorimer softly.

"Run it through again," said Brotherhood.

"What's happened?" said Kate.

The boys rewound the spools and switched again to forward. The Morse resumed and stopped as before.

"Could it be a fault the other end?" Lorimer asked.

"Sure," Frankel said. "Possible his winder's on the blink, possible he hit some bad ionosphere. In a minute he comes through again. No problem."

The taller of the two boys was pulling off his headphones. "Mind if we decode, Mr. Frankel?" he said. "Sometimes when they've got a hitch they tell us about it in the message."

On a nod from Frankel he shifted a spool to a machine at the far end of the bank. The printer began chattering immediately. Nigel and Lorimer moved quickly towards the platform. The printer stopped. Nigel magisterially ripped out the sheet and held it for Lorimer and himself to read. Brotherhood was already striding down the aisle. Mounting the platform, he snatched the script from their unresisting hands.

"Jack, don't," said Kate under her breath.

"Don't what?" Brotherhood said, suddenly out of patience with her. "Don't care about my agents? Don't do what exactly?"

"Tell them to print another copy, will you, Frankel?" Nigel said smoothly. "Then we can all look at it together without shoving."

Brotherhood was holding the sheet before him. Nigel and Lorimer had meekly arranged themselves to either side of him and were reading it over his shoulder.

"Routine intelligence report, Bo," Nigel announced reading aloud. "Promised length, three hundred and seven groups. Actual length so far forty-one. Subject, restationing of Soviet missile bases in mountains north of Pilsen. Subsource Mirabeau reporting ten days ago. Mirabeau in turn reporting her Soviet Army boyfriend codename Leo—Leo's done us rather well in the past, I seem to remember. Message reads as follows: Subsource Talleyrand confirms empty low-loaders leaving area— message ends in midsentence. Obviously the winder. Unless, as you say, his signal hit freak conditions."

Frankel was already giving orders to the taller boy. "Send them 'Your signal garbled.' Do it immediately. Tell them we want a rerun. Tell them if they can't transmit now we'll remain on standby till they can. Tell them we want a roll-call of all members of the network. You got set phrases for that or you want I draft something?"

"Tell them damn all," Brotherhood ordered very loud. "And stop crying everybody. No one's hurt."

He had thrust his hands into his raincoat pockets. He was halfway down the aisle. Nigel and Lorimer were still on stage, a pair of choirboys clutching their hymn sheet between them. Brammel sat stoically upright in the auditorium. Kate was staring at him, not stoical at all.

"You can tell them you want a roll-call or a rerun, you can tell them to abort, you can tell them to jump in the Vistula. It doesn't make a dime of difference," said Brotherhood.

"Poor man," said Nigel to Lorimer. "They're his Joes, you see. It's the strain."

"They're not my Joes and they never were. You can have them with my blessing." He looked around him for men with sense. "Frankel. For Christ's sake. Lorimer. When this service catches someone else's Joe, if it ever does these days, what does it do? If he's willing to be played, we play him back. If he's not we send him to the Tower. Is it different now? I wouldn't know."

"So?" said Nigel, humouring him.

"If we decide to play him back, we do it as naturally and as fast as we can. Why? Because we want to show the opposition that nothing has changed. We want it seamless. We don't hide his car and close his house. We don't let him or his daughter or anybody else vanish into thin air. We don't ignore dead letter boxes or invent fatuous stories about people eating bad mushrooms. We don't sandbag radio operators in the middle of their high-speed transmissions. That is the last, the very last thing we do. Unless."

"I don't read you, Jack, old boy," Nigel said, whom Brotherhood had deliberately ignored. "I don't think anybody does, to be truthful. I think you are very naturally upset and you are getting a bit metaphysical, if you don't mind my saying."

"Unless what, Jack?" said Frankel.

"Unless we *want* the opposition to know we're rolling up their network."

"But why would anybody want that, Jack?" Frankel asked earnestly. "Explain to us. Please."

"Why not explain it another time?" said Nigel.

"There never was a bloody network. They owned those networks from day one. They paid the actors, wrote the script. They owned Pym and near enough they owned me. They owned all of you as well. You just haven't woken up to it."

"Then why do they bother to tell us anything at all?" Frankel objected. "Why send us a fake interrupted signal? Why rig the disappearance of the Joes?"

Brotherhood smiled. Not kindly, not with humour. But he did turn to Frankel and he did smile at him. "Because, old boy, they want us to think they've got Pym when they haven't," he said. "That is the only lie they've got left to sell us. They want us to call off the hunt and go home to our high tea. They want to find him for themselves. That's the good news of the day. Pym is still on the run and they want him as much as we do."

They watched him turn and stride down the aisle and slide the locks back on the padded door. Poor old Jack, they said to each other with their eyes as the light went up: his life's work. Lost all his Joes and can't face it. Dreadful to see him so cut up. Only Frankel seemed to wish he hadn't gone.

"Have you ordered the rerun yet?" said Nigel. "I said have you ordered a rerun?"

"I'll do it now," said Frankel.

"Good man," said Bo appreciatively from the stalls.

In the corridor, Brotherhood paused to light himself a cigarette. The door opened and closed again. It was Kate.

"I can't go on," she said. "It's mad."

"Well it's going to get a damn sight madder," snapped Brotherhood, still angry. "That was just the trailer."

It was night once more and Mary had got through another day without throwing herself politely from a top-floor window or scrawling filthy words on the dining-room walls. Seated on her bed still moderately sober, she stared at the book and then at the phone. The phone had a second wire fed into it. The wire led to a grey box and seemed to stop. Since my time, she thought. Can't be doing with these modern gadgets. She poured another generous tot of whisky and set the glass on the table at her elbow in order to end the argument she had been having with herself for the last ten minutes. There you are, damn you. If you want one, have one. If you don't, leave the bloody thing where it is. She was fully dressed. She was supposed to have a headache but the headache was a lie to escape the excruciating company of Fergus and the girl Georgie who had begun to treat her with the deference of warders before her hanging. "How about a nice game of Scrabble, Mary? . . . Not in the mood are we? Never mind. . . . I say, that shepherd's pie *did* go down a treat, didn't it, Georgie? I haven't had a shepherd's pie like that since my man went. Do you think it's the freezing that does it? Sort of ripens it, does it, the freezing?" At eleven o'clock, screaming inside, she had left them to the washing-up and brought herself up here to the book and to the note that had accompanied it. A deckled card.

Silver-edged, my wedding anniversary. In a deckled envelope. Vile cherub blowing trumpet top left.

"Dear Mary,

"So sorry to hear about M's calamity. Picked this up for pennies this morning and wondered whether you would like to bind it for me, same as all the others, full hide, buckram and the title printed in gold capitals between the first and second band on the spine. The end-papers look kind of new to me, maybe just rip them out? Grant's away too so I guess I know how you feel. Could you do it quickly, as a surprise for him? Usual fee, of course!

"My love, darling,

Bee"

Keeping her hand away from the whisky and her mind clear of thoughts of a certain moustached phantom, Mary applied her training to the note. The handwriting was not Bee Lederer's. It was a forgery and to anyone who knew the game a dismal one. The writer had paid lip-service to Bee's all-American copperplate but the Germanic influence was clear in the spiky "u"s and "n"s and the "t"s without tails. "Whether" instead of "if," she thought: when did an American write "whether"? The spelling wasn't Bee's either: a word like "calamity." Bee couldn't spell for toffee. She doubled every consonant on sight. Her letters to Mary in Greece, penned on similar stationery, had contained such family gems as menipullate and phallassy. As to "full hide": Mary had bound just three books for Bee, and Bee hadn't known from green apples how she wanted them, except she thought they looked great on Grant's shelf, just like the old libraries you have in England. Full hide, buckram, the placing of the lettering: these were the writer talking, not Bee. And if Bee suspected that the end-papers might not be original—well bully for Bee because a month ago she had asked Mary wherever had she bought that cute wallpaper stuff she stuck on the inside of her covers?

The note was so bad, Mary concluded—and so unlike Bee—that it was almost deliberately bad: good enough to fool Fergus when it was delivered to the door this afternoon, bad enough to be a signal to Mary that it meant something different.

Something she had been warned of, for instance.

She had read the clues from the moment she opened the door to the vanman, while Fergus the idiot lurked in the coat cupboard with a bloody great Howitzer in his hand in case the vanman turned out to be a Russian in disguise—which perhaps on reflection he was, because Bee had never used a private delivery service in her life. Bee would have dropped the book in herself on the way back from Becky's school, cooeeing through the letter box. Bee would have buttonholed Mary at the International Ladies on Tuesday, leaving her to hump the damn thing home as best she could.

"Mind if I read the card, Mary?" Fergus had said. "It's just routine, only you know what they're like in London. Bee. That'll be Mrs. Lederer, wife of the American gentleman?"

"That's who it will be," Mary had confirmed.

"Well it's a nice book, I will say. In English too. Looks really old, it does." He was turning through it with practised fingers, pausing at pencil marks, holding occasional pages to the light.

"It's 1698," Mary had said, pointing to the Roman numerals.

"My goodness, you can read that stuff."

"Can I have it back now, please?"

The grandfather clock in the hall was striking twelve. Fergus and Georgie were by now no doubt lying blissfully in each other's arms. Over the interminable days of her secret imprisonment Mary had watched their romance ripen. Tonight when she came down to dinner George had the indisguisable glow of someone who had been screwing minutes before. In a year's time the two of them would become yet another his-and-hers couple in one of the resources sections where the Other Ranks held sway: surveillance, microphone installation, sweeping, steaming mail. A year later when they had pooled their fiddled overtime and their cooked-up mileage and inflated their out-of-town subsistence they would make a down payment on a house in East Sheen, have two children and become eligible for the Firm's subsidised education scheme. I'm being a jealous bitch, thought Mary, unrepentant. Right now, I wouldn't mind an hour with Fergus myself. She picked up the receiver and waited.

"Who are you ringing, Mary?" said Fergus's voice immediately.

Wherever he was in his love-life just then, Fergus was very awake indeed when it came to cutting in on Mary's outgoing phone calls.

"I'm lonely," Mary replied. "I want to have a chat with Bee Lederer. Anything wrong with that?"

"Magnus is still in London, Mary. He's been delayed."

"I know where he is. I know the story. I am also grown up."

"He's been contacting you regular by phone, you've had nice chats with him, he'll be back in a day or two. Head Office has nabbed him for a briefing while he's over there. That's all that happened."

"I'm all right, Fergus. I'm word perfect."

"Would you normally ring her as late as this?"

"If both Magnus and Grant are away, yes I would."

Mary heard a click and then the dialling tone. She dialled the number and Bee started moaning at once. She was having her damned period, she said, a real bastard, cramps, the bends, you name it. It always grabbed her this way in winter, specially when Grant wasn't there to service her. Giggle. "Oh shit, Mary, I really miss it. Does that make me a whore?"

"I've had a lovely long letter from Tom," said Mary. A lie. It was a letter and it was long but it was not lovely. It was an account of the great time Tom had had with Uncle Jack last Sunday and it had made Mary's flesh creep.

Bee declared that Becky just adored Tom so much it was indecent. "Can you imagine what is going to happen the day those kids wake up and discover *la différence*?"

Yes, I can, thought Mary. They're going to hate each other's guts. She took Bee through her day. Hell, just screwing around, said Bee. She'd had a squash date with Cathie Krane from the Canadian Embassy but they'd agreed on a coffee instead because of Bee's condition. Salad at the Club, and Jesus somebody *really* ought to teach these damned Austrians how to make a decent salad. This afternoon a cruddy Bring and Buy at the Embassy in aid of the Contras in Nicaragua and who gives a fly's elbow about the Contras in Nicaragua?

"You should go out and buy yourself something," Mary suggested. "A dress or an antique or something."

"Listen, I can't even *move*. You know what he did, the little runt? He turned the Audi in for servicing on his way to the airport. I don't get the car, I don't get a lay."

"I'd better ring off," Mary said. "I've got a feeling Magnus is going to pull one of his dead-of-night calls and there'll be all hell if the number is engaged."

"Yeah, how's he taken it?" said Bee vaguely. "Is he all weepy or is he sort of reconciled? Some men, I think they really want to castrate their fathers all their lives. You should hear Grant sometimes."

"I'll know when he's back," said Mary. "Before he left he hardly spoke a word."

"Too cut up, huh? Grant never gets cut up about anything, the creep."

"It hit him badly at first," Mary confessed. "He sounds much better now." She had scarcely rung off before the phone gave its in-house buzz.

"Why didn't you mention the beautiful book she sent you, Mary?" Fergus complained. "I thought that was why you'd be ringing."

"I told you why I was ringing. I was ringing because I was lonely. Bee Lederer sends me about fifteen books a week. Why should I talk to her about a bloody book to please you?"

"I wasn't meaning to offend, Mary."

"She didn't mention the book so why should I? She gave me all the necessary instructions in her bloody note." I'm protesting too much, she thought, cursing herself. I'm putting questions in his mind. "Listen, Fergus. I'm tired and liable to bite, okay? Leave me alone and go back to what you both do best."

She picked up the book. Nothing, not a book on earth, could have authenticated the sender so perfectly. "De Arte Graphica. The Art of Painting by C. A. DU FRESNOY with REMARKS. Translated into English together with an Original Preface containing a Parallel between Painting and Poetry. By Mr. DRYDEN." She drained the glass of whisky. It was the same book. She had no doubt. The same book Magnus brought to me in Berlin when I still belonged to Jack. Came bounding up the stairs with it. Knocking on the steel door of Special Ordnance which was our cover while he clutched it in his hand. "Hey, Mary, open up!" It was before we had become lovers. Before he had started to call me Mabs. "Listen I want you to do a rush job for me. Can you put a CD into the binding of this? It's to take one standard sheet of code cloth. Can you do it by tonight?" Then I staged a misunderstanding because we were already flirting. I pretended I hadn't heard of CDs except on diplomatic cars, which allowed Magnus to explain to me in his earnest way that CD meant concealment device and Jack Brotherhood had told him Mary was the best person for the job. "We're using a bookshop as a dead letter box," Magnus explained. "I've got this Joe who's an antiquarian-book fiend." Case officers were not usually so generous about their operations.

And I took off the end-paper, she remembered as she began gently prodding the covers. I scraped away a patch of cover board until I was nearly at the hide. Other people would have taken off the hide and gone under it from the front. Not our Mary. For Magnus nothing but perfection would do. Next night he gave me dinner. The night after that we went to bed together. Next morning I told Jack what had happened and he was gallant and sweet and said we were both very lucky, and that

he'd withdraw from the field and let us get on with it, if that was what I wanted.
I said it was. And I told Jack in my happiness that what had brought me and
Magnus together was de Arte Graphica, a Parallel between Painting and Poetry,
which was rather extraordinary when you remembered that I was mad about
painting and Magnus was hell-bent on writing the great novel of his life.

"Where are you going, Mary?" Fergus said, looming before Mary in the corridor. She had the book in her hand. She shoved it at him. "I can't sleep. I'm going
down to the cellar to fool around with this. Now go back to your nice lady and leave
me alone."

Closing the cellar door she went quickly to the workbench. In minutes Georgie
is going to saunter in with a nice cup of tea for me in order to make sure I haven't
defected or cut my wrists. Filling a bowl with warm water damped a rag and set
to work soaking off the endpaper. The writer of the note knew what he was talking
about. On a book of that age the original glue was animal and would have
crystallised. Mary, when she had doctored it for Magnus, had used animal glue too.
But the new paper had been stuck on with flour paste which responded quickly to
water. She was using a cloth and scrubbing. Normally she would have used blotting
paper and a pressing tin. The endpaper came away. The board remained. Taking
a scalpel she began scuffing it with the blade. If they've used rope board, I've had
it. Rope board was made of real old rope taken from a man-of-war. It was tarred
and twisted and packed solid. To scrape into it would take hours. She need not have
worried. It was modern millboard and disintegrated like dry earth. She kept scuffing
and suddenly the code cloth lay before her, flat against the inside of the hide, exactly
where she had put it for Magnus. Except that this one had capital letters instead of
figure groups. This one began "Dear Mary." She stuffed it quickly down her front,
retrieved the scalpel, and set about removing the rest of the endpaper as if she were
going to rebind from the beginning, full hide as Bee had requested.

"I just thought I had to come and see how you do it," Georgie explained, sitting
down beside her. "I really need a hobby like that myself, Mary. I just don't ever
seem able to relax."

"Poor you," said Mary.

It was night and Brotherhood was angry. Though he was out in the streets and away
from the Firm and the Firm's ken, though he had work to do and action to relieve
him, he was angry. His anger had been mounting for two days. This morning's
outburst about the Joes was not the start of it. It had been kindled yesterday, like
a slow-burning fuse, as he was leaving the conference room in St. John's Wood after
perjuring himself to save Brammel's neck. It had stuck with him like a faithful friend
through his meeting with Tom and his excursion to Reading station: Pym has
broken the moral laws. He has outlawed himself by choice. It had touched flash-
point in the signals room this morning and gathered more heat with every pointless
conference and frittered hour since. From his position of half-pitied and wholly
blamed has-been, Brotherhood had listened to his own arguments being used
against him and had looked on as, under his very eyes, his old defence of Pym had
been adopted and updated into a policy of institutionalised inertia.

"But, Jack, it's all so circumstantial—you said so yourself," Brammel brayed,
never stronger than when demonstrating that two positives made a negative. " 'If

you run any succession of coincidences through a computer, you will find that everything looks possible and most things look highly likely.' Who said that, pray? I'm quoting you deliberately, Jack. We're sitting at your feet, remember? Good heavens, I never thought I'd have to defend Pym against *you!*"

"I was wrong," said Brotherhood.

"But who says you were? Only you, I think. So Pym has a Czech code pad in his chimney place," Brammel conceded. "He has a camera we didn't know about with a document-copying attachment or whatever. Good heavens, Jack, think of all the bits of equipment you've picked up in your time, just in the ordinary way of playing agents back and forth! Gold bars, cameras, microdot lenses, concealment devices, I don't know what. You could have started your own pawnbroker's shop with them. All right I grant you he should have turned the stuff in. I see him as being rather in the position of a police detective who has taken a lot of swag off one of his informants. He shoves it in a drawer—or in the fireplace—hides it from his family and one day it's all discovered. But it doesn't make him a burglar. It makes him an efficient policeman who's been cavalier or at worst careless."

"He's not careless," said Brotherhood. "He's not a risk taker."

"All right, so now he is. The fellow's had a nervous breakdown, he's acting clean out of character, he's hidden himself away somewhere, he's putting out the usual cries for help," Brammel reasoned, in a note of saintly tolerance. "Probably a girlfriend, knowing him. We shall find out soon enough. But look at the scenario, Jack. His father dies. He's the artistic type of officer, always wanting to write the great novel, paint, sculpt, take sabbaticals, I don't know what. He's hit a menopausal age in life. He's been living under a cloud of suspicion for far too long. Do you wonder he's had a bit of a crack-up? Be a wonder if he hadn't, if you ask me. All right, I don't condone it. And I shall want to know why he took that burnbox, though you tell me he knew everything that was in it anyway and wrote most of it himself, so what's the difference? And when we find him, I may pull him out of the field for a while. There is still no justification for me to raise a public hue and cry. To go to my Minister and say 'We've found another one.' Least of all to the Americans. Bang go the barter treaties. Bang goes the intelligence pooling and the private line to Langley that often means so much more than normal diplomatic links. Do you want me to risk all that until we *know?*"

"Bo feels you should stop flying solo," Nigel said when they were back on the servants' side of Brammel's door. "I'm afraid I agree. From now on you'll make no field enquiries without my personal authority. You're to remain on call and you're to start nothing. Is that clear?"

It is clear, thought Brotherhood, examining the house from across the road. It is clear that the rewards of my old age are dangerously threatened. He tried to remember who it was in mythology who was cursed to live long enough to witness the consequences of his bad advice. The house was in the best of Chelsea's many beautiful backwaters, set at the end of a long garden only partly visible above the gate. An air of decadence pervaded its genteel shabbiness, an unworldly languor inhabited its flaking stucco. Brotherhood walked past it several times, checking the upper windows, studying the skyline for sight of a church, for Pym's mental substitutions were becoming rooted in his mind like spy talk. On the fourth floor a dormer window was lit and curtained. As he watched he saw a figure pass across it, too quickly and too far away for him to tell whether it was man or woman.

He took a last look up and down the road. A brass bellpush was set into the gatepost. He pressed it and waited but not long. He shoved the gate, it creaked and opened, he stepped inside and closed it after him. The garden was a secret patch of English countryside walled on three sides. Nothing overlooked it. The sounds of traffic ceased miraculously. The flagstone path was slippery with unswept leaves. Home, he rehearsed again. Home in Scotland, home in Wales. Home by the sea. Home as an upper window and a church. Home as an aristocratic mother who took him visiting great houses. He passed the statue of a draped woman, one stone breast offered to the autumn night. Home as a series of concentric fantasies, all with the same truth at the centre. Who had said that?—Pym or himself? Home as promises to women he didn't love. The front door was opening as he reached it. A young manservant was watching him approach. His monkey jacket had a regimental cut. Behind him, unrestored gilt mirrors and a chandelier glinted against dark wallpaper. "He's got a boy name of Stegwold living there," Superintendent Bellows of police liaison had reported. "If you were old enough, I'd read you his record of convictions."

"Sir Kenneth in, son?" said Brotherhood pleasantly as he wiped his shoes on the mat and shook off his raincoat.

"I don't know, do I? Who shall I say?"

"Mr. Marlow, son, and I'd like ten minutes with him alone on a mutual matter."

"From?" said the boy.

"His constituency, son," said Brotherhood just as pleasantly.

The boy tripped quickly upstairs. Brotherhood's gaze skimmed the hall. Hats, idiosyncratic. Coaching overcoat, green with age. One Guards bowler, ditto. Army service cap with Coldstream badge. Blue china urn stuffed with ancient golf clubs, walking-sticks and warped tennis racquets. The boy came mincing down the stairs again, trailing one hand on the banisters, unable to resist an entrance.

"He'll see you now, Mr. Marlow," he said.

The stairs were lined with portraits of rude men. In a dining-room, two places were laid with enough silver for a banquet. A decanter, cold meats, and cheeses lay on the sideboard. It was not till Brotherhood noticed a couple of dirty plates that he realised the meal was already over. The library smelled of mildew and the fumes of paraffin from a stove. A gallery ran along three walls. Half the balustrade was missing. The stove had been shoved into the fireplace and in front of it stood a clothes-horse hung with socks and underpants. In front of the clotheshorse stood Sir Kenneth Sefton Boyd. He wore a velvet smoking jacket and an open-necked shirt and old satin slippers with gold-stitched monograms worn away. He was burly and thick-necked, with uneven pads of flesh round his jaw and eyes. His mouth was bent to one side as if by a clenched fist. He spoke with the bent side while the other stayed still.

"Marlow?"

"How do you do, sir," said Brotherhood.

"What do you want?"

"I'd like to speak to you alone if I may, sir."

"Policeman?"

"Not quite, sir. Something like."

He handed Sir Kenneth a card. This is to certify that the bearer is engaged in enquiries affecting the national security. For confirmation please ring Scotland Yard extension so-and-so. The extension led to Superintendent Bellows's department, which knew all Brotherhood's names. Unimpressed, Sir Kenneth handed the card back.

"So you're a spy."

"Of a sort, I suppose. Yes."

"Want a drink? Beer? Scotch? What do you want to drink?"

"A scotch would be very welcome, sir, now you mention it."

"Scotch, Steggie," said Sir Kenneth. "Get him a scotch, will you? Ice? Soda? What do you want in your scotch?"

"A little water would be welcome."

"All right. Give him water. Bring him a jug. Put it on the table. Over there by the tray. Then he can help himself. You can go away. And top mine up, while you're about it. Want to sit down, Marlow? Over there do you?"

"I thought we were going to the Albion," said Steggie from the door.

"Can't now. Got to talk to this chap."

Brotherhood sat. Sir Kenneth sat opposite him; his gaze was yellowed and unresponsive. Brotherhood had seen dead men whose eyes were more alive. His hands had fallen into his lap and one of them kept flipping like a beached fish. On the table between them lay a backgammon board with the pieces in mid-battle. Who was he playing with? thought Brotherhood. Who dined with him? Who was sharing his music with him? Who warmed my chair before I sat in it?

"You surprised to see me, sir?" said Brotherhood.

"Take a bit more than that to surprise me, old boy."

"Anyone else been here recently, making funny enquiries? Foreign gentlemen? Americans?"

"Not that I know of. Why should they?"

"There's a bunch going round from our own vetting side as well, I'm told. I wondered whether any of them had been here. I tried to find out before I left the office but there's a lack of coordination, it's all moving so fast."

"What is?"

"Well, sir, it seems that your old school friend Mr. Magnus Pym has disappeared. They're looking into everyone who might have knowledge of his whereabouts. That will include you naturally."

Sir Kenneth's eye lifted to the door.

"Something out there bothering you, sir?" said Brotherhood.

Sir Kenneth rose, went to the door and pulled it open. Brotherhood heard a scuffle of footsteps on the stairs but he was too late to see who it was, though he jostled Sir Kenneth aside in his haste to look.

"Steggie, I want you to go to the Albion ahead of me," Sir Kenneth called into the well. "Go now. I'll join you later. I don't want him hearing this stuff," he told Brotherhood as he closed the door. "What he doesn't know can't hurt him."

"With his record I don't blame you," said Brotherhood. "Mind if I look upstairs now we're standing?"

"Yes I damn well do. And don't lay hands on me again. I don't fancy you. Got a warrant?"

"No."

Resuming his chair, Sir Kenneth took a spent matchstick from the pocket of his smoking jacket and set to work on his fingernails with its charred end. "Get a warrant," he advised. "Get a warrant and I might let you look. Other hand I mightn't."

"Is he here?" said Brotherhood.

"Who?"

"Pym."

"Don't know. Didn't hear. Who's Pym?"

Brotherhood was still standing. He was unnaturally pale, and it took him a moment to steady his voice before he spoke again.

"I've got a deal for you," he said.

Sir Kenneth still did not hear.

"Hand him over to me. You go upstairs. Or you ring him. You do whatever you've agreed to do between you. And you hand him over to me. In return I'll keep your name out of it, and Steggie's name out of it. The alternative is 'Baronet M.P. shelters very old friend on the run.' It's also a serious possibility that you will be charged as an accomplice. How old is Steggie?"

"Old enough."

"How old was he when he started here?"

"Look it up. Don't know."

"I'm Pym's friend too. There are worse people than me coming looking for him. Ask him. If he agrees, I agree. I'll keep your name out of it. Just give him to me and you and Steggie need never hear from him or me again."

"Sounds to me as though you've more to lose than we have," said Sir Kenneth, surveying the results of his manicure.

"I doubt it."

"Question of what we've all got left, I suppose. Can't lose what you haven't got. Can't miss what you don't care about. Can't sell what isn't yours."

"Pym can, apparently," said Brotherhood. "He's been selling his nation's secrets by the looks of it."

Sir Kenneth continued to admire his fingernails. "For money?"

"Probably."

Sir Kenneth shook his head. "Didn't care about money. Love was all he cared about. Didn't know where to find it. Clown really. Tried too hard."

"Meanwhile he's wandering around England with a lot of papers that aren't his to give away, and you and I are supposed to be patriotic Englishmen."

"Lot of chaps do a lot of things they shouldn't do. That's when they need their chums."

"He wrote to his son about you. Do you know that? Some drivel about a penknife. Does that ring a bell?"

"Matter of fact it does."

"Who's Poppy?"

"Never heard of her."

"Or him?"

"Nice thought, but no."

"Wentworth?"

"Never been there. Hate the place. What about it?"

"There was a girl called Sabina he apparently got caught up with in Austria. He ever mention her?"

"Not that I remember. Pym got caught up with a lot of girls. Not that it did him much good."

"He rang you, didn't he? On Monday night, from a callbox."

With startling abruptness, Sir Kenneth flung up one arm in pleasure and gave a hoot of merriment. "Pissed out of his skull," he declared, very loud. "Ossified. Haven't heard him so pissed since Oxford when six of us put away a case of his father's port. Pretended some queen from Merton gave it to him, I don't know why. There weren't any queens in Merton in those days. Not rich ones. We were all at Trinity."

It was after midnight. Back in the confinement of his Shepherd Market flat with the pigeons on the parapet Brotherhood poured himself another vodka and added orange juice from a carton. He had thrown his jacket on the bed, his pocket tape-recorder lay before him on the desk. He was jotting as he listened.

". . . don't go to Wiltshire a lot as a rule while Parliament's in session but Sunday was my second wife's birthday and our boy was down from school so I went and did my stuff and thought I'd stay on for a day or two and see what gives in the constituency. . . ."

Forward again: ". . . don't normally answer the phone in Wiltshire but Monday's her bridge night and I was in the library playing a game of backgammon so when the phone rang I thought I might as well take it rather than spoil her four. Half past eleven it must have been but Jean's bridge nights go on for ever. Chap's voice. Must be her boyfriend, I thought. Bloody cheek, really, this time of night. 'Hullo? Sef? That Sef?' 'Who the hell's that?' I said. 'It's me. Magnus. My father's died. Over here to bury him.' I thought, Poor old chap. Nobody likes to have his old man die on him. . . . That right for you? More water? Help yourself."

Brotherhood hears himself roar "Thanks" as he leans towards the water jug. Then the sounds of a flood as he pours.

" 'How's Jem?' he says. Jemima's my sister. They had a ding-dong once, never came to much. Married a florist. Extraordinary thing. Chap grows flowers all along the road to Basingstoke. Puts his name up on a board. Doesn't seem to bother her. Not that she sees much of him. Navigational problems, our Jem. Same as me."

Forward again: ". . . pissed. Couldn't tell whether he was laughing or crying. Poor chap, I thought. Drowning his sorrows. I'd do the same. Next thing I know, he's prosing on about our private school. I mean Christ, we'd done two or three schools together, Oxford, not to mention a couple of holidays, yet all he wants to talk about forty years later, on the blower middle of the night, party going on, is how he carved my initials in the staff loo at our private and got me flogged for it. 'Sorry I carved your initials, Sef.' All right. He did it. He carved 'em. I never doubted he carved 'em. Cocked it up too. He would. Know what he did? Bloody fool put a hyphen between the 'S' and the 'B' where we don't have one. I told old Grimble, the headmaster. 'Why would I put a hyphen in?' I said. 'Not how I spell my name,' I said. 'No hyphen in it. Look at the school list.' Not a blind bit of difference, flogged me. Way it goes, you see. No justice. I don't know I minded much. Everybody flogged everybody in those days. Besides, I wasn't very nice to him myself. Always ragging him about his people. Father was a con man, you know. Nearly ruined my aunt. Had a go at my mother too. Tried to bed her but she was too fly. Some scheme to build a new airport in Scotland somewhere. He'd squared the locals, all he needed was buy the land, get the formal permission, make a fortune. Cousin of mine owns half Argyll. I asked him about it. Hokum, the whole thing. Extraordinary. I stayed with 'em once. Tarts' parlour in Ascot. All these crooks hanging about and Magnus calling them 'sir.' Father tried to get into Parliament once. Pity he didn't. He'd have been good company. . . ."

Forward again: ". . . banging in the cash. I asked him where he was, he said London but he had to use phone boxes, he was being followed. I said, 'Whose initials have you been carving now?' Joke actually, but he didn't see it. I was sorry about his old man, you see. Didn't want him moping. Dramatic chap, always has been. Nothing going on in his life unless he's got some frightful problem on his hands. You could have sold him the Egyptian pyramids long as you said they were falling down. I said, give me the number of your phone, I'll ring you back. He said somebody must have told me to say that. I said 'Absolute bilge, hell are you talking about? Half my friends are on the run.' He said his father was dead and he was looking at his life for the first time. Fundamental. Always has been. Then he went back to these initials he'd carved. 'I'm really sorry, Sef.' I said, 'Look here, old boy, I always knew it was you and I don't think we should go through life wearing hairshirts about what we did at our private. Do you need cash? Want a bed? Take a cottage on the estate.' 'I'm really sorry, Sef. Really sorry.' I said, 'You tell me what I can do, I'll do it. I'm in the book in London, give me a buzz if I can help.' Well I mean damn it, he'd been on for twenty minutes. I put the phone down and half an hour later he's back. 'Hullo, Sef. Me again.' Jean was pretty shirty this time. Thought it was Steggie having a tantrum. 'Got to talk to you, Sef. Listen to me.' Well, you can't ring off on an old chum when he's down, can you?"

Brotherhood heard Sir Kenneth's clock chime twelve. He was jotting fast. Concentric fantasies, he repeated to himself, defining the truth at the centre. He had reached the passage he was waiting for.

". . . said he was in secret work. That didn't surprise me, who isn't these days? . . . Said there was this Englishman he worked for, called him the Brotherhood. I don't think I listened to all of it, to be honest. There was the Brotherhood and there was this other chap. Said he was working for both of 'em. They were like two parents for him. Kept him going. I said bully for you, if they keep you going, you stick to them. Said he had to write this book about them, put the record right. What record? God knows. He'd write to the Brotherhood, write to the other chap, then he'd take himself off to a secret place and do his number." Brotherhood heard his own patient murmur in the background. ". . . Well maybe I got that one a bit wrong then. Maybe he was going to hunker down in his secret place first and write to them from there. I wasn't listening to all of it. Drunks bore me. I'm one myself."

Prompt from Brotherhood.

Long pause.

Renewed prompt from Brotherhood.

Sir Kenneth indistinct: "Said he was his runner."

"Who was whose runner?"

"Pym was t'other chap's runner. Not the Brotherhood's. The other fellow's. Said he'd crippled him somehow. Pissed, I told you."

Brotherhood again, riding him a little harder: ". . . name for this person?"

"Don't think so. Don't think it stuck. Sorry. No, it didn't."

"And the secret place? Where was that?"

"Didn't say. His business."

Brotherhood let the tape continue. Avalanche as Sefton Boyd lights himself a cigarette. Cannon-blast of the front door being slammed open and shut again, signalling Steggie's petulant return.

Brotherhood and Sir Kenneth are on the landing.

"What's that, old boy?" Sir Kenneth very loud.

"I said, so where do you think he might be?" says Brotherhood.

"Upstairs, old boy. That's what you said." In his memory's eye, Brotherhood sees Sir Kenneth's pouch face approach close to his own, smiling its downward twist. "Get a warrant, maybe you can have a look. Maybe you can't. Don't know. Have to see."

Brotherhood heard his own heels clumping down Sir Kenneth's stairs. He heard himself reach the hall and Steggie's lighter footsteps mingle with his own. He heard Steggie's pointed "Good night" and the clatter of bolts as he unlocks the door for him. Followed by Steggie's muffled shriek as Brotherhood hauls him out of the house, one hand over his mouth, the other at the back of his head. Then the thump as he taps Steggie's head against the plaster pillar of Sir Kenneth's gracious porch, and his own voice, very near to Steggie's ear.

"Have they done this before to you, have they? Put you up against a wall?"

A whimper for an answer.

"Who else is living in the house, son?"

"No one."

"Who was on the top floor this evening, back and forth in front of the window."

"Me."

"Why?"

"It's my room!"

"I thought you two would share the bridal chamber."

"I've still got my own room, haven't I? I'm entitled to my privacy, same as he is."

"Nobody else in the house at all?"

"No!"

"Not all week?"

"No. I told you. Hey, stop!"

"What's the matter?" says Brotherhood, already halfway down the path.

"I haven't got my key. How do I get back in?"

A clang as Brotherhood slams the gate.

He phoned Kate. No answer.

He phoned his wife. No answer.

He phoned Paddington and wrote down the times and places along the route of the night sleeper from Paddington to Penzance via Reading.

For an hour he tried to sleep, then returned to his desk, pulled Langley's folder toward him and stared yet again at the eaten-out features of Herr Petz-Hampel-Zaworski, Pym's presumed controller, lately of Corfu. ". . . Real name unknown . . . query member Czech archaeological team visiting Egypt 1961 (Petz) . . . query

1966 att. Czech Military Mission East Berlin (Hampel) . . . height 6 ft., stoops, limps slightly with left leg . . .''

"There was the Brotherhood and there was this other chap," Sefton Boyd had said. "They were like two parents for him. Said he was his runner."

"You brought it on yourselves," he heard Belinda say. "You invented him."

He continued to stare at the photograph. The down-turned eyelids. The down-turned moustache. The twinkly eyes. The hidden Slav smile. Who the devil are you? Why do I recognise you when I have never set eyes on you?

Grant Lederer had never stood so high in the world, or felt so rounded as a human being. Justice lives! he assured himself in the perfect peacefulness of his triumph. My masters are worthy of their authority. A noble service has tried me to the limit and found me worthy of my hire. All round him the sealed operations room on the sixth floor of the American Embassy in Grosvenor Square was filling up with people he had not known existed. They came from the remote corners of London Station, yet each as he entered appeared to bestow a glance of kinship on him. As fine a looking bunch of Americans as you'd wish to meet, he thought. The Agency really knows how to pick us these days. They had hardly settled before Wexler began speaking.

"Time to wrap this thing up," he said grimly as the door was locked. "Meet Gary, everybody. Gary's head of SISURP. He's here to report an important break-through on Pym and discuss action."

SISURP, Lederer had recently learned, was the acronym for Surveillance Intelligence, Southern Europe. Gary was your typical Kentuckian—tall, spare and amusing. Lederer already admired him intensely. An aide sat at his elbow with a heap of papers, but Gary did not refer to them. Our quarry, he said baldly, was Petz-Hampel-Zaworski, now known to the indoctrinated familiarly as PHZ. A SISURP team picked him up Tuesday 10:12 A.M. emerging from the Czech Embassy in Vienna. Lederer listened enthralled as Gary noted each tiny detail of PHZ's day. Where PHZ took his coffee. Where PHZ took his leaks. The bookshops where PHZ browsed. Who PHZ lunched with. Where. What he ate. PHZ's limp. His ready smile. His charm, particularly with women. His cigars, where he lit them, bought them. PHZ's ease of association, his apparent unawareness that he was being observed by a field force eighteen strong. The two occasions when "wittingly or otherwise" PHZ placed himself in the vicinity of Mrs. Mary Pym. On one of these occasions, said Gary, eye contact was confirmed. On the other, surveillance was inhibited by the presence of a British pair believed to be the escorts of Mrs. Pym. And thence at last to the crowning moment of the operation and the high point of Grant Lederer's brilliant marriage and dazzling career so far, when at 8 A.M. local time today three members of Gary's team found themselves stuck in the rear pews of the English church in Vienna, while twelve more were staked out around the outside of it—mobile units, necessarily, because this was diplomatic-land where loiterers were not well regarded—and PHZ and Mary Pym were placed either side of the aisle. Lederer's cue had arrived. Gary was looking expectantly towards him.

"Grant, I guess you should take over here. We're a little out of our depth," he said, with pleasing gruffness.

As heads at the table shifted in curiosity, Lederer felt the warmth of their interest bear him to new heights. He began speaking at once. Modestly.

"Well hell, I mean I see this whole thing as Bee's achievement and not mine. Bee is Mrs. Lederer," he explained to an older man across the table from him, then realised too late that it was Carver, Head of London Station, never a Lederer fan. "She's Presbyterian. Her parents were Presbyterian too. Mrs. Lederer latterly has been able to reconcile her spirituality with organised religion and has been attending regularly at the Christchurch Anglican church, Vienna, known as the English church, and frankly just the sexiest little church you ever saw. Right, Gary? Cherubs, angels—more like a religious boudoir than a regular church at all. You know, Mick, if anybody's name is going up in lights at Langley over this, I guess it should be Bee's," he added, still somehow not quite able to get to his story.

The rest came out faster. It was Bee after all and not the surveillance team who had managed to slide out into the aisle after PHZ and stand in line right behind him as he and Mary queued for the Sacrament. It was Bee who from a distance of maybe five feet had watched as PHZ leaned forward and whispered real words into Mary's ear, and watched again as Mary first leaned back to catch them, then went ahead with her devotions as if nothing in the world had happened.

"So I mean it was actually my wife, my helpmate throughout all of this long operation, who witnessed the spoken contact." He shook his head in marvel. "And it was Bee again who, the first moment the service ended, raced back to our apartment to phone me right here at the Embassy and describe the whole amazing occurrence, using the domestic codewords the two of us had hashed out together for just such a contingency. And I mean Bee did not even *know* that an Agency surveillance team was present in that church at all. She just went because Mary was going, as much as anything. Yet she scooped SISURP singlehanded by like six *hours,* more. Harry," said Lederer a little breathlessly, finding Wexler as he put the finishing touch to his narrative, "my only regret is that Mrs. Lederer never learned to lip-read."

Lederer had not expected applause. It was in the nature of the community he had joined that there should be none. The pregnant silence struck him as a more fitting tribute.

Artelli the cryptographer was the first to break it. "Here at the Embassy," he repeated, not quite as a question.

"Pardon me?" said Lederer.

"Your wife called you here at the Embassy? From Vienna? Directly after the happening in the church? On the open phone from your apartment?"

"Yes, sir, and I took her news straight upstairs to Mr. Wexler. He had it on his desk by 9 A.M."

"Nine-thirty," Wexler said.

"And what were these domestic codewords that she used, please?" said Artelli while he wrote.

Lederer was happy to explain: "Well really what we did in *fact* was borrow the names of Bee's aunts and uncles. We have always considered there was a similarity in the psychological profiles of Mary Pym and Bee's Aunt Edie. So we kind of worked it up from there. 'You know what Aunt Edie did in church today?' . . . Bee is very subtle."

"Thanks," said Artelli.

Next Carver spoke, and his question did not seem entirely friendly.

"You mean your wife is *conscious* to this operation, Grant? I thought the Pym case was strictly a no-wives thing. Harry, didn't we make a ruling on that a little while back?"

"Strictly it is no wives," Lederer agreed handsomely. "However since Mrs. Lederer has effectively been out in the field with me on this one it would be somewhat illusory to suppose she would not be aware of the general level of suspicion in relation to the Pyms. Well, to Magnus anyway. And I may add that it was always Bee's contention that somewhere at the bottom of this heap we are going to find Mary playing a very deep and laid-back rôle. Mary is a rôle-player."

Carver again. "Is Mrs. Lederer also conscious to PHZ? He's a pretty hot addition to the cast, Grant. He could be a big fish. But she's in on that, huh?"

There was nothing Lederer could do to stop the colour rushing to his face, or his voice developing its strident edge: "Mrs. Lederer had an instinct regarding that encounter and she acted on it. You want to censure her for that, Carver, you censure me first, okay?"

Artelli again, with his damned French drawl. "What was your domestic code-name for PHZ?"

"Uncle Bobby," Lederer snapped.

"But then Bobby is more than instinct, Grant," Carver objected. "Bobby is an agreed thing between you. How could you have agreed Bobby if you hadn't given her the story on Petz-Hampel-Zaworski?"

Wexler had taken back the meeting. "Okay, okay, okay," he growled unhappily. "Cope with that later. Meantime what do we do? SISURP splits and stays with the both of them. PHZ and Mary. That right, Gary? Wherever they go."

"I'm calling for fresh horses right now," said Gary. "Should have two full teams by this time tomorrow."

"Next question, what the hell do we tell the Brits and when and how?" said Wexler.

"Looks like we told them already," said Artelli, with a lazy glance at Lederer. "That's unless the Brits have given up tapping U.S. Embassy telephone lines these days, which I tend to doubt."

Justice lives, but justice, as Grant Lederer discovered before morning, also dies. His health was found to have suffered a sudden lapse, his appointment in Vienna terminated for him in his absence. His wife, far from receiving the commendations Lederer dreamed of, was ordered to follow him back to Langley, Virginia, at once.

"Lederer overheats and overrelates," wrote one of the Agency's ever-expanding team of house psychiatrists. "He requires a less hysterical environment."

The prescribed calm was eventually found for him in Statistics, and it drove him nearly mad.

13

The green cabinet stood in the centre of Pym's room like a discarded fieldpiece that had once been its regiment's pride. Its chrome was peeling from the handles, a heavy boot or fall had stove in one corner, so that the slightest touch could set it trembling and worrying. The chips had rusted into sores, the rust had spread to the screw holes and underneath the paintwork, causing it to lift in humiliating pimples. Pym walked round it with the awe and loathing of a primitive. It has arrived from Heaven. It is destined to return there. I should have put it in the incinerator with him so that he can show it to his Maker as he intended. Four dense drawers of innocence, the Gospel according to Saint Rick.

He gave the cabinet a push and heard a sagging sound from inside as the files slipped obediently to his command.

I should write you witches along his path, Tom. The full moon should be turning red and the owl doing whatever the owl did that was so unnatural when foul murder was afoot. But Pym is deaf and blind to them. He is Second Lieutenant Magnus Pym riding in his private train across occupied Austria, entering by way of that very border town where, long ago, in the less mature existence of a different Pym, E. Weber's fictitious crock of gold had supposedly awaited Mr. Lapadi's collection. He is a Roman conqueror on his way to taking up his first appointment. He is oven-fired against human frailty and his own destiny, as you may observe from the scowls of military abstinence he bestows upon the bare breasts of the Barbarian peasant women harvesting corn in the sunlit fields. His preparation has passed with the ease of an English Sunday, not that Pym ever asked for ease. The privileged English assets of good manners and bad learning have never been more to his advantage. Even his murky political affiliations at Oxford have turned out to be a blessing. "If the Pongos ask you whether you are now or ever have been a member of the clan, look 'em slap in the eye and tell 'em *never*," the last of the Michaels advised him, over a sporting lunch beside the swimming-pool at the Lansdowne, as they watched the pure bodies of suburban girls wriggle through the disinfected water.

"Pongos?" said Pym, mystified.

"Licentious soldiery, old boy. The War Office. Wood from here up. The Firm is fixing your clearance direct. Tell them to mind their damn business."

"Thanks terribly," said Pym.

The same evening, glowing from the best of nine games of squash, Pym was led to the presence of a Very Senior Member of the service, in a plain, forgettable office not far from Rick's newest Reichskanzlei. Was this the Colonel Gaunt who had first approached him? He's higher, Pym was told. Don't ask.

"We want to thank you," said the Senior Member.

"I really enjoyed it," said Pym.

"It's a filthy job, mixing with those people. Somebody has to do it."

"Oh, it's not that bad, sir."

"Look here. We're leaving your name on the books. I can't promise you anything, we've got a selection board these days. Besides, you belong to those chaps across the park and we make it a rule not to fish in one another's preserves. All the same if you ever do decide that protecting your country at home is more to your liking than playing Mata Hari abroad, let us know."

"I will, sir. Thank you," said Pym.

The Very Senior Member was crisp and brown and ostentatiously nondescript like one of his own envelopes. He had the testy manners of a country solicitor, which was what he had been before answering the Great Call. Leaning across his desk he pulled a puzzled smile. "Don't tell me if you don't want. How ever did you get mixed up with that crowd in the first place?"

"The Communists?"

"No, no, no. Our sister service."

"In Bern, sir. I was a student there."

"In Switzerland," said the great man, consulting a mental map.

"Yes, sir."

"My wife and I went skiing near Bern once. Little place called Mürren. The British run it so there aren't any cars. We rather liked it. What did you do for them?"

"Much the same as for you, sir, really. It was just a bit more dangerous."

"In what way?"

"You don't feel you have the protection out there. It's eyeball to eyeball, I suppose."

"Seemed such a peaceful spot to me. Well good luck to you, Pym. Look out for those chaps. They're good but they're slippery. We're good but we've got a bit of honour left. That's the difference."

"He's brilliant," Pym told his guide. "He pretends to be completely ordinary but he sees right into you."

His elation had not left him when a few days later he presented himself, suitcase in hand, at the guardroom of his basic-training regiment where for two months he reaped the plentiful rewards of his upbringing. While Welsh miners and Glaswegian cut-throats wept unashamedly for their mothers, went absent without leave and were carted off to a place of punishment, Pym slept soundly and wept for no one. Long before reveille had dragged his comrades smoking and cursing from their beds, he had polished his boots and belt-brasses and cap badge, made his bed and dressed his bedside locker, and was all ready, should anybody ask it of him, to take a cold shower, dress again, and read the first of the Day Hours with Mr. Willow before a disgusting breakfast. On the parade ground and the football ground he excelled. He neither took fright at being shouted at nor expected logic of authority.

"Where's Gunner Pym?" the colonel barked one day, in the middle of a lecture on the battle of Corunna, and looked up angrily as if someone else had spoken. Every sergeant in the drill hall screamed Pym's name until he stood.

"Are you Pym?"

"Sir!"

"See me after this lecture."

"Sir!"

Company Headquarters lay on the other side of the parade ground. Pym marched there and saluted. The colonel's aide-de-camp left the room.

"At ease, Pym. Sit down."

The colonel spoke carefully, with a soldier's mistrust of words. He had a soft honey-coloured moustache and the limpid gaze of an entirely stupid man.

"It has been put to me by certain people that, assuming you are commissioned, you would do well to attend a certain training course at a certain establishment, Pym."

"Yes, sir."

"I am therefore to submit a personal report on you."

"Yes, sir."

"Which I shall do. Favourable, as a matter of fact."

"Thank you, sir."

"You are keen. You are not cynical. You are not marred, Pym, by the luxuries of peace. You are somebody this country needs."

"Thank you, sir."

"Pym."

"Yes, sir."

"If ever those people you're mixed up with happen to be looking for a rather fit retired army colonel with a certain amount of *je ne sais quoi,* I trust you to remember me. I speak some French. I ride decently. I know my wines. Tell them that."

"I shall, sir. Thank you, sir."

Possessing little in the way of memory, the colonel had a habit of returning to conversations as if they were new to him.

"Pym."

"Yes, sir."

"Pick your moment. Don't rush in with it. They don't like that. Be subtle. That's an order."

"I will, sir."

"You know my name?"

"Yes, sir."

"Spell it."

Pym did.

"I'll change it if they want. They've only to let me know. I hear you took a First, Pym."

"Yes, sir."

"Carry on."

In the evenings, seated beside lonely men, Pym the ever-willing obliged by dictating letters of love to their girlfriends. Where the physical feat of writing eluded them, he acted as their amanuensis, adding personalised endearments to their specification. Sometimes, fired by his own rhetoric, he would burst into song on his own account, in the lyrical style of a Blunden or a Sassoon:

"Dearest Belinda,

"I cannot tell you what fun and simple human goodness are to be found among one's working-class comrades. Yesterday—great excitement—we drove our twenty-five-pounders to a remote firing range. Somewhere in England for our first Shoot, embussing before dawn and not reaching the r.v. till eleven.

The slatted seats of a fifteen-hundredweight are designed to split the spine in several places. We had no cushions and only iron rations to munch. Yet the chaps whistled and sang in tremendous spirits all the way, acquitted themselves superbly and endured the journey back with only the most cheerful grumbles. I felt privileged to be one of them and am seriously considering refusing a commission. . . ."

When a commission came his way, however, Pym contrived without difficulty to accept it, as witness the erogenous hillocks of khaki thread backed on green cloth, one to each shoulder of his battledress, whose existence he covertly confirms whenever the train enters another tunnel. The bare breasts of the peasant girls are his first since the election. With each new valley, he strains his disapproving gaze to see more of them and is seldom disappointed. "We'll send you to Vienna first," his commanding officer at the Intelligence Depot had said. "Chance to get the feel of the place before you're pushed out into the field."

"It sounds ideal, sir," said Pym.

Austria in those days was a difficult country from the one we have come to love, Tom, and Vienna was a divided city like Berlin or your father. A few years later to everyone's lasting amazement the diplomats agreed they wouldn't bother with a sideshow while there was Germany to squabble over, so the occupying powers signed a treaty and went home, thus notching up the British Foreign Office's one positive achievement in my lifetime. But in Pym's day the sideshow was going great guns. The Americans had Salzburg as their capital, the French Innsbruck and the Brits Graz, and everyone had a piece of Vienna to play with. At Christmastime the Russians gave us wooden buckets of caviar and we gave the Russians plum puddings, and there was a story still going the rounds when Pym arrived that when the caviar was served to the men as a prelude to their dinner, a corporal of Argylls complained to the duty officer that the jam tasted of fish. The brains of British Vienna was a sprawling villa called Div. Int., and that was where Second Lieutenant Pym was launched upon his duties, which consisted of reading reports on the movements of everything from Soviet mobile laundries to Hungarian horse cavalry, and pushing coloured pins into maps. His most exciting map showed the Soviet Zone of Austria which began a mere twenty minutes' drive from where he worked. Pym had only to look at its borders to feel intrigue and danger prickle on his skin. At other times, when he was tired or forgot himself, his eye would lift to the western tip of Czechoslovakia, to Karlovy Vary formerly Carlsbad, the charming eighteenth-century spa once favoured by Brahms and Beethoven. But he knew of no personal connection with the place and his interest was purely historical.

He lived an odd life those first months, for his destiny did not lie in Vienna, and it seems to me in fanciful moments now that the capital was itself waiting to release him to the sterner laws of nature. Too lowly to be taken seriously by his brother officers, prevented by protocol from mixing with the Other Ranks, too poor to revel in the swagman's restaurants and nightclubs, Pym floated between his commandeered hotel room and his maps, much as he had floated round Bern in the days of his illegality. And I will admit now but never then that, more than once, listening to the Viennese chattering their zany German on the pavements, or taking himself to one of the struggling small theatres that were cropping up in cellars and bombed houses, he had a pang of nostalgic longing to turn his head and discover a good friend limping at his side. But he knew of none. It is merely my German soul reviving, he told himself; it is the German nature to feel incomplete. On other nights, the great secret agent would take himself on reconnaissance through the Soviet Sector disguised in a green Tyrolean hat he had bought specially for the purpose, to observe from beneath its brim the stubby Russian sentries with their submachine guns posted outside the Soviet headquarters at twenty-yard intervals down the street. If they challenged him Pym had only to show his military pass for their Tartar faces to crack in friendly recognition as they took a pace back in their soft leather boots and tossed up a grey-gloved hand in salute.

"English good."

"But Russian good too," Pym would insist with a laugh. "Russian very good, honestly."

"Kamarad!"

"Tovarich. Kamarad," the great internationalist responded.

He would offer a cigarette and take one. He would light them with his big-flamed American Zippo lighter obtained from one of the many clandestine merchants operating inside Div. Int. He would let it glow on the sentry's features and his own. Then Pym in his goodheartedness had half an urge, though fortunately not the language, to explain that although he had spied on the Communists at Oxford, and was spying on them again in Vienna, he was still a Communist at heart and cared more for the snows and cornfields of Russia than ever he did for the musical cocktail cabinets and roulette wheels of Ascot.

And sometimes, very late, returning through empty squares to his monkish little bedroom with its army fire extinguisher and photograph of Rick, he would pause, and drink the clean night air in gusts until he was elated, and gaze down misted cobble streets, and pretend that he saw Lippsie walking towards him through the lamplight in her refugee's headscarf, carrying her cardboard suitcase. And he would smile at her and valiantly congratulate himself that, whatever his outward longings, he was still living in the world inside his head.

He had been in Vienna three months when Marlene asked him for his protection. Marlene was a Czech interpreter and celebrated beauty.

"You are Mr. Pym?" she enquired one evening with a civilian's delightful shyness as he descended the great staircase behind a bevy of high-ranking officers. She wore a baggy mackintosh nipped at the waist and a hat with little horns.

Pym confessed that he was.

"You are walking to the Weichsel Hotel?"

Pym said that he did so every evening.

"You allow I walk with you, please, once? Yesterday a man tried to rape me. You will guide me to my door? I am not trouble?"

Soon the intrepid Pym was guiding Marlene to her door each evening and collecting her from it in the mornings. His day unfolded between these radiant interludes. But when he invited her to have dinner with him after payday, he was summoned by a furious captain of Fusiliers who had charge of new arrivals.

"You are a lecherous little swine, do you hear?"

"Yes, sir."

"Div. Int. subalterns do not, repeat not, fraternise in public with civilian person-nel. Not unless they've put a lot more service in than you have. D'you hear?"

"Yes, sir."

"Do you know what a shit is?"

"Yes, sir."

"No, you don't. A shit, Pym, is an officer whose tie is of a lighter khaki than his shirt. Have you seen your tie recently?"

"Yes, sir."

"Have you seen your shirt?"

"Yes, sir."

"Compare them, Pym. And ask yourself what sort of young officer you are. That woman isn't even cleared above restricted."

It's all training, thought Pym, as he changed his tie. I'm being hardened for the field. Nevertheless it worried him that Marlene had asked him so many questions about himself and he wished that he had not been quite so frank in his replies.

Not long after this, Pym was mercifully deemed to have got the feel of the place. Before departing he was again summoned by the captain who showed him two photographs. One depicted a pretty young man with soft lips, the other a chubby drunk with a sneer.

"If you see either of these men you will report that information to a senior officer immediately, do you hear?"

"Who are they?"

"Hasn't anyone taught you not to ask questions? If you can't find a senior officer, arrest them yourself."

"How?"

"Use your authority. Be courteous but firm. 'You men are under arrest.' Then bring them to the nearest senior officer."

Their names, Pym learned a few days later from the *Daily Express,* were Guy Burgess and Donald Maclean and they were members of the British Foreign Service. For several weeks, he continued to look for them everywhere, but he never found them because they had already defected to Moscow.

So which of us is responsible, Tom, tell me? Is it Pym's wistful soul or God's wry humour that contrives to deal him a spell of Paradise before every Fall? I told you of the Ollingers in Bern that it was given to us once only in a lifetime to know a truly happy family, but I had forgotten Major Harrison Membury, formerly of the British Library in Nairobi and one-time officer in the Education Corps, who had strayed by a delicious caprice of military logic into the ragtag ranks of Field Security. I had forgotten his beautiful wife and their many grimy daughters who were Fräulein Ollingers in the making, except that they kept goats and a boisterous piglet in preference to making music, which made mayhem of their military hiring, to the rage of the garrison Administration officer, who was powerless because the Memburys were Intelligence and immune. I had forgotten Number 6 Field Interro-gation Unit, Graz, a pink baroque villa in a wooded cleft of hills a mile from the city's edge. Bunches of telephone cable led into it, aerials desecrated the spired roof. It had a gateway with a gatehouse and a wild-eyed blond mess waiter called Wolfgang who rushed down the steps in a pressed white coat to hand you out of your jeep. But the best thing about it as far as Membury was concerned was the lake, which he spent his days stocking, for he was mad on fish and lavished a sizable part of our secret imprest on encouraging rare breeds of trout. You must imagine a big, genial man, quite strengthless, with the elegant gestures of an invalid. And of a dreamy religious eye and disposition. A civilian to his soft fingertips if ever I met one, yet when I see him now it is always in army battledress with worn suède boots and a webbing belt either above his belly or below it, standing amid the dragonflies at the edge of his beloved lake in the heat of a scorching afternoon, exactly as Pym discovered him on the day he reported for duty, poking a thing like a shrimping net into the water while he muttered shy imprecations against a marauding pike.

"Oh my goodness. You're Pym. Yes, well, so glad you've come. Look here, I'm going to clear away the weed and drag the whole bed to see exactly what we've got. What do you think of that?"

"It sounds great, sir," said Pym.

"I'm so glad. Are you married?"

"No, sir."

"Marvellous. Then you'll be free at weekends."

And I think of him for some reason as one of a pair of brothers, though I don't recall ever hearing he had a brother. His home-based staff consisted of a sergeant whom I barely remember and a cockney driver called Kaufmann who had a degree in Economics at Cambridge. His second in command was a pink-cheeked young banker named Lieutenant McLaird who was returning to the City. In the cellars, dutiful Austrian clerks tapped telephones, steamed open mail and dumped their unread product in a row of army dustbins which were emptied by the Graz authorities punctiliously once a week because it was a nightmare of Membury's that some fish-hating vandal would tip them in the lake. On the ground floor he kept his stable of locally recruited lady interpreters who ranged from the maternal to the nubile, and Membury, when he remembered their existence, admired them all. And finally he had his wife Hannah, a painter of trees, and Hannah, as is so often the way with the wives of very large men, was as fragile as a wisp. Hannah made painting attractive to me, and I remember her best seated at her easel in a low white dress while the girls roll shrieking down a grass bank and Membury and myself in bathing costumes toil in the brown water. Even today it is impossible to imagine her as the mother of all those daughters.

The rest of Pym's life could scarcely have been more to his liking. For commodities he had Naafi whisky at seven shillings a bottle and cigarettes at twelve shillings a hundred. He could barter or, if he preferred, convert them without effort into the local currency, though it was safest to rely on the services of an elderly Hungarian Rittmeister who sat around Registry reading secret files and gazing lovingly at Wolfgang, much as Mr. Cudlove liked to gaze at Ollie. All of it was familiar, all of it was necessary to Pym for the continuation of his unlived orthodox childhood. On Sundays, he escorted the Memburys to mass and over lunch looked down the front of Hannah's dress. Membury is a genius, Pym exulted as he moved his desk into the great man's anteroom. Membury is Renaissance Man made spy. Within weeks he had his own imprest. Within a few more he had a second pip for Wolfgang to sew on his shoulder, for Membury said he looked silly with only one.

And he had his Joes.

"This is Pepi," McLaird explained with a droll smile, over a discreet dinner out of town. "Pepi fought the Reds for the Germans and now he's fighting them for us. You're a fanatic anti-Communist, aren't you, Pepi? That's why he takes his motorbike into the Zone and sells pornographic photographs to the Russian soldiery. Four hundred Players Medium a month. In arrears."

"This is Elsa," McLaird said, presenting a dumpy Carinthian housewife with four children, in the grill-room of the Blue Rose. "Her boyfriend runs a café in St. Pölten. Sends her the registration numbers and insignia of the Russian lorries that go past his window, doesn't he, Elsa? All in secret writing on the back of his love letters. Three kilos of medium-roast coffee a month. In arrears."

There were a dozen of them and Pym set to work immediately to develop and welfare them in every way he knew. Today when I play them through my memory they are as fine a bunch of neverwozzers as ever came the way of an aspiring spymaster. But to Pym they were simply the best scouts ever and he would see them right if it killed him.

And I have left till last Sabina, Jack, who like her friend Marlene in Vienna was an interpreter, and like Marlene was the most beautiful girl in the world, plucked straight from the pages of *Amor and Rococo Woman*. She was small like E. Weber, with broad, fluid hips and intense demanding eyes. Her breasts in summer or winter were high and very strong and, like her buttocks, pushed their way through the most workaday clothes, insistently demanding Pym's attention. Her features were those of a gloomy Slav elf haunted by sadness and superstition but capable of amazing bursts of sweetness, and if Lippsie had been reincarnated and made twenty-three again, she could have done a great deal worse than take Sabina's form.

"Marlene says you are respectable," she informed Pym with contempt as she clambered aboard Corporal Kaufmann's jeep, not bothering to conceal her Rococo legs.

"Is that a crime?" Pym asked.

"Don't worry," she replied ominously, and away they drove to the camps. Sabina spoke Czech and Serbo-Croat as well as German. In her spare time she was studying econmics at Graz University, which gave her an excuse to talk to Corporal Kaufmann.

"You are believing in mixing agrarian economy, Kaufmann?"

"I don't believe in any of it."

"You are Keynesian?"

"I wouldn't be one with my own money, I'll tell you that," said Kaufmann.

Thus the conversation went back and forth while Pym searched for ways of brushing carelessly against her white shoulder, or causing her skirt to open a fraction further to the north.

Their destination on these journeys was the camps. For five years the refugees of Eastern Europe had been pouring into Austria through every fast-closing gap in the barbed wire: crashing frontiers in stolen cars and lorries, across minefields, clinging to the underneath of trains. They brought their hollow faces and their shorn children and their puzzled old and their frisky dogs, and their Lippsies in the making, to be corralled and questioned and decided over in their thousands, while they played chess on wooden packing cases and showed each other photographs of people they would never see again. They came from Hungary and Rumania and Poland and Czechoslovakia and Yugoslavia and sometimes Russia, and they hoped they were on their way to Canada and Australia and Palestine. They had travelled by devious routes and often for devious reasons. They were doctors and scientists and bricklayers. They were truck drivers, thieves, acrobats, publishers, rapists and architects. All passed across Pym's vision as he rode in his jeep from camp to camp with Kaufmann and Sabina, questioning, grading and recording, then hastening home to Membury with his booty.

At first his sensitivity was offended by so much misery and he had a hard time disguising his concern for everyone he spoke to: yes, I will see you to Montreal if it kills me; yes, I will send word to your mother in Canberra that you are safely here. At first Pym was also embarrassed by his lack of suffering. Everyone he questioned had had more experience in a day than he had in his whole young life and he resented them. Some had been crossing borders since they were children. Others spoke of death and torture so casually that he became indignant at their unconcern, until his disapproval sparked their anger and they flung back at him with mockery. But Pym the good labourer had work to do, and a commanding officer to please and, when he armed himself, a quick and covert mind to do it with. He had only to consult his own nature to know when someone was writing in the margin of his memory and excluding the main text. He knew how to make small talk while he was watching, and how to read the signals that came back to him. If they described a night crossing over the hills, Pym crossed with them, lugging their Lippsie suit-cases and feeling the icy mountain air cutting through their old coats. When one of them told a lie direct, Pym rapidly took back-bearings on likely versions of the truth with the aid of his mental compass. Questions teemed in him and, budding lawyer that he was, he learned quickly to shape them into a pattern of accusation. "Where do you come from? What troops did you see there? What colour shoulder boards did they wear? What did they drive around in, what weapons did they have? Which route did you take, what guards, obstructions, dogs, wire, minefields did you meet along your way? What shoes were you wearing? How did your mother manage, your grandmother, if the mountain pass was so steep? How did you cope with two suitcases and two small children when your wife was so heavily pregnant? Is it not more likely that your employers in the Hungarian secret police drove you to the border and wished you luck as they showed you where to cross? Are you a spy and if so, would you not prefer to spy for us? Or are you merely a criminal, in which case you would surely like to take up spying, rather than be tossed back across the border by the Austrian police?" Thus Pym drew from his own criss-cross lives in order to unravel theirs, and Sabina with her scowls and moods and occasional gorgeous smiles became the sultry voice in which he did it. Sometimes he let her translate into German for him, in order to give himself the secret advantage of hearing everything twice.

"Where you learn to play these stupid games?" she asked him sternly one evening as they danced together at the Hotel Wiesler, to the disapproval of the army wives.

Pym laughed.

On the brink of manhood, with Sabina's thigh riding against his own, why should he owe anything to anybody? So he invented a story for her about this cunning German he'd known at Oxford who had turned out to be a spy.

"We had a rather weird battle of wits," he confessed, drawing upon hastily created memories. "He used all the tricks in the book and to start with I was as innocent as a babe and believed everything he told me. Gradually the contest got a bit more even."

"He was Communist?"

"As it turned out, yes. He made a show of hiding it, but it slipped out when you really went for him."

"He was hommsexual?" Sabina asked, voicing an ever-ready suspicion as she squirmed more deeply into him.

"Not so far as I could see. He had women in regiments."

"He slept only with military women?"

"I meant he had large quantities of them. I was using a metaphor."

"I think he was wishing to disguise his hommsexuality. This is normal."

Sabina spoke of her own life as if it belonged to someone she hated. Her stupid Hungarian father had been shot at the border. Her fool mother had died in Prague attempting to produce a baby for a worthless lover. Her older brother was an idiot and studying to be a doctor in Stuttgart. Her uncles were drunkards and had got themselves shot by the Nazis and the Communists.

"You want I give you Czech lesson Saturday?" she asked him one evening in an even stricter tone than usual, as they drove home three abreast.

"I would like that very much," Pym replied, holding her hand at her side. "I'm really beginning to enjoy it."

"I think we make love this time. We shall see," she said severely, at which Kaufmann nearly drove into a ditch.

Saturday came and neither Rick's shadow nor Pym's terrors could prevent him from ringing Sabina's doorbell. He heard a footstep softer than her usual practical tread. He saw the lightspots of her eyes regard him through the eye-slit in the door, and did his best to smile in a rugged, reassuring manner. He had brought enough Naafi whisky to banish the guilt of ages, but Sabina had no guilt and when she opened the door to him she was naked. Incapable of speech he stood before her clutching his carrier bag. In a daze he watched her reset the security chain, take the bag from his lifeless hands, stalk to the sideboard and unpack it. The day was warm but she had lit a fire and turned back the bedcovers.

"You have had many women, Magnus?" she demanded. "Women in regiments like your bad friend?"

"I don't think I have," said Pym.

"You are hommsexual like all English?"

"I'm really not."

She led him to the bed. She sat him down and unbuttoned his shirt. Severely, like Lippsie when she needed something for the laundry van outside. She unbuttoned the rest of him and arranged his clothes over a chair. She guided him on to his back and spread herself over him.

"I didn't know," said Pym aloud.

"Please?"

He started to say something, but there was too much to explain and his interpreter was already occupied. He meant: I didn't know, for all my longing, what I was longing for till now. He meant: I can fly, I can swim on my front and on my back and on my side and on my head. He meant: I'm whole and I've joined the men at last.

It was a balmy Friday afternoon in the villa six days later. In the gardens below the windows of Membury's enormous office, the Rittmeister in his lederhosen was shelling peas for Wolfgang. Membury sat at his desk, his battledress unbuttoned to the waist while he drafted a questionnaire for trawler captains that he proposed to send in hundreds to the major fishing fleets. For weeks now he had set his heart on tracing the winter routes of sea trout, and the unit's resources had been hard pressed to accommodate him.

"I've had a rather rum approach made to me, sir," Pym began delicately. "Somebody claiming to represent a potential defector."

"Oh but how interesting for you, Magnus," Membury said politely, prising himself with difficulty from his preoccupations. "I hope it's not another Hungarian frontier guard. I've rather had my fill of them. So has Vienna, I'm sure." Vienna was a growing worry to Membury, as Membury was to Vienna. Pym had read the painful correspondence between them that Membury kept safely locked at all times in the top left drawer of his flimsy desk. It might be only a question of days before the captain of Fusiliers arrived in person to take charge.

"He's not Hungarian, actually, sir," said Pym. "He's Czech. He's attached to HQ Southern Command based outside Prague."

Membury tilted his large head to one side as if shaking water out of his ear. "Well that's heartening," he remarked doubtfully. "Div. Int. would give their eye-teeth for some good stuff about Southern Czecho. Or anywhere else in Czecho for that matter. The Americans seem to think they have a monopoly of the place. Somebody said as much to me on the telephone only the other day, I don't know who."

The telephone line to Graz ran through the Soviet Zone. In the evenings Russian technicians could be heard on it, singing drunken Cossack music.

"According to my source he's a disgruntled clerk sergeant working in their strongroom," Pym persisted. "He's supposed to be coming out tomorrow night. If we're not there to receive him he'll go to the Americans."

"You didn't hear of him through the Rittmeister, did you?" said Membury nervously.

With the skill of long habitation, Pym entered the risky ground. No, it was not the Rittmeister, he assured Membury. At least it didn't sound like the Rittmeister. The voice sounded younger and more positive.

Membury was confused. "Could you possibly explain?" he said.

Pym did.

It was just an ordinary Thursday evening, he said. He'd been to the movies to see *Liebe 47*, and on his way back he thought he'd drop in at the Weisses Ross for a beer.

"I don't think I know the Weisses Ross."

"It's just another pub, sir, really, but the Czech émigrés use it a lot and everyone sits at long tables. I'd been there literally two minutes when the waiter called me to the phone. '*Herr Leutnant, für Sie.*' They know me a bit there so I wasn't too surprised."

"Good for you," said Membury, impressed.

"It was a man's voice, speaking High German. 'Herr Pym? Here is an important message for you. If you do exactly as I tell you, you will not be disappointed. Have you pen and paper?' I had, so he started reading to me at dictation speed. He checked it back with me and rang off before I could ask him who he was."

From his pocket Pym produced the very sheet of paper, torn from the back of a diary.

"But if this was last night, why on earth didn't you tell me earlier?" Membury objected, taking it from him.

"You were at the Joint Intelligence Committee meeting."

"Oh my hat, so I was. He asked for you by name," Membury remarked with pride, still looking at the paper. " 'Only Lieutenant Pym will do.' That's rather flattering, I must say." He pulled at a protruding ear. "Well look here, you take jolly good care," he warned, with the sternness of a man who could refuse Pym nothing. "And don't go too near the border in case they try and haul you over."

This was not by any means the first advance tip-off of a defector's arrival that had come Pym's way in recent months, not even the sixth, though it was the first that had been whispered to him by a naked Czech interpreter in a moonlit orchard. Only a week before, Pym and Membury had sat out a night in the Carinthian lowlands waiting to receive a captain of Rumanian Intelligence and his mistress who were supposedly approaching in a stolen aeroplane crammed with priceless secrets. Membury had the Austrian police close off the area, Pym fired coloured Very lights into the empty air as they had been instructed in secret messages. But when dawn came no aeroplane had arrived.

"What are we supposed to do now?" Membury had complained with pardonable irritation as they sat shivering in the jeep. "Sacrifice a bloody goat? I do wish the Rittmeister were more precise. It makes one look so silly."

A week before that, disguised in green loden coats, they had taken themselves to a remote inn on the Zonal border in search of a Heimkehrer from a Soviet uranium mine who was expected any moment. As they pushed open the door the conversation in the bar stopped dead and a score of peasants gawped at them.

"Billiards," Membury ordered with rare decisiveness, from under his hand. "There's a table over there. We'll get a game going. Fit in."

Still in his green loden, Membury stooped to play his ball, only to be interrupted by the resounding clang of heavy metal striking the tiled floor close at hand. Glancing down, Pym saw his commanding officer's .38 service revolver lying at his large feet. He had recovered it for him in a moment, never quicker. But not quick enough to prevent the stampede to the door as the terrified peasants scattered in the darkness and the landlord locked himself in the cellar.

"Can I go back now, sir?" said Kaufmann. "I'm not a soldier at all, you see. I'm a coward."

"No you can't," said Pym. "Now be quiet."

The barn stood by itself as Sabina had said it would, at the centre of a flat field lined with larches. A yellow path led to it; behind it lay a lake. Behind the lake a hill and on the hill, as the evening darkened, a single watchtower overlooked the valley.

"You will wear civilian clothes and park your car at the crossroads to Klein

Brandorf," Sabina had whispered to his thighs as she kissed and fondled and revived him. The orchard had a brick wall and was occupied by a family of large brown hares. "You will leave sidelights burning. If you cheat and bring protection he will not appear. He will stay in the forest and be angry."

"I love you."

"There is a stone, painted white. This is where Kaufmann must stand. If Kaufmann passes the white stone, he will not appear, he will stay in the forest."

"Why can't you come too?"

"He does not wish it. He wishes only Pym. Perhaps he is hommsexual."

"Thanks," said Pym.

The white stone glinted ahead of them.

"Stay here," Pym ordered.

"Why?" said Kaufmann.

Evening mist lay in strips across the field. The surface of the lake popped with rising fish. With the sun setting, the larches threw mile-long shadows across the golden meadow. Sawn logs lay beside the barn door, boxes of geraniums adorned the windows. Pym thought again of Sabina. Her enfolding flanks, the broad spaces of her back. "What I tell you I have not told to any Englishman. In Prague I have a younger brother who is called Jan. If you tell this to Membury he will already dismiss me immediately. The British do not allow us to have close family inside a Communist country. Do you understand?" Yes, Sabina, I understand. I have seen the moonlight on your breasts, your moisture is on my lips, it is sticking to my eyelids. I understand. "Listen. My brother sends me this message for you. Only for Pym. He trusts you because of me and because I have told him only good things about you. He has a friend who wishes to come out. This friend is very gifted, very brilliant, top access. He will bring you many secrets about the Russians. But first you must invent a story for Membury to explain how you received this information. You are clever. You can invent many stories. Now you must invent one for my brother and his friend." Yes, Sabina, I can invent. For you and your beloved brother I can invent a million stories. Get me my pen, Sabina. Where did you put my clothes? Now tear me a piece of paper from your diary and I will invent a story about a strange man who telephoned me at the Weisses Ross and made me an irresistible proposal.

Pym unbuttoned his loden. "Always draw across the body," his weapons instructor had advised at the sad little depot in Sussex where they had taught him how to fight Communism. "It gives you better protection when the other laddie shoots first." Pym was not sure this was good advice. He reached the door and it was closed. He walked round the barn, trying to find a place to peep in. "His information will be good for you," Sabina had said. "It will make you very famous in Vienna, Membury also. Good intelligence from Czechoslovakia is extremely rare at Div. Int. Mostly it comes from the Americans and is therefore corrupt."

The sun had set and the dusk was gathering fast. From across the lake Pym heard the yelping of a fox. Rows of chicken coops stood at the back of the barn and the straw in them was clean. Chickens in no-man's-land, he thought frivolously. Stateless eggs. The chickens tucked their necks at him and blew out their feathers. A grey heron lifted from the lake and set course toward the hills. He returned to the front of the barn.

"Kaufmann!"

"Sir?"

A hundred metres lay between them but their voices were as close as lovers in the evening stillness.

"Did you cough?"

"No, sir."

"Well, don't."

"I expect I was sobbing, sir."

"Keep guard, but whatever you see, don't come any nearer unless I order you."

"I'd like to desert, if I may, sir. I'd rather be a defector than this, honestly. I'm a sitting target. I'm not a human being at all."

"Do some mental sums or something."

"I can't. I've tried. Nothing comes."

Pym lifted the door latch, stepped inside and smelt cigar smoke and horse. St. Moritz, he thought, lightheaded in his apprehension. The barn was cavernous and beautiful and raised at one end like an old ship. On the dais stood a table and on the table, to Pym's surprise, a lighted oil lamp. By its glow he admired the ancient beams and roof. "Wait inside and he will come," Sabina had said. "He will want to see you go in first. My brother's friend is very cautious. Like many Czechs, he has a great and cautious mind." Two high-backed wooden chairs were pulled to the table and magazines were strewn on it like in a dentist's waiting-room. Must be where the farmer does his paperwork. At the end of the barn, he noticed a rustic ladder leading to a loft. At the weekend I'll bring you here. I'll bring wine and cheese and bread, and blankets in case it's prickly, and you can wear your flouncy skirt with nothing underneath. He climbed halfway up the ladder and peered over. Sound floor, dry hay, no sign of rats. An admirable location for rustic Rococo. He returned to the ground floor and made his way towards the dais where the light burned, intending to settle down in one of the chairs. "You must be patient, if necessary all night," Sabina had said. "Crossing the border is extremely dangerous now. It is late summer and the doubters are coming over before the passes close. Therefore they have many guards and spies." A stone pathway ran between two cattle drains. His feet echoed thickly in the roof. The echo stopped, his feet with it. A slender figure was seated at the head of the table. He was leaning alertly forward, posing for something. He held a cigar in one hand and an automatic pistol in the other. His gaze, like the barrel of the automatic, was fixed on Pym.

"Keep walking towards me, Sir Magnus," Axel urged in a tone of considerable anxiety. "Put your arms up and for heaven's sake don't go imagining you are a great cowboy or a war hero. Neither of us is a member of the shooting classes. We put our guns away and we have a nice chat. Be reasonable. Please."

It would take our Maker himself, Tom, with help from all of us, to describe the range of thoughts and emotions charging at that moment through Pym's poor head. His first response, I am sure, was disbelief. He had encountered Axel very often in the last few years and this was merely another example of the phenomenon. Axel watching him in his sleep, Axel standing at his bedside with his beret on—"Let's take another look at Thomas Mann." Axel laughing at him for his addiction to Old High German and remonstrating with him for his bad habit of protesting loyalty to everyone he met: to the Oxford Communists, to all women, to the Jacks and

Michaels and to Rick. "You are a serious fool, Sir Magnus," he had warned him once, when Pym returned to his rooms after a particularly deft night of juggling girls and social opposites. "You think that by dividing everything you can pass between." Axel had limped at his side along the Isis towpath and watched him dash his knuckles against the wall in order to impress Jemima. At the election Pym could not have told you how often Axel's glistening white dome had popped up in the audience, or his long, restive hands flapped in sarcastic applause. With Axel so much upon his conscience, therefore, Pym knew for a fact that Axel did not exist. And with this certainty in his head it was perfectly reasonable that his next response to seeing Axel was downright indignation that someone so thoroughly forbidden, someone who had been literally, for whatever reason, banished out of sight or mention over the borders of Pym's kingdom, should presume to be sitting here, smoking and smiling and pointing a pistol at him—at me, Pym, a bulletproof, fornicating member of the British Occupational classes gifted with supernatural powers. And after that, of course, paradoxical as ever, Pym was more exultant, more thrilled and more happy to see Axel than anyone since the day Rick rode round the corner on his bicycle singing "Underneath the Arches."

Pym walked then ran to Axel's side. He kept his arms above his head as Axel ordered him. He waited impatiently while Axel flashed his army revolver from his waistband and laid it with his own respectfully at the further end of the table. Then at last he dropped his arms far enough to fling them round Axel's neck. I don't remember that they had ever embraced before or did so afterwards. But I remember that evening as the last of childish sentiments between them, the last day of Bern, because I see them hugging and laughing chest to chest, Slav style, before they hold one another at a distance to see what damage the years of separation have done to each of them. And we may assume from contemporary photographs and from my own memories of the mirror in those days, which still played a large part in the young officer's contemplations, that Axel saw the typical, uncut Anglo-Saxon features of a good-looking, fair young man still trying hard to put on the mantle of experience, whereas in Axel's face Pym witnessed at once a hardening, a hollowing-out, a shaping that was there for ever. Axel would look like this for the rest of his days. Life had had its say. He had the manly, human face that he deserved. The softer contours had gone, leaving an etched jauntiness and assurance. His hairline had retreated but consolidated. Streaks of grey had joined the black, giving it a practical and military appearance. The clown's moustache, the clown's hooped eyebrows had acquired a sadder humour. But the twinkling dark eyes, peering beneath their languid eyelids, were as merry as ever, while everything around them seemed to give depth to their perception.

"You look well, Sir Magnus!" Axel declared exuberantly, still holding him. "You are a fine fellow, my God. We should buy you a white horse and give you India."

"But who are you?" Pym cried in equal excitement. "Where are you? What are you doing here? Should I arrest you?"

"Maybe I arrest you. Maybe I did already. You put your hands up, do you remember? Listen. We are in no-man's-land here. We can arrest each other."

"You're under arrest," Pym said.

"You too," said Axel. "How's Sabina?"

"Fine," Pym said with a grin.

"She knows nothing, you understand? Only what her brother told her. You will protect her?"

"I promise I will," Pym said.

Here a slight pause as Axel pretended to clap his hands over his ears. "Don't promise, Sir Magnus. Just don't promise."

For a frontier crosser Axel had come well equipped, Pym noticed. There was not a trace of mud on his boots, his clothes were pressed and official-looking. Releasing Pym, he grabbed a briefcase, plonked it on the table and drew from it a pair of glasses and a bottle of vodka. Then gherkins, sausage and a loaf of the black bread he used to send Pym out to buy in Bern. They toasted each other gravely, the way Axel had taught him. They refilled their glasses and drank again, a drink for each man. And it is my recollection that by the time they separated they had finished the bottle, for I remember Axel chucking it out into the lake to the outrage of about a thousand moorhens. But if Pym had drunk a case of the stuff it would not have affected him, such was the intensity of his feeling. Even while they began to talk, Pym kept secretly blinking into corners to make sure everything was how it was when he had last looked, so eerily similar at times was the barn to the Bern attic, right down to the soft wind that used to whirr in the skylights. And when he heard the fox again in the distance, he had the certain feeling it was Bastl barking on the wooden staircase after everyone had gone. Except that, as I say, those sentimental days were over. Magnus had killed them dead; the manhood of their friendship was beginning.

Now it is the way of old friends when they bump into each other, Tom, to put aside the immediate cause of their meeting until last. They prefer as a prelude to account for the years between, which gives a kind of rightness to whatever they have met to discuss. And that is what Pym and Axel did, though you will understand, now that you are familiar with the workings of Pym's mind, that it was he and not Axel who led this passage of the conversation, if only in order to show to himself as well as to Axel that he was totally without sin in the tricky matter of Axel's disappearance. He did it well. He was a polished performer these days.

"Honestly, Axel, nobody ever went out of my life so abruptly," he complained in a tone of jocular reproach as he sliced sausage, buttered the bread and generally occupied himself with what actors call business. "You were there all safely tucked up in the evening, we'd got a bit drunk, said good night. Next morning I hammered on your wall, no answer. I go downstairs and walk into poor old Frau O crying her heart out. 'Where's Axel? They've taken away our Axel! The Fremdenpolizei carried him down the stairs and one of them kicked Bastl.' From all they said, I must have been sleeping like the dead."

Axel smiled his old warm smile. "If we only knew how the dead sleep," he said.

"We held a sort of wake, hung around the house, half expecting you to come back. Herr Ollinger made some useless phone calls and got absolutely nowhere, naturally. Frau O remembered she had a brother in one of the Ministries, *he* was no good. In the end I thought, To hell with it, what have we got to lose? So I went down to the Fremdenpolizei myself. Passport in hand. 'My friend's missing. Some men dragged him from the house early this morning, said they came from you.

Where is he?' I banged the table a bit and got nowhere. Then two rather creepy gentlemen in raincoats took me into another room and told me that if I made any more trouble the same thing would happen to me."

"That was brave of you, Sir Magnus," said Axel. Reaching out a pale fist he tapped Pym lightly on the shoulder to say thanks.

"No, it wasn't. Not really. I mean I did have somewhere to go. I was British and I had rights."

"Sure. And you knew people at the Embassy. That's true also."

"And they'd have helped me out too. I mean they tried to. When I went to them."

"You did?"

"Absolutely. Later, of course. Not immediately. Rather as a last resort. But they had a go. . . . So anyway, back I went to the Länggasse and we—honestly, we buried you. It was awful. Frau O was up in your room still crying, trying to sort out whatever you'd left behind without looking at it. Which wasn't much. The Fremdenpolizei seemed to have pinched most of your papers. I took your library books back. Your gramophone records. We hung your clothes in the cellar. Then we sort of wandered round the house as if it had been bombed. 'To think this could happen in Switzerland,' we kept saying. Really just like a death."

Axel laughed. "It was good of you to mourn me at least. Thank you, Sir Magnus. Did you hold a funeral service also?"

"With no body and no forwarding address? All Frau O wanted to do was look for the culprit. She was convinced you'd been informed against."

"Who did she think did it?"

"Everyone in turn really. The neighbours. The shopkeepers. Maybe someone from the Cosmo. One of the Marthas."

"Which one did she choose?"

Pym picked the prettiest and frowned. "I seem to remember there was a leggy blonde one who was reading English."

"*Isabella?* Isabella informed against *me?*" said Axel incredulously. "But she was in love with me, Sir Magnus. Why would she do that?"

"Maybe that was the reason," said Pym boldly. "She came round a few days after you'd gone, you see. Asked for you. I told her what had happened. She howled and wept and said she was going to kill herself. But when I mentioned to Frau O that she'd called, she promptly said, 'Isabella is the one. She was jealous of his other women so she informed against him.' "

"What did you think?"

"Seemed a bit far-fetched to me, but then everything else did too. So yes, maybe Isabella did it. She did seem a bit crazy sometimes, to be honest. I could sort of imagine her doing something awful out of jealousy—on an impulse, you know—then persuading herself she hadn't done it in the first place. It's a sort of syndrome, isn't it, with jealous people?"

Axel took his time to reply. For a defector in the throes of negotiating his terms, Pym reflected, he was remarkably relaxed. "I don't know, Sir Magnus. I don't have your gifts of imagination sometimes. Do you have any other theories?"

"Not really. It could have happened so many ways."

In the silence of the night, Axel replenished their glasses, smiling broadly. "You all seem to have thought about it far more than I have," he confessed. "I'm very touched." He lifted his palms, Slav style, languidly. "Listen. I was illegal. I was a bum. No money, no papers. On the run. So they caught me, they threw me out. That's what happens to illegals. A fish gets a hook in its throat. A traitor gets a bullet in his head. An illegal gets marched across the border. Don't frown so much. It's over. Who gives a damn who did it? To tomorrow!"

"Tomorrow," Pym said, and they drank. "Hey—how did the great book go by the way?" he asked in the secret euphoria of his absolution.

Axel laughed louder. "Go? My God, it went! Four hundred pages of immortal philosophising, Sir Magnus. Imagine the Fremdenpolizei wading their way through that!"

"You mean they kept it—stole it? That's outrageous!"

"Maybe I was not too polite about the good Swiss burghers."

"But you've written it again since?"

Nothing could quench his laughter. "Written it again? It would have been twice as bad next time. Better we bury it with Axel H. You still have *Simplicissimus?* You haven't sold him?"

"Of course not."

A pause intervened. Axel smiled at Pym. Pym smiled at his hands, then raised his eyes to Axel.

"So here we both are," said Pym.

"That's right."

"I'm Lieutenant Pym and you're Jan's intelligent friend."

"That's right," Axel agreed, still smiling.

Having thus, in his own estimation, skilfully circumvented the one awkwardness that might have stood between them, the intelligence predator in Pym now artfully advanced upon the pertinent question of what had become of Axel since his eviction, and what his access had been, and so by extension—as Pym hoped—what cards he held, and what price he proposed to put on them as a reward for favouring the British over the Americans or even—dreadful thought—the French. In this he met at first with no unpleasant inhibition on Axel's part since, doubtless out of deference to Pym's position of authority, he seemed resigned to take the passive rôle. Nor could Pym fail to notice that his old friend in rendering account of himself assumed the familiar meekness of the displaced person in the presence of his betters. The Swiss had marched him across the German border, he said—and for ease of reference he mentioned the frontier point in case Pym wished to check. They had handed him over to the West German police who, having dealt him a ritual beating, handed him to the Americans, who beat him again, first for escaping, then for returning, and finally of course for being the red-toothed war criminal that he was not, but whose identity he had unwisely purloined, The Americans put him in prison while they prepared a fresh case against him, they brought in fresh witnesses who were too frightened not to identify him, they set a date to try him, and still Axel could reach nobody who would vouch for him or say he was just Axel from Carlsbad and not a Nazi monster brother. Worse still, as the rest of the evidence began to look increasingly thin, said Axel with an apologetic smile, his own confession became increasingly important, so they had naturally beaten him harder in order to obtain it. No trial was held, however. War crimes, even fictitious ones, were becoming out of date, so one day the Americans had thrown him on another train and handed him over to the Czechs who, not to be outdone, beat him for the double crime of having been a German soldier in the war and an American prisoner after it.

"Then one day they stopped beating me and let me out," he said, smiling and opening his hands once more. "For this, it seems, I had my dear dead father to thank. You remember the great Socialist who had fought in the Thälmann brigade in Spain?"

"Of course I do," said Pym, and it occurred to him as he watched Axel's quick hands gesticulating and his dark eyes twinkling that Axel had put aside the German in him and put on the Slav for good. "I had become an aristocrat," he said. "In the new Czechoslovakia I was Sir Axel suddenly. The old Socialists had loved my father. The new ones had been my friends at school and were already in the Party apparatus. 'Why do you beat up Sir Axel?' they asked my guards. 'He's got a good brain, stop hitting him and let him out. Okay, so he fought for Hitler. He's sorry. Now he'll fight for us, won't you, Axel?' 'Sure,' I said. 'Why not?' So they sent me to university."

"But what did you study?" said Pym amazed. "Thomas Mann? Nietzsche?"

"Better. How to use the Party to advance oneself. How to rise in the Youth Union. Shine in the committees. How to purge the faculties and students, climb over the backs of friends and the reputation of one's father. Which arses to kick and which to kiss. Where to talk too much and where to shut your mouth. Maybe I should have learned that earlier."

Feeling he was close to the heart of things, Pym wondered whether it was time for him to take notes but decided not to destroy Axel's flow.

"Somebody had the nerve to call me a Titoist the other day," Axel said. "Since '49 it's the latest insult." Pym secretly wondered whether this was why Axel had come over. "Know what I did?"

"What?"

"I informed against him."

"No! What for?"

"I don't know. Something bad. It's not what you say, it's who you say it to. You should know that. You're a big spy, I hear. Sir Magnus of the British Secret Service. Congratulations. Is Corporal Kaufmann all right out there? Maybe you should take him something?"

"I'll deal with him later, thank you."

There was a hiatus while each in his separate way savoured the effect of this disciplinary note. They drank another toast, shaking their heads at one another over their luck. But inside himself Pym was less at ease than he let on. He had a sense of slipping standards and complicated undertones.

"So what work have you actually been up to these last days?" Pym asked, struggling to reclaim the ascendancy. "How does a sergeant from HQ Southern Command come to be wandering round the Soviet Zone of Austria, planning his defection?"

Axel was lighting himself a fresh cigar so Pym had to wait a minute for his answer.

"A sergeant I don't know. In my unit we have only aristos. Like you, I am also a great spy, Sir Magnus. It's a boom industry these days. We did well to select it."

Needing suddenly to tend his outward appearance, Pym smoothed his hair back in a reflective gesture he was working on. "But you are still proposing to come over to us—assuming that we can offer you the right sort of terms of course?" he asked, with hard-edged courtesy.

Axel waved away such a stupid idea. "I've paid my ticket same as you. So it's not perfect but it's my country. I've crossed my last frontier. They've got to put up with me."

Pym had a sensation of dangerous disconnection. "Then why are you here— if you don't want to defect—if I may ask."

"I heard about you. The great Lieutenant Pym of Div. Int., more latterly of Graz. Linguist. Hero. Lover. I was so excited to think of you spying on me. And me spying on you. It was so beautiful to think we were back in our old attic together, just that little thin wall between us—knock, knock! 'I've got to get in touch with this fellow,' I thought. Shake his hand. Give him a drink. Maybe we can set the world to rights, same as we used to in the old days."

"I see," said Pym. "Great."

" 'Maybe we can put our heads together. We are reasonable men. Maybe he doesn't want to fight any more wars. Maybe I don't. Maybe we are tired of being heroes. Good men are scarce,' I thought. 'How many people in the world have shaken hands with Thomas Mann?' "

"Nobody but me," said Pym with a burst of real laughter and they drank again.

"I owe you so much, Sir Magnus. You were so generous. I never knew a better heart. I yelled at you, cursed you. What did you do? Held my head when I threw up. Cooked me tea, cleaned the vomit and the shit off me, fetched me books—back and forth to the library—read to me all night. I owe this man, I thought. I owe this man a step or two forward in his career. I should make him a gesture that is painful to me. If I can help him achieve a position of influence in the world, that's rare, that's already good. For the world as well as for him. Not many good men achieve a position of influence today. So I'll play a little trick and go and see him. And shake his hand. And say, thank you, Sir Magnus. And take him a gift to pay my debt to him and help him in his career, I thought. Because I love this man, do you hear?"

He had brought no straw hat filled with coloured packages but from the briefcase at his side he drew a folder and handed it to Pym across the table.

"You have landed a great coup, Sir Magnus," he declared proudly as Pym lifted the cover. "Took me a lot of spying to get it for you. A lot of risks. Never mind. It's better than Grimmelshausen, I think. If they ever find out what I've done, I can bring you my balls as well."

Pym closes his eyes and opens them again, but it is the same night in the same barn. "I'm a little fat Czech sergeant who loves his vodka," Axel is explaining while Pym continues in a dream to turn the pages of his gift. "I'm a good soldier Schweik. Did we read that book? My name is Pavel. Hear me? Pavel."

"Of course we read it. It was great. Is this genuine, Axel? It isn't a joke or anything?"

"You think fat Pavel takes a risk like this to bring you a joke? He has a wife who beats him, kids who hate him, Russian bosses who treat him worse than a dog. Are you listening?"

With half his head, yes, Pym is listening. He is reading too.

"Your good friend Axel H, he doesn't exist. You never met him tonight. In Bern long ago, sure, you met a sickly German soldier who was writing a great book and maybe his name was Axel, what's a name? But Axel vanished. Some bad guy informed against him, you never knew what happened. Tonight you are meeting fat Sergeant Pavel of Czech Army Intelligence who likes garlic and screwing and betraying his superiors. He speaks Czech and German, and the Russians use him as a dogsbody because they don't trust the Austrians. One week he's hanging around their headquarters in Wiener Neustadt playing messenger boy and interpreter, the next he's freezing his arse off on the zonal border looking for small spies. The week after that he's back in his garrison in Southern Czecho being kicked around by more Russians." Axel is tapping Pym's arm. "See this? Pay attention. Here's a copy of his paybook. Look at it, Sir Magnus. Concentrate. He brought it for you because he doesn't expect anybody ever to believe anything he says unless it is accompanied by *Unterlagen*. You remember *Unterlagen*? Papers? They are what I didn't have in Bern. Take it with you. Show it to Membury."

Reluctantly Pym lifts his eyes from his reading long enough to notice the wad of glossy paper Axel is holding up for him to admire. A photocopy in those days is a big matter: plate photographs, tied into a looseleaf book with bootlaces through the holes. Axel presses it upon Pym and again rouses him sufficiently from the material in the folder to make him study the portrait of the bearer: a piggy, part-shaven little man with puffy eyes and a pout.

"That is *me*, Sir Magnus," Axel says, and bangs Pym on the shoulder quite hard to assure his attention, exactly as he used to in Bern. "Look at him, will you? He's a greedy, grubby fellow. Farts a lot, scratches his head, steals his Commandant's chickens. But he doesn't like his country to be occupied by a bunch of sweating Ivans who swagger round the streets of Prague and tell him he's a stinking little Czech, and he doesn't like being packed down to Austria at somebody's whim to play toady to a lot of drunk Cossacks. So he's brave too, you follow me? He's a brave little greasy coward."

Pym again pauses in his reading, this time to register a bureaucratic complaint which later causes him some shame. "It's all very well inventing this delightful character, Axel, but what am I to do with him?" he reasons in an aggrieved tone. "I'm supposed to produce a defector, not a paybook. They want a warm body back there in Graz. I haven't got one, have I?"

"You idiot!" cries Axel, pretending to be exasperated by Pym's obtuseness. "You guileless English baby! Have you never heard of a defector in place? Pavel *is* a defector! He's defecting but staying where he is. In three weeks' time he'll come here again, bring you more material. He'll defect not just once but if you are sensible twenty times, a hundred. He's an intelligence clerk, a courier, a low-grade fieldman, a bottlewasher, a coding sergeant and a pimp. Don't you understand what that means in terms of access? He will bring you wonderful intelligence again and again. His friends in the frontier unit will help him cross. Next time we meet you will have Vienna's questions for him. You will be at the centre of a fantastic industry: 'Can you get us this, Pavel? What does this mean, Pavel?' If you're polite to him, if you come alone, bring him a nice present, maybe he'll answer them."

"And will it be you—will I see you?"

"You will see Pavel."

"And will you be Pavel?"

"Sir Magnus. Listen." Pushing aside the briefcase that lay between them, Axel bangs his glass beside Pym's and yanks his chair so close that his shoulder is nudging against Pym's shoulder and his mouth is at Pym's ear. "Are you being very, very attentive now?"

"Of course I am."

"Because I think you are so fantastically stupid you better not play this game at all. Listen." Pym is grinning exactly as he used to grin when Axel was explaining why he was a *Trottel* for not understanding Kant. "What Axel is doing for you tonight, he can never undo in his whole life. I am risking my bloody neck for you. Like Sabina gave you her brother, Axel gives you Axel. Do you understand? Or are you too shit-stupid to recognise that I am putting my future in your hands?"

"I don't want it, Axel. I'd rather give it back."

"It's too late. I have stolen the papers, I have come over, you have seen them, you know what they contain. Pandora's box cannot be closed again. Your nice Major Membury—those clever aristos in Div. Int.—none of them ever saw such information. Do you follow this?"

Pym nods, Pym shakes his head. Pym frowns, smiles, and tries to look in every way he can the worthy and mature custodian of Axel's destiny.

"In return, you must swear me one thing. I told you earlier you must not promise. Now I tell you you must. To me, Axel, you must promise loyalty. Sergeant Pavel, he's a different matter. Sergeant Pavel you can betray and invent as much as you like—he is an invention anyway. But I Axel—this Axel here—look at me— *I do not exist*. Not for Membury, not for Sabina, not even for yourself. Even when you are lonely and bored and you need to impress somebody or buy somebody or sell somebody, I am not a creature in your game. If your own people threaten you, if they torture you, you must still deny me. If they put you on the cross in fifty years from now, will you lie for me? Answer."

Pym finds time to marvel that after energetically denying Axel's existence for so long he should be promising him to deny it for still longer. And that it must be a very rare thing indeed to be offered a second chance to prove one's loyalty after failing so miserably at the first attempt.

"I will," says Pym.

"What will you?"

"I will keep you secret. I'll lock you in my memory and give you the key."

"For always. Sabina's brother Jan also?"

"For always. Jan too. That's the whole Soviet Order of Battle in Czechoslovakia you've given me," says Pym in a trance. "If it's genuine."

"It's a little bit old, but you British know how to value antiquity. Your maps in Vienna and Graz are older. And they are not so genuine. You like Membury?"

"I think so. Why?"

"Me too. You are interested in fish? You are helping him to restock the lake?"

"Sometimes. Yes."

"That's important work. Do it with him. Help him. It's a lousy world, Sir Magnus. A few happy fish will make it better."

It was six in the morning when Pym left. Kaufmann had long ago put himself to bed in the jeep. Pym could see his boots sticking over the tailboard. Pym and Axel walked as far as the white stone. Axel leaning on his arm the way he used to when they walked beside the Aare. As they reached it Axel stooped and picked a harvest poppy and handed it to Pym. Then he picked another for himself which on reflection he handed to Pym also.

"There is one of me and one of you, Sir Magnus. There will never be another of either of us. You are the keeper of our friendship. Give my love to Sabina. Tell her that Sergeant Pavel sends her a special kiss to thank her for her help."

A man with a highly regarded source is an admired man and a well-fed one, Tom, as Pym quickly discovered in the next few weeks. Visiting Very Senior Officers from Vienna take him to dinner just for the touch of him and the vicarious feel of his achievement. Membury comes too, a grinning, loping Caesar dwarfing his Antony, hauling on his ear, dreaming of fish and smiling at the wrong people. Other officers less senior but still substantial alter their opinion of Pym overnight and send him smarmy notes by interzonal bag. "Marlene sends her love and is so sad that you had to leave Vienna without saying goodbye to her. It looked for a moment as if I might become your C.O. but fate decreed otherwise. M and I hope to be engaged as soon as we get clearance from the War Office." He is a cult of one and to know him is to be an insider: "The fantastic work young Pym is doing—if I had my way, I'd give him a third pip, national serviceman or not." "You should have heard London on the scrambler, they're sending it to the top." On London's orders, no less, Sergeant Pavel receives the codename Greensleeves and Pym a commendation. Voluptuous Czech interpreters are proud of him, and demonstrate their pleasure in refined ways.

"You must never tell me what happened, it is a rule," Sabina ordered him, biting him half to death between her deep sad lips.

"I never will."

"He is handsome, Jan's friend? He is beautiful? Like you? I would love him immediately, yes?"

"He is tall and beautiful and very intelligent."

"Sexy also?"

"Very sexy."

"Hommsexual like you?"

"Totally."

The description pleased her in some deep and satisfying way.

"You are good man, Magnus," she assured him. "You have good taste that you protect this man like my brother."

The due day came round when Sergeant Pavel was to make his second appearance. As Axel had predicted, Vienna had prepared a dense crop of follow-up questions for him concerning his first offering. Pym arrived with them written out in a shorthand notebook. He also brought brown smoked-salmon sandwiches and an excellent Sancerre from Membury. He brought cigarettes and Naafi mint chocolates and everything else the gastronomic experts of Div. Int. could think of to fill the tummy of a brave defector in place. While they ate the smoked salmon and drank vodka, they cleared up the outstanding points.

"So what have you got for me this time round?" Pym enquired cheerfully when they had reached a natural break in the proceedings.

"Nothing," Axel replied comfortably, helping himself to more vodka. "We let them starve a little. Gives them a better appetite next time."

"Pavel's having a crisis of conscience," Pym reported next day to Membury, obeying Axel's instructions to the letter. "He's having wife trouble and his daughter is going to bed with a no-good Russian officer every time Pavel is sent down to Austria. I didn't press him. I told him we were there and he could trust us and we're not adding to his pressures. I believe in the long run he's going to thank us for that. But I did ask him our questions about the concentrated armour east of Prague and he was interesting."

A visiting colonel from Vienna was sitting in. "What did he say?" asked the colonel, following Pym closely.

"He said he thinks it's guarding something."

"Any idea what?"

"Weaponry of some sort. Could be rockets."

"Stay with him," the colonel advised, and Membury puffed out his cheeks and looked like the proud father he had become.

At their third meeting source Greensleeves solved the mystery of the concentrated armour and produced in addition a breakdown of the total Soviet air strength in Czechoslovakia as of November last. Or nearly total. Vienna was in any case amazed, and London authorised the payment of two small gold bars on condition that the British assay marks first be removed for reasons of deniability. Sergeant Pavel was thus characterised as a greedy man which made everybody feel easier. For several months after this Pym scampered back and forth between Axel and Membury like a butler serving two masters. Membury wondered whether he should meet Greensleeves in person: Vienna seemed to think it would be a good idea. Pym tried for him but came back with the sad news that he would treat only with Pym. Membury resigned himself. It was the breeding season for trout. Vienna summoned Pym and dined him. Colonels, air commodores, and naval persons vied to stake their claim to him. But it was Axel, as it turned out, who was his true proprietor and parent company.

"Sir Magnus," Axel whispered. "Something very terrible has happened." His smile had lost its bounce. His eyes were haunted and there were heavy shadows under them. Pym had brought any number of Naafi delicacies but he refused them all. "You have to help me, Sir Magnus," he said, darting scared looks towards the barn door. "You're my only hope. Help me, for Christ's sake. Do you know what they do to people like me? Don't look at me like that! Think of something for a change! It's your turn!"

I am in the barn at this moment, Tom. I have lived there these thirty and more years. Miss Dubber's stippled ceiling has rolled away, leaving the old rafters and the upside-down bats dangling from the roof. I can smell his cigar smoke as I sit here and I can see the holes of his dark eyes in the lamplight as he whispers Pym's name like the invalid he used to be: get me music, get me painting, get me bread, get me secrets. But there is no self-pity in his voice, no supplication or regret. That was never Axel's way. He demands. His voice is sometimes soft, it is true. But it is never less than powerful. He is his man, as ever. He is Axel, he is owed. He has crossed frontiers and been beaten. Of myself I am thinking nothing at all. Not now, not then.

"They are arresting my friends back home, did you hear? Two of our group were dragged from their beds yesterday morning in Prague. Another vanished on his way to work. I had to tell them about us. It was the only way."

The import of this statement takes a moment to penetrate Pym's worried understanding. Even when it has done so, his voice remains mystified: "About us? Me? What did you say? Who to, Axel?"

"Not in detail. In principle. Nothing bad. Not your name. It's okay, just more complicated, takes more handling. I've been more cunning than the others. In the end it may be better."

"But what did you tell them about *us?*"

"Nothing. Listen. For me it's different. The others, they work in factories, in the universities, they've no back door. When they're tortured they tell the truth and the truth kills them. But me, I'm a big spy, I've got a strong position, same as you. 'Sure,' I say to them. 'I go over the border. That's my job. I collect intelligence, remember?' . . . I act indignant, I demand to see my senior officer. He's not bad, this senior officer. Not a hundred percent, maybe sixty. But he hates the Ivans too. 'I'm cultivating a British traitor,' I tell him. 'He's a big fish. An army officer. I have kept it secret from you because of the many Titoists inside our organisation. Get the secret police off my back and you can share his product with me when I put the heat on him.' "

Pym has given up speech by now. He doesn't bother to ask what the senior officer says in reply, or to what extent the real life of Axel may be compared with the fictitious life of Sergeant Pavel. The cells are dying all over him, in his head, his groin, his bone marrow. His loving thoughts about Sabina are as old as childhood memories to him. There is only Pym and Axel and disaster in the world. He is changing into an old man even while he listens. The ignorance of ages is descending on him.

"He says I've got to bring him proof," says Axel a second time.

"Proof?" Pym mumbles. "What sort of proof? Proof? I don't follow you."

"Intelligence." Axel rubs his finger against his thumb, exactly as E. Weber once did. "Pinka-pinka. Product. Money. Something a British traitor like you could give me when I blackmailed him. It doesn't have to be the secrets of the atom bomb but it has to be good. Good enough to keep him quiet. No junk, you understand? He's got senior officers too." Axel smiles, though it is not a smile I care to recollect even now. "There's always one guy higher up the ladder, isn't there, Sir Magnus? Even when you think you're at the top. Then when you reach the top, there they are again below you, swinging on your boots. That's how it is in a system like ours. 'No fabrication,' he says to me. 'Whatever it is, it's got to have quality. Then we can fix it.' Steal for me, Sir Magnus. As you love my freedom, get me something wonderful."

"You look as though you've been seeing things," Corporal Kaufmann says as Pym returns to the jeep.

"It's my stomach," says Pym.

But on the journey back to Graz he began to feel better. Life is duty, he reflected. It's just a question of establishing which creditor is asking loudest. Life is paying. Life is seeing people right if it kills you.

* * *

There were half a dozen reconstructed Pyms wandering the streets of Graz that night, Tom, and there isn't one of them I need now feel ashamed of, or wouldn't happily embrace as a long-lost son who had paid his debt to society and come home, if he knocked on Miss Dubber's door at this moment and said, Father, it's me. I don't think there was a night in his life when he thought less about himself and more about his obligation to others than when he was patrolling his city kingdom under the shadows of crumbling Hapsburg glories, pausing now at the leafy gates of Membury's spacious married quarters, now at the doorway to Sabina's unprepossessing apartment house, while he made his plan and flashed them reassuring promises. "Don't worry about a thing," he told Membury in his heart. "You will suffer no humiliation, your lake will continue to be stocked and your post will be safe for as long as you care to adorn it. The Highest in the Land will continue to respect you as the presiding genius of the Greensleeves operation." "Your secrets are in my hands," he whispered to Sabina's unlit window. "Your employment by the British, your heroic brother Jan, your exalted opinion of your lover Pym are all secure. I shall cherish them as I cherish your soft warm body sleeping its troubled sleep."

He took no decisions because he had no doubts. The lone crusader had identified his mission, the skilled spy would take care of the detail, the loyal attacher would never again betray his friend in exchange for the illusion of being a servant of national necessity. His loves, his duties and allegiances had never been clearer. Axel, I owe you. Together we can change the world. I will bring you gifts as you brought gifts to me. I will never again send you to the camps. If he contemplated alternatives, then it was only to reject them as disastrous. Over the last months the inventive Pym had built Sergeant Pavel into a figure of joy and admiration in the secret corridors of Graz, Vienna and Whitehall. Under his skilful hand the choleric little hero's drinking, womanising and quixotic bursts of courage had become a legend. Even if Pym were prepared to break Axel's trust a second time, how could he go to Membury and say: "Sir. Sergeant Pavel does not exist. Greensleeves is my friend Axel, who requires that we give him genuine British secrets"? Membury's kindly eyes would pop open, his innocent face would collapse in lines of sadness and despair. His trust in Pym would wither, his reputation with it: Membury to the lantern, sack Membury; Membury, his wife and all his daughters, go home. An even worse disaster would result if Pym were to strike a compromise by visiting Axel's dilemma upon the fictitious Sergeant Pavel. He had played that scene, too, in his imagination: "Sir. Sergeant Pavel's frontier-crossings have been noticed. He has told the Czech secret police that he has a British agent in play. We must therefore give him chickenfeed to back his story." Div. Int. had no mandate to run double agents. Graz even less so. Even a defector in place was stretching things. Only Greensleeves' insistence on being handled by Pym personally had prevented a takeover by London long ago, and there was already a lot of earnest talk going on about who would get Pavel when Pym's military service expired. To place Sergeant Pavel in the position of a double agent would unloose a string of immediate consequences, all frightful: Membury would lose Greensleeves to London; Pym's successor would discover the deception in five minutes; Axel would once more be betrayed and his chances of survival forfeit; the Memburys would be posted to Siberia.

No, Tom. As Pym walked the momentous night away under a canopy of unreachable ideals, eschewing Sabina's bed in his purity of soul, he was not tormenting himself over great choices. He was not examining his immortal spirit in anticipation of what purists might call a treasonable act. He did not consider that tomorrow was the day set for his irrevocable execution—the day on which all hope for Pym would die and your father would be born. He was watching the dawn rise on a day of beauty and harmony. A day when a bad record could be put straight, when the fate of everyone he was responsible for rested in his care, when the electors of his secret constituency would go down on their knees and thank Pym and his Maker that he had been born to see them right. He was glowing and exulting. He was letting his goodwill and self-faith fill him up with courage. The secret crusader had placed his sword upon the altar and was transmitting fraternal messages to the God of Battles.

"Axel, come over!" Pym had begged him. "Forget about Sergeant Pavel. You can be an ordinary defector. I'll look after you. I'll get you everything you need. I promise."

But Axel was as fearless as he was determined. "Do not advise me to betray my friends, Sir Magnus. I am the only one who can save them. Did I not tell you I have crossed my last frontier? If you help me, we can win a great victory. Be here on Wednesday at the same time."

Briefcase in hand Pym makes quickly for the top floor of the villa and unlocks the door to his office. I am a morning man, it is known of me. Pym is an early riser, Pym is keen, Pym has done a day's work while most of us are still shaving. Membury's office is linked to his own by a pair of grand doors. Pushing them open, Pym steps inside. As he does so, his sense of well-being becomes unbearable: a dizzying blend of resolution, rightness and release. I am blessed. Membury's tin desk is no Reichstag desk. It has an old tin back and Pym's Swiss Army penknife knows the four screws well. In the third drawer down, on the left side, Membury keeps his basic works of reference: standing orders for the unit, *Brown Fish of the World,* classified telephone directory, *Lakes and Waterways of Austria,* Order of Battle of Military Intelligence in London, a list of leading aquaria and a chart for Div. Int., Vienna, showing units and their functions but no names. Pym reaches a hand in. Not an invasion. Not a retribution. No initials are being carved into the panelling. I am here to administer a caress. Folders, loose-leaf manuals. Signals instructions marked "Top Secret, Guard" which Pym has never seen. I am here to borrow, not to steal. Opening his briefcase he extracts an army-issue Agfa camera with a one-foot measuring chain fastened to the lens front. It is the same camera that he uses when Axel brings out raw material and Pym has to photograph it on the spot. He cocks it and sets it on the desk. This is what I was born for, he thinks, not for the first time. In the beginning was the spy.

From a file with the word "Vertebrates" crossed out on the cover, he selects the Order of Battle of Div. Int. Axel knows it anyway, he reasons. Nevertheless, there are impressive "Top Secret" stamps at top and bottom, and a distribution stamp to guarantee authenticity. As you love my freedom, get me something wonderful. He photographs it once, then again, and is left with a feeling of anticlimax. There are thirty-six frames on this film. Why do I cheesepare and give him only two? I could do something for our mutual understanding. Axel, you deserve better. He remembers a recent War Office assessment of the Soviet threat. If they will read that, they'll read anything. It is in the top drawer, beside *A Handbook of Water Mammals,* and begins with a summary of conclusions. He photographs each page and finishes the film nicely. Axel, I've done it! We're free. We've put the world to rights, exactly as you said we would! We are men of the middle ground—we have founded our own country with a population of two!

"Promise you will never bring me anything so good again, Sir Magnus," said Axel at their next meeting. "If you do, they will make me a general and we shall not be able to meet any more."

"Dear Father"—Pym wrote to the Majestic Hotel, Karachi, where Rick appeared to be living for his health—"Thanks for your two letters. I am so glad to hear you are hitting it off with the Aga Khan. I believe I am doing good work out here and you would be proud of me."

When Mary Pym at the age of sixteen decided it was time to lose her virginity she faked a heavy dose of adolescent vapours and had herself put to bed by Matron instead of playing hockey. There she lay in the sick wing staring at the wall till the three-o'clock bell rang, telling her that Matron was off duty until five. She waited five more minutes exactly by her Confirmation watch, held her breath for thirty seconds which always helped to get her courage up, then tiptoed down the stone back stairs past the kitchens and the laundry and across a bit of sour grass to an old brick potting shed where the under-gardener had made a provisional bed of blankets and old sacking. The results were more spectacular than she had reason to hope, but what she relished afterwards was not the event so much as the anticipation of it: the lying boldly in the bed with her skirt rucked round her waist knowing nothing was going to stop her now she had made up her mind; the sense of freedom as she took herself across the border into a state of sin.

And that was the feeling she had now, sitting demurely in the centre row in Caroline Lumsden's overfurnished drawing-room, with her hideous Thai tables and her garish Chinese paintings and her shelf full of factory-made Buddhas, listening to Caroline trying to sound like the Queen as she moaned out the minutes of the last meeting of the Vienna Branch of the Diplomatic Wives Association in her plummy swansong. I'll do it, Mary told herself, dead calm. If it doesn't work one way, I'll make it work another. She glanced to the window. In their hired Mercedes across the street, Georgie and Fergus were sitting with their heads together, two lovers pretending to study a street map while they kept an eye on the front door and her Rover parked in Caroline's drive. I'll take the back way out. It worked then, it'll work now.

"It was therefore *unanimously* agreed," Caroline was lamenting, "that the Foreign Office Inspectors' *report* on the local cost of living was both distorted *and* unfair, and that a Finance subcommittee would be formed *immediately,* headed, I am pleased to say, by *Mrs. McCormick*"—respectful hush. Ruth McCormick was the wife of the Economic Minister and therefore a financial genius. Nobody mentioned that she was screwing the Dutch military attaché. "The subcommittee will itemise *all* our points and, having done so, submit a *written* objection to our association in London for submission *through* the proper channels to the Head of the Inspectorate *himself*."

Patter of soprano applause from fourteen pairs of female hands, Mary's included. Great, Caroline, great. In another life, it will be your turn to be the rising young diplomat and your husband's to stay home and imitate you.

Caroline had turned to Any Other Business. "Next *Monday,* our weekly transatlantic lunch at Manzi's. Twelve-thirty *sharp* and four hundred schillings a head, cash, please, to include two glasses of wine, and please *don't* be late as Herr Manzi took an *awful* lot of persuading to give us a private *room*." Pause. Say it, you fool, Mary urged her. Caroline didn't. Not yet. "Then on Friday, one week today, please, Marjory de Weever will be giving her really *fascinating* lantern lecture *here* on aerobics which she taught *very* successfully to an all-ranks class in the Sudan where her husband was second *man*. Right, Marjory?"

"Well, chargé really," Marjory roared from the front row. "The Ambassador was only there for three months out of fourteen. Not that Brian got paid for it but that's beside the point."

For pity's sake! thought Mary furiously. *Now!* But she had forgotten about Penny Sharlow's bloody husband landing a medal.

"And I'm sure we'd *all* like to congratulate Penny on the fantastic support she's given to James over the years, without which I'll bet he wouldn't have got anything at *all*."

This was apparently a joke because there was hysterical laughter by too few voices, which Caroline quelled with a mournful stare into the middle distance. She put on her Official Mourning voice.

"And Mary darling—you did say you wouldn't mind if I mentioned it." Mary looked hastily downward to her lap. "I'm sure *everyone* would like me to say how *sorry* we are about the death of your *father*-in-law. We know Magnus has been hit *very* hard and we do hope he will get over it *soon*, and be back among us in his usual *high* spirits that we *all* find so refreshing."

Sympathetic murmurs. Mary whispered "Thank you" and keeled forward not too far. She sensed the anxious pause while everyone waited for her head to come up, but it didn't. She began to shake and was impressed to see real tears flopping on to her clenched hands. She let out a little choke and from her willed darkness heard cheerful Mrs. Simpson, wife of the Chancery guard, say "Come here, lovely," as she put an enormous arm round Mary's back. She choked again, pushed Mrs. Simpson halfheartedly away and struggled to her feet, tears everywhere: tears for Tom, tears for Magnus, tears for being deflowered in the potting shed and I bet I'm pregnant. She let Mrs. Simpson take her arm, she shook her head and stammered "I'm fine." She reached the hall to find that Caroline Lumsden had followed her out. "No thanks . . . really I don't want to lie down. Far rather just take a walk . . . get my coat, please? . . . Blue with a foul fur collar . . . Rather be alone if you don't mind . . . You've been so kind. Oh Christ, I'm going to cry again. . . ."

Once in the Lumsdens' long back garden, she wandered, still hunched, along the path until it dropped out of sight behind the trees. Then she moved fast. Training, she thought gratefully, as she unlatched the back gate; nothing quite like it for cooling the blood. She headed quickly for the bus stop. There was one every fourteen minutes. She had looked them up.

"How terribly good of them!" cried Mrs. Membury, with the greatest satisfaction, as she topped up Brotherhood's glass with her homemade elderflower wine. "Oh I do think that's farsighted and sensible. I'd never supposed the War Office would have *half* the wit. Would *you*, Harrison? Not deaf," she explained to Brotherhood while they waited. "Just slow-thinking. Would you, darling?"

Harrison Membury had come up from the stream at the end of the garden where he had been cutting reeds, and he was still wearing his waders. He was large and loping and at seventy still boyish, with pink immature cheeks and silk white hair. He sat at the far end of the table washing down homemade cake with tea from a huge pottery mug with "Gramps" written on it. He moved, Brotherhood reckoned, at exactly half his wife's pace and spoke at half the volume.

"Oh I don't know," he said when everyone else had forgotten the question. "There were some quite clever chaps scattered around the place. Here and there."

"Ask him about fish and you'll get a *far* quicker answer," said Mrs. Membury, hurtling off to the corner of the room and pulling out some albums from among the collected works of Evelyn Waugh. "How are the trout, Harrison?"

"Oh they're all right," said Membury with a grin.

"We're not allowed to eat them, you know. Only the pike can do that. Now would it be fun to look at my photographs? I mean is it going to be an *illustrated* history? Don't tell me. It doubles the cost. It said so in the *Observer*. Pictures double the cost of a book. But then I do think they double the attractiveness too. Specially with biographies. I can't be doing with biography if I can't *look* at the people who are being biogged. Harrison can. He's cerebral. I'm visual. Which are you?"

"I think I must be more your way," said Brotherhood with a smile, playing his ponderous role.

The village was one of those half-urbanised Georgian settlements on the edge of Bath where English Catholics of a certain standing have elected to gather in their exile. The cottage lay at the country end of it, a tiny sandstone mansion with a steep narrow garden descending to a stretch of river, and they sat in the cluttered kitchen on wheelback chairs, surrounded by washing-up, and vaguely votive bric-a-brac: a cracked ceramic plaque of the Virgin Mary from Lourdes; a disintegrating rush cross jammed behind the cooker; a child's paper mobile of angels rotating in the draught; a photograph of Ronald Knox. While they talked, filthy grandchildren wandered in and stared at them before tall mothers swept them off. It was a household in permanent and benevolent disorder, pervaded by the gentle thrill of religious persecution. A white morning sun was poking through the Bath mist. There was a sound of slow water dripping in the gutters.

"You an academic chap?" Membury enquired suddenly, from the end of the table.

"Darling, I *told* you. He's an *historian*."

"Well, more a retired trooper, I suppose, sir, to be honest," Brotherhood replied. "I was lucky to get the job. I'd have been on the shelf by now, if this hadn't come along."

"Now when will it come out?" Mrs. Membury shouted, as if everyone were deaf. "I've got to know *months* in advance so that I can put my name down with Mrs. Lanyon. Tristram, don't tug. We have a mobile library here, you know. Magda darling, do something about Tristram, he's trying to tear a page out of history. They come once a week and they're an absolute godsend as long as you don't mind waiting. Now this is Harrison's villa where he had his office and everyone worked for him. The main bit's 1680, the wing's new. Well nineteenth. This is his pond. He stocked it from scratch. The Gestapo had thrown grenades into it and blown up all the fish. They would. Pigs."

"From what my masters say, it will start out as a work of internal reference," Brotherhood said. "Then afterwards they'll publish a sanitised version for the open market."

"You're not M. R. D. Foot, are you?" said Mrs. Membury. "No, you can't be. You're Marlow. Well I think they're inspired, anyway. So sensible to get hold of the actual people before they peg out."

"Who did you troop with?" Membury said.

"Let's just say I did a little of this and a little of that," Brotherhood suggested with deliberate coyness, while he pulled on his reading glasses.

"There he is," said Mrs. Membury, stabbing a tiny finger at a group photograph. "There. That's the young man you were asking about. Magnus. He did all the really brilliant work. That's the old Rittmeister, he was an absolute darling. Harrison, what was the mess waiter's name—the one who ought to have become a novice but didn't have the gump?"

"Forget," said Membury.

"And who are the girls?" said Brotherhood, smiling.

"Oh my dear, they were all sorts of trouble. Each one dottier than the next and if they weren't pregnant they were running off with unsuitable lovers, cutting their wrists. I could have opened a Marie Stopes clinic for them full time if we'd believed in birth control in those days. Now we're hybrids. Our girls are on the pill, but they still get pregnant by mistake."

"They did the interpreting for us," Membury said, filling himself a pipe.

"Was there an interpreter involved in the Greensleeves operation?" Brotherhood said.

"No need," said Membury. "Chap spoke German. Pym handled him alone."

"Completely alone?"

"Solo. Greensleeves insisted on it. Why don't you talk to Pym?"

"But who took him over when Pym left?"

"I did," said Membury proudly, brushing wet tobacco from the front of his disgraceful pullover.

There is nothing like a red-backed notebook to instill order into desultory conversation. Having spread one very deliberately among the débris of several meals, and shaken out his big right arm as a prelude to becoming what he called a little bit official, Brotherhood drew a pen from his pocket with as much ceremony as a village policeman at the scene of the occurrence. The grandchildren had been removed. From an upper room came the sounds of someone trying to coax religious music from a xylophone.

"If we could get it all down first I can come back to the individual specifics later," said Brotherhood.

"Jolly good idea," said Mrs. Membury sternly. "Harrison, darling, listen."

"Unfortunately, as I have already told you, most of the raw material on Greensleeves has been destroyed, lost or misplaced, which puts even greater responsibility on the shoulders of surviving witnesses. That's you. Now then."

For a while after this forbidding warning there was relative sanity while Membury with surprising accuracy recalled the dates and content of Greensleeves' principal triumphs and the part played by Lieutenant Magnus Pym of the Intelligence Corps. Brotherhood wrote diligently and prompted little, only pausing to wet his thumb and turn the pages of his notebook.

"Harrison, darling, you're being slow again," Mrs. Membury interposed occasionally. "Marlow hasn't got all day." And once: "Marlow's got to get back to *London,* darling. He's not a fish."

But Membury continued swimming at his own good pace, now describing Soviet military emplacements in southern Czechoslovakia; now the laborious procedure for prising small gold bars out of the Whitehall war chests which Greensleeves insisted on receiving in payment; now the fights he had had with Div. Int. to protect his pet agent from being overused. And Brotherhood, despite the little tape-recorder that nestled once more in his wallet pocket, set it all out for them to see, dates left, material centre.

"Greensleeves didn't have any other codename at any time, did he?" he asked casually as he jotted. "Sometimes a source gets rechristened for security reasons or because the name's already been bagged."

"Think, Harrison," Mrs. Membury urged.

Membury took his pipe from his mouth.

"Source Wentworth?" Brotherhood suggested, turning a page.

Membury shook his head.

"There was also a source"—Brotherhood faltered slightly as if the name had nearly escaped him—"Serena, that was it—no it wasn't—Sabina. Source Sabina, operating out of Vienna. Or was it Graz? Maybe it was Graz before your time. Used to be a popular thing that, anyway, mixing up the sexes with the cover names. A quite general trick of disinformation, I'm told."

"Sabina?" cried Mrs. Membury. "Not *our* Sabina?"

"He's talking about a source, darling," Membury said firmly, coming in much more quickly than was his habit. "Our Sabina was an interpreter, not an agent. Quite different."

"Well *our* Sabina was an absolute—"

"She wasn't a source," said Membury firmly. "Now, come on, don't tittle-tattle. Poppy."

"I beg your pardon?" said Brotherhood.

"Magnus wanted to call him Poppy. We did for a bit. Source Poppy. I rather liked it. Then up came Remembrance Day and some ass in London decided Poppy was derogatory to the fallen—poppies are for heroes, not traitors. Absolutely typical of those chaps. Probably got promoted for it. Total buffoon. I was furious, so was Magnus. 'Poppy *is* a hero,' he said. I liked him for that. Nice chap."

"That's the bare bones done, then," said Brotherhood, surveying his handiwork. "Now let's flesh them out, can we?" He was reading from the subject headings he had written at the beginning of his notebook before he came. "Personalities, well, we're touching on that. Value or otherwise of national servicemen to the peacetime intelligence effort, were they a help or a hindrance—we'll come to it. Where they all went afterwards—did they attain positions of interest in their chosen walk of life? Well, you may have kept up with them, and there again you may not. That's more for us to worry about than you."

"Yes, well now, whatever *did* happen to Magnus?" Mrs. Membury demanded. "Harrison was so upset he never wrote. Well so was I. He never even told us whether he converted. He was awfully *close,* we felt. All he needed was one more shove. Harrison was exactly like that for years. It took a jolly good talking to from Father D'Arcy before Harrison saw the light, didn't it, darling?"

Membury's pipe had gone out and he was peering disappointedly into the bowl.

"I never liked the chap," he explained with a kind of embarrassed regret. "Never thought much of him."

"Darling, don't be silly. You adored Magnus. You practically adopted him. You know you did."

"Oh Magnus was a splendid chap. The other chap. The source. The Greensleeves chap. I thought he was a bit of a fraud, to be honest. I didn't say anything —it didn't seem useful. With Div. Int. and London waving their caps in the air, why should we complain?"

"Nonsense," said Mrs. Membury, very firmly indeed. "Marlow, don't listen. Darling, you're being far too modest, as usual. You were the linchpin of the operation, you know you were. Marlow's writing a *history,* darling. He's going to write about *you.* You mustn't spoil it for him, must he, Marlow? That's the fashion these days. Put down, put down. I get absolutely sick of it. Look at what they did to poor Captain Scott on the television. Daddy knew Scott. He was a marvellous man."

Membury continued as if she hadn't spoken. "All the brigadiers from Vienna beaming away like sand boys. Roars of applause from the War Office. No point in me killing the golden goose if they were all happy, was there? Young Magnus cock-a-hoop. Well I didn't want to spoil *his* fun."

"*And* he was taking instruction," said Mrs. Membury pointedly. "Harrison had arranged for him to go to Father Moynihan twice a week. *And* he was running garrison cricket. *And* he was learning Czech. You can't do that in a day."

"Ah now, that's interesting. About the learning Czech, I mean. Was this because he had a Czech source then?"

"It's because Sabina set her cap at him, the little minx," said Mrs. Membury, but this time her husband actually spoke through her.

"His stuff was all so flashy, somehow," he was saying, undeterred. "Always looked good on the plate, but when you came to chew it over, nothing really there. That's how it seemed to me." He gave a puzzled giggle. "Same as trying to eat a pike. All bones. You'd get a report in, look it over. I say, that's jolly good, you'd think. But when you took a closer look it was boring. Yes, that's true because we already know it. . . . Yes, that's possible but we can't verify it because we've nothing on that region. I didn't like to say anything, but I think the Czechs could have been batting and bowling at the same time. I always thought that was why Greensleeves didn't show up after Magnus went back to England. He wasn't so sure he could hoodwink an older chap. Mean of me, I expect. I'm just a failed fish freak, aren't

I, Hannah? That's what she calls me. Failed fish freak."

The description pleased them both so much that they broke out laughing for some while, so that Brotherhood had to laugh with them and keep back his question until Membury was able to hear him clearly.

"You mean you never met Greensleeves? He never came to the rendezvous? I'm sorry, sir," he said, returning to his notebook, "but didn't you say just now you yourself took over source Greensleeves when Pym left Graz?"

"I did."

"And now you say you never met him."

"Perfectly true. I didn't. Stood me up at the altar, didn't he, Hannah? She got me into my best suit, packed together all these stupid special foods he was supposed to like—how that started, God knows—he never turned up."

"Harrison probably got the wrong night," said Mrs. Membury, with a fresh gust of laughter. "Harrison's frightful about time, aren't you, darling? He was never *trained* for Intelligence, you know. He was librarian in Nairobi. A jolly good one too. Then he met someone on the ship and got roped in."

"And out," said Membury cheerfully. "Kaufmann came along. He was the driver. Charming chap. Well he knew the meeting place like the back of his hand. I didn't get the wrong night, darling. I got the right one, I know I did. Sat in an empty barn all night. No word from him, nothing. We'd no means of getting hold of him, it was all one way. Ate a bit of his stupid food. Drank some of his booze, I enjoyed that. Went home. Same again the next night and the next. I waited for a message of some sort, phone call like the first time. Absolute blank. Chap was never heard of again. We should have had a formal handover with Pym present, of course, but Greensleeves wouldn't allow it. Prima donna, you see, like all agents. 'One chap at a time.' Iron rule." Membury absently helped himself from Brotherhood's glass. "Vienna was furious. Blamed it all on me. Then I told them he was no good anyway and that didn't help." He gave another rich laugh. "I should think it got me sacked if truth were known. They didn't say so, but I'll bet it jolly well helped!"

Mrs. Membury had made a tuna-fish risotto because it was Friday, and a trifle with cherries on it which she refused to let Membury eat. When lunch was over she and Brotherhood stood on the river bank watching Membury hacking cheerfully at the reeds. Nets and fine wires were stretched all ways across the water. Among the breeding boxes, an old punt was sinking at its mooring. The sun, freed of the mist, beat brightly.

"So tell us about the wicked Sabina," Brotherhood suggested artfully, out of Membury's earshot.

Mrs. Membury couldn't wait. An absolute minx, she repeated: "One look at Magnus and she saw herself with a British passport, a jolly good British husband and nothing to worry about for the rest of her life. But Magnus was a bit too sly for her, I'm pleased to say. He must have stood her up. He never said so, but that was the way we read it. In Graz one day. Gone the next."

"Where did she go then?" Brotherhood said.

"Home to Czechoslovakia, that was the story. With her tail between her legs was our theory. Left a note for Harrison saying she was homesick and she was going back to her old boyfriend, despite the beastly régime. Well *that* didn't please London, as you can imagine. It didn't raise Harrison's stock one bit. They said he should have seen it coming and done something about it."

"I wonder what became of her," Brotherhood mused with an historian's dreaminess. "You don't remember her other name, do you?"

"Harrison. What was Sabina's other name?"

With surprising swiftness the answer rang back across the water. "Kordt. K-O-R-D-T. Sabina Kordt. Very beautiful girl. Charming."

"Marlow says what became of her?"

"God knows. Last we heard she'd changed her name and landed herself a job in one of the Czech Ministries. One of the defectors said she'd been working for 'em all along."

Mrs. Membury was not so much astonished as proved right. "Now there you are! Married getting on for fifty years, thirty-something years since Austria, and he doesn't even tell me she turned up in Czechoslovakia working for one of the Ministries! I expect Harrison had an affair with her himself if truth were known. Practically everybody did. Well my dear she must have been a spy, mustn't she? It sticks out a mile. They'd never have taken her back if they hadn't their hooks on her all along, they're far too vindictive. So Magnus was well rid of her then, wasn't he? Are you sure you won't stay for tea?"

"If I could take a few of those old photographs," Brotherhood said. "We'll give you a credit in the book, naturally."

Mary knew the technique exactly. In Berlin she had watched Jack Brotherhood use it a dozen times, and helped him often. At training camp they had called it paperchasing: how to make an encounter with someone you don't trust. The only difference was, today it was Mary who was the subject of the operation, and the anonymous writer of the note who didn't trust her:

> "I have information that could lead us both to Magnus. You will please do the following. Any morning between ten and twelve, you will sit in the lobby of the Hotel Ambassador. Any afternoon between two and six you will take a coffee at the Café Mozart. Any evening between nine and midnight, the lounge of the Hotel Sacher. Mr. König will collect you."

The Mozart was half empty. Mary sat at a centre table where she could be seen and ordered herself a coffee and a brandy. They've watched me arrive and now they're watching to see whether I am followed. Pretending to consult her diary, she took covert note of the people round her and the parked charabancs and fiacres in the street outside the big windows, looking for anything that could resemble a stake-out. When you've got a conscience like mine, everything stinks anyway, she thought: from the two nuns frowning at the stock exchange prices in the window of the bank to the huddle of bowler-hatted young coachmen stamping their feet and watching the girls go by. In a corner of the café, a fat Viennese gentleman was expressing interest in her. I should have worn a hat, she thought. I'm not a respectable single woman. She got up, went to the newspaper rack and without thinking chose Die Presse. Now I suppose I roll it up and take it for a walk in my stockinged feet, she thought stupidly, as she opened it at the film page.

"Frau Pym?"

A woman's voice, a woman's bosom. A woman's deferentially smiling face. It was the girl from the cash desk.

"That's right," said Mary, smiling in return.

From behind her back she produced an envelope with "Frau Pym" written on it in pencil. "Herr König left this message for you. He is very sorry."

Mary gave her fifty schillings and opened the envelope.

"Please pay your bill and leave the café at once, turning right into the Maysedergasse, and remaining on the right-hand pavement. When you reach the pedestrian precinct turn left, and keep to the left side, walking slowly and admiring the shop windows."

She wanted the loo but she didn't like to go in case he thought she was tipping someone off. She put the note in her handbag, finished her coffee and took her bill to the cash desk where the girl gave her another smile.

"These men are all the same," the girl said while the change rattled down the chute.

"You're telling me," said Mary. They both laughed.

As she left the café a young couple entered and she had a feeling they were disguised Americans. But then a lot of Austrians were. She turned right and came at once to the Maysedergasse. The two nuns were still at their stock prices. She kept to the right-hand pavement. It was twenty past three and the Wives' meeting was sure to end by five so that they could all get home to change into halter dresses and sequin handbags for the evening cattle market. But even when everyone had gone and only Mary's car remained in the Lumsdens' drive, Fergus and Georgie might well assume she had stayed on for a quiet drink with Caroline on her own. If I make it back by quarter to six I stand a chance, she reckoned. She paused before a woman's lingerie shop and found herself admiring a pair of tart's black cami-knickers in the window. Who buys that stuff anyway? Bee Lederer, a pound to a penny. She hoped something would happen soon, before the Ambassadress came out with an armful of the stuff, or one of the many unattached men tried to pick her up.

"Frau Pym? I am from Herr König. Please come quickly."

The girl was pretty and badly dressed and nervous. Following her Mary had an overwhelming memory of being back in Prague visiting a painter the authorities did not approve of. The side street was one minute packed with shoppers, the next empty. All Mary's senses were alight. She smelt delicatessen, frost and tobacco. She glanced into a shop doorway and recognised the man from the Café Mozart. The girl turned left then right, then left again. Where am I? They entered a paved square. We're in the Kärntnerstrasse. We're not. A hippie boy took Mary's photograph and tried to press a card on her. She brushed him aside. A red plastic bear was holding his mouth open for contributions to some charity. An Asian pop group was singing Beatles music. Across the square lay a dual carriageway and at the near side of it a brown Peugeot waited with a man at the wheel. As they approached, he pushed the back door open at them. The girl grabbed the door and said, "Get in, please." Mary got in and the girl followed. Must be the Ring, she thought. If so it was not a part of the Ring she recognised. She saw a black Mercedes dawdling behind them. Fergus and Georgie, she thought, knowing that it wasn't. Her driver glanced both ways, then pointed the car straight at the central reservation—bump, it's the front tyres, bump, that was my backside you just broke. Everything hooted and the girl peered anxiously through the back window. They left the carriageway and shot down a side street, across a square and as far as the Opera where they stopped. The door on Mary's side opened. The girl ordered her out. Mary had hardly made the pavement before a second woman squeezed past her and took her place. The car drove away at speed, as neat a substitution as Mary had seen. A black Mercedes followed it but she didn't think it was the same one. A dapper, embarrassed young man was guiding her through a wide doorway to a courtyard.

"Take the lift, please, Mary," said the young man, in Euro-American, handing her a piece of paper. "Apartment six, please. Six. You go up alone. You have that?"

"Six," Mary said.

He smiled. "Sometimes when we are scared we kind of forget everything."

"Sure," she said. She walked to the doorway and he smiled and waved at her. She pushed it open and saw an old lift waiting with its doors open, and an old janitor smiling too. They've all been to the same charm school, she thought. She got into the lift and told the janitor, "Six, please," and the janitor launched her on her climb. As the doorway sank below her she had a last glimpse of the boy standing in the courtyard still smiling and a couple of well-dressed girls standing behind him, consulting some bit of paper. The bit of paper in her own hand read "Six, Herr König." Odd, she thought as she slipped it into her handbag. With me it works the other way. When I'm scared I don't forget a damn thing. Like the car number. Like the number of the second Mercedes behind us. Like the fringe of dyed black hair on the driver's neck. Like the Opium perfume that the girl was wearing and Magnus always insists on bringing me when he goes on air journeys. Like the fat gold ring with the red seal on the boy's left hand.

The door to number 6 stood open. A brass plate beside it read "Interhansa Austria A.G." She walked in and the door closed behind her. A girl again but not pretty. A sullen, strong girl with a flat Slav face and resentful, anti-Party manner. With a scowl she nodded Mary forward. She entered a dark drawing-room and saw nobody. At the far end of it stood another pair of doors, also open. The furnishings were old Vienna, phoney. Phoney old chests and oil paintings slipped by her as she advanced. Phoney lamp brackets reached at her from phoney imperial wallpaper. As she kept walking she had a reprise of the erotic expectation she had felt at the Wives' meeting. He's going to order me to undress and I shall obey. He's going to lead me to a red fourposter and have me raped by footmen for his pleasure. But the second room contained no fourposter, it was a drawing-room like the first, with a desk and two armchairs and a heap of out-of-date *Vogues* on the coffee table. It was otherwise empty. Angry, Mary swung round intending to say something rude to the flat-faced Slav. Instead she found herself staring at him. He was standing in the doorway smoking a cigar and for a second she was puzzled she couldn't smell it, but in some eerie way she knew that nothing about him was ever going to surprise her. The next moment the aroma had reached her and she was shaking his lazy hand as if this was the way they always greeted each other when they met fully dressed in Viennese apartments.

"You are a courageous woman," he remarked. "Are they expecting you back soon or what is the arrangement? What can we do to make life easier for you?"

That's perfectly right, she thought in absurd relief. The first thing you always ask your agent is how long you've got him for. The second is whether he needs immediate help. Magnus is in good hands. But she knew that already.

"Where is he?" she said.

He had the authority that enabled him to own to failure. "If only we knew, how happy we would both be!" he agreed as if her question had been a statement of despair, and with his long hand showed her to the chair that he required her to sit on. We, she thought. We are equals yet you are in command. No wonder Tom fell in love with you on sight.

They were sitting opposite one another, she on the gilded sofa, he on the gilded chair. The Slav girl had brought a tray of vodka and some gherkins and black bread and her devotion to him was obscene, she preened and smirked so. She's one of his Marthas, thought Mary, which was what Magnus called his Station secretaries. He poured two stiff ones, holding each glass carefully by turn. He drank to her, looking over the brim. That's what Magnus does, she thought. And it's you he learned it from.

"Has he telephoned?" he asked.

"No. He can't."

"Of course not," he agreed sympathetically. "The house is bugged and he knows that. Has he written?"

She shook her head.

"He's wise. They are watching for him everywhere. They are immoderately angry with him."

"Are you?"

"How can I be angry when I owe the man so much? His last message to me was that he didn't want to see me any more. He said he was free and goodbye. I felt a genuine pang of jealousy. What freedom has he found so suddenly that he cannot share it with us?"

"He said the same to me—I mean about being free. I think he said it to several people. To Tom as well."

Why do I talk to you as if you were an old lover? What sort of whore am I that I can throw off my loyalties with my clothes? If he had reached out to her and taken her hand she would have let him. If he had drawn her to him—

"He should have come to me when I told him," he said in the same philosophically reproachful tone. "It's over, Sir Magnus,' I said to him. That's my name for him. Forgive me."

"In Corfu," she said.

"In Corfu, in Athens, everywhere I could speak to him. 'Come with me. We are passé, you and I. It's time for us oldies to leave the field to the next anguished generation.' He wouldn't see it. 'Do you want to be like one of those poor old actors one has literally to drag from the stage?' I said. He wouldn't listen. He was so adamant they would clear him."

"They almost did. Maybe they did. He thought so."

"Brotherhood won a little time and that was all. Not even Jack could sweep back the tide for ever. Besides—Jack has joined the bad guys now. Hell hath no fury like a deceived protector."

He taught Magnus his style, she thought, in another spurt of recognition. The style he was always wanting for his novel. He taught him how to be superior to human foibles and how to give a Godlike laugh at himself as a way of fending off morbidity. He did all the things for him that a woman is grateful for, except that Magnus is a man.

"His father seems to have been quite a mystery man," he said, lighting himself another cigar. "What's all that about, do you think?"

"I don't know. I never met him. Did you?"

"Many times. In Switzerland when Magnus was a student, his father was a great British sea captain who had gone down with his ship."

She laughed. Heaven help me, I'm actually laughing. Now it's me who's found the style.

"Oh yes. Then when I next heard of him he was a great financial baron. His tentacles extended to every banking house in Europe. He had miraculously recovered from being drowned."

"Oh Christ," she said. And burst out again in cathartic, uncontrollable laughter.

"Since I was German at the time I naturally felt greatly relieved. I had had a really bad conscience about sinking his father until then. What is it about your husband, do you know, that gives us such a bad, bad conscience?"

"His potential," she said unthinkingly, and took a long pull of vodka. She was trembling and her cheeks were burning hot. He watched her calmly, helping her to steady.

"You're his other life," she said.

"He always told me I was his oldest friend. If you know different, please don't destroy my illusions."

She was getting it back. Her head. The room was clearing and her head with it. "I understood that position was reserved for somebody called Poppy," she said.

"Where did you hear that name?"

"It's in the great book he's been writing. 'Poppy, my dearest, oldest friend.'"

"Is that all?"

"Oh no. There's much more. Poppy gets a big hand on every fifth page. Poppy this, Poppy that. When they found the camera and the codebook they found dried poppies with them, as a keepsake."

She had hoped to disconnect him, but all she drew from him was a smile of gratification.

"I'm flattered. Poppy is the fanciful codename he awarded me many years ago. I have been Poppy for most of our lives."

Somehow she stayed in there fighting. "So what is he?" she demanded. "Is he a Communist? He can't be. It's too ridiculous."

He opened his long hands. He smiled again, infectiously, offering an immediate bond of his bewilderment. He was invulnerable. "I've asked myself the same question many times. And then I think—well, who believes in marriage these days? He's a searcher. Isn't that enough? In our profession I am sure we should not ask for more. Can you imagine being married to a sedentary ideologist? I had an uncle once who was a Lutheran pastor. He bored us all to death."

She was getting stronger. Less mad. More indignant. "What did Magnus do for you?" she asked.

"He spied. Selectively, it is true. But treasonably it is also true. And often very energetically—something you will understand about him. When his life is happy he believes in God and wants everyone to have a gift. When he is down he will sulk and refuse to go to church. Those of us who run him have to live with that."

Nothing had happened to her. She was upright and drinking vodka in a stranger's safe flat. He has pronounced the sentence, she thought calmly, as if she were attending someone else's trial. Magnus is dead. Mary is dead. Their marriage is dead. Tom is an orphan with a traitor for a father. Everybody's absolutely fine.

"But then I don't run him," she objected, answering his point quite calmly.

He appeared not to notice the new coldness in her voice. "Allow me to sell myself to you a little. I am fond of your husband."

And so you should be, she thought. After all, he sacrificed us to you.

"I also owe him," he continued. "Whatever he wants for the rest of his life, I can give it to him. I am greatly to be preferred to Jack Brotherhood and his service."

You're not, she thought. You are absolutely not.

"Did you say something?" he asked.

She smiled sadly for him and shook her head.

"Brotherhood wishes to catch your husband and punish him. I am the opposite. I wish to find him and reward him. Whatever he will allow us to give, we will give it." He drew on his cigar.

You're a sham, she thought. You seduce my husband and call yourself his friend and mine.

"You know this trade, Mary. I don't need to tell you that a man in his position is a most desirable commodity. Put more frankly, we cannot afford to lose him. The last thing we want is to have him sitting in an English prison for the rest of his useful life, telling the authorities what he's been doing these thirty and more years. Nor do we particularly want him to write a book."

You want, she thought. What about us?

"We would much prefer him to enjoy a well-earned retirement with us— distinction, medals, his family around him if they wish it—where we can still consult him as we need. I can't guarantee that we will permit him to lead the double life he is accustomed to but in every other respect we shall do our best to meet his needs."

"He doesn't want you any more though, does he? That's why he's hiding."

He puffed at his cigar, flapping a hand between them to stop the smoke from bothering her. But it bothered her anyway. It would shame and disgust and accuse her for the rest of her life. He was talking again. Reasonably.

"I am at my wits' end, to be frank. I have done all I can to put Brotherhood and everyone else off the scent and to find your husband ahead of them. I still have not the least idea where he is and I feel a complete fool."

"What happened to the people he betrayed?" she said.

"Magnus? Oh he hates bloodshed. He always made that clear."

"That never stopped anybody yet from shedding blood."

Once more a pause for his private gravity. "You are right," he agreed. "And he chose a hard profession. I'm afraid it's a little late for us all to ponder our moralities."

"Some of us are rather new to them," she said. But she could not move him. "Why did you ask me here?"

She met his gaze and saw that though nothing had changed in his expression his face was indifferent, which was what happened sometimes when she looked at Magnus.

"Before you came I had ideas that you and your son might care to start a new life in Czechoslovakia and that Magnus would therefore be strongly tempted to join you." He indicated a briefcase at his side. "I brought passports for you and all that nonsense. I was absurd. Having met you, I realise you are not defector material. However, it still occurs to me as a possibility that you do know where he is, and that you have managed, because you are a capable woman, not to tell anybody. You cannot suppose he is better off with his pursuers than he would be with me. So if you do know, I think you should tell me now."

"I don't know where he is," she said. And closed her mouth before she could add: and if I did, you would be the last person on earth I would ever tell.

"But you have theories. You have ideas. You have been thinking of nothing else night and day ever since he left, surely. Magnus, where are you? It's your one thought, isn't it?"

"I don't know. You know more about him than I do."

She was beginning to hate his sanctimony. His manner of pondering before he spoke to her, as if wondering whether she was up to his next question.

"Did he ever talk to you about a woman called Lippsie?"

"No."

"She died when he was young. She was Jewish. All her friends and relations had been killed by the Germans. It seems she adopted Magnus as some kind of support. Then changed her mind and killed herself instead. The reasons, as usual with Magnus, are clouded. It was a curious example for a child, nonetheless. Magnus is a great imitator, even when he doesn't know it. Really I sometimes think he is entirely put together from bits of other people, poor fellow."

"He never told me about her," she repeated doggedly.

He brightened. Just as Magnus might. "Come, Mary. Do you not have the consoling feeling there is someone looking after him? I am sure there is. My understanding of him has always been that he is attracted only to human beings, not to ideas at all. He hates to be alone because then his world is empty. So who is looking after him? Let us try to think whom he would like—I'm not talking of women, you see. Only of friends."

She was smoothing her skirt, looking for her coat. "I'll take a cab," she said. "You don't need to ring for one. There's a stand just on the corner. I saw it as I came."

"Why not his mother? She would be a good person."

She stared at him, unable for a moment to believe her ears.

"Not long ago he talked to me about his mother for the first time," he explained. "He said he had taken to visiting her again. I was surprised. Also flattered, I confess. He unearthed her somewhere and put her in a house. Does he see her much?"

She had the wit. Still in the nick of time she felt her cunning come rushing back to take command of her. Magnus hasn't got a mother, you idiot. She's dead, he hardly knew her, and he doesn't care. The one true thing I know of him, and will swear for him on the Last Day, is that Magnus Pym is not now and never has been the adult son of any woman. But Mary kept her head. She didn't fling insults at him, or sneer at him, or laugh out loud in relief that Magnus had lied to his oldest, dearest friend with the same precision with which he had lied to his wife, his child and his country. She spoke reasonably and sensibly as a good spy always does.

"He likes to chat with her now and then, certainly," she conceded. Picking up her handbag she peered inside it as if to make sure she had money for her taxi.

"Then might he not have taken himself off to Devon and stayed with her? She was so grateful to have her bit of sea air at last. And Magnus was so proud he had been able to work the magic for her. He spoke interminably of the wonderful walks they had together on the beach. How he took her to church on Sundays and fixed her garden for her. Maybe he is doing something as innocent as that?"

"Her house was the first place they looked," Mary lied, closing her handbag. "They frightened the poor old lady out of her skin. How do I get in touch with you if I need you? Throw a newspaper over the wall?"

She stood up. He stood up also, though not so easily. His smile was still in place, his eyes were still as wise and sad and merry in the style that Magnus envied so.

"I don't think you will need me, Mary. And perhaps you are right that Magnus does not want me any more either. Just as long as he wants someone. That's all we must worry about if we love him. There are so many ways of taking vengeance on the world. Sometimes literature is simply not enough."

The alteration in his tone momentarily halted her in her hurry to get out.

"He'll find an answer," she said carelessly. "He always does."

"That's what I'm afraid of."

They walked towards the front door, slowly in order to allow for his limp. He summoned the lift for her and held back the grille. She got in. Her last sight of him was through the bars, still watching her. By then she was liking him again, and frightened stiff.

She had worked out what she would do. She had her passport and she had her credit card. She had checked both when she looked inside her handbag. She had her plan, because it was the one she had used on training exercises in little English towns, and later with modifications in Berlin. In the world of ordinary mortals it was dusk. In the courtyard, two priests were talking in low voices with their heads together, swinging their rosaries behind their backs. The street was packed with shoppers. A hundred people could have been watching her, and when she began to count the possibilities in her mind, a hundred seemed about the likely figure. She imagined a kind of Vienna Quorn, with Nigel as Master and Georgie and Fergus as Whips, and bearded little Lederer heading up the bunch, and teams of Czech hoods in hot pursuit. And poor old Jack, unhorsed, plodding over the horizon after them.

She chose the Imperial which Magnus loved for its pomp.

"I've no luggage, I'm afraid, but I'd like a room for the night," she said to the silver-haired receptionist, handing him the credit card, and the receptionist, who recognised her at once, said, "How is your husband, madam?"

A chasseur showed her to a magnificent bedroom on the first floor. Room 121 that everybody asks for, she thought; the very room I brought him to on his birthday for dinner and a night of love. The memory did not move her in the least. She phoned down to the same receptionist and asked him to book her on tomorrow morning's flight to London: "Of course, Frau Pym." Smoke, she remembered. Smoke was what we called deception. She sat on the bed listening to the footsteps go quiet in the corridor as the dinner hour drew nearer. Double doors, twelve foot high. Painting called *Evening on the Bosphorus* by Eckenbrecher. "I'll love you till we're both too old," he'd said, with his head on that very pillow. "Then I'll go on loving you." The phone rang. It was the concierge to say only club class was available. Mary said, then take club. She kicked her shoes off and held them in her hand while she softly opened the door and peered out. If I think I'm being watched I'll put my shoes out to be cleaned. Burble and canned music from the bar. A whiff of dill sauce from the dining-room. Fish. They have such good fish. She stepped onto the landing, waited but still no one came. Marble statues. Portrait of bewhiskered nobleman. She pulled her shoes on, climbed one staircase, called the lift and descended to the ground floor, emerging in a side corridor out of sight of the reception area. A darkened passage led towards the rear of the hotel. She followed it, heading for a service door at the far end. The door was ajar. She pushed it, already smiling apologetically. An elderly waiter was adding the finishing touches to a private dinner table. Another door stood open behind him, leading to a side street. With a jolly *"Guten Abend"* to the waiter, Mary stepped quickly into the fresh air and hailed a cab. "Wienerwald," she told the driver and heard him announce it over the intercom: "Wienerwald." Nothing was following. Approaching the Ring she gave him a hundred schillings, hopped out at a pedestrian crossing and took a second cab to the airport where she sat reading in the ladies' loo for an hour until the last flight to Frankfurt.

It was earlier on the same evening.

The house was semi-detached and backed on to a railway embankment exactly as Tom had described. Once again Brotherhood reconnoitred it before making his approach. The road was as straight as the railway and seemingly as long. Nothing but the setting autumn sun disturbed the skyline. There was the road, there was the embankment with its telegraph lines and water tower, and there was the huge sky of Brotherhood's raggedy-arsed childhood which was always filled with white cloud left by the stop-go trains as they trundled across the fens to Norwich. The houses were all of the same design, and as he studied them their symmetry became beautiful to him without his understanding why. This was the order of life, he thought. This line of little English coffins is what I thought I was preserving. Decent white men in ordered rows. Number 75 had replaced his wooden gate with a wrought-iron one, with "Eldorado" done in curly handwriting. Number 77 had laid himself a concrete path with seashells bedded in it. Number 81 had faced himself in rustic teak. And number 79, upon which Brotherhood now advanced, was resplendent with a Union Jack fluttering from a fine white flagpole planted just inside his territory. The tyre marks of a heavy vehicle were cut into the little gravel drive. An electric speaker was set beside the polished doorbell. Brotherhood pressed and waited. A gasp of atmospherics greeted him, followed by a wheezing male voice.

"Who the bloody hell's that?"

"Are you Mr. Lemon?" Brotherhood said into the microphone.

"What if I am?" said the voice.

"My name is Marlow. I wondered whether I might have a quiet word with you on a private matter."

"I've got two of them and they both work. Piss off."

In the window bay the net curtain parted far enough for Brotherhood to glimpse a bronzed, shiny little face, very wrinkled, observing him from the darkness.

"Let me put it this way," said Brotherhood more softly, still into the microphone. "I'm a friend of Magnus Pym."

A further crackling while the voice the other end seemed to regather strength.

"Well why the hell didn't you say so in the first place? Come in and have a wet."

Syd Lemon was a tiny, thickset old man these days, dressed all in brown like a rabbit. His brown hair, without a fleck of grey, was parted down the centre of his skull. His brown tie had horses' heads looking doubtfully at his heart. He wore a trim brown cardigan and pressed brown trousers and his brown toecaps shone like conkers. From amid a maze of sun-baked wrinkles two bright animal eyes shone merrily, though his breath came hard to him. He carried a blackthorn stick with a rubber ferrule, and when he walked he swung his little hips like a skirt to get himself along.

"The next time you press that bell, just say you're an Englishman," he advised as he led the way down the tiny, spotless hall. On the walls Brotherhood saw photographs of racehorses, and a younger Syd Lemon wearing Ascot rig. "After that you state your business clearly and I'll tell you to piss off again," he ended with a gush of laughter and pivoted awkwardly on his stick so that he could wink at Brotherhood and show him it was just his joke.

"How is the young tyke then?" said Syd.

"In excellent shape, thank you," said Brotherhood.

Without warning Syd sat himself abruptly on a high-backed chair, then leaned cautiously forward on his stick like a tiny dowager until he had the angle that cost him least discomfort. Brotherhood saw dark shadows under his eyes and a film of sweat on his forehead.

"You'll have to do the honours for us today, squire, I'm not myself," he said. "It's in the corner. Lift the lid. I'll take a drop of the scotch one for my health and you'll please yourself."

A thick maroon carpet ran wall to wall. A lurid painting of a Swiss scene hung above the tiled fireplace, to one side of which stood a fine burr-walnut cocktail cabinet. As Brotherhood lifted the lid, a music box began playing a tune, which was what Syd had been waiting for it to do.

"Know that one, do you?" said Syd. "Listen to it. Put the lid down again— that's right—now pull it up. There we go."

"It's 'Underneath the Arches,' " Brotherhood said with a smile.

"Course it is. His dad give it me. 'Syd,' he says. 'I can't afford a gold watch just now, and I'm afraid there's a temporary problem of liquidity about your pension. But there's an article of furniture I possess which has given us a lot of fun down the corridor of years which is worth a bob or two and I'd like you to have it as a small token.' So we run the van up, me and Meg, before the repossession artists got their hands on it. Five years ago that was. He'd bought six of them from Harrods to see his contacts right. There was this one left. He never asked for it back, not once. 'Still playing, is she, Syd?' he'd say. 'Many a good tune played on an old fiddle, you know. I can still surprise them myself.' He could too. The bloody keyholes wasn't safe when he was around. Right till the end. I couldn't get to the funeral. I was indisposed. How was it?"

"I'm told it was beautiful," said Brotherhood.

"Well it would be. He'd made his mark. They weren't burying just anybody, you know. That man had shaken hands with some of the Highest in the Land. He called the Duke of Edinburgh 'Philip.' Did they write about him when he died? I looked in a few papers but I didn't see a lot. Then I thought, Well they're probably saving it up for the Sundays. Of course you can never tell with Fleet Street. I'd have slipped up there if I'd been well, offered them a few bob to make sure. Are you a bogey, sir?"

Brotherhood laughed.

"You look like a bogey. I did time for him, you know. A lot of us did as a matter of fact. 'Lemon,' he says—always called me by my surname when he wanted something very badly, I never knew why—'Lemon, they'll get me on my signature on those documents. Now if I was to deny it was my signature, and you was to say you'd forged it, nobody would be the wiser, would they?' 'Well,' I said, 'I would. I'd do a lot of time for it,' I said to him. 'If doing time makes you wise, I'm going to be as wise as Methuselah,' I said. I still did it, mind. I don't know why. He said I'd have fifty grand when I come out. I knew I wouldn't. I suppose you could call it friendship really. A cocktail cabinet like that, you couldn't get one to save your life these days. Here's to him. Mud in your eye."

"Cheers," said Brotherhood and drank while Syd looked on approvingly.

"So what are you if you're not a bogey? Are you one of his airy-fairy Foreign Office friends? You don't look like an airy-fairy. More like a boxer to me, if you're not a bogey. Ever do that at all, did you, the fight game? Ringside seats we used to have, every time. We was there the night Joe Baksi said goodbye to poor old Bruce Woodcock. We had to have a bath afterwards, get the blood off. Then round to the Albany Club and there was Joe standing at the bar without a mark on him, a couple of Lovelies beside him there, and Rickie says to him, 'Why didn't you finish him off, Joe? Why did you spin it out like that, round after round?' Wonderful way with words he had. 'Rickie,' says Joe, 'I couldn't do it. I hadn't got the heart and that's a fact. Every time I hit him he was going "oooh—oooh"—like that—I couldn't put the finisher in and that's a fact.' "

While he continued to listen, Brotherhood allowed his eye to fall idly upon the imprint of an absent piece of furniture in a corner of the room. The shape of it was square, perhaps two foot by two, and it had cut through the carpet pile to the canvas backing underneath. "Did Magnus come along that night as well?" he enquired jovially, turning the conversation delicately back upon the purpose of his visit.

"He was too young, sir," Syd replied stoutly. "Too tender he was. Rickie would have took him but Meg she said no. 'You leave him with me,' she said. 'You boys can go out, you can have your fun. But Titch stays here with me and we'll go to a flick and have a nice evening and that's it.' Well, you didn't quarrel with Meg when she said a thing like that, not twice you didn't. I'd be broke today without her. I'd have given him every penny I had. But Meg, she put a bit away. She knew her Syd. Knew her Rickie too—a bit too well, I thought sometimes. Still you can't blame her. He was bent, you see. We was all bent, but Titch's dad was very bent indeed. Took me a long time to realise that. Still, if he came back, I suppose we'd all do the same." He laughed though it hurt him to do so. "We'd do the same and more, I'll bet we would. Is Titch in trouble, then?"

"Why should he be?" said Brotherhood, lifting his gaze away from the corner of the room.

"You tell me. You're the bogey, not me. You could run a prison with a face like that. I shouldn't be talking to you. I can feel it. I'd walk into the office one day. Audley Street. Mount Street. Chester Street. Old Burlington. Conduit. Park Lane.

Always the best addresses. Nothing altered. Everything nice and tidy. Receptionist there, sitting at her desk like the Mona Lisa. 'Morning, Mr. Lemon.' 'Morning, sweetheart.' But I'd know. I'd see it in her face. I'd hear the quiet. Hullo, I'd say to myself. It's the bogies. They've been having a word with Rickie. Off you go, Syd, it's out the back door fast. I was never wrong. Not once. Even if it was another twelve months without the option when they nicked me, I always had the nose for when the trouble started."

"When did you last see him then?"

"Couple of years ago. Maybe more. He stayed away after Meg went, I don't know why. I'd have thought he'd come more but he didn't like it. Didn't like people dying on him, I suppose. Didn't like people being poor, or no-hopers. He stood for Parliament once, you know. He'd have got in too if we'd started a week earlier. Same as his horses. Always leaving it too late at the finish. He'd ring up of course. Loved the telephone, always did. Never happy if the blower wasn't ringing."

"I was meaning Magnus," said Brotherhood patiently. "Titch."

"I thought you might be," said Syd. He began coughing. His whisky stood on the table in front of him but he hadn't touched it although it was in reach. He doesn't drink any more, thought Brotherhood. It's there for the decorum. The coughing ended and left him breathless.

"Magnus came and saw you," said Brotherhood.

"Did he? I didn't notice. When was that?"

"On his way to see Tom. After the funeral."

"How did he do that then?"

"Drove out here. Sat with you. Chatted about old times. He was pleased he came. He told young Tom afterwards. 'I had a lovely talk with Syd,' he said. 'It was just like old times.' He wanted everyone to know."

"Did he tell you that?"

"He told Tom."

"Didn't tell you though. Or you wouldn't need to come here. I always reasoned that. I was never wrong. 'If the bogies ask, it's because they don't know. So don't tell them. If they ask and they do know, they're trying to catch you out. So don't tell 'em either.' I used to say the same to Rickie but he wouldn't listen. It was being a Mason partly. It made him feel immune if he talked enough. That's how they got him, nine times out of ten. He talked himself into it." He barely paused. "Listen, squire. I'll do a deal with you. You tell me what you want and I'll tell you to piss off. How's that?"

A long silence followed but Brotherhood's patient smile did not tire. "Tell me something. What's that Union Jack doing out there?" he suggested. "Does it have a meaning at all, or is it just a big flower for the garden?"

"It's a scarecrow for keeping off foreigners and bogies."

As if he were producing a photograph of his family, Brotherhood drew out his green card, the one he had shown to Sefton Boyd. Syd drew a pair of spectacles from his pocket and read it back and front. A train thundered past but he appeared not to hear it.

"Is this a con?" he asked.

"I'm in the same business as that flag," Brotherhood said. "If that's a con."

"Could be. Everything could be."

"You were Eighth Army, weren't you? I understand you picked up a small medal at Alamein as well. Was that a con, too?"

"Could have been."

"Magnus Pym is in a little bit of trouble," said Brotherhood. "To be perfectly honest with you, which I always am with people, he seems to have temporarily disappeared."

Syd's small face had tightened. His breathing became harsh and quick. "Who's disappeared him, then? You? He hasn't been messing with Muspole's boys, has he?"

"Who's Muspole?"

"Friend of Rickie's. He knew people."

"He may have been lifted, he may have gone into hiding. He was playing a dangerous game with some very bad foreigners."

"Foreigners eh? Well he had the parley-voo, didn't he?"

"He was working under cover. For his country. And for me."

"Well he's a silly little bugger then," said Syd angrily and, hauling a perfectly ironed handkerchief from his pocket, dusted his shiny face. "I've no patience with him. Meg saw it. 'He'll go to the bad,' she said. 'There's a copper in that boy, you mark my words. He's a natural grass. Born to it.'"

"This wasn't grassing, this was risking his neck," said Brotherhood.

"That's what you say. That's what you think perhaps. Well you're wrong. Never satisfied, that boy wasn't. God wasn't half good enough for him. Ask Meg. You can't. She's gone. She was a wise one, Meg was. She was a woman, but she had more sense in one eye than you and me and half the world together. He's been playing both ends against the middle, I know. Meg always said he would."

"How did he look when he came and saw you?"

"Healthy. Everyone does. Roses in his nasty little cheeks. I always know when he wants something. He's charming, like his dad. I said, 'A bit more mourning would become you by the look of you.' He wouldn't hear of it. 'It was a beautiful service, Syd,' he says. 'You'd have loved it.' Well that was smoke up my arse for a start. 'They was packed together like sardines and there still wasn't room for them in the church.' 'Moonshine,' I said. 'They was in the square outside, they were queuing down the street, Syd. There must have been a thousand people there. If the Irish had let a bomb off, they'd have deprived this country of its finest brains.' 'Was Philip there?' I said. 'Course he was.' Well, I mean he couldn't have been, could he, or they'd have had it in the papers and the telly. Well, I suppose he could have gone incognito. I'm told they do that a lot these days, thanks to the Irish. He had a friend once. Kenny Boyd. His mum was a lady. Rick had a how d'you do with his aunt. Maybe he went to young Kenny. He might."

Brotherhood shook his head.

"Belinda? She was straight, always, although he bilked her. He could go to Belinda any time."

Brotherhood shook it again.

"I mean, a thousand mourners," Syd objected. "*Creditors,* if you like. Not mourners. You don't mourn Rick. Not really. You heave a bit of a sigh of relief, to be frank. Then you look in your wallet and thank old Meg there's still a bit left over for yourself. I didn't tell Titch that. It wouldn't have been appropriate. . . . Did Philip go? Did *you* hear anything about Philip going?"

"It was a lie," said Brotherhood.

Syd was shocked. "Ah now, that's a bit hard, that is. That's copper's talk. Magnus was conning me, put it that way, same as his dad did."

"Why?" said Brotherhood.

Syd didn't hear.

"What did he want?" said Brotherhood. "Why would he take so much trouble to con you?"

Syd was overacting. He frowned. He pursed his lips. He dusted the tip of his brown nose. "Wanted to see me right, didn't he?" he said too brightly. "Flannel me along. 'I'll go and chat up old Syd. Make him feel nice.' Oh we was always friends. Great friends. A father to him I was, quite often. And Meg was a truly incredible mother." Perhaps with old age he had lost the liar's art. Or perhaps he had never quite had it in the first place. "He just wanted a social, that's all. Comfort, that's what it comes down to. I'll comfort you, you comfort me. He was always fond of Meg, you see. Even when she saw through him. Loyal. I'll say that."

"Who's Wentworth?" Brotherhood said.

Syd's face had slammed tight as a prison door. "Who's who, old boy?"

"Wentworth."

"No. No, I don't think so. I don't think I know a Wentworth. More a place. Why, is a Wentworth giving him trouble then?"

"Sabina. Did he ever mention a Sabina?"

"That's a racehorse, isn't it? Wasn't there a Princess Sabina who was fancied for the Gold Cup last year?"

"Who's Poppy?"

"Here. Is Magnus playing the Lovelies again? Mind you, he wouldn't be his dad's son if he didn't."

"What did he come here for?"

"I told you. Comfort." Then, by a kind of cruel magnetism, Syd's gaze slid to the spot where a piece of furniture had stood, before returning, too brazenly, to Brotherhood.

"Well then," said Syd.

"Tell us something, do you mind?" said Brotherhood. "What was in that corner there?"

"Where?"

"There."

"Nothing."

"Furniture? Keepsakes?"

"Nothing."

"Something of your wife's you've sold?"

"Meg's? I wouldn't sell anything of Meg's if I was starving."

"What made those lines then?"

"What lines?"

"Where I'm pointing. In the carpet. What made them?"

"Fairies. What's it to do with you?"

"What's it to do with Magnus?"

"Nothing. I told you. Don't repeat things. It annoys me."

"Where is it?"

"Gone. It isn't anything. It's nothing."

Leaving Syd sitting in his chair, Brotherhood ran up the narrow stairs two at a time. The bathroom was ahead of him. He looked inside then stepped to the main bedroom left. A frilly pink divan filled most of the room. He looked under it, felt beneath the pillows, looked under them. He pulled open the wardrobe and swept aside rows of camel-hair coats and costly women's dresses. Nothing. A second bedroom lay across the landing but it contained no piece of heavy furniture two feet by two, just heaps of very beautiful white hide suitcases. Returning to the ground floor he inspected the dining-room and kitchen and, from the rear window, the tiny garden leading to the embankment. There was no hut, no garage. He returned to the parlour. Another train was passing. He waited for the sound of it to fade before he spoke. Syd was sitting hard forward in his chair. His hands were clasped over the handle of his blackthorn, his chin rested passively upon them.

"And the tyre marks in your drive," said Brotherhood. "Did the fairies make them too?"

Then Syd spoke. His lips were tight and the words seemed to hurt him. "Do you swear to me, Scout's honour, copper, that this is for his country?"

"Yes."

"Is what he done, which I don't believe and don't want to know, unpatriotic or could be?"

"It could be. The most important thing for all of us is to find him."

"And may you rot if you're lying to me?"

"And may I rot."

"You will, copper. Because I love that boy but I never did wrong by my country. He come here to con me, that's true. He wanted the filing cabinet. Old green filing cabinet Rick gave me to look after when he went off on his travels. 'Now Rick's dead, you can release his papers. It's all right,' he says. 'It's legal. They're mine. I'm his heir, aren't I?' "

"What papers?"

"His dad's life. All his debts. His secrets, you might say. Rickie always kept them in this special cabinet. What he owed us all. One day he was going to see everybody right, we'd never want for anything again. I said no at first. I'd always said no when Rickie was alive, and I didn't see nothing had changed it. 'He's dead,' I said. 'Let him have his peace. Nobody never had a better pal than your old dad and you know it, so just you stop asking questions and get on with your own life,' I says. There's some bad things in that cabinet. Wentworth was one of them. I don't know the other names you said. Maybe they're in there too."

"Maybe they are."

"He argued around and so finally I said 'Take it.' If Meg had been here, he'd never have had it off me, legal heir or not, but she's gone. I couldn't refuse him, that's the truth. I never could, no more than what I could his dad. He was going to write a book. I didn't like that either. 'Your dad never held with books, Titch,' I said. 'You know that. He was educated in the university of the world.' He didn't listen. He never would when he wanted something. 'All right,' I said. 'Take it. And maybe that'll get him off your back. Shove it in the car and piss off,' I said, 'I'll get the big Mick from next door to help you lift it.' He wouldn't. 'The car's not right for it,' he says. 'It's not going where the cabinet's going.' 'All right,' I says, 'then leave it here and shut up.' "

"Did he leave anything else here?"

"No."

"Was he carrying a briefcase?"

"A black airy-fairy job with the Queen's badge on it and two keyholes."

"How long did he stay?"

"Long enough to con me. An hour, half an hour, what do I know? Wouldn't even sit down. Couldn't. He walked back and forth all the time in his black tie, smiling. Kept looking out of the window. 'Here,' I said, 'which bank have you robbed, then? I'll go and take my money out.' He used to laugh at jokes like that. He didn't, but he was smiling all the time. Well, funerals, they take you in a lot of ways, don't they? I could have done without his smiling all the same."

"So then he left. With the cabinet?"

"Course he didn't. He sent the lorry, didn't he?"

"Of course he did," said Brotherhood, cursing himself for his stupidity.

He was seated close to Syd and he had put his whisky beside Syd's on the beaten-brass Indian table that Syd kept polished till it shone like the Eastern sun. Syd was speaking very reluctantly, and his voice had almost died.

"How many?"

"Two blokes."

"Did you give them a cup of tea?"

"Course I did."

"See their lorry?"

"Course I did. I was looking out for them, wasn't I? That's a major entertainment, that is, round here, a lorry."

"What was the firm?"

"I don't know. It wasn't written, was it? It was a plain lorry. More like a hired one."

"Colour?"

"Green."

"Hired from who?"

"How should I know?"

"Did you sign anything?"

"Me? You're daft. They had a tea, loaded up, and buggered off."

"Where were they taking it?"

"The depot, weren't they?"

"Where's the depot?"

"Canterbury."

"You sure?"

"Course I'm sure. Canterbury. Package for Canterbury. Then they complained about the weight. They always do that, they think it gets them more dropsy."

"Did they say package for Pym?"

"Canterbury. I told you."

"Did they have a name at all?"

"Lemon. Call at Lemon's, get the package for Canterbury. I'm Lemon. The answer is a Lemon."

"Did you see the number of the lorry?"

"Oh yes. Wrote it down. I mean that's my hobby, lorry numbers."

Brotherhood managed a smile. "Well, can you at least remember what make of lorry it might have been?" he asked. "Distinguishing marks and whatnot?"

It was a harmless enough question, harmlessly put. Brotherhood himself had little expectation of it. It was the kind of question that unasked leaves a gap, but asked produces no dividend: part of the necessary luggage of the interrogator's trade. Yet it was the last that Brotherhood put to Syd on that dying autumn evening, and as a matter of fact it was the last in his short but desperate search for Magnus Pym, because after it he had only answers to concern him. Yet Syd refused point-blank to address himself to it. He started to speak, but then he changed his mind and clapped his mouth shut with a little pop. His chin came off his hands, his head lifted, then by degrees his whole little body lifted too, painfully but strictly from the chair, as if a distant bugle had summoned him to a last parade. His back arched, he held his stick to his side.

"I don't want that boy doing prison," he said with a husk to his voice. "Do you hear me? And I'm not going to help you put him there. His dad did prison. I did prison. And I don't want the boy there. It bothers me. Nothing personal, copper, but on your way."

It's over, thought Brotherhood calmly, staring round the crowded conference table in Brammel's suite on the Fifth Floor. This is my last feast with you. I shall walk out of this door a gamekeeper's son of sixty. A dozen pairs of hands lay under the downlight like corpses waiting to be identified. To his left languished the tailor-made worsted sleeves of the Foreign Office representative named Dorney. Heraldic lions postured on his gold cufflinks. Beyond Dorney reposed the unspoiled fingertips of his master Brammel, whose mid-Surrey heredity needed no advertisement. Beyond Bo sat Mountjoy from Cabinet. Then the rest. In his mood of increasing alienation Brotherhood found it difficult to put the voices to the hands. Not that it mattered any more because tonight they were one voice and one dead hand. They are the body corporate I once believed was greater than the sum of its parts, he thought. In my lifetime I have witnessed the birth of the jet airplane and the atom bomb and the computer, and the demise of the British institution. We have nothing to clear away but ourselves. The musty midnight air smelt of decay. Nigel was reading the death certificate.

"They waited outside the Lumsden house till six-twelve, then telephoned the house from a callbox down the road. Mrs. Lumsden replied that she and her maid were looking for Mrs. Pym at this moment. Mary had taken herself for a walk in the back garden and not returned. She'd been out more than an hour. The garden was empty. Lumsden himself was at the Residence. The Ambassador apparently required him."

"I hope nobody's going to try and blame the Lumsdens for this," said Dorney.

"I'm sure not," said Bo.

"She left no note, no word to anyone," Nigel continued. "She'd been preoccupied during the day but that was natural. We checked the airlines and found she was booked to London on tomorrow morning's British Airways flight club class. She gave her address as the Imperial Hotel, Vienna."

"This morning's," somebody corrected, and Brotherhood saw Nigel's gold watch tilt sharply towards him.

"This morning's flight then," Nigel agreed testily. "When we checked the

Imperial she wasn't in her room and when we tried the airport a second time we established she'd taken a standby seat on the last flight of the day, Lufthansa to Frankfurt. Unfortunately we did not come by this information until after the Frankfurt flight had landed at its destination."

She diddled you, thought Brotherhood with a satisfaction bordering on pride. She's a good girl and knows the game.

"Isn't it rather a pity you couldn't have found out about Frankfurt the *first* time you went to the airport?" said an unbeliever boldly from the end of the table.

"Of course it's a pity," Nigel snapped. "But if you had been listening a little more closely, I think you would have heard me say that she took a standby seat. The official flight list bearing her name was therefore not complete until literally the moment when the plane took off."

"Sounds a bit of a muddle all the same," said Mountjoy. "What about the unofficial flight list?"

No, thought Brotherhood. It is not a muddle. To make a muddle you must first have order. This is inertia, this is normality. What was once a great service has become an immovable hybrid—half bureaucrat, half freebooter, and using the arguments of the one to negate the other.

"So where is she?" somebody asked.

"We don't know," said Nigel with satisfaction. "And short of asking the Germans—and incidentally of course the Americans—to search every hotel in Frankfurt, which seems a long shot to say the least, I fail to see what more we can do. Or could have done. Frankly."

"Jack?" said Brammel.

Brotherhood heard an older version of his own voice ebb into the darkness. "God knows," he said. "Probably sitting on her backside in Prague by now."

Nigel again. "She's done nothing *wrong* as far as anyone knows. We can't keep her prisoner against her will, you know. She's a free citizen. If her son wants to join her there next week there's not much we can do about *that* either."

Mountjoy voiced a previous worry. "I do think the telephone intercept from the American Embassy *is* fairly extraordinary. This woman Lederer, sitting in Vienna, screaming to her husband in London about two people exchanging messages in church. That was our church she was talking about. Mary was *there*. Couldn't we have made a few deductions from that?"

Nigel had his answer pat: "Only long after the event, I'm afraid. Perfectly understandably, the transcribers saw nothing dramatic in the intercept and passed it to us twenty-four hours after the phone call had taken place. The information that *would* have put us on the alert—namely that Mary had been seen *possibly* emerging from a Czech safe flat where this man Petz and so forth had previously been housed—therefore reached us *before* the intercept. You can hardly blame us because we didn't put the cart before the horse, can you?"

Nobody seemed to know whether they could or couldn't.

Mountjoy said it was time to take a view. Dorney said they really must decide whether to call in the police and circulate Pym's photograph, and be damned. At this Brammel came sharply to life.

"If we do that, we may as well put up the shutters," he said. "We're so nearly there. We're so *warm*, aren't we, Jack?"

"I'm afraid we're not," said Brotherhood.

"But of course we are!"

"It's guesswork. Still. We need the furniture van. That won't be a simple job either. He'll have used cut-outs, halfway houses. The police know how to do those things. We don't have a chance. He's using the name of Canterbury. Or we think he is. That's because in the past all his worknames have been places—he's got a tic about that. Colonel Manchester, Mr. Hull, Mr. Gulworth. On the other hand they just may have taken the cabinet to Canterbury and Canterbury is where he is. Or they've taken it to Canterbury and Canterbury is where he isn't. We need a square beside the sea and a house with a woman in it whom he apparently loves. She's not in Scotland or Wales because that's where he says she is. We are not in a position to comb every seaside town in the United Kingdom. The police are."

"He's mad," said a ghost.

"Yes, he's mad. He's been betraying us for more than thirty years and so far we have failed to certify him. Our error. So we may as well agree that he makes a pretty decent show of being sane when he needs to, and that his tradecraft is damn good. Is anybody nearer to him than I am?"

The door opened and closed. Kate was standing before them with an armful of red striped folders. She was pale and very steady, like a sleepwalker. She laid one folder before each guest.

"These have just come up from Sig. Int.," she said, to Bo only. "They ran the *Simplicissimus* bookcode across the Czech transmissions. The results are positive."

At seven in the morning the London streets were empty but Brotherhood marched in them as if they were full, keeping a straight back among the falterers and weaklings, a man of bearing in a crowd. A solitary policeman wished him good morning. Brotherhood was the kind of man policemen greeted. Thank you, Officer, he thought, striding yet more purposefully. You have just smiled on the man who befriended tomorrow's newest traitor—the man who fought off criticism of him until the case became unanswerable, then fought off his apologists when it became unfaceable. Why do I begin to understand him? he wondered, marvelling at his own tolerance. Why is it that in my heart if not my intellect I sense a stirring of sympathy for the man who all his life has made a failure of my successes? What I made him do, he made me pay for.

You brought it on yourself, Belinda had said. Then why was it that, as with his dangling arm at the moment it was shot to pieces, he had yet to feel the pain?

He's in Prague, he thought. The chase game of the last few days was a Czech fan dance to keep us looking the wrong way while they smuggled him to safety. Mary would never have gone there unless Magnus was ahead of her. Mary would never have gone there, period.

Would she? Wouldn't she? He didn't know and he wouldn't have trusted anybody who said they did. To leave Plush and all her Englishness behind? For Magnus now?

She'd never do it.

She'd do it for Magnus.

Tom will come first for her.

She'll stay.

She'll take Tom with her.

I need a woman.

An all-night coffee shop stood at the corner of Half Moon Street and on other early mornings Brotherhood might have stopped there and let the tired whores make a fuss of his dog, and Brotherhood in return would have made a fuss of the whores, bought them a coffee and chatted them up, because he liked their tradecraft and their guts and their mixture of human canniness and stupidity. But his dog was dead and so for the time being was his sense of fun. He unlocked his door and headed for the sideboard where the vodka was. He poured himself a warm half tumbler and drank it down. He ran a bath, switched on his transistor radio and took it to the bathroom. The news reported disasters everywhere but no British diplomatic couple surfacing in Prague. If the Czechs want to blow the whistle they'll do it at midday in order to catch the evening television and tomorrow's papers, he thought. He began shaving. The phone was ringing. It's Nigel saying we've found him, he was at his club all the time. It's the duty officer reporting that the Prague Foreign Ministry has put out a midday press call for foreign correspondents. It's Steggie, saying he likes strong men.

He switched off the radio, walked naked to the drawing-room, snatched up the receiver, said "Yes?" and heard a ping, then nothing. He pressed his lips together as a warning to himself not to speak. He was praying. He was definitely praying. Speak, he prayed. Say something. Then he heard it: three short taps of a coin or a nail-file on the drum of the mouthpiece: *Prague procedures.* Casting round for something metal, he saw his fountain pen on the writing table and managed to seize it without relinquishing the telephone. He tapped once in return: *I am reading you.* Two more taps, then three again. *Stay where you are,* said the message. *I have information for you.* With his pen he gave four taps to the mouthpiece and heard two in reply before the caller rang off. He ran his fingers through his stubble hair. He took his vodka to the desk and sat down, put his face in his hands. Keep alive, he prayed. It's the networks. It's Pym, putting it all right. Keep clever. I'm here, if that's what you're asking. I'm here and waiting for your next signal. Don't call again until you're ready.

The phone screamed a second time. He lifted the receiver but it was only Nigel. Pym's description and photograph were on their way to every police station in the country, he said. The Firm was switching to the operational telephone lines only. Bo had ordered the Whitehall lines disconnected. The press contacts were already beating down the doors. Why is he talking to me? Brotherhood wondered. Is he lonely or is he giving me a chance to say I've just had this funny phone call from a Joe using Prague procedures? It's the funny call, he decided.

"Some joker just phoned me with a Czech call sign," he said. "I gave him the signal to speak but he wouldn't. God alone knows what it was about."

"Well if anything comes through, let us know at once. Use the operational line."

"So you said," said Brotherhood.

Waiting again. Thinking of every Joe who had ever come through badland. Take your time. Move carefully and with confidence. Don't panic. Don't run. Take your time. Pick your phone box. He heard a knock at the door. It's some bloody hawker. Kate's taken her overdose. It's that fool Arab boy who lives downstairs and always thinks my bathroom's leaking on him. He pulled on a dressing-gown, opened the door and saw Mary. He hauled her inside and slammed the door. Whatever seized him after that he didn't know. Relief or fury, remorse or indignation. He slapped her once, then he slapped her again and on a clear day he would have taken her straight to bed.

"There's a place called Farleigh Abbott near Exeter," she said.

"What of it?"

"Magnus told him he'd put his mother in a house beside the sea in Devon."

"Told who?"

"Poppy. His Czech controller. They were students together in Bern. He thinks Magnus is going to kill himself. I suddenly realised. That's what's in the burnbox with the secrets. The Station gun. Isn't it?"

"How do you know it's Farleigh Abbott?"

"He talked about his mother in Devon. He hasn't got a bloody mother. His only place in Devon is Farleigh Abbott. 'When I was in Devon,' he'd say. 'Let's go to Devon for a holiday.' It was Farleigh Abbott, always. We never went and he stopped talking about it. Rick used to take him there from school. They used to picnic and bicycle on the beach. It's one of his ideal places. He's there with a woman. I know he is."

15

You will imagine, Tom, with what glory in his youthful heart the brilliant intelligence officer and lover celebrated the completion of his two years of devoted service to the flag in distant Austria and set about returning to civilian England. His leave-taking from Sabina was not as heart-rending as he had feared, for as the day approached she feigned a Slav indifference to his departure.

"I shall be happy woman, Magnus. Your English wives will not make sour faces at me. I shall be economist and free woman, not the courtesan of a frivolous soldier." Nobody had ever called Pym frivolous before. She even took herself on leave ahead of him to forestall the agony of parting. She is being brave, Pym told himself. His farewell from Axel, though haunted by rumours of fresh purges, had a similarly rounded feel to it.

"Sir Magnus, whatever happens to me, we have done a great work together," he said as, in the evening light, they faced each other outside the barn that had become Pym's second home. "Never forget you owe me two hundred dollars."

"I never will," Pym said.

He began the long walk back to Sergeant Kaufmann's jeep. He turned to wave but Axel had vanished into the forest.

The two hundred dollars were a reminder of their increasing closeness during the final months of their relationship.

"My father's pressing me for money again," Pym had said one evening while they photographed a codebook he had borrowed from Membury's cricket locker. "The Burmese police are proposing to arrest him."

"Then send it to him," Axel had replied, winding back the film of his camera.

He slipped the film in his pocket and inserted a fresh one. "How much does he want?"

"Whatever it is, I haven't got it. I'm a subaltern on thirteen shillings a day, not a millionaire."

Axel had appeared to pay no further interest, and they turned instead to the topic of Sergeant Pavel. Axel said it was time to stage a fresh crisis in Pavel's life.

"But he had a crisis only last month," Pym had objected. "His wife threw him out of his apartment for drunkenness and we had to help him buy his way in again."

"We need a crisis," Axel had repeated firmly. "Vienna is beginning to take him for granted and I do not care for the tone of their follow-up questions."

Pym found Membury sitting at his desk. The afternoon sun was shining on one side of his friendly head while he read a fish book.

"I'm afraid Greensleeves wants a bonus of two hundred dollars cash," he said.

"But my dear chap, we've paid him a pot of money this month already! What on earth can he want two hundred dollars for?"

"He's got to buy his daughter an abortion. The doctor only takes U.S. dollars and it's getting urgent."

"But the child's a mere fourteen. Who's the man? They ought to throw him into prison."

"It's that Russian captain from headquarters."

"The pig. The utter swine."

"Pavel's a Roman Catholic too, you know," Pym reminded him. "Not a very good one, I agree. But it's not easy for him either."

The next night Pym counted two hundred dollars across the barn table. Axel tossed them back at him.

"For your father," he said. "A loan from me to you."

"I can't do that. Those are operational funds."

"Not any more. They belong to Sergeant Pavel." Pym still did not pick up the money. "And Sergeant Pavel lends them to you as your friend," Axel said, tearing a sheet of paper from his notebook. "Here—write me an I.O.U. Sign it and one day I shall make you pay it back."

Pym rode away in good heart, confident that Graz and all its responsibilities, like Bern, would cease to exist the moment he entered the first tunnel.

Laying down his arms at the Intelligence Corps Depot in Sussex, Pym was handed the following PRIVATE & CONFIDENTIAL letter by the demobilisation officer:

> The Government Overseas Research Group
> P.O. Box 777
> The Foreign Office
> London, S.W. 1

Dear Pym,

Mutual friends in Austria have passed your name to me as someone who might be interested in longer term employment. If this is so, would you care to lunch with me at the Travellers' Club for an informal chat on Friday the nineteenth at 12:45?

(Signed) Sir Alwyn Leith, C.M.G.

For several days a mysterious squeamishness held Pym back from replying. I need new horizons, he told himself. They are good people but limited. Feeling strong one morning, he wrote regretting he was considering a career in the Church.

"There's always Shell, Magnus," said Belinda's mother, who had taken Pym's future much to heart. "Belinda's got an uncle in Shell, haven't you, darling?"

"He wants to do something *worthwhile*, Mummy," Belinda said, stamping her foot and making the breakfast table rattle.

"Time somebody did," said Belinda's father from behind his *Telegraph*, and for some reason found this very funny, and went on laughing through his gapped teeth while Belinda stormed into the garden in a rage.

A more interesting contender for Pym's services was Kenneth Sefton Boyd, who had come into an inheritance and was proposing that he and Pym should open a nightclub. Keeping this intelligence from Belinda, who had views on nightclubs and the Sefton Boyds, Pym pleaded an engagement at his old school and took himself to the family estate in Scotland, where Jemima met him at the station. She was driving the very Land Rover from which she had glowered at him when they were children. She was more beautiful than ever.

"How was Austria?" she asked as they bumped cheerfully over purple Highlands towards a monstrous Victorian castle.

"Super," said Pym.

"Did you box and play rugger all the time?"

"Well not all the time, actually," Pym confessed.

Jemima cast him a look of protracted interest.

The Sefton Boyds lived in a parentless world. A disapproving retainer served them dinner. Afterwards they played backgammon until Jemima was tired. Pym's bedroom was as large as a football field and as cold. Sleeping lightly, he woke without stirring to see a dismembered red spark switching like a firefly across the darkness. The spark descended and disappeared. A pale shape advanced on him. He smelt cigarette and toothpaste and felt Jemima's naked body arrange itself softly around him, and Jemima's lips find his own.

"You won't mind if we turf you out on Friday, will you?" said Jemima while the three breakfasted in bed from a tray brought in by Sefton Boyd. "Only we've got Mark coming for the weekend."

"Who's Mark?" said Pym.

"Well I'm going to sort of marry him, actually," said Jemima. "I'd marry Kenneth if I could, but he's so conventional about those things."

Renouncing women, Pym wrote to the British Council offering to distribute culture among primitives, and to his old housemaster, Willow, asking for a position teaching German. "I greatly miss the school's discipline and have felt a keen loyalty towards it ever since my father failed to pay my fees." He wrote to Murgo booking himself in for an extended retreat, though he had the prudence to be vague about dates. He wrote to the Catholics of Farm Street asking to continue the instruction he had begun in Graz. He wrote to an English school in Geneva and an American school in Heidelberg, and to the BBC, all in a spirit of self-negation. He wrote to the Inns of Court about opportunities for reading law. When he had thus surrounded himself with a plethora of choices, he filled in an enormous form detailing his brilliant life till now and followed it to the Oxford Appointments Board in search of more. The morning was sunny; his old university city dazzled him with carefree memories of his days as a Communist informer. His interlocutor was whimsical if not downright fey. He pushed his spectacles to the top of his nose. He shoved them into his greying locks like an effeminate racing driver. He gave Pym sherry and put a hand on his backside in order to propel him to a long window that gave on to a row of council houses.

"How about a life in filthy industry?" he suggested.

"Industry would be fine," said Pym.

"Not unless you like eating with the crew. Do you like eating with the crew?"

"I'm really not very class-conscious actually, sir."

"How charming. And do you like having grease up to your elbows?"

Pym said he didn't mind grease either, actually, but by then he was being guided to a second window that gave on to spires and a lawn.

"I've a menial librarianship at the British Museum and a sort of third assistant clerkship to the House of Commons, which is the proletarian version of the Lords. I've bits and bobs in Kenya, Malaya, and the Sudan. I can do you nothing in India, they've taken it away from me. Do you like abroad or hate it?"

Pym said abroad was super, he had been to university in Bern. His interlocuter was puzzled. "I thought you went to university here."

"Here too," said Pym.

"Ah. Now do you like danger?"

"I love it, actually."

"You poor boy. Don't keep saying 'actually.' And will you give unquestioning allegiance to whoever is rash enough to employ you?"

"I will."

"Will you adore your country right or wrong so help you God and the Tory Party?"

"I will again," said Pym, laughing.

"Do you also believe that to be born British is to be born a winner in the great lottery of life?"

"Well, yes, to be honest, that too."

"Then be a spy," his interlocutor suggested and drew from his desk yet another application form and handed it to Pym. "Jack Brotherhood sends his love, and says why on *earth* haven't you been in touch with him, and why won't you have lunch with his nice recruiter?"

I could write whole essays for you, Tom, on the voluptuous pleasures of being interviewed. Of all the arts of affiliation Pym mastered, and throughout his life improved upon, the interview must stand in first place. We didn't have Office trick-cyclists in those days, as your Uncle Jack likes to call them. We didn't have anybody who wasn't himself a citizen of the secret world, blessed with the unlined innocence of privilege. The nearest they had come to life's experience was the war, and they saw the peace as its continuation by other means. Yet in the terms of the world outside their heads they had led lives so untested, so childlike and tender in their simplicities, so inward in their connections, that they required echelons of cut-outs to reach the society they honestly believed they were protecting. Pym sat before them, calm, reflective, resolute, modest. Pym composed his features in one mould after another, now of reverence, now of awe, zeal, passionate sincerity or spiritual good humour. He paraded pleasurable surprise when he heard that his tutors thought the world of him, and a stern-jawed pride on learning that the army loved him too. He modestly demurred or modestly boasted. He weeded out the half-believers from the believers and did not rest until he had converted the pack of them to paid-up life membership of the Pym supporters' club.

"Now tell us about your father, will you, Pym?" said a man with a droopy moustache uncomfortably reminiscent of Axel's. "Sounds a bit of a colourful sort of type to me."

Pym smiled ruefully, sensing the mood. Pym delicately faltered before rallying.

"I'm afraid he's a bit *too* colourful sometimes, sir," he said amid a hubble-bubble of male laughter. "I don't see a lot of him to be honest. We're still friends, but I rather steer clear of him. I have to, actually."

"Yes. Well, I don't think we can hold you responsible for the sins of your old man, can we?" said the same questioner indulgently. "It's you we're interviewing, not your papa."

How much did they know of Rick, or care? Even today I can only guess, for the question was never raised again and I am sure that in any formal way it went forgotten within days of Pym's acceptance. English gentlemen, after all, do not discriminate against each other on the grounds of percentage, only of breeding. Occasionally they must have read of one of Rick's more lurid collapses, and perhaps allowed themselves an amused smile. Here and there, presumably, word trickled down to them by way of their commercial contacts. But my suspicion is that Rick was an asset. A healthy streak of criminality in a young spy's background never did him any harm, they reasoned. "Grown up in a hard school," they told one another. "Could be useful."

The last question of the interview and Pym's answer echo for ever in my head. A military man in tweeds put it.

"Look here, young Pym," he demanded, with a thrust of his bucolic head. "You're by way of being a Czech buff. Speak their language a bit, know their people. What d'you say to these purges and arrests they're having over there? Worry you?"

"I think the purges are quite appalling, sir. But they are to be expected," said Pym, fixing his earnest gaze upon a distant, unreachable star.

"Why *expected?*" demanded the military man, as if nothing ought to be.

"It's a rotten system. It's superimposed on tribalism. It can only survive by the exercise of oppression."

"Yes, yes. Granted. So what would you do about it—*do?*"

"In what capacity, sir?"

"As one of us, you fool. Officer of this service. Anyone can talk. We *do.*"

Pym had no need to think. His patent sincerity was out there speaking for him already.

"I'd play their game, sir. I'd divide them against themselves. Spread rumour, false accusation, suspicion. I'd let dog eat dog."

"You mean you wouldn't mind getting innocent chaps chucked into prison by their own police, then? Being a bit harsh, aren't you? Bit immoral?"

"Not if it shortens the life of the system. No, sir, I don't think I am. And I'm not persuaded about the innocence of these men of yours either, I'm afraid."

In life, says Proust, we end up doing whatever we do second best. What Pym might have done better, I shall never know. He accepted the Firm's offer. He opened his *Times* and read with a similar detachment of his engagement to Belinda. That's me taken care of, then, he thought. With the Firm getting one half of me and Belinda the other, I'll never want for anything again.

Turn your eye to Pym's first great wedding, Tom. It occurs largely without his participation, in his last months of training, in a break between silent killing and a three-day seminar entitled Know Your Enemy, led by a vibrant young tutor from the London School of Economics. Imagine Pym's enjoyment of this unlikely preparation for his married state. The fun of it. The free-wheeling unreality! He has chased Buchan's ghost across the moors of Argyll. He has messed about in rubber boats, made night landings on sandy shores, with hot chocolate awaiting him in the vanquished enemy's headquarters. He has fallen out of aeroplanes, dipped into secret inks, learned Morse and tapped scatological radio signals into the bracing Scottish air. He has watched a Mosquito aeroplane glide a hundred feet above him through the darkness, dropping a boxful of boulders in place of genuine supplies. He has played secret games of fox-and-geese in the streets of Edinburgh, photographed innocent citizens without their knowledge, fired live bullets at pop-up targets in simulated drawing-rooms, and plunged his dagger into the midriff of a swinging sandbag, all for England and King Harry. In spells of quiet he has been dispatched to genteel Bath to improve his Czech at the feet of an ancient lady called Frau Kohl, who lives in a crescent house of impoverished splendour. Over tea and muffins, Frau Kohl shows him albums of her childhood in Carlsbad, now called Karlovy Vary.

"But you know Karlovy Vary very well, Mr. Sanderstead!" she cries when Pym shows off his knowledge. "You have been there, yes?"

"No," says Pym. "But I have a friend who has."

Then back to base camp Somewhere in Scotland to resume the red thread of violence that has been spun into every new thing he is learning. This violence is not only of the body. It is the ravishment that must be done to truth, friendship and, if need be, honour in the interest of Mother England. We are the chaps who do the dirty work so that purer souls can sleep in bed at night. Pym of course has heard these arguments before from the Michaels, but now he must hear them again, from his new employers, who make pilgrimages from London in order to warn the uncut young of the wily foreigners they will one day have to tangle with. Do you remember your own visit, Jack? A gala night it was, close to Christmas: the great Brotherhood is coming! We had streamers hanging from the rafters. You sat at the directing staff's table in the excellent canteen, while we young 'uns craned our necks to catch a glimpse of one of the great players of the Game. After dinner we gathered round you in a half circle, clutching our subsidised port, and you told us tales of derring-do until we crept off to bed and dreamed of being like you—though alas we could never really have your lovely war, even if that was what we were rehearsing for. Do you remember how in the morning, before you left, you called on Pym while he was shaving, and congratulated him on a damn good showing so far?

"Nice girl you're marrying, too," you said.

"Oh, do you know her, sir?" said Pym.

"Just good reports," you said complacently.

Then off you went, confident you had scattered a pinch more stardust in Pym's eyes. Which you had, Jack. You had. Except that what goes up with Pym has a way of coming down, and it annoyed him to discover that his impending marriage had received the Firm's approval while it still awaited his.

"So what *exactly* are you doing for a living, old boy? Don't quite understand," Belinda's father asked, not for the first time, during a discussion about whom to invite.

"It's a government-sponsored language lab, sir," said Pym, in accordance with the Firm's sketchy guidelines on cover. "We work out exchanges of academics from various countries and arrange courses for them."

"Sounds more like the Secret Service to me," said Belinda's father, with that queer cracked laugh of his that always seemed to know too much.

To his future spouse, on the other hand, Pym told everything he knew about his work, and more. He showed her how he could break her windpipe with a single blow, and put her eyes out with two fingers easily. And how she could smash the small bones in someone's foot if they were annoying her under the table. He told her everything that made him a secret hero of England, seeing the world right single-handed.

"So how many people have you killed?" Belinda asked him grimly, discounting those that he had merely maimed.

"I'm not allowed to say," said Pym, and with a crisping of the jaw stared away from her towards the stark wastelands of his duty.

"Well don't then," Belinda said. "And don't tell Daddy *anything*, or he'll tell Mummy."

"Dear Jemima"—Pym wrote on an off chance, a week before his great day—

"It seems so odd we are both getting married within a month of each other. I keep wondering whether we are doing the right thing. I'm sick of the boring work I'm doing, and considering a change. I love you. Magnus."

Pym waited eagerly for the mail and scanned the moors around the training camp for a sight of her Land Rover as she dashed over the horizon to save him. But nothing came, and by the eve of his wedding he was left with himself again, walking the night streets of London, and pretending they reminded him of Karlovy Vary.

And what a husband he was, Tom! What a match was celebrated! Priests of upper-class humility, the great church famed for its permanence and previous successes, the frugal reception in a tomblike Bayswater hotel, and there at the centre of the throng, our Prince Charming himself, chatting brilliantly to the crowned heads of suburbia. Pym forgot no one's name, was fluent and informative on the subject of government-sponsored language laboratories, vouchsafed Belinda long and tender glances. All this, at least, until somebody switched off the soundtrack, Pym's included, and the faces of his audience turned mysteriously way from him, looking for the cause of breakdown. Suddenly the interconnecting doors at the far end of the room, until now locked, were flung open by unseen hands. And Pym knew in his toes at once, just by the timing and the pause, and by the way people parted before the empty space, that somebody had rubbed the lamp. Two waiters entered with the grace of well-tipped men, bearing trays of uncorked bubbly and chargers of smoked salmon, though Belinda's mother had not ordered smoked salmon, and had decreed that no champagne be served before the toast to the bride and groom. After that it was the Gulworth election all over again, because first Mr. Muspole appeared, followed by a thin man with a razor slash, and each commandeered a doorpost as Rick swept between them in full Ascot rig, leaning backwards and holding his arms wide, and smiling everywhere at once. "Hullo, old son! Don't you recognise your old pal? Have this one on me, boys! Where's that bride of his? By Jove, son, she's a beauty! Come here, my dear. Give your old father-in-law a kiss! My God, there's some flesh here, son. Where have you been hiding her all these years?"

One on each arm, Rick marched the nuptial pair to the hotel forecourt, where a brand-new Jaguar car, painted Liberal yellow, stood parked in everybody's way, with white wedding ribbons tied to the bonnet, and a mile-high bunch of Harrods gardenias crammed into the passenger seat, and Mr. Cudlove at the wheel with a carnation in his mulberry buttonhole.

"Seen one of those before then, son? Know what it is? It's your old man's gift to both of you and nobody will ever take it away from you as long as I'm spared. Cuddie's going to drive you wherever you want to go and leave it with you, aren't you, Cuddie?"

"I wish you both all good fortune in your chosen walk of life, sir," Mr. Cudlove said, his loyal eyes filling with tears.

Of Rick's long speech, I remember only that it was beautiful and modest, and free of all hyperbole, and rested upon the theme that when two young people love each other, us old 'uns who have had our day should stand aside, because if anyone has deserved it, they have.

Pym never saw the car again, and it was a long while before he saw Rick either, because when they went back outside Mr. Cudlove and the yellow Jaguar had vanished, and two very obvious plainclothes police detectives were talking in low tones to the confused hotel manager. But I have to tell you, Tom, that it was the best of our wedding presents, barring perhaps the posy of red poppies, thrust into Pym's arms, without a card of explanation, by a man in a Polish-looking Burberry raincoat as Pym and Belinda rode into the sunset for a week at Eastbourne.

"Put him into the field while he's unsullied," says Personnel, who has a way of speaking about people as if they weren't seated across the desk from him.

Pym is trained. Pym is complete. Pym is armed and ready and only one question remains. What mantle shall he wear? What disguise shall cover the secret frame of his maturity? In a series of unconsummated interviews reminiscent of the Oxford Appointments Board, Personnel unlocks a bedlam of possibilities. Pym will be a freelance writer. But can he write and will Fleet Street have him? With disarming openness Pym is marched through the offices of most of our great national newspapers, whose editors inanely pretend they do not know where he has come from, or why, though henceforth they will know him for ever as a creature of the Firm, and he them. He is already halfway to stardom with the *Telegraph* when a Fifth Floor genius has a better plan: "Look here, how would you like to join up with the Coms again, trade on your old allegiances, get yourself a billet in the international left wing set? We've always wanted to chuck a stone into that pond."

"It sounds fascinating," says Pym as he sees himself selling *Marxism Today* on street corners for the rest of his life.

A more ambitious plan is to get him into Parliament where he can keep an eye on some of these fellow-travelling M.P.s: "Any particular preference as to party, or aren't we fussy?" asks Personnel, still in tweeds from his weekend in Wiltshire.

"I'd rather prefer it not to be the Liberals if it's all the same to you," says Pym.

But nothing lasts long in politics and a week later Pym is destined for one of the private banks whose directors wander in and out of the Firm's Head Office all day long, moaning about Russian gold and the need to protect our trade routes from the Bolsheviks. At the Institute of Directors, Pym is lunched by a succession of captains of finance who think they may have an opening.

"I knew a Pym," says one, over a second brandy or a third. "Kept a dirty great office in Mount Street somewhere. Best man at his job I ever knew."

"What was his job, sir?" Pym asks politely.

"Con man," says his host with a horsy laugh. "Any relation?"

"Must be my distant wicked uncle," says Pym, laughing also, and hurries back to the sanctuary of the Firm.

On goes the dance, how seriously I'll never know, for Pym is not yet privy to these backstage deliberations, though it isn't for want of peeking into a few desk drawers and locked steel cupboards. Then suddenly the mood changes.

"Look here," says Personnel, trying to hide his aggravation. "Why the devil didn't you remind us you spoke Czech?"

Within a month, Pym is attached to an electrical-engineering company in Gloucester as a management trainee, no previous experience necessary. The managing director, to his lasting regret, was at school with the Firm's reigning Chief, and has made the mistake of accepting a series of valuable government contracts at a time when he needed them. Pym is given to the exports department, charged with opening up the East European market. His first mission is nearly his last.

"Well, why don't you just sort of take a general swing through Czecho and test the market?" says Pym's notional employer wanly. And beneath his breath: "And do *please* remember that whatever else you get up to is *nothing* to do with *us*, will you?"

"A quick in and out," Pym's controller tells him gaily, in the safe house in Camberwell where cub agents receive their operational briefing before cutting their milk-teeth. He hands Pym a portable typewriter with hidden cavities in the carriage.

"I know it seems silly," says Pym, "but I can't actually type."

"Everyone can type a *bit*," says Pym's controller. "Practise over the weekend."

Pym flies to Vienna. Memories, memories. Pym hires a car. Pym crosses the border without the smallest difficulty, expecting to see Axel waiting for him the other side.

The countryside was Austrian and beautiful. Many barns lay beside many lakes. In Plzeň Pym toured a despondent factory in the company of square-faced men. In the evening he kept the safety of his hotel, watched by a pair of secret policemen who drank one coffee apiece until he went to bed. His next calls were in the north. On the road to Ústí he saw army lorries and memorised their unit insignia. To the east of Ústí lay a factory that the Firm suspected of producing isotope containers. Pym was unclear what an isotope was, or what it should be contained in, but he drew a sketch of the main buildings and hid it in his typewriter. Next day he continued to Prague and at the arranged hour sat himself in the famous Tyn church, which has a window looking into Kafka's old apartment. Tourists and officials wandered about unsmiling.

"So K. began to move off slowly," Pym read as he sat in the south aisle, third row from the altar, pretending to study his guidebook. *"K. felt forlorn and isolated as he advanced between the rows of empty pews, with the priest's eyes fixed on him for all he knew. . . ."*

Needing a rest, Pym knelt down and prayed. With a grunt and a puff, a heavy man shuffled in beside him and sat down. Pym smelt garlic and thought of Sergeant Pavel. Through a crack in his fingers, he identified the recognition signals: smear of white paint on left fingernail, splash of blue on left cuff, a mass of disgraceful black hair, black coat. My contact is an artist, he realised. Why didn't I think of that before? But Pym did not sit back, he did not ease the little package from his pocket as a prelude to laying it between them on the pew. He remained kneeling and soon discovered why he had done so. The sound of trained feet was crunching towards him down the aisle. The footsteps stopped. A male voice said, "Come with us, please," in Czech. With a sigh of resignation, Pym's neighbor clambered wearily to his feet and followed them out.

"Sheer coincidence," Pym's controller assured him, much amused, when he got back. "He's already been on to us. They were pulling him in for a routine questioning. He comes up for one every six weeks. Never even crossed their minds he might be making a clandestine pickup. Let alone with a chap your age."

"You don't think he's—well, told them?" Pym said.

"Old Kyril? Blown *you?* You must be joking. Don't worry. We'll give you another shot in a few weeks' time."

Rick was not pleased to hear of Pym's contribution to the British export drive, and told him so on one of his secret visits from Ireland, where he had established his winter quarters while he cleared up certain misunderstandings with Scotland Yard, and fought his way into the crowded new profession of West End property evictions.

"Working as a commercial traveller—my own boy?" he exclaimed, to the alarm of the adjoining tables. "Selling electric shavers to a bunch of foreign Communists? We *did* all that, son. It's over. What did I pay your education for? Where's your patriotism?"

"They're not electric shavers, Father. I sell alternators, oscillators and sparking plugs. How's your glass?"

Hostility towards Rick was a new and giddying notion for Pym. He vented it cautiously, but with growing excitement. If they ate a meal, he insisted on paying in order to savour Rick's disapproval at seeing his own boy put down good money where a signature would have done the trick.

"You're not mixed up with some racket out there, are you?" said Rick. "The doors of tolerance only open a certain distance, you know, son. Even for you. What are you up to? Tell us."

The pressure on Pym's arm was suddenly dangerous. He made a joke of it, smiling broadly. "Hey, Father, that hurts," he said, awfully amused. It was Rick's thumbnail that he was most aware of, boring into an artery. "Could you possibly stop doing that, Father?" he said. "It really is uncomfortable." Rick was too busy pursing his lips and shaking his head. He was saying it was a damned shame when a father who had given up everything for his own son was treated like a "poor ayah." He meant pariah but the notion had never properly formed in him. Placing his elbow on the table, Pym relaxed his whole arm and let it ride about with Rick's pressure—flop one way, flop the other. Then abruptly stiffened it and, exactly as he had been taught, smacked the fat of Rick's knuckles on to the table-edge, causing the glasses to jump and the cutlery to dance and slide off the table. Taking back his bruised hand, Rick turned away to bestow a resigned smile on his subjects feasting around him. Then with his good hand he lightly pinged the edge of his Drambuie glass to indicate that he required another nice touch. Just as, by unlacing his shoes, he used to let it be known that somebody should fetch his bedroom slippers. Or by rolling on to his back, after a lengthy banquet, and spreading his knees, he declared a carnal appetite.

Yet, as ever, nothing is one thing for long with Pym, and soon a strange calm begins to replace his early nervousness as he continues his secret missions. The silent, unlit country that at first sight appeared so threatening to him becomes a secret womb where he can hide himself, rather than a place of dread. He has only to cross the border for the walls of his English prisons to fall away: no Belinda, no Rick—and very nearly no Firm either. I am the travelling executive of an electronic company. I am Sir Magnus, roving free. His solitary nights in unpeopled provincial towns, where at first the yapping of a dog had been enough to bring him sweating to his window, now inspire him with a sense of protection. The air of universal oppression that hangs over the entire country enfolds him in its mysterious embrace. Not even the prison walls of his public school had given him such a sense of security. On car and train rides through river valleys, over hills capped by Bohemian castles, he drifts through realms of such inner contentment that the very cattle seem to be his friends. I shall settle here, he decides. This is my true home. How foolish of me to have supposed that Axel could ever leave it for another! He begins to relish his stilted conversations with officials. His heart leaps when he unlocks a smile from their faces. He takes pride in his slowly filling order book, feels a fatherly responsibility for his oppressors. Even his operational detours, when he is not blocking them from his mind, can be squeezed beneath the broad umbrella of his munificence: "I am a champion of the middle ground," he tells himself, using an old phrase of Axel's, as he prises a loose stone from a wall, fishes out one package and replaces it with another. "I am giving succour to a wounded land."

Yet even with all this preliminary self-conditioning, it takes another six journeys on Pym's part before he can coax Axel out of the shadows of his perilous existence.

"Mr. Canterbury! Are you all right, Mr. Canterbury? Answer!"

"Of course I'm all right, Miss D. I'm always all right. What is it?"

Pym pulled back the door. Miss Dubber was standing in the darkness, her hair in papers, holding Toby for protection.

"You thump so, Mr. Canterbury. You grind your teeth. An hour ago you were humming. We're worried that you're ill."

"Who's *we?*" said Pym sharply.

"Toby and me, you silly man. Do you think I've got a lover?"

Pym closed the door on her and went swiftly to the window. One parked van, probably green. One parked car, white or grey, Devon registration. An early milkman he had not seen before. He returned to the door, put his ear to it and listened intently. A creak. A slippered footstep. He pulled the door open. Miss Dubber was halfway down the corridor.

"Miss D?"

"Yes, Mr. Canterbury?"

"Has anybody been asking you questions about me?"

"Why should they, Mr. Canterbury?"

"I don't know. Sometimes people just do. Have they?"

"It's time you slept, Mr. Canterbury. I don't mind how much the country needs you, it can always wait another day."

The town of Strakonice is more famous for its manufacture of motorcycles and Oriental fezzes than for any great cultural gem. Pym made his way there because he had filled a dead letter box in Pisek, nineteen kilometres to the north-east, and Firm tradecraft required he should not register his presence in a target town where a dead letter box was waiting to be cleared. So he drove to Strakonice feeling flat and bored, which was how he always felt after a bit of Firm's business, and booked himself into an ancient hotel with a grand staircase, then drifted round the town trying to admire the old butchers' shops on the south side of the square, and the Renaissance church which, according to his guidebook, had been changed to baroque; and the church of St. Wenceslaus which, though originally Gothic, had been altered in the nineteenth century. Having exhausted these excitements, and feeling even wearier from the long heat of the summer's day, he trudged up the stairs to his bedroom thinking how pleasant it would be if they were leading him to Sabina's apartment in Graz, in the days when he had been a penniless young double agent without a care in the world.

He put his key in the keyhole but it was not locked. He was not unduly surprised by this for it was still the evening hour when servants turned back bedcovers, and secret policemen took a last look round. Pym stepped inside and discerned, half hidden behind a sloping shaft of sunlight from the window, the figure of Axel, waiting as the old wait, his domed head propped against the chair's back, pitched a little sideways so that he could make out, among the lights and shades, who was coming in. And not in all the Firm's unarmed combat lessons, and dagger-play lessons, and close-contact shooting lessons, had anybody thought to teach Pym how to terminate the life of an emaciated friend seated behind a sunbeam.

Axel was prison-pale and a stone lighter. Pym could not have supposed, from his parting memory of him, that he had more flesh to give. But the purgers and interrogators and gaolers had managed to find it, as they usually do, and they had helped themselves to it in handfuls. They had taken it from his face, his wrists, his finger-joints and ankles. They had drained the last blood from his cheeks. They had also helped themselves to one of his teeth, though Pym did not discover this immediately, because Axel had his lips tight shut, and one twiglike forefinger raised to them in warning while he waved the other at the wall of Pym's hotel bedroom, indicating microphones at work. They had smashed his right eyelid too, which drooped over its parent eye like a cocked hat, adding to his piratical appearance. But his coat, for all that, still hung over his shoulders like a musketeer's cape, his moustache flourished, and he had inherited a marvellous pair of boots from somewhere, rich as timber, with soles like the running-boards of a vintage car.

"Magnus Richard Pym?" he demanded with theatrical gruffness.

"Yes?" said Pym after a couple of unsuccessful attempts to speak.

"You are charged with the crimes of espionage, provocation of the people, incitement to treason and murder. Also sabotage on behalf of an imperialist power."

Still slouched languidly in his chair, Axel drove his hands together with improbable vigour, producing a thwack that echoed round the great bedroom, and no doubt impressed the microphones. After it, he offered the prolonged grunt of a man coming to terms with a heavy punch in the stomach. Delving in his jacket pocket, he then detached a small automatic pistol from the lining and, finger to his lips again, waved it about so that Pym got a healthy sight of it.

"Face the wall!" he barked, clambering with difficulty to his feet. "Place your hands on your head, you Fascist swine! March."

Laying a hand gently round Pym's shoulder, Axel guided him towards the door. Pym stepped ahead of him into the gloomy corridor. Two burly men in hats ignored him.

"Search his room!" Axel commanded them. "Find what you can but do not remove anything! Pay attention to the typewriter, his shoes and the lining of his suitcase. Do not leave his room until you receive orders from me personally. Walk slowly down the stairs," he told Pym, prodding him in the small of the back with the gun.

"This is an outrage," Pym said lamely. "I demand to see a British consul immediately."

At the reception desk the female concierge sat knitting like a hag at the guillotine. Axel prodded Pym past her to a waiting car outside. A yellow cat had taken shelter underneath it. Pulling open the passenger door, Axel nodded Pym to get in and, having shooed the cat into the gutter, climbed in after him and started the engine.

"If you collaborate completely you will not be harmed," Axel announced in his official voice, indicating a patch of crude perforations in the dashboard. "If you attempt to escape you will be shot."

"This is a ridiculous and scandalous act," Pym muttered. "My government will insist that those responsible be punished."

But once again, his words had none of the confident ring they had possessed in the cosy barrack hut in Argyll where he and his colleagues had practised the skills of resisting interrogation.

"You have been watched from the moment you arrived here," said Axel loudly. "All your movements and contacts have been observed by the protectors of the people. You have no alternative but to make an immediate admission of your guilt on all charges."

"The free world will see this senseless act as the latest evidence of the brutality of the Czech régime," Pym declared, with increasing strength. Axel nodded approvingly.

The streets were empty, the old houses also. They entered what had once been a rich suburb of patrician villas. Sprawling hedges hid the lower windows. The iron gateways, wide enough to ride a coach through, were blocked with ivy and barbed wire.

"Get out," Axel commanded.

The evening was young and beautiful. The full moon shed a white, unearthly light. Watching Axel lock the car, Pym smelt hay and heard the clamour of insects. Axel guided him down a narrow path between two gardens until they came to a gap in the yew hedge to his right. Grabbing Pym's wrist, he led him through it. They were standing on the terrace of what had once been a great garden. A many-towered castle lifted into the sky behind them. Ahead, almost lost to a thicket of roses, stood a decrepit summerhouse. Axel wrestled with the door but it refused to yield.

"Kick it for me, Sir Magnus," he said. "This is Czechoslovakia."

Pym drove his foot against the panel. The door gave, they stepped inside. On a rusted table stood the familiar bottle of vodka and a tray of bread and gherkins. Grey stuffing was bleeding from the ripped covers of the wicker chairs.

"You are a very dangerous friend, Sir Magnus," Axel complained as he stretched out his thin legs and surveyed his fine boots. "Why in God's name couldn't you have used an alias? Sometimes I think you have been put on earth in order to be my black angel."

"They said I would be better being me," Pym replied stupidly as Axel twisted the cap from the vodka bottle. "They call it natural cover."

For a long time after that, Axel appeared unable to think of anything useful to say at all, and Pym did not feel it was his place to interrupt his captor's reverie. They were sitting legs parallel and shoulder to shoulder like a retired couple on the beach. Below them, squares of cornfield stretched towards a forest. A heap of broken cars, more than Pym had ever seen on the Czech roads, littered the lower end of the garden. Bats wheeled decorously in the moonlight.

"Do you know this was my aunt's house?" said Axel.

"Well, no, I didn't, actually," said Pym.

"Well, it was. My aunt was a witty woman. She once described to me how she broke the news to her father that she wished to marry my uncle. 'But why do you want to marry him?' said her father. 'He has no money. He is very small and you are small too. You will have small children. He is like the encyclopedias you make me buy you every year. They look pretty but once you have opened them and seen inside, you don't bother with them any more.' He was wrong. Their children were large and she was happy." He scarcely paused. "They want me to blackmail you, Sir Magnus. That is the only good news I have for you."

"Who do?" said Pym.

"The aristos I work for. They think I should show you the photographs of the two of us coming out of the barn together in Austria, and play you the recordings of our conversations. They say I should wave the I.O.U. in your face that you signed to me for the two hundred dollars we tricked out of Membury for your father."

"How did you answer them?" said Pym.

"I said I would. They don't read Thomas Mann, these guys. They're very crude. This is a crude country, as you no doubt noticed in your journeys."

"Not at all," said Pym. "I love it."

Axel drank some vodka and stared into the hills. "And you people don't make it any better. Your hateful little department has been seriously interfering in the running of my country. What are you? Some kind of American butler? What are you doing, framing our officials, sowing suspicion, and seducing our intellectuals? Why do you cause people to be beaten unnecessarily, when a few years in prison would be enough? Do they teach you no reality over there? Have you no reality at all, Sir Magnus?"

"I didn't know the Firm was doing that," said Pym.

"Doing what?"

"Interfering. Causing people to be tortured. That must be a different section. Ours is just a sort of postal service for small agents."

Axel sighed. "Maybe they're not doing it. Maybe I have been brainwashed by our own stupid propaganda these days. Maybe I'm blaming you unfairly. Cheers."

"Cheers," said Pym.

"So what will they find in your room?" Axel asked when he had lit himself a cigar and puffed at it several times.

"Pretty well everything, I suppose."

"What's everything?"

"Secret inks. Film."

"Film from your agents?"

"Yes."

"Developed?"

"I assume not."

"From the dead letter box in Pisek?"

"Yes."

"Then I wouldn't bother to develop it. It's cheap pedlar material. Money?"

"A bit, yes."

"How much?"

"Five thousand dollars."

"Codebooks?"

"A couple."

"Anything I might have forgotten? No atom bomb?"

"There's a concealed camera."

"Is that the talcum-powder tin?"

"If you peel the paper off the lid, it makes a lens."

"Anything else?"

"A silk escape map. In one of my neckties."

Axel drew on his cigar again, his thoughts seemingly far away. Suddenly he drove his fist on to the iron table. "We have got to get ourselves *out* of this, Sir Magnus!" he exclaimed angrily. "We have got to get ourselves *out*. We've got to rise in the world. We've got to help each other until we become aristos ourselves and we can kick the other bastards goodbye." He stared into the gathering darkness. "You make it so difficult for me, you know that? Sitting in that prison, I had bad thoughts about you. You make it very, very difficult to be your friend."

"I don't see why."

"Oh, oh! He doesn't see why! He does not see that when the bold Sir Magnus Pym applies for a business visa, even the poor Czechs can look in their card index and discover there was a gentleman of the same name who was a Fascist imperialist militarist spy in Austria, and that a certain running dog named Axel was his fellow conspirator." His anger reminded Pym of the days of his fever in Bern. His voice had acquired the same unpleasant edge. "Are you really so ignorant of the manners of the country you are spying on that you do not understand what it means these days for a man like me even to have been in the same continent as a man like you, let alone his fellow conspirator in a spying game? Do you really not know that in this world of whispers and accusers, I may literally die of you? You've read George Orwell, haven't you? These are the people who can rewrite yesterday's weather!"

"I know," said Pym.

"Do you also know then, that I may be fatally contaminated like all those poor agents and informers you are showering with money and instructions? Do you not know that you are delivering them to the scaffold, unless they belong to us already? You know at least what they will do with you, I assume, unless I make them hear me, these aristos of mine, if we can't satisfy their appetites by other means? They mean to arrest you and parade you before the world's press with your stupid agents and associates. They plan to have another show trial, hang some people. When they start to do that, it will be sheer oversight if they don't hang me too. Axel, the imperialist lackey who spied for you in Austria! Axel, the revanchist Titoist Trotskyist typist who was your accomplice in Bern! They would prefer an American but in the meantime they will stretch a point and hang an Englishman until they can get hold of the real thing." He flopped back, his fury exhausted. "We've got to get *out* of this, Sir Magnus," he repeated. "We've got to rise, rise, *rise*. I am sick of bad superiors, bad food, bad prisons and bad torturers." He drew angrily on his cigar again. "It's time I looked after your career and you looked after mine. And this time properly. No bourgeois shrinking back from the big scoops. This time we are professionals, we make straight for the biggest diamonds, the biggest banks. I mean it."

Suddenly, Axel turned his chair until it was facing Pym, then sat on it again and laughed, and tapped Pym smartly on the shoulder with the back of his hand to cheer him up.

"You got the flowers okay, Sir Magnus?"

"They were super. Someone handed them into our cab as we were leaving the reception."

"Did Belinda like them?"

"Belinda doesn't know about you. I never told her."

"Who did you say the flowers were from?"

"I said I'd no idea. Probably for another wedding altogether."

"That was good. What's she like?"

"Super. We were childhood sweethearts together."

"I thought Jemima was your childhood sweetheart."

"Well, Belinda was too."

"At the same time—both of them? That's quite a childhood you had," Axel said with a fresh laugh as he refilled Pym's glass.

Pym managed to laugh too, and they drank together.

Then Axel began speaking, kindly and gently without irony or bitterness, and it seems to me that he spoke for about thirty years because his words are as loud in my ear now as they ever were in Pym's then, never mind the din of the cicadas and the cheeping of the bats.

"Sir Magnus, you have in the past betrayed me but, more important, you have betrayed yourself. Even when you are telling the truth, you lie. You have loyalty and you have affection. But to what? To whom? I don't know all the reasons for this. Your great father. Your aristocratic mother. One day maybe you will tell me. And maybe you have put your love in some bad places now and then." He leaned forward and there was a kindly, true affection in his face and a warm long-suffering smile in his eyes. "Yet you also have morality. You search. What I am saying is, Sir Magnus: for once nature has produced a perfect match. You are a perfect spy. All you need is a cause. I have it. I know that our revolution is young and that sometimes the wrong people are running it. In the pursuit of peace we are making too much war. In the pursuit of freedom we are building too many prisons. But in the long run I don't mind. Because I know this. All the junk that made you what you are: the privileges, the snobbery, the hypocrisy, the churches, the schools, the fathers, the class systems, the historical lies, the little lords of the countryside, the little lords of big business, and all the greedy wars that result from them, we are sweeping that away for ever. For your sake. Because we are making a society that will never produce such sad little fellows as Sir Magnus." He held out his hand. "So. I've said it. You are a good man and I love you."

And I remember that touch always. I can see it any time by looking into my own palm: dry and decent and forgiving. And the laughter: from the heart as it always was, once he had ceased to be tactical and become my friend again.

16

How appropriate, Tom, that looking back over all the years that follow our meeting in the Czech summerhouse, I see nothing but America, America, her golden shores glittering on the horizon like the promise of freedom after the repressions of our troubled Europe, then leaping towards us in the summer joy of our attainment! Pym still has more than a quarter of a century in which to serve his two houses according to the best standards of his omnivorous loyalty. The trained, married, case-hardened, elderly adolescent has still to become a man, though who will ever break the genetic code of when a middle-class Englishman's adolescence ends and his manhood takes over? Half a dozen dangerous European cities, from Prague to Berlin to Stockholm to the occupied capital of his native England, lie between the two friends and their goal. Yet it seems to me now they were no more than staging places where we could provision and refurbish and watch the stars in preparation for our journey. And consider for a moment the dreadful alternative, Tom: the fear of failure that blew like a Siberian wind on our unprotected backs. Consider what it would have meant, to two men such as ourselves, to have lived out our lives as spies without ever having spied on America!

It must be said quickly, lest there is any doubt of it left in your mind, that after the summerhouse Pym's path was set for life. He had renewed his vow and in the terms your Uncle Jack and I have always lived by, Tom, there was no way out. Pym was owned and hooked and pledged. Finish. After the barn in Austria, well, yes, there had been a little latitude still, though never any prospect of redemption. And you have seen how, if feebly, he did try to jump clear of the secret world and brave the hazards of the real one. Not with any conviction, true. But he made a stab at it, even if he knew he would be about as much use out there as a beached fish dying of too much oxygen. But after the summerhouse, God's brief to Pym was clear: no more dithering; stay put in your proper station, in the element to which nature has appointed you. Pym needed no third telling.

"Make a clean breast of it," I hear you cry, Tom. "Hurry home to London, go to Personnel, pay the penalty, begin again!" Well now, Pym thought of that, naturally he did. On the drive back to Vienna, on the aeroplane home, on the bus to London from Heathrow, Pym did a lot of energetic agonising along those lines, for it was one of the occasions when the whole of his life was pinned up in a vivid strip cartoon inside his skull. Begin where? he asked himself, not unreasonably. With Lippsie, whose death, in his gloomier hours, he was still determined to take upon himself? With Sefton Boyd's initials? With poor Dorothy whom he had driven off her head? With Peggy Wentworth, screaming her dirt at him, another victim for sure? Or with the day he first picked the locks of Rick's green cabinet or Membury's desk? How many of the systems of his life exactly are you proposing that he bare to the guilt-bestowing gaze of his admirers?

"Then resign! Bolt to Murgo! Take the teaching job at Willow's." Pym thought of that too. He thought of half a dozen dark holes where he could bury his leftover life and hide his guilty charm. Not one of them attracted him for five minutes.

Would Axel's people really have exposed Pym if he had cut and run? I doubt it, but that isn't the point. The point is, Pym quite frequently loved the Firm as much as he loved Axel. He adored its rough, uncomprehending trust in him, its misuse of him, its tweedy bear-hugs, flawed romanticism and cock-eyed integrity. He smiled to himself each time he stepped inside its Reichskanzleis and safe palaces, accepted the unsmiling salute of its vigilant janitors. The Firm was home and school and court to him, even when he was betraying it. He really felt he had a lot to give it, just as he had a lot to give to Axel. In his imagination, he saw himself with cellars full of nylons and black-market chocolate, enough to see everybody right in every shortage—and intelligence is nothing if not an institutionalised black market in perishable commodities. And this time Pym himself was the hero of the fable. No Membury stood between himself and the fraternity.

"Suppose that on a lonely drive to Plzeň, Sir Magnus, you stopped your car to give a lift to a couple of workmen on their way to work. You would do that?" Axel had suggested, in the small hours of the morning in the summerhouse, when he had put Pym back together again.

Pym conceded that he might.

"And suppose, Sir Magnus, that as simple fellows will, they had confided to you, as you drove along, their fears about handling radioactive material without suffi-cient protective clothing. You would prick up your ears?"

Pym laughed and agreed that he would.

"And suppose also that as a great operator and a generous spirit, Sir Magnus, you had written down their names and addresses and promised to bring them a pound or two of good English coffee next time you visited their region?"

Pym said he would certainly have done this.

"And suppose," Axel continued, "that having driven these fellows to the outer perimeter of the protected area where they work, you had the courage, and the initiative, and the officer qualities—as you assuredly have—to park your car in a discreet spot and climb this hill." Axel was indicating the very hill on a military map he happened to have brought along with him and spread over the iron table. "And from its apex you photographed the factory, using the convenient protection of a thicket of lime trees whose lower branches are later discovered to have slightly marked the pictures? Your aristos would admire your enterprise? They would applaud the great Sir Magnus? They would instruct him to recruit the two loquacious workmen and obtain further details of the factory's output and purpose?"

"They surely would," said Pym vigorously.

"Congratulations, Sir Magnus."

Axel drops the very film into Pym's waiting palm. The Firm's own issue. Wrapped in anonymous green. Pym secretes it in his typewriter. Pym hands it to his masters. The wonder does not stop there. When the product is rushed to the Whitehall analysts, the factory turns out to be the very plant recently photographed from the air by an American overflight! With a show of reluctance, Pym supplies the personal particulars of his two innocent and, thus far, fictitious informants. The names are filed, carded, checked, processed and bandied round the senior officers' bar. Until finally, under the divine laws of bureaucracy, they are the subject of a special committee.

"Look here, young Pym, what makes you think these chaps aren't going to turn you in next time you show up on their doorstep?"

But Pym is in interview mode, he has a large audience and is invincible: "It's a hunch, sir, that's all." Count two slowly. "I think they trusted me. I think they're keeping their mouths shut and hoping I'll show up one evening exactly as I said I would."

And events prove him right, as they would, wouldn't they, Jack? Braving all, our hero returns to Czecho and repairs, regardless of risk, to their very doorsteps—how can he fail to, since he is escorted there by Axel, who makes the introductions? For this time there will be no Sergeant Pavels. A loyal, bright-eyed repertory company of actors has been born, Axel is its producer and these are its founder-members. Painfully and dangerously, the network is built upon. By Pym, a cool number if ever we knew one. Pym, the latest hero of the corridors, the chap who put Conger together.

The Firm's system of natural selection, accelerated by Jack Brotherhood's promptings, can no longer be resisted.

"Joined the *Foreign Office?*" Belinda's father echoes, in heavy, artificial mystification. "Posted it to *Prague?* How do you do *that* from a deadbeat electronics firm? Well, well, I must say."

"It's a contract appointment. They need Czech speakers," says Pym.

"He's boosting British trade, Daddy. You wouldn't understand. You're just a stockbroker," says Belinda.

"Well they might at least give him a decent cover story, mightn't they?" says Belinda's father, laughing his infuriating laugh.

In the Firm's newest and most secret safe flat in Prague, Pym and Axel drink to Pym's instatement as Second Secretary Commercial and Visa Officer at the British Embassy. Axel has fattened, Pym observes with pleasure. The lines of suffering are clearing from his haggard features.

"To the land of the free, Sir Magnus."

"To America," says Pym.

"My dearest Father,

"I am so glad you approve of my appointment. Unfortunately, I am not yet in a position to persuade Pandit Nehru to grant you an audience so that you can put your football pool scheme to him, though I can well imagine the boost it might give to the struggling Indian economy."

So were there no genuine Joes at all? I hear you asking, Tom, in a tone of disappointment. Were they *all* pretend? Indeed there were genuine Joes. Never fear! And very good they were too, the best. And every one of them profited from Pym's improved tradecraft, and looked up to Pym as he looked up to Axel. And Pym and Axel looked up to the genuine Joes also, in their fashion, regarding them as the unwitting ambassadors of the operation, testifying to its smooth running and integrity. And used their good offices to shield and advance them, arguing that every improvement in their circumstances brought glory to the networks. And smuggled them to Austria for clandestine training and rehabilitation. The genuine Joes were our mascots, Tom. Our stars. We made sure they would never want for anything again, so long as Pym and Axel were there to see them right. Which, as a matter of fact, is how it all went wrong. But later.

I wish I could adequately describe to you, Jack, the pleasure of being really well run. Of jealousy, of ideology, nothing. Axel was as keen for Pym to love England as he was to direct him at America, and it was part of his genius throughout our partnership to praise the freedoms of the West while tacitly implying that Pym had it within his reach, if not his duty as a free man, to bring some of this freedom to the East. Oh, you may laugh, Jack! And you may shake your grey hairs at the depths of Pym's innocence! But can you not imagine how easily it came to Pym to take a tiny, impoverished country into his protection, when his own was so favoured, so victorious and wellborn? And, from where he saw it, so absurd? To love poor Czecho like a rich protector through all her terrible vicissitudes, for Axel's sake? To forgive her lapses in advance? And blame them on the many betrayals that his parent England had perpetrated against her? Does it honestly amaze you that Pym, by making bonds with the forbidden, should be once more escaping from what held him? That he who had loved his way across so many borders should now be loving his way across another, with Axel there to show him how to walk and where to cross?

"I'm sorry, Bel," Pym would say to Belinda as he abandoned her yet again to the Scrabble board in their dark apartment in Prague's diplomatic ghetto. "Got to go up country. May be a day or two. Come on, Bel. Kiss-kiss. You wouldn't rather be married to a nine-till-five man, would you?"

"I can't find *The Times*," she said, shaking him aside. "I suppose you left it at the bloody Embassy again."

But however frayed Pym's nerves when he arrived at the rendezvous, Axel reclaimed him every time they met. He was never hasty, never importunate. He was never anything but respectful of the pains and sensibilities of his agent. It was not stasis one side and all movement the other either, Tom, far from it. Axel's ambitions were for himself as well as Pym. Was not Pym his ricebowl, his fortune in all its meanings, his passport to the privileges and status of a paid-up Party aristo? Oh, how he studied Pym! Such obsessive, flattering concentration on a single man! How delicately he coaxed and gentled him! How meticulous he was, always to put on the clothes Pym needed him to wear—now the mantle of the wise and steady father Pym had never had, now the bloody rags of suffering that were the uniform of his authority, now the soutane of Pym's one confessor, his Murgo absolute. He had to learn Pym's codes and evasions. He had to read Pym faster than ever he could read himself. He had to scold and forgive him like the parents who would never slam the door in his face, laugh where Pym was melancholy and keep the flame of all Pym's faiths alive when he was down and saying, I can't, I'm lonely and afraid.

Above all, he had to keep his agent's wits constantly alert against the seemingly limitless tolerance of the Firm, for how could we ever dare believe, either of us, that the dear, dead wood of England was not a cladding for some masterly game being played inside? Imagine the headaches Axel had, as Pym went on producing his mountains of intelligence material, to persuade his masters they were not the victims of some grand imperialist deception! The Czechs admired you so much, Jack. The old ones knew you from the war. They knew your skills and respected them. They knew the dangers, every day, of underestimating their wily adversary. Axel had to fight toe to toe with them, more than once. He had to argue with the very henchmen who had tortured him, in order to prevent them from pulling Pym out of the field and giving him a little of the medicine they periodically dished out to one another, on the off chance of extracting a true confession from him: "Yes, I am Brotherhood's man!" they wanted him to scream. "Yes, I am here to plant disinformation on you. To distract your eye from our anti-Socialist operations. And yes, Axel is my accomplice. Take me, hang me, anything but this." But Axel prevailed. He begged and bullied and slammed the table, and when still more purges were planned to explain the chaos left behind by the last ones, he scared his enemies into silence by threatening to expose them for their insufficient appreciation of the historically inevitable imperialist decay. And Pym helped him every inch of the distance. Sat again at his sickbed—if only metaphorically—gave him nourishment and courage, held up his spirits. Ransacked the Station files. Armed him with outrageous examples of the Firm's incompetence worldwide. Until, fighting thus for their mutual survival, Pym and Axel drew still closer together, each laying the irrational burdens of his country at the other's feet.

And once in a while, when a battle was over and won, or a great scoop had been achieved on one side or the other, Axel would put on the play clothes of the libertine and arrange a midnight dash to his frugal equivalent of St. Moritz, which was a small white castle in the Giant Mountains, set aside by his service for people they thought the world of. The first time they went there was for an anniversary celebration, in a limousine with blackened windows. Pym had been in Prague two years.

"I have decided to present you with an excellent new agent, Sir Magnus," Axel announced as they zigzagged contentedly up the gravel road. "The Watchman network is lamentably short of industrial intelligence. The Americans are pledged to the collapse of our economy, but the Firm is providing nothing to support their optimism. How would you regard a middle executive from our great National Bank of Czechoslovakia, with access to some of our most serious mismanagements?"

"Where am I supposed to have found him?" Pym countered cautiously, for these were delicate decisions, requiring lengthy correspondence with Head Office before the approach to a new potential source was licensed.

The dinner table was laid for three, the candelabra lit. The two men had taken a long, slow walk in the forest and now they were drinking an apéritif before the fire, waiting for their guest.

"How is Belinda?" said Axel.

This was not a subject they often discussed, for Axel had little patience with unsatisfactory relationships.

"Fine, thank you, as always."

"That's not what our microphones tell us. They say you fight like two dogs day and night. Our listeners are becoming thoroughly depressed by you both."

"Tell them we'll mend our ways," said Pym with a rare flash of bitterness.

A car was coming up the hill. They heard the footsteps of the old servant crossing the hall, and the rattle of bolts.

"Meet your new agent," Axel said.

The door banged open and Sabina marched in. A little more matronly, perhaps, at the hips: one or two hard lines of officialdom around the jaw; but his delicious Sabina all the same. She was wearing a stern black dress with a white collar, and clumpy black court shoes that must have been her pride, for they had green brilliants on the straps and the sheen of imitation suède. Seeing Pym, she drew up sharply and scowled at him in suspicion. For a moment, her manner reflected the most radical disapproval. Then to his delight she burst out laughing her crazy Slav laugh, and ran to cover him with her body, much as she had done in Graz when he took his first faltering lessons in Czech.

And so it was, Jack. Sabina rose and rose until she became the head agent of the Watchman network, and the darling of her successive British case officers, though you knew her either as Watchman One or as the intrepid Olga Kravitsky, secretary to the Prague Internal Committee on Economic Affairs. We retired her, if you remember, when she was expecting her third baby by her fourth husband, at a special dinner for her in West Berlin while she was attending her last conference of Comecon bankers in Potsdam. Axel kept her on a little longer, before he decided to follow your example.

"I've been posted to Berlin," Pym told Belinda, in the safety of a public park, at the end of his second tour in Prague.

"Why are you telling me?" said Belinda.

"I wondered whether you'd like to come," Pym replied, and Belinda began coughing again, her long unquenchable cough that she must have picked up from the climate.

Belinda went back to London and took an Open University course in journalism, though none in silent killing. Eventually, in her thirty-seventh year, she launched herself upon the hazardous path of fashionable liberal causes, where after encountering several Pauls, she married one, and had an unruly daughter who criticised her for everything she did, which gave Belinda the feeling of being reconciled with her own parents. And Pym and Axel embarked on the next leg of their pilgrims' voyage. In Berlin, a brighter future awaited them, and a maturer treason.

c/o Colonel Evelyn Tremaine, D.S.O.
Pioneer Corps, ret.
P.O. Box 9077
MANILA

To His Excellency Sir Magnus Richard Pym, Decorations
The British High Mission
BERLIN

My dearest Son,
      Merely a note which I hope does not Inconvenience you on your way to the Top, since none should expect gratitude until it is his turn to stand before the Father of us all which I expect to be doing at an early Date. Medical Science being still at a primitive Stage here, it appears notwithstanding that this Cruel summer is likely to be the writer's Last, despite Sacrifice of Alcohol and other Comforts. If you are Sending for Treatment or Funeral be sure to make out cheque and envelope to the Colonel, not Self, as the name of Pym is Persona non Gratis to the natives, and anyway may be Dead.
      Praying to be Spared,
                                                Rick T. Pym
P.S. Am advised that 916 Gold may be had in Berlin at knockdown price, the Diplomatic Bag being available to those in High Position seeking opportunity for informal Reward. Perce Loft is at old Address and will assist for ten percent but watch him.

Berlin. What a garrison of spies, Tom! What a cabinet full of useless, liquid secrets, what a playground for every alchemist, miracle-worker, and rat-piper that ever took up the cloak and turned his face from the unpalatable constraints of political reality! And always at the centre, the great good American heart, bravely drumming out its honourable rhythms in the name of liberty, democracy, and setting the people free.

      In Berlin, the Firm had agents of influence, agents of disruption, subversion, sabotage and disinformation. We even had one or two who supplied us with intelligence, though these were an underprivileged crowd, kept on more out of a traditional regard than any intrinsic professional worth. We had tunnellers and smugglers, listeners and forgers, trainers and recruiters and talent-spotters and couriers and watchers and seducers, assassins and balloonists, lip-readers and disguise artists. But whatever the Brits had, the Americans had more, and whatever the Americans had the East Germans had five of it and the Russians ten of it. Pym stood before these marvels like a child let loose in a sweet shop, not knowing what to grab first. And Axel, slipping in and out of the city on any number of false passports, padded softly behind him with his basket. In safe flats and dark restaurants, never the same one twice, we ate quiet meals, exchanged our goods and gazed upon each other with the incredulous contentment that passes between mountaineers when they are standing on the peak. But even then, we never forgot the bigger peak that lay ahead of us as we raised our vodka glasses to each other and whispered, "Next year in America!" across the candlelight.

And the committees, Tom! Berlin was not safe enough to contain them. We assembled in London, in gilded imperial chambers appropriate to players of the world's game. And such a bold, diverse, brilliantly inventive cross-section of our society's leaders we were, for these were the new years of England, when the country's hidden talent would be winkled from its shell and harnessed to the nation's service. Spies are blinkered! went the cry. Too incestuous. For Berlin we must open the doors to the real world of dons, barristers and journalists. We need bankers and trade unionists and industrialists, chaps who put their money where their mouths are and know what makes the world tick. We need Members of Parliament who can supply a whiff of the hustings and utter stern words about taxpayers' money!

And what happened to these wise men, Tom, these shrewd no-nonsense outsiders, watchdogs of the secret war? They rushed in where even the spies might have feared to tread. Too long frustrated by the limitations of the overt world, these brilliant, unfettered minds fell overnight in love with every conspiracy, skulduggery and short cut you can imagine.

"Do you know what they're dreaming up now?" Pym raged, pacing the carpet of the service flat in Lowndes Square which Axel had rented for the duration of an Anglo-American conference on unofficial action.

"Calm yourself, Sir Magnus. Have another drink."

"Calm myself? When these lunatics are seriously proposing to plug themselves into the Soviet ground control, talk a MiG over American airspace, blow it out of the sky and, if the pilot by any chance survives, offer him the choice of being put on trial for espionage or staging a public defection in front of the microphones? That's the defence editor of the *Guardian* newspaper speaking, for Christ's sake! He'll start a war. He wants to. It will give him something to report at last. He was backed by a nephew of the Archbishop of Canterbury and a deputy director general of the BBC."

But Axel's love of England would not be spoiled by Pym's prissiness. Through the passenger window of a self-drive Ford from the Firm's carpool, he gazed at Buckingham Palace and softly clapped his hands when he saw the royal pennant fluttering in its arclight.

"Go back to Berlin, Sir Magnus. One day it will be the Stars and Stripes."

His Berlin apartment was in the centre of Unter den Linden, on the top floor of a sprawling Biedermeier house that had miraculously survived the bombing. His bedroom was on the garden side so he didn't hear their car pull up, but he heard their spongy footsteps on the stairs and had a memory of the Fremdenpolizei stealing up Herr Ollinger's wooden staircase in the early hours of the morning that policemen like the best. Pym knew it was the end, though of all the ways he had imagined the end he hadn't expected it to come this way. Fieldmen feel those things and learn to trust them, and Pym was a fieldman twice over. So he knew it was the end and in a quiet way he was neither surprised nor disconcerted. He was out of bed and into the kitchen in a second, because the kitchen was where he had been concealing the rolls of film for his next rendezvous with Axel. By the time they pressed the doorbell he had unrolled six reels and exposed them, and touched off the instant-ignition code pad that he had hidden in an oilskin inside the lavatory cistern. In his clear-eyed acceptance of his fate, he even contemplated something rather more drastic, for Berlin was no Vienna and he kept a pistol in his bedside locker and another in a drawer in the hall. But something about the apologetic way they murmured "Herr Pym, wake up, please," through the letter box discouraged him, and when he looked through the peephole and saw the amiable shape of Police Lieutenant Dollendorf and the young sergeant at his side, a shaming awareness came over him of the shock he would cause them if he took that path. So they're pulling a soft entry, he thought as he opened the door: first you spread your wolf-children round the building, then you put in Mr. Nice Guy by the front door.

Lieutenant Dollendorf, like most people in Berlin, was a client of Jack Brotherhood, and earned a small retainer by looking the other way when agents were being hustled back and forth across the profitable stretch of Wall in his district. He was a cosy Bavarian fellow with all the Bavarian appetites, and his breath smelt permanently of *Weisswurst*.

"Forgive us, Herr Pym. Excuse the disturbances, so late," he began, smiling too broadly. He was in uniform. His gun was still in its holster. "Our Herr Kommandant asks that you come immediately to headquarters on a personal and urgent matter," he explained, still not touching his gun.

There was resolution in Dollendorf's voice as well as embarrassment, however, and his sergeant was peering sharply up and down the stairwell. "The Herr Kommandant assures me that everything can be arranged discreetly, Herr Pym. He wishes at this stage to be delicate. He has made no approach to your superiors," Dollendorf insisted, as Pym still hesitated. "The Kommandant has high respect for you, Herr Pym."

"I have to dress."

"But quickly, if you are so kind, Herr Pym. The Kommandant would like the matter dealt with before he has to hand it over to the day shift."

Pym turned and walked carefully to his bedroom. He waited to hear the policemen following him, or a barked order, but they preferred to remain in the hall, looking at the Cries of London prints, courtesy of the Firm's accommodation section.

"May I use your telephone, Herr Pym?"

"Go ahead."

He dressed with the door open, hoping to overhear the conversation. But all he heard was: "Everything in order, Herr Kommandant. Our man is coming immediately."

They walked down the broad stairs three abreast, to a parked police car with its light flashing. Nothing behind it, no late-night loiterers in the street. How typical of the Germans to disinfect the entire area before arresting him. Pym sat in the front with Dollendorf. The sergeant sat tensely behind. It was raining and two in the morning. A red sky was seething with black cloud. Nobody spoke any more.

And at the police station Jack will be waiting, thought Pym. Or the Military Police. Or God.

The Kommandant rose to receive him. Dollendorf and his sergeant had faded away. The Kommandant considered himself a man of supernatural subtlety. He was tall and grey and hollow-backed, with staring eyes and a narrow rattling mouth that operated at self-destructive speed. He leaned back in his chair and put his fingertips together. He spoke in an anguished monotone to an etching of his birthplace in East Prussia that was hanging on the wall above Pym's head. He spoke, in Pym's calm estimation, for about six hours without a break and without appearing to draw breath, which for the Kommandant was the equivalent of a quick warm-up before they got down to a serious discussion. The Kommandant said that he was a man of the world and a family man, conversant with what he called the "intimate sphere." Pym said he respected this. The Kommandant said he was not didactic, he was not political, though he was a Christian Democrat. He was Evangelical but Pym could rest assured that he had no quarrel with Roman Catholics. Pym said he would have expected no less. The Kommandant said that misdeeds were a spectrum that ran between pardonable human error and calculated crime. Pym agreed, and heard a footfall in the corridor. The Kommandant begged Pym to bear in mind that foreigners in a strange country frequently felt a sense of false security when contemplating what might strictly be regarded as a felonious act.

"I may speak frankly, Herr Pym?"

"Please do," said Pym, in whom by now a fearful premonition was beginning to form that it was Axel, not himself, who was under arrest.

"When they brought him to me, I looked at him. I listened to him. I said, 'No, this cannot be. Not Herr Pym. The man is an impostor,' I said. 'He is trading upon a distinguished connection.' However as I continued to listen to him, I detected a sense of, shall I say, vision? There is an energy here, an intelligence, I may say also a charm. Possibly, I thought, this man is who he says he is. Only Herr Pym can tell us, I thought." He pressed a button on his desk. "I may confront him with you, Herr Pym?"

An old turnkey appeared, and waddled ahead of them down a painted brick corridor that stank of carbolic. He unlocked a grille and closed it behind them. He unlocked another. It was the first time I had seen Rick in prison, Tom, and I have made sure ever since that it was the last. In future times, Pym sent him food, clothes, cigars, and, in Ireland, Drambuie. Pym emptied his bank account for him, and if he had been a millionaire he would have bankrupted himself rather than see him there again, even in his mind's eye. Rick sat in the corner and Pym knew at once that he did this in order to give himself a bigger view of the cell, for ever since I had known him he always needed more space than God had given him. He sat with his great head tipped forward, scowling with a convict's sullenness, and I swear he had closed off his hearing with his thinking and hadn't heard us coming.

"Father," said Pym. "It's me."

Rick came to the bars and put a hand each side and his face between. He stared first at Pym, then at the Kommandant and the turnkey, not understanding Pym's position. His expression was sleepy and bad-tempered.

"So they got you too, did they, son?" he said—not, I thought, without a certain satisfaction. "I always thought you were up to something. You should have read your law like I told you." Slowly the truth began to dawn on him. The turnkey unlocked his door, the good Kommandant said, "Please, Herr Pym," and stood aside for Pym to enter. Pym went to Rick, and put his arms round him, but delicately, in case they had been beating him and he was sore. Gradually the puff began to fill Rick up again.

"God in heaven, old son, what the devil are they doing to me? Can't an honest fellow do a bit of business in this country? Have you seen the food they give you here, these German sausages? What do we pay our taxes for? What did we fight the war for? What's the good of a son who's head of the Foreign Office if he can't keep these German thugs away from his old man?"

But by then Pym was bear-hugging Rick, slapping his shoulders and saying it was good to see him in whatever circumstances. So Rick took to weeping also, and the Kommandant delicately removed himself to another room while, reunited, each pal celebrated the other as his saviour.

I don't mean to disappoint you, Tom, but I do honestly forget, perhaps deliberately, the details of Rick's Berlin transactions. Pym was expecting his own judgment at the time, not Rick's. I remember two sisters and that they were of noble Prussian stock and lived in an old house in Charlottenburg, because Pym called on them to pay them off for the usual missing paintings Rick was selling for them, and the diamond brooch he was getting cleaned for them, and the fur coats that were being remodelled by a first-rate tailor friend of his in London who would do it free because he thought the world of Rick. And I remember the sisters had a bent nephew who was involved in a shady arms racket, and that somewhere in the story Rick had an aeroplane for sale, the finest, best-preserved fighter-bomber you could wish for, in mint condition inside and out. And for all I know it was being painted by those lifelong Liberals, Balham's of Brinkley, and guaranteed to fly everyone to Heaven.

It was in Berlin also that Pym courted your mother, Tom, and took her away from his boss and hers, Jack Brotherhood. I am not sure that you or anybody else has a natural right to know what accident conceived you, but I'll try to help you as best I can. There was mischief in Pym's motive, I won't deny it. The love, what there was of it, came later.

"Jack Brotherhood and I seem to be sharing the same woman," Pym remarked impishly to Axel one day, during a callbox-to-callbox conversation.

Axel required to know immediately who she was.

"An aristo," said Pym, still teasing him. "One of ours. Church and spy Establishment, if that means anything to you. Her family's connections with the Firm go back to William the Conqueror."

"Is she married?"

"You know I don't sleep with married women unless they absolutely insist."

"Is she amusing?"

"Axel, we are talking of a lady."

"I mean is she social?" Axel demanded impatiently. "Is she what you call diplomatic geisha? Is she bourgeois? Would Americans like her?"

"She's a top Martha, Axel. I keep telling you. She's beautiful and rich and frightfully British."

"Then maybe she is the ticket that will get us to Washington," said Axel, who had recently been expressing anxieties about the number of random women drifting through Pym's life.

Soon afterwards, Pym received similar advice from your Uncle Jack.

"Mary has told me what's going on between you, Magnus," he said, taking him aside in his most avuncular manner. "And if you ask me you could travel further and fare a damned sight worse. She's one of the best girls we've got, and it's time you looked a little less disreputable."

So Pym, with both his mentors pushing in the same direction, followed their advice and took Mary, your mother, to be his truly wedded partner at the High Table of the Anglo-American alliance. And really, after all that he had given away already, it seemed a very reasonable sacrifice.

"Hold his hand, Jack"—Pym wrote—"He's the dearest thing I had."

"Mabs, forgive"—Pym wrote—"Dear, dear Mabs, forgive. If love is whatever we can still betray, remember that I betrayed you on a lot of days."

He began a note to Kate and tore it up. He scribbled "Dearest Belinda" and stopped, scared by the silence around him. He looked sharply at his watch. Five o'clock. Why hasn't the clock chimed? I've gone deaf. I'm dead. I'm in a padded cell. From across the square the first chime sounded. One. Two. I can stop it any time I want, he thought. I can stop it at one, at two, at three. I can take any part of any hour and stop it dead. What I cannot do is make it chime midnight at one o'clock. That's God's trick, not mine.

A shocked stillness had descended over Pym and it was the literal stillness of death. He was standing at the window once more, watching the leaves drift across the empty square. An ominous inactivity marked everything he saw. Not a head in a window, not an open doorway. Not a dog or cat or squirrel or a single squawking child. They have taken to the hills. They are waiting for the raiders from the sea. But in his head he is standing in the cellar flat of a run-down office block in Cheapside, watching the two faded Lovelies on their knees as they tear open the last of Rick's files and lick their crabbed fingertips to speed them in their paperchase. Paper lies in growing mounds around them, it flutters through the air like swirling petals as they rummage and discard what they have vainly plundered: bank statements written in blood, invoices, furious solicitors' letters, warrants, summonses, love letters dripping with reproach. The dust of them is filling Pym's nostrils as he watches, the clang of the steel drawers is like the clang of his prison grilles, but the Lovelies heed nothing; they are avid widows ransacking Rick's record. At the centre of the débris, drawers and cupboard askew, stands Rick's last Reichskanzlei desk, its serpents twining themselves round its bombé legs like gilded garters. On the wall hangs the last photograph of the great TP in mayoral regalia and on the chimney piece, above a grate stuffed with false coals and the last of Rick's cigar butts, stands the bronze bust of your Founder and Managing Director himself, beaming out the last of his integrity. On the open door at Pym's back hangs the memorial tablet to Rick's last dozen companies, but a sign beside the bell reads "Press here for attention," because when Rick has not been saving his nation's faltering economy, he has been working as night porter for the block.

"What time did he die?" says Pym, before remembering that he knows.

"Evening, dearie. The pubs was just opening," says one of the Lovelies through her cigarette as she heaves another batch of paper on to the rubbish heap.

"He was having a nice drop next door," says the other, who like the first has not for one moment relaxed her labours.

"What's next door?" says Pym.

"Bedroom," says the first Lovely, tossing aside another spent file.

"So who was with him?" Pym asks. "Were you with him? Who was with him, please?"

"We both were, dearie," says the second. "We was having a little cuddle, if you want to know. Your dad loved a drink and it always made him amorous. We'd had a nice tea early because of his commitments, steak with onion, and he'd had a bit of a barney on the blower with the telephone exchange about a cheque that was in the post to them. He was depressed, wasn't he, Vi?"

The first Lovely, if reluctantly, suspends her researches. The second does likewise. Suddenly they are decent London women, with kindly faces and puffed, overworked bodies.

"It was over for him, dearie," she says, pushing away a hank of hair with her chubby wrist.

"What was?"

"He said if he couldn't have that phone no more, he'd have to go. He said that phone was his lifeline and if he couldn't have it, it was a judgment on him, how would he do his business without a blower and a clean shirt?"

Mistaking Pym's silence for rebuke, her companion flares at him. "Don't look at us like that, darling. He'd had all we've got long ago. We done the gas, we done the electric, we cooked his dinners, didn't we, Vi?"

"We done all we could," says Vi. "And given him the comfort, too."

"We pulled tricks for him more than was natural, didn't we, Vi? Three a day for him, sometimes."

"More," says Vi.

"He was very lucky to have you," says Pym sincerely. "Thank you very much for looking after him."

This pleases them, and they smile shyly.

"You haven't got a nice bottle in that big black briefcase of yours, I suppose, dearie?"

"I'm afraid not."

Vi goes to the bedroom. Through the open doorway Pym sees the great imperial bed from Chester Street, its upholstery ripped and stained with use. Rick's silk pyjamas lie sprawled across the coverlet. He smells Rick's body lotion and Rick's hair oil. Vi returns with a bottle of Drambuie.

"Did he talk about me at all, in the last days?" says Pym while they drink.

"He was proud of you, dear," says Vi's friend. "Very proud." But she seems dissatisfied with her reply. "He was going to catch you up, mind. That was nearly his last words, wasn't it, Vi?"

"We was holding him," says Vi, with a sniff. "You could see he was going from the breathing. 'Tell them I forgive them at the telephone exchange,' he says. 'And tell my boy Magnus we'll both be ambassadors soon.' "

"And after that?" says Pym.

" 'Give us another touch of the Napoleon, Vi,' " says Vi's friend, now weeping also. "It wasn't Napoleon though, it was the Drambuie. Then he says: 'There's enough in those files, girls, to see you right till you join me.' "

"He just nodded off really," says Vi, into her handkerchief. "He mightn't have been dead at all, if it hadn't been for his heart."

There is a rustle at the door. Three knocks. Vi opens it an inch, then all the way, then stands back disapprovingly to admit Ollie and Mr. Cudlove, armed with buckets of ice. The years have not been kind to Ollie's nerves, and the tears at the corners of his eyes are stained with mascara. But Mr. Cudlove is unchanged, down to his chauffeur's black tie. Transferring the bucket to his left side, Mr. Cudlove seizes Pym's right hand in a manly grip. Pym follows them down a narrow corridor lined with photographs of neverwozzers. Rick is lying in the bath with a towel round his middle, his marbled feet crossed over each other as if in accordance with some Oriental ritual. His hands are curled and cupped in readiness to harangue his Maker.

"It's just that there wasn't the funds, sir," Mr. Cudlove murmurs while Ollie pours in the ice. "Not a penny piece anywhere, to be frank, sir. I think those ladies may have taken a liberty."

"Why didn't you close his eyes?" says Pym.

"We did, sir, to be frank, but they would open again, and it didn't seem respectful."

On one knee before his father, Pym writes out a cheque for two hundred pounds, and nearly makes it dollars by mistake.

Pym drives to Chester Street. The house has been in other hands for years but tonight it stands in darkness, as if once more waiting for the Distraining Bailiffs. Pym approaches gingerly. On the doorstep, a nightlight burns despite the rain. Beside it like a dead animal lies an old boa in the mauve of half mourning, similar to the one belonging to Aunt Nell that he had used to block the lavatory at The Glades so long ago. Is it Dorothy's? Or Peggy Wentworth's? Is it some child's game? Is it put there by Lippsie's ghost? No card attaches to its dew-soaked feathers. No sequestrator has pinned his claim to it. The only clue is the one word "Yes," scrawled in trembling chalklines on the door, like a safety signal in a target town.

Turning his back on the deserted square Pym strode angrily to the bathroom and opened the skylight that years ago he had daubed with green paint for Miss Dubber's greater decency. Through a gun slit, he examined the gardens at the side of the house and concluded that they too were unnaturally empty. No Stanley, the Alsatian, tethered to the rain tub of number 8. No Mrs. Aitken, the butcher's wife, who spends every waking hour at her roses. Closing the skylight with a bang, he stooped over the basin and sluiced water in his face, then glowered at his reflection till it gave him a false and brilliant smile. Rick's smile, put on to taunt him, the one that is too happy even to blink. The one that cuddles up against you and presses into you like a thrilled child. The one Pym hated most.

"Fireworks, old son," said Pym, mimicking Rick's cadences at their holy worst. "Remember how you loved a firework? Remember dear old Guy Fawkes night, and the great setpiece there, with your old man's initials on it, RTP, going up in lights all over Ascot? Well then."

Well then, Pym echoed in his soul.

* * *

Pym is writing again. Joyously. No pen can take the strain of this. Reckless free letters are careering over the paper. Light-paths, rocket tails, stars and stripes are zipping above his head. The music of a thousand transistor radios plays around him; the bright faces of strangers laugh into his own, and he is laughing back at them. It is July 4th. It is Washington's night of nights. The diplomatic Pyms have arrived a week ago to take up his appointment as Deputy Head of Station. The island of Berlin is sunk at last. They have a spell in Prague behind them, Stockholm, London. The path to America was never easy, but Pym has gone the distance, Pym has made it, he is assumed and almost risen into the reddened dark that is repeatedly blasted into whiteness by the floodlights, fireworks and searchlights. The crowd is bobbing round him and he is part of it, the free people of the earth have taken him among them. He is one with all these grown-up happy children celebrating their independence of things that never held them. The Marine Band, the Breckenridge Boys Choir and the Metropolitan Area Symposium Choral Group have wooed and won him unopposed. At party after party Magnus and Mary have been celebrated by half the intelligence aristos of Georgetown, have eaten swordfish by candlelight in red-brick yards, chatted under lights strung in overhanging branches, have embraced and been embraced, shaken hands and filled their heads with names and gossip and champagne. Heard a lot about you, Magnus—Magnus, welcome aboard! Jesus, is that your wife? That's *criminal!* Till Mary, worried about Tom —the fireworks have over-excited him—is determined to go home and Bee Lederer has gone with her.

"I'll join you soon, darling," Pym murmurs as she leaves. "Must pop in on the Wexlers or they'll think I'm cutting them."

Where am I? In the Mall? On the Hill? Pym has no idea. The bare arms and thighs and unhampered breasts of young American womanhood are brushing contentedly against him. Friendly hands make space for him to pass; laughter, pot-smoke, din pack the scalding night. "What's your name, man?" "You British? Here, let's shake your hand—take a swig of this." Pym adds a mouthful of bourbon to the impressive mixture he has already taken in. He is climbing a slope, whether of grass or tarmac he cannot determine. The White House glistens below him. Before it, erect and floodlit, the white needle of the Washington Monument cuts its light-path to the unreachable stars. Jefferson and Lincoln, each in his eternal patch of Rome, lie to either side of him. Pym loves them both. All the patriarchs and founding fathers of America are mine. He crests the slope. A black man offers him popcorn. It is salt and hot like his own sweat. Further up the valley, the harmless battles of other firework shows boom and splash into the sky. The crowd is denser up here but still they smile at him and part for him while they ooh and aah at the fireworks, call friendship to each other, break into patriotic song. A pretty girl is teasing him. "Hey, man, why won't you dance?" "Well, thank you, I will with pleasure but just let me take off my coat," Pym replies. His answer is too woody, she has found another partner. He is shouting. At first he does not hear himself but as he enters a quieter place his own voice bursts on him with startling distinctness. "Poppy! Poppy! Where are you?" Helpfully, the good people round him take up the cry. "Hurry on over, Poppy, your boyfriend's here!" "Come on, Poppy, you bad bitch, where you bin?" Behind and above him the rockets become a ceaseless fountain against the swirling crimson clouds. Before him a gold umbrella opens, embracing the whole white mountain and lighting the emptying street. Instructions are ringing remotely in Pym's head. He is reading the numbers of the streets and doorways. He finds the door and with a final surge of joy feels the familiar bony hand close round his wrist and the familiar voice admonishing him.

"Your friend Poppy cannot come tonight, Sir Magnus," says Axel softly. "So will you please stop shouting her name?"

Shoulder to shoulder the two men sit on the steps of the Capitol, gazing down into the Mall on the uncountable thousands they have taken into their protection. Axel has a basket containing a thermos flask of ice-cold vodka, and the best gherkins and brown bread America can supply.

"We made it, Sir Magnus," he breathes. "We are home at last."

"My dearest Father,

"I am very pleased to be able to tell you of my new appointment. Cultural Counsellor may not sound much to you, but it is a post that commands a deal of respect among the highest circles here, and even gets me into the White House. I am also the proud owner of what is called a Cosmic Pass, which means literally that no doors are closed to me any more."

17

Oh my heaven, Tom, the fun we had! The glorious free-wheeling last honeymoon, even as the clouds gathered!

You would be pardoned for thinking that the duties of a Deputy Head of Station, though elevated, are inferior to those of his boss. Not so. The Head of Station in Washington floats in the upper air of intelligence diplomacy. His task is to massage the corpse of the Special Relationship and convince everybody, including himself, that it is alive and well. Every morning, poor Hal Tresider rose early, put on his old Shirburnian tie and sweat-patched tropical suit, and pedalled his pushbike earnestly away to the sodden dreamland of the committee rooms, leaving your father free to ransack the Station Registry, supervise the outstations in San Francisco, Boston, and Chicago, or dart off to welfare a field agent in transit to Central America, China, or Japan. Another chore was shepherding grey-faced British boffins through the battery farms of American high technology, where the scientific secrets that are traded in Washington have their artificial conception. Dining the poor souls, Tom, where others would have left them mouldering in their motels. Consoling them in their womanless, under-financed foreign exile. Chatting hastily memorised jargon at them, about nose cones, turning radius, underwater communication and captive-carry. Borrowing their working documents from them to give back in the morning. "Hullo—*that* looks interesting. Mind if I sneak a sight of that for our Naval Attaché? He's been badgering the Pentagon about that one for years, but they've been holding out on him."

The Naval Attaché had a sight, London had a sight, Prague had a sight. For what use is a Cosmic Pass without a Cosmic readership?

Poor stolid, worthy Hal! How meticulously Pym misused your trust and torpedoed your innocent ambitions! Never mind. If the National Trust won't have you, you can always count on the Royal Automobile Club or a favoured City company.

"I say, Pymmie, there's some ghastly group of physicists visiting the Livermore weapons laboratory next month," you would say, all apology and diffidence. "You don't think you could pop down there and feed and water a few of them and see they don't blow their noses on the tablecloth, could you? Why on earth this service has to behave like a lot of flat-footed security officers these days, I really don't know. I've a good mind to do a letter to London about it, if I can squeeze a moment."

No country was ever easier to spy on, Tom, no nation so open-hearted with its secrets, so quick to air them, share them, confide them, or consign them too early to the junk heap of planned American obsolescence. I am too young to know whether there was a time when Americans were able to restrain their admirable passion to communicate, but I doubt it. Certainly the path has been downhill since 1945, for it was quickly apparent that information which ten years ago would have cost Axel's service thousands of dollars in precious hard currency could by the mid-seventies be had for a few coppers from the *Washington Post*. We could have resented this sometimes, if we had been smaller natures, for there are few things more vexing in the spy world than landing a great scoop for Prague and London one week, only to read the same material in *Aviation Weekly* the next. But we did not complain. In the great fruit garden of American technology, there were pickings enough for everyone and none of us need ever want for anything again.

Cameos, Tom, little tiles for your mosaic are all I need to give you now. See the two friends romping under a darkening sky, catching the last rays of the sunlight before the game is over. See them thieving like children, knowing the police are round the corner. Pym did not take to America in a night, not in a month, for all the splendid fireworks of the Fourth. His love of the place grew with Axel's. Without Axel he might never have seen the light. Pym set out, believe it or not, determined to disapprove of everything he saw. He found no holding point, no stern judgment to revolt against. These vulgar pleasure-seeking people, so frank and clamorous, were too uninhibited for his shielded and involuted life. They loved their prosperity too obviously, were too flexible and mobile, too little the slaves of place, origin and class. They had no sense of that hush which all Pym's life had been the background music of his inhibition. In committee, it was true, they reverted soon enough to type, and became the warring princelings of the European countries they had left behind. They could run you up a cabal that would make mediaeval Venice blush. They could be Dutch and stubborn, Scandinavian and gloomy, Balkan and murderous and tribal. But when they mixed with one another they were American and loquacious and disarming, and Pym was hard put to find a centre to betray.

Why had they done him no harm? Why had they not cramped him, frightened him, forced his limbs into impossible positions from the cradle up? He found himself longing for the empty, darkened streets of Prague and the reassuring embrace of chains. He wanted his dreadful schools back. He wanted anything but the marvellous horizons that led to lives he had not lived. He wanted to spy upon hope itself, look through keyholes at the sunrise and deny the possibilities he had missed.

And all this time, ironically, Europe was coming to get him. He knew that. So did Axel. Not a year had passed before the first insidious whispers of suspicion began to reach their ears. Yet it was this very intimation of mortality that shook Pym out of his reluctance, and inspired him to take the upper hand in their relationship just as Axel was saying, "End it, get out." A mysterious gratitude for America the Just and her impending retribution seized him as, like a ponderous, puzzled giant, she bore steadily down on him, clutching in her great soft fist the multiplying evidence of his duplicity.

"Certain aristos in Langley and London are getting worried about our Czecho networks, Sir Magnus," Axel warned him in his stiff, dry English at a crash meeting at the carpark of the Robert F. Kennedy Stadium. "They have begun to discern certain unfortunate patterns."

"What patterns? There are no patterns."

"They have noticed that the Czecho networks provide better intelligence when we are running them and almost nothing when we are not. That is the pattern. They have computers these days. It takes them five minutes to turn everything upside down and wonder what is the right way up. We have been careless, Sir Magnus. We were too greedy. Our parents were right. If you want a thing done well, you must do it yourself."

"Jack Brotherhood can run those networks as well as we can. The head agents are genuine, they report whatever they can get hold of. All networks go moribund now and then. It's normal."

"These networks only go moribund when we are not there, Sir Magnus," Axel repeated patiently. "That is Langley's perception. It bothers them."

"Then give the networks better material. Signal Prague. Tell your aristos we need a scoop."

Axel sadly shook his head. "You know Prague, Sir Magnus. You know my aristos. The man who is absent is the man they conspire against. I have no power to persuade them."

Calmly Pym contemplated the option that remained to him. Over dinner in their smart house in Georgetown, while Mary played gracious hostess, gracious English lady, gracious diplomatic geisha, Pym wondered whether it was time to persuade Poppy to cross one more frontier after all. He saw himself free of taint, a husband, son and father in good standing at last. He remembered an old Revolutionary farmhouse he and Poppy had admired in Pennsylvania, set among rolling fields and stone fences, with thoroughbred horses that loomed at them out of the sun-stained morning fog. He remembered the whitewashed churches, so sparkling and hopeful after the musty crypts of his childhood, and imagined the resettled family Pym at work and prayer there, and Axel rocking on the garden swing while he drank vodka and shelled peas for lunch.

I shall sell Axel to Langley and buy my freedom, he thought as he dazzled a pearly-toothed matron with a witty anecdote. I shall negotiate an administrative amnesty for myself, and put the record straight.

He never did, he never would. Axel was his keeper and his virtue, he was the altar on which Pym had laid his secrets and his life. He had become the part of Pym that was not owned by anybody else.

* * *

Do I need to tell you, Tom, how bright and dear the world looks when we know our days are numbered? How all life swells and opens to you, and says "Come in" just when you had thought you were unwanted? What a paradise America became once Pym knew the writing was on the wall. All his childhood, rushing back to him! He took Mary to point-to-points at Winterthur in the château country and dreamed of Switzerland and of Ascot. He wandered Georgetown's beautiful Oak Hill Cemetery and imagined he was with Dorothy at The Glades, confined to the dripping orchard where his guilty face could be hidden from the passers-by. Minnie Wilson was our letter box at Oak Hill, Tom. Our first in all America—go and take a look at her one day. She lies on a curled plinth a short way down the terraced bowl, a small dead Victorian girl in marble drapes. We left our messages in a leafy recess between Minnie's backside and her protector, one Thomas Entwistle, who had died in later age. The doyen of the graveyard rested higher up, near the gravel sweep where Pym parked his diplomatic car. Axel found him, Axel made sure Pym found him too. He was Stefan Osusky, co-founder of the Czechoslovak Republic, died in exile, 1973. No concealed offering to Axel seemed complete without a silent prayer of greeting to our brother Stefan. After Minnie, as the volume of our business grew, we were obliged to appoint postmen nearer to the centre of the town. We selected forgotten bronze generals, mostly French, who had fought on the American side in order to annoy the British. We relished their soft hats and telescopes and horses, and the flowers in red uniform at their feet. Their battlefields were grass squares filled with lounging students, our letter boxes anything from the stubby cannon that protected them to the stunted conifers whose inner branches made convenient brown nests of pine needles. But Axel's favourite place of all was the newly opened Air and Space Museum, where he could gaze his heart out at the *Spirit of St. Louis* and John Glenn's *Friendship 7,* and touch the Moon Relic with his forefinger as devoutly as if he were taking water from a holy shrine. Pym never saw him do these things. He could only hear about them afterwards. The trick was to leave their packages in separate lockers in the cloakroom, and swap keys in the darkness of the Samuel P. Langley projection theatre while the audience gasped and clutched the handrails as the screen dazzled them with the thrills of flight.

And away from the eyes and ears of Washington, Tom? What shall I give you first? Silicon Valley, perhaps, and the little Spanish village south of San Francisco where Murgo's monks sang plainsong to us after dinner. Or the Dead Sea landscape of Palm Springs, where the golf carts had Rolls-Royce grilles, and the Mountains of Moab looked down on the pastel stucco and artificial-rock pools of our walled motel while illegal Mexicans wandered the lawns with backpacks, blowing away unsightly leaves that could offend the sensibilities of our fellow millionaires. Can you imagine Axel's ecstasy as he beheld the outdoor air-conditioning machines that moistened the desert air and blew micro-mist over the sunbathers with faces covered in green mud? Shall I tell you of the Palm Springs Humane Society's dog-adoption dinner we attended to celebrate Pym's acquisition of the very latest blueprint for the nose cone of the Stealth bomber? How the dogs were led on stage groomed and ribboned, to be auctioned to humane ladies, while everybody wept as if they were Vietnamese orphans? Of the all-day Bible-thumpers' radio channel that portrayed the Christian God as the champion of wealth, since wealth was the enemy of

Communism? "God's waiting room" is what they call Palm Springs. It has one swimming-pool for every five inhabitants, and lies a couple of hours' drive from the biggest killing factories in the world. Its industries are charity and death. That night, unknown to the retired bandits and senile comedians who made up its geriatric court, Pym and Axel added espionage to the list of its accomplishments.

"We shall never fly so high again, Sir Magnus," Axel said as he reverently surveyed Pym's offering in the silence of their six-hundred-dollar-a-night suite. "I think we may retire also."

Shall I give you Disneyland and another projection room, with a circular screen that showed us the American dream? Can I convince you that Pym and Axel wept sincere tears as they watched the refugees from European persecution set foot on American soil while the commentator spoke of a Nation of Nations and the Land of the Free? We believed it, Tom. And Pym believes it still. Pym never felt more free in his life until the night Rick died. Everything he still contrived to love in himself was here to love in the people round him. A willingness to open themselves to strangers. A guile that was only there to protect their innocence. A fantasy that fired but never owned them. A capacity to be swayed by everything, while still remaining sovereign. And Axel loved them too, but he was not so confident that his affection was reciprocated.

"Wexler is setting up an investigation team, Sir Magnus," he warned one night in Boston as they dined in the Colonial dignity of the Ritz Hotel. "Some bad defector has been telling stories. It's time we got out."

Pym said nothing at all. They walked through the park and watched the swan boats on the pond. They sat in a tense, bare Irish pub that seethed with crimes the English had forgotten. But Pym still refused to speak. A few days later, however, visiting an English don at Yale who occasionally supplied the Firm with tidbits, he found himself in front of the effigy of the American hero Nathan Hale, who was hanged by the British as a spy. His hands were bound behind his back. Below him were inscribed his last words: "I only regret that I have but one life to lose for my country." For several weeks after this, Pym went to ground.

Pym was talking. Pym was on the move. Pym was somewhere in the room, arms locked at his sides, palms splayed like someone wishing to fly or swim. He was sinking into his knees, rolling his shoulders against the wall. He was clutching the green cabinet and shaking it and the cabinet was hobbling in his grasp like an old grandfather clock about to flatten him with its embrace, and the burnbox was bobbing and swaying on top of it saying, "Take me." He was swearing, all in his head. He was talking, all in his head. He wanted calm from his surroundings but they wouldn't give it him. He was at his desk again and the sweat was patting on the paper round him. He was writing. He was calm, but the damned room still wouldn't settle, it was interfering with his prose.

Boston again.

Pym has been visiting the golden semicircle that lies along Route 128. Welcome to America's Technological Highway. It is a place like a crematorium without a smokestack. Discreet, low-lying factories and laboratories crouch amid shrubberies and landscaped mounds. He has picked the brains of a British delegation and taken a few forbidden photographs with a concealed camera in his briefcase. He has lunched privately at the home of a great American patriarch of industry named Bob, whom he has befriended for his indiscretion. They have sat on the verandah, they have gazed across a garden of descending lawns which a black man is sedately mowing with a triple cutter. After lunch Pym drives to Needham, where Axel is waiting for him beside a bend in the Charles River, which serves them as their local Aare. A heron skims over the blue-green rushes. Red-tailed hawks eye them from dead trees. Their path climbs deep into the woods, along a raised esker.

"So what's the matter?" says Axel finally.

"Why should anything be the matter?"

"You are tense and you are not speaking. It is reasonable to assume something is the matter."

"I'm always tense for a debriefing."

"Not tense like this."

"He wouldn't talk to me."

"Bob wouldn't?"

"I asked him how the *Nimitz* refitting contract was going. He replied that his corporation was making great strides in Saudi Arabia. I asked him about his discussions with the Admiral of the Pacific Fleet. He asked me when I was going to bring Mary up to Maine for the weekend. His face has changed."

"How?"

"He's angry. Somebody's warned him about me. I think he's more angry with them than he is with me."

"What else?" says Axel patiently, knowing that with Pym there is always one more door.

"I was followed to his house. A green Ford, smoked windows. There's nowhere to hang around and American watchers don't walk, so they left again."

"What else?"

"Stop asking what else!"

"What else?"

Suddenly a great gulf of caution and mistrust separated them.

"Axel," said Pym finally.

It was unusual for Pym to address him by name; the proprieties of espionage normally restrained him.

"Yes, Sir Magnus."

"When we were in Bern together. When we were students. You weren't, were you?"

"Not a student?"

"You weren't spying on anyone. On the Ollingers. On the Cosmo. On me. You hadn't got people running you in those days. You were just you."

"I was not spying. Nobody was running me. Nobody owned me."

"Is that true?"

But Pym knew already that it was. He knew it by the rare glow of anger that shone in Axel's eyes. By the solemnity and distaste in his voice.

"It was your idea that I was a spy, Sir Magnus. It was never mine."

Pym watched him light a fresh cigar and noticed how the flame of the match trembled.

"It was Jack Brotherhood's idea," Pym corrected him.

Axel drew on the cigar and his shoulders slowly relaxed. "It doesn't matter," he said. "It is simply unimportant at our age."

"Bo's authorised a hostile interrogation," said Pym. "I'm flying back to London on Sunday to face the music."

Who should talk to Axel of interrogation? And of a hostile one at that? Who should dare compare the nocturnal posturings of a couple of the Firm's tame barristers in a safe house in Sussex with the beatings and electric shocks and deprivations that for two decades had been Axel's irregular fare? I blush now to think I used the word to him at all. In '52, as I learned later, Axel had denounced Slansky and demanded the death sentence for him—not very loud because he was half dead himself.

"But that's terrible!" Pym had cried. "How can you serve a country that does that to you?"

"It was not terrible at all, thank you. I should have done it earlier. I secured my survival and Slansky would have died whether I denounced him or not. Give me another vodka."

In '56 he went down again: "That time it was less problematic," he explained, lighting himself a fresh cigar. "I denounced Tito and nobody even bothered to go and kill him."

In the early sixties, while Pym was in Berlin, Axel had rotted for three months in a mediaeval dungeon outside Prague. What he promised that time has always been unclear to me. It was the year when the Stalinists themselves were purged, if only halfheartedly, and Slansky was declared alive again, if only posthumously. (Though he was still ruled to be guilty of his offences, you will remember, if only innocently.) In any case, Axel came back looking ten years older, and for some months had a soft "r" in his speech that was very like a stammer.

Beside experience like this, the inquisition of Pym was watery stuff indeed. Jack Brotherhood was there to defend him. Personnel fussed over him like an old hen, assuring him it was just a matter of answering a few questions. Some chinless flunkey from Treasury kept warning my persecutors they were in danger of exceeding their brief, and my two gaolers insisted on talking to me about their children. After five days and nights of it, Pym felt as spry as if he had been taking a country holiday, and his interrogators were out on their feet.

"Good trip, darling?" Mary asked, back in Georgetown, after a morning in bed in which Pym had temporarily slaked the tension.

"Great," said Pym. "And Jack sends love."

But on his walk to the Embassy he saw a new white arrow chalked on the brickwork of the Fayre-deal wine shop, which was Axel's warning to attempt no contact until further notice.

And here, Tom, it is time for me to tell you what Rick was doing, for your grandfather had one last trick to play before the end. It was his best, as you would suppose. Rick shrank. He abandoned monstrosity as a way of life, and came weeping and cringing to me like a whipped animal. And the smaller and more encompassable he became, the less secure Pym felt. It was as if the Firm and Rick were closing in on him from either side, each with his regretful, hangdog banality, and Pym, like an acrobat on the high wire between them, suddenly had nothing to support him. Pym implored him in his mind. He screamed at him: Stay bad, stay monstrous, keep your distance, don't give up! But on Rick came, shuffling and smirking like a pauper, knowing his power was greatest now that he was weak. "I did it all for you, son. It's thanks to me you've taken your place among the Highest in the Land. Got a few coppers for your old man, have you? How about a nice mixed grill, or are you ashamed to take your old pal out?"

He struck first one Christmas Day, not six weeks after Pym had received a formal apology from Head Office. Georgetown had two feet of snow and we had asked the Lederers to lunch. Mary was putting the food on the table as the phone rang. Will Ambassador Pym accept a collect call from New Jersey? He will.

"Hullo, old son. How's the world using you?"

"I'll take this upstairs," says Pym grimly to Mary, and everybody looks understanding, knowing that the secret world never sleeps.

"Happy Christmas, old son," says Rick as Pym picks up the bedroom phone.

"And Happy Christmas to you, too, Father. What are you doing in New Jersey?"

"God's the twelfth man on the cricket team, son. It's God who tells us to keep the left elbow up through life. No one else."

"So you always said. But it's not the cricket season. Are you drunk?"

"He's umpire, judge and jury rolled into one and never you forget it. There's no conning God. There never was. Are you glad I paid for your education, then?"

"I'm not conning God, Father, I'm trying to celebrate with my family."

"Say hullo to Miriam," says Rick, and there is muffled protest before Miriam comes on the line.

"Hullo, Magnus," says Miriam.

"Hullo, Miriam," says Pym.

"Hullo," says Miriam a second time.

"They feed you all right in that Embassy of yours, son, or is it all Thousand Island and French fries?"

"We have a perfectly decent canteen for the lower staff but at the moment I'm trying to eat at home."

"Turkey?"

"Yes."

"English bread sauce?"

"I expect so."

"That grandson of mine all right then, is he? He's got the forehead, has he, the one I gave you that everybody talks about?"

"He's got a very good brow."

"Blue eyes, same as mine?"

"Mary's eyes."

"I hear she's first class, son. I hear first-rate reports of her. They say she's got a fine piece of property down in Dorset that's worth a bob or two."

"It's in trust," says Pym sharply.

But Rick has already begun drowning in the gulf of his own self-pity. He weeps, the weep becomes a howl. In the background, Miriam is weeping, too, in a high-pitched whimper, like a small dog locked in a big house.

"But darling," says Mary as Pym resumes his place as head of the family. "Magnus. You're upset. What's the matter?"

Pym shakes his head, smiling and crying at once. He grabs his wineglass and lifts it.

"To absent friends," he calls out. "To *all* our absent friends!" And later, for a wife's ears only: "Just an old, old Joe, darling, who managed to track me down and wish me happy bloody Yule."

Would you ever have supposed, Tom, that the greatest country in the world could be too small for one son and his old man? Yet that is what happened. That Rick should head for wherever he could use his son's protection was, I suppose, only natural and after Berlin, probably inevitable. He went first, as I now know, to Canada, unwisely trusting in the bonds of Commonwealth. The Canadians quickly tired of him and when they threatened to repatriate him he made a small down payment on a Cadillac and headed south. In Chicago, my enquiries show that he succumbed to the many enticing offers from property companies to move into new developments on the edge of town and live rent-free for three months as an inducement. A Colonel Hanbury resided at Farview Gardens, a Sir William Forsyth graced Sunleigh Court, where he extended his tenancy by conducting protracted negotiations to buy the penthouse for his butler. What either of them did for liquidity is, as ever, a mystery, though no doubt there were grateful Lovelies in the background. The one clue is a prickly letter from the stewards of a local turf club, advising Sir William that his horses will be welcome when his stable fees have been settled. Pym was still only vaguely aware of these distant rumblings, and his absences from Washington gave him a false sense of protection. But in New Jersey something changed Rick for ever, and whatever it was, from then on Pym became his only industry. Was the same wind of reckoning blowing over both men simultaneously? Was Rick really ill? Or was he, like Pym, merely conscious of impending judgment? Certainly Rick thought he was ill. Certainly he thought he ought to be:

"Am obliged to use strong walking-stick (twenty-nine dollars cash) at all times owing to Heart and other more sinister Ailments"—he wrote—"My doctor keeps the Worst from me and recommends that Frugal diet (plain foods and Champagne only, no Californian) could Prolong this Meagre existence and enable me to Fight back for a few more Months before I am Called."

Certainly he took to wearing liver-coloured spectacles like Aunt Nell. And when he fell foul of the law in Denver, the prison doctor was so impressed by him that he was released the moment Pym had paid the medical fees.

And after Denver you decided you were already dead, didn't you, and set out to haunt me with your smallness? Every town I went to, I walked in fear of your pathetic ghost. Every safe house I entered, I expected to see you waiting at the gate, parading your willed, deliberate littleness. You knew where I would be before I got there. You would con a ticket and travel five thousand miles just to show me how small you had become. And off we'd go to the best restaurant in town, and I would buy you your treat and boast to you about my diplomatic doings and listen to your boastings in return. I would shower you with all the money I could afford, praying that it would enable you to add a few more Wentworths to the green cabinet. But even while I fawned on you and exchanged radiant smiles with you and held hands with you and bolstered you in your idiotic schemes, I knew that you had pulled the best con of them all. You were nothing any more. Your mantle had passed to me, leaving you a naked little man, and myself the biggest con I knew.

"Why don't those fellows give you your knighthood, then, old son? They tell me you ought to be Permanent Under Secretary by now. Got a skeleton in your cupboard, have you? Maybe I should slip over to London and have a word with those Personnel boys of yours."

How did he find me? How could it be that his systems of intelligence were better than those of the Agency's leash dogs who were fast becoming my regular, unwelcome companions? At first I thought he was using private detectives. I began collecting the numbers of suspicious cars, noting the times of dead-end phone calls, trying to distinguish them from Langley's. I bearded my secretary: has someone calling himself my sick father been pestering you for information? Eventually I discovered that the Embassy travel clerk had an addiction to playing English snooker at some Masonic hostel in the dirty part of town. Rick had found him there and pitched him a fatuous cover story: "I've got this dicky heart," he'd said to the fool. "It could get me any time, you see, but don't you go telling my boy. I don't like to bother him when he's got enough on his plate as it is. What you're to do, you're to get on the blower to me and give me the wink whenever that boy of mine leaves town, so that I know where to find him when the end comes." And no doubt there was a gold watch in it somewhere. And tickets for next year's Cup Final. And seeing the boy's dear old mother right next time Rick slipped home for a drop of English air.

But my discovery had come too late. We had had San Francisco by then, and Denver, and Seattle, and Rick had homed on every one of them, weeping and shrinking before my very eyes, until all that was left of Rick was what he owned of Pym; and all that was left of Pym, it seemed to me, as I wove my lies and blandished, and perjured myself before one kangaroo court after another, was a failing con man tottering on the last legs of his credibility.

And that's how it was, Tom. Betrayal is a repetitive trade and I will not bother you with more of it. We have reached the end, though it seems from here to look quite like the beginning. The Firm pulled Pym out of Washington and sent him to Vienna so that he could take back his networks and so that his growing army of accusers could draw its wretched computer pattern tighter round his neck. There was no saving him. Not in the end. Poppy knew that. So did Pym, though he would never admit it, even to himself. Just one more con, Pym kept saying to himself; one more con will see me right. Poppy pressed him, begged him, threatened him. Pym was adamant: Leave me in place, I'll win through, they love me, I've given my life to them.

But the truth is, Tom, that Pym preferred to test the limits of the tolerance of those he loved. He preferred to sit here in Miss Dubber's upper room and wait for God to come, while he looked down the gardens to the beach where the best pals ever had kicked a football from one end of the world to the other, and ridden their Harrods bicycles across the sea.

18

It's fireworks night at Plush, thought Mary, staring into the darkness of the square. It's an unlit bonfire waiting for Tom. Through the windscreen of their parked car she gazed at the empty bandstand and pretended she saw the last of her family and retainers crammed into the old cricket pavilion. The muffled footsteps were the footsteps of the gamekeepers as they gathered to her brother Sam, back for his last leave. She pretended she could hear her brother's voice, a little too parade-ground for her liking, still scratchy from the strain of Ireland. "Tom?" he calls. "Where's old Tom?" . . . Not a move. Tom is stuck inside Mary's sheepskin coat, his head jammed against her thigh and nothing short of Christmas is going to lure him out. "Come on, Tom Pym, you're the youngest!" cries Sam. "Where is he? . . . You'll be too old next year, you know, Tom." Then his brutal dismissal. "Fuck it. Let's have someone else." Tom is shamed, the Pyms are disgraced, Sam as usual is angry that Tom has no taste for blowing up the universe. A braver child puts the match and the world ignites. Her brother's military rockets race over it in perfect salvoes. Everyone is small, looking at the night sky.

She sat at Brotherhood's side and he was holding her wrist the way the doctor held it when she was about to bear her little coward. To reassure her. To steady her. To say "I am in charge here." The car was parked in a side street and behind them stood the police van and behind the police van stood a caravan of about six hundred parked police cars and radio vans and ambulances and bomb lorries, all occupied by Sam's familiars who spoke soundlessly to one another without moving their eyes. Beside her was a shop called Sugar Novelties with a neon-lit window and a plastic gnome pushing a wheelbarrow laden with dusty sweets, and next to it a granite workhouse with "Public Library" engraved over a funereal door. Across the street stood a hideous Baptist church that told you God was no fun either. Beyond the church lay God's square and His bandstand and His monkey-puzzle trees, and between the fourth and fifth tree from the left, as she had counted twenty times, and three-quarters of the way up, hung an arched lighted window with the orange curtains drawn, which my officers advise me is where your husband's room is situated, madam, though our enquiries indicate that he is known locally by the name of Canterbury and is well liked in the community.

"He's always liked," Mary snapped.

But the superintendent was saying this to Brotherhood. He was speaking through Brotherhood's window and deferring to Brotherhood as her keeper. And Mary knew that the superintendent had been ordered to speak to her as little as possible, which came hard to him. And that Brotherhood had given himself the job of answering for her, which the superintendent seemed to accept was as near to godliness as he was likely to get without having his ears blasted off. The superintendent was a Devon man, and ponderously traditional. I'm so *frightfully* glad he's being arrested by a *Devon* man, she thought cruelly, in Caroline Lumsden's Sloane-Ranger twitter. I always think it's *so* much *nicer* to be taken prisoner by a man of the soil.

"Are you quite sure you wouldn't like to come into the Church Hall, madam?" the superintendent was saying for the hundredth time. "It's much warmer in the Church Hall and there's some quite fine company. Cosmopolitan, counting the Americans."

"She's best here," Brotherhood murmured in reply.

"Only we can't allow the gentleman to switch on the engine, you see, to be truthful, madam. And if he can't switch on the engine, well you can't have the heating, if you see what I mean."

"I'd like you to go away," Mary said.

"She's all right as she is," said Brotherhood.

"Only it could be all night, you see, madam. Could be all tomorrow too. If our friend decides to stick it out, kind of thing, to be truthful."

"We'll play it as it comes," Brotherhood said. "When you need her, this is where she'll be."

"Well I'm afraid she won't, sir, to be truthful, not when we go in, if we have to. I'm afraid she'll have to withdraw to a somewhat safer position, to be truthful, same as you. Only the rest of them are back in the Church Hall, if you follow me, sir, and the chief constable says that's where all non-combatants have got to be at that stage in the proceedings including the Americans."

"She doesn't want to be with the rest of them," said Mary before Brotherhood could speak. "And she's not American. She's his wife."

The superintendent went away and came back almost immediately. He's the go-between. They've chosen him for his bedside manner.

"Message from the roof, sir," he began apologetically, crouching yet again to Brotherhood's window. "Do you happen to know, please, the precise type and calibre of the weapon our friend is alleged to have in his possession?"

"Standard Browning three-eight automatic. An old one. Shouldn't think it's been cleaned for years."

"Any theories regarding the type of ammunition at all, sir? Only it would be nice for them to know the carry, you see."

"Short nose, I should think."

"But not a stopper, for instance, or a dumdum?"

"Why the hell should he want a dumdum?"

"I don't know, sir, do I? Information is gold dust on this one, the way it's being passed around, if I may say so. I haven't seen so many tight lips in one room for, oh, a long time. How many rounds has our friend got, do you think?"

"One magazine. Maybe a spare."

Mary was suddenly furious. "For God's sake. He's not a maniac! He's not going to start a—"

"Start a what?" said the superintendent, whose country manners had a way of slipping when he wasn't spoken to respectfully.

"Just assume it's one magazine and one spare," Brotherhood said.

"Well, then, perhaps you can tell us how our friend's marksmanship is," the superintendent suggested as if stepping on to safer ground. "You can't blame them for asking that, can you?"

"He's been trained and topped up all his life," said Brotherhood.

"He's good," Mary said.

"Now how do you know that, madam, if I may be allowed to ask a simple question?"

"He shoots Tom's air pistol with him."

"Rats and that? Or something larger?"

"Paper targets."

"Does he now? And gets a high score then, does he, madam?"

"Tom says so."

She glanced at Brotherhood and knew what he was thinking. Just let me go in and get him, gun or no. She was thinking much the same herself: Magnus, come out of there and stop making yourself so bloody ridiculous. The superintendent was speaking again, this time to Brotherhood directly.

"Now there's a query from our disposal people this time, sir," he said, as if it were all a little bit unreasonable but we must humour them. "Regarding this box device our friend is carrying with him. I've tried them in the Church Hall but they're all a bit above the technicalities like, and they said to ask you. Our boys do appreciate they're not allowed to know too much about it, but they would like the benefit of your wisdom regarding the charge it contains."

"It's self-consuming," Brotherhood replied. "It's not a weapon."

"Ah, but could it be used as a weapon, put it that way, if it got into the hands of one who might for instance have lost the balance of his mind?"

"Not unless he put somebody inside it," Brotherhood replied and the superintendent let out a mellow country laugh.

"I'll tell that one to the boys," he promised. "They like a joke up there, the boys do, it gets the tension out of them." His voice fell and he spoke to Brotherhood alone. "Has our friend ever fired his gun in anger, sir?"

"It's not his gun."

"Ah, now you didn't quite answer the question there, sir, did you?"

"To my knowledge he's never been in a shoot-out."

"Our friend doesn't get angry," Mary said.

"Has he ever taken anybody prisoner, sir?"

"Us," Mary said.

Pym had made the cocoa and Pym had put the new shawl over Miss Dubber's shoulders although she said she didn't feel the chill. Pym had chopped up the piece of chicken for Toby that he had bought at the supermarket as a treat for him, and if she had let him he would have cleaned out the canary's cage as well; for the canary was his secret pride ever since a night when he had found it dead after Miss Dubber had gone to bed, and contrived, unknown to her, to exchange it for a live one with Mr. Loring of the pet shop. But Miss Dubber wanted no more fussing from him. She wanted him sitting beside her where she could keep an eye on him and listen to him reading Aunt Al's latest letter from distant Sri Lanka, which came in yesterday, Mr. Canterbury, but you never had the interest.

"Is that Ali the dhobi who stole her lace last year?" she enquired sharply, interrupting him. "Why does she go on employing him if he stole from her? I thought we'd seen the last of Ali long ago."

"I expect she forgave him," said Pym. "He had all those wives, if you remember. She probably couldn't bear to chuck him into the street." His voice was very clear to him and beautiful. It was good to speak aloud.

"I do wish she'd come home," Miss Dubber said. "It can't be good for her, the heat, after all these years."

"Ah but then she'd have to do her own washing, wouldn't she, Miss D?" said Pym. And his smile warmed him as he knew it was warming her.

"You're better now, aren't you, Mr. Canterbury? I'm so glad. It's got out of you, whatever it is. You can have a nice rest now."

"What from?" said Pym gently, still smiling at her.

"Whatever you've been doing all these years. You can let somebody else run the country for a while. Did he leave you a lot of work to do, the poor gentleman who died?"

"I suppose he did really. It's always difficult when you don't have a proper handover."

"But you'll be all right now, won't you? I can see."

"I will when you say you'll take that holiday, Miss D."

"Only if you come."

"I can't *do* that. I told you! I've run out of leave!"

His voice had lifted more than he intended. She looked at him and he saw the scare in her face, which was how he had caught her looking at him ever since the green cabinet had arrived, or when he had smiled and pampered her too much.

"Well I'm not going," she replied tartly. "I don't like putting Toby into prison and Toby doesn't like going to prison and we're not going to do it just to please you, are we, Toby? You're very kind but don't mention it again. Is that all she says?"

"The rest is about the race riots. She thinks there are more on the way. I don't think you'd like it."

"You're quite right, I would *not*," said Miss Dubber firmly and her eyes stayed on him as he crossed the room, folded the letter and put it in the ginger jar. "You can read it to me in the morning when I don't mind so much. Why's the square quiet? Why isn't Mrs. Peel playing her television next door? She should be watching that announcer she's in love with."

"Probably gone to bed," said Pym. "More cocoa, Miss D?" he asked, taking the mugs to the scullery. The curtains were drawn, but beside the window was an extractor fan that Pym had built into the wooden wall and it was made of transparent plastic. Putting his eye to it he quickly surveyed the square but saw no sign of life.

"Don't be so silly, Mr. Canterbury," Miss Dubber was saying. "You know I never have a second cup. Come back and watch the news."

At the far end of the square, in the shadow of the church, a small light went on and off.

"Not tonight, Miss D, if you don't mind," he called to her. "I've had nothing but politics all week." He ran the tap and waited till the Crimean war geyser caught before he rinsed the mugs. "I'm going to put myself to bed and give the world a rest, Miss D."

"Well you'd better answer the telephone first," she replied. "It's for you."

She must have lifted the receiver at once for he had not heard it above the sobbing of the geyser. It had never rung for him before. He returned to the kitchen and she was holding the receiver out to him and he saw the scare in her face again, accusing him, as he reached out a steady hand to take it. He put the phone to his ear and said "Canterbury." The line went dead but he kept the phone to his ear and gave a quick bright smile of recognition to the middle distance of Miss Dubber's kitchen, somewhere between the picture of Pilgrim slogging up the hill past the hookers, and the picture of the little girl in bed with her hair brushed, about to eat her boiled egg.

"Thank you," he said. "Well thank you very much indeed, Bill. Well that's very handsome of you. And of the Minister. Thank him for me, will you, Bill? Let's have lunch about it next week. On me."

He rang off. There was a lot of heat in his face and he was no longer quite sure, now that he looked at Miss Dubber, what her expression was doing, or whether she was aware of the pains he was getting around the shoulders and neck and in the right knee, which he had ricked when he was skiing at Lech with Tom.

"Apparently the Minister's rather pleased with the work I did for him," he explained to her a little blindly. "He wanted me to know that my efforts hadn't been in vain. That was his private secretary, Bill. Sir William Wells. Friend of mine."

"I see," Miss Dubber said. But she was not enthusiastic.

"The Minister's not terribly appreciative as a rule, to be honest. Doesn't let it show. Hard man to please. Practically never been known to hand out a compliment in his life. But we're all rather devoted to him. Warts and all, as you might say. We do all rather tend to be a bit fond of him notwithstanding, if you follow. We've all rather decided to accept that he's part of life's rich pageant, and not some sort of monster. Yes, well I'm tired, Miss D. Let's put you to bed."

She had not moved. He talked harder.

"It wasn't Himself of course. He's in all-night session. Liable to be there on and off for a long while. This was his private secretary."

"So you told me."

" 'That's medal material, Pym dear boy,' he said. 'The old man actually smiled.' The old man, that's what we call the Minister. Sir William to his face, but 'the old man' behind his back. Be nice to have a gong, wouldn't it, Miss D? Put it over the fireplace. Polish it at Easter and Christmas. Our own private medal. Earned on the premises. If anyone's deserved it, you have."

He stopped speaking for a while because he was blurting a bit and his mouth was dry and he had the worst ear-and-throat thing he could remember. I really ought to go to one of those private health clinics and have the complete sheep-dip. So instead of speaking he stood over her with his hands dangling so that he could haul her to her feet and give her the old good-night bear-hug that meant so much to her. But Miss Dubber did not oblige. She did not want the hug.

"Why do you call yourself Canterbury if your name is Pym?" she demanded sternly.

"That's my first name. Pym. Like Pip. Pym Canterbury."

She had thought for a long time about that. She studied his dried-up eyes and his cheek muscles that were writhing for no known reason. And he noticed that she didn't like much what she saw, and was disposed to quarrel. But as he strained his smile at her, and willed her with all the life that was left in him, he was rewarded by a strict nod of acceptance.

"Well we're both too old for Christian names now, Mr. Canterbury," she said. After which she did finally hold out her arms and he did gently take hold of them above the elbows, and he did have to remember not to pull too hard, because he was so keen to have her against him and get himself off to bed where he belonged.

"Now I'm glad about that medal," she announced as he led her along the passage. "I've always admired a man who gets a medal, Mr. Canterbury. Whatever he's done."

The stairs belonged to the houses of his childhood so he skipped up them lightly and forgot his aches and pains. The star-of-Bethlehem lampshade on the landing, though it shed a lousy light, was an old friend from The Glades. Everything is kind to me, he noticed. When he pushed open the door of his room, everything winked and laughed at him like a surprise party. The parcels were all as he had prepared them but it never did any harm to check. So he checked them now. Envelope for Miss Dubber, lots of money and apologies. Envelope to Jack, no money and come to think of it, precious few apologies. Poppy, how odd that you are such a distant sound at last. That stupid filing cabinet, I don't know why I bothered with it all these years. I haven't even looked inside. The burnbox, what a weight it is for so few secrets. Nothing to Mary but he'd really nothing much more to say to her: "Sorry I married you for cover. Glad I managed a bit of love along the way. Hazards of the trade, m'dear. You're a spy too, remember? Rather better than Pym was, come to think of it. Class will tell in the end." Only the envelope to Tom bothered him, and he tore open the sealed flap feeling that a last word of explanation was after all required.

"You see, Tom, I am the bridge," he wrote in a hand that was irritatingly sluggish. "I am what you must walk over to get from Rick to life."

Then he added his initials, as one always should with a postscript, and addressed a fresh envelope and put the old one in the waste-paper basket because he had been taught from early in his life that untidiness was the sister of insecurity.

Then he hauled the burnbox from the top of the cabinet to the desk and with the two keys from his chain disarmed it and fished out first the files which were too secret to be classified at all and which gave a lot of bogus information about the networks he and Poppy had so painstakingly composed. He chucked them in the waste-paper basket too. When he'd done that he pulled out the gun and loaded it and cocked it, all rather swiftly, and set it on the desk thinking of the many times he had carried a gun and not fired it. He heard a scraping sound from the roof, and said to himself: must be a cat. He shook his head as if to say those damned cats, they get everywhere these days, don't give the birds a chance. He glanced at his gold watch, a wide gesture, remembering that Rick had given it to him and that he might forget to take it off in the bath. So he took it off now and laid it on Tom's envelope and drew a cheerful moon face right next to it, the sign they drew for one another to say "Smile." He undressed and laid his clothes neatly by the bed, then he put on his dressing-gown and took both his towels from the clothes-horse, the big one for the bath, the small one for hands and face. He slipped the gun into the dressing-gown pocket, leaving the safety catch in the "off" position because it was the laborious ethic of the trainers that a safed gun was more dangerous than a live one. He was only going across the corridor but it's a violent world these days and you can't be too careful. About to open the bathroom door he was annoyed to discover that the porcelain knob had stiffened up and scarcely turned. Damned doorknob. Look at that. It took him all the strength of both his hands to twist it and, more annoying still, some idiot must have left soap on it, because his hands kept slithering and he had to use a towel to get a grip. It's probably dear old Lippsie, he thought with a smile: always living in that world inside her head. Placing himself for the last time before the shaving mirror, he arranged the towels around his head and shoulders, making a bonnet of the small one and a cape of the large one, because if there was one thing Miss Dubber hated above another, it was mess. Then he held the gun to where his right ear was, forgetting, as anybody might in the circumstances, whether the trigger of your Browning .38 automatic had two pressures or just the one. And he noticed how he was leaning: not away from the gun, but into it, like someone a little deaf, straining for a sound.

Mary never heard the shot. The superintendent was crouching at Brotherhood's window again, this time to tell him that Magnus's presence inside the house had now been positively confirmed by a ruse and that he had orders to assemble non-combatants in the Church Hall without delay. Brotherhood was contesting this, and Mary still had her eye on the four men playing Grannie's Footsteps among the chimney-pots across the square. For half an hour now they had been reeling out rope to one another and adopting classic postures of stealth, and Mary loathed the lot of them more than she could have imagined possible. A society that admires its shock troops had better be bloody careful about where it's going, Magnus liked to say. The superintendent was confirming that there were no other male lodgers on the premises apart from the said Canterbury, and he was asking Mary whether she would hold herself in readiness to speak to her husband on the telephone in a conciliatory manner if this became necessary during the course of operations. And Mary was retorting: "Of *course* I will," in an overbold whisper intended to deflate all this theatrical nonsense. All those things in her later memory were taking place or had just done so as Brotherhood shoved open the driver's door, sending the superintendent flying to one side, one boot for ever frozen in the window frame. After that she had a forward image of Jack pelting towards the house at a young man's pace because sometimes she had a dream of him doing exactly that, and the house was always Plush and he was coming to make love to her. But with the clamour all around him he was standing still. Lights had come on, ambulances were racing to the spot without apparently knowing where the spot was, police and plainclothesmen were falling over each other and the fools on the roof were shouting at the fools in the square and England was being saved from things it didn't know were threatening it. But Jack Brotherhood was standing to attention like a dead centurion at his post, and everyone was watching a dignified little lady in a dressing-gown coming down the steps of her house.

For Bob Gottlieb,
a great editor and a long-suffering friend

Indeed, I think that people want peace so much that one of these days governments had better get out of their way and let them have it.

DWIGHT D. EISENHOWER

One must think like a hero to behave like a merely decent human being.

MAY SARTON

FOREWORD

Acknowledgements in novels can be as tedious as credits at the cinema, yet I am constantly touched by the willingness of busy people to give their time and wisdom to such a frivolous undertaking as mine, and I cannot miss this opportunity to thank them.

I recall with particular gratitude the help of Strobe Talbott, the illustrious Washington journalist, Sovietologist and writer on nuclear defence. If there are errors in this book, they are surely not his, and there would have been many more without him. Professor Lawrence Freedman, the author of several standard works on the modern conflict, also allowed me to sit at his feet, but must not be blamed for my simplicities.

Frank Gerrity, for many years an agent of the Federal Bureau of Investigation, introduced me to the mysteries of the lie detector, now sadly called the polygraph, and if my characters are not as complimentary about its powers as he is, the reader should blame them, not him.

I must also offer a disclaimer on behalf of John Roberts and his staff at the Great Britain–USSR Association, of which he is Director. It was he who accompanied me on my first visit to the USSR, opening all sorts of doors for me that might otherwise have stayed shut. But he knew nothing of my dark intent, neither did he probe. Of his staff, I may mention particularly Anne Vaughan.

My Soviet hosts at the Writers' Union showed a similar discretion, and a largeness of spirit that took me by surprise. Nobody who visits the Soviet Union in these extraordinary years, and is privileged to conduct the conversations that were granted me, can come away without an enduring love for its people and a sense of awe at the scale of the problems that face them. I hope that my Soviet friends will find reflected in this fable a little of the warmth that I felt in their company, and of the hopes we shared for a saner and more companionable future.

Jazz is a great unifier and I did not want for friends when it came to Barley's saxophone. Wally Fawkes, the celebrated cartoonist and jazz player, lent me his musician's ear, and John Calley his perfect pitch both in words and music. If such men would only run the world, I should have no more conflicts to write about.

1

In a broad Moscow street not two hundred yards from the Leningrad station, on the upper floor of an ornate and hideous hotel built by Stalin in the style known to Muscovites as Empire During the Plague, the British Council's first ever audio fair for the teaching of the English language and the spread of British culture was grinding to its excruciating end. The time was half past five, the summer weather erratic. After fierce rain showers all day long, a false sunlight was blazing in the puddles and raising vapour from the pavements. Of the passers-by, the younger ones wore jeans and sneakers, but their elders were still huddled in their warms.

The room the Council had rented was not expensive but neither was it appropriate to the occasion. I have seen it.—Not long ago, in Moscow on quite another mission, I tiptoed up the great empty staircase and, with a diplomatic passport in my pocket, stood in the eternal dusk that shrouds old ballrooms when they are asleep.—With its plump brown pillars and gilded mirrors, it was better suited to the last hours of a sinking liner than the launch of a great initiative. On the ceiling, snarling Russians in proletarian caps shook their fists at Lenin. Their vigour contrasted unhelpfully with the chipped green racks of sound cassettes along the walls, featuring *Winnie-the-Pooh* and *Advanced Computer English in Three Hours*. The sackcloth sound-booths, locally procured and lacking many of their promised features, had the sadness of deck chairs on a rainy beach. The exhibitors' stands, crammed under the shadow of an overhanging gallery, seemed as blasphemous as betting shops in a tabernacle.

Nevertheless a fair of sorts had taken place. People had come, as Moscow people do, provided they have the documents and status to satisfy the hard-eyed boys in leather jackets at the door. Out of politeness. Out of curiosity. To talk to Westerners. Because it is there. And now on the fifth and final evening the great farewell cocktail party of exhibitors and invited guests was getting into its stride. A handful of the small *nomenklatura* of the Soviet cultural bureaucracy was gathering under the chandelier, the ladies in their beehive hairstyles and flowered frocks designed for slenderer frames, the gentlemen slimmed by the shiny French-tailored suits that signified access to the special clothing stores. Only their British hosts, in despondent shades of grey, observed the monotone of Socialist austerity. The hubbub rose, a brigade of pinafored governesses distributed the curling salami sandwiches and warm white wine. A senior British diplomat who was not quite the Ambassador shook the better hands and said he was delighted.

Only Niki Landau among them had withheld himself from the celebrations. He was stooped over the table in his empty stand, totting up his last orders and checking his dockets against expenses, for it was a maxim of Landau's never to go out and play until he had wrapped up his day's business.

And in the corner of his eye—an anxious blue blur was all that she amounted to—this Soviet woman he was deliberately ignoring. *Trouble,* he was thinking as he laboured. *Avoid.*

The air of festivity had not communicated itself to Landau, festive by temperament though he was. For one thing, he had a lifelong aversion to British officialdom, ever since his father had been forcibly returned to Poland. The British themselves, he told me later, he would hear no wrong of them. He was one of them by adoption and he had the poker-backed reverence of the convert. But the Foreign Office flunkies were another matter. And the loftier they were, and the more they twitched and smirked and raised their stupid eyebrows at him, the more he hated them and thought about his dad. For another thing, if he had been left to himself, he would never have come to the audio fair in the first place. He'd have been tucked up in Brighton with a nice new little friend he had, called Lydia, in a nice little private hotel he knew for taking little friends.

"Better to keep our powder dry till the Moscow book fair in September," Landau had advised his clients at their headquarters on the Western by-pass. "The Russkies love a book, you see, Bernard, but the audio market scares them and they aren't geared for it. Go in with the book fair, we'll clean up. Go in with the audio fair, we're dead."

But Landau's clients were young and rich and did not believe in death. "Niki boy," said Bernard, walking round behind him and putting a hand on his shoulder, which Landau didn't like, "in the world today, we've got to show the flag. We're patriots, see, Niki? Like you. That's why we're an offshore company. With the *glasnost* today, the Soviet Union, it's the Mount Everest of the recording business. And you're going to put us on the top, Niki. Because if you're not, we'll find somebody who will. Somebody younger, Niki, right? Somebody with the drive and the class."

The drive Landau had still. But the class, as he himself was the first to tell you, the class, forget it. He was a card, that's what he liked to be. A pushy, short-arsed Polish card and proud of it. He was Old Nik the cheeky chappie of the Eastward-facing reps, capable, he liked to boast, of selling filthy pictures to a Georgian convent or hair tonic to a Roumanian billiard ball. He was Landau the undersized bedroom athlete, who wore raised heels to give his Slav body the English scale he admired, and ritzy suits that whistled "here I am." When Old Nik set up his stand, his travelling colleagues assured our unattributable enquirers, you could hear the tinkle of the handbell on his Polish vendor's barrow.

And little Landau shared the joke with them, he played their game. "Boys, I'm the Pole you wouldn't touch with a barge," he would declare proudly as he ordered up another round. Which was his way of getting them to laugh with him. Instead of at him. And then most likely, to demonstrate his point, he would whip a comb from his top pocket and drop into a crouch. And with the aid of a picture on the wall, or any other polished surface, he'd sweep back his too black hair in preparation for fresh conquest, using both his little hands to coax it into manliness. "Who's that comely one I'm looking at over there in the corner then?" he'd ask, in his godless blend of ghetto Polish and East End cockney. "Hullo there, sweetheart! Why are we suffering all alone tonight?" And once out of five times he'd score, which in Landau's book was an acceptable rate of return, always provided you kept asking.

But this evening Landau wasn't thinking of scoring or even asking. He was thinking that yet again he had worked his heart out all week for a pittance—or, as he put it more graphically to me, a tart's kiss. And that every fair these days, whether it was a book fair or an audio fair or any other kind of fair, took a little more out of him than he liked to admit to himself, just as every woman did. And gave him a fraction too little in return. And that tomorrow's plane back to London couldn't come too soon. And that if this Russian bird in blue didn't stop insinuating herself into his attention when he was trying to close his books and put on his party smile and join the jubilant throng, he would very likely say something to her in her own language that both of them would live to regret.

That she was Russian went without saying. Only a Russian woman would have a plastic perhaps-bag dangling from her arm in readiness for the chance purchase that is the triumph of everyday life, even if most perhaps-bags were of string. Only a Russian would be so nosy as to stand close enough to check a man's arithmetic. And only a Russian would preface her interruption with one of those fastidious grunts, which in a man always reminded Landau of his father doing up his shoe laces, and in a woman, Harry, bed.

"Excuse me, sir. Are you the gentleman from Abercrombie & Blair?" she asked.

"Not here, dear," said Landau without lifting his head. She had spoken English, so he had spoken English in return, which was the way he played it always.

"Mr. Barley?"

"Not Barley, dear. Landau."

"But this is Mr. Barley's stand."

"This is not Barley's stand. This is my stand. Abercrombie & Blair are next door."

Still without looking up, Landau jabbed his pencil-end to the left, towards the empty stand on the other side of the partition, where a green-and-gold board proclaimed the ancient publishing house of Abercrombie & Blair of Norfolk Street, Strand.

"But that stand is empty. No one is there," the woman objected. "It was empty yesterday also."

"Correct. Right on," Landau retorted in a tone that was final enough for anybody. And he ostentatiously lowered himself further into his account book, waiting for the blue blur to remove itself. Which was rude of him, he knew, and her continuing presence made him feel ruder.

"But where is Scott Blair? Where is the man they call Barley? I must speak to him. It is very urgent."

Landau was by now hating the woman with unreasoning ferocity.

"*Mr.* Scott Blair," he began as he snapped up his head and stared at her full on, "more commonly known to his intimates as Barley, is *awol,* madam. That means absent without leave. His company booked a stand—yes. And Mr. Scott Blair is chairman, president, governor-general and for all I know lifetime dictator of that company. However, he did not occupy his stand—" But here, having caught her eye, he began to lose his footing. "Listen, dear, I happen to be trying to make a living here, right? I am not making it for Mr. Barley Scott Blair, love him as I may."

Then he stopped, as a chivalrous concern replaced his momentary anger. The woman was trembling. Not only with the hands that held her brown perhaps-bag but also at the neck, for her prim blue dress was finished with a collar of old lace and Landau could see how it shook against her skin and how her skin was actually whiter than the lace. Yet her mouth and jaw were set with determination and her expression commanded him.

"Please, sir, you must be very kind and help me," she said as if there were no choice.

Now Landau prided himself on knowing women. It was another of his irksome boasts but it was not without foundation. "Women, they're my hobby, my life's study and my consuming passion, Harry," he confided to me, and the conviction in his voice was as solemn as a Mason's pledge. He could no longer tell you how many he had had, but he was pleased to say that the figure ran into the hundreds and there was not one of them who had cause to regret the experience. "I play straight, I choose wisely, Harry," he assured me, tapping one side of his nose with his forefinger. "No cut wrists, no broken marriages, no harsh words afterwards." How true this was nobody would ever know, myself included, but there can be no doubt that the instincts that had guided him through his philanderings came rushing to his assistance as he formed his judgments about the woman.

She was earnest. She was intelligent. She was determined. She was scared, even though her dark eyes were lit with humour. And she had that rare quality which Landau in his flowery way liked to call the Class That Only Nature Can Bestow. In other words, she had quality as well as strength. And since in moments of crisis our thoughts do not run consecutively but rather sweep over us in waves of intuition and experience, he sensed all these things at once and was on terms with them by the time she spoke to him again.

"A Soviet friend of mine has written a creative and important work of literature," she said after taking a deep breath. "It is a novel. A great novel. Its message is important for all mankind."

She had dried up.

"A novel," Landau prompted. And then, for no reason he could afterwards think of, "What's its title, dear?"

The strength in her, he decided, came neither from bravado nor insanity but from conviction.

"What's its message then, if it hasn't got a title?"

"It concerns actions before words. It rejects the gradualism of the *perestroika*. It demands action and rejects all cosmetic change."

"Nice," said Landau, impressed.

She spoke like my mother used to, Harry: chin up and straight into your face.

"In spite of *glasnost* and the supposed liberalism of the new guidelines, my friend's novel cannot yet be published in the Soviet Union," she continued. "Mr. Scott Blair has undertaken to publish it with discretion."

"Lady," said Landau kindly, his face now close to hers. "If your friend's novel is published by the great house of Abercrombie & Blair, believe me, you can be assured of total secrecy."

He said this partly as a joke he couldn't resist and partly because his instincts told him to take the stiffness out of their conversation and make it less conspicuous to anybody watching. And whether she understood the joke or not, the woman smiled also, a swift warm smile of self-encouragement that was like a victory over her fears.

"Then, Mr. Landau, if you love peace please take this manuscript with you back to England and give it immediately to Mr. Scott Blair. Only to Mr. Scott Blair. It is a gift of trust."

What happened next happened quickly, a street-corner transaction, willing seller to willing buyer. The first thing Landau did was look behind her, past her shoulder. He did that for his own preservation as well as hers. It was his experience that when the Russkies wanted to get up to a piece of mischief, they always had other people close by. But his end of the assembly room was empty, the area beneath the gallery where the stands were was dark and the party at the centre of the room was by now in full cry. The three boys in leather jackets at the front door were talking stodgily among themselves.

His survey completed, he read the girl's plastic name badge on her lapel, which was something he would normally have done earlier but her black-brown eyes had distracted him. Yekaterina Orlova, he read. And underneath, the word "October," given in both English and Russian, this being the name of one of Moscow's smaller State publishing houses specialising in translations of Soviet books for export, mainly to other Socialist countries, which I am afraid condemned it to a certain dowdiness.

Next he told her what to do, or perhaps he was already telling her by the time he read her badge. Landau was a street kid, up to all the tricks. The woman might be as brave as six lions and by the look of her probably was. But she was no conspirator. Therefore he took her unhesitatingly into his protection. And in doing so he spoke to her as he would to any woman who needed his basic counsel, such as where to find his hotel bedroom or what to tell her hubby when she got home.

"Got it with you then, have you, dear?" he asked, peering down at the perhaps-bag and smiling like a friend.

"Yes."

"In there, is it?"

"Yes."

"Then give me the whole bag normally," Landau said, talking her through her act. "That's the way. Now give me a friendly Russian kiss. The formal sort. Nice. You've brought me an official farewell gift on the last evening of the fair, you see. Something that will cement Anglo-Soviet relations and make me overweight on the flight home unless I dump it in the dustbin at the airport. Very normal transaction. I must have received half a dozen such gifts today already."

Part of this was spoken while he crouched with his back to her. For, reaching into the bag, he had already slipped out the brown-paper parcel that was inside it and was dropping it deftly into his briefcase, which was of the home filing variety, very compendious, with compartments that opened in a fan.

"Married, are we, Katya?"

No answer. Maybe she hadn't heard. Or she was too busy watching him.

"Is it your husband who's written the novel, then?" said Landau, undeterred by her silence.

"It is dangerous for you," she whispered. "You must believe in what you are doing. Then everything is clear."

As if he had not heard this warning at all, Landau selected, from a pile of samples that he had kept to give away tonight, a four-pack of the Royal Shakespeare Company's specially commissioned reading of *A Midsummer Night's Dream*, which he placed ostentatiously on the table and signed for her on the plastic casing with a felt-tip pen: "From Niki to Katya, Peace," and the date. Then he put the four-pack ceremoniously into the perhaps-bag for her, and gathered the handles of the bag together and pressed them into her hand, because she was becoming lifeless and he was worried she might break down or cease to function. Only then did he give her the reassurance that she seemed to be asking for, while he continued to hold her hand, which was cold, he told me, but nice.

"All of us have got to do something risky now and then, haven't we, dear?" Landau said lightly. "Going to adorn the party, are we?"

"No."

"Like a nice dinner out somewhere?"

"It is not convenient."

"You want me to take you to the door?"

"It doesn't matter."

"I think we've got to smile, dear," he said, still in English as he walked her across the room, chatting to her like the good salesman he had once again become.

Reaching the great landing, he shook her hand. "See you at the book fair, then? September. And thanks for warning me, okay? I'll bear it in mind. Still, the main thing is, we've got a deal. Which is always nice. Right?"

She took his hand and seemed to draw courage from it, for she smiled again and her smile was dazed but grateful, and almost irresistibly warm.

"My friend has made a great gesture," she explained as she pushed back an unruly lock of hair. "Please be sure that Mr. Barley is aware of this."

"I'll tell him. Don't you worry," said Landau jauntily.

He would have liked another smile just for himself, but she had lost interest in him. She was delving in her bag for her card, which he knew she had forgotten till this moment. "ORLOVA, Yekaterina Borisovna," it read, in Cyrillic one side and Roman the other, again with the name "October" in both renderings. She gave it to him, then walked stiffly down the pompous staircase, head up and one hand on the broad marble balustrade, the other hand trailing the perhaps-bag. The boys in leather jackets watched her all the way down to the hall. And Landau, while he popped the card into his top pocket with the half-dozen others he'd collected in the last two hours, saw them watch her and gave the boys a wink. And the boys after due reflection winked back at him, because this was the new season of openness when a pair of good Russian hips could be acknowledged for what they were, even to a foreigner.

For the fifty minutes of revelry that remained, Niki Landau threw his heart into the party. Sang and danced for a grim-faced Scottish librarian in pearls. Recited a witty political anecdote about Mrs. Thatcher for a pair of pale listeners from the State Copyright Agency, VAAP, till they suddenly emitted wild laughter. Buttered up three ladies from Progress Publishers and, in a series of nimble journeys to his briefcase, presented each with a memento of his stay, for Landau was a natural giver and remembered names and promises, just as he remembered so many other things, with the directness of an unencumbered mind. But all the while he kept the briefcase unobtrusively in view, and even before the guests had left, he was holding it in his spare hand while he made his farewells. And when he boarded the private bus that was waiting to take the reps back to their hotel, he sat with it on his knees while he joined in a tuneful unison of rugby songs, led as usual by Spikey Morgan.

"Ladies present now, boys," Landau warned and, standing up, commanded silence at the passages that he considered too broad. But even when he was playing the great conductor he contrived to keep a firm grip on the briefcase.

At the hotel entrance the usual gaggle of pimps, drug-pushers and currency dealers hung around and, together with their KGB minders, watched the group enter. But Landau saw nothing in their behaviour to concern him, whether over-watchful or over-casual. The crippled old warrior who guarded the passageway to the lifts demanded as usual to see his hotel pass, but when Landau, who had already presented him with a hundred Marlboros, asked him accusingly in Russian why he wasn't out flirting with his girlfriend tonight, he gave a rasping laugh and punched him on the shoulder in goodfellowship.

"If they're trying to frame me, I thought, they'd better be quick about it or the trail will be cold, Harry," he told me, taking the part of the opposition rather than his own. "When you frame, Harry, you've got to move in fast while the evidence is still planted on the victim," he explained, as if he had been framing people all his life.

"Bar of the National, nine o'clock then," Spikey Morgan said to him wearily when they had fought their way out at the fourth floor.

"Could be, could be not, Spikey," Landau replied. "I'm not quite myself, to be honest."

"Thank God for that," said Spikey through a yawn, and plodded off into his own dark corridor watched by the evil-eyed floor concierge in her horsebox.

Reaching his bedroom door Landau braced himself before putting the key into the lock. They'd do it now, he thought. Here and now would be the best time to snatch me and the manuscript.

But when he stepped inside, the room was empty and undisturbed and he felt foolish for having suspected it of being any different. Still alive, he thought, and set the briefcase on the bed.

Then he pulled the handkerchief-sized curtains as close as they would go, which was halfway, and hung the useless "Do Not Disturb" notice on the door, which he then locked. He emptied the pockets of his suit, including the pocket where he stored incoming business cards, pulled off his jacket and tie, his metal armbands, finally his shirt. From the fridge he poured himself half an inch of lemon vodka and took a sip. Landau was not a drinker really, he explained to me, but when in Moscow he did like a nice lemon vodka to end his day. Taking his glass to the bathroom, he stood before the mirror and for a good ten minutes anxiously examined the roots of his hair for signs of white, touching out offending spots with the aid of a new formula that was working wonders. Having completed this labour to his satisfaction, he bound his skull with an elaborate rubber turban like a bathing cap and showered, while he sang "I am the very model of a modern major-general" rather well. Then he towelled himself, vigorously for the sake of his muscle-tone, slipped into a bold flowered bathrobe and marched back to the bedroom still singing.

And he did these things partly because he always did them and needed the steadying familiarity of his own routines, but partly also because he was proud of having thrown caution to the winds for once and not found twenty-five sound reasons for doing nothing, which these days he might have done.

She was a lady, she was afraid, she needed help, Harry. When did Niki Landau ever refuse a lady? And if he was wrong about her, well then she'd made a crying fool of him and he might as well pack up his toothbrush and report himself at the front door of the Lubyanka for five years' study of their excellent graffiti without the option. Because he'd rather be made a fool of twenty times over than turn away that woman without a reason. And so saying, if only in his mind, for he was always alert to the possibility of microphones, Landau drew her parcel from the briefcase and with a certain shyness set to work untying the string but not cutting it, just the way he had been taught by his sainted mother, whose photograph at this moment nestled faithfully in his wallet. They've got the same glow, he thought in pleasant recognition as he worried patiently at the knot. It's the Slav skin. It's the Slav eyes, the smile. Two nice Slav girls together. The only difference was that Katya hadn't finished up in Treblinka.

The knot finally yielded. Landau coiled up the string and laid it on the bed. I have to know, you see, dear, he explained to the woman Yekaterina Borisovna in his mind. I don't want to pry, I'm not the nosy one, but if I've got to con my way through Moscow customs, I'd better know what I'm conning them out of, because it helps.

Delicately so as not to tear it, using both hands, Landau parted the brown paper. He did not see himself as any sort of a hero, or not yet. What was a danger to a Moscow beauty might not be a danger to him. He had grown up hard, it was true. The East End of London had been no rest cure for a ten-year-old Polish immigrant, and Landau had taken his share of split lips, broken noses, smashed knuckles and hunger. But if you had asked him now or at any time in the last thirty years what his definition of a hero was, he would have replied without a second's thought that a hero was the first man out of the back door when they started yelling for volunteers.

One thing he did know as he stared at the contents of that brown-paper parcel: he had the buzz on him. Why he had it was something he could sort out later when there weren't better things to do. But if dodgy work needed to be done tonight, Niki Landau was your man. Because when Niki has the buzz, Harry, no one buzzes better, as the girls all know.

The first thing he saw was the envelope. He registered the three notebooks underneath it and saw that the envelope and notebooks were joined with a thick elastic band, the kind he always saved but never found a use for. But it was the envelope that held him because it had her writing on it—a strict copybook kind of writing that confirmed his pure image of her. One square brown envelope, glued rather messily and addressed "Personal for Mr. Bartholomew Scott Blair, urgent."

Slipping it free of the elastic band, Landau held it to the light but it was opaque and revealed no shadow. He explored it with his finger and thumb. One sheet of thin paper inside, two at most. *Mr. Scott Blair has undertaken to publish it with discretion,* he remembered. *Mr. Landau, if you love peace . . . give it immediately to Mr. Scott Blair. Only to Mr. Scott Blair . . . it is a gift of trust.*

She trusts me too, he thought. He turned the envelope over. The back was blank.

And there being only so much that one may learn from a sealed brown envelope, and since Landau drew the line at reading Barley's or anybody else's personal mail, he opened his briefcase again and, having searched the stationery compartment, extracted from it a plain manila envelope of his own, with the words "From the desk of Mr. Nicholas P. Landau" inscribed tastefully on the flap. Then he popped the brown envelope inside the manila one and sealed it. Then he scribbled the name "Barley" on it and filed it in the compartment marked "Social," which contained such oddities as visiting cards that had been pressed on him by strangers and notes of odd commissions he had undertaken to perform for people—such as the publishing lady who needed refills for her Parker pen or the Ministry of Culture official who wanted a Snoopy T-shirt for his nephew or the lady from October who simply happened to be passing while he was wrapping up his stand.

And Landau did this because with the tradecraft that was instinctive in him, if totally untaught, he knew that his first job was to keep the envelope as far away as possible from the notebooks. If the notebooks were trouble, then he wanted nothing that would link them with the letter. And vice versa. And in this he was entirely right. Our most versatile and erudite trainers, dyed in all the oceans of our Service folklore, would not have told it to him one whit differently.

Only then did he take up the three notebooks and slip off the elastic band while he kept one ear cocked for footfalls in the corridor. Three grubby Russian notebooks, he reflected, selecting the top one and turning it slowly over. Bound in crudely illustrated board, the spine in fraying cloth. Two hundred and twenty-four pages of poor-quality, feint-ruled quarto, if Landau remembered correctly from the days when he peddled stationery, Soviet price around twenty kopeks retail from any good stationer, always provided that the delivery had arrived and that you were standing in the right queue on the right day.

Finally he opened the notebook and stared at the first page.

She's daft, he thought, fighting off his disgust.

She's in the hands of a nutter. Poor kid.

Meaningless scribblings, done by a lunatic with a mapping pen, in India ink at

breakneck speed and furious angles. In the margins, sideways, longways. Diagonally across itself like a doctor's writing on the blink. Peppered with stupid exclamation marks and underlinings. Some of it Cyrillic, some English. "The Creator
creates creators," he read in English. "To be. Not to be. To counter-be." Followed
by a burst of stupid French about the warfare of folly and the folly of warfare,
followed by a barbed-wire entanglement. Thank you very much, he thought, and
flipped to another page, then another, both so dense with crazy writing you could
hardly see the paper. "Having spent seventy years destroying the popular will, we
cannot expect it suddenly to rise up and save us," he read. A quote? A night
thought? There was no way to tell. References to writers, Russian, Latin and
European. Talk of Nietzsche, Kafka and people he'd never heard of, let alone read.
More talk of war, this time in English: "The old declare it, the young fight it, but
today the babies and old people fight it too." He turned another page and came on
nothing but a round brown stain. He lifted the notebook to his nose and sniffed.
Booze, he thought with contempt. Stinks like a brewery. No wonder he's a mate of
Barley Blair's. A double page devoted to a series of hysterical proclamations.

OUR GREATEST PROGRESS IS IN THE FIELD OF BACKWARDNESS!
SOVIET PARALYSIS IS THE MOST PROGRESSIVE IN THE WORLD!
OUR BACKWARDNESS IS OUR GREATEST MILITARY SECRET!
IF WE DON'T KNOW OUR OWN INTENTIONS AND OUR OWN
   CAPACITIES, HOW CAN WE KNOW YOURS?
THE TRUE ENEMY IS OUR OWN INCOMPETENCE!

And on the next page, a poem, painstakingly copied from Lord knew where:

> He wires in and wires out,
> And leaves the people still in doubt
> Whether the snake that made the track
> Was going south or coming back.

Scrambling to his feet, Landau strode angrily to the window, which gave on to
a glum courtyard full of uncollected rubbish.

"A blooming word-artist, Harry. That's what I thought he was. Some long-
haired, drug-ridden, self-indulgent genius, and she's gone and thrown herself away
on him same as they all do."

She was lucky there was no Moscow telephone directory or he'd have rung her
up and told her what she'd got.

To stoke his anger, he took up the second book, licked his fingertip and whisked
contemptuously through it page by page, which was how he came upon the drawings. Then everything went blank for him for a moment, like a flash of empty screen
in the middle of a film, while he cursed himself for being an impetuous little Slav
instead of a cool calm Englishman. Then he sat down on the bed again, but gently,
as if there were someone resting in it, someone he had hurt with his premature
condemnations.

For if Landau despised what too often passed for literature, his pleasure in
technical matters was unconfined. Even when he didn't follow what he was looking
at, he could relish a good page of mathematics all day long. And he knew at one
glance, as he had known of the woman Katya, that what he was looking at here was

quality. Not your ruled drawing, it was true. Light sketches but all the better for it. Drawn freehand without instruments by somebody who could think with a pencil. Tangents, parabolas, cones. And in between the drawings, businesslike descriptions that architects and engineers use, words like "aimpoint" and "captive carry" and "bias" and "gravity" and "trajectory." "Some in your English, Harry, and some in your Russian."

Though Harry is not my real name.

Yet when he began to compare the lettering of these beautifully written words in the second book with the rambling jungle in the first, he discovered to his astonishment certain unmistakable similarities. So that he had the sensation of looking at a kind of schizophrenic's diary with Dr. Jekyll writing one volume and Mr. Hyde the other.

He looked in the third notebook, which was as orderly and purposeful as the second but arranged like a kind of mathematical log with dates and numbers and formulae, and the word "error" repeating itself frequently, often underlined or lifted with an exclamation mark. Then suddenly Landau stared, and continued staring, and could not remove his eyes from what he was reading. The cosy obscurity of the writer's technical jargon had ended with a bang. So had his philosophical ramblings and elegant annotated drawings. The words came off the page with a blazoned clarity.

"The American strategists can sleep in peace. Their nightmares cannot be realised. The Soviet knight is dying inside his armour. He is a secondary power like you British. He can start a war but cannot continue one and cannot win one. Believe me."

Landau looked no further. A sense of respect, mingled with a strong instinct for self-preservation, advised him that he had disturbed the tomb enough. Taking up the elastic band, he put the three notebooks together and snapped it back over them. That's it, he thought. From here on I mind my business and do my duty. Which is to take the manuscript to my adopted England and give it immediately to Mr. Bartholomew *alias* Barley Scott Blair.

Barley Blair, he thought in amazement as he opened his wardrobe and hauled out the large aluminium hand-case where he kept his samples. Well, well. We often wondered whether we were nurturing a spy in our midst and now we know.

Landau's calm was now absolute, he assured me. The Englishman had once more taken command of the Pole. "If Barley could do it, I could, Harry, that's what I said to myself." And it was what he said to me too, when for a short spell he appointed me his confessor. People do that to me sometimes. They sense the unrealised part of me and talk to it as if it were the reality.

Lifting the case on to the bed he snapped the locks and drew out two audio-visual kits that the Soviet officials had ordered him to remove from his display— one pictorial history of the twentieth century with spoken commentary, which they had arbitrarily ruled to be anti-Soviet, and one handbook of the human body with action photographs and a keep-fit exercise cassette, which, after gazing longingly at the pliant young goddess in the leotard, the officials had decided was pornographic.

The history kit was a glossy affair, built as a coffee-table book and containing a quantity of interior pockets for cassettes, parallel texts, progressive vocabulary cards and students' notes. Having emptied the pockets of their contents, Landau offered the notebooks to each in turn but found none large enough. He decided to convert two pockets into one. He fetched a pair of nail scissors from his sponge bag and set to work with steady hands, easing the steel staples out of the centre divide.

Barley Blair, he thought again as he inserted the point of the nail scissors. I should have guessed, if only because you were the one it couldn't possibly be. Mr. Bartholomew Scott Blair, surviving scion of Abercrombie & Blair—spy. The first staple had come loose. He gingerly extracted it. Barley Blair, who couldn't sell hay to a rich horse to save his dying mother on her birthday, we used to say: spy. He began prising the second staple. Whose principal claim to fame was that two years ago at the Belgrade book fair he had drunk Spikey Morgan under the table on straight vodkas, then played tenor sax with the band so beautifully that even the police were clapping. Spy. Gentleman spy. Well, here's a letter from your lady, as they say in the nursery rhyme.

Landau picked up the notebooks and offered them to the space he had prepared but it was still not big enough. He would have to make one pocket out of three.

Playing the drunk, thought Landau, his mind still on Barley. Playing the fool and fooling us. Burning up the last of your family money, running the old firm deeper into the ground. Oh yes. Except that somehow or another you always managed to find one of those smart City banking houses to bail you out in the nick of time, didn't you? And what about your chess-playing then? *That* should have been a clue, if Landau had only had eyes for it! How does a man who's drunk himself silly beat all comers at chess then, Harry—straight games—if he isn't a trained spy?

The three pockets had become one pocket, the notebooks fitted more or less inside, the printed indication above them still read "Student Notes."

"Notes," Landau explained in his mind to the inquisitive young customs officer at Sheremetyevo airport. "Notes, you see, son, like it says. Student's notes. That's why there's a pocket here for notes. And these notes that you are holding in your hand are the work of an actual student following the course. That's why they're here, son, do you see? They are *demonstration notes*. And the drawings here, they're to do with the—"

With socio-economic patterns, son. With demographic population shifts. With vital statistics that you Russkies can never get enough of, can you? Here, seen one of these? It's called a body book.

Which might or might not save Landau's hide, depending on how smart the boy was, and how much they knew, and how they felt about their wives that day.

But for the long night ahead of him, and for the dawn raid when they kicked the door down and burst in on him with drawn pistols and shouted, "All right, Landau, give us the notebooks!"—for that happy moment, the kit wouldn't do at all. "Notebooks, Officer? Notebooks? Oh, you mean that bunch of junk some loony Russian beauty pressed on me at the fair tonight. I think you'll probably find them in the rubbish basket, Officer, if the maid hasn't emptied it for once in her life."

For this contingency also, Landau now meticulously set the scene. Removing the notebooks from the pocket of the history kit, he placed them artistically in the wastepaper basket exactly as if he had flung them there in the rage he had felt when he had taken his first look. To keep them company, he tossed in his surplus trade literature and brochures, as well as a couple of useless farewell gifts he had received: the thin volume of yet another Russian poet, a tin-backed blotter. As a final touch, he added a pair of undarned socks that only your rich Westerner throws away.

Once again I must marvel, as later we all did, at Landau's untutored ingenuity.

Landau did not go out and play that night. He endured the familiar imprisonment of his Moscow hotel room. From his window he watched the long dusk turn to darkness and the dim lights of the city reluctantly brighten. He made himself tea in his little travelling kettle and ate a couple of fruit bars from his iron rations. He dwelt gratefully upon the most rewarding of his conquests. He smiled ruefully at others. He braced himself for pain and solitude and summoned up his hard childhood to help him. He went through the contents of his wallet and his briefcase and his pockets and took out everything that was particularly private to him which he would not wish to answer for across a bare table—a hot letter a little friend sent him years ago that could still revive his appetites, membership of a certain video-by-mail club that he belonged to. His first instinct was to "burn them like in the movies" but he was restrained by the sight of the smoke detectors in the ceiling, though he'd have laid any money they didn't work.

So he found a paper bag and, having torn up everything very small, he put the pieces in the bag, dropped the bag out of the window and saw it join the rubbish in the courtyard. Then he lay on the bed and watched the dark go by. Sometimes he felt brave, sometimes he was so scared that he had to drive his fingernails into his palms to hold himself together. Once he turned on the television set, hoping for nubile girl gymnasts, which he liked. But instead he got the Emperor himself telling his bemused children for the umpteenth time that the old order had no clothes. And when Spikey Morgan, half drunk at best, telephoned from the bar of the National, Landau kept him on the line for company till old Spikey fell asleep.

Only once, at his lowest point, did it cross Landau's mind to present himself at the British Embassy and seek the assistance of the diplomatic bag. His momentary weakness angered him. "Those flunkies?" he asked himself in scorn. "The ones who sent my dad back to Poland? I wouldn't trust them with a picture postcard of the Eiffel Tower, Harry."

Besides, that wasn't what she had asked him to do.

In the morning he dressed himself for his own execution, in his best suit, with the photograph of his mother inside his shirt.

And that is how I see Niki Landau still, whenever I dip into his file, or receive him for what we call a six-monthly top-up, which is when he likes to relive his hour of glory before signing yet another declaration of the Official Secrets Act. I see him stepping jauntily into the Moscow street with the metal suitcase in his hand, not knowing from Adam what's in it, but determined to risk his brave little neck for it anyway.

How he sees me, if he ever thinks of me, I dare not wonder. Hannah, whom I loved but failed, would have no doubt at all. "As another of those Englishmen with hope in their faces and none in their hearts," she would say, flushing with anger. For I am afraid she says whatever comes to her these days. Much of her old forbearance is gone.

T he whole of Whitehall was agreed that no story should ever begin that way again. Indoctrinated ministers were furious about it. They set up a frightfully secret committee of enquiry to find out what went wrong, hear witnesses, name names, spare no blushes, point fingers, close gaps, prevent a recurrence, appoint me Chairman and draft a report. What conclusions our committee reached, if any, remains the loftiest secret of them all, particularly from those of us who sat on it. For the function of such committees, as we all well knew, is to talk earnestly until the dust has settled, and then ourselves return to dust. Which, like a disgruntled Cheshire cat, our committee duly did, leaving nothing behind us but our frightfully secret frown, a meaningless interim working paper, and a bunch of secret annexes in the Treasury archives.

It began, in the less sparing language of Ned and his colleagues at the Russia House, with an imperial cock-up, between the hours of five and eight-thirty on a warm Sunday evening, when one Nicholas P. Landau, travelling salesman and taxpayer in good standing, if of Polish origin, with nothing recorded against, presented himself at the doors of no fewer than four separate Whitehall ministries to plead an urgent interview with an officer of the British Intelligence Branch, as he was pleased to call it, only to be ridiculed, fobbed off and in one instance physically manhandled. Though whether the two temporary doormen at the Defence Ministry went so far as to grab Landau by the collar and the seat of his pants, as he maintained they did, and frogmarch him to the door, or whether they merely assisted him back into the street, to use *their* words, is a point on which we were unable to achieve a consensus.

But why, our committee asked sternly, did the two doormen feel obliged to provide this assistance in the first place?

Mr. Landau refused to let us look inside his briefcase, sir. Yes, he offered to let us take charge of the briefcase while he waited, provided he kept charge of the key, sir. But that wasn't regulations. And yes, he shook it in our faces, patted it for us, tossed it about in his hands, apparently in order to demonstrate that there was nothing in it that any of us needed to be afraid of. But that wasn't regulations either. And when we tried with a minimum of force to relieve him of the said briefcase, this *gentleman*—as Landau in their testimony had belatedly become—resisted our efforts, sir, and shouted loudly in a foreign accent, causing a disturbance.

But what did he shout? we asked, distressed by the notion of anybody shouting in Whitehall on a Sunday.

Well, sir, so far as we were able to make him out, him in his emotional state, he shouted that this briefcase of his contained highly secret papers, sir. Which had been entrusted to him by a Russian, sir, in Moscow.

And him a rampageous little Pole, sir, they might have added. On a hot cricketing Sunday in London, sir, and us watching the replay of the Pakistanis against Botham in the back room.

Even at the Foreign Office, that freezing hearth of official British hospitality, where the despairing Landau presented himself as a last resort and with the greatest of reluctance, it was only by dint of high entreaty and some honest-to-God Slav tears that he fought his way to the rarefied ear of the Honourable Palmer Wellow, author of a discerning monograph on Liszt.

And if Landau had not used a new tactic, probably the Slav tears would not have helped. Because this time he placed the briefcase open on the counter so that the doorman, who was young but sceptical, could crane his pomaded head to the recently installed armoured glass and scowl down into it with his indolent eyes, and see for himself that it was only a bunch of dirty old notebooks in there and a brown envelope, not bombs.

"Come-back-Monday-ten-to-five," the doorman said through the wonderfully new electric speaker, as if announcing a Welsh railway station, and slumped back into the darkness of his box.

The gate stood ajar. Landau looked at the young man, and looked past him at the great portico built a hundred years earlier to daunt the unruly princes of the Raj. And the next thing anyone knew, he had picked up his briefcase and, defeating all the seemingly impenetrable defences set up to prevent exactly such an onslaught, was pelting hell-for-leather with it—"like a bloomin' Springbok, sir"—across the hallowed courtyard up the steps into the enormous hall. And he was in luck. Palmer Wellow, whatever else he was, belonged to the appeasement side of the Foreign Office. And it was Palmer's day on.

"Hullo, *hullo*," Palmer murmured as he descended the great steps and beheld the disordered figure of Landau panting between two stout guards. "Well you *are* in a muck. My name's Wellow. I'm a resident clerk here." He held his left fist to his shoulder as if he hated dogs. But his right hand was extended in greeting.

"I don't want a clerk," said Landau. "I want a high officer or nothing."

"Well, a clerk is *fairly* high," Palmer modestly assured him. "I expect you're put off by the language."

It was only right to record—and our committee did—that nobody could fault Palmer Wellow's performance thus far. He was droll but he was effective. He put no polished foot wrong. He led Landau to an interviewing room and sat him down, all attention. He ordered a cup of tea for him with sugar for his shock, and offered him a digestive biscuit. With a costly fountain pen given him by a friend, he wrote down Landau's name and address and those of the companies that hired his services. He wrote down the number of Landau's British passport and his date and place of birth, 1930 in Warsaw. He insisted with disarming truthfulness that he had no knowledge of intelligence matters, but undertook to pass on Landau's material to the "competent people," who would no doubt give it whatever attention it deserved. And because Landau once again insisted on it, he improvised a receipt for him on a sheet of Foreign Office blue draft, signed it and had the janitor add a date-and-time stamp. He told him that if there was anything further the authorities wished to discuss they would very probably get in touch with him, perhaps by means of the telephone.

Only then did Landau hesitatingly pass his scruffy package across the table and watch with lingering regret as Palmer's languid hand enfolded it.

"But why don't you simply give it to Mr. Scott Blair?" Palmer asked after he had studied the name on the envelope.

"I tried, for Christ's sake!" Landau burst out in fresh exasperation. "I told you. I rang him everywhere. I've rung him till I'm blue in the face, I tell you. He's not at his home, he's not at work, he's not at his club, he's not at anywhere," Landau protested, his English grammar slipping in despair. "From the airport I tried. All right, it's a Saturday."

"But it's Sunday," Palmer objected with a forgiving smile.

"So it was a Saturday yesterday, wasn't it! I try his firm. I get an electronic howl. I look in the phone book. There's one in Hammersmith. Not his initials but Scott Blair. I get an angry lady, tells me to go to hell. There's a rep I know, Archie Parr, does the West Country for him. I ask Archie: 'Archie, for Christ's sake, how do I get hold of Barley in a hurry?' 'He's skedaddled, Niki. Done one of his bunks. Hasn't been seen in the shop for weeks.' Enquiries, I try. London, the Home Counties. Not listed, not a Bartholomew. Well he wouldn't be, would he, not if he's a—"

"Not if he's a what?" said Palmer, intrigued.

"Look, he's vanished, right? He's vanished before. There could be reasons why he vanishes. Reasons that you don't know of because you're not meant to. Lives are at stake, could be. Not only his either. It's top urgent, she told me. And top secret. Now get on with it. Please."

The same evening, there being not much doing on the world front apart from a dreary crisis in the Gulf and a squalid television scandal about soldiers and money in Washington, Palmer took himself off to a rather good party in Montpelier Square that was being thrown by a group of his year from Cambridge—bachelors like himself, but fun. An account of this occasion, too, reached our committee's ears.

"Have any of you heard of a Somebody Scott Blair, by the by?" Wellow asked them at a late hour when his memory of Landau happened to have been revived by some bars of Chopin he was playing on the piano. "Wasn't there a Scott Blair who was up with us or something?" he asked again when he failed to get through the noise.

"Couple of years ahead of us. Trinity," came a fogged reply from across the room. "Read History. Jazz fiend. Wanted to blow his saxophone for a living. Old man wouldn't wear it. Barley Blair. Pissed as a rat from daybreak."

Palmer Wellow played a thunderous chord that stunned the garrulous company to silence. "I said, is he a poisonous spy?" he enunciated.

"The father? He's dead."

"The son, ass. Barley."

Like someone stepping from behind a curtain, his informant emerged from the crowd of young and less young men and stood before him, glass in hand. And Palmer to his pleasure recognised him as a dear chum from Trinity a hundred years ago.

"I really don't know whether Barley's a poisonous spy or not, I'm afraid," said Palmer's chum, with an asperity habitual to him, as the background babel rose to its former roar. "He's certainly a failure, if that's a qualification."

His curiosity whetted still further, Palmer returned to his spacious rooms at the Foreign Office and to Landau's envelope and notebooks, which he had entrusted to the janitor for safekeeping. And it is at this point that his actions, in the words of our interim working paper, took an unhelpful course. Or in the harsher words of

Ned and his colleagues in the Russia House, this was where, in any civilised country, P. Wellow would have been strung by his thumbs from a high point in the city and left there in peace to reflect upon his attainments.

For what Palmer did was have a nice time with the notebooks. For two nights and one and a half days. Because he found them so amusing. He did not open the buff envelope—which was by now marked in Landau's handwriting "Extremely Private for the attention of Mr. B. Scott Blair or a top member of the Intelligence" —because like Landau he was of a school that felt it unbecoming to read other people's mail. In any case, it was glued at both ends, and Palmer was not a man to grapple with physical obstacles. But the notebook—with its crazed aphorisms and quotations, its exhaustive loathing of politicians and soldiery, its scatter-shot references to Pushkin the pure Renaissance man and to Kleist the pure suicide—held him fascinated.

He felt little sense of urgency, none of responsibility. He was a diplomat, not a Friend, as the spies were called. And Friends in Palmer's zoology were people without the intellectual horsepower to be what Palmer was. Indeed it was his outspoken resentment that the orthodox Foreign Office to which he belonged resembled more and more a cover organisation for the Friends' disgraceful activities. For Palmer too was a man of impressive erudition, if of a random kind. He had read Arabic and taken a First in Modern History. He had added Russian and Sanskrit in his spare time. He had everything but mathematics and common sense, which explains why he passed over the dreary pages of algebraic formulae, equations and diagrams that made up the other two notebooks, and in contrast to the writer's philosophical ramblings had a boringly disciplined appearance. And which also explains—though the committee had difficulty accepting such an explanation —why Palmer chose to ignore the Standing Order to Resident Clerks Relating to Defectors and Offers of Intelligence, whether solicited or otherwise, and to do his own thing.

"He makes the most frantic connections right across the board, Tig," he told a rather senior colleague in Research Department on the Tuesday, having decided that it was finally time to share his acquisition. "You simply must read him."

"But how do we know it's a he, Palms?"

Palmer just felt it, Tig. The vibes.

Palmer's senior colleague glanced at the first notebook, then at the second, then sat down and stared at the third. Then he looked at the drawings in the second book. Then his professional self took over in the emergency.

"I think I'd get this lot across to them fairly sharpish if I were you, Palms," he said. But on second thoughts he got it across to them himself, very sharpish indeed, having first telephoned Ned on the green line and told him to stand by.

Upon which, two days late, hell broke loose. At four o'clock on the Wednesday morning the lights on the top floor of Ned's stubby brick out-station in Victoria known as the Russia House were still burning brightly as the first bemused meeting of what later became the Bluebird team drew to a close. Five hours after that, having sat out two more meetings in the Service's headquarters in a grand new high-rise block on the Embankment, Ned was back at his desk, the files gathering around him as giddily as if the girls in Registry had decided to erect a street barricade.

"God may move in a mysterious way," Ned was heard to remark to his redheaded assistant, Brock, in a lull between deliveries, "but it's nothing to the way He picks his joes."

A joe in the parlance is a live source, and a live source in sane English is a spy. Was Ned referring to Landau when he spoke of joes? To Katya? To the unchristened writer of the notebooks? Or was his mind already fixed upon the vaporous outlines of that great British gentleman spy, Mr. Bartholomew Scott Blair? Brock did not know or care. He came from Glasgow but of Lithuanian parents, and abstract concepts made him angry.

As to myself, I had to wait another week before Ned decided with a proper reluctance that it was time to haul in old Palfrey. I've been old Palfrey since I can remember. To this day I have never understood what happened to my Christian names. "Where's old Palfrey?" they say. "Where's our tame legal eagle? Get the old lawbender in! Better chuck this one at Palfrey!"

I am quickly dealt with. You need not stumble on me long. Horatio Benedict dePalfrey are my names but you may forget the first two immediately, and somehow nobody has ever remembered the "de" at all. In the Service I am Harry, so quite often, being an obedient soul, I am Harry to myself. Alone in my poky little bachelor flat of an evening, I am quite inclined to call myself Harry while I cook my chop. Legal adviser to the illegals, that's me, and sometime junior partner to the extinct house of Mackie, Mackie & dePalfrey, Solicitors and Commissioners for Oaths, of Chancery Lane. But that was twenty years ago. For twenty years I have been your most humble secret servant, ready at any time to rob the scales of the same blind goddess whom my young heart was brought up to revere.

A palfrey, I am told, was neither a warhorse nor a hunter, but a saddle horse deemed suitable for ladies. Well, there's only one little lady who ever rode this Palfrey any distance, but she rode him nearly to his grave and her name was Hannah. And it was because of Hannah that I scurried for shelter inside the secret citadel where passion has no place, where the walls are so thick I cannot hear her beating fists or tearful voice imploring me to let her in and brave the scandal that so terrified a young solicitor at the threshold of a respectable career.

Hope in my face and nothing in my heart, she said. A wiser woman might have kept such observations to herself, it has always seemed to me. Sometimes the truth is by way of being a self-indulgence. "Then why do you pursue a hopeless case?" I would protest to her. "If the patient is dead, why keep trying to revive him?"

Because she was a woman, seemed to be the answer. Because she believed in the redemption of male souls. Because I had not paid enough for being inadequate.

But I have paid now, believe me.

It is because of Hannah that I walk the secret corridors to this day, calling my cowardice duty and my weakness sacrifice.

It is because of Hannah that I sit here late at night, in my grey box of an office with LEGAL on the door, files and tapes and films stacked around me like the case of Jarndyce v. Jarndyce without the pink string, while I draft our official whitewash of the operation we called the Bluebird and of its protagonist, Bartholomew, alias Barley, Scott Blair.

It is because of Hannah also that even while he scribbles at his exculpation, this old Palfrey now and then puts down his pen and lifts his head and dreams.

* * *

Niki Landau's recall to the British colours, if he had ever seriously abandoned them, took place exactly forty-eight hours after the notebooks hit Ned's desk. Ever since his miserable sojourn through Whitehall, Landau had been sick with anger and mortification. He hadn't gone to work, he hadn't bothered with his little flat in Golders Green which he normally buffed and pampered as if it were the lantern of his life. Not even Lydia could rouse him from his melancholy. I myself had hastily arranged the Home Office warrant to tap his phone. When she telephoned, we listened to him putting her off. And when she made a tragic appearance at his front door, our watchers reported that he let her stay for a cup of tea and then dismissed her.

"I don't know what I've done wrong but whatever it is, I'm sorry," they heard her remark sadly as she left.

She was hardly in the street before Ned rang. Afterwards, Landau shrewdly wondered to me whether that was a coincidence.

"Niki Landau?" Ned enquired in a voice you didn't feel like fooling with.

"I could be," said Landau, sitting up straight.

"My name's Ned. I think we have a mutual friend. No need to mention names. You kindly dropped a letter in for him the other day. Rather against the odds, I'm afraid. A package too."

Landau thrilled to the voice immediately. Capable and commanding. The voice of a good officer, not a cynic, Harry.

"Well, yes, I did," he said, but Ned was already talking again.

"I don't think we need to go into a lot of details over the telephone, but I do think you and I need to have a long chat and I think we need to shake your hand. Rather soon. When can we do that?"

"Whenever you say," said Landau. And had to stop himself from saying "sir."

"I always think now's a good time. How do you feel about that?"

"I feel a whole lot better, Ned," said Landau with a grin in his voice.

"I'm going to send a car for you. Won't be at all long, so perhaps you'd just stay where you are and wait for your front doorbell to ring. It's a green Rover, B registration. The driver's name is Sam. If you're worried, ask him to show you his card. If you're still worried, phone the number on it. Think you'll manage?"

"Our friend's all right, is he?" said Landau, unable to resist asking, but Ned had rung off.

The doorbell pealed a couple of minutes afterwards. They had the car waiting round the corner, thought Landau as he floated downstairs in a dream. This is it. I'm in the hands of the professionals. The house was in smart Belgravia, one of a terrace recently restored. Its newly painted white front glistened wholesomely at him in the evening sun. A palace of excellence, a shrine to the secret powers that rule our lives. A polished-brass sign on the pillared doorway said FOREIGN LIAISON STAFF. The door was already opening as Landau climbed the steps. And as the uniformed janitor closed it behind him Landau saw a slender, straight-built man in his early forties advance towards him through the sunbeams, first the trim silhouette, then the no-nonsense handsome healthy features, then the handshake: discreet but loyal as a naval salute.

"Well done, Niki. Come on in."

Good voices do not always belong to good faces, but Ned's did. As Landau followed him into the oval study, he felt he could say anything in the world to him and Ned would still be on his side. Landau in fact saw a whole lot of things in Ned that he liked at once, which was Ned's Pied Piper gift: the careful charm, the restrained good looks, the power of quiet leadership and the "Come on in." Landau also sniffed the polyglot in him, for he was one himself. He had only to drop a Russian name or phrase for Ned to reach out for it and smile, and match it with a phrase of his own. He was one of us, Harry. If you had a secret, this was the man to tell it to, not that flunky in the Foreign Office.

But then Landau had not realised, until he began talking, how desperately he had been needing to confide. He opened his mouth, he was away. All he could do from then on was listen to himself in amazement, because he wasn't just talking about Katya and the notebooks, and why he had accepted them, and how he had hidden them, but about his whole life till now, his confusions about being a Slav, his love of Russia despite everything, and his feeling of being suspended between two cultures. Yet Ned did not lead him or check him in any way. He was a born listener. He hardly stirred except to write himself neat notes on bits of card, and if he interrupted, it was only to clear up a rare point of detail—the moment at Sheremetyevo, for example, when Landau was waved through to the departure lounge without a glance.

"Now did all your group receive that treatment or only you?"

"The lot of us. One nod, we were through."

"You didn't feel singled out in any way?"

"What for?"

"You didn't have the impression you might be getting a different kind of treatment from other people? A better one, for instance?"

"We went through like a bunch of sheep. A flock," Landau corrected himself. "We handed in our visas, that was it."

"Were other groups going through at the same rate, did you notice?"

"The Russkies didn't seem to be bothering at all. Maybe it was the summer Saturday. Maybe it was the *glasnost*. They pulled a few out to inspect and let the others through. I felt a fool, to be truthful. I didn't need to have taken the precautions that I did."

"You were no sort of fool. You did marvellously," said Ned, without a hint of patronising while he wrote again. "And on the plane, who did you sit next to, remember?"

"Spikey Morgan."

"Who else?"

"No one. I had the window."

"Which seat was that?"

Landau knew the seat number off pat. It was the one he pre-booked whenever he could.

"Did you talk much on the flight?"

"Quite a lot, as a matter of fact."

"What about?"

"Women, mainly. Spikey's moved in with a pair of freewheelers in Notting Hill."

Ned gave a pleasant laugh. "And did you tell Spikey about the notebooks? In your relief, Niki? It would have been perfectly natural in the circumstances. To confide."

"I wouldn't dream of it, Ned. Not to a soul. I never did, I never will. I'm only telling you because he's vanished and you're official."

"How about Lydia?"

The offence to Landau's dignity momentarily outweighed his admiration of Ned, and even his surprise at Ned's familiarity with his affairs.

"My ladies, Ned, they know a little about me. They may even think they know more than they do," he replied. "But they do not share my secrets because they are not invited to."

Ned continued writing. And somehow the trim movement of the pen, coupled with the suggestion that he could have been indiscreet, provoked Landau into chancing his hand, because he had noticed already that every time he started to talk about Barley, a kind of freeze settled over Ned's quietly reassuring features.

"And Barley's really all right, is he? He hasn't had an accident or anything?"

Ned seemed not to hear. He took a fresh card and resumed his writing.

"I suppose Barley would have used the Embassy, wouldn't he?" said Landau. "Him being a professional. Barley. It's the chess that gives him away, if you want to know. He shouldn't play it, in my opinion. Not in public."

Then and only then did Ned's head rise slowly from the page. And Landau saw a stony expression in his face that was more frightening than his words. "We never mention names like that, Niki," said Ned very quietly. "Not even among ourselves. You couldn't know, so you've done nothing wrong. Just please don't do it again."

Then, seeing perhaps the effect that he had had on Landau, he got up and strolled to a satinwood sidetable and poured two glasses of sherry from a decanter and handed one to Landau. "And yes, he's all right," he said.

So they drank a silent toast to Barley, whose name Landau had by then sworn to himself ten times already would never again cross his lips.

"We don't want you to go to Gdansk next week," said Ned. "We've arranged a medical certificate and compensation for you. You're ill. Suspected ulcer. And stay away from work in the meantime, do you mind?"

"I'll do whatever you say," said Landau.

But before he left he signed a declaration of the Official Secrets Act while Ned benignly looked on. It's a weasely document in legal terms, calculated to impress the signatory and no one else. But then the Act itself is scarcely a credit to its drafters either.

After that, Ned switched off the microphones and the hidden video cameras that the twelfth floor had insisted on because it was becoming that kind of operation.

And this far, Ned did everything alone, which was his good right as head of the Russia House. Fieldmen are nothing if not loners. He didn't even call in old Palfrey to read the riot act. Not yet.

If Landau had felt neglected until that afternoon, for the rest of the week he was swamped with attention. Early the next morning, Ned telephoned asking him with his customary courtesy to present himself to an address in Pimlico. It turned out to be a nineteen-thirties block of flats, with curved steel-framed windows painted green and an entrance that should have led to a cinema. In the presence of two men whom he did not introduce, Ned took Landau crisply through his story a second time, then threw him to the wolves.

The first to speak was a distraught, floating man with baby-pink cheeks and baby-clear eyes and a flaxen jacket to match his straggling flaxen hair. His voice floated too. "You said a blue dress, I think? My name's Walter," he added, as if himself startled by the news.

"I did, sir."

"You're sure?" he piped, rolling his head and peering crookedly at him from under his silken brow.

"Totally, sir. A blue dress with a brown perhaps-bag. Most perhaps-bags are made of string. Hers was brown plastic. 'Now, Niki,' I said to myself, 'today is not the day, but if you were ever thinking of having a tumble with this lady at a future date, which you might, you could always bring her a nice blue handbag from London to match her blue dress, couldn't you?' That's how I remember, you see. I have the connection in my head, sir."

And it is always an oddity of the tapes when I replay them that Landau called Walter "sir," while he never called Ned anything but Ned. But this was no great sign of respect in Landau so much as of a certain squeamishness that Walter inspired. After all, Landau was a ladies' man and Walter was quite the opposite.

"And the hair *black*, you say?" Walter sang, as if black hair strained credulity.

"Black, sir. Black and silky. Verging towards the raven. Definitely."

"Not dyed, you don't think?"

"I know the difference, sir," said Landau, touching his own head, for he wanted to give them everything by now, even the secret of his eternal youth.

"You said earlier she was Leningrad. Why did you say that?"

"The bearing, sir. I saw quality, I saw a Russian woman of Rome. That's how I think of her. Petersburg."

"But you didn't see Armenian? Or Georgian? Or Jewish, for example?"

Landau dwelt on the last suggestion but rejected it. "I'm Jewish myself, you see. I won't say it takes one to know one but I'll say I didn't go ting-a-ling inside."

A silence that could have been embarrassment seemed to encourage him to continue. "I think being Jewish is overdone, to be frank. If that's what you want to be, good luck I say. But if you don't need it, nobody should make you have it. Myself, I'm a Brit first, a Pole second and everything else comes afterwards. Never mind there's a lot would have it the other way round. That's their problem."

"Oh well said!" Walter cried energetically, flapping his fingers and giggling. "Oh that *does* put it in a nutshell. And you say her English was really rather good?"

"More than good, sir. Classic. A lesson to us all."

"Like a schoolteacher, you said."

"That was my impression," said Landau. "A teacher, a professor. I felt the learning. The intellect. The will."

"Could she not be an interpreter, you see?"

"Good interpreters efface themselves, in my opinion, sir. This lady projected herself."

"Oh well I say, that's rather a good answer," said Walter, shooting his pink cuffs. "And she was wearing a wedding ring. Well done."

"She certainly was, sir. A betrothal ring and a marriage ring. That's the first thing I look at after the usual, and in Russia it's not England, you have to look the wrong way round because the girls wear their wedding rings on the right hand. Single Russian women are a pest and divorce is off the peg. Give me a nice solid hubby and a couple of little ones for them to go home to any day. Then I might oblige."

"Let's ask you about that. You think she had children as well, do you, or not?"

"I am convinced of it, sir."

"Oh come, you can't be," Walter said peevishly, with a sudden downturn of the mouth. "You're not psychic, are you?"

"The hips, sir. The hips, the dignity even when she was scared. She was not a Juno, she was not a sylph. She was a mother."

"Height?" Walter shrieked in a descant as his hairless eyebrows bucked upwards in alarm. "Can you do her height for us? Think of yourself. Measure her against you. Are you looking up or down?"

"Above the normal. I told you."

"Taller than you, then?"

"Yes."

"Five six? Five seven?"

"More like the second," said Landau sullenly.

"And her age again? You fumbled it before."

"If she's over thirty-five, she doesn't know it. A lovely skin, a fine form, a fine woman in her prime, especially the spirit, sir," Landau replied with a defeated grin, for while he might find Walter unsavoury in some way, he still had the Pole's weakness for eccentrics.

"It's a Sunday. Imagine she's English. Would you expect her to be going to church?"

"She'd definitely have given the problem a good going over," said Landau to his great surprise before he had time to think of an answer. "She might have said there was *no* God. She might have said there *was* a God. But she wouldn't have let it drift away from her like most of us. She'd have gone for it and come to a decision and done something about it if she thought she should."

Suddenly all Walter's quaint ways had resolved themselves into a long rubbery smile. "Oh you *are* good," he declared enviously. "Now do you know any science?" he continued as his voice again soared into the clouds.

"A bit. Kitchen science, really. What I pick up."

"Physics?"

"O-level, not more, sir. I used to sell the course books. I'm not sure I'd scrape through the exam, mind, even now. But they did enable me to improve myself, put it that way."

"What does telemetry mean?"

"Never heard of it."

"Not in English, not in Russian?"

"Not in any language, sir, I'm afraid. Telemetry has passed me by."

"How about CEP?"

"The what, sir?"

"Circular-error-probable. My goodness, he wrote enough about it, didn't he, in those funny notebooks that you brought us? Don't tell me CEP hasn't stuck in your mind."

"I didn't notice it. I skipped. That's all I did."

"Until you came to his point about the Soviet knight dying inside his armour. Where you stopped. Why?"

"I didn't come to it. I *happened* to come to it."

"All right, you happened to come to it. And you formed a view. Is that right? Of what the writer was telling us. What view?"

"Incompetence, I suppose. They're no good at it. The Russkies. They're duff."

"Duff at what?"

"The rockets. They make errors."

"What sort of errors?"

"All sorts. *Magnetic* errors. *Bias* errors, whatever those are. I don't know. That's your job, isn't it."

But Landau's defensive surliness only emphasised his virtue as a witness. For where he wished to shine and could not, his failure reassured them, as Walter's airy gesture of relief now testified.

"Well I think he's done terribly well," he declared as if Landau were nowhere within earshot, flinging up his hands again, this time in a theatrical gesture of conclusion. "He tells us what he remembers. He doesn't make things up to spin a better tale. You won't do that, will you, Niki?" he added anxiously, uncrossing his legs as if his crotch were nipping him.

"No, sir, you may rest assured."

"And you haven't? I mean, because sooner or later we'd find out. Then everything you've given us would lose its lustre."

"No, sir. It's the way I told it. No more, no less."

"I'm sure it is," said Walter to his colleagues in a tone of simple trust as he again sat back. "The hardest thing in our trade or anybody else's is to say 'I believe.' Niki's a natural source and rare as hen's teeth. If there were more of *him*, nobody would need *us*."

"This is Johnny," Ned explained, playing the aide-de-camp.

Johnny had wavy greying hair and a broad jaw and a file full of official-looking telegrams. With his gold watch-chain and tailored charcoal suit, he might have been a foreign barmaid's vision of an Englishman but he certainly wasn't Landau's.

"Niki, first we have to thank you, pal," Johnny said, in lazy East Coast American. We the larger beneficiaries, his munificent tone suggested. We the majority shareholders. I'm afraid Johnny is like that. A good officer, but unable to keep his American supremacy inside its box. I sometimes think that is the difference between American spies and our own. Americans, with their frank enjoyment of power and money, flaunt their luck. They lack the instinct to dissemble that comes so naturally to us British.

Anyway, Landau's hackles went up in a flash.

"Mind if I ask you a couple of questions?" Johnny said.

"If it's all right by Ned," said Landau.

"Of course it is," said Ned.

"So we're at the audio fair that night. Okay, pal?"

"Well, evening really, Johnny."

"You escort the woman Yekaterina Orlova across the room to the top of the staircase. Where the guards are. You say goodbye to her."

"She's holding my arm."

"She's holding your arm, great. In front of the guards. You watch her down the stairs. Do you also watch her into the street, pal?"

I had not heard Johnny use "pal" before, so I took it that he was trying to needle Landau somehow, a thing that Agency people learn from their in-house psychologists.

"Correct," Landau snapped.

"Right into the street? Pause and think," he suggested, with the attorney's false expansiveness.

"Into the street and out of my life."

Johnny waited till he was sure everyone was aware that he was waiting, and Landau more aware than anybody. "Niki, pal, we've had people stand at the top of that staircase in the last twenty-four hours. No one sees the street from the top of that staircase."

Landau's face darkened. Not in embarrassment. In anger. "I saw her walk down the stairs. I saw her cross the lobby to where the street is. She did not return. So unless somebody has moved the street in the last twenty-four hours, which I grant you under Stalin was always possible—"

"Let's go on, shall we?" said Ned.

"See anyone walk out after her?" Johnny asked, riding Landau a little harder. "Down the stairs or into the street?"

"Both, pal. Both."

"No, I didn't. I didn't see her go into the street, did I, because you just told me I didn't. So why don't you answer the questions and I'll ask them?"

While Johnny sat idly back, Ned intervened. "Niki, some things have to be very carefully examined. There's a lot at stake and Johnny has his orders."

"I'm at stake too," said Landau. "My word's on the line and I don't like having it made a fool of by an American who's not even British."

Johnny had returned to the file. "Niki, will you please describe the security arrangements for the fair, as you yourself observed them?"

Landau took a tense breath. "Well then," he said, and started again. "We had these two young uniformed policemen hanging about the hotel lobby. Those are the boys who keep the lists of all the Russians who come and go, which is normal. Then upstairs inside the hall we had the nasties. Those are the plainclothes boys. The dawdlers, they call them, the *toptuny*," he added for Johnny's enlightenment. "After a couple of days you know the *toptuny* by heart. They don't buy, they don't steal the exhibits or ask for freebies and there's always one of them with the butter-blond hair, don't ask me why. We had three boys and they didn't change all week. They were the ones who watched her go down the stairs."

"That everyone, pal?"

"As far as I know it is everyone but I'm waiting to be told I'm wrong."

"Were you not also aware of two ladies of indeterminate age, grey-haired persons who were also present every day of the fair, came early, left late, who also didn't buy, didn't enter negotiations with any of the standholders or exhibitors, or appear to have any legitimate purpose for attending the fair?"

"You're talking about Gert and Daisy, I suppose."

"Excuse me?"

"There was two old biddies from the Council of Libraries. They came for the beer. Their main pleasure was whipping brochures off the stands and cadging free handouts. We christened them Gert and Daisy after a certain British radio show popular in the war years and after."

"It did not occur to you that these ladies might also be performing a surveillance function?"

Ned's powerful hand was already out to restrain Landau but he was too late.

"Johnny," said Landau, boiling over. "This is Moscow, right? Moscow, Russia, *pal*. If I stopped to consider who had a surveillance function and who didn't, I wouldn't get out of bed in the morning and I wouldn't get into it at night. The birds in the trees are wired, for all I know."

Yet again Johnny was at his telegrams. "You say that Yekaterina Borisovna Orlova referred to the adjoining stand of Abercrombie & Blair as having been empty on the previous day, correct?"

"I do say so, yes."

"But you didn't see her the day before? Is that also correct?"

"It is."

"You also say that you have an eye for a pretty lady."

"I do, thank you, and may it long remain vigilant."

"Don't you think you should have noticed her then?"

"I do sometimes miss one," Landau confessed, colouring again. "If my back is turned, if I am bent over a desk or relieving myself in the toilet, it is possible my attention may flag for a moment."

But Johnny's nervelessness was acquiring its own authority. "You have relatives in Poland, do you not, Mr. Landau?" The "pal" had evidently done its work, for listening to the tape I noticed he had dropped it.

"I do."

"Do you not have an elder sister highly placed in the Polish administration?"

"My sister works in the Polish Health Ministry as a hospital inspector. She is not highly placed and she is past retiring age."

"Have you at any time directly or indirectly been the witting target of pressure or blackmail by Communist bloc agencies or third parties acting in their behalf?"

Landau turned to Ned. "A what target? My English isn't very good, I'm afraid."

"Conscious," said Ned with a warning smile. "Aware. Knowing."

"No I haven't," said Landau.

"In your travels to Eastern bloc countries, have you been intimate with women of those countries?"

"I've been to bed with some. I haven't been intimate."

Like a naughty schoolboy, Walter let out a squeak of choked laughter, lifting his shoulders to his neck and cupping his hand over his dreadful teeth. But Johnny soldiered doggedly on: "Mr. Landau, have you ever prior to this time had contacts with any intelligence agency of any hostile or friendly country anywhere?"

"Negative."

"Have you ever sold information to any person of whatever status or profession —newspaper, enquiry agency, police, military—for any purpose, however innocuous?"

"Negative."

"And you are not and never have been a member of a Communist party or any peace organisation or group sympathetic to its aims?"

"I'm a British subject," Landau retorted, thrusting out his little Polish jaw.

"And you have no idea, however vague, however mistily formed, of the overall message contained in the material you handled?"

"I didn't handle it. I passed it on."

"But you read it along the way."

"What I could, I read. Some. Then I gave up. As I told you."

"Why?"

"From a sense of decency, if you want to know. Something which I begin to suspect you are not troubled by."

But Johnny, far from blushing, was digging patiently in his file. He drew out an envelope and from the envelope a pack of postcard-sized photographs, which he dealt on to the table like playing-cards. Some were fuzzy, all were grainy. A few had foreground obstructions. They showed women coming down the steps of a bleak office building, some in groups, some singly. Some carried perhaps-bags, some had their heads down and carried nothing. And Landau remembered hearing that it was Moscow practice for ladies slipping out for lunchtime shopping to stuff whatever they needed into their pockets and leave their handbags lying on their desks in order to show the world they had only gone down the corridor.

"This one," said Landau suddenly, pointing with his forefinger.

Johnny played another of his courtroom tricks. He was really too intelligent for all this nonsense but that didn't stop him. He looked disappointed and mighty unbelieving. He looked as if he had caught Landau in a lie. The video film shows him overacting quite outrageously. "How can you be so damn sure, for God's sake? You never even *saw* her in an overcoat."

Landau is undismayed. "That's the lady. Katya," he says firmly. "I'd recognise her anywhere. Katya. She's done her hair up, but it's her. Katya. That's her bag too, plastic." He continues staring at the photograph. "And her wedding ring." For a moment he seems to forget he is not alone. "I'd do the same for her tomorrow," he says. "*And* the day after."

Which marked the satisfactory end to Johnny's hostile examination of the witness.

As the days progressed and one enigmatic interview followed another, never the same place twice, never the same people except for Ned, Landau had increasingly the feeling that things were advancing to a climax. In a sound laboratory behind Portland Place, they played him women's voices, Russians speaking Russian and Russians speaking English. But he didn't recognise Katya's. Another day, to his alarm, was devoted to money. Not theirs but Landau's. His bank statements—where the hell did they get them from? His tax returns, salary slips, savings, mortgage, endowment policy, worse than the Inland Revenue.

"Trust us, Niki," said Ned—but with such an honest, reassuring smile that Landau had the feeling that Ned had been out there fighting for him somehow, and that things were on the verge of coming right.

They're going to offer me a job, he thought on the Monday. They're going to turn me into a spy like Barley.

They're trying to put it right about my father twenty years after his death, he thought on the Tuesday.

Then on the Wednesday morning, Sam the driver pressed his doorbell for the last time and everything came clear.

"Where is it today then, Sam?" Landau asked him cheerfully. "The Bloody Tower?"

"Sing Sing," said Sam, and they had a good laugh.

But Sam delivered him not to the Tower and not to Sing Sing either, but to the side entrance of one of the very Whitehall ministries that Landau only eleven days earlier had attempted unsuccessfully to storm. The grey-eyed Brock guided him up a back staircase and disappeared. Landau entered a great room that looked on to the Thames. A row of men sat at a table facing him. To the left sat Walter with his tie set straight and his hair slicked down. To the right sat Ned. Both looked solemn. And between them, with his cuffed hands resting flat on the table and lines of refusal round his neat jaw, sat a younger, sharp-suited man whom Landau rightly assumed to be senior in rank to both of them, and who, as Landau later put it, looked as though he had stepped out of a different movie. He was sleek and tight-lipped and groomed for television. He was rich in more than money. He was forty and rising, but the worst thing about him was his innocence. He looked too young to be charged with adult crimes.

"My name's Clive," he said in an underpowered voice. "Come in, Landau. We've got a problem about what to do with you."

And beyond Clive—beyond all of them, in fact—Niki Landau as an after-thought saw me. Old Palfrey. And Ned saw him see me and Ned smiled and made a pleasant show of introducing us.

"Ah now, Niki, this is Harry," he said untruthfully.

Nobody else had earned a trade description till then but Ned provided one for me: "Harry's our in-house umpire, Niki. He makes sure everyone gets a fair deal."

"Nice," said Landau.

Which is where, in the history of the affair, I made my own modest entrance, as legal errand boy, as fixer and bit player, and pleaser, and finally as chronicler; now Rosencrantz, now Guildenstern, and just occasionally Palfrey.

And to take even more care of Landau there was Reg, who was big and ginger and reassuring. Reg led Landau to a dunce's chair at the centre of the room, then sat beside him on another. And Landau took to Reg at once, which was usual, for Reg was by trade a welfarer and his clients included defectors, grounded fieldmen and blown agents, and other men and women whose bonds to England might have worn a little thin if old Reg Wattle and his cosy wife Berenice had not been there to hold their hands.

"You've done a good job but we can't tell you why it's good, because that would be insecure," Clive continued in his arid voice when Landau was comfortably settled. "Even the little you know is too much. And we can't let you wander round Eastern Europe with our secrets in your head. It's too dangerous. For you and the people involved. So while you've performed a valuable service for us, you've also become a serious worry. If this were wartime, we could lock you up or shoot you or something. But it isn't, not officially."

Somewhere on his prudent little journey to power, Clive had taught himself to smile. It was an unfair weapon to use on friendly people, rather like silence on the telephone. But Clive knew nothing of unfairness because he knew nothing of its opposite. As to passion, it was what you used when you needed to persuade people.

"After all, you could point the finger at some very important people, couldn't you?" he continued so quietly that everyone kept still to hear him. "I know you wouldn't do that deliberately but when one's handcuffed to a radiator one doesn't have much choice. Not in the end."

And when Clive thought he had scared Landau just enough he glanced to me, and nodded to me, and watched me while I opened up the pompous leather folder I had brought with me and handed Landau the long document I had prepared, of which the purport was that Landau renounce in perpetuity all travel behind the Iron Curtain, that he never leave the country without first advising Reg so many days in advance, the details to be arranged between the two of them, and that Reg should look after Landau's passport in order to prevent mishaps. And that he accept irrevocably into his life the role of Reg or whomever the authorities should appoint in Reg's place as confidant, philosopher and discreet arbiter of his affairs of every kind—including the ticklish problem of how to handle the taxation on the cashier's cheque attached, drawn on the Fulham branch of a very boring British bank, in the sum of a hundred thousand pounds.

And that, in order that he be regularly scared by Authority, he should present himself every six months to the Service's Legal Adviser, Harry, for a top-up on the subject of Secrecy—to old Palfrey, Hannah's sometime lover, a man so bowed by life that he can be safely charged with keeping others upright. And that further to the above and pursuant to it and consequent upon it, the whole matter relating to a certain Russian woman and to her friend's literary manuscript, and to the contents of said manuscript—however much or little he may have understood their import—and to the part played by a certain British publisher, be as of this moment solemnly declared void, dead, inoperative and expunged, henceforth and for all time. Amen.

There was one copy and it would live in my safe till it was shredded or fell apart of old age. Landau read it twice while Reg read it over his shoulder. Then Landau disappeared into his own thoughts for a while without much regard for who was watching him or who was willing him to sign and cease to be a problem. Because Landau knew that in this instance he was the buyer, not the seller.

He saw himself standing at the window of his Moscow hotel room. He remembered how he had wished he could hang up his travellers' boots and settle to a less arduous life. And the amusing notion came to him that his Maker must have taken him at his word and fixed things accordingly, which to everyone's unease caused him to break out in a little burst of laughter.

"Well I hope old Johnny the Yank is footing the bill for this, Harry," he said.

But the joke did not receive the applause it deserved, since it happened to be true. So Landau took Reg's pen and signed, and handed me the document and watched me add my own signature as a witness, Horatio B. dePalfrey, which after twenty years has such a practised illegibility that if I had signed it Heinz's Tomato Sauce neither Landau nor anybody else could have told the difference, and put it back inside its leather coffin and patted down the lid. There was handshaking, mutual assurances were exchanged, and Clive murmured, "We're grateful to you, Niki," just like in the movie that Landau periodically convinced himself he was part of.

Then everybody shook Landau's hand yet again and, having watched him ride nobly into the sunset or more accurately walk jauntily off down the corridor chatting away at Reg Wattle, who was twice his size, they waited fretfully for the "take" on the intercepts for which I had already obtained the warrants under the infallible plea of intense American interest.

They tapped his office and home telephones, read his mail and fitted an electronic limpet to the rear axle of his beloved drop-head Triumph.

They followed him in his leisure hours and recruited a typist in his office to keep an eye on him as a "suspect foreigner" while he served out the last weeks of his notice.

They put potential lady-friends alongside him in the bars where he liked to do his hunting. Yet despite these cumbersome and needless precautions, dictated by that same intense American interest, they drew a blank. No hint of bragging or indiscretion reached their ears. Landau never complained, never boasted, never attempted to go public. He became, in fact, one of the few finished and perfectly happy short stories of the trade.

He was the perfect prologue. He never came back.

He never attempted to get in touch with Barley Scott Blair, the great British spy. He lived in awe of him for ever. Even for the grand opening of the video shop, when he would have loved more than anything in the world to bask in the presence of this real-life secret British hero, he never tried to stretch the rules. Perhaps it was satisfaction enough for him to know that, one night in Moscow when the old country had called on him, he too had behaved like the English gentleman he sometimes longed to be. Or perhaps the Pole in him was content to have cocked a snook at the Russian bear next door. Or perhaps it was the memory of Katya that kept him faithful, Katya the strong, the virtuous, Katya the brave and beautiful, who even in her own fear had taken care to warn him of the dangers to himself. "You must believe in what you are doing."

And Landau had believed. And Landau was proud as Punch that he had, as any of us should be.

Even his video shop flourished. It was a sensation. A little rich for some people's blood now and then, including that of the Golders Green police, with whom I had to have a friendly word. But for others pure balm.

Above all, we were able to love him, because he saw us as we wished to be seen, as the omniscient, capable and heroic custodians of our great nation's inner health. It was a view of us that Barley never quite seemed able to share—any more, I have to say, than Hannah could, though she only ever knew it from outside, as the place to which she could not follow me, as the shrine of ultimate compromise and therefore, in her unrelenting view, despair.

"They are definitely not the cure, Palfrey," she had told me only a few weeks before, when for some reason I was trying to extol the Service. "And they sound to *me* more likely to be the disease."

There is no such thing, we older hands like to say, as an intelligence operation that does not occasionally run to farce. The bigger the operation, the bigger the belly laughs, and it is a matter of Service history that the week-long manhunt for Bartholomew alias Barley Scott Blair generated enough frenzy and frustration to power a dozen secret networks. Orthodox young novices like Brock from the Russia House learned to hate Barley's life before they even found the man who led it.

After five days of chasing after him, they thought they knew everything about Barley except where he was. They knew his free-thinking parentage and his expensive education, both wasted, and the unedifying details of his marriages, all broken. They knew the café in Camden Town where he played his chess with any layabout spirit who happened to drift in. A regular gentleman, even if he was the guilty party, they told Wicklow, who was posing as a divorce agent. Under the usual tacky but effective pretexts, they had doorstepped a sister in Hove who despaired of him, tradesmen in Hampstead who were writing to him, a married daughter in Grantham who adored him and a grey-wolf son in the City who was so withdrawn he might have taken a vow of silence.

They had talked to members of a scratch jazz band for whom he had occasionally played saxophone, to the almoner at the hospital where he was enrolled as a visitor and to the vicar at the Kentish Town church where to everyone's amazement he sang tenor. "Such a lovely voice when he shows up," said the vicar indulgently. But when they tried, with old Palfrey's help again, to tap his phone to get more of this lovely voice, there was nothing to tap because he hadn't paid his bill.

They even found a trace on him in our own records. Or rather the Americans found it for them, which did not add to their enchantment. For it turned out that in the early sixties, when any Englishman who had the misfortune to possess a double-barrelled name was in danger of being recruited to the Secret Service, Barley's had been passed to New York for vetting under some partially observed bilateral security treaty. Furious, Brock checked again with Central Registry, who, after first denying all knowledge of Barley, dug up his card from a cut in the white index that was still waiting to be transferred to the computer. And from the white card, behold a white file containing the original vetting form and correspondence. Brock rushed into Ned's room as if he had found the clue to everything. Age, 22! Hobbies, theatre and music! Sports, nil! Reasons for considering him, a cousin named Lionel in the Life Guards!

The payoff alone was lacking. The recruiting officer had lunched Barley at the Athenaeum and stamped his file "No Further Action," taking the trouble to add the word "ever" in his own hand.

Nevertheless this quaint episode of more than twenty years ago had a certain oblique effect on their attitude towards him, just as they had puzzled uneasily for a while over the bizarre left-wing attachments of old Salisbury Blair, his father. It undermined Barley's independence in their eyes. Not in Ned's, for Ned was made of stronger stuff. But in the others, Brock and the younger ones. It led them to feel they owned him somehow, if only as the unsuccessful aspirant to their mystique.

A further frustration was provided by Barley's disgraceful car, which the police found parked illegally in Lexham Gardens with the offside wing bashed in and the licence out of date and a half bottle of Scotch stuck in the glove compartment with a sheaf of love letters in Barley's hand. Neighbours had been complaining about it for weeks.

"Tow it, boot it, charge it or just crush it?" the obliging superintendent of traffic asked Ned over the phone.

"Forget it," Ned replied wearily. Nevertheless he and Brock hastened round there in the vain hope of a clue. The love letters turned out to have been written to a lady of the Gardens but she had given them back to him. She was the last person in the world, she assured them with a tragic air, to know where Barley was now.

It wasn't till the following Thursday, when Ned was patiently checking Barley's monthly bank statements, that he discovered among the overdrawn columns a quarterly standing order in favour of a property company in Lisbon, a hundred and something pounds to Real Somebody Limitada. He stared at it unbelievingly. He kept staring. Then he said a foul word where normally he never swore. Then he phoned Travel in a hurry and had them check old flightlists from Gatwick and Heathrow. When Travel phoned back, Ned swore again. They were home. Days of phone calls, interviews and banging on doors, the rules bent in all directions, watch lists, cables to friendly liaison services in half the capitals of the world, their vaunted Records Section humiliated in front of the Americans. Yet nobody they had spoken to and no researches had revealed the one crucial, indispensable, idiotic fact they needed to know: that ten years ago on a whim Barley Blair, having inherited a stray couple of thousand from a remote aunt, bought himself a scruffy pied-à-terre in Lisbon, where he was accustomed to take periodic rests from the burden of his many-sided soul. It could have been Cornwall, it could have been Provence or Timbuktu. But Lisbon by an accident had got him, down on the waterfront, next to a bit of rough parkland, and too near the fish market for a lot of people's sensitivities.

An embattled calm settled over the Russia House with this discovery and Brock's bony face took on a sallow fury.

"Who's our Brother Lisbon these days?" Ned asked him, light as a summer breeze once more.

Then he telephoned old Palfrey alias Harry and put him on permanent standby, which, as Hannah would have said, described my situation nicely.

Barley was sitting at the bar when Merridew walked in on him. He was perched on a stool and shooting his mouth off about human nature to a drink-sodden expatriate major of artillery named Graves: Major Arthur Winslow Graves, later whitelisted as a Barley contact, his only claim on history and he never knew it. Barley's long pliant back was arched away from the open door and the door led off the courtyard, so Merridew, who was a fat boy of thirty, was able to collect some much-needed breath before he made his pitch. He had been chasing Barley half the day, missing him everywhere and getting more furious with each rebuff:

At Barley's flat, not five minutes' walk from here, where an Englishwoman with a common accent had told him through the letterbox to get stuffed.

At the British Library, where the lady librarian had reported that Barley had spent an afternoon browsing, by which she appeared to imply—though promptly denied it when directly asked—that he was in an alcoholic stupor.

And at a revolting Tudor tavern in Estoril, where Barley and friends had enjoyed a liquid supper under plastic muskets and noisily departed not half an hour before.

The hotel—it prefers to call itself a humble *pensão*—was an old convent, a place the English loved. To reach it Merridew had to scale a cobbled stairway overhung with vines and, having scaled it and taken a first cautious look, he had to hurry down it again in order to tell Brock to run, "and I mean really run," and telephone Ned from the café on the corner. Then scale it yet again, which was why he was feeling so puffed and even more than usually put-upon. Smells of cool sandstone and fresh-ground coffee mingled with the night plants. Merridew was impervious to them. He lacked breath. The sob of distant trams and the honking of boats provided the only background sounds to Barley's monologue. Merridew had no awareness of them.

"Blind children cannot *chew,* Gravey, my dear old charmer," Barley was explaining patiently while he rested the point of his spidery forefinger on the major's navel and his elbow on the bar beside an unfinished game of chess. "Fact of science, Gravey. Blind children have to be taught to bite. Come here. Close your eyes."

Tenderly taking hold of the major's head in both his hands, Barley guided it towards him, parted the unresisting jaws, and popped in a couple of cashews. "There's a lad. On the command champ, champ. Mind your tongue. Champ. Repeat."

Taking this as his cue Merridew hoisted his hail-fellow smile and ventured a step into the bar, where he was surprised by two life-sized carvings of mulatto ladies in court dress standing either side of him at the doorway. Colour of hair chestnut, colour of eyes green, he rehearsed, checking off Barley's points as if he were a horse. Height six foot nothing, clean-shaven, well-spoken, slender build, idiosyncratic dress. Idiosyncratic, my foot, thought tubby Merridew, still winded, while he examined Barley's linen bush-jacket, grey flannels and sandals. What do the fools in London expect him to wear on a hot night in Lisbon? Mink?

"Ah, excuse me," Merridew said pleasingly. "I'm actually *looking* for someone. I wonder if you can help me."

"Which proves, my dear old mother's arse," Barley resumed, when he had carefully restored the major to an upright position, "quoting the celebrated song, that notwithstanding the fact that the big juju man made us of meat, eating people is wrong."

"I say, do pardon me, but I rather think you're Mr. Bartholomew Scott Blair," said Merridew. "Yes? Correct?"

Keeping a grasp upon the major's lapel in order to avert a military disaster, Barley cautiously turned himself half-circle on his stool and looked Merridew over, beginning with his shoes and ending with his smile.

"My name's Merridew from the Embassy, you see. Only I'm the Commercial Second Secretary here. I'm frightfully sorry. We've received a rather pressing telegram for you over our link. We think you should pop round and read it straight away. Would you mind?"

Then unwisely Merridew permitted himself a mannerism peculiar to plump officials. He flung an arm out, cupped his hand and passed it officiously over the top of his head as if to confirm that his hair and his cover were still in their proper places. And this large gesture, performed by a fat man in a low room, seemed to raise fears in Barley that might otherwise have slumbered, for he became disconcertingly sober.

"Are you telling me somebody's dead, old boy?" he asked with a smile so tense it looked ready for the worst of jokes.

"Oh my dear sir. Don't be so Gothic, please. It's a commercial thing, not consular. Why else would it come over our link?" He tried a placatory giggle.

But Barley had not yielded. Not by an inch. He was still looking into the pit, wherever Merridew might choose to look himself. "So what the hell are we telling ourselves, actually?" he asked.

"Nothing," Merridew retorted, scared. "A pressing telegram. Don't take it so personally. Diplomatic wireless."

"Who's doing the pressing?"

"No one. I can't give you a précis in front of everyone. It's confidential. Our eyes only."

They forgot his spectacles, thought Merridew, while he returned Barley's stare. Round. Black-framed. Too small for his eyes. Slips them to the tip of his nose when he scowls at you. Gets you in his sights.

"Never knew an honest debt that couldn't wait till Monday," Barley declared, returning to the major. "Loosen your girdle, Mr. Merridew. Take a drink with the unwashed."

Merridew might not have been the slenderest of men or the tallest. But he had grip, he had cunning and like many fat men he had unexpected resources of indignation which he was able to turn on like a flood when they were needed.

"Look here, Scott Blair, your affairs are not my concern, I am glad to say. I am not a bailiff, I am not a common messenger. I am a diplomat and I have a certain standing. I've spent half the day traipsing round after you, I have a car and a clerk waiting outside and I have certain rights over my own life. I'm sorry."

Their duet might have continued indefinitely had not the major staged an unexpected revival. Jerking back his shoulders, he thrust his fists to the seams of his trousers and tucked his chin into a rictal grimace of respect. "Royal summons, Barley," he barked. "Embassy's the local Buck House. Invitation's a command. Mustn't insult Her Majesty."

"He's not Her Majesty," Barley objected patiently. "He isn't wearing a crown."

Merridew wondered whether he should summon Brock. He tried smiling winningly but Barley's attention had wandered to the alcove, where a vase of dried flowers hid an empty grate. He tried calling, "Okay? All set?" much as he might have called to a wife when she was keeping him waiting for a dinner party. But Barley's haggard gaze remained on the dead flowers. He seemed to see his whole life in them, every wrong turning and false step from there to here. Then just as Merridew was giving up hope, Barley began loading his junk into his bush-jacket pockets, ritualistically, as if setting off on a safari: his bent wallet, full of uncashed cheques and cancelled credit cards; his passport, mildewed with sweat and too much travel; the notebook and pencil he kept handy for penning gems of alcoholic wisdom to himself for contemplation when he was sober. And when he had done all this he dumped a large banknote on the bar like somebody who wouldn't be needing money for a long while.

"See the major into his cab, Manuel. That means help him down the steps and into the back seat and pay the driver in advance. When you've done that, you can keep the change. So long, Gravey. Thanks for the laughs."

Dew was falling. A young moon lay on its back among the moist stars. They descended the stairway, Merridew first, urging Barley to be sure and mind his step. The harbour was filled with roving lights. A black saloon with CD plates waited at the curbside. Brock lurked restively beside it in the darkness. A second unmarked car lay further back.

"Ah now, this is Eddie," said Merridew, making the introductions. "Eddie, I'm afraid we took our time. I trust you have made your phone call?"

"All done," said Brock.

"And everybody at home is happy, I trust, Eddie? The little ones all tucked up and so forth? You won't get flak from the missus?"

"It's all right," Brock growled in a tone that said shut up.

Barley sat in the front seat, his head pitched back on the rest, eyes closed. Merridew drove. Brock sat very still in the back. The second car pulled out slowly, in the way good watchers do.

"This the way you usually go to the Embassy?" Barley asked in his seeming doze.

"Ah now, the duty dog took the telegram to his house, you see," Merridew explained lavishly, as if responding to a particularly well-taken point. "I'm afraid that, come weekends, we have to batten down the Embassy against the Irish. Yes." He switched on the radio. A deep-throated woman began sobbing a succulent lament. "Fado," he declared. "I adore Fado. I think it's why I'm here. I'm sure it is. I'm sure I put Fado on my post request." He began conducting with his spare hand. "Fado," he explained.

"Are you the people who've been snooping round my daughter, asking her a lot of stupid questions?" Barley asked.

"Oh we're just commercial, I'm afraid," Merridew said, and kept conducting for all that he was worth. But inside himself he was by now gravely disturbed by Barley's want of innocence. Sooner them than me, he thought, feeling Barley's untamed gaze upon his right cheek. If this is what Head Office has to reckon with these days, God preserve me from a home posting.

They had rented the town house of a former member of the Service, a British banker with a second house in Cintra. Old Palfrey had clinched the deal for them. They wanted no official premises, nothing that could afterwards be held against them. Yet the sense of age and place had its own particular eloquence. A wrought-iron coaching lamp lit the vaulted entrance. The granite flagstones had been hacked to stop the horses slipping. Merridew rang the bell. Brock had closed in tight in case of accidents.

"Hullo. Come on in," said Ned pleasantly, opening the huge scrolled door.

"Well I'll be off, won't I," said Merridew. "Marvellous, terrific." Still burbling covering fire, he scampered back to his car before anyone could contradict him. And as he did so the second car cruised by like one good friend who has seen another to his doorstep on a dangerous night.

For a long moment, while Brock stood off observing them, Ned and Barley appraised one another as only Englishmen can who are of the same height and class and shape of head. And though Ned in appearance was the very archetype of quiet British self-command and balance, and in most ways therefore the exact reverse of Barley—and though Barley was loose-limbed and angular with a face that even in repose seemed determined to explore beyond the obvious—there was still enough of the other in each of them to permit a recognition. Through a closed door came the murmur of male voices, but Ned made as though he hadn't heard it. He led Barley down the passage to a library and said, "In here," while Brock stayed in the hall.

"How drunk are you?" Ned asked, lowering his voice and handing Barley a glass of iced water.

"Not," said Barley. "Who's hijacking me? What goes on?"

"My name's Ned. I'm about to move the goalposts. There's no telegram, no crisis in your affairs beyond the usual. No one's being hijacked. I'm from British Intelligence. So are the people waiting for you next door. You once applied to join us. Now's your chance to help."

A silence settled between them while Ned waited for Barley to respond. Ned was Barley's age exactly. For twenty-five years, in one guise or another, he had been revealing himself as a British secret agent to people he needed to obtain. But this was the first time that his client had failed to speak, blink, smile, step back or show the smallest sign of surprise.

"I don't know anything," said Barley.

"Maybe we want you to find something out."

"Find it out for yourselves."

"We can't. Not without you. That's why we're here."

Drifting over to the bookshelves, Barley tilted his head to one side and peered over the top of his round spectacles at the titles while he went on drinking his water.

"First you're commercial, now you're spies," he said.

"Why don't you have a word with the Ambassador?"

"He's a fool. I was at Cambridge with him." He took down a bound book and glanced at the frontispiece. "Crap," he pronounced with contempt. "Must buy them by the yard. Who owns this place?"

"The Ambassador will verify me. If you ask him whether he can manage golf on Thursday, he'll tell you not till five o'clock."

"I don't play golf," said Barley, taking down another volume. "I don't play anything actually. I've retired from all games."

"Except chess," Ned suggested, holding out the open telephone directory to him. With a shrug Barley dialled the number. Hearing the Ambassador he gave a raffish if rather puzzled smile. "Is that Tubby? Barley Blair, here. How about a spot of the golf on Thursday for your liver?"

An acid voice said it was engaged till five o'clock.

"Five won't do at all," Barley retorted. "We'll be playing in the dark at that rate —bugger's rung off," he complained, shaking the dead receiver. Then he saw Ned's hand on the telephone cradle.

"It isn't a joke, I'm afraid," said Ned. "It's actually very serious."

Lost once more in his own contemplations, Barley slowly replaced the receiver. "The line between actually very serious and actually very funny is actually very thin," he remarked.

"Well let's cross it, shall we?" said Ned.

The talk behind the door had ceased. Barley turned the handle and walked in. Ned followed. Brock stayed in the hall to guard the door. We had been listening to everything over the relay.

If Barley was curious as to what he would face in there, so were we. It's an odd game, turning a man's life inside out without meeting him. He entered slowly. He took a few paces into the room and stopped, his long arms dangling wide of his sides while Ned, halfway to the table, made the all-male introductions.

"This is Clive, this is Walter, and over here is Bob. This is Harry. Meet Barley, everyone."

Barley scarcely nodded as the names were spoken. He seemed to prefer the evidence of his eyes to anything he was being told.

The ornate furniture and the coppice of vulgar indoor plants interested him. So did an orange tree. He touched a fruit, caressed a leaf, then delicately sniffed his thumb and finger as if assuring himself that they were real. There was a passive anger about him that went ahead of finding out the cause. Anger at being woken, I thought. At being singled out and named—a thing that Hannah said I always feared the most.

I also remember thinking he was elegant. Not, God knows, by virtue of his shabby clothes. But in his gestures, in his faded chivalry. In his natural courtesy, even if he resisted it.

"You don't run to surnames, by any chance, do you?" Barley enquired when he had completed his inspection of the room.

"I'm afraid not," said Clive.

"Because a Mr. Rigby called on my daughter Anthea last week. Said he was a tax inspector. Some bilge about wanting to adjust an unfair assessment. Was he one of you clowns?"

"By the sound of him I should think he probably was," said Clive, with the arrogance of someone who can't be bothered to lie.

Barley looked at Clive, who had one of those English faces that seemed to have been embalmed while he was still a boy king, at his hard clever eyes with nothing behind them, at the ash beneath his skin. He turned to Walter, so round, wispy and amused, a teased-out Falstaff of the richer common rooms. And from Walter his gaze moved on to Bob, taking in the patrician scale of him, his greater age, his avuncular ease, the browns he wore instead of greys and blues. Bob was lounging with his legs stretched out, one arm flung proprietorially over a chair. Gold-framed half-glasses peeked from his handkerchief pocket. The soles of his cracked mahogany shoes were like flat-irons.

"Barley, I am the odd man out in this family," Bob announced comfortably in a rich Bostonian drawl. "I guess I am also the oldest and I don't want to be sitting here under a false flag. I am fifty-eight years old, God help me, I work for the Central Intelligence Agency, which as you probably know is based in Langley in the state of Virginia. I do have a surname but I will not insult you by offering you one because it surely would not be much like the real thing." He raised a liver-spotted hand in leisurely salute. "Proud to meet you, Barley. Let's have fun. Let's do some good."

Barley turned back to Ned. "Now that *is* jolly," he said, though with no detectable animus. "So where are we all off to? Nicaragua? Chile? Salvador? Iran? If you want a Third World leader assassinated, I'm your man."

"Don't rant," Clive drawled, though ranting was about the last thing Barley had been guilty of. "We're as bad as Bob's lot and we do the same things. We also have an Official Secrets Act, which they don't, and we expect you to sign it."

At which Clive nodded in my direction, causing Barley to take proper if belated notice of my existence. I always try to sit a little apart on these occasions and I was doing so that night. Some residual fantasy, I suppose, about being an Officer of the Court. Barley looked at me and I was momentarily disconcerted by the animal straightness of his stare. It somehow did not fit our untidy portrait of him. And Barley, after running his eye over me and seeing I know not what, undertook a more detailed examination of the room.

It was plush and perhaps he thought Clive owned it. It would certainly have been Clive's taste, for Clive was only middle class in the sense that he was unaware there was a better taste. It had carved thrones and chintz sofas and electric candles on the walls. The team's table, which could have sat an entire Armistice ceremony, stood in a raised alcove lined with sprawling rubber-plants in Ali Baba jars.

"Why didn't you go to Moscow?" Clive asked without waiting any longer for Barley to settle. "You were expected. You rented a stand, booked your flight and your hotel. But you didn't show up and you haven't paid. You came to Lisbon with a woman instead. Why?"

"Would you rather I came here with a man?" Barley asked. "What's it got to do with you and the CIA whether I came here with a woman or a Muscovy duck?"

He pulled back a chair and sat down, more in protest than obedience.

Clive nodded to me and I did my routine number. I rose, I walked round the preposterous table and set the Official Secrets Act form in front of him. I drew an important pen from my waistcoat pocket and offered it to him with funereal gravity. But his eyes were fixed on a spot outside the room, which was a thing that tonight and in the months that followed I noticed in him often, his way of looking beyond the present company into some troubled private territory of his own; of bursting into noisy talk as a means of exorcising ghosts that no one else had seen; of snapping his fingers without cause, as if to say, "That's settled then," where, so far as anybody else knew, nothing had been proposed in the first place.

"Are you going to sign that thing?" said Clive.

"What do you do if I don't?" Barley asked.

"Nothing. Because I'm telling you now, formally and in front of witnesses, that this meeting and everything that passes between us is secret. Harry's a lawyer."

"I'm afraid that's true," I said.

Barley pushed the unsigned form away from him across the table. "And I'm telling you that if I feel the urge I'll paint it on the rooftops," he said with equal calm.

I resumed my place, taking my important pen with me.

"You seem to have made a pretty good mess of London too, before you left,"

Clive remarked as he returned the form to his folder. "Debts everywhere. No one knowing where you are. Trails of weeping mistresses. Are you trying to destroy yourself or what?"

"I inherited a romantic list," Barley said.

"What on earth does that mean?" said Clive, unabashed by his own ignorance. "Are we using a smart word for dirty books?"

"My grandfather made a corner in novels for the housemaid. In those days people had housemaids. My father called them 'Novels for the Masses' and continued the tradition."

Bob alone felt moved to offer solace. "God damn it, Barley," he cried, "what's so wrong with romantic literature? Better than some of the horse manure they put out. My wife reads the stuff in bucketfuls. Never did *her* any harm."

"If you don't like the books you publish, why don't you change them?" Clive asked, who never read anything except Service files and the right-wing press.

"I have a Board," Barley replied wearily, as if to a tiresome child. "I have Trustees. I have family shareholders. I have aunts. They like the old safe lines. How-to's. Romances. Tie-ins. Birds of the British Empire." A glance at Bob. "Inside the CIA."

"Why didn't you go to the Moscow audio fair?" Clive repeated.

"The aunts cancelled the match."

"Will you explain that?"

"I thought I'd take the firm into audio cassettes. The family found out and thought I wouldn't. End of story."

"So you ran away," said Clive. "Is that what you normally do when somebody thwarts you? Perhaps you'd better tell us what this letter's about," he suggested and, without looking at Barley, slid it along the table to Ned.

Not the original. That was in Langley, being tested for everything from fingerprints to Legionnaires' disease by the unchallengeable forces of technology. A facsimile, prepared to Ned's meticulous instruction, down to the sealed brown envelope marked "Personal for Mr. Bartholomew Scott Blair, urgent," in Katya's hand, then slit with a paperknife to show it had been opened along the way. Clive handed it to Ned. Ned handed it to Barley. Walter scrabbled at his scalp with his paw and Bob looked on magnanimously like the nice guy who had donated the money. Barley shot a look in my direction, as if he had appointed himself my client. What do I do with this? he was asking with his glance. Do I read it or do I chuck it back at them? I remained, I hope, impassive. I didn't have clients any more. I had the Service.

"Read it slowly," Ned warned.

"Take all the time in the world, Barley," said Bob.

How often had we all of us not read the same letter during the last week? I wondered, watching Barley examine the envelope front and back, hold it away from him, hold it close, his round spectacles raised like goggles to his forehead. How many opinions had they not listened to and discarded? It was written in a train, six experts in Langley had pronounced. In bed, said three more in London. In the back of a car. In haste, in jest, in love, in terror. By a woman, by a man, they had said. The writer is left-handed, right-handed. Is someone whose script of origin is Cyrillic, is Roman, is both, is neither.

As a final twist of the comedy, they had even consulted old Palfrey. "Under our own copyright law the recipient owns the physical letter but the writer owns the copyright," I had told them. "I don't imagine anyone will take you through the Soviet courts." I couldn't tell whether they were worried or relieved by my opinion.

"Do you recognise the handwriting or not?" Clive asked Barley.

Poking his long fingers into the envelope, Barley finally fished out the letter—but disdainfully, as if still half expecting it to be a bill. Then paused. And removed his quaint round spectacles and laid them on the table. Then turned his chair and himself away from everyone. And as he began to read, his face buckled into a frown. He finished the first page then glanced at the end of the letter for the signature. He turned to the second page and read the rest of the letter clean through. Then he read the whole of it over again in one run from "My beloved Barley" to "Your loving K." After which he clutched the letter jealously into his lap with both hands and craned his trunk over it so that by design or accident his face was hidden from everyone and his forelock hung down like a hook and his private prayers stayed private to himself.

"She's potty," he pronounced into the blackness below him. "Certifiably, totally barmy. She wasn't even there."

Nobody asked, who's *she?* or where's *there?* Even Clive knew the value of a good silence.

"K short for Katya, short for Yekaterina, I take it," piped Walter after a further wait. "The patronymic is Borisovna." He was wearing a crooked bow tie, yellow, with a brown-and-orange motif.

"Don't know a K, don't know a Katya, don't know a Yekaterina," Barley said. "Borisovna ditto. Never screwed one, never flirted with one, never proposed to one, never even married one. Never *met* one, far as I remember. Yes, I did."

They waited, I waited; and we would have waited all night and there would not have been the creak of a chair or the clearing of a throat while Barley ransacked his memory for a Katya.

"Old cow in Aurora," Barley resumed. "Tried to flog me some art prints of Russian painters. I didn't bite. Aunts would have blown their corks."

"Aurora?" Clive asked, not knowing whether it was a city or a State agency.

"Publishers."

"Do you remember her other name?"

Barley shook his head, his face still out of sight. "Beard," he said. "Katya of the beard. Ninety in the shade."

Bob's rich voice had a stereophonic quality, and a knack of changing things simply by its reach. "Want to read it aloud, Barley?" he called with the hominess of an old scouting buddy. "Maybe reading it aloud will freshen up your memory. Want to try, Barley?"

Barley, Barley, everyone his friend except Clive, who never once, to my memory, called him anything but Blair.

"Yes, do that, will you. Read it aloud," said Clive, making an order of it, and Barley to my surprise seemed to think it a good idea. Sitting himself up with one jointless movement of his back, he arranged his torso in such a way that both the letter and his face were in the light. Frowning as before, he started reading aloud in a tone of studied mystification.

"*My beloved Barley.*" He tilted the letter and began again. "*My beloved Barley, Do you remember a promise you made to me one night in Peredelkino as we lay on the verandah of our friends' dacha and recited to each other the poetry of a great Russian mystic who loved England? You swore to me that you would always prefer humanity to nations and that when the day came you would act like a decent human being.*"

He had stopped again.

"Is none of that true?" said Clive.

"I told you. I never *met* the hag!"

There was a force in Barley's denial that was not there before. He was shoving back something that was threatening him.

"*So now I am asking you to redeem your promise, though not in the way we might have imagined that night when we agreed to become lovers.* Total balls," he muttered. "Silly cow's got it all mixed up. *I ask you to show this book to English people who think as we do. Publish it for me, using the arguments you expressed with so much fire. Show it to your scientists and artists and intelligentsia and tell them it is the first stone of a great avalanche and they must throw the next stone for themselves. Tell them that with the new openness we can move together to destroy the destruction and castrate the monster we have created. Ask them which is more dangerous to mankind: to conform like a slave or resist like a man? Act like a decent human being, Barley. I love Herzen's England and you. Your loving K.* Who the hell is she? She's off her tree. They both are."

Leaving the letter on the table, Barley wandered off into the dark end of the room, softly cursing, hammering his right fist downward on to the air. "Hell's the woman up to?" he protested. "She's taken two completely different stories and twisted them together. Anyway, where's the book?" He had remembered us and was facing us again.

"The book is safe," said Clive, with a sideways glance at me.

"Where is it, please? It's mine."

"We rather thought it was her friend's," said Clive.

"I've been charged with it. You saw what he wrote. I'm his publisher. It's mine. You've no right to it."

He had landed with both feet in the very ground we wished him not to enter. But Clive was quick to distract him.

"*He?*" Clive repeated. "You mean Katya's a man? Why do you say *he?* You really are confusing us, you know. You're a confusing person, I suppose."

I had been expecting the outburst sooner. I had sensed already that Barley's submissiveness was a truce and not a victory, and that each time Clive reined him in he brought him nearer to revolt. So that when Barley sauntered up to the table, leaned across it and slackly raised his hands, palms forward, from his sides, in what might well have been a docile gesture of helplessness, I did not necessarily expect him to offer Clive a sweetly reasoned answer to his question. But not even I had reckoned with the scale of the detonation.

"You have no damned right!" Barley bellowed straight into Clive's face, smashing his palms on to the table so hard that my papers bounced up and down in front of me. Brock came rushing from the hall. Ned had to order him back. "That's *my* manuscript. Sent to me by *my* author. For *my* consideration in *my* good time. You have no right to steal it, read it or keep it. So give me the book and go home to your squalid island." He flung out an arm at Bob. "And take your Boston Brahmin with you."

"*Our* island," Clive reminded him. "The book, as you call it, is not a book at all and neither you nor we have any right to it," he continued frigidly and untruthfully. "I'm not interested in your precious publishing ethics. Nobody here is. All we know is, the manuscript in question contains military secrets about the Soviet Union that, assuming they are true, are vital to the defence of the West. To which hemisphere you also belong—I take it, thankfully. What would you do in our place? Ignore it? Throw it into the sea? Or try to find out how it came to be addressed to a derelict British publisher?"

"He wants it published! By me! Not hidden in your vaults!"

"Quite," said Clive with another glance at me.

"The manuscript has been officially impounded and classified as top secret," I said. "It's subject to the same restrictions as this meeting. But even more so." My old law tutor would have turned in his grave—not, I am afraid, for the first time. But it's always wonderful what a lawyer can achieve when nobody knows the law.

One minute and fourteen seconds was how long the silence lasted on the tape. Ned timed it with his stopwatch when he got back to the Russia House. He had been waiting for it, even relishing it, but he still began to fear that he had hit one of those maddening faults that always seem to happen with recorders at the crucial moment. But when he listened harder he caught the grumble of a distant car and a scrap of girl's laughter carrying to the window, because Barley by then had thrown the curtains open and was staring down into the square. For one minute and fourteen seconds, then, we watched Barley's strangely articulate back silhouetted against the Lisbon night. Then comes a most frightful crash like the shattering of several window panes at once, followed by an oil gush, and you would suppose that Barley had staged his long-delayed breakout, taking the ornamental Portuguese wall plates and curly flower vases with him. But the truth is, the whole rumpus is only the sound of Barley discovering the drinks table and dumping three cubes of ice into a crystal tumbler and pouring a decent measure of Scotch over them, all within a couple of inches' range of a microphone that Brock with his characteristic over-production had concealed in one of the richly carved compartments.

He had made a base camp at his own end of the room on a stiff school chair as far away from us as he could get. He perched on it sideways to us, stooped over his whisky glass, which he held in both hands, peering into it like a great thinker or at least a lonely one. He spoke not to us but to himself, emphatically and scathingly, not stirring except to take a sip from his glass or buck his head in affirmation of some private and usually abstracted point of narrative. He spoke in the mixture of pedantry and disbelief that people use to reconstruct a disastrous episode, such as a death or a traffic accident. So I was *here* and you were *there* and the other chap came from over *there*.

"It was last Moscow book fair. The Sunday. Not the Sunday before, the Sunday after," he said.

"September," Ned suggested, at which Barley rolled his head around and muttered "Thanks," as if genuinely grateful to be prodded. Then he wrinkled his nose and fussed his spectacles and began again.

"We were knackered," he said. "Most of the exhibitors had got out on the Friday. It was only a bunch of us who hung around. Those who had contracts to tidy up, or no particular reason to get back in a hurry."

He was a compelling man and he had centre stage. It was difficult not to attach to him a little, stuck out there on his own. It was difficult not to think, There but for the grace of God go I. And the more so since none of us knew where he was going.

"We got drunk on Saturday night and on the Sunday we all drove out to Peredelkino in Jumbo's car." Once again he seemed to have to remind himself that he had an audience. "Peredelkino is the Soviet writers' village," he said as if none of us had heard of it. "They get dachas there for as long as they behave themselves. Writers' Union runs it on a members-only basis—who gets a dacha, who writes best in prison, who doesn't write at all."

"Who's Jumbo?" said Ned—a rare interjection.

"Jumbo Oliphant. Peter Oliphant. Chairman of Lupus Books. Closet Scottish Fascist. Black-belt Freemason. Thinks he's got a special wavelength to the Sovs. Gold card." Remembering Bob, he tilted his head at him. "Not American Express, I'm afraid. A Moscow book fair gold card, dished out by the Russian organisers, saying what a big boy he is. Free car, free translator, free hotel, free caviar. Jumbo was born with a gold card in his mouth."

Bob grinned too broadly in order to show the joke was taken in good part. Yet he was a large-hearted man and Barley had spotted this. Barley, it occurred to me, was one of those people from whom good natures cannot hide, just as he could not disguise his own accessibility.

"So off we all went," Barley resumed, returning to his reverie. "Oliphant from Lupus, Emery from the Bodley Head. And some girl from Penguin, can't remember her name. Yes, I can. Magda. How the hell could I forget a Magda? And Blair from A. & B."

Riding like nabobs in Jumbo's stupid limo, said Barley, tossing out short sentences like old clothes from his memory box. Ordinary car not good enough for our Jumbo, had to be a damn great Chaika with curtains in the bedroom, no brakes and a gorilla with bad breath for a driver. The plan was to take a look at Pasternak's dacha, which rumour had it was about to be declared a museum, though another rumour insisted that the bastards were about to pull it down. Maybe his grave as well. Jumbo Oliphant didn't know who Pasternak was at first but Magda murmured "Zhivago" and Jumbo had seen the film, said Barley. There was no earthly hurry, all they wanted was a bit of a walk and a peck of country air. But Jumbo's driver used the special lane reserved for official roadhogs in Chaikas, so they did the journey in about ten seconds flat instead of an hour, parked in a puddle and shlepped up to the cemetery still trembling with gratitude from the drive.

"Cemetery on a hillside among a lot of trees. Driver stays in the car. Raining. Not much, but he's worried about his awful suit." He paused, in contemplation of the driver. "Mad ape," he muttered.

But I had the feeling Barley was railing at himself and not the driver. I seemed to hear a whole self-accusing chorus in Barley, and I wondered whether the others were hearing it as well. He had people inside himself who really drove him mad.

Point was, Barley explained, that as luck would have it they had hit a day when the liberated masses were out in force. In the past, he said, whenever he'd been there, the place had been deserted. Just the fenced-in tombs and the creepy trees. But on that September Sunday with the unfamiliar smells of freedom in the air, there were about two hundred fans crammed round the grave and more by the time they left, all shapes and sizes. Grave was knee-deep in flowers, Barley said. Offerings pouring in all the time. People passing bouquets over the heads to get them on the heap.

Then the readings began. Little chap read poetry. Big girl read prose. Then a filthy little aeroplane flew so low overhead you couldn't hear a thing. Then it flew back the other way. Then back the same way.

"Wang, wang!" Barley yelled, his long wrist whipping back and forth through the air. "Wee-ah, wee-ah," he whined through his nose in disgust.

But the plane couldn't damp the enthusiasm of the crowd any more than the rain could. Someone began singing, the punters took up the refrain and it became a knees-up. Finally the plane pushed off, presumably because it was low on fuel. But that wasn't what you felt, said Barley. Not a bit. You felt the singing had shot the little swine out of the sky.

The singing grew stronger and deeper and more mystical. Barley knew three words of Russian and the others none. Didn't stop them joining in. Didn't stop the girl Magda from crying her eyes out. Or Jumbo Oliphant from swearing to God, through lumps in his throat, as they walked away down the hill that he was going to publish every word Pasternak had written, not just the film but the other stuff, so help me, and subsidise it out of his very own personal pocket as soon as he got back to his damask castle in the docklands.

"Jumbo has these hot flushes of enthusiasm," Barley explained with a disarming grin, returning to his audience, but principally to Ned. "Sometimes they don't die down for minutes on end." Then he paused and frowned again and pulled off his strange round spectacles that seemed to be more an infliction than a help, and peered at everybody in turn as if to remind himself of his situation.

They were still walking down the hill, he said, and still having a good cry when this same little Russian chap came darting up to them holding his cigarette to one side of his face like a candle, asking in English whether they were Americans.

Once again Clive was ahead of all of us. His head slowly lifted. There was a knife-edge to his managerial drawl. "Same? What same little Russian chap? We haven't had one."

Unpleasantly reminded of Clive's presence, Barley screwed up his face in a renewal of distaste. "He was the reader, for goodness' sake," he said. "Chap who'd read Pasternak's poetry at the graveside. He asked if we were American. I said no, thank God, British."

And I noticed, as I supposed we all did, that it was Barley himself, not Oliphant or Emery or the girl Magda, who had become the appointed spokesman of their group.

Barley had fallen into direct dialogue. He had the mynah bird's ear. He had a

Russian accent for the little chap and a Scottish woof-woof voice for Oliphant. The mimicry slipped out of him as if he were unaware of it.

"You are writers?" the little chap asked, in Barley's voice for him.

"No, alas. Just publishers," said Barley, in his own.

"English publishers?"

"Here for the Moscow book fair. I run a corner shop called Abercrombie & Blair and this is the Chairman Himself of Lupus Books. Very rich bloke. Be a knight one day. Gold card and bar. Right, Jumbo?"

Oliphant protested that Barley was saying *far* too much. But the little chap wanted more.

"May I ask then what were you doing at Pasternak's grave?" said the little chap.

"Chance visit," Oliphant said, barging in again. "Total chance. We saw a crowd, we came up to see what was going on. Pure chance. Let's go."

But Barley had no intention of going. He was annoyed by Oliphant's manners, he said, and he wasn't going to stand by while a fat Scottish millionaire gave the brush-off to an undernourished Russian stranger.

"We're doing what everyone else here's doing," Barley replied. "We're paying our respects to a great writer. We liked your reading too. Very moving. Great stuff. Ace."

"You respect Boris Pasternak?" the little chap asked.

Oliphant again, the great civil rights activist, rendered by a gruff voice and a twisted jaw: "We have no position on the matter of Boris Pasternak or any other Soviet writer," he said. "We're here as guests. Solely as guests. We have no opinions on internal Soviet affairs."

"We think he's marvellous," Barley said. "World class. A star."

"But why?" asked the little chap, provoking the conflict.

Barley needed no urging. Never mind he wasn't totally convinced that Pasternak was the genius he was cracked up to be, he said. Never mind that, as a matter of fact, he thought Pasternak quite seriously overpraised. That was publisher's opinion, whereas this was war.

"We respect his talent and his art," Barley replied. "We respect his humanity. We respect his family and his culture. And tenthly or whatever it is, we respect his capacity to reach the hearts of the Russian people despite the fact that he had the daylights hounded out of him by a bunch of bureau-rats who are very probably the same little beasts who sent us that aeroplane."

"Can you quote him?" the little chap asked.

Barley had that kind of memory, he explained to us awkwardly. "I gave him the first couplet of 'Nobel Prize.' I thought it was appropriate after that foul aeroplane."

"Give it to us now, please, will you?" said Clive, as if everything had to be checked.

Barley mumbled, and it crossed my mind that he might actually be a very shy man.

> "Like a beast in the pen, I'm cut off
> From my friends, freedom, the sun,

But the hunters are gaining ground.
I've nowhere else to run.''

The little chap was frowning at the lighted end of his cigarette while he listened to this, said Barley, and for a moment he really did wonder whether they had walked into a provocation as Oliphant feared.

"If you respect Pasternak so much, why don't you come and meet some friends of mine?" the little chap suggested. "We are writers here. We have a dacha. We would be honoured to talk to distinguished British publishers."

Oliphant had only to hear the first half of this speech to develop a severe case of the bends, said Barley. Jumbo knew all about accepting invitations from strange Russians. He was an expert on it. He knew how they ensnared you, drugged you, compromised you with disgraceful photographs and obliged you to resign your directorships and give up your chances of a knighthood. He was also in the middle of an ambitious joint publishing deal through VAAP, and the last thing he needed was to be found in the company of undesirables. Oliphant boomed all this to Barley in a theatrical whisper that assumed the little stranger was deaf.

"Anyway," Oliphant ended triumphantly, "it's raining. What are we going to do about the car?"

Oliphant looked at his watch. The girl Magda looked at the ground. The bloke Emery looked at the girl Magda and thought there could be worse things to do on a Sunday afternoon in Moscow. But Barley, as he told it, took another look at the stranger and decided to like what he saw. He had no designs on the girl or on a knighthood. He had already decided he would rather be photographed in the raw with any number of Russian tarts than fully dressed on the arm of Jumbo Oliphant. So he waved them all off in Jumbo's limo and stayed behind with the stranger.

"Nezhdanov," Barley declared abruptly to the silent room, interrupting his own flow. "I've remembered the chap's name. Nezhdanov. Playwright. Ran one of these studio theatres, couldn't put on his own plays."

Walter spoke, his soaring voice shattering the momentary lull. "My dear boy, Vitaly Nezhdanov is a latterday *hero*. He has *three* one-acters opening in Moscow just five weeks from now, and everyone has the most exotic hopes for them. Not that he's a blind bit of good, but we're not allowed to say that because he's a dissident. Or was."

For the first time since I had set eyes on him, Barley's face took on a sublimely happy aspect, and at once I had the feeling that this was the real man, whom the clouds till now had hidden. "Oh, now that's really great," he said with the simple pleasure of someone able to enjoy another man's success. "Fantastic. That's just what Vitaly needed. Thanks for telling me," he said, looking a fraction of his age.

Then once again his face darkened over and he began drinking his whisky in little nips. "Well, there we all were," he murmured vaguely. "More the merrier. Meet my cousin. Have a sausage roll." But his eyes, I noticed, like his words, had acquired a remote quality, as if he were already looking forward to an ordeal.

I glanced along the table. Bob smiling. Bob would smile on his deathbed, but with an old scout's sincerity. Clive in profile, his face keen as an axe and about as profound. Walter never at rest. Walter with his clever head thrown back, twisting a hank of hair around his spongy forefinger while he smirked at the ornate ceiling, writhed and sweated. And Ned, the leader—capable, resourceful Ned—Ned the linguist and the warrior, the doer and the planner—sitting as he had sat from the beginning, to attention, waiting for the order to advance. Some people, I reflected, watching him, are cursed with too much loyalty, for a day could come when there was nothing left for them to serve.

Big, rambling house, Barley was reciting in the telegraphese he had resorted to. Edwardian clapboard, fretted verandahs, overgrown garden, birch forest. Rotting benches, charcoal fire, smell of a cricket ground on a rainy day, ivy. About thirty people, mostly men, sitting and standing around in the garden, cooking, drinking, ignoring the bad weather just like the English. Lousy old cars parked along the roadside, just like English cars used to be before Thatcher's pigs in clover took over the ship. Good faces, fluent voices, arty *nomenklatura*. Enter Nezhdanov leading Barley. No heads turn.

"Hostess was a poet," Barley said. "Tamara something. Dikey lady, white hair, jolly. Husband editor of one of the science magazines. Nezhdanov was his brother-in-law. Everyone was someone's brother-in-law. The lit. scene has clout over there. If you've got a voice and they let you use it, you've got a public."

In his arbitrary memory, Barley now split the occasion into three parts. Lunch, which began around two-thirty when the rain stopped. Night, which followed immediately upon lunch. And what he called "the last bit," which was when whatever happened had happened, and which so far as any of us could ever fathom occurred in the blurred hours between about two and four when Barley, to use his own words, was drifting painlessly between nirvana and a near-terminal hangover.

Until lunch came along, Barley had pottered from group to group, he said—first with Nezhdanov, then alone, having a shmooze with whoever felt like talking to him.

"Shmooze?" Clive repeated suspiciously, as if he had learned of a new vice.

Bob hastened to interpret. "A chat, Clive," he explained in his friendly way. "A chat and a drink. Nothing sinister."

But when lunch was called, said Barley, they sat themselves at a trestle table with Barley up one end and Nezhdanov the other and bottles of Georgian white between them, and everyone talking their best English about whether truth was truth if it was not convenient to the great proletarian so-called Revolution, and whether we should revert to the spiritual values of our ancestors and whether the *perestroika* was having any positive effect on the lives of the common people, and how if you really wanted to know what was wrong with the Soviet Union the best way to find out was to try sending a refrigerator from Novosibirsk to Leningrad.

To my secret irritation, Clive again cut in. Like a man bored by irrelevances, he wanted names. Barley slapped his forehead with his palm, his hostility to Clive forgotten. Names, Clive, God. One chap a professor at Moscow State but I never caught his name, you see. Another chap in chemical procurement—that was Nezhdanov's half-brother, they called him the Apothecary. Somebody in the Soviet Academy of Sciences, Gregor, but I didn't get round to finding out what his name was, let alone his angle.

"Any women at the table?" Ned asked.

"Two, but no Katya," said Barley, and Ned like myself was visibly impressed by the pace of his perception.

"But there was *someone* else, wasn't there?" Ned suggested.

Barley leaned himself slowly backwards to drink. Then forward again as he planted the glass between his knees and stooped over it, nose down, inhaling its wisdom.

"Sure, sure, sure, there was someone else," he agreed. "There always is, isn't there?" he added enigmatically. "Not Katya. Someone else."

His voice had changed. From what to what I couldn't fathom. A shorter ring. A hint of regret or remorse. I waited as we all did. I think we all sensed even then that something extraordinary was appearing on the horizon.

"Thin bearded chap," Barley went on, staring into the gloom as if he were making him out at last. "Tall. Dark suit, black tie. Hollow face. Must be why he grew a beard. Sleeves too short. Black hair. Drunk."

"Did he have a name?" asked Ned.

Barley was still staring at the half-dark, describing what none of us could see.

"Goethe," he said at last. "Like the poet. They called him Goethe. Meet our distinguished writer Goethe. Could have been fifty, could have been eighteen. Thin as a boy. These dabs of colour on his cheeks, very high up. Beard."

Which, as Ned remarked later, when he was playing over the tape to the team, was operationally speaking the moment when the Bluebird spread his wings. It is not marked by any awesome silence or the intake of breath around the table. Instead, Barley chose this moment to be assailed by a sneezing fit, his first of many in our experience of him. It began as a series of single rounds, then accelerated to a grand salvo. Then it slowly petered out again while he beat his face with his handkerchief and cursed between convulsions.

"Bloody kennel cough," he explained apologetically.

"I was brilliant," Barley resumed. "Couldn't put a hoof wrong."

He had refilled his glass, this time with water. He was sipping from it in slow rhythmic movements like one of those plastic drinking birds that used to bob up and down between the miniatures on every gloomy English bar in the days before television sets replaced them.

"Mr. Wonderful, that was me. Star of stage and screen. Western, courteous and specious. That's why I go there, isn't it? Sovs are the only people daft enough to listen to my bullshit." His forelock dipped towards his glass again. "It's the way it happens there. You go for a walk in the countryside and end up arguing with a bunch of drunk poets about freedom versus responsibility. You take a leak in some filthy public loo, somebody leans over from the next stall and asks you whether there's life after death. Because you're a Westerner. So you know. And you tell them. And they remember. Nothing goes away."

He seemed to be in danger of ceasing to talk at all.

"Why don't you just tell us what happened and leave the reproaches to us?" Clive suggested, somehow implying that the reproaches were above Barley's station.

"I shone. That's what happened. A glib mind had a field day. Forget it."

But forgetting was the last thing anybody intended, as Bob's cheerful smile showed. "Barley, I think you are being too hard on yourself. Nobody should blame themselves for being entertaining, for Pete's sake. All you did was sing for your supper, by the sounds of it."

"What did you talk about?" said Clive, undeflected by Bob's goodheartedness.

Barley shrugged. "How to rebuild the Russian Empire between lunch and teatime. Peace, progress and *glasnost* by the bottleful. Instant disarmament without the option."

"Are these subjects you frequently enlarge upon?"

"When I'm in Russia, yes they are," Barley retorted, provoked again by Clive's tone, but never for long.

"May we know what you said?"

But Barley was not telling his story to Clive. He was telling it to himself and to the room and whoever was in it, to his fellow passengers, point for point, an inventory of his folly. "Disarmament was not a military matter and not a political one, I said. It was a matter of human will. We had to decide whether we wanted peace or war and prepare for it. Because what we prepared for was going to be what we got." He broke off. "It was top-of-my-head stuff," he explained, again selecting Ned. "Warmed-up arguments I'd read around the place."

As if he felt more explanation was required, he started again. "It so happened I was an expert that week. I'd thought the firm might commission a quick book. Some tout at the book fair wanted me to take UK rights in a book on *glasnost* and the crisis of peace. Essays by past and present hawks, reappraisals of strategy. Could real peace break out after all? They'd signed up some of the old American warhorses from the sixties and shown how a lot of them had turned full circle since they left office."

He was apologising and I wondered why. What was he preparing us for? Why did he feel he should lessen the shock in advance? Bob, who was no kind of fool, for all his candour, must have been asking himself the same question.

"Sounds a fine enough idea to me, Barley. *I* can see money in that. Might even take a piece of it myself," he added with a locker-room chuckle.

"So you had the patter," Clive said in his barbed undertone. "And you regurgitated it. Is that what you're telling us? I'm sure it isn't easy to reconstruct one's alcoholic flights of fancy but we'd be grateful if you'd do your best."

What had Clive studied, I wondered, if he ever had? Where? Who bore him, sired him? Where did the Service find these dead suburban souls with all their values, or lack of them, perfectly in place?

Yet Barley remained compliant in the face of this renewed onslaught. "I said I believed in Gorbachev," he said equably, giving himself a sip of water. "They mightn't, I did. I said the West's job was to find the other half of him, and the East's was to recognise the importance of the half they had. I said that if the Americans had ever bothered as much about disarmament as they had about putting some fool on the moon or pink stripes into toothpaste, we'd have had disarmament long ago. I said the West's great sin was to believe we could bankrupt the Soviet system by raising the bidding on the arms race, because that way we were gambling with the fate of mankind. I said that by shaking our sabres the West had given the Soviet leaders the excuse to keep their gates locked and run a garrison state."

Walter let out a whinnying laugh and cupped his gappy teeth with his hairless hand. "Oh my Lord! So *we're* to blame for Russia's ills. Oh, I think that's *marvellously* rich! You don't think that by any chance they did it to themselves, for instance? Locked themselves up inside their own paranoia? No, he doesn't. I can see."

Undeterred, Barley resumed his confession. "Somebody asked me, didn't I think nuclear weapons had kept the peace for forty years? I said that was Jesuitical bollocks. Might as well say gunpowder had kept the peace between Waterloo and Sarajevo. Anyway, I said, what's peace? The bomb didn't stop Korea and it didn't stop Vietnam. It didn't stop anyone from pinching Czecho or blockading Berlin or building the Berlin Wall or going into Afghanistan. If that's peace, let's try it without the bomb. I said what was needed was not experiments in space but experiments in human nature. The superpowers should police the world together. I was flying."

"And did you *believe* any of this nonsense?" Clive asked.

Barley didn't seem to know. He seemed suddenly to regard himself as facile by definition, and became shamefaced. "Then we talked about jazz," he said. "Bix Beiderbecke, Louis Armstrong, Lester Young. I played some."

"You mean somebody had a *saxophone?*" Bob cried in spontaneous amusement. "What else did they have? Bass drums? A ten-piece band? Barley, I'm not believing this!"

I thought at first that Barley was walking out. He unwound himself and clambered to his feet. He peered round for the door, then headed apologetically towards it, so that Ned rose in alarm, afraid that Brock would get to him first. But Barley had halted halfway across the room where a low carved table stood. Stooping before it, he began lightly slapping his fingertips on the edge while he sang "pah-pah-paah, pah-pah-pah-pah," through his nose, to the simulated accompaniment of cymbals, wire brushes and drums.

Bob was already applauding, Walter too. So was I, and Ned was laughing. Clive alone found nothing to entertain him. Barley took a sobering pull from his glass and sat down again.

"Then they asked me what could be done," he said as if he'd never left his chair.

"Who did?" said Clive, with that maddening note of disbelief he had.

"One of the people at the table. What does it matter?"

"Let's assume everything matters," said Clive.

Barley was doing his Russian voice again, clogged and pressing. " 'All right, Barley. Given is all as you say. Who will conduct these experiments in human nature?' You will, I said. They were very surprised. Why us? I said because, when it came to radical change, the Sovs had it easier than the West. They had a small leadership and an intelligentsia with great traditional influence. In a Western democracy it was much harder to make yourself heard above the crowd. They were pleased by the paradox. So was I."

Not even this frontal assault upon the great democratic values could ruffle Bob's genial forbearance. "Well, Barley, that's a broad-brush judgment but I guess there's some truth in it at that."

"But did you suggest what should be *done?*" Clive insisted.

"I said there was only Utopia left. I said that what had looked like a pipe dream twenty years ago was today our only hope, whether we're talking disarmament or ecology or plain human survival. Gorbachev understood that, the West didn't want to. I said that Western intellectuals must find their voice. I said the West should be setting the example, not following it. It was everyone's duty to start the avalanche."

"So unilateral disarmament," said Clive, clamping his hands together in a knot.

"Aldermaston, here we come. Well, well. Yes." Except that he didn't say "yes" so much as "ears," which was how he said yes when he meant no.

But Bob was impressed. "And all this eloquence just from reading around the subject a little?" he said. "Barley, I think that's extraordinary. Why, if I could absorb that way, I'd be a proud man."

Perhaps *too* extraordinary, he was also suggesting, but the implications evidently passed Barley by.

"And while you were saving us from our worst instincts, what was the man called Goethe doing?" asked Clive.

"Nothing. The others joined in. Goethe didn't."

"But he listened? Wide-eyed, I should imagine."

"We were redesigning the world by then. Yalta all over again. Everyone was talking at once. Except Goethe. He didn't eat, he didn't talk. I kept tossing ideas at him, simply because he wasn't joining in. All he did was grow paler and drink more. I gave him up."

And Goethe never spoke, Barley continued in the same tone of mystified self-recrimination. All through the afternoon not a dickybird, Barley said. Goethe would listen, he'd glare into some invisible crystal ball. He'd laugh, though not by any means when there was anything much to laugh about. Or he'd get up and cut a straightish line to the drinks table to fetch himself another vodka when everyone else was drinking wine, and come back with a tumbler of the stuff, which he knocked off in a couple of swigs whenever anyone proposed a fitting toast. But Goethe, he proposed no toasts at all, said Barley. He was one of those people who exert a moral influence by their silence, he said, so that you end up wondering whether they're dying of a secret illness or riding on some great accomplishment.

When Nezhdanov led the group indoors to listen to Count Basie on the stereo, Goethe tagged obediently along. It wasn't till late into the night, when Barley had given up all thought of him, that he finally heard Goethe speak.

Once again Ned permitted himself a rare question. "How did the others behave towards him?"

"They respected him. He was their mascot. 'Let's see what Goethe thinks.' He'd raise his glass and drink to them and we'd all laugh except Goethe."

"The women too?"

"Everyone. They deferred to him. Practically made way for him. The great Goethe, here he comes."

"And no one told you where he lived or worked?"

"They said he was on holiday from somewhere where drinking wasn't approved of. So it was a drinking holiday. They kept drinking to his drinking holiday. He was someone's brother. Tamara's, I don't know. Maybe cousin. I didn't catch it."

"Do you think they were protecting him?" said Clive.

Barley's pauses are like nobody else's, I thought. He has his own tenuous hold on present things. His mind leaves the room and you wait on tenterhooks to see whether it will come back.

"Yes," said Barley suddenly, sounding surprised by his own answer. "Yes, yes, they were protecting him. That's right. They were his supporters' club, of course they were."

"Protecting him from what?"

Another pause.

"Maybe from having to explain himself. I didn't think that at the time. But I think it now. Yes I do."

"And why should he not explain himself? Can you suggest a reason without inventing one?" asked Clive, determined apparently to hold Barley to the angry edge.

But Barley didn't rise. "I don't invent," he said, and I think we all knew that was true. He was gone again. "He was high-powered. You felt it in him," he said, returning.

"What does that mean?"

"The eloquent silence. All you hear at a hundred miles an hour is the ticking of the brain."

"But no one told you, 'He's a genius,' or whatever?"

"No one told me. No one needed to."

Barley glanced at Ned to find him nodding his understanding. A fieldman to his fingertips, if necessarily a grounded one, Ned had a way of popping up ahead of you when you thought he was still trying to catch you up.

Bob had another question. "Anyone take you by the elbow and explain to you just *why* Goethe had a drinking problem, Barley?"

Barley let out an unfettered laugh. His momentary freedoms were a little frightening. "You don't have to have a *reason* to drink in Russia, for Christ's sake! Name me a single Russian worth his salt who could face the problems of his country sober!"

He dropped into silence again, grimacing into the shadows. He wrinkled up his eyes and muttered an imprecation of some kind, I assumed against himself. Then snapped out of it. "Woke with a jolt round midnight." He laughed. " 'Christ. Where am I?' Lying in a deck chair on a verandah with a bloody blanket over me! Thought I was in the States at first. One of those New England screened porches with panels of mosquito gauze and the garden beyond. Couldn't think how I'd got to America so fast after a pleasant lunch in Peredelkino. Then I remembered they'd stopped talking to me and I'd got bored. Nothing personal. They were drunk and they were tired of being drunk in a foreign language. So I'd settled on the verandah with a bottle of Scotch. Somebody had thrown a blanket over me to keep the dew off. The moon must have woken me, I thought. Big full moon. Bloodshot. Then I heard this chap talking to me. Very sombre. Immaculate English. Christ, I thought, new guests at this hour. 'Some things are necessary evils, Mr. Barley. Some things are more evil than necessary,' he says. He's quoting me from lunch. Part of my world-shaking lecture on peace. I don't know who I was quoting. Then I take a closer look around and I make out this nine-foot-tall bearded vulture hovering over me, clutching a bottle of vodka, hair flapping round his face in the breeze. Next thing I know he's crouching beside me with his knees up round his ears, filling up his glass. 'Hullo, Goethe,' I say. 'Why aren't you dead yet? Nice to see you about.' "

Whatever had set Barley free had put him back in prison again, for his face had once more clouded over.

"Then he gives me back another of my lunchtime pearls. 'All victims are equal. None are more equal than others.'

"I laugh. But not too much. I'm embarrassed, I suppose. Queasy. Feel I've been spied on. Chap sits there all through lunch, drunk, doesn't eat, doesn't say a word. All of a sudden ten hours later he's quoting me like a tape recorder. It's not comfortable.

" 'Who are you, Goethe?' I say. 'What do you do for a living when you're not drinking and listening?'

" 'I'm a moral outcast,' he says. 'I trade in defiled theories.'

" 'Always nice to meet a writer,' I say. 'What sort of stuff are you turning out these days?'

" 'Everything,' he says. 'History, comedy, lies, romances.' Then off he goes into some drivel he wrote about a lump of butter melting in the sun because it lacked a consistent point of view. Only thing was, he didn't talk like a writer. Too diffident. He was laughing at himself, and for all I knew he was laughing at me too. Not that he hadn't every right to, but that didn't make it any funnier."

Once more we waited, watching Barley's silhouette. Was the tension in us or in him? He took a sip from his glass. He rolled his head around and muttered something like "not well" or possibly "to hell" which neither his audience nor the microphones ever completely caught. We heard his chair crackle like wet firewood. On the tape it sounds like an armed attack.

"So then he says to me, 'Come on, Mr. Barley. You're a publisher. Aren't you going to ask me where I get my ideas from?' And I thought, That's not what publishers ask actually, old boy, but what the hell? 'Okay, Goethe,' I say. 'Where do you get your ideas from?'

" 'Mr. Barley. My ideas are obtained from—one'—he starts counting."

Barley too had spread his long fingers and was counting on them, using only the lightest Russian intonations. And once again I was struck by the delicacy of his musical memory, which he seemed to achieve less by repeating words than by retrieving them from some cursed echoing chamber where nothing ever faded from his hearing.

" 'My ideas are obtained from—one, the paper tablecloths of Berlin cafés in the nineteen-thirties.' Then he takes a heave of vodka and a great noisy snort of night air both at once. He creaks. Know what I mean? Those chaps with bubbling chests? 'Two,' he says, 'from the publications of my more gifted competitors. Three, from the obscene fantasies of generals and politicians of all nations. Four, from the liberated intellects of press-ganged Nazi scientists. Five, from the great Soviet people, whose every democratic wish is filtered upwards by means of consultation at all levels, then dumped in the Neva. And six, very occasionally from the mind of a distinguished Western intellectual who happens to drop into my life.' That's me, apparently, because he glues his eyes on me to see how I take it. Staring and staring like a precocious child. Transmitting these life-important signals. Then suddenly he changes and becomes suspicious. Russians do that. 'That was quite a performance you gave at lunch,' he says. 'How did you persuade Nezhdanov to invite you?' It's a sneer. Saying I don't believe you.

" 'I didn't persuade him,' I say. 'It was his idea. What are you trying to hang on me?'

" 'There is no ownership of ideas,' he says. 'You put it into his head. You are a clever fellow. Cunning work, I would say. Congratulations.'

"Then instead of sneering at me he's clutching on to my shoulders as if he's drowning. I don't know whether he's ill or he's lost his balance. I've got a nasty feeling he may want to be sick. I try to help him but I don't know how. He's hot as hell and sweating. His sweat's dripping on to me. Hair's all wet. These wild childish eyes. I'll loosen his collar, I think. Then I get his voice, shoved right down my ear, lips and hot breath all at once. I can't hear him at first, he's too near. I back away but he comes with me.

" 'I believe every word you said,' he whispers. 'You spoke into my heart. Promise me you are not a British spy and I'll make you a promise in return.'

"His words exactly," Barley said, as if he were ashamed of them. "He remembered every word I'd said. And I remember every word of his."

It was not the first time that Barley had spoken of memory as if it were an affliction, and perhaps that is why I found myself, as so often, thinking of Hannah.

"Poor Palfrey," she had taunted me in one of her cruel moods, studying her naked body in the mirror as she sipped her vodka and tonic and prepared to go back to her husband. "With a memory like yours, how will you ever forget a girl like me?"

Did Barley have that effect on everyone? I wondered—touch their central nerve unconsciously, send them rushing to their closest thoughts? Perhaps that was what he had done to Goethe too.

The passage that followed was never paraphrased, never condensed, never "reconstrued." For the initiated, either the unedited tape was played or else the transcript was offered in its entirety. For the uninitiated, it never existed. It was the crux of everything that followed and it was called with deliberate obfuscation "the Lisbon Approach." When the alchemists and theologians and end-users on both sides of the Atlantic had their turn, this was the passage they picked out and ran through their magic boxes to justify the preselected arguments that characterised their artful camps.

" 'Not a spy actually, Goethe, old boy. Not now, never have been, never will. May be your line of country, not mine. How about chess. Fond of chess? Let's talk about chess.'

"Doesn't seem to hear. 'And you are not an American? You are nobody's spy, not even ours?'

" 'Goethe, listen,' I say. 'I'm getting a bit jumpy, to be honest. I'm nobody's spy. I'm me. Let's either talk about chess or you try a different address, okay?' I thought that would shut him up, but it didn't. Knew all about chess, he said. In chess, one chap has a strategy, and if the other chap doesn't spot it or if he relaxes his watch, you win. In chess, the theory is the reality. But in life, in certain types of life, you can have a situation where a player has such grotesque fantasies about another one that he ends up by inventing the enemy he needs. Do I agree? Goethe, I agree totally. Then suddenly it's not chess any more and he's explaining himself the way Russians do when they're drunk. Why he's on the earth, for my ears only. Says he was born with two souls, just like Faust, which is why they call him Goethe. Says his mother was a painter but she painted what she saw, so naturally she wasn't allowed to exhibit or buy materials. Because anything we see is a State secret. Also if it's an illusion it's a State secret. Even if it doesn't work and never will, it's a State secret.

And if it's a lie from top to bottom, then it's the hottest State secret of the lot. Says his father did twelve years in the camps and died of a surfeit of intellectual ability. Says the problem with his father was, he was a martyr. Victims are bad enough, saints are worse, he says, but martyrs are the living end. Do I agree?

"I agree. Don't know why I agree but I'm a polite soul and when a chap who is clutching my head tells me his father's done twelve years then died, I'm not about to quarrel with him even when I'm tight.

"I ask him his real name. Says he hasn't got one. His father took it with him. Says that in any decent society they shoot the ignorant, but in Russia it's the other way around, so they shot his father because, unlike his mother, he refused to die of a broken heart. Says he wants to make me this promise. Says he loves the English. The English are the moral leaders of Europe, the secret steadiers, the unifiers of the great European ideal. Says the English understand the relationship between words and action whereas in Russia nobody believes in action any more, so words have become a substitute, all the way up to the top, a substitute for the truth that nobody wants to hear because they can't change it, or they'll lose their jobs if they change it, or maybe they simply don't know *how* to change it. Says the Russians' misfortune is that they long to be European but their destiny is to become American, and that the Americans have poisoned the world with materialistic logic. If my neighbour has a car, I must have two cars. If my neighbour has a gun, I must have two guns. If my neighbour has a bomb, I must have a bigger bomb and more of them, never mind they can't reach their targets. So all I have to do is imagine my neighbour's gun and double it and I have the justification for whatever I want to manufacture. Do I agree?"

It is a miracle that nobody interrupted here, not even Walter. But he didn't, he held his tongue, as they all did. You don't even hear a chair creak before Barley goes on.

"So I agree. Yes, Goethe, I agree with you to the hilt. Anything's better than being asked whether I'm a British spy. Starts talking about the great nineteenth-century poet and mystic Piturin."

"Pecherin," says a high sharp voice. Walter has finally brimmed over.

"That's right. Pecherin," Barley agrees. "Vladimir Pecherin. Pecherin wanted to sacrifice himself for mankind, die on the cross with his mother at his feet. Have I heard of him? I haven't. Pecherin went to Ireland, became a monk, he says. But Goethe can't do that because he can't get a visa and anyway he doesn't like God. Pecherin liked God and didn't like science unless it took account of the human soul. I ask him how old he is. Goethe, not Pecherin. He looks about seven by now, going on a hundred. He says he's nearer to death than life. He says he's fifty but he's just been born."

Walter chimes in, but softly, like someone in church, not his usual squeak at all. "Why did you ask him his *age*? Of all the questions you could have asked? What on earth does it matter at that moment how many teeth he's got?"

"He's unsettling. Not a wrinkle on him till he scowled."

"And he said science. Not physics. Science?"

"Science. Then he starts reciting Pecherin. Translating as he goes. The Russian first, then the English. *How sweet it is to hate one's native land and avidly await its ruin . . . and in its ruin to discern the dawn of universal renaissance.* I may not have got it quite right but that's the gist. Pecherin understood that it was possible to love your country at the same time as hating its system, he says. Pecherin was nuts about England, just as Goethe is. England as the home of justice, truth and liberty. Pecherin showed there was nothing disloyal in betrayal provided you betrayed what you hated and fought for what you loved. Now supposing Pecherin had possessed great secrets about the Russian soul. What would he have done? Obvious. He'd have given them to the English.

"I'm wanting him out of my hair by now. I'm getting panicky. He's coming close again. Face against face. Wheezing and grinding like a steam engine. Heart breaking out of his chest. These big brown saucer eyes. 'What have you been drinking?' I said. 'Cortisone?'

" 'You know what else you said at lunch?' he says.

" 'Nothing,' I say. 'I wasn't there. It was two other blokes and they hit me first.' He's not hearing me again.

" 'You said, "Today one must think like a hero to behave like a merely decent human being." '

" 'That's not original,' I say. 'None of it is. It's stuff I picked up. It's not me. Now just forget everything I said and go back to your own people.' Doesn't listen. Grabs my arm. Hands like a girl's but they grip like iron. 'Promise me that if ever I find the courage to think like a hero, you will act like a merely decent human being.'

" 'Look,' I say. 'Leave this out and let's get something to eat. They've got some soup in there. I can smell it. You like soup? Soup?'

"He's not crying as far as I can tell but his face is absolutely soaked. Like a pain sweat all over this white skin. Hanging on to my wrist as if I were his priest. 'Promise me,' he says.

" 'But what am I supposed to be promising, for God's sake?'

" 'Promise you'll behave like a gentleman.'

" 'I'm not a gentleman. I'm a publisher.'

"Then he laughs. First time. Huge laughter with a sort of weird click in it. 'You cannot imagine how much confidence I derive from your rejection,' he says.

"That's where I stand up. Nice and easy, not to alarm him. While he goes on clutching me.

" 'I commit the sin of science every day,' he says. 'I turn ploughshares into swords. I mislead our masters. I mislead yours. I perpetuate the lie. I murder the humanity in myself every day. Listen to me.'

" 'Got to go now, Goethe, old lad. All those nice lady concierges at my hotel sitting up and worrying about me. Let me loose, will you, you're breaking my arm.'

"Hugs me. Pulls me right on to him. Makes me feel like a fat boy, he's so thin. Wet beard, wet hair, this burning heat.

" 'Promise,' he says.

"Squeezed it out of me. Fervour. Never saw anything like it. 'Promise! Promise!'

" 'All right,' I say. 'If you ever manage to be a hero, I'll be a decent human being. It's a deal. Okay? Now let me go, there's a good chap.'

" 'Promise,' he says.

" 'I promise,' I say, and shove him off me."

Walter is shouting. None of our preliminary warnings, no furious glares from

Ned or Clive or myself, could switch him off any longer. "But did you *believe* him, Barley? Was he conning you? You're a sharp cookie underneath the flannel. What did you *feel?*"

Silence. And more silence. Then finally, "He was drunk. Maybe twice in my life I've been as drunk as he was. Call it three times. He'd been on the white stuff all day long and he was still drinking it like water. But he'd hit one of those clear spells. I believed him. He's not the kind of chap you don't believe."

Walter again, furious. "But *what* did you believe? What did you think he was talking to you about? What did you think he *did?* All this chatter about things not reaching their targets, lying to his masters and yours, chess that isn't chess but something else? You can *add,* can't you? Why didn't you come to us? I know why! You put your head in the sand. 'Don't know because don't *want* to know.' That's you."

And the next sound on the tape after that is Barley cursing himself again as he stomps round the room. "Damn, damn, damn," he whispers. On and on. Until, cutting through him, we hear Clive's voice. If it ever falls to Clive to order the destruction of the universe, I imagine him using this same deserted tone.

"I'm sorry but I'm afraid we're going to need your rather serious help," he says.

Ironically I believe Clive *was* sorry. He was a technology man, not at ease with live sources, a suburban espiocrat of the modern school. He believed that facts were the only kind of information and he despised whoever was not ruled by them. If he liked anything at all in life apart from his own advancement and his silver Mercedes car, which he refused to take out of the garage if it had so much as a scratch on it, then it was hardware and powerful Americans, in that order. For Clive to sparkle, the Bluebird should have been a broken code, a satellite or an Inter Agency committee. Then Barley need never have been born.

Whereas Ned was all the other way, and more at risk on account of it. He was by temperament and training an agent-runner and captain of men. Live sources were his element and, so far as he knew the word, his passion. He despised the in-fighting of intelligence politics and left all that happily to Clive, just as he left the analysis to Walter. In that sense he was the determined primitive, as people who deal in human nature have to be, while Clive, to whom human nature was one vast unsavoury quagmire, enjoyed the reputation of a modernist.

5

We had moved to the library where Ned and Barley had begun. Brock had set up a screen and projector. He had put chairs in a horseshoe with a special person in his mind for each chair, for Brock, like other violent minds, had an exaggerated appetite for menial labour. He had been listening to the interview over the relay and despite his sinister inklings about Barley a glow of excitement smouldered in his pale Baltic eyes. Barley, deep in thought, lounged in the front row between Bob and Clive, a privileged, if distracted, guest at a private screening. I watched his head in silhouette as Brock switched on the projector, first turned downward in contemplation, then sharply upward as the first frame struck the screen. Ned sat beside me. Not a word, but I could feel the disciplined intensity of his excitement. Twenty male faces flicked across our vision, most of them Soviet scientists who on a first hasty search around the Registries of London and Langley were deemed to have had possible access to the Bluebird information. Some were featured more than once: first with beards, then with their beards touched out. Others were shown when they were twenty years younger because that was all the archives had of them.

"Not among those present," Barley pronounced when the parade was over, suddenly shoving his hand to his head as if he had been stung.

Bob just couldn't believe this. His incredulities were as charming as his credulities. "Not even a perhaps or a maybe, Barley? You sound pretty sure of yourself for a man who was drinking well when he made the original sighting. Jesus, I've been to parties where I couldn't remember my own name."

"Not a tickle, old boy," said Barley, and returned to his thoughts.

Now it was Katya's turn, though Barley couldn't know it. Bob advanced on her cautiously, a Langley professional showing us his footwork.

"Barley, these are some of the boys and girls around the Moscow publishing scene," he said over-casually as Brock ran up the first stills. "People you might have bumped into during your Russian travels, people at receptions, book fairs, people on the circuit. If you see anybody you know, holler."

"Bless us, that's Leonora!" Barley cut in with pleasure while Bob was still talking. On the screen a splendid burly woman with a backside like a football field was marching across a stretch of open tarmac. "Leni's top gun with SK," Barley added.

"SK?" Clive echoed as if he had unearthed a secret society.

"Soyuzkniga. SK order and distribute foreign books throughout the Soviet Union. Whether the books get there is another matter. Leni's a riot."

"Know her other name?"

"Zinovieva."

Confirmed, said Bob's smile to the knowing.

They showed him others and he picked the ones they knew he knew, but when they showed him the photograph of Katya that they had shown to Landau—Katya in her overcoat with her hair up, coming down the steps with her perhaps-bag—Barley muttered, "Pass," as he had to all the others he didn't know.

But Bob was delightfully upset. Bob said, "Hold her there, please," so unhappily that a babe in arms would have guessed that this picture had unrecognised significance.

So Brock held, as we all did: held our breath.

"Barley, the little lady here with the dark hair and big eyes in this picture is with the October Publishing Company, Moscow. Speaks a fine English, classical like yours and Goethe's. We understand she's a *redaktor*, commissioning and approving English-language translations of Soviet works. No bells?"

"No such luck," said Barley.

At which Clive handed him to me. With a tip of his head. Take him, Palfrey. Your witness. Scare him.

*　*　*

I do a special voice for my indoctrination sessions. It's supposed to instil the terror of the marriage vow and I hate it because it is the voice that Hannah hates. If my profession had a false white coat, this would be the moment where I administered the wicked injection. But that night as soon as I was alone with him, I chose a more protective tone and became a different and perhaps rejuvenated Palfrey, the one that Hannah used to swear could overcome. I addressed Barley not as I would some raw probationer but as a friend I was seeking to forewarn.

Here's the deal, I said, using the most non-legal jargon I could think of. Here's the noose we're putting round your neck. Take care. Consider.

Other people, I make them sit. I let Barley roam because I had seen that he was more at ease when he was able to pace and fidget and chuck his arms back in a luxurious stretch. Empathy is a curse even when it is short-lived, and not all the bad law in England can protect me from it.

And while I temporarily warmed to him I noticed a number of things about him I had not registered in the larger company. How his body leaned away from me, as if he were guarding himself against his deep-rooted disposition to give himself to the first person who asked for him. How his arms, despite their striving for self-discipline, remained unruly, particularly at the elbows, which like renegades seemed to be wanting to break free of whatever uniform they were pressed into.

And I noticed my own frustration that I could still not observe him closely enough, but cast round for other glimpses of him in the gilded mirrors as he passed them. Even to this day, I think of him as being a long way off.

And I noticed the pensiveness in him as he dipped in and out of my homily, taking a point or two, then swinging away from me in order to digest it, so that suddenly I was facing a breadth of powerful back that was not to be reconciled with the unreconciled front.

And how, as he returned to me, his eyes lacked the subservience that in other recipients of my wise words so often sickened me. He was not daunted. He was not even touched. His eyes disturbed me nonetheless, as they had the first time they appraised me. They were too truthful, too clear, too undefended. None of his milling gestures could protect them. I felt that I or anyone else could have waded into them and claimed possession of him, and the feeling scared me as if it were a threat. It made me fear for my own security.

I thought about his file. So many headlong crashes, acts of seeming self-destruction, so little prudence. His frightful school record. His efforts to earn himself a few laurels by boxing, for which he ended up in the school sanatorium with a broken jaw. His expulsion for being drunk while reading the Epistle at Sung Eucharist. "I was drunk from the night before, sir. It was not intentional." Flogged and expelled.

How convenient, I thought, for him and me, if I could have pointed to some great crime that haunted him, some act of cowardice or omission. But Ned had shown me his entire life, secret annexes and all, medical history, money, women, wives, children. And it was small stuff all the way. No big bang, no big crime. No big anything—which may have been the explanation of him. Was it for want of a greater sea that he had repeatedly wrecked himself against life's little rocks, challenging his Maker to come up with something bigger or stop bothering him? Would he be so headlong when faced with greater odds?

Then abruptly, before I am aware of it, our rôles are reversed. He is standing over me, peering down. The team is still waiting in the library and I hear sounds of their restlessness. The declaration form lies before me on the table. But it is me that he is reading, not the form.

"So have you any questions?" I ask up at him, conscious of his height. "Anything you want to know before you sign?" I am using my special voice after all, for self-protection.

He is at first puzzled, then amused. "Why? Have you got more answers you want to tell me?"

"It's an unfair business," I warn him sternly. "You've had a big secret thrust on you. You didn't ask for it but you can't unknow it. You know enough to hang a man and probably a woman. That places you in a certain category. It brings obligations you can't escape."

And, God help me, I think of Hannah again. He has woken the pain of her in me as if she were a brand-new wound.

He shrugs, brushing off the burden. "I don't know what I know," he says.

There is a thump on the door.

"The point is, they may want to tell you more," I say, softening again, trying to make him aware of my concern for him. "What you know already may be only the beginning of what they want you to find out."

He is signing. Without reading. He is a nightmare client. He could be signing his life away and he wouldn't know it and wouldn't care. They are knocking but I have still to add my name as witness.

"Thanks," he says.

"What for?"

I put away my pen. Got him, I think, in ice-cold triumph, just as Clive and the rest of them march in. A tricky customer but I signed him up.

But the other half of me is ashamed and mysteriously alarmed. I feel I have lit a fire inside our own camp, and there is no knowing how it will spread or who will put it out.

The only merit of the next act was that it was brief. I was sorry for Bob. He was never a sly man and he was certainly not a bigot. He was transparent, but that is not yet a crime, even in the secret world. He was more in Ned's stamp than Clive's, and nearer to the Service's way of doing things than to Langley's. There was a time when Langley had a lot of Bob's sort, and was the better for it.

"Barley, do you have any concept at all of the nature of the material that the source you call Goethe has so far provided? Of its overall message, shall we say?" Bob enquired awkwardly, putting up his broad smile.

Johnny had pitched the same sort of question at Landau, I remembered. And burned his fingers.

"How can I?" Barley replied. "I haven't set eyes on the stuff. You won't let me."

"Are you quite certain Goethe himself gave you no advance indication? No whispered word, author to publisher, of what he *might*—one day, if you both kept your promises—supply? Beyond what you have already accounted for in Peredelkino—the broad talk of weaponry and unreal enemies?"

"I've told you everything I remember," said Barley, shaking his head in confusion.

Also like Johnny before him, Bob began squinting at the brief he held below the table. But in Bob's case with genuine discomfort. "Barley, in the six visits you have made to the Soviet Union over the last seven years have you formed any connection, however briefly, with peaceniks, dissidents or other unofficial groups of that nature?"

"Is that a crime?"

Clive cut in. "Answer the question, will you?"

Amazingly, Barley obliged. Sometimes Clive was simply too small to reach him. "You meet all sorts, Bob. Jazz people, book people, intellectuals, journalists, artists —it's an impossible question. Sorry."

"Then can I turn it around a little and ask whether you are acquainted with any peace people back in England at all?"

"I've no idea."

"Barley, would you be aware that two members of a certain blues group you played with between 1977 and 1980 were involved with the Campaign for Nuclear Disarmament, as well as other peace outfits?"

Barley seemed puzzled but a little enchanted. "Really? Do they have names?"

"Would it amaze you if I said Maxi Burns and Bert Wunderley?"

To the amusement of everyone but Clive, Barley broke out in jolly laughter. "Oh my Lord! Forget the peace label, Bob. Maxi was a red-toothed Com. He'd have blown up the Houses of Parliament if he'd had a bomb. And Bert would have held his hand while he did it."

"I take it they were homosexual?" said Bob, with an old dog's smile.

"Gay as trivets," Barley agreed contentedly.

At which, with evident relief, Bob folded up his piece of paper and gave Clive a glance to say he'd finished, and Ned proposed to Barley that they take some air. Walter moved invitingly to the door and opened it. Ned must have wanted him as a foil, for Walter would never have dared otherwise. Barley hesitated a moment, then picked up a bottle of Scotch and a glass and dropped them one into each side pocket of his bush-jacket, in what I suspect was a gesture designed to shock us. Thus equipped he ambled after them, leaving the three of us alone without a word between us.

"Were those Russell Sheriton's questions you were shooting at him?" I asked Bob amiably enough.

"Russell's too bright for all that damn stuff these days, Harry," Bob replied with evident distaste. "Russell's come a long way."

Langley's power struggles were a mystery even to those who were involved in them, and certainly—however much we pretended otherwise—to our barons of the twelfth floor. But in the seethings and jockeyings, Sheriton's name had featured frequently as the man likely to come out at the top of the heap.

"So who authorised them?" I asked, still upon the questions. "Who drafted them, Bob?"

"Maybe Russell."

"You just said Russell was too bright!"

"Maybe he has to keep his boyars quiet," Bob said uncomfortably, lighting up his pipe and swinging out the match.

We settled down to wait on Ned.

* * *

The shade tree is in a public garden near the waterfront. I have stood under it and sat under it and watched the dawn rise over the harbour while the dew made teardrops on my grey raincoat. I have listened, without understanding, to an old mystic with a saintly face who likes to receive his disciples there, in that self-same spot by daylight. They are of all ages, and call him The Professor. The bench is built round its trunk and divided by iron arm-rests into seats. Barley sat at the centre with Ned and Walter either side of him. They had talked first in a sleepy sailors' tavern, then on a hilltop, Barley said, but Ned for some reason refuses to remember the hilltop. Now they had come back into the valley for their final place. Brock sat wakefully in the hired car keeping a view of them across the grass. From the warehouses on the other side of the road came a whine of cranes, a pumping of lorries and the yells of fishermen. It was five in the morning but the harbour is awake from three. The first clouds of dawn were shaping and breaking like the First Day.

"Choose somebody else," Barley said. He had said it before in several different ways. "I'm not your man."

"We didn't choose you," Ned said. "Goethe did. If we knew a way of getting back to him without you, we'd jump at it. He's taken a fix on you. Probably been waiting ten years for someone like you to turn up."

"He chose me because I wasn't a spy," said Barley. "Because I sang my bloody aria."

"And you won't be a spy now," said Ned. "You'll be a publisher. His. All you'll be doing is collaborating with your author and with us at the same time. What's wrong with that?"

"You've got the draw, you've got the wits," said Walter. "No wonder you drink. You've been under-used for twenty years. Now's your chance to shine. You're lucky."

"I shone at Peredelkino. Every time I shine, the lights go out."

"You might even be solvent," said Ned. "Three weeks of preparation back in London while you're waiting for your visa, a jolly week in Moscow and you'll be off the hook for ever."

With the prudence that was innate in him, Ned had avoided the word "training."

Back comes Walter, a touch of the whip, a piece of flattery, both over the top, but Ned let him run. "Oh never mind the money, Barley's *far* too grand! It's one shot for your country and a lot of people never get the chance. They dream of it, they write in for it but it never comes their way. And afterwards, when you've done your bit, you can sit back and enjoy the benefits of being British, knowing you've earned them even if you sneer at them, which is your good right, something that has to be fought for like everything else."

And Ned had judged rightly. Barley laughed and told Walter "Come off it," or something of the kind.

"One shot for your author too, if you think about it," Ned cut in, with his plain man's talk. "You'll be saving his neck for him. If he's going to hand over State secrets, the least you can do for him is put him on to the competent people. You're a Harrow man, aren't you?" he added as if he had just remembered this. "Didn't I read somewhere you'd been educated at Harrow?"

"I just went to school there," Barley said and Walter let out one of his hoots of laughter, in which Barley out of politeness joined.

"Why did you apply to us all those years ago? Do you remember what prompted you?" Ned asked. "Some sense of duty, was it?"

"I wanted to stay out of my father's firm. My tutor said teach at a prep school. My cousin Lionel said join the spies. You turned me down."

"Yes, well I'm afraid we can't do you the favour a second time," said Ned.

Like old companions the three men silently surveyed the waterfront. A chain of naval ships straddled the harbour mouth, their rigging drawn in necklaces of lights.

"Do you know, I've always dreamed there'd be one?" Walter sang suddenly, talking out to sea. "I'm a God man at heart, I'm sure I am. Or else a failed Marxist. I always believed that sooner or later their history had to throw one up. How much science have you got? None. You wouldn't. You're that generation—the last of the arts virgins. If I asked you what a rate of burn was, you'd probably think I was talking about baking a cake."

"Probably," Barley agreed, laughing again despite himself.

"CEP? Not a concept?"

"Don't like initials, I'm afraid."

"Circular-error-probable then. How's that?"

"Illiterate," Barley snapped, in one of his unpredictable fits of tetchiness.

"Recalibrate? Whom or what do I recalibrate, and what with?"

Barley didn't bother to reply.

"Very well, then. What's the Big Motherfucker, familiarly known in circles as the BMF? That won't offend your ear for English, will it? Nice Anglo-Saxon words?"

Barley shrugged.

"The BMF was the Soviet SS9 super rocket," Walter said. "It was wheeled out at a May Day parade in the dark years of the Cold War. Its dimensions were breathtaking and it was later credited with a notorious *footprint*. Also not a name to you? Footprint? Never mind, it will be. The footprint in this case was three huge holes in the Russian wastes that looked like the pattern of the Minuteman silo group with its command centre. The argument was whether they were made by independently targetable warheads, and could the Sovs therefore hit three American silos at once? Those who didn't want to believe they could called the footprints a fluke. Those who did upped the ante and said the warheads were for destroying cities not silos. The believers won the day and got themselves a green light for the ABM program. Never mind their theory was discredited three years later. They squeezed through. I'm losing you, I see."

"You never had me," Barley said.

"But he's a fast learner, of course he is," Walter assured Ned contentedly across Barley's body. "Publishers can get their minds halfway round anything."

"What's wrong with *finding out?*" Ned complained in the tone of a good man confused by smart talk. "That's what I never understand. We're not asking you to build the beastly rockets or push the button. We're asking you to help us improve our knowledge of the enemy. If you don't like the nuclear business, so much the better. And if the enemy turns out to be a friend where's the harm?"

"I thought the Cold War was supposed to be over," Barley said.

At which Ned, in what appeared to be genuine alarm, exclaimed, "Oh my dear Lord," under his breath.

But Walter showed no such restraint. Walter pretended to be indignant, and perhaps he was. He could be anything at any moment and often several things at once. "Cheap political theatricals and feigned friendships!" he snorted. "Here we are, locked into the biggest ideological face-off in history, and you tell me it's all over because a handful of statesmen find it convenient to hold hands in public and scrap a few obsolete toys. The evil empire's on its knees, oh yes! Their economy's a disaster, their ideology's up the spout and their back-yard's blowing up in their faces. Just don't tell me that's a reason for unbuckling our guns, because I won't believe a word of you. It's a reason for spying the living daylights out of them twenty-five hours a day and kicking them in the balls every time they try to get off the floor. God *knows* who they won't think they are ten years from now!"

"I suppose you do realise that if you walk out on Goethe you'll be leaving him to the Americans?" said Ned, on a practical point of information. "Bob won't let him go, why should he? Don't be fooled by those old Yalie manners of his. How will you live with yourself *then?*"

"I don't want to live with myself," said Barley. "I can't think of anybody worse to live with."

A slate-coloured cloud slid across the red sunpath before shattering into fragments.

"It comes down to this," said Ned. "It's crude and un-English but I'll say it anyway. Do you want to be a passive or an active player in the defence of your country?"

Barley was still hunting for an answer when Walter supplied it for him, and with an air of finality that brooked no contradiction. "You're from a free society. You've got no choice," he said.

The din of the harbour rose with the advancing daylight. Barley slowly stood up and rubbed his back. He seemed to have a permanent patch of pain there, just above the waistband. Perhaps it accounted for his slope.

"Any decent Church would have burned you bastards at the stake long ago," he remarked wearily. He turned to Ned, peering down at him through his too small spectacles. "I'm the wrong man," he warned him. "And you're a fool for using me."

"We're all the wrong men," said Ned. "We're dealing with wrong things."

Barley walked across the grass, beating his pockets for his keys. He entered a side street and vanished from their view as Brock went softly after him. The house was a wedge, narrow on the street, broad at the back. Barley unlocked the front door and closed it behind him. He pressed the time switch and began climbing the stairs, keeping an even pace because he had a long way to go.

She was a good woman and nothing was her fault. They were all good women. They were women with a mission to him, just as Hannah once had a mission to me —to save him, to straighten him out, to get his oh-so-many talents working in one direction, to help him make the fresh start that would get him clear of all the fresh starts he had made before. And Barley had encouraged her as he had encouraged all of them. He had stood beside them at the patient's bedside as if he were not himself the patient but a member of the healing team. "So what shall we do about this poor old chap that will get him up and functioning again?"

The only difference was, he had never believed in the remedy, any more than I had.

She lay face down, exhausted and possibly asleep. She had cleaned the flat. As prisoners clean cells and the bereaved tend tombs, she had scoured the surface of a world she couldn't alter. Other people might tell Barley he was too hard on himself. Women said it to him often. How he mustn't hold himself responsible for both halves of every relationship that collapsed on him. Barley knew better. He knew the distance between himself and everything. In those days he was still the unequalled expert on his own incurability.

He touched her shoulder but she didn't stir, so he knew she was awake.

"I had to go to the Embassy," he said. "People in London baying for my blood. I've got to go back and face the music or they'll take away my passport."

He fished a suitcase from under the bed and began filling it with the shirts she'd ironed for him.

"You said this time you weren't going back," she told him. "You'd served your English stretch, you said. You'd done your time."

"They've put me on the early flight. There's nothing I can do. There's a car coming for me in a few minutes." He went to the bathroom for his toothbrush and shaving gear. "They're throwing the whole book at me," he called. "There's nothing I can do."

"And I go back to my husband," she said.

"Stay here. Use the flat. Whatever. It'll only take a few weeks. Then it's done."

"If you just hadn't said all that stuff, we'd have been fine. I'd have been happy just having an affair. You should see your letters. Hear yourself."

Barley didn't look at her. He was stooped over his suitcase.

"Just don't do it to anyone else," she said.

That was as far as her calm could stretch. She began sobbing and was sobbing when he left, and she was still sobbing next morning when I pitched her some line and pushed a declaration form under her nose as I asked her how much he'd told her. Nothing. She blabbed out the whole story yet defended him to the death. Hannah would have done the same. Does it still, a surfeit of loyalty to this day, even though her illusions are destroyed.

Three weeks were all that Ned and his Russia House people had to knock Barley into shape. Three weekends, and fifteen days that didn't start till five when Barley slipped away from his office.

But Ned drove the job through as only Ned was able. Ned would have kept the trainers up all night and himself all night and day. And Barley, with the changefulness that was innate in him, swung and turned with every breeze, until he settled down and found a steady face and, as the day of his departure approached, a serious one as well. Often he seemed to embrace the entire ethic of our trade without demur. After all, he declared to Walter, was not seeming the only kind of being? Oh my *God*, yes! Walter cried, delighted—and not only in our trade! And was not the whole of man's identity a cover? Barley insisted: and was not the only world worth living in the secret one? Walter assured him that it was, and advised him to take up permanent residence there before prices rose.

Barley had loved Walter from the start, loved the fragility in him and, as I see it now, the transience. He seemed to know from the outset that he was holding the hand of a man who was on his way to the breaker's yard. At other times Barley's own face became as empty as the open grave. He would not have been Barley if he hadn't been a pendulum.

Most of all he took to the family atmosphere which Ned, with his instinct for the unanchored joe, assiduously tended—the chatty suppers, the sharing and being the star of the family, the games of chess with old Palfrey, whom Ned cunningly harnessed to Barley's wagon to redress the disturbingly ephemeral influence of Walter.

"Drop in whenever you're in the mood," Ned told me, with a friendly pat.

So I became Barley's old Harry.

Old Harry, give us a game of chess, damn you! Old Harry, why aren't you staying for supper? Old Harry, where's your bloody glass, man?

Ned invited Bob sparingly and Clive not at all. It was Ned's show, Ned's joe. And he had a shrewd eye for Barley's flashpoints.

For the safe house Ned had chosen a pretty Edwardian cottage in Knightsbridge, an area of London where Barley had no connection. Clive winced at the cost but the Americans were paying so his fastidiousness was misplaced. The house lay in a cul-de-sac not five minutes' walk from Harrods and I rented it in the name of the Ethical Research & Action Group, a charitable body I had registered years before and locked away for a rainy day. A cosy Service housekeeper named Miss Coad was placed in charge, and I duly swore her on to the Bluebird indoctrination list. The top-floor nursery was converted into a modest lecture room and, like the rest of the rooms, which were snug and well furnished, it was microphoned.

"This is your home from home for the duration," Ned told Barley as we showed him round. "Here's your bedroom when you need one, here's your key. Use the phone as much as you like but I'm afraid we'll be listening, so if it's private you'd do better from the box across the road."

For good measure, I had extended the Home Office warrant to cover the phone box too. Intense American interest.

Since Barley and I were not long sleepers, we played our chess when the others had turned in. He was an impulsive opponent and often a brilliant one, but there is a calculating streak in me that he never possessed and I was more attuned to his weaknesses than he to mine. After all, I had read his file. But I still remember games where he saw a whole campaign at a glance and with three or four moves and a bellow of amusement forced me to resign.

"Got you, Harry! Say you're sorry! Hang your head!"

But when we set them up again, I could feel the patience drain out of him. He would start to prowl and flick his hands around and let his mind take one of its journeys.

"Married, Harry?"

"Not so's you'd notice," I replied.

"Hell does that mean?"

"I have a wife in the country. I live in the town."

"Had her long?"

"Couple of lifetimes," I said carelessly, already wishing I had given him a different answer.

"Love her?"

"My dear chap!" But he was staring at me, wanting to know. "From a distance, I suppose. Yes," I added grudgingly.

"She love you back?"

"I assume so. It's some time since I asked her."

"Kiddywinks?"

"A boy. Man, I suppose."

"Ever see him?"

"A card at Christmas. Funerals and weddings. We're good enough friends in our way."

"What's he do?"

"He flirted with the law. Now he makes money."

"Is he happy?"

I was angry, which these days is unusual in me. Definitions of happiness and love were none of his damned business. He was a joe. It was my right to come close to him, not the other way around. But it was more unusual still that I should let my anger show. Yet I must have done, for I caught him gazing at me with concern, wondering no doubt whether he had accidentally touched upon some family tragedy. Then he coloured and swung away, looking for a distraction that would get us off the hook.

"He's not fighting it, sir, I'll put it that way," a Mr. Candyman, specialist in the latest thing in body microphones, told Ned. "I won't say he's a natural but he does listen and my goodness he does remember."

"He's a gentleman, Mr. Ned, which is what I like," said a lady watcher entrusted with teaching Barley the rudiments of streetcraft. "He's got the brains and he's got a sense of humour, which I often say is halfway to an eye." Later she confessed that she had declined his advances in accordance with Service rules, but that he had successfully introduced her to the work of Scott Fitzgerald.

"Whole thing's a load of hocus-pocus," Barley pronounced raucously at the end of a wearying session on the techniques of secret writing. But he clearly enjoyed it, all the same.

And as the day of reckoning drew nearer, his submissiveness became total. Even when I wheeled in the Service accountant, a dreary stick called Christopher, who had devoted five days to an awed inspection of the Abercrombie & Blair books, Barley showed none of the rebelliousness I had expected.

"But every last swine in publishing is broke, Chris old boy!" he protested, pacing the pretty drawing-room to the rhythms of his own humming, holding his whisky glass wide while he dipped at the knees for the long steps. "The big fellows like Jumbo eat the leaves and we gnaw the bark." A German voice: "You hef your methods, ve hef ours."

But neither Ned nor I gave a cuss about every last swine. Neither did Chris. We cared about the operation and were haunted by the nightmare that Barley might go bankrupt on us in the middle of it.

"But I don't *want* a bloody editor!" Barley cried, waving his longsuffering spectacles at us. "I can't *pay* a bloody editor. My sainted aunts in Ely will pop their *garters* if I hire a bloody editor!"

But I had already squared the sainted aunts. Over luncheon at Rules I had wooed and won the Lady Pandora Weir-Scott, better known to Barley as the Sacred

Cow on account of her High Anglican beliefs. Posing as a Foreign Office Pontiff, I had explained to her in the greatest confidence that the house of Abercrombie & Blair was about to be the recipient of an under-the-counter Rockefeller grant to promote Anglo-Soviet cultural relations. But not a word, or the money would be whisked away and given to another deserving house.

"Well *I'm* a bloody sight more deserving than *anybody*," Lady Pandora averred, spreading her elbows wide to get the last scrap out of her lobster. "*You* try running Ammerford on thirty thousand a year."

Mischievously, I asked her whether I could safely approach her nephew.

"Not on your nelly. Leave him to me. He doesn't know money from muck and he can't lie for toffee."

The need to provide Barley with a minder seemed suddenly more pressing. "You advertised for him," Ned explained, brandishing a small ad from a recent edition of the cultural press in Barley's face. *Old Established British Publisher seeks qualified Russian reader for promotion to editor, 25–45, fiction and technical, curriculum vitae.*

And on the next afternoon Leonard Carl Wicklow presented himself for interview at the much mortgaged premises of Abercrombie & Blair of Norfolk Street, Strand.

"I have an angel for you, Mr. Barley," boomed Mrs. Dunbar's gin-soaked voice over the ancient intercom. "Shall I ask him to fly in?"

An angel in bicycle clips, a webbing kitbag slung across his chest. A high angelic brow, not a worry on it, blond angelic curls. Angelic blue eyes that knew no evil. An angelic nose, so mysteriously knocked off course that your first instinct on meeting him was to reach out and switch it straight again. Interview him as you would anybody, Ned had told Barley. Leonard Carl Wicklow, born Brighton 1964, honours graduate, School of Slavonic & East European Studies, University of London.

"Oh yes, you. Marvellous. Sit down," Barley grumbled. "Hell brings you to publishing? Lousy trade." He had lunched with one of his more strident lady novelists, and was still digesting the experience.

"Well it's been kind of an on-going thing of mine for years, actually, sir," said Wicklow, with a smile of angelic enthusiasm.

"Well if you do come to us you certainly won't *on-go*," Barley warned, bridling at this unprovoked assault on the English language. "You may *continue*. You may *endure*. You may even *prevail*. But you jolly well won't *on-go* while *I'm* in the driving seat."

"Don't know whether the bugger barks or purrs," he growled to Ned, the same evening back in Knightsbridge, as the three of us loped up the narrow stairs for our evening tryst with Walter.

"He does both rather well, actually," said Ned.

And Walter's seminars held Barley in their thrall, a sell-out every time. Barley loved anyone whose hold on life was tenuous, and Walter looked as if he were in danger of falling off the edge of the world each time he left his chair. They would talk tradecraft, they would talk nuclear theology, they would talk the horror story of Soviet science that the Bluebird, whoever he might be, was inescapably heir to. Walter was too good a tutor to reveal what his subject was, and Barley was too interested to enquire.

"*Control?*" Walter the ultimate hawk shouted at him indignantly. "Can you honestly not distinguish between *control* and *disarmament,* you ninny? Defuse world crisis, did I hear? What *Guardian* bilge is that? Our leaders *adore* crisis. Our leaders *feast* on crisis. Our leaders spend their lives quartering the globe in search of crisis to revive their flagging libidos!"

And Barley, far from taking offence, would crane forward in his chair, groan and clap and bay for more. He would challenge Walter, leap to his feet and pound the room shouting "*But*—hang on, damn you—*but!*" He had the memory, he had the aptitude, as Walter had predicted. And his scientific virginity yielded at the first assault, when Walter delivered his introductory lecture on the balance of terror, which he had contrived to turn into an inventory of all the follies of mankind.

"There's no way out," he announced with satisfaction, "and no amount of wishful dreaming will produce one. The demon won't go back in its bottle, the face-off is for ever, the embrace gets tighter and the toys cleverer with every generation, and there's no such thing for either side as enough security. Not for the main players, not for the nasty little newcomers who each year run themselves up a suitcase bomb and join the club. We get tired of believing that, because we're human. We may even con ourselves into believing the threat has gone away. It never will. Never, never, never."

"So who'll save us, Walt?" Barley asked. "You and Nedsky?"

"Vanity, if anything will, which I doubt," Walter retorted. "No leader wants to go down in history as the ass who destroyed his country in an afternoon. And funk, I suppose. Most of our gallant politicians do have a narcissistic objection to suicide, thank God."

"Otherwise no hope?"

"Not for man alone," said Walter contentedly, who more than once had seriously considered taking holy orders rather than the Service's.

"So what's Goethe trying to achieve?" Barley asked another time, with a hint of exasperation.

"Oh, save the world, I'm sure. We'd all like to do *that.*"

"*How* save it? What's his message?"

"That's for you to find out, isn't it?"

"What's he told us so far? Why can't I know?"

"My dear boy, don't be so childish," Walter exclaimed petulantly, but Ned stepped quickly in.

"You know all you need to know," he said with a calming authority. "You're the messenger. It's what you're equipped to be, it's what he wants you to be. He's told us that a lot of things on the Soviet side don't work. He's painted a picture of failure at every level—inaccuracy, incompetence, mismanagement and, on top of that, falsified test results sent to Moscow. Perhaps it's true, perhaps he's made it up. Perhaps somebody made it up for him. It's a beguiling enough story as it stands."

"Do *we* think it's true?" Barley persisted stubbornly.

"You can't know."

"Why not?"

"Because under interrogation everybody talks. There are no heroes any more. You talk, I talk, Walter talks, Goethe talks, she talks. So if we tell you what we know about them, we risk compromising our capacity to spy on them. Do we know a particular secret about them? If the answer is no, then they know we lack the software, or the device, or the formula, or the super-secret ground station to find it out. But if the answer is yes, they'll take evasive action to make sure we can't go on watching and hearing them by that method."

Barley and I played chess.

"Do you reckon marriage only works from a distance then?" he asked me, resuming our earlier conversation as if we had never abandoned it.

"I'm quite sure love does," I replied with an exaggerated shudder, and quickly moved the subject to less intimate paths.

For his last evening, Miss Coad prepared a salmon trout and polished the silver plate. Bob was commanded, and produced a rare malt whisky and two bottles of Sancerre. But our festivities caught Barley in the same introspective mood, until Walter's spirited Final Sermon rescued him from the doldrums.

"The issue is *why*," Walter trilled suddenly, his cranky voice flying all over the room, while he helped himself to my glass of Sancerre. "That's what we're after. Not the substance, but the motive. *Why?* If we trust the motive, we trust the man. Then we trust his material. In the beginning was not the word, not the deed, not the silly serpent. In the beginning was *why?* Why did she pluck the apple? Was she bored? Was she inquisitive? Was she paid? Did Adam put her up to it? If not, who did? The Devil is every girl's cover story. Ignore him. Was she fronting for somebody? It's not enough to say, 'Because the apple is there.' That may do for Everest. It may even do for Paradise. But it won't do for Goethe and it won't do for us and it *certainly* won't do for our gallant American allies, will it, Bobby?"

And when we all burst out laughing he squeezed his eyes shut and raised his voice still higher.

"Or take the ravishing Katya! Why does Goethe pick on *her*? Why does he put *her* life at risk? And why does she let him? We don't know. But we must. We must know everything we can about her because in our profession the couriers are the message. If Goethe is genuine, the girl's head is on the block. That's a given. If he's not, what does that make her? Did she invent the stuff herself? Is she really in touch with him? Is she in touch with someone different and if so who?" He thrust a strengthless forefinger at Barley's face. "Then there's *you,* sir. Does Goethe think you're a spy or doesn't he? Did other people *tell* him you were a spy? Be a hamster. Store every nugget you can get. God bless you and all who sail in you."

I discreetly filled another glass and we drank. And I remember how in the deep quiet we distinctly heard the chimes of Big Ben floating up the river from Westminster.

It was not till early next morning when Barley's departure was only hours off that we granted him a limited sight of the documents he had so stridently demanded in Lisbon—Goethe's notebooks, re-created in facsimile by Langley under draconian conditions of secrecy, down to the thick Russian board backs and line-block drawings of jolly Soviet schoolkids on the covers.

Silently accepting them in both hands, Barley became pure publisher while the rest of us watched the transformation. He opened the first notebook, peered at the gutter, felt the weight and flipped to the back, seeming to work out how long it would take him to read it. He reached for the second, sliced it open at a random page and, seeing tightly written lines, pulled a face that as good as complained that the script was single-spaced and handwritten.

Then he ranged across all three notebooks at once, puzzling his way from illustration to text and text to literary effusion, while he kept his head stiffly backwards and to one side, as if determined to reserve his judgment.

But I noticed how, when he raised his eyes, they had lost their sense of place, and appeared to be fixed on some far mountain of his own.

A routine search of Barley's Hampstead flat conducted by Ned and Brock after his departure revealed no hard clues to his state of mind. An old notebook in which he was accustomed to make his jottings was found amid the litter of his desk. The last entries looked recent. The most apt was probably a couplet he had culled from the later work of Stevie Smith.

> I am not so afraid of the dark night
> As the friends I do not know . . .

Ned conscientiously entered it on the file but refused to make anything of it. Name him a joe who didn't get butterflies in his stomach on the eve of his first run.

And on the back of an old bill tossed into the wastepaper basket Brock came on a quotation which he eventually traced to Roethke, and which for his own dark reasons he only mentioned weeks later.

> I learn by going where I have to go.

6

Katya woke sharply and, as she afterwards persuaded herself, with an immediate awareness that today was the day. She was an emancipated Soviet woman but superstition died hard in her.

"It was meant," she told herself later.

Through the threadbare curtains a white sun was appearing over the cement parade grounds of her north Moscow suburb. All round her the brick apartment blocks, decked with washing, rose like tattered pink giants into an empty sky.

It's Monday, she thought. I'm in my own bed. I'm free of the street after all. She was thinking of her dream.

Having woken she lay still a moment, patrolling her secret world and trying to shake her mind free of its bad thoughts. And when this didn't work she sprang from her bed and impulsively, as she did most things, ducked with practised deftness between the hanging clothes and crumbling bathroom fittings and showered herself.

She was a beautiful woman as Landau had observed. Her tall body was full but not plump, with a fine neat waist and strong legs. Her black hair was luxuriant and, when she was in a mood to neglect it, rampant. Her face was puckish but intelligent and seemed to animate everything around her. Whether clothed or naked she could make no gesture that did not have its grace.

When she had showered, she turned the taps as hard as they would go, then finished them off with a wallop of the wooden mallet that said, "Take that!"

Humming to herself, she picked up the little mirror and strode back to her bedroom to dress. The street again: where was it? In Leningrad or Moscow? The shower had not washed her dream away.

Her bedroom was very small, the smallest of the three rooms that made up her tiny apartment, an alcove with a cupboard and a bed. But Katya was accustomed to these confinements and her swift movements as she brushed out her hair, twisted it and pinned it for the office, had a sensual, if haphazard, elegance. Indeed the apartment might have been a lot smaller had not Katya been entitled to an extra twenty metres for her work. Uncle Matvey was worth another nine; the twins and her own resourcefulness accounted for the rest. She had no quarrel with the apartment.

Maybe the street was in Kiev, she thought, recalling a recent visit there. No. The Kiev streets are wide but mine was narrow.

While she dressed, the block began to wake up and Katya gratefully counted off the rituals of the normal world. First through the adjoining wall came the Goglidzes' alarm clock sounding six-thirty, followed by their crazy borzoi howling to be let out. The poor Goglidzes, I must take them a gift, she thought. Last month Natasha had lost her mother and on Friday Otar's father had been rushed to hospital with a brain tumour. I'll give them some honey, she thought—and in the same instant found herself smiling a wry greeting to a former lover, a refusenik painter who against all the odds of Nature had contrived to keep a swarm of illegal bees on a rooftop behind the Arbat. He had treated her disgracefully, her friends assured her. But Katya always defended him in her mind. He was an artist, after all, perhaps a genius. He was a beautiful lover and between his rages he had made her laugh. Above all, she had loved him for achieving the impossible.

After the Goglidzes came the grizzling of the Volkhovs' baby daughter cutting her first teeth and a moment later through the floorboards the beat of their new Japanese stereo thumping out the latest American rock. How on earth could they afford such things, Katya wondered in another leap of empathy—Elizabeth always pregnant and Sasha on a hundred and sixty a month? After the Volkhovs came the unsmiling Karpovs, nothing but Radio Moscow for them. A week ago, the Karpovs' balcony had fallen down, killing a policeman and a dog. The wits in the block had wanted to get up a collection for the dog.

She became Katya the provider. On Mondays there was a chance of fresh chickens and vegetables brought privately from the country over the weekend. Her friend Tanya had a cousin who functioned informally as a dealer for smallholders. Phone Tanya.

Thinking this, she also thought about the concert tickets. She had taken her decision. As soon as she got to the office she would collect the two tickets for the Philharmonic which the editor Barzin had promised her as amends for his drunken advances at the May Day party. She had never even noticed his advances, but Barzin was always torturing himself about something, and who was she to stand in the way of his guilt—particularly if it took the form of concert tickets?

At lunchtime after shopping she would trade the tickets with the porter Morozov, who had pledged her twenty-four bars of imported soap wrapped in decorative paper. With the fancy soap she would buy the bolt of green check cloth of pure wool that the manager of the clothing shop was keeping locked in his storeroom for her.

Katya resolutely refused to wonder why. This afternoon after the Hungarian reception she would hand the cloth to Olga Stanislavsky, who, in return for favours to be negotiated, would make two cowboy shirts on the East German sewing machine she had recently traded for her ancient family Singer, one for each twin in time for their birthday. And there might even be enough cloth left over to squeeze them both a private check-up from the dentist.

So goodbye concert. It was done.

The telephone was in the living room where her Uncle Matvey slept, a precious red one from Poland. Volodya had smuggled it from his factory and had the goodness not to take it with him when he made his final exit. Tiptoeing past the sleeping Matvey—and vouchsafing him a tender glance along the way, for Matvey had been her father's favourite brother—she carried the phone across the corridor on its long flex, set it on her bed and began dialling before she had decided whom to talk to first.

For twenty minutes she rang round her friends, trading gossip mostly about where things might be had, but some of it more intimate. Twice when she put the phone down, somebody rang her. The newest Czech film director was at Zoya's last night. Alexandra said he was devastating and today she would take her life in her hands and ring him up, but what could she use for a pretext? Katya racked her brains and came up with a suggestion. Three avant-garde sculptors, till now banned, were to hold their own exhibition at the Railway Workers' Union. Why not invite him to accompany her to the exhibition? Alexandra was delighted. Katya always had the best ideas.

Black-market beef could be bought every Thursday evening from the back of a refrigeration van on the road to Sheremetyevo, said Lyuba; ask for a Tartar named Jan, but don't let him near you! Cuban pineapples were on sale from a shop behind Kropotkin Street, said Olga; mention Dimitri and pay double what they ask.

Ringing off, Katya discovered she was being persecuted by the American book on disarmament that Nasayan had lent her, blue with Roman lettering. Nasayan was October's new non-fiction editor. Nobody liked him, nobody understood how he had got the job. But it was noted that he kept the key to the one copying machine, which placed him squarely in the murkier ranks of officialdom. Her bookshelves were in the corridor, crammed from floor to ceiling and overflowing. She hunted hard. The book was a Trojan horse. She wanted it out of her house, and Nasayan with it.

"Is somebody going to translate it then?" she had asked him sternly as he padded round her office, squinting at her letters, poking through her heap of unread manuscripts. "Is this why you wish me to read it?"

"I thought it was something that might interest you," he had replied. "You're a mother. A liberal, whatever that means. You got on your high horse over Chernobyl and the rivers and the Armenians. If you don't want to borrow it, don't."

Discovering his wretched book jammed between Hugh Walpole and Thomas Hardy, she wrapped it in newspaper, stuffed it in her perhaps-bag, then hung the bag on the front doorknob because, just as she remembered everything these days, so she forgot everything.

The doorknob that we bought together from the flea market! she thought with a surge of compassion. Volodya, my poor dear intolerable husband, reduced to nursing your historical nostalgia in a communal flat with five ill-smelling grass widowers like yourself!

Her telephoning over, she hastily watered her plants, then went to wake the twins. They were sleeping diagonally in their single bed. Standing over them, Katya gazed at them in awe, for a moment not brave enough to touch them. Then she smiled so that they would be sure to see her smile as they woke.

For an hour after that, she gave herself to them totally, which was how she planned each day. She cooked their *kasha,* peeled their oranges and sang daft songs with them, ending with the "Enthusiasts' March," their absolute favourite, which they growled in unison, chins on chests, like heroes of the Revolution—not knowing, though Katya knew and was repeatedly amused by it, that they were also singing the melody of a Nazi marching song. While they drank their tea she made their packed lunch, white bread for Sergey, black bread for Anna, a meat-cake inside for each of them. And after that she fastened Sergey's button-on collar and straightened Anna's red neckerchief and kissed them both before she brushed their hair because their school principal was a Pan-Slavist who preached that tidiness was an act of homage to the State.

And when she had done all this, she dropped into a crouch and gathered the twins into her arms, as she had each Monday for the last four weeks.

"So what do you do if Mummy doesn't come back one evening, if she's had to dash off to a conference or visit somebody who is ill?" she asked brightly.

"Telephone Daddy and tell him to come and stay with us," said Sergey, tugging himself free.

"And I look after Uncle Matvey," said Anna.

"And if Daddy is away too, what do you do then?"

They began giggling, Sergey because the notion unsettled him and Anna because she was thrilled by the prospect of disaster.

"Go to Auntie Olga's!" Anna cried. "Wind up Auntie Olga's clockwork canary! Make it sing!"

"And what is Auntie Olga's telephone number? Can you sing that too?"

They sang it, hooting with laughter, all three of them. The twins were still laughing as they clattered ahead of her down the stinking stairwell that served the adolescents as a love-nest and the alcoholics as a bar, and seemingly everybody except themselves as a lavatory. Stepping into the sunlight, they marched hand in hand with her across the park to school, Katya in the middle.

"And what is the objective purpose of your life today, Comrade?" Katya demanded of Sergey with mock ferocity as she straightened his collar once more.

"To serve the people and the Party with all my strength."

"And?"

"Not to let Vitaly Karpov pinch my lunch!"

More laughter as the twins ran away from her up the stone steps, Katya waving till they had disappeared.

In the metro she saw everything too brightly and from a distance. She noticed how glum the passengers were, as if she were not one of them herself; and how they all seemed to be reading Moscow newspapers, a sight that would have been unthinkable a year ago when newspapers were good for nothing but toilet paper and closing off draughts. On other days Katya might have read one too; or if not, a book or manuscript for work. But today, despite her efforts to rid herself of her stupid dream, she was living too many lives at once. She was cooking fish soup for her father to make up for some act of wilfulness. She was enduring a piano lesson at the elderly Tatyana Sergeyevna's and being rebuked for levity. She was running in the street, unable to wake. Or the street was running after her. Which was probably why she almost forgot to change trains.

Reaching her office, which was a half-heartedly modern affair of flaking wood and weeping concrete—more suited to a public swimming pool, she always thought, than to a State publishing house—she was surprised by the sight of workmen hammering and sawing in the entrance hall, and for a second she gave way to the disgusting notion that they were building a scaffold for her public execution.

"It's our *appropriation*," wheezed old Morozov, who always had to steal a word with her. "The money was allocated to us six years ago. Now some bureaucrat has consented to sign the order."

The lift was being repaired as usual. Lifts and churches, she thought, in Russia always under repair. She took the stairs, climbing swiftly without knowing what the hurry was, yelling cheerful good mornings at whoever needed one. Thinking afterwards about her haste, she wondered whether the ringing of her telephone had drawn her forward subconsciously, because as she entered her room there it was on her desk howling to be put out of its pain.

She grabbed the receiver and said "Da," out of breath, but evidently she spoke too soon, for the first thing she heard was a man's voice asking in English for Madame Orlova.

"This is Madame Orlova," she said, also in English.

"Madame Yekaterina Orlova?"

"Who is this, please?" she asked, smiling. "It is Lord Peter Wimsey perhaps? Who is this?"

One of my silly friends playing a joke. Lyuba's husband again, hoping for a date. Then her mouth dried.

"Ah well, you don't know me, I'm afraid. My name's Scott Blair. Barley Scott Blair from Abercrombie & Blair in London, publishers, over here on a business trip. I think we have a mutual friend in Niki Landau. Niki was very insistent I should give you a call. How do you do?"

"How do you do," Katya heard herself say, and felt a hot cloud come over her and a pain start at the centre of her stomach just below the rib cage. At the same moment Nasayan strolled in, hands in pockets and unshaven, which was his way of showing intellectual depth. Seeing her talking, he hunched his shoulders and stuck his ugly face at her in a resentful pout, willing her to get off the line.

"*Bonjour* to you, Katya Borisovna," he said sarcastically.

But the voice in the telephone was already talking again, pressing itself upon her. It was a strong voice so she assumed someone tall. It was confident so she assumed someone arrogant, the kind of Englishman who wears expensive suits, has no culture and walks with his hands behind his back.

"Look, I'll tell you why I'm calling," he was saying. "Apparently Niki promised to look out some old editions of Jane Austen for you with the original drawings, is that right?" He gave her no time to say whether it was right or wrong. "Only I've brought a couple over with me—rather nice ones, actually—and I wondered whether we could possibly arrange a handover at some mutually convenient point?"

Tired of glowering, Nasayan was picking through the papers in her in-tray after his usual habit.

"You are very kind," she said into the mouthpiece, using her dullest voice. She had closed her face, making it lifeless and official. That was for Nasayan. She had closed her mind. That was for herself.

"Niki's also sent you about a ton of Jackson's tea," the voice continued.

"A *ton?*" said Katya. "What are you talking about?"

"I didn't even know Jackson's were still in business, to be honest. They used to have a marvellous shop in Piccadilly a few doors down from Hatchard's. Anyway, I've got three different kinds of their tea sitting here in front of me—"

He had disappeared.

They have arrested him, she thought. He never rang. It's my dream again. God in Heaven, what do I do next?

"—Assam, Darjeeling and Orange Pekoe. What on earth's a pekoe? Sounds more like an exotic bird to me."

"I don't know. I suspect it will be a plant."

"I suspect you'll be right at that. Anyway, the question is, how can I give them to you? Can I bring them to you somewhere? Or can you drop in at the hotel and could we have a quick drink and a formal presentation?"

She was learning to appreciate his long-windedness. He was giving her time to steady herself. She pushed her fingers through her hair, discovering to her surprise that it was tidy.

"You have not told me which hotel you are staying at," she objected severely.

Nasayan's head jerked round to her in disapproval.

"Well, neither I did now. How ridiculous of me. I'm at the Odessa, know the Odessa? Just up the road from the old bath house? I've become quite fond of it. Always ask for it, don't always get it. My daytimes are rather taken up with meetings—always the way when one's over on a flying visit—but evenings are relatively free at the moment, if that's any good to you. I mean how about tonight —no time like the present—would tonight be any good for you?"

Nasayan was lighting one of his filthy cigarettes, though the whole office knew she hated smoking. Having lit it, he hoisted it in the air and sucked from it with his woman's lips. She grimaced at him but he ignored her.

"That is actually quite convenient," Katya said in her most military manner. "Tonight I have to attend an official reception in your district. It is for an important delegation from Hungary," she added, not sure whom she was meaning to impress. "We have been looking forward to it for many weeks."

"Great. Marvellous. Suggest a time. Six? Eight? What suits you best?"

"The reception is at six o'clock. I shall come at perhaps eight-fifteen."

"Perhaps-eight-fifteen it is. You got the name, did you? Scott Blair. Scott like the Antarctic, Blair like a trumpet. I'm tall and seedy, about two hundred years old, with spectacles I can't see through. But Niki tells me you're the Soviet answer to the Venus de Milo so I expect I'll recognise you anyway."

"That is most ridiculous!" she exclaimed, laughing despite herself.

"I'll be hanging around the lobby looking out for you, but why don't I give you my room telephone number just in case. Got a pencil?"

As she rang off, the contrary passions that had been gathering in her burst their banks and she turned on Nasayan with flashing eyes.

"Grigory Tigranovich. Whatever your position here, you have no right to haunt my room like this, inspect my correspondence and listen to my telephone conversations. Here is your book. If you have something to say to me, say it later."

Then she scooped up a sheaf of translator's manuscript on the achievements of Cuban agricultural cooperatives and with cold hands began leafing through the pages, pretending to count them. A full hour passed before she telephoned Nasayan.

"You must forgive my anger," she said. "A close friend of mine died at the weekend. I was not myself."

By lunchtime she had changed her plans. Morozov could wait for his tickets, the shopkeeper for his bars of fancy soap, Olga Stanislavsky for her cloth. She walked, she took a bus, not a cab. She walked again, crossing one courtyard after another until she found the down-at-heel blockhouse she was looking for and the alley that ran beside it. "This is how you get hold of me when you need me," he had said. "The janitor is a friend of mine. He will not even know who made the sign."

You have to believe in what you are doing, she reminded herself.

I do. I absolutely do.

She had the picture postcard in her hand, a Rembrandt from the Hermitage in Leningrad. "Love to you all," her message read, signed "Alina," and a heart.

She had found the street. She was standing in it. It was the street of her bad dream. She pressed the bell, three rings, then shoved the card under the door.

A perfect Moscow morning, alight and beckoning, the air alpine, a day to forgive all sins. The telephone call behind him, Barley stepped out of his hotel and, standing on the warm pavement, loosened his wrists and shoulders and rolled his head round his collar while he turned his mind outward and let the city drown his fears with its conflicting smells and voices. The stink of Russian petrol, tobacco, cheap scent and river water—hullo! Two more days here I shan't know I'm smelling you. The sporadic cavalry charges of the commuter cars—hullo! The belching brown lorries thundering through the pot-holes in pursuit. The eerie emptiness between. The limousines with their blackened windows, the unmarked buildings splitting before their time—are you a block of offices, a barracks or a school? The dough-faced boys smoking in the doorways, waiting. The chauffeurs, reading newspapers in their parked cars, waiting. The unspeaking group of solemn men in hats, staring at a closed door, waiting.

Why did it always draw me? he wondered, contemplating his life in the past tense, which had recently become his habit. Why did I keep coming back here? He was feeling high and bright, he couldn't help it. He was not used to fear.

Because of their making do, he decided. Because they can rough it better than we can. Because of their love of anarchy and their terror of chaos, and the tension in between.

Because God always found excuses not to come here.

Because of their universal ignorance, and the brilliance that bursts through it. Because of their sense of humour, as good as ours and better.

Because they are the last great frontier in an over-discovered world. Because they try so hard to be like us and start from so far back.

Because of the huge heart beating inside the huge shambles. Because the shambles is my own.

I shall come at perhaps-eight-fifteen, she had said. What had he heard in her voice? Guardedness? Guarding whom? Herself? Him? Me? In our profession, the couriers are the message.

Look outwards, Barley told himself. Outwards is the only place to be.

From the metro a group of teenage girls in cotton frocks and boys in denim jackets trotted purposefully to work or instruction, their glum expressions switching to laughter at a word. Spotting the foreigner they studied him with cool glances —his rounded, pop-eye spectacles, his shabby handmade shoes, his old imperialist suit. In Moscow, if nowhere else, Barley Blair observed the bourgeois proprieties of dress.

Joining the stream he let it carry him, not caring which way he went. By contrast with his determinedly contented mood the early food queues had a restless and unsettled look. The grim-suited labour heroes and war veterans, their breastplates of medals jingling in the sunlight as they waded through the crowds, had an air of being late for wherever they were marching. Even their sloth seemed to have an air of protest. In the new climate, doing nothing was itself an act of opposition. Because by doing nothing we change nothing. And by changing nothing we hang on to what we understand, even if it is the bars of our own jail.

I shall come at perhaps-eight-fifteen.

Reaching the wide river Barley again dawdled. On the far bank the fairytale domes of the Kremlin lifted into a cloudless heaven. A Jerusalem with its tongue pulled out, he thought. So many towers, scarcely a bell. So many churches, barely a spoken prayer.

Hearing a voice close beside him he swung round too sharply and discovered an old couple in their best clothes asking him the way to somewhere. But Barley of the perfect memory had few words of Russian. It was a music he had listened to often without summoning the nerve to penetrate its mysteries.

He laughed and made an apologetic face. "Don't speak it, old boy. I'm an imperialist hyena. English!"

The old man grasped his wrist in friendship.

In every foreign city he had ever been, strangers asked him the way to places he didn't know in languages he didn't understand. Only in Moscow did they bless him for his ignorance.

He retraced his steps, pausing at unswept windows, pretending to examine what they offered. Painted wooden dolls. Who for? Dusty tins of fruit, or were they fish? Battered packets hanging from red string, contents a mystery, perhaps pekoes. Jars of pickled medical samples, lit by ten-watt bulbs. He was approaching his hotel again. A drunk-eyed peasant woman pushed a bunch of dying tulips at him, wrapped in newspaper.

"Awfully kind of you," he cried and, rummaging through his pockets, found among the junk a rouble note.

A green Lada was parked outside the hotel entrance, the radiator smashed. A hand-inked card in the windscreen said VAAP. The driver was leaning over the bonnet detaching the wiper blades as a precaution against theft.

"Scott Blair?" Barley asked him. "You looking for me?" The driver paid him not the slightest attention but continued with his work. "Blair?" said Barley. "Scott?"

"Those for me, dear?" Wicklow enquired, coming up behind him. "You're fine," he added quietly. "Clean as a whistle."

Wicklow will watch your back for you, Ned had said. Wicklow, if anybody, will know whether you're being followed. Wicklow and who else? Barley wondered. Last night, as soon as they had checked in to the hotel, Wicklow had vanished until after midnight, and as Barley had put himself to bed he had seen him from his window, standing in the street talking to two young men in jeans.

They got into the car. Barley tossed the tulips on to the back ledge. Wicklow sat in the front seat chatting cheerily to the driver in his perfect Russian. The driver let out a great bellow of laughter. Wicklow laughed too.

"Want to share it?" Barley asked.

Wicklow was already doing so. "I asked him whether he'd like to drive the Queen when she came here on her State visit. There's a saying here. If you steal, steal a million. If you screw, screw a queen."

Barley lowered his window and tapped out a tune on the sill. Life was a romp till perhaps-eight-fifteen.

"Barley! Welcome to Barbary, my dear chap. For God's sake, man, don't shake hands with me across the threshold, we have enough troubles as it is! You look positively healthy," Alik Zapadny complained in alarm when they had time to examine each other. "Why have you no hangover, may I ask? Are you in love, Barley? Are you divorced again? What have you been up to that you require to confess to me?"

Zapadny's drawn face examined him with desperate intelligence, the shadows of confinement stamped for ever in his hollowed cheeks. When Barley had first known him, Zapadny had been a dubious translator in disgrace working under other names. Now he was a dubious hero of the Reconstruction, dressed in a larger man's white collar and black suit.

"I've heard the Voice, Alik," Barley explained, with a rush of the old fondness as he slipped him a bunch of back-numbers of the *Times* wrapped in brown paper. "In bed with a good book every night at ten. Meet Len Wicklow, our Russian specialist. Knows more about you than you do, don't we, Leonard Carl?"

"Well, thank God somebody does!" Zapadny protested, careful not to acknowledge the gift. "We are becoming so unsure of ourselves these days, now that our great Russian mystery is being held up to public view. How much do you know about your new boss, by the way, Mr. Wicklow? Have you heard, for instance, how he undertook the re-education of the Soviet Union single-handed? Oh yes. He had a charming vision of a hundred million under-educated Soviet workers longing to improve themselves in their leisure. He was going to sell them a great range of titles about how to teach themselves Greek and trigonometry and basic housekeeping. We had to explain to him that the Soviet man-in-the-street regards himself as finite and in his leisure hours he is drunk. Do you know what we bought from him instead to keep him happy? A golf book! You would not imagine how many of our worthy citizens are fascinated by your capitalist golf." And in haste, still a dangerous joke —"Not that we have any capitalists *here*. Oh my God, no."

They sat ten strong at a yellow table under an icon of Lenin made in wood veneers. Zapadny was the speaker, the others were listeners and smokers. Not one of them, so far as Barley knew, was competent to sign a contract or approve a deal.

"Now, Barley, what is this total nonsense you are putting about that you have come here in order to buy Soviet books, please?" Zapadny demanded by way of opening courtesies, lifting his hooped eyebrows and placing the tips of his fingers together like Sherlock Holmes. "You British *never* buy our books. You make us buy yours instead. Besides, you are broke, or so our friends from London tell us. A. & B. are living off God's good air and Scotch whisky, they say. Personally I consider that an excellent diet. But why have you come? I think you only wanted an excuse to visit us again."

Time was passing. The yellow table floated in the sunbeams. A pall of cigarette smoke floated over it. Black-and-white images of Katya in photographic form came and went in Barley's mind. The Devil is every girl's cover story. They drank tea out of pretty Leningrad cups. Zapadny was delivering his standard caveat against trying to make deals directly with Soviet publishers, selecting Wicklow as his audience: the day-and-night war between VAAP and the rest of the world was evidently raging well. Two pale men wandered in to listen and wandered out again. Wicklow was earning favour by handing round blue Gauloises.

"We've had an injection of capital, Alik," Barley heard himself explaining from a long way off. "Times have changed. Russia's top of the pops these days. I've only got to tell the money boys I'm building up a Russian list and they come rushing after me as fast as their short fat legs will carry them."

"But, Barley, these *boys,* as you call them, can grow into *men* very quickly," Zapadny, the great sophisticate, warned to a fresh burst of docile laughter. "Particularly when they are wishing to be repaid, I would say."

"It's the way I described it in my telex, Alik. Maybe you haven't had time to read it," said Barley, showing a little muscle. "If things work out as we plan, A. & B. will be launching a brand-new imprint devoted entirely to things Russian within the year. Fiction, non-fiction, poetry, juveniles, the sciences. We've got a new line in popular medicine, all paperback. The subjects travel, so do the reputations of the authors. We'd like real Soviet doctors and scientists to contribute. We don't want sheep farming in Outer Mongolia or fish farming in the Arctic Circle but if you have sensible subjects you want to suggest we're here to listen and buy. We'll announce our list at the next Moscow book fair, and if things go well we'll bring out our first six titles next spring."

"And have you, forgive me, a sales force these days, Barley, or are you relying on divine intervention as before?" Zapadny enquired with his showy delicacy.

Resisting the temptation to tell Zapadny to watch his manners, Barley struggled on. "We're negotiating a distribution deal with several major publishers and we'll make an announcement soon. Except for fiction. For the fiction we'll use our own expanded team," he said, unable to remember for the life of him why they had settled on this bizarre arrangement or indeed whether they had.

"Fiction is still the A. & B. flagship, sir," Wicklow explained devoutly, helping Barley out.

"Fiction should *always* be one's flagship," Zapadny corrected him. "I would say that the novel is the greatest of all marathons. That is only my personal opinion, naturally. It is the highest form of art. Higher than poetry, higher than the short story. But please don't quote me."

"Well, it is for us literary superpowers, sir, put it that way," said Wicklow smarmily.

Very gratified, Zapadny turned to Barley. "On fiction, we should like in this special case to provide our own translator and take a further five percent royalty on the translation," he said.

"No problem," Barley said genially in his sleep. "These days, that's the kind of money A. & B. puts under the plate."

But to Barley's amazement Wicklow briskly intervened: "Excuse me, sir, that means a double royalty. I don't think we can swallow that and live. You must have misheard what Mr. Zapadny was saying."

"He's right," said Barley, sitting up sharply. "How the hell can we afford another five percent?"

Feeling like a conjuror who is proceeding to his next bogus act, Barley fished a folder from his briefcase and scattered half a dozen copies of a glossy prospectus at the sunbeams. "Our American connection is described on page two," he announced. "Potomac Boston is our partner in the project, A. & B. to buy full English-language rights in any Soviet work, and sell off North America to Potomac. They have a sister company in Toronto, so we'll throw in Canada. Right, Wickers?"

"Yes, sir."

How the hell did Wicklow learn all this junk so quickly? Barley thought.

Zapadny was still studying the prospectus, turning one stiff, immaculate page after another. "Did *you* print this shit, Barley?" he enquired politely.

"Potomac did," said Barley.

"But the Potomac River is so far from the city of Boston," Zapadny objected, airing his knowledge of American geography for the few who shared it. "Unless they have recently moved it, it is in Washington. What mutual attraction can they have, I ask myself, the city of Boston and this river? Are we speaking of an *old* company, Barley, or a *new* one?"

"New in the field. Old in business. They're merchants, ex-Washington now in Boston. Venture capital. Diversified portfolio. Film production, carparks, slot machines, call-girls and cocaine. All the usual. Publishing's just one of their sidelines."

But in his mind's ear as the laughter rose it was Ned who was doing the talking. "Congratulations, Barley. Bob here has come up with a wealthy Boston chum who's willing to take you on as a partner. All you have to do is spend his money."

And Bob, with his flat-iron feet and tweedy jacket, smiling the buyer's smile.

Eleven-thirty. Eight hours and forty-five minutes until perhaps-eight-fifteen.

"The driver wants to know what to expect when he meets the Queen," Wicklow was yelling enthusiastically over the back of his seat. "It's really getting to him. Does she take bribes? Does she have people executed for small offences? How does it feel to live in a country ruled by two fierce women?"

"Tell him it's exhausting but we're equal to it," Barley said with a huge yawn. And having refreshed himself with a nip from his flask he leaned back in the cushions and woke to find himself following Wicklow down a prison corridor. Except that instead of the cries of the incarcerated, it was the whistle of a tea kettle that he heard and the clicking of an abacus echoing through the gloom. A moment later, Wicklow and Barley are standing in the offices of a British railway company, vintage 1935. Flyblown light bulbs and defunct electric fans dangle from the cast-iron rafters. Amazons in headscarves preside over antiquated Cyrillic typewriters large as ovens. Ledgers cram the dusty shelves. Stacks of shoe boxes stuffed with buff folders rise from the floorboards to the sills.

"Barley! Jesus! Welcome to Prometheus Unbound! They tell me you got some money finally. Who gave it you?" yells a middle-aged figure in Fidel Castro battle gear leaping at them through the clutter. "We deal direct, okay? To hell with those arseholes in VAAP?"

"Yuri, marvellous to see you! Meet Len Wicklow, our Russian-speaking editor."

"You a spy?"

"Only in my spare time, sir."

"Jesus! Nice chap! Reminds me of my kid brother."

They are in Madison Avenue. Venetian blinds, wall charts and armchairs. Yuri is fat, exuberant and Jewish. Barley has brought him a bottle of Black Label and tights for his beautiful new wife. Tossing away the whisky cap, Yuri insists on pouring tots into the teacups. They enter the Russian ether. Talk of Bulgakov, Platonov, Akhmatova. Will Solzhenitsyn be permitted? Will Brodsky? Talk of a ragtag list of contemporary British writers who have arbitrarily found official favour and therefore fame in Russia. Barley has not heard of some, loathes others. Gusts of laughter, toasts, news of English friends, death to the arseholes in VAAP. Russia is changing by the hour, has Barley heard? Did he see that piece in *Moscow News* last Thursday about the neo-Fascist crazies in Pamyat, with their way-out nationalism and their anti-Semitism and their anti-everyone except themselves? And how about that piece in *Ogonyok* about Sigmund Freud? And *Novy Mir*'s stand on Nabokov? Editors, designers, translators proliferate in the usual amazing numbers, but no Katyas. Everyone is drunk, even those who have declined the alcohol. A great writer named Misha is presented and seated where his audience can watch him.

"Misha hasn't been to prison yet," Yuri explains apologetically, to huge laughter. "But maybe if he's lucky, they'll send him before it's too late, so that he can get published in the West!"

They talk the latest Soviet masterpieces of fiction. Yuri has chosen a mere eight from his own list—every one of them a sure bestseller, Barley. Publish them and you will be able to open a Swiss bank account for me. A hunt for plastic carrier bags before Wicklow takes charge of the carbon copies of eight unpublishable manuscripts, for this is a world in which the photocopier and electric typewriter are still the forbidden instruments of sedition.

They talk theatre and Afghanistan. Soon we shall all meet in London! Yuri cries, like a mad gambler staking all. "I send you my son, okay? Will you send me yours? Listen, we exchange hostages and that way nobody bombs each other!"

Everyone falls silent when Barley speaks, and stays silent for Misha the great writer. Wicklow translates while Yuri and three others object to Wicklow's translation. Misha objects to the objections. The downturn has begun.

Somebody demands to know why Britain is still run by the Fascist Conservative

Party. Why doesn't the proletariat kick the bastards out? Barley offers something unoriginal about democracy being the worst of systems except for the others. No one laughs. Perhaps they have heard it, perhaps they don't like it. In the wake of the whisky it is time to get out while the smiles are still fading. How can the English preach human rights, somebody sullenly demands, when they are enslaving the Irish and the Scots? Why do you support the disgusting government in South Africa? yells a ninety-year-old blonde in a ball-dress. I don't, says Barley. I truly don't.

"Listen," says Yuri, at the door. "Stay away from that bastard Zapadny, okay? I don't say he's KGB. All I say is, he needed some damn good friends to get him back into circulation. You're a nice fellow. Know what I mean?"

They have already embraced many times.

"Yuri," says Barley. "My old mother brought me up to believe that all of you were KGB."

"Me too?"

"You specially. She said you were the worst."

"I love you. Hear me? Send me your son. What's his name?"

One-thirty and they are an hour late for their next step along the hard road to perhaps-eight-fifteen.

Dark timber, splendid food, respectful menials, the atmosphere of a baronial hunting lodge. They are sitting at the long table below the balcony in the Writers' Union, Alik Zapadny once again presiding. Several promising young writers of sixty stroll over, listen and stroll away again, taking their great thoughts with them. Zapadny points out those recently released from prison and those who he hopes will soon replace them. Literary bureaucrats pull up chairs and practise their English. Wicklow interprets, Barley sparkles, all on fruit juice and the residue of Black Label. The world is going to be a better place, Barley assures Zapadny, as if he were an expert on the world.

Rashly he quotes Zinoviev. "When will it all end? When people stop queuing for the Tomb?"—a reference to Lenin's mausoleum.

The applause this time is not so deafening.

At two o'clock in conformity with the new drinking laws and in the nick of time, the waiter brings a carafe of wine, and Zapadny in Barley's honour extracts a bottle of pepper vodka from his worm-eaten briefcase.

"Did Yuri tell you I was KGB?" he asks mournfully.

"Of course he didn't," says Barley stoutly.

"Please do not regard yourself as singled out. He tells it to all Westerners. As a matter of fact, I sometimes worry a little bit about Yuri. He's a nice fellow but everyone knows he is a lousy publisher, so how does a Jew like him get his position? His little boy was christened at Zagorsk last week. How do you explain this?"

"It's not my problem, Alik. Live and let live. Finito." And aside: "Wickers, get me out of here, I'm getting sober."

By six, after two more enormously eloquent meetings, and having miraculously succeeded in declining half a dozen invitations for the evening, Barley is back in his hotel room, fighting with the shower to sober up while Wicklow shouts cheerful publishing talk at him through the door for the benefit of the microphones. For Wicklow has Ned's orders to stay with Barley till the last moment in case he gets stage fright or fluffs his lines.

7

The Odessa Hotel in that third year of the Great Soviet Reconstruction was not the jewel of Moscow's rugged tourist trade but it was not the worst piece either. It was dilapidated, it was down-at-heel, it was selective in its favours. Tied to the rouble rather than to the dollar, it lacked such refinements as foreign-currency bars and groups of travel-weary Minnesotans appealing tearfully for their missing luggage. It was so ill-lit that the brass lamps and blackamoors and galleried dining room recalled the bad old past at the point of its collapse rather than the Socialist phoenix rising from the ashes. And when you stepped from the juddering lift and braved the frown of your floor concierge, crouching in her box surrounded by blackened room-keys and mossy telephones, you were quite likely to have the sensation of being returned to the vilest institutions of your youth.

But then the Reconstruction was not yet a visual medium. It was strictly in the audio stage.

Nevertheless, for those who looked for it, the Odessa in those days had soul, and with luck has it still. The good ladies of reception keep a kindly heart behind their iron stares; the porters have been known to wink you to the lift without demanding to see your hotel pass for the fifth time in one day. The restaurant manager, given the right encouragement, will usher you graciously to your alcove and likes a good face in return. And in the evenings between six and nine the lobby becomes an impromptu pageant of the hundred nations of the Empire. Smartly dressed administrators from Tashkent, flaxen schoolteachers from Estonia, fiery-eyed Party functionaries from Turkmenia and Georgia, factory managers from Kiev, naval engineers from Archangel—not to mention Cubans, Afghans, Poles, Roumanians and a platoon of dowdily arrogant East Germans—pour out of their airport charabancs and descend from the sunlight of the street into the quelling darkness of the lobby in order to pay their homage to Rome and shift their luggage in metric stages towards the tribune.

And Barley, himself a reluctant emissary though from a different empire, that evening took his place among them.

First he sat, only to have an old lady thump him on the shoulder and demand his seat. Then he hovered in an alcove near the lift until he risked being walled in by a rampart of cardboard suitcases and brown parcels. Finally he removed himself to the protection of a central pillar and there he remained, apologising to everyone, watching the glass door turn off and on and shuffling out of everybody's light, then into it again, while he brandished Jane Austen's *Emma* at his chest and in his other hand a lurid carrier bag from Heathrow airport.

It was a good thing that Katya arrived to save him.

There was no secret to their meeting, nothing secretive in their behaviour. Each caught the other's eyes at the same instant, while Katya was still being buffeted through the door. Barley threw up an arm, waving Jane Austen.

"Hullo, it's me. Blair. Jolly good!" he yelled.

Katya vanished and reappeared victorious. Did she hear him? She smiled anyway and lifted her eyes to Heaven in mute show, making excuses for her lateness. She shoved back a lock of black hair and Barley saw Landau's wedding and betrothal rings.

"You should have seen me trying to get away," she was signalling across the heads. Or: "Couldn't get a cab for love nor money."

"Doesn't matter a bit," Barley was signalling back.

Then she cut him dead while she scowled and rummaged in her handbag for her identity card to show to the plainclothes boy, whose agreeable job that night was to challenge all attractive ladies entering the hotel. It was a red card that she produced so Barley divined the Writers' Union.

Then Barley himself was distracted while he tried in his passable, if clotted, French to explain to a tall Palestinian that no, he was afraid he was *not* a member of the Peace Group, old boy, and alas *not* the manager of the hotel either, and he doubted very much whether there was one.

Wicklow, who had observed these events from halfway up the staircase, reported later that he had never seen an overt encounter better done.

As actors Barley and Katya were dressed for different plays: Katya for high drama in her blue dress and old lace collar that had so taken Landau's fancy; and Barley for low English comedy in a pinstripe suit of his father's that was too short for him in the sleeve, and a pair of very scuffed buckskin boots by Ducker's of Oxford that only a collector of bygones could have regarded as still splendid.

When they met they surprised each other. After all, they were still strangers, closer to the forces that had brought them here than to one another. Discarding the impulse to give her a formal peck on the cheek, Barley found himself instead puzzling over her eyes, which were not only very dark and full of light at the same time but heavily fringed, so that he couldn't help wondering whether she was endowed with a double set of eyelashes.

And since Barley on his side wore that indefinably foolish expression which overcomes certain Englishmen in the presence of beautiful women, it was Katya's suspicion that her first instinct on the telephone had been right and he was haughty.

Meanwhile they were standing close enough to feel the warmth of each other's bodies and for Barley to smell her make-up. The babel of foreign languages continued round them.

"You are Mr. Barley, I think," she told him breathlessly and laid a hand along his forearm, for she had a way of touching people as if seeking to assure herself that they were real.

"Yes indeed, the same, hullo, well done, and you're Katya Orlova, Niki's friend. Wonderful you could make it. Masterpiece of timing. How are you?"

Photographs don't lie but they don't tell the truth either, Barley was thinking, watching her breast rise and fall with her breathing. They don't catch the glow of a girl who looks as though she's just witnessed a miracle and you're the person she's chosen to tell first.

The restless crowd in the lobby brought him to his senses. No two people, however purposefully united, could have survived for long exchanging pleasantries in the centre of that turmoil.

"Tell you what," he said, as if he had had a bright idea on the spur of the moment. "Why don't I buy you a bun? Niki was determined I should make a fuss of you. You met each other at that fair, he tells me. What a character. Heart of gold," he continued cheerfully as he led her towards the staircase and a sign that read BUFFET. "Salt of the earth. A pain in the neck as well, of course, but who isn't?"

"Oh Mr. Landau is a *very* kind man," she said, speaking much as Barley was for the benefit of an unidentified audience, but sounding very persuasive nevertheless.

"And reliable," Barley called approvingly as they gained the first-floor landing. Now Barley too was for some reason out of breath. "Ask Niki to do a thing, he does it. In his own way, it's true. But he does it and keeps his thoughts to himself. I always think that's a sign of a good friend, don't you?"

"I would say that without discretion there can be no friendship," she replied as if quoting from a marriage book. "True friendship must be based on mutual trust."

And Barley while responding warmly to such profundity could not fail to recognise the similarity of her cadences to those of Goethe.

In a curtained area stood a thirty-foot food counter with a single tray of sugar biscuits on it. Behind it three bulky ladies in white uniforms and helmets of transparent plastic had mounted guard over a regimental samovar while they argued among themselves.

"Sound judge of a book too, in his own way, old Niki," Barley observed, stretching out the topic as they took up their places before the rope barrier. *"Bête intellectuelle,* as the French say. Tea, please, ladies. Marvellous."

The ladies went on haranguing each other. Katya stared at them with no expression on her face. Suddenly to Barley's astonishment she drew out her red pass and snarled—there was no other word for it—with the result that one of them detached herself from her companions long enough to yank two cups from a rack and slap them viciously on two saucers as if she were breech-loading an old rifle. Still furious, she filled a huge kettle. And having with further signs of rage unearthed a modern box of matches, she turned up a gas ring and dumped the kettle on it before returning to her comrades.

"Care for a biscuit?" Barley asked. *"Foie gras?"*

"Thank you. I ate cake already at the reception."

"Oh my God. Good cake?"

"It was not very interesting."

"But nice Hungarians?"

"The speeches were not significant. I would say they were banal. I blame our Soviet side for this. We are not sufficiently relaxed with foreigners even when they are from Socialist countries."

Both for a moment had run out of lines. Barley was remembering a girl he had known at university, a general's daughter with skin like rose petals who lived only for the rights of animals until she hurriedly married a groom from the local hunt. Katya was staring gloomily into the further end of the room where a dozen stand-up tables were placed in strict lines. At one of them stood Leonard Wicklow sharing a joke with a young man his own age. At another an elderly *Rittmeister* in riding boots was drinking lemonade with a girl in jeans and throwing out his arms as if to describe his lost estates.

"Can't think why I didn't offer you dinner," Barley said, meeting her eyes again with the feeling of falling straight into them. "One doesn't want to be too forward, I suppose. Not unless one can get away with it."

"It would not have been convenient," she replied, frowning.

The kettle began chugging but the war-hardened women of the buffet kept their backs to it.

"Always so difficult, performing on the telephone, don't you think?" Barley said, for small talk. "Addressing oneself to a sort of plastic flower, I mean, instead of a human face. Hate the beastly thing personally, don't you?"

"Hate what, please?"

"The telephone. Talking at a distance." The kettle began spitting on the gas. "You get the silliest ideas about people when you can't see them."

Jump, he told himself. *Now.*

"I was saying the very same thing to a publishing friend of mine only the other day," he went on, at the same jolly, conversational level. "We were discussing a new novel someone sent me. I'd shown it to him, strictly confidentially, and he was absolutely knocked out by it. Said it was the best thing he'd seen for years. Dynamite, in fact." Her eyes fixed on his own and they were scaringly direct. "But so *odd* not to have any sort of picture of the writer," he continued airily. "I don't even know the chap's name. Let alone where he gets all his information from, learnt his craft and so forth. Know what I mean? Like hearing a bit of music and not being sure whether it's Brahms or Cole Porter."

She was frowning. She had drawn in her lips and seemed to be moistening them inside her mouth. "I do not regard such personal questions as appropriate to an artist. Some writers can work only in obscurity. Talent is talent. It does not require explanations."

"Well I wasn't talking so much about explanations, you see, as about authenticity," Barley explained. A path of down followed the line of her cheekbone but unlike the hair on her head it was gold. "I mean, *you* know publishing. If a fellow's written a novel about the hill tribes of Northern Burma, for instance, one's entitled to ask whether he's ever been south of Minsk. Specially if it's a really important novel, which this one is. A potential world-beater, according to my chum. In a case like that, I reckon you're entitled to insist that the writer should stand up and declare his qualifications."

Bolder than the others, the senior lady was pouring boiling water into the samovar. A second was unlocking the regimental cash box. A third was scooping rations of tea into a handscale. Searching in his pockets Barley came up with a three-rouble note. At the sight of it the woman at the cash box broke into a despairing tirade.

"I expect she wants change," Barley said stupidly. "Don't we all?"

Then he saw that Katya had put thirty kopeks on the counter and that she had two very small dimples when she smiled. He took the books and bag. She followed him with the teacups on a tray. But as they reached their table she addressed him with an expression of challenge.

"If an author is obliged to prove that he is saying the truth, so also is his publisher," she said.

"Oh, I'm for honesty on all sides. The more people put their cards on the table, the better off we'll *all* be."

"I am informed that the author was inspired by a Russian poet."

"Pecherin," Barley replied. "Looked him up. Born 1807 in Dymerka, province of Kiev."

Her lips were near the brim of her cup, her eyes down. And though he had plenty of other things on his mind, Barley noticed that her right ear, protruding from her hair, had become transparent in the evening light from the window.

"The author was also inspired by certain opinions of an Englishman concerning world peace," she said with the utmost severity.

"Do you think he would like to meet that Englishman again?"

"This can be established. It is not known."

"Well the Englishman would like to meet *him*," said Barley. "They've got an awful lot to say to each other. Where do you live?"

"With my children."

"Where are your children?"

A pause while Barley again had the uncomfortable sensation of having offended against some unfamiliar ethic.

"We live close to the Aeroport metro station. There is no airport there any more. There are apartments. How long are you staying in Moscow, please, Mr. Barley?"

"A week. Any address for your apartment?"

"It is not convenient. You are staying all the time here at the Hotel Odessa?"

"Unless they chuck me out. What does your husband do?"

"It is not important."

"Is he in publishing?"

"No."

"Is he a writer?"

"No."

"So what is he? A composer? A frontier guard? A cook? How does he maintain you in the style to which you are accustomed?"

He had made her laugh again, which seemed to please her as much as it did him. "He was manager of a timber concern," she said.

"What's he manager of now?"

"His factory prefabricates houses for rural areas. We are divorced, like everyone else in Moscow."

"What are the kids? Boys? Girls? How old?"

And that put an end to laughter. For a moment he thought she would walk out on him. Her head lifted, her face closed and an angry fire filled her eyes. "I have a boy and a girl. They are twins, eight years old. It is not relevant."

"You speak beautiful English. Better than I do. It's like well water."

"Thank you, I have a natural comprehension of foreign languages."

"It's better than that. It's unearthly. It's as if English had stopped at Jane Austen. Where did you learn it?"

"In Leningrad. I was at school there. English is also my passion."

"Where were you at university?"

"Also in Leningrad."

"When did you come to Moscow?"

"When I married."

"How did you meet him?"

"My husband and I knew each other from childhood. While we were at school, we attended summer camps together."

"Did you catch fish?"

"Also rabbits," she said as her smile came back again to light the whole room. "Volodya is a Siberian boy. He knows how to sleep in the snow, skin a rabbit and catch fish through the ice. At the time I married him I was in retreat from intellectual values. I thought the most important thing a man could know was how to skin a rabbit."

"I was *really* wondering how you met the author," Barley explained.

He watched her wrestle with her indecision, noticing how readily her eyes reflected her changing emotions, now coming to him, now retreating. Until he lost her altogether as she stooped below the level of the table, pushed away her flying hair and picked up her handbag. "Please thank Mr. Landau for the books and the tea," she said. "I shall thank him myself next time he comes to Moscow."

"Don't go. Please. I need your advice." He lowered his voice and it was suddenly very serious. "I need your instructions about what to do with that crazy manuscript. I can't fly solo. Who wrote it? Who's Goethe?"

"Unfortunately I have to return to my children."

"Isn't somebody looking after them?"

"Naturally."

"Ring up. Say you're running late. Say you've met a fascinating man who wants to talk literature to you all night. We've hardly met. I need time. I've got masses of questions for you."

Gathering up the volumes of Jane Austen she started towards the door. And like a persistent salesman Barley stumbled at her side.

"Please," he said. "Look. I'm a lousy English publisher with about ten thousand enormously serious things to discuss with a beautiful Russian woman. I don't bite, I don't lie. Have dinner with me."

"It is not convenient."

"Is another night convenient? What do I do? Burn joss? Put a candle in my window? You're what I came here for. Help me to help you."

His appeal had confused her.

"Can I have your home number?" he insisted.

"It is not convenient," she muttered.

They were descending the wide staircase. Glancing at the sea of heads Barley saw Wicklow and his friend among them. He grasped Katya's arm, not fiercely but nevertheless causing her to stand still.

"When?" he said.

He was still holding her arm at the bicep, just above the inside of the elbow where it was firmest and most full.

"Perhaps I shall call you late tonight," she replied, relenting.

"Not perhaps."

"I shall call you."

Remaining on the stair he watched her approach the edge of the crowd, then seem to take a breath before spreading her arms and barging her way to the door. He was sweating. A damp shawl hung over his back and shoulders. He wanted a drink. Above all he wanted to get rid of the microphone harness. He wanted to smash it into very small pieces and trample on them and send them registered and personal to Ned.

Wicklow, with his crooked nose, was skipping up the stairs at him, grinning like a thief and talking some bilge about a Soviet biography of Bernard Shaw.

She walked quickly, looking for a taxi but needing movement. Clouds had gathered and there were no stars, just the wide streets and the glow of arc-lights from Petrovka. She needed distance from him and from herself. A panic born not of fear but of a violent aversion was threatening to seize hold of her. He should not have mentioned the twins. He had no right to knock down the paper walls between one life and another. He should not pester her with bureaucratic questions. She had trusted him: why did he not trust her?

She turned a corner and kept walking. He is a typical imperialist, false, importunate and untrusting. A taxi passed, not heeding her. A second slowed down long enough to hear her call her destination, then sped away in search of a more lucrative assignment—to ferry whores, to carry furniture, to deliver black-market vegetables, meat and vodka, to work the tourist traps. The rain was beginning, big drops, well aimed.

His humour, so ill-placed. His inquisitions, so impertinent. I shall never go near him again. She should take the metro but dreaded the confinement. Attractive, naturally, as many Englishmen are. That graceful clumsiness. He was witty and without doubt sensitive. She had not expected him to come so close. Or perhaps it was she who went too close to him.

She kept walking, steadying herself, looking for a taxi. The rain fell harder. She pulled a folding umbrella from her bag and opened it. East German, a present from a short-lived lover she had not been proud of. Reaching a crossroads, she was about to step into the street when a boy in a blue Lada pulled up beside her. She had not hailed him.

"How's business, sister?"

Was he a taxi, was he a freebooter? She jumped in and gave her destination. The boy started to argue. The rain was thundering on the car roof.

"It's urgent," she said, and handed him two three-rouble notes. "It's urgent," she repeated and glanced at her watch, at the same time wondering whether glancing at watches was something people did when they were in a hurry to get to hospital.

The boy seemed to have taken her cause to heart. He was driving and talking at breakneck speed while the rain poured through his open window. His sick mother in Novgorod had fainted while picking apples from a ladder and woken up with both legs in plaster, he said. The windscreen was a torrent of gushing water. He had not stopped to attach the wipers.

"How is she now?" Katya asked, tying a scarf round her hair. A woman in a hurry to get to hospital does not exchange small talk about the plight of others, she thought.

The boy hauled the car to a halt. She saw the gates. The sky was calm again, the night warm and sweet-smelling. She wondered whether it had rained at all.

"Here," said the boy, holding out her three-rouble notes. "Next time, okay? What's your name? You like fresh fruit, coffee, vodka?"

"Keep it," she snapped, and pushed the money back at him.

The gates stood open, leading to what could have been an office block with a few lights dimly burning. A flight of stone steps, half-buried in mud and rubbish, rose to an overhead walkway. The walkway led across a sliproad. Looking down, Katya saw parked ambulances, their blue lights lazily rotating, drivers and attendants smoking in a group. At their feet lay a woman on a stretcher, her smashed face wrenched to one side as if to escape a second blow.

He took care of me, she thought as her mind returned to Barley for a moment.

She hurried towards the grey block that rose ahead of her. A clinic designed by Dante and built by Franz Kafka, she remembered. The staff go there to steal medicines and sell them on the black market; the doctors are all moonlighting to feed their families, she remembered. A place for the lowlife and riffraff of our empire, for the luckless proletariat with neither the influence nor connections of the few. The voice in her head had a rhythm that marched with her as she strode confidently through the double doors. A woman snapped at her, and Katya, rather than show her card, handed her a rouble. The lobby echoed like a swimming pool. Behind a marble counter, more women ignored everyone except one another. An old man in blue uniform sat dozing in a chair, his open eyes staring at a defunct television set. She strode past him and entered a corridor lined with patients' beds. Last time there had been no beds in the corridor. Perhaps they cleared them out to make room for someone important. An exhausted trainee was giving blood to an old woman, assisted by a nurse in open overalls and jeans. Nobody groaned, nobody complained. Nobody asked why they must die in a corridor. An illuminated sign gave the first letters of the word "Emergency." She followed it. Look as though you own the place, he had advised her the first time. And it had worked. It still did.

The waiting-room was a discarded lecture hall lit like a night ward. On the platform, a matron with a saintly face sat at the head of a line of applicants as long as a retreating army. In the auditorium, the wretched of the earth growled and whispered in the twilight, nursed their children. Men with half-dressed injuries lay on benches. Drunks lolled and swore. The air stank of antiseptic, wine and old blood.

Ten minutes to wait. Yet again she found her mind slipping back to Barley. His straight familiar eyes, his air of hopeless valour. Why would I not give him my home telephone number? His hand on her arm as if it had been there for ever. "You're what I came here for." Selecting a broken bench near the rear door marked "Lavatories," she sat and peered ahead of her. You can die there and nobody will ask your name, he had said. There is the door, there is the alcove for the cloakroom, she rehearsed. Then there are the lavatories. The telephone is in the cloakroom but it is never used because nobody knows it is there. Nobody can get through to the hospital on the open line, but this line was put in for a bigwig doctor who wanted to keep in touch with his private patients and his mistress, until he got himself transferred. Some idiot installed it out of sight behind a pillar. It's been there ever since.

How do you know about such places? she had asked him. This entrance, this wing, this telephone, sit down and wait. How do you know?

I walk, he had replied, and she had had a vision of him striding the Moscow streets without sleep, food or herself, walking. I am the wandering Gentile, he had told her. I walk to keep company with my mind, I drink to hide from it. When I walk, you are beside me; I can see your face at my shoulder.

He will walk until he falls, she thought. And I shall follow him.

On the bench beside her a peasant woman in a saffron headscarf had begun to pray in Ukrainian. She was holding a small icon in both hands and bowing her head over it, deeper each time, till she was prodding her hairless forehead with the tin frame. Her eyes grew bright and as they closed, Katya saw tears come out from between the lids. In the blink of a star I shall look like you, she thought.

She remembered how he had told her about visiting a mortuary in Siberia, a factory for the dead, situated in one of the phantom cities where he worked. How the corpses came out of a chute and were passed around a carousel, male and female mixed, to be hosed and labelled and stripped of their gold by the old women of the night. Death is a secret like any other, he had told her; a secret is something that is revealed to one person at a time.

Why do you always try to educate me to the meaning of death? she had demanded of him, sickened. Because you have taught me how to live, he had replied.

The telephone is the safest in Russia, he had said. Even our lunatics in the security *Organs* would not think of tapping the unused telephone of an emergency hospital.

She remembered their last meeting in Moscow, in the deepest part of winter. He had picked up a slow train at a backwater station, a place with no name in the centre of nowhere. He had bought no ticket and travelled hard class, pushing ten roubles into the conductor's palm like everybody else. Our gallant competent *Organs* are so bourgeois these days they no longer know how to mix with the workers, he had said. She pictured him a waif in his thick underclothes, lying in semi-darkness on the top berth reserved for luggage, listening to the smokers' coughing and the grumble of the drunks, suffocating from the stink of humanity and the leaky water-heater while he stared at the appalling things he knew and never spoke of. What kind of hell must that be, she wondered, to be tormented by your own creations? To know that the absolute best you can do in your career is the absolute worst for mankind?

She saw herself waiting for him to arrive, bivouacked among the thousands of other waiting-wounded at the Kazansky railway station under the foul fluorescent lights. The train is delayed, is cancelled, is derailed, said the rumours. Heavy snowfalls all the way to Moscow. The train is arriving, it never started, I need never have bothered to tell so many lies. The station staff had poured formaldehyde into the lavatories and the whole concourse stank of it. She was wearing Volodya's fur hat because it hid more of her face. Her mohair scarf covered her chin, her sheepskin coat the rest of her. She had never known such desire for anyone. It was a heat and a hunger at once inside the fur.

When he stepped off the train and walked towards her through the slush, her body was stiff and embarrassed like a boy's. As she stood beside him in the crowded metro, she nearly screamed in the silence as he pressed against her. She had borrowed Alexandra's apartment. Alexandra had gone to the Ukraine with her husband. She unlocked the front door and made him go ahead. Sometimes he seemed not to know where he was or, after all her planning, not to care. Sometimes she was scared to touch him, he was too frail. But not today. Today she ran at him, grasped him with all her force, gathering him to her without skill or tenderness, punishing him for her months and nights of fruitless longing.

But he? He embraced her as her father used to, keeping his waist clear of her and his shoulders firm. And as she pulled away from him she knew that the time was past when he could bury his torment in her body.

You are the only religion I have, he whispered, kissing her brow with closed lips. Listen to me, Katya, while I tell you what I have decided to do.

The peasant woman was kneeling on the floor, loving her icon, pressing it to her breast and lips. Katya had to climb over her to reach the gangway. A pale young man in a leather jacket had sat himself at the end of the bench. He had one arm tucked into his shirt, so she supposed it was his wrist that was broken. His head had fallen forward and as she squeezed past him she noticed that his nose was broken too, though healed.

The alcove was in darkness. A broken light bulb dangled uselessly. A massive wooden counter barred her way to the cloakroom. She tried to lift the flap but it was too heavy so she wriggled under it. She was standing among empty coat-racks and hangers and uncollected hats. The pillar was a metre across. A handwritten sign said NO CHANGE GIVEN and she read it by the light of an opening and closing door. The telephone was in its usual place on the other side, but when she placed herself before it she could hardly see it in the dark.

She stared at it, willing it to ring. Her panic was over. She was strong again. Where are you? she wondered. In one of your postal numbers, one of your blurs on the map? In Kazakhstan? In the Middle Volga? In the Urals? He visited all of them, she knew. In the old days she had been able to tell by his complexion when he had been working outdoors. At other times he looked as though he had been underground for months. Where are you with your dreadful guilt? she wondered. Where are you with your terrifying decision? In a dark place like this? In a small-town telegraph office that is open round the clock? She imagined him arrested, the way she sometimes dreamed of him, trussed and white in a hut, tied to a wooden horse, scarcely bucking any more as they went on beating him. The phone was ringing. She lifted the receiver and heard a flat voice.

"This is Pyotr," he said, which was their code to protect each other—if I am in their hands, and they force me to call you, I shall tell them a different name so that you can hide.

"And this is Alina," she replied, amazed that she could speak at all. After that she didn't care. He's alive. He hasn't been arrested. They are not beating him. They have not tied him to a wooden horse. She felt lazy and bored. He was alive, he was speaking to her. Facts, no emotion, his voice at first remote and only half familiar. Backwards and forwards, only facts. Do this. He said this. I said this. Tell him I thank him for coming to Moscow. Tell him he is behaving like a reasonable human being. I am well. How are you?

She rang off, too weak to talk any more. She returned to the lecture hall and sat on a bench with the rest of them, reaching for breath, knowing nobody would care.

The boy in the leather jacket was still lounging on the bench. She noticed his bent nose again, perfect yet off-true. She remembered Barley again and was grateful for his existence.

He lay on his bed in his shirt-sleeves. His bedroom was an airless box hacked from a grand bedchamber and filled with the water-chorus of every Russian hotel, the snuffle of the taps, the trickle of the cistern from the tiny bathroom, the gulping of the huge black radiator, the groan of the refrigerator as it flung itself upon a fresh cycle of convulsions. He was sipping whisky from a toothmug, pretending to read by the useless bedlight. The telephone lay at his elbow, and beside the telephone lay his notebook for messages and great thoughts. Phones can be alive whether or not they're on their cradles, Ned had warned him. Not this one, it isn't, thought Barley. This one's dead as a dodo till she rings. He was reading wonderful García Márquez but the print was like barbed wire to him; he kept stumbling and having to go back.

A car went by in the street, then a pedestrian. Then it was the turn of the rain, cracking like tired shot against the window panes. Without a scream or a laugh or a cry of anger, Moscow had returned herself to the great spaces.

He remembered her eyes. What did they see in me? A relic, he decided. Dressed in my father's suit. A lousy actor concealed by his own performance, and behind the greasepaint nothing. She was looking for the conviction in me and saw instead the moral bankruptcy of my English class and time. She was looking for future hope and finding vestiges of a finished history. She was looking for connection and saw the notice on me saying RESERVED. So she took one look at me and ran.

Reserved for whom? For what great day or passion have I reserved myself?

He tried to imagine her body. With a face like that, who needs a body anyway?

He drank. She's courage. She's trouble. He drank again. Katya, if that's who you are, I am reserved for you.

If.

He wondered what else there was to know of her. Nothing except the truth. There had been an epoch, long forgotten, when he had mistaken beauty for intelligence, but Katya was so obviously intelligent there could be no problem this time of confusing the two qualities. There had been another epoch, God help him, when he had mistaken beauty for virtue. But in Katya he had sensed such iridescent virtue that if she were to pop her head round the door at this moment and tell him she had just murdered her children, he would instantly find six ways of assuring her she was not to blame.

If.

He took another pull of Scotch and with a jolt remembered Andy.

Andy Macready, trumpeter, lying in hospital with his head cut off. Thyroid, said his missus vaguely. When they'd first discovered it, Andy didn't want the surgery. He'd prefer to take the long swim and not come back, he said, so they got drunk together and planned the trip to Capri, one last great meal, a gallon of red and the long swim to nowhere through the filthy Mediterranean. But when the thyroid really got to him Andy discovered he preferred life to death, so he voted for the surgery instead. And they cut his head off his body, all but the vertebrae, and kept him going on tubes. So Andy was alive still, with nothing to live for and nothing to die of, cursing that he hadn't done the swim in time, and trying to find a meaning for himself that death wouldn't take away.

Phone Andy's missus, he thought. Ask her how her old man is. He peered at his watch, calculating what time it was in the real or unreal world of Mrs. Macready. His hand started for the phone but didn't pick it up in case it rang.

He thought of his daughter Anthea. Good old Ant.

He thought of his son Hal in the City. Sorry I screwed it up for you, Hal, but you've still got a bit of time left to get it right.

He thought of his flat in Lisbon and the girl crying her heart out, and he wondered with a shudder what had become of her. He thought of his other women, but his guilts weren't quite up to their usual, so he wondered about that too. He thought of Katya again and realised he had been thinking of her all the time.

A tap at the door. She has come to me. She is wearing a simple housecoat and is naked underneath. Barley, she whispers, darling. Will you still love me afterwards?

She does nothing of the kind. She has no precedent and no sequel. She is not part of the familiar, well-thumbed series.

It was Wicklow, his guardian angel, checking on his ward.

"Come on in, Wickers. Care for a spot?"

Wicklow raised his eyebrows, asking has she phoned? He was wearing a leather jacket and there were drops of rain on it. Barley shook his head. Wicklow poured himself a glass of mineral water.

"I've been running through some of the books they pushed at us today, sir," he said, in the fancy tone they both adopted for the microphones. "I wondered whether you'd like an update on some of the non-fiction titles."

"Wickers, date me up," said Barley hospitably, stretching himself on the bed again while Wicklow took the chair.

"Well there is just *one* of their submissions I'd like to share with you, sir. It's that fitness handbook on dieting and exercises. I think we might consider it for one of our co-production splashes. I wondered whether we could sign one of their top illustrators and raise the Russian impact level."

"Raise it. Sky's the limit."

"Well I'll have to ask Yuri first."

"Ask him."

Hiatus. Let's run that through again, thought Barley.

"Oh, by the way, sir. You were asking why so many Russians use the word 'convenient.' "

"Well now, so I was," said Barley, who had been asking nothing of the kind.

"The word they're thinking of is *udobno*. It means convenient but it also means proper, which must be a bit confusing sometimes. I mean it's one thing not to be convenient. It's another not to be proper."

"It is indeed," Barley agreed after long thought while he sipped his Scotch.

Then he must have dozed because the next thing he knew he was sitting bolt upright with the receiver to his ear and Wicklow standing over him. This was Russia, so she didn't say her name.

"Come round," he said.

"I am sorry to call so late. Do I disturb you?"

"Of course you do. All the time. That was a great cup of tea. Wish it could have lasted longer. Where are you?"

"You invited me for dinner tomorrow night, I think."

He was reaching for his notebook. Wicklow held it ready.

"Lunch, tea, dinner, all three of them," he said. "Where do I send the glass coach?" He scribbled down an address. "What's your home telephone number, by the way, in case I get lost or you do?" She gave him that too, reluctantly, a departure from principle, but she gave it all the same. Wicklow watched him write it all down, then softly left the room as they continued talking.

You never know, Barley thought, steadying his mind with another long pull of Scotch when he had rung off. With beautiful, intelligent, virtuous women, you simply never know where they stand. Is she pining for me, or am I a face in her crowd?

Then suddenly the Moscow fear hit him at gale force. It sprang out at him when he was least expecting it, after he had fought it off all day. The muffled terrors of the city burst thundering upon his ears and after them the piping voice of Walter.

"Is she really in touch with him? Did she invent the stuff herself? Is she in touch with someone different, and if so who?"

8

In the situation room in the basement of the Russia House the atmosphere was of a tense and permanent night air-raid. Ned sat at his command desk before a bank of telephones. Sometimes one winked and he spoke into it in terse monosyllables. Two female assistants softly put round the telegrams and cleared the out-trays. Two illuminated post-office clocks, one London time, one Moscow time, shone like twin moons from the end wall. In Moscow it was midnight. In London nine. Ned scarcely looked up as his head janitor unlocked the door to me.

It was the earliest I had been able to get away. I had spent the morning at the Treasury solicitors' and the afternoon with the lawyers from Cheltenham. Supper was helping to entertain a delegation of espiocrats from Sweden before they were packed off to the obligatory musical.

Walter and Bob were bowed over a Moscow street map. Brock was on the internal telephone to the cypher room. Ned was immersed in what seemed to be a lengthy inventory. He waved me to a chair and shoved a batch of incoming signals at me, scribbled messages from the front.

0954 hrs Barley has successfully telephoned Katya at October. They have made an appointment for 2015 at the Odessa tonight. More.

1320 hrs irregulars have followed Katya to number 14 so-and-so street. She posted a letter at what appears to be an empty house. Photographs to follow soonest by bag. More.

2018 hrs Katya has arrived at the Odessa Hotel. Barley and Katya are talking in the canteen. Wicklow and one irregular observing. More.

2105 hrs Katya departs Odessa. Summary of conversation to follow. Tapes to follow soonest by bag. More.

2200 hrs interim. Katya has promised to telephone Barley tonight. More.

2250 hrs Katya followed to the so-and-so hospital. Wicklow and one irregular covering. More.

2325 hrs Katya receives phone call on disused hospital telephone. Speaks three minutes twenty seconds. More.

And now suddenly, no more.

Spying is normality taken to extremes. Spying is waiting.

"Is Clive Without India receiving tonight?" Ned asked, as if my presence had reminded him of something.

I replied that Clive would be in his suite all evening. He had been locked up in the American Embassy all day, and he had told me he proposed to be on call.

I had a car so we drove to Head Office together.

"Have you seen this bloody document?" Ned asked me, tapping the folder on his lap.

"Which bloody document is that?"

"The Bluebird distribution list. Bluebird readers and their satraps."

I was cautiously non-committal. Ned's bad temper in mid-operation was legendary. The light on the door of Clive's office was green, meaning come in if you dare. The brass plate said "Deputy" in lettering to outshine the Royal Mint.

"What the devil's happened to the need-to-know, Clive?" Ned asked him, waving the distribution list as soon as we were in the presence. "We give Langley one batch of highly sensitive, unsourced material and overnight they've recruited more cooks than broth. I mean what is this? Hollywood? We've got a live joe out there. We've got a defector in place we've never met."

Clive toured the gold carpet. He had a habit when he was arguing with Ned of turning his whole body at once, like a playing-card. He did so now.

"So you think the Bluebird readership list too long?" he enquired in the tone of one taking evidence.

"Yes, and so should you. And so should Russell Sheriton. Who the devil are the Pentagon Scientific Liaison Board? What's the White House Academic Advisory Team when it's at home?"

"You would prefer me to take a high line and insist Bluebird be confined to their Inter-Agency Committee? Principals only, no staff, no aides? Is that what you are telling me?"

"If you think you can get the toothpaste back in the tube, yes."

Clive affected to consider this on its merits. But I knew, and so did Ned, that Clive considered nothing on its merits. He considered who was in favour of something and who was against it. Then he considered who was the better ally.

"Firstly, not a single one of those elevated gentlemen I have mentioned is capable of making head or tail of the Bluebird material without expert guidance," Clive resumed in his bloodless voice. "Either we let them flounder in ignorance or we admit their appendages and accept the price. The same goes for their Defense Intelligence team, their Navy, Army, Air Force and White House evaluators."

"Is this Russell Sheriton speaking or you?" Ned demanded.

"How can we tell them not to call in their scientific panels when we offer them immensely complex material in the same breath?" Clive persisted, neatly letting Ned's question pass him by. "If Bluebird's genuine, they're going to need all the help they can get."

"*If*," Ned echoed, flaring. "*If* he's genuine. My God, Clive, you're worse than they are. There are two hundred and forty people on that list and every one of them has a wife, a mistress and fifteen best friends."

"And *secondly*," Clive went on, when we had forgotten there had been a firstly, "it's not *our* intelligence to dispose of. It's Langley's." He had swung on me before Ned could get in his reply. "Palfrey. Confirm. Under our sharing treaty with the Americans, is it not the case that we give Langley first rights on all strategic material?"

"In strategic matters our dependence on Langley is total," I conceded. "They give us what they want us to know. In return we are obliged to give them whatever we find out. It isn't often much but that's the deal."

Clive listened carefully to this and approved it. His coldness had an unaccustomed ferocity and I wondered why. If he had possessed a conscience, I would have said it was uneasy. What had he been doing at the Embassy all day? What had he given away to whom for what?

"It is a common misapprehension of this Service," Clive continued, talking straight at Ned now, "that we and the Americans are in the same boat. We're not. Not when it comes to strategy. We haven't a defence analyst in the country who is capable of holding a candle to his American counterpart on matters of strategy. Where strategy is concerned, we are a tiny, ignorant British coracle and they are the *Queen Elizabeth*. It is not our place to tell them how to run their ship."

We were still marvelling at the vigour of this declaration when Clive's hot line began ringing and he went for it greedily, for he always loved answering his hot line in front of his subordinates. He was unlucky. It was Brock calling for Ned.

Katya had just phoned Barley at the Odessa and they had agreed a meeting for tomorrow evening, said Brock. Moscow station required Ned's urgent approval of their operational proposals for the encounter. Ned left at once.

"What are you brewing with the Americans?" I asked Clive, but he didn't bother with me.

All next day I spent talking to my Swedes. In the Russia House, life was scarcely more enlivening. Spying is waiting. Around four I slipped back to my room and telephoned Hannah. Sometimes I do that. By four she is back from the Cancer Institute where she works part time, and her husband never comes home before seven. She told me how her day had gone. I scarcely listened. I gave her some story about my son, Alan, who was in deep water with a nurse up in Birmingham, a nice enough girl but really not Alan's class.

"I may ring you later," she said.

Sometimes she said that, but she never rang.

Barley walked at Katya's side and he could hear her footsteps like a tighter echo of his own. The flaking mansions of Dickensian Moscow were bathed in stale twilight. The first courtyard was gloomy, the second dark. Cats stared at them from the rubbish. Two long-haired boys who might have been students were playing tennis across a row of packing cases. A third leaned against the wall. A door stood ahead of them, daubed with graffiti and a red crescent moon. "Watch for the red marks," Wicklow had advised. She was pale and he wondered if he was pale too, because it would be a living miracle if he wasn't. Some men will never be heroes, some heroes will never be men, he thought, with urgent acknowledgements to Joseph Conrad. And Barley Blair, he'll never be either. He grabbed the doorhandle and yanked it. She kept her distance. She was wearing a headscarf and a raincoat. The handle turned but the door wouldn't budge. He shoved it with both hands, then shoved harder. The tennis players yelled at him in Russian. He stopped dead, feeling fire on his back.

"They say you should please kick it," Katya said, and to his amazement he saw that she was smiling.

"If you can smile now," he said, "how do you look when you're happy?"

But he must have said it to himself because she didn't answer. He kicked it and it gave, the grit beneath it screaming. The boys laughed and went back to their game. He stepped into the black and she followed him. He pressed a switch but no light came. The door slammed shut behind them and when he groped for the handle he couldn't find it. They stood in deep darkness, smelling cats and onions and cooking oil and listening to bits of music and argument from other people's lives. He struck a match. Three steps appeared, then half a bicycle, then the entrance to a filthy lift. Then his fingers burned. You go to the fourth floor, Wicklow had said. Watch for the red marks. How the devil do I watch for red marks in the dark? God answered him with a pale light from the floor above.

"Where are we, please?" she asked politely.

"It's a friend of mine," he said. "A painter."

He pulled back the lift door, then the grille. He said "Please" but she was already past him, standing in the lift and looking upward, willing it to rise.

"He's away for a few days. It's just somewhere to talk," he said.

He noticed her eyelashes again, the moisture in her eyes. He wanted to console her but she wasn't sad enough.

"He's a painter," he said again, as if that legitimised a friend.

"Official?"

"No. I don't think so. I don't know."

Why hadn't Wicklow told him which kind of bloody painter the man was supposed to be?

He was about to press the button when a small girl in tortoiseshell spectacles hopped in after them hugging a plastic bear. She called a greeting and Katya's face lit up as she greeted her in return. The lift juddered upwards, the buttons popping like cap pistols at each floor. At the third the child politely said goodbye, and Barley and Katya said goodbye in unison. At the fourth the lift bumped to a halt as if it had hit the ceiling and perhaps it had. He shoved her ashore and leapt after her. A passage opened before them, filled with the stench of baby, perhaps a lot of babies. At the end of it, on what seemed to be a blank wall, a red arrow directed them left. They came on a narrow wooden staircase leading upwards. On the bottom step Wicklow crouched like a leprechaun reading a weighty book by the aid of a mechanic's light. He did not lift his head as they climbed past him but Barley saw Katya stare at him all the same.

"What's the matter? Seen a ghost?" he asked her.

Could she hear him? Could he hear himself? Had he spoken? They were in a long attic. Chinks of sky pierced the tiles, bats' mess smeared the rafters. A path of scaffolders' boards had been laid over the joists. Barley took her hand. Her palm was broad and strong and dry. Its nakedness against his own was like the gift of her entire body.

He advanced cautiously, smelling turpentine and linseed and hearing the tapping of an unexpected wind. He squeezed between a pair of iron cisterns and saw a life-sized paper sea-gull in full flight strung from a beam, turning on its thread. He pulled her after him. Beyond it, fixed to a shower-rail, hung a striped curtain. If there's no sea-gull there's no meeting, Wicklow had said. No sea-gull means abort. That's my epitaph, thought Barley. "There was no sea-gull, so he aborted." He swept the curtain aside and entered a painter's studio, once more drawing her after him. At its centre stood an easel and a model's upholstered box. An aged Chesterfield rested on its stuffing. It's a one-time facility, Wicklow had said. So am I, Wickers, so am I. A homemade skylight was cut into the slope of the roof. A red mark was daubed on its frame. Russians don't trust walls, Wicklow had explained, she'll talk better in the open air.

The skylight opened, to the consternation of a colony of doves and sparrows. He nodded her through first, noticing the easy flow of her long body as she stooped. He clambered after her, barking his spine and saying "Damn" exactly as he knew he would. They were standing between two gables in a leaded valley only wide enough for their feet. The pulse of traffic rose from streets they couldn't see. She was facing him and close. Let's live up here, he thought. Your eyes, me, the sky. He was rubbing his back, screwing up his eyes against the pain.

"You are hurt?"

"Just a fractured spine."

"Who is that man on the stairs?" she said.

"He works for me. He's my editor. He's keeping a lookout while we talk."

"He was at the hospital last night."

"What hospital?"

"Last night after seeing you, I was obliged to visit a certain hospital."

"Are you ill? Why did you go to hospital?" Barley asked, no longer rubbing his back.

"It is not important. He was there. He appeared to have a broken arm."

"He can't have been there," Barley said, not believing himself. "He was with me the whole evening after you left. We had a discussion about Russian books."

He saw the suspicion slowly leave her eyes. "I am tired. You must excuse me."

"Let me tell you what I've worked out, then you can tell me it's no good. We talk, then I take you out to dinner. If the People's custodians were listening to our call last night they'll expect that anyway. The studio belongs to a painter friend of mine, a jazz nut like me. I never told you his name because I couldn't remember it and perhaps I never knew it. I thought we could bring him a drink and look at his pictures but he didn't appear. We went on to dinner, talked literature and world peace. Despite my reputation I did not make a pass at you. I was too much in awe of your beauty. How's that?"

"It is convenient."

Dropping into a crouch, he produced a half bottle of Scotch and unscrewed the cap. "Do you drink this stuff?"

"No."

"Me neither." He hoped she would settle beside him but she remained standing. He poured a tot into the cap and set the bottle at his feet.

"What's his name?" he said. "The author's. Goethe. Who is he?"

"It is not important."

"What's his unit? Firm? Postbox number? Ministry? Laboratory? Where's he working? We haven't time to fool around."

"I don't know."

"Where's he stationed? You won't tell me that either, will you?"

"In many places. It depends where he is working."

"How did you meet him?"

"I don't know. I don't know what I may tell you."

"What did he tell you to tell me?"

She faltered, as if he had caught her out. She frowned. "Whatever is necessary. I should trust you. He was generous. It is his nature."

"So what's holding you up?" Nothing. "Why do you think I'm here?" Nothing. "Do you think I enjoy playing cops-and-robbers in Moscow?"

"I don't know."

"Why did you send me the book if you don't trust me?"

"It was for him that I sent it. I did not select you. He did," she replied moodily.

"Where is he now? At the hospital? How do you speak to him?" He looked up at her, waiting for her answer. "Why don't you just start talking and see how it goes?" he suggested. "Who he is, who you are. What he does for a living."

"I don't know."

"Who was in the woodshed at 3 a.m. on the night of the crime." More nothing. "Tell me why you've dragged me into this. You started this. I didn't. Katya? It's me. I'm Barley Blair. I do jokes, I do bird noises, I drink. I'm a friend."

He loved her grave silences while she stared at him. He loved her listening with her eyes and the sense of recovered companionship each time she spoke.

"There has been no crime," she said. "He is my friend. His name and occupation are unimportant."

Barley took a sip while he thought about this. "So is this what you usually do for friends? Smuggle their illicit manuscripts to the West for them?" She thinks with her eyes as well, he thought. "Did he happen to mention to you what his manuscript was about?"

"Naturally. He would not endanger me without my consent."

He caught the protectiveness in her voice and resented it. "What did he tell you was in it?" he asked.

"The manuscript describes my country's involvement in the preparation of anti-humanitarian weapons of mass destruction over many years. It paints a portrait of corruption and incompetence in all fields of the defence-industrial complex. Also of criminal mismanagement and ethical shortcomings."

"That's quite a mouthful. Do you know any details beyond that?"

"I am not acquainted with military matters."

"So he's a soldier."

"No."

"So what is he?"

Silence.

"But you approve of that? Passing that stuff out to the West?"

"He is not passing it to the West or to any bloc. He respects the British but that is not important. His gesture will ensure true openness among scientists of all nations. It will help to destroy the arms race." She had still to come to him. She was speaking flatly as if she had learned her lines by heart. "He believes there is no time left. We must destroy the abuse of science and the political systems responsible for it. When he speaks philosophy, he speaks English," she added.

And you listen, he thought. With your eyes. In English. While you wonder whether you can trust me.

"Is he a scientist?" he asked.

"Yes. He is a scientist."

"I hate them all. What branch? Is he a physicist?"

"Perhaps. I don't know."

"His information comes from across the board. Accuracy, aimpoints, command and control, rocket motors. Is he one man? Who gives him the material? How does he know so much?"

"I don't know. He is one man. That is obvious. I do not have so many friends. He is not a group. Perhaps he also supervises the work of others. I don't know."

"Is he high up? A big boss? Is he working here in Moscow? Is he a headquarters man? What is he?"

She shook her head at each question. "He does not work in Moscow. Otherwise I have not asked him and he does not tell me."

"Does he test things?"

"I don't know. He goes to many places. All over the Soviet Union. Sometimes he has been in the sun, sometimes he has been very cold, sometimes both. I don't know."

"Has he ever mentioned his unit?"

"No."

"Box numbers? The names of his bosses? The name of a colleague or subordinate?"

"He is not interested to tell me such things."

And he believed her. While he was with her, he would believe that north was south and babies grew on jacaranda trees.

She was watching him, waiting for his next question.

"Does he understand the consequences of publishing this stuff?" he asked. "To himself, I mean? Does he know what he's playing with?"

"He says that there are times when our actions must come first and we must consider consequences only when they occur." She seemed to expect him to say something but he was learning to slow down. "If we see one goal clearly we may advance one step. If we contemplate all goals at once we shall not advance at all."

"How about you? Has he thought about the consequences to you at all if any of this comes to light?"

"He is reconciled."

"Are you?"

"Naturally. It was my decision also. Why else would I support him?"

"And the children?" he asked.

"It is for them and for their generation," she said with a resolution bordering on anger.

"What about the consequences to Mother Russia?"

"We regard the destruction of Russia as preferable to the destruction of all mankind. The greatest burden is the past. For all nations, not only Russia. We regard ourselves as the executioners of the past. He says that if we cannot execute our past, how shall we construct our future? We shall not build a new world until we have got rid of the mentalities of the old. In order to express truth we must also be prepared to be the apostles of negation. He quotes Turgenev. A nihilist is a person who does not take anything for granted, however much that principle is revered."

"And you?"

"I am not a nihilist. I am a humanist. If it is given to us to play a part for the future, we must play it."

He was searching her voice for a hint of doubt. He found none. She was tone perfect.

"How long's he been talking like this? Always? Or is it only recent?"

"He has always been idealistic. That is his nature. He has always been extremely critical in a constructive sense. There was a time when he was able to convince himself that the weapons of annihilation were so terrible they would have the effect of abolishing war. He believed they would produce an alteration in the mind of the military establishments. He was persuaded by the paradox that the greatest weapons contained within them the greatest capacity for peace. He was in this regard an enthusiast of American strategic opinions."

She was starting towards him. He could feel it in her, the stirring of a need. She was waking and approaching him. Under the Moscow sky, she was shedding her mistrust after too much loneliness and deprival.

"So what changed him?"

"He has experienced for many years the incompetence and arrogance of our military and bureaucratic organisations. He has seen how it drags on the feet of progress. That is his expression. He is inspired by the *perestroika* and by the prospect of world peace. But he is not Utopian, he is not passive. He knows that nothing will come of its own accord. He knows that our people are deluded and lack collective power. The new revolution must be imposed from above. By intellectuals. By artists. By administrators. By scientists. He wishes to make his own irreversible contribution in accordance with the exhortations of our leadership. He quotes a Russian saying: 'If the ice is thin, one must walk fast.' He says we have lived too long in an era we no longer need. Progress can only be achieved when the era is finished."

"And you agree?"

"Yes and so do you!" Heat, now. Fire in her eyes. An English too perfect, learned in the cloister, from permitted classics of the past. "He says that he heard you criticise your own country in similar terms!"

"Does he have any small thoughts?" Barley asked. "I mean, does he like the movies? What car does he drive?"

She had turned away from him and he had the side view of her face cut against the empty sky. He took another nip of Scotch.

"You said he might be a physicist," he reminded her.

"He was trained as a physicist. I believe he has also qualified in aspects of engineering. In the field in which he works, I believe that the distinctions are not always closely observed."

"Where was he trained?"

"Already at school he was regarded as a prodigy. At fourteen he won a Mathematics Olympiad. His success was printed in the Leningrad newspapers. He went to the Litmo, afterwards to post-graduate studies at the University. He is extremely brilliant."

"When I was at school those were the people I hated," said Barley, but to his alarm she scowled.

"But you did not hate Goethe. You inspired him. He often quotes his friend Scott Blair. 'If there is to be hope, we must all betray our countries.' Did you really say this?"

"What's a Litmo?" said Barley.

"Litmo is the Leningrad Institute for Mechanical and Optical Science. From university he was sent to Novosibirsk to study at the scientific city of Akademgorodok. He made candidate of sciences, doctor of sciences. He made everything."

He wanted to press her about the everything, but he was scared of rushing her so he let her speak about herself instead. "So how did you get mixed up with him?"

"When I was a child."

"How old was the child?"

He felt her reticence collect again and then dissolve as if she had to remind herself she was in safe company—or in company so unsafe that to be further compromised made little difference.

"I was a great intellectual of sixteen," she said, with a grave smile.

"How old was the prodigy?"

"Thirty."

"What year are we talking about?"

"Nineteen sixty-eight. He was still an idealist for peace. He said they would never send in the tanks. 'The Czechs are our friends,' he said. 'They are like the Serbs and the Bulgarians. If it were Warsaw, perhaps they would send in the tanks. But against our Czechs, never, never.' "

She had turned her whole back to him. She was too many women at once. She had her back to him and was talking to the sky, yet she was drawing him into her life and appointing him her confidant.

It was August in Leningrad, she said, she was sixteen and studying French and German in her last year at school. She was a star pupil and a peace-dreamer and a revolutionary of the most romantic kind. She was on the brink of womanhood and thought herself mature. She was speaking of herself with irony. She had read Erich Fromm and Ortega y Gasset and Kafka and seen *Dr. Strangelove*. She regarded Sakharov as right in his thinking but wrong in his method. She was concerned about the Russian Jews but shared her father's view that they had brought their troubles on themselves. Her father was Professor of Humanities at the University, and her school was for sons and daughters of the Leningrad *nomenklatura*. It was August, 1968, but Katya and her friends were still able to live in political hope. Barley tried to remember whether he had ever lived in political hope and decided it was unlikely. She was talking as if nothing would ever stop her talking again. He wished he could hold her hand again as he had held it on the stairs. He wished he could hold any part of her but best of all her face, and kiss her instead of listening to her love story.

"We believed that East and West were drawing closer together," she said. "When the American students demonstrated against Vietnam, we were proud of them and regarded them as our comrades. When the students of Paris rioted, we wished we could be beside them at the barricades, wearing their nice French clothes."

She turned and smiled at him again over her shoulder. A horned moon had appeared above the stars at her left side and Barley had some vague literary memory that it boded bad luck. A flock of gulls had settled on a roof across the street. I'll never leave you, he thought.

"There was a man in our courtyard who had been absent for nine years," she was saying. "One morning he was back, pretending he had never been away. My father invited him to dinner and played him music all evening. I had never consciously met anyone who had been freshly persecuted so I naturally hoped that he would talk of the horrors of the camps. But all he wished to do was listen to Shostakovich. I did not understand in those days that some suffering cannot be described. From Czechoslovakia we heard of extraordinary reforms. We believed that these reforms would soon come to the Soviet Union and that we would have hard currency and be free to travel."

"Where was your mother?"

"Dead."

"How did she die?"

"Of tuberculosis. She was already ill when I was born. On the twentieth of August there was a closed showing of a Godard film at the Club of Scientists." Her voice had become strict against herself. "The invitations were for two persons. My father, after making enquiries about the moral content of the film, was reluctant to take me but I insisted. In the end he decided I should accompany him for the sake of my French studies. Do you know the Club of Scientists in Leningrad?"

"I can't say I do," he said, leaning back.

"Have you seen À Bout de Souffle?"

"I starred in it," he said, and she broke out laughing while he sipped his Scotch.

"Then you will remember that it is a very tense film. Yes?"

"Yes."

"It was the most powerful film I had ever seen. Everyone was greatly impressed by it, but for me it was a thunderbolt. The Club of Scientists is on the embankment of the river Neva. It is full of old glory, with marble staircases and very low sofas which are difficult to sit on in a tight skirt." She was sideways to him again, her head forward. "There is a beautiful winter-garden and a room like a mosque with heavy curtains and rich carpets. My father loved me very much but he was concerned for me and he was strict. When the film was over we moved to a dining room with wood panels. It was beautiful. We sat at long tables and that was where I met Yakov. My father introduced us. 'Here is a new genius from the world of physics,' he said. My father had the fault of sometimes being sarcastic with young men. Also Yakov was beautiful. I had heard something about him but nobody had told me how vulnerable he was, more like an artist than a scientist. I asked him what he was doing and he replied that he had returned to Leningrad to recover his innocence. I laughed and for a girl of sixteen produced an impressive response. I said I found it strange that a scientist of all people should be seeking innocence. He explained that in Akademgorodok he had shown too much brilliance in certain fields and had made himself too attractive to the military. It appears that in matters of physics the distinction between peaceful and military research is often very small. Now they were offering him everything—privileges, money to make his researches—but he was still refusing them because he wished to preserve his energies for peaceful means. This made them angry because they customarily recruit the cream of our scientists and do not expect refusal. So he had returned to his old university in order to recover his innocence. He proposed initially to study theoretical physics and was looking for influential people to support him, but they were reluctant because of his attitude. He had no permit to reside in Leningrad. He spoke very freely, as our scientists may. Also he was full of enthusiasm for the Gorodok. He spoke of the foreigners who in those days passed through, the brilliant young Americans from Stanford and MIT, also the English. He described the painters who were forbidden in Moscow but permitted to exhibit in the Gorodok. The seminars, the intensity of life, the free exchanges of ideas—and, as I was sure, of love. 'In what other country but Russia would Richter and Rostropovich come and play their music specially for the scientists, Okudzhava sing and Voznesensky read his poems! This is the world that we scientists must build for others!' He made jokes and I laughed like a mature woman. He was very witty in those days but also vulnerable, as he is today. There is a part of him that refuses to grow up. It is the artist in him, but it is the perfectionist also. Already in those days he was an outspoken critic of the incompetence of the authorities. He said there were so many eggs and sausages in the Gorodok supermarket that the shoppers poured out by bus from Novosibirsk and emptied the shelves by ten in the morning. Why could not the eggs make the journey instead of the people? This would be much better! Nobody collected the rubbish, he said, and the electricity kept cutting off. Sometimes the rubbish was knee-deep in the streets. And they call it a scientific Paradise! I made another precocious comment. 'That's the trouble with Paradise,' I said. 'There is nobody to collect the rubbish.' Everyone was very amused. I was a success. He described the old guard trying to come to grips with the ideas of the new men and going away shaking their heads like peasants who have seen a tractor for the first time. Never mind, he said. Progress will prevail. He said that the armoured train of the Revolution which Stalin had derailed was at last in motion again and the next stop would be Mars. That was when my father interrupted with one of his cynical opinions. He was finding Yakov too vociferous. 'But, Yakov Yefremovich,' he said, 'was not Mars the god of war?' Immediately Yakov became reflective. I had not imagined a man could change so quickly, one minute bold, the next so lonely and distressed. I blamed my father. I was furious with him. Yakov tried to recover but my father had thrown him into despair. Did Yakov talk to you about his father?"

She was sitting across the valley from him, propped against the opposing slope of the rooftiles, her long legs stretched before her, her dress drawn tightly over her body. The sky was darkening behind her, the moon and stars were growing.

"He told me his father died of an overdose of intelligence," Barley replied.

"He took part in a camp uprising. He was in despair. Yakov did not know of his father's death for many years. One day an old man came to Yakov's house and said he had shot Yakov's father. He had been a guard at the camp and was ordered to take part in the execution of the rebels. They were shot down in dozens by machine guns near the Vorkuta railway terminal. The guard was weeping. Yakov was only fourteen at the time but he gave the old man his forgiveness and some vodka."

I can't do this, Barley thought. I'm not equal to these dimensions.

"What year was his father shot?" he asked. Be a hamster. It's about the only thing you're fit for.

"I think it was the spring of 1952. While Yakov remained silent, everybody at the table began to talk vehemently about Czechoslovakia," she continued in her perfect archaeological English. "Some said the ruling gang would send in the tanks. My father was sure of it. Some said they would be justified in doing so. My father said they would do it whether they were justified or not. The red Czars would do exactly as they pleased, he said, just as the white Czars had done. The system would win because the system always won and the system was our curse. This was my father's conviction as it later became Yakov's. But Yakov was at that time still determined to believe in the Revolution. He wished his own father's death to have been worthwhile. He listened intently to what my father had to say but then he became aggressive. 'They will never send in the tanks!' he said. 'The Revolution will survive!' He beat the table with his fist. You have seen his hands? Like a pianist's, so white and thin? He had been drinking. So had my father and my father also became angry. He wished to be left in peace with his pessimism. As a distinguished humanist, he did not like to be contradicted by a young scientist whom he regarded as an upstart. Perhaps also my father was jealous, because while they quarrelled, I fell completely in love with Yakov."

Barley took another sip of Scotch.

"You don't find that shocking?" she demanded indignantly as her smile leapt back to her face. "A girl of sixteen, for an experienced man of thirty?"

Barley wasn't feeling very quick-witted, but she seemed to need his reassurance. "I'm speechless but on the whole I'd say they were both very lucky," he said.

"When the reception ended I asked my father for three roubles to go to the Café Sever to eat ice-cream with my companions. There were several daughters of academics at the reception, some were my school comrades. We made a group and I invited Yakov to join us. On the way I asked him where he lived and he told me: in the street of Professor Popov. He asked me, 'Who was Popov?' I laughed. Everyone knows who Popov is, I said. Popov was the great Russian inventor of radio who transmitted a signal even before Marconi, I told him. Yakov was not so sure. 'Perhaps Popov never existed,' he replied. 'Perhaps the Party invented him in order to satisfy our Russian obsession with being the first to invent everything.' From this I knew that he was still struggling with doubts about what they would do concerning Czechoslovakia."

Feeling anything but wise, Barley gave a wise nod.

"I asked him whether his apartment was a communal or a separate one. He said it was a room which he shared with an old acquaintance from the Litmo who was working in a special night laboratory, so they seldom met. I said, 'Then show me where you live. I wish to know that you are comfortable.' He was my first lover," she said simply. "He was extremely delicate, as I had expected him to be, but also passionate."

"Bravo," said Barley so softly that perhaps she didn't hear.

"I stayed with him three hours and took the last metro home. My father was waiting up for me and I talked to him like a stranger visiting his house. I did not sleep. Next day I heard the news in English on the BBC. The tanks had gone into Prague. My father, who had predicted this, was in despair. But I was not concerned for my father. Instead of going to school I went back to look for Yakov. His room-mate told me I would find him at the Saigon, which was the informal name of a cafeteria on the Nevsky Prospekt, a place for poets and drug-pedlars and speculators, not professors' daughters. He was drinking coffee but he was drunk. He had been drinking vodka since he heard the news. 'Your father is right,' he said. 'The system will always win. We talk freedom but we are oppressors.' Three months later he had returned to Novosibirsk. He was bitter with himself but he still went. 'It is a choice between dying of obscurity or dying of compromise,' he said. 'Since that is a choice between death and death, we may as well choose the more comfortable alternative.' "

"Where did that leave you?" Barley asked.

"I was ashamed of him. I told him that he was my ideal and that he had disappointed me. I had been reading the novels of Stendhal, so I addressed him like a great French heroine. Nevertheless I believed that he had taken an immoral decision. He had talked one thing and done the opposite. In the Soviet Union, I told him, too many people do this. I told him I would never speak to him again until he had corrected his immoral choice. I reminded him of E. M. Forster, whom we both admired. I told him that he must connect. That his thoughts and actions must be one. Naturally I soon relented and for a while we resumed our relationship, but it was no longer romantic and when he took up his new work we corresponded without warmth. I was ashamed for him. Perhaps also for myself."

"And so you married Volodya," Barley said.

"That is correct."

"And you kept Yakov going on the side?" he suggested, as if it were the most normal thing in the world.

She was blushing and scowling at once. "For a while, it is true, Yakov and I maintained a clandestine relationship. Not often, but sometimes. He said we were a novel that had not been finished. Each of us was looking to the other to complete his destiny. He was correct, but I had not realised the strength of his influence over me or of mine over him. I thought that if we met more we might become free of each other. When I realised this was not the case I ceased to see him. I loved him but I refused to see him. Also I was pregnant from Volodya."

"When did you get together again?"

"After the last Moscow book fair. You were his catalyst. He had been on vacation and drinking very heavily. He had written many internal papers and registered many official complaints. None of them had made any impression on the system, though I think he had succeeded in annoying the authorities. Now you had spoken into his heart. You had put his thoughts into words at a crucial moment in his life, and you had related words to actions, which Yakov does not find easy. The next day, he telephoned me at my office, using a pretext. He had borrowed the apartment of a friend. My relationship with Volodya was by then disintegrating, although we were still living together because Volodya had to wait for an apartment. While we sat in the room of Yakov's friend, he spoke very much about you. You had made everything come clear for him. That was his phrase to me. 'The Englishman has given me the solution. From now on, there is only action, there is only sacrifice,' he said. 'Words are the curse of our Russian society. They are a substitute for deeds.' Yakov knew that I had contact with Western publishers, so he told me to look for your name among our lists of foreign visitors. He set to work at once to prepare a manuscript. I should give it to you. He was drinking a great deal. I was scared for him. 'How can you write if you are drunk?' He replied that he drank to survive."

Barley took another nip of whisky. "Did you tell Volodya about Yakov?"

"No."

"Did Volodya find out?"

"No."

"So who does know?"

It seemed she had been asking herself the same question, for she replied with great promptness.

"Yakov tells his friends nothing. This I know. If I am the one who borrows the apartment, I say only that it is for a private matter. In Russia we have secrecy and we have loneliness, but we have no word for privacy."

"What about your girlfriends? Not a hint to them?"

"We are not angels. If I ask them for certain favours, they make certain assumptions. Sometimes it is I who provide the favours. That is all."

"And nobody helped Yakov compile his manuscript?"

"No."

"None of his drinking friends?"

"No."

"How can you be certain?"

"Because I am certain that in his thoughts he is completely alone."

"Are you happy with him?"

"Please?"

"Do you like him—as well as love him? Does he make you laugh?"

"I believe that Yakov is a great and vulnerable man who cannot survive without me. To be a perfectionist is to be a child. It is also to be impractical. I believe that without me he would break."

"Do you think he's broken now?"

"Yakov would say, which one is sane? The one who plans the extermination of mankind, or the one who takes steps to prevent it?"

"How about the one who does both?"

She didn't reply. He was provoking her and she knew it. He was jealous, wanting to erode the edges of her faith.

"Is he married?" he asked.

An angry look swept across her face. "I do not believe he is married but it is not important."

"Has he got kids?"

"These are ridiculous questions."

"It's a pretty ridiculous situation."

"He says that human beings are the only creatures to make victims of their children. He is determined to provide no victims."

Except yours, Barley thought: but he managed not to say it.

"So, you followed his career with interest," he suggested roughly, returning to the question of Goethe's access.

"From a distance, and without detail."

"And all that time you didn't know what work he did? Is that what you're saying?"

"What I knew, I deduced only from our discussions of ethical problems. 'How much of mankind should we exterminate in order to preserve mankind? How can we talk of a struggle for peace when we plan only terrible wars? How can we speak of selective targets when we have not the accuracy to hit them?' When we discuss these matters, I am naturally aware of his involvement. When he tells me that the greatest danger to mankind is not the reality of Soviet power but the illusion of it, I do not question him. I encourage him. I urge him to be consistent and if necessary brave. But I do not question him."

"Rogov? He never mentioned a Rogov? Professor Arkady Rogov?"

"I told you. He does not discuss his colleagues."

"Who said Rogov was a colleague?"

"I assumed this from your questions," she retorted hotly and yet again he believed her.

"How do you communicate with him?" he asked, recovering his gentler tone.

"It is not important. When a certain friend of his receives a certain message, he informs Yakov and Yakov telephones me."

"Does the certain friend know who the certain message is from?"

"He has no reason. He knows it is a woman. That is all."

"Is Yakov afraid?"

"Since he talks so much about courage, I assume he is afraid. He quotes Nietzsche. 'The ultimate goodness is not to be afraid.' He quotes Pasternak. 'The root of beauty—' "

"Are you?" he interrupted.

She stared away from him. In the houses across the streets, home lights were appearing in the windows.

"I must think not of my children but of *all* children," she said, and he noticed two tears lying neglected on her cheeks. He took another pull of whisky and hummed a few bars of Basie. When he looked again, the tears had gone.

"He talks about the great lie," she said, as if she had just remembered.

"What great lie?"

"Everything is part of the same great lie, down to the smallest spare part of the least significant weapon. Even the results that are sent to Mosców are subject to the great lie."

"Results? What results? Results of what?"

"I don't know."

"Of testing?"

She seemed to have forgotten her denial. "I believe, of testing. I believe he is saying that the results of testing are deliberately distorted in order to satisfy the orders of the generals and the official production requirements of the bureaucrats. Perhaps it is he personally who distorts them. He is very complicated. Sometimes he talks about his many privileges of which he has become ashamed."

The shopping list, Walter had called it. With a deadened sense of duty, Barley crossed off the last items. "Has he mentioned particular projects?"

"No."

"Has he mentioned being involved in command systems? How the field commander is controlled?"

"No."

"Has he ever told you what steps are taken to prevent mistaken launches?"

"No."

"Has he ever suggested he might be engaged in data processing?"

She was tired. "No."

"Does he get promoted now and then? Medals? Big parties as he moves up the ladder?"

"He does not speak of promotion except that it is all corrupt. I told you already that maybe he has been too loud in his criticisms of the system. I do not know."

She had withdrawn from him. Her face was out of sight behind the curtain of her hair.

"You will do best to ask him all further questions for yourself," she said, in the tone of someone packing up to leave. "He wishes you to meet him in Leningrad on Friday. He is attending an important conference at one of the military scientific institutions."

First the sky swayed, then Barley became aware of the evening chill. It had closed over him like an icy cloud, though the sky was dark and clear and the new moon, when it finally kept still, shed a warming glow.

"He has proposed three places and three times," she continued in the same flat tone. "You will please keep each appointment until he is successful. He will keep one of them if he can. He sends you his greetings and his thanks. He loves you."

She dictated three addresses and watched him while he wrote them in his diary, using his apology for a code. Then she waited while he had a sneezing fit, watching him as he heaved and cursed his Maker.

They dined like exhausted lovers in a cellar with an old grey dog and a gypsy who sang blues to a guitar. Who owned the place, who allowed it to exist or why, were mysteries Barley had never troubled to solve. All he knew was that in some previous incarnation, at some forgotten book fair, he had arrived here drunk with a group of crazy Polish publishers and played "Bless This House" on someone's saxophone.

They talked stiffly, and as they talked the gap between them widened until it seemed to Barley to engulf the totality of his insignificance. He gazed at her and felt that he had nothing to offer her that she did not have tenfold. In the ordinary way, he would have made a passionate declaration of love to her. A lunge into absolutes would have been essential to his need to break the tension of a new relationship. But in Katya's presence he could find no absolutes to put opposite her own. He saw his life as a series of useless resurrections, one failure supplanted by another. He was appalled to think that he belonged to a society that existed only in materialism and gave so little thought to its great themes. But he could tell her none of this. To tell her anything was to assail the image that she had of him, and he had nothing to offer in its place.

They discussed books and he watched her slipping away from him. Her face became distracted, her voice prosaic. He went after her, he sang and danced, but she had gone. She was making the same flat statements he had been listening to all day long while he had been waiting to meet her. In a minute, he thought, I'll be telling her about Potomac Boston and explaining how the river and the city are not joined. And God help him, he was doing just that.

It was not till eleven o'clock, when the management put the lights out and he walked her down the lifeless street to the metro station, that it dawned on him against all sane reckoning that he might have made an impression upon her that in some modest way compared with the impression she had made on him. She had taken his arm. Her fingers lay along the inside of his forearm and she had fallen into a wide stride in order to keep pace with him. The white mouth of the elevator shafts stood open to receive her. The chandeliers twinkled above them like inverted Christmas trees as he took her in the formal Russian embrace: left cheek, right cheek, left cheek and goodnight.

"Mr. Blair, sir! Thought I spotted you! Quite a coincidence! Come aboard, we'll run you home!"

Barley climbed in and Wicklow with his acrobat's agility spirited himself into the back seat where he set to work to dislodge the recorder from the small of Barley's back.

They drove him to the Odessa and dropped him. They had work to do. The lobby was like an airport terminal in thick fog. In every sofa and armchair, unofficial guests who had paid the going rate slumbered in the gloom. Barley peered benignly round them, wrinkling his nose. Some wore jumpsuits. Others were more formally dressed.

"Snoot, anybody?" he called, quite loud. No response. "Anyone care for a glass of *whisky* at all?" he enquired, fishing his bottle, still two-thirds full, from the poacher's pocket of his raincoat. He gave himself a long pull by way of example, then passed the bottle along the line.

And that was how Wicklow found him two hours later—in the lobby, squatted companionably among a group of grateful night souls, enjoying a last one before turning in.

⑨

"Who on earth are Clive's new Americans?" I murmured to Ned as we assembled like early worshippers round Brock's tape recorder in the situation room.

The London clock said six. Victoria Street had not yet begun its morning growl. The squeaking of the spool sounded like a chorus of starlings as Brock wound the tape in place. It had arrived by courier half an hour ago, having travelled overland by bag to Helsinki, then by special plane to Northolt. If Ned had been willing to listen to the technological tempters, we could have avoided the whole costly process, for the Langley wizards were swearing by a new device that transmitted spoken word securely. But Ned was Ned and he preferred his own tried methods.

He sat at his desk and was putting his signature to a document which he was shielding with his hand. He folded the paper, put it in its envelope and sealed the flap before handing it to tall Emma, one of his assistants. By then I had given up expecting a reply, so that his vehemence startled me.

"They're bloody carpetbaggers," he snapped.

"From Langley?"

"God knows. Security."

"Whose?" I insisted.

He shook his head, too furious to answer. Was it the document he had just signed that was annoying him, or the presence of the American interlopers? There were two of them. Johnny from their London station was escorting them. They wore navy blazers and short hair, and they had a Mormon cleanliness that I found slightly revolting. Clive stood between them, but Bob had sat himself demonstratively at the far end of the room with Walter, who looked wretched—I supposed at first because of the hour. Even Johnny seemed discomfited by their presence, and so immediately was I. These dull, unfamiliar faces had no place at the heart of our operation, and at such a crucial moment. They were like a gathering of mourners in advance of an anticipated death. But whose? I looked again at Walter, and my anxieties were compounded.

I looked again at the new Americans, so slight, so trim, so characterless. Security, Ned had said. Yet why? And why *now*?

Why did they look at everyone except Walter? Why did Walter look at everyone except them? And why did Bob sit apart from them, and Johnny go on staring at his hands? I was grateful to have my thoughts interrupted. We heard the boom of footsteps on wood stairs. Brock had started the recorder. We heard clunks and Barley's oath as he barked his back on the window frame. Then the shuffling of feet again as they clambered on to the rooftop.

It's a séance, I thought as their first words reached us. Barley and Katya are addressing us from the great beyond. The immobile strangers with their executioners' faces were forgotten.

Ned was the only one of us with earphones. They made a difference, I later discovered when I tried them. You hear the Moscow doves shuffling on the gable and the rapid breathing inside Katya's voice. You hear the beating of your own joe's heart through the body mikes.

Brock played the whole rooftop scene before Ned ordered a break. Only our new Americans seemed unaffected. Their brown glances brushed each one of us but settled nowhere. Walter was blushing.

Brock played the dinner scene and still no one stirred: not a sigh or a creak or a handclap, not even when he stopped the spool and wound it back.

Ned pulled off his earphones.

"Yakov Yefremovich, last name unknown, physicist, aged thirty in 1968, ergo born 1938," he announced as he grabbed a pink trace request from the pile before him and scribbled on it. "Walter, offers?"

Walter had to gather himself. He seemed distraught, and his voice had none of its usual flightiness. "Yefrem, Soviet scientist, other names unknown, father of Yakov Yefremovich q.v., shot in Vorkuta after an uprising in the spring of '52," he declared without looking at his pad. "There can't be *that* many scientific Yefrems who were executed for an overdose of intelligence, even in dear Stalin's day," he added rather pathetically.

It was absurd, but I fancied I saw tears in his eyes. Perhaps someone really *has* died, I thought, glancing once more at our two Mormons.

"Johnny?" said Ned, writing.

"Ned, we think we'll take Boris, other names unknown, widower, Professor of Humanities, Leningrad University, late sixties, one daughter Yekaterina," said Johnny, still to his hands.

Ned seized another trace form, filled it in and tossed it into his out-tray like money he was pleased to throw away.

"Palfrey. Want to play?"

"Put me down for the Leningrad newspapers, will you please, Ned?" I said as airily as I could, given that the Mormons had turned their brown gaze full upon me. "I'd like runners, starters and winners of the Mathematics Olympiad of 1952," I said amid laughter. "And for safety's sake perhaps you'd throw in '51 and '53 as well. And shall we add his academic medals, please, somewhere along the line? 'He made candidate of sciences, he made doctor of sciences. He made everything,' she said. Can we have that, please? Thank you."

When all the bids were in, Ned glared around for Emma to take the trace forms down to Registry. But that wasn't good enough for Walter, who was suddenly determined to be counted—for, leaping to his feet, he marched fussily to Ned's desk, all five foot nothing of him, his little wrists flying out in front of him.

"I shall do *all* the ferreting myself," he announced in far too grand a tone, as he grabbed the pink bundle to his breast. "This war is *far* too important to be left to our blue-rinse generals of Registry, irresistible though they may be."

And I remember noticing how our Mormons watched him all the way to the door, then watched each other as we listened to his merry little heels prinking down the corridor. And I do not think I am speaking with hindsight when I tell you that my blood ran chill for Walter, without my having the smallest idea why.

"A breath of country air," Ned told me on the internal telephone an hour later when I was barely back at my desk at Head Office. "Tell Clive I need you."

"Then you'd better go, hadn't you?" said Clive, still closeted with his Mormons.

We had borrowed a fast Ford from the car pool. As Ned drove, he brushed aside my few attempts at conversation and handed me the file to read instead. We entered the Berkshire countryside but he still didn't talk. And when Brock rang on the carphone to give him some elliptical confirmation he required, he merely grunted, "Then tell him," and returned to his brooding.

We were forty miles from London, on the foulest planet of man's discovery. We were in the slums of modern science, where the grass is always nicely cut. The ancient gateposts were mastered by eroded sandstone lions. A polite man in a brown sports jacket opened Ned's door. His colleague poked a detector underneath the chassis. Politely, they patted us both down.

"Taking the briefcase, are we, gentlemen?"

"Yes," said Ned.

"Care to open it, sir?"

"No."

"Dip it in the box, can we, gentlemen? We're not talking unexposed film, I presume, sir?"

"Please," I said. "Dip it in the box."

We watched while they lowered the briefcase into what looked like a green coal bin, and took it out again.

"Thank you," I said, taking it back.

"It's my pleasure, sir. Not at all, I'm sure."

The blue van said FOLLOW ME. An Alsatian dog frowned at us from its barred rear window. The gates opened electronically and beyond them lay mounds of clipped grass like mass graves grown over. Olive downs stretched towards the sunset. A mushroom-shaped cloud would have looked entirely natural. We entered parkland. A pair of buzzards wheeled in the cloudless sky. High wire fenced off the hay fields. Smokeless brick buildings nestled in artful hollows. A noticeboard urged protective clothing in Zones D to K. A skull and crossbones said "You Have Been Warned." The van ahead of us was moving at a funeral's pace. We lumbered round a bend and saw empty tennis courts and aluminium towers. Lanes of coloured pipe jogged beside us, guiding us to a cluster of green sheds. At their centre, on a hilltop, stood the last vestige of the pre-nuclear age: a Berkshire cottage of brick and flint with "Administrator" stencilled on the gate. A burly man came tripping down the crazy-paving path to greet us. He wore a blazer of British racing green and a tie with gold squash rackets on it, and a handkerchief shoved into his cuff.

"You're from the Firm. Well done. I'm O'Mara. Which of you is who? I've told him to kick his heels in the lab till we whistle for him."

"Good," said Ned.

O'Mara had grey-blond hair and an offhand regimental voice cracked by alcohol. His neck was puffy and his athlete's fingers were stained mahogany with nicotine. "O'Mara keeps the long-haired scientists in line," Ned had told me in one of our rare exchanges during the drive. "He's half personnel, half security, all shit."

The drawing-room had the air of being tended by Napoleonic prisoners of war. Even the bricks of the fireplace had been polished and the plaster lines between them picked out in loving white. We sat in rose-patterned armchairs drinking gin and tonic, lots of ice. Horse-brasses twinkled from the glistening black beams.

"Just come back from the States," O'Mara recalled, as if accounting for our recent separation. He raised his glass and ducked his mouth to it, meeting it halfway. "You fellows go there a lot?"

"Occasionally," said Ned.

"Now and then," I said. "When duty calls."

"We send quite a few of our chaps out there on loan, actually. Oklahoma. Nevada. Utah. Most of them like it pretty well. A few get the heebie-jeebies, run for home." He drank and took a moment to swallow. "Visited their weapons laboratory at Livermore, out in California. Nice enough place. Decent guest house. Money galore. Asked us to attend a seminar on death. Bloody macabre if you think about it, but the shrinks seemed to believe it would do everybody good and the wines were extraordinary. I suppose if you're planning to consign large chunks of humanity to the flames you might as well know how it works." He drank again, all the time in the world. The hilltop at that hour was a very quiet place. "Surprising how many people hadn't given the subject much thought. Specially the young. The older ones were a bit more squeamish. They could remember the age of innocence, if it ever existed. You're a prompt fatality if you die straight off, and a soft one if you do it the slow way. I never realised. Gives a new meaning to the value of being at the centre of things, I suppose. Still, we're into the fourth generation now. Dulls the pangs. You chaps golfers?"

"No," said Ned.

"I'm afraid not," I said. "I used to take lessons but they somehow never made much difference."

"Marvellous courses but they made us hire bloody Noddy carts. Wouldn't be seen dead in the things over here." He drank again, the same slow ritual. "Wintle's an oddball," he explained when he had swallowed. "They're all oddballs but Wintle's got odder balls than most. He's done Socialism, he's done Jesus. Now he's into contemplation and Tai Chi. Married, thank God. Grammar school but talks proper. Three years to go."

"How much have you told him?" Ned asked.

"They always think they're under suspicion. I've told him he isn't, and I've told him to keep his stupid mouth shut when it's over."

"And do you think he will?" I asked.

O'Mara shook his head. "Don't know how to, most of 'em, however hard we boot 'em."

There was a knock at the door and Wintle came in, an eternal student of fifty-seven. He was tall but crooked, with a curly grey head that shot off at an angle, and an air of brilliance almost extinguished. He wore a sleeveless Fair Isle pullover, Oxford bags and moccasins. He sat with his knees together and held his sherry glass away from him like a chemical retort he wasn't sure of.

Ned turned professional. His tantrums were set aside. "We're in the business of tracking Soviet scientists," he said, managing to make himself sound dull. "Watching the snakes and ladders of their defence establishment. Nothing very sexy, I'm afraid."

"So you're Intelligence," said Wintle. "I thought as much, though I didn't say anything."

It occurred to me that he was a very lonely man.

"Mind your own fucking business what they are," O'Mara advised him perfectly pleasantly. "They're English and they've got a job to do, same as you."

Ned fished a couple of typed sheets from a folder and handed them to Wintle, who put down his glass to take them. His hands had a way of finishing knuckles down and fingers curled, like a man begging to be freed.

"We're trying to maximalise some of our neglected old material," Ned said, falling into a jargon he would otherwise have eschewed. "This is an account of your debriefing when you returned from a visit to Akademgorodok in August, 1963. Do you remember a Major Vauxhall? It's not exactly a literary masterpiece but you mention the names of two or three Soviet scientists we'd be grateful to catch up with, if they're still around and you remember them."

As if to protect himself from a gas attack, Wintle pulled on a pair of extraordinarily ugly steel-framed spectacles.

"As *I* recall that debriefing, *Major* Vauxhall gave me his *word* of honour that everything I said was *entirely* voluntary and confidential," he declared with a didactic jerkiness. "I am therefore *very* surprised to see my name *and* my words lying about in open Ministerial archives a full twenty-five *years* after the event."

"Well it's the nearest you'll ever get to immortality, sport, so I should shut up and enjoy it," O'Mara advised.

I interposed myself like somebody separating belligerents in a family row. If Wintle could just expand a little on the interviewer's rather bald account, I suggested. Maybe flesh out one or two of the Soviet scientists whose names are listed on the final page, and perhaps throw in some account of the Cambridge team while he was about it? If he wouldn't mind answering just one or two questions which might tilt the scales?

" 'Team' is *not* a word I would use in this context, thank you," Wintle retorted, pouncing on the word like some bony predator. "Not on the British side anyway. *Team* suggests common purpose. We were a Cambridge *group*, yes. A *team*, no. Some went for the ride, some went for the self-aggrandisement. I refer particularly to Professor Callow, who had a *highly* exaggerated opinion of his work on accelerators, since refuted." His Birmingham accent had escaped from its confinement. "A very small minority *indeed* had ideological motives. They happened to believe in science without borders. A free exchange of knowledge for the common benefit of mankind."

"Wankers," O'Mara explained to us helpfully.

"We'd the French there, Americans galore, the Swedes, Dutch, even one or two Germans," Wintle continued, oblivious to O'Mara's gibe. "All of them had hope, in my opinion, and the Russians had it in bucketfuls. It was us British who were dragging our feet. We still are."

O'Mara groaned and took a restorative pull of gin. But Ned's good smile, even if a little battered, encouraged Wintle to run on.

"It was the height of the Khrushchev era, as you will doubtless recall. Kennedy this side, Khrushchev that side. A golden age was beckoning, said some. People in those days talked about Khrushchev very much as they talk of Gorbachev now, I'm sure. Though I do have to say that, in my opinion, our enthusiasm *then* was more genuine and spontaneous than the so-called enthusiasm *now*."

O'Mara yawned and fixed his pouchy gaze disconcertingly upon myself.

"*We* told them whatever *we* knew. *They* did the same," Wintle was saying as his voice gathered assurance. "*We* read *our* papers. *They* read *theirs*. Callow didn't cut any ice, I'm bound to say. They rumbled *him* in no time. But we'd Panson on cybernetics and *he* flew the flag all right, and we had me. *My* modest lecture was quite a success, though I do say it myself. I haven't heard applause like it since, to be frank. I wouldn't be surprised if they still talk about it over there. The barricades came down so fast you could *literally* hear them crashing in the lecture hall. 'Flow, not demarcation.' That was our slogan. 'Flow' wasn't the word for it either, not if you saw the vodka that was drunk at the late-night parties. *Or* the girls there. *Or* heard the chat. The KGB was listening, of course. We knew *all* about that. We'd had the pep talk before we left, though several objected to it. Not me, I'm a patriot. But there wasn't a blind thing that any of them could do, not *their* KGB and not *ours*." He had evidently hit a favourite theme for he straightened himself to deliver a prepared speech. "I'd like to add here that *their* KGB is greatly misjudged, in my opinion. I have it on *good* authority that the Soviet KGB has very *frequently* sheltered some of the most tolerant elements of the Soviet intelligentsia."

"Jesus—well don't tell me ours hasn't," O'Mara said.

"Furthermore I've no doubt whatever that the Soviet authorities very *rightly* argued that in any trade-off of scientific knowledge with the West, the Soviet Union had more to *gain* than *lose*." Wintle's slanted head was switching from one to another of us like a railway signal, and his upturned hand was resting on his thigh in anguish. "They had the culture too. None of your arts-sciences divide for *them*, thank you. They had the Renaissance dream of rounded man, still do have. I'm not much of a one for culture myself. I don't have the time. But it was all there for those who had the *interest*. And reasonably charged too, I understand. Some of the events were complimentary."

Wintle needed to blow his nose. And to blow his nose Wintle needed first to spread his handkerchief on his knee, then poke it into operational mode with his febrile fingertips. Ned seized upon the natural break.

"Well now, I wonder whether we could take a look at one or two of those Soviet scientists whose names you kindly gave to Major Vauxhall," he suggested, taking the sheaf of papers I was holding out to him.

We had arrived at the moment we had come for. Of the four of us in the room, I suspected, only Wintle was unaware of this, for O'Mara's yellowed eyes had lifted to Ned's face and he was studying him with a dyspeptic shrewdness.

Ned led with his discards, as I would have done. He had marked them for himself in green. Two were known to be dead, a third was in disgrace. He was testing Wintle's memory, rehearsing him for the real thing when it came. Sergey? said Wintle. My goodness yes, Sergey! But what was his other name then? Popov? Popovich? That's right, Protopopov! Sergey Protopopov, engineer specialising in fuels!

Ned coaxed him patiently along, three names, a fourth, guiding his memory, exercising it: "Well now, just think about him a second before you say no again. Really no? Okay. Let's try Savelyev."

"Come again?"

Wintle's memory, I noticed, had the Englishman's embarrassment with Russian surnames. It preferred first names that it could anglicise.

"Savelyev," Ned repeated. Again I caught O'Mara's eye upon him. Ned peered at the report in his hand, perhaps a mite too carelessly. "That's it. Savelyev." He spelt it. " 'Young, idealistic, talkative, called himself a humanitarian. Working on particles, brought up in Leningrad.' Those were your words, according to Major Vauxhall all those lifetimes ago. Anything more I might add? You didn't keep up with him, for instance? Savelyev?"

Wintle was smiling in marvel. "Was that his name, then? Savelyev? Well I'm blowed. There you are. I'd forgotten. To me he's still Yakov, you see."

"Fine. Yakov Savelyev. Remember his patronymic?"

Wintle shook his head, still smiling.

"Anything to add to your original description?"

We had to wait. Wintle had a different sense of time from ours. And to judge by his smirk, a different sense of humour.

"Very sensitive fellow, Yakov was. Wouldn't dare ask his questions in the plenum. Had to hang back and pluck your sleeve when it was over. 'Excuse me, sir, but what do you think of so-and-so?' Good questions, mind. A very cultural man too, they say, in his way. I'm told he cut quite a dash at some of the poetry readings. And the art shows."

Wintle's voice trailed off and I feared he was about to fabricate, which is a thing people do often when they have run out of information but want to keep their ascendancy. But to my relief he was merely retrieving memories from his store— or rather milking them out of the ether with his upright fingers.

"Always going from one group to another, Yakov was," he said, with the same irritating smile of superiority. "Standing himself at the edge of a discussion, very earnest. Perching on the edge of a chair. There was some mystery about his father, I never knew what. They say he was a scientist too, but executed. Well a lot were, weren't they, scientists. They killed them off like fruit flies, I've read about it. If they didn't kill them, they kept them in prison. Tupolev, Petliakov, Korolev—some of their greatest stars of aircraft technology designed their best stuff in prison. Ramzin invented a new boiler for heat engines in prison. Their first rocketry research unit was set up in prison. Korolev ran it."

"Bloody well done, old boy," said O'Mara, bored again.

"Gave me this piece of rock," Wintle continued.

And I saw his hand, upward on his knee again, opening and closing round the imaginary gift.

"*Rock?*" said Ned. "Yakov gave it to you? Do you mean music? No, you mean a geological sample of some kind."

"When we Westerners left Akadem," Wintle resumed, as if launching himself and us upon an entirely new story, "we *stripped* ourselves of our possessions. *Literally*. If you'd seen our group on that last day, you would *not* have believed it. We'd our Russian hosts crying *their eyes* out, hugging and embracing, flowers on the buses, even Callow was having a weep if you can believe it. And us Westerners unloading everything we had: books, papers, pens, watches, razors, toothpaste, even our *toothbrushes*. Gramophone records if we'd brought them. Spare underclothes, ties, shoes, shirts, socks, everything except the minimum we needed for our decency to fly home in. We didn't *agree* to do it. We hadn't even *discussed* it. It happened *spontaneously*. There was some did more, of course. Particularly the Americans, being impulsive. I heard of one fellow offering a marriage of convenience to a girl who was desperate to get out. I didn't do that. I wouldn't. I'm a patriot."

"But you gave some of your goodies to Yakov," Ned suggested, while he affected to write painstakingly in a diary.

"I started to, yes. It's a bit like feeding birds in the park, handing out your treasures is. You pick the one who's not getting his share and you try to fatten him up. Besides, I'd taken to young Yakov, you couldn't help it, him being so soulful."

The hand had frozen round the empty shape, the fingertips striving to unite. The other hand had risen to his brow and taken hold of a sizable pinch of flesh.

" 'Here you are, Yakov,' I said. 'Don't be slow in coming forward. You're too shy for your own health, you are.' I'd an electric shaver in those days. Plus batteries, transformer, all in a nice carrying case. But he didn't seem to be that comfortable with them. He put them aside sort of thing, and kept shuffling about. Then I realised he was trying to give something to *me*. It was this rock, wrapped in newspaper. They'd no fancy wrapping, naturally. 'It's a piece of my country,' he says. 'To thank you for your lecture,' he says. He wanted me to love the good in it always, however bad it might sometimes seem from outside. Spoke a beautiful English, mind, better than half of *us*. I was a bit embarrassed, frankly, if you want to know. I kept that piece of old rock for very many years. Then my wife threw it out during one of her spring-cleans. I thought of writing to him sometimes, I never did. He was arrogant, mind, in his way. Well a lot of them were. I dare say *we* were in *our* way, too. We all thought science could rule the world. Well I suppose it does now, though not in the way it was meant to, I'm sure."

"Did he write to you?" said Ned.

Wintle wondered about this for a long time. "You can never tell, can you? You never know what's been stopped in the post. Or who by."

From the briefcase I passed Ned the bunch of photographs. Ned passed them to Wintle while O'Mara watched. Wintle leafed through them and suddenly let out a cry.

"That's him! Yakov! The man who gave me the rock." He thrust the pictures back at Ned. "Look for yourself! Look at those eyes! *Then* tell me he's not a dreamer!"

Extracted from the Leningrad evening paper dated 5th January 1954 and reconstituted by Photographic Section, Yakov Yefremovich Savelyev as a teenaged genius.

There were other names, and Ned took Wintle laboriously through each one of them, laying false trails, brushing over his tracks until he was satisfied that in Wintle's mind at least Savelyev meant no more than the rest.

"Clever of you to hide your trump in the middle of your hand," O'Mara remarked as, glass in hand, he walked us down the drive to the car. "Last time I heard of Savelyev he was running their testing range in darkest Kazakhstan, dreaming up ways to read their own telemetry without everyone reading it over their shoulder. What's he up to now? Selling the shop?"

It is not often I take pleasure in my work but our meeting and the place had sickened me, and O'Mara had sickened me more than both. It is not often that I seize someone by the arm either, and have to recoil, and loosen my grip.

"I take it you have signed the Official Secrets Act?" I asked him quietly enough.

"Practically wrote the bloody thing," O'Mara retorted, very surprised.

"Then you will know that all knowledge that comes to you officially and all speculation based upon that knowledge are the perpetual property of the Crown." Another legal distortion, but never mind. I released him. "So if you like your job here, and you are hoping for promotion, and if you are looking forward to your pension, I suggest you never think of this meeting again or of any name associated with it. Thank you so much for the gin. Goodbye."

On the journey back, with the identification of Bluebird confirmed and phoned ahead of us in word code to the Russia House, Ned remained withdrawn. Yet when we reached Victoria Street he was suddenly determined not to let me go. "You stick around," he ordered me, and guided me ahead of him down the basement steps.

At first glance the scene in the situation room was one of purest joy. The centrepiece was Walter, poised like an artist before a whiteboard as big as he was, drawing up the details of Savelyev's life in coloured crayons. If he had been wearing a broad-brimmed hat and smock, he could not have looked more rakish. Only at second glance did I recall my eerie apprehensions of that morning.

Around him—which meant behind him, for the whiteboard was propped against the wall beneath the clocks—stood Brock and Bob, and Jack our cypher clerk, and Ned's girl Emma, and a senior girl called Pat who was one of the mainstays of Soviet Registry. They held glasses of champagne and each of them in his different way was smiling, though Bob's smile was more like a grimace of pain suppressed.

"A lonely decider," Walter declaimed rhapsodically. He froze a moment as he heard us, but did not turn his head. "A fifty-year-old achiever shaking his mid-life bars, looking at mortality and a wasted life. Well, aren't we all?"

He stood back. Then skipped forward again and chalked in a date. Then took a swig of champagne. And I sensed something ghoulish and scaring about him, like make-up on the dying.

"Living at their secret centre all his adult life," he continued gaily. "But keeping his mouth shut. Taking his own decisions, all by himself in the dark, bless him. Getting his own back on history if it kills him, which it probably will." Another date, and the word OLYMPIAD. "He's the vintage year. Any younger, he'd be brainwashed. Any older, he'd be looking for an old fart's sinecure."

He drank, his back still turned to us. I glanced at Bob for enlightenment but he was looking studiously at the floor. I glanced at Ned. His eyes were on Walter but his face was expressionless. I glanced at Walter again and saw that his breath was coming to him in defiant gasps.

"I invented him, I'm sure I did," Walter puffed, seemingly oblivious to the dismay around him. "I've been predicting him for years." He wrote the words FATHER EXECUTED. "Even after they'd drafted him, the poor lamb tried so *hard* to be good. He wasn't sneaky. He wasn't resentful. He had his doubts but, as scientists go, he was a good soldier. Until one day—*bingo!* He wakes up and discovers it's all a load of junk and he's wasted his genius on a bunch of incompetent gangsters and brought the world to the edge of ruin into the bargain." He was writing in fierce strokes while the sweat ran over his temples: WORKING UNDER ROGOV AT 109 TESTING SITE KAZAKHSTAN. "He doesn't know it but he's joined the great Russian male menopausal revolution of the eighties. He's had all the lies, he's had Stalin, the Khrushchev chink of light and the long dark of Brezhnev. But he's still got one last shot in him, one last menopausal chance to print himself on the world. And the new buzz-words are ringing in his ears: revolution from above, openness, peace, change, courage, reconstruction. He's even being *encouraged* to revolt."

He was writing faster than ever, shortwinded or not: TELEMETRY, ACCURACY. "Where will they land?" he was asking rhetorically between gasps. "How close will how many get to how many targets when? What's the expansion and temperature of the skin? What's gravity up to? Crucial questions and the Bluebird knows the answers. He knows because he's in charge of making the missiles talk while they go along—without the Americans hearing, which is his skill. Because he's contrived the encryption systems that dodge the American super-listeners in Turkey and mainland China. He sees all the answers in clear, before Brother Rogov fudges them for his lords and masters in Moscow. Which, according to the Bluebird, is Rogov's speciality. 'Professor Arkady Rogov is an arse-licking toady,' he tells us in notebook two. A fair judgment. That's what Arkady Rogov is. A verifiable, fully paid-up, spineless, arse-licking toady, meeting his norms and earning his medals and his privileges. Who does that remind us of? No one. Certainly not our own dear Clive. So Bluebird blows his lid. He confesses his agony to Katya and Katya says, 'Don't just whimper, do something.' And by golly, he does it. He gives us every bloody thing he can lay his hands on. The Crown Jewels doubled and re-doubled. Encryptions decrypted. Telemetry *en clair*. Retrospective code-breaks to help us check it out. The unbuggered, head-on truth, before it gets repainted for Moscow consumption. All right, he's potty. Who isn't, who's any good?" He took a last swig from his glass, and I saw that the centre of his face was a crimson mass of pain and embarrassment and indignation. "Life's a botch," he explained as he shoved the glass into my hand.

The next I knew, he had slipped past us up the stairs and we heard the steel doors successively opening and slamming shut, one after another, till he had reached the street.

"Walter was a liability," Clive explained to me tersely next morning when I bearded him. "To us, he was merely eccentric, perhaps. But to others—" It was the nearest I had ever known him come to acknowledging the existence of sex. He quickly censored himself. "I've given Walter to Training Section," he continued, with a return to his most frigid manner. "He raised too many eyebrows on the other side."

He meant on the other side of the Atlantic.

So Walter, wonderful Walter, disappeared and I was right—we never saw the Mormons again and Clive never once referred to them. Were they mere messengers from Langley, or had they formed their verdict and exacted their punishment? Were they from Langley at all, or from one of the mushrooming groups of initials that Ned had so objected to when he complained to Clive about the Bluebird distribution list? Or were they Ned's greatest of all pet hates—tame psychiatrists?

Whatever they were, the effect of them was felt all through the Russia House, and Walter's absence yawned at us like a shell-hole made by our best ally's guns. Bob felt it and was ashamed. Even hard-faced Johnny remained ill at ease.

"I'll want you nearer to the operation," Ned told me.

It seemed a wretched consolation for Walter's disappearance.

"You're on edge again," said Hannah as we walked.

It was lunchtime. Her office was close to Regent's Park. Sometimes on warm days we would share a sandwich together. Sometimes we even did a bit of zoo. Sometimes she gave the Cancer Institute a rest and we ended up in bed.

I asked after her husband, Derek. He was one of the few subjects we had in common. Had Derek lost his temper again? Had he beaten her up? Sometimes, in the days when we had been full-time lovers, I used to think it was Derek who held us together. But today she didn't want to talk about Derek. She wanted to know why I was on edge.

"They sacked a man I rather liked," I said. "Well, not sacked, but threw him on the rubbish heap."

"What did he do wrong?"

"Nothing at all. They just decided to see him in a different light."

"Why?"

"Because it suited them. They withdrew their tolerance of him in order to satisfy certain requirements."

She thought about this. "You mean that convention got the better of them," she suggested. Like you, she was saying. Like us.

Why do I keep coming back to her, I wondered. To visit the scene of the crime? To seek, for the thousandth time, her absolution? Or do I visit her as we visit our old schools, trying to understand what happened to our youth?

Hannah is still a beautiful woman, which is a consolation. The greying and the broadening have yet to come. When I catch her face backlit, and glimpse her valiant, vulnerable smile, I see her as I saw her twenty years ago, and tell myself I have not ruined her after all. "She's all right. Look at her. She's smiling and undamaged. It's Derek, not you, who kicks her around."

But I am never sure. Never sure at all.

The Union Jack that had so enraged the dictator Stalin when he observed it from the battlements of the Kremlin dangled dispiritedly from its mast in the British Embassy forecourt. The cream-coloured palace behind it resembled an old wedding cake waiting to be cut, the river lay docile as the morning downpour flailed its oily back. At the iron gates two Russian policemen studied Barley's passport while the rain smeared the ink. The younger copied out his name. The elder dubiously compared his harrowed features with his photograph. Barley was wearing a drenched brown mackintosh. His hair was plastered to his scalp. He looked a little shorter than his usual height.

"Well, *honestly* what a day!" cried the well-bred girl in a pleated tartan skirt, waiting in the lobby. "Hullo, I'm Felicity. You *are* who I think you are, aren't you? A jolly wet Scott Blair? The Economic Counsellor *is* expecting you."

"I thought the Economic people were in the other building."

"Oh, that's Commercial. They're *quite* different."

Barley followed her swinging tail up the ancestral staircase. As always when he entered a British mission, a sense of dislocation overtook him, but this morning it was absolute. The tuneless whistling came from his local paper boy in Hampstead. The huffing and bumping of the floor polisher was the Co-op milk van. It was eight in the morning, and official Britain was not yet officially awake. The Economic Counsellor was a stubby Scotsman with silver hair. His name was Craig.

"Mr. Blair, sir! How do you do? Sit you down! Do you take the tea or the coffee? They both taste the same, I'm afraid, but we're working on it. Gradually, but we'll get there."

Seizing Barley's mackintosh, he impaled it on a Ministry of Works coat-tree. Above the desk a framed photograph showed the Queen in riding habit. A notice beside her warned that speech in this room was not secure. Felicity brought tea and Garibaldi biscuits. Craig talked vigorously, as if he couldn't wait to get rid of his news. His red face was shiny from shaving.

"Oh and I hear you've been having the most *fantastic* runaround from those brigands in VAAP! Have they been making any sense at all? Are you getting anywhere, or are they just giving you the usual Moscow flannel? It's all *makework* here, you see. Seldom but seldom is anything actually transacted. The profit motive, somewhat like diligence, is unknown to them. It's all Brownie points and scratching one another's you-know-whats. The impossible combination, I always say, of incurable idleness harnessed to unattainable visions. The Ambassador used my very phrase in a despatch recently. No credit given, none asked. How do they ever come to grips, I ask you, with an economy built upon sloth, tribalism and hidden unemployment? Answer, they don't! When will they ever break free? What will happen if they do? Answer, God alone knows. I'm seeing the book-world here as a microcosm for their entire dilemma, follow me?"

He roared on until he seemed to decide that Barley and the microphones had had their fill. "Well, I've surely relished our little conversation here this morning. You've given me much food for thought, I don't mind telling you. There's a great danger in our business of getting cut off from the source here. Will you allow me to pass you around a little now? Our Chancery people will never forgive me if I don't."

With a nod of command, he led the way along a passage to a metal door with an evil eyehole in it. The door opened as they reached it and closed as Barley stepped inside.

Craig is your link, Ned had said. He's hell on earth but he'll take you to your leader.

Barley's first impression was that he was in a darkened ward, his next that the ward was a sauna, for the only light came from a corner of the floor and there was a smell of resin. Then he decided that the sauna was suspended, for he detected a rocking underfoot.

Seating himself gingerly on a bridge chair, he discerned two figures behind a table. Above the first hung a curling poster of a Beefeater defending London Bridge. Above the second, Lake Windermere languished under a British Rail sunset.

"Bravo, Barley," exclaimed a sturdy English voice, not unlike Ned's, from below the Beefeater. "My name's Paddy, short for Patrick, and this gent is Cy. He's American."

"Hi, Barley," said Cy.

"We're just the local messenger boys here," Paddy explained. "We're rather limited in what we can do, naturally. Our main job is to supply the camels and hot meals. Ned sends his very special greetings. So does Clive. If they weren't so sullied they'd have come over and done their nail-biting with us. Hazard of the profession. Comes to us all, I'm afraid."

As he spoke, the poor light released him. He was shaggy but lithe, with the craggy brows and faraway eyes of an explorer. Cy was sleek and urban and younger by a dozen years. Their four hands lay on a street map of Leningrad. Paddy's shirtcuffs were frayed. Cy's were drip dry.

"I'm to ask you whether you want to go on, by the by," Paddy said, as if that were a rather good joke. "If you want to bail out that's your good right and no hard feelings. Want to bail out? What do you say?"

"Zapadny will kill me," Barley muttered.

"Why's that?"

"I'm his guest. He's footing my bill, fixing my program." Lifting his hand to his forehead, he scrubbed at it as a way of reviving communication with his brain. "What do I tell him? I can't just up-sticks, bye-bye, I'm off to Leningrad. He'd think I was loony."

"But you *are* saying Leningrad, not London?" Paddy persisted kindly enough.

"I haven't got a visa. I've got Moscow. I haven't got Leningrad."

"But assuming."

Another lengthy delay.

"I need to talk to him," Barley said, as if that were an explanation.

"To Zapadny?"

"Goethe. Got to talk to him."

Dragging the back of his right wrist across his mouth in one of his habitual gestures, Barley looked at it as if expecting blood. "I won't lie to him," he muttered.

"There's no question of your lying to him. Ned wants a partnership, not a deception."

"That goes for us too," said Cy.

"I won't be sly with him. I'll talk to him straight or not at all."

"Ned wouldn't wish it any other way," said Paddy. "We want to give him everything he needs."

"Us too," said Cy.

"Potomac Boston, Incorporated, Barley, your new American trading partner," Paddy proposed in a fresh voice, glancing at a paper before him. "The head of their publishing operation is a Mr. Henziger, is that right?"

"J.P.," Barley said.

"Ever met him?"

Barley shook his head and winced. "Name on the contract," he said.

"That the nearest you've got to him?"

"We've spoken on the phone a couple of times. Ned thought we ought to be heard on the transatlantic line. Cover."

"But you've no mental portrait of him otherwise?" Paddy persisted, in the way he had of forcing clear replies even if it made a pedant of him. "He's not a drawn character for you in some way?"

"He's a name with money and offices in Boston and he's a voice on the phone. That's all he's ever been."

"And in your conversations with local third parties—with Zapadny, say—J. P. Henziger has not featured as some kind of horror figure? You haven't given him a false beard or a wooden leg or a lurid sexlife? Nothing one might have to take into account if one were making him flesh, as it were?"

Barley considered the question but seemed to lose hold of it.

"No?" asked Paddy.

"No," Barley said, and again unwisely shook his head.

"So a situation that might have arisen is this," said Paddy. "Mr. J. P. Henziger of Potomac Boston, young, dynamic, pushy, is presently to be found on holiday in Europe with his wife. It's the season. They are at this moment, let us say, at the Marski Hotel in Helsinki. Know the Marski?"

"I've had a drink there," Barley said, as if he were ashamed of it.

"And in this impulsive American way they have, the Henzigers have taken it into their heads to make a lightning trip to Leningrad. Over to you, I think, Cy."

Cy unlocked his smile and obliged. He had a sharp face when it came alive and an intelligent, if snappish, way of talking.

"The Henzigers take a three-day guided tour, Barley. Visas at the Finnish border, the guide, the bus, the whole nine yards. They're straightforward people, decent. This is Russia and it's their first time. *Glasnost* is news back home in Boston. He has money invested in you. Knowing you are in Moscow spending it, he requires you to drop everything, hurry to Leningrad, carry his bags for him and report progress. That's normal practice, typical of a young tycoon. You see a problem? Some way it doesn't play for you?"

Barley's head was clearing and his vision with it.

"No. It plays. I can make it work if you can."

"First thing this morning UK time, J.P. calls your London office from the Marski, gets your machine," Cy continued. "J.P. does not talk to machines. An hour from now he telexes you care of Zapadny at VAAP, copy to Craig here at the British Embassy, Moscow, requesting you to meet with him this Friday at the Hotel

Evropeiskaya, alias the Europe, Leningrad, which is where his tour-group is staying. Zapadny will wriggle, maybe raise a cry of pain. But since you are spending J.P.'s cash it's our prediction Zapadny will have no choice but to bow to market forces. Figure?"

"Yes," said Barley.

Paddy took back the story. "If he's got any sense he'll help you get your visas changed. If he sulks, Wicklow can whisk them across to OVIR and they'll change them while he waits. You wouldn't make too much of it to Zapadny, in our view. You wouldn't grovel or apologise, not to Zapadny. You'd make a virtue of it. Tell him that's how life is lived these days in the fast lane."

"J. P. Henziger is family," Cy said. "He's a fine officer. So's his wife."

He stopped abruptly.

Like an umpire who has spotted a foul, Barley had flung out an arm and was pointing it at Paddy's chest.

"Hang on, you two! Hold your water. Half a mo! What use will *either* of them be, however *fine* they are, if they're riding round Leningrad locked in a bloody tour-bus all day?"

Paddy took only a moment to recover from this unexpected onslaught. "You tell him, Cy," he said.

"Barley, on their arrival at the Hotel Europe Thursday evening Mrs. Henziger will contract a severe dose of Leningrad tummy. J.P. will have no taste for sightseeing while his lovely lady is laid low with the runs. He'll dig in with her at the hotel. No problem."

Paddy set the lamp and power-pack next to the map of Leningrad. Katya's three addresses were ringed in red.

It was late afternoon before Barley telephoned her, about the time when he reckoned she would be locking away her paperclips. He had taken a nap and followed it with a couple of Scotches to bring himself up to par. But when he started talking he discovered that his voice was too high, and he had to bring it down.

"Ah. Hullo! You got home all right," he said, sounding like someone he'd never met. "Train didn't turn into a pumpkin or anything?"

"Thank you, it was not a problem."

"Great. Well, I just rang to find out, really. Yes. Say thank you for a marvellous evening. Mmhmh. And goodbye for the time being."

"Thank you also. It was productive."

"Hoped we might have had another chance to meet, you see. Trouble is, I've got to go to Leningrad. Some stupid bit of business has cropped up and made me change my plans."

A prolonged silence. "Then you must sit down," she said.

Barley wondered which of them had gone mad. "Why?"

"It is our custom, when we are preparing for a long journey, first to sit down. You are sitting now?"

He could hear the happiness in her voice and it made him happy too.

"I'm lying down, actually. Will that do?"

"I have not heard of it. You are supposed to sit on your luggage or a bench, sigh a little and then cross yourself. But I expect that lying down will have the same effect."

"It does."

"Will you come back to Moscow from Leningrad?"

"Well, not on this trip. I think we'll fly straight back to school."

"School?"

"England. Stupid expression of mine."

"What does it denote?"

"Obligations. Immaturity. Ignorance. The usual English vices."

"You have many obligations?"

"Suitcases of 'em. But I'm learning to sort them out. I actually said no yesterday and astonished everybody."

"Why do you have to say no? Why not say yes? Perhaps they would be even more astonished."

"Yes, well that was the trouble with last night, wasn't it? I never got round to talking about myself. We talked about you, the great poets down the ages, Mr. Gorbachev, publishing. But we left out the main topic. Me. I'll have to make a special trip just to come and bore you."

"I am sure you will not bore me."

"Is there anything I can bring you?"

"Please?"

"Next time I come. Any special wishes? An electric toothbrush? Paper curlers? More Jane Austen?"

A long delicious pause.

"I wish you a good journey, Barley," she said.

The last lunch with Zapadny was a wake without a corpse. They sat fourteen, all men, the only guests in the enormous upstairs restaurant of an unfinished new hotel. Waiters brought food and vanished to the distant outskirts. Zapadny had to send scouts to find them. There was no drink and precious little conversation unless Barley and Zapadny contrived it between them. There was canned music of the fifties. There was a lot of hammering.

"But we have arranged a great party for you, Barley," Zapadny protested. "Vassily is bringing his drums, Viktor will lend you his saxophone, a friend of mine who makes his own moonshine has promised us six bottles, there will be some mad painters and writers. It has all the makings of a most disreputable evening and you have the weekend to recover. Tell your American Potomac bastard to go to hell. We do not like you so serious."

"Our tycoons are your bureaucrats, Alik. We ignore them at our peril. So do you."

Zapadny's smile was neither warm nor forgiving. "We even thought you might have lost your heart a little to one of our celebrated Moscow beauties. Can't the delicious Katya persuade you to stay?"

"Who's Katya?" Barley heard himself reply while he was still wondering why the ceiling hadn't fallen in.

A buzz of eager amusement rose from around the table.

"This is Moscow, Barley," Zapadny reminded him, very pleased with himself. "Nothing happens without something happening. The intelligentsia is small, we are all broke and local telephone calls are free. You cannot dine with Katya Orlova in an intimate and rather crazy restaurant without at least fifteen of us being advised of it next morning."

"It was strictly business," Barley said.

"Then why didn't you take Mr. Wicklow along with you?"

"He's much too young," said Barley, and scored another peal of Russian merriment.

The night sleeper to Leningrad leaves Moscow at a few minutes before midnight, traditionally so that Russia's numberless bureaucrats may claim a second day's subsistence for the journey. The compartment had four berths, and Wicklow and Barley had the lower pair until a heavyweight blond lady insisted Barley exchange places with her. The fourth berth was occupied by a quiet man of apparent means who spoke elegant English and carried an air of private grief about him. First he wore a lawyer's dark suit, then he wore wildly striped pyjamas that would have graced a clown, but his mood did not brighten with his costume. There was more business when the blond lady refused to take off even her hat until the three men had removed themselves to the corridor. Harmony was restored when she called them back and, clad in a pink tracksuit with pompoms on the shoulders, fed them homemade pastries in gratitude for their gallantry. And when Barley produced whisky she was so impressed she made them eat her sausage too, insisting they drink the health of Mrs. Thatcher more than once.

"Where do you come from?" the sad man asked Barley across the divide as they settled for the night.

"London," said Barley.

"London in England. Not from the moon, not from the stars, but London in England," the sad man confirmed and, unlike Barley, soon appeared to fall asleep. But a couple of hours later as they pulled into a station, he resumed their conversation. "Do you know where we are now?" he asked without bothering to establish whether Barley was awake.

"I don't think I do."

"If Anna Karenina were travelling with us tonight and had her wits about her, this would be the place where she would abandon the unsatisfactory Vronsky."

"Marvellous," said Barley, quite mystified. His whisky was gone but the sad man had Georgian brandy.

"It was a swamp before, it is a swamp today," the sad man said. "If you are studying the Russian disease, you must live in the Russian swamp."

He was talking about Leningrad.

A low cottonwool sky hung over the imported palaces, making them dreary in their fancy dress. Summer music played in the parks but the summer clung behind the clouds, leaving a chalky Nordic mist to trick and tremble on the Venetian waterways. Barley walked and, as always when he was in Leningrad, he had the sensation of walking through other cities, now Prague, now Vienna, now a bit of Paris or a corner of Regent's Park. No other city that he knew hid its shame behind so many sweet façades or asked such terrible questions with its smile. Who worshipped in these locked, unreal churches? And whose God? How many bodies had choked these graceful canals or floated frozen to the sea? Where else on earth has so much barbarism built itself such pretty monuments? Even the people in the street, so slow spoken, decorous, reserved, seemed joined to one another by their monstrous dissembling. And Barley, as he loitered and gazed like any tourist—and like any spy counted off the minutes—Barley felt himself a part of their duplicity.

He had shaken hands with an American tycoon who was not a tycoon, and commiserated with him about his sick wife who was not sick and probably not his wife.

He had instructed a subordinate who was not his subordinate to give succour in an emergency that did not exist.

He was on his way to keep a rendezvous with an author who was not an author but was seeking martyrdom in a city where martyrdom could be had free across the counter, whether or not you happened to stand in line for it.

He was scared numb and had a hangover for the fourth day running.

He was a citizen of Leningrad at last.

Finding himself in the Nevsky Prospekt he realised he was looking for the cafeteria called informally the Saigon, a place for poets, drug-pedlars and speculators, not professors' daughters. "Your father is right," he heard her say. "The system will always win."

He had his own street map, courtesy of Paddy—German, with a multi-lingual text. From Cy he had a copy of *Crime and Punishment,* a battered Penguin paperback in a translation to drive him to despair. He had put them both in a plastic carrier bag. Wicklow had insisted. Not just any bag but this bag, advertising some beastly American cigarette and recognisable at five hundred metres. Now his only mission in life was to trail Raskolnikov on his fateful journey to murder the old lady, which was why he was searching for a courtyard leading off the Griboyedev Canal. Iron gates opened to it, a spreading tree gave it shade. He wandered in it slowly, peering at his Penguin book, then guardedly at the grimy windows as if expecting the old pawnbroker's blood to come seeping down the yellowing paintwork. Only occasionally did he allow his gaze to stray into that unfocussed middle distance which is the preserve of the English upper classes, and which comprises such extraneous objects as passers-by, or those not passing by but doing nothing; or the gate that led to Plekhanova Street which only very local people knew of, said Paddy, such as scientists who in their youth had studied at the Litmo around the corner, but who, so far as Barley could see from his casual searching of the approaches, showed no sign of returning.

He was out of breath. A bubble of nausea like an airpocket filled his lower chest. He reached the gate and opened it. He passed through an entrance hall. He climbed the short flight of steps to the street. He glanced both ways and made another show of comparing his findings while Wicklow's hated microphone harness sawed his back. He turned round and sauntered back through the courtyard and under the spreading tree until he was once more alongside the canal. He sat on a bench and unfolded the street map. Ten minutes, Paddy had said, handing him a scratched sports-watch in place of his unreliable heirloom. Five before, five after, then abort.

"You are lost?" asked a pale man who looked too old to be a tout. He was wearing Italian racing-driver glasses and Nike sneakers. His Russian English had an American accent.

"I'm always lost, old boy, thank you," said Barley politely. "It's the way I like it."

"You want to sell me something? Cigarettes? Scotch? Fountain pen? You want to trade drugs or currency or something like this?"

"Thanks, but I'm very nice as I am," Barley replied, relieved to hear himself speaking normally. "If you'd just move out of the sun a little, I'll be even nicer."

"You want to meet an international group of people including girls? I can show you the real Russia nobody ever gets to see."

"Old boy, to be perfectly honest, I don't believe you'd know the real Russia if it got up and bit you in the balls," said Barley, returning to his map. The man drifted away.

On Fridays even the great scientists will be doing what everyone else is doing, Paddy had said. They'll be closing down the week and getting drunk. They'll have had their three-day knees-up, they'll have shown each other their achievements and traded their researches. Their Leningrad hosts will be feeding them a lavish lunch but leaving them time to get at the shops before they return to their postbox numbers. That will be your friend's first chance to slip away from the group if he's going to.

My friend. *My* Raskolnikov friend. Not *his* friend. Mine. In case I come unstuck.

One rendezvous down and two to go.

Barley stood up, rubbed his back and with time to waste continued his literary tour of Leningrad. Recrossing the Nevsky Prospekt, he gazed at the weathered faces of the shoppers and in a rush of empathy prayed to be assumed into their ranks: "I'm one of you! I share your confusions! Accept me! Hide me! Ignore me!" He steadied himself. Look round. Look foolish. Gawp.

Behind him stood the Kazan Cathedral. Ahead of him rose the House of Books, where as a good publisher Barley now lingered, squinting into the windows and upwards at the stubby tower with its vile globe. But he did not stay for long in case he was recognised by somebody from one of the editorial offices upstairs. He entered Zhelyabova Street and approached one of the great department stores of Leningrad, with its wartime English fashions in the window and fur hats out of season. He placed himself conspicuously at the main entrance, hooking the carrier bag over his middle finger and unfolding his map for refuge.

Not here, he thought. For Christ's sake, not here. Give us a decent privacy, Goethe, please. Not here.

"If he selects the shop, he's reckoning on a very public meeting," Paddy had said. "He's got to fling up his arms and shout, 'Scott Blair, can it be you?'"

For the next ten minutes Barley thought of nothing. He stared at the map, lifted his head and stared at buildings. He stared at girls, and in Leningrad that summer's day the girls were staring back. But their alertness did not reassure him and he ducked back into his map. Sweat was running like marbles over his rib cage. He had a fantasy that the microphones would short-circuit. Twice he cleared his throat because he feared he wouldn't be able to speak. But when he tried to moisten his lips he discovered that his tongue had withered.

The ten minutes were up but he waited another two because he owed them: to himself, to Katya, to Goethe. He folded the map, not making the right folds, but then he had never managed that anyway. He stuffed the map into the gaudy plastic bag. He rejoined the crowds and discovered that after all he could walk like everybody else, no sudden lurches, no bone-cracking falls headlong to the pavement.

He strolled back down the Nevsky towards the Anichkov Bridge, looking for the No. 7 trolleybus to Smolny for his third and final appearance before the assembled spies of Leningrad.

Two boys in jeans stood ahead of him in the queue. Three babushkas stood behind him. The trolleybus arrived and the boys leapt in. Barley followed them aboard. The two boys chatted noisily. An old man stood up in order to let one of the babushkas sit. We're a good crowd in here, Barley thought in another lurch of dependence upon those he was deceiving; let's stay together all day and enjoy each other. A small boy was frowning into his face, asking him something. On an inspiration, Barley pulled back his sleeve and showed him Paddy's steel wristwatch. The boy studied it and gave a hiss of rage. The trolleybus clanged to a halt.

He's funked it, thought Barley in relief as he entered into the park. The sun broke clear of the clouds. He's chickened and who can blame him?

But by then he had spotted him. Goethe, precisely as advertised. Goethe, the great lover and thinker, seated on the third bench to your left as you enter the gravel path, a nihilist who takes no principle for granted.

Goethe. Reading his newspaper. Sober and half his original size, dressed in a black suit certainly, but looking like his smaller, older brother. Barley's heart sank, then leapt, at the sight of such sheer ordinariness. The shadow of the great poet was extinct. Lines of age marked the once-smooth face. The mercurial had no place in this clerkish, bearded Russian taking his midday air on a park bench.

But Goethe nonetheless, and seated amid a cluster of warring Russian shrines: not a pistol shot from the fiery statues of Marx, Engels and Lenin, who forced their bronze scowls on him from strangely separated plinths; not a musket shot from the sacred Room 67, where Lenin had set up his revolutionary headquarters in a boarding school for the better class of Petersburg girl; not a funeral march from Rastrelli's blue baroque cathedral built to ease the declining years of an empress; not a blindfold walk from the Leningrad Party Headquarters with its oversize policemen glowering at the liberated masses.

Smola means tar, Barley recalled stupidly in this continuing moment of monstrous normality. In Smolny, Peter the Great stored his tar for the first Russian Navy.

Those nearest to Goethe were as normal as the man himself. The day might have started dull but the new sunlight had worked miracles and the good citizens were stripping off as if a common urge had seized them. Boys bare to the waist, girls like thrownaway flowers, hulking women in satin brassières lay sprawled at Goethe's feet, playing radios, munching sandwiches and discussing whatever it was that made them grimace, ponder and laugh in swift succession.

A chip path ran close to the bench. Barley launched himself upon it studying the *Informationen* at the back of the folded map. In the field, Ned had said, in a session devoted to the macabre etiquette of tradecraft, the source is the star and the star decides whether to make the meeting or abort.

Fifty yards separated Barley from his star but the path joined them like a ruled line. Was he walking too fast or too slowly? One moment he was pressing up against the couple in front of him, the next he was being shoved aside from behind. If he ignores you, wait five minutes then try a second pass, Paddy had said. Squinting over his map, Barley saw Goethe's face lift as if he had scented his approach. He saw the whiteness of his cheeks and the unlit hollows of his eyes; then the whiteness of the newspaper as he folded it together like a camper's blanket. He saw that there was something angular and not quite reconciled about his movements, so that he resembled in Barley's racing mind a figure of over-orderly clockwork in a Swiss town: now I will lift my white face, now I strike twelve with my white flag, now I stand up and march away. The newspaper folded, Goethe put it in his pocket and gave a pedagogic glance at his wristwatch. Then with the same mechanical air of being someone else's invention, he took his place in the army of pedestrians and loped among them towards the river.

Now Barley's pace was set, for it was Goethe's. His quarry was following the path towards a row of parked cars. Eyes and brain clear, Barley walked after him and, reaching the cars, saw him standing against the fast-flowing Neva, his jacket puffed out by the river breeze. A pleasure steamer passed but the passengers gave no sign of pleasure. A coaling boat hobbled by, dappled in red lead, and the filthy smoke from its funnel was beautiful in the dancing river light. Goethe leaned over the balustrade and peered down at the current as if calculating its speed. Barley headed towards him, slurring his feet while he orientated himself from his map with increasing diligence. Even when he heard himself addressed, in the immaculate English that had woken him on the verandah in Peredelkino, he did not immediately respond.

"Sir? Excuse me, sir. I think we are acquainted."

But Barley at first refused to hear. The voice was too nervous, too tentative. He went on frowning at his *Informationen*. Must be another tout, he was saying to himself. Another of those drug-pedlars or pimps.

"Sir?" Goethe repeated, as if he himself were now unsure.

Only now, won over by the stranger's insistence, did Barley reluctantly raise his head.

"I think you are Mr. Scott Blair, sir, the distinguished publisher from England."

At which Barley finally persuaded himself to recognise the man addressing him, first with doubt, then unfeigned but muted pleasure as he thrust out his hand.

"Well, I'm damned," he said quietly. "Good God. The great Goethe, as I live and breathe. We met at that disgraceful literary party. We were the only two people sober. How are you?"

"Oh, I am *very* well," Goethe said as his strained voice gathered courage. But his hand when Barley shook it was slippery with sweat. "I do not know how I could be better at this moment. Welcome to Leningrad, Mr. Barley. What a pity I have an appointment this afternoon. You can walk a little? We can exchange ideas?" His voice barely fell. "It is safest to keep moving," he explained.

He had grasped Barley's arm and was propelling him swiftly along the embankment. His urgency had driven every tactical thought from Barley's mind. Barley glanced at the bobbing figure beside him, at the pallor of his racked cheeks, the tracks of pain or fear or worry that ran down them. He saw the hunted eyes flicking nervously at every passing face. And his only instinct was to protect him: for Goethe's own sake and for Katya's.

"If we could walk for half an hour, we would see the battleship *Aurora*, which fired the blank shot to launch the Revolution. But the next revolution shall begin with a few gentle phrases of Bach. It is time. Do you agree?"

"And no conductor," said Barley, with a grin.

"Or maybe some of that jazz you play so beautifully. Yes, yes! I have it! You shall announce our revolution by playing Lester Young on the saxophone. You have read the new Rybakov novel? Twenty years suppressed and therefore a great Russian masterpiece? It is a rape of time, I think."

"It hasn't appeared in English yet."

"You have read mine?" The thin hand had tightened on his arm. The pressed-in voice had fallen to a murmur.

"What I could understand of it, yes."

"What do you think?"

"It's brave."

"No more than that?"

"It's sensational. What I could understand of it. Great."

"We recognised each other that night. It was magic. You know our Russian saying 'One fisherman always sees another from afar'? We are fishermen. We shall feed the thousands with our truth."

"Maybe we will at that," said Barley doubtfully, and felt the gaunt head swing round to him. "I have to discuss it with you a bit, Goethe. We've got one or two problems."

"That's why you have come. I too. Thank you for coming to Leningrad. When will you publish? It must be soon. The writers here, they wait three, five years for publication even if they are not Rybakov. I can't do that. Russia has no time. Neither have I."

A line of tugs drew by, a two-man scull flicked cheekily in their wake. Two lovers were embracing at the parapet. And in the shadow of the cathedral a young woman stood rocking a pram while she read from the book she was holding in her spare hand.

"When I didn't show up at the Moscow audio fair, Katya gave your manuscript to a colleague of mine," Barley said cautiously.

"I know. She had to take a chance."

"What you don't know is that the colleague couldn't find me when he got back to England. So he gave it to the authorities. People of discretion. Experts."

Goethe turned sharply to Barley in alarm and the shadow of dismay spread swiftly over his fraught features. "I do not *like* experts," he said. "They are our jailers. I despise experts more than anyone on earth."

"You're one yourself, aren't you?"

"Therefore I know! Experts are addicts. They solve nothing! They are servants of whatever system hires them. They perpetuate it. When we are tortured, we shall be tortured by experts. When we are hanged, experts will hang us. Did you not read what I wrote? When the world is destroyed, it will be destroyed not by its madmen but by the sanity of its experts and the superior ignorance of its bureaucrats. You have betrayed me."

"Nobody's betrayed you," Barley said angrily. "The manuscript went astray, that's all. Our bureaucrats are not your bureaucrats. They've read it, they admire it, but they need to know more about you. They can't believe the message unless they can believe the source."

"But do they want to publish it?"

"First of all they need to reassure themselves you're not a trick, and their best way to do that is to talk to you."

Goethe was striding too fast, taking Barley with him. He was staring out ahead of him. Sweat was running down his temples.

"I'm an arts man, Goethe," Barley said breathlessly to his averted face. "All I know about physics is *Beowulf,* girls and warm beer. I'm out of my depth. So's Katya. If you want to go this road, go it with the experts and leave us out. That's what I came to tell you."

They crossed a path and struck out across another segment of lawn. A group of schoolchildren broke ranks to let them through.

"You came to tell me that you refuse to publish me?"

"How *can* I publish you?" Barley retorted, in turn fired by Goethe's desperation. "Even if we could knock the material into shape, what about Katya? She's your courier, remember? She's passed Soviet defence secrets to a foreign power. That's not exactly a laugh a minute over here. If they ever find out about the two of you, she'll be dead the day the first copy hits the stands. What sort of part is that for a publisher to play? Do you think I'm going to sit in London and press the button on the two of you here?"

Goethe was panting, but his eyes had ceased to scan the crowds and were turned to Barley.

"Listen to me," Barley pleaded. "Just hold on a minute. I understand. I really think I understand. You had a talent and it was put to unfair uses. You know all the ways the system stinks and you want to wash your soul. But you're not Christ and you're not Pecherin. You're out of court. If you want to kill yourself, that's your business. But you'll kill her too. And if you don't care who you kill, why should you care who you save?"

They were heading for a picnic place with chairs and tables cut from logs. They sat side by side and Barley spread his map. They bent over it, pretending to examine it together. Goethe was still measuring Barley's words, matching them against his purposes.

"There is only *now,*" he explained finally, his voice not above a murmur. "There is no other dimension but *now.* In the past we have done everything badly for the sake of the future. Now we must do everything right for the sake of the present. To lose time is to lose everything. Our Russian history does not give us second chances. When we leap across an abyss, she does not give us the opportunity for a second step. And when we fail she gives us what we deserve: another Stalin, another Brezhnev, another purge, another ice age of terrified monotony. If the present momentum continues, I shall have been in the vanguard. If it stops or goes back, I shall be another statistic of our post-Revolutionary history."

"So will Katya," Barley said.

Goethe's finger, unable to stay still, was travelling across the map. He glanced round him, then continued. "We are in Leningrad, Barley, the cradle of our great Revolution. Nobody triumphs here without sacrifice. You said we needed an experiment in human nature. Why are you so shocked when I put your words into practice?"

"You got me wrong that day. I'm not the man you took me for. I'm the original useless mouth. You just met me when the wind was in the right direction."

With a frightening control Goethe opened his hands and spread them palms downward on the map. "You do not need to remind me that man is not equal to his rhetoric," he said. "Our new people talk about openness, disarmament, peace. So let them have their openness. And their disarmament. And their peace. Let us call their bluff and give them what they ask. And make sure that this time they cannot put the clock back." He was standing, no longer able to bear the confinement of the table.

Barley stood beside him. "Goethe, for God's sake. Take it easy."

"To the devil with easy! It is easy that kills!" He began striding again. "We do not break the curse of secrecy by passing our secrets from hand to hand like thieves! I have lived a great lie! And you tell me to keep it secret! How did the lie survive? By secrecy. How did our great vision crumble to this dreadful mess? By secrecy. How do you keep your own people ignorant of the insanity of your war plans? By secrecy. By keeping out the light. Show my work to your spies if that's what you must do. But publish me as well. That is what you promised and I shall believe your promise. I have dropped a notebook containing further chapters into your carrier bag. No doubt it answers many of the questions the idiots wish to put to me."

The breeze of the river washed over Barley's heated face as they strode along. Glancing at Goethe's glistening features, he fancied he glimpsed traces of the hurt innocence that seemed to be the source of his outrage.

"I shall wish a book jacket that is only letters," he announced. "No drawing, please, no sensational design. You heard me?"

"We haven't even got a title," Barley objected.

"You will please use my own name as the author. No evasions, no pseudonyms. To use a pseudonym is to invent another secret."

"I don't even *know* your name."

"They will know it. After what Katya told you, and with the new chapters, they will have no problem. Keep correct accounts. Every six months, please send the money to a deserving cause. Nobody shall say I did this for my own profit."

Through the approaching trees the strains of martial music vied with the clatter of invisible trams.

"Goethe," said Barley.

"What is the matter? Are you afraid?"

"Come to England. They'll smuggle you out. They're smart. Then you can tell the world everything you want. We'll rent the Albert Hall for you. Put you on television, radio—you name it. And when it's over, they'll give you a passport and money and you can live happily ever after in Australia."

They had stopped again. Had Goethe heard? Had he understood? Still nothing stirred behind his unblinking stare. His eyes were fixed on Barley as if he were a distant spot upon a vast horizon.

"I am not a defector, Barley. I am a Russian, and my future is here, even if it is a short one. Will you publish me or not? I need to know."

Buying time, Barley reached into his jacket pocket and pulled out Cy's worn paperback. "I'm to give you this," he said. "A memento of our meeting. Their questions are bound into the text, together with an address in Finland you can write to and a phone number in Moscow with instructions on what to say when you call. If you'll do business with them direct, they've got all sorts of clever toys they can give you to make communication easier." He placed the paperback in Goethe's open hand and it remained there.

"Will you publish me? Yes or no."

"How do they get hold of you? They have to know."

"Tell them I can be reached through my publisher."

"Take Katya out of the equation. Stay with the spies and keep away from her."

Goethe's gaze had descended to Barley's suit and remained there, as if the sight of it troubled him. His sad smile was like a last holiday.

"You are wearing grey today, Barley. My father was sent to prison by grey men. He was shot by an old man who wore a grey uniform. It is the grey men who have ruined my beautiful profession. Take care or they will ruin yours too. Will you publish me or must I start again in my search for a decent human being?"

For a while Barley could not answer. His mechanisms of evasion had run out.

"If I can get control of the material, and find a way through it to a book, I'll publish you," he replied.

"I asked you, yes or no."

Promise him anything he asks within reason, Paddy had said. But what was reason? "All right," he replied. "Yes."

Goethe handed Barley back the book and Barley in a daze returned it to his pocket. They embraced and Barley smelt sweat and stale tobacco smoke and felt again the desperate strength of their farewell in Peredelkino. As abruptly as Goethe had seized him, so he now released him and with another nervous glance round him set off quickly towards the trolleybus stop. And as Barley watched him he noticed how the old couple from the outdoor café was watching his departure too, standing in the shadow of the dark blue trees.

Barley sneezed, then started sneezing seriously. Then really sneezed. He walked back into the park, his face buried in his handkerchief while he shook his shoulders and sneezed and shook again.

"Why, *Scott!*" J. P. Henziger exclaimed, with the overbright enthusiasm of a busy man kept waiting, as he snatched back the door on the largest bedroom in the Hotel Europe. "Scott, this is a day when we discover who our friends are. Come in, please. What kept you? Say hullo to Maisie."

He was mid-forties, muscular and prehensile, but he had the kind of ugly friendly face that Barley would normally have warmed to instantly. He wore an elephant hair round one wrist and a gold-link bracelet round the other. Half-moons of sweat blackened his denim armpits. Wicklow appeared behind him and quickly closed the door.

Twin beds, draped in olive counterpanes, commanded the centre of the room. In one of them languished Mrs. Henziger, a thirty-five-year-old kitten without her make-up, her combed-out tresses spread tragically over her freckled shoulders. A man in a black suit hovered uneasily at her side. He wore liver-coloured spectacles. A medical practitioner's case lay open on the bed. Henziger continued vamping for the microphones.

"Scott, I want you to meet Dr. Pete Bernstorf from the U.S. Consulate General here in Leningrad, a fine physician. We are indebted to him. Maisie is improving fast. We are indebted to Mr. Wicklow also. Leonard fixed the hotel, the tour people, the pharmacy. How was your day?"

"One bloody long laugh," Barley blurted, and for a moment the script threatened to go badly wrong.

Barley tossed the carrier bag on to the bed and with it the rejected paperback book from his jacket pocket. With shaking hands he pulled off his jacket, tore the microphone harness out of his shirt and flung it after the bag and the book. He reached behind him into his waistband and, brushing aside Wicklow's offer of assistance, extracted the grey recording box from the small of his back and threw that on the bed as well, so that Maisie let out a stifled "shit" and moved her legs quickly to one side. Marching to the washbasin, he emptied his whisky flask into a toothmug, hugging one arm across his chest as if he had been shot. Then he drank and went on drinking, oblivious to the perfect drill unfolding round him.

Henziger, light as a cat for all his bulk, grabbed the carrier bag, picked out the notebook and shoved it at Bernstorf, who spirited it into his medical case among the phials and instruments, where it mysteriously disappeared. Henziger passed him the paperback, which also vanished. Wicklow swept up the recorder and harness. They too went into the case, which Bernstorf snapped shut while he issued departing instructions to the patient: no solids for forty-eight hours, Mrs. Henziger, tea, a piece of brown bread if you must, make sure you complete the course of antibiotics whether or not you feel better. He had not finished before Henziger chimed in.

"And, Doctor, if ever you are in Boston, and you need anything, because I mean *anything,* here's my card and here's my promise and here's . . ."

Toothmug in hand, Barley remained facing the washbasin, glowering in the mirror as the Good Samaritan's case made its journey to the door.

Of all his nights in Russia and, come to think of it, of all his nights anywhere in the world, this was Barley's worst.

Henziger had heard that a cooperative restaurant had just opened in Leningrad, cooperative being the new codeword for private. Wicklow had tracked it down and reported it full, but rejection for Henziger was challenge. By dint of heavy telephoning and heavier tipping, an extra table was laid for them, three feet from the worst and noisiest gypsy opera Barley ever hoped to hear.

And there they now sat, celebrating Mrs. Henziger's miraculous recovery. The mewing of the singers was amplified by electronic bullhorns. There was no remission between numbers.

And all round them sat the Russia that the slumbering puritan in Barley had long hated but never seen: the not-so-secret czars of capitalism, the industrial parvenus and conspicuous consumers, the Party fat-cats and racketeers, their jewelled women reeking of Western perfumes and Russian deodorant, the waiters doting on the richest tables. The singers' frightful voices rose, the music rose to drown them, the voices rose again and Henziger's voice rose above them all.

"Scott, I want you to know something," he bellowed to Barley, leaning excitedly across the table. "This little country is on the move. I smell hope here, I smell change, I smell commerce. And we in Potomac are buying ourselves a piece of it. I'm proud." But his voice had been taken away from him by the band. "Proud," his lips repeated soundlessly to a million gypsy decibels.

And the trouble was, Henziger was a nice fellow and Maisie was a sport, which made it worse. As the agony dragged on, Barley entered the blessed state of deafness. Inside the cacophony he discovered his own safe room. From its arrow-slit windows his secret self stared into the white Leningrad night. Where have you gone, Goethe? he asked. Who stands in for her when she isn't there? Who darns your black socks and cooks your washed-out soup for you while you drag her by the hair along your noble altruistic path to self-destruction?

Somehow without his being aware of it they must have returned to the hotel, for he woke to discover himself propped on Wicklow's arm among the Finnish alcoholics stumbling shamefacedly round the lobby.

"Great party," he told anyone who would hear him. "Splendid band. Thank you for coming to Leningrad."

But as Wicklow patiently hauled him up to bed the undrunk part of Barley glanced over his shoulder, down the wide staircase. And in the darkness near the entrance, he saw Katya, seated with her legs crossed, her perhaps-bag on her lap. She was wearing a pinched black jacket. A white silk scarf was knotted under her chin, and her face was pressed towards him with that tense smile she had, sad and hopeful, open to love.

But as his gaze cleared he saw her say something saucy out of the corner of her mouth to the porter, and he realised she was just another Leningrad tart looking for a trick.

And next day, to the fanfare of the most discreet of British trumpets, our hero came home.

Ned wanted no display, no Americans and certainly no Clive, but he was determined on a gesture, so we drove to Gatwick and, having posted Brock at the Arrivals barrier with a card saying "Potomac," we installed ourselves in a hospitality lounge that the Service shared uneasily with the Foreign Office amid endless argument about who had drunk the gin.

We waited, the plane was delayed. Clive phoned from Grosvenor Square to ask "Has he arrived, Palfrey?" as if he half expected him to stay in Russia.

Another half-hour passed before Clive phoned again and this time Ned himself took the call. He had scarcely slammed the phone down before the door opened and Wicklow slipped in grinning like a choirboy but contriving at the same time to shoot his eyes in warning.

Seconds after him, enter Barley looking like his own surveillance photographs, except that he was white-faced. "Buggers cheered!" he blurted before Brock had got the door shut. "That prissy captain with his Surrey vowels! I'll kill the swine."

While Barley stormed on, Wicklow discreetly explained the cause of his distress.

Their charter flight out of Leningrad had been occupied by a delegation of young British traders whom Barley had arbitrarily branded yuppies of the vilest sort, which by the sound of them they were. Several were drunk by the time they boarded, the rest were quick to catch up. They had not been more than a few minutes in the air when the captain, who in Barley's view was the provocateur of the incident, announced that the plane had left Soviet airspace. A roar went up while the air hostesses scampered up and down the aisle doling out champagne. Then they all broke into "Rule, Britannia!"

"Give me Aeroflot every time," Barley raged at the assembled faces. "I'm going to write to the airline. I'm going to—"

"You're going to do nothing of the kind," Ned kindly interrupted him. "You're going to let us make an enormous fuss of you. You can have your tantrum later."

As he said this, he went on shaking Barley's hand until Barley eventually smiled.

"Where's Walt?" he asked, peering round.

"I'm afraid he's off on a job," said Ned, but Barley had already lost interest. His hand trembled violently as he drank and he wept a bit, which Ned assured me was par for the course for joes coming back from the field.

11

The pattern of the next three days, like the wreck of a smashed aeroplane, was afterwards minutely examined for technical faults, though few were found.

After his outburst at the airport Barley entered the bright stage, smiling a lot to himself on the car journey, greeting familiar landmarks with his habitual shy affection. He also had a sneezing fit.

As soon as we reached the Knightsbridge house, where Ned was determined Barley should spend the night before returning to his flat, he dumped his luggage in the hall, flung his arms round Miss Coad and, declaring his undying love for her, presented her with a splendid lynx-fur hat which neither Wicklow nor anyone else could afterwards remember him buying.

At this point I removed myself. Clive had commanded me to the twelfth floor for what he termed "a crucial discussion," though it turned out that what he really wanted was to tap me. Was Scott Blair nervous? Was he above himself? How was he, Palfrey? Johnny was there, listening but scarcely speaking. Bob, he said, had been recalled to Langley for consultations. I told them what I had seen, no less, certainly no more. Both were puzzled by Barley's tears.

"You mean he said he was going back?" said Clive.

The same night Ned dined with Barley alone. This was not yet the debriefing. It was the coming down. The tapes reveal Barley in staccato mood and his voice a key higher than usual. By the time I joined them for coffee he was talking about Goethe but with artificial objectivity.

Goethe had aged, had lost his bounce.

Goethe was really shot up.

Goethe seemed to have stopped drinking. He was getting his highs elsewhere.

"You should have seen his hands, Harry, shaking over that map."

You should have seen yours, I thought, when you were drinking champagne at the airport.

He referred to Katya only once that evening, also in a deliberately unemotional way. I think he was determined we should know that he had no feelings that were not ours to control. That was not deviousness on Barley's part. With the exception of what we had taught him, he was incapable of it. It was his fear of where his feelings might end up if they were no longer anchored to us.

Katya was more scared for her kids than she was for herself, he said, again with studied detachment. He supposed most mothers were. On the other hand her children were the cyphers for the world she wished to save. So in a sense what she was doing was a kind of absolute version of mother love, don't you agree, Nedsky?

Ned agreed. Nothing harder than to experiment with one's own children, Barley, he said.

But a marvellous girl, Barley insisted, now in patronising mode. A bit too hell-bent for Barley's personal taste these days, but if you liked your women to have the moral fibre of Joan of Arc, then Katya was for you. And she was beautiful. No question. A bit too haywire to be classical, if we knew what he meant, but undeniably striking.

We couldn't tell him we had been admiring photographs of her for the last week, so we took his word for it.

At eleven, complaining of the time difference, Barley flopped. We stood in the hall watching him haul himself upstairs to bed.

"Anyway it was good stuff, was it?" he asked as he clung to the banister and grinned down at us through his little round spectacles. "The new notebook he gave us. You've looked at it."

"The boffins are burning the midnight oil over it at this moment," Ned replied. He could hardly say they were fighting over it like cats and dogs.

"Experts are addicts," Barley said, with another grin.

But he remained on the half-landing swaying, while he seemed to search for an appropriate exit line.

"Somebody ought to do a bit of work on those body microphones, Nedsky. Bloody saddle-sores all over my back. The next bloke you send had better have a thicker hide. Where's Uncle Bob, by the by?"

"He sends love," said Ned. "Business is brisk at the moment. He hopes to catch up with you soon."

"Is he out hunting with Walt?"

"If I knew I wouldn't tell you," said Ned, and we all laughed.

That night, I remember, I received a particularly irrelevant phone call from Margaret, my wife, about a parking ticket she had picked up in Basingstoke—in her view, unfairly.

"It was *my* space, I had put my indicator out when this bloody little man in a brand-new Jaguar, a white one, with slicked black hair—"

Unwisely I laughed, and suggested to her that Jaguars with slicked black hair had no special dispensation at parking meters. Humour was never Margaret's strong point.

The next morning, the Sunday, Clive again required my attendance, first to pump me about the previous night, then to hear me "talk turkey" with Johnny on such esoteric matters as whether Barley could legally be styled an employee of our Service and, if so, whether by taking our shilling he had renounced certain rights —his right to legal representation in the event of a dispute with us, for instance. I was Delphic, which annoyed them, but basically I said the answer was yes. Yes, he had renounced those rights. Or more exactly, yes, we could gull him into thinking he had, whether he had in law or not.

Johnny, if I have not mentioned it already, had graduated from Harvard Law School, so for once it was not necessary for Langley to send us a chorus of legal advisers.

In the afternoon, Barley being restless and the day sunny, we drove to Maidenhead and walked the towpath beside the Thames. By the time we returned, I suppose you could say Barley had been debriefed: for what with no questions coming down to us from our analysts, and his operational encounters already covered by technical means, there was really very little left to debrief him about.

Was Barley affected by our worries? We were as jolly as we could be, but I couldn't help wondering whether the atmosphere of menacing stagnation was getting through to him. Or perhaps his feelings were such a maelstrom of confusion and anticlimax that he merely lumped us in with them.

On the Sunday night we ate supper together in Knightsbridge and Barley was so mild-mannered and reposed that Ned decided—as I would have done—that it was safe to send him back to Hampstead.

His flat was in a Victorian block off East Heath Road and the static surveillance post was situated directly below it, manned by a bright young Service couple. The rightful tenants had been temporarily resettled elsewhere. Around eleven the couple reported that Barley was in his flat alone but prowling. They could hear but not see him. Ned had drawn the line at video. He was doing a lot of talking to himself, they said, and when he opened his mail, curses and groans came over the monitors.

Ned was unbothered. He had read Barley's mail already and knew it contained no horrors beyond the usual.

Around 1 a.m., Barley rang his daughter Anthea in Grantham.

"What's an ig?"

"An Eskimo house without a loo. How was Moscow?"

"What do you get if you cross the Atlantic with the *Titanic?*"

"About halfway. How was Moscow?"

"What do you get if you cross a sheep with a kangaroo?"

"I asked you how Moscow was."

"A woolly jumper. How's your boring husband?"

"Asleep, trying to be. What became of the cream bun you took to Lisbon?"

"Rained off."

"I thought she was permanent."

"She is. I'm not."

Barley next telephoned two women, the first a former wife over whom he had retained visiting rights, the second not previously listed. Neither could oblige him at such short notice, not least because they were in bed with their men.

At one-forty the couple reported that Barley's bedroom lights were out. Ned gratefully went to sleep, but I was already in my little flat and sleep was the last thing in my mind. Memories of Hannah were teeming through my head, mixed with images of Barley in the Knightsbridge house. I remembered his falsely casual way of talking about Katya and her children and I kept comparing it with my own repeated denials of my love for Hannah, back in the days when it endangered me. *Hannah looks a bit down in the mouth,* some innocent would remark every five minutes of my day. *Is that husband of hers leading her a dance or what?* And I'd smile. *I gather he likes to knock her around a bit,* I'd say, with exactly that same superior tone of detachment that I had heard in Barley, while the cancerous secret fires inside me ate away my heart.

Next morning Barley went to his office to resume work, but it was agreed that he would drop by the Knightsbridge house on his way home from work in case there were points to clear up. This was not quite the loose arrangement that it sounds, for Ned by now was locked in a serious shoot-out with the twelfth floor, and it was likely that by evening he would either have to give ground or face a full-scale battle with the mandarins.

But by then Barley had disappeared.

According to Brock's watchers, Barley left his office in Norfolk Street a little earlier than expected, at four-forty-three, carrying his saxophone in its case. Wicklow, who was in Abercrombie & Blair's back office typing up an account of the Moscow trip, was unaware of his departure. But a pair of Brock's boys in jeans followed Barley west down the Strand and, when he changed his mind, crossed with him into Soho where he went to earth in an afternoon watering-hole frequented by publishers and agents. He spent twenty minutes there, emerged still carrying his saxophone and looking perfectly steady. He hailed a cab, and one of the boys was close enough to hear him give the address of the safe house. The same boy bleeped Brock, who called Ned in Knightsbridge to say "Stand by, your guest is on his way." I was elsewhere, fighting other wars.

Thus far nobody was to blame, except that neither of the boys thought to take the cab's number, an oversight that later cost them dear. It was rush hour. A trip between the Strand and Knightsbridge could take an age. It was not till seven-thirty that Ned gave up waiting and, worried but not yet alarmed, returned to the Russia House.

At nine when nobody had any sensible suggestions Ned reluctantly declared an in-house alert, which by definition excluded the Americans. As usual, Ned was operational cool. Perhaps subconsciously he had steeled himself for such a crisis, for Brock later commented that he slipped into a prepared routine. He did not inform Clive, but as he explained to me later, telling Clive in the present poisoned atmosphere was as good as sending a singing telegram to Langley.

Ned drove himself first to Bloomsbury where the Service listeners owned a run of cellars under Russell Square. He used a car from the pool and must have driven like the wind. The head duty listener was Mary, a compulsive eater of forty, rose-faced and spinsterish. Her only known loves were unattainable voices. Ned handed her a list of Barley's contacts, compiled by the departed Walter from intercepts and watch reports. Could Mary cover them immediately? Like now?

Mary damn well could not. "Stretching regulations is one thing, Ned. A dozen illegal taps is completely another, can't you even *see?*"

Ned might have argued that the extra numbers were covered by the existing Home Office warrant but he didn't bother. He phoned me in Pimlico just as I was uncorking the bottle of Burgundy with which I proposed to console myself after a dirty day. It's a rather awful little flat and I had the window open to get out the smell of frying. I remember closing the window while we talked.

Phone warrants are in theory signed by the Home Secretary or in his absence by his Minister. But there is a trick to this, for he has provided the Legal Adviser with a delegated authority to be used only in emergency and accounted for in writing within twenty-four hours. I scribbled out my authority, signed it, turned off the gas —I was still boiling the Brussels sprouts—clambered into a cab and twenty minutes later handed the authority to Mary. Within the hour the telephones of Barley's twelve contacts were covered.

What was I thinking as I did all this? Did I think Barley had done away with himself? No, I did not. His concerns were for the living. The last thing he wished to do was leave them to their fate.

But I considered the possibility that he had broken ranks, and I suppose my worst fantasy was of Barley loudly clapping as the Aeroflot pilot announced that his plane had re-entered Soviet airspace.

In the meantime, on Ned's orders, Brock had persuaded the police to put out an emergency call for any metropolitan cab-driver who had picked up a tall man with a saxophone on the corner of Old Compton Street at five-thirty, destination Knightsbridge but probably changed en route. Yes, a tenor saxophone—a baritone sax was twice the size. By ten they had their man. The cab had started out for Knightsbridge but at Trafalgar Square Barley had indeed changed his mind and asked to be driven to Harley Street. The fare came to three pounds. Barley gave the driver a fiver and told him to keep the change.

By a small miracle of quick thinking, assisted by the late Walter's records, Ned made the connection—Andrew George Macready, alias Andy, former jazz trumpeter and listed Barley contact, had been admitted to the Sisters of Mercy Hospice, Harley Street, three weeks ago, see scrawled letter intercept in pencil, Mrs. Macready to Hampstead, serial 47A, and Walter's lapidary comment on the minute sheet: *Macready is Barley's guru on mortality.*

I still remember how I clung to the grab handle of Ned's car with both hands. We arrived at the hospice to be told Macready was under sedation. Barley had sat with him for an hour and they had managed to exchange a few words. The night matron, who had just come on duty, had taken Barley a cup of tea, no milk or sugar. Barley had topped it up with whisky from a flask. He had offered the matron a dram but she declined. He asked her whether he might "play old Andy a couple of his favourite numbers." He played softly for ten minutes exactly, which was what she had allowed him. Several of the nuns had gathered in the corridor to listen, and one of them recognised the tune as Basie's "Blue and Sentimental." He left his phone number and a cheque for a hundred pounds "for the croupier" on a brass collection plate at the door. The matron had told him he could come back whenever he wanted.

"You're not police, are you?" she asked me unhappily as we made for the door.

"Good Lord, no. Why ever should we be?"

She shook her head and would not answer, but I thought I knew what she had seen in him. A man in flight, hiding from his own actions.

Using the car telephone as we sped back to the Russia House, Ned ordered Brock to list all clubs, concert halls and pubs in the London area where jazz was being played tonight. He should distribute as many watchers as he could muster over these events.

For good measure I added the lawyer's ten cents' worth. In no circumstance was Brock or any watcher physically to restrain Barley or close with him. Whatever other rights Barley might have waived, he had not waived his right to defend himself and he was a powerful man.

We were settling for a long wait when Mary the head listener rang, this time all sweetness and oil. "Ned, I think you ought to get round here a tiny bit fastish. Some of your eggs have hatched."

We tore back to Russell Square, Ned leaning the car against the curves at sixty miles an hour.

In her cellar lair Mary received us with the doting smile she reserved for moments of disaster. A favourite girl called Pepsi stood beside her, dressed in green overalls. A tape recorder turned on the desk.

"Who the hell's *that* at this hour?" a stentorian voice demanded and I recognised immediately Barley's formidable Aunt Pandora, the Sacred Cow whom I had entertained to lunch. Hiatus while coins were fed into the machine. Followed by Barley's courteous voice.

"I'm rather afraid I've had it, Pan. I'm kissing the firm goodbye."

"Don't talk cock," Aunt Pandora retorted. "Some fool girl's been getting at you again."

"I'm serious, Pan. This time it's for real. I had to tell you."

"You're *always* serious. That's why you're such a fraud pretending to be frivolous."

"I'm going to talk to Guy in the morning." Guy Solomons, family solicitor, listed Barley contact. "Wicklow, the new man, can take it over. He's a tough little runt and he's a fast learner."

"Did you trace the phone box?" Ned asked Mary as Barley rang off.

"No time," said Mary proudly.

From the tape we heard the renewed ring of a phone. Barley again. "Reggie? I'm having a blow tonight. Come and play."

Mary handed us a piece of card on which she had written, *Canon Reginald Cowan, drummer and clerk in holy orders.*

"Can't," said Reggie. "Bloody Confirmation class."

"Ditch them," said Barley.

"Can't. Buggers are here with me now."

"We need you, Reggie. Old Andy's dying."

"So are we all. All the bloody time."

As the tape was ending, Brock came through on a live call from the Russia House asking for Ned urgently. His watchers had reported that Barley had looked in on his Soho drinking club an hour ago, drunk five whiskies then moved on to the Noah's Arch at King's Cross.

"Noah's *Arch?* You mean Ark."

"Arch. It's an arch under the railway line. Noah's an eight-foot West Indian. Barley's joined the band."

"Alone?"

"So far."

"What sort of place?"

"Diner and boozer. Sixty tables, stage, brick walls, whores, the usual."

Brock thought all pretty girls were whores.

"How full?" said Ned.

"Two-thirds and rising."

"What's he playing?"

" 'Lover Man,' Duke Ellington."

"How many exits?"

"One."

"Put together one team of three men and park them at a table near the door. If he leaves, straddle him but don't touch him. Call Resources and tell them I want Ben Lugg to get his cab over to the Noah's Arch immediately and wait with his flag down. He'll know what to do." Lugg was the Service's tame cabby. "Are there any public phones in the club?"

"Two."

"Have them occupied till I get there. Has he seen you?"

"No."

"Don't let him. What's across the road?"

"A launderette."

"Is it open?"

"No."

"Wait for me in front of it." He swung round on Mary, who was still smiling. "There are two phones at the Noah's Arch, King's Cross," he said, speaking very slowly. "Have them faulted *now*. If the management's got its own line, have that faulted too. *Now*. I don't care how short-staffed the engineers are, fault them *now*. If there are phone boxes in the street outside, fault the lot. *Now*."

We abandoned the Service car and hailed a cab. Brock was waiting as ordered in the doorway of the launderette. Ben Lugg was parked at the curbside. Tickets were five ninety-five at the door. Ned led me past the watchers' table without a glance and shoved his way to the front.

Nobody was dancing. The band's front line was taking a break. Barley was standing centre stage in front of a gold chair, playing with the gentle backing of the double bass and drums. A brick arch made a sound chamber over him. He was still wearing his publishing suit and seemed to have forgotten to remove his jacket. Rotating coloured lights wandered over him, occasionally closing on his face which was running sweat. His expression was nerveless and remote. He was holding the long notes and I knew they were a requiem for Andy and for whoever else was occupying his beleaguered mind. A couple of girls had sat themselves in the band seats and were staring at him with unblinking eyes. A line of beers was also awaiting his attention. Beside him stood the immense Noah with his arms folded across his chest, listening with his head down. The piece ended. Deliberately and tenderly, as if he were dressing a friend's wound, Barley cleaned out his sax and laid it to rest in its case. Noah did not allow applause but there was a scuffling noise while everyone snapped their fingers and there were calls of "encore" but Barley didn't bother with them. He drained a couple of the beers, gave a wave round and picked his way delicately through the crowd to the door. We went after him and as we stepped into the street Ben Lugg drew alongside with his flag up.

"Mo's," Barley ordered as he flopped into the back seat. He had another flask of Scotch from somewhere and was unscrewing the cap. "Hullo, Harry. How's love at a distance?"

"Great, thanks. I recommend it."

"Where on earth's Mo's?" Ned asked as he settled beside him and I parked myself on the jump seat.

"Tufnell Park. Underneath the Falmouth Arms."

"Good sound?" Ned asked.

"The best."

But it was not Barley's false cheerfulness that alarmed me. It was the remoteness of him, the deadness of his eyes, the way he kept himself confined inside the fastness of his English courtesy.

Mo was a blonde in her fifties and she spent a long time kissing Barley before she would let us sit at her table. Barley played blues and Mo wanted him to stay, I think for the night, but Barley could stay nowhere long, so we went to a music pizza house in Islington where he played another solo and Ben Lugg came in with us to have a cup of tea and a listen. Ben was a boxer in his day and still talked about the fight game. From Islington we crossed the river to the Elephant to hear a black group playing soul in a bus garage. It was four-fifteen but Barley was showing no sign of sleep; he preferred to sit with the group drinking spiked cocoa out of pint-sized china mugs. When we at last gentled him towards Ben's cab, the two girls from Noah's reappeared from nowhere and sat themselves either side of him in the back seat.

"Now then, you girls," said Ben while Ned and I waited on the pavement. "Hop it."

"Stay where you are, I should," Barley advised them.

"It's not your cab, dears. It's this bloke's"—indicating Ned—"now piss off, like good girls."

Barley swung his fist at Ben's head, which was adorned with a black Homburg hat. Ben blocked the blow like a man waving away a cobweb, and in the same movement drew Barley carefully out of the cab and handed him over to Ned, who took him equally carefully in an armlock.

Still in his Homburg, Ben disappeared into the back of the cab and came out with a girl in each hand.

"Why don't we all get a bit of fresh air?" Ned suggested while Ben gave the girls a tenner each to get lost.

"Good idea," said Barley.

So we crossed the river in slow procession, with Brock's watchers bringing up the rear and Ben Lugg's cab crawling along behind us. A dirty brown dawn was rising over dockland.

"Sorry about that," said Barley after a while. "No harm done, is there, Nedsky?"

"None that I know of," said Ned.

"Be alert," Barley advised. "Your Country Needs Lerts. Right, Nedsky? Just felt like making a spot of music," he explained to me. "You a musical man, Harry? Chum of mine used to play to his girl over the phone. Only piano, mind, not sax, but he said it did the trick. You could try it out on your Missus."

"We're leaving for America tomorrow," said Ned.

Barley took the news conversationally. "Nice for you. Nice time of year. Country looking at its best, I'd say."

"It's nice for you too, actually," said Ned. "We thought we'd take you along."

"Casual, is it?" Barley asked. "Or better pack a dinner jacket to be on the safe side?"

12

We flew to the island in a small plane, arriving at dusk. The small plane belonged to a grand American corporation. Nobody said who owned the island. It was narrow and wooded, its middle sagged into the sea and its ends were propped up by conical peaks, so that my impression from the air was of a Bedouin tent collapsing into the Atlantic. I put it at two miles long. We saw the New England mansion and its grounds at one end, and the tiny white dock at the other, though I learned later that the mansion was called a summer house because nobody went there in winter. It had been built at the turn of the century by a rich Bostonian, in the days when such people called themselves rusticators. We felt the wings rock and smelt salt sea through the rattling cabin windows. We saw sunspots flicking over the waves like searchlights at a tattoo, and cormorants warring in the wind. We saw a light-beacon on the mainland to the west. We had been following the coast of Maine for fifty-eight minutes by my watch. The trees came up either side of us, the sky vanished, and suddenly we were bouncing and swinging along a grass avenue with Randy and his boys waiting with a jeep at the end of it. Randy was wholesome as only privileged Americans can be. He wore a windcheater and a tie. I felt I knew his mother.

"I'm your host here, gentlemen, for as long as you elect to stay, and welcome to our island." He shook Barley's hand first. They must have shown him photographs. "Mr. Brown, sir, this is a real honour. Ned? Harry?"

"Jolly nice of you," said Barley.

The pine trees, as we wound down the hillside, stood black against the sea. The boys followed in a second car.

"You gentlemen fly British? Mrs. Thatcher really got a hold of that line!" said Randy.

"Time she went down with the ship," Barley growled.

Randy laughed as if laughing were something he'd learned on the course. Brown was Barley's workname for the trip. Even his passport, which Ned carried, said that he was Brown.

We bumped across a causeway to the gatehouse. The gates opened and closed behind us. We were on our own headland. At the top of it stood the mansion lit by arc-lights hidden in the bushes. Lawns and wind-burned shrubs fell away from it to either side. The posts of a broken jetty stepped precariously out to sea. Randy parked the jeep and, taking Barley's luggage, led us along an illuminated path between hydrangeas to a boat-house. On our crossing to Boston, Barley had dozed and drunk and groaned at the film. On our small plane he had frowned at the New England landscape as if its beauty troubled him. But once we landed he seemed to re-enter his own world.

"Mr. Brown, sir, my orders are to accommodate you in the bridal suite," said Randy.

"Can't think of anywhere nicer, old boy," said Barley politely.

"You really *say* that, Mr. Brown: *old boy?*"

Randy ushered us through a stone-flagged hall to a captain's cabin. The style was designer homestead. A reproduction brass bed stood in a corner, a reproduction scrubwood writing desk at the window. Doubtful ship's fittings hung on the walls. In the alcove where the all-American kitchen was, Barley identified the refrigerator, pulled it open and peered hopefully inside.

"Mr. Brown likes a bottle of Scotch in his room of an evening, Randy. If you've such a thing in your locker he'd be grateful."

The summer house was a museum of golden childhoods. In the porch, honey-coloured croquet mallets lay propped against a dusty goat-cart laden with lobster buoys gathered from the beach. There were smells of beeswax and leather. In the hall, portraits of young men and women in broad hats hung beside primitive paintings of whalers. We followed Randy up a wide polished staircase, Barley trailing behind us. On each landing, arched windows bordered with stained glass made jewelled gateways to the sea. We entered a corridor of blue bedrooms. The largest was reserved for Clive. From our balconies we could look down the gardens to the boat-house and across the sea to the mainland. The dusk was turning to dark.

In a white-raftered dining room, a Langley vestal managed not to look at us while she served Maine lobster and white wine.

While we ate, Randy explained the rules of the house. "No fraternising with the staff, please, gentlemen, just a good morning and hullo. Anything needs saying to them, best let me say it for you. The guards are for your convenience and safety, gentlemen, but we would like you to remain within the confines of the property. Please. Thank you."

Dinner and speeches over, Randy took Ned to the communications room and I walked Barley back to the boat-house. A fierce wind was ripping over the gardens. As we passed in and out of the light-cones Barley seemed to be smiling into it recklessly. Boys with handsets watched us pass.

"How about chess?" I asked him as we reached his door.

I wished I could see his face more clearly but I had lost it, just as I had lost his mood. I felt a pat on the arm as he wished me goodnight. His door opened and closed again, but not before I had glimpsed the spectral figure of a sentry standing not two yards from us in the darkness.

"A wise lawyer, a fine officer," Russell Sheriton advised me next morning in a reverential murmur, knowing I was neither, as his strong, soft palms enveloped my hand. "One of the true greats. Harry, how are you doing?"

Little had changed in him since his tour of duty in London: the rings beneath the eyes a little doggier, a little sadder, the blue suit a size or two larger, the same white-shirted paunch. The same mortician's aftershave, six years on, anointed the Agency's newest head of Soviet operations.

A group of his young men stood respectfully apart from him, clutching their travel bags and looking like stranded passengers at an airport. Clive and Bob were mounted either side of him like cohorts. Bob looked older by ten years. A chastened smile had replaced his old-world self-assurance. He greeted us too effusively, as if he had been warned to stay away from us.

The Island Conference, as it euphemistically became known, was about to begin.

There is an underlying pleasantness to the events of the next days, an air of good men going about their business, which I am in danger of forgetting as I recall the rest.

It is the hardest point for me to make, yet I owe it to Barley to try, for he never took against our hosts—he never blamed them for anything that happened to him, then or later. He could grumble about Americans in general, but no sooner had he met them individually than he spoke of them as decent fellows all. There was not a man among them he wouldn't have been happy to swap a drink with any evening at the local, if we'd had one. And of course Barley always saw the force of any argument that was directed against him, just as he was always vastly impressed by other people's industry.

And my goodness, were they industrious! If numbers, money and sheer endeavour alone could have produced intelligence, the Agency would have had it by the cartload—except that, alas, the human head is not a cart, and there is such a thing as unintelligence as well.

And how deeply they yearned to be loved!—and Barley warmed immediately to their need. Even as they tore into him, they needed to be loved. And by Barley, too! Just as to this day they need to be loved for all their staged putsches, destabilisations and wild adventures against The Enemy Out There.

Yet it was this very mystery of good hearts turned inside out that gave our week its underlying terror.

Years ago I talked to a man who had been flogged, an English mercenary who was doing us a few favours in Africa and needed paying off. What he remembered most was not the lash but the orange juice they gave him afterwards. He remembers being helped back to his hut, he remembers being laid face down on the straw. But what he really remembers is the glass of fresh orange juice that a warder set at his head, then crouched beside him, waiting patiently, till he was strong enough to drink some. Yet it was this same warder who had flogged him.

We too had our glasses of orange juice. And we had our decent warders, even if they were disguised behind headsets and a surface animosity that quickly melted before Barley's warmth. Within a day of our arrival, the same guards with whom we were forbidden to fraternise were tiptoeing at any odd moment in and out of Barley's boat-house, stealing a Coke or a Scotch from him before slipping back to their posts. They sensed he was that kind of man. And as Americans they were fascinated by his celebrity.

There was one old hand called Edgar, an ex-Marine, who gave him quite a run for his money at chess. Barley, I learned later, got his name and address out of him, against every known canon of the trade, so that they could play a contest by post "when all this is over."

Not only warders either. In Sheriton's chorus of young men, as in Sheriton himself, there was a moderation that was like an even beat of sanity against the hysterical highs and lows of those whom Sheriton himself dubbed collectively the egomaniacs.

But that, I suppose, is the tragedy of great nations. So much talent bursting to be used, so much goodness longing to come out. Yet all so miserably spoken for that sometimes we could scarcely believe it was America speaking to us at all.

But it was. The lash was real.

The interrogations took place in the billiards room. The wooden floor had been painted dark red for dancing and the billiards table replaced by a ring of chairs. But an ivory scorer and a row of initialled cue-cases still lined the wall, and the long downlight made a pool at the centre where Barley was obliged to sit. Ned fetched him from the boat-house.

"Mr. Brown, sir, I am proud to shake your hand and I have just decided that my name for the duration of our relationship is Haggarty," Sheriton declared. "I took one look at you, I felt Irish. Don't ask me why." He was leading Barley at a good pace across the room. "Most of all, I wish to congratulate you. You have all the virtues: memory, observation, British grit, saxophone."

This in one hypnotic flow while Barley grinned sheepishly and allowed himself to be settled in the place of honour.

But Ned already sat stiffly, arms folded across his chest, and Clive, though he was of the circle, had managed to paint himself out of the picture. He sat among Sheriton's young men and had pushed his chair back till they hid him.

Sheriton remained standing before Barley and was talking down at him, even when his words said he was addressing someone else. "Clive, would you permit me to bombard Mr. Brown with some impertinent questions? Ned, will you tell Mr. Brown, please, that he is in the United States of America and that if he doesn't care to answer anything he needn't, because his silence will be taken as clear evidence of his guilt?"

"Mr. Brown can look after himself," Barley said—but still grinning, still not quite believing in the tension.

"He can? That's great, Mr. Brown! Because for the next couple of days that's exactly what we hope you'll do!"

Sheriton went to the sideboard and poured himself some coffee and came back with it. His voice struck the calmer note of common sense. "Mr. Brown, we are buying a Picasso, okay? Everybody round this room is buying the same Picasso. Blue, seignant, well-done, what the fuck? There are about three people in the world who understand it. But when you get to the bottom line there's one question counts. Did Picasso paint it, or did J. P. Shmuck, Jr., of South Bend, Indiana, or Omsk, Russia, paste it together in his potato barn? Because remember this." He was prodding his own soft chest and holding his coffee cup in his spare hand. "No resale. This is not London. This is Washington. And for Washington, intelligence has to be useful, and that means it has to be used, not contemplated in Socratic detachment." He lowered his voice in reverent commiseration. "And you're the guy who's selling it to us, Mr. Brown. Like it or not, you personally are the nearest we shall get to the source until the day we persuade the man you call Goethe to change his ways and work to us direct. If we ever do. Doubtful. Very, very doubtful."

Sheriton took a turn and moved to the edge of the ring. "You are the linchpin, Mr. Brown. You are *the man*. You are *it*. But how much of *it, are* you? A little of it? Some of it? Or all of it? Do you write the script, act, produce and direct? Or are you the bit part you say you are, the innocent bystander we all have yet to meet?"

Sheriton sighed, as if it were a little hard on a man of his tender sensitivities. "Mr. Brown, do you have a regular girl these days, or are you screwing the backlist?"

Ned was halfway to his feet but Barley had already answered. Yet his voice was not abrasive, even now, it was not hostile. It was as if he were unwilling to disturb the good atmosphere all of us were enjoying.

"Well now, how about you, sunshine? Does Mrs. Haggarty oblige or are we reduced to the habits of our youth?"

Sheriton was not even interested.

"Mr. Brown, we are buying *your* Picasso, not mine. Washington doesn't like its assets cruising the singles bars. We have to play this very frank, very honest. No English reticence, no old-school persiflage. We've fallen for that horse manure before and we will never, *never* fall for it again."

This, I thought, for Bob, whose head was once again turned downward to his hands.

"Mr. Brown is not cruising the singles bars," Ned cut in hotly. "And it's not his material. It's Goethe's. I don't see that his private life has the least to do with it."

Keep your thoughts to yourself, Clive had told me. His eyes repeated the message to Ned now.

"Oh, Ned, come on now, come *on!*" Sheriton protested. "The way Washington is these days, you have to be married and born again before you can get on a fucking bus. What takes you to Russia every five minutes, Mr. Brown? Are you buying property there?"

Barley was grinning, but no longer so pleasantly. Sheriton was getting to him, which was exactly what Sheriton intended.

"As a matter of fact, old boy, it's a rôle I rather inherited. My old father always preferred the Soviet Union to the United States, and went to a lot of trouble publishing their books. He was a Fabian. A kind of New Dealer. If he'd been one of your people he'd have been blacklisted."

"He'd have been framed, fried and immortalised. I read his record. It's awful. Tell us more about him, Mr. Brown. What did he bequeath to you that you inherited?"

"What the devil's that to anyone?" said Ned.

He was right. The matter of Barley's eccentric father had been aired and dismissed as irrelevant by the twelfth floor long ago. But not apparently by the Agency. Or not any more.

"And in the thirties, as you no doubt also know then," Barley continued in his calmer tone, "he started up a Russian Book Club. It didn't last long but he had a go. And in the war when he could get the paper he'd publish pro-Soviet propaganda, most of it glorifying Stalin."

"And after the war what did he do then? Go help them build the Berlin Wall on weekends?"

"He had hopes, then he packed them in," Barley replied after reflection. The contemplative part of him had regained the upper hand. "He could have forgiven the Russians most things, but not the Terror, not the camps and not the deportations. It broke his heart."

"Would his heart have been broken if the Sovs had used less muscular methods?"

"I don't expect so. I think he'd have died a happy man."

Sheriton wiped his palms on his handkerchief and like an overweight Oliver Twist carried his coffee cup in both hands back to the refreshments table, where he unscrewed the thermos jug and peered mournfully inside before pouring himself a fresh cup.

"Acorns," he complained. "They gather acorns and press them and make coffee out of them. That's what they do out here." There was an empty chair beside Bob. Sheriton lowered himself into it and sighed. "Mr. Brown, will you let me spell it out for you a little? There is no longer the space in life to take each humble member of the human family on his merits, okay? So everybody who is anybody has a record. Here's yours. Your father was a Communist sympathiser, latterly disenchanted. In the eight years since he died you have made no fewer than six visits to the Soviet Union. You have sold the Sovs precisely four very lousy books from your own list and published precisely three of theirs. Two awful modern novels which didn't do a damn thing, a piece of crap about acupuncture which did eighteen copies in the trade edition. You're on the verge of bankruptcy yet we calculate your outlay for these trips at twelve thousand pounds and your revenue at nineteen hundred. You're divorced, freestyle and British public school. You drink like you're watering the desert single-handed and you pick jazz friends with records that make Benedict Arnold look like Shirley Temple. Seen from Washington, you're rampant. Seen from here, you're very nice, but how will I explain this to the next Congressional sub-committee of Bible-belt knuckle-draggers who take it into their heads to pillory Goethe's material because it endangers Fortress America?"

"Why does it do that?" said Barley.

I think we were all surprised by his calm. Sheriton certainly was. He was looking at Barley over his shoulder until then, affecting a slightly pitiful stance as he explained his dilemma. Now he straightened up, and faced Barley full on with an alert and quizzical directness.

"Pardon me, Mr. Brown?"

"Why does Goethe's material scare them? If the Russians can't shoot straight, Fortress America should be jumping for joy."

"Oh we are, Mr. Brown, we are. We're ecstatic. Never mind that the entire American military might is invested in the belief that the Soviet hardware is accurate as hell. Never mind that a perception of Soviet accuracy is *all* in this game. That with accuracy, you can sneak up on your enemy while he's out playing golf, take out his ICBMs unawares and leave him unable to respond in kind. Whereas without accuracy, you'd damn well better not try it, because that's when your enemy turns right around and takes out your twenty favourite towns. Never mind that zillions of taxpayers' dollars and whole junk-yards of political rhetoric have been lavished on the fond nightmare of a Soviet first strike and the American window of vulnerability. Never mind that even today the idea of Soviet supremacy in the matter of ICBMs is the main argument in favour of Star Wars, and the principal strategic fun-game at Washington cocktail parties." To my astonishment, Sheriton abruptly changed voices and broke into the accents of a Deep South hillbilly. "Time we blew those mothers apart before they do the same to us, Mr. Brown. This li'l ole planet just ain't big enough for two superpowers, Mr. Brown. Which one do *you* favour, Mr. Brown, when poo-ush comes to sheu-uve?"

Then he waited, while his pouchy face resumed its contemplation of life's many injustices.

"And I *believe* in Goethe," he went on in a startled voice. "I am on record as buying Goethe outright from the day he stepped out of the closet. Retail. Goethe for my money is a source whose time has come. And do you know what that tells me? It tells me that I also have to believe in Mr. Brown here and that Mr. Brown needs to be very candid with me or I'm dead." He cupped a paw reverently over his left breast. "I believe in Mr. Brown, I believe in Goethe, I believe in the material. And I'm scared shitless."

Some people change their minds, I was thinking. Some people have a change of heart. But it takes Russell Sheriton to announce that he has seen the light on the road to Damascus. Ned was staring at him in disbelief. Clive had chosen to admire the cue-cases. But Sheriton remained pouting at his coffee, reflecting on his bad luck. Of his young men, one had his chin in his hand while he studied the toe-cap of his Harvard shoe. Another was peering at the sea through the window as if the truth might rather lie out there.

But nobody was looking at Barley, nobody seemed to have the nerve. He was sitting still and looking young. We had told him a little, but nothing like this. Least of all had we told him that the Bluebird material had set the industrial-military factions at one another's throats and raised roars of outrage from some of Washington's most sleazy lobbies.

Old Palfrey spoke for the first time. As I did so, I had a sense of performing in the theatre of the absurd. It was as if the real world were slipping out from under our feet.

"What Haggarty is asking you is this," I said. "Will you voluntarily submit to questioning by the Americans so that they can take a view of the source once and for all? You can say no. It's your choice. Is that right, Clive?"

Clive didn't like me for that but he gave his reluctant assent before once more ducking below the horizon.

The faces round the ring had turned to Barley like flowers in the sun.

"What do you say?" I asked him.

For a while he said nothing. He stretched, he drew the back of his wrist across his mouth, he looked vaguely embarrassed. He shrugged. He looked towards Ned but could not find his eye, so he looked back at me, rather foolishly. What was he thinking, if anything? That to say "no" would be to cut him off from Goethe for good? From Katya? Had he even got that far in his mind? To this day I have no idea. He grinned, apparently in embarrassment.

"What do *you* think, Harry? In for a penny? What does my mouthpiece say?"

"It's more a question of what the client says," I answered glossily, smiling back at him.

"We'll never know if we don't give it a try, will we?"

"I suppose we never will," I said.

Which seems to be the nearest he ever came to saying, "I'll do it."

* * *

"Yale has these secret societies, you see, Harry," Bob was explaining to me. "Why, the place is shot through with them. If you've heard of Skull and Bones, Scroll and Key, you've still only heard the tip of the iceberg. And these societies, they emphasise the team. Harvard now—why, Harvard goes all the other way and puts its money on individual brilliance. So the Agency, when it's fishing for recruits in those waters, has a way of picking its team players from Yale and its high flyers from Harvard. I won't go so far as to say that every Harvard man is a prima donna or every Yale man gives blind obedience to the cause. But that's the broad tradition. Are you a Yale man, Mr. Quinn?"

"West Point," said Quinn.

It was evening and the first delegation had just flown in. We sat in the same room with the same red floor under the same billiards light, waiting for Barley. Quinn sat at the head and Todd and Larry sat to either side of him. Todd and Larry were Quinn's people. They were clean-limbed and pretty and, for a man of my age, ludicrously youthful.

"Quinn's from way up there," Sheriton had told us. "Quinn talks to Defense, he talks to the corporations, he talks to God."

"But who hires him?" Ned had asked.

Sheriton seemed genuinely puzzled by the question. He smiled as if pardoning a solecism in a foreigner.

"Well now, Ned, I guess we all do," he said.

Quinn was six foot one, wide-shouldered and big-eared. He wore his suit like body armour. There were no medals on it, no badges of rank. His rank was in his stubborn jaw and shaded empty eyes, and in the smile of enraged inferiority that overcame him in the presence of civilians.

Ned entered first, then came Barley. Nobody stood up. From his deliberately humble place in the centre of the American row, Sheriton meekly made the introductions.

Quinn likes them plain, he had warned us. Tell your man not to be too damn clever. Sheriton was following his own advice.

It was right that Larry should open the questioning because Larry was the outgoing one. Todd was virginal and withdrawn, but Larry wore an overlarge wedding ring and had the colourful tie and did the laughing for them both.

"Mr. Brown, sir, we have to think this thing through from the point of view of your detractors," he explained with elaborate insincerity. "In our business, there's unverified intelligence and there's verified intelligence. We'd like to verify your intelligence. That's our job and that's what we're paid for. Please don't take any hint of suspicion personally, Mr. Brown. Analysis is a science apart. We have to respect its laws."

"We have to imagine it's an organised put-together," Todd blurted belligerently from Larry's side. *"Smoke."*

Amusement, until Larry laughingly explained to Barley that he was not being offered a cigarette: "smoke" was the trade word for deception.

"Mr. Brown, sir, whose idea was it, please, to go out to Peredelkino that day after the book fair?" asked Larry.

"Mine, probably."

"Are you sure of that, sir?"

"We were drunk when we made the plan, but I'm pretty sure it was me who proposed it."

"You drink quite a lot, don't you, Mr. Brown?" said Larry.

Quinn's enormous hands had settled round a pencil as if they proposed to strangle it.

"Fair amount."

"Does drinking make you forget things, sir?"

"Sometimes."

"And sometimes not. After all, we have long verbatims between you and Goethe when you were both totally inebriated. Had you ever been to Peredelkino before that day, sir?"

"Yes."

"Often?"

"Two or three times. Maybe four."

"Did you visit with friends out there?"

"I visited friends, yes," said Barley, instinctively bridling at the American usage.

"Soviet friends?"

"Of course."

Larry paused long enough to make Soviet friends sound like a confession.

"Care to identify these friends, please, sir, names?"

Barley identified the friends. A writer. A woman poet. A literary bureaucrat. Larry wrote them down, moving his pencil slowly for effect. Smiling as he wrote, while Quinn's shadowed eyes continued glowering at Barley on fixed lines down the table.

"On the day of your trip then, Mr. Brown," Larry resumed, "on this Day One, as we may call it, did it not occur to you to press a few doorbells of your old acquaintance, see who was around, sir, say hullo?" Larry asked.

Barley didn't seem to know whether it had occurred to him or not. He shrugged and performed his habitual trick of pulling the back of his hand across his mouth, the perfect untruthful witness.

"Didn't want to saddle them with Jumbo, I suppose. Too many of us to cope with. Didn't occur to me really."

"Sure," said Larry.

Three excuses, I noted unhappily. Three where one would have been enough. I glanced at Ned and knew he was thinking the same. Sheriton was busy not thinking at all. Bob was busy being Sheriton's man. Todd was murmuring in Quinn's ear.

"So was it also *your* idea to visit Pasternak's tomb, Mr. Brown, sir?" Larry enquired, as if it were an idea anyone could be proud of having had.

"Grave," Barley corrected him testily. "Yes, it was. Shouldn't think the others knew it was there till I told them."

"And Pasternak's dacha too, I believe." Larry consulted his notes. " 'If the bastards hadn't pulled it down.' " He made *bastards* sound particularly dirty.

"That's right, his dacha too."

"But you didn't visit the Pasternak dacha, am I right? You didn't even establish whether the dacha still existed. The Pasternak dacha disappeared totally from the agenda."

"It was raining," Barley said.

"But you did have a car. And a driver, Mr. Brown. Even if he was malodorous."

Larry smiled again and opened his mouth just wide enough to let the point of his tongue caress his upper lip. Then he closed it and allowed a further pause for uncomfortable thoughts.

"So *you* mustered the party, Mr. Brown, and *you* identified the aims of the journey," Larry resumed in a tone of whimsical regret. "You rode point, you led the group up the hill to the tomb. Grave, forgive me. It was you personally, no one else, that Mr. Nezhdanov spoke to as you all came down the hill. He asked if you were American. You said, *'No, thank God, British.'* "

No laughter, not even a smile from Larry himself. Quinn looked as though he were concealing an abdominal wound with difficulty.

"It was you too, Mr. Brown, who quite by chance were able to quote the poet, speak out for the company during a discussion of his merits, and almost *by magic* to detach yourself from your companions and find yourself seated next to the man we call Goethe during lunch. 'Meet our distinguished writer Goethe.' Mr. Brown, we have a field report from London regarding the girl Magda from Penguin Books. We understand it was obtained unobtrusively, in non-suspicious social circumstances, by a non-American third party. Magda had the impression you wished to handle the Nezhdanov interview on your own. Can you explain that, please?"

Barley had disappeared again. Not from the room but from my understanding. He had left suspicion to the dreamers and entered his own realms of reality. It was Ned not Barley who, unable to contain himself in the face of this admission of Agency skulduggery, produced the desired outburst.

"Well, she's not going to tell your informant she was panting to tuck her boyfriend into bed for the afternoon, is she?"

But again that single answer might have done the trick if Barley had not capped it with his own. "Maybe I *did* pack them off," he conceded in a remote but friendly enough voice. "After a week of book fair any reasonable soul has had enough of publishers to last him a lifetime."

Larry's smile had a doubtful slant. "Well hell," he said, and shook his pretty head before handing over his witness to Todd.

But not yet, because Quinn was speaking. Not to Barley, not to Sheriton, not even to Clive. Not really to anyone. But he was speaking all the same. The captive little mouth was writhing like a hooked eel.

"This man been fluttered?"

"Sir, we have protocol problems," Larry explained, with a glance at me.

At first I honestly did not understand. Larry had to explain.

"What we used to call a lie detector, sir. A polygraph. Known in the business as a flutterer. I don't think you have them over there."

"We do in certain cases," said Clive hospitably from beside me before I had a chance to answer. "Where you insist on it, we bend towards you and apply it. They're coming in."

Only then did the troubled, inward Todd take over. Todd was not prolix; he was at first bite not anything. But I had met counsel like Todd before: men who make a crusade of their charmlessness and learn to use their verbal clumsiness as a bludgeon.

"Describe your relationship with Niki Landau, Mr. Brown."

"I haven't one," Barley said. "We've been pronounced strangers till Doomsday. I had to sign a paper saying I'd never speak to him. Ask Harry."

"Prior to that arrangement, please?"

"We had the odd jar together."

"The odd what?"

"Jar. Drink. Scotch. He's a nice chap."

"But not socially your class, surely? He did not go to Harrow and Cambridge, I take it?"

"What difference does that make?"

"Do you disapprove of the British social structure, Mr. Brown?"

"One of the crying pities of the modern world, it always seemed to me, old boy."

" 'He's a nice chap.' That means you like him?"

"He's an irritating little sod but I liked him, yes. Still do."

"You never did deals with him? Any deal?"

"He worked for other houses. I was my own boss. What deals could we do?"

"Ever *buy* anything from him?"

"Why should I?"

"I would like to know, please, what you and Niki Landau transacted together on the occasions when you were alone, often in Communist capital cities."

"He boasted about his conquests. He liked good music. Classical stuff."

"He ever discuss his *sister* with you? His *sister* still in Poland?"

"No."

"He ever express his resentment to you regarding the alleged ill-treatment of his father by the British authorities?"

"No."

"When was your last intimate conversation with Niki Landau, please?"

Barley finally allowed himself to betray a certain irritation. "You make us sound like a pair of queens," he complained.

Quinn's face did not flicker. Perhaps he had made that deduction already.

"The question was *when*, Mr. Brown," said Todd, in a tone suggesting that his patience was being stretched.

"Frankfurt, I suppose. Last year. Couple of belts in the Hessischer Hof."

"That the Frankfurt book fair?"

"One doesn't go to Frankfurt for fun, old boy."

"No dialogue with Landau since?"

"Don't recall one."

"Nothing at the London book fair this spring?"

Barley appeared to rack his brains. "Oh my hat. Stella. You're right."

"I beg your pardon?"

"Niki had spotted a girl who used to work for me. Stella. Decided he fancied her. He fancied everybody, really. By way of being a stoat. Wanted me to introduce them."

"And you did?"

"Tried to."

"You pimped for him. That the term?"

"That's right, old boy."

"What transpired, please?"

"I asked her for a drink at the Roebuck round the corner, six o'clock. Niki turned up, she didn't."

"So you were left alone with Landau? One on one?"

"That's right. One to one."

"What did you talk about?"

"Stella, I suppose. The weather. Might have been anything."

"Mr. Brown, do you have anything very much to do with past or former Soviet citizens in the United Kingdom?"

"Cultural Attaché, now and then. When he can be bothered to answer, which isn't often. If a Sov writer comes over and the Embassy gives a binge for him, I'll probably go along."

"We understand you like to play chess at a certain café in the area of Camden Town, London."

"So?"

"Is this not a café frequented by Russian exiles, Mr. Brown?"

Barley raised his voice but otherwise held steady. "So I know Leo. Leo likes to lead from weakness. I know Josef. Josef charges at anything that moves. I don't go to bed with them and I don't trade secrets with them."

"You do have a very selective memory, though, don't you, Mr. Brown? Considering the extraordinarily detailed accounts you give of other episodes and persons?"

Still Barley did not flare, which made his reply all the more devastating. For a moment, indeed, it seemed he would not even answer; the tolerance that was now so deeply seated in him seemed to tell him not to bother.

"I remember what's important to me, old boy. If I haven't got a dirty enough mind to match yours, that's your bloody business."

Todd coloured. And went on colouring. Larry's smile widened till it nearly split his face. Quinn had put on a sentry's scowl. Clive had not heard a thing.

But Ned was pink with pleasure and even Russell Sheriton, sunk in a crocodile's sleep, seemed to be remembering, among so many disappointments, something vaguely beautiful.

The same evening as I was taking a walk along the beach, I came on Barley and two of his guards, out of sight of the mansion, skimming flat stones to see who could get the most bounces.

"Got you! Got you!" he was shouting, leaning back and flinging his arms at the clouds.

"The mullahs are smelling heresy," Sheriton declared over dinner, regaling us with the latest state of play. Barley had pleaded a headache and asked for an omelette in the boat-house. "Most of these guys came to town on a Margin of Safety ticket. That means raise military spending and develop any new system however crazy that will bring peace and prosperity to the arms industry for the next fifty years. If they're not sleeping with the manufacturers, they're sure as hell eating with them. The Bluebird is telling them a very bad story."

"And if it's the truth?" I asked.

Sheriton sadly helped himself to another piece of pecan pie. "The truth? The

Sovs can't play? They're cost-cutting at every corner and the buffoons in Moscow don't know one half of the bad news because the buffoons in the field cheat on them so they can earn their gold watches and free caviar? You think *that's* the truth?" He took a huge mouthful but it didn't alter the shape of his face. "You think that certain unpleasant *comparisons* aren't made?" He poured himself some coffee. "You know what's the worst thing for our democratically elected neanderthals? The total worst? It's the implications against *us*. Moribund on the Sov side means moribund *our* side. The mullahs hate that. So do the manufacturers." He shook his head in disapproval. "To hear the Sovs can't do solid fuel from shit, their rocket motors suck instead of blow? Their early-warning errors worse than ours? Their heavies can't even get out of the kennel? That our intelligence estimates are ludicrously exaggerated? The mullahs get terrible vibes from these things." He reflected on the inconstancy of mullahs. "How do you peddle the arms race when the only asshole you have to race against is yourself? Bluebird is life-threatening intelligence. A lot of highly paid favourite sons are in serious danger of having their rice-bowls broken, all on account of Bluebird. You want truth, that's it."

"So why stick your neck out?" I objected. "If it's not a popular ticket, why run on it?"

And suddenly I didn't know where to put myself.

It isn't often that old Palfrey stops a conversation, causes every head to swing round at him in amazement. And I certainly hadn't meant to this time. Yet Ned and Bob and Clive were staring at me as if I had taken leave of my senses, and Sheriton's young men—we had two of them, if I remember rightly—independently put down their forks and began independently wiping their fingers on their napkins.

Only Sheriton didn't seem to have heard. He had decided that a little cheese wouldn't hurt him after all. He had pulled the trolley to him, and was morosely examining the display. But none of us imagined that cheese was uppermost in his mind, and it was clear to me that he was buying time while he wondered whether to reply and how.

"Harry," he began carefully, addressing not me but a piece of Danish blue. "Harry, I swear to God. You have before you a man committed to peace and brotherly love. By this I mean that my primary ambition is to knock so much shit out of the Pentagon firebreathers that they will never again tell the President of the United States that twenty rabbits make a tiger, or that every fucking sardine fisherman three miles out of port is a Soviet nuclear submarine in drag. I also wish to hear no more bullshit about digging little holes in the ground and surviving nuclear war. I am a glasnostic, Harry. I have made certain discoveries about myself. I was born a glasnostic, my parents are old glasnostics from way back. For me, glasnosticism is a way of life. I want my children to live. Quote me and enjoy me."

"I didn't know you had any children," said Ned.

"Figurative," said Sheriton.

But Sheriton, if you pulled away the wrapping, was telling us a truthful version of his new self. Ned sensed it, I sensed it. And if Clive didn't, that was only because he had deliberately abbreviated his perceptions. It was a truth that lay not so much in his words, which as often as not were designed to obscure his feelings rather than express them, but in a new and irrepressible humility that had entered his manner since his cut-throat days in London. At the age of fifty, after quarter of a century as a Cold War brawler, Russell Sheriton, to use Walter's expression, was shaking his mid-life bars. It had never occurred to me that I could like him, but that evening I began to.

"Brady's bright," Sheriton warned us with a yawn as we turned in. "Brady can hear the grass growing."

And Brady, parse him how you would, was bright as boot-buttons.

You spotted it in his clever face and in the nerveless immobility of his courteous body. His ancient sports coat was older than he was, and as he came into the room you knew he took pleasure in being unspectacular. His young assistant wore a sports coat too and, like his master had a classy dowdiness.

"Looks like you've done a fine thing, Barley," Brady said cheerfully in his Southern lilt, setting his briefcase on the table. "Anybody say thank you along the way? I'm Brady and I'm too damned old to fool around with funny names. This is Skelton. *Thank you*."

The billiards room again but without Quinn's table and upright chairs. Instead, we lounged gratefully in deep cushions. A storm was brewing. Randy's vestals had closed the shutters and put on lights. As the wind rose, the mansion began clinking like restless bottles on a shelf. Brady unpopped his briefcase, a gem from the days when they knew how to make them. Like the university professor he occasionally was, he wore a polka-dot blue tie.

"Barley, did I read somewhere, or am I dreaming, you once played sax in the great Ray Noble's band?"

"Beardless boy in those days, Brady."

"Wasn't Ray just the sweetest man you ever knew? Didn't he make the best sound ever?" Brady asked as only Southerners can.

"Ray was a prince." Barley hummed a few bars from "Cherokee."

"Too bad about his politics," Brady said, smiling. "We all tried to talk him out of that nonsense, but Ray would go his way. Ever play chess with him?"

"Yes I did, as a matter of fact."

"Who won?"

"Me, I think. Not sure. Yes, me."

Brady smiled. "So did I."

Skelton smiled too.

They talked London and which part of Hampstead Barley lived in: "Barley, I just love that area. Hampstead is my idea of civilization." They talked the bands Barley had played. "My God, don't tell me *he's* still around! At his age I wouldn't even buy unripe bananas!" They talked British politics and Brady just *had* to know what it was that Barley thought so wrong with Mrs. T.

Barley appeared to have to think about that, and at first came up with no suggestions. Perhaps he had caught Ned's warning eye.

"Hell, Barley, it's not *her* fault she hasn't any worthwhile opponents, is it?"

"Woman's a bloody Red," Barley growled, to the secret alarm of the British side.

Brady didn't laugh, just raised his eyebrows and waited, as we all did.

"Elective dictatorship," Barley continued, quietly gathering steam. "God bless the corporation and bugger the individual."

He seemed to be about to enlarge on this thesis, then to our relief changed his mind and let it rest.

Nevertheless it was a light enough beginning, and after ten minutes Barley must have been feeling pretty much at ease. Until in his languid way Brady came to "this present thing you've gotten yourself into, Barley," and proposed that Barley should go over the turf again in his own words, "but homing in on that historic eye-to-eye you two fellows had in Leningrad."

Barley did as Brady wanted, and though I like to think I listened quite as sharply as Brady, I heard nothing in Barley's narrative that seemed to me contradictory or particularly revealing beyond what was already on the record.

And at first blush Brady didn't seem to hear anything surprising either, for when Barley had finished, Brady gave him a reassuring smile and said, "Well now, thank you, Barley," in a voice of apparent approval. His slender fingers poked among his papers. "Worst thing about spying, I always say, is the hanging around. Must be like being a fighter pilot," he said, selecting a page and peering at it. "One minute sitting home eating your chicken dinner, next minute frightening the hell out of yourself at eight hundred miles an hour. Then it's back home in time to wash the dishes." He had apparently found what he was looking for. "Is that how it felt to you, Barley, stuck out there in Muscovy without a prayer?"

"A bit."

"Hanging around waiting for Katya? Hanging around waiting for Goethe? You seemed to do quite some hanging around after you and Goethe had finished your little pow-wow, didn't you?"

Perching his spectacles on the tip of his nose, Brady was studying the paper before passing it to Skelton. I knew the pause was contrived but it scared me all the same, and I think it scared Ned for he glanced at Sheriton, then anxiously back to Barley. "According to our field reports, you and Goethe broke up around fourteen thirty-three Leningrad time. Seen the picture? Show it to him, Skelton."

All of us had seen it. All but Barley. It portrayed the two men in the gardens of the Smolny after they had said goodbye. Goethe had turned away. Barley's hands were still held out to him from their farewell embrace. The electronic timeprint in the top left corner said fourteen thirty-three and twenty seconds.

"Remember your last words to him?" Brady asked, with an air of sweet reminiscence.

"I said I'd publish him."

"Remember *his* last words to *you?*"

"He wanted to know whether he should look for another decent human being."

"One hell of a goodbye," Brady remarked comfortably while Barley continued to look at the photograph, and Brady and Skelton looked at Barley. "What did you do then, Barley?"

"Went back to the Europe. Handed over his stuff."

"What route did you take? Remember?"

"Same way I got there. Trolleybus into town, then walked a bit."

"Have to wait long for the trolleybus?" Brady asked, while his Southern accent became, to my ear at least, more of a mocking-bird than a regional digression.

"Not that I remember."

"How long?"

"Five minutes. Maybe longer."

I could not remember one occasion until now when Barley had pleaded an imperfect memory.

"Many people in line?"

"Not many. A few. I didn't count."

"The trolleybus runs every ten minutes. The ride into town takes another ten. The walk to the Europe, at your pace, ten. Our people have timed it all ways up. Ten's the outside. But according to Mr. and Mrs. Henziger, you didn't show up in their hotel room till fifteen fifty-five. That leaves us with quite a tidy hole, Barley. Like a hole in time. Mind telling me how we're going to fill it? I don't expect you went on a drinking spree, did you? You were carrying some pretty valuable merchandise. I'd have thought you wanted to unload it pretty quick."

Barley was becoming wary and Brady must have seen that he was, for his hospitable Southern smile was offering a new kind of encouragement, the kind that said "come clean."

As to Ned, he was sitting stock still with both feet flat on the ground, and his straight gaze was fixed on Barley's troubled face.

Only Clive and Sheriton seemed to have pledged themselves to display no emotions at all.

"What were you doing, Barley?" Brady said.

"I mooched," said Barley, not lying at all well.

"Carrying Goethe's notebook? The notebook he had *entrusted* to you with his life? Mooched? You picked a damned odd afternoon to mooch for fifty minutes, Barley. Where d'you go?"

"I wandered back along the river. Where we'd been. Paddy had told me to take my time. Not to rush back to the hotel but to go at a leisurely speed."

"That's true," Ned murmured. "Those were my instructions via Moscow station."

"For fifty minutes?" Brady persisted, ignoring Ned's intervention.

"I don't know how long it was. I wasn't looking at my watch. If you take time, you take time."

"And it didn't cross your mind that with a tape and a power-pack in your pants, and a notebook full of potentially priceless intelligence material in your carrier bag, the shortest distance between two points might *just* be a straight line?"

Barley was getting dangerously angry but the danger was to himself as Ned's expression, and I fear my own, could have warned him.

"Look, you're not listening, are you?" he said rudely. "I told you. Paddy told me to take time. They trained me that way in London, on our stupid little runs. Take time. Never hurry if you're carrying something. Better to make the conscious effort to go slowly."

Yet again, brave Ned did his best. "That's what he was taught," he said.

But he was watching Barley as he spoke.

Brady was also watching Barley. "So you mooched *away* from the trolleybus stop, *towards* the Communist Party Headquarters in the Smolny Institute—not to mention the Komsomol and a couple of other Party shrines—*carrying* Goethe's notebook—in your bag? Why did you do that, Barley? Fellows in the field do some damned strange things, you don't have to tell *me* that, but this strikes me as plain suicidal."

"I was obeying orders, blast you, Brady! I was taking my time! How often do I have to tell you?"

But even as he flared it occurred to me that Barley was caught not so much in a lie as in a dilemma. There was too much honesty in his appeal, too much loneliness in his assailed eyes. And Brady to his credit seemed to understand this too, for he showed no sign of triumph at Barley's distress, preferring to befriend him rather than to goad.

"You see, Barley, a lot of people around here would attach a heap of suspicion to a gap like that," Brady said. "They would have a picture of you sitting in somebody's office or car while that somebody photographed Goethe's notebook or gave you orders. Did you do any of that? I guess now's the time to say so if you did. There's never going to be a good time, but this is about as good as we're likely to get."

"No."

"No, you won't tell?"

"That's not what happened."

"Well, something happened. Do you remember what was in your mind while you mooched?"

"Goethe. Publishing him. Bringing down the temple if he had to."

"What temple's that, exactly? Can we get away from the metaphysical a little?"

"Katya. The children. Taking them with him if he gets caught. I don't know who has the right to do that. I can't work it out."

"So you mooched and tried to work it out."

Maybe Barley did mooch, maybe he didn't. He had clammed up.

"Wouldn't it have been more normal to hand over the notebook first and try to work out the ethics afterwards? I'm surprised you were able to think clearly with that damn thing burning a hole in your carrier bag. I'm not suggesting we're any of us very logical in these situations, but even by the laws of *un*logic, I would feel you had put yourself in a damned uncomfortable situation. I think you did something. I think you think so too."

"I bought a hat."

"What kind of hat?"

"A fur hat. A woman's hat."

"Who for?"

"Miss Coad."

"That a girlfriend?"

"She's the housekeeper at the safe house in Knightsbridge," Ned cut in before Barley could reply.

"Where'd you buy it?"

"On the way between the tram stop and the hotel. I don't know where. A shop."

"That all?"

"Just a hat. One hat."

"How long did that take you?"

"I had to queue."

"How long did it take?"

"I don't know."

"What else did you do?"

"Nothing. I bought a hat."

"You're lying, Barley. Not gravely, but you are undoubtedly lying. What else did you do?"

"I phoned her."

"Miss Coad?"

"Katya."

"Where from?"

"A post office."

"Which one?"

Ned had put a hand across his forehead as if to shield his eyes from the sun. But the storm had taken hold, and outside the window both sea and sky were black.

"Don't know. Big place. Phone cabins under a sort of iron balcony."

"You called her at her office or at her home?"

"Office. It was office hours. Her office."

"Why don't we hear you do that on the body tapes?"

"I switched them off."

"What was the purpose of the call?"

"I wanted to make sure she was all right."

"How did you go about that?"

"I said hullo. She said hullo. I said I was in Leningrad, I'd met my contact, business was going along fine. Anyone listening would think I was talking about Henziger. Katya would know I was talking about Goethe."

"Makes pretty good sense to me," said Brady with a forgiving smile.

"I said, so goodbye again till the Moscow book fair and take care. She said she would. Take care, I mean. Goodbye."

"Anything else?"

"I told her to destroy the Jane Austens I'd given her. I said they were the wrong edition. I'd bring her some new ones."

"Why'd you do that?"

"The Jane Austens had questions for Goethe printed into the text. They were duplicates of the questions in the paperback he wouldn't take from me. In case she got to him and I didn't. They were a danger to her. Since he wasn't going to answer them anyway, I didn't want them lying around her house."

Nothing stirred in the room. Just the sea wind making the shutters crack, and puffing in the eaves.

"How long did your call with Katya take, Barley?"

"I don't know."

"How much money did it cost you?"

"I don't know. I paid at the desk. Two roubles something. I talked a lot about the book fair. So did she. I wanted to listen to her."

This time it was Brady's turn to keep quiet.

"I had a feeling that as long as I was talking, life was normal. She was all right."

Brady took a while, then against all our expectation closed the show: "So, small talk," he suggested as he began to pack his wares into his grandfather's attaché case.

"That's it," Barley agreed. "Small talk. Chit chat."

"As between acquaintances," Brady suggested, popping the case shut. "Thank you, Barley. I admire you."

We sat in the huge drawing room, Brady at our centre, Barley gone.

"Drop him down a hole, Clive," Brady advised, in a voice still steeped in courtesy. "He's flakey, he's a liability and he thinks too damn much. Bluebird is making waves you would not believe. The fiefdoms are up in arms, the Air generals are in spasm, Defense says he's a charter to give away the store, the Pentagon's accusing the Agency of promoting bogus goods. Your only hope is throw this man out and put in a professional, one of ours."

"Bluebird won't deal with a professional," said Ned, and I heard the fury simmering in his voice and knew it was about to boil over.

Skelton too had a suggestion. It was the first time I had heard him speak, and I had to crane my head to catch his cultured college voice.

"Fuck Bluebird," he said. "Bluebird's got no business calling the shots. He's a traitor and a guilt-driven crazy and who knows what else he is besides? Hold his feet to the fire. Tell him if he stops producing we'll sell him to his own people and the girl with him."

"If Goethe's a good boy, he gets the jackpot, I'll see to it," Brady promised. "A million's no problem. Ten million's better. If you frighten him enough and pay him enough, maybe the neanderthals will believe he's on the level. Russell, give my love. Clive, it's been a pleasure. Harry. Ned."

With Skelton at his side he started to move towards the door.

But Ned wasn't saying goodbye. He didn't raise his voice or bang the table but neither did he hold back the dark glow in his eyes or the edge of outrage in his words.

"Brady!"

"Something on your mind, Ned?"

"Bluebird won't be bullied. Not by them, not by you. Blackmail may look nice in the planning room but it won't play on the ground. Listen to the tapes if you don't believe me. Bluebird's in search of martyrdom. You don't threaten martyrs."

"So what do I do with them, Ned?"

"Did Barley lie to you?"

"Not unduly."

"He's straight. It's a straight case. Do you remember straight? While you're thinking round corners, Bluebird's going straight for goal. And he's chosen Barley as his running mate. Barley's the only chance we have."

"He's in love with the girl," said Brady. "He's complicated. He's a liability."

"He's in love with hundreds of girls. He proposes to every girl he meets. That's who he is. It's not Barley who thinks too much. It's your people."

Brady was interested. Not in his own conviction, if he had any, but in Ned's.

"I've done all kinds," Ned went on. "So have you. Some cases are never straight, even when they're over. This one was straight from the first day, and if anyone is shoving it off course, we are."

I had never heard him speak with so much fervour. Neither had Sheriton, for he was transfixed, and perhaps it was for this reason that Clive felt obliged to interpose himself with a fanfare of civil servants' exit music. "Yes, well I think we have ample food for thought here, Brady. Russell, we must talk this through. Perhaps there's a middle way. I rather think there may be. Why don't we take soundings? Kick it around a little. Run over it one more time."

But nobody had left. Brady, for all Clive's ushering platitudes, had remained exactly where he was, and I observed a raw kindliness in his features that was like the real man beneath the mask.

"Nobody hired us for our brotherly love, Ned. That's just not what they put us spooks on earth for. We knew that when we signed up." He smiled. "Guess if plain decency was the name of the game, you'd be running the show in place of Deputy Clive here."

Clive was not pleased by this suggestion, but it did not prevent him from escorting Brady to his jeep.

For a moment I thought I was alone with Ned and Sheriton, until I saw Randy our host framed in the doorway, wearing an expression of star-struck disbelief. "Was that *the* Brady?" he asked breathlessly. "The Brady who did like *everything?*"

"It was Greta Garbo," Sheriton said. "Go away, Randy. Please."

I should play you more of that steadying music while Sheriton's young men take Barley back again, and walk with him on the beach and joke with him and produce the street map of Leningrad for him, and painstakingly log the very shop where Miss Coad's lynx hat was bought, and how he paid for it and where the receipt might have got to if there ever was one, and whether Barley had declared the hat to customs at Gatwick, and the very post office where he must have made his telephone call.

I should describe to you the spare hours Ned and I spent sitting around Barley's boat-house in the evenings, hunting for ways to shake him from his introspections and finding none.

For Barley's journey away from us—I felt it even then—had not flagged from the moment when he first agreed to be interrogated.

Then comes the morning following—a real sparkler, as they call it there; I think it must have been the Thursday—when the little plane from Logan airport brought us Merv and Stanley in time for their favourite breakfast of pancakes and bacon and pure maple syrup.

Randy's kitchen was well acquainted with their tastes.

They were bearish, kindly men of the soil, with pumice-stone faces and big hands, and they arrived looking like a vaudeville duo, wearing dark trilby hats and humping a salesman's suitcase which they kept close to them while they ate and later set down gingerly on the red-painted floor of the billiards room.

Their profession had made their faces dull, but they were the type our own Service likes best—straightforward, loyal, uncomplicated foot-soldiers with a job to do and kids to feed, who loved their country without making a to-do of it.

Merv's hair was cropped to a moleskin fuzz. Stanley had bandy legs and wore some sort of loyal badge.

"You can be Jesus Christ, Mr. Brown. You can be a fifteen-hundred-a-month typist," Sheriton had said as we stood around in Barley's boat-house in a state of shifty supplication. "It's voodoo, it's alchemy, it's the Ouija board, it's reading fucking tea-leaves. And if you don't go through with it, you're dead."

Clive spoke next. Clive could find reasons for anything. "If he's nothing to hide, why should he be bothered?" he said. "It's their version of the Official Secrets Act."

"What does Ned say?" Barley asked.

Not Nedsky any more. Ned.

There was a defeat in Ned's reply that I shall never forget, and in his eyes as well. Brady's interrogation of Barley had shaken his faith in himself, and even in his joe.

"It's your choice," he said lamely. And as if to himself, "A pretty disgusting one too, if you ask me."

Barley turned to me, exactly as he had done before, when I had first asked him whether he would submit to the American questioning. "Harry? What do I do?"

Why did he insist on my opinion? It was unfair. I expect I looked as uncomfortable as Ned. I certainly felt so, though I managed a light-hearted shrug. "Either humour them and go along with it or tell them to go to hell. It's up to you," I replied, much as I had on the first occasion.

Thus the eternal lawyer.

Barley's stillness again. His indecision slowly giving way to resignation. His separation from us as he stares through the window at the sea. "Well, let's hope they don't catch me telling the truth," he says.

He stands up and flips his wrists around, loosening his shoulders, while the rest of us like so many butlers confirm among ourselves by furtive looks and nods that our master has said yes.

At their work Merv and Stanley had the respectful nimbleness of executioners. Either they had brought the chair with them or the island kept one for them as a permanency, an upright wooden throne with a scalloped arm-rest on the left side. Merv set it handy for the electric socket while Stanley spoke to Barley like a grandfather.

"Mr. Brown, sir, this is not a situation where you should expect hostility. It is our wish you should not be troubled by a relationship with your examiners. The examiner is not adversarial, he is an impartial functionary, it's the machine that does the work. Kindly remove your jacket, no need to roll back your sleeves, sir, or unbutton your shirt, thank you. Very easy now, please, nice and relaxed."

Meanwhile with the greatest delicacy Merv slipped a doctor's blood-pressure cuff over Barley's left bicep until it was flush with the artery inside his elbow. Then he inflated the cuff until the dial said fifty milligrams while Stanley, with the devotion of a boxing second, fitted a one-inch-diameter rubberised tube round Barley's chest, careful to avoid the nipples so that it didn't chafe. Then Stanley fitted a second tube across Barley's abdomen while Merv slipped a double finger stall over the two central fingers of Barley's left hand, with an electrode inside it to pick up the sweat glands and the galvanised skin response and the changes of skin temperature over which the subject, provided he has a conscience, has no control—or so preach the converted, for I had had it all explained to me by Stanley beforehand, much as a concerned relative will inform himself in advance about the details of a loved one's surgical operation. Some polygraphers, Harry, they liked an extra band around the head like an encephalograph. Not Stanley. Some polygraphers, Harry, they liked to shout and rage at the subject. Not Stanley. Stanley reckoned that a lot of people got disturbed by an accusatory question, whether or not they were guilty.

"Mr. Brown, sir, we ask you to make no movement, fast or slow," Merv was saying. "If you do make such a movement we are liable to get a violent disturbance in the pattern which will necessitate further testing and a repetition of the questions. Thank you. First we like to establish a norm. By norm we mean a level of voice, a level of physical response—imagine a seismograph, you are the earth, you provide the disturbance. Thank you, sir. Answer to be 'yes' or 'no' only, please, always answer truthfully. We break off after every eight questions, that will be to loosen the pressure cuff in order to prevent discomfort. While the cuff is loosened we shall engage in normal conversation, but no humour, please, no undue excitation of any kind. Is your name Brown?"

"No."

"Do you have a different name from the one you are using?"

"Yes."

"Are you British born, Mr. Brown?"

"Yes."

"Did you fly here, Mr. Brown?"

"Yes."

"Did you come here by boat, Mr. Brown?"

"No."

"Have you truthfully answered my questions so far, Mr. Brown?"

"Yes."

"Do you intend to answer my questions truthfully throughout the remainder of this test, Mr. Brown?"

"Yes."

"Thank you," said Merv, with a gentle smile, while Stanley released the air from the cuff. "Those are what we call the non-relevant questions. Married?"

"Not at the moment."

"Kids?"

"Two, actually."

"Boys or girls?"

"One of each."

"Wise man. Alrighty?" He began pumping up the cuff again. "Now we go relevant. Easy now. That's nice. That's very nice."

In the open suitcase, the four spectral wire claws described their four mauve skylines across the graph paper while the four black needles nodded inside their dials. Merv had taken up a sheaf of questions and settled himself at a small table at Barley's side. Not even Russell Sheriton had been allowed to know the questions the faceless desk inquisitors in Langley had selected. No casual tampering by Barley's terrestrial co-habitants was to be allowed to breathe upon the mystic powers of the box.

Merv spoke tonelessly. Merv, I was sure, prided himself upon the impartiality of his voice. He was the March of Time. He was Houston Control.

"I am knowingly engaged in a conspiracy to supply untrue information to the intelligence services of Britain and the United States of America. Yes, I am so engaged. No, I am not so engaged."

"No."

"My motive is to promote peace between nations. Yes or no?"

"No."

"I am operating in collusion with Soviet Intelligence."

"No."

"I am proud of my mission on behalf of world Communism."

"No."

"I am operating in collusion with Niki Landau."

"No."

"Niki Landau is my lover."

"No."

"Was my lover."

"No."

"I am homosexual."

"No."

A break while Stanley once more eased the pressure. "How's it feeling, Mr. Brown? Not too much pain?"

"Never enough, old boy. I thrive on it."

But we didn't look at him in these breaks, I noticed. We looked at the floor or at our hands, or at the beckoning wind-bent trees outside the window. It was Stanley's turn. A cosier tone, but the same mechanical flatness.

"I am operating in collusion with the woman Katya Orlova and her lover."

"No."

"The man I call Goethe is known to me as a plant of Soviet Intelligence."

"No."

"The material he has passed to me has been prepared by Soviet Intelligence."

"No."

"I am the victim of sexual entrapment."

"No."

"I am being blackmailed."

"No."

"I am being coerced."

"Yes."

"By the Soviets?"

"No."

"I am being threatened with financial ruin if I do not collaborate with the Soviets."

"No."

Another break. Round Three. Merv's turn.

"I lied when I said I had telephoned Katya Orlova from Leningrad."

"No."

"From Leningrad I called my Soviet Control and told him of my discussion with Goethe."

"No."

"I am the lover of Katya Orlova."

"No."

"I have been the lover of Katya Orlova at some time."

"No."

"I am being blackmailed regarding my relationship with Katya Orlova."

"No."

"I have told the truth so far throughout this interview."

"Yes."

"I am an enemy of the United States of America."

"No."

"My aim is to undermine the military preparedness of the United States of America."

"Do you mind running that one by me again, old boy?"

"Hold it," said Merv, and Stanley at the suitcase held it, while Merv made a pencilled annotation on the graph paper. "Don't break the rhythm, please, Mr. Brown. We have people do that on purpose when they want to shake off a bad question."

Round Four and Stanley's turn again. The questions droned on and it was clear they would not stop until they had reached the nadir of their vulgarity. Barley's "no"s had acquired a deadened rhythm and a mocking passivity. He remained sitting exactly as they had placed him. I had never seen him so still for so long.

They broke again but Barley no longer relaxed between rounds. His stillness was becoming unbearable. His chin was lifted, his eyes were closed and he appeared to be smiling, God alone knew what about. Sometimes his "no" fell before the end of a sentence. Sometimes he waited so long that the two men paused and looked up, the one from his dials and the other from his papers, and they seemed to me to have the torturer's anxiety that they might have taxed their man too hard. Till the "no" finally fell again, neither louder nor quieter, a letter delayed in the mail.

Where does he get his stoicism from? No, no, to everything. Why does he sit there like a man preparing himself for the indignities of age, meekly mouthing "no"? What does this meekness mean, *no, yes, no, no,* till lunchtime, when they take him off the machine?

But in another part of my head, I think I knew the answer, even if I could not yet put it into words: his reality had moved elsewhere.

Spying is waiting.

We waited three days, and you may still count the hours in my grey hairs. We had split on lines of seniority: Sheriton to go with Bob and Clive to Langley; Ned to stay on the island with his joe, Palfrey to remain with them on standby, though what I was standing by for was a mystery to me. I hated the island by then and I suspected that Ned and Barley did too, though I could get no nearer to Ned than I could to Barley. He had become remote and for the time being humourless. Something had happened to his pride.

So we waited. And played distracted chess, seldom finishing a game. And listened to Randy talk about his yacht. And listened for the telephone. And to the screaming of the birds and the pulse of the sea.

It was a mad time, and the vagaries of the isolated place with its fuming skies and storms and patches of idyllic beauty made it madder. A "dungeon fog," as Randy called it, enveloped us and with it a mindless fear that we would never leave the island. The fog cleared but we were still there. The shared intimacy should have drawn us closer, but both men had withdrawn to their kingdoms, Ned to his room and Barley to the outdoors. With the rain whipping over the island like grapeshot I would peer through the streaming window and glimpse him pounding over the cliff in his oilskins, picking up his knees as if wrestling with uncomfortable shoes

—or once, playing solitary cricket on the beach with Edgar the guard, a piece of driftwood and a tennis ball. In sunny spells he sported an old blue sailing cap which he had unearthed from a sea-chest in his room. He wore it with a grim face, eyes upon unconquered colonies. One day Edgar appeared with an old yellow dog he had unearthed from somewhere and they made it run back and forth between them. On another day there was a regatta off the mainland and a shoal of white yachts clustered in a ring like tiny teeth. Barley stood watching them interminably, seemingly delighted by the carnival, while Edgar stood off watching Barley.

He's thinking of his Hannah, I thought. He's waiting for life to provide him with the moment of choice. It did not occur to me till much later that some people do not take their decisions in quite that way.

My last image of the island has the convenient distortions of a dream. I had spoken to Clive only twice on the telephone, which for him was virtually a blackout. Once he wished to know "how your friends are bearing up" and I gathered from Ned that he had already asked him the same question. And once he needed to hear about the arrangements I had made for Barley's compensation, including the subsidies to his company, and whether the monies would come from our own funds or in the form of a supplementary estimate. I had a few notes with me and was able to enlighten him.

It is midday and *The New York Times* and *Washington Post* have just arrived on the table in the sunroom. I am stooped over them when I hear Randy yelling at the guards to get Ned to the telephone. As I turn, I see Ned himself entering from the garden side and striding across the hall to the communications room. I glance beyond him, up to the first-floor landing, and I see Barley, a motionless silhouette. There are some old bookcases up there, and that morning he has persuaded Randy to unlock them so that he can browse. It is the landing with the semi-circular window, the one that looks over the hydrangeas to the sea.

He is standing with his back turned and a book hanging from one long hand, and he is staring at the Atlantic. His feet are apart, his spare hand is raised, as it often is, to somewhere near his head, as if to fend off a blow. He must have heard everything that is going on—Randy's yell, then Ned's hasty footsteps across the hall, followed by the slam of the communications room door. The landing floor is tiled and footsteps come chiming up that stairwell like squeaky church bells. I can hear them now as Ned emerges from the communications room, goes a few steps and halts.

"Harry! Where's Barley?"

"Up here," says Barley quietly over the banister.

"They've given you the thumbs-up!" Ned shouts, jubilant as a schoolboy. "They apologise. I spoke to Bob, I spoke to Clive, I spoke to Haggarty. Goethe's is the most important stuff they've handled for years. Official. They'll go for him a hundred percent. There'll be no turning back any more. You've beaten their whole apparatus."

Ned was used to Barley's distracted ways by then, so he should not have been surprised when Barley gave no sign of having heard him. His gaze was still fixed on the Atlantic. Did he think he saw a small boat founder? Everybody does. Watch the Maine seas for long enough and you see them everywhere, a sail, a hull, now the speck of a survivor's head or hand, ducking under the sea's swell never to resurface.

You must go on watching for a long time to know you are looking at ospreys and cormorants going about their hunting.

But Ned in his excitement manages to be wounded. It is one of those rare moments in him when the professional drops his guard and reveals the unfinished man inside.

"You're going back to Moscow, Barley! That's what you wanted, isn't it? To see it through?"

And Barley at last, concerned that he has hurt Ned's feelings: Barley half turning so that Ned can see his smile. "Yes, old boy. Of course it is. Just what I wanted."

Meanwhile it is my turn in the communications room. Randy is beckoning me in.

"Is that you, Palfrey?"

It is I.

"*Langley* are taking over the case," says Clive, as if this were the other part of the great news. "They're giving it a full-facility grading, Palfrey. That's the highest they go," he adds quellingly.

"Oh well. Congratulations," I say and, taking the telephone from my ear, stare at it in disbelief while Clive's drawl continues to ooze out of it like a tap nothing can turn off. "I want you to draw up a document of understanding immediately, Palfrey, and prepare a full-length agreement to cover the usual contingencies. We've got them eating out of our hand, so I expect you to be firm. Firm but fair. We're dealing with very realistic people, Palfrey. Hard-nosed."

More. Still more. And more yet. Langley to take over Barley's pension and resettlement as earnest of their total operational control. Langley to share equally in the running of the source, but to have a casting vote in the event of disagreement.

"They're preparing a full-scale shopping list, Palfrey, a grand slam. They're taking it to State, Defense, the Pentagon and the scientific bodies. All the biggest questions of the day will be canvassed and set down for the Bluebird to respond to. They know the risks but that isn't deterring them. Nothing ventured, nothing gained, they reason. That takes courage."

It is his Despatch Box voice. Clive has India at last. "In the great offence-defence stand-off, Palfrey, nothing exists in a vacuum," he explains loftily, quoting, I had no doubt, what somebody had said to him an hour before. "It's a matter of the finest tuning. Every question is as important as every answer. They know that. They see it clearly. They can pay the source no higher compliment than to prepare a no-holds-barred questionnaire for him. It's a thing they haven't done for many, many years. It breaks precedent. Recent precedent anyway."

"Does Ned know?" I ask when I can get a word in.

"He can't. None of us can. We're talking the highest strategic classifications."

"I meant, does he know you've made them a present of his joe?"

"I want you to come down to Langley immediately and thrash out terms with your opposite numbers here. Randy will arrange transport. Palfrey?"

"Does he know?" I repeat.

Clive makes one of his telephone silences, in which you are supposed to work out all the ways in which you are at fault.

"Ned will be brought up to date when he gets back to London, thank you. That will be quite soon enough. Until then I shall expect you to say nothing. The rôle of the Russia House will be respected. Sheriton values the link. It will even be enlarged in certain ways, perhaps permanently. Ned should be grateful."

The news was nowhere more joyfully received than in the British trade press. *Marriage with a Future,* trumpeted *Booknews* a few weeks later in its trailer for the Moscow book fair. *The long-rumoured engagement between Abercrombie & Blair of Norfolk Street, Strand, and Potomac Traders, Inc., of Boston, Mass., is* ON! *Seventeen-stone entrepreneur Jack Henziger has finally weighed in beside Bartholomew Scott Blair of A. & B. with a new joint company titled Potomac & Blair, which plans an aggressive campaign in the fast-opening East Bloc markets. "This is a shop window on tomorrow," declares confident Henziger.*

Moscow Book Fair, here they come!

The newsflash was accompanied by a warming photograph of Barley and Jack Henziger shaking hands across a bowl of flowers. The photograph was taken by the Service photographer in the safe house in Knightsbridge. Flowers by Miss Coad.

I met Hannah the day following my return from the island and I assumed we would make love. She looked tall and golden, which is the way she always looks when I have not seen her for a while. A Thursday, so she was taking her fourteen-year-old son Giles to some spurious consultant behind Harley Street. I have never cared for Giles, probably because I know that he was conceived on the rebound, on one of the occasions when I had sent her back to Derek. We sat in our usual evil café drinking rancid tea, while she waited for him to come out, and smoked, a thing I hate. But I wanted her, and she knew it.

"Whereabouts in America?" she said, as if it mattered.

"I don't know. Some island full of ospreys and bad weather."

"I bet they weren't real ospreys."

"They were, actually. They're common there."

And I saw by the strain in her eyes that she wanted me too.

"Anyway, I've got to take Giles home," she said when we had sufficiently read each other's thoughts.

"Put him in a cab," I suggested.

But by then we were opposed to each other once more, and the moment was dead.

13

Katya collected Barley at ten o'clock on the Sunday morning from the forecourt of the immense Mezhdunarodnaya, which was where Henziger had insisted on staying. Westerners know it familiarly as "the Mezh." Both Wicklow and Henziger, seated in the hotel's preposterous Great Hall, contrived to witness their happy reunion and departure.

The day was fine and Barley had started waiting for her early, hovering in the forecourt amid the blind limousines that fetched and disgorged their Third World chieftains in a steady flow. Then at last her red Lada popped up among them like a burst of fun at a funeral, with Anna's white hand streaming out of the rear window like a handkerchief and Sergey, upright as a commissar beside her, clutching his fishing net.

It was important to Barley to notice the children first. He had thought about it and told himself it was what he would do, because nothing was insignificant any more, nothing could be left to chance. Only when he had waved enthusiastically at both of them therefore and pulled a face at Anna through the back window, did he allow himself to peer into the front, where Uncle Matvey sat squarely in the passenger seat, his polished brown face glowing like a chestnut and his sailor's eyes twinkling under the brim of his plaid cap. Sunshine or storm, Matvey had put on his best things to honour the great Englishman: his twill jacket, his best boots and bow tie. The crossed enamelled flags of the Revolution were pinned to his lapel. Matvey lowered his window and Barley reached through it, grasping his hand and yelling "Hullo, *hullo*" at him several times. Only then did he venture to look at Katya. And there was a kind of hiatus as if he had forgotten his lines or his cover story, or simply how beautiful she was, before he hoisted his smile.

But Katya showed no such reticence.

She leapt out of the car. She was wearing badly cut slacks and looked marvellous in them. She rushed round to him beaming with happiness and trust. She yelled "Barley!" And by the time she reached him she had flung her arms so wide that her body was cheerfully and unthinkingly open to him for his embrace—which as a good Russian girl she then decorously curtailed, standing back from him but still holding on to him, examining his face, his hair, his ancient outdoor gear, while she chatted away in a flood of spontaneous goodfellowship.

"It is so *good*, Barley. Really so good to see you!" she was exclaiming. "Welcome to the book fair, welcome to Moscow again. Matvey could not believe it, your phone call from London! 'The English were always our friends,' he said. 'They taught Peter how to sail, and if he had not known how to sail, we would not today have a navy.' He is speaking of Peter the Great, you see. Matvey lives only for Leningrad. Do you not admire Volodya's fine car? I am so grateful he has something he can love at last."

She released him and, like the happy idiot he by now was looking, Barley let out a cry of "God, nearly forgot!" He meant the carrier bags. He had propped them against the wall of the hotel beside the entrance, and by the time he reappeared with them, Matvey was trying to climb out of the car to make room for him in the front, but Barley would have none of it.

"No, no, no, *no!* I'll be absolutely fine with the twins! Bless you all the same, Matvey." Then he threaded and backed his long body into the rear seat as if he were parking an articulated lorry, while he handed round his parcels and the twins giggled at him in awe: this giant Westerner with so many joints and bits left over, who has brought us English chocolates, and Swiss crayons, and drawing books, one each, and the works of Beatrix Potter in English to share, and a beautiful new pipe for Uncle Matvey, which Katya is saying will make him happier than is possible to imagine, with a pouch of English tobacco to smoke in it.

And for Katya everything she could want for the rest of her life—lipsticks and a pullover and scents and a French silk scarf too beautiful to wear.

All this by the time Katya drove out of the Mezh forecourt and bumped on to a pockmarked highway, chatting about the book fair that was opening tomorrow, and steering inaccurately between the flooded craters.

They were heading roughly east. The friendly gold September sun hung ahead of them, making even the Moscow suburbs beautiful. They entered the sad flatland of Moscow's outskirts, with its proprietorless fields, desolate churches and fenced-in transformers. Clusters of old dachas were scattered like ancient beach-huts along the roadside, and their sculptured gables and boxed gardens reminded Barley as always of the English country railway stations of his youth. From his seat in the front, Matvey was poisoning them all with his new pipe and proclaiming his ecstasy through the clouds of smoke. But Katya was too busy pointing out the sights to pay him much attention.

"Over *that* hill lies the so-and-so metal foundry, Barley. The shabby cement building to your left is a collective farm."

"Great!" said Barley. "Fascinating! What a day, though, wow!"

Anna had emptied her crayons on to her lap and discovered that if she licked the points they left wet trails of paint. Sergey was urging her to put them back in their tin and Barley was trying to keep the peace by drawing animals in her sketch book for her to colour, but Moscow road surfaces are not kind to artists.

"Not *green,* you chump," he told her. "Who ever saw a green cow? Katya, for heaven's sake, your daughter thinks cows are green."

"Oh Anna is *completely* impractical!" Katya cried laughing, and spoke quickly to Anna over her shoulder, who giggled up at Barley.

And all this had to be heard over Matvey's continued monologue and Anna's immense hilarity and Sergey's troubled interjections, not to mention the anguished thunder of the little engine, until nobody could hear anything except themselves. Suddenly they swung off the road, across a grass field and up a hill without even a track to guide them, to huge laughter from the children and from Katya too, while Matvey clutched his hat with one hand, and his pipe with the other.

"You see?" Katya was demanding of Barley above the din, as if she had proved a long-contested point between lovers. "In Russia we may go *exactly* where our fancy takes us, provided we do not trespass into the estates of our millionaires or government officials."

They crested the hill amid more riotous laughter and plunged into a grass dip, then rose again like a brave little boat on a wave to join a farm track that ran beside a stream. The stream entered a birch grove, the track raced beside it. Katya somehow hauled the car to a halt, heaving on the handbrake as if she were slowing down a sledge. They were alone in Paradise with the stream to dam, and a bank to picnic on, and space to play *lapta* with Sergey's stick and ball from the boot of the car, which required everybody to stand in a ring, and one to bowl and one to bat.

Anna, it quickly became apparent, was frivolous about *lapta*. Her ambition was to get through it with as much laughter as possible, then settle down to lunch and flirt with Barley. But Sergey the soldier was a believer and Matvey the sailor was a zealot. While Katya spread out the picnic, she explained the mystical importance of *lapta* to the development of Western culture.

"Matvey assures me it is the origin of American baseball and your English cricket. He believes it was introduced to you by Russian immigrants. I am sure he also believes that it was invented by Peter the Great."

"If it's true, it's the death of the Empire," said Barley gravely.

Lying in the grass, Matvey is still talking volubly while he puffs at his new pipe. His generous blue eyes, receding into their glorious Leningrad past, are filled with a heroic light. But Katya hears him as if he were a radio that can't be switched off. She picks on the odd point and is deaf to all the rest. Marching across the grass, she climbs into the car and closes the door behind her, to reappear in shorts, carrying the picnic in an oilcloth bag, with sandwiches wrapped in newspaper. She has prepared cold *kotleti* and cold chicken and meat pies. She has salted cucumber and hard-boiled eggs. She has brought bottles of Zhiguli beer, Barley has brought Scotch, with which Matvey fervently toasts some absent monarch, perhaps Peter himself.

Sergey stands on the bank, raking the water with his net. His dream, Katya explains, is to catch a fish and cook it for everyone who depends on him. Anna is drawing. Ostentatiously, leaning away from her work so that others may admire it. She wishes to give Barley a portrait of herself to hang in his room in London.

"She is asking, are you married?" Katya says, yielding to her daughter's importuning.

"No, not at present, but I'm always available."

Anna asks another question but Katya blushes and rebukes her. His loyalist duties completed, Matvey is lying on his back with his cap over his eyes, rattling on about heaven knows what, except that, whatever it is, it is all delightful to him.

"Soon he will describe the siege of Leningrad," Katya calls with a fond smile.

A pause while she glances at Barley. She means, "Now we can talk."

The grey lorry was leaving, and high time too. Barley had been resenting it over her shoulder for quite a while, hoping it was friendly but wishing it would leave them alone. The side windows of its cab were dark with dust. Gratefully he saw it lumber to the road, then lumber out of sight and mind.

"Oh, he is *very* well," Katya was saying. "He wrote me a long letter and everything is excellent with him. He was ill but he is completely recovered, I am sure. He has many matters to discuss with you and he will make a special visit to Moscow during the fair in order to meet you and hear the progress concerning his book. He would like to see some prepared manuscript soon, perhaps only a page. My opinion is that this would be dangerous but he is so impatient. He wants proposals about the title, translations, even illustrations. I think he is becoming a typical dictatorial writer. He will confirm everything very soon and he will also find an apartment where you can meet. He wishes to make all the arrangements himself, can you imagine? I think you have been a very good influence for him."

She was searching in her handbag. A red car had parked on the other side of the birch grove but she seemed oblivious to everything but her own good spirits. "Personally I believe his work will soon be regarded as redundant. With the disarmament talks advancing so rapidly and the new atmosphere of international cooperation, all these terrible things will shortly belong to the past. Naturally the Americans are suspicious of us. Naturally we are suspicious of them. But when we have joined our forces, we can disarm completely and between us prevent all further trouble in the world." It was her didactic voice, brooking no argument.

"How do we prevent all further trouble in the world if we haven't got any arms to prevent it with?" Barley objected, and won a sharp look for his temerity.

"Barley, you are being Western and negative, I think," she retorted as she drew the envelope from her handbag. "It was you, not I, who told Yakov that we required an experiment in human nature."

No stamp, Barley noticed. No postmark. Just "Katya" in Cyrillic, in what looked like Goethe's handwriting, but who could tell? He felt a sudden sense of warning in his head and shoulders, like a poison, or an allergy coming on.

"What's he been recovering from?" he asked.

"Was he nervous when you met him in Leningrad?"

"We both were. It was the weather," Barley replied, still waiting for an answer. He was feeling slightly sick as well. Must be something he had eaten.

"It was because he was ill. Quite soon after your meeting he had a bad collapse and it was so sudden and severe that even his colleagues did not know where he had disappeared to. They had the worst suspicions. A trusted friend told me they feared he might be dead."

"I didn't know he had any trusted friends except you."

"He has appointed me his representative to you. He naturally has other friends for other things." She drew out the letter but did not give it to him.

"That's not quite what you told me before," he said feebly, while he continued to battle with his multiplying symptoms of mistrust.

She was unmoved by his objection. "Why should one tell everything at a first encounter? One has to protect oneself. It is normal."

"I suppose it is," he agreed.

Anna had finished her self-portrait and needed immediate recognition. It showed her picking flowers on a rooftop.

"Superb!" Barley cried. "Tell her I'll hang it above my fireplace, I know just the spot. There's a picture of Anthea skiing on one side, and Hal sailing on the other. Anna goes in the middle."

"She asks how old is Hal?" Katya said.

He really had to think. He had first to remember Hal's birth year, then the year it was now, then laboriously subtract the one from the other while he fought off the singing in his ears. "Ah well now, Hal's twenty-four. But I'm afraid he's made a rather foolish marriage."

Anna was disappointed. She stared reproachfully at them as Katya resumed their conversation.

"As soon as I heard he had disappeared I tried to contact him by all the usual means but I was not successful. I was extremely distressed." She passed him the letter at last, her eyes alight with pleasure and relief. As he took it from her, his hand distractedly closed over hers and she let it. "Then eight days ago, a week ago yesterday which was Saturday, just two days after you telephoned from London, Igor telephoned me at my house. 'I have some medicine for you. Let us have a coffee and I will give it to you.' Medicine is our code for a letter. He meant a letter from Yakov. I was amazed and very happy. It is even years since Yakov has sent me a letter. And such a letter!"

"Who's Igor?" Barley said, speaking rather loudly in order to defeat the uproar inside his head.

There were five pages of it, written on good white unobtainable writing paper, in an orderly, regular script. Barley had not imagined Goethe capable of such a conventional-looking document. She took back her hand, but gently.

"Igor is a friend of Yakov from Leningrad. They studied together."

"Great. What does he do now?"

She was annoyed by his question and impatient to have his good reaction to the letter, even if he could only judge it by appearance. "He is a scientist of some kind with one of the ministries. What does it matter how Igor is employed? Do you wish me to translate it to you or not?"

"What's his other name?"

She told him, and in the midst of his confusion he was exalted by her abrasiveness. We should have had years, he thought, not hours. We should have pulled each other's hair when we were kids. We should have done everything we never did, before it was too late. He held the letter for her and she knelt herself carelessly behind him on the grass, steadying herself with one hand on his shoulder, while with the other she pointed past him at the lines as she translated. He could feel her breasts brushing against his back. He could feel his world steady itself inside him, as the monstrosity of his first suspicions made way for a more analytical frame of mind.

"Here is the address, just a box number, that is normal," she said, her fingertip on the top right corner. "He is in a special hospital, perhaps in a special town. He wrote the letter in bed—you see how well he writes when he is sober?—he gave it to a friend who was on his way to Moscow. The friend gave it to Igor. It is normal. 'My darling Katya,'—that is not exactly how he begins, it is a different endearment, never mind. 'I have been struck down with some variety of hepatitis but illness is very instructive and I am alive.' That is so typical of him, to draw at once the moral lesson." She was pointing again. "This word makes the hepatitis worse. It is 'irritated.' "

"Aggravated," Barley said, quite calmly.

The hand on his shoulder gave him a reproving squeeze. "What does it matter what is the right word? You want me to fetch a dictionary? 'I have had a high temperature and much fantasy—' "

"Hallucination," Barley said.

"The word is *gallutsinatsiya*—" she began furiously.

"Okay, let's stick with that."

" '—but now I am recovered and in two days I shall go to a convalescent unit for a week by the sea.' He does not say which sea, why should he? 'I shall be able to do everything except drink vodka, but that is a bureaucratic limitation which as a good scientist I shall quickly ignore.' Is that not typical also? That after hepatitis he thinks immediately of vodka?"

"Absolutely," Barley agreed, smiling in order to please her—and perhaps to reassure himself.

The lines were dead straight as if written on a ruled page. There was not a single crossing out.

" 'If only all Russians could have hospitals like this, what a healthy nation we would soon become.' He is always the idealist, even when he is ill. 'The nurses are so beautiful and the doctors are young and handsome, it is more a house of love here than a house of sickness.' He says this to make me jealous. But do you know something? It is most unusual that he comments on anybody happy. Yakov is a tragedian. He is even a sceptic. I think they have cured his bad moods as well. 'Yesterday I took exercise for the first time but I soon felt exhausted like a child. Afterwards I lay on the verandah and got quite a suntan before sleeping like an angel with nothing on my conscience except how badly I have treated you, always exploiting you.' Now he writes love talk, I shall not translate it."

"Does he always do that?"

She laughed. "I told you. It is not even normal that he writes to me, and it is many months, I would say years, since he spoke of our love, which is now entirely spiritual. I think the illness has made him a little sentimental, so we shall forgive him." She turned the page in his hand, and again their hands met, but Barley's was as cold as winter, and he was secretly surprised that she did not comment on it. "Now we come to Mr. Barley. You. He is extremely cautious. He does not mention you by name. At least the illness has not affected his discretion. 'Please tell our good friend that I shall try my best to see him during his visit, provided that my recovery continues. He should bring his materials and I shall try to do the same. I have to deliver a lecture in Saratov that week'—Igor says that is the military academy where Yakov always gives a lecture in September, so many things one learns when somebody is ill—'and I shall come to Moscow as soon as possible from there. If you speak to him before I do, please tell him the following. Tell him to bring all further questions because after this I do not wish to answer any more questions for the grey men. Tell him his list should be final and exhaustive.' "

Barley listened in silence to Goethe's further instructions, which were as emphatic as they had been in Leningrad. And as he listened, the black clouds of his disbelief swept together to make a secret dread inside him, and his nausea returned.

A sample page of translation, but in print, please, print is so much more revealing, she was saying on Goethe's behalf.

I wish for an introduction by Professor Killian of Stockholm, please approach him as soon as possible, she was saying.

Have you had further reactions from your intelligentsia? Kindly advise me.

Publishing dates. Goethe had heard that autumn was the best market, but must one really wait a whole year? she asked, for her lover.

The title again. How about *The Biggest Lie in the World?*

The blurb, please let me see a draft. And please send an early copy to Dr. Dagmar Somebody at Stanford and Professor Herman Somebody-else at MIT. . . .

Barley painstakingly wrote all this down in his notebook on a page he headed BOOK FAIR.

"What's in the rest of the letter?" he asked.

She was returning it to its envelope. "I told you. It is love talk. He is at peace with himself and he wishes to resume a full relationship."

"With you."

A pause while her eyes considered him. "Barley, I think you are being a little childish."

"Lovers then?" Barley insisted. "Live happily ever after. Is that it?"

"In the past he was scared of the responsibility. Now he is not. That is what he writes and naturally it is out of the question. What has been has been. It cannot be restored."

"Then why does he write it?" said Barley stubbornly.

"I don't know."

"Do you believe him?"

She was about to be seriously angry with him when she caught something in his expression that was not envy and not hostility but an intense, almost frightening concern for her safety.

"Why should he spin you the talk just because he's ill? He doesn't usually fool around with people's emotions, does he? He prides himself on speaking the truth."

And still his penetrating gaze would not relinquish her or the letter.

"He is lonely," she replied protectively. "He is missing me so he exaggerates. It is normal. Barley, I think you are being a little bit—"

Either she could not find the word, or on second thought she decided against using it, so Barley supplied it for her. "Jealous," he said.

And he managed what he knew she was waiting for. He smiled. He composed a good, sincere smile of disinterested friendship and squeezed her hand and clambered to his feet. "He sounds fantastic," he said. "I'm very happy for him. For his recovery."

And he meant it. Every word. He could hear the true note of conviction in his voice as his eye moved quickly to the parked red car on the other side of the birch grove.

Then to the common delight Barley hurls himself upon the business of becoming a weekend father, a rôle for which his torn life has amply prepared him. Sergey wants him to try his hand at fishing. Anna wants to know why he hasn't brought his swim suit. Matvey has gone to sleep, smiling from the whisky and his memories. Katya stands in the water in her shorts. She looks more beautiful to him than ever before, and more remote. Even collecting rocks to build a dam, she is the most beautiful woman he has ever seen.

Yet nobody ever worked harder on a dam than Barley that afternoon, nobody had a clearer vision of how the waters should be held at bay. He rolls up his stupid grey flannel trousers and soaks himself to the crotch. He heaves sticks and stones till he is half dead, while Anna sits astride his shoulders directing operations. He pleases Sergey with his businesslike approach, and Katya with his romantic flourish. A white car has replaced the red one. A couple sit in it with the doors open, eating whatever they are eating, and at Barley's suggestion the children stand on the hilltop and wave to them, but the couple in the white car don't wave back.

Evening falls and a tang of autumn fires drifts through the dying birch leaves. Moscow is made of wood again, and burning. As they load the car, a pair of wild geese fly over them and they are the last two geese in the world.

On the journey back to the hotel, Anna sleeps on Barley's lap while Matvey chatters and Sergey frowns at the pages of *Squirrel Nutkin* as if they are the Party Manifesto.

"When do you speak to him again?" Barley asks.

"It is arranged," she says enigmatically.

"Did Igor arrange it?"

"Igor arranges nothing. Igor is the messenger."

"The new messenger," he corrects her.

"Igor is an old acquaintance and a new messenger. Why not?"

She glances at him and reads his intention. "You cannot come to the hospital, Barley. It is not safe for you."

"It's not exactly a holiday for you either," he replies.

She knows, he thought. She knows but does not know she knows. She has the symptoms, a part of her has made the diagnosis. But the rest of her refuses to admit there's anything amiss.

The Anglo-American situation room was no longer a shabby basement in Victoria but the radiant pent-house of a smart new baby skyscraper off Grosvenor Square. It styled itself the Inter-Allied Conciliation Group and was guarded by shifts of conciliatory American Marines in military plainclothes. An air of thrilled purpose pervaded it as the expanded team of trim young men and women flitted between clean desks, answered winking telephones, spoke to Langley on secure lines, passed papers, typed at silent keyboards or lounged in attitudes of eager relaxation before the rows of television monitors that had replaced the twin clocks of the old Russia House.

It was a deck on two levels, and Ned and Sheriton were seated side by side on the closed bridge, while below them on the other side of the sound-proofed glass their unequal crews went about their duties. Brock and Emma had one wall, Bob, Johnny and their cohorts the other wall and centre aisle. But all were travelling in the same direction. All wore the same obediently purposeful expressions, faced the same banks of screens that rolled and flickered like stock-exchange quotations as the automatic decodes came in.

"Truck's safely back in dock," said Sheriton as the screens abruptly cleared and flashed the codeword BLACKJACK.

The truck itself was a miracle of penetration.

Our own truck! In Moscow! Us! In English it would have been a lorry but here it was a truck in deference to the American proprietorship. An enormous separate operation lay behind its acquisition and deployment. It was a Kamaz, dirty grey and very big, one of a fleet of trucks belonging to SOVTRANSAVTO, hence the acronym daubed in Roman letters across its filthy flank. It had been recruited, together with its driver, by the Agency's enormous Munich station during one of the truck's many forays to West Germany to collect luxury commodities for Moscow's privileged few with access to a special distribution store. Everything from Western shoes to Western tampons to spare parts for Western cars had been shuttled back and forth inside the truck's bowels. As to the driver, he was one of the Long Distance Gunners, as these luckless creatures are known in the Soviet Union—State employees, miserably underpaid, with neither medical nor accident insurance to protect them against misfortune in the West, who even in deepest winter huddle stoically in the lee of their great charges, munching sausage before sharing another night's sleep in their comfortless cabins—but making for themselves in Russia, nevertheless, vast fortunes out of their opportunities in the West.

And now, for yet more immense rewards, this particular Long Distance Gunner had agreed to "lend" his truck to a "Western dealer" here in the very heart of Moscow. And this same dealer, who was one of Cy's own army of *toptuny,* lent it to Cy, who in turn stuffed inside it all kinds of ingeniously portable surveillance and audio equipment, which was then swept away again before the truck was returned through intermediaries to its legal driver.

Nothing of the sort had ever happened before. Our own mobile safe room, in Moscow!

Ned alone found the whole idea unsettling. The Long Distance Gunners worked in pairs, as Ned knew better than anyone. By KGB edict, these pairs were deliberately incompatible, and in many cases each man had a responsibility to report upon the other. But when Ned asked if he could read the operational file, it was denied him under the very laws of security he himself held dear.

But the most impressive piece of Langley's new armoury had still to be unveiled, and once again Ned had not been able to hold out against it. From now onwards, sound tapes in Moscow would be encrypted into random codes and transmitted in digital pulses in one-thousandth of the time that the tapes would take to run if you were listening to them in your drawing room. Yet when the pulses were restored to sound by the receiving station, the Langley wizards insisted, you could never tell the tapes had had such a rough time.

The word WAIT was forming in pretty pyramids. Spying is waiting.

The word SOUND replaced it. Spying is listening.

Ned and Sheriton put on their headsets as Clive and I slipped into the spare seats behind them and put on ours.

Katya sat pensively on her bed staring at the telephone, not wanting it to ring again.

Why do you give your name when none of us give names? she asked him in her mind.

Why do you give mine?

Is that Katya? How are you? This is Igor speaking. Just to tell you I have heard nothing more from him, okay?

Then why do you ring me to tell me nothing?

The usual time, okay? The usual place. No problem. Just like before.

Why do you repeat what needs no repetition, after I have already told you I will be at the hospital at the agreed time?

By then he'll know what his position is, he'll know which plane he can catch, everything. Then you don't have to worry, okay? How about your publisher? Did he show up all right?

"Igor, I do not know which publisher you are referring to."

And she rang off before he could say more.

I am being ungrateful, she told herself. When people are ill it is normal that old friends should rally. And if they promote themselves overnight from casual acquaintance to old friend, and take centre stage when for years they have hardly spoken to you, it is still a sign of loyalty and there is nothing sinister about it, even if only six months ago Yakov declared Igor to be unredeemable—"Igor has continued along the path I left behind," he had remarked after meeting him by chance in the street. "Igor asks too many questions."

Yet here was Igor acting as Yakov's closest friend and putting himself out for him in risky and invaluable ways. *"If you have a letter for Yakov, you have only to give it to me. I have established an excellent line of communication to the sanatorium. I know somebody who makes the journey almost every week,"* he had told her at their last meeting.

"The sanatorium?" she had cried excitedly. "Then where is he? Where is it located?"

But it was as if Igor had not yet thought of the answer to this question, for he had scowled and looked uncomfortable and pleaded State secrecy. Us, State secrecy, when we are flaunting the State's secrets!

I am being unfair to him, she thought. I am starting to see deception everywhere. In Igor, even in Barley.

Barley. She frowned. He had no business to criticise Yakov's declaration of affection. Who does he think he is, this Westerner with his attaching manners and cynical suspicions? Coming so close so quickly, playing God to Matvey and my children?

I shall never trust a man who was brought up without dogma, she told herself severely.

I can love a believer, I can love a heretic, but I cannot love an Englishman.

She switched on her little radio and ran through the shortwave bands, having first put in the earpiece so as not to disturb the twins. But as she listened to the different voices clamouring for her soul—Deutsche Welle, Voice of America, Radio Liberty, Voice of Israel, Voice of God knew whom, each one so cosy, so superior, so compelling—an angry confusion came over her. I'm a Russian! she wanted to shout back at them. Even in tragedy, I dream of a better world than yours!

But *what* tragedy?

The phone was ringing. She grabbed the receiver. But it was only Nasayan, an altered man these days, checking on tomorrow's plans.

"Listen, I am confirming privately that you really wish to be at the October stand tomorrow. Only we must begin early, you see. If you have to get your kids to school or something of that sort, I can easily instruct Yelizavyeta Alexeyevna to come instead of you. It is no hardship. You have only to tell me."

"You are very kind, Grigory Tigranovich, and I appreciate your call. But having spent most of last week helping to put up the exhibits, I should naturally like to be present at the official opening. Matvey can manage very well to see the children off to school."

Thoughtfully, she put the receiver back on its cradle. Nasayan, my God—why do we address each other like characters on the stage? Who do we think is listening to us who requires such rounded sentences? If I can talk to an English stranger as if he is my lover, why can't I talk normally to an Armenian who is my colleague?

He rang, and she knew at once that she had been waiting all this while for his call, because she was already smiling. Unlike Igor, he did not say his name or hers.

"Elope with me," he said.

"Tonight?"

"Horses are saddled, food for three days."

"But are you also sober enough to elope?"

"Amazingly, I am." A pause. "It's not for want of trying but nothing happened. Must be old age."

He sounded sober too. Sober and close.

"But what about the book fair? Are you going to desert it as you deserted the audio fair?"

"To hell with the book fair. We've got to do it before or never. Afterwards we'll be too tired. How are you?"

"Oh, I am furious with you. You have completely bewitched my family, and now they ask only when you will come back with more tobacco and crayons."

Another pause. He was not usually so thoughtful when he was joking.

"That's what I do. I bewitch people, then the moment they're under my spell I cease to feel anything for them."

"But that's terrible!" she cried, deeply shocked. "Barley, what are you telling me?"

"Just repeating the wisdom of an early wife, that's all. She said I had impulses but no feelings and I shouldn't wear a duffle coat in London. Anyone tells you something like that, you believe it for the rest of your life. I've never worn a duffle coat since."

"Barley, that woman—Barley, that was a totally cruel and irresponsible thing for her to say. I am sorry but she is completely wrong. She was provoked, I am sure. But she is wrong."

"She is, is she? So what do I feel? Enlighten me."

She broke out laughing, realising she had walked straight into his trap.

"Barley, you are a very, very bad man. I shall have nothing to do with you."

"Because I don't feel anything?"

"For one thing, you feel protection for people. We all noticed that today, and we were grateful."

"More."

"For another, you feel a sense of honour, I would say. You are decadent, naturally, because you are a Westerner. That is normal. But you are redeemed because you feel honour."

"Are there any pies left over?"

"You mean you feel hunger too?"

"I want to come and eat them."

"Now?"

"Now."

"That is completely impossible! We are all in bed already and it's nearly midnight."

"Tomorrow."

"Barley, this is too ridiculous. We are about to begin the book fair, both of us have a dozen invitations."

"What time?"

A beautiful silence was settling between them.

"You may come at perhaps-half-past-seven."

"I may be early."

For a long while after that neither of them spoke. But the silence joined them more closely than words could have done. They became two heads on a single pillow, ear to ear. And when he rang off it was not his jokes and self-ironies that stayed with her but the tone of contented sincerity—she would almost say solemnity—that he had seemed unable to keep out of his voice.

He was singing.

Inside his head, and outside it too. In his heart and all over his body at last, Barley Blair was singing.

He was in his big grey bedroom at the gloomy Mezh on the eve of the Moscow book fair, and he was singing "Bless This House" in the recognisable manner of Mahalia Jackson while he pirouetted round the room with a glass of mineral water in his hand, glimpsing his reflection in the immense television screen that was the room's one glory.

Sober.

Hot sober.

Barley Blair.

Alone.

He had drunk nothing. In the safe truck for his debriefing, though he had sweated like a racehorse, nothing. Not even a glass of water while he had regaled Paddy and Cy with a sweetened, unworried version of his day.

At the French publishers' party at the Rossiya with Wicklow, where he had positively shone with confidence, nothing.

At the Swedes' party at the National with Henziger, where he had shone yet more brightly, he had grabbed a glass of Georgian *shampanskoye* in self-protection because Zapadny was so pointedly amazed he was not drinking. But he had contrived to leave it undrunk behind a flower vase. So still nothing.

And at the Doubleday party at the Ukraina with Henziger again, shining like the North Star by now, he had clutched a mineral water with a bit of lemon floating in it to look like gin and tonic.

So nothing. Not out of highmindedness. Not a reformed spirit, God forbid. He had not signed the Pledge or turned over a new leaf. It was merely that he wished nothing to mar the clear-headed, reasoned ecstasy that was collecting in him, this unfamiliar sense of being at dreadful risk and equal to it, of knowing that whatever was happening he had prepared himself for it, and that if nothing was happening he was ready for that too, because his preparedness was an all-round defence with a sacred absolute at its centre.

I have joined the tiny ranks of people who know what they will do first if the ship catches fire in the middle of the night, he thought; and what they will do last, or not do at all. He knew in ordered detail what he considered worth saving and what was unimportant to him. And what was to be shoved aside, stepped over and left for dead.

A great house-cleaning had taken place inside his mind, comprising quite humble details as well as grand themes. Because, as Barley had recently observed, it was in humble detail that grand themes wrought their havoc.

The clarity of his view amazed him. He peered round him, took a turn or two, sang a few bars. He came back to where he was, and knew that nothing had been left out.

Not the momentary inflection of uncertainty in her voice. Or the shadow of doubt flitting across the dark pools of her eyes.

Or Goethe's straight lines of handwriting instead of wild scrawls.

Or Goethe's cumbersome, untypical jokes about bureaucrats and vodka.

Or Goethe's guilty dirge about the way he had treated her, when for twenty years he had treated her however he had damn well felt like, including using her as a throwaway delivery-girl.

Or Goethe's callow promise to make it all up to her in the future, so long as she'll stay in the game for the time being, when it is an article of Goethe's faith that the future no longer interests him, that his whole obsession is with now. "There is only *now!*"

Yet from these spindrift theories that were most likely nothing more than theories, Barley's mind flew effortlessly to the grandest prize of his clarified perception: that in the context of Goethe's notion of what he was achieving, Goethe was *right,* and that for most of his life Goethe had stood on one side of a corrupt and anachronistic equation while Barley in his ignorance had stood on the other.

And that if Barley were ever called upon to choose, he would rather go Goethe's path than Ned's or anybody else's, because his presence would be urgently required in the extreme middle ground of which he had elected himself a citizen. ·

And that everything that had happened to Barley since Peredelkino had delivered the proof of this. The old isms were dead, the contest between Communism and capitalism had ended in a wet whimper. Its rhetoric had fled underground into the secret chambers of the grey men, who were still dancing away long after the music had ended.

As to his loyalty to his country, Barley saw it only as a question of which England he chose to serve. His last ties to the imperial fantasy were dead. The chauvinist drumbeat revolted him. He would rather be trampled by it than march with it. He knew a better England by far, and it was inside himself.

He lay on his bed, waiting for the fear to seize him, but it wouldn't. Instead, he found himself playing a kind of mental chess, because chess was about possibilities, and it seemed best to contemplate them in tranquillity rather than try and sort through them when the roof was falling in.

Because if Armageddon didn't strike, there was nothing lost. But if Armageddon did, there was much to save.

So Barley began to think. And Barley began to make his preparations with a cool head, exactly as Ned would have advised if Ned were still holding the reins. ·

He thought till early morning and dozed a bit and when he woke he went on thinking, and by the time he strode cheerfully into breakfast already looking round for the fun of the fair, there was an entire section of his head that was given over full time to thinking what the fools who do it describe as the unthinkable.

14

Oh come, Ned," said Clive airily, still elated by the wizardry of the transmission. "The Bluebird's been ill before. Several times."

"I know," said Ned distractedly. "I know." And then, "Maybe I don't mind him being ill. Maybe I mind him writing."

Sheriton was listening chin in hand, as he had been listening to the tape. An affinity had grown up between Ned and Sheriton, as in an operation it must. They were handling the transfer of power as if it had happened long ago.

"But my dear man, that's what we all do when we're ill," Clive exclaimed in a misjudged demonstration of human understanding. "We *write* to the whole world!"

It had never occurred to me that Clive was capable of illness, or that he had friends to write to.

"I mind him handing chatty letters to mysterious intermediaries. And I mind him talking about trying to bring more materials for Barley," Ned said. "We know he never normally writes to her. We know he's security conscious to a fault. Suddenly he falls ill and writes her a gushing five-page love letter via Igor. Igor who? Igor when? How?"

"He should have photographed the letter," said Clive, becoming disapproving of Barley. "Or taken it off her. One or the other."

Ned was too wrapped up in his thoughts to give this suggestion the contempt it deserved.

"How could he? She knows him as a publisher. That's all she knows him as."

"Unless the Bluebird told her otherwise," said Clive.

"He wouldn't," Ned retorted, and returned to his thoughts. "There was a car," he said. "A red car, then a white car. You saw the watch report. The red car went in first, then the white car took over."

"That is pure speculation. On a warm Sunday the whole of Moscow takes to the countryside," said Clive knowledgeably.

He waited for a reaction but in vain, so he returned to the subject of the letter. "*Katya* didn't have any problems with it," he objected. "*Katya*'s not crying foul. She's jumping for joy. If she didn't smell a rat, and Scott Blair didn't, why should *we*—sitting here in London, doing their worrying for them?"

"He asked for the shopping list," said Ned, as if still hearing distant music. "A final and exhaustive list of questions. Why did he do that?"

Sheriton had finally stirred himself. He was flagging Ned down with his big paw. "Ned, Ned, Ned, Ned. Okay? It's Day One again, so we're jumpy. Let's get some sleep."

He stood up. So did Clive and so did I. But Ned stayed doggedly rooted where he was, his hands clasped before him on his desk.

Sheriton spoke down at him. With affection, but with force as well. "Ned, just hear me, Ned, okay? Ned?"

"I'm not deaf."

"No, but you're tired. Ned, if we bad-mouth this operation one more time, it will never come back. We are going with *your* man, the one *you* brought to *us* in order to persuade *us*. We moved hell on earth to get this far. We have the source. We have the appropriation. We have the influential audience. We are within pissing distance of filling gaps in our knowledge that no smart machines, no electronic heavy breathers, no Pentagon Jesuits can get within light-years of. If we keep our nerve, and Barley does, and Bluebird does, we will have landed a bonanza beyond the dreams of the most accomplished fantasists. If we stay in there."

But Sheriton was speaking with too much conviction, and his face, for all its pudgy inscrutability, was betraying an almost desperate need.

"Ned?"

"Hearing you, Russell. Loud and clear."

"Ned, this is no longer a cottage industry, for Christ's sake. We played big, now we have to think big. You don't get bigger than this. Presidential findings are not an invitation to doubt our own good judgment. They are in the way of being orders. Ned, I really think you should get some sleep."

"I don't think I'm tired," said Ned.

"I think you are. I think everyone will say you are. I think they may even say Ned was very bullish for the Bluebird until the big bad American wolf came and took his joe away. Then all of a sudden the Bluebird was a very iffy source. I think people are going to say you are tired as hell."

I glanced at Clive.

Clive too was looking down at Ned, but with eyes so cold they chilled my blood. Time to move you on, they were saying. Time to measure you for the drop.

Both Henziger and Wicklow kept a close eye on Barley that day and reported on him frequently, Henziger to Cy by whatever means they used, Wicklow by way of an irregular to Paddy. Both attested to his high spirits and relaxed manner, and in differing language to his sovereignty. Both described how at breakfast he had enchanted a couple of Finnish publishers who were showing interest in the Trans-Siberian Railway project.

"They were eating out of his hand," said Wicklow, providing an unconsciously comic picture of breakfast, but at the Mezh anything is possible.

Both recorded with amusement Barley's determination to act as their tour-guide when they reached the permanent exhibition site, and how he obliged their taxi to drop them at the end of the grand avenue so that, as first-time pilgrims from the world of capitalism, they could make their approach on foot.

So the two professional spies strolled contentedly through the wet autumn sunshine with their jackets over their shoulders and their joe between them while Barley favoured them with his own eccentric guided tour, extolling the "late Essoldo period" architecture and the "Revolutionary Rococo" gardens. He doted on the immense ornamental pool and its golden fish spewing jets of water at the rumps of fifteen naked golden nymphs, one for each of the Socialist republics. He insisted that they dawdle at the white-pillared love bowers and temples of delight—whose portals, he pointed out, were dedicated not to Venus or Bacchus but to the fallen goddesses of the Soviet economy—coal, steel and even atomic energy, Jack!

"He was witty but he wasn't high," reported Henziger, who had already taken fondly to Barley in Leningrad. "He was damn funny."

And from the temples Barley marched them up the triumphal avenue itself, the Emperor's Ride, perhaps a mile of it and heaven knows how broad, celebrating the People's Achievements in the Service of Mankind. And surely no vision of popular power was ever portrayed in such despotic images! he proclaimed. Surely no Revolution had so perfectly enshrined everything it had set out to raze to the ground! But by then Barley had to bellow his irreverences over the din of the loudspeakers, which all day long pour floods of self-congratulatory messages on to the heads of the benighted crowds below.

Finally they arrived, as they had to, at the two pavilions housing the fair.

"On my right, the publishers of Peace, Progress and Goodwill," Barley announced, playing the referee at a prize fight. "On my left, the distributors of Fascist imperialist lies, the pornographers, the poisoners of truth. Seconds out. Time."

They showed their passes and walked in.

* * *

The exhibition stand of the newly inaugurated and geographically confusing house of Potomac & Blair was a small but satisfactory sensation of the fair. Langley's lovingly created P. & B. symbol shone resplendent between the dowdier displays of Astral Press and Purbeck Media. The stand's interior design, characterised by its Langley architects as tough but tasty, was a model of instant impact. The exhibits —many of them, as is customary, dummies of books still to enter the production line—were prepared with all the attention to detail that intelligence services traditionally bestow on fakes. The only good coffee at the fair was to be found bubbling on an ingenious machine in the rear cubby-hole. There was Langley's own Mary Lou to serve it. For the favoured, there was even a forbidden shot of Scotch to help them through the day—forbidden, indeed, by special edict of the organisers, for even literary reconstruction must be the work of sober men.

And Mary Lou, with her homespun schoolgirl smile and billowing tweed skirt, made a natural product of the nicer side of Madison Avenue. Nobody need ever have guessed she had a little of Langley's thread woven into her as well.

Neither was Wicklow, with his polished patter, anything other than the quick-eyed, upwardly mobile young publisher they make these days.

As to honest Jack Henziger, he was the archetype of the settled buccaneer of the modern American book trade. He made no secret of his antecedents. Pipelines in the Middle East, humanity in Afghanistan, red beans to opium-growing hill-tribes in Thailand—Henziger had sold them all, whatever he had sold for Langley on the side. But publishing was where his heart was, and he was here to prove it.

And Barley seemed to revel in the artifice. He threw himself upon it as if it were his long-lost reality, shaking hands, receiving the congratulations of his competitors and colleagues, until around eleven he professed himself restless and proposed to Wicklow that they tour the lines and take comfort to the troops.

So off they set, Barley bearing in his arms a bunch of white envelopes of which he occasionally pressed one into a chosen hand as he yelled and greeted his way along the packed alleys of visitors and exhibitors.

"Well blow me over, if it isn't Barley Bloody Blair," a familiar voice declared from the centre of a multi-lingual display of illustrated Bibles. "Remember me, do you? Third from the left in the mink jock-strap, back in your humble days?"

"Spikey. They let you in again," said Barley with pleasure, and handed him his envelope.

"It's when they won't let me *out* I'm worried. This your dad, then?"

Barley presented the distinguished editor Wicklow, and Spikey Morgan bestowed a priestly blessing on him with his nicotine-stained fingers.

They pressed on, only to stumble into Dan Zeppelin a few yards later. Dan did not talk. Dan conspired in a gravedigger's murmur, leaning across his counter at you over folded arms.

"So I mean tell me something, Barley. Okay? Are we pioneers or are we the fucking Mitford sisters? So a few unbooks are books this year. So a few unwriters have been sprung from jail. Big deal. I walk into my own stand this morning, there's some asshole pulling the books out of my shelves. 'May I ask you a personal question?' I says. 'What the fuck are you doing with my books?' 'Orders,' he says. Six books, he confiscated. Mary G. Ambleside on fucking *Black Consciousness in Song and Word*. Orders! I mean who are we, Barley? Who are they? What do they think they're restructuring when there was never a structure in the first place? How do you restructure a corpse?"

At Lupus Books they were directed to the coffee room, where our Chairman Himself, the newly knighted Sir Peter Oliphant, had upstaged even the Russians by reserving a table. A handwritten notice in both languages confirmed his triumph. The flags of Britain and the Soviet Union warned off doubters. Flanked by interpreters and high officials, Sir Peter was dilating on the many advantages to the Soviet Union of subsidising his generous purchases from them.

"It's the Earl!" cried Barley, handing him an envelope. "Where's the coronet?"

With scarcely a flicker of his dusty eyelids, the great man continued his dissertation.

At the Israeli stand an armed peace reigned. The dark queue was orderly but mute. Boys in jeans and sneakers lounged against the walls. Lev Abramovitz was white-haired and overpoweringly tall. He had served in the Irish Guards.

"Lev. How's Zion?"

"Maybe we're winning, maybe the happy ending's at the beginning," Lev said, pocketing Barley's envelope.

And from Israel, with Barley leading at a canter, they pounded across the concourse to the Pavilion of Peace, Progress and Goodwill, where there could no longer be any doubt of the massive historical upheaval taking place, or of who was doing the heaving.

Every banner and spare bit of wall screamed the new Gospel. In every stand of every Republic, the thoughts and writings of the no-longer-new prophet, with his birthmark turned away and his jaw raised, were blazoned alongside those of his colourless master, Lenin. At the VAAP stand, where Barley and Wicklow shook a few hands and Barley shed a batch of envelopes, the Leader's speeches, wrapped in shiny covers and rendered into English, French, Spanish and German, made a totally resistible appeal.

"How much more of this shit do we have to take, Barley?" a blond-faced Moscow publisher demanded *sotto voce* as they went by. "When will they start repressing us again to make us comfortable? If our past's a lie, who's to say our future isn't a lie as well?"

They continued along the stands, Barley leading, Barley greeting, Wicklow following.

"Joseph! Great to see you! Envelope for you. Don't eat it all at once."

"Barley! My friend! Didn't they give you my message? Maybe I didn't leave one."

"Yuri. Great to see you! Envelope for you."

"Come and drink tonight, Barley! Sasha is coming, so is Rosa. Rudi's giving a concert tomorrow so he wants to stay sober. You heard about the writers they let out? Listen, it's Potemkin village stuff. They let them out, they give them a few meals, show them off and throw them back inside till next year. Come over here, I got to sell you a couple of books to annoy Zapadny."

At first Wicklow didn't even realise they had arrived at their destination. He saw a Roman standard hung with faded flags and some gold lettering stitched on red bunting. He heard Barley's yell of "Katya, where are you?" But nothing said who owned the stand and probably that was a part of the display that hadn't arrived.

He saw the usual unreadable books on agricultural development in the Ukraine and the traditional dances of Georgia expiring on their shelves under the strain of previous exhibitions. He saw the usual half-dozen broad-hipped women standing around as if they were waiting for a train, and a small unshaven fellow clutching his cigarette in front of him like a conjuror's wand, scowling at Barley's nametag.

Nasayan, Wicklow read in return. *Grigory Tigranovich. Senior Editor, October Publishing.*

"You are looking for Miss Katya Orlova, I think," Nasayan told Barley in English, holding his cigarette still higher as if to get a clearer look at his visitor.

"I'll say I am!" Barley replied with enthusiasm, and a couple of the women smiled.

A grin of frightful courtesy had spread over Nasayan's face. With a flourish of his cigarette he stepped aside and Wicklow recognised Katya's back as she talked with two very small Asians whom he took to be Burmese. Then an instinct made her turn and she caught sight of Barley first, then Wicklow, then Barley again, while a splendid smile lit her face.

"Katya. Fantastic," said Barley shyly. "How are the kids? Did they survive?"

"Oh thank you, they are *very* well!"

Watched by Nasayan and his ladies, as well as by Wicklow, Barley handed her an invitation to the great *glasnost* launch party of Potomac & Blair.

"Oh by the way, I may skip some of the gay whirl tonight," Barley remarked as they made their way back to the Western pavilion. "You and Jack and Mary Lou will have to manage on your own. I'm dining with a beautiful lady."

"Anyone we know?" Wicklow asked. They both laughed. It was a sunny day.

She's fine, Barley was thinking contentedly. If something is happening, it hasn't happened to her yet.

How much did we know or guess, any of us, of Barley's feelings towards Katya? In a case so scrupulously monitored and controlled, the question of love received diffident handling.

Wicklow, diligently promiscuous in his own life, was puritanical about Barley's. Perhaps as a young man he still could not take seriously the notion of an older passion. For Wicklow, Barley was merely infatuated, which he usually was anyway. People of Barley's age were not in love.

Henziger, who was Barley's rough contemporary, regarded sex as an unsung perquisite of the secret life, and took it for granted that a square-shooter like Barley would put his body where his duty lay. Like Wicklow, but for different reasons, he found nothing exceptional in Barley's tender feelings towards Katya and operationally much to recommend them.

And in London? There was no sharply defined view. On the island Brady had said a mouthful, but Brady's assault had been repelled and his advice with it.

And Ned? Ned had a wife as soldierly as himself, and as unawakened. Name me a joe in a bad country, Ned liked to say with a rueful smile, who doesn't fall for a pretty face if she's on his side against the world.

And Bob, Sheriton and Johnny seem all to have assumed in different ways that Barley's private life and his appetites generally were of such a seedy complexity that they were best left out of the equation.

And Palfrey, what was old Palfrey thinking—hurrying up to Grosvenor Square in any spare hour and, if he couldn't make it, phoning Ned to ask, "How's the boy?"

Palfrey was thinking about Hannah. The Hannah he had loved and loves still, as only cowards may. The Hannah whose smile was once as warm and deep as Katya's. "You're a good man, Palfrey," she will say with terrible control on the days when she is trying to understand me. "You'll find a way. Maybe not now, but one day." And oh, Palfrey found a way all right! He pleaded the code—that convenient code that rules that a young solicitor caught in adultery is *ipso facto* excluded from doing anything about it. He pleaded children, hers and his—so many people involved, dear. He pleaded marriage, curse him—how will they cope without us, dear, Derek can't even boil an egg? He pleaded the partnership and, when it was dissolved, he buried his stupid head in the sands of the secret desert where no Hannah would ever be able to threaten him again. And he had the nerve to plead duty—the Service would never forgive me a mucky divorce, dear—not its legal adviser, it couldn't.

I was thinking about the island too. About the evening Barley and I had stood on the shingle beach watching the fog-bank roll at us across the grey Atlantic.

"They'd never get her out, would they?" Barley said. "Not if things went wrong."

I didn't answer and I don't think he expected me to, but he was right. She was a thoroughbred Soviet national and she had committed a thoroughbred Soviet crime. She was nowhere near the swappable class.

"Anyway, she'd never leave her children," he said, confirming his own doubts.

We watched the sea for a while, his eyes on Katya and mine on Hannah, who would never leave her children either, but wanted to bring them with her, and make an honest man out of a career-obsessed Chancery Lane hack who was sleeping with his senior partner's wife.

"Raymond Chandler!" Uncle Matvey yelled from his chair, over the clamour of neighbours' television sets.

"Terrific," Barley said.

"Agatha Christie!"

"Ah well, now, *Agatha*."

"Dashiell Hammett! Dorothy Sayers. Josephine Tey."

Barley sat on the sofa where Katya had settled him. The living room was tiny. The span of his arms could have bridged the width of it. A glass-fronted corner cupboard contained the family treasures. Katya had already given him the tour of them. The pottery mugs, made by a friend for her wedding, their medallions portraying the bride and groom. The Leningrad coffee set, no longer complete, that had belonged to the lady in the wood frame on the top shelf. The old sepia photograph of a Tolstoyan couple, the man bearded and resolute in his stiff white collar, the girl in her bonnet and fur muff.

"Matvey is passionate for English detective fiction," Katya called from the kitchen, where she had last things to do.

"Me too," said Barley untruthfully.

"He is telling you it was not permitted under the Czars. They would never have tolerated such an intrusion into their police system. Do you have vodka? No more for Matvey, please. You must take some food. We are not alcoholics like you Westerners. We do not drink without food."

Under the pretext of examining her books, Barley stepped into the tiny passage from where he could see her. Jack London, Hemingway and Joyce, Dreiser and John Fowles. Heine, Remarque and Rilke. The twins were in the bathroom chattering. He gazed at her through the open kitchen door. Her gestures had an air of timeless and deliberate delay. She's become a Russian again, he thought. When something works, she's grateful. When it doesn't work, it's life. From the living room Matvey was still talking gaily.

"What's he saying now?" Barley asked.

"He is talking about the siege."

"I love you."

"The Leningraders refused to accept that they were beaten." She was preparing cakes of liver on rice. Her hands kept still a moment, then went on with their work. "Shostakovich still composed even if the ink froze in his inkwell. The novelists went on writing, you could hear a chapter of a new novel any week if you knew the right cellars to go to."

"I love you," he repeated. "All my failures were preparations for meeting you. Fact."

She breathed out sharply and they both fell silent, for a moment deaf to Matvey's jolly monologue from the sitting room, and to the sounds of splashing from the bathroom.

"What else does he say?" Barley asked.

"Barley—" she protested.

"Please. Tell me what he's saying."

"The Germans were four kilometres from the city on the south side. They covered the outskirts with machine-gun fire and shelled the centre with artillery." She handed him mats and knives and forks and followed him to the living room. "Two hundred and fifty grams of bread for a labourer, others a hundred and twenty-five. Are you really so fascinated by Matvey, or are you pretending to be polite as usual?"

"It's a mature, unselfish, absolute, thrilling love. I've never known anything approaching it. I thought you ought to be the first to know."

Matvey was beaming at Barley in unalloyed adoration. His new English pipe gleamed from his top pocket. Katya held Barley's stare, started to laugh, shook her head, not in negation but in daze. The twins rushed in wearing their dressing-gowns and swung on Barley's hands. Katya settled them to the table and put Matvey at the head. Barley sat beside her while she poured the cabbage soup. With a prodigious show of power Sergey drew the cork from a wine bottle, but Katya would take no more than a half-glass and Matvey was permitted only vodka. Anna broke ranks to fetch a drawing she had made after a visit to the Timiryasev Academy: horses, a real wheatfield, plants that could survive the snow. Matvey was telling the story of the old man in the machine shop across the road, and once more Barley insisted on hearing every word.

"There was an old man Matvey knew, a friend of my father's," Katya said. "He had a machine shop. When he was too weak from starving, he strapped himself to the machinery so that he would not collapse. That was how Matvey and my father found him when he died. Strapped to the machinery. Frozen. Matvey also wishes you to know that he personally wore a luminous badge on his coat"—Matvey was proudly indicating the very spot on his pullover—"so that he didn't knock into his friends in the dark when they took their buckets to fetch water from the Neva. So. That is enough of Leningrad," she said firmly. "You have been very generous, Barley, as usual. I hope you are sincere."

"I have never been so sincere in my life."

Barley was in the middle of toasting Matvey's health when the telephone started ringing beside the sofa. Katya sprang up but Sergey was ahead of her. He put the receiver to his ear and listened, then replaced it on the cradle with a shake of his head.

"So many misconnections," Katya said, and handed round plates for the liver cakes.

There was only her room. There was only her bed.

The children had gone to their bed and Barley could hear them snuffling in their sleep. Matvey lay on his army bedroll in the living room, already dreaming of Leningrad. Katya sat upright and Barley sat beside her, holding her hand while he watched her face against the uncurtained window.

"I love Matvey too," he said.

She nodded and gave a short laugh. He put his knuckles against her cheek and discovered that she was weeping.

"Just not in the same way I love you," he explained. "I love children, uncles, dogs, cats and musicians. The entire Ark is my personal responsibility. But I love you so profoundly that I am ashamed to be articulate. I would be very grateful if we could find a way to silence me. I look at you, and I am absolutely sick of the sound of my own voice. Do you want that in writing?"

Then with both hands he turned her face to him and kissed her. Then he guided her towards the top of the bed and laid her head on the pillow and kissed her again, first her lips and then her closed wet eyelashes while her arms gathered round his back and drew him down on her. Then she pushed him away from her and sprang up and went to look at the twins before returning. Then she slid the bolt inside her bedroom door.

"If the children come, you must dress and we must be very serious," she warned, kissing him.

"Can I tell them I love you?"

"If you do I shall not interpret."

"Can I tell you?"

"If you are very quiet."

"Will you interpret?"

She was no longer weeping. She was no longer smiling. Black, logical eyes, searching like his own. An embrace without reservation, no hidden codicils, no small print to the agreement.

I had never known Ned in such a mood. He had become the Jonah of his own operation and his rugged stoicism only made his forebodings harder to take. In the situation room he sat at his desk as if he were presiding at a court martial, while

Sheriton lolled beside him like an intelligent Teddy bear. And when as a reckless throw I walked him down the road to the Connaught where I occasionally took Hannah and, to ease the waiting, fed him a magical dinner in the Grill, I still could not penetrate the mask of his forbearance.

For the truth was, his pessimism was seriously affecting my own spirits. I was on a see-saw. Clive and Sheriton were up one end, Ned was the dead weight at the other. And since I am no great decision-taker, it was all the more disturbing to watch a man normally so incisive resign himself to ostracism.

"You're seeing ghosts, Ned," I told him with little of Sheriton's conviction. "You've gone far beyond whatever anybody else is thinking. All right, it's not your case any more. That doesn't mean it's a shipwreck. And your credibility is—well, ebbing."

"A final and exhaustive list," Ned said again, as if the phrase had been dinned into him by a hypnotist. "Why final? Why exhaustive? Answer me that. When Barley saw him in Leningrad, he wouldn't even accept our preliminary questionnaire. He threw it back in Barley's face. Now he's asking for the whole shopping list in one go. *Asking* for it. The *final* list. The grand slam. We're to get it all together for the weekend. After that the Bluebird will answer no more questions from the grey men. 'This is your last chance,' he's saying. *Why?*"

"Look at it the other way round a minute," I urged him in a desperate murmur when the wine waiter had brought us a second decanter of priceless claret. "All right. The Bluebird has been turned by the Sovs. He's bad. The Sovs are running him. So why do they close it down? Why not sit back and play us along? *You* wouldn't close it down if you were in their shoes. You wouldn't hand us an ultimatum, create deadlines. Would you?"

His reply put paid to the best and most expensive meal I had ever given a fellow officer in my life.

"I might have to," he said. "If I were Russian."

"Why?"

His words were the more chilling for being spoken with a leaden dispassion. "Because he might not be presentable any more. He might not be able to speak. Or pick up his knife and fork. Or pour salt on his grouse. He might have made a couple of voluntary statements about his charming mistress in Moscow who had no idea, but really no idea, what she was doing. He might have—"

We walked back to Grosvenor Square. Barley had left Katya's apartment at midnight Moscow time and returned to the Mezh, where Henziger had sat up for him in the lobby, ostensibly reading a manuscript.

Barley was in high spirits but had nothing new to report. Just a family evening, he had told Henziger, but good fun all the same. And the hospital visit still on, he added.

The whole of the next day nothing. A space. Spying is waiting. Spying is worrying yourself sick while you watch Ned sink into a decline. Spying is taking Hannah to your flat in Pimlico between the hours of four and six when she is supposed to be having a German lesson, God knows why. Spying is imitating love, and making sure she's home in time to give dear Derek his dinner.

15

They went in Volodya's car. She had borrowed it for the evening. He was to wait for her outside the Aeroport metro station at nine, and at nine exactly the Lada pulled up precariously beside him.

"You should not have insisted," she said.

The tower blocks glowed above them but in the streets there was already the menacing atmosphere of curfew. Scents of autumn filled the damp night air. A half-moon, draped in shrouds of mist, hung ahead of them. Occasionally their hands brushed. Occasionally their hands grasped each other in a strong embrace. Barley was watching the wing mirror. It was smashed and some of the bits were missing but he could see enough in it to watch the cars that followed without overtaking. Katya turned left but still nothing passed them.

She wasn't speaking so he wasn't either. He wondered how they learned it, where is safe to speak, where isn't. At school? From older girls as they grew up? Or was it your earnest little lecture from the family doctor somewhere round the second year of puberty? "It's time you learned that cars and walls have ears just like people . . ."

They were bumping over a pitted sliproad into a half-finished carpark.

"Imagine you are a doctor," she warned him as they faced each other across the roof of the car. "You must look very strict."

"I'm a doctor," Barley said. Neither of them was joking.

They picked their way between a maze of moonlit puddles to a pathway covered in asbestos awning, leading to double doors and an empty reception desk. He caught the first alarming smells of hospital: disinfectant, floor polish, surgical spirit. At a crisp pace she marched him across a circular hallway of mottled concrete, down a linoleum corridor and past a marble counter staffed by sullen women. A clock said ten-twenty-five. Making a consciously officious gesture, Barley compared it with his watch. The clock was ten minutes slow. The next corridor was lined with figures slumped on kitchen chairs.

The waiting room was a gloomy catacomb supported by immense pillars with a raised platform at one end. At the other, swing doors gave on to the lavatories. Somebody had rigged a temporary light to show the way. By its pale light, Barley could make out empty coat-racks behind a wooden counter, parked stretcher trolleys and, fixed to the nearest pillar, an ancient telephone. A bench stood against the wall. Katya sat on it, so Barley sat beside her.

"He tries always to be punctual. Sometimes he is delayed by the connection," she said.

"Can I speak to him?"

"He would be angry."

"Why?"

"If they hear English on a long-distance line they will immediately pay attention. It is normal."

A man in a head-bandage looking like a blinded soldier from the front wandered into the women's lavatory as two women emerged. They grabbed hold of him and redirected him. Katya unclipped her handbag and took out a notebook and a pen.

He will try at ten-forty, she had said. At ten-forty he will attempt the first connection. He will not speak for long, she had said. To speak too long even between safe telephones is unwise.

She stood up and walked to the telephone, ducking like a regular under the cloakroom counter.

Will he tell her he loves her? Barley wondered—"I love you enough to risk your life for me"? Will he give her the love talk he gave her in his letter? Or will he tell her that she is an acceptable price for the cleansing of his uneasy soul?

She was standing sideways to him, gazing keenly through the swing doors. Had she seen something bad? Had she heard something? Or was her mind already far away with Yakov?

It's how she stands when she's waiting for him, he thought—like someone who is prepared to wait all day.

The telephone rang hoarsely, as if it had dust in its larynx. A sixth sense had already guided her towards it, so it had no chance to give a second squawk before she had it in her hand. Barley was only a few feet from her but he was hard put to it to hear her voice above the background clatter of the hospital. She had turned away from him, presumably for privacy, and she had boxed her hand over her free ear so that she could hear her lover in the earpiece. Barley could just hear her say "yes" and "yes" again, submissively.

Leave her alone! he thought angrily. I've told you before and I'm going to tell you again at the weekend. Leave her alone, keep her out of this. Deal with the grey men or me!

The notebook lay open on a rickety shelf attached to the pillar, the pen on top of it, but she hadn't touched either one of them. *Yes. Yes. Yes.* I did that on the island. *Yes. Yes. Yes.* He saw her shoulders rise into her neck and stay there and her back stretch as if she had taken a deep breath or enjoyed some pleasurable moment within herself. Her elbow rose from her side to cram the earpiece more firmly into her head. *Yes. Yes.* What about *no* for once? *No, I won't lie down for you!*

Her spare hand had found the pillar and he could see the fingers part and brace themselves as the tips pressed into the dark plaster. He saw the back of her hand whiten as it stiffened, but it didn't move, and suddenly her hand alarmed him. It had found a climbing hold and was clinging to it for grim life. She was on the cliff face and the fingerhold was all she had between her lover and the abyss.

She turned, the receiver still pressed to her ear, and he saw her face. Who was she? What had she become? For the first time since he had met her she was without expression, and the telephone jammed against her temple was the gun that somebody was holding there.

She had the hostage stare.

Then her body began sliding down the pillar as if she couldn't be bothered any more to hold it upright. At first it was only her knees that gave way, then she crumpled at the waist as well, but Barley was there to hold her. He flung one arm round her waist and with the other he snatched the phone from her. He held it to his ear and shouted "Goethe!" but all he got was a dialling tone so he rang off.

It was an odd thing, but Barley had forgotten until now that he was strong. They started to move but as they did so she was seized with a violent revulsion against him and lashed out silently with her clenched fist, cracking him so hard over the cheekbone that for a moment he saw nothing but a dazzling light. He grappled her hands to her sides and held them there while he pulled her under the counter and frogmarched her through the hospital and across the carpark. "She's a disturbed patient," he was explaining in his mind. "A disturbed patient in a doctor's care."

Still holding her, he tipped her handbag on to the roof of the car, found the key, unlocked the passenger door and bundled her inside. Then he ran round to the driver's side in case she had ideas of taking over after all.

"I shall go home," she said.

"I don't know the way."

"Take me home," she repeated.

"I don't know the way, Katya! You'll have to tell me right and left, do you hear?" He grabbed her shoulders. "Sit up. Look out of the window. Where's reverse on this bloody thing?"

He fiddled with the gears. She grabbed the lever and slammed it in reverse, making the gearbox scream.

"Lights," he said.

He had already found them, but he made her turn them on for him, willing her by his anger to respond. As he bumped across the carpark, he had to swerve to avoid an ambulance entering at speed. Mud and water blacked out the windscreen, but there were no wipers because it wasn't raining. Stopping the car, he sprang out and smeared the windscreen halfway clean with his handkerchief, then back into the car.

"Go left," she ordered. "Be quick, please."

"We came the other way before."

"It's one way. Be quick."

Her voice was dead and he couldn't rouse it. He offered her his flask. She pushed it aside. He drove slowly, ignoring her instruction to be quick. Headlights in the driving mirror, not gaining or losing. It's Wicklow, he thought. It's Paddy, Cy, Henziger, Zapadny, the whole Guards Armoured of them. Her face lit and went out again under the sodium streetlamps but it was lifeless. She was staring into her own head at whatever frightful things she saw in her imagination. Her clenched fist was in her mouth. Its knuckles were wedged between her teeth.

"Do I turn here?" he asked her roughly. And again he shouted at her. "Tell me where to turn, will you?"

She spoke first in Russian, then in English. "Now. Right. Go faster."

Nothing was familiar to him. Every empty street was like the next one and the last one.

"Turn now."

"Left or right?"

"*Left!*"

She screamed the word at the top of her voice, then screamed it again. After the scream came her tears and they went on coming between choking hopeless sobs. Then gradually the sobs began to falter and by the time he drew up at her apartment block they had ceased. He pulled the handbrake but it was broken. The car was still rolling as she shoved her door open. He reached for her but she was too quick.

Somehow she had scrambled on to the pavement and was running across the forecourt with her handbag open, foraging for her keys. A boy in a leather jacket was lounging in the doorway and he appeared to want to block her. But by then Barley was level with her, so the boy leapt aside for them to pass. She wouldn't wait for the lift or perhaps she'd forgotten that there was one. She ran up the stairs and Barley ran after her, past a couple embracing. On the first landing an old man sat drunk in the corner. They climbed and kept climbing. Now it was an old woman who was drunk. Now it was a boy. They climbed so many flights that Barley began to fear she had forgotten which floor she was supposed to live on. Then suddenly she was turning the locks and they were inside her apartment again, and Katya was in the twins' room, kneeling on their bed with her head struck forward and panting like a desperate swimmer, one arm flung across the body of each sleeping child.

Once more there was only her bedroom. He led her to it because even in that tiny space she no longer knew the way. She sat on the bed unsurely, seeming not to know how high it was. He sat beside her, staring into her dull face, watching her eyes close, half open and close again, not venturing to touch her because she was rigid and appalled and apart from him. She was clasping her wrist as if it were broken. She gave a deep sigh. He said her name but she didn't seem to hear him. He peered round the room searching. A minuscule worktop was fixed along one wall, a make-up table and writing desk combined. Tossed among old letters lay a ring-backed writing block similar to the sort that Goethe used. A framed Renoir reproduction hung above the bed. He unhooked it and set it on his lap. The trained spy ripped a page out of the notebook, laid it on the picture glass, took a pen from his pocket and wrote.

Tell me.

He put the paper before her and she read it with indifference without relinquishing her wrist. She gave a faint shrug. Her shoulder was leaning against his, but she was unaware of it. Her blouse was open and her rich black hair was tousled from the running. He wrote again, *Tell me,* then he grabbed her by the shoulders while his eyes implored her with a desperate love. Then he stabbed his forefinger at the sheet of paper. He picked up the picture and rammed it into her lap for her to press on. She stared at the paper and at *Tell me,* then she gave a long heartbreaking choke and put her head down until he lost sight of her behind the chaotic curtain of her hair.

They have taken Yakov, she wrote.

He took back the pen.

Who told you?

Yakov, she replied.

What did he say?

He will come to Moscow on Friday. He will meet you at Igor's apartment at eleven o'clock on Friday night. He will bring you more material and answer your questions. Please have a precise list ready. It will be the last time. You should bring him news of publication, dates, details. You should bring good whisky. He loves me.

He grabbed back the pen.

Was it Yakov talking?

She nodded.

Why do you say they've taken him?

He used the wrong name.

What name?

Daniil. It was our rule. Pyotr if he is safe, Daniil if he is taken.

The pen had been passing urgently between them. Now Barley held on to it as he wrote question after question. *He made a mistake,* he wrote.

She shook her head.

He has been ill. He has forgotten your code, he wrote.

She shook her head again.

Has he never got it wrong before? he wrote.

At this she shook her head, took back the pen and wrote in an angry hand. *He called me Mariya. He said, Is that Mariya? Mariya is how I should call myself if there was danger. If I am safe, Alina.*

Write his words.

This is Daniil. Is that Mariya speaking? My lecture was the greatest success of my career. That was a lie.

Why?

He says always, in Russia the only success is not to win. It is a joke we have. He spoke deliberately against our joke. He was telling me we are dead.

Barley went to the window and looked steeply down at the concourse and the street. The whole dark world inside him had fallen into silence. Nothing moved, nothing breathed. But he was prepared. He had been prepared all his life, and never known it. She is Goethe's woman, therefore she is as dead as he is. Not yet, because this far Goethe has protected her with the last bit of courage left in him. But dead as dead can be, any time they care to reach out their long arm and pick her off the tree.

For perhaps an hour he remained there at the window before returning to the bed. She was lying on her side with her eyes open and her knees drawn up. He put his arm round her and drew her into him and he felt her cold body break inside his grasp as she began sobbing with convulsive, soundless heaves, as if she was afraid even to weep within the hearing of the microphones.

He began writing to her again, in bold clear capitals: PAY ATTENTION TO ME.

The screens were rolling every few minutes. Barley has left the Mezh. More. They have arrived at the metro station. More. Have exited (*sic*) the hospital, Katya on Barley's arm. More. Men lie but the computer is infallible. More.

"Why on earth's he driving?" Ned asked sharply as he read this.

Sheriton was too absorbed to reply but Bob was standing behind him and Bob picked up the question.

"Men like to drive women, Ned. The chauvinist age is still upon us."

"Thank you," said Ned politely.

Clive was smiling in approval.

Intermission. The screens slip out of sequence as Anastasia takes back the story. Anastasia is an angry old Latvian of sixty who has been on the Russia House books for twenty years. Anastasia alone has been allowed to cover the vestibule.

The legend speaks:

She made two passes, first to the lavatory, then back to the waiting room.

On her first pass, Barley and Katya were sitting on a bench waiting.

On her second, Barley and Katya were standing beside the telephone and appeared to be embracing. Barley had a hand to her face, Katya also had a hand up, the other hung at her side.

Had Bluebird's call come through by then?

Anastasia didn't know. Though she had stood in her lavatory cubicle listening as hard as she could, she hadn't heard the phone ring. So either the call had failed to come through or it was over by the time she made her second pass.

"Why on earth should he be embracing her?" said Ned.

"Maybe she had a fly in her eye," Sheriton said sourly, still watching the screen.

"He drove," Ned insisted. "He's not allowed to drive over there, but he drove. He let her drive all the way out to the country and back. She drove him to the hospital. Then all of a sudden he takes over the wheel. Why?"

Sheriton put down his pencil and ran his forefinger round the inside of his collar. "So what's the betting, Ned? Did Bluebird make his call or didn't he? Come on."

Ned still had the decency to give the question honest thought. "Presumably he made it. Otherwise they would have gone on waiting."

"Maybe she heard something she didn't like. Some bad news or something," Sheriton suggested.

The screens had gone out, leaving the room sallow.

Sheriton had a separate office done in rosewood and instant art. We decamped to it, poured ourselves coffee, stood about.

"Hell's he doing in her flat for so long?" Ned asked me aside. "All he has to do is get the time and place of the meeting out of her. He could have done that two hours ago."

"Maybe they're having a tender moment," I said.

"I'd feel better if I thought they were."

"Maybe he's buying another hat," said Johnny unpleasantly, overhearing us.

"Geronimo," said Sheriton as the bell rang, and we trooped back to the situation room.

An illuminated street map of the city showed us Katya's apartment marked by a red pinlight. The pick-up point lay three hundred metres east of it, at the south-east corner of two main streets marked green. Barley must now be heading along the south pavement, keeping close to the curb. As he reached the pick-up point, he should affect to slow down as if hunting for a car. The safe car would pull alongside him. Barley had been instructed to give the driver the name of his hotel in a loud voice and negotiate a price with his hands.

At the second roundabout the car would take a side turning and enter a building site where the safe truck was parked without lights, its driver appearing to doze in his cab. If the truck's wing aerial was extended, the car would make a right-hand circle and return to the truck.

If not, abort.

Paddy's report hit the screens at 1 a.m. London time. The tapes were available for us less than an hour later, blasted from the roof of the US Embassy. The report has since been torn to pieces in every conceivable way. For me it remains a model of factual field reporting.

Naturally the writer needs to be known, for every writer under the sun has limitations. Paddy was not a mindreader but he was a lot of other things, a former Gurkha turned special forces man turned intelligence officer, a linguist, a planner and improviser in Ned's favourite mould.

For his Moscow persona, he had put on such a skin of English silliness that the uninitiated made a joke of him when they described him to each other: his long shorts in the summer when he took himself on treks through the Moscow woods; his langlaufing in the winter, when he loaded up his Volvo with ancient skis and bamboo poles and iron rations and finally his own egregious self, clad in a fur cap that looked as though it had been kept over from the Arctic convoys. But it takes a clever man to act the fool and get away with it for long, and Paddy was a clever man, however convenient it later became to take his eccentricities at face value.

Also in controlling his motley of pseudo language students, travel clerks, little traders and third-flag nationals, Paddy was first rate. Ned himself could not have bettered him. He tended them like a canny parish priest, and every one of them in his lonely way rose to him. It was not his fault if the qualities that made men come to him also made him vulnerable to deception.

So to Paddy's report. He was struck first by the precision with which Barley gave his account, and the tape bears him out. Barley's voice is more self-assured than in any previous recording.

Paddy was impressed by Barley's resolve and by his devotion to his mission. He compared the Barley he saw before him in the truck with the Barley he had briefed for his Leningrad run and warmed to the improvement. He was right. Barley was an enlarged and altered man.

Barley's account to Paddy tallied also with every checkable fact at Paddy's disposal, from the pick-up at the metro and the drive to the hospital, to the wait on the bench and the stifled bell. Katya had been standing over the phone when it rang, Barley said. Barley himself had scarcely heard it. Then no wonder Anastasia hadn't heard it either, Paddy reasoned. Katya must have been quick as light to grab that receiver.

The conversation between Katya and the Bluebird had been short, two minutes at most, said Barley. Another neat fit. Goethe was known to be scared of long telephone conversations.

With so much collateral available to him therefore, and with Barley navigating his way through it, how on earth can anybody afterwards maintain that Paddy should have driven Barley straight to the Embassy and shipped him back to London bound and gagged? But of course Clive maintained just that, and he was not the only one.

Thus to the three mysteries that by now were sticking in Ned's throat—the embrace, the drive from the hospital with Barley at the wheel, the two hours they spent together in the flat. For Barley's answers, we must see him as Paddy saw him, bowed over the low light on the table in the truck, his face glistening from the heat. There is the whirr from the bafflers in the background. Both men are wearing earphones, a closed-circuit microphone lies between them. Barley whispers his story, half to the microphone, half to his station chief. Not all Paddy's nights of adventure on the North-West Frontier could have yielded a more dramatic atmosphere.

Cy sits in the shadows in a third pair of earphones. It is Cy's truck but he has orders to let Paddy host the feast.

"Then she goes and gets the wobblies," says Barley, with enough of the man-to-man in his voice to make Paddy smile. "She'd been winding herself up all week for his call and suddenly it was over and she went pop. Probably didn't help her, me being there. Without me around, I reckon she'd have held it back till she got home."

"Probably would at that," Paddy agrees understandingly.

"It was too much for her. Hearing his voice, hearing he'll be in town in a couple of days, her worries about her kids—and about him, and about herself as well—it was just too much for her."

Paddy understood perfectly. He had known emotional women in his day, and was experienced in the sorts of thing they cried over.

From there everything else flowed naturally. The deception became a symphony. Barley had done what he could to comfort her, he said, but she was in bad shape so he put his arm round her and lugged her to the car and drove her home.

In the car she did some more crying but she was on the mend by the time they got to her flat. Barley made her a cup of tea and patted her hand, until he was confident she was able to cope.

"Well done," said Paddy. And if, as he says this, he sounds like a nineteenth-century Indian Army officer congratulating his men after a futile cavalry charge, that is only because he is impressed and his mouth is too near the microphone.

There is lastly Barley's question, which is where Cy came in. With hindsight, no doubt, it sounds like a straight declaration of larcenous intent. But Cy didn't hear it that way and neither did Paddy. Neither, in fact, did anyone in London except Ned, whose impotence was by now unnerving. Ned was becoming the pariah of the situation room.

"Oh yes—that's it—what about the shopping list?" says Barley as he prepares to leave. The question emerges as one of several small administrative worries, not a solo. "When do you get to press the shopping list into my hot little hand?" he asks repetitiously.

"Why?" says Cy from the shadows.

"Well I don't know. Shouldn't I bone up on it a bit or something?"

"There's nothing to bone up," says Cy. "It's written questions, yes-or-no answers, and it is positively important that you do not know any part of it, thank you."

"So when do I get it?"

"The shopping list we do as late as possible," says Cy.

Of Cy's own opinion of Barley's state of mind, one nugget is recorded. "With the Brits," he is reported to have said, "you never know what the hell they're thinking anyway."

That night at least, Cy had a certain justice on his side.

"There was no bad news," Ned insisted while Brock played the truck tapes for the third or thirtieth time.

We were back in our own Russia House. We had taken refuge there. It was like the early days all over again. It was dawn, but we were too wakeful to remember sleep.

"There was no *bad* news," Ned repeated. "It was all *good* news. 'I'm well. I'm safe. I gave a great lecture. I'm catching the plane. See you on Friday. I love you.' So she weeps."

"Oh, I don't know," I said, talking against my own mood. "Haven't *you* ever cried when *you* were happy?"

"She weeps so much he has to cart her down the hospital corridor. She weeps so much she can't drive. When they get to her apartment she runs ahead of him to the door as if Barley doesn't exist, because she's so *happy* that the Bluebird's flying in on time. And he comforts her. For all the good news she's had." Barley's recorded voice had come on again. "And he's calm. Totally calm. Not a worry in the world. 'We're bang on target, Paddy. Everything's fine. That's why she's weeping.' Of course it is."

He sat back and closed his eyes while Barley's trustworthy voice continued to talk to him from the recorder.

"He doesn't belong to us any more," said Ned. "He's gone away."

As also, in a different sense, had Ned. He had launched a great operation. Now all he could do by his own reckoning was watch it hurtle out of control. In my whole life I never saw a man so isolated, with the possible exception of myself.

Spying is waiting.
   Spying is worrying.
   Spying is being yourself but more so.
The nostrums of the extinct Walter and the living Ned rang in Barley's ears. The apprentice had become heir to the spells of his masters but his magic was more potent than theirs had ever been.

He was on a plateau none of them had ascended. He had the goal, he had the means to reach it and he had what Clive would have called the motivation, which in better mouths was purpose. Everything they had taught him was paying off as he rode calmly into battle to deceive them. But he was not their trickster.

Their flags were nothing to him. They could wave in any wind. But he was not their traitor. He was not his own cause. He knew the battle he had to win and whom he had to win it for. He knew the sacrifice he was prepared to make. He was not their traitor. He was complete.

He did not need their scared labels and their weakling systems. He was one man alone but he was greater than the sum of those who had presumed to take control of him. He knew them as the worst of all bad weapons, because their existence justified their targets.

In a gentle way that was not even all that gentle, he had discovered anger. He could smell its first kindling and hear the crackle of its brushwood.

There was only now. Goethe was right. There was no tomorrow because tomorrow was the excuse. There was now or there was nowhere, and Goethe, even nowhere, was still right. We must cut down the grey men inside ourselves, we must burn our grey suits and set our good hearts free, which is the dream of every decent soul, and even—believe it or not—of certain grey men too. But how, with what?

Goethe was right, and it was not his fault or Barley's that each by accident had set the other in motion. With the radiance of spirit that was rising in him, Barley's sense of kinship with his unlikely friend was overwhelming. He brimmed with allegiance to Goethe's frantic dream of unleashing the forces of sanity and opening the doors on dirty rooms.

But Barley did not dwell long on Goethe's agony. Goethe was in hell and very likely Barley would soon be following him. I'll mourn him when I have the time, he thought. Until then his business was with the living whom Goethe had put so shamefully at risk, and in a brave last gesture had attempted to preserve.

For his immediate business Barley must use the grey men's wiles. He must be himself but more so than he has ever been before. He must wait. He must worry. He must be a man reversed, inwardly reconciled, outwardly unfulfilled. He must live secretly on tiptoe, arch as a cat inside his head while he acts the Barley Blair they wish to see, their creature all the way.

Meanwhile the chess-player in him reckons his moves. The slumbering negotiator is becoming unobservably awake. The publisher is achieving what he has never achieved before, he is becoming the cool-headed broker between the necessity and the far vision.

Katya knows, he reasons. *She knows Goethe is caught.*

But they do not know she knows, because she kept her wits about her on the telephone.

And they do not know I know that Katya knows.

In the whole world I am the only person apart from Katya and Goethe who knows that Katya knows.

Katya is still free.

Why?

They have not stolen her children, ransacked her flat, thrown Matvey in the madhouse or displayed any of the delicacy traditionally reserved for Russian ladies playing courier to Soviet defence physicists who have decided to entrust their nation's secrets to a derelict Western publisher.

Why?

I too this far am free. They have not chained my neck to a brick wall.

Why?

Because they do not know we know they know.

So they want more.

They want us, but more than us.

They can wait for us, because they want more.

But what is the more?

What is the clue to their patience?

Everybody talks, Ned had said, stating a fact of life. *With today's methods everybody talks.* He was telling Barley not to try and hold out if he was caught. But Barley was not thinking about himself any more. He was thinking about Katya.

Each night, each day that followed, Barley moved the pieces round in his mind, honing his plan while he waited, as we all did, for Friday's promised meeting with the Bluebird.

At breakfast, Barley punctually on parade, a model publisher and spy. And each day, all day long, the life and soul of the fair.

Goethe. Nothing I can do for you. No power on earth will prise you from their grip.

Katya, still savable. Her children, still savable. Even though everybody talks and Goethe in the end will be no exception.

Myself, unsavable as ever.

Goethe gave me the courage, he thought, as his secret purpose grew in him, *and Katya the love.*

No. Katya gave me both. And gives them to me still.

And the day as quiet as the days before, the screens near-blank, as Barley steers himself methodically towards the evening's grand Potomac & Blair Launch Party in the Spirit of Goodwill and Glasnost, as our flowery invitations have it, printed in triptych with deckle edges on the Service's own printing press not two weeks ago.

And intermittently, with a seeming casualness, Barley assures himself of Katya's continuing welfare. He rings her whenever he can. He chats to her and makes her use the word "convenient" as a safety signal. In return he includes the word "frankly" in his own careless chatter. Nothing heavy; nothing on the matter of love or death or great German poets. Just:

How are you doing?

Is the fair wearing you out, frankly?

How are the twins?

Is Matvey still enjoying his pipe?

Meaning, I love you, and I love you, and I love you, and I love you frankly.

For further assurance regarding her safety, Barley despatches Wicklow to take a passing look at her in the Socialist pavilion. "She's fine," Wicklow reports with a smile, humouring Barley's nervousness. "She's steady as she goes."

"Thanks," says Barley. "Jolly nice of you, old boy."

The second time, again at Barley's bidding, Henziger himself goes. Perhaps Barley is saving himself for the evening. Or perhaps he does not trust his own emotions. But she is still there, still alive, still breathing, and she has changed into her party frock.

Yet all the while, even driving back early to town in order to be ahead of his guests, Barley continues to muster his private army of alterable and unalterable facts with a clarity that the most trained and compromised lawyer would be proud of.

"Gyorgy! Marvellous! Fantastic! Where's Varenka?"

"Barley, my friend, for Christ's sake save us! We don't like the twentieth century any better than you English. Let's run away from it together! We leave tonight, okay? You buy the tickets?"

"Yuri. My God, is this your new wife? Leave him. He's a monster."

"Barley! Listen! Everything is fine! We have no more problems! In the old days we had to assume that everything was a mess! Now we can look in our newspapers and confirm it!"

"Misha! How's the work going? Super!"

"It's war, for Christ's sake, Barley, open war. First we got to hang the old guard, then we got to fight another Stalingrad!"

"Leo! Great to see you! How's Sonya?"

"Barley, pay attention to me! Communism is not a threat! It's a parasite industry that lives off the mistakes of all you stupid assholes in the West!"

The reception was in the mirrored upstairs room of an elderly mid-town hotel.

Plainclothes guards stood outside on the pavement. More hovered in the hall and on the staircase and at the entrance to the room.

Potomac & Blair had invited a hundred people. Eight had accepted, nobody had refused, and so far a hundred and fifty had arrived. But until Katya was among them Barley preferred the spaces near the door.

A flock of Western girls swept in, escorted by the usual dubious official interpreters, all men. A portly philosopher who played the clarinet arrived with his newest boyfriend.

"Aleksander! Fantastic! Marvellous!"

A lonely Siberian called Andrey, already drunk, needed to speak to Barley on a matter of vital urgency. "One-party Socialism is a disaster, Barley. It has broken our hearts. Keep your British variety. You will publish my new novel?"

"Well I don't know about that, Andrey," Barley replied cautiously, glancing towards the door. "Our Russian editor admires it but he doesn't see an English market. We're thinking about it."

"You know why I came tonight?" Andrey asked.

"Tell me."

Another jolly group arrived, but still with no Katya among them.

"In order to wear my fine clothes for you. We Russians know each other's tricks too well. We need your Western mirror. You come here, you depart again with our best images reflected in you and we feel noble. If you have published my first novel, it is only logical that you publish my second."

"Not if the first one didn't make any money, it isn't, Andrey," said Barley with rare firmness, and to his relief saw Wicklow slipping towards them across the room.

"You have heard that Anatoly died in prison of a hunger strike in December? After two years of this Great New Russia we are enjoying?" Andrey continued, taking another enormous pull of whisky, supplied courtesy of the American Embassy in support of a more sober Russia.

"Of course we heard about him," Wicklow cut in soothingly. "It was disgusting."

"So why don't you publish my novel?"

Leaving Wicklow to cope, Barley spread his arms and hastened beaming to the door. The superb Natalie of the All-Union State Library of Foreign Literature had arrived, a wise beauty of sixty. They fell into an adoring embrace.

"So whom shall we discuss tonight, Barley? James Joyce or Adrian Mole? Why are you looking so intelligent, suddenly? It is because you have become a capitalist."

A stampede flung half the company to the further end of the room and caused the guards to peer through the doorway in alarm. The roar of conversation dipped and recovered. The buffet had been unveiled.

But still no Katya.

"Today under the *perestroika* it is all much easier," Natalie was saying through her irresistible smile. "Foreign travel is no problem. For example to Bulgaria. All we have to do is describe to our bureaucrats what kind of person we think we are. Naturally the Bulgarians need to know this before we arrive. They must be warned what to expect. Are we an intelligent person, medium intelligent or normal intelligent? The Bulgarians need to prepare themselves, perhaps even train themselves a little. Are we calm or excitable, plain-minded or full of imagination? When we have answered these simple questions and a thousand more of the same sort, we may proceed to the more important issues, such as the address and full names of our maternal grandmother, the date of her death and the number of her death certificate and, if they are feeling like it, perhaps also the name of the doctor who signed it. So you may see that our bureaucrats are doing everything possible to introduce the new, relaxed regulations quickly, and send us all abroad on holiday with our children. Barley, whom are you staring round for? Have I lost my looks or are you bored with me already?"

"So what did you tell them?" Barley asked with a laugh, and willed himself to keep his eyes on her.

"Oh, I said I was very intelligent, I was a calm, amusing person and the Bulgarians would be delighted with my company. The bureaucrats are testing our determination, that is all. They hope that if we have to satisfy so many different departments we shall lose courage and decide to stay at home. But it is getting better. Everything is getting a little better. Maybe you don't believe it, but the *perestroika* is not being run for foreigners. It is run for us."

"How is your dog, Barley?" a man's gloomy voice murmured at Barley's side. It was Arkady, unofficial sculptor, with his beautiful unofficial girlfriend.

"I haven't got a dog, Arkady. Why do you ask?"

"Because from this moment it has become safer to discuss one's dog than one's fellow human beings, I would say."

Barley turned his head to follow Arkady's gaze and saw Alik Zapadny standing on the far side of the room in earnest conversation with Katya.

"We Muscovites are talking too dangerously these days," Arkady continued, his eyes still fixed upon Zapadny. "We are becoming careless in our excitement. The informers will have a good harvest this autumn, even if nobody else does. Ask him. He is at the peak of his profession, I would say."

"Alik, you old devil, what are you pestering this poor girl about?" Barley demanded as he embraced Katya first and then Zapadny. "I could see her blushing from across the room. You want to watch him, Katya. His English is almost as good as yours, and he talks it a lot faster. How are you?"

"Oh thank you," she said softly. "I am *very* well."

She was wearing the dress she had worn at their meeting at the Odessa. She was withdrawn but in command of herself. Her face had the battered eagerness of bereavement. Dan Zeppelin and Mary Lou stood with them.

"We were having rather an interesting discussion on human rights, as a matter of fact, Barley," Zapadny explained, waving his glass in a circular gesture round the company as if he were taking a collection. "Weren't we, Mr. Zeppelin? We are always so grateful when Westerners preach to us about how to behave towards our criminals, you see! But then what is the difference, I am asking myself, between a country that locks a few extra people in prison, and a country that leaves its gangsters at large? I think I have just found a negotiating point here for our Soviet leaders, actually. Tomorrow morning we shall announce to the so-called Helsinki Watch Committee that we can have nothing further to do with them until they have put the American Mafia behind bars. How would that be, Mr. Zeppelin? We let ours out, you put yours inside. It's a fair deal, I would say."

"You want the polite answer or the real one?" Dan snapped over Mary Lou's shoulder.

Another polyglot group of guests swept past, followed after a theatrical pause by none other than the great Sir Peter Oliphant himself, surrounded by a retinue of Russian and English bag-carriers. The noise grew, the room filled. Three sickly-looking British correspondents inspected the depleted buffet and departed. Somebody opened the piano and began playing a Ukrainian song. A woman sang well and others joined her.

"No, Barley, I do not know what terrifies you," Katya was replying, to Barley's surprise, so he must have asked her. "I am sure you are very brave, like all English."

In the heat of the room and the swirl of the occasion, his own excitement had turned suddenly against him. He felt drunk but not from alcohol, for he had been nursing one tired Scotch all evening.

"Maybe there's nothing there," he ventured, addressing not just Katya but a ring of unfamiliar faces. "Out in the woodwork. Talent." Everyone was waiting, Barley too. He was trying to look at all of them while his eyes saw only Katya. What had he been saying? What had they been hearing? Their faces were still turned to him but there was no light in them, not even Katya's; there was only concern. He stumbled on. "We had this vision, all of us, for years, of great Russian artists waiting to be discovered." He faltered. "Well, didn't we? Epic novels, plays? Great painters, banned, working in secrecy? Attics full of wonderful illegal stuff? Musicians the same? We talked about it. Dreamed about it. The secret continuation of the nineteenth century. 'And when the thaw comes, they'll all come out of the ice and dazzle us,' we told each other. So where the hell are they, all these geniuses? What if they froze to death in the ice? Maybe the repression worked. That's all I'm saying."

A spellbound silence followed before Katya came to his aid. "The Russian talent exists and has always existed, Barley, even in the worst times. It cannot be destroyed," she declared with a hint of her old strictness. "Perhaps it will first have to adjust itself to the new circumstances, but soon it will express itself brilliantly. I am sure that is what you wish to say."

Henziger is making his speech. It is a masterpiece of unconscious hypocrisy. "May the pioneering venture of Potomac & Blair provide a modest addition to the great new era of East-West understanding!" he declares, puffed up by his conviction. His voice lifts and with it his glass. He is the honest trader, he is every decent American with his heart in the right place. And no doubt that he is precisely what he thinks he is, for the ham actor in him lies just below the surface. "Let's make each other rich!" he cries, raising his glass still higher. "Let's make each other free! Let's trade together, and let's talk together and let's drink together, and let's make the world a better place. Ladies and gentlemen—to you and to Potomac & Blair and to our mutual profit—and to the *perestroika*—good health! Amen!"

They are yelling for Barley. Spikey Morgan starts it, Yuri and Alik Zapadny take it up, all the old hands who know the game yell, "Barley, Barley!" Soon the whole room is yelling for Barley, some of them without even knowing why, and for a moment none of them sees him anyway. Then suddenly he is standing on the buffet table holding a borrowed saxophone and playing "My Funny Valentine," which he has played at every Moscow book fair since the first, while Jack Henziger accompanies him on the piano in the unmistakable style of Fats Waller.

The guards at the door creep into the room to listen, the guards from the stairs come to the doorway and the guards from the hall come to the stairs as the first notes of Barley's swansong gather clarity and then a splendid power.

"We're going to the new Indian, for Christ's sake," Henziger protests as they stand on the pavement under the stodgy gaze of the *toptuny*. "Bring Katya with you! We've booked a table!"

"Sorry, Jack. We're bespoke. Longstanding date."

Henziger is only putting on a show. "She needs welfaring," Barley has confided to him. "I'm going to take her off and give her a quiet supper somewhere."

But Barley did not take Katya to dinner for their farewell evening, as the irregulars confirmed before they were stood down. And it was Katya, not Barley this time, who did the taking. She took him to the place known to every urban Russian boy and girl from adolescence, and it is to be found at the top of every purpose-built apartment block in every major city. There is not a Russian of Katya's generation who does not count such places among her memories of early love. And such a place was to be found at the top of Katya's staircase also, at the point where the last flight ends and the attics begin, though it was more sought after in winter than in summer because it included the suppurating hot-water tank and steaming black-bandaged pipes.

First it was necessary for her to inspect Matvey and the twins and establish that they were still safe, while Barley stood on the landing and waited for her. Then she led him by the hand up several flights until the last, which was of wood. She had a key and it fitted the rusted steel door that ordered all trespassers to keep their distance. And when she had unlocked it and relocked it, she led him across the rafters to the bit of hard floor where she had prepared a makeshift bed, with a muddied view of the stars through the filthy skylight and the chugging of the pipes and the stench of drying clothes for company.

"The letter you gave to Landau went astray," he said. "It ended up in the hands of our officials. It was the officials who sent me to you. I'm sorry about that."

But there was no more time for either of them to be shocked by anything. He had told her little of his plan and he told her no more now. It was understood between them that she knew too much already. And besides, they had more important matters to discuss, for it was on this night also that Katya told Barley the things that afterwards constituted the rest of his knowledge of her. And she confessed her love for him in terms simple enough to sustain him through the separation they both knew lay ahead of them.

Nevertheless Barley did not outstay his welcome. He did not give the men in the field or the men in London cause to be anxious for him. He was back at the Mezh by midnight, in good time for a last one with the boys.

"Oh, Jack, Alik Zapadny's summoned me to his traditional farewell snoot for old hands tomorrow afternoon," he confided to Henziger over a nightcap in the first-floor bar.

"Want me to come along?" asked Henziger. For like the Russians themselves, Henziger harboured no illusions about Zapadny's regrettable connections.

Barley smiled regretfully. "Your knees aren't brown enough, Jack. It's for us golden oldies from the days when there was no hope."

"What time?" asked Wicklow, ever practical.

"Four o'clock, I think he said. Seems a damned odd time for a drink. Yes, I'm sure he did. Four."

Then he wished them all an affectionate goodnight and rode to Heaven in the lift, which in the Mezh is a glass cage that slides up and down the outside of a steel rod, to the private worry of many honest souls below.

It was lunchtime and after all our sleepless nights and wakeful dawns there was something indecent about a sensation that occurred at lunchtime. But a sensation it was. A hand-carried sensation. A sensation inside a yellow envelope inside a locked steel briefcase. Gaunt Johnny from their London station ran into the situation room with it, having brought it under guard from the Embassy across the square. He ran right through the lower level and up the little staircase to the command area before he realised we had moved to Sheriton's rosewood parlour for our sandwiches and coffee.

He handed it to Sheriton and stood over him like a stage messenger while Sheriton read first the covering letter, which he stuffed into his pocket, then the message itself.

Then he stood over Ned while Ned read the message too. It wasn't till Ned passed it back to me that Johnny seemed to decide he had read it enough times: a signals intercept, transmitted by the Soviet military out of Leningrad, intercepted in Finland by the Americans and decrypted in Virginia by a bank of computers powerful enough to light London for a year.

Leningrad to Moscow, copy to Saratov.

Professor Yakov Savelyev is authorized to take a recreational weekend in Moscow following his lecture to the military academy in Saratov this Friday. Please arrange transport and facilities.

"Well thank you, Mr. Administration Officer, Leningrad," Sheriton murmured.

Ned had taken back the signal and was re-reading it. Of all of us, he seemed to be the only one who was not impressed.

"Is this all they broke?" he asked.

"I don't know, Ned," said Johnny, not bothering to conceal his hostility.

"It says here 'one over one.' What's that supposed to mean? Find out whether it's the only one in the batch. If it isn't, perhaps you'd be good enough to find out what else they picked up on the same trawl that was worth a damn." He waited till Johnny had left the room. "Perfect," he said acidly. "Copybook. My God, you'd think we were dealing with the Germans."

We stood about, nibbling distractedly at our food. Sheriton had shoved his hands into his pockets and turned his back to us while he stared out of the smoked-glass window at the silent traffic. He was wearing a long-haired black cardigan. Through the interior window the rest of us could watch Johnny talking on one of the supposedly safe telephones. He rang off and we watched him come back across the room to us.

"Zero," he announced.

"What's zero?" Ned said.

" 'One over one' means one over one. It's a solo. Nothing either side."

"A fluke then?" Ned suggested.

"A solo," Johnny repeated stubbornly.

Ned swung round to Sheriton, who still had his back to us. "Russell. Read the signs. That intercept is completely on its own. There's nothing anywhere near it and it stinks. They're tossing us a piece of bait."

Now it was Sheriton's turn to make a second study of the sheet. When he finally spoke, he affected a deep weariness and it was clear he was reaching the limits of his tolerance.

"Ned, I am confidently assured by the cryptographers that the intercept came from lowgrade military crap put out on an army squeezebox vintage 1921. Nobody plants deception that way any more. Nobody does those things. It's not the Bluebird that's going off course. It's you."

"Maybe that's *why* they planted it that way! Isn't that what you and I might do? Come in on the blind side?"

"Well, maybe we would at that," Sheriton conceded, as if it scarcely mattered to him. "Once you start thinking that way, it's pretty hard to think any other way."

Clive at his worst. "We can hardly ask Sheriton to break off the operation on the grounds that everything is going *well,* Ned," he said silkily.

"On the grounds of pixie voices," Sheriton corrected him, his temper gathering as he wandered moodily back into the room. "On the grounds that anything going our way is a Kremlin plot, and everything we fuck up is evidence of our integrity. Ned, my Agency damn nearly died of that ailment. So did you guys. We're not going that route today. It's my operation and my ass."

"And my joe," said Ned. "We've blown him. And we've blown the Bluebird."

"Sure, sure," said Sheriton with icy affability. "No question." He glanced unlovingly at Clive. "Mr. Deputy?"

Clive had his own ways of sitting on the fence, and they were all of them well tried. "Russell—if I may say so—Ned. I think you are both being slightly egotistical. We are a service. We live corporate lives. It is our masters, not we ourselves alone, who have given the Bluebird their blessing. There is a corporate will here that is bigger than any of us."

Wrong again, I thought. It is smaller than all of us. It is an insult to the powers of each of us, except perhaps of Clive, who therefore needs it.

Sheriton turned back to Ned, but still did not raise his voice. "Ned, do you have any idea what will happen in Washington and Langley if I abort *now?* Can you imagine the peals of hyena laughter that will resound across the Atlantic from Defense, the Pentagon and the neanderthals? Can you guess what view might be taken of the Bluebird material until now?" He pointed without apparent rancour at Johnny, who sat skull-eyed, watching each of them in turn. "Can you see this guy's report? This Judas? We were sowing a little moderation around town, remember? Now you tell me I've got to throw Bluebird to the jackals."

"I'm telling you not to give him the shopping list."

Sheriton inclined his ear as if he were a little deaf. *"Barley* the shopping list? Or *Bluebird* the shopping list?"

"Neither of them. Abort."

Finally Sheriton became very angry indeed. He had been winding himself up for this moment, and now it had arrived. He stood himself before Ned and not two feet from him, and when he flung up his palms in remonstration he wrenched half his fluffy cardigan with him so that he resembled an overweight bat in a fury.

"So okay! Here's our worst-case situation. Cooked Ned-style. Okay? We show Bluebird the shopping list and he turns out to be their asset, not ours. Have I considered that possibility? Ned, night and day I have considered little else. If Bluebird is their guy and not ours, if Barley is, if the girl is, if all or any of the players is less than strictly kosher, the shopping list will shine a very bright light up the anal orifice of the United States of America." He began pacing. "It will show the Sovs what has been given away by their own man. So they'll know what we know. Already bad. It will show the Sovs what we *don't* know, and *how* we don't know it. More bad, but there's worse to come. Cleverly analysed, the shopping list can show them the gaps in our intelligence-gathering machinery and, if they're cleverer still, in our own grotesque, fucking ridiculous, incompetent, ludicrously over-stocked arsenal. Why? Because in the end we concentrate on what scares us, which is what we can't do and they can. That's the down side. Ned, I have looked at the bank balance. I know the stakes. I know what we can earn ourselves from Bluebird and what he stands to cost us if we screw up. Losing disenchants me. I've seen it done. I am not impressed. If we're wrong, it's shit city. We knew that back on Nowhere Island and we know it a little better now because it's live-ammunition time. But this is *not* the moment to start looking over our shoulders unless we have a cast-iron reason!"

He came back to Ned. *"Bluebird is straight,* Ned! Remember? Your words. I loved you for them! I still do! Bluebird is telling the unpolluted truth as he knows it. And my myopic masters are going to have it shoved up their asses even if it turns their balls to water. Do you read me, Ned? Or have I put you to sleep already?"

But Ned would not rise to Sheriton's black rage. "Don't give it to him, Russell. We've lost him. If you give him anything at all, give him smoke."

"Smoke? Play Barley *back,* you mean? Admit the Bluebird's bad? Are you joking? Give me *proof,* Ned! Don't give me *hunches!* Give me fucking *proof!* Everybody in Washington who hasn't got hair between his toes tells me that Bluebird is the Holy Bible, the Talmud and the Koran! Now *you* tell me, give him smoke! You got us into this, Ned! Don't try and jump off the tiger at the first fucking stop!"

Ned pondered this for a while, and Clive pondered Ned. Finally Ned gave a shrug as if to say perhaps it made no difference anyway. Then he returned to his desk where he sat alone seeming to read papers, and I remember wondering suddenly whether he had a Hannah too, whether we all did, some life unled that kept him to the wheel.

Perhaps it was true that VAAP had no small rooms or perhaps Alik Zapadny, after his years in prison, had an understandable aversion to them.

In any case, the room he had singled out for their encounter seemed to Barley big enough for a regimental dance, and the only thing small about it was Zapadny himself, who crouched at one end of a long table like a mouse on a raft, watching his visitor with darting eyes as he ambled down the parquet floor at him, his long arms dangling at his sides, elbows up a little, and an expression on his face such as neither Zapadny nor perhaps anyone else had ever seen in him before: not apologetic, not vague, not wilfully foolish, but of an almost menacing firmness of intention.

Zapadny had arranged some papers before him, and a heap of books beside the papers and a jug of drinking water and two glasses. It was evident that he wished to offer Barley an impression of being discovered in the midst of his duties, rather than facing him in cold blood without props or the protection of his numberless assistants.

"Barley, my dear chap, look here it's most kind of you to call by and say your farewells like this, you must be as busy as I am at this moment, my hat," he began, speaking much too quickly. "I would say that if our publishing industry continues to expand like this, then I see no way out of it, though it is only my personal and unofficial opinion, we shall have to employ a hundred more staff and most likely apply for larger offices also." He hummed and fussed his papers and pulled back a chair in what he imagined to be a gesture of old-style European courtesy. But Barley as usual preferred to stand. "Well it's more than my life is worth to offer you a drink on the premises, when the sun is not even over the yardarm as we say, but I mean do sit down and let us kick a few thoughts around for a few minutes"—raising his eyebrows and looking at his watch—"my God, we should have a month of it, not five days! How is the Trans-Siberian Railway progressing? I mean I see no basic difficulties there, provided our own position is respected, and the rules of fair play are observed by all the contracting parties. Are the Finns being too greedy? Perhaps your Mr. Henziger is being greedy? He is certainly a hard-nosed character, I would say."

He caught Barley's eye again and his discomfort increased. Standing over him, Barley bore no resemblance to a man who wished to discuss the Trans-Siberian Railway.

"I find it actually a little odd that you insisted so dogmatically on speaking to me completely alone, you see," Zapadny continued rather desperately. "After all, this one is fairly and squarely in Mrs. Korneyeva's court. It is she and her staff who are directly responsible for the photographer and all the practical arrangements."

But Barley also had a prepared speech, though it was not marred by any of Zapadny's nervousness. "Alik," he said, still declining to sit down. "Does that telephone work?"

"Of course."

"I need to betray my country and I'm in a hurry. And what I would like you to do is put me in touch with the proper authorities, because there are certain things that have to be hammered out in advance. So don't start telling me you don't know who to get hold of, just do it, or you'll lose a lot of Brownie points with the pigs who think they own you."

It was mid-afternoon but a wintery dusk had settled over London, and Ned's little office in the Russia House was bathed in twilight. He had put his feet on his desk and was sitting back in his chair, eyes closed and a dark whisky at his elbow—not by any means, I quickly realised, his first of the day.

"Is Clive Without India still cloistered with the Whitehall nobles?" he asked me, with a tired levity.

"He's at the American Embassy settling the shopping list."

"I thought no mere Brit was allowed near the shopping list."

"They're talking principle. Sheriton has to sign a declaration appointing Barley an honorary American. Clive has to add a citation."

"Saying what?"

"That he's a man of honour and a fit and proper person."

"Did you draft it for him?"

"Of course."

"Silly fellow," said Ned with an air of dreamy reproof. "They'll hang you." He leaned back and closed his eyes.

"Is the shopping list really worth so much?" I asked. I had a sense, for once, of being more practically disposed than Ned was.

"Oh it's worth everything," Ned replied carelessly. "If any of it's worth anything, that is."

"Do you mind telling me why?"

I had not been admitted to the inmost secrets of the Bluebird material, but I knew that if I ever had been I would not have been able to make head or tail of them. But conscientious Ned had taken himself to night-school. He had sat at the feet of our in-house boffins and lunched our grandest defence scientists at the Athenaeum in order to bone up.

"Interface," he said with contempt. "Mutually assured bedlam. We track their toys. They track ours. We watch each other's archery contests without either of us knowing which targets the other side is aiming at. If they're aiming for London, will they hit Birmingham? What's error? What's deliberate? Who's approaching zero-CEP?" He caught my bewilderment and was pleased with himself. "We watch them lob their ICBMs into the Kamchatka Peninsula. But can they lob them down a Minuteman silo? We don't know and they don't. Because the big stuff on either side has never been tested under war conditions. The test trajectories are not the trajectories they'll use when the fun starts. The earth, God bless her, is not a perfect globe. How can she be at her age? Her density varies. So does the old girl's gravitational pull when things fly over her, like missiles and warheads. Enter bias. Our targeteers try to compensate for it in their calibrations. Goethe tried. They pour in data from earth-watch satellites, and perhaps they succeed better than Goethe did. Perhaps they don't. We won't know till the blessed balloon goes up, and nor will they, because you can only try the real thing once." He stretched luxuriously as if the topic pleased him. "So the camps divide. The hawks cry, 'The Sovs are pinpoint! They can knock the smile off the arse of a fly at ten thousand miles!' And all the doves can reply is 'We don't know what the Sovs can do, and the Sovs don't know what the Sovs can do. And nobody who doesn't know whether his gun works or not is going to shoot first. It's the uncertainty that keeps us honest,' say the doves. But that is not an argument that satisfies the literal American mind, you see, because the literal American mind does not like to grapple with fuzzy concepts or grand visions. Not at its literal field level. And what Goethe was saying was an even larger heresy. He was saying that the uncertainty was all there was. Which I rather agree with. So the hawks hated him and the doves had a ball and hanged themselves from the chandelier." He drank again. "If Goethe had only backed the pinpoint boys instead, everything would have been fine," he said reprovingly.

"And the shopping list?" I asked him again.

He peered whimsically into his glass. "The targeting of one side, my dear Palfrey, is based on that side's assumptions about the other side. And vice versa. *Ad infinitum*. Do we harden our silos? If the enemy can't hit them, why should we bother? Do we superharden them—even if we know how—at a cost of billions? We're already doing so, as a matter of fact, though it's not much sung about. Or do we protect them imperfectly with SDI at a cost of more billions? Depends what our prejudices are and who signs our pay cheque. Depends whether we're manufacturers or taxpayers. Do we put our rockets on trains or autobahns or park them in country lanes, which happens to be this month's flavour? Or do we say it's all junk anyway, so to hell with it?"

"So is it ending or beginning?" I asked.

He shrugged. "When did it ever end? Turn on your television set, what do you see? The leaders of both sides hugging each other. Tears in their eyes. Looking more like each other every day. *Hooray, it's all over!* Bollocks. Listen to the insiders and you realise the picture hasn't altered by a brush-stroke."

"And if I turn my television off? What will I see then?"

He had ceased to smile. Indeed his good face was more serious than I had ever seen it before, though his anger—if such it was—seemed to be directed at no one but himself.

"You'll see *us*. Hiding behind our grey screens. Telling each other we keep the peace."

17

The elusive truth that Ned was speaking of came out slowly and in a series of distorted perceptions, which is generally the case in our secret overworld.

At 6 p.m. Barley was seen to "exit" the VAAP offices, as our screens now insisted on advising us, and there was a flurry of apprehension that he might be drunk, for Zapadny was a drinking buddy and a farewell vodka with him was likely to be just that. Barley emerged, Zapadny with him. They embraced fulsomely on the doorstep, Zapadny flushed and a little excitable in his movements and Barley rather rigid, hence the watchers' worry that he was drunk, and their rather odd decision to photograph him—as if by freezing the moment they might somehow sober him up. And since this is the last photograph of him on the file, you may imagine how much attention has been paid to it. Barley has Zapadny in his arms, and there is strength to their embrace, at least on Barley's side. In my imagination, if no one else's, it is as if Barley is holding the poor fellow up in order to give him the courage to keep his half of the bargain; as if he is literally breathing courage into him. And the pink is weird. VAAP is a former school on Bolshaya Bronnaya Street in the centre of Moscow. It was built, I guess, at the turn of the century, with large windows and a plaster façade. And this plaster was painted in that year a light pink, which in the photograph is transformed to a flaming orange, presumably by the last rays of a red sun. The entwined men are thus caught in an unholy scarlet halo like a red flash. One of the watchers even gained the entrance hall on the pretext of visiting the cafeteria, and tried to achieve the reverse shot. But a tall man stood in his way, watching the scene on the pavement. Nobody has identified him. At the news-stand, a second man, also tall, is drinking from a mug, but not with much conviction, for his eyes too are turned to the two embracing figures outside.

The watchers took no note of the scores of people who had passed in and out of the VAAP building during the two hours Barley had been in the place—how could they? They had no idea whether the visitors had come to buy copyrights or secrets.

Barley returned to his hotel where he had a drink in the bar with a bunch of publishing cronies, among them Henziger, who was able to confirm, to London's relief, that Barley was not drunk—to the contrary, that he was calm and in thoughtful spirits.

Barley did mention in passing that he was expecting a phone call from one of Zapadny's outriders—"We're still trying to stitch up the Trans-Siberian thing." And at about 7 p.m. he suddenly confessed himself ravenous, so Henziger and Wicklow took him through to the Japanese restaurant, together with a couple of jolly girls from Simon & Schuster whom Wicklow was counting on for light relief to ease Barley's passage to his late-evening rendezvous.

Over dinner Barley sparkled so brightly that the girls tried to persuade him to come back to the National with them, where a party was being thrown by a group of American publishers. Barley replied that he had a date but might come on afterwards if it didn't run too long.

Exactly at 8 p.m. by Wicklow's watch, Barley was summoned to the telephone and took the call in the restaurant, not five yards from where the party was sitting. Wicklow and Henziger strained, as a matter of routine, to catch his words. Wicklow recalls hearing "That's all that matters to me." Henziger thinks he heard "We've got a deal" but it might have been *not* a deal" or even "not yet real."

Either way, Barley was cross when he resumed his seat and complained to Henziger that the bastards were still holding out for too much money, which Henziger regarded more as a sign of his internal stress than of any great concern for the Trans-Siberian project.

Quarter of an hour later the phone rang again and Barley returned from his conversation smiling. "We're on," he told Henziger jubilantly. "Sealed, signed and delivered. They never go back on a handshake." At which Henziger and Wicklow broke out clapping and Henziger remarked that "we could do with a few more of *them* in Moscow."

It seems not to have occurred to either man that Barley had never before shown so much enthusiasm for a publishing agreement. But then what were they supposed to be looking for, except the night's great coup?

Barley's dinner conversation was later painstakingly reconstructed, without result. He was talkative but not excitable. His subject was jazz, his idol was Slim Gaillard. The great ones were always outlaws, he maintained. Jazz was nothing if not protest. Even its own rules had to be broken by the real improvisers, he said.

And everyone agreed with him, yes, yes, long live dissent, long live the individual over the grey men! Except nobody saw it that way. And again, why should they?

At 9:10 p.m., with less than two hours to kill, Barley announced that he would stretch out in his room for a bit, he had letters to write and business to clear up. Both Wicklow and Henziger offered to give him a hand because they had orders not to leave him to himself if they could avoid it. But Barley declined their offers and they could not insist.

So Henziger took up his post in the next-door room and Wicklow placed himself in the lobby while Barley stretched out, though in reality he cannot have stretched out even for a second, for what he accomplished verges on the heroic.

Five letters were traced to this short span, not to mention two telephone calls to England, one to each of his children, both monitored within the United Kingdom and bounced through to Grosvenor Square but neither of operational consequence. Barley was merely concerned to catch up with family news and enquire after his grand-daughter, aged four. He insisted she be brought to the telephone, but she was too shy or too tired to talk to him. When his daughter Anthea asked him how his love-life was, he replied "complete," which was held to be an unusual sort of reply, but then the circumstances were not usual.

Ned alone remarked that Barley had said nothing about returning to England the next day, but Ned was by now a voice in the wilderness and Clive was seriously considering taking him off the case altogether.

Barley also wrote two shorter letters, one to Henziger, one to Wicklow. And since they were not tampered with, so far as the laboratories could afterwards determine, and since—even more remarkable—the hotel delivered them to the correct room numbers promptly at eight o'clock next morning, it was assumed that these letters were in some way part of the package that Barley had negotiated while he was inside the VAAP building.

The letters advised the two men that if they left the country quietly that day, taking Mary Lou with them, no harm would come to them. Barley had a warm word for each.

"Wickers, there's a real publisher in you. Go for it!"

And for Henziger, "Jack, I hope this won't mean you take premature retirement in Salt Lake City. Tell them you never trusted me anyway. I didn't trust me, so why should you?"

No homilies, no apt quotations from his large, untidy store. Barley, it seemed, was coping very well without the assistance of other people's wisdom.

At ten o'clock, he left the hotel accompanied by Henziger only, and they had themselves dropped on the northern outskirts of the town where Cy and Paddy were once more waiting in the safe truck. This time Paddy was driving. Henziger sat beside him and Barley got in the back with Cy, slipped off his coat and let Cy put on the microphone harness and give him the latest operational intelligence: that Goethe's plane from Saratov had arrived in Moscow on time, and that a figure answering Goethe's description had been observed entering Igor's apartment block forty minutes ago.

Soon afterwards, lights had come up in the windows of the target flat.

Cy then handed Barley two books, one a paperback copy of *From Here to Eternity* which contained the shopping list, the other a fatter volume, leather bound, which was a concealment device containing a sound-baffler to be activated by pulling open the front cover. Barley had played with one in London and was proficient in its use. His body microphones were tuned to defeat the impulses of the device, but normal wall microphones were not. The disadvantage of the baffler was also known to him. Its presence in the room was detectable. If Igor's flat was microphoned, then the listeners would at once be aware that a baffler was being used. This risk had been passed by both London and Langley as acceptable.

The other risk had not been considered, namely that the device might fall into the hands of the opposition. It was still in the prototype stage and a small fortune and several years of research had been lavished on its development.

At 10:54 p.m., just as Barley was leaving the safe truck, he handed Paddy an envelope and said, "This is for Ned personally in case anything happens to me." Paddy slipped the envelope in his inside jacket pocket. He noticed that it was a fat envelope and, so far as he could see in the half-light, it was not addressed.

The most lively account of Barley's walk to the foot of the apartment block was provided not by the military reportese of Paddy, still less by the Haig-speak of Cy, but in the boisterous tones of his good friend Jack Henziger, who escorted him to the entrance. Barley did not utter, he said. Neither did Jack. They'd no wish to be identified as foreigners.

"We walked alongside of each other out of step," Henziger said. "He has this long step, mine's short. It bothered me we couldn't keep step. The apartment house was one of these brick monsters they have out there with like a mile of concrete around them, and we kept on walking without getting anywhere. It's like one of those dreams, I thought. You keep on running but you don't make any distance. Very hot, the air. Sweaty. I'm sweating, but Barley's cool. He was collected, no question. He looked great. He looked straight into my eyes. He wished me a lot of luck. He was at peace with himself. I felt it."

Shaking hands, Henziger nevertheless had a momentary impression that Barley was angry about something. Perhaps angry against Henziger, for now in the half-dark he seemed determined to avoid Henziger's eye.

"Then I thought, Maybe he's mad at Bluebird for getting him into this. Then I thought, Maybe he's mad at all of us, but too polite to say it. Like he was being very British somehow, very laid back, very understated, keeping it all inside."

Ninety seconds later, as they were preparing to leave, Cy and Paddy saw a silhouette at Igor's window and took it to be Barley's. The right hand was adjusting the top of the curtain, which was the agreed signal to say "All's well." They drove away and left the surveillance of the apartment to the irregulars, who covered each other in shifts all night, but the light in the apartment stayed burning and Barley didn't come out.

One theory out of hundreds is that he never went up to the apartment at all, and that they took him straight through the building and out the other side, and that the figure in the window was one of their own people—for instance, one of the tall men in the photograph taken in the VAAP foyer that afternoon. It never seemed to me to matter, but to the experts for some reason it did. When a problem threatens to engulf you, there's nothing like irrelevant detail to keep your head above water.

Speculation about Barley's disappearance began slowly and built throughout the night. Optimists like Bob, and for a while Sheriton, clung on till dawn and after. Barley and Bluebird had drunk themselves under the table again, they kept insisting in order to keep each other's spirits up. It was Peredelkino all over again—a re-run, no question, they told each other.

Then for a short while they worked up a kidnap theory, until soon after five-thirty in the morning—thanks to the time difference—when Henziger and Wicklow had their letters and Wicklow without further fuss took a cab to the British Embassy, where the Soviet guards at the gate did not obstruct him. The result was a flash signal to Ned, decypher yourself, from Paddy. Meanwhile, Cy was putting through a similar message to Langley, Sheriton and anyone else who was still willing to listen to a man whose Moscow days looked like being over very soon.

Sheriton took the news with his customary phlegm. He read Cy's telegram, he looked around the room and realised that the whole team was watching him—the smart girls, the boys in ties, loyal Bob, ambitious Johnny with his gunman's eyes. And of the Brits, Ned, myself and Brock, for Clive had prudently discovered urgent business elsewhere. There was a lot of the actor in Sheriton, just as there was in Henziger, and he used it now. He stood up, he hauled at his waistband, he massaged his face like a man reckoning he needed a shave.

"Well, boys. Better put the chairs on the tables till next time."

Then he walked over to Ned, who was still sitting at his desk studying Paddy's telegram, and he laid a hand on Ned's shoulder.

"Ned, I owe you dinner some time," he said.

Then he walked over to the door and unhooked his new Burberry and buttoned himself into it and departed, followed after a moment by Bob and Johnny.

Others did not bow out so elegantly, least of all the barons of the twelfth floor.

Once again, a committee of enquiry was formed.

Names should be named. Nobody should be spared. Heads must roll.

The Deputy to chair it, Palfrey to be secretary.

Another purpose of such committees, I discovered, is to impart a sense of ceremony to events that have passed off without any. We were extremely solemn.

The first to be heard, as usual, were the conspiracy theorists, who were recruited in short order from the Foreign Office, the Defence Ministry and a rather unlovely body called the Informal Consultants, which consisted of industrial and academic scientists who fancied themselves as Sunday spies. These amateur espiocrats commanded huge influence around the Whitehall bazaars, and were heard at inordinate length by the committee. A professor from Edinburgh addressed us for five full pipe-loads and nearly gassed us all, but nobody had the nerve to tell him to put the damn thing out.

The first great question was, what would happen next? Would there be expulsions, a scandal? What would become of our Moscow station? Had any of the irregulars been compromised?

The audio truck, though Soviet property, was an American problem, and its abrupt disappearance caused hushed concern among those who had favoured its use.

The question of who is expelled for what is never a plain one, for heads of station in Moscow, Washington and London are these days declared to their host countries. Nobody in Moscow Centre had any illusions about Paddy's activities, or Cy's. Their cover was not designed to protect them from the opposition, but from the gaze of the real world.

In any case, they were not expelled. Nobody was expelled. Nobody was arrested. The irregulars, who were stood down indefinitely, went peaceably about their cover jobs.

The absence of a retaliatory gesture was quickly seen by Western pundits as vastly significant.

A conciliatory move in the season of *glasnost?*

A clear signal to us that the Bluebird was a gambit to obtain the American shopping list?

Or a less clear signal to us that the Bluebird material was accurate, but too embarrassing to acknowledge?

The battle-lines were set. Somewhat along the principle that Ned had already explained to me, doves and hawks on both sides of the Atlantic once more gleefully parted company.

If the Sovs are sending us a signal that the material is accurate, why then clearly the material is inaccurate, said the hawks.

And vice versa, said the doves.

And vice versa again, said the hawks.

Papers written, feuds waged. Promotions, sackings, pensions, medals, lateral postings and downgradings. But no consensus. Just the usual triumph of the fattest, disguised as rational deduction.

In our committee Ned alone refused to join the dance. He seemed cheerfully determined to accept the blame. "The Bluebird was straight and Barley was straight," he repeated to the committee over and again, without once losing his good humour. "There was no deception by anyone, except where we deceived ourselves. It was we who were crooked. Not the Bluebird."

Soon after he had delivered himself of this judgment, it was agreed he was under mental stress and his attendance was required more sparingly.

Oh, and note was taken. Passively, since active verbs have an unpleasant way of betraying the actor. Very serious note. Taken all over the place.

Note was taken that Ned had failed to advise the twelfth floor of Barley's drunken breakout after his return from Leningrad.

Note was taken that Ned had requisitioned all manner of resources on that same night, for which he had never accounted, among them Ben Lugg and the services of the head listener Mary, who sufficiently overcame her loyalty to a brother officer to give the committee a lurid account of Ned's high-handedness. Demanding illegal taps! Imagine! Faulting telephones! The liberty!

Mary was pensioned off soon after this and now lives in a rage in Malta, where it is feared she is writing her memoirs.

Note was also taken, if regretfully, of the questionable conduct of our Legal Adviser dePalfrey—I even got my "de" back—who had failed to justify his use of the Home Secretary's delegated authority in the full knowledge that this was required of him by the secretly agreed Procedures Governing the Service's Activities as Amended by et cetera, and in accordance with paragraph something of a deniable Home Office protocol.

The heat of battle was, however, taken into account. The Legal Adviser was not pensioned off, neither did he take himself to Malta. But he was not exonerated either. A partial pardon at best. A Legal Adviser should not have been so close to an operation. An inappropriate use of the Legal Adviser's skills. The word "injudicious" was passed around.

It was also noted with regret that the same Legal Adviser had drafted a glowing testimonial of Barley for Clive's signature not forty-eight hours before Barley's disappearance, thus enabling Barley to take possession of the shopping list, though presumably not for long.

In my spare hours, I drew up Ned's terms of severance and thought nervously about my own. Life inside the Service might have its limitations but the thought of life outside it terrified me.

The announcement of Bluebird's passing provided a temporary setback to our committee's deliberations, but it soon recovered. The offending item was a six-line affair in *Pravda,* carefully pitched to be neither too much nor too little, reporting the death after illness of the distinguished physicist Professor Yakov Savelyev of Leningrad and listing his several decorations. He had died of natural causes—the bulletin assured us—soon after delivering an important lecture to the military academy at Saratov.

Ned took the day off when this news reached him, and the day became three days, "a light flu." But the conspiracy theorists had a ball.

Savelyev was not dead.

He had been dead all along, and the version we had dealt with was an imposter.

He was doing what he had always been doing, running the Scientific Disinformation Section of the KGB.

His material was vindicated, was not vindicated.

It was worthless.

It was pure gold.

It was smoke.

It was a truthful message of peace sent to us at immense risk by the moderates inside Moscow's ruling ranks in order to show us that the Soviet nuclear sword had rusted in its scabbard and the Soviet nuclear shield had more holes in it than a colander.

It was a fiendish plot to persuade the American faint-hearts to take their fingers off the nuclear trigger.

In short, there was enough for everyone to get his teeth into.

And, because in the symbiotic relationship that exists between belligerent states nothing can take place in the one without setting off a mirror reaction in the other, a counter-industry grew up and the history of the American part in the Bluebird affair was hastily rewritten.

Langley knew all along that the Bluebird was bad, said the counter-industry.

Or that Barley was.

Or that both of them were.

Sheriton and Brady were playing double-double games, said the counter-industry. Their one aim was to plant the smoke convincingly and steal another march on the Russians in the endless struggle for the Margin of Safety.

Sheriton was a genius.

Brady was a genius.

They were all, all geniuses!

Sheriton had scored a brilliant coup. Brady had.

The Agency was staffed by nothing but brilliant strategists who were quite unlike their dismal counterparts in the overt world. God preserve the Agency. Where would we be without it?

As if all this were not enough, new tiers of possibility were added to the old. For example, that Sheriton had been the unwitting instrument of the Pentagon and Defense. It was they who had prepared the phoney shopping list and they who had known all along that the Bluebird was a plant.

And each fresh rumour had to be taken seriously in its turn, even if the only real mystery was who had fabricated it or why. The answer, in many cases, appeared to be Russell Sheriton, who was fighting for his hide.

As to the Bluebird, if he had not died of natural causes, he was certainly doing so now.

Ned alone, returned from his self-imposed vigil, was once more so crass as to speak the likely truth. "The Bluebird was straight and we killed him," he said roundly, at the first meeting he attended. He was not invited to the next one.

And all this while our search for Barley did not let up, even if there were those of us who were glad not to find him. We edged towards him, round him and, too often, away from him. But we were honourable men. We never let up.

But what had Barley traded—and for what?

What were the Russians prepared to buy from him—from Barley, who till now had only needed an expensive lunch, paid for most likely out of his own pocket, to talk himself into an irreversible loss?

He was blown, after all! To smithereens! Already by the time he went to them! And knew it!

What had he got to offer them that they couldn't help themselves to? We are talking after all of torture, of the foulest methods, and registers of agony from which even the return is unimaginable hell. The Russians might be improving their image, but nobody seriously supposed that they were going to abandon overnight methods that had stood them in good stead for thousands of years.

The first and most obvious answer was the shopping list. Barley could tell the Russians baldly he would not obtain it from his masters until he had the necessary assurances. And that he would sooner boil in oil for the rest of his life than fetch the shopping list for free.

And they believed him. They saw that they would have to go without the shopping list if they didn't play his game. And because the grey men of either side are as scared of self-sacrifice as they are of love, the tender sages of the KGB evidently preferred to deal with the part of him they understood, rather than meddle with the part they didn't.

They knew he had the power to refuse them, to say, "No, I will not fetch the shopping list. No, I will not walk into Igor's apartment until you have given me your more than solemn word."

They knew, when they had listened to him, that he had the strength. And, like us, they were a little embarrassed by it.

And Barley—as he had told Henziger and Wicklow at dinner—had never met a Russian yet who could give his solemn word and walk away from it. He was not talking of politics, of course—just business.

And in return? What did Barley buy with what he sold?

Katya.

Matvey.

The twins.

Not a bad deal. Real people in exchange for unreal arguments.

For himself? Nothing. Nothing that could conceivably modify the strength of his demand on account of those whom he had taken into his protection.

And little by little it became clear that Barley for once in his life had hammered out a first-rate contract. If the Bluebird was a lost cause, Katya and her children showed every sign of being a saved one. She remained at October, she was sighted at the occasional reception, she answered her telephone at home and at her office. The twins still went to school and sang the same daft songs. Matvey wandered his amiable ways.

Soon, therefore, another great theory added itself to the rest. "The Sovs are engaging in an internal cover-up," it ran. "They do not wish to give currency to Bluebird's revelations of incompetence."

So the needle swung the other way for a while and Bluebird's material was deemed genuine. But not for long.

"This is what they *want* us to believe!" a man of power cried.

So the needle swung hastily back to where it was before, because nobody wants to be made a fool of.

But Barley's deal held. Katya did not lose her privileges, her red card, her apartment, her job or even, as the months went by, her looks. At first, it was true, the reports spoke of the pallor of widowhood, of an unkempt appearance and long absences from work. And clearly nobody had promised Barley that she would not be invited to make a voluntary statement about her relationship with the late Bluebird.

But gradually, after a becoming period of withdrawal, her ebullience reasserted itself and she was seen about.

And of Barley himself?

The trail went hot, then cold, then very cold indeed.

Formal letters of resignation, postmark Lisbon, were received by his aunts within a few days of the book fair and bore the marks of Barley's earlier style—a general weariness of publishing, the industry has outgrown itself, time to turn his hand to other things while he still has a few good years ahead of him.

As to his immediate plans, he proposed "to lose himself for a while" and explore unusual places. So it was clear that he was not in Russia any more.

Seemingly clear, that is.

And after all, he said so himself. So did the pretty girl in the Barry Martin Travel Agency, which has its offices in the Mezhdunarodnaya. Mr. Scott Blair had decided he would fly to Lisbon instead of back to London, she said. A courier from VAAP brought his ticket. She rewrote it and booked him on the Aeroflot direct flight, leaving on the Monday at 1120 hours, arriving Lisbon 1530, stopping Prague.

And somebody used that ticket. A tall man, spoke to nobody, a Barley to the life, or nearly. Tall like the men in the VAAP lobby perhaps, but we checked him anyway. We checked him all along the line and the line only stopped when it reached Tina, Barley's Lisbon housekeeper. Yes, yes! Tina had heard from him, she told Merridew—a nice postcard from Moscow saying he'd met a lady-friend and they were going to take a holiday!

Merridew was profoundly relieved to learn that Barley had not, after all, returned to his patch.

Then over the next months a picture of Barley's after-life began to form before it disappeared again.

A West German drug-smuggler while in detention heard that a man of Barley's description was under interrogation in a prison near Kiev. A cheerful fellow, said the German. Popular with the inmates. Free. Even the guards gave him the odd grudging smile.

An adventurous French motoring couple returning home had been assisted by a "tall friendly Englishman" who spoke some French to them when they were involved in a traffic pile-up with a Soviet limousine near Smolensk. Nobody was hurt. Six foot, brown floppy hair, polite, with a big laugh, and tended by these burly Russians.

And one day near Christmas, not long after Ned had formally handed over the Russia House, a signal came in from Havana reporting a Cuban source to the effect that an Englishman was under special detention at a political jail near Minsk, and that he sang a lot.

Sang? went the outraged signal back. Sang about *what?*

Sang Satchmo, came Havana's reply. Source was a jazz fiend, like the Englishman.

And the text of Barley's letter to Ned?

It remains a small mystery of the affair that it never reached the file, and there is no record of it in the official history of the Bluebird case. I think Ned hung on to it as something he cared about too much to file.

So that should be the end of the story, or rather the story should have no end. Barley, in the judgment of the knowing, was all set to take his place among the other shadows that haunt the darker byways of Moscow society—the trodden-out defectors and spies, the traded ones and the untrusted ones with their pathetic wives and pallid minders, sharing out their dwindling rations of Western treats and Western memories.

He should have been spotted after a few years, accidentally but on purpose, at a party where a lucky British journalist was mysteriously present. And perhaps, if times remained the same, he would be fitted out with some taunting piece of disinformation, or invited to throw a little pepper into the eyes of his former masters.

And indeed that was the very ritual that seemed to be unfolding when a flash telegram from Paddy's successor reported that a tall sandy Englishman had been sighted—not only sighted, heard—playing tenor saxophone at a newly opened club in the old town, one year to the day after his disappearance.

Clive was hauled from his bed, signals flew between London and Langley, the Foreign Office was asked to take a view. They did, and it was unequivocal for once —*not our problem and not yours.* They seemed to feel the Russians were better equipped to muzzle Barley than we were. After all, the Russians had obliged before.

Next day a second telegram arrived, this time from fat Merridew in Lisbon. Barley's housekeeper, Tina, with whom Merridew had reluctantly maintained relations, had been instructed to prepare the flat for the arrival of her master.

But *how* instructed? asked Merridew.

By telephone, she replied, Senhor Barley had telephoned her.

Telephoned you where *from,* you stupid woman?

Tina hadn't asked and Barley hadn't said. Why should she ask where he was, if he was coming to Lisbon any day?

Merridew was appalled. He was not the only one. We advised the Americans, but Langley had suffered a collective loss of memory. They near as nothing asked us, Barley who? There is a public notion that services such as ours take violent retribution against those who have betrayed their secrets. Well, and sometimes it is true, they do—though seldom against people of Barley's class. But in this case it was immediately clear that nobody, and least of all Langley, had any wish to make a shining beacon out of somebody they would greatly prefer to forget. Better to square him, they agreed—and keep the Americans out of it.

I mounted the staircase apprehensively. I had declined the protective services of Brock, and Merridew's half-hearted offer of support. The stairwell was dark and steep and inhospitable, and unpleasantly silent. It was early evening but we knew he was at home. I pressed the bell but did not hear it ring, so I rapped the door with my knuckles. It was a stubby little door, thickly panelled. It reminded me of the boat-house on the island. I heard a step inside and at once stood back, I still don't know quite why, but I suppose it was a kind of fear of animals. Would he be fierce, would he be angry or over-effusive, would he throw me down the stairs or fling his arms round me? I was carrying a briefcase and I remember transferring it to my left hand as if to be ready to protect myself. Though, God knows, I am not a fighting man. I smelt fresh paint. There was no eyehole in the door, and it was flush against its iron lintel. He had no way of knowing who was there before he opened to me. I heard a latch slip. The door swung inward.

"Hullo, Harry," he said.

So I said, "Hullo, Barley." I was wearing a lightweight dark suit, blue in preference to grey. I said, "Hullo, Barley," and waited for him to smile.

He was thinner, he was harder and he was straighter, with the result that he had become very tall indeed, taller than me by a head. You're a nerveless traveller, I remember thinking as I waited. It was what Hannah in her early days used to say we should both of us learn to become. The old untidy gestures had left him. The discipline of small spaces had done its work. He was trim. He was wearing jeans and an old cricket shirt with the sleeves rolled to the elbow. He had splashes of white paint on his forearms and a smear of it across his forehead. I saw a step-ladder behind him and a half-whited wall, and at the centre of the room heaps of books and gramophone records partly protected with a dustsheet.

"Come for a game of chess, Harry?" he asked, still not smiling.

"If I could just talk to you," I said, as I might have said to Hannah, or anybody else to whom I was proposing a half-measure.

"Officially?"

"Well . . ."

He studied me as if he hadn't heard me, frankly and in his own time, of which he seemed to have a lot—much, I suppose, as one studies cellmates or interrogators in a world where the common courtesies tend to be dispensed with.

But his gaze had nothing downward or shameful in it, nothing of arrogance or shiftiness. It seemed, to the contrary, even clearer than I remembered it, as if it had settled itself permanently in the far regions to which it used occasionally to drift.

"I've got some cold plonk, if that'll do you," he said, and stood back to let me pass him while he watched me, before he closed the door and dropped the latch.

But he still didn't smile. His mood was a mystery to me. I felt I could understand nothing of him unless he chose to tell it me. Put another way, I understood everything about him that was within my grasp to understand. The rest, infinity.

There were dustsheets on the chairs as well but he pulled them off and folded them as if they were his bedding. Prison people, I have noticed over the years, take a long time to shake off their pride.

"What do you want?" he asked, pouring us each a glass from a flagon.

"They've asked me to tidy things up," I said. "Get some answers out of you. Assurances. Give you some in return." I had lost my way. "Whether we can help," I said. "Whether you need things. What we can agree on for the future and so on."

"I've got all the assurances I need, thanks," he said politely, lighting on the one word that seemed to catch his interest. "They'll move at their own pace. I've promised to keep my mouth shut." He smiled at last. "I've followed your advice, Harry. I've become a long-distance lover, like you."

"I was in Moscow," I said, fighting hard to find the flow to our conversation. "I went to the places. Saw the people. Used my own name."

"What is it?" he asked with the same courtliness. "Your name. What is it?"

"Palfrey," I said, leaving out the "de."

He smiled as if in sympathy, or recognition.

"The Service sent me over there to look for you. Unofficially but officially, as it were. Ask the Russians about you. Tidy things up. We thought it was time we found out what had happened to you. See if we could help."

And make sure they were observing the rules, I might have added. That nobody in Moscow was going to rock the boat. No silly leaks or publicity stunts.

"I told you what happened to me," he said.

"You mean in your letters to Wicklow and Henziger and people?"

"Yes."

"Well, naturally we knew the letters had been written under duress, if you wrote them at all. Look at poor Goethe's letter."

"Balls," he said. "I wrote them of my own free will."

I edged a little nearer to my message. And to the briefcase at my side.

"As far as we're concerned, you acted very honourably," I said, drawing out a file and opening it on my lap. "Everybody talks under duress and you were no exception. We're grateful for what you did for us and aware of the cost to you. Professionally and personally. We're concerned that you should have your full measure of compensation. On terms, naturally. The sum could be large."

Where had he learned to watch me like that? To withhold himself so steadily? To impart tension in others, when he seemed impervious to it himself?

I read him the terms, which were somewhat like Landau's in reverse. To stay out of the United Kingdom, and only to enter with our prior consent. Full and final settlement of all claims, his silence in perpetuity expressed *ex abundanti cautela* in half a dozen different ways. And a lot of money to sign here, provided—always and only provided—he kept his mouth shut.

He didn't sign, though. He was already bored. He waved the important pen away.

"What did you do with Walt, by the way? I brought a hat for him. Kind of tea-cosy in tiger stripes. Can't find the damn thing."

"If you send it to me, I'll see he gets it," I said.

He caught my tone and smiled at me sadly. "Poor old Walt. They've given him the push, eh?"

"We peak early in our trade," I said, but I couldn't look him in the eye, so I changed the subject. "I suppose you heard that your aunts have sold out to Lupus Books."

He laughed—not his old wild laughter, it was true, but a free man's laugh, all the same. "Jumbo! The old devil! Conned the Sacred Cow! Trust him!"

But he was at ease with the idea. He seemed to take genuine pleasure in the rightness of it. I am scared, as we all are in my trade, of people of good instinct. But I was able to share vicariously in his repose. He seemed to have developed universal tolerance.

She'll come, he told me as he gazed out at the harbour. They promised that one day she would come.

Not at once, and in their time, not in Barley's. But she would come, he had no doubt. Maybe this year, maybe next, he said. But something inside the mountainous bureaucratic Russian belly would heave and give birth to a mouse of compassion. He had no doubt of it. It would be gradual but it would happen. They had promised him.

"They don't break their promises," he assured me, and in the face of such trust it would have been churlish in me to contradict him. But something else was preventing me from voicing my customary scepticism. It was Hannah again. I felt she was begging me to let him live with his humanity, even if I had destroyed hers. "You think people never change because you don't," she had once said to me. "You only feel safe when you're disenchanted."

I suggested I take him out for food but he seemed not to hear. He was standing at the long window, staring at the harbour lights while I stared at his back. The same pose that he struck when we had first interviewed him here in Lisbon. The same arm holding out his glass. The same pose as on the island when Ned told him he had won. But straighter. Was he talking to me again? I realised he was. He was watching their ship arrive from Leningrad, he said. He was watching her hurry down the gangway to him with her children at her side. He was sitting with Uncle Matvey under the shade tree in the park below his window, where he had sat with Ned and Walter in the days before his manhood. He was listening to Katya's rendering of Matvey's heroic tales of endurance. He was believing in all the hopes that I had buried with me when I chose the safe bastion of infinite distrust in preference to the dangerous path of love.

I succeeded in persuading him to come to dinner, and as a kindness he let me pay. But I could buy nothing else from him, he signed nothing, he accepted nothing, he wanted nothing, he conceded nothing, he owed nothing and he wished the living lot of us, without anger, to the Devil.

But he had a splendid quiet. He wasn't strident. He was considerate of my feelings, even if he was too courteous to enquire what they were. I had never told him about Hannah, and I knew I never could, because the new Barley would have no patience with my unaltered state.

For the rest, he seemed concerned to make me a gift of his story, so that I would have something to take home to my masters. He brought me back to his flat and insisted I have a nightcap, and that nothing was my fault.

And he talked. For me. For him. Talked and talked. He told me the story as I have tried to tell it to you here, from his side as well as ours. He went on talking till it was light, and when I left at five in the morning, he was wondering whether he might as well finish that bit of wall before turning in. There was a lot to get ready, he explained. Carpets. Curtains. Bookshelves.

"It's going to be all right, Harry," he assured me as he showed me off the premises. "Tell them that."

Spying is waiting.

THE

SECRET

PILGRIM

*For Alec Guinness
with affection and thanks*

1

Let me confess to you at once that if I had not, on the spur of the moment, picked up my pen and scribbled a note to George Smiley inviting him to address my passing-out class on the closing evening of their entry course—and had Smiley not, against all my expectations, consented—I would not be making so free to you with my heart.

At the most, I would be offering you the sort of laundered reminiscence with which, if I am honest, I was a bit too inclined to regale my students: feats of secret chivalry, of the dramatic, the resourceful and the brave. And always, of course, the useful. I would be enthralling you with memories of night drops into the Caucasus, hazardous crossings by fast boat, beach landings, winking shore lights, clandestine radio messages that ceased in mid-transmission. Of silent heroes of the Cold War who, having made their contribution, modestly went to earth in the society they had protected. Of defectors-in-place snatched in the nick of time from the jaws of the opposition.

And to a point, yes, that is the life we lived. In our day we did those things, and some even ended well. We had good men in bad countries who risked their lives for us. And usually they were believed, and sometimes their intelligence was wisely used. I hope so, for the greatest spy on earth is worth nothing when it isn't.

And for the lighter note, over a second whisky in the Probationers' Mess, I would have picked out for them the occasion when a three-man reception team from the Circus, operating inside East Germany, and gallantly led by myself, lay freezing on a ridge in the Harz Mountains, praying for the flutter of an unmarked plane with its engines cut, and the blessed black parachute floating in its wake. And what did we find when our prayer was answered and we had slithered down an icefield to claim our treasure? Stones, I would tell my wide-eyed students. Chunks of honest Argyll granite. The despatchers at our Scottish airbase had sent us the training cannister by mistake.

That tale, at least, found a certain echo, even if some of my other offerings tended to lose their audience halfway through.

I suspect that my impulse to write to Smiley had been brewing in me longer than I realised. The idea was conceived during one of my regular visits to Personnel to discuss the progress of my students. Dropping in on the Senior Officers' Bar for a sandwich and a beer, I had bumped into Peter Guillam. Peter had played Watson to George's Sherlock Holmes in the long search for the Circus traitor, who turned out to be our Head of Operations, Bill Haydon. Peter had not heard from George for—oh, a year now, more. George had bought this cottage in North Cornwall somewhere, he said, and was indulging his dislike of the telephone. He had some kind of sinecure at Exeter University, and was allowed to use their library. Sadly I pictured the rest: George the lonely hermit on an empty landscape, taking his solitary walks and thinking his thoughts. George slipping up to Exeter for a little human warmth in his old age while he waited to take his place in the spies' Valhalla.

And Ann, his wife? I asked Peter, lowering my voice as one does when Ann's name comes up—for it was an open secret, and a painful one, that Bill Haydon had counted among Ann's many lovers.

Ann was Ann, said Peter, with a Gallic shrug. She had bits of family with grand houses on the Helford Estuary. Sometimes she stayed with them, sometimes she stayed with George.

I asked for Smiley's address. "Don't tell him I gave it you," said Peter as I wrote it down. With George, there had always been that certain kind of guilt about passing on his whereabouts—I still don't quite know why.

Three weeks later Toby Esterhase came down to Sarratt to give us his celebrated talk on the arts of clandestine surveillance on unfriendly soil. And of course he stayed for lunch, which was greatly enhanced for him by the presence of our first three girls. After a battle lasting as long as I had been at Sarratt, Personnel had finally decided that girls were all right after all.

And I heard myself trailing Smiley's name.

There have been times when I would not have entertained Toby in the wood-shed, and others when I thanked my Maker I had him on my side. But with the years, I am pleased to notice, one settles to people.

"Oh look here, my God, Ned!" Toby cried in his incurably Hungarian English, smoothing back his carefully pomaded mane of silver hair. "You mean you haven't heard?"

"Heard what?" I asked patiently.

"My dear fellow, George is chairing the Fishing Rights Committee. Don't they tell you anything down here in the sticks? I think I better take this up with the Chief actually, one to one. A word in his ear at the Club."

"Perhaps you'd tell me first what the Fishing Rights Committee is," I suggested.

"Ned, you know what? I think I get nervous. Maybe they took you off the list."

"Maybe they did at that," I said.

He told me anyway, as I knew he would, and I duly acted astonished, which gave him an even greater sense of his importance. And there is a part of me that remains astonished to this day. The Fishing Rights Committee, Toby explained for the benefit of the unblessed, was an informal working party made up of officers from Moscow Centre and the Circus. Its job, said Toby—who I really believe had lost any capacity to be surprised—was to identify intelligence targets of interest to both services and thrash out a system of sharing. "The idea actually, Ned, was to target the world's trouble spots," he said with an air of maddening superiority. — "I think they fix first the Middle East. Don't quote me, Ned, okay?"

"And you're telling me Smiley *chairs* this committee?" I asked incredulously when I had attempted to digest this.

"Well, maybe not much longer, Ned—Anno Domini and so forth. But the Russians were so frightfully keen to meet him, we brought him in to snip the tape. Give the old fellow a treat, I say. Stroke him a bit. Bunch of fivers in an envelope."

I didn't know which to marvel at the more: the notion of Toby Esterhase tripping to the altar with Moscow Centre, or of George Smiley presiding over the marriage. A few days later, with Personnel's permission, I wrote to the Cornish address Guillam had given me, adding diffidently that if George loathed public speaking half as much as I did, he should on no account accept. I had been a bit in the dumps till then, but when his prim little card arrived by return declaring him delighted, I felt a probationer myself, and just as nervous.

Two weeks after that, wearing a brand-new country suit for the occasion, I was standing at the barrier at Paddington Station, watching the elderly trains disgorge their middle-aged commuters. I don't think I had ever been quite so aware of Smiley's anonymity. Wherever I looked, I seemed to see versions of him: tubby, bespectacled gentlemen of a certain seniority, and every one of them with George's air of being slightly late for something he would rather not be doing. Then suddenly we had shaken hands and he was sitting beside me in the back of a Head Office Rover, stockier than I remembered him, and white-haired, it was true, but of a vigour and good humour I had not seen in him since his wife had her fatal fling with Haydon.

"Well, well, Ned. How do you like being a schoolmaster?"

"How do you like retirement?" I countered, with a laugh. "I'll be joining you soon!"

Oh, he loved retirement, he assured me. Couldn't get enough of it, he said wryly; I should have no fears of it at all. A little tutoring here, Ned, the odd paper to deliver there; walks, he'd even acquired a dog.

"I hear they hauled you back to sit on some extraordinary committee," I said. "Conspiring with the Bear, they say, against the Thief of Baghdad."

George does not gossip, but I saw his smile broaden. "Do they now? And your source would be Toby, no doubt," he said, and beamed contentedly upon the

dismal subtopian landscape while he launched into a diversionary story about two
old ladies in his village who hated each other. One owned an antique shop, the other
was very rich. But as the Rover continued its progress through once-rural Hertford-
shire, I found myself thinking less about the ladies of George's village than about
George himself. I was thinking that this was a Smiley reborn, who told stories about
old ladies, sat on committees with Russian spies and gazed on the overt world with
the relish of someone who has just come out of hospital.

That evening, squeezed into an elderly dinner jacket, the same man sat at my
side at Sarratt high table, peering benignly round him at the polished plate candle-
sticks and old group photographs going back to God knows when. And at the fit,
expectant faces of his young audience as they waited on the master's word.

"Ladies and gentlemen, Mr. George Smiley," I announced severely as I rose to
introduce him. "A legend of the Service. Thank you."

"Oh, I don't think I'm a legend at all," Smiley protested as he clambered to his
feet. "I think I'm just a rather fat old man wedged between the pudding and the
port."

Then the legend began talking, and I realised that I had never heard Smiley address
a social gathering before. I had assumed it was a thing he would be congenitally bad
at, like forcing his opinions on people, or referring to a joe by his real name. So the
sovereign way in which he addressed us surprised me before I had begun to fathom
the content. I heard his first few sentences and I watched my students' faces—not
always so obliging—lift and relax and light to him as they gave him first their
attention, then their trust and finally their support. And I thought, with an inner
smile of belated recognition: yes, yes, of course, this was George's other nature.
This was the actor who had always lain hidden in him, the secret Pied Piper. This
was the man Ann Smiley had loved and Bill Haydon had deceived and the rest of
us had loyally followed, to the mystification of outsiders.

There is a wise tradition at Sarratt that our dinner speeches are not recorded and
no notes are taken, and that no official reference may afterwards be made to what
was said. The guest of honour enjoyed what Smiley in his Germanic way called "the
fool's freedom," though I can think of few people less qualified for the privilege. But
I am nothing if not a professional, trained to listen and remember, and you must
understand also that Smiley had not spoken many words before I realised—as my
students were not slow to notice—that he was speaking straight into my heretical
heart. I refer to that other, less obedient person who is also inside me and whom,
if I am honest, I had refused to acknowledge since I had embarked on this final lap
of my career—to the secret questioner who had been my uncomfortable companion
even before a reluctant joe of mine called Barley Blair had stepped across the
crumbling Iron Curtain and, for reasons of love, and some sort of honour, had
calmly kept on walking, to the incredulity of the Fifth Floor.

The better the restaurant, we say of Personnel, the worse the news. "It's time
you handed on your wisdom to the new boys, Ned," he had told me over a
suspiciously good lunch at the Connaught. "*And* to the new *girls*," he added, with
a loathsome smirk. "They'll be letting them into the Church next, I suppose." He
returned to happier ground. "You know the tricks. You've kicked around. You've
had an impressive last lap running Secretariat. Time to put it all to advantage. We

think you should take over the Nursery and pass the torch to tomorrow's spies."

He had used a rather similar set of sporting metaphors, if I remembered rightly, when in the wake of Barley Blair's defection he had removed me from my post as Head of the Russia House and consigned me to that knacker's yard, the Interrogators' Pool.

He ordered up two more glasses of Armagnac. "How's your Mabel, by the way?" he continued, as if he had just remembered her. "Somebody told me she'd got her handicap down to twelve—ten, by God! Well. I trust you'll keep her away from me! So what do you say? Sarratt in the week, home to Tunbridge Wells at weekends, sounds to me like the triumphant crowning of a career. What do you say?"

So what *do* you say? You say what others have said before you. Those who can, do. Those who can't, teach. And what they teach is what they can't do any more, because either the body or the spirit or both have lost their singleness of purpose; because they have seen too much and suppressed too much and compromised too much, and in the end tasted too little. So they take to rekindling their old dreams in new minds, and warming themselves against the fires of the young.

And that brings me back to the opening bars of Smiley's speech that night, for suddenly his words were reaching out and grasping me. I had invited him because he was a legend of the past. Yet to the delight of all of us, he was turning out to be the iconoclastic prophet of the future.

I'll not bother you with the finer points of Smiley's introductory tour of the globe. He gave them the Middle East, which was obviously on his mind, and he explored the limits of colonial power in supposedly post-colonialist times. He gave them the Third World and the Fourth World and posited a Fifth World, and pondered aloud whether human despair and poverty were the serious concern of any wealthy nation. He seemed pretty confident they weren't. He scoffed at the idea that spying was a dying profession now that the Cold War had ended: with each new nation that came out of the ice, he said, with each new alignment, each rediscovery of old identities and passions, with each erosion of the old status quo, the spies would be working round the clock. He spoke, I discovered afterwards, for twice the customary length, but I didn't hear a chair creak or a glass clink—not even when they dragged him to the library and sat him in the throne of honour before the fire for more of the same, more heresy, more subversion. My children, hardened cases all of them, in love with George! I didn't hear a sound beyond the confident flow of Smiley's voice and the eager burst of laughter at some unexpected self-irony or confession of failure. You're only old once, I thought, as I listened with them, sharing their excitement.

He gave them case histories I had never heard, and which I was certain nobody in Head Office had cleared in advance—certainly not our Legal Adviser Palfrey, who in response to the openness of our former enemies had been battening down and double-locking every useless secret he could lay his obedient hands on.

He dwelt on their future rôle as agent-runners and, applying it to the altered world, vested in it the traditional Service image of mentor, shepherd, parent and befriender, as prop and marriage counsellor, as pardoner, entertainer and protector; as the man or woman who has the gift of treating the outrageous premise as an everyday affair, and so becomes his agent's partner in illusion. None of that had changed, he said. None of it ever would. He paraphrased Burns: "A spy's a spy for all that."

But no sooner had he lulled them with this sweet notion than he warned them of the death of their own natures that could result from the manipulation of their fellow men, and the truncation of their natural feeling.

"By being all things to all spies, one does rather run the risk of becoming nothing to oneself," he confessed sadly. "Please don't ever imagine you'll be unscathed by the methods you use. The end may justify the means—if it wasn't supposed to, I dare say you wouldn't be here. But there's a price to pay, and the price does tend to be oneself. Easy to sell one's soul at your age. Harder later."

He mixed the deadly serious with the deadly frivolous and made the difference small. Betweenwhiles he seemed to be asking the questions I had been asking of myself for most of my working life, but had never managed to express, such as: "Did it do any good?" And "What did it do to me?" And "What will become of us now?" Sometimes his questions were answers: George, we used to say, never asked unless he knew.

He made us laugh, he made us feel and, by means of his inordinate deference, he shocked us with his contrasts. Better still, he put our prejudices at risk. He got rid of the acceptance in me and revived the slumbering rebel that my exile to Sarratt had silenced. George Smiley, out of a clear sky, had renewed my search and confused me wonderfully.

Frightened people never learn, I have read. If that is so, they certainly have no right to teach. I'm not a frightened man—or no more frightened than any other man who has looked at death and knows it is for him. All the same, experience and a little pain had made me a mite too wary of the truth, even towards myself. George Smiley put that right. George was more than a mentor to me, more than a friend. Though not always present, he presided over my life. There were times when I thought of him as some kind of father to replace the one I never knew. George's visit to Sarratt gave back the dangerous edge to my memory. And now that I have the leisure to remember, that's what I mean to do for you, so that you can share my voyage and ask yourself the same questions.

2

There are some people," Smiley declared comfortably, favouring with his merry smile the pretty girl from Trinity Oxford whom I had thoughtfully placed across the table from him, "who, when their past is threatened, get frightened of losing everything they thought they had, and perhaps everything they thought they were as well. Now I don't feel that one bit. The purpose of *my* life was to end the time I lived in. So if my past were still around today, you could say I'd failed. But it's not around. We won. Not that the victory matters a damn. And perhaps we didn't win anyway. Perhaps they just lost. Or perhaps, without the bonds of ideological conflict to restrain us any more, our troubles are just beginning. Never mind. What matters is that a long war is over. What matters is the hope."

Removing his spectacles from his ears, he fumbled distractedly with his shirt front, looking for I could not imagine what, until I realised that it was the fat end of the necktie on which he was accustomed to polish his lenses. But an awkwardly assembled black bow tie provides no such conveniences, so he used the silk handkerchief from his pocket instead.

"If I regret anything at all, it's the way we wasted our time and skills. All the false alleys, and bogus friends, the misapplication of our energies. All the delusions we had about who we were." He replaced his spectacles and, as I fancied, turned his smile upon myself. And suddenly I felt like one of my own students. It was the sixties again. I was a fledgling spy, and George Smiley—tolerant, patient, clever George—was observing my first attempts at flight.

We were fine fellows in those days, and the days seemed longer. Probably no finer than my students today, but our patriotic vision was less clouded. By the end of my new-entry course I was ready to save the world if I had to spy on it from end to end. We were ten in my intake and after a couple of years of training—at the Sarratt Nursery, in the glens of Argyll and battle camps of Wiltshire—we waited for our first operational postings like thoroughbreds pining for the chase.

We too in our way had come to maturity at a great moment in history, even if it was the reverse of this one. Stagnation and hostility stared at us from every corner of the globe. The Red Peril was everywhere, not least on our own sacred hearth. The Berlin Wall had been up two years and by the looks of it would stay up for another two hundred. The Middle East was a volcano, just as it is now, except that in those days Nasser was our chosen British hate object, not least because he was giving Arabs back their dignity and playing hookey with the Russians into the bargain. In Cyprus, Africa and South East Asia the lesser breeds without the law were rising against their old colonial masters. And if we few brave British occasionally felt our power diminished by this—well, there was always Cousin America to cut us back into the world's game.

As secret heroes in the making, therefore, we had everything we needed: a righteous cause, an evil enemy, an indulgent ally, a seething world, women to cheer us, but only from the touchline, and best of all the Great Tradition to inherit, for the Circus in those days was still basking in its wartime glory. Almost all our leading men had earned their spurs by spying on the Germans. All of them, when questioned at our earnest, off-the-record seminars, agreed that when it came to protecting mankind against its own excesses, World Communism was an even darker menace than the Hun.

"You gentlemen have inherited a dangerous planet," Jack Arthur Lumley, our fabled Head of Training, liked to tell us. "And if you want my personal opinion, you're bloody lucky."

Oh, we wanted his opinion all right! Jack Arthur was a derring-do man. He had spent three years dropping in and out of Nazi-occupied Europe as if he were a regular house-guest. He had blown up bridges single-handed. He had been caught and escaped and caught again, no one knew how many times. He had killed men with his bare fingers, losing a couple in the fray, and when the Cold War came along to replace the hot one, Jack hardly noticed the difference. At the age of fifty-five he could still shoot you a grin on a man-sized target with a 9-millimetre Browning at twenty paces, pick your door lock with a paper clip, booby-trap a lavatory chain in thirty seconds or pin you helpless to the gym-mat in one throw. Jack Arthur had despatched us by parachute from Stirling bombers and landed us in rubber boats on Cornish beaches and drunk us under the table on mess nights. If Jack Arthur said it was a dangerous planet, we believed him to the hilt!

But it made the waiting all the harder. If I hadn't had Ben Arno Cavendish to share it with, it would have been harder still. There are only so many attachments you can serve around Head Office before your enthusiasm turns to gall.

Ben and I had been born under the same star. We were the same age, the same schooling, the same build, and within an inch of the same height. Trust the Circus to throw us together—we told each other excitedly; they probably knew it all along! We both had foreign mothers, though his was dead—the Arno came from his German side—and were both, perhaps by way of compensation, determinedly of the English extrovert classes—athletic, hedonistic, public-school, male, born to administer if not to rule. Though, as I look at the group photographs of our year, I see that Ben made a rather better job of the part than I did, for he possessed an air of maturity that in those days eluded me—he had the widow's peak and the confirmed jaw, a man superior to his youthfulness.

Which, for all I knew, was why Ben got the coveted Berlin job instead of me, running flesh-and-blood agents inside East Germany, while I was once more put on standby.

"We're lending you to the watchers for a couple of weeks, young Ned," said Personnel, with an avuncular complacency I was beginning to resent. "Be good experience for you, and they can do with a spare pair of hands. Plenty of cloak-and-dagger stuff. You like that."

Anything for a change, I thought, putting a brave face on it. For the past month I had bent my ingenuity to sabotaging the World Peace Conference in—let's say—Belgrade, from a dark desk on the Third Floor. Under the instruction of a slow-spoken superior who lunched for hours on end in the Senior Officers' Bar, I had enthusiastically re-routed delegates' trains, blocked their hotel plumbing and made anonymous bomb threats to their conference hall. For the month before that, I had crouched bravely in a stinking cellar next to the Egyptian Embassy at six every morning, waiting for a venal charlady to bring me, in exchange for a five-pound note, the contents of the Ambassadorial wastepaper basket from the previous day. By such modest standards, a couple of weeks riding around with the world's best watchers sounded like a free holiday.

"They're assigning you to Operation Fat Boy," Personnel said, and gave me the address of a safe house off Green Street in the West End. I heard the sound of ping-pong as I walked in, and a cracked gramophone record playing Gracie Fields. My heart sank, and once again I sent a prayer of envy to Ben Cavendish and his heroic agents in Berlin, the spy's eternal city. Monty Arbuck, our section leader, briefed us the same evening.

Let me apologise for myself in advance. I knew very little of other ranks in those days. I was of the officer caste—literally, for I had served with the Royal Navy—and found it perfectly natural that I had been born into the upper end of the social system. The Circus is nothing if not a little mirror of the England it protects, so it seemed equally right to me that our watchers and allied trades, such as burglars and eavesdroppers, should be drawn from the artisan community. You cannot follow a man for long in a bowler hat. A honed BBC voice is no passport to unobtrusiveness once you are outside London's golden mile, least of all if you are posing as a street hawker or a window cleaner or a post-office engineer. So you should see me, at best, as a callow young midshipman seated among his more experienced and less privileged shipmates. And you should see Monty not as he was, but as I saw him that evening, as a taut-minded gamekeeper with a chip on his shoulder. We were ten, including Monty: three teams of three, therefore, with a woman to each so that we could cover ladies' lavatories. That was the principle. And Monty our controller.

"Good evening, College," he said, placing himself before a blackboard and talking straight at me. "Always nice to have a touch of quality to raise the tone, I say."

Laughter all round, loudest from myself, a good sport to his men.

"Target for tomorrow, College, is His Right Royal Sovereign Highness Fat Boy, otherwise known as—"

Turning to the blackboard, Monty helped himself to a piece of chalk and laboriously scratched up a long Arab name.

"And the nature of our mission, College, is PR," he resumed. "I trust you know what PR is, do you? I have no doubt they teach you that at the spies' Eton?"

"Public Relations," I said, surprised to occasion so much merriment. For alas it turned out that in the watchers' vernacular the initials stood for Protect and Report, and that our task for tomorrow, and for as long as our royal visitor chose to remain our charge, was to ensure that no harm came to him, and to report to Head Office on his activities, whether social or commercial.

"College, you're with Paul and Nancy," Monty told me, when he had provided us with the rest of our operational intelligence. "You'll be number three in the section, College, and you'll kindly do *exactly* as you are told, irregardless."

But here I prefer to give you the background to Fat Boy's case not in Monty's words but in my own, and with the benefit of twenty-five years of hindsight. Even today, I can blush to think who I thought I was, and how I must have appeared to the likes of Monty, Paul and Nancy.

Understand first that licensed arms dealers in Britain regard themselves as some kind of rough-edged élite—did then, do now—and that they enjoy quite disproportionate privileges at the hands of the police, the bureaucracy and the intelligence services. For reasons I have never understood, their grisly trade puts them in a relationship of confidence with these bodies. Perhaps it's the illusion of reality they impart, of guns as the earthy truth of life and death. Perhaps, in the tethered minds of our officials, their wares suggest the same authority that is exerted by those who use them. I don't know. But I've seen enough of the street side of life in the years between to know that more men are in love with war than ever get a chance to fight one, and that more guns are bought to satisfy this love than for a pardonable purpose.

Understand also that Fat Boy was a most valued customer of this industry. And that our task of Protecting and Reporting was only one small part of a far larger undertaking; namely, the care and cultivation of a so-called friendly Arab state. By which was meant, and is meant to this day, currying favour, suborning and flattering its princelings with our English ways, wheedling favourable concessions in order to satisfy our oil addiction—and, along the way, selling enough British weaponry to keep the Satanic mills of Birmingham turning day and night. Which may have accounted for Monty's rooted distaste for our task. I like to think so anyway. Old watchers are famous for their moralising—and with reason. First they watch, later they think. Monty had reached the thinking stage.

As to Fat Boy, his credentials for this treatment were impeccable. He was the wastrel brother of the ruler of an oil-rich sheikdom. He was capricious, and prone to forget what he had bought before. And he arrived as billed, in the ruler's Boeing jet, at a military airport near London specially cleared for him, to have himself a little fun and do a little shopping—which we understood would include such fripperies as a couple of armoured Rolls-Royces for himself, half the trinkets at Cartier's for his women friends around the globe, a hundred or so of our not quite latest ground-to-air missile launchers, and a squadron or two of our not quite latest combat fighters for his royal brother. Not forgetting a succulent British government contract for spares, services and training which would keep the Royal Air Force and the arms manufacturers in clover for years to come. —Oh, and oil. We would have oil to burn. Naturally.

His retinue, apart from private secretaries, astrologers, flatterers, nannies, children and two tutors, comprised a personal doctor and three bodyguards.

Lastly there was Fat Boy's wife, and her codename is irrelevant because from Day One Monty's watchers dubbed her "the Panda" on account of the dark circles round her eyes when she was unveiled, and her wistful and solitary deportment, which gave the air of an endangered species. Fat Boy had a string of wives, but the Panda, though the oldest, was the most favoured, and perhaps the most tolerant of her husband's pleasures around town, for he liked nightclubs and he liked to gamble —tastes for which my fellow watchers cordially loathed him before he arrived, since it was known of him that he seldom went to bed before six in the morning, and never without losing about twenty times their combined annual salaries.

The party had rooms at a grand West End hotel, on two floors linked by a specially installed lift. Fat Boy, like many forty-year-old voluptuaries, was worried about his heart. He was also worried about microphones, and liked to use the lift as his safe room. So the Circus listeners had thoughtfully provided a microphone in the lift for him as well, which was where they reckoned to pick up their tidbits about the latest palace intrigues, or any unforeseen threat to Fat Boy's military shopping list.

And everything was running smoothly until Day Three, when one small unknown Arab man in a black overcoat with velvet collars appeared silently on our horizon. Or more accurately, in the ladies' lingerie department of a great Knightsbridge department store, where the Panda and her attendants were picking their way through a stack of frilly white undergarments spread over the glass counter. For the Panda also had her spies. And word had reached her that, on the day before, the Fat Boy himself had brooded fondly over the same articles, and even ordered a few dozen to be sent to an address in Paris where a favoured lady friend constantly awaited him in subsidised luxury.

Day Three, I repeat, and the morale of our three-strong unit under strain. Paul was Paul Skordeno, an inward man with a pocked complexion and a talent for ferocious invective. Nancy told me he was under a cloud, but wouldn't say what for.

"He *hit* a girl, Ned," she said, but I think now that she meant more than merely hit.

Nancy herself was all of five feet tall and in appearance a kind of licensed bag-lady. For her standard, as she called it, she wore lisle stockings and sensible rubber-soled walking shoes, which she seldom changed. What more she needed— scarves, raincoats, woollen hats of different colours—she took in a plastic carrier.

On surveillance duty our section worked eight-hour shifts always in the same formation, Nancy and Paul playing forward, young Ned trailing along behind as sweep. When I asked Skordeno whether we could vary the formation, he told me to get used to what I'd got. On our first day we had followed Fat Boy to Sandhurst, where a lunch had been organised in his honour. The three of us ate egg-and-chips in a café close to the main gates while Skordeno railed first against the Arabs, then against the Western exploitation of them, then to my distress against the Fifth Floor, whom he described as Fascist golfers.

"You a Freemason, College?"

I assured him I was not.

"Well, you'd best hurry up and join then, hadn't you? Haven't you noticed the saucy way Personnel shakes your hand? You'll never get to Berlin if you're not a Mason, College."

Day Two had been spent hanging around Mount Street while Fat Boy had himself measured for a pair of Purdy shotguns, first precariously brandishing a try-gun round the premises, then throwing a tantrum when he discovered he would have to wait two years before they were ready. Paul ordered me twice into the shop while this scene was unfolding, and seemed pleased when I told him the staff were becoming suspicious of my frivolous enquiries.

"I'd have thought it was your kind of place," he said, with his skull-like grin. "Huntin', shootin' and fishin'—they like that on the Fifth Floor, College."

The same night had found us sitting three up in a van outside a shuttered whorehouse in South Audley Street, and Head Office in a state of near panic. Fat Boy had only been holed up there two hours when he had telephoned the hotel and ordered his personal doctor to attend immediately. His heart! we thought in alarm. Should we go in? While Head Office dithered, we entertained visions of our quarry dead of a heart attack in the arms of some over-conscientious whore before he had signed the cheque for his obsolete fighter planes. It was not till four o'clock that the listeners laid our fears to rest. Fat Boy had been afflicted by a spell of impotence, they explained, and his doctor had been summoned to inject an aphrodisiac into the royal rump. We returned home at five, Skordeno drunk with anger, but all of us consoled by the knowledge that Fat Boy was due in Luton at midday to attend a grand demonstration of the nearly latest British tank, and we could count on a day's rest. But our relief was premature.

"The Panda wants to buy herself some pretties," Monty announced to us benignly on our arrival in Green Street. "Your lot's on. Sorry about that, College."

Which brings us to the lingerie department of the great Knightsbridge store, and to my moment of glory. Ben, I was thinking; Ben, I would trade one day of yours for five of mine. Then suddenly I wasn't thinking of Ben any more and I had ceased to envy him. I had drawn back into the privacy of a doorway and was speaking into the mouthpiece of the cumbersome radio set, which in those days was the best there was. I had selected the channel which gave me a direct line to base. It was the one Skordeno had told me not to use.

"The Panda's got a monkey on her back," I informed Monty in my calmest voice, using the approved watchers' jargon to describe a mysterious follower. "Five five, black curly hair, heavy moustache, aged forty, black overcoat, rubber-soled black shoes, Arab appearance. He was at the airport when Fat Boy's plane came in. I remember him. It's the same man."

"Stay on him" came Monty's laconic reply. "Paul and Nancy stick with the Panda, you stick with the monkey. Which floor?"

"One."

"Stay on him wherever he goes, keep talking to me."

"He could be carrying," I said as my eyes again fixed surreptitiously on the subject of my call.

"You mean he's pregnant?"

I didn't think that very funny.

Let me set the scene precisely, for it was more complicated than you may suppose. Our trio was not alone in following the Panda's retinue on its snail-paced shopping expedition. Wealthy Arab princesses do not arrive unannounced at great Knightsbridge stores. In addition to a pair of floorwalkers in black jackets and striped trousers, two very obvious house detectives had placed themselves at either archway with their feet apart and their hands curled at their sides, ready at any moment to grapple with whirling dervishes. As if that were not enough, Scotland Yard had that morning taken upon itself to provide its own brand of protection in the form of an iron-faced man in a belted raincoat who insisted on placing himself beside the Panda and glowering at anyone who came near. And finally, you must see Paul and Nancy in their Sunday best, their backs turned to everyone while they affected to study trays of negligés, and watched our quarry in the mirrors.

And all of this again, you understand, set in the hushed and scented privacy of the harem; in a world of flimsy undergarments, deep-pile carpets and languorous half-naked dummies—not to mention those kindly grey-haired lady attendants in black crêpe who, at a certain age, are deemed to have achieved a sufficiently unthreatening demeanour to preside over shrines of female intimacy.

Other men, I noticed, preferred not to enter the lingerie department at all, or hurried through it with averted gaze. My instinct would have been the same, had it not been for my recognition of this melancholy little man with his black moustache and passionate brown eyes, who unswervingly trailed the Panda's retinue at fifteen paces. If Monty had not appointed me sweep, I might not have seen him at all—or not then. But it was quickly clear that both he and I, by virtue of our different trades, were obliged to keep the same distance from our target—I with nonchalance, he with a kind of intense and mystical dependence. For his gaze never wavered from her. Even when he was unsighted by a pillar or a customer, he still contrived to crane his dark head this way or that until he had locked her once more in his zealous and—I was now convinced—fanatical gaze.

I had first sensed this fervour in him when I had spotted him in the arrivals hall at the airport, pressing himself on tiptoe against the long window as he wriggled to get a better view of the royal couple's approach. I had made nothing so special of him then. I was subjecting everyone to the same critical examination. He had seemed to be just another of the gaggle of diplomats, retainers and hangers-on who formed the royal welcome party. Nevertheless his intensity had struck a chord in me: So this is the Middle East, I had mused as I watched him squeeze his hollowed face against the glass. These are the heathen passions my Service must contain if we are to drive our cars and heat our houses and sell our weaponry in peace.

The monkey had taken a couple of steps forward and was peering at a cabinet of ribbons. His gait—exactly like that of his namesake—was wide but stealthy; he seemed to move entirely from the knees, in conspiratorial strides. I selected a display of garters next to him and peered into it while I again furtively examined him for tell-tale bulges round the waist and armpits. His black overcoat was of the classic gunman's shape: voluminous and without a belt, the kind of coat that covers effortlessly a long-barrelled pistol fitted with a suppressor, or a semi-automatic slung beneath the arm.

I studied his hands, my own nervously prickling. His left hung loosely at his side, but his right, which looked the stronger, kept travelling towards his chest and withholding, as if he were preparing himself to pluck up courage for the final act.

A right-handed cross draw, I thought; most likely to the armpit. Our weapons trainers had taught us all the combinations.

And his eyes—those dark, slow-burning, soulful zealot's eyes—even in profile they seemed fixed upon the afterlife. Had he sworn vengeance on her? On her household? Had fanatical mullahs promised him a place in Heaven if he did the deed? My knowledge of Islam was scant, and what there was of it was drawn from a couple of background lectures and the novels of P. C. Wren. Yet it was enough to warn me that I was in the presence of a desperate fanatic who counted his own life cheap.

As to myself, alas, I was unarmed. It was a sore point with me. Watchers would never dream of carrying weapons on normal duty, but covert protection work is a different type of watching, and Paul Skordeno had been allocated a sidearm from Monty's safe.

"One's enough, College," Monty had told me, with his old man's smile. "We don't want you starting World War Three, now do we?"

All that was left to me, therefore, as I rose and softly followed him again, was to select in advance one of the blows we had been taught to master in our silent-killing classes. Should I count on attacking him from behind—with a rabbit punch? —with a double simultaneous blow over the ears? Either method could kill him instantly, whereas a live man can still be questioned. Then would I do better breaking his right arm first, hoping to take him with his own weapon? Yet if I let him draw, might I myself not go down in a hail of bullets from the several bodyguards around the room?

She had seen him!

The Panda had looked straight into the eyes of the monkey, and the monkey had returned her stare!

Had she recognised him? I was certain she had. But had she recognised his purpose? And was she, perhaps, in some strange turn of Oriental fatalism, preparing herself for death? The lurid possibilities went racing through my mind as I continued to observe their mysterious exchange. Their eyes met, the Panda froze in mid-gesture. Her jewelled, crabby little hands, plundering the clothing on the counter, kept still—and then, as if to his command, slipped passively to her sides. After which she stood motionless, without will, without even the strength to detach herself from his penetrating stare.

At last, with a forlorn and strangely humble air, she turned away from him, murmured something to her lady companions and, holding out her hand to the counter, released whatever frilly thing she was still clutching in it. She was wearing brown that day—if she had been a man, I would be tempted to say a Franciscan habit—with wide sleeves longer than her arms, and a brown headband bound tightly across her brow.

I saw her sigh, then slowly and, I was sure, resignedly, she led her entourage towards the archway. After her went her personal bodyguard; after him the Scotland Yard policeman. Then came the ladies of her train, followed by the floorwalkers. And finally came Paul and Nancy, who, with a show of indecision, had torn themselves away from their study of the negligés and were sauntering like any shoppers in the party's wake. Paul, who had surely overheard my conversations with Monty, vouchsafed me not the smallest glance. Nancy, who prided herself on her amateur dramatics, was pretending to pick a marital dispute with him. I tried to see whether Paul had unbuttoned his jacket, for he too favoured the cross draw. But his broad back was turned away from me.

"All right, College, show me," said Monty brightly into my left ear, appearing beside me as if by magic. How long had he been there? I had no idea. It was past midday and our time for standing down, but this was no moment to change the guard. The monkey was not five yards from us, stepping lightly but determinedly after the Panda.

"We can take him at the stairs," I murmured.

"Speak louder," Monty advised me, in the same unabashed voice. "Speak normally, no one listens to you. Mutter, mutter out of the corner of your mouth, they think you've come to rob the till."

Since we were on the first floor, the Panda's party was sure to take the lift, whether they went up or down. Beside the lift stood a pair of swing doors opening on to what in those days was a stone emergency staircase, rather dank and insanitary, with linoleum treads. My plan, which I outlined to Monty in staccato sentences as we followed the monkey towards the archway, was simplicity itself. As the party approached the lift, Monty and I would close on him from either side, grab an arm each and sweep him into the staircase. We would subdue him with a blow to the groin, remove his weapon, then spirit him to Green Street where we would invite him to make a voluntary statement. In training exercises we had done such things a dozen times—once, to our embarrassment, to an innocent bank clerk who was hurrying home to his wife and family, and whom we had mistaken for a member of the training staff.

But if Monty heard me, to my frustration he gave no sign of having done so. He was watching the floorwalkers clear a path through the crowd to the lift so that the Panda's party could ride in privacy. And he was smiling like any casual commoner who stumbles on a glimpse of royalty.

"She's going down," he declared with satisfaction. "Pound to a penny it's the costume jewellery she's after. You'd think the Gulfies wouldn't bother with the artificial stuff, but they can't get enough of it; they think it's got to be a bargain. Come on, son. This is fun. Let's go and take a look."

I like to think that even in my perplexity I recognised the excellence of Monty's tradecraft. The Panda's exotic entourage, mostly in Arab dress, was arousing lively curiosity among the shoppers. Monty was just another punter, enjoying the spectacle. And yes, he was right again, their destination was the costume jewellery department, as the monkey also had divined, for as we emerged from our lift the monkey scampered ahead of the party to take up a favoured place alongside the glittering displays, his left shoulder nearest to the wall, exactly as required of a right-handed gunman who draws across his chest.

Yet, far from choosing a strategic position from which to return fire, Monty merely wandered after him, and, having placed himself next to him, beckoned me to join them, and in such a way that I had no alternative but to leave Monty, not the monkey, at the centre of our trio.

"This is why I always come to Knightsbridge, son," Monty was explaining, loudly enough for half the floor to hear. "You never know who you're going to meet. I brought your mother last time—*you* remember—we'd gone to the Harrods Food Hall. I thought: '*Hullo,* I know you, you're Rex Harrison.' I could have held out my hand and touched him but I didn't. It's the crossroads of the world, Knightsbridge is, don't you agree, sir?"—lifting his hat to the monkey, who smiled wanly in return. "Now I wonder where this lot would be from. Arabs, by the look of them, with the wealth of Solomon at their fingertips. And they don't even pay taxes, I dare say. Not royalty, well they wouldn't have to. There isn't a royal household in the world pays taxes to itself, it wouldn't be logical. See the big policeman there, son? He'll be Special Branch, you can tell by his stupid scowl."

The Panda's party meanwhile was distributing itself among the illuminated glass counters while the Panda, in barely concealed agitation, was requiring that the trays be taken out for her inspection. And soon, as in the lingerie department, she was picking out one object after another, turning it critically under the inspection light, then setting it down and taking up another. And yet again, as she continued to appraise and relinquish each piece in turn, I saw her worried gaze slip towards us, first to the monkey, then to myself, as if she had seen in me her one hope of protection.

Yet Monty, when I glanced at him for confirmation, was still smiling.

"That's exactly what happened in the lingerie department," I whispered, forgetting his instruction to speak normally.

But Monty continued his noisy monologue. "But underneath, son—I always say this—underneath, royals or not, they're the same as what we are, through and through. We're all born naked, we're all on our way to the grave. Your wealth is your health, better to be rich in friends than money, I say. We've all got the same appetites, the same little weaknesses and naughty ways." And on he ran, as if in deliberate contrast to my extreme alertness.

She had ordered up more trays. The counter was covered with sumptuous paste tiaras, bracelets and rings. Selecting a three-string necklace of imitation rubies, she held it to her throat, then took up a hand mirror to admire herself.

And was it my imagination? It was not! She was using the mirror to observe the monkey and ourselves! First one dark eye, then the other fixed upon us; then the two of them together, warning us, imploring us, before she set the mirror down again and turned her back to us, and swept as if in anger along the edge of the glass counter, where a fresh display awaited her.

At the same moment, the monkey took a step forward and I saw his hand rise to the opening of his overcoat. Throwing caution aside, I too stepped forward, my right arm drawn back, the fingers of my right hand flexed, palm parallel to the ground in the approved Sarratt manner. I had decided on an elbow to the heart, followed by a side-of-hand to the upper lip, to the point where the nose cartilage joins the top half of the jaw. A complicated network of nerves has its meeting point here, and a well-aimed blow can immobilise the victim for some while. The monkey was opening his mouth and breathing in. I anticipated a cry to Allah, or perhaps the screamed slogan of some fundamentalist sect—though I am no longer sure how much we knew or cared in those days about fundamentalist Arabs. I at once determined to scream myself, not only in order to confuse him, but because a deep breath would put more oxygen into my bloodstream and so increase my striking power. I was actually drawing this breath when I felt Monty's hand lock like an iron ring round my wrist and, with unpredicted power, immobilise me as he drew me back to him.

"Now don't do that, son, this gentleman was before you," he said in a matter-of-fact voice. "He's got a little confidential business to transact, haven't you, sir?"

He had indeed. And Monty's grasp did not release me until I had observed the nature of it. The monkey was speaking. Not to the Panda, not to her retinue, but to the two floorwalkers in striped trousers who were inclining their heads to listen to him, at first condescendingly, then with startled interest as their gaze switched to the Panda.

"Alas, gentlemen, Her Royal Highness prefers to make her purchases informally, you see," he was saying. "Without the inconvenience of a wrapping or an invoice, let us put it that way. It is her time of life. Three and four years ago, she was a most expert bargainer, you know. Oh yes. She would negotiate a most competitive discount for everything she wished to buy. But today, at her time of life, she is taking matters most literally into her own hands, you see. Or should I say into her sleeve, oh dear? I am therefore charged by His Royal Highness to make a most bountiful settlement for all such informal purchases, on the very clear understanding that no breath of publicity reaches the public ear, gentlemen, whether in the written or the spoken word, if you understand me."

Then from his pocket he drew not, alas, a deadly Walther automatic, not a Heckler & Koch sub-machine gun, not even one of our beloved standard Browning 9-millimetres, but a tooled Moroccan leather wallet stuffed with his master's banknotes in a variety of denominations.

"I counted, I believe, three fine rings, sir, one in artificial emerald, two in paste diamond, also a fine artificial ruby necklace, gentlemen, three strings. It is the wish of His Royal Highness that our settlement should take generous account of any inconvenience suffered by your most excellent staff, you see. Also commission to your good selves, on the understanding already stated regarding publicity."

Monty's grip on me had at last relaxed, and as we walked towards the hall I dared to glance at him, and saw to my relief that his expression, though thoughtful, was surprisingly gentle.

"That's the trouble in our job, Ned," he explained contentedly, using my Christian name for the first time. "Life's looking one way, we're looking the other. I like an honest-to-God enemy myself sometimes, I don't mind admitting. Take a lot of finding, though, don't they? Too many nice blokes about."

3

"Now do please remember," Smiley piously exhorted his young audience, in much the tone he might have selected if he had been asking them to put their offerings in the collection box as they were leaving, "that the privately educated Englishman—and Englishwoman, if you will allow me—is the greatest dissembler on earth." He waited for the laughter to subside. "Was, is now and ever shall be for as long as our disgraceful school system remains intact. Nobody will charm you so glibly, disguise his feelings from you better, cover his tracks more skilfully or find it harder to confess to you that he's been a damned fool. Nobody acts braver when he's frightened stiff, or happier when he's miserable; nobody can flatter you better when he hates you than your extrovert Englishman or woman of the supposedly privileged classes. He can have a Force Twelve nervous breakdown while he stands next to you in the bus queue, and you may be his best friend, but you'll never be the wiser. Which is why some of our best officers turn out to be our worst. And our worst, our best. And why the most difficult agent you will ever have to run is yourself."

In his own mind, I had no doubt, Smiley was talking about the greatest deceiver of us all, Bill Haydon. But for me, he was talking about Ben—and yes, though it's harder to admit, about the young Ned, and perhaps the old one too.

It was the afternoon of the day I had failed to immolate the Panda's bodyguard. Tired and dispirited, I arrived at my flat in Battersea to find the door on the latch and two men in grey suits sifting through the papers in my desk.

They barely looked at me as I burst in. The nearer of them was Personnel and the second an owlish, ageless, tubby man in circular spectacles who eyed me with a sort of baleful commiseration.

"When did you last hear from your friend Cavendish?" said Personnel, scarcely glancing at me before returning to my papers.

"He *is* your friend, isn't he?" said the owlish man unhappily while I struggled to collect myself. "Ben? Arno? Which do you call him?"

"Yes. He is. Ben is. What is this?"

"So when did you last hear from him?" Personnel repeated, shoving aside a pile of letters from my girlfriend of the time. "Does he ring you? How do you keep in touch?"

"I had a postcard from him a week ago. Why?"

"Where is it?"

"I don't know. I destroyed it. If it isn't in the desk. Will you kindly tell me what's going on?"

"Destroyed it?"

"Threw it away."

"*Destroy* sounds deliberate, doesn't it? What did it look like?" Personnel said, pulling out another drawer. "Stay where you are."

"It had a picture of a girl on one side and a couple of lines from Ben on the other. What does it matter what it had on it? Please get out of here."

"Saying?"

"Nothing. It said, this is my latest acquisition. 'Dear Ned, this is my new catch, so glad you're not here. Love, Ben.' Now get out!"

"What did he mean by that?"—pulling out another drawer.

"Glad I wouldn't cut him out with the girl, I suppose. It was a joke."

"Do you usually cut him out with his women?"

"We've no women in common. We never have had."

"What *do* you have in common?"

"Friendship," I said angrily. "What the hell are you looking for actually? I think you'd better leave at once. Both of you."

"I can't find it," Personnel complained to his fat companion as he tossed aside another wad of my private letters. "No postcard of any kind. You're not lying, are you, Ned?"

The owlish man had not taken his eyes off me. He continued to regard me with a wretched empathy, as if to say it comes to all of us and there's nothing we can do. "How was the postcard *delivered*, Ned?" he asked. His voice, like his demeanour, was tentative and regretful.

"By post, how else?" I replied rudely.

"The open mail, you mean?" the owlish man suggested sadly. "Not by Service bag, for instance?"

"By Forces mail," I replied. "Field Post Office. Posted Berlin with a British stamp on it. Delivered by the local postman."

"Do you remember the Field Post Office *number*, by any chance, Ned?" the owlish man enquired with enormous diffidence. "On the postmark, I mean?"

"It was the ordinary Berlin number, I imagine," I retorted, struggling to keep up my indignation in the face of someone so exquisitely deferential. "Forty, I think. Why's it so important? I've had enough of this."

"But you'd say it was definitely posted in Berlin anyway? I mean, that was your impression at the time? So far as you recall it now? The Berlin number—you're sure?"

"It looked exactly like the others he'd sent me. I didn't submit it to a minute examination," I said, my anger rising again as I saw Personnel yank yet another drawer from my desk and tip out its contents.

"A *pin-up* sort of girl, Ned?" the owlish man enquired, with a hangdog smile, which was evidently intended to apologise for Personnel as well as for himself.

"A nude, yes. A tart, I assume, looking over her bare backside. That's why I threw it away. Because of my cleaning lady."

"Oh, so you remember now!" Personnel cried, swinging round to face me. " 'I threw it away.' Pity you didn't bloody say so at once!"

"Oh, I don't know, Rex," said the owlish man placatingly. "Ned was very confused when he came in. Who wouldn't be?" His worried gaze settled once more upon myself. "You're doing a stint with the watchers, isn't that right? Monty says you're rather good. Was she in colour, by the way? Your nude?"

"Yes."

"Did he always send postcards, or sometimes letters?"

"Only postcards."

"How many?"

"Three or four since he's been there."

"Always in colour?"

"I don't remember. Probably. Yes."

"And always of girls?"

"I think so."

"Oh, but you remember, really. Of course you do. And always naked too, I expect?"

"Yes."

"Where are the others?"

"I must have thrown them away too."

"Because of your cleaning lady?"

"Yes."

"To protect her sensitivities?"

"Yes!"

The owlish man took his time to consider this. "So the dirty postcards—forgive me, I don't mean that offensively, really not—they were a sort of running joke between you?"

"On his side, yes."

"But you didn't send him any in return? Please say if you did. Don't be embarrassed. There isn't time."

"I'm not embarrassed! I didn't send him any. Yes, they were a running joke. And they were getting increasingly *risqué*. If you want to know, I was becoming slightly bored with seeing them laid out on the hall table for my collection. So was Mr. Simpson. He's the landlord. He suggested I write to Ben and tell him to stop sending them. He said it was getting the house a bad name. Now will you please, one of you, tell me what the hell's going on?"

This time Personnel replied. "Well, that's what we thought you might be able to tell *us*," he said in a mournful voice. "Ben Cavendish has disappeared. So have his agents, in a manner of speaking. A couple of them are featured in this morning's *Neues Deutschland*. British spy ring caught red-handed. The London evening papers are running the story in their late editions. He hasn't been seen for three days. This is Mr. Smiley. He wants to talk to you. You're to tell him whatever you know. And that means anything. I'll see you later."

I must have lost my bearings for a moment, because when I saw Smiley again he was standing at the centre of my carpet, gloomily peering round him at the havoc he and Personnel had wreaked.

"I've a house across the river in Bywater Street," he confessed, as if it were a great burden to him. "Perhaps we ought to pop round there, if it's all the same to you. It's not *terribly* tidy, but it is better than this."

* * *

We drove there in Smiley's humble little Austin, so slowly you would have supposed he was conveying an invalid, which was perhaps how he regarded me. It was dusk. The white lanterns of Albert Bridge floated at us like waterborne coachlights. Ben, I thought desperately, what have we done? Ben, what have they done to you?

Bywater Street was jammed, so we parked in a mews. Parking for Smiley was as complicated as docking a liner, but he managed it and we walked back. I remember how impossible it was to keep alongside him, how his thrusting round-arm waddle somehow ignored my existence. I remember how he steeled himself to turn the key of his own front door, and his alertness as he stepped into the hall. As if home were a dangerous place for him, as I know now that it was. There was a couple of days' milk in the hall and a half-eaten plate of chop and peas in the drawing room. The turntable of a gramophone was silently revolving. It didn't take a genius to surmise that he had been called out in a hurry—presumably by Personnel yesterday evening—while he was tucking into his chop and listening to a spot of music.

He wandered off to the kitchen in search of soda for our whiskies. I followed him. There was something about Smiley that made you responsible for his solitude. Open tins of food lay about and the sink was crammed with dirty plates. While he mixed our whiskies, I started clearing up, so he fished a teacloth from the back of the door and set to work drying and putting away.

"You and Ben were considerable partners, weren't you?" he asked.

"We shared a cabin at Sarratt, yes."

"So that's what—kitchen, couple of bedrooms, bathroom?"

"No kitchen."

"But you were twinned for your training course as well?"

"For the last year of it. You choose an oppo and learn to work to each other."

"Choose? Or have chosen for you?"

"Choose first, then they approve or break you up."

"And after that, you're landed with each other for better for worse?"

"Pretty much, yes."

"For the whole of the last year? For half the course, in fact? Day and night, as it were? A total marriage?"

I could not understand why he was pressing me about things he must have known.

"And you do everything together?" he continued. "Forgive me but it's some time since I was trained. Written, practical, physical, you mess together, share a cabin—a whole life, in fact."

"We do the syndicate work together, and the strongarm stuff. That's automatic. It begins with being roughly the same weight and physical aptitude." Despite the disturbing tendency of his questions, I was beginning to feel a great need to talk to him. "Then the rest sort of follows naturally."

"Ah."

"Sometimes they split us up—say, for a special exercise or if they think one person is relying too much on his oppo. But as long as it's fifty-fifty they're happy for you to keep together."

"And you won everything," Smiley suggested approvingly, helping himself to another wet plate. "You were the best pair. You and Ben."

"It was just that Ben was the best student," I said. "Whoever had him would have won."

"Yes, of course. Well, we all know people like that. Did you know each other before you joined the Service?"

"No. But we'd run parallel. We were at the same school, different houses. We were at Oxford, different colleges. We both read languages but we still never met. He did a short service commission in the army, I did the same in the navy. It took the Circus to bring us together."

Taking up a delicate bone-china cup, he peered doubtfully into it, as if searching for something I had missed. "Would *you* have sent Ben to Berlin?"

"Yes, of course I would. Why not?"

"Well, why?"

"He's got perfect German from his mother. He's bright. Resourceful. People do what he wants them to do. His father had this terrific war."

"So did your mother, as I remember." He was referring to my mother's work with the Dutch Resistance. "What did *he* do—Ben's father, I mean?" he continued, as if he really didn't know.

"He broke codes," I said, with Ben's pride. "He was a wrangler. A mathematician. A genius, apparently. He helped organise the double-cross system against the Germans—recruit their agents and play them back. My mother was very small beer by comparison."

"And Ben was impressed by that?"

"Who wouldn't be?"

"He talked of it, I mean," Smiley insisted. "Often? It was a big matter for him. You had that impression?"

"He just said it was something he had to live up to. He said it was the up-side of having a German mother."

"Oh dear," said Smiley unhappily. "Poor man. And those were his words? You're not embellishing?"

"Of course I'm not! He said that with a background like his, in England you had to run twice as fast as everyone else, just to keep up."

Smiley seemed genuinely upset. "Oh dear," he said again. "How unkind. And do you think he has the stamina, would you say?"

He had once more stopped me short. At our age, we really didn't think of stamina as being limited.

"What for?" I asked.

"Oh, I don't know. What kind of stamina would one need for running twice as fast as everyone else in Berlin? A double ration of nerves, I suppose—always a strain. A doubly good head for alcohol—*and* where women are concerned—never easy."

"I'm sure he's got whatever it takes," I said loyally.

Smiley hung his teacloth on a bent nail which looked like his own addition to the kitchen. "Did you ever talk politics, the two of you?" he asked as we took our whiskies to the drawing room.

"Never."

"Then I'm sure he's sound," he said, with a sad little laugh, and I laughed too.

Houses always seem to me, at first acquaintance, to be either masculine or feminine, and Smiley's was undoubtedly feminine, with pretty curtains and carved mirrors and clever woman's touches. I wondered who he was living with, or wasn't. We sat down.

"And is there any reason why you *mightn't* have sent Ben to Berlin?" he resumed, smiling kindly over the top of his glass.

"Well, only that I wanted to go myself. Everybody wants a Berlin break. It's the front line."

"He simply disappeared," Smiley explained, settling back and appearing to close his eyes. "We're not keeping anything from you. I'll tell you what we know. Last Thursday he crossed into East Berlin to meet his head agent, a gentleman named Hans Seidl—you can see his photograph in *Neues Deutschland*. It was Ben's first solo meeting with him. A big event. Ben's superior in the Berlin Station is Haggarty. Do you know Haggarty?"

"No."

"Have you heard of him?"

"No."

"Ben never mentioned him to you?"

"No. I told you. I've never heard his name."

"Forgive me. Sometimes an answer can vary with a context, if you follow me." I didn't.

"Haggarty is second man in the Station under the Station Commander. Did you not know that either?"

"No."

"Has Ben a regular girlfriend?"

"Not that I know of."

"Irregular?"

"You only had to go to a dance with him, they were all over him."

"And after the dance?"

"He didn't brag. He doesn't. If he slept with them, he wouldn't say. He's not that kind of man."

"They tell me you and Ben took your bits of leave together. Where did you go?"

"Twickenham. Lord's. Bit of fishing. Mainly we stayed with one another's people."

"Ah."

I couldn't understand why Smiley's words were scaring me. Perhaps I was so scared for Ben that I was scared by everything. Increasingly I had the feeling Smiley assumed I was guilty of something, even if we had still to find out what. His recitation of events was like a summary of the evidence.

"First comes *Willis*," he said, as if we were following a difficult trail. "Willis is the Berlin Head of Station, Willis has overall command. Then comes *Haggarty,* and Haggarty is the senior field officer under Willis and Ben's direct boss. Haggarty is responsible for the day-to-day servicing of the Seidl network. The network is twelve agents strong, or was—that is to say, nine men and three women, now all under arrest. An illegal network of that size, communicating partly by radio and partly by secret writing, requires a base team of at least the same number to maintain it, and I'm not talking about evaluating or distributing the product."

"I know."

"I'm sure you do, but let me tell you all the same," he continued at the same ponderous pace. "Then you can help me fill in the gaps. Haggarty is a powerful personality. An Ulsterman. Off duty, he drinks, he's noisy and unpleasant. But when he's working he's none of those things. He's a conscientious officer with a prodigious memory. You're sure Ben never mentioned him to you?"

"I told you. No."

I had not intended this to sound so adamant. There's always a mystery about how often you can deny a thing without beginning to sound like a liar, even to yourself; and of course this was the very mystery Smiley was playing upon in order to bring hidden things to the surface in me.

"Yes, well you *did* tell me no," he agreed with his habitual courtesy. "And I did *hear* you say no. I merely wondered whether I had jogged your memory."

"No."

"Haggarty and Seidl were *friends*," he continued, speaking, if it were possible, even more slowly. "So far as their business allowed, they were *close* friends. Seidl had been a prisoner of war in England, Haggarty in Germany. While Seidl was working as a farm labourer near Cirencester in 1944, under the relaxed conditions for German prisoners of war that prevailed by then, he succeeded in courting an English landgirl. His guards at the camp took to leaving a bicycle for him outside the main gates with an army greatcoat tossed over the handlebar to cover Seidl's prisoner-of-war tunic. As long as he was back in his own bed by reveille, the guards turned a blind eye. Seidl never forgot his gratitude to the English. When the baby came along, Seidl's guards and fellow prisoners came to the christening. Charming, isn't it? The English at their best. But the story doesn't ring a bell?"

"How could it? You're talking about a joe!"

"A blown joe. One of Ben's. Haggarty's experiences of German prison camp were not so uplifting. Never mind. In 1948, while Haggarty was nominally working with the Control Commission, he picked up Seidl in a bar in Hannover, recruited him and ran him back into East Germany, to his home town of Leipzig. He has been running him ever since. The Haggarty-Seidl friendship has been the linchpin of the Berlin Station for the last fifteen years. At the time of his arrest last week, Seidl was fourth man in the East German Foreign Ministry. He had served as their Ambassador in Havana. But you've never heard of him. Nobody ever mentioned him to you. Not Ben. Not anyone."

"No," I said, as wearily as I could manage.

"Once a month Haggarty was accustomed to going into East Berlin and debriefing Seidl—in a car, in a safe flat, on a park bench, wherever—the usual thing. After the Wall there was a suspension of service for a while, before the meetings were cautiously resumed. The game was to cross in a Four Power vehicle—say, an army jeep—introduce a substitute, hop out at the right moment and rejoin the vehicle at an agreed point. It sounds perilous and it was, but with practice it worked. If Haggarty was on leave or sick, there was no meeting. A couple of months ago Head Office ruled that Haggarty should introduce Seidl to a successor. Haggarty is past retiring age, Willis has had Berlin so long he's blown sky high, and besides he knows far too many secrets to go wandering round behind the Curtain. Hence Ben's posting to Berlin. Ben was untarnished. Clean. Haggarty in person briefed him— I gather exhaustively. I'm sure he was not merciful. Haggarty is not a merciful man, and a twelve-strong network can be a complicated matter: who works to whom and why; who knows whose identity; the cut-outs, codes, couriers, covernames, symbols, radios, dead-letter boxes, inks, cars, salaries, children, birthdays, wives, mistresses. A lot to get into one's head all at once."

"I know."

"Ben told you, did he?"

I did not rise to him this time. I was determined not to. "We learned it on the course. *Ad infinitum*," I said.

"Yes. Well, I suppose you did. The trouble is, the theory's never quite the same as the real thing, is it? Who's his best friend, apart from you?"

"I don't know." I was startled by his sudden change of tack. "Jeremy, I suppose."

"Jeremy who?"

"Galt. He was on the course."

"And women?"

"I told you. No one special."

"Haggarty wanted to take Ben into East Berlin with him, make the introduction himself," Smiley resumed. "The Fifth Floor wouldn't wear that. They were trying to wean Haggarty away from his agent, and they don't hold with sending two men into badland where one will do. So Haggarty took Ben through the rendezvous procedures on a street map, and Ben went into East Berlin alone. On the Wednesday, he did a dry run and reconnoitred the location. On the Thursday he went in again, this time for real. He went in legally, driven in a Control Commission Humber car. He crossed at Checkpoint Charlie at three in the afternoon and slipped out of the car at the agreed spot. His substitute rode in it for three hours, all as planned. Ben rejoined the car successfully at six-ten, and recrossed into West Berlin at six-fifty in the evening. His return was logged by the checkpoint. He had himself dropped at his flat. A faultless run. Willis and Haggarty were waiting for him at Station Headquarters, but he telephoned from his flat instead. He said the rendezvous had gone to plan, but he'd brought nothing back except a high temperature and a ferocious stomach bug. Could they postpone their debriefing till morning? Lamentably they could. They haven't seen him or heard from him since. He sounded cheerful despite his ailment, which they put down to nerves. Has Ben ever been ill on you?"

"No."

"He said their mutual friend had been in great form, a real character and so forth. Obviously he could say no more on the open telephone. His bed wasn't slept in, he took no extra clothes with him. There's no proof that he was in his flat when he rang, there's no proof he's been kidnapped, there's no proof he hasn't been. If he was going to defect, why didn't he stay in East Berlin? They can't have turned him round and played him back at us or they wouldn't have arrested his network. And if they wanted to kidnap him, why not do it while he was their side of the Wall? There's no hard evidence that he left West Berlin by any of the approved corridors —train, autobahn, air. The controls are not efficient, and as you say, he was trained. For all we know, he hasn't left Berlin at all. On the other hand, we thought he might have come to you. Don't look so appalled. You're his friend, aren't you? His best friend? Closer to him than anyone? Young Galt doesn't compare. He told us so himself. 'Ben's great buddy was Ned,' he said. 'If Ben was going to turn to any of us, it would have to be Ned.' The evidence rather bears that out, I'm afraid."

"What evidence?"

No pregnant pause, no dramatic change of tone, no warning of any kind: just dear old George Smiley being his apologetic self. "There's a letter in his flat, addressed to you," he said. "It's not dated, just thrown in a drawer. A scrawl rather than a letter. He was probably drunk. It's a love letter, I'm afraid." And, having handed me a photocopy to read, he fetched us both another whisky.

Perhaps I do it to help me look away from the discomfort of the moment. But always when I set that scene in my memory I find myself switching to Smiley's point of view. I imagine how it must have felt to be in his position.

What he had before him is easy enough to picture. See a striving trainee trying to look older than his years, a pipesmoker, a sailor, a wise nodder, a boy who could not wait for middle age, and you have the young Ned of the early sixties.

But what he had behind him was not half so easy, and it was capable of altering his reading of me drastically. The Circus, though I couldn't know it at the time, was in low water, dogged by unaccountable failure. The arrest of Ben's agents, tragic in itself, was only the latest in a chain of catastrophes reaching across the globe. In northern Japan, an entire Circus listening station and its three-man staff had vanished into thin air. In the Caucasus, our escape lines had been rolled up over-night. We had lost networks in Hungary, Czechoslovakia and Bulgaria, all in a space of months. And in Washington our American Cousins were voicing ever-louder dissatisfaction with our reliability, and threatening to cut the special cord for good.

In such a climate, monstrous theories become daily fare. A bunker mentality develops. Nothing is allowed to be accident, nothing random. If the Circus tri-umphed, it was because we were allowed to do so by our opponents. Guilt by association was rife. In the American perception, the Circus was nurturing not one mole but burrows of them, each cunningly advancing the career of every other. And what joined them was not so much their pernicious faith in Marx—though that was bad enough—it was their dreadful English homosexuality.

I read Ben's letter. Twenty lines long, unsigned, on white unwatermarked Service stationery, one side. Ben's handwriting but awry, no crossings out. So yes, probably he was drunk.

It called me "Ned my darling." It laid Ben's hands along my face and drew my lips to his. It kissed my eyelids and my neck and, thank God, on the physical front it stopped there.

It was without adjectives, without art, and the more appalling for its lack of them. It was not a period piece, it was not affected. It was not arch, Greek or nineteen-twenties. It was an unobstructed cry of homosexual longing from a man I had known only as my good companion.

But when I read it, I knew it was the real Ben who had written it. Ben in torment confessing feelings I had never been aware of, but which when I read them I accepted as true. Perhaps that already made me guilty—I mean, to be the object of his desire, even if I had never consciously attracted it, and did not desire him in return. His letter said sorry, then it ended. I didn't think it was unfinished. He had nothing more to say.

"I didn't know," I said.

I handed Smiley back the letter. He returned it to his pocket. His eyes didn't leave my face.

"Or you didn't know you knew," he suggested.

"I didn't know," I repeated hotly. "What are you trying to make me say?"

You must try to understand Smiley's eminence, the respect his name awoke in someone of my generation. He waited for me. I shall remember all my life the compelling power of his patience. A sudden shower of rain fell, with the handclap that London rain showers make in narrow streets. If Smiley had told me he commanded the elements, I would not have been surprised.

"In England you can't tell anyway," I said sulkily, trying to collect myself. God alone knows what point I was trying to make. "Jack Arthur's not married, is he? Nowhere to go in the evenings. Drinks with the lads till the bar closes. Then drinks a bit more. No one says Jack Arthur's queer. But if they arrested him tomorrow in bed with two of the cooks, we'd say we'd known it all along. Or I would. It's imponderable." I stumbled on, all wrong, groping for a path and finding none. I knew that to protest at all was to protest too much, but I went on protesting all the same.

"Anyway, where was the letter found?" I demanded, trying to recover the initiative.

"In a drawer of his desk. I thought I told you."

"An empty drawer?"

"Does it matter?"

"Yes, it does! If it was jammed in among old papers, that's one thing. If it was put there to be found by you people, that's another. Maybe he was forced to write it."

"Oh, I'm sure he was forced," said Smiley. "It's just a question of what by. Did you know he was so lonely? If there was no one in his life but you, I'd have thought it would have been rather obvious."

"Then why wasn't it obvious to Personnel?" I said, bridling again. "My God, they grilled us for long enough before they appointed us. Sniffed round our friends and relations and teachers and dons. They know far more about Ben than I do."

"Why don't we just assume that Personnel fell down on the job? He's human, this is England, we're the clan. Let's begin again with the Ben who's disappeared. The Ben who wrote to you. There was no one close to him but you. Not anyone that you knew of, anyway. There could have been lots of people you *didn't* know of, but that's not your fault. As far as you knew, there was no one. We have that settled. Don't we?"

"Yes!"

"Very well then, let's talk about what you *did* know. How's that?"

Somehow he brought me down to earth and we talked into the small grey hours. Long after the rain had stopped and the starlings had begun, we were talking. Or I was—and Smiley was listening as only Smiley can, eyes half closed, chins sunk into his neck. I thought I was telling him everything I knew. Perhaps he thought I was too, though I doubt it, for he understood far better than I the levels of self-deception that are the means of our survival. The phone rang. He listened, muttered "Thank you" and rang off. "Ben's still missing and there are no new pointers," he said. "You're still the only clue." He took no notes that I remember and I don't know to this day whether he had a recorder running. I doubt it. He hated machines, and besides, his memory was more reliable than theirs.

I talked about Ben but I talked as much about myself, which was what Smiley wanted me to do: myself as the explanation for Ben's actions. I described again the parallel nature of our lives. How I had envied him his heroic father—I, who had no father to remember. I made no secret of our shared excitement, Ben's and mine, when we began to discover how much we had in common. No, no, I said again, I knew of no one woman—except his mother, who was dead. And I believed myself, I am sure I did.

In childhood, I told Smiley, I used to wonder whether somewhere in the world there was not another version of myself, some secret twin who had the same toys and clothes and thoughts that I did, even the same parents. Perhaps I'd read a book based on this story. I was an only child. So was Ben. I told Smiley all this because I was determined to talk directly to him from my thoughts and memories as they came to me, even if they incriminated me in his eyes. I only know that, consciously, I held nothing back from him, even if I reckoned it potentially ruinous to myself. Somehow Smiley had convinced me that this was the least I owed to Ben. Unconsciously—well, that's another matter altogether. Who knows what a man hides, even from himself, when he is telling the truth for his survival?

I told him of our first meeting—mine and Ben's—in the Circus training house in Lambeth where the newly selected entrants were convened. Until then, none of us had met any of his fellow novices. We had hardly met the Circus either, for that matter, beyond the recruiting officer, the selectors and the vetting team. Some of us had only the haziest notion of what we'd joined. Finally we were to be enlightened —about each other, and about our calling—and we gathered in the waiting room like so many characters in a Foreign Legion novel, each with his secret expectations and his secret reasons for being there, each with his overnight bag containing the same quantity of shirts and underpants, marked in Indian ink with his personal number, in obedience to the printed instructions on the unheaded notepaper. My number was nine and Ben's was ten. There were two people ahead of me when I walked into the waiting room, Ben and a stocky little Scot called Jimmy. I nodded at Jimmy, but Ben and I recognised each other at once—I don't mean from school or university but as people who bear a physical and temperamental similarity to one another.

"Enter the third murderer," he said, shaking my hand. It seemed a wonderfully inappropriate moment to be quoting Shakespeare. "I'm Ben, this is Jimmy. Apparently we've got no surnames any more. Jimmy left his in Aberdeen."

So I shook Jimmy's hand as well, and waited on the bench beside Ben to see who came through the door next.

"Five to one he's got a moustache, ten to one a beard, thirty to one green socks," said Ben.

"And evens on a cloak," I said.

I told Smiley about the training exercises in unfamiliar towns when we had to invent a cover story, meet a contact and withstand arrest and interrogation. I let him sense how such exploits deepened our companionship, just as sharing our first parachute jumps deepened it, or compass-trekking at night across the Scottish Highlands, or looking out dead-letter boxes in godforsaken inner cities, or making a beach landing by submarine.

I described to him how the directing staff would sometimes drop a veiled reference to Ben's father, just to emphasise their pride in having the son to teach. I told him about our leave weekends, how we would go once to my mother's house in Gloucestershire and once to his father's in Shropshire. And how, each parent being widowed, we had amused ourselves with the notion that we might broker a marriage between them. But the chances in reality were small, for my mother was stubbornly Anglo-Dutch, with jolly sisters and nephews and nieces who all looked like Breughel models, whereas Ben's father had become a scholarly recluse whose only known surviving passion was for Bach.

"And Ben reveres him," said Smiley, prodding again at the same spot.

"Yes. He adored his mother but she's dead. His father has become some sort of icon for him."

And I remember noticing to my shame that I had deliberately avoided using the word "love," because Ben had used it to describe his feelings for me.

I told him about Ben's drinking, though again I think he knew. How Ben normally drank little and often nothing at all, until an evening would come along —say, a Thursday and the weekend already looming—when he would drink insatiably, Scotch, vodka, anything, a shot for Ben, a shot for Arno. Then reel off to bed, speechless but inoffensive. And how on the morning after, he looked as if he had undergone a fortnight's cure at a health farm.

"And there was really nobody but you?" Smiley mused. "Poor you, what a burden, coping with all that charm alone."

I reminisced, I wandered, I told him everything as it came to me, but I knew he was still waiting for me to tell him something I was keeping back, if we could find out what it was. Was I conscious of withholding? I can only reply to you as I afterwards replied to myself: I did not know I knew. It took me a full twenty-four hours more of self-interrogation to winkle my secret out of its dark corner. At four a.m., he told me to go home and get some sleep. I was not to stray from my telephone without telling Personnel what I was up to.

"They'll be watching your flat, naturally," he warned me as we waited for my cab. "You won't take it personally, will you? If you imagine being on the loose yourself, there are really very few ports you'd feel safe to head for in a storm. Your flat could rank high on Ben's list. Assuming there isn't anybody else except his father. But he wouldn't go to him, would he? He'd be ashamed. He'd want you. So they watch your flat. It's natural."

"I understand," I said as a fresh wave of disgust swept over me.

"After all, there's no one of his age whom he seems to like better than you."

"It's all right. I understand," I repeated.

"On the other hand of course, he's not a fool, so he'll know how we're reasoning. And he could hardly imagine you would hide him in your priest-hole without telling us. Well, you wouldn't, would you?"

"No. I couldn't."

"Which if he's halfway rational he would also know, and that would rule you out for him. Still, he might drop by for advice or assistance, I suppose. Or a drink. It's unlikely, but it's not an assumption we can ignore. You must be far, far and away his best friend. Nobody to compare with you. Is there?"

I was wishing very much he would stop talking like this. Until now, he had shown the greatest delicacy in avoiding the topic of Ben's declared love for me.

Suddenly he seemed determined to reopen the wound.

"Of course he *may* have written to other people apart from you," he remarked speculatively. "Men or women, both. It's not so unlikely. There are times when one's so desperate that one declares one's love to all sorts of people. If one knows one's dying or contemplating some desperate act. The difference in their case would be, he posted the letters. Still, we can't go round Ben's chums asking them whether he's written them a steamy letter recently—it wouldn't be secure. Besides, where would one start? That's the question. You have to put yourself in Ben's position."

Did he deliberately plant the germ of self-knowledge in me? Later, I was certain he did. I remember his troubled, perspicacious gaze upon me as he saw me to the cab. I remember looking back as we turned the corner, and seeing his stocky figure standing in the centre of the street as he peered after me, ramming his last words into my departing head. "You have to put yourself in Ben's position."

I was in vortex. My day had begun in the small hours in South Audley Street and continued with barely pause for sleep through the Panda's monkey and Ben's letter until now. Smiley's coffee and my sense of being the prisoner of outrageous circumstance had done the rest. But the name of Stefanie, I swear it, was still nowhere in my head—not at the front, not at the back. Stefanie still did not exist. I have never, I am sure, forgotten anyone so thoroughly.

Back in my flat, my periodical spurts of revulsion at Ben's passion gave way to concern for his safety. In the living room I stared theatrically at the sofa where he had so often stretched out after a long day's street training in Lambeth: "Think I'll bunk down here if you don't mind, old boy. Jollier than home tonight. Arno can sleep at home. Ben sleeps here." In the kitchen I laid the palm of my hand on the old iron oven where I had fried him his midnight eggs: "Christ Almighty, Ned, is that a stove? Looks more like what we lost the Crimean War with!"

I remembered his voice, long after I had switched out my bedside light, rattling one crazy idea after another at me through the thin partition—the shared words we had, our insider language.

"You know what we ought to do with Brother Nasser?"

"No, Ben."

"Give him Israel. Know what we ought to do with the Jews?"

"No, Ben."

"Give them Egypt."

"Why, Ben?"

"People are only satisfied with what doesn't belong to them. Know the story of the scorpion and the frog crossing the Nile?"

"Yes, I do. Now shut up and go to sleep."

Then he'd tell me the story, nevertheless, as a Sarratt case history. The scorpion as penetration agent, needing to contact his stay-behind team on the opposite bank. The frog as double agent, pretending to buy the scorpion's cover story, then blowing it to his paymasters.

And in the morning he was gone, leaving behind him a one-line note saying, "See you at Borstal," which was his name for Sarratt. "Love, Ben."

Had we talked about Stefanie on those occasions? We hadn't. Stefanie was someone we discussed in motion, glancingly, not side by side through a stationary wall. Stefanie was a phantom shared on the run, an enigma too delightful to dissect. So perhaps that's why I didn't think of her. Or not yet. Not knowingly. There was no dramatic moment when a great light went up and I sprang from my bath shouting, *"Stefanie!"* It simply didn't happen that way, for the reason I am trying to explain to you; somewhere in the no-man's-land between confession and self-preservation, Stefanie floated like a mythic creature who only existed when she was owned up to. As best I remember, the notion of her first came back to me as I was tidying up the mess left by Personnel. Stumbling on my last year's diary, I began flipping through it, thinking how much more of life we live than we remember. And in the month of June, I came on a line drawn diagonally through the two middle weeks, and the numeral "8" written neatly beside it—meaning Camp 8, North Argyll, where we did our paramilitary training. And I began to think—or perhaps merely to sense—yes, of course, Stefanie.

And from there, still without any sudden Archimedean revelation, I found myself reliving our night drive over the moonlit Highlands: Ben at the wheel of the open Triumph roadster, and myself beside him making chatty conversation in order to keep him awake, because we were both happily exhausted after a week of pretending we were in the Albanian mountains raising a guerrilla army. And the June air rushing over our faces.

The rest of the intake were travelling back to London on the Sarratt bus. But Ben and I had Stefanie's Triumph roadster because Steff was a sport, Steff was selfless, Steff had driven it all the way from Oban to Glasgow just so that Ben could borrow it for the week and bring it back to her when the course restarted. And that was how Stefanie came back to me—exactly as she had come to me in the car—amorphously, a titillating concept, a shared woman—Ben's.

"So who or what *is* Stefanie, or do I get the usual loud silence?" I asked him as I pulled open the glove compartment and looked in vain for traces of her.

For a while I got the loud silence.

"Stefanie is a light to the ungodly and a paragon to the virtuous," he replied gravely. And then, more deprecatingly: "Steff's from the Hun side of the family." He was from it himself, he liked to say in his more acerbic moods. Steff was from the Arno side, he was saying.

"Is she pretty?" I asked.

"Don't be vulgar."

"Beautiful?"

"Less vulgar, but still not there."

"What is she, then?"

"She is perfection. She is luminous. She is peerless."

"So beautiful, then?"

"No, you lout. Exquisite. *Sans pareil*. Intelligent beyond the dreams of Personnel."

"And otherwise—to you—what is she? Apart from being a Hun and the owner of this car?"

"She is my mother's eighteenth cousin dozens of times removed. After the war she came and lived with us in Shropshire and we grew up together."

"So she's your age, then?"

"If the eternal is to be measured, yes."

"Your proxy sister, as it were?"

"She was. For a few years. We ran wild together, picked mushrooms in the dawn, touched wee-wees. Then I went off to boarding school and she returned to Munich to resume being a Hun. End of childhood idyll and back to Daddy and England."

I had never known him so forthcoming about any woman, nor about himself.

"And now?"

I feared he had switched off again, but finally he answered me. "Now is less funny. She went to art school, took up with a mad painter and settled in a dower house in the Western Isles of Scotland."

"Why's it less funny? Doesn't her painter like you?"

"He doesn't like anyone. He shot himself. Reasons unknown. Left a note to the local council apologising for the mess. No note to Steff. They weren't married, which made it more of a muddle."

"And now?" I asked him again.

"She still lives there."

"On the island?"

"Yes."

"In the dower house?"

"Yes."

"Alone?"

"Most of the time."

"You mean you go and see her?"

"I *see* her, yes. So I suppose I *go* too. Yes. I go and see her."

"Is it serious?"

"Everything to do with Steff is massively serious."

"What does she do when you're not there?"

"Same as she does when I'm there, I should think. Paints. Talks to the dickie birds. Reads. Plays music. Reads. Plays music. Paints. Thinks. Reads. Lends me her car. Do you want to know any more of my business?"

For a while we remained strangers, until Ben once more relented. "Tell you what, Ned. Marry her."

"Stefanie?"

"Who else, you idiot? That's a bloody good idea, come to think of it. I propose to bring the two of you together to discuss it. You shall marry Steff, Steff shall marry you, and I shall come and live with you both, and fish the loch."

My question sprang from a monstrous, culpable innocence: "Why don't you marry her yourself?" I asked.

Was it only now, standing in my flat and watching the slow dawn print itself on the walls, that I had the answer? Staring at the ruled-out pages of last June and remembering with a jolt his dreadful letter?

Or was it given to me already in the car, by Ben's silence as we sped through the Scottish night? Did I know even then that Ben was telling me he would never marry any woman?

And was this the reason why I had banished Stefanie from my conscious memory, planting her so deep that not even Smiley, for all his clever delving, had been able to exhume her?

Had I looked at Ben as I asked him my fatal question? Had I looked at him as he refused, and went on refusing, to reply? Had I deliberately *not* looked at him at all? I was used to his silences by then, so perhaps, having waited in vain, I punished him by entering my own thoughts.

All I knew for certain was that Ben never answered my question, and that neither of us ever mentioned Stefanie again.

Stefanie his dream woman, I thought as I continued to examine the diary. On her island. Who loved him. But should marry me.

Who had the taint of death about her that Ben's heroes always seemed to need.

Eternal Stefanie, a light to the ungodly, luminous, peerless, German Stefanie, his paragon and proxy sister—mother too, perhaps—waving to him from her tower, offering him sanctuary from his father.

You have to put yourself in Ben's position, Smiley had said.

Yet even now, the open diary in my hands, I did not allow myself the elusive moment of revelation. An idea was forming in me. Gradually it became a possibility. And only gradually again, as my state of physical and mental siege bore in on me, did it harden into conviction, and finally purpose.

It was morning at last. I hoovered the flat. I dusted and polished. I considered my anger. Dispassionately, you understand. I reopened the desk, pulled out my desecrated private papers and burned in the grate whatever I felt had been irrevocably sullied by the intrusion of Smiley and Personnel: the letters from Mabel, the exhortations from my former tutor to "do something a bit more fun" than mere research work at the War Office.

I did these things with the outside of myself while the rest of me grappled with the correct, the moral, the decent course of action.

Ben, my friend.

Ben, with the dogs after him.

Ben in anguish, and God knew what more besides.

Stefanie.

I took a long bath, then lay on my bed watching the mirror on the chest of drawers because the mirror gave me a view of the street. I could see a couple of men whom I took to be Monty's, dressed in overalls and doing something longwinded with a junction box. Smiley had said I shouldn't take them personally. After all, they only wanted to put Ben in irons.

It is ten o'clock of the same long morning as I stand purposefully to one side of my rear window, peering down into the squalid courtyard, with its creosoted shed that used to be the old privy, and its clapboard gate that opens on the dingy street. The street is empty. Monty is not so perfect after all.

The Western Isles, Ben had said. A dower house on the Western Isles.

But which isle? And Stefanie who? The only safe guess was that if she came from the German side of Ben's family and lived in Munich, and that since Ben's German relatives were grand, she was likely to be titled.

I rang Personnel. I might have rung Smiley but I felt safer lying to Personnel. He recognised my voice before I had a chance to state my business.

"Have you heard anything?" he demanded.

"Afraid not. I want to go out for an hour. Can I do that?"

"Where to?"

"I need a few things. Provisions. Something to read. Thought I'd just pop round to the library."

Personnel was famous for his disapproving silences.

"Be back by eleven. Ring me as soon as you get in."

Pleased by my cool performance, I went out by the front door, bought a newspaper and bread. Using shop windows, I checked my back. Nobody was following me, I was sure. I went to the public library and from the reference section drew an old copy of *Who's Who* and a tattered *Almanach de Gotha*. I did not pause to ask myself who on earth, in Battersea of all places, could have worn out the *Almanach de Gotha*. I consulted the *Who's Who* first and turned up Ben's father, who had a knighthood and a battery of decorations: *"1936, married the Gräfin Ilse Arno zu Lothringen, one son Benjamin Arno."* I switched to the *Almanach* and turned up the Arno Lothringens. They rated three pages, but it took me no time to identify the distant cousin whose first name was Stefanie. I boldly asked the librarian for a telephone directory for the Western Isles of Scotland. She hadn't one, but allowed me to call enquiries on her telephone, which was fortunate for I had no doubt my own was being tapped. By ten-forty-five I was back at the telephone in my flat talking to Personnel in the same relaxed tone as before.

"Where did you go?" he asked.

"To the newsagent. And the baker's."

"Didn't you do the library?"

"Library? Oh yes. Yes, I did."

"And what, pray, did you take out?"

"Nothing, actually. For some reason I find it hard to settle to anything at the moment. What do I do next?"

Waiting for him to reply, I wondered whether I had given too many answers but decided I had not.

"You wait. The same as the rest of us."

"Can I come in to Head Office?"

"Since you're waiting, you might as well wait there as here."

"I could go back to Monty, if you like."

It was probably my over-acute imagination at work, but I had a mental image of Smiley standing at his elbow, telling him how to answer me.

"Just wait where you are," he said curtly.

I waited, Lord knows how. I pretended to read. I dramatised myself and wrote a pompous letter of resignation to Personnel. I tore up the letter and burned the pieces. I watched television, and in the evening I lay on the bed observing the changing of Monty's guard in the mirror and thinking of Stefanie, then Ben, then Stefanie again, who was now firmly lodged in my imagination, always outside my reach, dressed in white, Stefanie the immaculate, Ben's protector. I was young, let me remind you, and in matters of women less experienced than you would have suspected if you had heard me speak of them. The Adam in me was still pretty much a child, not to be confused with the warrior.

I waited till ten, then slipped downstairs with a bottle of wine for Mr. Simpson and his wife, and sat with them while we drank it, watching more television. Then I took Mr. Simpson aside.

"Chris," I said. "I know it's daft but there's a jealous lady stalking me and I'd like to leave by the back way. Would you mind letting me out through your kitchen?"

An hour later, I was on the night sleeper to Glasgow. I had obeyed my counter-surveillance procedures to the letter and I was certain I was not being followed. At Glasgow Central Station, all the same, I took the precaution of dawdling over a pot of tea in the buffet while I cocked an eye for potential watchers. As a further precaution, I hired a cab to Helensburgh on the other side of the Clyde, before joining the Campbeltown bus to West Loch Tarbert. The ferry to the Western Isles sailed three days a week in those days, except for the short summer season. But my luck held: a boat was waiting, and she sailed as soon as I had boarded her, so that by early afternoon we had passed Jura, docked at Port Askaig and were heading out to the open sea again under a darkening northern sky. We were down to three passengers by then, an old couple and myself, and when I went up on deck to fend off their questions, the first mate cheerfully asked me more of his own: Was I on holiday now? Was I a doctor then? Was I married at all? Nevertheless, I was in my element. From the moment I take to the sea, everyone is clear to me, everything possible. Yes, I thought excitedly, surveying the great crags as they approached, and smiling at the shrieking of the gulls, yes, this is where Ben would hide! This is where his Wagnerian demons would find their ease!

You must understand and try to pardon my callow susceptibility in those days to all forms of Nordic abstraction. What Ben was driven by, I pursued. The mythic island—it should have been Ossian's!—the swirling clouds and tossing sea, the priestess in her solitary castle—I could not get enough of them. I was in the middle of my Romantic period, and my soul was lost to Stefanie before I met her.

The dower house was on the other side of the island, they told me at the shop, better ask young Fergus to take you in his jeep. Young Fergus turned out to be seventy, if a day. We passed between a pair of crumbling iron gates. I paid off young Fergus and rang the bell. The door opened; a fair woman stared at me.

She was tall and slim. If it was really true that she was my own age—and it was —she had an authority it would take me another lifetime to acquire. She wore, instead of white, a paint-smeared smock of dark blue. She held a palette knife in one hand, and as I spoke she raised it to her forehead and pushed away a stray bit of hair with the back of her wrist. Then lowered it again to her side, and stood listening to me long after I had finished speaking, while she pondered the resonance of my words inside her head and compared them with the man or boy who stood before her. But the strangest part of this moment is also the hardest for me to relate. It is that Stefanie came closer to the figure of my imagination than made sense. Her pallor, her air of uncorrupted truthfulness, of inner strength, coupled with an almost pitiable fragility, corresponded so exactly with my expectation that, had I bumped into her in another place, I would have known that she was Stefanie.

"My name's Ned," I said, speaking to her eyes. "I'm a friend of Ben's. Also a colleague. I'm alone. No one knows I'm here."

I had meant to go on. I had a pompous speech in my head that said something like "Please tell him that whatever he's done, it makes no difference to me." But the steadiness of her gaze prevented me.

"Why should it matter who knows that you are here and who does not?" she asked. She spoke without accent, but with a German cadence, making tiny hesitations before the open vowels. "He is not hiding. Who is looking for him except you? Why should he hide?"

"I understood he might be in some kind of trouble," I said, following her into the house.

The hall was half studio, half makeshift living room. Dustsheets covered much of the furniture. The remains of a meal lay on the table: two mugs, two plates, both used.

"What kind of trouble?" she demanded.

"It's to do with his work in Berlin. I thought perhaps he would have told you about it."

"He has told me nothing. He has never talked to me about his work. Perhaps he knows I am not interested."

"May I ask what he does talk about?"

She considered this. "No." And then, as if relenting, "At present he does not talk to me at all. He seems to have become a Trappist. Why not? Sometimes he watches me paint, sometimes he fishes, sometimes we eat something or drink a little wine. Quite often he sleeps."

"How long's he been here?"

She shrugged. "Three days?"

"Did he come straight from Berlin?"

"He came on the boat. Since he does not speak, that's all I know."

"He disappeared," I said. "There's a hue and cry for him. They thought he might come to me. I don't think they know about you."

She was listening to me again, listening first to my words and then my silence. She seemed to be without embarrassment, like a listening animal. It's the authority of suffering, I thought, remembering her lover's suicide; she cannot be reached by small worries.

"*They,*" she repeated with puzzlement. "Who are *they?* What is there to *know* about me that is so particular?"

"Ben was doing secret work," I said.

"*Ben?*"

"Like his father," I said. "He was tremendously proud of following in his father's steps."

She was shocked and agitated. "Why? Who for? *Secret* work? What a fool!"

"For British Intelligence. He was in Berlin, attached to the Military Adviser's office, but his real work was intelligence."

"*Ben?*" she said as the disgust and disbelief gathered in her face. "All those *lies* he must tell? Ben?"

"Yes, I'm afraid so. But it was duty."

"How *terrible.*"

Her easel stood with its back to me. Placing herself the other side of it, she began mixing her paints.

"If I could just talk to him," I said, but she pretended to be too much lost to her painting to hear me.

The back of the house gave on to parkland, then a line of pines hunchbacked by the wind. Beyond the pines lay a loch surrounded by small mauve hills. On its far bank I made out a fisherman standing on a collapsed jetty. He was fishing but not casting. I don't know how long I watched him, but long enough to know that it was Ben, and that he had no interest in catching fish. I pushed open the French windows and stepped into the garden. A cold wind was ruffling the surface of the loch as I tiptoed along the jetty. He was wearing a tweed jacket that was too full for him. I guessed it had belonged to her dead lover. And a hat, a green felt hat that, like all hats with Ben, looked as though it had been made for him. He didn't turn, though he must have felt my footsteps. I placed myself beside him.

"The only thing you'll catch like that is pneumonia, you German ass," I said.

His face was turned against me, so I remained standing beside him, watching the water with him and sensing the nudge of his shoulder as the rocking jetty threw us carelessly together. I watched the water thicken and the sky turn grey behind the mountains. A few times I watched the red float of his line vanish below the oily surface. But if a fish had struck, Ben made no effort to play it or reel it in. I saw the lights go on in the house, and the figure of Stefanie standing at her easel, adding a brush stroke, then backing her wrist against her brow. The air turned cold and the night gathered, but Ben didn't move. We were in competition with each other, as we had been during our strongarm training. I was demanding, Ben was refusing. Only one of us could have his way. If it took me all night and all tomorrow, and if I starved in the process, I wasn't going to yield till he'd acknowledged me.

A half moon came up, and stars. The wind dropped and a silver ground mist formed across the blackened heather. And still we stood there, waiting for one of us to surrender. I was nearly sleeping on my feet when I heard the rattle of his reel and saw the float lift from the water and the bare line after it, flashing in the moonlight. I didn't move and didn't speak. I let him reel in and make his hook fast. I let him turn to me, because he had to if he wanted to walk past me down the jetty.

We stood face to face in the moonlight. Ben looked downwards, apparently studying my feet to see how he could step round them. His gaze travelled up to my face, but nothing changed in his expression. His locked features stayed locked. If they betrayed anything, it was anger.

"Well," he said. "Enter the third murderer."

This time neither of us laughed.

She must have sensed our approach and removed herself. I heard music playing in another part of the house. When we reached the hall, Ben headed for the stairs but I grabbed his arm.

"You've got to tell me," I said. "There's never going to be anyone better to tell. I broke ranks to come here. You've got to tell me what happened to the network."

There was a long drawing room beyond the hall, with shuttered windows and more dustsheets over the sofas. It was cold, but Ben still had his jacket on and I my greatcoat. I opened the shutters and let the moonlight in. I had an instinct that anything brighter would disturb him. The music was not far away from us. I thought it was Grieg. I wasn't sure. Ben spoke without remorse and without catharsis. He had confessed enough to himself, all day and night, I knew. He talked in the dead tone of somebody describing a disaster he knows that nobody can understand who was not part of it, and the music kept playing below his voice. He had no use for himself. The glamorous hero had given up as one of life's contenders. Perhaps he was a little tired of his guilt. He spoke tersely. I think he wanted me to go.

"Haggarty's a shit," he said. "World class. He's a thief, he drinks, he rapes a bit. His one justification was the Seidl network. Head Office were trying to wheedle him away from it and give Seidl to new people. I was the first new person. Haggarty decided to punish me for taking away his network."

He described the studied insults, the successive night duties and weekends, the hostile reports passed back to Haggarty's supporters' club in Head Office.

"At first he wouldn't tell me anything about the network. Then Head Office bawled him out, so he told me everything. Fifteen years of it. Every tiny detail of their lives, even the joes who'd died on the job. He'd send files to me in pyramids, all flagged and cross-referred. Read this, remember that. Who's she? Who's he? Note this address, this name, these covernames, those symbols. Escape procedures. Fallbacks. The recognition codes and safety procedures for the radio. Then he'd test me. Take me to the safe room, sit me across the table, grill me. 'You're not up to it. We can't send you in till you know your stuff. You'd better stay in over the weekend and mug it up. I'll test you again on Monday.' The network was his life. He wanted me to feel inadequate. I did and I was."

But Head Office did not give in to Haggarty's bullying, neither did Ben. "I put myself on an exam footing," he said.

As the day of his first meeting with Seidl approached, Ben assembled for himself a system of mnemonics and acronyms that would enable him to encompass the network's fifteen years of history. Seated night and day in his office at Station Headquarters, he drew up consciousness charts and communications charts and devised systems for memorising the aliases, covernames, home addresses and places of employment of its agents, sub-agents, couriers and collaborators. Then he transferred his data to plain postcards, writing on one side only. On the other, in one line, he wrote the subject: "dead-letter boxes," "salaries," "safe houses." Each night, before going back to his flat or stretching out in the Station sickroom, he would play a game of memory with himself, first putting the cards face downward on his desk, then comparing what he had remembered with the data on the reverse side.

"I didn't sleep a lot but that's not unusual," he said. "As the day came up, I didn't sleep at all. I spent the whole night mugging up my stuff, then I lay on the couch staring at the ceiling. When I got up I couldn't remember any of it. Sort of paralysis. I went to my room, sat down at the desk, put my head in my hands and started to ask myself questions. 'If covername Margaret-stroke-two thinks he's under surveillance, whom does he contact how, and what does the contact then do?' The answer was a total blank.

"Haggarty wandered in and asked how I was feeling and I said 'fine.' To do him justice, he wished me luck and I think he meant it. I thought he'd shoot some trick question at me and I was going to tell him to go to hell. But he just said, '*Komm gut Heim*,' and patted my shoulder. I put the cards in my pocket. Don't ask me why. I was scared of failure. That's why we do everything, isn't it? I was scared of failure and I hated Haggarty and Haggarty had put me to the torture. I've got about two hundred other reasons why I took the cards, but none of them help a great deal. Perhaps it was my way of committing suicide. I quite like that idea. I took them and I went across. We used a limousine, specially converted. I sat in the back with my double hidden under the seat. The Vopos weren't allowed to search us, of course. All the same, switching with a double as you turn a sharp corner is a bloody hairy game. You've got to sort of roll out of the car. Seidl had provided a bike for me. He believes in bicycles. His guards used to lend him one when he was a prisoner of war in England."

Smiley had told me the story already, but I let Ben tell it to me again.

"I had the cards in my jacket pocket," he went on. "My inside jacket pocket. It was one of those blazing-hot Berlin days. I think I unbuttoned my jacket while I bicycled. I don't know. When I try to remember, I sometimes unbuttoned it and I sometimes didn't. That's what happens to your memory when you work it to death. It does all the versions for you. I got to the rendezvous early, checked the cars, the usual bullshit, went in. It had all come back to me by then. Taking the cards with me had done the trick. I didn't need them. Seidl was fine. I was fine. We did our business, I briefed him, gave him some money—all just like Sarratt. I rode back to the pickup point, ditched the bike, dived into the car and as we crossed into West Berlin I realised I hadn't got the cards. I was missing the weight of them, or the pressure or something. I was in a panic but I always am. Deep down, I'm in a panic all the time. That's who I am. This was just a bigger panic. I made them drop me at my flat, rang Seidl's emergency number. No one answered. I tried the fallback. No answer. I tried his stand-in, a woman called Lotte. No answer. I took a cab to Tempelhof, made a discreet exit, came here."

Suddenly there was only Stefanie's music to listen to. Ben had finished his story. I didn't realise at first that this was all there was. I waited, staring at him, expecting him to go on. I had been wanting a kidnapping at least—savage East German secret police rising from the back of his car, sandbagging him, forcing a chloroformed mask on him while they rifled his pockets. It was only gradually that the appalling banality of what he had told me got through to me: that you could lose a network as easily as you could lose a bunch of keys or a cheque book or a pocket handkerchief. I was craving for a greater dignity, but he had none to offer me.

"So where did you last have them?" I said stupidly. I could have been talking to a child about his lost schoolbooks, but he didn't mind, he had no pride any more.

"The cards?" he said. "Maybe on the bicycle. Maybe rolling out of the car. Maybe getting back into it. The bike has a security chain to lock round the wheel. I had to stoop down to put it on and take it off. Maybe then. It's like losing anything. Till you find it, you never know. Afterwards, it's obvious. But there hasn't been an afterwards."

"Do you think you were followed?"

"I don't know. I just don't know."

I wanted to ask him when he had written his love letter to me, but I couldn't bring myself to. Besides, I thought I knew. It was in one of his drinking sessions when Haggarty was riding him hardest and he was in despair. What I really wanted him to tell me was that he had never written it. I wanted to put the clock back and make things the way they had been until a week ago. But the simple questions had died with the simple answers. Our childhoods were over for good.

They must have surrounded the house, and certainly they never rang the bell. Monty was probably standing outside the window when I opened the shutters to let the moonlight in, because when he needed to, he just stepped into the room, looking embarrassed but resolute.

"You did ever so nicely, Ned," he said consolingly. "It was the public library gave you away. Your nice librarian lady took a real shine to you. I think she'd have come with us if we'd let her."

Skordeno followed him, and then Smiley appeared in the other doorway, wearing the apologetic air that frequently accompanied his most ruthless acts. And I recognised with no particular surprise that I had done everything he had wanted me to do. I had put myself in Ben's position and led them to my friend. Ben didn't seem particularly surprised either. Perhaps he was relieved. Monty and Skordeno moved into place either side of him, but Ben remained sitting among the dustsheets, his tweed jacket pulled round him like a rug. Skordeno tapped him on the shoulder; then Monty and Skordeno stooped and, like a pair of furniture removers used to one another's timing, lifted him gently to his feet. When I protested to Ben that I had not knowingly betrayed him, he shook his head to say it didn't matter. Smiley stepped aside to let them by. His myopic gaze was fixed on me enquiringly.

"We've arranged a special sailing," he said.

"I'm not coming," I replied.

I looked away from him and when I looked again he was gone. I heard the jeep disappearing down the track. I followed the music across the empty hall into a study crammed with books and magazines and what appeared to be the manuscript of a novel spread over the floor. She was sitting sideways in a deep chair. She had changed into a housecoat and her pale golden hair hung loose over her shoulders. She was barefoot, and did not lift her head as I entered. She spoke to me as if she had known me all her life, and I suppose in a way she had, in the sense that I was Ben's familiar. She switched off the music.

"Were you his lover?" she asked.

"No. He wanted me to be. I realise that now."

She smiled. "And I wanted him to be *my* lover, but that wasn't possible either, was it?" she said.

"It seems not."

"Have you had women, Ned?"

"No."

"Had Ben?"

"I don't know. I think he tried. I suppose it didn't work."

She was breathing deeply and tears were trickling down her cheeks and neck. She climbed to her feet, eyes pressed shut, and, like a blind woman, stretched out her arms for me to embrace her. Her body squeezed against me as she buried her head in my shoulder and shook and wept. I put my arms round her but she pushed me away and led me to the sofa.

"Who made him become one of you?" she said.

"No one. It was his own choice. He wanted to imitate his father."

"Is that a choice?"

"Of a sort."

"And you too, you are a volunteer?"

"Yes."

"Whom are *you* imitating?"

"No one."

"Ben had no capacity for such a life. They had no business to be charmed by him. He was too persuasive."

"I know."

"And you? Do you need them to make a man of you?"

"It's something that has to be done."

"To make a man of you?"

"The work. It's like emptying the dustbins or cleaning up in hospitals. Somebody has to do it. We can't pretend it isn't there."

"Oh, I think we can." She took my hand and wound her fingers stiffly into mine. "We pretend a lot of things aren't there. Or we pretend that other things are more important. That's how we survive. We shall not defeat liars by lying to them. Will you stay here tonight?"

"I have to go back. I'm not Ben. I'm me. I'm his friend."

"Let me tell you something. May I? It is very dangerous to play with reality. Will you remember that?"

I have no picture of our leavetaking, so I expect it was too painful and my memory has rejected it. All I know now is, I had to catch the ferry. There was no jeep waiting so I walked. I remember the salt of her tears and the smell of her hair as I hurried through the night wind, and the black clouds writhing round the moon and the thump of the sea as I skirted the rocky bay. I remember the headland and the stubby little lighted steamer starting to cast off. And I know that for the entire journey I stood on the foredeck and that for the last part of it Smiley stood beside me. He must have heard Ben's story by then, and come up on deck to offer me his silent consolation.

I never saw Ben again—they kept me from him as we disembarked—but when I heard he had been discharged from the Service I wrote to Stefanie and asked her to tell me where he was. My letter was returned marked "Gone Away."

I would like to be able to tell you that Ben did not cause the destruction of the network, because Bill Haydon had betrayed it long before. Or better, that the network had been set up for us by the East Germans or the Russians in the first place, as a means of keeping us occupied and feeding us disinformation. But I am afraid the truth is otherwise, for in those days Haydon's access was limited by compartmentation, and his work did not take him to Berlin. Smiley even asked Bill, after his capture, whether he had had a hand in it, and Bill had laughed.

"I'd been wanting to get my hooks on that network for years," he'd replied. "When I heard what had happened, I'd a bloody good mind to send young Cavendish a bunch of flowers, but I suppose it wouldn't have been secure."

The best I could tell Ben, if I saw him today, is that if he hadn't blown the network when he did, Haydon would have blown it for him a couple of years later. The best I could tell Stefanie is that she was right in her way, but then so was I, and that her words never left my memory, even after I had ceased to regard her as the fountain of all wisdom. If I never understood who she was—if she belonged, as it were, more to Ben's mystery than my own—she was nevertheless the first of the siren voices that sounded in my ear, warning me that my mission was an ambiguous one. Sometimes I wonder what I was for her, but I'm afraid I know only too well: a callow boy, another Ben, unversed in life, banishing weakness with a show of strength, and taking refuge in a cloistered world.

* * *

I went back to Berlin not long ago. It was a few weeks after the Wall had been declared obsolete. An old bit of business took me, and Personnel was pleased to pay my fare. I never was formally stationed there, as it worked out, but I had been a frequent visitor, and for us old cold warriors a visit to Berlin is like returning to the source. And on a damp afternoon I found myself standing at the grimy little bit of fencing known grandly as the Wall of the Unknown Ones, which was the memorial to those killed while trying to escape during the sixties, some of whom did not have the foresight to give their names in advance. I stood among a humble group of East Germans, mostly women, and I noticed that they were examining the inscriptions on the crosses: unknown man, shot on such-and-such a date, in 1965. They were looking for clues, fitting the dates to the little that they knew.

And the sickening notion struck me that they could even have been looking for one of Ben's agents who had made a dash for freedom at the eleventh hour and failed. And the notion was all the more bewildering when I reflected that it was no longer we Western Allies, but East Germany itself, which was struggling to snuff out its existence.

The memorial is gone now. Perhaps it will find a corner in a museum somewhere, but I doubt it. When the Wall came down—hacked to pieces, sold—the memorial came down with it, which strikes me as an appropriate comment on the fickleness of human constancy.

4

Somebody asked Smiley about interrogation, yet again. It was a question that cropped up often as the night progressed—mainly because his audience wanted to squeeze more case histories out of him. Children are merciless.

"Oh, there's *some* art to faulting the liar, of course there is," Smiley conceded doubtfully, and took a sip from his glass. "But the real art lies in recognising the truth, which is a great deal harder. Under interrogation, nobody behaves normally. People who are stupid act intelligent. Intelligent people act stupid. The guilty look innocent as the day, and the innocent look dreadfully guilty. And just occasionally people act as they are and tell the truth as they know it, and of course they're the poor souls who get caught out every time. There's nobody less convincing to our wretched trade than the blameless man with nothing to hide."

"Except possibly the blameless woman," I suggested under my breath.

George had reminded me of Bella and the ambiguous sea captain Brandt.

He was a big, rough flaxen fellow, at first guess Slav or Scandinavian, with the roll of a landed seaman and the far eyes of an adventurer. I first met him in Zurich where he was in hot water with the police. The city superintendent called me in the middle of the night and said, "Herr Konsul, we have somebody who says he has information for the British. We have orders to put him over the border in the morning."

I didn't ask which border. The Swiss have four, but when they are throwing somebody out they're not particular. I drove to the district prison and met him in a barred interviewing room: a caged giant in a roll-neck pullover who called himself Sea Captain Brandt, which seemed to be his personal version of *Kapitän zur See*.

"You're a long way from the sea," I said as I shook his great, padded hand.

As far as the Swiss were concerned, he had everything wrong with him. He had swindled a hotel, which in Switzerland is such a heinous crime it gets its own paragraph in the criminal code. He had caused a disturbance, he was penniless and his West German passport did not bear examination—though the Swiss refused to say this out loud, since a fake passport could prejudice their chances of getting rid of him to another country. He had been picked up drunk and vagrant and he blamed it on a girl. He had broken someone's jaw. He insisted on speaking to me alone.

"You British?" he asked in English, presumably in order to disguise our conversation from the Swiss, though they spoke better English than he did.

"Yes."

"Prove, please."

I showed him my official identity card, describing me as Vice-Consul for Economic Affairs.

"You work for British Intelligence?" he asked.

"I work for the British government."

"Okay, okay," he said, and in sudden weariness sank his head into his hand so that his long blond hair flopped forward, and he had to toss it back again with a sweep of his arm. His face was chipped and pitted like a boxer's.

"You ever been in prison?" he asked, staring at the scrubbed white table.

"No, thank God."

"Jesus," he said, and in bad English told me his story.

He was a Latvian, born in Riga of Latvian and Polish parents. He spoke Latvian, Russian, Polish and German. He was born to the sea, which I sensed immediately, for I was born to it myself. His father and grandfather had been sailors, he had served six years in the Soviet navy, sailing the Arctic out of Archangel, and the Sea of Japan out of Vladivostok. A year back he had returned to Riga, bought a small boat and taken up smuggling along the Baltic coast, running cheap Russian vodka into Finland with the help of Scandinavian fishermen. He was caught and put in prison near Leningrad, escaped and stowed away to Poland, where he lived illegally with a Polish girl student in Cracow. I tell you this exactly as he told it to me, as if stowing away to Poland from Russia were as self-evident as catching a number 11 bus or popping down the road for a drink. Yet even with my limited familiarity with the obstacles he had overcome, I knew it was an extraordinary feat—and no less so when he performed it a second time. For when the girl left him to marry a Swiss salesman, he headed back to the coast and got himself a ride to Malmö, then down to Hamburg where he had a distant cousin, but the cousin was distant indeed, and told him to go to hell. So he stole the cousin's passport and headed south to Switzerland, determined to get back his Polish girl. When her new husband wouldn't let her go, Brandt broke the poor man's jaw for him, so here he was, a prisoner of the Swiss police.

All this still in English, so I asked him where he'd learned it. From the BBC, when he was out smuggling, he said. From his Polish girl—she was a language student. I had given him a packet of cigarettes and he was devouring them one after another, making a gaschamber of our little room.

"So what's this information you've got for us?" I asked him.

As a Latvian, he said in preamble, he felt no allegiance to Moscow. He had grown up under the lousy Russian tyranny in Latvia, he had served under lousy Russian officers in the navy, he had been sent to prison by lousy Russians and hounded by lousy Russians, and he had no compunction about betraying them. He hated Russians. I asked him the names of the ships he had served on and he told me. I asked him what armament they carried and he described some of the most sophisticated stuff they possessed at that time. I gave him a pencil and paper and he made surprisingly impressive drawings. I asked him what he knew about signals. He knew a lot. He was a qualified signalman and had used their latest toys, even if his memory was a year old. I asked him, "Why the British?" and he replied that he had known "a couple of you guys in Leningrad"—British sailors on a goodwill visit. I wrote down their names and the name of their ship, returned to my office and sent a flash telegram to London because we only had a few hours' grace before they put him over the border. Next evening Sea Captain Brandt was undergoing rigorous questioning at a safe house in Surrey. He was on the brink of a dangerous career. He knew every nook and bay along the south Baltic coast; he had good friends who were honest Latvian fishermen, others who were black marketeers, thieves and disaffected drop-outs. He was offering exactly what London was looking for after our recent losses—the chance to build a new supply line in and out of northern Russia, across Poland into Germany.

I have to set the recent history for you here—of the Circus, and of my own efforts to succeed in it.

After Ben, it had been touch and go for me whether they promoted me or threw me out. I think today that I owed more to Smiley's backstairs intervention than I gave him credit for at the time. Left to himself, I don't think Personnel would have kept me five minutes. I had broken bounds while under house arrest, I had withheld my knowledge of Ben's attachment to Stefanie, and if I was not a willing recipient of Ben's amorous declarations, I was guilty by association, so to hell with me.

"We rather thought you might like to consider the British Council," Personnel had suggested nastily, at a meeting adorned not even by a cup of tea.

But Smiley interceded for me. Smiley, it appeared, had seen beyond my youthful impulsiveness, and Smiley commanded what amounted to his own modest private army of secret sources scattered around Europe. A further reason for my reprieve was provided—though not even Smiley could have known it at the time—by the traitor Bill Haydon, whose London Station was rapidly acquiring a monopoly of Circus operations worldwide. And if Smiley's questing eye had not yet focussed on Bill, he was already convinced that the Fifth Floor was nursing a Moscow Centre mole to its bosom, and determined to assemble a team of officers whose age and access placed them beyond suspicion. By a mercy, I was one.

For a few months I was kept in limbo, devilling in large back rooms, evaluating and distributing low-grade reports to Whitehall clients. Friendless and bored, I was seriously beginning to wonder whether Personnel had decided to post me to death, when to my joy I was summoned to his office and in Smiley's presence offered the post of second man in Zurich, under a capable old trooper named Eddows, whose stated principle was to leave me to sink or swim.

Within a month I was installed in a small flat in the Altstadt, working round the clock eight days a week. I had a Soviet naval attaché in Geneva who loved Lenin but loved a French air hostess more, and a Czech arms dealer in Lausanne who was having a crisis of conscience about supplying the world's terrorists with weapons and explosives. I had a millionaire Albanian with a chalet in St. Moritz who was risking his neck by returning to his homeland and recruiting members of his former household, and a nervous East German physicist on attachment to the Max Planck Institute in Essen who had secretly converted to Rome. I had a beautiful little microphone operation running against the Polish Embassy in Bern and a telephone tap on a pair of Hungarian spies in Basel. And I was by now beginning to fancy myself seriously in love with Mabel, who had recently been transferred to Vetting Section, and was the toast of the Junior Officers' Bar.

And Smiley's faith in me was not misplaced, for by my own exertions in the field, and his insistence upon rigid need-to-know at home, we succeeded in netting valuable intelligence and even getting it into the right hands—and you would be surprised how rarely that combination is achieved.

So that when after two years of this the Hamburg slot came up—a one-man post, and working directly to London Station, now willy-nilly the operational hub of the Service—I had Smiley's generous blessing to apply for it, whatever his private reservations about Haydon's widening embrace. I angled, I was not brash, I re-minded Personnel of my naval background. I let him infer, if I did not say it in as many words, that I was straining at the bonds of Smiley's old-world caution. And it worked. He gave me Hamburg Station on the Haydon ticket, and the same night, after a romantic dinner at Bianchi's, Mabel and I slept together, the first time for each of us.

My sense of the rightness of things was further increased when, on looking over my new stocklist, I saw to my amusement that one Wolf Dittrich, alias Sea Captain Brandt, was a leading player in my new cast of characters. We are talking of the late sixties now. Bill Haydon had three more years to run.

Hamburg had always been a good place to be English, now it was an even better place to spy. After the lakeside gentility of Zurich, Hamburg crackled with energy and sparkled with sea air. The old Hanseatic ties to Poland, northern Russia and the Baltic states were still very much alive. We had commerce, we had banking— well, so had Zurich. But we had shipping too, and immigrants and adventurers. We had brashness and vulgarity galore. We were the German capital of whoredom and the press. And on our doorstep we had the secretive lowlands of Schleswig-Holstein, with their horizontal rainstorms, red farms, green fields and cloudstacked skies. Every man has his price. To this day, my soul can be bought for a jar of Lübeck beer, a pickled herring and a glass of schnapps after a trudge along the dykes.

Everything else about the job was equally pleasing. I was Ned the Assistant Shipping Consul; my humble office was a pretty brick cottage with a brass plate, handy enough for the Consulate General, yet prudently apart from it. Two clerks on secondment from the Admiralty performed my cover work for me, and kept their mouths shut. I had a radio and a Circus cypher clerk. And if Mabel and I were not yet engaged to be married, our relationship had reached a stage when she was ready to clear her decks for me whenever I popped back to London for a consultation with Bill or one of his lieutenants.

To meet my joes, I had a safe flat in Wellingsbüttel overlooking the cemetery, on the upper floor of a flower shop managed by a retired German couple who had belonged to us in the war. Their busiest days were Sundays, and on Monday mornings a queue of kids from the housing estate sold them back the flowers they had sold the day before. I never saw a safer spot. Hearses, covered vans and funeral cortèges rolled past us all day long. But at night the place was literally as quiet as the grave. Even the exotic figure of my sea captain became unremarkable when he donned his black hat and dark suit and swung into the brick archway of our shop and, with his commercial traveller's briefcase bouncing at his side, stomped up the stairs to our innocent front door marked *"Büro."*

I shall go on calling him Brandt. Some people, however much they change their names, have only one.

But the jewel in my crown was the *Margerite*—or, as we called her in English, the *Daisy*. She was a fifty-foot clinker-built, double-ended fishing boat converted to a cabin cruiser, with a wheelhouse, a main saloon and four berths in the foc'sle. She had a mizzen mast and sail to steady her from rolling. She had a dark-green hull with light-green gunnels and a white cabin roof. She was built for stealth, not speed. In poor light and choppy water, she was invisible to the naked eye. She had sparse top-hamper, and lay close to the water, which gave her a harmless image on the radar screens, particularly in heavy weather. The Baltic is a vengeful sea, shallow and tideless. Even in a mild wind, the waves come steep and nasty. At ten knots and full throttle, the *Daisy* pitched and rolled like a pig. The only speedy thing about her was the fourteen-foot Zodiac dinghy hoisted as the ship's lifeboat and lashed to the cabin roof, with a Johnson 50-horsepower to whisk our agents in and out.

For her berth she had the old fishing village of Blankenese on the river Elbe, just a few short miles out of Hamburg. And there she lay contentedly among her equals, as humble an example of her kind as you could wish. From Blankenese, when she was needed, she could slip upriver to the Kiel Canal, and crawl its sixty miles at five knots before hitting open sea.

She had a Decca navigator that took readings from slave stations on the shore, but so did everyone. She had nothing inside or out that was not consistent with her modesty. Each of her three-man crew could turn his hand to everything. There were no specialists, though each had his particular love. When we needed expert despatchers or fitters, the Royal Navy was on hand to help us.

So you can see that, what with a new dynamic team to back me up at London Station, and a full hand of sources to test my versatility, and the *Daisy* and her crew to manage, I had everything that a Head of Station with salt water in his blood could decently inherit.

And of course I had Brandt.

Brandt's two years before the Circus mast had altered him in ways I at first found hard to define. It was not so much an aging or a hardening I observed in him, as that wearying alertness, that overwakefulness, which the secret world with time imprints upon even the most relaxed of its inhabitants. We met at the safe flat. He entered. He stopped dead and stared at me. His jaw fell open and he let out a great shout of recognition. He seized my arms in a sultan's greeting and nearly broke them. He laughed till the tears came, he held me away to look at, then hauled me back to hug against his black overcoat. But his spontaneity was strained by watchfulness. I knew the signs. I had seen them in other joes.

"God damn, why they don't tell me nothing, Herr Konsul?" he cried as he embraced me yet again. "What damn game they playing? Listen, we do some good things over there, hear me? We got good people, we beat those damn Russians to death, okay?"

"I know," I said, laughing back at him. "I heard."

And when night fell he insisted on seating me among the coils of rope in the back of his van and driving me at breakneck speed to the remote farmhouse that London had acquired for him. He was determined to introduce me to his crew and I looked forward to it. And I looked forward even more to getting a sight of his girlfriend Bella, because London Station was feeling a little queasy about her recent arrival in his life. She was twenty-two years old and had been with him three months. Brandt was looking hard at fifty. It was midsummer, I remember, and the inside of the van smelt of freesias, for he had bought her a bunch at the market.

"She's a number one girl," he told me proudly as we entered the house. "Cooks good, makes good love, learns English, everything. Hey, Bella, I brought you new boyfriend!"

Painters and sailors make the same kind of houses, and Brandt's was no exception. It was scant but homely, with brick floors and low, white-raftered ceilings. Even in the darkness it seemed to usher in the outside light. From the front door we stepped straight down into the drawing room. A wood fire smouldered in the hearth and a ship's lamp shone on the naked flank of a girl as she lay reading on a heap of cushions. Hearing us enter, she sprang excitedly to her feet. Twenty-two and going on eighteen, I thought as she grabbed my hand and gaily pumped it up and down. She was wearing a man's shirt and very short shorts. A gold amulet glinted at her throat, declaring Brandt's possession of her: this is my woman, wearing my badge of ownership. Her face was peasant and Slav and naturally happy, with clear, wide eyes, high cheeks and a tipped-up smile even when her lips were in repose. Her bare legs were long and tanned to the same gold colour as her hair. She had a small waist, high breasts and full hips. It was a very beautiful, very young body, and whatever Brandt was thinking, it belonged to no one of his age, or even mine.

She set his freesias in a vase and fetched black bread and pickles and a bottle of schnapps. She was carelessly provocative in her movements. Either she knew exactly, or not at all, the power of each slight gesture she made. She sat beside him at the table, smiled at me and threw her arm around him, letting her shirt gape. She took possession of his hand and showed me by comparison the slenderness of her own, while Brandt talked recklessly about the network, mentioning joes and places by name, and Bella measured me with her frank eyes.

"Listen," Brandt said, "we got to get Aleks another radio, hear me, Ned? They take it apart, they put new spares, batteries, that radio's lousy. That's a bad-luck radio."

When the phone rang, he answered it imperiously: "Listen, I'm busy, okay? . . . Leave the package with Stefan, I said. Listen, have you heard from Leonids?"

The room gradually filled up. First to enter was a darting, bandy-legged man with a drooping moustache. He kissed Bella rapturously but chastely on the lips, punched Brandt's forearm and helped himself to a plateful of food.

"That's Kazimirs," Brandt explained, with a jab of his thumb. "He's a bastard and I love him. Okay?"

"Very okay," I said heartily.

Kazimirs had escaped three years ago across the Finnish border, I remembered. He had killed two Soviet frontier guards along his way, and he was crazy about engines—never happier than when he was up to his elbows in oil. He was also the respected ship's cook.

After Kazimirs came the Durba brothers, Antons and Alfreds, stocky and pert like Welshmen, and blue-eyed like Brandt. The Durbas had sworn to their mother that they would never go to sea together, so they took it in turns, for the *Daisy* handled best with three, and we liked to leave space for cargo and unexpected passengers. Soon everyone was talking at once, shooting questions at me, not waiting for the answers, laughing, proposing toasts, smoking, reminiscing, conspiring. Their last run had been bad, really bad, said Kazimirs. That was three weeks ago. *Daisy* had hit a freak storm off the Gulf of Danzig and lost her mizzen. At Ujava on the Latvian coast, they had missed the light signal in the fog, said Antons Durba. They had fired a rocket and God help them, there was this whole damned reception party of crazy Latvians standing on the beach like a delegation of city fathers! Wild laughter, toasts, then a deep Nordic silence while everyone but myself was struck by the same solemn memory.

"To Valdemars," said Kazimirs, and we drank a toast to Valdemars, a member of their group who had died five years ago. Then Bella took Brandt's glass and drank too, a separate ceremony while she watched me over the brim. "Valdemars," she repeated softly, and her solemnity was as beguiling as her smile. Had she known Valdemars? Had he been one of her lovers? Or was she simply drinking to a brave fellow countryman who had died for the Cause?

But I have to tell you a little more about Valdemars—not whether he had slept with Bella or even how he had died, for no one knew for sure. All that was known was that he had been put ashore and never heard of again. One story said he had managed to swallow his pill, another that he had given orders to his bodyguard to shoot him if he walked into a trap. But the bodyguard had disappeared too. And Valdemars was not the only one who had disappeared during what was now remembered by the group as "the autumn of betrayal." In the next few months, as the anniversaries of their deaths came round, we drank to four other Latvian heroes who had perished unaccountably in the same ill-starred period—delivered, it was now believed, not to partisans in the forest, nor loyal reception parties on the beach, but straight into the hands of Moscow Centre's chief of Latvian operations. And if new networks had been cautiously rebuilt meanwhile, five years later the stigma of these betrayals still clung to the survivors, as Haydon had been at pains to warn me.

"They're a careless bunch of sods," he had said with his usual irreverence, "and when they're not being careless, they're duplicitous. Don't be fooled by all that Nordic phlegm and backslapping."

I was remembering his words as I continued my mental reconnaissance of Bella. Sometimes she listened resting her head on her clenched fist, sometimes she laid her head on Brandt's forearm, dreaming his thoughts for him while he plotted and drank. But her big, light eyes never ceased visiting me, working me out, this Englishman sent to rule our lives. And occasionally, like a warm cat, she shook herself free of Brandt and took time to groom herself, recrossing her legs and primly correcting the fit of her shorts, or twisting a hank of hair into a plait, or drawing her gold amulet from between her breasts and examining it front and back. I waited for a spark of complicity between herself and other members of the crew, but it was clear to me that Brandt's girl was holy ground. Even the ebullient Kazimirs deadened his face to talk to her. She fetched another bottle, and when she returned she sat down beside me and took hold of my hand and opened my palm on the table, examining it while she spoke in Latvian to Brandt, who broke into a gust of laughter which the rest of them took up.

"You know what she say?"

"I'm afraid I don't."

"She says English make damn good husband. If I die, she going to have you instead!"

She clambered back to him and, laughing, wriggled into his embrace. She didn't look at me after that. It was as if she didn't need to. So I avoided her eyes in return, and thought dutifully about her history as told to London Station by Sea Captain Brandt.

She was the daughter of a farmer from a village near Jelgava, who had been shot dead when security police raided a secret meeting of Latvian patriots, Brandt had said. The farmer was a founder member of the group. The police wanted to shoot the girl as well, but she escaped into the forest and joined up with a band of partisans and outlaws who passed her round among them for a summer, which did not seem to have upset her. By stages she had made her way to the coast and, by a route that was still mysterious to us, got word to Brandt, who, without troubling to mention her to London in advance, picked her off a beach while he was landing a new radio operator to replace another who had had a nervous breakdown. Radio operators are the opera stars of every network. If they don't have breakdowns, they have shingles.

"Great guys," said Brandt enthusiastically as he drove me back to town. "You like them?"

"They're terrific," I said, and meant it, for there is no better company anywhere than men who love the sea.

"Bella want to work with us. She want to kill the guys who shoot her father. I say no. She's too young. I love her."

A fierce white moon shone on the flat meadows, and by its light I saw his craggy face in profile, as if set against the storm to come.

"And you knew him," I suggested, affecting to recapitulate something I vaguely remembered. "Her father. Feliks. He was a friend of yours."

"Sure I knew Feliks! I love him! He was a great guy! The bastards shot him dead."

"Did he die immediately?"

"They shoot him to pieces. Kalashnikovs. They shoot everybody. Seven guys. All shot."

"Did anyone see it happen?"

"One guy. He see it, run away."

"What became of the bodies?"

"Secret police take them. They're scared, those police guys. Don't want no trouble from the people. Shoot the partisans, throw them in a truck, drive away to hell."

"How well did you know him—her father?"

Brandt made his sweeping gesture with his forearm. "Feliks? He was my friend. Fought at Leningrad. Prisoner of war in Germany. Stalin didn't like those guys. When they came home from Germany, he sent them to Siberia, shot them, gave them a bad time. What the hell?"

But London Station had picked up a different story, even if at this stage it was only a whisper. The father had been the informant, said the whisper. Recruited in Siberian captivity and sent back to Latvia to penetrate the groups. He had called the meeting, tipped off his masters, then climbed out of the back window while the partisans were being slaughtered. As a reward, he was now managing a collective farm near Kiev, living under a different name. Somebody had recognised him and told somebody else who had told somebody else. The source was delicate, checking would be a lengthy process.

So I was warned. Watch out for Bella.

I was more than warned. I was disturbed. In the next weeks I saw Bella several times, and each time I was obliged to record my impressions on the encounter sheet which London Station now insisted must be completed each time she was sighted. I made a rendezvous with Brandt at the safe flat, and to my alarm he brought her with him. She had spent the day in town, he said. They were on their way back to the farmhouse, why not?

"Relax. She don't speak no English," he reminded me with a laugh, noticing my discomfort.

So I kept our business short, while she lounged on the sofa and smiled and listened to us with her eyes, but mostly she listened to me.

"My girl's studying," Brandt told me proudly, patting her on the backside as we prepared to separate. "One day she be a big professor. *Nicht wahr, Bella? Du wirst ein ganz grosser Professor, du!*"

A week later, when I took a discreet look at the *Daisy* at her berth in Blankenese, Bella was there again, wearing her shorts and scampering over the deck in her bare feet as if we were planning a Mediterranean cruise.

"For heaven's sake. We can't have girls aboard. London will go mad," I told Brandt that night. "So will the crew. You know how superstitious they are about having women on the ship. You're the same yourself."

He brushed me aside. My predecessor had raised no objection, he said. Why should I?

"Bella makes the boys happy," he insisted. "She's from home, Ned, she's a kid. She's a family for them, come on!"

When I checked the file, I discovered he was half right. My predecessor, a seconded naval officer, had reported that Bella was "conscious to" the *Daisy,* even adding that she seemed to "exert a benign influence as ship's mascot." And when I read between the lines of his report of the *Daisy*'s most recent operational mission, I realised that Bella had been there on the dockside to wave them off—and no doubt to wave them safely back as well.

Now of course operational security is always relative. I had never imagined that everything in the Brandt organisation was going to be played by Sarratt rules. I was aware that in the cloistered atmosphere of Head Office it was too easy to mistake our tortuous structures of codenames, symbols and cut-outs for life on the ground. Cambridge Circus was one thing. A bunch of volatile Baltic patriots risking their necks was another.

Nevertheless the presence of an uncleared, unrecruited camp-follower at the heart of our operation, privy to our plans and conversations, went beyond anything I had imagined—and all this in the wake of the betrayals five years earlier. And the more I worried over it, the more proprietorial, it seemed to me, did Brandt's devotion to the girl become. His endearments grew increasingly lavish in my presence, his caresses more demonstrative. "A typical older man's infatuation for a young girl," I told London, as if I had seen dozens of such cases.

Meanwhile a new mission was being planned for the *Daisy,* the purpose to be revealed to us later. Twice, three times a week, I found myself of necessity driving out to the farmhouse, arriving after dark, then sitting for hours at the table while we studied charts and weather maps and the latest shore observation bulletins. Sometimes the full crew came, sometimes it was just the three of us. To Brandt it made no difference. He clasped Bella to him as if the two of them were in the throes of constant ecstasy, fondling her hair and neck, and once forgetting himself so far as to slip his hand inside her shirt and cup her naked breast while he gave her a prolonged kiss. Yet as I discreetly looked away from these disturbing scenes, what remained longest in my sight was Bella's gaze on me, as if she were telling me she wished that it was I, not Brandt, who was caressing her.

"Explicit embraces appear to be the norm," I wrote drily on the encounter sheet, Hamburg to London Station, late that night in my office. And in my nightly log: "Route, weather and sea conditions acceptable. We await firm orders from Head Office. Morale of crew high."

But my own morale was fighting for survival as one calamity followed upon another.

There was first the unfortunate business of my predecessor, full name Lieutenant Commander Perry de Mornay Lipton, D.S.O., R.N., retd., sometime hero of Jack Arthur Lumley's wartime irregulars. For ten years until my arrival, Lipton had cultivated the rôle of Hamburg character, by day acting the English bloody fool, sporting a monocle and hanging around the expatriate clubs ostensibly to pick up free advice on his investments. But come nightfall, he put on his secret hat and went to work briefing and debriefing his formidable army of secret agents. Or so the legend, as I had heard it from Head Office.

The only thing that had puzzled me was that there had been no formal handover between us, but Personnel had told me tersely Lipton was on a mission elsewhere. I was now admitted to the truth. Lipton had departed, not on some life-and-death adventure in darkest Russia, but to southern Spain, where he had set up house with a former Corporal of Horse named Kenneth, and two hundred thousand pounds of Circus funds, mainly in gold bars and Swiss francs, which he had paid out over several years to brave agents who did not exist.

The mistrust shed by this sad discovery now spilled into every operation Lipton had touched, including inevitably Brandt's. Was Brandt too a Lipton fiction, living high on our secret funds in exchange for ingeniously fabricated intelligence? Were his networks, were his vaunted collaborators and friends, many of whom were drawing liberal salaries?

And Bella—was Bella part of the deception? Had Bella softened his head and weakened his will? Was Brandt too feathering his nest before retiring with his loved one to the south of Spain?

A procession of Circus experts passed through the doors of my little shipping office. First came an improbable man called Captain Plum. Crouched in the privacy of my safe room, Plum and I pored over the *Daisy*'s old fuel dockets and mileage records and compared them with the perilous routes that Brandt and the crew claimed to have steered on their missions along the Baltic coast. The ship's logs were sketchy at best, as most logs are, but we read them all, alongside Plum's records of signals intercepts, radar stations, navigational buoys and sightings of Soviet patrol boats.

A week later Plum was back, this time accompanied by a foul-mouthed Mancunian called Rose, a former Malayan policeman who had made himself a name as a Circus sniffer dog. Rose questioned me as roughly as if I were myself a part of the deception. But when I was about to lose my temper he disarmed me by declaring that, on the evidence available, the Brandt organisation was innocent of misdoing.

Yet in the minds of such people as this, suspicions of one kind only fired suspicions of another, and the question mark hanging over Bella's father, Feliks, had not gone away. If the father was bad, then the daughter must know it, went the reasoning. And if she knew and had not said it, then she was bad as well. Moscow Centre, like the Circus, was well known for recruiting entire families. A father-and-daughter team was eminently plausible. Soon, without any solid evidence I was aware of, London Station began to peddle the notion that Feliks had been responsible for the betrayals five years ago.

Inevitably, this placed Bella in an even more sinister light. There was talk of ordering her to London and grilling her, but here my authority as Brandt's case officer held sway. Impossible, I advised London Station. Brandt would never stand for it. Very well, came the answer—typical of Haydon's cavalier approach—bring them both over and Brandt can sit in while we interrogate the girl. This time I was sufficiently moved to fly back to London myself, where I insisted on stating my case personally to Bill. I entered his room to find him stretched out on a chaise longue, for he affected the eccentricity of never sitting at his desk. A joss stick was burning from an old ginger jar.

"Maybe Brother Brandt isn't as prickly as you think, Master Ned," he said accusingly, peering at me over his half-framed spectacles. "Maybe *you're* the prickly one?"

"He's besotted with her," I said.

"Are you?"

"If we start accusing his girl in front of him, he'll go crazy. He lives for her. He'd tell us to go to hell and dismantle the network, and I doubt whether anyone else could run it."

Haydon pondered this: "The Garibaldi of the Baltic. Well, well. Still, Garibaldi wasn't much bloody good, was he?" He waited for me to answer but I preferred to take his question as rhetorical. "Those jokers she shacked up in the forest with," he drawled finally. "Does she talk about them?"

"She doesn't talk about any of it. Brandt does, she doesn't."

"So what does she talk about?"

"Nothing much. If she says anything of significance, it's usually in Latvian and Brandt translates or not as he thinks fit. Otherwise she just smiles and looks."

"At you?"

"At him."

"And she's quite a looker, I gather."

"She's attractive, I suppose. Yes."

Once more he took his time to consider this. "Sounds to me like the ideal woman," he pronounced. "Smiles and looks, keeps quiet, fucks—what more can you ask?" He again examined me quizzically over his spectacles. "Do you mean she doesn't even speak *German?* She must do, coming from up there. Don't be daft."

"She speaks German reluctantly when she's got no choice. Speaking Latvian's a patriotic act. German isn't."

"Good tits?"

"Not bad."

"Couldn't you get alongside her a bit more? Without rocking the lovers' boat, obviously. Just the answers to a few basic questions would be a help. Nothing dramatic. Just whether she's the real thing, or whether Brother Brandt smuggled her into the nest in a warming pan—or whether Moscow Centre did, of course. See what you can get out of her. He's not her natural father, you realise that, I suppose. He can't be."

"Who isn't?" For a confused moment I had thought he was still talking about Brandt.

"Her daddy. Feliks. The one who got shot or didn't. The farmer. According to the record, she was born January '45, wasn't she?"

"Yes."

"Ergo, conceived around April '44. At which time—if Brother Brandt's to be believed—her supposed daddy was languishing in a prisoner-of-war camp in Germany. Mind you, we shouldn't be too straitlaced about it. No great feat of skill, I suppose, to get yourself knocked up while your old man's in the pen. Still every little helps when we're trying to decide whether to abort a network which may have run its course."

I was grateful for Mabel's company that night, even if we had not yet found our form as the great lovers we were so anxious to become. But of course I didn't tell her anything of my business, least of all about Bella. As a Vetting girl, Mabel was on the routine side of the Circus. It would have been quite improper for me to share my problems with her. If we had already been married—well, that might have been a different thing. Meanwhile, Bella must remain my secret.

And she did. Back in my solitary bed in Hamburg I thought of Bella and little else. The double mystery of her—as a woman and as a potential traitor—elevated her to an object of almost unlimited danger to me. I saw her no longer as a fringe figure of our organisation but its destiny. Her virtue was ours. If Bella was pure, so was the network. But if she was the plaything of another service—a deceiver planted on us to tempt and weaken and ultimately betray us—then the integrity of those round her was soiled with her own, and the network would indeed, as Haydon put it, have run its course.

I closed my eyes and saw her gaze upon me, sunny and beckoning. I felt again the softness of her kisses each time we greeted one another—always, as it seemed to me, held for a fraction longer than formality required. I pictured her liquid body in its different poses, and turned it over and over in my imagination in the same way that I contemplated the possibilities of her treason. I remembered Haydon's suggestion that I should try to "get alongside her," and discovered I was incapable of separating my sense of duty from my desires.

I retold myself the story of her escape, questioning it at every stage. Had she got away before the shooting or during it? And how? Had some lover among the security troops tipped her off? Had there been a shooting at all? And why did she not grieve more for her dead father, instead of making love to Brandt? Even her happiness seemed to speak against her. I imagined her in the forest, with the cut-throats and outlaws. Did each man take her at his will, or did she live now with this one, now with that? I dreamed of her, naked in the forest, and myself naked with her. I awoke ashamed of myself and put through an early-morning call to Mabel.

Did I understand myself? I doubt it. I knew little about women, beautiful women least of all. I am sure it never occurred to me that finding fault with Bella might be my way of weakening her sexual hold on me. Determined on the straight path, I wrote to Mabel daily. Meanwhile I fixed on the *Daisy*'s forthcoming mission as the perfect opportunity to undertake a hostile questioning of Bella. The weather was turning foul, which was what suited the *Daisy* best. It was autumn and the nights were lengthening. The *Daisy* liked the dark too.

"Crew stand by to sail Monday," said London Station's first signal. The second, which did not arrive till Friday evening, gave their destination as the Narva Bay in northern Estonia, not a hundred miles west of Leningrad. Never before had the *Daisy* ventured so far along the Russian seaboard; only rarely had she been used in support of non-Latvian patriots.

"I would give my eyes," I told Brandt.

"You're too damn dangerous, Ned," he replied, clapping me on the shoulder. "Be seasick four days, lie in your bunk, get in the way, what the hell?"

We both knew it was impossible. The most Head Office had ever granted me was a night spin round the island of Bornholm, and even that had been like drawing teeth.

On the Saturday night we gathered in the farmhouse. Kazimirs and Antons Durba arrived together in the van. It was Antons's turn to go to sea. With such a small operational crew, everyone had to know everything, everyone had to be interchangeable. There was no more drink. From now on, they were a dry ship. Kazimirs had brought lobsters. He cooked them elaborately, with a sauce that he was famous for, while Bella played cabin girl to him, fetching and carrying and being decorative. When we had eaten, Bella cleared the table and I spread the charts under the hanging overhead lamp.

Brandt had said six days. It was an optimistic guess. From the Kieler Förde the *Daisy* would make for open sea, passing Bornholm on the Swedish side. On reaching the Swedish island of Gotland she would put in at Sundre on the southern tip, refuel and top up her provisions. While refuelling, she would be approached by two men, one of whom would ask if they had any herring. They were to reply: "Only in tins. There have been no herring in these waters for years." All such exchanges sound fatuous in cold blood, and this one reduced Antons and Kazimirs to fits of nervous laughter. Returning from the kitchen, Bella joined in.

One of the men would then ask to come aboard, I continued. He was an expert —I did not say in sabotage, because the crew had mixed feelings on the matter. His name for the trip would be Volodia. He would be carrying a leather suitcase and, in his coat pocket, a brown button and a white button as proof of his good faith. If he did not know his name, or carried no suitcase, or did not produce the buttons, they were to put him back on shore alive, but return to Kiel at once. There was an agreed radio signal for this eventuality. Otherwise they should make no signals whatever. A moment's silence gripped us, and I heard the sound of Bella's bare feet on the brick floor as she fetched more firewood.

From Gotland they should head northeast through international waters, I said, and steer a central course up the Gulf of Finland, until they were lying off the island of Hogland, where they should idle till dusk, then head due south for Narva Bay, reckoning to make landfall by midnight.

I had brought large-scale charts of the Bay and photographs of the sandy coastline. I spread them on the table and the men gathered to my side to look at them. As they did so, something made me glance up and I caught sight of Bella, curled up in her own corner of the room, her excited eyes full upon me in the firelight.

I showed them the point on the beach that the Zodiac should make for, and the point on the headland where they should watch for signals. The landing party would be wearing ultra-violet glasses, I said; the Estonian reception party would be using an ultra-violet lamp. Nothing would be visible to the naked eye. After the passenger and his suitcase had been landed, the dinghy should wait no more than two minutes for any possible replacement before heading back for the *Daisy* at full speed. The dinghy should be crewed by one man only, so that if necessary he could take a second passenger on the return run. I recited the recognition signals to be exchanged with the reception party, and this time nobody laughed. I gave the shelving and gradients of the landing beach. There would be no moon. Bad weather was expected, and surely hoped for. Bella brought us tea, brushing carelessly against us as she set out the mugs. It was as if she were harnessing her sexuality to our cause. Reaching Brandt, who was still stooped over the beach chart, she gravely caressed his broad back with both her hands as if filling him with her youthful strength.

I returned to my flat at five in the morning with no thought of sleep. In the afternoon I rode with Brandt and Bella to Blankenese in the van. Antons and Kazimirs had been with the boat all day. They were dressed for the voyage, in bobble hats and oilskin trousers. Orange life jackets were airing on the deck. Shaking hands with each man in turn, I passed round the seaproofed capsules that contained their lethal pills of pure cyanide. A grey drizzle was falling; the little quay was deserted. Brandt walked to the gangway, but when Bella made to follow him, he stopped her.

"No more," he told her. "You stay with Ned."

She was wearing his old duffle coat, and a woollen hat with earflaps, which I suspected she had been wearing when he rescued her. He kissed her and she hugged him till he pushed her off and went aboard, leaving her at my side. Antons stepped into the engine house and we heard the engine cough and come to life. Brandt and

Kazimirs cast off. Nobody looked at us any more. The *Daisy* cleared the quay and headed sedately for the centre of the river. The three men's backs remained turned against us. We heard the hoot of her ship's horn, and watched her until she had slipped behind the curtain of grey mist.

Like abandoned children, Bella and I walked hand in hand up the ramp to Brandt's parked van. Neither of us spoke. Neither of us had anything to say. I glanced back for a last sight of the *Daisy,* but the mist had swallowed her. I looked at Bella and saw that her eyes were unusually bright, and that she was breathing fast.

"He'll be all right," I assured her, releasing her hand while I unlocked the door. "They're very experienced. He's a great man." Even in German, it sounded rather silly.

She got into the van beside me and took back my hand. Her fingers were like separate lives inside my palm. Get alongside her, Haydon had kept insisting. In my most recent signal, I had assured him I would try.

At first we drove in companionable silence, joined and separated by our shared experience. I was driving cautiously because I was taut, but my hand still held hers to give her comfort, and when I was obliged to take a firmer grasp of the steering wheel, I saw that her hand stayed beside me, fingers upward, waiting for me to come back. Suddenly I was terribly concerned about where to take her. Absurdly so. I thought of an elegant basement restaurant with tiled alcoves where I took my banking joes. The elderly waiters would provide her with the kind of reassurance she needed. Then I remembered she was wearing Brandt's duffle coat, jeans and rubber boots. I was no better dressed myself. So where? I wondered anxiously. It was getting late. Through the mist, lights were coming on in the cottages.

"Are you hungry?" I asked.

She put her hand back on her lap.

"Should I find us somewhere to eat?" I asked.

She shrugged.

"Shall I take you to the farmhouse?" I suggested.

"What for?"

"Well I mean, how are you going to spend the next few days? What did you do the last time he was away?"

"I rested from him," she said, with a laugh I had not expected.

"Then tell me how you would like to wait for him," I suggested magnanimously, with a hint of rank. "Do you prefer to be alone? Meet up with other exiles and have gossips? What's best?"

"It's not important," she said, and moved away from me.

"Tell me all the same. Help me."

"I shall go to cinemas. Look at shops. Read magazines. I shall listen to music. Try to study. Get bored."

I decided on the safe flat. There would be food in the fridge, I told myself. Give her a meal, a drink, get her talking. Then either drive her to the farmhouse or send her by cab.

We entered the city. I parked two streets away from the safe flat and took her arm as we walked along the tree-lined pavement. I would have done the same for any woman in a dark street, but there was something disturbing about feeling her bare arm inside Brandt's sleeve. The city was unfamiliar to me. In the lighted windows of the houses, people talked and laughed as if we didn't exist. She clasped my arm and drew my hand against her breast—to be precise, the underside of it, I could feel its shape precisely through the layers of clothing. I was remembering the Circus bar-room jokes about certain officers who picked up their best intelligence in bed. I was remembering Haydon asking me whether she had good tits. I felt ashamed, and took back my hand.

There was a man-door to one side of the cemetery gates. As I unlocked it and ushered her ahead of me, she turned and kissed me on the eyes, one after the other, while she held my face in both her hands. I gripped her waist and she seemed weightless. She was very happy. I could see her smile by the yellow cemetery lights.

"Everyone is dead," she whispered excitedly. "But we are alive."

I went ahead of her up the stairs. Halfway, I looked back to make sure she was following me. I was scared that she might have changed her mind. I was scared altogether—not because I was without experience—thanks to Mabel I was not—but because I knew already that I was encountering a different category of woman from any I had known before. She was standing right behind me, holding her shoes in her hands, still smiling.

I opened the door for her. She stepped through and kissed me again, laughing in merriment, just as if I had lifted her up and carried her across the threshold on our wedding day. I remembered stupidly that Russians never shake hands in door-ways, and perhaps Latvians didn't either, and perhaps her kisses were some kind of ceremony of exorcism. I would have asked her, except that, near enough, I had lost my voice. I closed the door, then crossed the room to turn up the fire, an electric convector affair which, as long as the room was cold, blew out warm air with enormous vigour, but afterwards only fitfully, like an old dog dreaming.

I went to the kitchen to fetch some wine. When I returned she had disappeared and the light was on under the bathroom door. I set the table carefully with knives and forks and spoons and cheese and cold meat and glasses and paper napkins and anything else that I could possibly think of, because I was taking refuge in the distancing formalities of hospitality.

The bathroom door opened and she emerged wearing Brandt's coat wrapped round her as a dressing-gown and, to judge by her bare legs, little else. Her hair was brushed. In our safe flats, we always keep a brush and comb for hospitality.

And I remember thinking that if she was as bad as Haydon seemed to think she was, it was a pretty terrible thing for her to be wearing Brandt's coat in order to deceive the man she was already betraying; and a pretty terrible thing for me to be the man she had selected, while my agents were heading for high danger with lethal pills in their coat pockets. But I had no sense of guilt. I mention this in order to try to explain that my mind was zigzagging in any number of directions in its effort to still my desire for her.

I kissed her and took off her coat, and I never saw before or since anyone so beautiful. And the truth is that, at that moment and at that age, I had not yet acquired the power to distinguish between truth and beauty. They were one and the same to me, and I could only feel awe for her. If I had ever suspected her of anything, the sight of her naked body convinced me of her innocence.

After that, the images of my memory must tell you their own tale. Even today I see us as two other people, never as ourselves.

Bella naked by the half light of the fire, lying on her side as I had first seen her by the fire in the farmhouse. I had fetched the duvet from the bedroom.

"You're so beautiful," she whispered.

It had not occurred to me that I could fill her with a comparable wonder.

Bella at the window, the light from the cemetery making a perfect statue of her body, gilding her fleece and drawing light patterns on her breasts.

Bella kissing Ned's face, hundreds of small kisses as she brings him back to life. Bella laughing at the limitless beauty of herself, and of the two of us together. Bella taking laughter into love, a thing that had never happened to me before, until every part of each of us was a matter for celebration, to be kissed and suckled and admired in its own way.

Bella turning away from Ned to offer herself, thrusting back to accept him as she continues whispering to him. Her whispering stops. She begins her ascent, arching backward until she is upright. And suddenly she is crying out, crying to me and the dead, and she is the most living thing on earth.

Ned and Bella calm at last, standing at the window and gazing down into the graveyard.

There is Mabel, I say, but it seems too early to get married.

"It is always too early," she replies as we start to make love again.

Bella in the bath and myself crammed happily against the taps the other end while she lazily fondles me under the water and talks about her childhood.

Bella on the duvet, drawing my head between her legs.

Bella above me, riding me.

Bella kneeling over me, her secret garden open to my face as she transports me to places I have never imagined, not even lying in my wretched single bed, dreaming over and over of this moment and trying with far too little knowledge to ward off the unknown.

And betweenwhiles you may see Ned dozing on Bella's breast, our untouched food still on the table that I had set so formally in self-protection. With a mind made lucid by our lovemaking, I ask whatever else I can think of that will satisfy Bill Haydon's curiosity, and my own.

I drove her home and reached my flat around seven in the morning. In no mood to sleep for the second night running, I sat down and wrote my encounter report instead, my pen flying because I was still in paradise. There was no message from the *Daisy* but I expected none. Come evening, I received an interim report on her progress. She had passed Kiel and was heading for the Kieler Förde. She would be hitting open sea in a couple of hours. I had a tame German journalist to see that night and a consular meeting in the morning, but I passed the news in veiled terms to Bella on the telephone and promised to come to her soon, for she was determined I should visit her at the farmhouse. When Brandt returned, she said, she wanted to be able to look at all the places in the house where we had made love, and think of me. I suppose it testifies to the power of love's illusion that I found nothing underhand in this, or paradoxical. We had created a world together and she wished to have it round her when I was taken away from her. That was all. She was

Brandt's girl. She expected nothing of me but my love.

When I arrived, we made straight for the long drawing room, where this time it was she who had laid the table. We sat at it quite naked, which was what she wanted. She wanted to see me among the familiar furniture. Afterwards we made love in their bed. I suppose I should have been ashamed, but I felt only the excitement of being appointed to the most secret places of their lives. "These are his hairbrushes," she said. "These are his clothes, you are on his side of the bed." One day I will understand what this means, I thought. And then, more grimly: or is this the pleasure that she takes in betrayal?

Next evening I had arranged to visit an old Pole in Lübeck who had established a clandestine correspondence with a distant nephew in Warsaw. The boy was being trained for cypher work in the Polish diplomatic service, and wanted to spy for us in exchange for resettlement in Australia. London Station was considering a direct approach to him. I returned to Hamburg and slept like the dead. Next morning, while I was still writing my report, a signal from London announced that the *Daisy* had successfully refuelled in Sundre and was on course for the Finnish Gulf with passenger Volodia aboard. I phoned Bella and told her all was still well, and she said, "Please come to me."

I spent the morning in the Reeperbahn police station extricating a pair of drunk British merchant sailors who had broken up a brothel, and the afternoon at a ghastly consular wives' tea party to rally support for the Week of the Political Prisoner. I wished the merchant sailors had broken up that brothel too. I arrived at the farmhouse at eight in the evening and we went straight to bed. At two in the morning the phone rang and Bella answered it. It was my cypher clerk calling me from the shipping office: a decypher yourself, flash priority; I was required at once. I drove like the wind and made the office in forty minutes. As I sat down to the codebooks, I realised that Bella's smells were on my face and hands.

The signal had been transmitted over Haydon's symbol, personal to Head of Station, Hamburg. The *Daisy*'s landing party had come under heavy fire from prepared positions, it said. The dinghy was unaccounted for, and so was everyone aboard it, which meant Antons Durba and his passenger, and very likely whoever was waiting on the beach. There was no word of the Estonian patriots. The *Daisy* had sighted ultra-violet-light signals from the shore, but only one completed series of the agreed pattern, and the assumption was that the Estonian team had been taken captive as soon as they had lured the landing party to its fate. It was a familiar story, even if it was five years old. The fallback radio in Tallinn was not replying.

I was to pass this information to nobody and return to London on the first flight of the morning. A seat had been reserved for me. Toby Esterhase would meet me at Heathrow. I drafted an acknowledgement and handed it to my clerk, who accepted it without comment. He knows, I thought. How could he not? He had telephoned me at the farmhouse and spoken to Bella. The rest he could see in my face and, for all I knew, he could smell it too.

This time there was no joss burning in Haydon's room and he was sitting at his desk. Roy Bland, his Head of Eastern Europe, sat one side of him, Toby Esterhase the other. Toby's jobs were never easily defined, for he liked to keep them vague in the hope that they would multiply. But in practice he was Haydon's poodle, a rôle which later cost him dear. And I was surprised to see George Smiley sitting unhappily apart from them on the edge of Haydon's chaise longue, even if the symbolism of his posture did not dawn on me till three years later.

"It's an inside job," Haydon said without preliminaries. "The mission was blown sky high in advance. If Durba hasn't gone down with the ship, he's already swinging by his thumbs, telling his all. Volodia doesn't know a lot, but that may be his tough luck, because his interrogators aren't going to believe him and he's got a hamper full of explosives to explain. Maybe he took the pill, but I doubt it—he's a ninny."

"Where's Brandt?" I said.

"Sitting under a bright light in the Sarratt interrogation wing and roaring like a bull. Somewhere somebody blundered. We're asking Brandt whether it might possibly be him. If not, who? It's a carbon-copy fuck-up from the last time round. Each member of the crew is being grilled separately."

"Where's the *Daisy*?"

"In Helsinki. We've put a navy crew aboard and they're under orders to get her out tonight. The Finns don't fancy being seen providing safe harbour for people teasing the Bear. If the press don't get to hear about it, it'll be a bloody miracle."

"I see," I said stupidly.

"Good. I don't. What do we do? You tell me. You've got thirty Baltic agents waiting on your every word. What do you say? Abort? Apologise? Act natural and look busy? All suggestions gratefully acknowledged."

"The Durbas weren't conscious to the Estonian network," I objected. "Antons can't blow what he doesn't know."

"So who blew Antons, pray? Who blew the landing party, the coordinates, the beach, the time? Who set us up? We asked Brandt the same question, funnily enough. We thought he might suggest Bella, the Baltic strumpet. He suggested it was one of us lot instead, the cheeky bastard."

He was furious and his fury was directed at me. I would never have imagined that lethargy could convert to such violent anger. Yet he still spoke quietly, in the nasal, upper-class drawl he had. He still managed to remain offhand. Even in passion he conveyed a deadly casualness, which made him all the more formidable.

"So what do *you* say?" he demanded of me.

"What about?"

"About *her*, sweetheart. Pouting Miss Latvia." He was holding up the encounter report that I had written after our first night together. "Christ Almighty, I asked for an assessment, not a bloody aria."

"I think she's innocent," I said. "I think she's a simple peasant kid. That's my assessment. I expect it's Brandt's too. She answered my questions, she gave a plausible account of herself."

Haydon had found his charm again. He could do that at the drop of a hat. He drew you and he repelled you. I remember that exactly. He danced all ways for you, playing your emotions against each other, because he had none of his own.

"Most spies *do* give a plausible account of themselves," he retorted as he turned the pages of my report. "The better ones do, anyway. Don't they, Tobe?"—favouring Esterhase.

"Absolutely, Bill. All the way, I would say," said Esterhase the pleaser.

The others had a copy too. Silence settled while they studied it, pausing at the passages Haydon had sidelined. Roy Bland lifted his head and peered at me. Bland had lectured to us at Sarratt. He was a North Countryman and former don who had spent years behind the Curtain under academic cover. His accent was broad and very flat.

"Bella admits her father's not her father, right, Ned? Her mother was raped by the Germans and got pregnant from it, so she's half German by origin. Right, Ned?"

"Yes. Right, Roy. That's what she told me."

"So when her father, as she calls him, when Feliks comes back from prisoner-of-war camp, and hears what's happened, he adopts the child. Her. Bella. Nice of him. She volunteered that to you. She made no secret of it. Right, Ned?"

"Yes. Right, Roy."

"Then why the fuck doesn't she tell Brandt the same tale as she tells you?"

I had asked her this myself, and so was able to answer him at once. "When he brought her to the West, she was afraid he wouldn't take her in if he knew she wasn't his best friend's natural daughter. They weren't lovers then. He was offering protection and a life. She was scared. She took it. She'd been living in the forest. It was her first time in the West. Her own father was dead, so she needed another father figure."

"Brandt, you mean?" said Bland slyly.

"Yes, of course."

"Well, don't you think it's pretty bloody odd then, Ned, that Brandt didn't know the truth about her *anyway?*" he demanded triumphantly. "If Brandt was her father's close buddy like he says he was, wouldn't he be bound to know all that? Come on, Ned!"

Smiley cut in, I thought in order to help me: "Brandt very probably *does* know, Roy. Would *you* tell your best friend's daughter that she was the illegitimate child of a German soldier if you thought she wasn't aware of it? I'm sure *I* wouldn't. *I'd* go to quite some lengths to protect her. Specially if the father was dead and I was in love with the daughter."

"Bugger love," said Haydon, turning another page of my report. "Brandt's a randy old goat. Who's this Tadeo she keeps talking about? 'Tadeo saw the bodies being loaded into the truck. Tadeo says he saw my father's body go in last. They'd shot most of the men in the face, but my father was shot in the chest and stomach, a machine gun had nearly cut him in two.' I mean, Christ, for a wilting violet she's bloody explicit when it helps her story, I will say."

"Tadeo was her first lover," I said.

"Jealous, are we?" Haydon asked me, drawing laughter from the satraps either side of him.

But not from Smiley. And not from me.

"Tadeo was a boy at her school," I said. "He'd been ordered to keep guard outside the house while the meeting took place, but he was making love with Bella in a field nearby. That's how she managed to escape. Tadeo told her to run for it, and who to ask for when she reached the partisans. Then he hid in a nearby house and watched what happened before joining her. It's in my report."

Toby Esterhase added his own kind of sneer, in his own kind of Austro-Hungarian English. "And Tadeo is most conveniently dead, of course, Ned. Being a witness in Bella's story is actually quite a risk business, I would say."

"He was shot by a frontier guard," I said. "He wasn't even trying to cross. He was making a reconnaissance. She has the feeling everyone she touches dies," I added, thinking involuntarily of Ben.

"She could be right, at that," said Haydon.

Perversely, it seemed to me, Roy Bland now joined in my defence—for increasingly I had the feeling I was in the dock. "Mind you, Tadeo could be kosher *and* wrong about Feliks's death. Maybe the police faked his death. After all, he did go into the truck last. He'd have been covered with blood anyway in that slaughterhouse. They wouldn't have needed to splash the tomato ketchup on him, would they? It would have been done for them already."

Smiley took up Bland's cudgels. I was beginning to regret I had lobbied so hard to be posted out of his care.

"Is the father *really* so important to us, Bill?" he objected. "Feliks can be the Judas of all time, and still have a perfectly honest daughter, can't he?"

"I believe that too," I said. "She admires her father. She has no problem talking about him. She honours him. She's still in mourning for him."

I was remembering how she had looked down into the graveyard. I was remembering her determination to celebrate the gift of life. I refused to believe she had been pretending.

"All right," said Haydon impatiently, shoving a full-plate photograph at me across the desk. "We'll stretch a point and trust you. What the hell are we supposed to make of this lot?"

It was a much enlarged photograph and out of register. I guessed it was a photograph of a photograph. It was stamped in red along the top left corner with the one word "Witchcraft," which I had heard on the grapevine was London Station's most secret source.

Toby Esterhase's warning to me confirmed this: "You never saw this photograph actually, Ned," he told me over Haydon's shoulder, with the kind of smarminess people reserve for the young. "Also you never saw the word 'Witchcraft.' When you leave this room, your mind will be a blank, totally."

It was a group photograph of young men and women arranged against a background of what could have been a barracks, or the campus of a university. They were about sixty strong, and in civilian uniform, the men in suits and ties, the women in high white blouses and long skirts. A group of older men and an evil-looking woman stood to one side of them. The mood, like the clothes and the building and the background, was sullen.

"Second row of the chorus, third from the right," said Haydon, handing me a magnifying glass. "Good tits, same as the young man said."

It was Bella, there was no doubt of it. Bella three or four years younger it was true, and Bella with her hair swept back in what I guessed to be a bun. But Bella's broad, fair eyes and Bella's irrepressible smile, and the high, firm cheeks I adored.

"Did Bella ever whisper in your tiny shell-like that she'd been at language school in Kiev?" Haydon asked me.

"No."

"Did she give any account of her education at all, apart from how she'd had it off with Tadeo in the hay?"

"No."

"Of course Kiev *is* more of a holiday school than a school. Not a place many chaps talk about afterwards much. Unless they're confessing. Theoretically it's a school for tomorrow's interpreters but I'm afraid that in practice it's more a spawning ground for Moscow Centre hopefuls. Centre owns it, Centre staffs it, Centre skims the cream. The slops go to their Foreign Office, same as here."

"Has Brandt seen this?" I asked.

His levity fell from him. "You're joking, aren't you? Brandt's a hostile witness, so are they all."

"Can I see Brandt?"

"I wouldn't recommend it."

"Does that mean no?"

"Yes. It means no."

"Was Witchcraft also the source of the report against Bella's father?"

"Mind your own bloody business," he said, but I had caught Toby's startled eye and sensed that I was right.

"Does Moscow Centre always take class photographs of its white hopes?" I asked, emboldened as Smiley's head lifted to me in what I again took to be support.

"We take 'em at Sarratt," Haydon retorted. "Why shouldn't Moscow Centre?"

I could feel the sweat running down my back, and I knew my voice was slipping. But I floundered on. "Has anyone else in this photograph been identified?"

"As a matter of fact, yes."

"What as?"

"Never mind."

"What languages did she learn?"

Haydon had had enough of me. He lifted his eyes to Heaven as if appealing for the gift of patience. "Well, they *all* learn English, darling, if *that's* what you're asking," he drawled and, putting his chin in his hand, gave Smiley a long look.

I am not clairvoyant and I had no way of knowing what was passing between the two men, or what had passed already. But even allowing for the advantages of hindsight, I am sure I had the sensation of being caught between hostile camps. Even somebody as remote from Head Office politics as I was could not help hearing the rumble of the battle that was raging: how the great X had walked clean past the great Y in the corridor without so much as a "Good morning"; how A had refused to sit at the same table with B in the canteen. And how Haydon's London Station was becoming a service within a service, gobbling up the regional directorates, taking over the special sections, the watchers, the listeners, right the way down to such humble beings as our postmen, who sat in dripping sorting offices, loyally steaming open mail with gas kettles permanently on the boil. It was even hinted that the true clash of Titans was between Bill Haydon and the reigning Chief, the last to call himself Control, and that Smiley as Control's cupbearer was more on his master's side than Haydon's.

But then it was also hinted that Smiley himself was under sentence—or, put more tactfully—contemplating an academic appointment so that he could take more care of his marriage.

Haydon looked jauntily at Smiley, but the jaunty look became a chill stare as he waited for Smiley to return it. The rest of us waited too. The embarrassment was that Smiley didn't return it. He was like a man declining to acknowledge a salute.

He sat on the chaise longue with his eyebrows lifted, and his long eyelids turned down, and his round head tilted, seeming to study the Persian prayer mat that was another eccentric feature of Bill's room. And he simply went on studying it as if he were unaware of Haydon's interest in him, though we all knew—even I knew— that he wasn't. Then he puffed out his cheeks and pulled a frown of disapproval. And finally he stood—not dramatically, for George never had that far to go—and gathered up his papers.

"Well, I think we've had the meat of this, don't you, Bill?" he said. "Control will see indoctrinated officers in one hour, please, if that's convenient, and we'll try to take a view. Ned, you and I have a small piece of Zurich history to clear up. Perhaps you'd drop by when Bill has done with you."

Twenty minutes later I was sitting in Smiley's office.

"Do you believe that photograph?" he asked, with no pretence of talking about Zurich.

"I suppose I have to."

"Why do you suppose that? Photographs can be faked. There is such a thing as disinformation. Moscow Centre has been known to go in for it now and then. They've even stooped to discrediting innocent people, I'm told. They have an entire department, as a matter of fact, devoted to little else. It runs to about five hundred officers."

"Then why frame Bella? Why not go for Brandt or one of the crew?"

"What's Bill told you to do?"

"Nothing. He says I'll get my orders in due course."

"You never answered his question. Do you think we should abort the network?"

"It's hard for me to say. I'm just the local link. The network's run direct from London Station."

"Nevertheless."

"We can't exfiltrate thirty agents. We'd start a war. If the supply lines are blown and the escape routes are closed, I don't see there's anything we can do for them at all."

"So they're dead anyway," he suggested, more in confirmation than question. A phone was ringing on his desk but he didn't pick it up. He continued to look at me with a merciful concern. "Well, if they *are* dead, will you please remember it's not your fault, Ned?" he added kindly. "Nobody expects you to take on Moscow Centre single-handed. It may be the Fifth Floor's fault, it may be mine. It certainly isn't yours."

He nodded me to the door. I closed it after me and heard his phone stop ringing.

I returned to Hamburg the same night. Bella sounded excited when I rang, and sad that I wasn't rushing round to her at once.

"Where's Brandt?" she asked. She had no notion of telephone security. I said Brandt was fine, just fine. I felt guilty talking to her when I knew so much and she so little. I was to be natural towards her, Haydon had said: "Whatever you did before, keep doing it or do it better. I don't want her guessing anything." I should tell her that Brandt loved her, which he was apparently insisting on. I guessed that in his travail he was asking to see me. I hoped so, because I trusted him and he was my responsibility.

I tried not to feel upset for myself when there were so many larger tragedies round me, but it was hard. Until a few days ago, Brandt and the crew had been mine to care for. I had been their spokesman and champion. Now one of them was dead or worse, and the rest had been taken out of my hands. The network, though it had worked to London, had been my proxy family. Now it was like the remnants of a ghostly army, out of touch, floating between life and death.

Worst of all was my sense of dislocation, of holding a dozen conflicting theories in my head at once, and favouring each in turn. One minute I was insisting to myself that Bella was innocent, just as I had maintained to Haydon. The next I was asking myself how she could have communicated with her masters. The answer was, only too easily. She shopped, she went to cinemas, she went to school. She could meet couriers, fill and empty dead-letter boxes to her heart's content.

But no sooner had I gone this far than I ran to her defence. Bella was not *bad*. The photograph was a plant and the story about her father amounted to nothing. Smiley had said as much. There were a hundred ways in which the mission could have been blown without Bella having the least thing to do with it. Our operational security was tight, but not as tight as I would have wished. My predecessor had turned out to be corrupt. Might he not, in addition to inventing agents, have sold a few as well? And even if he hadn't, was it really so unreasonable of Brandt to suggest that the leak could have come from our side of the fence, not his?

Now I would not have you think that, alone in his cot that night, the young Ned unravelled single-handed the skein of treachery that later took all George Smiley's powers to expose. A source can be a plant, a plant can be ignored, an experienced intelligence officer can take a wrong decision—all without the assistance of a traitor within the Fifth Floor's gates. I knew that. I was not a child, and not one of your grey-cheeked Circus conspiracy-theorists either.

Nevertheless I did ponder, as any of us might when he is stretched to the limits of his allegiance to his Service. I pieced together from my worm's-eye view all the rumours that had reached me on the Circus grapevine. Stories of unaccountable failure and repeated scandal, of the mounting anger of our American Cousins. Of meaningless reorganisations, wasteful rivalries between men who were today immortals and tomorrow had resigned. Horror stories of incompetence being taken as proof of grand betrayal—and unnerving evidence of betrayal dismissed as incompetence.

If there is such a thing as growing up, you may say that sometime that night I made one of those leaps into maturity. I realised that the Circus was much the same as any other British institution, except that it was more so, since it played its games in the safety of sealed rooms, with other people's lives for counters. Yet I was pleased to have made my recognition. It gave me back the responsibility for my actions, which hitherto I had been a little too willing to lay at other people's feet. If my career till now had been a constant battle between submission and identity, then you might say that submission had maintained the upper hand. But that night I crossed some sort of border. I decided that from then on, I would pay more heed to my own instincts and desires, and less to the harness that I seemed unable to dispense with.

*   *   *

We met at the safe flat. If there was neutral ground to be found anywhere, it was there. She still knew nothing of the catastrophe. I had told her only that Brandt had been summoned to England. We made love at once, blindly and hungrily; then I waited for the clarity of after-love to begin my interrogation.

I began playfully stroking her hair, smoothing it against her head. Then I swept it back with both my hands, and scooped it into a rough bun.

"This way you look *very* stern," I said, and kissed her, still holding it in place. "Have you ever worn it like this?" I kissed her again.

"When I was a girl."

"When was that?" I said, between our joined lips. "You mean before Tadeo? When?"

"Until I went to the forest. Then I cut it off. Another woman did it with a knife."

"Have you got a photograph of yourself like this?"

"In the forest we did not take photographs."

"I mean before. When you wore it like a stern lady."

She sat up. "Why?"

"Just tell me."

She was watching me with her almost colourless eyes. "At school, they took our photographs. Why?"

"In groups? In classes? What sort of photographs?"

"Why?"

"Just tell me, Bella. I need to know."

"They took photographs of us in our class, and they took photographs for our documents."

"What documents?"

"For identity. For our passports."

She did not mean a passport as we understand it. She meant a passport for moving about inside the Soviet Union. No free citizen could cross the road without one.

"A full-face photograph? Not smiling?"

"Yes."

"What did you do with your old passport, Bella?"

She didn't remember.

"What did you wear for it—for the photograph?" I kissed her breasts. "Not these. What did you wear?"

"A blouse and tie. What nonsense are you talking?"

"Bella, listen to me. Is there anyone you can think of, back at home, a school-friend, an old boyfriend, a relation, who would have a photograph of you with your hair back? Someone you could write to, perhaps, who could be contacted?"

She considered for a moment, staring at me. "My aunt," she said grumpily.

"What's her name?"

She told me.

"Where does she live?"

In Riga, she said. With Uncle Janek. I seized an envelope, sat her still naked at a table and made her write out their full address. Then I put a piece of plain writing paper before her and dictated a letter which she translated as she wrote.

"Bella." I lifted her to her feet and kissed her tenderly. "Bella, tell me something else. Did you ever go to any school, of any kind, except the schools in your own town?"

She shook her head.

"No holiday schools? Special schools? Language schools?"

"No."

"Did you learn English at school?"

"Of course not. Otherwise I would speak English. What's happening to you, Ned? Why are you asking me these stupid questions?"

"The *Daisy* sailed into trouble," I said, still face to face with her. "There was shooting. Brandt wasn't hurt but others were. That's all I'm allowed to tell you. We're to fly back to London tomorrow, you and I together. They need to ask us some questions and find out what went wrong."

She closed her eyes and began shaking. She opened her mouth and made a silent scream.

"I believe in you," I said. "I want to help you. And Brandt. That's the truth."

Gradually she came back to me and put her head on my chest while she wept. She was a child again. Perhaps she had always been one. Perhaps, by helping me to grow up, she had increased the distance between us. I had brought a British passport for her. She had no nationality of her own. I made her stay the night with me and she clutched me like a drowning girl. Neither of us slept.

On the plane she held my hand but we were already continents apart. Then she spoke in a voice that I had not heard from her before. A firm, adult voice of sadness and disillusionment that reminded me of Stefanie's when she had delivered her Sibyl's warning to me on the island.

"*Es ist ein reiner Unsinn,*" she said. It is a pure nonsense.

"What is?"

She had taken away her hand. Not in anger, but in a kind of worldly despair. "You tell them to put their feet into the water and you wait to see what happens. If they are not shot, they are heroes. If they are shot, they are martyrs. You gain nothing that is worth having and you encourage my people to kill themselves. What do you want us to do? Rise up and kill the Russian oppressor? Will you come and help us if we try? I don't think so. I think you are doing something because you cannot do nothing. I think you are not useful to us at all."

I could never forget what Bella said, for it was also a dismissal of my love. And today I think of her each morning as I listen to the news before walking my dog. I wonder what we thought we were promising to those brave Balts in those days, and whether it was the same promise which we are now so diligently breaking.

This time it was Peter Guillam who was waiting at the airport, which was a relief to me, because his good looks and breezy manners seemed to give her confidence. For a chaperone he had brought Nancy from the watchers, and Nancy had made herself motherly for the occasion. Between them they led Bella through immigration to a grey van which belonged to the Sarratt inquisitors. I wished that someone could have thought to send a less formidable vehicle, because when she saw the van she stopped and looked back to me in accusation before Nancy grabbed her by the arm and shoved her in.

In the turbulent life of a case officer, I was learning, there was not always such a thing as an elegant goodbye.

* * *

I can only tell you what I next did, and what I later heard. I made for Smiley's office, and spent most of my day trying to catch him between meetings. Circus protocol required me to go first to Haydon, but I had already exceeded Haydon's brief by the questions I had put to Bella, and I suspected Smiley would give me a more sympathetic hearing. He listened to me; he took charge of Bella's letter and examined it.

"If we have it posted in Moscow and give a Finnish safe address for them to write back to, it might just work," I urged him.

But, as so often with Smiley, I had the impression that he was thinking beyond me into realms from which I was excluded. He dropped the letter in a drawer and closed it.

"I rather think it won't be necessary," he said. "Let us hope not anyway."

I asked him what they would do with Bella.

"I suppose much the same as they have done with Brandt," he replied, waking sufficiently from his absorption to give me a sad smile. "Take her through every detail of her life. Try to trip her up. Wear her down. They won't hurt her. Not physically. They won't tell her what they have against her. They'll just hope to break her cover. It seems that most of the men who looked after her in the forest were rounded up recently. That won't speak well for her, naturally."

"What will they do with her afterwards?"

"Well, I think we can still prevent the worst, even if we can't prevent much else these days," he replied, returning to his papers. "Time you went on to Bill, isn't it? He'll be wondering what you're up to."

And I remember the expression on his face as he dismissed me: the pain and frustration in it, and the anger.

Did Smiley have the letter posted as I suggested? Did the letter produce a photo-graph and did the photograph turn out to be the very one that Moscow Centre's forgers had dropped into their group photograph? I wish it were so neat, but in reality it never is, though I like to believe that my efforts on Bella's behalf had some influence on her release and resettlement in Canada, which occurred a few months later in circumstances that are a puzzle to me.

For Brandt refused to take her back, let alone go with her. Had Bella told him of our affair? Had someone else? I hardly think it possible, unless Haydon himself did it out of mischief. Bill hated all women and most men too, and liked nothing better than to turn people's affections inside out.

Brandt too was given a clean ticket and, after some resistance from the Fifth Floor, a gratuity to start him in a respectable walk of life. That is to say, he was able to buy a boat and take himself to the West Indies, where he resumed his old trade of smuggling, except that this time he chose arms to Cuba.

And the betrayal? The Brandt network had simply been too efficient for Hay-don's stomach, Smiley told me later, so Bill had betrayed it as he had betrayed its predecessor, and tried to fix the blame on Bella. He had arranged for Moscow Centre to fake the evidence against her, which he then presented as coming from his spurious source Merlin, the provider of the Witchcraft material. Hard on the mole's tracks by then, Smiley had voiced his suspicions in high places, only to be sent into exile for being right. It took another two years for him to be brought back to clean the stable.

* * *

And there the story stood until our own internal *perestroika* began in earnest—in the winter of '89—when Toby Esterhase, the ubiquitous survivor, conducted a middle-ranking Circus delegation to Moscow Centre as a first step to what our blessed Foreign Office insisted on calling a "normalisation of the relationship between the two services."

Toby's team was welcomed at Dzerzhinsky Square and shown many of the appointments, though not, one gathers, the torture chambers of the old Lubyanka, or the roof on which certain careless prisoners had occasionally lost their footing. Toby and his men were wined and dined. They were shown, as the Americans say, a time. They bought fur hats and pinned facetious badges on them and had themselves photographed in Dzerzhinsky Square.

And on the last day, as a special gesture of goodwill, they were escorted to the gallery of Centre's huge communications hall, where reports from all sources are received and processed. And it was here, as they were leaving the gallery, says Toby, that he and Peter Guillam in the same moment spotted a tall, flaxen, thickset fellow in half silhouette at the further end of the corridor, emerging from what was apparently the men's lavatory, for there was only one other door in that part of the corridor, and it was marked for women.

He was a man of some age, yet he strode out of the doorway like a bull. He paused, and for a long beat stared straight at them, as if in two minds whether to come towards them and greet them or retreat. Then he lowered his head and, as it seemed to them, with a smile, swung away from them and disappeared into another corridor. But not before they had ample opportunity to remark his seamanly roll and wrestler's shoulders.

Nothing goes away in the secret world; nothing goes away in the real one. If Toby and Peter are right—and there are those who still maintain that Russian hospitality had got the better of them—then Haydon had an even stronger reason to point the finger of suspicion at Bella, and away from Sea Captain Brandt.

Was Brandt bad from the beginning? If so, I had unwittingly furthered his recruitment and our agents' deaths. It is a dreadful thought and sometimes in the cold grey hours as I lie at Mabel's side, it comes home to haunt me.

And Bella? I think of her as my last love, as the right turning I never took. If Stefanie had unlocked the door of doubt in me, Bella pointed me towards the open world while there was still time. When I think of my women since, they are aftercare. And when I think of Mabel, I can only explain her as the lure of domesticity to a man returned from the front line. But the memory of Bella remains as fresh for me as on our first night in the safe flat overlooking the cemetery— though in my dreams she is always walking away from me, and there is reproach even in her back.

5

A re you saying we could be housing another Haydon *now?*" a student named
Maggs called out amid the groans of his colleagues. "What's his motivation, Mr.
Smiley? Who's paying him? What's his bag?"

I had had my doubts about Maggs ever since he had joined. He was earmarked
for a cover career in journalism, and already had the worst characteristics of his
future trade. But Smiley was unruffled.

"Oh well, I'm sure that in retrospect we owe Bill a great debt of thanks," he
replied calmly. "He administered the needle to a Service that had been far too long
a-dying." He made a fussy little frown of perplexity. "As to *new* traitors, I'm sure
our present leader will have sown her discontents, won't she? Perhaps I'm one. I do
find I become a great deal more radical in my old age."

But believe me, we didn't thank Bill at the time.

There was Before the Fall and there was After the Fall and the Fall was Haydon,
and suddenly there was not a man or woman in the Circus who could not tell you
where he was and what he was doing when he heard the dreadful news. Old hands
tell each other to this day of the silence in the corridors, the numbed, averted faces
in the canteen, the unanswered telephones.

The greatest casualty was trust. Only gradually, like dazed people after an air
attack, did we step shyly, one by one, from our shattered houses, and set to work
to reconstruct the citadel. A fundamental reform was deemed necessary, so the
Circus abandoned its ancient nickname and the warren of Dickensian corridors and
crooked staircases in Cambridge Circus that had housed its shame, and built itself
instead a vile steel-and-glass affair not far from Victoria, where the windows still
blow out in a gale and the corridors reek of stale cabbage from the canteen, and
typewriter-cleaning fluid. Only the English punish themselves with quite such
dreadful prisons. Overnight we became, in formal parlance, the Service, though the
name "Circus" still occasionally crosses our lips in the same way as we speak of
pounds, shillings and pence long after decimalisation.

The trust was broken because Haydon had been part of it. Bill was no upstart
with a chip on his shoulder and a pistol in his pocket. He was exactly who he had
always sneeringly described himself to be: Church and Spy Establishment, with
uncles who sat on Tory Party committees, and a rundown estate in Norfolk with
tenant farmers who called him "Mr. William." He was a strand of the finely spun
web of English influence of which we had perceived ourselves the centre. And he had
caught us in it.

In my own case—I still claim a certain distinction for this—I actually succeeded
in hearing the news of Bill's arrest twenty-four hours after it had reached the rest
of the Circus, for I was incarcerated in a windowless mediaeval cell at the back of
a run of grand apartments in the Vatican. I was commanding a team of Circus
eavesdroppers under the guidance of a hollow-eyed friar supplied to us by the

Vatican's own secret service, who would rather have gone to the Russians themselves than seek the assistance of their secular colleagues a mile up the road in Rome. And our mission was to winkle a probe microphone into the audience room of a corrupt Catholic bishop who had got himself involved in a drugs-for-arms deal with one of our disintegrating colonies—well, why be coy? It was Malta.

With Monty and his boys flown in for the occasion, we had tiptoed through vaulted dungeons, up underground staircases, until we had reached this vantage point, from which we proposed to drill a fine hole through a course of old cement that ran between the blocks of a three-foot party wall. The hole by agreement was to be no more than two centimetres in diameter, wide enough for us to insert the elongated plastic drinking straw that would conduct the sound from the target room to our microphone, small enough to spare the hallowed masonry of the Papal palace. Today we would use more sophisticated equipment, but the seventies were the last of the steam age and probes were still the fashion. Besides, with the best will in the world, you don't show off your prize gadgets to official Vatican liaison, let alone to a friar in a black habit who looks as though he has stepped straight out of the Inquisition.

We drilled, Monty drilled, the friar watched. We poured water onto red-hot drill-heads, and onto our sweating hands and faces. We muffled the drone of our drills with liquid foam, and every few minutes we took readings to make sure we hadn't drilled our way into the holy man's apartment by mistake. For the aim was to stop the drill-head a centimetre short of entry, and listen from inside the membrane of the wallpaper or surface plaster.

Suddenly we were through, but worse than through. We were in thin air. A hasty sampling by vacuum produced only exotic threads of silk. A bemused silence descended on us. Had we struck furniture? Drapes? A bed? Or the hem of some unsuspecting prelate's robe? Had the audience room been altered since we had taken the reconnaissance photographs?

At which low point the friar was inspired to remember, in an appalled whisper, that the good bishop was a collector of priceless needlework, and we realised that the shreds of cloth we were staring at were not pieces of sofa or curtain, or even some priest's finery, but fragments of Gobelin tapestry. Excusing himself, the friar fled.

Now the scene changes to the old Kentish town of Rye, where two sisters named the Misses Quayle ran a tapestry-restoration business, and by a mercy—or, you may say, by the ineluctable laws of English social connection—their brother Henry was a retired member of the Service. Henry was run to earth, the sisters were roused from their beds, an RAF jet plane wafted them to Rome's military airport, from where a car sped them to our side. Then Monty calmly returned to the front of the building and ignited a smoke bomb which cleared half the Vatican and gave our augmented team four desperate hours in the target room. By mid-afternoon of the same day, the Gobelin was passably patched and our probe microphone snugly in place.

The scene changes yet again to the grand dinner given by our Vatican hosts. Swiss Guards stand menacingly at the doors. Monty, a white napkin at his throat, is seated between the sedate Misses Quayle and wiping the last of his cannelloni from his plate with a piece of bread while he regales them with accounts of his daughter's latest accomplishments at her riding school.

"Now you won't know this, Rosie, and there's no reason why you should, but my Beckie has the best pair of hands for her age in the whole of South Croydon—"

Then Monty stops dead in his tracks. He is reading the note I have passed him, delivered to me by hand of a messenger from our Rome Station: *Bill Haydon, Director of Circus Clandestine Operations, has confessed to being a Moscow Centre spy.*

Sometimes I wonder whether that was the greatest of all Bill's crimes: to steal for good the lightness we had shared.

I returned to London to be told that when there was more to tell me I would be told. A few mornings later Personnel informed me that I had been classified "Tailor Halftone," which was Circus jargon for "unpostable to all but friendly countries." It was like being told I would spend the rest of my life in a wheelchair. I had done nothing wrong, I was in no disgrace, quite the contrary. But in the trade, cover is virtue, and mine was blown.

I packed up my desk and gave myself the rest of the day off. I drove into the country and I still don't remember the drive, but there is a walk I do on the Sussex Downs, over whaleback chalk hills with cliffs five hundred feet high.

It took another month before I heard my sentence: "You'll be back with the émigrés, I'm afraid," Personnel said, with his customary distaste. "And it's Germany again. Still, the allowances are quite decent, and the skiing isn't bad either, if you go high enough."

⑥

It was approaching midnight but Smiley's good spirits had increased with every fresh heresy. He's like a jolly Father Christmas, I thought, who hands round seditious leaflets with his gifts.

"Sometimes I think the most *vulgar* thing about the Cold War was the way we learned to gobble up our own propaganda," he said, with the most benign of smiles. "I don't *mean* to sound didactic, and of course in a way we'd done it all through our history. But in the Cold War, when our enemies lied, they lied to conceal the wretchedness of their system. Whereas when *we* lied, we concealed our virtues. Even from ourselves. We concealed the very things that made us right. Our respect for the individual, our love of variety and argument, our belief that you can only govern fairly with the consent of the governed, our capacity to see the other fellows' view—most notably in the countries we exploited, almost to death, for our own ends. In our supposed ideological rectitude, we sacrificed our compassion to the great god of indifference. We protected the strong against the weak, and we perfected the art of the public lie. We made enemies of decent reformers and friends of the most disgusting potentates. And we scarcely paused to ask ourselves how much longer we could defend our society by these means and remain a society worth defending." A glance to me again. "So it wasn't much wonder, was it, Ned, if we opened our gates to every con-man and charlatan in the anti-Communist racket? We got the villains we deserved. Ned knows. Ask Ned.''

At which Smiley, to the general delight, burst out laughing—and I, after a moment's hesitation, joined in and assured my students that I would tell them about it some day.

Perhaps you caught the show, as they say in the States. Perhaps you were part of the appreciative audience at one of the many rousing performances they gave on their tireless trail through the American mid-West, as they pressed the flesh and worked the rubber-chicken luncheons of the lecture circuit, a hundred dollars a plate and every plate a sell-out. We called it the Teodor-Latzi show. Teodor was the Professor's first name.

Perhaps you joined in one of the numberless standing ovations as our two heroes humbly took centre stage, the Professor tall and resplendent in one of several costly new suits purchased for his tour, and the diminutive Latzi his chubby mute, his shallow eyes brimming with ideals. There were ovations before they started speaking and ovations when they had finished. No applause was loud enough for "two great American Hungarians who, single-handed, kicked themselves a hole in the Iron Curtain." I am quoting the Tulsa *Herald*.

Perhaps your all-American daughter dressed herself in the becoming costume of a Hungarian peasant girl and put flowers in her hair for the occasion—such things happened too. Perhaps you sent a donation to the League for the Liberation, Post Box something or other, Wilmington. Or did you read about our heroes in the *Reader's Digest* in your dentist's waiting room?

Or perhaps, like Peter Guillam, who was based in Washington at the time, you were honoured to be present at their grand world *première,* jointly stage-managed by our American Cousins, the Washington city police and the FBI, at no less a shrine of right-thinking than the austere and panelled Hay-Adams Hotel, just across the square from the White House. If so, you must have been rated a serious influence-maker. You had to be a front-line journalist or lobbyist at least to be admitted to the hushed conference room where every understated word had the authority of an engraved tablet, and men in bulging blazers watched tautly over your comfort and convenience. For who knew when the Kremlin would strike back? It was still that kind of time.

Or maybe you read their book, slipped by the Cousins to an obedient publisher on Madison Avenue and launched to a fanfare of docile critical acclaim before occupying the lower end of the non-fiction bestseller list for a spectacular two weeks. I hope you did, for though it appeared over their joint names, the fact is I wrote a slice of it myself, even if the Cousins took exception to my original title. The title of record was *The Kremlin's Killer.* I'll tell you what mine was later.

As usual, Personnel had got it wrong. For anybody who has lived in Hamburg, Munich is not Germany at all. It is another country. I never felt the remotest connection between the two cities, but when it came to spying, Munich like Hamburg was one of the unsung capitals of Europe. Even Berlin ran a poor second when it came to the size and visibility of Munich's invisible community. The largest and nastiest of our organisations was a body known best by the place that housed it,

Pullach, where much too soon after 1945 the Americans had installed an unlovely assembly of old Nazi officers under a former general of Hitler's military intelligence. Their brief was to pay court to other old Nazis in East Germany and, by bribery, blackmail or an appeal to comradely sentiment, procure them for the West. It never seemed to occur to the Americans that the East Germans might be doing the same thing in reverse, though they did more of it and better.

So the German Service sat in Pullach, and the Americans sat with them, egging them on, then getting cold feet and egging them off. And where the Americans sat, there sat everybody else. And now and then frightful scandals broke, usually when one or other of this company of clowns literally forgot which side he was working for, or made a tearful confession in his cups, or shot his mistress or his boyfriend or himself, or popped up drunk on the other side of the Curtain to declare his loyalty to whomever he had not been loyal to so far. I never in my life knew such an intelligence bordello.

After Pullach came the codebreakers and security artists, and after these came Radio Liberty, Radio Free Europe and Radio Free Everywhere Else, and inevitably, since they were largely the same people, the émigré conspirators, who by now were feeling a little down on their luck but dared not say it. And much time was spent among these exiled bodies arguing out niceties about who would be Master of the Royal Horse when the monarchy was restored; and who would be awarded the Order of Saint Peter and the Hedgehog; or succeed to the Grand Duke's summer palace once the Communist chickens had been removed from its drawing rooms; or who would recover the crock of gold that had been sunk to the bottom of the Whatnotsee, always forgetting that the said lake had been drained thirty years ago by the Bolshevik usurpers, who had built a six-acre hydro-electric plant on the site before running out of water.

As if this were not enough, Munich played host to the wildest sort of All German aspiration, whose adherents regarded even the 1939 borders as a mere prelude to Greater German needs. East Prussians, Saxons, Pomeranians, Silesians, Balts and Sudeten Germans all protested the terrible injustice done to them, and drew fat pay-packets from Bonn for their grief. There were nights, as I trudged home to Mabel through the beery streets, when I fancied I could hear them singing their anthems behind Hitler's marching ghost.

Are they still in business as I write? Oh, I fear they are, and looking a lot less mad than in the days when it was my job to move among them. Smiley once quoted Horace Walpole to me, not a name that would otherwise have sprung naturally to my mind: This world is a comedy to those that think, said Walpole, a tragedy to those that feel. Well, for comedy Munich has her Bavarians. And for tragedy, she has her past.

My memory is patchy nearly twenty years later regarding the Professor's political antecedents. At the time, I fancied I understood them—indeed, I must have done, for most of my evenings with him were spent listening to his recitations of Hungarian history between the wars. And I am sure we put them into the book too —a chapter's worth, at least, if I could only lay my hands on a copy.

The problem was, he was so much happier evoking Hungary's past than her present. Perhaps he had learned, in a life of continual adjustment, that it is wise to limit one's concerns to issues safely consigned to history. There were the Legitimists, I remember, and they supported King Charles, who made a sudden return to Hungary in 1921, much to the consternation of the Allies, who ordered him smartly from the stage. I don't think the Professor could have been a day above five years old when this moving event occurred, but he spoke of it with tears in his enlightened eyes, and there was much in his bearing to suggest the transitory touch of monarchy. And when he mentioned the Treaty of Trianon, the refined white hand that held his wine glass trembled in restrained outrage.

"It was a *Diktat,* Herr Ned," he protested to me in courtly reproof. "Imposed upon us by you victors. You robbed us of two-thirds of our land under the Crown! You gave it to Czechoslovakia, Romania, Yugoslavia. Such scum you gave it to, Herr Ned! And we Hungarians were cultivated people! Why did you do it to us? For what?"

I could only apologise for my country's bad behaviour, just as I could only apologise for the League of Nations, which destroyed the Hungarian economy in 1931. Quite how the League achieved this reckless act I never understood, but I remember it had something to do with the wheat market, and the League's rigid policy of orthodox deflation.

Yet when we approached more contemporary matters, the Professor became strangely reticent in his opinions.

"It is another catastrophe" was all he would say. "It is all a consequence of Trianon and the Jews."

Shafts of evening sunlight sloped through the garden window on to Teodor's superb white head. He was a lion of a fellow, believe me, wide-browed and Socratic, like a grand conductor close to genius all the time, with sculpted hands and flowing locks, and a stoop of intellectual profundity. Nobody who looked so venerable could be shallow—not even when the learned eyes appeared a mite too small for their sockets, or slipped furtively to one side in the manner of a diner in a restaurant who catches sight of a better meal passing by.

No, no, he was a great, good man, and fifteen years our joe. If a man is tall, then clearly he has authority. If he has a golden voice, then his words are also golden. If he looks like Schiller, he must feel like Schiller. If the smile is remote and spiritual, then so for sure is the man within. Thus the visual society.

Except that just occasionally, as I think now, God amuses Himself by dealing us an entirely different man inside the shell. Some founder and are rumbled. Others expand until they meet the challenge of their looks. And a few do neither, but wear their splendours like a favour granted from above, blandly accepting the homage that is not their due.

The Professor's operational history is quickly told. Too quickly, for it was a mite banal. He was born in Debrecen, close to the Romanian border, an only son of indulgent parents of the small nobility who trimmed their sails to every wind. Through them, he inherited money and connections, a thing that happened more often in the so-called Socialist countries, even in those days, than you would suppose. He was a man of letters, a writer of articles for learned journals, a bit of a poet and a lover several times married. He wore his jackets like capes, the sleeves loose. All these luxuries he could well afford, on account of his privileges and discreet wealth.

In Budapest, where he taught a languid version of philosophy, he had acquired a modest following among his students, who discerned more fire in Teodor's words than he intended, for he was never cut out to be an orator, rhetoric being something for the rabble. Nevertheless, he had risen a certain distance to their needs. He had observed their passion, and as a natural conciliator he had responded by giving it a voice—moderate enough in all conscience, but a voice for all that, and one they respected, along with his beautiful manners and air of representing an older, better order. He was of an age, by then, to be warmed by youthful adulation, and he was always vain. And through vanity he allowed himself to be carried on the counter-revolutionary tide. So that when the Soviet tanks turned back from the border and surrounded Budapest on the terrible night of November 3, 1956, he had no choice but to run for his life, which he did, into the arms of British Intelligence.

The Professor's first act on arriving in Vienna was to telephone a Hungarian friend at Oxford, pressing him in his peremptory way for money, introductions and letters testifying to his excellence. This friend happened also to be a friend of the Circus, and it was the high season for recruitment.

Within months, the Professor was on the payroll. There was little courtship, no arch approach, no customary fan dance. The offer was made, and accepted as a due. Within a year, with generous American assistance, Professor Teodor had been set up in Munich, in a comfortable house beside the river, with a car and his devoted if distraught wife Helena, who had escaped with him—one suspected, somewhat to his regret. Henceforth, and for an extraordinary length of time, Professor Teodor had been the unlikely spearhead of our Hungarian attack, and not even Haydon had unseated him.

His cover job was Radio Free Europe's patrician-at-large on the subject of Hungarian history and culture, and it fitted him like a glove. He had never been much else. In addition, he lectured a little and gave private tuition—mainly, I noticed, to girls. His clandestine job, for which, thanks to the Americans, he was remarkably well paid, was to foster his links with the friends and former students he had left behind, to be a focus for them and a rallying point and, under guidance, to shape them into an operational network, though none, to my knowledge, had ever quite emerged. It was a visionary operation, and better on the page perhaps than on the ground. Yet it ran and ran. It ran for five years, and then another five and by the time I took up the great man's file, it had completed an extraordinary fifteen years. Some operations are like that, and stagnation favours them. They are not expensive, they are not conclusive, they don't necessarily lead anywhere—but then neither does political stalemate—they are free of scandal. And each year when the annual audit is taken, they are waved through without a vote, until their longevity becomes their justification.

Now I won't say the Professor had achieved nothing for us in all that time. To say so would not only be unfair, it would be derogatory to Toby Esterhase, himself of Hungarian origin, who on his reinstatement After the Fall had become the desk officer handling the Professor's case. Toby had paid a heavy price for his blind support of Haydon, and when he was given the Hungary desk—never the most exalted of Iron Curtain slots—the Professor promptly became the most important player in Toby's personal rehabilitation programme.

"Teodor, I would say, Ned—Teodor is our absolutely total star," he had assured me before I left London, over a lunch he nearly paid for. "Old school, total discretion, lot of years in the saddle, loyal like a leech. Teodor is our ace, totally."

And certainly one of the Professor's more striking accomplishments had been to escape the Haydon axe—either because he had been lucky or, less charitably, because the Professor had never produced enough intelligence to merit the interest of a busy traitor. For I could not help noticing as I prepared myself for the takeover —my predecessor having dropped dead of a stroke while on leave in Ibiza—that whereas Teodor's personal file ran to several volumes, his product file was unusually slender. Partly this could be explained by the fact that his main function had been to spot talent rather than exploit it, partly that the few sources he had guided into our net over the long period he had been working for us were still relatively unproductive.

"Hungary, Ned, that's actually a damned hard target, I would say," Toby assured me when I delicately pointed this out to him. "It's too open. An open target, you get a lot of crap you know already. If you don't get the Crown Jewels, you get the common knowledge—who needs it? What Teodor produces for the Americans, it's fantastic."

This seemed to be the nub. "So what *does* he produce for them actually?" I asked. "Apart from hearts and minds on the radio, and articles no one reads?"

Toby's smile became unpleasantly superior. "Sorry, Ned, old boy. 'Need to know,' I'm afraid. You're not on the list for this one."

A few days later, as protocol required, I called on Russell Sheriton in Grosvenor Square to say my goodbyes. Sheriton was the Cousins' Head of Station in London, but he was also responsible for their Western European operations. I bided my time, then dropped the name of Teodor.

"Ah now, that's for Munich to say, Ned," Sheriton said quickly. "You know me. Never trespass on another man's preserves."

"But is he doing you any good? That's all I want to know. I mean joes do burn out, don't they? Fifteen years."

"Well now, we thought he was doing *you* some good, Ned. To hear Toby speak, you'd think Teodor was propping up the free world single-handed."

No, I thought. To hear Toby speak, you'd think Teodor was propping up Toby single-handed. But I was not cynical. In spying, as in much of life, it is always easier to say no than yes. I arrived in Munich prepared to believe that Teodor was the star Toby had cracked him up to be. All I wanted was to be assured.

And I was. At first I was. He was magnificent. I thought my marriage to Mabel had ridded me of such swift enthusiasms, and in a way it had, until the evening when he opened the door to me and I decided I had walked in on one of those perfectly preserved relics of mid-European history, and that all I could decently do was sit at his feet like the rest of his disciples and drink in his wisdom. This is what the Service is for! I thought. Such a man is worth saving on his own account! The culture, I thought. The breadth. The years and years of service.

He received me warmly but with a certain distance, as became his age and distinction. He offered me a glass of fine Tokay and treated me to a discourse on its provenance. No, I confessed, I knew little about Hungarian wines, but I was keen to learn. He talked music, of which I am also sadly ignorant, and played a few bars for me on his treasured violin, the very one he had brought with him when he escaped from Hungary, he explained, and made not by Stradivarius but someone infinitely better, whose name has long escaped me. I thought it a wonderful privilege to be running an agent who had fled with his violin. He talked theatre. A Hungarian theatrical company was presently on tour in Munich with an extraordinary *Othello,* and though Mabel and I had yet to see the production, his opinion of it enchanted me. He was dressed in what Germans call a *Hausjacke,* black trousers and a pair of splendidly polished boots. We talked of God and the world, we ate the best *gulyás* of my life, served by the distraught Helena, who whispered her excuses and left us. She was a tall woman and must once have been beautiful, but she preferred to wear the signs of her neglect. We rounded off the meal with an apricot Palinka.

"Herr Ned, if I may call you so," said the Professor, "there is one matter which weighs heavily on my mind, and which you will permit me to raise with you at the outset of our professional relationship."

"Please do," I said generously.

"Unfortunately, your most recent predecessor—a good man, of course"—he broke off, evidently unable to speak ill of the recent dead—"and, like yourself, a man of culture—"

"Please," I repeated.

"It concerns my British passport."

"I didn't know you had one!" I exclaimed in surprise.

"That is the point. I haven't. One understands there are problems. It is so with all bureaucracies. Bureaucracies are the most evil of man's institutions, Herr Ned. They enshrine the worst of us and bring low the best of us. An exiled Hungarian living in Munich in the employment of an American organisation is not naturally eligible for British citizenship. I understand that. Nevertheless, after my many years of collaboration with your department, I am owed this passport. A temporary travel document is not a dignified alternative."

"But I understood the Americans were giving you a passport! Wasn't that the deal right from the beginning? The Americans to be responsible for your citizenship and resettlement? That includes a passport, surely. It must!"

I was upset that a man who had given us so much of his life should have been denied this simple dignity. But the Professor had learned a more philosophical attitude.

"The Americans, Herr Ned, are a young people and a mercenary people. Having used the best of me, they can scarcely regard me as a man of the future. For the Americans, I belong already to the garbage heap of obsolescence."

"But didn't they promise—subject to satisfactory service? I'm sure they did!"

He made a gesture I shall never forget. He lifted his hands from the table as if he were raising a prodigiously heavy rock. He brought them almost to the level of his shoulders, before letting them crash at full force back onto the table, the imaginary rock between them. And I remember his eyes, indignant from the exertion, accusing me in the silence. So much for your promises, he was saying. Yours and the Americans, both.

"Just get me my passport, Herr Ned."

As a loyal case officer, concerned to do the best for my joe, I threw myself upon the problem. Knowing Toby of old, I decided to take an official tone from the beginning: no half promises, no vaporous reassurances for me. I informed Toby of Teodor's request and asked for guidance. He was my desk officer after all, my

London anchor. If it was true that the Americans were sliding out of their undertaking to give the Professor citizenship, the matter would have to be dealt with in London or Washington, I said, not Munich. And if, for reasons outside my knowledge, a British passport was to be granted after all, this too would require the energetic endorsement of the Fifth Floor. The days were gone for good when the Home Office handed out free British citizenship to every ex-Circus Tom, Dick and Teodor. The Fall had seen to that.

I did not signal my request, but sent it by bag, which in Circus lore gives greater formality. I wrote a fighting letter and a couple of weeks later followed it with a reminder. But when the Professor asked for a progress report, I was non-committal. It's in the pipeline, I assured him; London does not take kindly to being hustled. But I still wondered why Toby took so long to answer.

Meanwhile, at my meetings with Teodor, I strove to unravel what precisely he was doing for us that made him the star of Toby's underpopulated firmament. My investigations were not made easier by the Professor's prickliness, and at first I wondered whether he was withholding his cooperation until the question of his passport was settled. Gradually I realised that where our secret work was concerned, this was his normal demeanour.

One of his more humdrum jobs was maintaining a one-roomed student flat in the Schwabing district, which he used as a safe address for receiving mail from certain of his Hungarian contacts. I persuaded him to take me there. He unlocked the door and there must have been a dozen envelopes lying on the mat, all with Hungarian stamps.

"My goodness, when did you last come here, Professor?" I asked him as I watched him gather them laboriously together.

He shrugged, I thought gracelessly.

"How many letters do you normally reckon to receive in a week, Professor?"

I took the envelopes from him and went through the postmarks. The oldest had been posted three weeks ago, the most recent, one. We moved to the tiny desk, which was covered in dust. With a sigh he settled himself in the chair, opened a drawer and withdrew a couple of bottles of chemicals and a paintbrush from a concealed recess. Taking up the first envelope, he examined it gloomily, then slit it open with a pocket knife.

"Who's it from?" I asked, with more curiosity than he appeared to consider warranted.

"Pali," he replied gloomily.

"Pali at the Agriculture Ministry?"

"Pali from Debrecen. He has been visiting Romania."

"What for? Not the toxic-weapons conference? That could be a scoop!"

"We shall see. An academic conference of some kind. His field is cybernetics. He is undistinguished."

I watched him dip the brush into the first bottle and paint the back of the handwritten letter with it. He rinsed the brush in water and applied the second chemical. And it seemed to me he was determined to demonstrate his disdain for such menial employment. He repeated the process for every letter, sometimes varying the routine by spreading open the envelope and treating the inside of it, or by painting between the lines of the visible handwriting. In the same slow motion, he sat himself at an upright Remington and wearily tapped out in translation the texts that had emerged: anticipated mineral and power deficiencies in the new industries . . . bauxite quotas for mines in the Bakony Mountains . . . low metal content of iron ore recently extracted in the region of Miskolc . . . projected yield of maize and sugar-beet harvests in the region of somewhere else . . . rumours of five-year plan to revitalise State railway network . . . disruptive action against Party officials in Sopron . . . I could almost hear the yawns of the Third Floor analysts as they waded through such turgid stuff. I remembered Toby's boast that Teodor was only interested in the highest quality of intelligence. If this was the highest, what in heaven's name was the lowest? Patience, I told myself. Great agents have to be humoured.

The next day I received a reply to my letter about the passport. The problem, Toby explained, was that there had been a lot of changes among the Cousins' Hungarian Section in recent years. An effort was now being made, he said—making suspicious use of the passive voice—to establish the terms of any undertakings given by the Americans or ourselves. Meanwhile I should avoid discussing the matter with Teodor, he added—as if it were I, not the Professor, who was making the running.

The matter was still in the air three weeks later when I lunched with Milton Wagner at the Cosmo. Wagner was an old hand and my American opposite number. Now he was winding up his career as the Cousins' Chief of Eastern Operations, Munich. The Cosmo was the kind of place Americans make anywhere, with crisp potato skins and garlic dip, and club sandwiches impaled on enormous plastic hairpins.

"How are you getting along with our distinguished academic friend?" he asked, in his southern drawl, after we had despatched our other business.

"Splendidly," I replied.

"Couple of our people seem to think Teodor's been having himself a free ride these how many years," said Wagner lazily.

This time I said nothing.

"The boys back home have been holding a retrospective of his work. Not good, Ned. Not good at all. Some of the 'Hello, Hungary' stuff he's been pushing out on the radio. It's been said before. They've found one passage makes a perfect fit with an article published in *Der Monat* back in '48. The original writer recognised his own words soon as he heard them on the air and flipped." He helped himself liberally to ketchup. "Could be any day now we haul him in for a full and frank exchange."

"Probably going through a bad patch," I said.

"Fifteen years is a long bad patch, Ned."

"Is he aware you're checking on him?"

"In Radio Free Europe, Ned? Among Hungarians? *Gossip?* You must be joking."

I could no longer contain my anxiety. "But why has nobody warned London? Why haven't *you?*"

"Understand we did, Ned. Understand the message fell on pretty deaf ears. Bad time for you boys. Don't we know it."

By now the momentous force of his news had got through to me. If the Professor was cheating with his broadcasts, whom else might he not be cheating?

"Milt, can I ask you a silly question?"

"Be my guest, Ned."

"Has Teodor *ever* done good work for you? In all his time? Secret work? Very secret work, even?"

Wagner pondered this, determined to give the Professor the benefit of the doubt. "Can't say he has, Ned. We did consider using him as an intermediary for one of our big fish one time, but we kind of didn't like the old man's manners."

"Can I believe that?"

"Would I ever lie to you, Ned?"

So much for the fantastic work he's doing for the Americans, I thought. So much for the years of loyal service nobody can quite recall.

I signalled Toby straight away. I wasted time drafting different texts because my anger kept getting in the way. I understood only too well now why the Americans were refusing to give the Professor his passport, and why he had turned to us for one instead. I understood his air of last things, his listlessness, his lack of urgency: he was waiting to be sacked. I repeated Wagner's information and asked whether it was known to Head Office. If not, the Cousins were in default of their sharing agreement with us. If, on the other hand, the Cousins *had* warned us, why hadn't I been warned too?

Next morning I had Toby's slippery reply. It took a regal tone. I suspected he had got somebody to write it for him, for it was accent-free. The Cousins had given London a "non-specific warning" he explained, that the Professor might be facing "disciplinary enquiries at some future date on the subject of his broadcasts." Head Office—by which I suspected he meant himself—had "adopted the view" that the Professor's relationship with his American employers was not of direct concern to the Circus. Head Office also "took the point"—who but Toby could have made it? —that with so much operational work to occupy him, the Professor could be excused for any "small defects" in his cover work. If another cover job had to be found for the Professor, Head Office would "take steps at the appropriate time." One solution would be to place him with one of the tame magazines to which he was already an occasional contributor. But that was for the future. The Professor had fallen foul of his employers before, Toby reminded me, and he had ridden out the storm. This was true. A woman secretary had complained of his advances, and elements of the Hungarian community had taken exception to his anti-Semitic views.

For the rest, Toby advised me to cool down, bide my time, and—always a maxim of Toby's—act as if nothing had happened. Which was how matters stood one week and twelve hours later when the Professor telephoned me at ten at night, using the emergency wordcode and asking me in a strangled but imperious voice to come round to his house immediately, entering by way of the garden door.

My first thought was that he had killed someone, possibly his wife. I could not have been more wrong.

The Professor opened the back door, and closed it swiftly after me. The lights inside the house were dimmed. Somewhere in the gloom, a Biedermeier grandfather clock ticked like a big old bomb. At the entrance to the living room stood Helena, her hands to her mouth, smothering a scream. Twenty minutes had passed since Teodor's call, but the scream still seemed to be on the point of coming out of her.

Two armchairs stood before a dying fire. One was empty. I took it to be the Professor's. In the other, somewhat obscured from my line of sight, sat a silky, rounded man of forty, with a cap of soft black hair, and twinkling round eyes that said we were all friends, weren't we? His winged chair was high-backed and he had fitted himself into the angle of it like an aircraft passenger prepared for landing. His rather circular shoes stopped short of the floor, and it occurred to me they were East European shoes: marbled, of an uncertain leather, with moulded, heavy-treaded soles. His hairy brown suit was like a remodelled military uniform. Before him stood a table with a pot of mauve hyacinths on it, and beside the hyacinths lay a display of objects which I recognised as the instruments of silent killing: two garottes made of wooden toggles and lengths of piano wire; a screwdriver so sharpened that it was a stiletto; a Charter Arms .38 Undercover revolver with a five-shot cylinder, together with two kinds of bullet, six soft-nosed, and six rifled, with congealed powder squashed into the grooves.

"It is cyanide," the Professor explained, in answer to my silent perplexity. "It is an invention of the Devil. The bullet has only to graze the victim to destroy him utterly."

I found myself wondering how the poisonous powder was supposed to survive the intense heat of a gun barrel.

"This gentleman is named Ladislaus Kaldor," the Professor continued. "He was sent by the Hungarian secret police to kill us. He is a friend. Kindly sit down, Herr Ned."

With ceremony, Ladislaus Kaldor rose from his chair and pumped my hand as if we had concluded a profitable deal.

"Sir!" he cried happily, in English. "Latzi. I am sorry, sir. Don't worry anything. Everybody call me Latzi. Herr Doktor. My friend. Please sit down. Yes."

I remember how the scent of the hyacinths seemed to go so nicely with his smile. It was only slowly I began to realise I had no sense of danger. Some people convey danger all the time; others put it on when they are angry or threatened. But Latzi, when I was able to consult my instincts, conveyed only an enormous will to please. Which perhaps is all you need if you're a professional killer.

I did not sit down. A chorus of conflicting feelings was yelling in my head, but fatigue was not among them. The empty coffee cups, I was thinking. The empty plates with cake crumbs. Who eats cake and drinks coffee when his life is being threatened? Latzi was sitting again, smiling like a conjuror. The Professor and his wife were studying my face, but from different places in the room. They've quarrelled, I thought; crisis has driven them to their separate corners. An American revolver, I thought. But not the spare cylinder that serious players customarily carried. East European shoes, and with soles that leave a perfect print on every carpet or polished floor. Cyanide bullets that would burn off their cyanide in the barrel.

"How long's he been here?" I asked the Professor.

He shrugged. I hated his shrugs. "One hour. Less."

"More than one hour," Helena contradicted him. Her indignant gaze was fixed upon me. Until tonight she had made a point of ignoring me, slipping past me like a ghost, smiling or scowling at the ground to show her disapproval. Suddenly she needed my support. "He rang the bell at eight-forty-five exactly. I was listening to the radio. The programme changed."

I glanced at Latzi. "You speak German?"

"*Jawohl,* Herr Doktor!"

Back to Helena. "Which programme?"

"The BBC World Service," she said.

I went to the radio and switched it on. A reedy Oxford academic of unknown gender was bleating about Keats. Thank you, BBC. I switched it off.

"He rang the bell—who answered it?" I said.

"I did," said the Professor.

"He did," said Helena.

"Please," said Latzi.

"And then?"

"He was standing on the doorstep, wearing a coat," said the Professor.

"A raincoat," Helena corrected him.

"He asked if I was Professor Teodor, I said yes. He gave his name, he said 'Forgive me, Professor, I have come to kill you with a garotte or cyanide bullet but I do not wish to, I am your disciple and admirer. I wish to surrender to you and remain in the West.' "

"He spoke Hungarian?" I asked.

"Naturally."

"So you invited him in?"

"Naturally."

Helena did not agree. "No! First Teodor asked for *me,*" she insisted. I had not heard her correct her husband before tonight. Now she had done so twice in as many minutes. "He calls to me and says, 'Helena, we have a guest.' I say, 'Good.' Then he asks Latzi into the house. I take his raincoat, I hang it in the hall, I make coffee. That is how it happened exactly."

"And cake," I said. "You made cake."

"The cake was made already."

"Were you afraid?" I asked—for fear, like danger, was something else that was missing.

"I was disgusted, I was shocked," she replied. "Now I am afraid—yes, I am very afraid. We are all afraid."

"And you?" I said to the Professor.

He shrugged again, as if to say I was the last man on earth to whom he would confide his feelings.

"Why don't you take your wife to the study?" I said.

He was disposed to argue, then changed his mind. Strangers arm in arm, they marched from the room.

I was alone with Latzi. I stood, he sat. Munich can be a very silent city. Even in repose his face smiled at me ingratiatingly. His small eyes still twinkled, but there was nothing I could read in them. He gave me a nod of encouragement, his smile broadened. He said "Please," and eased himself more comfortably into his chair. I made the gesture every Middle European understands. I held out my hand, palm upward, and passed my thumb across the tip of my forefinger. Still smiling, he rummaged in his inside jacket pocket and handed me his papers. They were in the name of Egon Braubach of Passau, born 1933, occupation artist. I never saw anyone who looked less like a Bavarian artist. They comprised one West German passport, one driver's licence and one social security document. None of them, it seemed to me, carried the least conviction. Neither did his shoes.

"When did you enter Germany?"

"This afternoon, Herr Doktor, this afternoon at five. Please."

"Where from?"

"Vienna, please. Vienna," he repeated, in a breathless rush, as if making me a gift of the entire city, and gave another wriggling motion of his rump, apparently to achieve greater subservience. "I caught the first train to Munich this morning, Herr Doktor."

"At what time?"

"At eight o'clock, sir. The eight-o'clock train."

"When did you enter Austria?"

"Yesterday, Herr Doktor. It was raining. Please."

"Which papers did you present at the Austrian border?"

"My Hungarian passport, Your Excellency. In Vienna I was given German papers."

Sweat was forming on his upper lip. His German was fluent but unmistakably Balkan. He had travelled by train, he said: Budapest, Györ, Vienna, Herr Doktor. His masters had given him a cold chicken and a bottle of wine for the journey. With best pickles, Your Honour, and paprika. More smiles. Arriving in Vienna, he had checked in at the Altes Kaiserreich Hotel, near the railway station, where a room had been reserved for him. A humble room, a humble hotel, Your Excellency, but I am a humble man. It was at the hotel, late at night, that he was visited by a Hungarian gentleman whom he had not seen before—"But I suspect he was a diplomat, Herr Doktor. He was distinguished like yourself!" This gentleman gave him his money and documents, he explained—and the arsenal that lay before us on the table.

"Where are you staying in Munich?"

"It is a modest guesthouse on the edge of town, Herr Doktor," he replied, with an apologetic smile. "More a brothel. Yes, a brothel. One sees many men there, coming and going all the time." He told me its name, and I had half a notion he was going to recommend a girl as well.

"Did they tell you to stay there?"

"For the discretion, Herr Doktor. The anonymity. Please."

"Do you have luggage there?"

He gave the poor man's shrug, quite unlike the Professor's. "A toothbrush," he said. "Some clothes. A bag, sir. Modest materials."

In Hungary he was by vocation an agricultural journalist, he said, but he had made himself a second living working for the secret police, first as an informer, and more recently, for the money, as assassin. He had performed certain duties inside Hungary but preferred—forgive him, Excellency—not to say what these were until he was assured he would not be prosecuted in the West. The Professor was his first "foreign duty," but the thought of killing him had offended his sense of decorum.

"The Professor is a man of format, Herr Doktor! Of reputation! He is not some

Jew or priest! Why should I kill this man? I'm a respectable human being, good heavens! I have my honour! Please!"

"Tell me your orders."

They were not complicated. He was to ring the Herr Professor's doorbell, they had said—so he had rung it. The Professor was sure to be at home, since on Wednesdays he gave private tuition until nine, they had said. —The Professor was indeed at home.— He should describe himself as a friend of Pali from Debrecen. —He had taken the liberty not to describe himself in these terms.— Once inside the house, he should kill the Herr Professor by whatever means seemed appropriate, but preferably the garotte, since it was sure and silent, though there was always a regrettable danger of decapitation. He should kill Helena also, they said—perhaps kill her first, depending on who opened the door to him, they were not particular. It was for this contingency that he had brought a second garotte. With a garotte, Herr Doktor, he explained helpfully, one could never be sure of being able to disentangle the instrument after use. He should then telephone a number in Bonn, ask for Peter, and report that "Susi will be staying with friends tonight"—Susi being the Professor's codename for the operation, Excellency. This was the signal for success, though in the present circumstance, Herr Doktor, it must be admitted that he had not been successful. Giggle.

"Telephone from here?" I asked.

"From this house, exactly. To Peter. Please. They are violent men, Herr Doktor. They threaten my family. I have no choice, naturally. I have a daughter. They gave me strict instructions: 'From the Professor's house you will telephone Peter.' "

This also surprised me. Since the Professor was identified to the Hungarian secret police as a Western asset—and had been for fifteen years—one might suppose they would be suspicious of his telephone.

"What do you do if you've failed?" I asked.

"If the duty cannot be fulfilled—if the Herr Professor has guests, or is for some reason not available—I am to ring from a phone box and say that Susi is on her way home."

"From any particular phone box?"

"All phone boxes are suitable, Herr Doktor, in the event of a non-completion. Peter may then give further instructions, he may not. If not, I return at once to Budapest. Alternatively, Peter may say, 'Try again tomorrow,' or he may say, 'Try in two days.' It is all in the hands of Peter in this case."

"What is the Bonn telephone number?"

He recited it.

"Turn out your pockets."

A khaki handkerchief, some badly printed family snaps, including some of a young girl, presumably his daughter, three East European condoms, an open packet of Russian cigarettes, a wobbly tin penknife of obvious Eastern manufacture, a stub of unpainted pencil, 960 West German marks, some small change. The return half of a second-class rail ticket, Vienna—Munich—Vienna. I never in my life saw such miserably assembled pockets. Did the Hungarian Service have no despatchers? Checkers? What the Devil were they thinking of?

"And your raincoat," I said, and watched him fetch it from the hall. It was brand-new. The pockets were empty. It was of Austrian manufacture and good quality. It must have cost serious Western money.

"Did you buy this in Vienna?"

"*Jawohl*, Herr Doktor. It was raining cats and dogs and I had no protection."

"When?"

"Please?"

"What with?"

"Please?"

I discovered he could anger me quite quickly. "You caught the first train this morning, right? It left Vienna before the shops opened, right? You didn't get your money till late last night when the Hungarian diplomat visited you. So when did you buy the coat and what did you use for money? Or did you steal it? Is that the answer?"

First he frowned; then he laughed indulgently at my breach of good manners. It was clear that he forgave me. He opened his hands to me in generosity. "But I bought it last night, Herr Doktor! When I arrived at the station! With my personal *Valuten* that I brought with me from Hungary for shopping, naturally! I am not a liar! Please!"

"Did you keep the receipt?"

He shook his head sagely, advice to a younger man. "To keep receipts, Herr Doktor? I give you this advice. To keep receipts is to invite questions about where you get your money. A receipt—it's like a spy in the pocket. Please."

Too many excuses, I thought, releasing myself from the brilliance of his smile. Too many answers in one paragraph. All my instincts told me to trust nobody and nothing about the story that was being told me. It was not so much the sloppiness of the assassination plan that strained my credulity—the implausible documents, the contents of the pockets, the shoes—not even the basic improbability of the mission. I had seen enough of low-level Soviet satellite operations to regard such amateurishness as the norm. What disturbed me about these people was the unreality of their behaviour in my company, the feeling there was one story for me and one for them; that I had been brought here to perform a function, and the collective will required me to shut up and get on with it.

Yet at the same time I was trapped. I had no choice, and no time, but to take everything they had told me at face value. I was in the position of a doctor who, while suspecting a patient of malingering, has no option but to treat his symptoms. By the laws of the game, Latzi was a prize. It was not every day that a Hungarian assassin offered to defect to the West, no matter how incompetent he was. By the same token, the man was in considerable danger, since it was unthinkable that an assassination operation of this consequence could be launched without separate surveillance.

When in doubt, says the handbook, take the operational line. Were they watching the house? It was necessary to assume so, though it was not an easy house to watch, which was what had commended it to Teodor's handlers fifteen years ago. It stood at the end of a leafy cul-de-sac and backed on to the river. The way into the garden led along a deserted tow-path. But the front porch was visible to anybody passing by, and Latzi could have already been observed entering it.

I went upstairs and from the landing window surveyed the road. The neighbouring houses were in darkness. I saw no sign of stray cars or people. My own car was parked in the next sidestreet, close to the river. I returned to the drawing room. The telephone was on the bookcase. I handed Latzi the receiver and watched him dial the number in Bonn. His hands were girlish and moist. Obligingly, he tilted the earpiece in my direction, and himself with it. He smelt of old blanket and Russian tobacco. The phone rang out, I heard a man's voice, very grumpy, speaking German. For somebody awaiting news of a killing, I thought, you're doing a good job of pretending you aren't.

A thick accent, presumably Hungarian: "Hullo? Yes? Who is it?"

I nodded to Latzi to go ahead.

"Good evening, sir. I wish, please to speak to Mr. Peter."

"What about?"

"Is this Mr. Peter, please? It is a private matter."

"What do you want?"

"Is this Peter?"

"My name is Peter!"

"It is regarding Susi, Mr. Peter," Latzi explained, with a sideways wink at me. "Susi will not be coming home tonight, Mr. Peter. She will be staying with friends, I am afraid. Good friends. She will be looked after. Good night, Mr. Peter."

He was about to replace the receiver, but I stayed his hand long enough to hear a growl of contempt or incomprehension the other end before he rang off.

Latzi smiled at me, very pleased with himself. "He plays it well, Herr Doktor. A true professional, I would say. A fine actor, you agree?"

"Did you recognise the voice?"

"No, Herr Doktor. Alas, the voice is not familiar to me."

I shoved open the study door. The Professor sat at his desk, his fists in front of him. Helena sat on the tutorial sofa. I felt a need to acquaint the Professor with my scepticism. I stepped into the room, closing the door behind me.

"The man Latzi, as you call him, is a criminal," I said. "Either he's some kind of confidence trickster, or he's a self-confessed murderer who came to Germany on false papers in order to kill you and your wife. Either way, you're within your rights to turn him over to the West German police and be done with him. Do you want to do that? Or do you want to leave the decisions to us? Which?"

To my surprise, he appeared for the first time that evening genuinely alarmed. Perhaps he had not expected to be challenged. Perhaps the proximity of his own death had dawned on him. Either way, I had the impression he was attaching more importance to my question than I understood. Helena had turned her eyes away from me and was watching him also. Critically. A woman waiting to be paid.

"Do whatever you must do," he muttered.

"Then you must do as I ask. Both of you."

"We are cooperative. We shall be—yes, cooperative. We have been—cooperative—for many years. Too many."

I glanced at Helena.

"It will be my husband's responsibility," she said.

I had no time to ponder the mysteries of this ominous statement. "Then please put together some night things and be ready at the garden door in five minutes," I said, and returned to the drawing room and Latzi.

I think he had been standing at the door, for he stepped quickly back as I entered, then clasped his hands to his chin and beamed at me, asking what was *gefällig*—what was my pleasure?

"Have you ever seen the Professor before tonight?"

"No, sir. Only photographs. One would admire him anywhere. A true aristocrat."

"And his wife?"

"She is known to me, sir. Naturally."

"How?"

"She was once an actress, Herr Doktor, one of the best in Budapest."

"And you saw her on the stage?"

Another pause. "No, sir."

"Then where did you see her?"

He was trying to read me. I had the impression he was wondering whether she might have told me something, and he was trimming his answers accordingly.

"Theatre bills, Your Excellency. When she was young, her famous face was on every street corner. All young men loved her—I was no exception."

"Where else?"

He saw that I had nothing. And I saw that he saw. "So sad about a woman's looks, Herr Doktor. A man, he can remain impressive until he is eighty. A woman —" he sighed.

I let him pack together his weapons, then took possession of them. I loaded the soft-nosed bullets into the revolver. As I did so, a thought occurred to me.

"When I walked in here, the cylinder was empty and the bullets were spread on the table."

"Correct, Excellency."

"When did you take the bullets out of the cylinder?" I asked.

"Before entering the house. So that I could demonstrate my peaceful intentions. Naturally."

"Naturally."

As we moved to the hall, I shoved the revolver into my waistband.

"If you take it into your head to run away, I shall shoot you in the back," I explained to him, and had the satisfaction of seeing his little eyes swivel in alarm. Professional assassins, it seemed, did not take kindly to their own medicine.

I tossed him his raincoat and glanced round the room for other traces of him. There were none. I ordered silence and led the three of them into the garden and along the tow-path to my car. A famous actress, I thought, and not a word about it on the file. I put the Professor and Helena in the back, and Latzi in the front beside me. Then we sat still for five minutes while I waited for the slightest sign that we were being watched. Nothing. I drove as far as the main road and stopped again. Nothing. It was by now midnight and a new moon had risen among the stars. I circled the town, keeping a watch on my mirror, then took the autobahn south-west to the Starnbergersee, where we kept a safe house for briefing and debriefing joes in passage. It lay close to the lake's edge and was manned by two murderous long-haired wonders left over from London Station's Lamplighters Section. They were called Jeffrey and Arnold. Arnold was hovering in the doorway by the time we reached it. One hand was in the pocket of his kaftan. The other hung threateningly to his side.

"It's me, you buffoon," I said softly.

Jeffrey showed the Professor and his wife to their bedroom while Arnold sat with Latzi in the drawing room. I went down the garden to the boat-house, where I was at last able to talk to Toby Esterhase on the safe telephone. He was amazingly composed. It was as if he had been expecting my call.

Toby arrived in Munich on the first flight from London next morning, wearing a beaver-lamb coat and a leather Trilby hat, and looking more the impresario than the beleaguered spy.

"Nedike, my God!" he cried, embracing me like a prodigal father. "Listen, you look fantastic, I would say. Congratulations, okay? Nothing like a little excitement to bring the blooms to your cheeks. How's Mabel, actually? A marriage, that's something you got to water, same as a flower."

I drove slowly and spoke, as best I could, dispassionately, giving him the fruits of my researches throughout the long night. I wanted him to know everything I knew by the time we reached the lake house.

Neither the Americans nor the West Germans had any trace of Latzi, I said. Neither, I gathered from Toby, had London.

"Latzi, that's an unwritten page, Ned. Totally," Toby agreed, surveying the passing landscape with every sign of approval.

There was also no trace of his Bavarian covername, or of any of the covernames that Latzi claimed to have used on his "duties" inside Hungary, I said.

Toby lowered his window to enjoy the fragrance of the fields.

Latzi's West German passport was a fake, I continued with determination, one of a batch recently run up by a low-grade forger in Vienna and sold on the private market.

Toby was mildly indignant. "I mean who buys that crap, for God's sake?" he protested, as we passed a pair of palomino horses grazing in a paddock. "With passports, these days, you get what you pay for actually. What you get for crap like that, it's six months in a stinking gaol." And he shook his head sadly like a man whose warnings go unheeded until it's too late.

I blundered on. The phone number in Bonn belonged to the Hungarian military attaché, I said, whose first name was indeed listed as Peter. He was an identified Hungarian Intelligence officer. I allowed myself a restrained irony:

"That's a new one for us, isn't it, Tobe? A spy using his own name as a covername? I mean why bother any more? You're Toby, so we'll keep it a secret and call you Toby instead. Great."

But Toby was too set on enjoying his day in Bavaria to be disturbed by the implications of my words. "Nedike, believe me, those army guys, they're total idiots. Hungarian military intelligence, that's the same as Hungarian military music, know what I mean? They blow it out their arses actually."

I continued my recitation. West German Security had a permanent tap running on the Hungarian attaché's telephone, I said. A cassette of Latzi's conversation with Peter was on its way to my office. From what I understood, it offered no surprises except to underline that Peter appeared genuinely unprepared for the call. Peter had neither made nor received further calls last night, I said, nor had there been any burst of diplomatic signals traffic from the roof of the Hungarian Embassy in Bonn. Peter had, however, complained to the Protocol Department of the West German Foreign Office about telephone harassment on his home line. This was not, I suggested, the act of a conspirator. Toby was less sure.

"Could be one thing, Ned, could be the other," he said, leaning back in his seat and languidly tilting the flat of his hand both ways. "A man thinks he's been compromised? So maybe it's not so stupid he makes a formal complaint once, brushes over his traces—why not?"

I gave him the rest. I was determined to. Latzi's description of the putative diplomat in Vienna tallied with that of one Leo Bakocs, Commercial Secretary and, like Peter, an identified Hungarian Intelligence officer, I said. Cousin Wagner was getting hold of a photograph for us to show to Latzi later in the day.

The name Bakocs brought a fond smile to Toby's lips. "They drag *Leo* in on this? Listen, Leo's so vain he spies only on duchesses." He laughed in jolly disbelief. "Leo in some lousy hotel, handing over garottes to a smelly assassin? Tell me another, Ned. I mean."

"It isn't me who's telling you," I said. "It's Latzi."

Lastly, I said, I had despatched Jeffrey to the Munich whore-house to pay Latzi's bill and collect his overnight bag. The only article of interest in his luggage was a set of pornographic photographs.

"It's the tension, Ned," Toby explained magnanimously. "In a foreign country, killing somebody you don't know, you need a little private company—know what I mean?"

In return, Toby had brought me nothing whatever, private or otherwise. I had imagined him on the phone all night, and perhaps he had been. But not in support of my enquiries.

"Maybe we have a party tonight," he proposed. "Harry Palfrey of Legal Department is coming over with a couple of guys from the Foreign Office. That's a nice fellow, Harry. Very English."

I was bewildered. "What branch of the Foreign Office?" I said. "Who? Why Palfrey?"

But as Toby would say, questions are never dangerous until you answer them. We arrived at the lake house to find Arnold cooking eggs and bacon. The Professor and Latzi sat at one end of the table. Helena, a vegetarian, sat at the other, eating a nut bar from her handbag.

Arnold was blond and lank. His hair was done in a knot at the back. "They had a bit of a dingdong, Ned," he confided to me disapprovingly while Toby fell about the Professor's neck. "The Professor and his missus, a real dogfight. I don't know who started it or what it was about, I wouldn't ask."

"Did Latzi join in?"

"He was going to, Ned, but I told him to keep quiet. I don't like a man who comes between husband and wife, I never did."

In retrospect, our discussions that day resemble an intricate minuet, beginning in our humble kitchen and ending in the courts of the Almighty Himself—more precisely in the beflagged conference room of the American Consulate General, where the inspiring features of President Nixon and Vice President Agnew smiled favourably on our endeavours.

For Toby, as I soon realised, far from doing nothing, had laid on an entire programme for himself, which he advanced from stage to stage with the dexterity of a ringmaster. In the kitchen, he listened to the whole story over again from Latzi and the Professor, while Helena chewed her nut bar. I had never seen Toby in full Hungarian flight before and found time to marvel at the transformation. With one sentence he had flung aside the unnatural corset of his Anglo-Saxon restraint and was back among his people. His eyes caught fire. He preened, and his back arched as if he were sitting on a parade horse.

"Ned, they say you have been quite fantastic actually," he called to me down the table in the midst of all this. "A tower of strength, they are saying, completely. I think maybe they will recommend you a Nobel prize!"

"Tell them to make it an Oscar, I'll accept," I said sourly, and took myself for a walk down to the lakeside to recover my temper.

I returned to the house to find Toby and the Professor closeted in the drawing room, talking volubly. Toby's high respect for the Professor seemed, if anything, to have increased. Latzi was helping Arnold with the washing-up and they were both sniggering. Latzi had evidently been telling a dirty joke. Helena was nowhere to be seen. Next, it was Latzi's turn to sit alone with Toby, while the Professor and his wife walked uneasily at the lakeside, pausing every few steps to remonstrate with each other, until the Professor turned on his heel and strode back to the house.

Seizing the moment, I slipped out and joined Helena. Her lips were pursed and her face was sickly-white—whether from fear, anger or fatigue, I couldn't tell. When she spoke, she had to stop and begin again before the words would come.

"He is a *liar*," she said. "It is all lies! Lie, lie! He is a liar!"

"Who is?"

"They are *both* liars. From the day of birth, they *lie*. On their deathbeds, they *lie*."

"So what's the truth?" I said.

"*Wait* is the truth!"

"Wait for what?"

"I have warned him. 'If you do this, I shall tell the English.' So we wait. If he does it, I shall tell you. If he repents, I shall spare him. I am his wife."

She walked to the house, a stately woman. As she entered it, a black limousine pulled up in the drive and Harry Palfrey, the Circus legal adviser, emerged, accompanied by two other members of the English governing classes. I recognised the taller of them as Alan Barnaby, luminary of the Foreign Office's misnomered Information and Research Department, which traded in Communist counter-propaganda at its sleaziest. Toby was shaking him warmly by the hand while with his other he beckoned me to join them. We went indoors and sat down.

At first I smouldered in silence. The players had been sent upstairs. Toby was doing the talking, the others listened to him with the special reverence their kind reserves for paupers or black men. I even found myself feeling a little protective of him—of Toby Esterhase, God help me, who protected no one but himself!

"What we are dealing with here, Alan, without talking out of turn actually, is a completely top source who is now expended," Toby explained. "A great joe, but his day is over."

"You mean the Prof," Barnaby said helpfully.

"They are on to him. They know his value too well. From certain clues I have obtained from Latzi, it's clear the Hungarians have a fat dossier on the Professor's operations. After all, I mean, why would they try to kill a fellow who is no use to us? A Hungarian assassination attempt—that's a *Good Housekeeping* certificate for the target, I would say."

"We can't be responsible for the Professor's safety indefinitely," Palfrey cautioned us with his loser's smile. "We can give him protection for a bit, naturally. But we can't accept a life interest in him. He has to know that. We may have to get him to sign something just to make the point."

The second Foreign Office man was round and shiny with a chain across his waistcoat. I had a childish urge to pull it and see if he squealed.

"Well, *I* think we may all be talking too much," he said silkily. "If the Americans agree to take the pair of 'em off our hands, the Prof and his missus, we shan't have to worry, shall we? Best keep our heads down and our powder dry, what?"

Palfrey demurred. "He should still sign a release for us, Norman. He has rather been playing us off against the Cousins in the last few years."

Ever the protector of his own, Toby gave a knowing smile. "All the best joes do this, I would say, Harry. One hand washes the other, even at Teodor's level. The question is, now that he is no longer usable, what have we got to lose except trouble actually? I mean, I am not the expert here," he added, with an ingratiating smile at Barnaby.

"What about the assassin fellow?" said the man called Norman. "Will he play ball as well? Bloody dangerous, isn't it, sitting up there like a duck in a tree?"

"Latzi is flexible," said Toby. "He is scared, he is also a complete patriot." I would not have backed him on either of these points, but I was too sickened to interrupt. "These *apparatchiks,* when they step out of the system, they are in shock. Latzi is coping with it. He agonises over his family, but he is reconciled. If Teodor accepts, Latzi will accept also. With guarantees, naturally."

"What *sort* of guarantees?" said the shiny Foreign Office man, so quickly that not even Harry Palfrey got in ahead of him.

Toby did not falter. "Well, naturally the usual. Latzi and Teodor don't want to be thrown on to the rubbish heap when this one's over, I would say. Nor does Helena. American passports, a good bit of money at the end of the road, assistance and protection—I mean, that's basic so to speak."

"The whole thing's a con," I blurted. I had had enough.

Everybody was smiling at me. They would have smiled whatever I had said. They were that sort of crowd. If I had said I was a Hungarian double agent, they would have smiled. If I had said I was Adolf Hitler's reincarnated younger brother, they would have smiled. All but Toby, that is, whose face had acquired the lifelessness of someone who knows that all he can safely be at this moment is nobody at all.

"Now why on earth do you say that, Ned?" Barnaby was asking, awfully interested.

"Latzi's not a trained killer," I said. "I don't know what he is, but he isn't a killer. He was carrying an unloaded gun. No professional in his right mind does that. He's posing as a Bavarian artist, but he's wearing Hungarian clothes and half the junk in his pockets is Hungarian. I was standing over him when he made his phone call to Bonn. Fine, the attaché's first name is Peter. It's in the diplomatic list as Peter. Peter wasn't expecting that call in a month of Sundays. Latzi laid it on him. Listen to the German tape of their conversation."

"Then what about the chap in Vienna, Ned?" said Barnaby, still determined to patronise me. "The chap who gave him his money and his hardware? Eh? Eh?"

"They never met. We showed Latzi the photograph and he was delighted. 'That's the man,' he said. Oh sure: he'd seen a photograph somewhere else. Ask Helena, she knows. She's not telling at the moment, but if we put pressure on her, I'm sure she will."

Toby came briefly alive. "Pressure, Ned? Helena? Pressure, that's something you use when you know you can squeeze harder than the other fellow. That woman is crazy about her husband. She defends him to the grave actually."

"The Professor's fallen foul of the Americans," I said. "They're rolling up his red carpet. He's desperate. If he didn't set up the assassination himself, Latzi did. The whole ploy is a device for him to cut his losses and make a new life."

They waited for me to continue, all of them. It was as if they were waiting for the punchline. Finally Toby spoke. He had rediscovered his form.

"Nedike, how long since you slept actually?" he asked with an indulgent smile. "Tell us, please."

"What's that got to do with it?"

Toby was ostentatiously studying his watch. "I think you have been now thirty hours without sleep, Ned. You took some pretty damn big decisions in that time —all good ones, I would say. I don't think we can blame you for having a bit of a reaction."

It was as if I had never spoken. All heads had turned back to Toby.

"Well, *I* think it's rather important we take a peek at the cast," Barnaby was saying as I headed for the door. "Can we whistle them down, Toby? Question of how they'll shape up under the spotlights."

"I think there's news value in doing this thing straight away, Barnaby," Palfrey was saying, as I headed for the garden and sanity. "Strike while the iron is hot. With me?"

"With you all the way, Harry. Hundred percent."

I refused to be present for the first audition. I sulked in the kitchen and let Arnold minister to me while I pretended to listen to some story about his mother walking out on the fellow she'd been with for twenty years and shacking up with her childhood sweetheart. I watched Toby skip upstairs to fetch his champions, and scowled when the three men descended some minutes later, Latzi with his black hair slicked into a parting, the Professor with his jacket outside his shoulders, his seer's head struck forward in contemplation and his white mane flowing becomingly.

Then Helena came into the kitchen with tears streaming down her cheeks, so Arnold gave her a hug and fetched a blanket for her, because the spring morning was crisp and she was shivering. Then Arnold made her a camomile tea, and sat with his arm round her till Toby bustled in to say we were all expected at the American Consulate in two hours.

"Russell Sheriton is flying in from London, Pete de May from Bonn. They are mustard for it, Ned. Totally mustard. Washington throws its cap in the air, completely." I do not recall whether Pete de May was grander than Sheriton or less grand. But grand enough. "Ned, that Teodor's fantastic," Toby assured me privately.

"Really? In what way?"

"You know what they told him? 'What you are doing is damn risky, Professor.

Do you think you can handle it?' You know what he replied? 'Mr. Ambassador, risks are what we all take to protect civilised society.' He's quiet, he's dignified. Latzi too. Ned, after this you get some sleep, okay? I phone Mabel."

We rode in two cars, Toby with the Hungarians, myself with Palfrey and the Foreign Office. Opening the car door for me, Palfrey touched my arm and offered me some steel-edged advice. "I think from now on, it's all hands pulling together, Ned. Tired is one thing. Talk about con-tricks is something else. Yes? Agreed?"

We must have numbered twenty head. The Consul General presided. He was a pallid mid-Westerner, an ex-lawyer like Palfrey, and kept talking anxiously about "reprocussions." Milton Wagner was seated between Sheriton and de May. It was clear to me that, whatever their private thoughts, Sheriton and Wagner had orders to keep their scepticism to themselves. Perhaps they too had recognised that there were worse ways of getting rid of useless agents than offloading them onto the U.S. Information Services, who were represented by a quartet of troubled believers whose names I never learned.

Pullach was spoken for, naturally. Though not involved, they had sent their own observer, so we could be confident that our determinations would be the gossip of Potsdam by afternoon. They also insisted on making a voluble complaint about Vienna. It seemed that Pullach had a running battle with the Austrian police about forged passports, and suspected them of selling them to the Hungarians. Quite a lot of the meeting was taken up by an Oberst von-und-zu somewhere or other moaning about Austrian duplicity.

The three champions did not, of course, attend our deliberations, but sat in the waiting room. When sandwiches were passed round, a generous plate was sent out to them. And when they were finally called in, several of the lay members of the meeting broke into applause, which must have been the first of many times from then on when they heard the roar of the greasepaint.

But it was Helena's tears that stole the show. The Professor said his few words, and his halting dignity worked its predictable magic. Latzi followed him, and a cold chill fell over the room as he explained why he had carried the two garottes, which were then passed gingerly round the table with the rest of the exhibits. But when Helena stepped forward on the Professor's arm, I felt a lump rise to my throat, and knew that everyone in the room was feeling the same.

"I support my husband," was all the great actress could declaim.

But it was enough to bring the room to its feet.

It was late evening before I managed to speak to her alone. We were washed out by then; even the irrepressible Latzi was exhausted. The captains and the kings had departed, Toby had departed. I was sitting with Arnold in the drawing room of the lake house. An American van, with blackened windows and two plainclothes marines aboard, was waiting in the drive, but our stars were learning to keep their public waiting. The day had been spent preparing afternoon press announcements and signing Palfrey's releases, which he turned out to have brought with him in his briefcase.

She entered hesitantly, as if she expected me to strike her, but the anger had been drained out of me.

"We shall get our passports," she said, sitting down. "It is the new world."

Arnold slipped tactfully from the room, closing the door behind him.

"Who's Latzi?" I said.

"He is a friend of Teodor."

"What else is he?"

"He is an actor. A bad, oh a *bad* actor from Debrecen."

"Did he ever work for the secret police?"

She made a gesture of deprecation. "He had connections. When Teodor needed to arrange himself with the authorities, Latzi was the go-between."

"You mean, when Teodor needed to inform on his students?"

"Yes."

"Did Latzi supply Teodor with his information while you were in Munich?"

"At first only a little. But when none came from other sources, more. Then much more. Latzi prepared the material for Teodor. Teodor sold it to the British and Americans. Otherwise we would have had no money."

"Was Latzi getting help from the secret police to do this?"

"It was private. Things are changing in Hungary. It is no longer prudent to be involved with the authorities."

I unlocked the door and watched her make her exit, head erect.

A few weeks later, back in London, I faced Toby with her story. He was neither surprised nor contrite.

"Women, Ned, that's a criminal class actually. Better we eat the soup, not stir it."

A few weeks more and the Teodor-Latzi show was riding high. So was Toby. How much was he a part of it? How much did he know when? The whole of it? Did he dream up the entire piece of theatre in order to make the best of his imperilled agent and get him off his hands? I have often secretly suspected that the play was a three-hander, at the least, with Helena as the reluctant audience.

"Know what, Nedike?" Toby declared, throwing an affectionate arm around my shoulder. "If you can't ride two horses at once, you better stay out of the Circus."

You remember the pseudonymous Colonel Weatherby in the book? The master of disguises, at ease in seven European languages? Pimpernel leader of the East European resistance fighters? The man who "flitted back and forth across the Iron Curtain as if it were of frailest gossamer"? That was me. Ned. I didn't write that part, thank God. It was the work of some venal sports journalist from Baltimore recruited by the Cousins. Mine was the introductory pen portrait of the great man, printed under the caption "The Real Professor Teodor as I Knew Him," and gouged out of me by Toby and the Fifth Floor. My working title for the book was *Tricks of the Trade,* but the Fifth Floor said that might be misunderstood. They promoted me instead.

But not before I had taken my indignation to George Smiley, who had just given up his job as acting chief and was on the point of removing himself for the nearly last time to the shadows of academia. I was back in London on a mid-tour break. It was a Friday evening and I ran him to earth in Bywater Street, packing for the weekend. He heard me out, he gave a small chuckle, then a larger chuckle. He muttered, *"Oh Toby,"* affectionately under his breath.

"But then they *do* assassinate, don't they, Ned," he objected as he laboriously folded a tweed suit. "The Hungarians, I mean. Even by East European standards, they're one of the foulest mobs there are, surely?"

Yes, I conceded, the Hungarians killed and tortured pretty much at will. But that didn't alter the fact that Latzi was a fake and Teodor was Latzi's accomplice, and as to Toby—

Smiley cut me short. "Now, Ned, I think you're being a little bit prissy. Every church needs its saints. The anti-Communist church is no exception. And saints as a bunch are a pretty bogus lot, when you come down to it. But no one would pretend they don't have their uses, once they get the job. Do you think this shirt will do, or must I give it another iron?"

We sat in his drawing room sipping our Scotches and listening to the clamour of party-goers in Bywater Street.

"And did the ghost of Stefanie stalk the Munich pavements for you, Ned?" Smiley enquired tenderly, just when I was beginning to wonder whether he had dozed off.

I had long ceased to marvel at his capacity to put himself in my shoes.

"Now and then," I replied.

"But not in the flesh? How sad."

"I once rang one of her aunts," I said. "I'd had some silly row with Mabel and gone to a hotel. It was late. I expect I was a bit drunk." I found myself wondering whether Smiley already knew, and decided I was being fanciful. "Or I *think* it was an aunt. It could have been a servant. No, it was an aunt."

"What did she say?"

" 'Fräulein Stefanie is not at home.' "

A long silence, but this time I did not make the mistake of thinking he had gone to sleep.

"Young voice?" he enquired thoughtfully.

"Quite."

"Then perhaps it was Stefanie who answered."

"Perhaps it was."

We listened again to the raised voices in the street. A girl was laughing. A man was cross. Somebody hooted a horn and drove away. The sounds died. Stefanie's my Ann, I thought, as I walked back across the river to Battersea, where I had kept my little flat: the difference is, I never had the courage to let her disappoint me.

7

Smiley had interrupted himself—some tale of a Central American diplomat with a passion for British model railways of a certain generation, and how the Circus had bought the man's lifelong allegiance with a Hornby Double-O shunting engine stolen from a London toy museum by Monty Arbuck's team. Everyone was laughing until this sudden reflective silence, while Smiley's troubled gaze fixed itself upon some point outside the room.

"And just occasionally we meet the reality we've been playing with," he said quietly. "Until it happens, we're spectators. The joes live out our dreams for us, and we case officers sit safe and snug behind our one-way mirrors, telling ourselves that seeing is feeling. But when the moment of truth strikes—if it ever does for you— well, from then on we become a little more humble about what we ask people to do for us."

He never once glanced at me as he said this. He gave no hint of who was in his mind. But I knew, and he knew. And each knew the other knew that it was Colonel Jerzy.

I saw him and I said nothing to Mabel. Perhaps I was too surprised. Or perhaps the old habits of dissembling die so hard that even today my first response at any unexpected event is to suppress the spontaneous reaction. We were watching the nine-o'clock news on television, which for Mabel and myself has become a kind of Evensong these days, don't ask me why. And suddenly I saw him. Colonel Jerzy. And instead of leaping from my chair and shouting, "My God! Mabel! Look, that fellow in the back there! That's Jerzy!"—which would have been the healthy reaction of any ordinary man—I went on watching the screen and sipping my whisky and soda. Then, as soon as I was alone, I slipped a fresh tape into the video machine so that I could be sure of catching the repeat when it came round on "Newsnight." Since when—the incident is now six weeks old—I must have watched it a dozen more times, for there is always some extra nuance to be relished.

But I shall leave that part of the story to the end where it belongs. Better to give you the events in the order they occurred, for there was more to Munich than Professor Teodor, and there was more to spying in the wake of Bill Haydon's exposure than waiting for the wounds to heal.

Colonel Jerzy was a Pole and I have never understood why so many Poles have a soft spot for us. Our repeated betrayals of their country have always seemed to me so disgraceful that if I were Polish, I would spit on every passing British shadow, whether I had suffered under the Nazis or the Russians—the British in their time having abandoned the poor Poles to both. And I would certainly be tempted to plant a bomb under the so-called "competent department" of the British Foreign Office. Dear heaven, what a phrase! As I write, the Poles are once more squeezed between the unpredictable Russian Bear and the rather more predictable German Ox. But you may be quite sure that if they should ever need a good friend to help them out, the same "competent department" of the British Foreign Office will send its treacly regrets and plead a more enticing function up the road.

Nevertheless, the record of my Service boasts a disproportionate rate of success in Poland, and an almost embarrassing number of Polish men and women who, with reckless Polish courage, have risked their necks and those of their families in order to spy for "England."

No wonder then if, in the aftermath of Haydon, the casualty rate among our Polish networks was correspondingly high. Thanks to Haydon, the British had added yet another betrayal to their long list. As each new loss followed the previous one with sickening inevitability, the air of mourning in our Munich Station became almost palpable, and our sense of shame was compounded by our helplessness.

None of us had any doubt of what had happened. Until the Fall, Polish Security—ably led by their Chief of Operations, Colonel Jerzy—had held Haydon's treachery close to their chests, contenting themselves with penetrating our existing networks and using them as channels of disinformation—or, where they succeeded in turning them, playing them back at us with skill.

But After the Fall, the Colonel felt no further need of delicacy, and in the course of a few days savagely silenced those of our loyal agents whom till then he had allowed to remain in place. "Jerzy's hitlist," we called it as the tally rose almost daily, and in our frustration we developed a personal hatred of the man who had murdered our beloved joes, sometimes not bothering with the formalities of a trial, but letting his interrogators have their fun until the end.

It may seem odd to think of Munich as a springboard to Poland. Yet for decades Munich had been the command centre for a range of Polish operations. From the roof of our Consular annexe in a leafy suburb, our antennae had listened night and day for our Polish agents' signals—often no more than a blip compressed between words spoken on the open radio. And in return, on pre-determined schedules, we had transmitted comfort and fresh orders to them. From Munich we had despatched our Polish letters, impregnated with secret writing. And if our sources managed to travel outside Poland, it was from Munich again that we flew off to debrief and feast them and listen to their worries.

It was from Munich also, when the need was great enough, that our Station officers would cross into Poland, always singly and usually in the guise of a visiting businessman bound for a trade fair or exhibition. And in some roadside picnic spot or backstreet café, our emissaries would come briefly face to face with our precious joes, transact their business and depart, knowing they had refilled the lamp. For nobody who has not led a joe's life can imagine what loneliness of faith it brings. A well-timed cup of bad coffee shared with a good case officer can raise a joe's morale for months.

Which is how it happened that, one winter's day soon after the beginning of the second half of my tour in Munich (and the welcome departure of Professor Teodor and his appendages to America), I found myself flying into Gdansk on a LOT Polish Airlines flight from Warsaw, with a Dutch passport in my pocket describing me as Franz Joost of Nijmegen, born forty years before. According to my businessman's visa application, my mission was to inspect prefabricated agricultural buildings on behalf of a West German farming consortium. For I have some basic grounding as an engineer, and certainly enough to exchange visiting cards with officials from their Ministry of Agriculture.

My other mission was more complicated. I was looking for a joe named Oskar, who had returned to life six months after being given up for dead. Out of the blue, Oskar had sent us a letter to an old cover address, using his secret writing equipment and describing everything he had done and not done from the day he had first heard of the arrests till now. He had kept his nerve. He had remained at his job. He had anonymously denounced some blameless *apparatchik* in his Archives Section in order to divert suspicion. He had waited, and after a few weeks the *apparatchik* disappeared. Encouraged, he waited again. Rumour reached him that the *apparatchik* had confessed. Given Colonel Jerzy's tender ministrations, this was not surprising. As the weeks went by, he began to feel safe again. Now he was ready to resume work if someone would tell him what to do. In earnest of this, he had stuck microdots to the third, fifth and seventh full stops of the letter, which were the pre-arranged positions. Blown up, they amounted to sixteen pages of top secret orders from the Polish Defence Ministry to Colonel Jerzy's department. The Circus analysts declared them "likely and presumed reliable," which, coming from them, was an ecstatic declaration of faith.

You must imagine now the excitement that Oskar's letter kindled in the Station, and even in myself, though I had never met him. Oskar! the believers cried. The old devil! Alive and kicking under the rubble! Trust Oskar to beat the rap! Oskar, our hardened Polish Admiralty clerk, based at Gdansk's coastal defence headquarters, one of the best the Station ever had!

Only the hardest-nosed, or those nearest to retirement, dismissed the letter as a lure. Saying "no" in such cases is easy. Saying "yes" takes nerve. Nevertheless, the nay-sayers are always heard the clearest, particularly after Haydon, and for a while there was a stalemate when no one had the nerve to jump either way. Buying time, we wrote to Oskar asking for more collateral. He wrote back angrily demanding to know whether he was trusted, and this time he insisted on a meeting. "A meeting or nothing," he said. And in Poland. Soon or never.

While Head Office continued to vacillate, I begged to be allowed to go to him. The unbelievers in my Station told me I was mad, the believers said it was the only decent thing to do. I was convinced by neither side, but I wanted clarity. Perhaps I also wanted it for myself, for Mabel had recently shown signs of withdrawing herself from our relationship and I was not disposed to rate myself too highly. Head Office sided with the noes. I reminded them of my naval background. Head Office dithered and said "no, but maybe." I reminded them of my bilinguality and the tested strength of my Netherlands identity, which our Dutch liaison condoned in exchange for favours in another field. Head Office measured the risks and the alternatives, and finally said, "Yes, but only for two days." Perhaps they had concluded that, after Haydon, I hadn't that many secrets to give away anyway. Hastily I put together my cover and set off before they could change their minds again. It was six below as my plane touched down at Gdansk airport; thick snow was lying in the streets, more was falling and the quiet gave me a greater sense of safety than was prudent. But I was taking no risks, believe me. I might be looking for clarity, but I was nobody's innocent any more.

Gdansk hotels are of a uniform frightfulness and mine was no exception. The lobby stank like a disinfected urinal; checking-in was as complicated as adopting a baby and took longer. My room turned out to be someone else's and she spoke no known language. By the time I had found another room, and a maid to remove the grosser traces of its previous inhabitant, it was dusk and time for me to make my arrival known to Oskar.

Every joe has his handwriting. In summer, said the file, Oskar liked to fish, and my predecessor had held successful conversations with him along the river bank. They had even caught a couple of fish together, though the pollution had made them inedible. But this was deep-frozen winter, when only children and masochists fished. In winter Oskar's habits changed and he liked to play billiards at a club for small officials near the docks. And this club had a telephone. To initiate a meeting, my predecessor, who spoke Polish, had only to call him there and conduct a cheery conversation built round the fiction that he was an old naval friend named Lech. Then Oskar would say, "All right, I'll meet you tomorrow at my sister's for a drink," which meant "Pick me up in your car on the corner of so-and-so street in one hour's time."

But I spoke no Polish. And besides, the rules of post-Haydon tradecraft dictated that no agent should be reactivated by means of past procedures.

In his letter, Oskar had provided the telephone numbers of three cafés, and the times at which he would try to be available in each of them—three because there was always the likelihood that one of the phones would be out of order or occupied. If none of the phone calls worked, then we would resort to a car pick-up, and Oskar had told me which tram stop I should stand at, and at what time. He had provided the registration number of his new blue Trabant.

And if all of this seems to place me in a passive rôle, that is because the iron rule for such meetings is that the agent in the field is king, and it's the agent who decides what is the safest course for him, and the most natural to his lifestyle. What Oskar was suggesting was not what I would have suggested, nor did I understand why we had to speak on the telephone before we met. But perhaps Oskar understood. Perhaps he was afraid of a trap. Perhaps he wanted to sample the reassurance of my voice before he took the plunge.

Or perhaps there was some sidelight I had yet to learn of: he was bringing a friend with him; he wished to be evacuated at once; he had changed his mind. For there is a second rule of tradecraft as rigid as the first, which says that the outrageous is to be regarded at all times as the norm. The good case officer *expects* the entire Gdansk telephone system to fail the moment he begins his call. He *expects* the tram stop to be at the centre of a road works, or that Oskar will that morning have driven his car into a lamp-post or developed a temperature of a hundred and four, or that his wife will have persuaded him to demand a million dollars in gold before resuming contact with us, or that her baby will have decided to be premature. The whole art—as I told my students till they hated me for it—is to rely on Sod's Law and otherwise nothing.

It was with this maxim in mind that, having spent a fruitless hour telephoning the three cafés, I placed myself at the agreed tram stop at ten past nine that night, and waited for Oskar's Trabant to grope its way towards me down the street. For though the snow had by now ceased to fall, the street was still no more than a pair of black tracks at one side of the tramlines, and the few cars that passed had the wariness of survivors returning from the front.

There is old Danzig the stately Hanseatic port, and there is Gdansk the Polish industrial slum. The tram stop was in Gdansk. To left and right of me as I waited, dour, low-lit concrete apartment houses hunched under the smouldering orange sky. Looking up and down the street, I saw not the smallest sign of human love or pleasure. Not a café, not a cinema, not a pretty light. Even the pair of drunks slumped in a doorway across the street seemed afraid to speak. One peal of laughter, one shout of goodfellowship or pleasure would have been a crime against the drabness of this outdoor prison. A car slipped by but it was not blue and it was not a Trabant. Its side windows were caked with snow, and even after it had passed I could not have told you how many people were inside. It stopped. Not at the side of the street, not on the pavement or in a turning or a layby, for mounds of snow blocked them all. It simply stopped in the twin black tracks of the road, and cut its engine, then its lights.

Lovers, I thought. If so, they were lovers blind to danger, for the road was two-way. A second car appeared, travelling in the same direction as the first. It too pulled up, but short of my tram stop. More lovers? Or merely a sensible driver allowing plenty of skidding distance between himself and the stationary car ahead of him? The effect was the same; there was one car to either side of me, and as I stood waiting, I saw that the two silent drunks were standing clear of their doorway and looking very sober. Then I heard the single footstep behind me, soft as a bedroom slipper in the snow, but close. And I knew that I must not make any sudden movement, certainly not a clever one. There was no springing free, there was no preemptive blow that would save me, because what I was beginning to fear in my imagination was either nothing or it was everything. And if it was everything, there was nothing I could do.

A man was standing to my left, close enough to touch me. He wore a fur coat and a leather hat and carried a collapsed umbrella that could have been a lead pipe shoved into a nylon sheath. Very well, like myself he was waiting for the tram. A second man was standing to my right. He smelt of horse. And very well, like his companion and myself, he too was waiting for the tram, even if he had ridden here on horseback. Then a man's voice spoke to me in mournful Polish English, and it came neither from my left nor my right, but from directly behind me, where I had heard the slippered footstep.

"Oskar will not be coming tonight, I am afraid, sir. He has been dead for six months."

But by then he had given me time to think. A whole age, in fact. I knew of no Oskar. Oskar who? Coming where? I was a Dutchman who spoke only a limited amount of English, with a thick Dutch accent like my uncles and aunts in Nijmegen. I paused while I let his words have their effect on me; then I turned—but slowly and incuriously.

"You are confusing me, sir, I think," I protested, in the slow singsong voice I had learned at my mother's knee. "My name is Frans Joost, from Holland, and I do not think that I am waiting for anyone except the tram."

And that was when the men on either side of me grabbed hold of me like good professionals, pinning my arms and knocking me off balance at the same moment, then dragging and toppling me all the way to the second car. But not before I had time to recognise the squat man who had addressed me, his damp grey jowls and sodden night-clerk's eyes. It was our very own Colonel Jerzy, the much publicised hero of the Protection of the Polish People's Republic, whose expressionless photograph had graced the front pages of several illustrious Polish newspapers around the time that he was gallantly arresting and torturing our agents.

There are deaths we unconsciously prepare for, depending on our choice of trades. An undertaker contemplates his funeral, the richman his destitution, the gaoler his imprisonment, the debauchee his impotence. An actor's greatest terror, I am told, is to watch the theatre empty itself while he wrestles in a void for his lines, and what else is that but a premature vision of his dying? For the civil servant, it is the moment when his protective walls of privilege collapse around him and he finds himself no safer than the next man, exposed to the gaze of the overt world, answering like a lying husband for his laxities and evasions. And most of my intelligence colleagues, if I am honest, came into this category: their greatest fear was to wake up one morning to read their real names *en clair* in the newspapers; to hear themselves spoken of on the radio and television, joked and laughed about and, worse yet, questioned by the public they believed they served. They would have regarded such public scrutiny as a greater disaster than being outwitted by the opposition, or blown to every kindred service round the globe. It would have been their death.

And for myself, the worst death, and therefore the greatest test, the one for which I had prepared myself ever since I passed through the secret door, was the one that was upon me now: to have my uncertain courage tested on the rack; to be reduced mentally and physically to my last component of endurance, knowing I had within me the power to stop the dying with a word—that what was going on inside me was mortal combat between my spirit and my body, and that those who were applying the pain were merely the hired mercenaries in this secret war within myself.

So that from the first blinding explosion of pain, my response was recognition: Hullo, I thought, you've come at last—my name is Joost, what's yours?

There was no ceremony, you see. He didn't sit me at a desk in the tried tradition of the screen and say, "Either talk to me or you'll be beaten. Here is your confession. Sign it." He didn't have them lock me in a cell and leave me to cook for a few days while I decided that confession was the better part of courage. They simply dragged me out of the car and through the gateway of what could have been a private house, then into a courtyard where the only footprints were our own, so that they had to topple me through the thick snow, slewing me on my heels, all three of them, punching me from one to the other, now in the face, now in the groin and stomach, now back to the face again, this time with an elbow or a knee. Then, while I was still double, kicking me like a half-stunned pig across the slithery cobble as if they couldn't wait to get indoors before they had me.

Then, once indoors, they became more systematic, as if the elegance of the old bare room had instilled in them a sense of order. They took me in turns, like civilised men, two of them holding me and one hitting me, a proper democratic rota, except that when it was Colonel Jerzy's fifth or fiftieth turn, he hit me so regretfully and so hard that I actually did die for a while, and when I came round I was alone with him. He was seated at a folding desk, with his elbows on it, holding his unhappy head between his grazed hands as if he had a hangover, and reviewing with disappointment the answers I had given to the questions he had put to me between onslaughts, first lifting his head in order to study with disapproval my altered appearance, then shaking it painfully and sighing as if to say life really wasn't fair to him, he didn't know what more he could do to me to help me see the light. It dawned on me that more time had passed than I realised, perhaps several hours.

This was also the moment when the scene began to take on a resemblance to the one I had always imagined, with my tormentor sitting comfortably at a desk, brooding over me with a professional's concern, and myself spreadeagled against a scalding waterpipe, my arms handcuffed either side of a black concertina-style radiator, with corners that bit into the base of my spine like red-hot teeth. I had been bleeding from the mouth and nose and, I thought, from one ear as well, and my shirt front looked like a slaughterer's apron. But the blood had dried and I wasn't bleeding any more, which was another way of calculating the passage of time. How long does blood take to congeal in a big empty house in Gdansk when you are chained to a furnace and looking into the puppyish face of Colonel Jerzy?

It was terribly hard to hate him, and with the burning in my back it was becoming harder by the moment. He was my only saviour. His face stayed on me all the time now. Even when he turned his head downward to the table in private prayer, or got up and lit himself a filthy Polish cigarette and took a stretch around the room, his lugubrious gaze seemed to stay on me without reference to where the rest of him had gone. He turned his squat back to me. He gave me a view of his thick bald head and the pitted nape of his neck. Yet his eyes—treating with me, reasoning with me and sometimes, as it seemed, imploring me to ease his anguish—never left me for a second. And there was a part of me that really wanted to help him and it was becoming more and more strident with the burning. Because the burning was not a burning any more, it was pure pain, a pain indivisible and absolute, mounting like a scale that had no upper limit. So that I would have given almost anything to make him feel better—except myself. Except the part of me that made me separate from him, and was therefore my survival.

"What's your name?" he asked me, still in his Polish English.

"Joost." He had to bend over me to hear me. "Frans Joost."

"From Munich," he suggested, using my shoulder as a prop while he put his ear closer to my mouth.

"Born Nijmegen. Working for farmers in the Taunus, by Frankfurt."

"You've forgotten your Dutch accent." He shook me a little to wake me.

"You just don't hear it. You're a Pole. I want to see the Dutch Consul."

"You mean British Consul."

"Dutch." And then I think I repeated the same word "Dutch" several times, and went on repeating it till he threw cold water over me, then poured a little of it into my mouth to let me rinse and spit. I realised I was missing a tooth. Lower jaw, front left. Two teeth perhaps. It was hard to tell.

"Do you believe in God?" he asked me.

When he stared down at me like this, his cheeks fell forward like a baby's and his lips formed themselves in a kiss, so that he looked like a puzzled cherub.

"Not at the moment," I said.

"Why not?"

"Get me the Dutch Consul. You've got the wrong man."

I saw that he didn't like being told this. He wasn't used to being given orders or contradicted. He passed the back of his right hand across his lips, a thing he sometimes did before he hit me, and I waited for the blow. He began patting his pockets, I assumed for some instrument.

"No," he remarked, with a sigh. "You are mistaken. I have got the right man."

He knelt to me and I thought he was preparing to kill me, because I had noticed that he was at his most murderous when he appeared most unhappy. But he was unlocking my handcuffs. When he had done so, he shoved his clenched fists under my armpits and hauled me—I almost thought helped me—to a spacious bathroom with an old, freestanding bath filled with warm water.

"Strip," he said, and watched me dejectedly while I dragged off what remained of my clothes, too exhausted to care about what he would do to me once I was in the water: drown me, or cook me or freeze me, or drop in an electric wire.

He had my suitcase from the hotel. While I lay in the bath, he picked out clean clothes and tossed them on to a chair.

"You leave on tomorrow's plane for Frankfurt via Warsaw. There has been a mistake," he said. "We apologise. We shall cancel your business appointments and say you were the victim of a hit-and-run car."

"I'll need more than an apology," I said.

The bath was doing me no good. I was afraid that if I lay flat any longer, I would die again. I hauled myself into a crouch. Jerzy held out his forearm. I clutched it and stood upright, swaying dangerously. Jerzy helped me out of the bath, then handed me a towel and watched me gloomily while I dried myself and pulled on the clean clothes he had laid out for me.

He led me from the house and across the courtyard, carrying my case in one hand and bearing my weight with the other, because the bath had weakened me as well as easing the pain. I peered round for the henchmen but saw none.

"The cold air will be good for you," he said, with the confidence of an expert.

He led me to a parked car, and it did not resemble either of the cars that had taken part in my arrest. A toy steering wheel lay on the back seat. We drove down empty streets. Sometimes I dozed. We reached a pair of white iron gates guarded by militia.

"Don't look at them," he ordered me, and showed them his papers while I dozed again.

We got out of the car and stood on a grass clifftop. An inshore wind froze our faces. Mine felt big as two footballs. My mouth had moved into my left cheek. One eye had closed. There was no moon and the sea was a growl behind the salt mist. The only light came from the city behind us. Occasionally phosphorous sparks slipped past us, or puffs of white spume spun away into the blackness. This is where I'm supposed to die, I thought as I stood beside him; first he beats me, then he gives me a warm bath, now he shoots me and shoves me over the cliff. But his hands were hanging glumly at his sides and there was no gun in them, and his eyes—what I could make out of them—were fixed on the starless darkness, not on me; so perhaps someone else was going to shoot me, someone already waiting in the dark. If I had had the energy, I could have killed Jerzy first. But I hadn't, and I didn't feel the need. I thought of Mabel, but without any sense of loss or gain. I wondered how she'd manage living on a pension, whom she'd find. *Fräulein Stefanie is not at home*, I remembered. . . . *Then perhaps it was Stefanie who answered*, Smiley was saying. . . . So many unanswered prayers, I was thinking. But so many never offered, either. I was feeling very drowsy.

At last Jerzy spoke, his voice no less despondent than before. "I have brought you here because there isn't a microphone on earth can hear us. I wish to spy for your country. I need a good professional to act as intermediary. I have decided to choose you."

Once more I lost my sense of time and place. But perhaps he had lost his too, for he had turned his back on the sea and, with his hand clutched to his leather hat to hold it against the wind, he had undertaken a mournful study of the inland lights, scowling at things that needed no scowling at, sometimes punching the wind-tears from his cheeks with his big fists.

"Why should anyone spy for Holland?" I asked him.

"Very well, I propose to spy for Holland," he replied wearily, indulging a pedant. "Therefore I need a good professional *Dutchman* who can keep his mouth shut. Knowing what fools you *Dutchmen* have employed against us in the past, I am understandably selective. However, you have passed the test. Congratulations. I select you."

I thought it best to say nothing. Probably I didn't believe him.

"In the false compartment of your suitcase you will find a wad of Polish secret documents," he continued, in a tone of dejection. "At Gdansk airport you will have no Customs problems, naturally. I have given orders for them not to examine your luggage. For all they know, you are by now my agent. In Frankfurt, you are on home ground. I shall work to you and nobody else. Our next meeting will be in Berlin on May 5th. I shall be attending the May Day celebrations to mark the glorious victory of the proletariat."

He was trying to light a fresh cigarette, but the wind kept putting out his matches. So he took his hat off and lit the cigarette inside the crown, lowering his fat face to it as if he were drinking water from a stream.

"Your people will wish to know my motive," he continued when he had taken a deep draught of cigarette smoke. "Tell them—" Suddenly at a loss, he sank his head into his shoulders and peered round at me as if pleading for advice on how to deal with idiots. "Tell them I'm bored. Tell them I'm sick of the work. Tell them the Party's a bunch of crooks. They know that anyway, but tell them. I'm a Catholic. I'm a Jew. I'm a Tartar. Tell them whatever the hell they want to hear."

"They may want to know why you have chosen to come to the *Dutch,*" I said. "Rather than to the Americans, or the French or whoever."

He thought about that too, puffing at his cigarette in the darkness. "You Dutch had some good joes," he said ruminatively. "I got to know some of them pretty well. They did a good job till that bastard Haydon came along." An idea occurred to him. "Tell them my father was a Battle of Britain pilot," he suggested. "Got himself shot down over Kent. That should please them. You know Kent?"

"Why should a Dutchman know Kent?" I said.

If I had weakened, I could have told him that, before our so-called "friendly" separation, Mabel and I had bought a house in Tunbridge Wells. But I didn't, which was as well, because when Head Office came to check the story out, there was no record of Jerzy's father having flown anything larger than a paper kite. And when I put this to Jerzy several years later—long after his loyalty to the perfidious British had been demonstrated beyond all doubt—he just laughed, and said his father was an old fool who cared for nothing but vodka and potatoes.

So why?

For five years Jerzy was my secret university of espionage, but his contempt for motive—his own particularly—never relaxed. First we idiots do what we want to do, he said; then we look round for justifications for having done it. All men were idiots to him, he told me, and we spies were the biggest idiots of all.

At first I suspected that he was spying for vengeance, and drew him out on the people above him in the hierarchy who might have slighted him. He hated them all, himself the most.

Then I decided he was spying for ideological reasons, and that his cynicism was a disguise for the finer yearnings he had discovered in his middle age. But when I attempted to use my wiles to break his cynicism down—"Your family, Jerzy, your mother, Jerzy. Admit you're proud to have become a grandfather"—I found only more cynicism beneath. He felt nothing for any of them, he retorted, but so icily that I concluded that he did indeed, as he maintained, hate the entire human race, and that his savagery, and perhaps his betrayal too, were the simple expression of this hatred.

As to the West, it was run by the same idiots who ran everything in the world, so what's the difference? And when I told him this simply was not so, he became as defensive of his nihilist creed as any other zealot, and I had to rein myself in for fear of angering him seriously.

So why? Why risk his neck, his life, his livelihood and the family he hated, to do something for a world he despised?

The Church? I asked him that too, and significantly, as I think now, he bridled. Christ was a manic depressive, he retorted. Christ needed to commit suicide in public, so he provoked the authorities until they did him the favour. "Those God-thumper guys are all the same," he said with contempt. "I've tortured them. I know."

Like most cynics, he was a Puritan, and this paradox repeated itself in him in several ways. When we offered to drop money for him, open a Swiss bank account, the usual, he flew into a rage and declared he was not some "cheap informant." When I picked a moment—on the instruction of Head Office—to assure him that if ever things went wrong, we would spare no effort to get him out and provide him with a new identity in the West, his contempt was absolute: "I'm a Polish creep, but I would rather face a firing squad of my fellow creeps than die a traitor in some capitalist pigsty."

As to life's other comforts, we could offer him nothing he had not got. His wife was a scold, he said, and going home after a heavy day at the office bored him. His mistress was a young fool, and after an hour with her he preferred a game of billiards to her conversation.

Then why? I kept asking myself when I had exhausted my checklist of the Service's standard-issue motives.

Meanwhile, Jerzy continued to fill our coffers. He was turning his Service inside out as neatly as Haydon had ever done with ours. When Moscow Centre gave him orders, we knew of them before he passed them to his underlings. He photographed everything that came within his reach; he took risks I begged him not to take. He was so heedless that sometimes he left me wondering whether, like the Christ he was so determined to deny, he was looking for a public death. It was only the unflagging efficiency of what we were pleased to call his cover work that protected him from suspicion. For that was the dark side of his balancing act: God help the Western agent, real or imagined, who was invited to make his voluntary confession at Jerzy's hands.

Only once in the five years that I ran him did he seem to let slip the clue I was searching for. He was tired to death. He had been attending a conference of Warsaw Pact Intelligence chiefs in Bucharest, in the midst of fighting off charges of brutality and corruption against his Service at home. We met in West Berlin, in a *pension* on the Kurfürstendamm which catered to the better type of representative. He was a really tired torturer. He sat on my bed, smoking and answering my follow-up questions about his last batch of material. He was red-eyed. When we had finished, he asked for a whisky, then another.

"No danger is no life," he said, tossing three more rolls of film on the counterpane. "No danger is dead." He took out a grimy brown handkerchief and carefully wiped his heavy face with it. "No danger, you do better stay home, look after the baby."

I preferred not to believe it was danger he was talking about. What he was talking about, I decided, was feeling, and his terror that by ceasing to feel he was ceasing to exist—which perhaps was why he was so devoted to instilling feeling in others. For that moment, I thought I caught a glimpse of why he was sitting with me in the room breaking every rule in his book. He was keeping his spirit alive at a time of his life when it was beginning to look like dying.

The same night I dined with Stefanie at an Armenian restaurant ten minutes' walk from the *pension* where Jerzy and I had met. I had wangled her telephone number from a sister in Munich. She was as tall and beautiful as I remembered her, and determined to convince me she was happy. Oh, life was *perfect*, Ned, she declared. She was living with this *terribly* distinguished academic, not in his first youth any more—but look here, nor are we—and completely adorable and wise. She told me his name. It meant nothing to me. She said she was pregnant by him. It didn't show.

"And *you*, Ned, how did it go for *you?*" she asked, as if we were two generals reporting to each other from successful, but separate, campaigns.

I gave her my most confident smile, the one that had earned me the trust of my joes and colleagues in the years since I had seen her.

"Oh, I think it worked out pretty well actually, thanks, yes," I said, with seeming British understatement. "After all, you can't expect one person to be everything you need, can you? It's a pretty good partnership, I'd say. Good parallel living."

"And you still do that work?" she said. "Ben's work?"

"Yes."

It was the first time either of us had mentioned him. He was living in Ireland, she said. A cousin of his had bought a tumbledown estate in County Cork. Ben sort of caretook for him while he wasn't there, stocking the river and looking after the farm and so on.

I asked whether she ever saw him.

"No," she said. "He won't."

I would have driven her home, but she preferred a cab. We waited in the street till it came, and it seemed to take a terribly long time. As I closed the door on her, her head tipped forward as if she had dropped something on the floor. I waved her out of sight but she didn't wave back.

* * *

The nine-o'clock news was showing us an outdoor meeting of Solidarity in Gdansk, where a Polish Cardinal was exhorting an enormous crowd to moderation. Losing interest, Mabel settled the *Daily Telegraph* on her lap and resumed her crossword. At first the crowd heard the Cardinal noisily. Then, with the devotion Poles are famous for, they fell silent. After his address, the Cardinal moved among his flock, bestowing blessings and accepting homage. And as one dignitary after another was brought to him, I picked out Jerzy hovering in the background, like the ugly boy excluded from the feast. He had lost a lot of weight since he had retired, and I guessed that the social changes had not been kind to him. His jacket hung on him like someone else's; his once-formidable fists were hardly visible inside the sleeves.

Suddenly the Cardinal has spotted him, just as I had.

The Cardinal freezes as if in doubt of his own feelings, and for a moment makes himself neater somehow, almost in obedience, pressing in his elbows and drawing back his shoulders to attention. Then slowly his arms lift again and he gives an order to one of his attendants, a young priest who seems reluctant to obey it. The Cardinal repeats the order, the priest clears a path to Jerzy; the two men face each other, the secret policeman and the Cardinal. Jerzy winces, as if he has digestion pains. The Cardinal leans forward and speaks in Jerzy's ear. Awkwardly, Jerzy kneels to receive the Cardinal's blessing.

And each time I replay this moment I see Jerzy's eyes close apparently in pain. But what is he repenting? His brutality? His loyalty to a vanished cause? Or his betrayal of it? Or is squeezing the eyes shut merely the instinctive response of a torturer receiving the forgiveness of a victim?

I fish. I drop into my little reveries. My love of English landscape has, if possible, increased. I think of Stefanie and Bella, and my other half-had women. I lobby our Member of Parliament about the filthy river. He's a Conservative, but what on earth does he imagine he's conserving? I've joined one of the sounder environmentalist groups; I collect signatures on petitions. The petitions are ignored. I won't play golf, I never would. But I'll walk round with Mabel on a Wednesday afternoon, provided she's playing alone. I encourage her. The dog enjoys himself. Retirement is no time to be wandering lost, or puzzling how to reinvent mankind.

8

My students had decided to give Smiley a rough ride, just as they'd done to me from time to time. We'd be running along perfectly smoothly—a double session on natural cover, say, in the late afternoon—when one of them would start hectoring me, usually by adopting an anarchic stance which nobody in his right mind could sustain. Then a second would chime in, then all of them, so that if I didn't have my sense of humour shining-ready—and I'm only human—they'd be trampling me till the bell rang for close of play. And next day all would be forgotten: they'd have fed whatever little demon had got hold of them, and now they'd like to go back to learning, please, so where were we? At first I used to brood over these occasions, suspect conspiracy, hunt for ringleaders. Then cautiously I came to recognise them as spontaneous expressions of resistance to the unnatural harness that these children had chosen to put on.

But when they started in on Smiley, their guest of honour and mine, even questioning the entire purpose of his life's work, my tolerance ended with a snap. And this time the offender was not Maggs, either, but the demure Clare, his girlfriend, who had sat so adoringly opposite Smiley throughout dinner.

"No, no, Ned," Smiley protested, as I leapt angrily to my feet. "Clare has a valid point. Nine times out of ten a good journalist *can* tell us quite as much about a situation as the spies can. Very often they're sharing the same sources anyway. So why not scrap the spies and subsidise the newspapers? It's a point that should be answered in these changeable times. Why not?"

Reluctantly I resumed my seat, while Clare, snuggling close against Maggs, continued to gaze angelically at her victim, while her colleagues smothered their grins.

But where I would have taken refuge in humour, Smiley elected to treat her sally seriously:

"It is perfectly true," he agreed, "that most of our work is either useless, or duplicated by overt sources. The trouble is, the spies aren't there to enlighten the public, but governments."

And slowly I felt his spell re-unite them. They had moved their chairs to him in a disordered half-circle. Some of the girls were sprawled becomingly on the floor.

"And governments, like anyone else, trust what they pay for, and are suspicious of what they don't," he said. Thus delicately passing beyond Clare's provocative question, he addressed a larger one: "Spying is eternal," he announced simply. "If governments *could* do without it, they never would. They adore it. If the day ever comes when there are no enemies left in the world, governments will invent them for us, so don't worry. Besides—who says we only spy on enemies? All history teaches us that today's allies are tomorrow's rivals. Fashion may dictate priorities, but foresight doesn't. For as long as rogues become leaders, we shall spy. For as long as there are bullies and liars and madmen in the world, we shall spy. For as long as nations compete, and politicians deceive, and tyrants launch conquests, and consumers need resources, and the homeless look for land, and the hungry for food, and the rich for excess, your chosen profession is perfectly secure, I can assure you."

And with the topic thus neatly turned back to their own future, he once more warned them of its perils:

"There's no career on earth more cockeyed than the one you've picked," he assured them, with every sign of satisfaction. "You'll be at your most postable while you're least experienced, and by the time you've learned the ropes, no one will be able to send you anywhere without a trade description round your necks. Old athletes know they've played their best games when they were in their prime. But spies in their prime are on the shelf, which is why they take so ungraciously to middle age, and start counting the cost of living how they've lived."

Though his hooded gaze to all appearance remained fixed upon his brandy, I saw him cast a sideways glance at me. "And then, at a certain age, you want the answer," he continued. "You want the rolled-up parchment in the inmost room that tells you who runs your lives and why. The trouble is, that by then you're the very people who know best that the inmost room is bare. Ned, you're not drinking. You're a brandy traitor. Fill him up, someone."

It is an uncomfortable truth of the period of my life that follows that I recall it as a single search the object of which was unclear to me. And that the object, when I found him, turned out to be the lapsed spy Hansen.

And that, although in reality I was pursuing quite other goals and people along my eastward journey, all of them in retrospect seem to have been stages on my journey to him. I can put it no other way. Hansen in his Cambodian jungle was my Kurtz at the heart of darkness. And everything that happened to me on the way was a preparation for our meeting. Hansen's was the voice I was waiting to hear. Hansen held the answer to the questions I did not know I was asking. Outwardly, I was my stolid, moderate, pipesmoking, decent self, a shoulder for weaker souls to rest their heads on. Inside, I felt a rampant incomprehension of my uselessness; a sense that, for all my striving, I had failed to come to grips with life; that in struggling to give freedom to others, I had found none for myself. At my lowest ebb, I saw myself as ridiculous, a hero in the style not of Buchan but of Quixote.

I took to writing down sardonic versions of my life, so that when, for instance, I reviewed the episodes I have described to you this far, I gave them picaresque titles that emphasised their futility: the Panda—I safeguard our Middle Eastern interests! Ben—I run to earth a British defector! Bella—I make the ultimate sacrifice! Teodor —I take part in a grand deception! Jerzy—I play the game to the end! Though with Jerzy, I had to admit, a positive purpose had been served, even if it was as shortlived as most intelligence, and as irrelevant to the human forces that have now engulfed his nation.

Like Quixote, I had set out in life vowing to check the flow of evil. Yet in my lowest moments I was beginning to wonder whether I had become a contributor to it. But I still looked to the world to provide me with the chance to make my contribution—and I blamed it for not knowing how to use me.

To understand this, you should know what had happened to me after Munich. Jerzy, whatever else he did to me, brought me a sort of prestige, and the Fifth Floor decided to invent a job for me as roving operational fixer, sent out on short assignments "to appraise, and where possible exploit opportunities outside the remit of the local Station"—thus my brief, signed and returned to maker.

Looking back, I realise that the constant travel this entailed—Central America one week, Northern Ireland the next, Africa, the Middle East, Africa again— soothed the restlessness that was stalking me, and that Personnel in all likelihood knew this, for I had recently embarked on a senseless love affair with a girl called Monica, who worked in the Service's Industrial Liaison Section. I had decided I needed an affair; I saw her in the canteen and cast her in the part. It was as banal as that. One night it was raining, and as I started to drive home, I saw her standing at a number 23 bus stop. Banality made flesh. I took her to her flat, I took her to her bed, I took her to dinner and we tried to work out what we had done, and came up with the convenient solution that we had fallen in love. It served us well for several months, until tragedy abruptly called me to my senses. By a mercy, I was back in London briefing myself for my next mission when word came that my mother was failing. By an act of divine ill taste, I was in bed with Monica when I took the call. But at least I was able to be present for the event, which was lengthy, but unexpectedly serene.

Nevertheless, I found myself entirely unprepared for it. Somehow I had taken for granted that, in the same way that I had managed to negotiate myself round awkward hurdles in the past, I would do the same in the case of my mother's death. I could not have been more mistaken. Very few conspiracies, Smiley once remarked, survive contact with reality. And so it was with the conspiracy that I had made with myself to let my mother's death slip past me as a timely and necessary release from pain. I had not taken into my calculations that the pain could be my own.

I was orphaned and elated both at once. I can describe it no other way. My father had long been dead. Without my realising it, my mother had done duty for both parents. In her death I saw the loss, not only of my childhood, but of most of my adulthood as well. At last I stood unencumbered before life's challenges, yet many of them were already behind me—fudged, missed or botched. I was free to love at last, but whom? Not, I am afraid, Monica, however much I might protest the contrary and expect the reality to follow. Neither Monica nor my marriage offered me the magic it was henceforth my duty as a survivor to pursue. And when I looked at myself in the mirror of the undertaker's rose-tinted lavatory after my night's vigil, I was horrified by what I saw. It was the face of a spy branded by his own deception.

Have you seen it too, around you? On you? That face? In my case it was so much my everyday companion that I had ceased to notice it until the shock of death brought it home to me. We smile, but our withholding makes our smile false. When we are exhilarated, or drunk—or, even as I am told, make love—the reserve does not dissolve, the gyroscope stays vertical, the monitory voice reminds us of our calling. Until gradually our very withholding becomes so strident it is almost a security risk by itself. So that today—if I go to a reunion, say, or we have a Sarratt old-boys' night—I can actually look round the room and see how the secret stain has come out in every one of us. I see the overbright face or the underlit one, but inside each I see the remnants of a life withheld. I hear the hoot of supposedly abandoned laughter and I don't have to mark down the source of it to know that nothing has been abandoned—not its owner, not its interior restrictions, nothing. In my younger days, I used to think it was just the inhibited British ruling classes who became that person. "They were born into captivity and had no option from then on," I would tell myself as I listened to their unconvincing courtesies, and returned their good-chap smiles. But, as only half a Briton, I had exempted myself from their misfortune—until that day in the undertaker's pink-tiled lavatory when I saw that the same shadow that falls across us all had fallen across me.

From that day on, I now believe, I saw only the horizon. I am starting so late! I thought. And from so far back! Life was to be a search, or nothing! But it was the fear that it was nothing that drove me forward. That's how I see it now. And so, please, must you see it, in the fragmented recollections that belong to this surreal passage of my life. In the eyes of the man I had become, every encounter was an encounter with myself. Every stranger's confession was my own, and Hansen's the most accusing—and therefore, ultimately, the most consoling. I buried my mother, I said goodbye to Monica and Mabel. The next day I departed for Beirut. Yet even that simple departure was attended by a disconcerting episode.

* * *

To brief myself for my mission, I had been sharing a room with a rather clever man called Giles Latimer, who had made a corner for himself in what was known as "the Mad Mullah department," studying the intricate and seemingly indecypherable web of Muslim fundamentalist groups operating out of Lebanon. The notion so beloved of the amateur terror industry that these bodies are all part of a superplot is nonsense. If only it were so—for then there might be some way to get at them! As it is, they slip about, grouping and regrouping like drops of water on a wet wall, and they are about as easy to pin down.

But Giles, who was an Arabist and a distinguished bridge player, had come as near to achieving the impossible as anyone was likely to, and my job was to sit at his feet in order to prepare myself for my mission. He was tall, angular and woolly. He was of my intake. His boyish manner was given extra youthfulness by the redness of his cheeks, though this was actually the consequence of clusters of tiny broken blood vessels. He was indefatigably, painfully gentlemanly, forever opening doors and leaping to his feet for women. In the spring weather I twice saw him get drenched to the skin on account of his habit of lending his umbrella to whoever was proposing to venture out of doors without one. He was rich but frugal, and a thoroughly good man, with a thoroughly good wife, who organised Service bridge drives and remembered the names of the junior staff and their families. Which made it all the more bizarre when his files started disappearing.

It was I, inadvertently, who first noticed the phenomenon. I was tracking a German girl called Britta on her odyssey through the terrorist training camps in the Shuf Mountains, and I requested a contingent file which contained sensitive intercept material about her. The material was American and limited by a subscription list, but when I had gone through the rigmarole of signing myself in, nobody could find it. Nominally it was marked to Giles, but so was almost everything, because Giles was Giles and his name was on every list around.

But Giles knew nothing of it. He remembered reading it, he could quote from it; he thought he had passed it on to me. It must have gone to the Fifth Floor, he said, or back to Registry. Or somewhere.

So the file was posted missing and the Registry bloodhounds were informed, and everything ran along normally for a couple of days until the same thing happened again, though this time it was Giles's own secretary who started the hunt when Registry called in all three volumes on a misty group called the Brothers of the Prophet, supposedly based in Damour.

Once again, Giles knew nothing: he had neither seen nor touched them. The Registry bloodhounds showed him his signature on the receipt. He flatly disowned it. And when Giles denied something, you didn't feel like challenging him. As I say, he was a man of transparent rectitude.

By now, the hunt was up in earnest and inventories were being taken left and right. Registry was in its last days before computerisation, and could still find what it was looking for, or know for sure that it was lost. Today somebody would shake his head and phone for an engineer.

What Registry discovered was that thirty-two files marked out to Giles were missing. Twenty-one of them were standard top secret, five had higher gradings, and six were of a category called RETAIN, which meant, I am afraid, that nobody of strong pro-Jewish sentiments should be admitted as a signatory. Parse that how you will. It was a squalid limitation and there were few of us who were not embarrassed by it. But this was the Middle East.

My first intimation of the scale of the crisis came from Personnel. It was a Friday morning. Personnel always liked the shelter of the weekend when he was about to wield his axe.

"Has Giles been *well* lately, Ned?" he asked me, with old-boy intimacy.

"Perfectly," I said.

"He's a Christian, isn't he? Christian sort of chap. Pious."

"I believe so."

"Well, I mean we all are in a way, but is he a *heavy* sort of Christian, would you say, Ned? What's your opinion?"

"We've never discussed it."

"Are you?"

"No."

"Would you say, for example, he could be sympathetic to something like—say —the British-Israelite sect, or one of those sort of things, at all? Nothing against them, mind. Every man to his convictions, me."

"Giles is very orthodox, very down the middle, I am sure. He's some sort of lay dignitary at his parish church. I believe he gives the odd Lenten Address, and that's about it."

"That's what I've got down here," Personnel complained, tapping his knuckles on a closed file. "That's the picture I've got of him exactly, Ned. So what's up? Not always easy, my job, you know. Not always pleasant at all."

"Why don't you ask him yourself?"

"Oh I know, I know, I must. Unless you would, of course. You could take him out to lunch—my expense, obviously. Feel his bones. Tell me what you think."

"No," I said.

His old-boy manner gave way to something a lot harder. "I thought you'd say that. I worry about you sometimes, Ned. You're putting yourself about with the women and you're a touch stubborn for your health. It's the Dutch blood in you. Well, keep your mouth shut. That's an order."

In the end it was Giles who took me out to lunch. Probably Personnel had played the game both ways, pitching some tale to Giles in reverse. Whether he had or not, at twelve-thirty Giles sprang suddenly to his feet and said, "To hell with it, Ned. It's Friday. Come on, I'll give you lunch. Haven't had a pissy lunch for years."

So we went to the Travellers', and sat at a table by the window and we drank a bottle of Sancerre very fast. And suddenly Giles began talking about a liaison trip he'd made recently to the FBI in New York. He kicked off quite normally; then his voice seemed to get stuck on one note, and his eyes got fixed on something only he could see. I put it down to the wine at first. Giles didn't look like a drinker and didn't drink like one. Yet there was great conviction in the way he spoke and—as he continued—a visionary intensity.

"Peculiar chaps actually, the Americans, Ned, you want to watch out for them. One doesn't think they're after one at first. One's hotel, for instance. You can always read the clues in a hotel. Too much smiling when you sign in. Too much interest in your luggage. They're watching you. Damned great highrise greenhouse. Swimming pool on the top floor. You can look down on the helicopters going up the river. 'Welcome, Mr. Lambert, and have a nice day, sir.' I was using Lambert. I always do for America. The fourteenth floor they'd put me on. I'm a methodical chap. Always have been. Shoe-trees and that kind of thing. Can't help it. My father was the same. Shoes here, shirts there. Socks there. Suits in a certain order. We never have lightweight suits, do we, the English? You think they're lightweight. You choose lightweight. Your tailor tells you they're lightweight. 'Lightest we've got, sir. We don't go any lighter.' You'd think they'd have learned by now, the amount of American business they do. But they haven't. Cheers."

He drank and I drank with him. I poured him some mineral water. He was sweating.

"Next day I come back to the hotel. Meetings all day long. Lot of trying to like each other. And I do, I mean they're nice chaps. Just—well, different. Different attitudes. Carry guns. Want results. There can't be any, though, can there? We all know that. The more fanatics you kill, the more there are of them. I know that, they don't. My father was an Arabist too, you know."

I said I didn't. I said, "Tell me about him." I wanted to deflect him. I felt I would feel much better if he talked about his father instead of the hotel.

"So I walk in and they hand me my key. 'Hey, hang on,' I say. 'This isn't floor fourteen. This is floor twenty-one. Mistake.' I smile, naturally. Anyone can make a mistake. It's a woman this time. Very strong-looking woman. 'It is not a mistake, Mr. Lambert. You're on the twenty-first floor. Your room is 2109.' 'No, no,' I say. 'It's 1409. Look here.' I had this identity card they give you somewhere and I looked for it. Turned out my pockets while she watched, but couldn't find it. 'Look,' I said. 'Believe me. I have that kind of memory. My room is 1409.' She gets out the guest list, shows it to me. Lambert, 2109. I go up in the lift, unlock the room, it's all there. Shoes here. Shirts there. Socks there. Suits in the same order. Everything where I'd put it in the other room, down on the fourteenth floor. Know what they'd done?"

Again I said I didn't.

"Photographed it. Polaroid."

"Why would they do that?"

"They wanted to mike me—2109 was miked, 1409 was clean. No good to them, so they moved me up. They thought I was an Arab spy."

"Why would they think that?"

"Because of my father. He was a Lawrence man. They knew that. They'd decided. That's what they do. Photograph your room."

I scarcely remember the rest of lunch. I don't remember what we ate or what else we drank or anything at all. I have a recollection of Giles extolling Mabel at great length as the perfect Service wife, but perhaps that was my conscience. All I really remember is the two of us side by side in Giles's room back at Head Office, and Personnel standing in front of Giles's steel cupboard with the door removed, and the thirty-two missing files crammed higgledy-piggledy into the shelves—all the files Giles hadn't been able to cope with while he was having what Smiley called his "Force Twelve nervous breakdown" in place.

And the reason for it, as I learned later? Giles too had found his Monica. What had unhinged him, ostensibly, was his passion for a twenty-year-old girl in his village. His love for her, his guilt and despair had dictated that he could no longer function. He had continued going through the day's motions—naturally, he was a soldier—but his mind wouldn't play any more. It had acquired its own preoccupations, even if he wouldn't own to them.

What else had unhinged him, I leave that to you, and to our in-house shrinks who seem to be daily gaining ground. Something to do, perhaps, with the gap between our dreams and our realities. Something to do with the gap between what Giles longed for when he was young, and what he'd got now that he was nearly old. And the hard truth was, Giles had frightened me. I felt he had gone ahead of me down the road I myself was treading. I felt it as I drove to the airport; I felt it on the plane while I thought about my mother. And downed several in-flight whiskies in order not to feel it more.

I was still feeling it as I set out my own meagre wardrobe in Room 607 at the Commodore Hotel, Beirut, and the telephone began ringing a few inches from my head. As I picked up the receiver, I had a wayward fancy I was going to hear Ahmed at the front desk telling me I had been allocated a new room on floor twenty-one. I was wrong. Surreal episode number two had just announced itself.

Shooting had started, semi-automatic on the move. Most likely a bunch of kids in a Japanese pickup hosing down the neighbourhood with AK 47s. It was one of those seasons in Beirut when you could set your watch by the first excitements of the evening. But I had never minded too much about the shooting. Shooting has a logic, if a haphazard one. It's directed at you, or away from you. My personal phobia was car bombs—never knowing, as you hurried along a pavement or dawdled in the sweating, crawling traffic, whether a parked car was going to take out the entire block with one huge heave, and leave you in such tiny shreds that there was nothing worth a body bag, let alone a burial. The thing you noticed about car bombs—I mean afterwards—was shoes. People blown clean out of them, but the shoes intact. So that even after the bits of body had been picked out and taken away, there was still the odd pair or two of wearable shoes among the broken glass and smashed false teeth and shreds of someone's suit. A little machine-gun fire, like now, or the odd hand-held rocket, didn't trouble me as much as it did some people.

I lifted the receiver and when I heard a woman's voice I quickened, not only because of my domestic ambiguities but because my errand was to trace a German woman—the same Britta who had been taking lessons in terror in the Shuf Mountains.

But it was not Britta. It was not Monica and not Mabel. The voice was middle-American and scared. And I was Peter, remember—Peter Carter, from a great British newspaper, even if its local correspondent had never heard of me. I was reminding myself of this as I listened to her.

"Peter, for Christ's sake, I need to be with you," she said in a single rush of breath. "Peter, where the fuck have you been?"

A rattle of heavy machine-gun fire broke out, to be promptly silenced by the smack of a rocket-propelled grenade. The voice on the phone resumed in greater agitation.

"Jesus, Peter, why don't you call me? Okay, I said some shitty things. I spoiled your copy. I'm sorry. I mean, Jesus, what are we? Children? You know how I hate this stuff."

A frenzy of rifle fire. Sometimes the kids just shot into the sky for effect.

Her voice rose steeply. "Talk to me, Peter! Tell me something funny, will you, please? Something funny must be happening *somewhere* in the world! Peter, will you please answer me? You're not dead are you? You're not lying on the floor with your head blown off? Just nod for no. I don't want to die alone, Peter. I'm sociable. I love sociably, I die sociably. Peter, answer me. Please."

"What room are you calling?" I said.

Dead silence. The really dead silence that gathers between bursts of gunfire.

"Who is this?" she demanded.

"This is Peter, but I don't think I'm your Peter. What room are you calling?"

"This room."

"What number?"

"Room 607."

"I'm afraid he must have checked out. I arrived in Beirut this afternoon. This is the room they gave me."

A grenade exploded, answered by another. Out in the street, perhaps three blocks away, somebody screamed seriously. The scream ended.

"Is he dead?" she whispered.

I didn't answer.

"Could have been a woman," she said.

"Could have been," I agreed.

"Who are you? You British?"

"Yes." Peter is too, I thought, without knowing why.

"What do you do?"

"For a living?"

"Just talk to me. Keep talking."

"I'm a journalist," I said.

"Like Peter?"

"I don't know what kind of journalist he is."

"He's tough. The danger school. Are you tough?"

"Some things scare me, some don't."

"Mice?"

"Mice scare me stiff."

"Are you good?"

"As good as the news, I suppose. I don't write much any more. I'm editorial these days."

"Married?"

"Are you?"

"Yes."

"To Peter?"

"No, not Peter."

"How long have you known him?"

"My husband?"

"No. Peter," I said. I did not ask myself why I was more interested in her adultery than her marriage.

"You don't time things like that out here," she said. "A year, a couple of years —you don't talk that way. Not in Beirut. You're married too, aren't you? You didn't want to tell me till I told you first."

"Yes, I am."

"So tell me about her."

"My wife?"

"Sure. Do you love her? Is she tall? Great skin? Very British, stiff upper lip?"

I told her some harmless things about Mabel and invented some others, hating myself.

"I mean, who on earth can believe in sex after fifteen years of the same person?" she said.

I laughed but didn't answer.

"Are you faithful to her, Peter?"

"Infallibly," I said, after a delay.

"Okay, let's do work. Go back to work. What are you doing out here? Something special? Tell me what you're doing."

The spy in me dodged the question: "I think it's time you told me what *you* do," I said. "Are you a journalist too?"

A stream of tracer tore into the sky. The firing followed.

Her voice turned weary, as if the fear had worn her out. "I file copy, sure."

"Who for?"

"A lousy wire service, what else? Fifty cents a line, till some big prick steals it and makes two grand in an afternoon. What's new?"

"What's your name?" I asked.

"I don't know. Maybe Annie. Call me Annie. Listen, you're real nice, know that? What do you do if a Doberman humps your leg?"

"Bark?"

"Fake an orgasm. I'm scared, Peter. Maybe I didn't make that clear. I need a drink."

"Where are you?"

"Right here."

"Where's here?"

"In the hotel, for Christ's sake. The Commodore. Standing in the lobby, smelling Ahmed's garlic and getting eyeballed by the Greek."

"Who's the Greek?"

"Stavros. He pushes hard drugs and swears up and down they're soft. He's serious sleaze."

I listened, and for the first time made out the babble of voices in the background. The shooting was over.

"Peter?"

"Yes."

"Peter, put that light out."

She must have known there was only one light working in the room, a rickety bedside light with a tilted parchment shade. It lay on a locker between the two divans. I turned it off. There were stars again.

"Unlock your door and leave it ajar. One inch. Got booze?"

"A bottle of Scotch," I said.

"Vodka?"

"No."

"Ice?"

"No."

"I'll bring some. Peter?"

"Yes?"

"You're a good man. Anybody ever told you that?"

"Not for a long time."

"Watch this space," she said, and rang off.

She never came to me.

You may imagine it any way you like, as I did, all ways, while I sat on the divan, watching the door in the darkness and watching my life go by while I waited to hear her tread in the corridor.

After an hour I went downstairs. I sat in the bar and listened to every female American voice I could find. None fitted. I looked for someone who might call herself Annie and proposition a man she had only talked to on the telephone. I bribed Ahmed to tell me who had used the house phone from the lobby at nine o'clock that night, but his memory, for whatever reason, did not stretch to an emotional American woman.

I went so far as to try to establish the identity of the previous occupant of my room, and whether his first name was Peter, but Ahmed became mysteriously vague and said he had been in Tripoli visiting his old mother, and the hotel kept no lists.

Did the real Peter return in the nick of time and sweep her off? Did Stavros the Greek? Was she a whore? Was I? Was Ahmed pimping her? Was the phone call some kind of elaborate trick she played on newcomers to the hotel, to hook them on their first nervous night alone?

Or was she, as I prefer to think, simply a frightened woman missing her boyfriend and craving a body to hold on to when the nightly thunder of the city started driving her mad?

Whatever mystery she presented, I had learned something about myself even if it disconcerted me. I had learned how perilous was my solitude, how available I was, how much I needed to give love and receive it; and how fickle in me was that virtue which the Service called "personal security," compared with my growing hunger for connection. I thought of Monica and my hollow protestations of love which so failed to move the gods they were addressed to. I thought of Giles Latimer and his hopeless passion. And somehow the woman who called herself Annie seemed to belong to the same line of anguished messengers, all speaking from inside myself.

After the faceless girl came the faceless boy. That happened the next evening.

Exhausted, I had settled myself in the hotel lobby and I was drinking my Scotch alone. I had been visiting the camps round Sidon and my hand was still shaking from just another day in southern Lebanon. Now it was the magic hour of dusk, when Beirut's human animal kingdom agreed to put aside its feuds and assemble at the common watering hole. I have seen the same thing happen in the jungle. Perhaps you have too. At a single command, elephants, wart-hogs, gazelles, lions and giraffes tiptoe from the protective darkness of the trees and, mostly in silence, arrange themselves on the muddy flats. You could observe the Commodore lobby at the same hour, when the journalists came back from their day's excursions. As the electric glass doors, always a little too slow on their feet, sighed and grunted from their exertions, so the dark of the early Beirut night disgorged its motley: a Swedish television unit, fronted by a grey-faced blonde in designer denims; a photographer and correspondent from an American weekly; the wire men always in pairs; an elderly and utterly mysterious East German with his Japanese mistress. All had the same self-consciously undramatic way of entering, and pausing, and setting down the day's burden.

Not that their day was over. For the real journalists, there were films to be despatched, stories to be written and telexed and telephoned. Someone was missing and must be accounted for. So-and-so had taken a bad bullet, did his wife know? Nevertheless, with the closing of the glass doors behind them, their day was won back from the enemy. The hackpack was battening down the hatches for the night.

And as I watched, I waited—to meet a man who knew a man who knew another man who just might know the woman I had been sent to find. My day till then had yielded nothing, except another tour of the wretched of the earth.

Elsewhere in the lobby, other species were gathering, less glamorous but frequently more interesting to the observer: carpetbaggers and arms dealers and drug dealers and dark-suited minor diplomats, the pedlars in influence and information, switching at their worry-beads as their restless eyes darted from face to face about the room. And the spies—everyone's spies—trading openly, because in Beirut their trade was everyone's. There was not a man or woman in the place who had not got his source of inside information, if it was only Ahmed behind the counter, who for a few dollars and a smile would tell you the secrets of the universe.

But the figure who had caught my eye was exotic even by the standards of the Commodore's menagerie. I did not see him enter. He must have come in behind a group. I saw him inside the lobby, framed against the darkness of the glass doors, dressed in a striped football shirt and a clean white nurse's scarf tied lightly round his head. If he had not been slender and flat-chested, I would not have been certain, at first sight, whether he was a woman pretending to be a man, or a man pretending to be a woman.

The security man had noticed him too. So had Ahmed the concierge behind his formidable counter. His two Kalashnikovs were propped against the wall behind him, just below the pigeon-holes where the room keys hung, and I saw Ahmed ease a half-step backward so that he had one within reach. A small hand-grenade in that lobby at that hour could have wiped out half the better rackets in the city.

But the apparition kept moving forward, either unaware or unheeding of the curiosity he was arousing. He was tall and young and agile, but rigid. He was like a person without will, summoned forward by his controller's voice. I saw him better now. He had dark glasses, black stubble and moustache. That was why his face had seemed so black. And the white nurse's scarf over his head. But it was the automaton's stiffness of his walk that set my skin tingling and made me wonder what kind of believer we might have on our hands.

He had reached the centre of the lobby. A few people made way for him. Some looked at him and looked away, others turned their backs in abstention, as if they knew and did not like him. Suddenly, under the brightness of the centre light, he seemed to be ascending. With his shrouded head forward and his arms barely moving, he was mounting his own scaffold on orders from above. I saw now that he was American. I saw it in the dipping knees and hanging wrists and slightly girlish hips. An all-American boy. His dark glasses were not dark enough, apparently, for a cloth eyeshade dangled from one long hand. It was of the kind that gamblers are supposed to wear, and night editors in forties films. He was six feet tall, at least. He wore sneakers, vestal white like his headscarf, and soundless.

An Arab freak? I wondered.

A crazed Zionist? There had been a few of those.

Stoned?

A high-school war tourist on the hippy trail, searching for kicks in the city of the damned?

Changing direction, he had begun talking to the receptionist, but at an angle facing into the lobby, already searching for the person he was enquiring for. Which was when I saw the red spots scattered over his cheeks and forehead, like hives or chicken pox, but more vivid. The bedbugs had eaten him in some stinking hostel, I decided. He had stuck his head through the windscreen of a clapped-out car. He started walking towards me. Stiffly again, without expression. Purposefully, a man used to being looked at. Angrily, the eyeshade dangling from his hand. Glowering at me blindly through his black glasses as I sat drinking. A woman had taken his arm. She wore a skirt and could have been the nurse who had given him his headscarf. They stood before me. Me and no one else.

"Sir? This is Sol, sir," she said—or Mort, or Syd, or whatever. "He's asking whether you're the journalist, sir."

I said I was a journalist.

"From London, sir, visiting? Are you the editor, sir? Are you influential, sir?"

Influential I doubted, I said with a deprecating smile. I was on the managerial side, here on a brief swing.

"And going back to London, sir? Soon?"

In Beirut you learn not to talk in advance about your movements. "Pretty soon," I conceded, though the truth was I was planning to return south again next day.

"Can Sol speak with you a moment, sir, just speak? Sol needs very much to speak with a person who has influence with the major Western newspapers. The journalists here, he feels they've seen it all, they're jaded. Sol needs a voice from outside."

I made space and she sat beside me while Sol very slowly lowered himself into a chair—this covered, silent, very clean man in his long football sleeves and headscarf. Seated finally, he laid his wrists over his knees, holding the eyeshade in both hands. Then he gave a long sigh and began to murmur to me.

"There's this thing I've written, sir. I'd like, please, to have it printed in your newspaper."

His voice, though soft, was educated and polite. But it was lifeless and, like his movements, economical, as if each word hurt him to produce. Inside the lenses of his very dark glasses, I saw that his left eye was smaller than his right. Narrower. Not swollen, not closed by a punch, just altogether smaller than its partner, taken from a different face. And the spots were not bites, not hives, not cuts. They were craters, like the pockmarks of small-arms fire on a Beirut wall, stamped with heat and speed. Like craters also, the skin around them had risen but not closed.

His story followed without my asking for it. He was a relief volunteer, sir, a third-year medical student from Omaha. He believed in peace, sir. And he had been in this bombing, sir, down by the Corniche, in this restaurant that had been one of the worst-hit places, just wiped out, you should go down there and take a look, a place called Akhbar's, sir, where a lot of Americans went, there was this car bomb and car bombs are the worst. You can't get worse than car bombs for surprise.

I said I knew that.

Almost everyone in the restaurant had died except himself, sir, the people nearest the wall just blew apart, he continued, unaware that he had painted my own worst nightmare for me. And now he had this thing he had written, he felt he had to say it, sir, a sort of mild statement about peace, which he needed to print in my newspaper, maybe it would do some good, he was thinking of like this weekend or maybe Monday. He'd like to donate the fee to charity. He guessed it could be like a couple of hundred dollars, maybe more. In the Beirut hospitals, that still bought people a piece of hope.

"We need a pause, sir," he explained, in his dead voice as the woman fished a wad of typescript from his pocket for him. "A pause for moderation. Just a break between wars to find the middle way."

Only in the Commodore in Beirut could it have seemed natural that a bomb-shocked peace-seeker should be pleading a hopeless cause to a journalist who wasn't one. Nevertheless I promised to do what I could. When I had done my business with the man I was waiting for—who knew nothing, of course, had heard nothing, but perhaps, sir, if I spoke to Colonel Asme in Tyre?—I settled in my room and with a glass at my elbow began to read his offering, determined that, if it had any reasonable chance of publication, I would twist the arm of one of our number-less Fleet Street friendlies when I returned to London, and see it done.

It was a tragic piece, and quickly it became unreadable: a rambling, emotional appeal to Jews, Christians and Muslims alike to remember their own mothers and children, and live together in love. It urged the middle ground of compromise and gave inaccurate examples from history. It proposed a new religion "like Joan of Arc would have given us only the English wouldn't let her, so they burned her alive, disregarding her screams and the will of the ordinary people." This great new movement, he said, would "bind the Semitic races in a spiritual brotherhood of love and tolerance." Then it lost its way completely, and resorted to capital letters, underlining, and rows of exclamation marks. So that by the time I reached the end, it had ceased to be what it set out to be at all, and was talking about "this whole family, kids and grandparents, that was sitting up beside the wall nearest to the epicentre." And how they had all been blown to pieces, not once, but over and over again, each time Sol allowed himself to look into his anguished memory.

Suddenly I was writing the piece for him. To her. To Annie. First in my mind, then in the margin of his pages, then on a fresh sheet of A4 paper from my briefcase, which was quickly covered so I took another. I was sweating, the sweat was pouring off me like rain; it was that kind of Beirut night, quiet till now but with a damp, itchy heat rolling off the mountains and an evil grey smog like gunsmoke draping itself across the sea. I was writing, and wondering if she would ring again. I was writing as the bombed boy, to a girl I didn't know. I was writing—as I saw to my dismay when I awoke next morning—pretentious junk. I was proclaiming maver-ick affections, mouthing great sentiments, pontificating about the unbreakable cycle of human evil, about man's endless search for reasons to do the wrong thing.

A pause, the boy had said. A pause for moderation, a break between wars. I put him right on that. I put Annie right on it too. I told them that the only pauses in the history of human conflict had been pauses not for moderation but excess, pauses for the world to redivide itself, for the thugs and the victims to find each other, for greed and deprival to regroup. I wrote like an adolescent bleeding heart, and when the morning came and I saw the pages of my handwriting strewn over the floor around the empty whisky bottle, I could not believe this was the work of anyone I knew.

So I did the only thing I could think of. I put them in the handbasin and cremated them, then broke up the ash and scattered it in the lavatory and flushed it into the body-blocked sewers of Beirut. And when I had done that, I took myself for a punishing pelt along the waterfront, running as hard as I could go from whatever was coming after me.

I was running towards Hansen, away from myself, but I had one more stop to make along the way.

My German girl, Britta, turned out to be in Israel, in the middle of the Negev Desert, in a compound of stark grey huts near a village called Revivim. The huts had a ploughed strip round them, and a double perimeter of barbed-wire fencing with a manned watchtower at each corner. If there were other European prisoners in the compound apart from her, I was not introduced to them. Her only companions that I saw were young Arab girls, mainly from poor villages in the West Bank or the Gaza, who had been talked or bullied by their Palestinian comrades into committing acts of savagery against the hated Zionist occupiers, most often planting bombs in marketplaces or tossing them into civilian buses.

I arrived there by jeep from Beersheeba, driven by a hardy young Colonel of Intelligence whose father, while still a boy, had been trained as a Night Raider by the eccentric General Wingate during the British Mandate. The Colonel's father remembered Wingate squatting naked in his tent by candlelight, drawing out the battle plan in the sand. Every Israeli soldier seems to talk about his father and a good few talk about the British. After the Mandate, they think they know us for what we probably still are: anti-Semitic, ignorant and imperialist, with just enough exceptions to redeem us. Dimona, where the Israelis store their nuclear arsenal, was up the road.

My sense of unreality had not left me. To the contrary, it had intensified. It was as if I had lost the distance from the human condition that is essential to our trade. My feelings and the feelings of others seemed to count more with me than my observations. It is quite easy in the Lebanon, if you drop your guard, to develop an unreasoning hatred of Israel. But I had succumbed to a serious dose of the disease. Trudging through the mud and stench of the shattered camps, crouching in the sandbagged hovels, I convinced myself that the Israeli thirst for vengeance would not be stilled until the accusing eyes of the last Palestinian child had been closed for good.

Perhaps my young Colonel got a hint of this, for though I had flown in from Cyprus it was still only a few hours since I had left Beirut, and something of what I felt may still have been legible in my face.

"You get to see Arafat?" he asked, with a moody smile as we drove along the straight road.

"No, I didn't."

"Why not? He's a nice guy."

I let that go.

"Why do you want to see Britta?"

I told him. There was no point in not doing so. It had taken all London's powers of persuasion to get me the interview with her at all, and my hosts were certainly not going to let me speak to her alone.

"We think she may be willing to talk to us about an old boyfriend," I said.

"Why would she do that?"

"He jilted her. She was angry with him."

"Who's the boyfriend?"—as if he didn't know.

"He's Irish. He has the rank of adjutant in the IRA. He briefs bombers, reconnoitres targets, supplies the equipment. She lived underground with him in Amsterdam and Paris."

"Like George Orwell, huh? *Down and Out?*"

"Like George Orwell."

"How long ago he jilted her?"

"Six months."

"Maybe she's not angry any more. Maybe she'll tell you go suck. For a girl like Britta, six months is a hell of a long time."

I asked whether she had talked much in her captivity. It was a delicate question, since the Israelis were still not saying how long they had been holding her, or how they had obtained her in the first place. The Colonel was broad-faced and brown-skinned. His family came originally from Russia. He wore parachute wings on his short-sleeved khaki shirt. He was twenty-eight, a Sabra, born in Tel Aviv, engaged to a Sephardi from Morocco. His father, the Night Raider, was now a dentist. All this he had told me in the first few minutes of our acquaintance, in a guttural English he had captured single-handed.

"Talked?" he repeated with a grim smile, in answer to my question. "Britta? That lady didn't stop talking since she became a resident."

Knowing a little of Israeli methods, I was not surprised, and I shuddered inwardly at the prospect of questioning a woman who had been subjected to them. It had happened to me in Ireland: a man buttoned to the neck who had stared at me like a dead man and confessed to everything.

"Do you interrogate her yourself?" I asked, noticing afresh his thick brown forearms and the uncompromising set of his jaw. And thinking, perhaps, of Colonel Jerzy.

He shook his head. "Impossible."

"Why?"

He seemed about to tell me something, then changed his mind. "We got experts," he said. "Shin Bet guys, smart like Britta. Take their time with her. Family."

I had heard about this loving family too, though I didn't say so. The Zionists had lured her into a trap, a bloodshot-eyed informant had whispered to me in Tyre. She had left the camps and gone to Athens with her new boyfriend, Said, and three of Said's friends, he said. Good boys. All able. The plan had been to shoot down an El Al plane as it made its approach to Athens airport. The boys had got themselves a hand-held rocket launcher and a rented house on the flightpath. Britta's job, as an unsuspicious-looking European, was to stand in a phone box at the airport with a thirty-dollar shortwave receiver and relay the control tower's instructions to the boys on the roof as the plane came in. Everything had been set fair, said my bone-weary informant. The rehearsals had gone like a dream. But on the day, the operation had fouled up.

Listening to him, I had filled in the rest of the story for myself, imagining how the Service would have done the job if we'd had the foreknowledge: two teams to assault the roof and the phone box simultaneously; the target plane, forewarned and empty, landing safely at Athens airport; the plane's homeward journey to Tel Aviv with the terrorists chained in their seats. I wondered what they would do with her. Whether they would put her on trial or trade her for favours in return.

"What happened to the boys she was with in Athens?" I asked the Colonel, ignoring London's injunction to show no curiosity in such matters.

"Boys? She knows nothing from boys. Athens? Where's Athens already? She's an innocent German tourist on vacation in Eilat. We kidnapped her, we drugged her, we imprisoned her, now we're framing her for propaganda. She invites us to prove the contrary because she knows we can't. You want any more information? Ask Britta, be our guest."

His mood mystified me, the more so when, as we got out of the jeep, he laid a hand on my shoulder and wished me a sort of luck. "She's all yours," he said. "*Mazel tov.*"

I was beginning to dread what I might find.

A dumpy little woman in army uniform received us in her clean office. Prison staff never go short of cleaners, I thought. She was Captain Levi and she was Britta's unlikely gaoler. She spoke English the way a small-town American schoolmistress might speak it, but more slowly, with greater care. She had twinkly eyes and short grey hair and a look of kindly resignation. She had the dusty complexion of prison life, but when she put her hands together you felt she ought to be knitting for her grandchildren.

"Britta is very intelligent," she said apologetically. "For an intelligent man to question an intelligent woman, that's sometimes difficult. Do you have a daughter, sir?"

I was not about to fill in my character profile for her so I said no, which happened also to be the truth.

"A pity. Never mind. Maybe you still get one. A man like you, you have time. You speak German?"

"Yes."

"Then you are lucky. You can communicate with her in her language. That way you get to know her better. Britta and I, we can speak only English together. I speak it like my late husband, who was American. Britta speaks it like her late lover, who was Irish. Tel Aviv says we are to allow you two hours. Will you be happy with two hours? If you need more, we shall ask them—maybe they say yes. Maybe two hours will be too much. We shall see."

"You are very kind," I said.

"Kind, I don't know. Maybe we should be less kind. Maybe we are making kind too much. You will see."

And with this, she sent for coffee and for Britta, while the Colonel and myself took up our places along one side of the plain wood table.

But Captain Levi did not sit at the table, I supposed because she was not part of the interview. She sat beside the door on a straight kitchen chair, her eyes lowered as if in preparation for a concert. Even when Britta walked in between two young wardresses, she only lifted her eyes as far as was necessary to watch the three women's feet pass her to the centre of the room and halt. One wardress pulled back a chair for Britta, the second unlocked her handcuffs. The wardresses left, and we settled to the table.

And I would like to paint for you the scene exactly as I saw it from where I sat: with the Colonel to my right, and Britta opposite us across the table, and the bowed grey head of Captain Levi almost directly behind her, but slightly to the left, wearing a reminiscent expression that was half a smile. Throughout our discussion she stayed like that, still as a waxwork. Her part-smile of familiarity never altered and never went away. There was concentration in her pose, and something of effort, so that I wondered whether she was straining to pick out phrases and words she could identify, perhaps from a combined knowledge of Yiddish and English, for Britta, being a Bremen girl, spoke a clear and authoritarian German, which makes comprehension easier.

And Britta, without a doubt, was a fine sample of her breed. She was "blond as a bread roll," as they say up there, tall and deep-shouldered and well-grown, with wide rather insolent blue eyes and a strong, attractive jaw. She had Monica's youth and Monica's height as well; and, as I could not avoid speculating, Monica's sensuality. My suspicion that they had been maltreating her vanished as soon as she walked in. She held herself like a ballerina, but with more intelligence and more of life's reality than is to be found in most dancers. She would have looked well in tennis gear or in a *dirndl* dress, and I suspected that in her time she had worn both. Even her prison tunic did not diminish her, for she had made herself a cloth belt out of something, and tied it at the waist, and she had brushed her fair hair over her shoulders in a cape. Her first gesture when her hands were freed was to offer me one, at the same time dropping a schoolgirl bob, whether out of irony or respect it was too soon to tell. Her grasp was like a boy's, but lingering. She wore no make-up but needed none.

"*Und mit wem hab' ich die Ehre?*" she enquired, either courteously or impishly. And whom do I have the honour to address?

"I'm a British official," I said.

"Your name, please?"

"It's unimportant."

"But you are very important!"

Prisoners when they are brought up from their cells often say silly things in their first flush, so I answered her with consideration.

"I'm working with the Israelis on aspects of your case. That's all you need to know."

"Case? I am a case? How amusing. I thought I was a human being. Please sit down, Mr. Nobody," she said, doing so herself.

So we sit as I have described, with Captain Levi's face behind her, a little out of focus like its expression. The Colonel had not stood up to greet Britta, and he barely bothered to look at her now she was sitting before him. He seemed suddenly to be without expectation. He glanced at his watch. It was of dull steel and like a weapon on his brown wrist. Britta's wrists were white and smooth like Monica's, but chafed with red rings from the handcuffs.

Suddenly she was lecturing me.

She began at once, as if she were resuming a tutorial, and in a sense she was, for I soon realised she lectured everyone this way, or everyone whom she had dismissed as bourgeois. She said she had a statement to make which she would like me to relay to my "colleagues," as she called them, since she felt that her position was not being sufficiently appreciated by the authorities. She was a prisoner of war, just as any Israeli soldier in Palestinian hands was a prisoner of war, and entitled to the treatment and privileges set out in the Geneva Convention. She was a tourist here, she had committed no crime against Israel; she had been arrested solely on the strength of her trumped-up record in other countries, as a deliberate act of provocation against the world proletariat.

I gave a quick laugh, and she faltered. She was not expecting laughter.

"But look here," I objected. "Either you're a prisoner of war or you're an innocent tourist. You can't be both."

"The struggle is between the innocent and the guilty," she retorted without hesitation, and resumed her lecture. Her enemies were not limited to Zionism, she said, but what she called the dynamic of bourgeois domination, the repression of natural instincts, and the maintenance of despotic authority disguised as "democracy."

Again I tried to interrupt her, but this time she talked straight through me. She quoted Marcuse at me and Freud. She referred to the rebellion of sons in puberty against their fathers, and the disavowal of this rebellion in later years as the sons themselves became the fathers.

I glanced at the Colonel, but he seemed to be dozing.

The purpose of her "actions" she said, and those of her comrades, was to arrest this instinctual cycle of repression in all its forms—in the enslavement of labour to materialism, in the repressive principle of "progress" itself—and to allow the real forces of society to surge, like erotic energy, into new, unfettered forms of cultural creation.

"None of this is faintly interesting to me," I protested. "Just stop, please, and listen to my questions."

Acts of so-called "terrorism" had therefore two clear purposes, she continued, as if I had never spoken, of which the first was to disconcert the armies of the bourgeois-materialist conspiracy, and the second to instruct, by example, the pit-ponies of the earth, who had lost all knowledge of the light. In other words, to introduce ferment and awaken consciousness at the most repressed human levels.

She wished to add that though she was not an adherent of Communism, she preferred its teachings to those of capitalism,since Communism provided a powerful negation of the ego-ideal which used property to construct the human prison.

She favoured free sexual expression and—for those who needed them—the use of drugs as a means of discovering the free self as contrasted with the unfree self that is castrated by aggressive tolerance.

I turned to the Colonel. There is an etiquette of interrogation as there is about everything else. "Do we have to go on listening to this nonsense? The lady is your prisoner, not mine," I said. For I could hardly lay the law down to her across his table.

The Colonel lifted his head high enough to glance at her with indifference. "You want to go back down, Britta?" he asked her. "You want bread and water for a couple of weeks?" His German was as bizarre as his English. He seemed suddenly a lot older than his age, and wiser.

"I have more to say, thank you."

"If you're going to stay up here, you answer his questions and you shut up," said the Colonel. "It's your choice. You want to leave now, it's fine by us." He added something in Hebrew to Captain Levi, who nodded distantly. An Arab prisoner entered with a tray of coffee—four cups and a plate of sugar biscuits—and handed them round meekly, a coffee cup for each of us and one for Captain Levi, the biscuits at the centre of the table. An air of lassitude had settled over us. Britta stretched out her long arm for a biscuit, lazily, as if she were in her own home. The Colonel's hand crashed on the table just ahead of her as he removed the plate from her reach.

"So what do you wish to ask me, please?" Britta enquired of me, as if nothing at all had happened. "Do you wish me to deliver the Irish to you? What other aspects of my case could interest the English, Mr. Nobody?"

"If you deliver us one particular Irishman, that will be fine," I said. "You lived with a man named Seamus for a year."

She was amused. I had provided her with an opening. She studied me, and seemed to see something in my face she recognised. "*Lived* with him? That is an exaggeration. I slept with him. Seamus was only for sex," she explained, with a mischievous smile. "He was a convenience, an instrument. A *good* instrument, I would say. I was the same for him. You like sex? Sometimes another boy would join us, maybe sometimes a girl. We made combinations. It was irrelevant but we had fun."

"Irrelevant to what?" I asked.

"To our work."

"What work?"

"I have already described our work to you, Mr. Nobody. I have told you of its aims, and of our motivations. Humanitarianism is not to be equated with non-violence. We must fight to be free. Sometimes even the highest causes can only be served by violent methods. Do you not know that? Sex also can be violent."

"What kind of violent methods was Seamus involved in?" I asked.

"We are speaking not of wanton acts but of the people's right of resistance against acts committed by the forces of repression. Are you a member of those forces or are you in favour of spontaneity, Mr. Nobody? Perhaps you should free yourself and join us."

"He's a bomber," I said. "He blows up innocent people. His most recent target was a public house in southern England. He killed one elderly couple, the barman and the pianist, and I give you my word he didn't liberate a single deluded worker."

"Is that a question or a statement, Mr. Nobody?"

"It's an invitation to you to tell me about his activities."

"The public house was close to a British military camp," she replied. "It was providing infrastructure and comfort to Fascistic forces of oppression."

Again her cool eyes held me in their playful gaze. Did I say she was attractive? What is attraction in such circumstances? She was wearing a calico tunic. She was an enforced penitent of crimes that she did not repent. She was alert in every part of herself, I could feel it, and she knew I felt it, and the divide between us enticed her.

"My department is considering offering you a sum of money on your release, payable, if you prefer, to somebody you nominate in the meantime," I said. "They want information that would lead to the arrest and conviction of your friend Seamus. They are interested in his past crimes, others he has yet to commit, safe addresses, contacts, habits and weaknesses." She waited for me to go on, so, perhaps unwisely, I did. "Seamus is not a hero. He's a pig. Not what you call a pig. A real pig. Nobody did bad things to him when he was young; his parents are decent people who run a tobacco shop in County Down. His grandfather was a policeman, a good one. Seamus is blowing people up for kicks because he's inadequate. That's why he treated you badly. He only exists when he's inflicting pain. The rest of the time he's a spoilt little boy."

I had not scratched the surface of her steady stare.

"Are you inadequate, Mr. Nobody? I think perhaps you are. In your occupation, that is normal. You should join us, Mr. Nobody. You should take lessons with us, and we shall convert you to our cause. Then you will be adequate."

You must understand that she did not raise her voice while she said this, or indulge in dramatics of any kind. She remained condescending and composed, even hospitable. The mischief in her lay deep and well-disguised. She had a healthy natural smile and it stayed with her all the time she spoke, while Captain Levi behind her continued to gaze into her own memories, perhaps because she did not understand what was being said.

The Colonel glanced at me in question. Not trusting myself to speak, I lifted my hands from the table, asking what's the point? The Colonel said something to Captain Levi, who in the disappointed manner of someone who has prepared a meal only to see it taken away uneaten, pressed a bell for the escort. Britta rose to her feet, smoothed her prison tunic over her breasts and hips and held out her hands for the handcuffs.

"How much money were they thinking of offering me, Mr. Nobody?" she enquired.

"None," I said.

She dropped me another bob and walked between her guards towards the door, her hips flowing inside her calico tunic, reminding me of Monica's inside her dressing-gown. I was afraid she would speak again but she didn't. Perhaps she knew she had won the day, and anything more would spoil the effect. The Colonel followed her out and I was alone with Captain Levi. The half smile had not left her face.

"There," she said. "Now you know a little what it feels like to hear Britta's music."

"I suppose I do."

"Sometimes we communicate too much. Perhaps you should have spoken English to her. So long as she speaks English, I can care for her. She is a human being, she is a woman, she is in prison. And you may be sure she is in agony. She is courageous, and so long as she speaks English to me I can do my duty for her."

"And when she speaks German to you?"

"What would be the point, since she knows I cannot understand her?"

"But if she did—and if you could understand her? What then?"

Her smile twisted and became slightly shameful. "Then I think I would be frightened," she replied in her slow American. "I think if she ordered something of me, I would be tempted to obey her. But I do not let her order me. Why should I? I do not give her the power over me. I speak English and I stay the boss. I was for two years in concentration camp in Buchenwald, you see." Still smiling at me, she delivered the rest in German, in the clenched, hushed whisper of the campnik: *"Man hört so scheussliche Echos in ihrer Stimme, wissen Sie."* One hears such dreadful echoes in her voice, you see.

The Colonel was standing in the doorway waiting for me. As we walked downstairs, he put his hand once more on my shoulder. This time I knew why.

"Is she like that with all the boys?" I asked him.

"Captain Levi?"

"Britta."

"Sure. With you a bit more, that's all. Maybe that's because you're English."

Maybe it is, I thought, and maybe it's because she saw more in me than just my Englishness. Maybe she read my unconscious signals of availability. But whatever she saw in me, or didn't, Britta had provided the summation of my confusion until now. She had articulated my sense of trying to hold on to a world that was slipping away from me, my susceptibility to every stray argument and desire.

The summons to find Hansen arrived the same night, in the middle of a jolly diplomatic party given by my British Embassy host in Herzliyya.

9

Earnest Perigrew was quizzing Smiley about colonialism. Sooner or later, Perigrew quizzed everyone who came to Sarratt about colonialism, and his questions always hovered at the edge of outrage. He was a troubled boy, the son of British missionaries to West Africa, and one of those people the Service is almost bound to employ, on account of their rare knowledge and linguistic qualifications. He was sitting as usual alone, amid the shadows at the back of the library, his gaunt face thrust forward and one long hand held up as if to fend off ridicule. The question had started reasonably, then degenerated into a tirade against Britain's indifference towards her former enslaved subjects.

"Yes, well I think I rather agree with you," said Smiley courteously, to the general surprise, when he had heard Perigrew to the end. "The sad answer is, I'm afraid, that the Cold War produced in us a kind of *vicarious* colonialism. On the one hand we abandoned practically every article of our national identity to American foreign policy. On the other we bought ourselves a stay of execution for our vision of our colonial selves. Worse still, we encouraged the Americans to behave in the same way. Not that they needed our encouragement, but they were pleased to have it, naturally."

Hansen had said much the same. And in much the same language. But where Smiley had lost little of his urbanity, Hansen had glared into my face with eyes lit by the red hells from which he had returned.

I flew from Israel to Bangkok because Smiley said Hansen had gone mad and knew too many secrets: a decypher yourself signal, care of the Head of Station, Tel Aviv. Smiley had charge of Service security at the time, with the courtesy rank of deputy chief. Whenever I heard of him, he seemed to be scuttling round plugging another leak or another scandal. I spent the weekend in a heatwave sweating my way through the stack of hand-delivered files and an hour on the telephone placating Mabel, who had fallen at the last fence of her annual race to become ladies' captain of our local golf club and was scenting intrigue.

I don't know why they're so hard on Mabel. Perhaps it's her way of plain talking that puts them off. I did what I could. I told her that nothing I had come upon in the Service could compare with the skulduggery of those Kent wives. I promised her a splendid holiday when I returned. I forget where the holiday was going to be because we never took it.

Hansen's file gave me a portrait of a type I had grown familiar with because we used a good few of them. I was one myself and Ben was another: the crossbred Englishman who adopts the Service as his country and endows it with a bunch of qualities it hasn't really got.

Like myself, Hansen was half a Dutchman. Perhaps that was why Smiley had chosen me. He was born in the long night of the German Occupation of Holland and raised in the shadow of Delft Cathedral. His mother, a counter clerk at Thomas Cook's, was of English parents who urged her to go back to London with them when the war broke out. She refused, choosing instead to marry a Delft curate, who a year afterwards got himself shot by a German firing squad, leaving his pregnant wife to fend for herself. Undaunted, she joined a British escape line and, by the time the war ended, had charge of a fully fledged network, with its own communications, informants, safe houses and the usual appointments. My mother's work with the Service had not been so different.

By what route the infant Hansen found his way to the Jesuits, the file did not relate. Perhaps the mother converted. Those were dark years still, and if expediency required it, she may have swallowed her Protestant convictions to buy the boy a decent education. Give the Jesuits his soul, she may have reasoned, and they will give him a brain. Or perhaps she sensed in her son from early on the mercurial nature that later ruled his life, and she determined to subordinate him to a stronger religious discipline than was offered by the easy-going Protestants. If so, she was wise. Hansen embraced the faith as he embraced everything else, with passion. The nuns had him, the brothers had him, the priests had him, the scholars had him. Till at twenty-one, schooled and devout but still a novice, he was packed off to a seminary in Indonesia to learn the ways of the heathen: Sumatra, Molucca, Java.

The Orient seems to have been an instinctive love of Hansen's as it is for many Dutchmen. The good Dutch, like Heine's proverbial pine tree, can stand on the shores of their flat little country and sniff the Asian scents of lemon grass and cooking pots on the chill sea air. Hansen arrived, he saw, he was conquered. Buddhism, Islam, the rites and superstitions of the remotest savages—he flung himself on all of them with a fervour that only intensified the deeper he penetrated into the jungle.

Languages also came naturally to him. To his native Dutch and English he had effortlessly added French and German. Now he acquired Tamil, Khmer, Thai, Sanskrit and more than a smattering of Cantonese, often hiking hundreds of miles of hill country in his quest for a missing dialect or ritualistic link. He wrote papers on philology, marriage rites, illumination and monkeys. He discovered lost temples in the depths of the jungle, and won prizes the Society forbade him to accept. After six years of fearless exploring and enquiring, he was not only the kind of academic showpiece Jesuits are famous for; he was also a full priest.

But few secrets can survive six years. Gradually the stories about him began to acquire a seamy edge. Hansen the skin artist. Hansen's appetites. Don't look now but here comes one of Hansen's girls.

It was the scale as well as the duration that did for him: the fact that once they started probing, they found no corner to his life that was immune, no journey that did not have its detour. A woman here or there—a boy or two—well, from what I have seen of priesthood round the globe, such peccadilloes are to be found more in the observance than the breach.

But this wholesale indulgence, in every kampong, in every tawdry sidestreet, this indefatigable debauchery, flaunted, as they now discovered, beneath their noses for more than a decade, with girls who by Western standards were barely eligible for their First Communion, let alone the marriage bed—and many of them under the Church's own protection—made Hansen suddenly and dramatically untenable. Faced with the evidence of such prolonged and dedicated sinning, his Superior responded more in grief than indignation. He ordered Hansen to return to Rome, and sent a letter ahead of him to the General of the Society. From Rome, he told Hansen sadly, he would most likely go to Loyola in Spain, where qualified Jesuit psychotherapists would help him come to terms with his regrettable weakness. After Loyola—well, a new beginning, perhaps a different hemisphere, a different decade.

But Hansen, like his mother before him, stubbornly declined to leave the place of his adoption.

At a loss, the Father Guardian packed him off to a distant mission in the hills run by a traditionalist of the sterner school. There Hansen suffered the barbarities of house arrest. He was watched over like a madman. He was forbidden to pass beyond the precincts of the house, denied books, paper, company, laughter. Men take to confinement in different ways, as they take differently to heights or cold or dying. Hansen took to it terribly, and after three months could bear no more. As his brother guardians escorted him to Mass, he hurled one of them down a staircase while the other fled. Then he headed back to Djakarta and, with neither money nor passport, went to ground in the brothels he knew well. The girls took him into their care, and in return he worked as pimp and bouncer. He gave out beer, washed glasses, ejected the unruly, heard confessions, gave succour, played with the children in the back room. I see him, as I know him now, doing all those things without fuss or complication. He was barely thirty and his desires burned bright as ever. Until one day, yielding as so often to an impulse, Hansen shaved, put on a clean shirt, and presented himself to the British Consul to claim his British soul.

And the Consul, being neither deaf nor blind, but a longstanding member of the Service, listened to Hansen's story, asked a humdrum question or two and, from behind a mask of apathy, sprang to action. For years he had been looking for a man of Hansen's gifts. Hansen's waywardness did not deter the Consul in the least. He liked it. He signalled London for background; he lent Hansen cautious sums of cash against receipts in triplicate, for he did not wish to show undue enthusiasm. When London came back with a white trace on Hansen's mother, indicating she was a former agent of the Service, the Consul's cup brimmed over.

Another month and Hansen was semi-conscious, which means he knew, but only half knew, but then again might not know, that he just could be half in touch with what one might loosely refer to as British Intelligence. Another two months and, restless as ever, he was taking a swing through southern Java ostensibly in search of ancient scrolls, in reality to report back to the Consul the strength of Communist subversion, which was his newly adopted anti-Christ. By the end of the year he was headed for London with the brand-new British passport he had wanted in his pocket, though not in his own name.

I turned to his potted training record, all six months of it. Clive Bellamy, a gangly, mischievous Etonian, was in charge of Sarratt. "Excellent at all things practical," he wrote in Hansen's end-of-course report. "Has a first-rate memory, fast reactions, is self-sufficient. Needs to be ridden hard. If there's ever a mutiny on my ship, Hansen will be the first man I'll flog. Needs a big canvas and a first-rate controller."

I turned to the operational record. No madness there either. Since Hansen was still Dutch, Head Office decided to keep him that way and play down his English-ness. Hansen bridled but they overruled him. At a time when the British abroad were being seen by everyone except themselves as Americans without the clout, Head Office would kill for a Swede and steal for a West German. Even Canadians, though more easily manufactured, were smiled on. Back in Holland, Hansen for-malised his severance from the Jesuits and set about looking for new employment back East. A score of Oriental academic bodies were spread around the capitals of Western Europe in those days. Hansen did his rounds of them, gaining a promise here and a commitment there. A French Oriental news agency took him on as a stringer. A London weekly, nudged by Head Office, made a berth for him on condition they got him free. Till bit by bit his cover was complete—wide enough for him to have a reason to go anywhere and ask what questions he wanted, varied enough to be financially inscrutable, since no one would ever be able to tell which of his several employers were paying him how much for what. He was ready to be launched. British interests in South East Asia might have dwindled with her Empire, but the Americans were in there knee-deep with an official war running in Vietnam, an unofficial one in Cambodia and a secret one in Laos. In our unlovely rôle as camp follower, we were delighted to offer them Hansen's precious talents.

Espionage technology can do a lot. It can photograph crops and trenches, tanks and rocket sites and tyre-marks and the migration of the reindeer. It can flinch at the sound of a Russian fighter pilot breaking wind at forty thousand feet or a Chinese general belching in his sleep. But it can't replace human understanding. It can't tell you what's in the heart of a Cambodian farmer whose hill crops have been blown to smithereens by Dr. Kissinger's unmarked bombers, whose daughters have been sold into prostitution in the city, and whose sons have been lured into leaving the fields and fighting for an American puppet army, or urged, by way of family insurance, into the ranks of the Khmer Rouge. It can't read the lips of jungle fighters in black pyjamas whose most powerful weapon is the perverted Marxism of a blood-hungry Sorbonne-educated Cambodian psychopath. It can't sniff the exhaust fumes of an army that is unmechanised. Or break the codes of an army without radio. Or calculate the supplies of men who can nourish themselves on ground beetles and wood bark; or the morale of those who, having lost all they possess, have only the future to win.

But Hansen could. Hansen, the adopted Asian, could trek without food for a week, squat in the kampongs and listen to the murmur of the villagers, and Hansen could read the rising wind of their resistance long before it stirred the Stars and Stripes on the Embassy roofs of Phnom Penh and Saigon. And he could tell the bombers—and, to his later remorse, he did—he could tell the American bombers which villages were playing host to the Vietcong. He was a fisher of men, too. He could recruit helpers from every walk of life and instruct them how to see and hear and remember and report. He knew how little to tell them and how much, how to reward them and when not to.

For months, then years, Hansen functioned that way in the so-called "liberated areas" of northern Cambodia where the Khmer Rouge nominally held sway, until the day he vanished from the village he had made his home. Vanished soundlessly, taking the inhabitants with him. Soon to be given up for dead, another jungle disappearance.

And remained dead until a short time ago, when he had come alive in a brothel in Bangkok.

"Take your time, Ned," Smiley had urged me on the telephone to Tel Aviv. "If you want to add a couple of days for jet-lag, it's quite all right by me."

Which was Smiley-speak for "Get to him as fast as you can and tell me I haven't got another king-sized scandal on my hands."

Our Station Head in Bangkok was a bald, rude, moustachioed little tyrant called Rumbelow, whom I had never warmed to. The Service offers precious few prospects for men of fifty. Most are blown; many are too tired and disenchanted to care whether they are or not. Others head for private banking or big business, but the marriage seldom lasts. Something has happened to their way of thinking that unsuits them to the overt life. But a very few, of whom Toby Esterhase was one and Rumbelow another, pull off the trick of holding the Service hostage to their supposed assets.

Exactly what Rumbelow's were I never knew. Seedy, I am sure, for if he specialised in anything, it was human baseness. One rumour said he owned a couple of corrupt Thai generals who would work to him and to no one else. Another that he had managed to perform a grimy favour for a member of the royal household that was not transferable. Whatever his hold on them, the barons of the Fifth Floor would hear no ill of him. "And for God's sake, don't rub up Rumbelow the wrong way, Ned," Smiley had begged me. "I'm sure he's a pain in the neck, but we do need him."

I met him in my hotel room. To the overt world I was Mark Seymour, occupation accountant, and had no wish to parade myself at the Embassy or his house. I had been flying twenty hours. It was early evening. Rumbelow spoke like an Etonian bookmaker. Come to think of it, he looked like one as well.

"It was *sheerest* bloody coincidence we bumped into the bastard at all," he told me huffily. "One puts out one's feelers, naturally. One keeps one's ear to the proverbial ground. One knows the score. One's heard of other cases. One isn't insensitive. One doesn't like to think of one's joe trussed to a stick, being carted through the jungle for weeks on end, while the Khmer Rouge torture the hell out of him, naturally. Not an ostrich. Know the score. Your brown man doesn't obey the Queensberry Rules, you know," he assured me, as if I had implied the opposite. And, plucking a handkerchief from the sleeve of his sweat-patched suit, he pummelled his stupid moustache with it. "Your *average* joe would be yelling for a quick bullet after one night of it."

"Are you sure that's what happened to him?"

"Not sure of anything, thank you, old boy. Rumour, that's all. How *can* I be sure, if the bastard won't even talk to us? Threatens violence if we try! For all *I* know, the KR never had sight nor sound of him. Never did trust a Dutchman, not out here—they think they own the bloody place. Hansen wouldn't be the first joe to lie doggo when things got too hot for him, then come bouncing back when it's all over, asking for his gong and his pension, not by any means. Still in possession of all his fingers and thumbs, by all accounts. Not missing any other part of his anatomy either, to judge by where he's holed out. Duffy Marchbanks spotted him. Remember Duffy? Good chap."

With a sinking heart, yes, I remembered Duffy. I had remembered him when I saw his name in the file. He was a flamboyant crook based in Hong Kong, with a taste for fast deals in anything from opium to shellcases. For a few misguided years we had financed his office.

"Purest chance, it was, on Duffy's part. He'd popped up here on a flying visit. One day, that's all. One day, one night, then back to the missus and a book. Offshore leisure consortium wanted him to buy a hundred acres of prime coastland for them. Did his business, then off they all go to this girlie restaurant, Duffy and a bunch of his traders—Duffy's not averse to a bit of the other, never has been. Place called The Sea of Happiness, slap in the middle of the red-light quarter. Upmarket sort of establishment, as they go, I'm told. Private rooms, decent food if you like Hunanese, a straight deal and the girls leave you alone unless you tell 'em not to."

At girlie restaurants, he explained, somehow contriving to suggest he had never personally been to one, young hostesses, dressed or undressed, sat between the guests and fed them food and drink while the men talked high matters of business. In addition, The Sea of Happiness offered a massage parlour, a discothèque and a live theatre on the ground floor.

"Duffy clinches the deal with the consortium, a cheque is passed, he's feeling his oats. So he decides to do himself a favour with one of the girls. Terms agreed, off they go to a cubicle. Girl says she's thirsty, how about a bottle of champagne to get her going? She's on commission, naturally—they all are. Never mind. Duffy's feeling expansive, so he says why not? Girl presses a bell, squawks into the intercom, next thing Duffy knows, in marches this bloody great European chap with an ice bucket and a tray. Sets it down, Duffy gives him twenty baht for himself, fellow says 'Thank you' in English, polite enough but no smiles, clears out. It's Hansen. Jungle Hansen. Not a portrait . . . himself!"

"How does Duffy know that?"

"Seen his photograph, hasn't he?"

"Why?"

"Because we showed Duffy the bloody photograph, for heaven's sake, when Hansen went missing! We showed it to everyone we knew, all over the bloody hemisphere! We didn't say why—we just said if you spot this man, holler. Head Office's orders, thank you, not *my* idea. *I* thought it was bloody insecure."

To calm himself, Rumbelow poured us both another whisky. "Duffy roars back to his hotel, phones me at home straight away. Three in the morning. 'It's your fellow,' he tells me. 'What fellow?' I say. 'Fellow you sent me that pretty picture of, back in Hongkers a year ago or more. He's potboy at a whorehouse called The Sea of Happiness.' You know how old Duffy talks. Loose. I sent Henry round next day. Bloody fool made a hash of it. You heard about that, I hope? Typical."

"Did Duffy speak to Hansen? Ask him who he was? Anything?"

"Not a dickie bird. Looked clean through him. Duffy's a trouper. Salt of the earth. Always was."

"Where's Henry?"

"Sitting downstairs in the lobby."

"Call him up."

Henry was Chinese, the son of a Kuomintang warlord in the Shan States and our resident chief agent, though I suspect he had long ago taken out reinsurance with the Thai police and was earning a quiet living playing both ends against the middle.

He was a podgy, over-eager, shiny fellow and he smiled too much. He wore a gold chain round his neck and carried a smart leather notebook with a gold pen in it. His cover work was translator. No translator I had ever met sported a Gucci notebook, but Henry was different.

"Tell Mark how you made a bloody fool of yourself at The Sea of Happiness last Thursday evening," Rumbelow ordered menacingly.

"Sure, Mike."

"Mark," I said.

"Sure, Mark."

"His orders were to take a look. That's *all* he was to do," Rumbelow barged in before Henry could tell anything at all. "Take a look, sniff, get out, call me. Right, Henry? He was to spin the tale, sniff, *see* if he could spot Hansen anywhere, *not* approach him, report back to me. A discreet, no-contact reconnaissance. Sniff and tell. Now tell Mark what you did."

First Henry had had a drink at the bar, he said; then he had watched the show. Then he had sent for the Mama San, who hurried over assuming he had a special wish. The Mama San was a Chinese lady from the same province as Henry's father, so they had an immediate bond.

He had shown the Mama San his translator's card and said he was writing an article about her establishment—the superb food, the romantic girls, the high standards of sensitivity and hygiene, particularly the hygiene. He said he had a commission from a German travel magazine that recommended only the best places.

The Mama San took the bait and offered him the run of the house. She showed him the private dining rooms, the kitchens, cubicles, toilets. She introduced him to the girls—and offered him one on the house, which he declined—to the head chef, the doorman and the bouncers, but not, as it happened, to the enormous round-eye whom Henry had by then spotted three times, once as he carried a tray of glasses from the private dining rooms to the kitchens, once crossing a corridor pushing a trolley of bottles and once emerging from an open steel doorway which apparently led to the drinks store.

"But who is your *farang* who carries the bottles for you?" Henry had cried out with amusement to the Mama San. "Must he stay behind and work because he cannot pay his bill?"

The Mama San laughed also. Against *farangs,* or Westerners, all Asians feel naturally united. "The *farang* lives with one of our Cambodian girls," she replied with contempt, for Cambodians are rated even lower than *farangs* and Vietnamese in the Thai zoology. "He met her here and fell in love with her, so he tried to buy her and make a lady out of her. But she refused to leave us. So he brings her to work every day, and stays until she is free to go home again."

"What kind of *farang* is he? German? English? Dutch?"

The Mama San shrugged. What was the difference? Henry pressed her. But a *farang* who brings his woman to the brothel and pushes drinks about while she goes with other men, he insisted, and then takes her home again to his bed? This must be quite some girl!

"She is number nineteen," said the Mama San, with a shrug. "Her house name is Amanda. Would you like her?"

But Henry was too excited by his journalistic *coup* to be sidetracked. "But the *farang,* what is his name? What is his history?" he cried in great amusement.

"He is called Ham Sin. He speaks Thai with us and Khmer with the girl but you must not put him in your magazine, because he is illegal."

"I can disguise him. I can make it all disguised. Does the girl love him in return?"

"She prefers to be here at The Sea of Happiness with her friends," the Mama San said primly.

Henry could not resist taking a look. The girls who were not with clients lounged on plush benches behind a glass wall, wearing numbers round their necks and nothing else, while they chatted to each other or tended their fingernails or stared vacuously at an ill-tuned television set. As Henry watched, number 19 stood up in response to a summons, picked up her little handbag and a wrap and walked from the room. She was very young. Many girls lied about their age in order to defeat the regulations—penniless Cambodians particularly. But this girl, said Henry, had looked no more than fifteen.

It was here that Henry's excess of zeal began to lead him astray. He said his goodbyes to the Mama San and drove his car into an alley opposite the rear entrance, where he settled down to wait. Soon after one o'clock the staff began leaving, among them Hansen, twice the height of anyone else, leading number 19 on his arm. In the square, Hansen and the girl looked round for a cab and Henry had the temerity to pull up his car beside them. Pimps and illegal cab drivers thrive at that hour of night, and Henry in his time had been both, so perhaps the move came naturally to him.

"Where you want to go, sir?" he called to Hansen in English. "You want me to drive you?"

Hansen gave an address in a poor suburb five miles north. A price was agreed, Hansen and his girl got into the back of the car; they set off.

Now Henry began to lose his head in earnest. Flushed by his success, he decided for no reason he could afterwards explain that his best course of action would be to deliver his quarry and the girl to Rumbelow's house, which lay not north but west. He had not of course prepared Rumbelow for this bold manoeuvre; he had hardly prepared himself for it. He had no assurance that Rumbelow was at home, or in any condition, at one-thirty in the morning, to conduct a conversation with a former spy who had disappeared off the map for eighteen months. But reason, at that moment, did not predominate in Henry's mind. He was a joe, and there is not a joe in the world who does not, at one time or another in his life, do something totally daft.

"You like Bangkok?" Henry asked Hansen gaily, hoping to distract his passengers from the route he was taking.

No answer.

"You been here long?"

No answer.

"That's a nice girl. Very young. Very pretty. She your regular girl?"

The girl had her head on Hansen's shoulder. From what Henry could see in the mirror, she was already asleep. For some reason, this knowledge excited Henry further.

"You want a tailor, sir? All-night tailor, very good? I take you there. Good tailor."

And he drove wildly into a sidestreet, pretending to look for his wretched tailor while he hurried towards Rumbelow's house.

"Why are you going west?" said Hansen, speaking for the first time. "I don't want to go this way. I don't want a tailor. Get back on the main road."

The last of Henry's commonsense deserted him. He was suddenly terrified by Hansen's size and Hansen's tactical advantage in sitting behind him. What if Hansen was armed? Henry jammed on the brakes and stopped the car.

"Mr. Hansen, sir, I am your friend!" he cried in Thai, much as he might plead for mercy. "Mr. Rumbelow is your friend too. He's proud of you! He wants to give you a lot of money. You come with me, please. No problem. Mr. Rumbelow will be very happy to see you!"

That was the last speech Henry made that night, for the next thing he knew, Hansen had pushed the back of Henry's driving seat so hard that Henry's head nearly went through the windscreen. Hansen got out of the car and hauled Henry into the street. After that, Hansen lifted Henry to his feet and flung him across the road, to the dismay of a group of sleeping beggars, who began whimpering and clamouring while Hansen strode to where Henry lay and glared down at him.

"You tell Rumbelow, if he comes for me, I'll kill him," he said in Thai.

Then he led the girl up the road in search of a better cab, one arm round her waist while she dozed.

By the time I had heard the two men's story to the end, I was suddenly dreadfully tired.

I sent them away, telling Rumbelow to call me next morning. I said that before I did anything else I was going to sleep off my jet-lag. I lay down and was at once wide awake. An hour later, I was presenting myself at The Sea of Happiness and buying a ticket for fifty dollars. I removed my shoes, as custom required, and moments later I was standing in a neon-lit cubicle in my stockinged feet, staring into the passive, much painted features of girl number 19.

She wore a cheap silk wrap with tigers on it, but it was open from the neck down. Underneath it she was naked. A heavy Japanese-style make-up covered her complexion. She smiled at me and thrust her hand swiftly towards my groin, but I replaced it at her side. She was so slight it seemed a mystery that she was equal to the work. She was longer-legged than most Asian girls and her skin was unusually pale. She threw off her wrap and, before I could stop her, sprang on to the frayed chaise longue, where she arranged herself in what she imagined to be an erotic pose, caressing herself and uttering sighs of desire. She rolled on to her side with her rump thrust out, draping her black hair across her shoulder so that her tiny breasts poked through it. When I did not advance on her, she lay on her back and opened her thighs to me and bucked her pelvis, calling me "darling" and saying "please." She flung herself away from me so that I could admire her back view, keeping her legs apart in invitation.

"Sit up," I said, so she sat up and again waited for me to come to her.

"Put on your wrap," I said.

When she appeared not to understand, I helped her into it. Henry had written the message for me in Khmer. "I want to speak to Hansen," it read. "I am in a position to obtain Thai papers for yourself and your family." I handed it to her and watched her study it. Could she read? I had no way of telling. I held out a plain white envelope addressed to Hansen. She took it and opened it. The letter was typed and its tone was not gentle. It contained two thousand baht.

"As an old friend of Father Vernon," I had written, using the wordcode familiar to him, "I must advise you that you are in breach of your contract with our company. You have assaulted a Thai citizen and your girlfriend is an illegal Cambodian immigrant. We may have no alternative but to pass this information to the authorities. My car is parked across the street. Give the enclosed money to the Mama San as payment to release you for the night, and join me in ten minutes."

She left the cubicle, taking the letter with her. I had not realised till then how much noise there was in the corridor: the jangling music, the tinny laughter, the grumbles of desire, the swish of water down the ramshackle pipes.

I had left the car unlocked and he was sitting in the back, the girl beside him. Somehow I had not doubted he would bring the girl. He was big and powerful, which I knew already, and haggard. In the half darkness, with his black beard and hollowed eyes and his flattened hands curled tensely over the back of the passenger seat, he resembled one of the saints he had once worshipped, rather than the photographs on his file. The girl sat slumped and close to him, sheltering against his body. We had not gone a hundred metres before a rainburst crashed on us like a waterfall. I pulled in to the kerb while each of us stared through the drenched windscreen, watching the torrents of water swarm over the gutters and potholes.

"How did you get to Thailand?" I yelled in Dutch. The rain was thundering on the roof.

"I walked," Hansen replied in English.

"Where did you come over?" I yelled, in English also.

He mentioned a town. It sounded like "Orania Prathet." The downpour ended and I drove for three hours while the girl dozed and Hansen sat guard over her, alert as a cat, and as silent. I had selected a beach hotel advertised in the Bangkok *Nation*. I wanted to get him out of his own setting, into one that I controlled. I drew the key and paid a night's lodging in advance. Hansen and the girl followed me down a concrete path to the beach. The bungalows stood in a half ring facing the sea. Mine was at one end. I unlocked the door and went ahead of them. Hansen followed, after him the girl. I switched on the light and the air-conditioning. The girl hovered near the door, but Hansen kicked off his shoes and placed himself at the centre of the room, casting round him with his hollowed eyes.

"Sit down," I said. I pulled open the refrigerator door. "Does she want a drink?" I asked.

"Give her a Coca-Cola," said Hansen. "Ice. Got any limes in there?"

"No."

He watched me on my knees in front of the refrigerator.

"How about you?" I asked.

"Water."

I searched again: glasses, mineral water, ice. As I did so, I heard Hansen say something tender to the girl in Khmer. She protested and he overrode her. I heard him go into the bedroom and come out again. Climbing to my feet, I saw the girl curled on the daybed that ran along one wall of the room, and Hansen bending over her with a blanket, tucking her up. When he had finished, he switched out the lamp above her and touched her cheek with his fingertips before striding to the French window to stare at the sea. A full red moon hung above the horizon. The rainclouds made black mountains across the sky.

"What's your name?" he asked me.

"Mark," I said.

"Is that your real name? Mark?"

The surest knowledge we have of one another comes from instinct. As I watched Hansen's figure framed in the window and gazing out to sea, and the moonlight picking out the lines and hollows of his ravaged face, I knew that the lapsed priest had appointed me his confessor.

"Call me whatever you like," I said.

You must think of a strong but uneasy English voice, the tone rich, the manner shocked, as if its owner never expected it to say the things he is hearing. The slight accent is East Indian Dutch. The bungalow is unlit, designed for fornication, and gives on to a tiny illuminated swimming pool and concrete rockery. Beyond this nonsense lies a superb and placid Asian sea, with a wide moon-path, and stars sparkling in the water like sunspots. A couple of fishermen stand upright in their sampans, tossing their round nets into the water and drawing them slowly out again.

In the foreground you must set the jagged, towering figure of Hansen as he prowls the room in his bare feet, now pausing at the French window, now perching himself on the arm of a chair before slipping soundlessly away to another corner. And always the voice, now fierce, now ruminative, now shaken, and now, like his body, resting itself for minutes on end while it gathers strength for the next ordeal.

Stretched on her daybed, the Cambodian girl lies wrapped in a blanket, her forearm crooked Asian style beneath her head. Was she awake? Did she understand what he was saying? Did she care? Hansen cared. He could not pass her without stopping to gaze down at her, or fiddle with the blanket at her neck. Once, dropping to the floor beside her, he stared ardently into her closed eyes while he laid his palm on her brow as if to test her temperature.

"She needs limes," he murmured. "Coca-Cola is nothing for her. Limes."

I had sent out for them already. They arrived, by hand of a boy from the front desk. There was business while Hansen squeezed them for her, then held her upright while she drank.

His first questions were a vague catechism about my standing in the Service. He wished to know with what authority I had been sent, with what instructions.

"I want no thanks for what I have done," he warned me. "There are no thanks for bombing villages."

"But you may need help," I said.

His response was to tell me formally that he would never again, in any circumstance, work for the Service. I could have told him that too, but I refrained. He had thought he was working for the British, he said, but he had been working for murderers. He had been another man when he did the things he did. He hoped the American pilots had been other men as well.

He asked after his sub-agents—the farmer so-and-so, the rice trader so-and-so. He asked about the staybehind network he had painstakingly built up against the certain day when the Khmer Rouge would break out of the jungle and help themselves to the cities, a thing that neither we nor the Americans, despite all the warnings, had ever quite believed would happen. But Hansen had believed it. Hansen was one of the warners. Hansen had told us time and again that Kissinger's bombs were dragon's teeth, even though Hansen had helped direct them to their targets.

"May I believe you?" he asked me when I assured him there had been no pattern of arrests among his sources.

"It's the truth," I said, responding to the supplication in his voice.

"Then I didn't betray them," he muttered in marvel. For a moment he sat and cupped his head in his hands, as if holding it together.

"If you were captured by the Khmer Rouge, nobody could expect you to stay silent, anyway," I said.

"Silent! My God." He almost laughed. "Silent!" And, standing sharply, he swung away to the window again.

By the moonlight I saw tears of sweat clinging to his great bearded face. I started to say something about the Service wishing to acquit itself honourably by him, but halfway through my speech he flung out his arms to their fullest extent, as if testing the limits of his confinement. Finding nothing to obstruct them, they fell back to his sides.

"The Service to hell," he said softly. "The West to bloody, bloody hell. We have no business making our wars here, peddling our religious recipes. We have sinned against Asia: the French, the British, the Dutch, now the Americans. We have sinned against the children of Eden. God forgive us."

My tape recorder lay on the table.

We are in Asia. Hansen's Asia. The Asia sinned against. Listen to the frenetic chatter of the insects. Thais and Cambodians alike have been known to bet large sums on the number of times a bullfrog will burp. The room is twilit, the hour forgotten, the room forgotten also; the moon has risen out of sight. The Vietnam War is back with us, and we are in the Cambodian jungle with Hansen, and modern comforts are few, unless we include the American bombers that circle miles above us, like patient hawks, waiting for the computers to tell them what to destroy next: for instance, a team of oxen whose urine has been misread by secret sensors as the exhaust fumes of a military convoy; for instance, children whose chatter has been mistaken for military commands. The sensors have been hidden by American commandos along the supply routes Hansen has indicated to them—but unfortunately the sensors are not as well informed as Hansen is.

We are in what the American pilots call badland, though in the jungle definitions of good and bad are fluid. We are in a Khmer Rouge "liberated area" that provides sanctuary for Vietcong troops who wish to attack the Americans in the flank rather than head-on from the north. Yet despite these appearances of war, we are among people with no collective perception of their enemies, in a region unmapped except by fighters. To hear Hansen speak, the region is as close to paradise as makes no difference, whether he speaks as priest, sinner, scholar or spy.

A few miles up the trail by jeep is an ancient Buddhist temple which, with the help of villagers, Hansen has excavated from the depths of vegetation, and which is the apparent reason for his being there, and for the notes he takes, and for the wireless messages he sends, and for the trickle of visitors who arrive usually just before nightfall, and depart at first light. The kampong where he lives is built on stilts in a clearing at the edge of a good river, in a plain of fertile fields that climb in steps to a rain forest. A blue mist is frequent. Hansen's house is set high up the slope in order to improve his radio reception and give a view of whatever enters and leaves the valley. In the wet season, it is his habit to leave the jeep in the village and trudge up to his house on foot. In the dry season, he drives into his compound, most often taking half the village children with him. As many as a dozen of them will be waiting to clamber over the tailboard for the five-minute ride from the village to his compound.

"Sometimes my daughter was among them," Hansen said.

Neither Rumbelow nor the file had mentioned that Hansen had a daughter. If he had hidden her from us, he was gravely in breach of Service rules—though heaven knows, Service rules were about the last thing that mattered to either of us by then. Nevertheless he stopped speaking and glared at me in the darkness as if waiting for my reproof. But I preserved my silence, wishing to be the ear he had been waiting for, perhaps for years.

"While I was still a priest, I visited the temples of Cambodia," he said. "While I was there, I fell in love with a village woman and made her pregnant. In Cambodia it was the best time still. Sihanouk ruled. I remained with her until the child was born. A girl. I christened her Marie. I gave the mother money and returned to

Djakarta, but I missed my child terribly. I sent more money. I sent money to the headman to look after them. I sent letters. I prayed for the child and her mother, and swore that one day I would care for them properly. As soon as I returned to Cambodia, I put the mother in my house, even though in the intervening years she had lost her beauty. My daughter had a Khmer name, but from the day she came to me I called her Marie. She liked that. She was proud to have me as her father."

He seemed concerned to make clear to me that Marie was at ease with her European name. It was not an American name, he said. It was European.

"I had other women in my household, but Marie was my only child and I loved her. She was more beautiful than I had imagined her. But if she had been ugly and ungracious I would have loved her no less." His voice acquired sudden strength and, as I heard it, warning. "No woman, no man, no child, ever claimed my love in such a way. You may say that Marie is the only woman I have loved purely except for my mother." He was staring at me in the darkness, challenging me to doubt his passion. But under Hansen's spell, I doubted nothing and had forgotten everything about myself, even my own mother's death. He was assuming me, occupying me.

"Once you have embarked upon the impossible concept of God, you will know that real love permits no rejection. Perhaps that is something only a sinner can properly understand. Only a sinner knows the scale of God's forgiveness."

I think I nodded wisely. I thought of Colonel Jerzy. I was wondering why Hansen needed to explain that he could not reject his daughter. Or why his sinfulness was a concern to him when he spoke of her.

"That evening when I drove home from the temple, there were no children waiting for me in the kampong, though it was the dry season. I was disappointed because we had made a good find that day and I wanted to tell Marie about it. They must be having a school festival, I thought, but I could not think which one. I drove up the hill to the compound and called her name. The compound was empty. The gatehouse empty. The women's cookpots empty under the stilts. I called Marie again, then my wife. Then anybody. No one came. I drove back to the village. I went into the house of one of Marie's friends, then another and another, calling Marie. Even the pigs and chickens had disappeared. I looked for blood, for traces of fighting. There were none. But I found footprints leading into the jungle. I drove back to the compound. I took a spade and cached my radio in the forest, halfway between two tall trees that made a line due west, close to an old ant-hill shaped like a man. I hated all my work for you, all my lies, for you and for the Americans. I still do. I walked back to the house, uncached my codepads and equipment and destroyed them. I was glad to. I hated them also. I put on boots and filled a rucksack with food for a week. With my revolver I sent three bullets through the jeep's engine to immobilise it; then I followed the footprints into the jungle. The jeep was an insult to me, because you had bought it."

Alone, Hansen had set off in pursuit of the Khmer Rouge. Other men—even men who were not Western spies—might have thought twice and a third time, even with their wife and daughter taken hostage. Not Hansen. Hansen had one thought and, absolutist that he was, he acted on it.

"I could not allow myself to be separated from God's grace," he said. He was telling me, in case I did not know, that beyond the girl's survival lay the survival of his immortal soul.

* * *

I asked him how long he had marched for. He didn't know. To begin with he had marched only at night and lain up by day. But the daylight gnawed at him and gradually, against all jungle sense, it drew him forward. As he marched, he recalled every event of Marie's life from the night when he had lifted her from her mother's womb and, with a ritual bamboo stave, cut the cord and ordered the women in attendance to give him water so that he could wash her; and with the water, by his authority as priest and father, had christened her Marie after his own mother and the mother of Christ.

He remembered the nights when she had lain sleeping in his arms or in the rush crib at his feet. He saw her at her mother's breast in the firelight. He flailed himself for the dreadful years of separation in Djakarta and on his training course in England. He flailed himself for all the falsity of his work for the Service, and for his weakness, as he described it, his treachery against Asia. He was referring to his work of directing the American bombers.

He relived the hours he had spent telling her stories and singing her to sleep with English and Dutch songs. He cared only for his love for her, and his need of her, and for her need of him.

He was following the tracks because he had nothing else to follow. He knew now what had happened. It had happened to other kampongs, though none in Hansen's region. The fighters had surrounded the kampong at night and waited till dawn, when the able-bodied left for the fields. They had taken the able-bodied, then crept into the village and taken the elderly and the children, afterwards the livestock. They were provisioning themselves but they were also adding to their ranks. They were in a hurry or they would have ransacked the houses, but they wanted to return to the jungle before they were discovered. Soon, by the light of a full moon, Hansen came upon the first grisly proofs of his theory: the naked bodies of an old storekeeper and his wife, their hands bound behind their backs. Had they been unable to keep up? Were they too ugly? Had they argued?

Hansen marched faster. He was thanking God that Marie looked like a full Asian. In most children of mixed blood, the European strain would have been there for every Asian to see, but Hansen, though a giant, was dark-skinned and slim-bodied, and somehow with his Asian soul he had succeeded in engendering an Asian girl.

Next night another corpse lay beside the trail and Hansen approached it fearfully. It was Ong Sai, the argumentative schoolmistress. Her mouth was wide open. Shot while protesting, Hansen diagnosed, and pressed anxiously forward. In search of Marie, his pure love, the earth mother who was his daughter, the only keeper of his grace.

He wondered which sort of unit he was following. The shy boys who banged on your door at night to ask a little rice for the fighters? The grim-jawed cadres who regarded the Asian smile as an emblem of Western decadence? And there were the zombies, he remembered: freebooting packs of homeless who had clubbed together from necessity, more outlaws than guerrillas. But already in the group ahead of him he had an intimation of discipline. A less organised gang would have stayed to loot the village. They would have made camp to eat a meal and congratulate themselves. On the morning after he found Ong Sai, Hansen took special care to conceal himself while he slept.

"I had a premonition," he said.

In the jungle you ignored premonition at your peril. He buried himself deep in the undergrowth and smeared himself with mud. He slept with his revolver in his hand. He woke at evening to the smell of woodsmoke and the shrill sound of shouting, and when he opened his eyes he found himself looking straight into the barrels of several automatic rifles.

He was talking about the chains. Jungle fighters, trained to travel light, humping a dozen sets of manacles for hundreds of kilometres—how had it happened? He was still mystified. Yet somebody had carried them, somebody had made a clearing and driven a stake into the centre of the clearing, and dropped the iron rings round the stake, and attached the twelve sets of chains to the twelve iron rings in order to tether twelve special prisoners to the rain and heat and cold and dark. Hansen described the pattern of the chains. To do so, he broke into French. I assumed he needed the protection of a different language. "... *une tringle collective sur laquelle étaient enfilés des étriers ... nous étions fixés par un pied ... j'avais été mis au bout de la chaîne parce que ma cheville trop grosse ne passait pas ...*"

I glanced at the girl. She lay, if it were possible, more inert than before. She could have been dead or in a trance. I realised Hansen was sparing her something he did not want her to hear.

By day, he said, still in French, our ankles were released, enabling us to kneel and even crawl, though never far, because we were tethered to the stake and had each other's bodies to contend with. Only by night, when our foot irons were fixed to heavy poles that made up the circumference of the enclosure, were we able to stretch full length. The availability of chains determined the number of special prisoners, who were drawn exclusively from the village bourgeoisie, he said. He recognised two village elders, and a stringy forty-year-old widow called Ra who had a reputation for prophecy. And the three rice-dealing brothers Liu, who were famous misers, one of whom looked already dead, for he lay curled round his chains like a hairless hedgehog. Only the sound of his sobbing proved he was alive.

And Hansen, with his horror of captivity? How had he responded to his chains?

"*Je les ai portées pour Marie,*" he answered in the swift, warning French I was learning to respect.

The prisoners who were not special were confined to a stockade at the clearing's edge, from which at intervals one of them was led or dragged to headquarters, a place out of sight behind a hillock. Questioning was brief. After a few hours' screaming, a single pistol shot would ring out and the uneasy quiet of the jungle would return. Nobody came back from questioning. The children, including Marie, were allowed to roam provided they did not approach the prisoners or venture up the hillock which hid the headquarters. The boldest of them had already struck up an acquaintance with the young fighters during the march, and were scurrying around them trying to perform errands or touch their guns.

But Marie had stayed apart from everyone. She sat in the dust of the clearing on the other side of the poles, watching over her father from dawn till night. Even when they hauled her mother from the stockade and her screams for Hansen rang out from behind the hillock, changing to screams for mercy and ending with the usual pistol shot, Marie's eyes never flinched from Hansen's face.

"Did she know?" I asked in French.

"The whole camp knew," he replied.

"Had she been fond of her mother?"

Was it my imagination or had Hansen closed his eyes in the darkness?

"I was the father of Marie," he replied. "I was not the father of their relationship."

How had I known that the mother and daughter had hated each other? Was it because I sensed that Hansen's love for Marie had been a jealous and demanding one—absolute, like all his loves, excluding rivals?

"I was not allowed to speak to her, nor she to me," he was saying. "Prisoners spoke to nobody on pain of death."

Even a groan was enough, as one of the luckless Liu brothers learned when the guards reduced him to permanent silence with their rifle butts, and replaced him next morning with a cringing leftover from the stockade. But between Marie and her father no words were necessary. The stoicism Hansen saw in his daughter's face was the impassioned determination of his own heart as he lay bound and helpless in his chains. With Marie to support him, he could bear anything. Each would be the salvation of the other. Her love for him was as fierce and single-minded as his for her. He did not doubt it. For all his loathing of captivity, he thanked God he had followed her.

A day passed and another, but Hansen remained chained to the stake, burning in the sun, shaking in the evening cold, stinking in his own filth, his gaze and spirit fixed always upon Marie.

In his head, meanwhile, he was wrestling with the tactics of his situation.

From the start it had been clear to him that he was a celebrity. If they had been planning to capture a European, they would have made their attack before Hansen left his house, and searched the house afterwards. He was unexpected treasure, and they were waiting to hear what should be done with him. Others on the stake were fetched and disappeared, all but the one surviving Liu brother and the woman fortune teller, who after days of noisy questioning reappeared as camp trusties, abusing their former companions and trying by every means to ingratiate themselves with the soldiers.

An indoctrination class was formed, and each evening the children and selected survivors sat in a circle in the shade to be harangued by a young commissar with a red headband. While Hansen burned and froze, he could hear the commissar's shrill squawk, hour by hour, as he ranted against the hated imperialists. At first he resented these classes because they took Marie away from him. But when he made the effort, he could still lift his head high enough to see her straight body seated strictly at the far side of the circle, staring at him across the clearing. I will be your mother and your father and your friend, he told her. I will be your life, if I have to give up my own.

At other times he reproached himself with her spectacular beauty, regarding it as a punishment for his random lusts. Marie at twelve was without doubt the most beautiful in the camp, and though sex was forbidden to the cadres on the grounds that it was a bourgeois threat to their revolutionary will, Hansen could not help observe the effect that her thinly clothed figure had on the young fighters as they watched her pass; how their dulled eyes drank in her sprouting breasts and swinging haunches beneath the torn cotton frock, and their scowls darkened when they yelled at her. Worse still, he knew she was aware of their desire, and that her emerging womanhood responded to it.

Then a morning came when the routine of Hansen's captivity unaccountably improved, and his apprehensions deepened, for his benefactor was the young commissar in the red headband. Escorted by two soldiers, the commissar ordered Hansen to stand. When he was unable, the soldiers lifted him to his feet and, taking an arm each, let him stagger to a point along the river bank where an inlet made a natural pool.

"Wash," the young commissar ordered.

For days—ever since they had bound him—Hansen had been vainly demanding the right to clean himself. On his first evening he had roared at them, "Take me to the river!" They had beaten him. The next morning he had flung himself about on his chains, risking more beatings, yelling for a responsible comrade, all to assert his right to remain a person whom his captors could respect and consequently preserve.

Under the gaze of the soldiers, Hansen sufficiently rallied his racked limbs to bathe and—though it was a crucifixion—rub himself with the fine river mud before being led back to the stake. On each journey, he passed within a few feet of his beloved Marie in her habitual place beyond the ring of poles. Though his heart leapt at her nearness and the courage in her eyes, he could not suppress the suspicion that it was his own child who had purchased the rare comfort he was now enjoying. And when the commissar grunted a greeting to her, and Marie lifted her head and gave half a smile in return, the anguish of jealousy added itself to Hansen's pains.

After his bathe, they brought him rice—more than they had given him in all the time he had been their prisoner. And instead of making him eat it from the bowl like a dog, they untied his hands and let him use his fingers, so that he was able to secrete a small amount in his palm, and drop it down the front of his tunic before they chained him again.

All day long he thought of nothing but the pellet of rice inside his shirt, making sure no movement of his body crushed it. I will win her back, he thought. I will supplant the commissar in her admiration. When evening came and they again led him to the river, he achieved the miracle he had been planning. Staggering more dramatically than was necessary, he succeeded in dropping a pellet of rice at Marie's feet, unnoticed by his guards. As he passed by her again on his way back, he saw to his secret ecstasy that it had vanished.

Yet her face told him nothing. Only her eyes, straight and sometimes lifeless in their devotion, told him she returned his absolute love. I was deluding myself, he decided as they refastened his chains. She is learning the prisoner's tricks. She is chaste and will survive. That evening he listened with a new tolerance to the commissar's indoctrination class. Lead him on, he urged her in the telepathic dialogue he conducted with her constantly; lull him, bewitch him, gain his trust but give him nothing. And Marie must have heard him, because as the class broke up he saw the commissar beckon her over to him and rebuke her while she remained cowed and silent. He saw her head fall forward. He saw her walk away from him, her head still lowered.

Next day and for a week, Hansen repeated his trick, convinced he was unobserved except by Marie. The pellet of rice, rolling lightly over his stomach each time he shifted his body, became a source of vital comfort to him. *I am nourishing her from my own breast. I am her guardian, the protector of her chastity. I am her priest, giving her Christ's Sacrament.*

The rice was all that mattered to him. His concern was to contrive new ways to smuggle it to her, waiting till he was past her and flicking the pellet backward, letting it fall down the inside of his tattered trouser leg.

"I was inordinate," he said softly, in the tone of a penitent.

And because he had been inordinate, God took Marie from him. Suddenly one morning when they unchained him and led him to the pool, there was no Marie waiting to receive her Sacrament. At the evening indoctrination class, he saw that she had been elevated to the commissar's side, and he thought he heard her voice above the rest, intoning the liturgical responses with a new self-confidence. When night fell, he picked out her silhouette among the soldiers' fires—an accepted member of their company, sharing their rice like a comrade. Next day he did not see her at all, nor the day after.

"I wished to die," he said.

But in the evening as he waited in despair, prone and motionless, for the guards to chain his feet, it was the young commissar who marched towards him, and Marie, dressed in a black tunic, who trotted at his side.

"Is this man your father?" the commissar asked as they reached Hansen.

Marie's stare did not falter, but she seemed to be searching her memory for her reply. "Angka is my father," she said finally. "Angka is the father of all oppressed."

"Angka was the Party," Hansen explained for me, without my asking. "Angka was the Organisation that the Khmer Rouge prayed to. In the Khmer Rouge's ladder of beings, Angka was God."

"So who is your mother?" the commissar asked Marie.

"My mother is Angka. I have no mother but Angka."

"Who is this man?"

"He is an American agent," Marie replied. "He drops bombs on our villages. He kills our workers."

"Why does he pretend he is your father?"

"He wishes to trick us by claiming to be our comrade."

"Test the spy's chains. See that they are tight enough," the commissar commanded.

Marie knelt to Hansen's feet, exactly as he had taught her to kneel in prayer. For a moment, like the healing touch of Christ, her hand closed over his festering ankles.

"Can you insert your fingers between the chain and ankle?" the commissar asked.

In his panic, Hansen behaved as he always did when his feet were being chained. He flexed his ankle muscles, hoping to give himself more freedom when he relaxed. He felt her finger probe the chain.

"I can insert my little finger," she replied, holding it up while she kept her body in the line of sight between the commissar and Hansen's feet.

"Can you insert it with difficulty or easily?"

"I can insert my finger only with difficulty," she lied.

Watching them march away, Hansen noticed something that alarmed him. With her black tunic, Marie had put on the stealthy waddle of the jungle fighter. All the same, for the first time since his capture, Hansen slept soundly in his chains. She is joining them in order to deceive them, he assured himself. God is protecting us. Soon we shall escape.

The official interrogator arrived by boat, a smooth-cheeked student with an earnest, frowning manner. In Hansen's mind, that was how he named him: the student. A reception committee led by the commissar met him at the river bank and escorted him over the hillock to headquarters. Hansen knew he was the interrogator because he was the only one who did not turn his head to look at the last remaining prisoner rotting in the heat. But he looked at Marie. He stopped in front of her, obliging everybody to stop with him. He stood before her; he held his studious face close to her while he asked her questions Hansen could not hear. He kept it there while he listened to her parrot answers. My daughter is the camp whore, thought Hansen in despair. But was she? Nothing he had ever heard about the Khmer Rouge suggested they appointed or even tolerated prostitutes in their midst. Everything suggested the contrary. *"Angka haït le sexuel,"* a French anthropologist had said to him once.

Then they are ravishing her with their puritanism, he decided. They have locked her to them in a passion that is worse than a debauching. He lay with his face in the earth, praying to be allowed to take her sins of innocence upon himself.

I have no coherent picture of Hansen's interrogation for the reason he had little himself. I remembered my own treatment at the hands of Colonel Jerzy, and it was child's play by comparison. But Hansen's recollections had the same imprecision. That they tortured him goes without saying. They had built a wooden grid for the purpose. Yet they were also concerned to keep him alive, because between sessions they gave him food and even, if he remembered rightly, allowed him visits to the river bank, though it may have been a single visit broken by spells of unconsciousness.

There were also the sessions of writing, for in the literal mind of the student, no confession was real until it was written down. And the writing grew harder and harder and became a punishment in itself, even though they unstrapped him from the grid to make him do it.

As an interrogator, the student seems to have proceeded simultaneously on two intellectual fronts. When he was checked on the one, he shifted to the other.

You are an American spy, he said, and an agent of the counter-revolutionary puppet Lon Nol, also an enemy of the revolution. Hansen disagreed.

But you're also a Roman Catholic masquerading as a Buddhist, a poisoner of minds, a promoter of anti-Party superstitions, and a saboteur of the popular enlightenment, the student screamed at him.

In general, the student seems to have preferred making statements to asking questions: "You will now please give all dates and places of your conspiratorial meetings with the counter-revolutionary puppet and American spy Lon Nol, naming all Americans present."

Hansen insisted that no such meetings had occurred. But this gave the student no satisfaction. As the agony increased, Hansen recalled the names from an English folksong that his mother had used to sing him: Tom Pearse . . . Bill Brewer . . . Jan Stewer . . . Peter Gurney . . . Peter Davey . . . Dan'l Whiddon . . . Harry Hawk . . .

"You will now please write down the ringleader of this rabble," the student said, turning a page of his notebook. The student's eyes, said Hansen, were often nearly closed. I remembered that about Jerzy too.

"Cobbleigh," Hansen whispered, lifting his head from the desk where they had sat him. *Thomas Cobbleigh,* he wrote. *Tom for short. Covername Uncle.*

The dates were important because Hansen was concerned he would forget them once he had invented them, and be accused of inconsistency. He chose Marie's birthday and his mother's birthday and the date of his father's execution. He altered the year to suit Lon Nol's accession to power. For a conspiratorial place, he selected the walled gardens of Lon Nol's palace in Phnom Penh, which he had often admired on his way to a favourite *fumerie.*

His fear while he was confessing to this rubbish was that he would reveal true information by mistake, for it was by now clear to him that the student knew nothing about his real intelligence-gathering activities, and that the charges against him were based on the fact that he was a Westerner.

"You will please write down the name of each spy paid by you in the last five years, also each act of sabotage committed by you against the people."

Not in all the days and nights that Hansen had passed anticipating his ordeal had he imagined he might fail on the score of creativity. He recited the names of martyrs whose agonies he had contemplated in order to prepare himself; of Oriental scholars safely dead; of authors of learned works on philology and linguistics. Spies, he said. All spies. And wrote them down, his hand jerking on the paper to the convulsions of the pain that continued to rack him long after they switched off the machine.

Writing desperately, he made a list of T. E. Lawrence's officers in the desert, which he remembered from his many readings of *The Seven Pillars of Wisdom.* He described how on Lon Nol's personal orders he had organised the poisoning of crops and cattle by Buddhist priests. The student put him back on the grid and increased the pain.

He described the clandestine classes he had held in imperialism, and how he had encouraged the spread of bourgeois sentiment and family virtues. The student opened his eyes, offered his commiserations and again increased the pain.

He gave them nearly everything. He described how he had lit beacons to guide American bombers, and distributed rumours that the bombers were Chinese. He was on the brink of telling them who had helped him to lead American commandos to the supply trails, when mercifully he fainted.

But throughout his ordeal it was still Marie with whom he lived in his heart, to whom he cried out in his pain, whose hands drew him back to life when his body was begging to relinquish it, whose eyes watched over him in love and pity. It was Marie to whom he sacrificed his suffering and for whom he swore to survive. As he lay between life and death, he had an hallucination in which he saw himself stretched out in the well of the student's boat and Marie in her black tunic seated over him, paddling them upriver to Heaven. But he still was not dead. They have not killed me. I have confessed to everything and they have not killed me.

But he had not confessed to everything. He had remained true to his helpers and he had not told them about his radio. And when they dragged him back next day and strapped him once more to the grid, he saw Marie sitting at the student's side, a copy of his confession lying before her on the table. Her hair was cropped, her expression closed.

"Are you familiar with the statements of this spy?" the student asked her.

"I am familiar with his statements," she replied.

"Do the spy's statements accurately depict his lifestyle as you were able to observe it in his company?"

"No."

"Why not?" the student asked, opening his notebook.

"They are not complete."

"Explain why the spy Hansen's statements are not complete."

"The spy Hansen kept a radio in his house which he used for signalling to the imperialist bombers. Also the names he has mentioned in his confession are fictitious. They are taken from a bourgeois English song which he sang to me when he was pretending to be my father. Also he received imperialist soldiers at our house at night and led them into the jungle. Also he has failed to mention that he has an English mother."

The student appeared disappointed. "What else has he failed to mention?" he asked, flattening a fresh page with the edge of his small hand.

"During his confinement, he has been guilty of many breaches of regulation. He has hoarded food and attempted to buy the collaboration of comrades in his plans to escape."

The student sighed and made more notes. "What else has he failed to mention?" he asked patiently.

"He has been wearing his foot chains improperly. When the chains were being fastened, he braced his feet illegally, leaving the chains loose for his escape."

Until that moment Hansen had managed to persuade himself that Marie was playing a cunning game. No longer. The game was the reality.

"He is a whoremonger!" she screamed through her tears. "He debauches our women by bringing them to his house and drugging them! He pretends to make a bourgeois marriage, then forces his wife to tolerate his decadent practices! He sleeps with girls of my own age! He pretends he is the father of our children and that our blood is not Khmer! He reads us bourgeois literature in Western languages in order to deprave us! He seduces us by taking us for rides in his jeep and singing imperialist songs to us!"

He had never heard her scream before. Nor evidently had the student, who appeared embarrassed. But she would not be checked. She persisted in denying him. She told them how he had forbidden her mother to love her. She was expressing a hatred for him that he knew was unfeigned, as absolute and inordinate as his love for her. Her body shook with the pent-up hatred of a misused woman, her features were crumpled with hatred and guilt. Her arm struck out and she pointed at him in the classic posture of accusation. Her voice belonged to someone he had never known.

"Kill him!" she screamed. "Kill the despoiler of our people! Kill the corrupter of our Khmer blood! Kill the Western liar who tells us we are different from one another! Avenge the people!"

The student made a last note and ordered Marie to be led away.

"I prayed for her forgiveness," Hansen said.

In the bungalow, I realised, it was dawn. Hansen was standing at the window, his eyes fixed on the misty plateau of the sea. The girl lay on the daybed where she had lain all night, her eyes closed, the empty Coca-Cola can beside her, her head still supported by her arm. Her hand, hanging down, looked worn and elderly. A terseness had entered Hansen's voice, and for a moment I feared that with morning he had decided to resent me. Then I realised it was not me he was at odds with but himself. He was remembering his anger as they carried him, bound but not chained, to the stockade to sleep—if sleep is what you do when your body is dying of pain, and the blood is filling your ears and nose. Anger against himself, that he had implanted in his child so much loathing.

"I was her father still," he said in French. "I blamed Marie for nothing, myself for everything. If only I had made my escape earlier, instead of counting on her to help me. If only I had fought my way out when I was strong, instead of placing my reliance in a child. I should never have worked for you. My secret work had endangered her. I cursed you all. I still do."

Did I speak? My concern was to say nothing that would obstruct his flow.

"She was drawn to them," he said, making her excuses for her. "They were her own people, jungle fighters with a faith to die for. Why should she reject them?"

"I was the last obstacle to her acceptance by her people," he said, explaining her. "I was an intruder, a corrupter. Why should she believe I was her father when they were telling her I was not?"

Still lying in the stockade, he remembered her on the day the young commissar dressed her in her bridal black. He remembered her expression of distaste as she stared down at him, fouled and beaten, a beggar at her feet, a cringing Western spy. And beside her, the handsome commissar with his red headband. "I am wedded to the Angka," she was saying to him. "The Angka answers all my questions."

"I was alone," he said.

Darkness fell in the stockade, and he supposed that if they were going to shoot him they would wait for daylight. But the notion that Marie would go through life knowing she had ordered her father's death appalled him. He imagined her in middle age. Who would help her? Who would confess her? Who would give her release and absolution? The idea of his death became increasingly alarming to him. It will be her death too.

At some point he must have dozed, he said, for when dawn came he found a bowl of rice on the floor of the stockade and he knew it had not been there the night before; even in his agony he would have smelt it. Not rolled into pellets, the rice, not hoarded against the naked skin, but a white mound of it, enough for five days. At first he was too tired to be surprised. Lying on his stomach to eat, he noticed the quiet. By this hour the clearing should have been alive with the sounds of soldiers waking for the day: singsong voices and washing noises from the river bank, the clatter of pans and rifles, the chant of slogans led by the commissar. Yet when he paused to listen, even the birds and monkeys seemed to have stopped their shrieking and he heard no human sounds at all.

"They had gone," he said, from somewhere behind me. "They had decamped in the night, taking Marie with them."

He ate more rice and dozed again. Why have they not killed me? Marie has talked them out of it. Marie has bought me my life. Hansen set to work chafing his bonds against the wall of the stockade. By nightfall, covered in sores and flies, he was lying on the river bank, washing his wounds. He crawled back to the stockade to sleep, and next morning, with the remainder of his rice, he set off. This time, having no prisoners or livestock, they had left no tracks.

All the same, he went in search of her.

For months, Hansen thinks five or six, he remained in the jungle, moving from village to village, never settling, trusting no one—I suspect a little crazed. Wherever he could, he enquired after Marie's unit, but there was too little to describe it by and his quest became indiscriminate. He heard of units that had fighting girls. He heard of units that consisted of girls only. He heard of girls being sent into the towns as whores to gather information. He imagined Marie in all these situations. One night he crept back to his old house hoping she had taken refuge there. The village had been burned.

I asked him whether his cached wireless had been disturbed.

"I didn't look," he replied. "I didn't care. I hated you all."

Another night he called on Marie's aunt, who lived in a remote village, but she hurled pans at him and he had to flee. Yet his determination to rescue his daughter was stronger than ever, for he knew now that he must rescue her from herself. She is cursed with my absolutism, he thought. She is violent and headstrong; it is I who am to blame. I have locked her in the prison of my own impulses. Only a father's love could ever have blinded him to this knowledge. Now his eyes were open. He saw her drawn to cruelty and inhumanity as a means of proving her devotion. He saw her reliving his own erratic quest, yet deprived of his intellectual and religious disciplines—vaguely believing, like himself, that her assumption into a great vision would bring her self-fulfilment.

Of his walk to the Thai border he said little. He headed south-west towards Pailin. He had heard there was a camp there for Khmer refugees. He crossed mountains and malarial marshes. Once arrived, he besieged the tracing centres and pinned her description on camp noticeboards. How he achieved this without papers, money or connections, yet kept his presence in Thailand secret, is a mystery to me still. But Hansen was a trained and hardened agent, even if he denied us. He was not disposed to let much stop him. I asked why he did not turn to Rumbelow for help, but he shook off the idea contemptuously.

"I was not an imperialist agent any more. I believed in nothing but my daughter."

One day in the office of a relief organisation, he met an American woman who thought she remembered Marie.

"She left," she said cautiously.

Hansen pressed her. Marie was one of a group of half a dozen girls, said the woman. They were whores but they had the assurance of fighters. When they were not entertaining men, they kept themselves apart from everyone and were tough to handle. One day they broke bounds. She had heard they were picked up by the Thai police. She never saw them again.

The woman who said this appeared unsure whether to say what else was on her mind, but Hansen gave her no choice.

"We were afraid for her," she said. "She gave different names for herself. She gave conflicting accounts of how she came to us. The doctors argued over whether she was mad. Somewhere along her journey, she had lost track of who she was."

Hansen presented himself to the Thai police and, by threats or animal persuasion, traced Marie to a police hostel run for the enjoyment of the officers. They never asked him who he was, it seems, or what he had for papers. He was a round-eye, a *farang*, who spoke Khmer and Thai. Marie had stayed three months, then vanished, they said. She was strange, said a kindly sergeant.

"What is strange?" Hansen asked.

"She would speak only English," the sergeant replied.

There was another girl, a friend of Marie's, who had stayed longer and married one of the corporals. Hansen obtained her name.

He had ceased speaking.

"And did you find her?" I asked after a long silence.

I knew the answer already, as I had known it from halfway through his story, without knowing that I knew. He was sitting at the girl's head, which he was gently stroking. Slowly she sat upright and with her little, old hands rubbed her eyes, pretending she had been asleep. I think she had listened to us all night.

"It was all she understood any more," Hansen explained in English, while he continued to stroke her head. He was speaking of the brothel where he had found her. "She wanted no big choices, did you, Marie? No big words, no promises." He pressed her to him. "She wishes only to be admired. By her own people. By us. All of us must love Marie. That is what comforts her."

I think he mistook my reticence for reproach, for his voice rose. "She wishes to be harmless. Is that so bad? She wishes to be left alone, as all of them wish. It would be a good thing if more of us wished the same. Your bombers and your spies and your big talk are not for her. She is not the child of Dr. Kissinger. She asks only for a small existence where she can give pleasure and hurt no one. Which is worse? Your brothel or hers? Get out of Asia. You should never have come, any of you. I am ashamed I ever helped you. Leave us alone."

"I shall tell Rumbelow very little of this," I said as I rose to leave.

"Tell him what you like."

From the doorway, I took a last look at them. The girl was staring at me as I believe she had stared at Hansen from outside the circle of chains, her eyes unflinching, deep and still. I thought I knew what was in her mind. I had paid for her and not had her. She was wondering whether I wanted my money's worth.

Rumbelow drove me to the airport. Like Hansen, I would have preferred to do without him, but we had matters to discuss.

"You promised him *how* much?" he cried in horror.

"I told him he was entitled to a resettlement grant and all the protection we can give him. I told him you would be sending him a cashier's cheque for fifty thousand dollars."

Rumbelow was furious. "*Me* give *him* fifty thousand dollars? My dear man, he'll be drunk for six months and spill his life story all over Bangkok. What about that Cambodian whore of his? She's in the know, I'll bet."

"Don't worry," I said. "He turned me down."

This news astonished Rumbelow so profoundly that he ran out of indignation altogether, preserving instead a wounded silence that lasted us the rest of the journey.

On the plane I drank too much and slept too little. Once, waking from a bad dream, I was guilty of a seditious thought about Rumbelow and the Fifth Floor. I wished I could pack off the whole tribe of them on Hansen's march into the jungle, Smiley included. I wished I could make them throw everything over for a flawed and impossible passion, only to see the object of it turn against them, proving there is no reward for love except the experience of loving, and nothing to be learned by it except humility.

Yet I was content, as I am content to this day whenever I think of Hansen. I had found what I was looking for—a man like myself, but one who in his search for meaning had discovered a worthwhile object for his life; who had paid every price and not counted it a sacrifice; who was paying it still and would pay it till he died; who cared nothing for compromise, nothing for his pride, nothing for ourselves or the opinion of others; who had reduced his life to the one thing that mattered to him, and was free. The slumbering subversive in me had met his champion. The would-be lover in me had found a scale by which to measure his own trivial preoccupations.

So that when a few years later I was appointed Head of the Russia House, only to watch my most valuable agent betray his country for his love, I could never quite muster the outrage required of me by my masters. Personnel was not all stupid when he packed me off to the Interrogators' Pool.

10

Maggs, my unpleasing crypto journalist, was trying to draw Smiley on the amoral nature of our work. He was wanting Smiley to admit that anything went, as long as you got away with it. I suspect he was actually wanting to hear this maxim applied to the whole of life, for he was ruthless as well as mannerless, and wished to see in our work some kind of licence to throw aside his few remaining scruples.

But Smiley would not give him this satisfaction. At first he appeared ready to be angry, which I hoped he would be. If so, he checked himself. He started to speak, but stopped again, and faltered, leaving me wondering whether it was time to call a halt to the proceedings. Until, to my relief, he rallied, and I knew he had merely been distracted by some private memory among the thousands that made up his secret self.

"You see," he explained—replying, as so often, to the spirit rather than the letter of the question—"it really is essential in a free society that the people who do our work should remain unreconciled. It's true that we are obliged to sup with the Devil, and not always with a very long spoon. And as everyone knows—" a sly glance at Maggs produced a gust of grateful laughter—"the Devil is often far better company than the Godly, isn't he? All the same, our obsession with virtue won't go away. Self-interest is so *limiting*. So is expediency." He paused again, still deep inside his own thoughts. "All I'm really saying, I suppose, is that if the temptation to humanity does assail you now and then, I hope you won't take it as a weakness in yourselves, but give it a fair hearing."

The cufflinks, I thought, in a flash of inspiration. George is remembering the old man.

For a long time I could not fathom why the story had continued to haunt me for so long. Then I realised I had happened upon it at a period when my relationship with my son Adrian had hit a low point. He was talking of not bothering with university, and getting himself a well-paid job instead. I mistook his restlessness for materialism and his dreams of independence for laziness, and one night I lost my temper and insulted him, and was duly ashamed of myself for weeks thereafter. It was during one of those weeks that I unearthed the story.

Then I remembered also that Smiley had had no children, and that perhaps his ambiguous part in the affair was to some extent explained by this. I was slightly chilled by the thought that he might have been filling an emptiness in himself by redressing a relationship he had never had.

Finally I remembered that just a few days after coming upon the papers, I had received the letter that anonymously denounced poor Frewin as a Russian spy. And that there were certain mystical affinities between Frewin and the old man, to do with dogged loyalty and lost worlds. All this for context, you understand, for I never knew a case yet that was not made up of a hundred others.

Finally there was the fact that, as so often in my life, Smiley turned out once again to have been my precursor, for I had no sooner settled myself at my unfamiliar desk in the Interrogators' Pool than I found his traces everywhere: in our dusty archives, in backnumbers of our duty officer's log and in the reminiscent smiles of our senior secretaries, who spoke of him with the old vestal's treacly awe, part as God, part as teddy bear and part—though they were always quick to gloss over this aspect of his nature—as killer shark. They would even show you the bone-china cup and saucer by Thomas Goode of South Audley Street—where else?—a present to George from Ann, they explained dotingly, which George had bequeathed to the Pool after his reprieve and rehabilitation to Head Office—and, of course, like the Grail itself, the Smiley cup could never possibly be *drunk* from by a mere mortal.

The Pool, if you have not already gathered as much, is by way of being the Service's Siberia, and Smiley, I was comforted to discover, had served out not one exile there but two: the first, for his gall in suggesting to the Fifth Floor that it might be nursing a Moscow Centre mole to its bosom; and the second, a few years later, for being right. And the Pool has not only the monotony of Siberia but its remoteness also, being situated not in the main building but in a run of cavernous offices on the ground floor of a gabled pile in Northumberland Avenue at the northern end of Whitehall.

And, like so much of the architecture around it, the Pool has seen great days. It was set up in the Second World War to receive the offerings of strangers, to listen to their suspicions and calm their fears or—if they had indeed stumbled on a larger truth—misguide or scare them into silence.

If you thought you had glimpsed your neighbour late at night, for instance, crouched over a radio transmitter; if you had seen strange lights winking from a window and were too shy or untrusting to inform your local police station; if the mysterious foreigner on the bus who questioned you about your work had reappeared at your elbow in your local pub; if your secret lover confessed to you—out of loneliness or bravado or a desperate need to make himself more interesting in your eyes—that he was working for the German Secret Service—why then, after a correspondence with some spurious assistant to some unheard-of Whitehall Under-Secretary, you would quite likely, of an early evening, be summoned to brave the blitz, and find yourself being guided heart-in-mouth down the flaking, sand-bagged corridor, on your way to Room 909, where a Major Somebody or a Captain Somebody Else, both bogus as three-dollar bills, would courteously invite you to state your matter frankly without fear of repercussion.

And occasionally, as the covert history of the Pool records, great things were born, and are still occasionally born today, of these inauspicious beginnings, though business is not a patch on what it used to be, and much of the Pool's work is now given over to such chores as unsolicited offers of service, anonymous denunciations like the one levelled at poor Frewin and even—in support of the despised security services—positive vetting enquiries, which are the worst Siberias of all, and about as far as you can get from the high-wire operations of the Russia House without quitting the Service altogether.

All the same, there is more than mere humility to be learned from these chastisements. An intelligence officer is nothing if he has lost the will to listen, and George Smiley, plump, troubled, cuckolded, unassuming, indefatigable George, forever polishing his spectacles on the lining of his tie, puffing to himself and sighing in his perennial distraction, was the best listener of us all.

Smiley could listen with his hooded, sleepy eyes; he could listen by the very inclination of his tubby body, by his stillness and his understanding smile. He could listen because with one exception, which was Ann, his wife, he expected nothing of his fellow souls, criticised nothing, condoned the worst of you long before you had revealed it. He could listen better than a microphone because his mind lit at once upon essentials; he seemed able to spot them before he knew where they were leading.

And that was how George had come to be listening to Mr. Arthur Wilfred Hawthorne of 12, The Dene, Ruislip, half a lifetime before me, in the very same Room 909 where I now sat, curiously turning the yellowed pages of a file marked "Destruction Pending" which I had unearthed from the shelves of the Pool's strongroom.

I had begun my quest idly—you may even say frivolously—much as one might pick up an old copy of the *Tatler* in one's club. And suddenly I realised I had stumbled on page after page of Smiley's familiar, guarded handwriting, with its sharp little German t's and twisted Greek e's, and signed with his legendary symbol. Where he was forced to appear in the drama in person—and you could feel him seeking any means to escape this vulgar ordeal—he referred to himself merely as "D.O.," short for Duty Officer. And since he was notorious for his hatred of initials, you are made once more aware of his reclusive, if not downright fugitive nature. If I had discovered a missing Shakespeare folio, I could not have been more excited. Everything was there: Hawthorne's original letter, transcripts of the microphoned interviews, initialled by Smiley himself, even Hawthorne's signed receipts for his travel money and out-of-pocket expenses.

My dull care was gone. My relegation no longer oppressed me, neither did the silence of the great empty house to which I was condemned. I was sharing them with George, waiting for the clip of Arthur Hawthorne's loyal boots as he was marched down the corridor and into Smiley's presence.

"Dear Sir," he had written to "The Officer in Charge of Intelligence, Ministry of Defence." And already, because we are British, his class is branded on the page —if only by the strangely imperious use of capitals so dear to uneducated people. I imagined much effort in the penning, and perhaps a dictionary at the elbow. "I wish, Sir, to Request an Interview with your Staff regarding a Person who has done Special Work for British Intelligence at the highest Level, and whose Name is as Important to my Wife and myself as it may be to your good Selves, and which I am accordingly forbidden to Mention in this Letter."

That was all. Signed "Hawthorne, A. W., Warrant Officer Class II, retired." Arthur Wilfred Hawthorne, in other words, as Smiley's researches revealed when he consulted the voters' list, and followed up his findings with an examination of the War Office files. Born 1915, Smiley painstakingly recorded on Hawthorne's personal particulars sheet. Enlisted 1939, served with the Eighth Army from Cairo to El Alamein. Ex-Sergeant Major Arthur Wilfred Hawthorne, twice wounded in battle, three commendations and one gallantry medal for his trouble, demobilised without a stain on his character, "the best example of the best fighting man in the world," wrote his commandant, in a glowing if hyperbolic commendation.

And I knew that Smiley, as a good professional, would have taken up his post well ahead of his client's arrival, just as I myself had done these last months: at the same scuffed yellow desk of wartime pine, singed brown along the leading edge— legend has it by the Hun; with the same mossy telephone, letters as well as numbers on the dial; the same hand-tinted photograph of the Queen, sitting on a horse when she was twenty. I see George frowning studiously at his watch, then pulling a sour face as he peered round him at the usual mess, for there had been a running battle for as long as anyone could remember about who was supposed to clean the place, the Ministry or ourselves. I see him tug a handkerchief from his sleeve—laboriously again, for no gesture ever came to George without a struggle—and wipe the grime off the seat of his wooden chair, then do the same in advance for Hawthorne on the other side of the desk. Then, as I had done myself a few times, perform a similar service for the Queen, setting her frame straight and bringing back the sparkle to her young, idealistic eyes.

For I imagined George already studying the feelings of his subject, as any good intelligence officer must. An ex-sergeant major would expect a certain order about him, after all. Then I see Hawthorne himself, punctual to the minute, as the janitor showed him in, his best suit buttoned like a battledress, the polished toecaps of his boots glistening like conkers in the gloom. Smiley's description of him on the encounter sheet was sparse but trenchant: height five seven, grey hair close cut, cleanshaven, groomed appearance, military bearing. Other characteristics: suppressed limp of the left leg, army boots.

"Hawthorne, sir," he snapped, and held himself to attention till Smiley with difficulty persuaded him to sit.

Smiley was Major Nottingham that day and had an impressive card with his photograph to prove it. In my pocket as I read his account of the case lay a similar card in the name of Colonel Ned Ascot. Don't ask me why Ascot except to note that, in choosing a place-name for my alias, I was yet again unconsciously copying one of Smiley's little habits.

"What regiment are you from, sir, if you don't mind my asking?" Hawthorne enquired of Smiley as he sat.

"The General List, I'm afraid," said Smiley, which is the only way we are allowed to answer.

But I am sure it came hard to Smiley, as it would to me, to have to describe himself as some kind of non-combatant.

As evidence of his loyalty, Hawthorne had brought his medals wrapped in a piece of gun cloth. Smiley obligingly went through them for him.

"It's about our son, sir," the old man said. "I've got to ask you. The wife—well, she won't hear of it any more, she says it's a load of his nonsense. But I told her I've got to ask you. Even if you refuse to answer, I told her, I won't have done my duty by my son if I didn't ask on his account."

Smiley said nothing but I am sure his silence was sympathetic.

"Ken was our only boy, you see, Major, so it's natural," said Hawthorne apologetically.

And still Smiley let him take his time. Did I not say he was a listener? Smiley could draw answers from you to questions he had never put, just by the sincerity of his listening.

"We're not asking for secrets, Major. We're not asking to know what can't be known. But Mrs. Hawthorne is failing, sir, and she needs to know whether it's true before she goes." He had prepared the question exactly. Now he put it. "Was our boy, or was he not—was Ken—in the course of what appeared to be a criminal career, operating behind enemy lines in Russia?"

And here you might say that for once I was ahead of Smiley, if only because after five years in the Russia House I had a pretty good idea of the operations we had conducted in the past. I felt a smile come to my face, and my interest in the story, if it was possible, increased.

But to Smiley's face, I am sure, came nothing at all. I imagine his features settling into a Mandarin immobility. Perhaps he fiddled with his spectacles, which always gave the impression of belonging to a larger man. Finally he asked Hawthorne— but earnestly, never a hint of scepticism—why he supposed this might be the case.

"Ken told me he was, sir, that's why." And still nothing on Smiley's side, except an ever-open door. "Mrs. Hawthorne wouldn't visit Ken in prison, you see. I would. Every month. He was doing five years for grievous bodily harm, plus three more for being habitual. We had PD in those days, preventive detention. We're in the prison canteen there, me and Ken, sitting together at a table. And suddenly Ken puts his head close to mine, and he says to me in this low voice he's got, 'Don't come here again, Dad. It's difficult for me. I'm not really locked up, you see. I'm in Russia. They had to bring me back special, just to show me to you. I'm working behind the lines, but don't tell Mum. Write to me—that's not a problem, they'll send it on. And I'll write back same as if I was a prisoner here, which is what I pretend to be, because you can't get better cover than a prison. But the truth is, Dad, I'm serving the old country just like you did when you was with the Desert Rats, which is why the best of us are put on earth.' I didn't ask to see Ken after that. I felt I had to obey orders. I wrote to him, of course. In the prison. Hawthorne and then his number. And three months later he'd write back on prison paper like it was a different boy writing to me every time. Sometimes the big heavy writing, like he was angry, sometimes small and quick, like he hadn't had the time. Once or twice there was even the foreign words in there that I didn't understand, crossed out mainly, like he was having difficulty with his own language. Sometimes he'd drop me a clue. 'I'm cold but safe,' he'd say. 'Last week I had a bit more exercise than I needed,' he'd say. I didn't tell the wife because he said I wasn't to. Besides, she wouldn't have believed him. When I offered her his letters, she pushed them away—they hurt too much. But when Ken died we went and saw his body all cut to pieces in the prison morgue. Twenty stab wounds and nobody to blame. She didn't weep, she doesn't, but they might as well have stabbed her. And on the way home on the bus I couldn't help it. 'Ken's a hero,' I said to her. I was trying to wake her up because she'd gone all wooden. I got hold of her by the sleeve and gave her a bit of a shake to make her listen. 'He's not a dirty convict,' I said. 'Not our Ken. He never was. And it wasn't convicts who done him in, either. It was the Red Russians.' I told her about the cufflinks too. 'Ken's romancing,' she said. 'Same as he always did. He doesn't know the difference, he never did, which has been his trouble all along.' "

Interrogators, like priests and doctors, have a particular advantage when it comes to concealing their feelings. They can ask another question, which is what I would have done myself.

"What cufflinks, Sergeant Major?" Smiley said, and I see him lowering his long eyelids and sinking his head into his neck as he once more prepared himself to listen to the old man's tale.

" 'There's no medals, Dad,' Ken says to me. 'Medals wouldn't be secure. You have to be gazetted to get a medal, there'd be too many in the know. Otherwise I'd have a medal same as you. Maybe an even better one, if I'm honest, like the Victoria Cross, because they stretch us as far as we can go and sometimes further. But if you do right in the job, you earn your cufflinks and they keep them for you in a special safe. Then once a year there's this big dinner at a certain place I'm not allowed to mention, with the champagne and butlers you wouldn't believe, and all us Russia boys go to it. And we put on our tuxedos and we wear the cufflinks, same as a uniform but secret. And we have this party, with the speeches and the handshakes, like a special investiture, same as you had for your medals, I expect, in this place I'm not allowed to mention. And when the party's over, we hand the cufflinks back. We have to, for the security. So if ever I go missing, or if something happens to me, just you write to them at the Secret Service and ask them for the Russia cufflinks for your Ken. Maybe they'll say they never heard of me, maybe they'll say, "What cufflinks?" But maybe they'll make you a compassionate exception and let you have them, because they sometimes do. And *if* they do—you'll know that everything I ever did wrong was more right than you can imagine. Because I'm my dad's boy, right down the line, and the cufflinks will prove it to you. That's all I'm saying, and it's more than I'm allowed.' "

Smiley asked first for the boy's full name. Then for the boy's date of birth. Then he asked about his schooling and qualifications, which were predictably dismal, both. I see him acting quiet and businesslike as he takes down the details: Kenneth Branham Hawthorne, the old soldier told him—Branham, that was his mother's maiden name, sir; he sometimes used it for what they called his crimes—born Folkestone, July 14, 1946, sir, twelve months after I came back from the war. I wouldn't have a child earlier, although the wife wanted it, sir, I didn't think it right. I wanted our boy brought up in peace, sir, with both his living parents to look after him, Major, which is the right of any child, I say, even if it's not as usual as it ought to be.

Smiley's next task was not half as easy as it might seem, whatever the improbabilities of Kenneth Hawthorne's story. Smiley was never one to deny a good man, or even a bad one, the benefit of the doubt. The Circus of those days possessed no such thing as a reliable central index of its resources, and what passed for one was shamefully and often deliberately incomplete, for rival outfits guarded their sources jealously and poached from their neighbours when they saw the chance.

True, the old man's story bristled with unlikelihoods. In purist terms it was grotesque, for example, to imagine a group of secret agents meeting once a year to dine, thus breaking the most elementary rule of "need to know." But worse things could happen in the lawless world of the irregulars, as Smiley was aware. And it took all his powers of ingenuity and persuasion to satisfy himself that Hawthorne was nowhere on their books: not as a runner, not as a lamplighter or a scalphunter, not as a signalman and not as any other of the beloved tradenames with which these seedy operators glamourised their ranks.

And when he had exhausted the irregulars he turned to the armed services, the security services and the Royal Ulster Constabulary, any one of which might conceivably have employed—if on some much more modest basis than the boy described—a violent criminal of Ken Hawthorne's character.

For one thing at least seemed certain: the boy's criminal record was a nightmare. It would have been hard to imagine a grimmer record of persistent and often bestial behaviour. As Smiley crossed and recrossed the boy's history, through childhood to adolescence, reform school to prison, there seemed to be no transgression, from pilfering to sadistic assault, that Kenneth Branham Hawthorne, born Folkestone 1946, had not stooped to.

Till at the end of a full week, Smiley appears reluctantly to have admitted to himself what in another part of his head he must have known all along. Kenneth Hawthorne, for whatever sad reasons, had been an unredeemable and habitual monster. The death he had suffered at the hands of his fellow prisoners was no more than he deserved. His past was written and complete, and his tales of heroism on behalf of some mythical British intelligence service were merely the last chapter in his lifelong effort to steal his father's glory.

It was mid-winter. It was a foul grey, sleet-driven evening on which to drag an old soldier back across London to a barren interviewing room in Whitehall. And Whitehall in the meagre lighting of those days was a citadel still at war, even if its guns were somewhere else. It was a place of military austerity, heartless and imperial; of lowered voices and blacked windows, of rare and hurried footsteps and averted eyes. Smiley was in the War too, remember, even if he was sitting behind

German lines. I can hear the puttering of the paraffin Aladdin stove which the Circus had grudgingly approved to supplement the faulty ministerial radiators. It has the sound of a wireless transmitter operated by a freezing hand.

Hawthorne had not come alone to hear Major Nottingham's reply. The old soldier had brought his wife, and I can even tell you how she looked, for Smiley had written of her in his log and my imagination has long painted in the rest.

She had a buckled sick body wrapped in Sunday best. She wore a brooch in the design of her husband's regimental badge. Smiley invited her to sit, but she preferred her husband's arm. Smiley stood across the desk from them, the same burned, yellowed desk where I had sat in exile these last months. I see him standing almost to attention, with his rounded shoulders uncharacteristically straightened, his stubby fingers curled at the seams of his trousers in traditional army manner.

Ignoring Mrs. Hawthorne, he addressed the old soldier, man to man. "You understand I have absolutely nothing to say to you at all, Sergeant Major?"

"I do, sir."

"I never heard of your son, you understand? Kenneth Hawthorne is not a name to me, nor to any of my colleagues."

"Yes, sir." The old man's gaze was fixed parade-ground style above Smiley's head. But his wife had her eyes fiercely turned on Smiley's all the time, even if she found it hard to fix on them through the thick lenses of his spectacles.

"He has never in his life worked for any British department of government, whether secret or otherwise. He was a common criminal all his life. Nothing more. Nothing at all."

"Yes, sir."

"I deny absolutely that he was ever a secret agent in the service of the Crown."

"Yes, sir."

"You understand also that I can answer no questions, give you no explanations, and that you will never see me again or be received at this building?"

"Yes, sir."

"You understand finally that you may never speak of this moment to a living soul? However proud you may be of your son? That there are others still alive who must be protected?"

"Yes, sir. I understand, sir."

Opening the drawer of our desk, Smiley took out a small red Cartier box, which he handed to the old man. "I happened to find this in my safe," he said.

The old man passed the box to his wife without looking at it. With firm fingers, she forced it open. Inside lay a pair of superb gold cufflinks with a tiny English rose set discreetly in a corner, hand-engraved, a marvel of fine work. Her husband still did not look. Perhaps he didn't have to; perhaps he didn't trust himself. Closing the box, she parted the clasp of her scuffed purse and popped it inside. Then snapped the purse shut again, so loudly you would think she was slamming down the lid on her son's tomb. I have listened to the tape; it too is waiting to be destroyed.

The old man still said nothing. They were too proud to bother with Smiley as they left.

And the cufflinks? you ask—where did Smiley get the cufflinks from? I had my answer not from the yellowing records of Room 909 but from Ann Smiley herself, quite by chance one evening in a splendid Cornish castle near Saltash where we both happened to be guests. Ann was on her own, and chastened. Mabel had a golf tournament. It was long after the Bill Haydon business, but Smiley still could not bear to have her near him. When dinner was over, the guests dispersed themselves in groups, but Ann stayed close to me, I supposed as a substitute for being close to George. And I asked her, half intuitively, whether she had ever given George a pair of cufflinks. Ann was always at her most beautiful when she was alone.

"Oh those," she said, as if she scarcely remembered. "You mean the ones he gave to the old man."

Ann had given them to George on their first anniversary, she said. After her fling with Bill, he had decided they should be put to better use.

But *why*, exactly, did George decide that? I wondered.

At first it seemed perfectly clear to me. This was Smiley's soft centre. The old cold warrior was revealing his bleeding heart.

Like most things with George—maybe.

Or an act of vengeance against Ann perhaps? Or against his other faithless love, the Circus, at a time when the Fifth Floor was locking him out of the house?

Gradually I arrived at a slightly different theory, which I may as well pass on to you, since one thing is certain, and that is that George himself will not enlighten us.

Listening to the old soldier, Smiley recognised one of those rare moments when the Service could be of real value to real people. For once, the mythology of espionage would be used not to disguise yet another tale of incompetence or betrayal, but to leave an old couple with their dreams. For once, Smiley could look at an intelligence operation and say with absolute confidence that it had worked.

11

A nd some interrogations," said Smiley, gazing into the dancing flames of the log fire, "are not interrogations at all, but communions between damaged souls."

He had been talking about his debriefing of the Moscow Centre spymaster, codename Karla, whose defection he had secured. But for me, he was talking only of poor Frewin, of whom, so far as I know, he had never heard.

The letter denouncing Frewin as a Soviet spy arrived on my desk on a Monday evening, posted first class in the S.W. 1 area of London on the Friday, opened by Head Office Registry on the Monday morning and marked by the Assistant Registrar on duty "HIP to see," HIP being the unlikely acronym of the Head of the Interrogators' Pool; in other words, myself, and in the opinion of some the "H" ought to be an "R"—you Rest in Peace at the Interrogators' Pool. It was five o'clock by the time the Head Office green van unloaded its humble package at Northumberland Avenue, and in the Pool such late intrusions were customarily ignored until next morning. But I was trying to change all that and, having anyway nothing else to do, I opened the envelope at once.

Two pink trace slips were pinned to the letter, each bearing a pencilled note.

Head Office's notes to the Pool always had the ring of instructions addressed to an idiot. The first read, "FREWIN C presumed identical with FREWIN Cyril Arthur, Foreign Office cypher clerk," followed by Frewin's positive vetting reference and white file number, which was a cumbersome way of telling me there was nothing recorded against him. The second said, "MODRIAN S presumed identical with MODRIAN Sergei," followed by a further string of references, but I didn't bother with them. After my five years in the Russia House, Sergei Modrian was plain Sergei to me, as he had been to the rest of us: old Sergei, the crafty Armenian, head boy of Moscow Centre's generously over-staffed residence at the Soviet Embassy in London.

If I had had any lingering wish to postpone my reading of the letter till tomorrow, Sergei's name dispelled it. The letter might be bunkum, but I was playing on home ground.

To the Director,
The Security Department,
The Foreign Office,
Downing Street, SW.

Dear Sir,

This is to inform you, that C. Frewin, a Foreign Office cypher clerk with constant and regular access to *Top Secret and Above,* has been keeping surreptitious company with S. Modrian, First Secretary at the Soviet Embassy in London, for the last four years, and has not revealed same in his annual vetting returns. Secret materials have been passed. Mr. Modrian's whereabouts are no longer known, in view of the fact that he has recently been recalled to the Soviet Union. The said Frewin still resides at the Chestnuts, Beavor Drive, Sutton, and Modrian has been present there at least on one occasion. C. Frewin is now living a *highly solitary life.*

Yours sincerely,
A. Patriot.

Electronically typed. Plain white A4 paper, no watermark. Dated, overpunctuated, accurately spelt and crisply folded. And no address of sender. There never is.

Having nothing much else to do that evening, I had a couple of Scotches at The Sherlock Holmes, then wandered round to Head Office, where I checked myself into the Registry reading room and drew the files. Next morning at the surgery hour of ten I took my place in Burr's waiting room, having first spelt my name to his glossy personal assistant, who seemed never to have heard of me. Brock, from Moscow Station, was ahead of me in the queue. We talked intently about cricket till his name was called, and managed not to refer to the fact that he had worked for me in the Russia House, most recently on the Blair case. A couple of minutes later, Peter Guillam drifted in clutching a bunch of files and looking hung-over. He had recently become Head of Secretariat for Burr.

"Don't mind if I squeeze ahead of you, do you, old boy? I've been sent for urgently. Bloody man seems to expect me to work in my sleep. What's your problem?"

"Leprosy," I said.

There is nowhere quite like the Service—except possibly Moscow—for becoming an unperson overnight. In the upheavals that had followed Barley Blair's defection, not even Burr's predecessor, the nimble Clive, had kept his foothold on the slippery Fifth Floor deck. When last heard of, he was on his way to take up the salubrious post of Head of Station, Guyana. Only our craven legal adviser, Harry Palfrey, seemed as usual to have weathered the changes, and as I entered Burr's shiny executive suite, Palfrey was slipping stealthily out of the other door—but not quite quickly enough, so he treated me to a rhapsodic smile instead. He had recently grown himself a moustache for greater integrity.

"Ned! Marvellous! We must do that lunch," he breathed in an excited whisper, and disappeared below the waterline.

Like his office, Burr was all modern man. Where he came from was a mystery to me, but then I was no longer in the swim. Someone had told me advertising, someone else the City, someone else the Inns of Court. One wit in the Pool mailroom said he came from nowhere at all: that he had been born as found, smelling of aftershave and power, in his two-piece executive blue suit and his patent black shoes with side buckles. He was big and floating and absurdly young. Grasping his soft hand, you at once relaxed your grip for fear of denting it. He had Frewin's file in front of him on his executive desk, with my loose minute—written late last night—pinned to the cover.

"Where does the letter come from?" he demanded in his dry North Country cadence, before I had sat down.

"I don't know. It's well informed. Whoever wrote it did his homework."

"Probably Frewin's best friend," said Burr, as if that was what best friends were known for.

"He's got Modrian's dates right, he's got Frewin's access right," I said. "He knows the positive vetting routine."

"Not a work of art, though, is it? Not if you're an insider? Most likely a colleague. Or his girl. What do you want to ask me?"

I had not expected this quickfire interrogation. After six months in the Pool, I wasn't used to being hurried.

"I suppose I need to know whether you want me to pursue the case," I said.

"Why shouldn't I?"

"It's outside the Pool's normal league. Frewin's access is formidable. His section handles some of the most delicate signals traffic in Whitehall. I assumed you'd prefer to pass it to the Security Service."

"Why?"

"It's their bailiwick. If it's anything at all, it's a straight security enquiry."

"It's our information, our shout, our letter," Burr retorted, with a bluntness that secretly warmed my heart. "To hell with them. When we know what we've got, we'll decide where we go with it. All that those churchy buggers across the Park can think of is a judgeproof prosecution and a bunch of medals to hand around. I collect intelligence for the marketplace. If Frewin's bad, maybe we can keep him going and turn him round. He might even get us alongside Brother Modrian back in Moscow. Who knows? The security artists don't, that's for sure."

"Then presumably you'd prefer to hand the case to the Russia House," I said doggedly.

"Why should I do that?"

I had assumed I would make an unappetising figure to him, for he was still of an age to find failure immoral. Yet he seemed to be asking me to tell him why he shouldn't count on me.

"The Pool has no charter to function operationally," I explained. "We run a front office and listen to the lonelyhearts. We've no charter to conduct clandestine investigations or run agents, and no mandate to pursue suspects with Frewin's sort of access."

"You can run a phone tap, can't you?"

"If you get me a warrant I can."

"You can brief watchers, can't you? You've done that a few times, they say."

"Not unless you authorise it personally."

"Suppose I do? The Pool's also empowered to make vetting enquiries. You can play Mr. Plod. You're good at it, by all accounts. This is a vetting matter, right? And Frewin's due for a vetting top-up, right? So vet him."

"In positive vetting cases, the Pool is obliged to clear all enquiries with the Security Service in advance."

"Assume it's done."

"I can't do that unless I have it in writing."

"Oh yes you can. You're not a Service hack. You're the great Ned. You've broken as many rules as you've stuck to, you have, I've read you up. You know Modrian, too."

"Not well."

"How well?"

"I had dinner with him once and played squash with him once. That's hardly knowing him."

"Squash where?"

"At the Lansdowne."

"How did that come about?"

"Modrian was formally declared to us as the Embassy's Moscow Centre link. I was trying to put together a deal with him on Barley Blair. A swap."

"Why didn't you succeed?"

"Barley wouldn't go along with us. He'd done his own deal already. He wanted his girl, not us."

"What's his game like?"

"Tricky."

"Did you beat him?"

"Yes."

He interrupted his own flow while he looked me over. It was like being studied by a baby. "And you can handle it, can you? You're not under too much stress? You've done some good things in your time. You've a heart too, which is more than I can say for some of the capons in this outfit."

"Why should I be under stress?"

No answer. Or not yet. He seemed to be chewing at something just behind his thick lips.

"Who believes in marriage these days, for Christ's sake?" he demanded. His regional drawl had thickened. It was as if he had abandoned restraint. "If you want to live with your girl, live with her is my advice. We've cleared her, she's nobody's worry, she's not a bomb thrower or a secret sympathiser or a druggie, what's your bother? She's a nice girl in a nice way of life, and you're a lucky fellow. Do you want the case, or do you not?"

For a moment I was robbed of an answer. There was nothing surprising in Burr knowing of my affair with Sally. In our world you put those things on record before the record puts them on you, and I had already endured my obligatory confessional with Personnel. No, it was Burr's capacity for intimacy that had silenced me, the speed with which he had got under my skin.

"If you'll cover me and give me the resources, of course I'll take it," I said.

"So get on with it, then. Keep me informed but not too much—don't bullshit me, always give me bad news straight. He's a man without qualities, our Cyril is. You've read Robert Musil, I dare say, haven't you?"

"I'm afraid I haven't."

He was pulling open Frewin's file. I say "pulling" because his doughy hands gave no impression of having done anything before: now we are going to see how this file opens; now we are going to address ourselves to this strange object called a pencil.

"He's got no hobbies, no stated interests beyond music, no wife, no girl, no parents, no money worries, not even any bizarre sexual appetites, poor devil," Burr complained, flipping to a different part of the file. When on earth had he found time to read it? I asked myself. I presumed the early hours. "And how the hell a man of your experience, whose job is dealing with modern civilisation and its discontentments, can manage without the wisdom of Robert Musil is a question which at a calmer moment I shall require you to answer." He licked his thumb and turned another page. "He's one of five," he said.

"I thought he was an only child."

"Not his brothers and sisters, you mug, his work. There's five clerks in his dreary cyphers office and he's one of them. They all handle the same stuff; they're all the same rank, work the same hours, think the same dirty thoughts." He looked straight at me, a thing he had not done before. "If he did it, what's his motive? The writer doesn't say. Funny, that. They usually do. Boredom—how about that? Boredom and greed, they're the only motives left these days. Plus getting even, which is eternal." He went back to the file. "Cyril's the only one not married, notice that? He's a poofter. So am I. I'm a poofter, you're a poofter. We're all poofters. It's just a question which bit of yourself ends on top. He's no hair, see that?" I caught a flash of Frewin's photograph as he waved it past me and talked on. He had a daunting energy. "Still that's no crime, I dare say, baldness, any more than marriage is. I should know, I've had three and I'm still not done. That's no normal denunciation, is it? That's why you're here. That letter knows what it's talking about. You don't think Modrian wrote it, do you?"

"Why should he have done?"

"I'm asking, Ned, don't fox with me. Wicked thoughts are what keep me going. Perhaps Modrian thought he'd leave a little confusion in his wake when he went back to Moscow. He's a scheming little monkey, Modrian, when he puts his mind to it. I've been reading him too."

When? I thought again. When on earth did you find the time?

For another twenty minutes he zigzagged back and forth, tossing possibilities at me, seeing how they came back. And when I finally stepped exhausted into the anteroom, I walked straight into Peter Guillam again.

"Who the hell is Leonard Burr?" I asked him, still dazed.

Peter was astonished that I didn't know. "Burr? My dear chap. Leonard was Smiley's Crown Prince for years. George rescued him from a fate worse than death at All Souls."

Of Sally, my reigning extramarital girlfriend, what should I tell you? She was free, and spoke to the captive in me. Monica had been within my walls. Monica was a woman of the Service, bound and not bound to me by the same set of rules. But to Sally I was just a middle-aged civil servant who had forgotten to have any fun. She was a designer and sometime dancer whose passion was theatre, and she thought the rest of life unreal. She was tall and she was fair and rather wise, and sometimes I think she must have reminded me of Stefanie.

"Meet you, skipper?" Gorst cried over the telephone. "Top up our Cyril? It'll be my pleasure, sir!"

We met the next day in a Foreign Office interviewing room. I was Captain York, another dreary vetting officer doing his rounds. Gorst was head of Frewin's Cypher Section, which was better known as the Tank: a lecher in a beadle's suit, a waddling, smirking man with prising elbows and a tiny mouth that wriggled like a worm. When he sat, he scooped up the skirts of his jacket as if he were exposing himself from behind. Then he kicked out a plump leg like a chorus girl, before laying it suggestively over the thigh of the other.

"Saint Cyril, that's what we call Mr. Frewin," he announced blithely. "Doesn't drink, doesn't smoke, doesn't swear, certified virgin. End of vetting interview." Extracting a cigarette from a packet of ten, he tapped the tip of it on his thumbnail, then moistened it with his busy tongue. "Music's his only weakness. Loves the *operah*. Goes to the *operah* regular as clockwork. Never cared for it myself. Can't make out whether it's actors singing or singers acting." He lit his cigarette. I could smell the lunchtime beer on his breath. "I'm not too fond of fat women, either, to be frank. Specially when they scream at me." He tipped his head back and blew out smoke rings, savouring them as if they were emblems of his authority.

"May I ask how Frewin gets on with the rest of the staff these days?" I said, playing the honest journeyman as I turned a page of my notebook.

"Swimmingly, your grace. Par-fectly."

"The archivists, registrars, secretaries—no trouble on that front?"

"Not a finger. Not a mini-digit."

"You all sit together?"

"In a big room and I'm the titular head of it. Very *tit*-ular indeed."

"And I've had it said to me he's something of a misogynist," I said, fishing.

Gorst gave a shrill laugh. "Cyril? A *misogynist*? Bollocks. He just hates the girls. Won't speak to them, not apart from good morning. Won't come to the pre-Christmas party if he can help it, in case he has to kiss them under the mistletoe." He recrossed his legs, indicating that he had decided to make a statement. "Cyril Arthur Frewin—Saint Cyril—is a highly reliable, eminently conscientious, totally bald, incredibly boring clerk of the old school. Saint Cyril, though punctilious to a fault, has in my view reached his natural promotion ceiling in his line of country or profession. Saint Cyril is set in his ways. Saint Cyril does what he does, one hundred percent. Amen."

"Politics?"

"Not in my house, thank you."

"And he's not workshy?"

"Did I say he was, squire?"

"No, to the contrary, I was quoting from the file. If there's extra work to be done, Cyril will always roll his sleeves up, stay on in the lunch hour, the evenings and so forth. That's still the case, is it? No slackening off of his enthusiasm?"

"Our Cyril is ready to oblige at all hours, to the pleasure of those who have families, wives or a nice piece of Significant Other to return to. He'll do the early mornings, he'll do lunch hours, he'll do evening watch, except for *operah* nights, of course. Cyril never counts the cost. Latterly, I will admit, he has been slightly less inclined to martyr himself, but that is no doubt a purely temporary suspension of service. Our Cyril does have his little moods. Who does not, your eminence?"

"So recently a slackening off, you would say?"

"Not of his work, never. Cyril is your total workslave, always has been. Merely of his willingness to be put upon by his more human colleagues. Come five-thirty these days, Saint Cyril packs up his desk and goes home with the rest of us. He does not, for instance, offer to replace the late shift and remain solo incommunicado till nine o'clock and lock up, which was what he used to do."

"You can't put a date to that change of habit, can you?" I enquired as boringly as I could manage, turning dutifully to a fresh page of my notebook.

Curiously enough, Gorst could. He pursed his lips. He frowned. He raised his girlish eyebrows and pressed his chins into his grimy shirt collar. He made a vast show of ruminating. And he finally remembered. "The last time Cyril Frewin did young Burton's evening watch was Midsummer's Day. I keep a log, you see. Security. I also have quite an impressive memory, which I don't always care to reveal."

I was secretly impressed, but not by Gorst. Three days after Modrian left London for Moscow, Cyril Frewin had ceased to work late, I was thinking. I had other questions that were clamouring to be asked. Did the Tank boast electronic typewriters? Did the cypher clerks have access to them? Did Gorst? But I was afraid of arousing his suspicions.

"You mentioned his love of opera," I said. "Could you tell me a little more about that?"

"No I could not, since we do not get blow-by-blow accounts, and we do not ask for them. However, he does come in wearing a pressed dark suit on his *operah* days, if he doesn't bring his dinner jacket in a suitcase, and he does impart what I would refer to as a state of high if controlled excitement somewhat similar to other forms of anticipation, which I will not mention."

"But he has a regular seat, for instance? A subscription seat? It's only for the record. As you say, he's a bit short of relaxing pastimes otherwise."

"As I think I told you, squire, alas, me and *operah* were not made for each other. Put down 'opera buff' on his form and you're covered for your relaxing pastime is my advice."

"Thank you. I will." I turned another page. "And really no enemies that you can think of?" I said, my pencil hovering over my notebook.

Gorst became serious. The beer was wearing off. "Cyril is laughed at, Captain, I'll admit. But he takes it in good part. Cyril is not disliked."

"No one who would speak ill of him, for instance?"

"I can think of no single reason whatever why anyone should speak ill of Cyril Arthur Frewin. The British civil servant, he may be sullen but he's not malicious. Cyril does his duty, as we all do. We're a happy ship. I wouldn't mind if you put that down, too."

"I gather he went to Salzburg for Christmas this year. And previous years too, is that right?"

"That is correct. Cyril always takes his leave at Christmas. He goes to Salzburg, he hears the music. It's the one point on which he will make no concession to the rest of the Tank. There's some of the young ones try to complain about it, but I won't let them. 'Cyril makes it up to you in other ways,' I tell them. 'Cyril's got his seniority, he loves his trip to Salzburg for the music, he has his little ways, and that's how it's going to stay.' "

"Does he leave a holiday address behind when he goes?"

Gorst didn't know, but at my request he telephoned his personnel department and obtained it. The same hotel, the last four years running. He's been keeping company with Modrian for four years too, I thought, remembering the letter. Four years of Salzburg, four years of Modrian, ending in a *highly solitary life*.

"Does he take a friend, would you know?"

"Cyril never had a friend in his life, skipper." Gorst yawned. "Not one he'd take on holiday, that's for sure. Shall we do a lunch next time? They tell me you boys have very nifty expense accounts when you care to give them a tickle."

"Does he talk about his Salzburg trips at all when he comes back? The fun he's had—the music he's heard—anything like that?" Thanks to Sally, I suppose, I had learned that people were expected to have fun.

Having made a brief show of thinking, Gorst shook his head. "If Cyril has fun, squire, it's very, very private," he said, with a last smirk.

That wasn't Sally's idea of fun at all.

From my office at the Pool I booked a secure line to Vienna and spoke to Toby Esterhase, who with his infinite talent for survival had recently been made Head of Station.

"I want you to shake out the Weisse Rose in Salzburg for me, Toby. Cyril Frewin, British subject. Stayed there every Christmas for the last four years. I want to know when he arrived, how long he stayed, whether he's stayed there before, who with, how much the bills come to and what he gets up to. Concert tickets, excursions, meals, women, boys, celebrations—anything you can get. But don't raise local eyebrows, whatever you do. Be a divorce agent or something."

Toby was predictably appalled. "Ned, listen to me. Ned, this is actually completely impossible. I'm in Vienna, okay? Salzburg, that's like the other side of the globe. This city is buzzing like a beehouse. I need more staff, Ned. You got to tell Burr. He doesn't understand the pressures here. Get me two more guys, we do anything you want, no problem. Sorry."

He asked for a week. I said three days. He said he'd try his best and I believed him. He said he had heard a rumour that Mabel and I had broken up. I denied it.

Ever since I can remember, watchers have been most at home in condemned houses handy for bus routes and the airport. Monty's choice for his own headquarters was an unlikely Edwardian palazzo in Baron's Court. From the tiled hall, a stone staircase curled grandly through five pokey floors to a stained-glass skylight. As I climbed, doors flew open and shut like a French farce as his strange crew, in varying stages of undress, scurried between changing room, cafeteria and briefing room, their eyes averted from the stranger. I arrived in a garret once a painter's studio. Somewhere a women's foursome was playing noisy ping-pong. Closer at hand, two male voices were singing Blake's "Jerusalem" under the shower.

I had not set eyes on Monty for a long time, but neither the years between nor his promotion to Head Watcher had aged him. A few grey hairs, a sharper edge to his hollow cheeks. He was not a natural conversationalist, and for a while we just sat and sipped our tea.

"Frewin, then," he said finally.

"Frewin," I said.

Like a marksman, Monty had a way of making his own particular area of quiet. "Frewin's a funny one, Ned. He's not being normal. Now of course we don't know what normal is, do we, not really, not for Cyril, not apart from what you pick up from hearsay and that. Postman, milkman, neighbours, the usual. Everyone talks to a window cleaner, you'd be amazed. Or a Telecom engineer who's lost his way with a junction box. We've only been on him two days, all the same."

With Monty, when he talked like this, you just pinned your ears back and bided your time.

"And nights, of course," he added. "If you count nights. Cyril's not sleeping, that's for sure. More prowling, judging by his windows and his teacups in the morning. And his music. One of his neighbours is thinking of complaining to him. She never has before, but she might this time. 'Whatever's come over him?' she says. 'Handel for breakfast is one thing, but Handel at three in the morning's a bit of another.' She thinks he's having his change. She says men get like that at his age, same as women. We wouldn't know about that, would we?"

I grinned. And again bided my time. "*She* does, though," Monty said reflectively. "Her old man's gone off with a supply teacher from the comprehensive. She's not at all sure she'll have him back. Nearly raped our pretty boy who'd come to read the meter. Here—how's Mabel?" he demanded.

I wondered whether he too had heard the rumour; but I decided that if he had, he would not have asked me.

"Fine," I said.

"Cyril used to take a newspaper on the train. The *Telegraph,* need you ask. Cyril doesn't hold with Labour—he says they're common. But he doesn't buy a paper any more. He sits. Sits and stares. That's all he does. Our bloke had to give him a nudge yesterday when they pulled up at Victoria. He'd gone off in a daydream. Going home last night, he tapped out the whole score of an opera on his briefcase. Nancy says it was Vivaldi. I suppose she knows. Remember Pauli Skordeno?"

I said I did. Diversions were part of Monty's way. Like, "How's Mabel?" for instance.

"Pauli's doing seven years in Barbados for bothering a bank. What gets into them, Ned? He never put a foot wrong while he was watching. Never late, never naughty with his expenses, lovely memory, lovely eye, good nose. Burglaries galore we did. London, the Home Counties, the Midlands, the civil-rights boys, the disarmers, the Party, the naughty diplomats—we did the lot. Did Pauli ever get rumbled? Not once. The moment he goes private, he's all fingers and thumbs and boasting to the bloke next door to him in the bar. I think they *want* to be caught, that's my opinion. I think it's wanting recognition after all the years of being nobody."

He sipped his tea. "Cyril's other kick, apart from music, is his radio. He loves his radio. Only receiving, mind, as far as anybody knows. But he's got one of those fancy German sets with the fine tuning and big speakers for his concerts, and he didn't buy it locally because when it went on the blink the local shop had to send it off to Wiesbaden. Three months it took, and cost a fortune. He doesn't run a car, he doesn't hold with them. He shops by bus Saturday mornings, he's a stay-at-home except for his Christmases in Austria. No pets, he doesn't mix. Entertaining, forget it. No house-guests, lodgers, receives no mail except the bills, pays everything regular, doesn't vote, doesn't go to church, doesn't have a television. His cleaning lady says he reads a lot, mainly big books. She only comes once a week, usually when he's not there, and we didn't dare get close to her. A big book for her is anything bigger than a Bible-study pamphlet. His phone bills are modest, he's got six thousand in a building society, owns his house and maintains a well-managed bank account fluctuating between six and fourteen hundred, except Christmas times when it drops to around two hundred because of his holiday."

Monty's sense of the proprieties again required us to make a detour, this time to discuss our children. My son Adrian had just won a modern languages scholar-ship to Cambridge, I said. Monty was hugely impressed. Monty's only son had just passed his law exam with flying colours. We agreed that kids were what made life worth living.

"Modrian," I said when the formalities were once more over. "Sergei."

"I remember the gentleman well, Ned. We all do. We used to follow him round the clock some days. Except at Christmas, of course, when he took his home leave. . . . Hullo! Are you thinking what I'm thinking? We all take leave at Christmas?"

"It had crossed my mind," I said.

"We didn't even bother to pretend with Modrian, not after a while, you couldn't. *Oh*, he was a slippery eel, though. I could have walloped him sometimes, I really could. Pauli Skordeno got so angry with him once he let his tyres down outside the Victoria and Albert while he was inside sussing out a dead-letter box. I never reported it, I didn't have the heart."

"Am I not right in thinking Modrian was also an opera buff, Monty?"

Monty's eyes became quite round, and I had the rare pleasure of seeing him surprised.

"Oh my Lord, Ned," he exclaimed. "Oh dear, oh dear. You're right. Sergei was a Covent Garden subscriber—of course he was, same as Cyril. We must have taken him there and fetched him—oh, a dozen times. He could have used a cab if he'd had any mercy, but he never did. He liked wearing us out in the traffic."

"If we could know the performances he went to, and where he sat—if you could get them—we could try and match them up with Frewin's."

Monty had fallen into a theatrical silence. He frowned, then scratched his head. "You don't think this is all a touch too *easy* for us, do you, Ned?" he asked. "I get suspicious when everything fits in a pretty pattern, don't you?"

"I won't be part of your pattern," Sally had said to me the night before. "Patterns are for breaking."

"He *sings,* Ned," Mary Lasselles murmured while she arranged my white tulips in a pickle jar. "He sings *all* the time. Night and day, it doesn't matter. I think he missed his vocation."

Mary was as pale as a nightnurse and as dedicated. A luminous virtue lit her unpowdered face and shone from her clear eyes. A shock of white, like the mark of early widowhood, capped her bobbed hair.

Of the many callings that comprise the over-world of intelligence, none requires as much devotion as that of the sisterhood of listeners. Men are no good at it. Only women are capable of such passionate espousal of the destiny of others. Condemned to windowless cellars, engulfed by tracks of grey-clad cable and banks of Russian-style tape recorders, they occupy a nether region populated by absent lives which they know more intimately than those of their closest friends or relations. They never see their quarries, never meet them, never touch them or sleep with them. Yet the whole force of their personalities is beamed upon these secret loves. On microphones and telephones they hear them blandish, weep, smoke, eat, argue and couple. They hear them cook, belch, snore and worry. They endure their children, in-laws and babysitters without complaint, as well as their tastes in television. These days, they even ride with them in cars, take them shopping, sit with them in cafés and bingo halls. They are the secret sharers of the trade.

Passing me a pair of earphones, Mary put on her own and, folding her hands beneath her chin, closed her eyes for better listening. So I heard Cyril Frewin's voice for the first time, singing himself a passage from *Turandot* while Mary Lasselles with her eyes shut smiled in her enchantment. His voice was mellow and, to my untutored ear, as pleasing as it clearly was to Mary.

I sat up straight. The singing had stopped. I heard a woman's voice in the background, then a man's, and they were speaking Russian.

"Mary, who the hell's that?"

"His teachers, darling. Radio Moscow's Olga and Boris, five days a week, 6 a.m. sharp. This is yesterday morning."

"You mean he's teaching himself *Russian?*"

"Well, he listens to it, darling. How much of it is going into his little head is anybody's guess. Every morning, sharp at six, Cyril does his Olga and Boris. They're visiting the Kremlin today. Yesterday they were shopping at Gum."

I heard Frewin mutter unintelligibly in the bath, I heard him call out "Mother" in the night, while he tossed restlessly in bed. FREWIN Ella, I remembered, deceased, mother to FREWIN Cyril Arthur, q.v. I have never understood why Registry insists on opening personal files for the dead relatives of suspected spies.

I listened to him arguing with the British Telecom engineers' department after he had waited the statutory twenty minutes to be connected with them. His voice was edgy, full of unexpected emphases.

"Well, *next* time you elect to identify a *fault* on my line, I would be *highly* grateful if you would kindly inform *me* as the subscriber *prior* to barging into my house when my *cleaning* woman happens to be in, and leaving particles of *wire* on the carpet and *boot*marks on the kitchen *floor* . . ."

I listened to him phone the Covent Garden opera house to say he would not be taking up his subscription ticket this Friday. This time his tone was self-pitying. He explained that he was ill. The kind lady the other end said there was a lot of it about.

I listened to him talking to the butcher in anticipation of my visit, which Foreign Office Personnel had set for tomorrow morning at his house.

"Mr. Steele, this is Mr. Cyril Frewin. Good morning. I shall *not* be able to come *in* to you on Saturday, owing to the fact that I have a conference at my *house*. I would therefore be *grateful* if you would kindly deliver four *good* lamb chops for me on the Friday evening as you pass by on your way home. Will that be convenient, Mr. Steele? Also a jar of your pre-mixed mint *sauce*. No, I have red currant jelly already, thank you. Will you attach your *bill*, please?"

To my over-acute ear, he sounded like a man preparing to abandon ship.

"I'll take the engineers again, please, Mary," I said. Having twice more listened to Frewin's dogmatic tones of complaint to British Telecom, I gave her a distracted kiss and stepped into the evening air. Sally had said, "Come round," but I was in no mood to spend an evening professing love to her and listening to music I secretly detested.

I returned to the Pool. The Service laboratories had completed their examination of the anonymous letter. A Markus electronic, model number so-and-so, probably Belgian manufacture, new or little used, was the best they could suggest. They believed they would be able to identify another document issuing from the same machine. Could I get one? End of report. The laboratories were still wrestling with the characteristics of the new generation of machines.

I rang Monty at his lair in Baron's Court. Frewin's complaint to the engineers was still ringing in my memory: his pauses, like unnatural commas, his use of the word *highly*, his habit of punching the unlikely word to achieve vindictive emphasis.

"Did your fellows notice a typewriter in Cyril's house, Monty, by any chance, while they were kindly mending his telephone?" I asked.

"No, Ned. There was no typewriter, Ned—not one they saw, put it that way."

"Could they have missed it?"

"Easily, Ned. It was soft-pedalling only. No opening desks or cupboards, no photographing, not too much familiarity with his cleaning lady either, or she'll worry afterwards. It was 'See what you can, get out fast, and be sure you leave a mess or he'll smell a rat.' "

I thought of phoning Burr, but I didn't. My case officer's possessiveness was taking over, and I was damned if I was going to share Frewin with anyone, not even the man who had entrusted him to me. A hundred twisted threads were running through my head, from Modrian to Gorst to Boris and Olga to Christmas to

Salzburg to Sally. In the end, I wrote Burr a minute setting out most of what I had discovered and confirming that I would "make a first reconnaissance" of Frewin tomorrow morning when I interviewed him for his routine vetting clearance.

To go home? To go to Sally? Home was a hateful little service flat in St. James's, where I was supposed to be sorting myself out—though that's the last thing any man does when he sits alone with a bottle of Scotch and a reproduction painting of "The Laughing Cavalier," dithering between his dreams of freedom and his addiction to what holds him prisoner. Sally was my Alternative Life, but I knew already I was too set to jump the wall and reach it.

Preferring to remain at my desk, therefore, I fetched myself a whisky from the safe and browsed through Modrian's file. It told me nothing I didn't already know, but I wanted him at the front of my head. Sergei Modrian, tried and tested Moscow Centre professional. A charmer, a bit of a dancer, a befriender, a smiling Armenian with a mercury tongue. I had liked him. He had liked me. In our profession, since we may like no one beyond a point, we can forgive a lot for charm.

My direct line was ringing. I thought for a moment it would be Sally, for contrary to regulations I had given her the number. It was Toby and he sounded pleased with himself. He usually did. He didn't mention Frewin by name. He didn't mention Salzburg. I guessed he was ringing from his flat, and I'd a shrewd notion he was in bed and not alone.

"Ned? Your man's a joke. Books himself a single room for two weeks, checks in, pays his two weeks in advance, gives the staff their Christmas box, pats the kids, makes nice to everybody. Next morning he disappears, does it every year. Ned, can you hear me? Listen, the guy's crazy. No phone calls out, one meal, two *Apfelsaft*, no explanations, taxi to the station. Keep my room, don't let it, maybe I'll be back tomorrow, maybe in a few days, I don't know. After twelve days, back he comes, no explanations, tips the staff some more, everybody happy like a heathen. They call him 'the ghost.' Ned, you got to talk nice to Burr for me. You owe me now. Toby works his fingers to the bone, tell him. Old star like you, a young fellow like Burr, he'll listen to you, costs you nothing. I need another man out here, maybe two. Tell him, Ned, hear me? Cheers."

I stared at the wall, the one I couldn't scale; I stared at Modrian's file, I remembered Monty's dictum about too easy. I suddenly wanted Sally terribly, and had some cloudy notion that by solving the mystery of Frewin I would convert my recurring spurts for freedom into one bold leap. But as I reached for the phone to talk to her, it started to ring again.

"They fit," said Monty in a flat voice. He had managed to check Frewin's opera attendance. "It's Sergei and Cyril every time. When *he* goes, so does *he*. When *he* doesn't, neither does *he*. Maybe that's why *he* doesn't go any more. Got it?"

"And the seats?" I asked.

"Side by side, darling. What do you expect? Front to back?"

"Thanks, Monty," I said.

Do I have to tell you how I spent that interminable night? Have you never telephoned your own son, listened to his unhappy jibes and had to remind yourself that he is yours? Talked frankly to an understanding wife about your inadequacies, not knowing what on earth they were? Have you never reached out for your mistress, cried "I love you" and remained a mystified spectator to her untroubled fulfilment, before leaving her once more, to walk the London streets as if they were a foreign city? Have you never, from all the other sounds of dawn, picked out the wet chuckle of a magpie and fixed on it for your whole life long while you lie wide-eyed on your beastly single bed?

I arrived at Frewin's house at half past nine, having dressed myself as boringly as I could contrive, and that must have been boringly indeed, for I am not a natty dresser at the best of times, though Sally has appalling ideas about how she might improve my style. Frewin and I had agreed on ten but I told myself I wanted the element of surprise. Perhaps the truth was, I needed his company. A postman's van was parked up the street. A builder's truck with an aerial stood beyond it, telling me Monty's men were at their posts.

I forget what month it was but I know it was autumn, both in my private life and in the prim cul-de-sac of steep brick houses. For I see a disc of white sun hanging behind the pollarded chestnut trees that had given the place its name, and I smell to this day the scent of bonfires and autumn air in my nostrils urging me to leave London, leave the Service, take to Sally and the world's real countryside. And I remember the whirr of small birds as they lifted from Frewin's telephone line on their way to somewhere better. And a cat in the next-door garden rising on its rear paws to box a drowsy butterfly.

I dropped the latch to the garden gate and crunched up the prim gravel path to the Seven Dwarfs semi-detached, with its bottle-glass windows and thatched porch. I reached out my hand for the bell, but the front door flew away from me. It was ribbed, and studded with fake coach bolts, and it shot back as if it had been blasted by a street bomb, almost sucking me after it into the dark tiled hall. Then the door stood still, and Frewin stood beside it, a bald centurion to his own endangered house.

He was taller than I had realised by a wrestler's head. His thick shoulders were braced to receive my attack, his eyes were fixed on me in scared hostility. Yet even at this first moment of encounter I sensed no contest in him, only a sort of heroic vulnerability made tragic by his bulk. I entered his house, and knew I was entering a madness. I had known it all night long. In desperation we find a natural kinship with the mad. I had known that for much longer.

"Captain York? Yes, well, welcome, sir. Welcome indeed. Personnel of their good-ness *did* advise me you were coming. They don't always. But this time they did. Come in, please. You have your *duty* to do, Captain, as I have mine." His vast, soggy hands were lifted for my coat but seemed unable to grapple with it. So they hovered above my neck as if to strangle or embrace me while he went on talking. "We're all on the same side and no hard feelings, I say. I liken your job to airport security, personally, it's the same parameters. If they don't search *me,* they won't search the villains either, will they? It's the logical approach to the matter, in my view."

Heaven knows what lost original he thought he was copying as he delivered these over-prepared words, but at least they freed him from his frozen state. His hands descended to my coat and helped me out of it, and I can feel now the reverence with which they did so, as if unveiling something exciting to us both.

"You fly a lot then, do you, Mr. Frewin?" I asked.

He hung my coat on a hanger, and the hanger on a vile reproduction coat-tree. I waited for an answer but none came. I was thinking of his air travel to Salzburg, and I wondered whether he was too, and whether his conscience was speaking out of him in the tension of my arrival. He marched ahead of me to the drawing room, where by the light of the leaded bay window I was able to examine him at my ease, for he was already busy with the next article of his urgent hospitality: this time, an electric coffee percolator filled but not switched on—did I want the milk, or the sugar or the both, Captain? And the milk, Captain, was it hot or cold? And how about a home-made biscuit for you, Captain?

"You really made them yourself?" I asked as I fished one from the jar.

"Any fool who can read can cook," said Frewin, with a chaotic grin of superiority, and I could see at once why Gorst would loathe him.

"Well, I can read, but I certainly can't cook," I replied, with a rueful shake of my head.

"What's your first name, Captain?"

"Ned," I replied.

"Well, that's because you're married, Ned, I expect. Your wife has robbed you of your self-sufficiency. I've seen it too often in my life. In comes the wife, out goes the independence. I'm Cyril."

And you're ducking my question about your air travel, I thought, refusing to allow him this attempted incursion into my private territory.

"If *I* ran this country," Frewin announced over his shoulder to me while he poured, "which I am *pleased* to say I shall never have the opportunity to *do*"—his voice was acquiring the didactic drumbeat of his conversation with the engineers —"I would make an *absolute* law that *everyone,* regardless of colour, sex or creed, would take *cooking* as an obligatory subject *while* at school."

"Good idea," I said, accepting a mug of coffee, "very sound," and helped myself to sugar from the yellow beehive pot, which nestled like a missile in his damp paw. He had turned to me all at once, shoulders, waist and head together. His bare eyes, unfringed and unprotected, gazed down on me with a radiant and doting innocence.

"Play any games at all, Ned?" he enquired softly, tipping his head to one side for added confidentiality.

"A spot of golf, Cyril," I lied. "How about you?"

"Hobbies at all, Ned?"

"Well, I do like to do the odd watercolour when I'm on holiday," I said, borrowing again from Mabel.

"Drive a car, do you, Ned? I expect you boys have to have all the skills at your fingertips, don't you?"

"Just an old Rover."

"What year is it, then? What vintage, Ned? There's many a good tune played on an old fiddle, they say."

His energy was not just in his person, I realised as I gave him the first date that occurred to me; it spilled into every object that came within his sphere. Into the reproduction horse-brasses that glistened like military cap-badges from his vigorous polishing. Into the polished fire grate and wood floor and the resplendent surface of his dining table. Into the very chair where I now sat and meekly sipped my coffee, for its arms were concealed in linen covers so pressed and spotless that I was reluctant to put hands on them. And I knew without his telling me that, cleaning woman or none, he tended all these things himself, that he was their servant and dictator, in the kingdom of his boundless wasted energy.

"Where do you live then, Ned?"

"Me? Oh well, London, really."

"What part then, Ned? What district? Somewhere nice, or do you have to be slightly anonymous for your work?"

"Well, we're not really allowed to say, I'm afraid."

"London born, are you? Hastings, me."

"Sort of suburbs. You know. Pinner, say."

"You must retain your discretion, Ned. Always. Your discretion is your dignity. Let nobody take it from you. It's your professional integrity, discretion is. Remember that. It could come in handy."

"Thanks," I said, affecting a sheepish laugh. "I will."

He was feeding on me with his eyes. He reminded me of my dog Lizzie when she watches me for a signal—unblinking, body ready to go. "Shall we start, then?" he said. "Want to sound the 'off'? As soon as it's official, tell me. 'Cyril. The red light's on.' That's all you have to say."

I laughed, shaking my head again, as if to say he was a card.

"It's only routine, Cyril," I said. "My goodness, you must know the questions by heart after all these years. Mind if I smoke?" I laboriously lit my pipe and dropped the match into the ashtray he was pressing on me. Then I resumed my study of his room. Along the walls, do-it-yourself shelves filled with do-it-yourself books, every one of them of global resonance: *The World's One Hundred Greatest Men*; *Gems of All the World's Literature*; *Music of the Great Ages in Three Volumes*. Next to them, his gramophone records in cases, all classical. And in the corner, the gramophone itself, a splendid teak affair with more control buttons than a simpleton like myself could master.

"Well now, if you like painting watercolours, Ned, why don't you try the music too?" he suggested, following my eye. "It's the finest consolation in the world, good music is, properly played, if you choose right. I could put you on the right lines if you wanted."

I puffed for a while. A pipe is a great weapon for playing slow against someone else's haste. "I rather think I'm tone deaf, actually, Cyril. I have made the occasional effort, but I don't know, I sort of lose heart really . . ."

My heresy—drawn, I am afraid, from inconclusive debates I had had with Sally —was already too much for him. He had sprung to his feet, his face a mask of horror and concern as he seized the biscuit jar and thrust it at me as if only food would save me.

"Now, Ned, that is not *right,* if I may say so! There is no such *thing* as a tone-deaf *person!* Take two, go on, there's plenty more in the kitchen."

"I'll stick to my pipe if you don't mind."

"Tone deafness, Ned, is merely a *term,* an expression, I will go so far as to say an *excuse,* designed to cover up, to disguise, a purely *temporary,* self-imposed *psychological* resistance to a certain world which your conscious mind is refusing you permission to enter! It is *merely* a fear of the unknown which is holding you *back.* Let me give you the example of certain acquaintances of mine . . ."

He ran on and I let him, while he dabbed at me with his forefinger, and with the other hand clutched the biscuit jar against his heart. I listened to him, I watched him, I expressed my admiration at the appropriate moments. I fished for my black notebook and removed the garter of black elastic from it as a signal to him that I was ready to begin, but he ignored me and ranted on. I imagined Mary Lasselles in her lair, smiling dreamily while her loved one lectured me. And Monty's boys and girls in their surveillance vans outside, cursing him and yawning while they waited to change shifts. And for all I knew, Burr too—all of them hostages to Frewin's endless anecdote about a married couple he had had for neighbours when he lived in Surbiton, whom he had taught to share his musical appreciation.

"Anyway, I can tell my masters at PVHQ that music is still your great love," I suggested with a smile when he had finished.

"PV" for Positive Vetting, you understand, and "HQ" for Headquarters. My part as the downtrodden security workhorse required a higher authority than my own. Then, opening the notebook on my knee, I spread the pages, and with my unpainted government-issue pencil wrote the name FREWIN at the top of the left-hand page.

"Ah well, if you're talking about *love,* Ned—you *could* say music *was* my great love, yes. And music, to quote the bard, is the *food* of love. However, I'd *prefer* to say, it depends how you *define* love. What *is* love? That's your real question, Ned. *Define love.*"

God's coincidences are sometimes too vulgar to be borne. "Well, I suppose *I* define it rather broadly," I said doubtfully, my pencil poised. "How do *you* define it?"

He shook his head and began energetically stirring his coffee, all his thick fingers gathered round the neck of one tiny Apostle spoon.

"Is this on the record?" he asked.

"It could be. Please yourself."

"Commitment is how *I* define love. A great *number* of people speak of *love* as if it were some kind of *nirvana.* It isn't. I happen to know that. Love is not *separate* from life. It's not *beyond* it or *superior* to it. Love is *within* life. Love is totally *integral* to life, and what you get *out* of it depends on the ways and means whereby you invest your *efforts* and your loyalty. Our Lord taught us that *perfectly* clearly, not that I'm a God-man personally, I'm a rationalist. Love is *sacrifice* and love is hard work. Love is *also* sweat and tears, exactly as your great music has to be in order to qualify. By that token, yes, I'll grant you, Ned, *music* is my first love, if you follow me."

I was following him only too well. I had made similar half-hearted representations to Sally, only to have them swept aside. I knew also that in his beleaguered state of mind there was no such thing to him as a casual question, let alone a casual answer—any more than there was to me, even if my systems of concealment were more sophisticated than his.

"I don't think I'll write that down," I said. "I think I'll regard it as what we call deep background." In earnest of which, I pencilled a couple of words in the notebook, as a memo to myself and a sign to him that we were going on the record. "All right, let's do the meat-and-potatoes work first," I suggested, "or PVHQ will say I'm dragging my feet as usual. Have you joined the Communist Party since you were last spoken to by one of our representatives, Cyril, or have you managed to restrain yourself?"

"I have not," he said, with a smirk.

"Haven't joined or haven't restrained yourself?"

A broader smirk. "The first. I like you, Ned. I cherish wit when I find it, I always have done. Not that we're overburdened with it at my place of work. Where wit's concerned, I'd be inclined to refer to the Tank as a total desert."

"No friendship or peace groups?" I continued, affecting disappointment. "Fellow-travelling organisations? Taken out membership to any homosexual or otherwise deviant-oriented clubs, formed a secret passion for any under-age choir-boys lately?"

"No to the lot, thank you," said Frewin, now smiling broadly.

"Run up vast debts, causing you to live beyond your means? Set up some tasteful redhead in the style to which she is not accustomed? Acquired a Ferrari motorcar on the hire purchase?"

"My needs remain as modest as they have always been, thank you. I am not of a materialist or self-indulgent nature, as you may have gathered. I rather abhor materialism, frankly. There's too much of it these days. Far."

"And no to the rest?"

"All no."

I was jotting all the time, making annotations against an imaginary checklist.

"So you wouldn't be flogging secrets for money then," I commented, turning a page and adding a couple of ticks. "And you have not launched yourself upon a course of foreign language instruction without first obtaining the consent of your employing department in writing, I take it?" My pencil was poised once more. "Sanskrit? Hebrew? Urdu? Serbo-Croat?" I suggested. "Russian?"

He was standing very still and staring at me, but I pretended to be unaware of this.

"Hottentot?" I continued facetiously. "Estonian?"

"Since when's *that* been on the list?" Frewin demanded aggressively.

"Hottentot?"

I waited.

"Languages. A language isn't a defect. It's an attribute. An accomplishment! You don't have to list all your accomplishments, just to get cleared!"

I tilted back my head in reminiscence. "Addendum to the Positive Vetting procedure, November 5, 1967," I recited. "I always remember that one. Fireworks Day. Special circular to all employing departments, yours included, requiring advance notice in writing of all intended language instruction courses. Recommended by Judicial Steering Committee, approved by Cabinet."

He had turned his back to me. "I regard this as a totally out-of-court question and I refuse to answer it in any shape or form. Write that down."

I puffed through my pipe smoke.

"I said write it down!"

"I wouldn't say that, Cyril, if I were you. They'll be cross with you."

"Let them be."

I drew on my pipe again. "I'll put it to you the way HQ put it to me, shall I?

'What's all this nonsense Cyril's been getting up to with his chums Boris and Olga?' they said. 'Ask him that one—then see what he comes up with.' "

Still turned away from me, he was scowling indignantly from place to place around the room, appealing to his polished world to witness my profanity. I waited for the explosion I was sure would come. But instead he peered at me in hurt reproach. *Us,* he was saying, *friends—and you do this to me.* And in the way that the brain in stress can handle a multitude of images at once, I saw before me, not Frewin, but a typist I had once interrogated in our Embassy in Ankara: how she had rolled back the sleeve of her cardigan and thrust out her arm at me and showed me the festering cigarette burns she had inflicted on herself the night before our interview. "Don't you think you have made me suffer enough?" she asked. Yet it was not I who had made her suffer; it was the twenty-five-year-old Polish diplomat for whom she had sacrificed every secret she possessed.

I took my pipe from my mouth and gave him a reassuring laugh. "Come on, Cyril. Aren't Boris and Olga two of the characters on this Russian course you're doing on the sly? Papering their house together? Going off to stay at Auntie Tanya's dacha, all that? You're doing the standard Radio Moscow language course, five days a week, 6 a.m. sharp, that's what they told me. 'Ask him about Boris and Olga,' they say. 'Ask him why he's learning Russian on the q.t.' So I'm asking you. That's all."

"They'd no business knowing I was doing that course," he muttered, still grappling with the implications of my question. "Bloody sniffer dogs. It was private. Privately selected, privately pursued. They can get lost. So can you."

I laughed. But I was also put out. "Now don't be like that, Cyril. You know the rules as well as I do. It's not your style to ignore a regulation. It's not mine either. Russian is Russian, and reporting is reporting. It's only a matter of getting it down in writing. I didn't make up the regulations. I get a brief, the same as anyone else." I was talking to his back again. He had taken refuge at the bay window, and was gazing out at the rectangle that was his garden.

"What's their names?" he demanded.

"Olga and Boris," I repeated patiently.

This enraged him. "The people who brief you, idiot! I'm going to enter a complaint about them! Snooping, that's what it is. It's bloody brutal in this day and age. I'm holding you to blame too, frankly. What's their names?"

I still didn't answer him. I preferred to let the fury bank up in him.

"Number one," he announced in a louder voice, still staring at his mud patch. "Are you writing this down? Number one, I am not taking a language course within the meaning of the Act. A language course is going to a school or class, it is sitting on a bench with a bunch of snivelling typists with bad breath, it is submitting to the sneers of an uncouth instructor. Number two. I *do,* however, listen to *radio,* it being one of my *continuing* pleasures to scan the wavebands for examples of the quaint or esoteric. Write that down and I'll sign it. Finish, okay? Then take yourself off. I'm done with you, thank you, up to here. Nothing personal. It's them."

"Which was how you stumbled on Boris and Olga," I suggested helpfully, writing again. "Got it. You scanned the wavebands and there they were. Boris and Olga. Nothing wrong in that, Cyril. Stick with it and you might even land yourself a language allowance, if you pass the test. It's only a few bob, I suppose, but it's better in your pocket than theirs, I always say." I continued writing, but slowly, letting him hear the maddening scratch of my government-issue pencil. "It's always the *not* reporting that bothers them most," I confided, apologising for the foibles of my masters. " 'If he hasn't told us about Olga and Boris, what else hasn't he told us?' You can't blame them, I suppose. Their jobs are on the line, same as ours."

Turn another page. Lick tip of pencil. Make another annotation. I was beginning to feel the excitement of the chase. Love as commitment, he had said, love as part of life, love as effort, love as sacrifice. But love for whom? I drew a heavy pencil line and turned a page.

"Can we pass on to your Iron Curtains, please, Cyril?" I asked in my weariest voice. "HQ are devils for Iron Curtains. I wondered whether you'd any fresh names to add to the list of those you've already given us these past years. The last one" —I flipped to the back of the notebook—"my goodness, that was aeons ago. A gentleman from East Germany, a member of a local choral society you joined. Is there no one you can think of since at all? They're a bit after you now, Cyril, I'll admit, now that they've caught you not reporting the language course."

His disillusionment in me was again sliding into anger. Once again he began punching the unlikely words. But this time it was as if he were punching me.

"You will find *all* my Iron Curtain contacts, past and present, *such* as they are, *duly* listed *and* submitted *to* my superiors, according to regulations. *If* you had troubled yourself to *obtain* this data from Foreign Office Personnel Department *prior* to this interview—and I mean why they send me a hack like you—"

I decided to cut him short. I did not think it useful that he should be allowed to reduce me to nothing. To insignificance, yes. But not to nothing, for I was the servant of a higher authority. I pulled a sheet of paper from the back of my notebook. "Look, now, here you are, I've got them. All your Iron Curtains on one page. There's only been five ever, in your whole twenty years. HQ-cleared, I see, the lot. Well, so they would be, as long as you report them." I put the sheet back in my notebook. "Anyone to add, then? Who's to add? Think now, Cyril. Don't be hasty. They know an awful lot, my people. They shock me sometimes. Take your time."

He took his time. And more time. And more. Finally he took the line of self-pity.

"I'm not a *diplomat,* Ned," he complained in a small voice. "I'm not out doing the gay hurrah every night, Belgravia, Kensington, St. John's Wood, medals and white tie, rubbing shoulders with the great, am I? I'm a clerk. I'm not that man at all."

"What man's that, Cyril?"

"I like a treat, that's different. I like a friend best."

"I know you do, Cyril. HQ knows too."

A fresh resort to anger to mask his rising panic. Deafening body language as he clenches his great fists and lifts his elbows. "There is not a single *name* on that list that has *crossed* my path since I reported the *persons* concerned. The names in that list related *entirely* to the most *completely* casual encounters, which had no follow-up *whatsoever.*"

"But what about new people since?" I pleaded patiently. "You'll not get past them, Cyril. I don't, so why should you?"

"If there *was* anyone to add, any contact at all, even a Christmas card from someone, you may *rest* assured I would have been the first to add him. Finish. Done. Over. Next question, thank you."

Diplomat, I noted. *Him,* I noted. *Christmas.* Salzburg. I became if anything more laborious.

"That's not quite the answer they want, Cyril," I said as I wrote in my note-book. "That sounds a bit too much like flannel, frankly. They want a 'yes' or a 'no,' or an 'if yes, who?' They want a straight answer and they're not settling for flannel. 'He didn't own up to his language, so why should we think he's owning up to his Iron Curtains?' That's what they're thinking, Cyril. That's what they're going to say to me too. It'll all come back on me in the end," I warned him, still writing.

Once again I could feel that my ponderousness was a torture to him. He was pacing, snapping his fingers at his sides. He was muttering, working his jaw menac-ingly, growling again about getting names. But I was far too busy writing in my notebook to notice any of this. I was old Ned, Burr's Mr. Plod, doing his duty by HQ.

"How's about this then, Cyril?" I said at last. And, holding up my notebook, I read aloud to him what I had written: " 'I, Cyril Frewin, solemnly declare that I have not made the acquaintance, however briefly, of any Soviet or Eastern Bloc citizen, other than those already listed by me, in the last twelve months. Dated and signed Cyril.' "

I relit my pipe and studied the bowl in order to make quite sure it was drawing. I put the burned-out match in the matchbox, and the matchbox in my pocket. My voice, already slowed to a walking pace, now became a crawl.

"Alternatively, Cyril, and I say this advisedly, if there *is* anyone like that in your life, now's your chance to tell me. And them. I'll treat everything you say in confidence; so will they, depending what I tell them of it, which isn't always everything, not by any means. Nobody's a saint, after all. And HQ probably wouldn't clear them if they were."

Intentionally or otherwise, I had touched the fuse in him. He had been waiting for an excuse and now I had delivered it.

"Saint? Who's talking *saint?* Don't *you* call me bloody saint, I won't have it! Saint Cyril, they call me, did you know that? Of course you did, you're taunting me!"

Taut-faced and rude. Battering me with words. Frewin against the ropes, slug-ging anything that came at him. "If there *were* such a person—which there is not —I would *not* have told *you* or your snooping PV lot—I would have reported the matter *in writing,* according to regulations, to personnel department *at the—*"

For the second time, I allowed myself to cut him short. I didn't like him conducting the rhythm of our exchanges. "But there really isn't anyone, is that right?" I said, as pressingly as my passive rôle allowed. "There's no one? You haven't been to any functions—parties, get-togethers, meetings—official, unofficial —in London, outside London, abroad even—at which a citizen of an Iron Curtain country was remotely present?"

"Do I have to continue saying no?"

"Not if the answer's yes," I replied, with a smile he didn't like.

"The answer is no. No, no, no. Repeat no. Got it?"

"Thank you. So I can put *none,* can I? That means no one, not even a Russian. And you can sign it. Yes?"

"Yes."

"Meaning no?" I suggested, making another weak joke. "I'm sorry, Cyril, but we do have to be crystal clear, otherwise HQ will fall on us from a great height. Look, I've written it down for you. Sign it."

I handed him my pencil and he signed. I wanted to instil the habit in him. He handed back my notebook, smiling tragically at me. He had lied to me and he needed my comfort in his wretchedness. So I granted it to him—if only, I am afraid, because I wanted to take it away again very soon. I stowed the notebook in my inside pocket, stood up, and gave a big stretch as if announcing a break in our discussions, seeing that a tricky point was behind us. I rubbed my back a bit, an old man's ache.

"What's all that digging you've been doing out there, Cyril?" I said. "Building your own deep shelter, are you? Hardly necessary these days, I'd have thought."

Looking past him, my eye had fallen on a pile of new bricks stacked in a corner of the mud patch, with a tarpaulin tied over the top of them. An unfinished trench, about two feet deep, cut across the lawn towards them.

"I am *building* a *pond*," Frewin retorted, seizing gratefully on my facetious diversion. "I *happen* to be very fond of *water*."

"A goldfish pond, Cyril?"

"An *ornamental* pond." His good humour came sailing back. He relaxed, he smiled, and his smile was so warm and unaffected that I found myself smiling in return. "What I intend to do, Ned," he explained, drawing near to me in friendship, "is construct three separate levels of water, beginning four feet above the existing ground, descending over eighteen-inch intervals to that trench. I shall then illuminate each pool from beneath with the aid of a concealed lamp. I shall then pump the water with an electric pump. And at night, instead of drawing the curtains, I shall be able to look out on to my own private display of illuminated pools and waterfalls!"

"And play your music!" I cried, responding in full measure to his enthusiasm. "I think that's splendid, Cyril. Genius. I'm most impressed, I really am. I'd like my wife to see that. How was Salzburg, by the way?"

He actually reels, I thought, watching his head swing away from me. I hit him and he reels, and I wait till he recovers consciousness before I hit him again.

"You go to Salzburg for the music, they tell me. Quite a Mecca for you musicians, they tell me, Salzburg. Do they do opera at Christmas, or is it all carols and anthems you go for?"

They must have closed off the street, I thought, listening to the enormous silence. I wondered whether Frewin was thinking the same as he went on staring into the garden.

"Why should you care?" he answered. "You're a musical ignoramus. You said so. As well as being a very considerable snooper."

"Verdi? I've heard of Verdi. Mozart? He was Austrian, wasn't he? I saw the film. I'll bet they do you Mozart for Christmas. They'd have to. Which ones do they do?"

Silence again. I sat down and once again prepared myself to write to his dictation.

"Do you go alone?" I asked.

"Of course I do."

"Do you always?"

"Of course I do."

"Last time too?"

"Yes!"

"Do you stay alone?" I asked.

He laughed loudly. "Me? Not for one minute. Not me. There's dancing girls waiting for me in my room when I arrive. They're changed every day."

"But music night after night after night, the way you like it?"

"Who says what I like?"

"Fourteen nights of it. Twelve, I suppose, if you count the travel."

"Could be twelve. Could be fourteen. Could be thirteen. What does it matter?" He was still concussed. He was talking from a long way off.

"Which is what you go for. To Salzburg. And what you pay for. Yes? Yes, Cyril? Give me a signal, please, Cyril. I keep thinking I'm losing you. And it was what you went for this Christmas too?"

He nodded.

"Concerts, night after night? Opera? Carols?"

"Yes."

"Only the trouble is, you see, HQ says you only stayed the one night. You arrived on the first day as booked, they say, and you were off again next morning. You paid the full whack for your room, all two weeks, but the hotel never saw hide nor hair of you from your second day till you came back at the end of your holiday. So quite reasonably, really, HQ are asking where the bloody hell you went." I took my boldest leap so far. "And who with. They're asking whether you've got someone on the side. Like Boris and Olga, but real."

I turned a couple more pages of my notebook, and in the deep silence the rustle was like falling bricks. His terror was infecting me. It was like a shared evil. The truth lay a membrane from us, yet the dread of it seemed to be as terrible to the man who was trying to keep it outside the door as to myself, who was trying to let it in.

"All we need to do is get it down on paper, Cyril," I said. "Then we can forget it. Nothing like writing something down for getting it out of the way, I say. It's no crime to have a friend. Even a foreign one isn't a crime, as long as he's written down. He *is* foreign, I take it? Only, I notice a certain hesitation in you here. He must be quite some friend, I will say, if you gave up all that music for him."

"He's nowhere. He doesn't exist. He's gone. I was in his way."

"Well, he hadn't gone at Christmas time, had he? Not if you were together with him. Was he Austrian, Cyril?"

Frewin was lifeless. He was dead with his eyes open. I had hit him once too often.

"All right, then, he's French," I suggested more loudly, trying to jerk him from his introspection. "Was he a Frenchie, Cyril, your chum? . . . They wouldn't mind about a Frenchie, even if they don't like them. Come on, Cyril, how about a Yank then? They can't object to a Yank!" No answer. "Not Irish, was he? I hope not, for your sake!"

I did the laughing for him, but nothing stirred him from his melancholy. Still at the window, he had crooked his thumb and was boring the knuckle joint into his forehead, as if trying to make a bullet hole. Had he whispered something?

"I didn't catch you, Cyril!"

"He's above all that."

"Above nationality?"

"He's above it."

"You mean he's a diplomat?"

"He didn't *come* to Salzburg, can't you bloody listen?" He swung round at me and began screaming. "You're bloody spastic, you know that? Never mind the answers, you can't even *ask* right! No wonder the country's in a mess! Where's your savvy gone? Where's your human understanding, for a change?"

I stood up again. Slowly. Keep him watching me. Give my back another rub. I wandered down the room. I shook my head as if to say this simply would not do.

"I'm trying to help you, Cyril. If you went to Salzburg and stayed there, that's one scenario. If you went on somewhere else—well, that's quite another. If your chum is Italian, say. And if you pretended to go to Salzburg but went—oh, I don't know—to Rome, say, or Milan, even Venice—well, that's another. I can't do it all for you. It's not fair and they wouldn't thank me if I did."

He was wide-eyed. He was transferring his madness to me, appointing himself the sane one. I refilled my pipe, giving it my entire attention while I went on talking.

"You're a hard man to please, Cyril"—tamping the tobacco with my forefinger —"you're a tease, if you want to know. 'Don't touch me here, take your hand away from there, you can do this but only once.' I mean, what *am* I allowed to talk about?"

I struck a match and held it to the bowl, and as I did so I saw that he had transferred his knuckles to his eyes in order not to be in the room. But I pretended not to notice. "All right, we'll forget Salzburg. If Salzburg is hurtful, put Salzburg aside and let's go back to your Iron Curtains. Yes? Agreed?"

His hands slipped slowly from his face. No answer, but no outright rejection either. I went on talking. He wanted me to. I could sense his reliance on my words as a bridge between the real world and the inner hell where he was living. He wanted me to do the talking for both of us. I felt I had to make his confession for him, which was why I decided to play my most perilous card.

"So suppose, for argument's sake, Cyril, we were to add the name of Sergei Modrian to this list and call it a day," I suggested carelessly, almost covering over my words in my efforts to sound unthreatening. "Just to be on the safe side," I added cheerfully. "What do you say?" His head was still hanging downward, his face cut off from me. Chatting cheerfully, I expanded on my latest helpful proposal for HQ. " 'All right,' we say to them, 'so take your wretched Mr. Modrian. Don't play around with us any more, we'll come clean. Have him and go home. Ned and Cyril have got work to do.' "

He was dangling, smiling like a hanged man. In the profound silence that had settled over the neighbourhood, I had the sensation of hearing my words resounding from the rooftops. But Frewin seemed barely to have heard them.

"Modrian's the one they want you to own up to, Cyril," I continued reasonably. "They told me. If you say *yes* to Modrian—and if I write him down, which I'm doing, and you allow me to, and I notice you're not stopping me, are you?—nobody can accuse either one of us of being less than frank with them. 'Yes, I am a chum of Sergei Modrian and screw the lot of you'—how's that? '*And* I went with him to wherever we went, *and* we did this, we did that, we agreed to do certain other things, and we had a lovely time, or we didn't. And anyway, what's all the *glasnost*

for, if I'm still being forbidden to associate with an extremely civilised Russian?'
... How's that? Never mind the gaps for the moment, we can fill all those in later.
Then, the way I see it, they can pack up the file for another year and we can all get
on with our weekend."

"Why?"

I affected not to understand.

"Why can they pack up the file then?" he demanded, as suspicions crowded in
on him. "When they've been who they are? They're not going to turn round and
say 'What's the point?' Nobody does. Not when they've been one thing. They stay
who they are. They don't become other people. They can't."

"Come off it, Cyril!" He had sunk into his own thoughts and was becoming
hard to reach. *"Cyril!"*

"What then? What's up? Don't shout."

"So what's wrong with being Russian these days? HQ would be *far* more
worried if Sergei was a Frenchie! I only suggested Frenchie as a trap. I regret that
now, I apologise. But a Russian these days—for heaven's sake, we're not just
talking friendly nations, we're talking partners! *You* know HQ. They're always
behind the times. So's Gorst. Our job's to set the trend. Are you hearing me, Cyril?"

And that was where, for a moment, I thought I had lost the whole game—lost
his complicity, lost his dependence, lost the willing suspension of his disbelief. He
wandered past me like a sleepwalker. He stood himself at his bay window again,
where he remained contemplating his half-dug pool and all the other half-built
dreams of his life, which he must have known by now would never be completed.

Then, to my relief, he started talking. Not about what he had done. Not about
who he had done it with. But why.

"You don't know what it means, do you, to be locked up all day with a bunch of
morons?"

I thought at first he was complaining of his future, till I realised he was talking
about the Tank.

"Listening to their filthy jokes all day, choking on their fags and their B.O.? Not
you, you're privileged, however humble you make yourself out. Day after day of it,
sniggers about tits and knickers and periods and little bits on the side? 'Come on,
Saint, tell us a naughty joke for a change! You're a deep one, I'll bet, Saint! What
are you into—gym slips? Bit of the rough? What's the Saint's little fancy of a
Saturday night?' " His energy had returned to him in full force, and with it, to my
astonishment, an unexpected gift for mimicry. He was mincing at me, playing the
music-hall queen, a ghastly soft grin twisting his hairless face. " 'Heard the one
about the Boy Scouts and the Girl Guides, Saint? The excitement was in tents. Get
you!' You wouldn't know about that, would you? 'Do you pull it now and then,
Saint? Give it a little jerk occasionally, just to make sure it's there? You'll go blind,
you know. It'll drop off. I'll bet you've got a big one, haven't you? A real donkey
knock, all the way down your leg and tucked into your garter.' . . . You've never
had that, have you, all day long, in the office, in the canteen? You're a gentleman.
Know what they gave me April Fool's Day? A top secret incoming from Paris,
Frewin's eyes only, decypher yourself, manual, ha ha. *Flash priority*, get the joke?
I didn't. So I go into the cubicle and get out the books, don't I? And I decypher it,

don't I? Manual. Everyone's got his head down. Nobody laughing or spoiling it. I do the first six groups and it's filth, some filthy joke all about a French letter. Gorst had done it. He'd had the boys at the Paris Embassy send it specially as a joke. 'Steady on, Saint, keep your hair on, give us a smile. It was only a joke, Saint, can't you take a joke?' That's what Personnel said too, when I complained. Horseplay, they said. Pranks are good for morale. Think of it as a compliment, they said, show a little sporting instinct. If I hadn't had my music, I'd have killed myself long ago. I considered it, I don't mind telling you. Trouble was, I wouldn't see their faces when they found out what they'd done."

A traitor needs two things, Smiley had once remarked bitterly to me at the time of Haydon's betrayal of the Circus: somebody to hate, and somebody to love. Frewin had told me whom he hated. Now he began to talk about whom he loved.

"I'd been all over the world that night—Puerto Rico, Cape Verde, Jo'burg—and there wasn't anything that took my fancy. I like the amateurs best, as a rule, the hacks. They've got more wit, which is what I like, I told you. I didn't even know it was morning. I've got these thick curtains up there, three hundred quids' worth, interlined. It's meat and drink to me after the Tank, the quiet is."

A different smile had come up on him, a small boy's smile on his birthday.

" 'Good morning to you, Boris, my friend,' says Olga. 'How are you feeling this morning?' Then she says it in Russian and Boris replies that he's feeling a bit low. He's often low, Boris is. He's prone to Slav depressions. Olga takes care of him, mind. She'll have a joke, but it's never cruelly meant. They have a fight now and then too—well, it's only natural, seeing they do everything together. But they always make it up in the same programme. They don't bear a grudge from day to day. Olga couldn't do that, to be frank. It's out with it and that's it, with Olga. Then they'll have a laugh together. That's how they are. Constructive. Friendly. Clean spoken. Musical too, naturally—well, they would be, being Russian. I wasn't that keen on Tchaikovsky till I heard them discussing him. But afterwards I came round to him straight away. Boris has got quite advanced tastes in music actually. Olga —well, she's a bit easy to please. Still, they're only actors, I suppose, reading their lines. But you forget that when you're listening to them, trying to learn the language. You believe in them."

And you send your written work in, he was saying.

For free correction and advice, he was saying.

You don't even have to write to Moscow after the first time. They've got this box number in Luxembourg.

He had fallen quiet but not dangerously so. Nevertheless I was becoming scared that his trance might end too soon. I took myself out of his line of sight, and stood in a corner of the room behind him.

"What address did you give them, Cyril?"

"This one, of course. What else have I got to give them, then? A country house in Shropshire? A villa in Capri?"

"Did you give them your own name too?"

"Of course I didn't. Well, Cyril, yes. I mean anyone can be Cyril."

"Good man," I said approvingly. "Cyril who?"

"Nemo," he announced proudly. "Mr. C. Nemo. 'Nemo' is Latin for 'nobody,' in case you didn't know."

Mr. C. Nemo. Like Mr. A. Patriot, perhaps.

"Did you put your occupation?"

"Not my real one. You're being stupid again."

"So what did you put?"

"Musician."

"Did they ask for your age?"

"Of course they did. They had to. They had to know you were eligible, in case you won the prize. They can't give prizes to minors, can they? No one can."

"And status—married or single—you told them that too?"

"I *had* to put my status, didn't I, with the prize being available to *couples!* They can't give a *prize* to *one* person and leave his wife out, it wouldn't be gracious."

"What work did you send in—the first time round, for instance—do you remember?"

He decided to take further exception to my stupidity.

"Thickhead. What do you think I sent them? Bloody logarithms? You write in, you get the forms, you enrol, you get the Luxembourg box number, you get the book, you're one of them. After that you do what Boris and Olga tell you to do in the programme, don't you? 'Complete the exercise on page 9. Answer the questions on page 12.' Haven't you been to school then?"

"And you were good. HQ says you've got a mind like an encyclopaedia when you use it. They told me." I was beginning to learn how much he relished flattery.

"I was *more* than good, as a matter of fact, thank you, HQ. If you *wish* to know, I was in the nature of being their *top pupil.* Certain *notes* were sent to me by certain *tutors,* and some of them had a highly congratulatory *tone,*" he added, with the wild grin that came over him when he was praised. "It gave me quite a filip, if you wish to know, walking into the Tank of a Monday morning with one of their little *notes* in my pocket and not saying anything. I thought, I could tell some of *you* a tale if I wanted. I didn't, though. I preferred my privacy. I preferred my friendships. I wasn't going to have those animals making filthy comments about Olga and Boris, thank you."

"And you wrote back to these tutors?"

"Only as Nemo."

"But you didn't fool with them otherwise?" I asked, trying to fathom what restraints, if any, were in his mind as he embarked on this first illicit love affair. "I mean, if they asked you a plain question, you'd give them a plain answer. You weren't coy."

"I was *not* coy! I had no *cause* to be! I took great care to be courteous, the same as my tutors were. They were high professors, some of them, academicians. I was *grateful* and I was *diligent.* That was the least they deserved, considering there was no fee and it was voluntary and in the interests of human understanding."

The hunter in me again. I was calculating the moves they would have made as they played him along. I was working out how I would have played him myself, if the Circus had dreamed up anything so perfect.

"And I suppose, as you improved, they passed you on from plain printed exercises to the more ambitious stuff—composition, essays?"

"When it was deemed by the Board of Tutors in Moscow that I was ripe for it, yes, they moved me up to freestyle."

"Do you remember the subjects they set you?"

He laughed his superior laugh. "You think I'd forget them? Five nights at each one of them with the dictionary? Two hours' sleep if I'm lucky? Wake up, will you, Ned!"

I gave a rueful little laugh as I wrote to his dictation.

" 'My Life' was the first one. I told them about the Tank, not mentioning names, of course, or the nature of our work, naturally. Nevertheless, a certain element of social comment was present, I won't deny it. I thought the Board had a right to know, specially with the *glasnost* in the pipeline and everything easing up for the benefit of all mankind."

"What was the next one?"

" 'My Home.' I told them about my plans for the pond. They liked that. And my cooking. One of them was quite a major cook. After that they gave me 'My Favourite Pastime,' which could have been redundant but wasn't."

"You described your love of music, I suppose?"

"Wrong."

The rest of his answer rings in my ears today: as an accusation, as a cry of sympathy from a fellow sufferer; as a blind prayer flung into the ether by a man who, like myself, was desperate for love before it was too late.

"I elected 'Good Company' as my favourite pastime, if you really wish to know," he said as the wild smile came racing back to his cheeks. "The fact that I had not *had* much good company in my life hitherto did not *deter* me from relishing the few occasions when it *had* come my way." He seemed to forget that he had spoken, for he began again, in words I might have used of Sally: "I had a feeling I had *renounced* something in my life which I *now* wished to reclaim," he said.

"And did they admire your advanced work too? Were they impressed by it?" I asked as I diligently wrote this down.

He was smirking again. "Moderately, I assume. Marginally. Here and there. With reservations, naturally."

"Why do you assume that?"

"Because, unlike some, they had the grace and generosity to show their appreciation. That's why."

And they showed it, said Frewin—I scarcely needed to press him further—they showed it in the person of one Sergei Modrian, First Secretary Cultural, of the Soviet Embassy in London, in his capacity as Radio Moscow's devoted local emissary despatched to answer Frewin's prayer.

Like all good angels, Modrian arrived without warning, on Frewin's doorstep one dank November Saturday, bearing with him the gifts of his high office: one bottle of Moskovskaya vodka, one tin of Sevruga caviar, and one foully printed artbook about the Bolshoi Ballet. And one grandly typed letter appointing Mr. C. Nemo to be an Honorary Student of Moscow State University, in recognition of his unique progress in the Russian language.

But the greatest gift of all was Modrian's own magical person, custom-trained to provide the good company Frewin had so loudly craved in his prize-winning essay for the Board.

* * *

We had arrived at our destination. Frewin was calm, Frewin was in triumph; Frewin, for however long, was fulfilled. His voice had broken free of its confinements; his plain face was lit with the smile of a man who had known true love and was longing to impart his luck. If there had been anyone in the world for whom I could ever have smiled in the same way, I would have been a different man.

"*Modrian,* Ned? Sergei Modrian? Oh, Ned, I mean we're talking the total top league here. One look at him, I knew. None of your half measures here, I thought. This one's the whole hog. We had the same sense of humour, of course, straight off. Acid. No wool across the eyes. The same interests too, right down to composers." He attempted a more detached tone, but in vain. "It is very *rare* in life, in my experience, for two human beings to be naturally compatible in each and every respect—bar women, where I have to admit that Sergei's experience far outran my own. Sergei's attitude to women"—he was trying hard to be disapproving—"I'll put it this way: if it had been anyone else behaving in that manner, I would have been hard put to it to approve."

"Did he introduce you to women, Cyril?"

His expression switched to one of adamant rejection. "He assuredly did not, thank you. Nor would I have permitted him to. Nor would he have regarded such introductions as coming within the ambit of our relationship."

"Not even on your trips to Russia together?" I ventured, taking another leap for him.

"Nowhere, thank you. It would have ruined them, as a matter of fact. Killed them stone dead."

"So it's all hearsay, what they say about his women?"

"No, it's not. It's what Sergei told me himself. Sergei Modrian had a totally ruthless attitude to women. His colleagues confirmed this to me privately. Ruthless."

I found time to marvel at Modrian's psychological dexterity—or was it the dexterity of his masters? Between Modrian the ruthless pursuer of women, and Frewin the ruthless rejecter of them, there was indeed a natural bond.

"So you met his colleagues too," I said. "In Moscow, presumably. At Christmas."

"Only the ones he trusted. Their respect for him was incredible. Or Leningrad. I wasn't fussy, I'd no right to be. I was an honoured guest. I went along with whatever they'd arranged for me."

I kept my eyes on my notebook. God knows what I was writing by then. Gobbledygook. Afterwards, there were whole tracts I couldn't read a word of. I selected my absolutely dullest tone.

"And was all this in honour of your remarkable linguistic abilities, Cyril? Or were you already providing informal services for Modrian by then? Like giving him information or whatever. Translating and so on. A lot do it, I'm told. They're not supposed to, of course. But you can't blame people—can you?—wanting to help the *glasnost* along, now it's come. We've waited long enough. Only, I've got to put the proper history to this, Cyril. They'll skin me otherwise."

I did not dare look up. I simply kept writing. I turned a page and wrote: *keep talking, keep talking, keep talking.* And still I did not look up.

I heard him whisper something I couldn't understand. I heard him mutter, "It's *not.* I didn't. I never bloody did." I heard him complain more loudly: "Don't *say* that, do you mind? Don't you ever say that again, you and your HQ. 'Giving him information'—what's all that about? They're wrong words. *I'm talking to you, Ned!*"

I looked up, sucking on my pipe and smiling. "Are you, Cyril? Of course you are. I'm sorry. You're my sixth in a week, to be honest. They're all doing the *glasnost* these days. It's the fashion. I'm beginning to feel my age."

He decided to comfort me. He sat down. Not in the chair, but on its arm. He put on an avuncular, friend-to-friend manner that reminded me of my preparatory-school headmaster.

"You're by way of being a liberal yourself, aren't you, Ned? You've got the face for it anyway, even if you are a bit of a toady for HQ."

"I suppose I'm a sort of free thinker in my way, yes," I conceded. "Though I do have my pension to consider, naturally."

"Of course you are! You favour a mixed economy, don't you? You don't like public poverty and private wealth any more than I do. Humanity above ideology, you believe in that? Stop the derailed train of capitalism destroying all before it in its path? Of course you do! You've got a sensible concern for the environment, I dare say. Badgers, whales, fur coats, power stations. Even a vision of sharing, where it doesn't impinge. Brothers and sisters marching together towards common goals, culture and music for all! Freedom of movement and choice of allegiance! Peace! Well, then."

"Makes good enough sense to me," I said.

"You're not old enough to have done the thirties; neither am I. I wouldn't have held with them if I had been. We're *good men*, that's all we are. *Reasonable men.* That's what Sergei was too. You and Sergei—I can see it in your face, Ned, it's no good your trying to hide it, you're birds of a feather. So don't go painting me black and you white, because we're like minds, same as me and Sergei were. On the same side against the wickedness, the lack of culture, the filth. 'We're "the unrecognised aristocracy" '—that's what Sergei called us. He was right. You're one too, that's all I'm saying. I mean, who else is there? Who's the alternative to what we see around us every day, the degradation, the waste, the disrespect? Who are we going to listen to, up there in the attic at night, twiddling the dials? Not the yuppies, that's for sure. Not the pigs-in-clover lot—what have they got to say? Not the make-more spend-more be-more school, they're no help. Not the knickers-and-tits brigade, either. And we're not going to convert to Islam in a hurry, are we, not while they go round pinching countries off each other and doing the poison gas. So I mean what's the alternative for a feeling man, a man of conscience, now the Russians are abandoning their responsibilities right and left and putting on the hair shirt? Who's out there for us? Where's the vision any more? Where's the relief? The friendship? Someone's got to fill the gap. I can't be left in the air. I can't be without. Not after Sergei, Ned—I'd die. Sergei was the most important man on earth to me. Drink, meat and laughter, Sergei was. He was my total meaning. What's going to happen? That's what I want to know. There's some heads could roll, in my view. Sergei had the ideology. I don't see it in you—I don't think I do anyway. I get a glimpse of it, a longing here and there, then I'm not at all sure. I don't know you've got the quality."

"Try me," I said.

"I don't know you've got the wit. The dance. I thought that as you came in. I compared you with Sergei in my mind, and I'm afraid I found you seriously wanting. Sergei didn't shuffle in like a deadbeat; he took me by storm. Rings the bell, marches in as if he's bought the place, sits down where you're sitting, but more awake—not that he ever sat anywhere long, Sergei didn't, he was a shocking fidget, even at the opera. Then he grins like an elf and lifts up a glass of his own vodka. 'Congratulations, Mr. Nemo,' he says. 'Or may I call you C? You've won the competition and I'm the first prize.' "

He passed the back of his hand across his mouth, and I realised that he was wiping away a grin. "He was a real flyer, Sergei was."

He was laughing, so I laughed with him. Modrian was his false freedom, I was thinking. As Sally is mine.

"He hadn't even taken his coat off," he continued. "He went straight into his pitch. 'Now the first thing we've got to talk about is the ceremony,' he says. 'Nothing flashy, Mr. Nemo, just a couple of friends of mine, who happen to be Boris and Olga, plus one or two high dignitaries from the Board, and a small reception for a few of your many admirers in Moscow.'

" 'At your Embassy?' I said. 'I'm not coming there. My office would kill me— you don't know Gorst.'

" 'No, no, Mr. Nemo,' he says. 'No, no, Mr. C. *I'm* not talking about the Embassy—who cares about the Embassy? *I'm* talking about Moscow State University foreign language school and the official inauguration of your honorary studentship with full civilian honours.'

"I thought I was dead at first. My heart had stopped beating. I could feel it. I'd never been beyond Dover in my life, let alone Russia, although I was Foreign Office. 'Come to Moscow?' I said. 'You're off your head,' I said. 'I'm a cypher clerk, not a trade union leader with an ulcer. I can't come to Moscow at the drop of a hat,' I said. 'Even if there is a prize at the end of it, and Olga and Boris waiting to shake my hand, and studentships and I don't know what. You don't seem to understand the position at all. I'm in highly sensitive work,' I said. 'The people aren't that sensitive, but the work is. I've got constant and regular access to top secret and above. I'm not just anybody off the street, into your plane to Moscow and nobody's the wiser. I thought I put that in my essays, some of them.'

" 'Then come to Salzburg,' he says. 'Who's counting? Take a plane to Salzburg, say you're doing the music there, slip up to Vienna, I'll have the air tickets ready —all right, it's Aeroflot but it's only two hours—no nonsense with the passports when we arrive, we'll keep the ceremony family, who's the wiser?' Then he hands me this document like a scroll, all with the burned edges and that, the full formal invitation, signed by the whole Board, English one side, Russian the other. I read the English, I don't mind telling you. I wasn't going to sit in front of him with a dictionary for an hour, was I? I'd have looked a total idiot, me a top language student." He paused—a little shamefully, I thought. "Then I told him my name," he said. "I shouldn't have done, really, but I'd had enough of being Nemo. I wanted to be me."

Now you must lose me for a minute, as I lost Cyril. Until now, I had managed to stay abreast of his references. Where I had dared, I had even led them. Now suddenly he was running free and I was struggling to keep up with him. He was in Russia, but I wasn't. He'd given me no warning that we'd gone there. He was talking about Boris and Olga, not how they sounded any more, but how they looked; and how Boris had flung his arms round him, and how Olga had given him a demure but heartfelt Russian kiss—he didn't hold with kissing as a rule, Ned, but with the Russians it wasn't Gorst's kind of kissing at all, so you didn't mind. You even got to expect it, Ned, it being all part of what Russians regard as comradely. Frewin was looking twenty years younger and talking about being made a fuss of, all the birthdays that he'd never had. Olga and Boris in the flesh, Ned, no side to them, just natural, same as they were in their lessons.

" 'Congratulations, Cyril,' she says to me, 'on your completely phenomenal progress in the Russian language.' Well, through interpreters, naturally, I wasn't *that* far on, as I told her. Then Boris puts his arm round me. 'We're proud to be of assistance, Cyril,' he says. 'There's a lot of our students fall by the wayside, to be truthful, but those as don't make up for all the rest.' "

And by then at last I had pieced together the scene that he was painting for me in such broad, unpredicated strokes: his first Christmas in Russia, and for Frewin, I had no doubt, his first good Christmas anywhere, and Sergei Modrian playing ringmaster at his side. They are in a great room somewhere in Moscow, with chandeliers and speeches and a presentation, and fifty handpicked extras from Moscow Central Casting, and Frewin in paradise, which is exactly where Modrian wishes him to be.

Then, as abruptly as Frewin had treated me to this memory, he abandoned it. The light went out of his eyes, his head tipped to one side, and he beetled his eyebrows as if in judgment at his own behaviour.

Prudently, I returned him to time present. "So where is it?" I said. "The scroll he gave you. Here? The scroll, Cyril. Appointing you. Where?"

He stared at me, slowly waking. "I had to give it back to Sergei. 'When we're in Moscow, Cyril,' he said, 'you shall have it hanging on your wall and framed in gold. Not here. I wouldn't put you in the danger.' He'd thought of everything, Sergei had, and he was quite right, what with you and your HQ snooping on me night and day."

I allowed no pause, no alteration in my voice, not even in the direction of casualness. I lowered my eyes again and dug once more in my inside pocket. I was his candidate as Sergei's replacement, and he was courting me. He was showing me his tricks and asking me to take him on. Instinct told me to make him work harder for me. I addressed myself to the notebook again, and I spoke exactly as if I were asking him the name of his maternal grandfather.

"So when did you start giving Sergei all these great British secrets?" I said. "Well, what we *call* secrets, anyway. Obviously what was secret a few years ago is not going to be the same as what's secret today, is it? We didn't win the Cold War by secrecy, did we? We won it with the openness. The *glasnost*."

It was the second time I had mentioned passing over secrets, but on this occasion, when I crossed the Rubicon for him, he came with me. Yet he seemed not even to notice he was on the other side.

"Correct. That's how we won it. And Sergei didn't even want the secrets at first, either. 'Secrets, Cyril, they're unimportant to me,' he said. 'Secrets, Cyril, in the changing world in which we live, I'm pleased to say, they're a drug on the market,' he said. 'I'd rather keep our friendship on a non-official basis. However, if I *do* require something in that line, you may count on me to let you know.' In the meantime, he said, it would be quite sufficient if I wrote him a few unofficial reports on the quality of Radio Moscow's programmes just to keep his bosses happy. Whether the reception was good enough, for example. You'd think they'd know that, really, but they don't. You never know with Russians where you're going to strike the ignorance in them, to be frank. That's not a criticism, it's a fact. He'd like my opinion of the course as well, he said, the standard of instruction generally, any suggestions I might have for Boris and Olga in the future, me being somewhat of an unusual pupil in my own right."

"So what changed it?"

"Changed what? Be lucid, please, Ned. I'm not nobody, you know. I'm not Mr. Nemo. I'm Cyril."

"What changed Sergei's reluctance to take secrets from you?" I said.

"His Embassy did. The diehards. The barbarians. They always do. They prevailed on him. They declined to recognise the course of history; they preferred to remain total troglodytes in their caves and continue with their ridiculous Cold War."

I said I did not understand him. I said he was a bit above my head.

"Yes, well I'm not surprised. I'll put it this way. There was a lot of them in that Embassy didn't like the time given over to cultural friendship, for a start. There was this internal rivalry going on between the camps. I was an impotent spectator. The *doves,* they were in favour of the culture, naturally, and above all they were in favour of the *glasnost*. They saw culture filling the vacuum left behind by the withdrawal of hostilities. Sergei explained that to me. But the hawks—*including* the Ambassador, I regret to say—wanted Sergei concentrating more on the continuation of old attitudes, what's left of them, gathering intelligence and generally acting in an aggressive and conspiratorial manner regardless of the changes in the world climate. The Embassy diehards didn't care about Sergei being an idealist, not at all. Well, they wouldn't, would they, any more than what Gorst does. Sergei had to tread a highly precarious path, frankly, a bit for one side, then a bit for the other. So did I, it was duty. We'd do our culture together, a bit of language, a bit of art or music; then we'd do some secrets to satisfy the hawks. We had to justify ourselves to all parties, same as you with your HQ and me with the Tank."

He was fading, I was losing him. I had to use the whip. "So *when?*" I asked impatiently.

"When what?"

"Don't be clever with me, Cyril, do you mind? I've got to get this down. Look at the time. *When* did you start giving Sergei Modrian information, *what* did you give him, what for, how *much* for, when did it stop, and why, when it could perfectly well have continued? I'd like a weekend, Cyril, if you don't mind. So would my wife. I'd like to put my feet up in front of the telly. I'm not paid overtime, you know. It's strictly piecework, what they offer. One candidate's the same as another, when it comes to payday. We're living in a time of cost effectiveness, in case you haven't noticed. They tell me we could be privatised if we're not careful."

He didn't hear me. He didn't want to. He was wandering, in his body and in his mind, looking for distraction, for somewhere to hide. My anger was not all simulated. I was beginning to hate Modrian. I was angry about how much we depended on the credulity of the innocent in order to survive. It was sickening me that a trickster like Modrian had contrived to turn Frewin's loneliness to treachery. I felt threatened by the notion of love as the antithesis of duty.

I stood up smartly, anger still my ally. Frewin was perched listlessly on the edge of a carved Arthurian stool with the Royal Navy's ensign stitched into the seat.

"Show me your toys," I ordered him.

"What toys? I'm a man, if you don't mind, not an infant. It's my house. Don't tell me what to do."

I was remembering Modrian's tradecraft, the stuff he used, the way he equipped his agents. I was remembering my own tradecraft, from the days when I had run Frewin's counterparts against the Soviet target, even if they were not quite as mad as Frewin. I was imagining how I would have handled a high-access walk-in like Frewin, living on borrowed sanity.

"I want to see your camera, don't I?" I said petulantly. "Your high-speed transmitter, right, Cyril? Your signals plan. Your one-time codepads. Your crystals. Your white carbons for your secret writing. Your concealment devices. I want to see them, Cyril, I want to put them in my briefcase for Monday; then I want to go home and watch Arsenal against United. That may not be your taste, but it happens to be mine. So can we move this along a bit and cut out the bullshit, *please?*"

The madness was running out, I could feel it. He was drained and so was I. He sat head down and knees spread, staring dully at his hands. I could sense the end beginning in him—the moment when the penitent grows tired of his confession and of the emotions that compelled it.

"Cyril, I'm getting a bit edgy," I said.

And when he still didn't respond, I strode to his telephone, the same one that Monty's fake engineer had made permanently live. I dialled Burr's direct line and heard his fancy secretary the other end, the same one who hadn't known my name.

"Darling?" I said. "I'm going to be about another hour, if I'm lucky. I've got a slow one. Yes, all right, I know, I'm sorry. Well, I said I'm sorry. Yes, of course."

I rang off and stared at him accusingly. He climbed slowly to his feet and led me upstairs. His attic was a spare bedroom, roof high. His radio receiver stood on a table in the corner—German, just as Monty had said. I switched it on while he watched me, and we heard an accented female Russian voice talking indignantly about Moscow's criminal mafia.

"Why do they *do* that?" Frewin burst out at me, as if I were responsible. "The Russians. Why do they run down their own country all the time? They never used to. They were proud. I was proud too. All the cornfields, the classlessness, the chess, the cosmonauts, the ballet, the athletes. It was paradise till they started running it down. They've forgotten the good in themselves. It's bloody disgraceful. That's what I told Sergei."

"Then why do you still listen to them?" I said.

He was almost weeping, but I pretended not to notice.

"For the message, don't I?"

"Make it snappy, will you, Cyril!"

"Telling me I'm reactivated. That I'm wanted again. 'Come back, Cyril. All is forgiven, love, Sergei.' That's all I need to hear."

"How would they say that?"

"White paint."

"Go on."

" 'There's white paint on the dog, Olga.' . . . 'We need a spot of white paint on the bookshelf, Boris.' . . . 'Oh dear, oh dear, Olga, look at the cat, someone has dipped her tail in white paint. I hate cruelty,' says Boris. Why don't they say it when I'm listening?"

"Let's just stick to the method, can we? All right, you hear the message. On the radio. Olga or Boris says 'white paint.' Or they both do. *Then* what do you do?"

"Look in my signals plan."

I held out my hand, commanding him with my snapping fingers. "Hurry!" I said.

He hurried. He found a wooden hairbrush. Pulling the bristles from the casing, he shoved his big fingers into the gap and hauled out a piece of soft, flammable paper with times of the day and wavebands printed in parallel. He offered it to me, hoping it would satisfy. I took it from him without pleasure and snapped it into my notebook, glancing at my watch at the same moment.

"Thanks," I said curtly. "More, please, Cyril. I need a codebook and a transmitter. Don't tell me you haven't got them, I'm not in the mood."

He was grappling with a tin of talcum powder, tugging at the base, trying desperately to please me. He talked nervously while he shook the powder into the handbasin.

"I was respected, you see, Ned, you don't get that a lot. There's three of these. Olga and Boris tell me which to use, like with the white paint except it was the composers. Tchaikovsky was number three, Beethoven was number two, Bach was one. They did them alphabetical to help me remember. You get the glimpses but you don't get the friends, not normally, do you? Not unless you meet Sergei or one of his lot."

The powder was all poured away. Three radio crystals lay in his palm, together with a tiny codepad and an eye-glass to enlarge it.

"He had all I'd got, Sergei did. I gave it to him. He'd tell me a thing, I'd add it to my life. I'd have a mood, he'd get me straight again. He understood. He could see right into me. It gave me a feeling of being known, which I liked. It's gone now. It's been posted back to Moscow."

His rambling was scaring me. So was his feverish desire to pacify me. If I had been his hangman, he would have been gratefully loosening his tie.

"Your transmitter," I snapped. "What the hell's the good of a crystal and a codepad if you can't send!"

At the same terrible pace, he bent his swelled body to the floor and rolled back a corner of the tufted Wilton carpet.

"I haven't got a knife actually, Ned," he confessed.

Neither had I, but I dared not leave him, I dared not break my command over him. I crouched beside him. He was peering vaguely at a loose floorboard, trying to raise it with his thick fingertips. Clenching my fist, I punched one end of the board, and had the satisfaction of seeing the other end lift.

"Help yourself," I said.

It was old stuff, I could have guessed, nothing they cared about any more—a rig of grey boxes, a squash transmitter, a lash-up to be fitted to his receiver. Yet he handed it to me proudly, in its tangled mess.

A terrible anxiety had entered his eyes. "All I am now, you see, Ned, I'm a hole," he explained. "I don't mean to be morbid, do I, but I don't exist. This house isn't anything either. I used to love it. It looked after me, same as I looked after it. We'd have been nothing without each other, this house and me. It's hard for you to understand that, I dare say, if you have a wife, what a house is. She'd come between you. You and the house, I mean. Your wife. You and him. Modrian. I loved him, Ned. I was infatuated. 'You're too much, Cyril,' he used to say. 'Cool down. Relax. Take a holiday. You're hallucinating.' I couldn't. Sergei was my holiday."

"Camera," I ordered.

He didn't read me at once. He was obsessed with Modrian. He looked at me, but it was Modrian he saw.

"Don't be like that," he said, not understanding.

"Camera!" I yelled. "For Christ's sake, Cyril, don't you *ever* have a weekend?"

He stood at his wardrobe. Camelot sword blades carved on oak doors.

"Camera!" I shouted louder as he still hesitated. "How can you slip film to a good friend at the opera if you haven't photographed your files in the first place?"

"Take it easy, Ned. Cool down, will you? Please." Grinning in a superior way, he reached a hand into the wardrobe. But his eyes were ogling me, saying "Now watch this." He groped in the wardrobe, smiling at me mysteriously. He pulled out a pair of opera glasses and trained them on me, first the right way, then back to front. Then he handed them to me so that I could do the same to him. I took them in my hands and felt their unnatural weight at once. I turned the central dial until it clicked. He was nodding at me, encouraging me, saying "Yes, Ned, that's the way." He grabbed a book from the bookshelf and opened it at the centre, *All the World's Dancers,* illustrated. A young girl was doing a *pas de chat.* Sally too had been at ballet school. He unbuckled the neck strap and I saw that the short end did duty as a measuring chain. He took the binoculars from me and trained them on the book, measured the distance and turned the dial till it clicked.

"See?" he said proudly. "*Comprenez,* do you? They made it specially. For me. For opera nights. Sergei designed it personally. There's a lot of idleness in Russia, but Sergei had to have the best. I'd stay in late at the Tank. I'd photograph the whole weekly float for him if I felt like it, then give him the film while we were sitting in the stalls. I'd give it to him in one of the arias, usually—it was a sort of joke between us." He handed the binoculars back to me and drifted down the room, scrabbling his fingertips on his bare scalp as if he had a full head of hair. Then he held out his hands like someone testing the atmosphere for rain.

"Sergei had the best of me, Ned, and he's gone. *C'est la vie,* I say. Now it's up to you. Have you got the courage? Have you got the wit? That's why I wrote to you. I had to. I was empty. I didn't know you, but I needed you. I wanted a good man who understood me. A man I could trust again. It's up to you, Ned. Now's your chance. Jump out of yourself and live, I say, while there is yet time. That wife of yours is a bit of a bully, by the sound of her. You'd be well advised to tell her to live her own life instead of yours. I should have advertised, shouldn't I?" A terrible smile, which he turned full upon me. "Single man, non-smoker, fond of music and wit. I peruse those columns sometimes—who doesn't? I contemplate replying sometimes, except I'd never know how to break it off if I wasn't suited. So I wrote you a letter, didn't I? It was like writing to God in a way, till you came along in your shabby coat and asked a lot of spotty questions, no doubt drafted by HQ. It's time you stood on your own feet, Ned, same as me. You're cowed, that's your trouble. Your wife is partly to blame, in my opinion. I listened to your voice while you were apologising and I was not impressed. You won't reach out to take. Still, I reckon I could make something of you, and you could make something of me, too. You could help me dig my pool. I could show you music. That's evens, right? Nobody's impervious to music. I only did it because of Gorst." His voice leapt in horror. "*Ned!* Leave that alone, do you mind! Take your thieving hands off my property, Ned. *Now!*"

I was fingering his Markus typewriter. It was in the wardrobe where he kept his opera glasses, stowed under a few shirts. Signed A. Patriot, I thought. *"A"* standing for *Anyone's,* I thought. Anyone who loved him. I'd guessed already and he'd told me already, but the sight of it had excited both of us with a sense of ending.

"So why did you break it off with Sergei?" I asked him, still fingering the keys.

But this time he didn't rise to my flattery. "*I* didn't break it off. *He* did. I haven't ended it now, not if you're stepping into his shoes. Put that away. Cover it over the way you found it, thank you."

I did as he asked. I hid the evidence of the typewriter.

"What did he say?" I asked carelessly. "How did he break it to you? Or did he write and run?" I was thinking of Sally again.

"Not a lot. You don't need a lot of words when someone's stuck in London and you're in Moscow. The silence speaks for itself."

He wandered over to his radio and sat before it. I followed close on his heels, ready to restrain him.

"Let's plug her in, shall we, have a nice listen. I could still get a 'Come back, Cyril,' you never know."

I watched him set up his transmitter, then fling open the leaded window and toss out the hairline-aerial, which was like a fishing line with a lead sinker but no hook. I watched him peer at his signals plan and type out SOS and his callsign on his squash recorder. Then he linked the recorder to the transmitter and, with a *whizz,* sent it into the ether. He did this several times before he switched over to receive, but nothing came and he didn't expect it to; he was showing me that it never would again.

"He did *tell* me it was over," he said, staring at the dials. "I'm not accusing him. He did *say.*"

"*What* was over? Spying?"

"Oh no, not spying, that'll go on for ever, won't it? Communism, really. He said Communism was just another minority religion these days, but we hadn't woken up to the fact. 'Time to hang up your boots, Cyril. Better not come to Russia if you're rumbled, Cyril. You'd be a bit of an embarrassment to the new climate. We might have to give you back as a gesture. We're out of date, you see, you and me. Moscow Centre's decided. It's hard currency that talks to Moscow these days. They need all the pounds and dollars they can get. So I'm afraid we're on the shelf, you and me, we're *de trop* and slightly *déjà vu,* not to say a rather large embarrassment to all concerned. Moscow can't afford to be seen running Foreign Office cypher clerks with access to top secret and above, and they rather regard you and me as more of a liability than an asset, which is the reason why they're calling me home. My advice to you, Cyril, therefore, is to take a nice long holiday, see a doctor and get some sun and rest, because between you and me you're showing signs of being slightly barking. We'd like to do right by you but we're a bit strapped for hard currency, to be frank. If you'd like a modest couple of thousand, I'm sure we can do you a small something in a Swiss bank, but the larger sums are unavailable till further notice.' He was like a different person talking to me, to be honest, Ned," he continued, in a tone of valiant incomprehension. "We'd been these great friends and he didn't want me any more. 'Don't take life so hard, Cyril,' he says. He keeps telling me I'm under strain, too many people inside my head. He's right really, I suppose. I lived the wrong life, that's all. You don't know till it's too late, though, do you, sometimes? You think you're one person, you turn out to be another, same as opera. Still, not to worry, I say. Fight another day. Say not the struggle naught availeth. All grist to the mill. Yes."

He had pulled back his soft shoulders and inflated himself somehow, seeing himself as a person superior to events. "Right, then," he said, and we returned spryly to the drawing room.

We had finished. All that remained was to mop up the missing answers and obtain an inventory of what he had betrayed.

We had finished, but it was I, not Frewin, who was resisting the final step. Sitting on the arm of the sofa, he turned his head away from me, smiling over-brightly and offering me his long neck for the knife. But he was waiting for a strike that I was refusing to deliver. His round bald head was craned tensely upward while he leaned away from me as if saying, "Do it now, hit me here." But I couldn't do it. I made no move towards him. I had the notebook in my hand, and enough written down for him to sign and destroy himself. But I didn't move. I was on his stupid side, not theirs. Yet what side was that? Was love an ideology? Was loyalty a political party? Or had we, in our rush to divide the world, divided it the wrong way, failing to notice that the real battle lay between those who were still searching, and those who, in order to prevail, had reduced their vulnerability to the lowest common factor of indifference? I was on the brink of destroying a man for love. I had led him to the steps of his own scaffold, pretending we were taking a Sunday stroll together.

"Cyril?"

I had to repeat his name.

"What is it?"

"I'm supposed to take a signed statement from you."

"You can tell HQ that I was furthering understanding between great nations," he said helpfully. I had the feeling that if he had been able, he would have told them for me. "Tell them I was putting an end to the mindless and incredible hostility I had observed for many years in the Tank. That should keep them quiet."

"Well, they did guess it would be something like that," I said. "It's just that there's a bit more to it than you understand."

"Also, put in that I wish for a posting. I should like to leave the Tank forthwith and earn out my retirement in a non-classified appointment. I'll accept demotion, I've decided. I'm not short of a bob or two. I'm not proud. A change of work is better than a holiday, I say. Where are you going, Ned? The facilities are the other way."

I was heading for the door. I was heading for sanity and escape. It was as if my world had reduced itself to this dreadful room. "Just back to the office, Cyril. For an hour or so. I can't produce your statement out of a hat for you, you know. It's got to be properly drawn up on the right forms and so forth. Never mind about the weekend. I never like weekends anyway, to be truthful. Holes in the universe, if you want my secret opinion, weekends are." Why was I speaking with his cadences? "Not to worry, Cyril. I'll see myself out. You get some rest."

I wanted to escape before they came. Looking past Frewin's head to the window, I could see Monty and two of his boys climbing out of their van, and a black police car pulling up outside the house—for the Service, thank God, has no powers of arrest.

But Frewin was talking again, the way the dying go on talking after you think they're dead.

"I can't be left alone, Ned, you see. Not any more. I can't explain it to a stranger, Ned, what I've done, not all over again, no one can."

I heard a footfall on the gravel, then the ring of the doorbell. Frewin's head came up and his eyes found mine and I watched the knowledge dawn in them, and fade in disbelief, and dawn again. I kept my gaze on him while I opened the front door. Palfrey was standing at Monty's shoulder. Behind them stood two uniformed police officers and a man called Redman, better known as Bedlam, from the Service's team of shrinks.

"Marvellous, Ned," Palfrey murmured, in a hasty aside to me as the others brushed past us into the drawing room. "An absolute *coup*. You'll get a medal, I'll see to it."

They had put handcuffs on him. It had not occurred to me that they would do that. They had handcuffed his hands behind his back, which made him lift his chin. I walked with him to the van and helped him into it, but by then he had found some kind of dignity of his own, and was no longer bothering whose hand was on his elbow.

"It's not everyone can crack a Modrian-trained spook between breakfast and lunchtime," said Burr with dour satisfaction. We were eating a muted dinner at Cecconi's, where he had insisted on taking me the same evening. "Our dear brethren across the Park are beside themselves with rage, anger, indignation and envy, which is never bad either." But he was speaking to me from a world I had temporarily taken leave of.

"He cracked himself," I said.

Burr looked sharply at me. "I won't have that, Ned. I've not seen a hand played better. You were a whore. You had to be. We're all whores. Whores who pay. I've had enough of your melancholy, come to think of it—sitting over there in Northumberland Avenue, sulking like a stormcloud, caught between your women. If you can't take a decision, that's a decision. Leave your little love and go back to Mabel, if you want my advice, which you don't. I went back to mine last week and it's bloody murder."

Despite myself I discovered I was laughing.

"So what I've decided is this," Burr continued when he had generously consented to another enormous plate of pasta. "You're to abandon sulking as a way of life, and you're to abandon the Interrogators' Pool, in which, in my humble opinion, you have been studying your own narcissistic reflection for somewhat too long. And you're to unroll your mat on the Fifth Floor and replace Peter Guillam as my Head of Secretariat, which will suit your Calvinist disposition and rid me of a thoroughly idle officer."

I did what he suggested—all of it. Not because he had suggested it, but because he had spoken into my mind. I told Sally of my decision the next night and, if nothing else, the wretchedness of the occasion served to ease my memories of Frewin. For a few months, at her request, I continued writing to her from Tunbridge Wells, but it became as difficult as writing home from school. Sally was the last of what Burr had called my little loves. Perhaps I had had a notion that, added together, they would make up one big one.

So it's over," said Smiley. The glow of the dying fire lit the panelled library, gilding its gappy shelves of dusty books on travel and adventure, and the old, cracked leather of its armchairs, and the foxed photographs of its vanished battalions of uniformed officers with walking sticks; and finally our own assorted faces, turned to Smiley on his throne of honour. Four generations of the Service lounged about the room, but Smiley's quiet voice and the haze of cigar smoke seemed to bind us in a single family.

I did not remember ever quite inviting Toby to join us, but certainly the staff had been expecting him and the mess waiters had scurried out to greet him as he arrived. In his wide, watered-silk lapels and waistcoat with its Balkan frogging, he looked every inch the *Rittmeister*.

Burr had hastened directly from Heathrow, changing into his dinner jacket in the back of his chauffeur-driven Rover in deference to George. He had entered almost unremarked, with that soundless dancer's walk of his that big men seem to manage naturally. Then Monty Arbuck spotted him and at once gave up his seat. Burr had recently become the first man to make Coordinator before the age of thirty-five.

And at Smiley's feet lounged my last intake of students, the girls like cut flowers in their evening dresses, the boys keen and fresh-faced after their end-of-course exertions in Argyll.

"It's over," Smiley repeated.

Was it his sudden stillness that alerted us? His altered voice? Or some almost priestly gesture that he made, a stiffening of his tubby body in piety or resolution? I couldn't have told you then, I can't tell you now. But I know I caught no one's eye, yet with his words I felt at once a kind of tensing among us, as if Smiley were calling us to arms—yet what he was talking about had as much to do with laying them down as taking them up.

"It's over, and so am I. Absolutely over. Time you rang down the curtain on yesterday's cold warrior. And please don't ask me back, ever again. The new time needs new people. The worst thing you can do is imitate us."

I think he had intended to end there, but with George you do better not to guess.

For all I know, he had committed his entire closing speech to memory before he came, worked on it, rehearsed it word for word. In either case our silence now commanded him, as did our need of ceremony. Indeed, so thorough was our dependence on him at that moment that if he had turned and walked from the room without offering us another word, our disappointment would have turned our love to gall.

"I only ever cared about the *man*," Smiley announced. And it was typical of his artfulness that he should have opened with a riddle, then waited a moment before setting out to explain it. "I never gave a fig for the ideologies, unless they were mad or evil, I never saw institutions as being worthy of their parts, or policies as much other than excuses for not feeling. *Man*, not the mass, is what our calling is about. It was *man* who ended the Cold War in case you didn't notice. It wasn't weaponry, or technology, or armies or campaigns. It was just *man*. Not even Western man either, as it happened, but our sworn enemy in the East, who went into the streets, faced the bullets and the batons and said: we've had enough. It was *their* emperor, not ours, who had the nerve to mount the rostrum and declare he had no clothes. And the ideologies trailed after these impossible events like condemned prisoners, as ideologies do when they've had their day. Because they have no heart of their own. They're the whores and angels of our striving selves. One day, history may tell us who really won. If a democratic Russia emerges—why then, Russia will have been the winner. And if the West chokes on its own materialism, then the West may still turn out to have been the loser. History keeps her secrets longer than most of us. But she has one secret that I will reveal to you tonight in the greatest confidence. Sometimes there are no winners at all. And sometimes nobody needs to lose. You asked me how we should think of Russia today."

Was that really what we had asked him? What else explained his change of direction? We had talked loosely of the crumbling Soviet Empire, it was true; we had pondered the rise and rise of Japan and the historical shifts of economic power. And in the to-and-fro after dinner, yes, there had been a few passing references to my time in the Russia House, and a few questions touching on the Middle East and Smiley's work with the Fishing Rights Committee, which, thanks to Toby, had become common knowledge. But I don't think that was the question George was choosing to answer now.

"You ask," he went on, "can we ever trust the Bear? You seem to be amused, yet a bit unseated, by the notion that we can talk to the Russians like human beings and find common cause with them in many fields. I will give you several answers at once.

"The first is no, we can never trust the Bear. For one reason, the Bear doesn't trust himself. The Bear is threatened and the Bear is frightened and the Bear is falling apart. The Bear is disgusted with his past, sick of his present and scared stiff of his future. He often was. The Bear is broke, lazy, volatile, incompetent, slippery, dangerously proud, dangerously armed, sometimes brilliant, often ignorant. Without his claws, he'd be just another chaotic member of the Third World. But he isn't without his claws, not by any means. And he can't pull his soldiers back from foreign parts overnight, for the good reason that he can't house them or feed them or employ them, and he doesn't trust them either. And since this Service is the hired keeper of our national mistrust, we'd be neglecting our duty if we relaxed for one second our watch on the Bear, or on any of his unruly cubs. That's the first answer.

"The second answer is yes, we can trust the Bear completely. The Bear has never been so trustworthy. The Bear is begging to be part of us, to submerge his problems in us, to have his own bank account with us, to shop in our High Street and be accepted as a dignified member of our forest as well as his—all the more so because his society and economy are in tatters, his natural resources are pillaged and his managers incompetent beyond belief. The Bear needs us so desperately that we may safely trust him to need us. The Bear longs to wind back his dreadful history and emerge from the dark of the last seventy or seven hundred years. We are his daylight.

"The problem is, we Westerners do not find it in us naturally to trust the Bear, whether he's a White Bear or a Red Bear, or both kinds of bear at once, which is what he is at the moment. The Bear may be in perdition without us, but there are lots of us who believe that's exactly where he belongs. Just as there were people in 1945 who argued that a defeated Germany should remain a rubble desert for the rest of human history."

Smiley paused and seemed to wonder whether he had said enough. He glanced towards me but I refused to catch his eye. The waiting silence must have convinced him to go on.

"The Bear of the future will be whatever we make of him, and the reasons for making something of him are several. The first is common decency. When you've helped a man to escape from wrongful imprisonment, the least you can do is provide him with a bowl of soup and the means to take his place in a free world. The second is so obvious it makes me a little intemperate to have to mention it at all. Russia—even Russia alone, shorn of all her conquests and possessions—is a vast country with a vast population in a crucial part of the globe. Do we leave the Bear to rot?—encourage him to become resentful, backward, an over-armed nation outside our camp? Or make a partner of him in a world that's changing its shape every day?"

He picked up his balloon glass and peered thoughtfully into it while he swirled the last of his brandy. And I sensed that he was finding it harder to take his leave than he had expected.

"Yes. Well," he muttered, as if somehow defending himself against his own assertions. "It's not only our minds we're going to have to reconstruct, either. It's the over-mighty modern State we've built for ourselves as a bastion against something that isn't there any more. We've given up far too many freedoms in order to be free. Now we've got to take them back."

He gave a shy grin, and I knew that he was trying to break his own spell upon us.

"So while you're out there striving loyally for the State, perhaps you'll do me a small favour and lean on its pillars from time to time. It's got a lot too big for its boots of late. It would be nice if you would cut it down to size. Ned, I'm a bore. Time you sent me home."

He stood up abruptly, as if shaking himself free of something that threatened to hold him too tight. Then, very deliberately, he treated himself to a last slow look round the room—not at the students any more, but at the old photographs and trophies of his time, apparently committing them to memory. He was taking leave of his house after he had bequeathed it to his heirs. Then, with a great flurry, he launched a search for his spectacles, before he discovered he was wearing them. Then he drew back his shoulders and marched purposefully to the door as two students hastened to open it for him.

"Yes. Well. Goodnight. And thanks. Oh, and tell them to spy on the ozone layer, will you, Ned? It's dreadfully hot in St. Agnes for the time of year."

He left without looking back.

13

The rituals of retirement from the Service are probably no more harrowing than any other professional leavetaking, but they have their own poignancy. There are the ceremonies of remembering—lunches with old contacts, office parties, brave handshakes with tearful senior secretaries, courtesy visits to friendly services. And there are the ceremonies of forgetting, where snip by snip you sever yourself from the special knowledge not given to other mortals. For someone who has spent a lifetime in the Service, including three years in Burr's inmost Secretariat, these can be lengthy and repetitive affairs, even if the secrets themselves have retired long before you. Closeted in Palfrey's musty lawyer's office, mercifully quite often in the glow of a good lunch, I signed away one piece after another of my past, obediently mumbling after him the same shy little English oath, and listening each time to his insincere warnings of retribution should I be tempted by vanity or money to transgress.

And I would be deceiving us both if I pretended that the cumulative burden of these ceremonies did not slowly weigh me down, and make me wish that my day of execution could be brought forward—or, better still, regarded as accomplished. For day by day I began to feel like the man who is reconciled to death but has to spend the last of his energies consoling those who will survive him.

It was a considerable relief to me, therefore, when seated once more in Palfrey's wretched lair with three days still to go before my final freedom or imprisonment, I received a peremptory summons to Burr's presence.

"I've got a job for you. You'll hate it," he assured me, and slammed down the phone.

He was still fuming when I reached his gaudy modern office. "You're to read his file, then drive into the country and reason with him. You're not to offend him, but if you should happen to break his neck by accident you'll not find me over-critical."

"Who is he?"

"Some leftover relic of Percy Alleline's. One of those beer-bellied tycoons from the City that Percy liked to play his golf with."

I glanced at the cover of the top volume. "BRADSHAW," I read, "Sir Anthony Joyston." And in small letters underneath: "asset index," meaning that the file-holder was perceived as an ally of the Service.

"You're to crawl to him, that's an order. Appeal to his better nature," said Burr in the same acid tone. "Strike the elder statesman's note. Bring him back into the fold."

"Who says I am?"

"The sainted Foreign Office. Who do you think?"

"Why don't they do their own crawling?" I said, peering curiously at the career synopsis on page 1. "I thought that was what they were paid for."

"They tried. They sent a Junior Minister, cap in hand. Sir Anthony is crawl-proof. He also knows too much. He can name names and point fingers. Sir Anthony Bradshaw"—Burr announced, raising his voice in a North Country salvo of indignation—"Sir Anthony *Joyston* Bradshaw," he corrected himself, "is one of England's natural shits, who in the course of affecting to be of service to his country has picked up more knowledge of the disreputable activities of Her Majesty's Government than HMG ever picked up from Sir Anthony in regard to her adversaries. He accordingly has HMG by the balls. Your brief is to invite him, very courteously, to relax his grip. Your weapons for this task are your grey locks and your palpable good nature, which I have observed that you are not above putting to perfidious use. He's expecting you at five this evening and he likes punctuality. Kitty's cleared a desk for you in the anteroom."

It was not long before Burr's outrage was explained to me. There are few things more riling in our trade than having to cope with the unappetising leftovers of one's predecessors, and Sir Anthony Joyston Bradshaw, self-styled merchant venturer and City magnate, was a gruesome example of the type. Alleline had befriended him—at his club, where else? Alleline had recruited him. Alleline had sponsored him through a string of shady transactions of dubious value to anybody but Sir Anthony, and there were uncomfortable suggestions that Alleline might have taken a cut. Where scandal had threatened, Alleline had sheltered Sir Anthony under the Circus's compendious umbrella. Worse still, many of the doors that Alleline had opened for Bradshaw appeared to have stayed open, for the reason that nobody had thought to close them. And it was through one of these that Bradshaw had now walked, to the shrill outrage of the Foreign Office and half of Whitehall.

I drew an Ordnance Survey map from Library and a Ford Granada from the car pool. At half past two, with the file pretty much in my head, I set off. Sometimes you forget how beautiful England is. I passed through Newbury and climbed a winding hill lined with beech trees whose long shadows were cut like trenches into the golden stubble. A smell of cricket fields filled the car. I mounted a crest, castles of white cloud waited to receive me. I must have been thinking of my childhood, I suppose, for I had a sudden urge to drive straight into them, a thing I had often dreamed of as a boy. The car dipped again and fell free, and suddenly a whole valley opened below me, strewn with hamlets, churches, folding fields and forests.

I passed a pub, and soon a great pair of closed and gilded gates appeared between stone gateposts capped by carved lions. Beside them stood a neat white gatehouse newly thatched. A fit young man lowered his face to my open window and studied me with sniper's eyes.

"To see Sir Anthony," I said.

"Name, sir?"

"Carlisle," I replied, using an alias for the last time.

The boy disappeared into the lodge; the gates opened, then closed as soon as I was through them. The park was bordered by a high brick wall—there must have been a couple of miles of it. Fallow deer lay in the shade of chestnut trees. The drive lifted and the house appeared before me. It was golden and immaculate and very large. The centre section was William and Mary. The wings looked later, but not much. A lake lay before it, vegetable gardens and greenhouses behind. The old stables had been converted to offices, with clever outside staircases and glazed external corridors. A gardener was watering the orangerie.

The drive skirted the lake and brought me to the front sweep. Two Arab mares and a llama eyed me over the fence of a lunging ring. A young butler came down the steps, dressed in black trousers and a linen jacket.

"Shall I park your car round the back, Mr. Carlisle, once you've been introduced?" he asked. "Sir Anthony does like a clear façade, when he can get one, sir."

I gave him the keys and followed him up the wide steps. There were nine, though I can't imagine why I counted, except that it was something we had taught on the Sarratt awareness course, and in recent weeks my life seemed to have become less a continuation than a mosaic of past ages and experiences. If Ben had come striding up to me and grasped my hand, I don't think I would have been particularly surprised. If Monica or Sally had appeared to accuse me, I would have had my answers ready.

I entered a huge hall. A splendid double staircase rose to an open landing. Portraits of noble ancestors, all men, stared down at me, but somehow I didn't believe they were of one family, or could have lived here long without their women. I passed through a billiards room and noticed that the table and cues were new. I suppose I saw everything so clearly because I was treating each experience as my last. I followed the butler through a stately drawing room and traversed a second room that was got up as a hall of mirrors, and a third that was supposed to be informal, with a television set the size of one of those old ice-cream tricycles that used to call at my preparatory school on sunny evenings just like this. I arrived at a pair of majestic doors and waited while the butler knocked. Then waited again for a response. If Bradshaw were an Arab, he would keep me standing here for hours, I thought, remembering Beirut.

Finally I heard a male voice drawl "Come," and the butler took a pace into the room and announced, "A Mr. Carlisle, Sir Anthony, from London."

I had not told him I had come from London.

The butler stepped aside and gave me a first view of my host, though it took a little longer before my host had his first view of Mr. Carlisle.

He was sitting at a twelve-foot desk with brass inlay and cabriole legs. Modern oil paintings of spoilt children hung behind him. His correspondence was stacked in trays of thick stitched hide. He was a big, well-nourished man, and clearly a big worker also, for he had stripped to his shirt, which was blue with a midwife's white collar, and he was working in his braces, which were red. Also he was too busy to acknowledge me. First he read, using a gold pen to guide his eye. Then he signed, using the gold pen to write. Then he meditated, still in a downward direction, using the tip of the gold pen as a focus for his great thoughts. His gold cufflinks were as big as old pennies. Then at last he laid the pen down and, with a wounded—even accusatory—air, he raised his head, first to discover me, then to measure me by standards I had yet to ascertain.

At the same moment, by a happy chance of nature, a shaft of low sunlight from the French windows landed on his face, and I was able to measure him in return: the self-sadness of his pouchy eyes, as if he should be pitied for his wealth, the straight small mouth set tense and crooked in the puckered chins, the air of resolution formed of weakness, of boyhood suspicions in a grown-up world. At forty-five, this fattened child was unappeased, blaming some absent parent for his comforts.

Suddenly, Bradshaw was walking towards me. Stalking? Wading? There is an English walk these days peculiar to men of power, and it is a confection of several things at once. Self-confidence is one, lazy sportiveness another. But there is also menace in it, and impatience, and a leisured arrogance, which comes with the crablike splaying of elbows that give way to nobody, and the boxer's slouch of the shoulders, and the playful springiness in the knees. You knew long before you shook his hand that he had no truck with a whole category of life that ranged from art to public transport. You were silently forewarned to keep your distance if you were that kind of fool.

"You're one of Percy's boys," he told me, in case I didn't know, while he sampled my hand, and was duly disappointed. "Well, well. Long time no see. Must be ten years. More. Have a drink. Have champagne. Have what you like." An order: "Summers. Get us a bottle of shampoo, bucket of ice, two glasses, then bugger off. And nuts!" he shouted after him. "Cashews. Brazils. Masses of fucking nuts—like nuts?" he enquired of me, with a sudden and disarming intimacy.

I said I did.

"Good. Me too. Love 'em. You've come to read me the riot act. Right? Go on. Not made of glass."

He was flinging open the French windows so that I could have a better view of what he owned. He had chosen a different walk for this manoeuvre, more march, more swinging of the arms to the rhythm of unheard martial music. When he had opened the doors, he gave me his back to look at, and kept his arms up, palms propped against the door posts, like a martyr waiting for the arrow. And the City haircut, I thought: thick at the collar and little horns above the ears. In golds and browns and greens, the valley faded softly into eternity. A nanny and a small child were walking among the deer. She wore a brown hat with the brim up all the way round and a brown uniform like a Girl Guide's. The lawn was set for croquet.

"We're just appealing to you, that's all, Sir Anthony," I said. "Asking you another favour, like the ones you did for Percy. After all, it was Percy who got you your knighthood, wasn't it?"

"Fuck Percy. Dead, isn't he? Nobody gives me anything, thank you. Help myself to it. What do you want? Spit it out, will you? I've had one sermon already. Portly Savoury from the Foreign Office. Used to flog him when he was my fag at school. Wimp then, wimp now."

The arms stayed up there, the back was braced and aggressive. I might have spoken, but I felt strangely off key. Three days before my retirement, I was beginning to feel I hardly knew the real world at all. Summers brought champagne, uncorked it and filled two glasses, which he handed to us on a silver tray. Bradshaw snatched one and strode into the garden. I trailed after him to the centre of a grass alley. Azaleas and rhododendrons grew high to either side of us. At the farther end, a fountain played in a stone pond.

"Did you get a lordship of the manor when you bought this house?" I asked, thinking a little small talk might give me time to collect myself.

"Suppose I did?" Bradshaw retorted, and I realised he did not wish to be reminded that he had bought his house rather than inherited it.

"Sir Anthony," I said.

"Well?"

"It's concerning your relationship with a Belgian company called Astrasteel."

"Never heard of 'em."

"But you are associated with them, aren't you?" I said, with a smile.

"Aren't now, never was. Told Savoury the same."

"But you have holdings in Astrasteel, Sir Anthony," I protested patiently.

"Zilch. Absolutely buggerall. Different bloke, wrong address. Told him."

"But you do have a one hundred percent holding in a company called Allmetal of Birmingham Limited, Sir Anthony. And Allmetal of Birmingham does own a company called Eurotech Funding & Imports Limited of Bermuda, doesn't it? And Eurotech of Bermuda does own Astrasteel of Belgium, Sir Anthony. So we may take it that a certain loose association might be said to exist between yourself on the one hand, and the company that is owned by the company you own on the other." I was still smiling, still reasoning with him, joking him along.

"No holdings, no dividends, no influence over Astrasteel's affairs. Arm's length, whole thing. Told Savoury, tell the same to you."

"Nevertheless, when you were invited by Alleline—back in the old days, I know, but not so long ago, was it?—to make deliveries of certain commodities to certain countries not strictly on the official shopping list for those commodities, Astrasteel *was* the company you used. And Astrasteel did what you told them to do. Because if they hadn't done, Percy would not have come to you—would he? You'd have been no use to him." My smile felt stiff on my face. "We're not *policemen,* Sir Anthony, we're not the *taxman.* I'm merely indicating to you certain relationships that stand—as you insist—beyond the law's reach, and were indeed designed—with Percy's active help—to do just that."

My speech sounded so ill composed to me, so unpointed, that I assumed at first that Bradshaw did not propose to bother with it at all.

And in a way I was right, for he merely shrugged and said, "Fuck's that got to do with anything?"

"Well quite a lot actually." I could feel my blood beginning to rise, and there was nothing I could do to check it. "We're asking you to lay off. Stop. You've got your knighthood, you're worth a fortune, you have a duty to your country today just as you had twelve years ago. So get out of the Balkans and stop stirring it with the Serbs and stop stirring it in Central Africa, stop offering them guns galore on tick, and stop trying to cash in on wars that may never happen if you and other like-minded spirits keep your fingers out of them. You're British. You've more money in your pocket than most of us will touch in a lifetime. Stop. Just stop. That's all we're asking. Times have changed. We're not playing those games any more."

For a moment I fancied I had impressed him, for he turned his unlit gaze on me, and looked me over as if I were someone who might after all be worth buying. Then his interest flickered out again and he relapsed into despondency.

"It's your country talking to you, Bradshaw," I said, now with real anger. "For

Christ's sake, man, what more do you *need*? Haven't you got even the vestige of a conscience?"

I will give you Bradshaw's reply as I transcribed it, for at Burr's request I had slipped a recorder into my jacket pocket, and Bradshaw's sawing nasal tones ensured a perfect reproduction. I will give you his voice too, as nearly as I can write it down. He spoke English as if it were his second language, but it was the only one he had. He spoke in what my son Adrian tells me is called "slur," which is a slack-mouthed Belgravia cockney that contrives to make *mice* out of *mouse* and dispenses almost entirely with the formality of pronouns. It has a vocabulary, naturally: nothing rises but it *escalates,* no opportunity is without a *window,* no minor event occurs that is not *sensational.* It also has a pedantic inaccuracy which is supposed to distinguish it from the unwashed, and explains gems like "as for you and I." But even without my tape recorder, I like to think I would have remembered every word, for his speech was like an evening war-cry from a world I was leaving to itself.

"I'm sorry," he began, which was a lie to start with. "Did I understand you were appealing to my *conscience?* Good. Right. Make a statement for the record. Mind? Statement begins here. Point One. There *is* only one point actually. *I don't give a fart.* The difference between me and other charlies is, *I* admit it. If a horde of niggers —yes, I said *niggers,* I meant *niggers*—if these *niggers* shot each other dead with my toys tomorrow and I made a bob out of it, great news by me. Because if *I* don't sell 'em the goods, some *other* charlie will. Government used to understand that. If they've gone soft, tough titty on 'em. Point Two. Question: heard what the tobacco boys are up to these days? Flogging off high-toxic tobacco to the fuzzy-wuzzies and telling 'em it makes 'em horny and cures the common cold. Tobacco boys give a fart? Sit at home having nervous breakdowns about spreading lung cancer among the natives? The fuck they do. Doing a little creative selling, period. Take drugs. Don't use 'em personally. Don't need 'em. Never mind. If willing seller is doing business with willing buyer, my advice is step aside, let them slug it out, and bloody good luck to 'em. If drugs don't kill 'em, the atmosphere will or they'll get barbecued by the global warming. British, you said. Matter of fact, rather proud of it. Also rather proud of one's *school.* Empire man. Happens to be the tradition one's inherited. When people get in one's way, I break 'em. Or they break me. Discipline is rather up one's street too, actually. *Order.* Accepting responsibilities of one's class and education, and beating the foreigner at his own game. Thought you people were rather committed to that one, too. Error, apparently. Failure of communication. What one cares about is quality of life. *This* life. *Standards* actu-ally. Old word. Don't care. *These* standards. Pompous, you're thinking. All right, I'm pompous. Fuck you. I'm Pharaoh, right? If a few thousand slaves have to die so that I can build this pyramid, nature. And if they can make *me* die for *their* fucking pyramid, bloody good on 'em. Know what I've got in my cellar? Iron rings. Rusty iron rings, built into the walls when this house was built. Know what they were for? Slaves. *That*'s nature too. Original owner of this house—man who *built* this house—man who *paid* for it, man who sent his architect to Italy, learn his trade —that man owned slaves, and had his slave quarters in the cellar of this house. Think there aren't slaves today? Think capital doesn't *depend* on slaves? Jesus Christ, what kind of shop do you run? One doesn't normally talk philosophy, but

I'm afraid one doesn't like being preached to either. Won't have it, you see. Not in my house, thank you. Annoys me. Don't bug easily, rather famous for one's cool. But one does have a certain view of nature; one gives work to people and one takes one's share."

I said nothing, and that is on the tape too.

In the face of an absolute, what can you say? All my life I had battled against an institutionalised evil. It had had a name, and most often a country as well. It had had a corporate purpose, and had met a corporate end. But the evil that stood before me now was a wrecking infant in our own midst, and I became an infant in return, disarmed, speechless and betrayed. For a moment, it was as if my whole life had been fought against the wrong enemy. Then it was as if Bradshaw had personally stolen the fruits of my victory. I remembered Smiley's aphorism about the right people losing the Cold War, and the wrong people winning it, and I thought of repeating it to him as some sort of insult, but I would have been beating the air. I thought of telling him that now we had defeated Communism, we were going to have to set about defeating capitalism, but that wasn't really my point: the evil was not in the system, but in the man. And besides, by then he was asking me whether I wanted to stay to dinner, at which I politely declined, and left.

In the event, it was Burr who gave me dinner, and I am pleased to say I don't remember much about it. Two days later, I turned in my Head Office pass.

You see your face. It's no one you remember. You wonder where you put your love, what you found, what you were after. You want to say: "I slew the dragon, I left the world a safer place." You can't really, not these days. Perhaps you never could.

We have a good life, Mabel and I. We don't talk about things we can't change. We don't cross each other. We're civilised. We've bought a cottage on the coast. There's a long garden there I'd like to get my hands on, plant a few trees, make a vista to the sea. There's a sailing club for poor kids I'm involved in; we bring them down from Hackney, they enjoy it. There's a move to draft me for the local council. Mabel does the church. I go back to Holland now and then. I still have a few relations there.

Burr drops in from time to time. I like that in him. He gets on well with Mabel, as you'd expect. He doesn't try to be wise. He chats to her about her watercolours. He's not judgmental. We open a good bottle, cook a chicken. He brings me up to date, drives back to London. Of Smiley, nothing, but that's the way he wanted it. He hates nostalgia, even if he's part of other people's.

There's no such thing as retirement, really. Sometimes there's knowing too much, and not being able to do much about it, but that's just age, I'm sure. I think a lot. I'm stepping out with my reading. I talk to people, ride on buses. I'm a newcomer to the overt world but I'm learning.

ABOUT THE AUTHOR

JOHN LE CARRÉ born in 1931, attended the universities of Berne and Oxford. He spent five years in the British Foreign Service. *The Spy Who Came in From the Cold,* his third book, secured his worldwide reputation. John le Carré lives in Cornwall, England.